THE FOUNDING

• GAUNT'S GHOSTS •
Dan Abnett

THE FOUNDING

BOOK 1: FIRST AND ONLY
BOOK 2: GHOSTMAKER
BOOK 3: NECROPOLIS

THE SAINT

BOOK 4: HONOUR GUARD
BOOK 5: THE GUNS OF TANITH
BOOK 6: STRAIGHT SILVER
BOOK 7: SABBAT MARTYR

THE LOST

BOOK 8: TRAITOR GENERAL
BOOK 9: HIS LAST COMMAND
BOOK 10: THE ARMOUR OF CONTEMPT
BOOK 11: ONLY IN DEATH

THE VICTORY

BOOK 12: BLOOD PACT
BOOK 13: SALVATION'S REACH
BOOK 14: THE WARMASTER
BOOK 15: ANARCH

More tales from the Sabbat Worlds

SABBAT WAR
Edited by Dan Abnett

SABBAT CRUSADE
Edited by Dan Abnett

SABBAT WORLDS
Edited by Dan Abnett

DOUBLE EAGLE
Dan Abnett

TITANICUS
Dan Abnett

BROTHERS OF THE SNAKE
Dan Abnett

THE FOUNDING

A GAUNT'S GHOSTS OMNIBUS

DAN ABNETT

BLACK LIBRARY

A BLACK LIBRARY PUBLICATION

'A Ghost Return' first published in 2013.
First and Only first published in 1999.
'Of Their Lives in the Ruins of Their Cities' first published in 2010.
Ghostmaker first published in 2000.
Necropolis first published in 2000.
'In Remembrance' first published in 2002.
This edition published in Great Britain in 2022 by
Black Library, Games Workshop Ltd.,
Willow Road, Nottingham, NG7 2WS, UK.

Represented by: Games Workshop Limited – Irish branch,
Unit 3, Lower Liffey Street, Dublin 1,
D01 K199, Ireland.

13

Produced by Games Workshop in Nottingham.
Cover illustration by K. D. Stanton.

A CIP record for this book is available from the British Library.

ISBN 13: 978 1 78496 617 1

See Black Library on the internet at

blacklibrary.com

Find out more about Games Workshop
and the worlds of Warhammer at

games-workshop.com

Printed and bound by CPI Group (UK) Ltd, Croydon, CR0 4YY

For more than a hundred centuries the Emperor has sat immobile on the Golden Throne of Earth. He is the Master of Mankind. By the might of His inexhaustible armies a million worlds stand against the dark.

Yet, He is a rotting carcass, the Carrion Lord of the Imperium held in life by marvels from the Dark Age of Technology and the thousand souls sacrificed each day so that His may continue to burn.

To be a man in such times is to be one amongst untold billions. It is to live in the cruellest and most bloody regime imaginable. It is to suffer an eternity of carnage and slaughter. It is to have cries of anguish and sorrow drowned by the thirsting laughter of dark gods.

This is a dark and terrible era where you will find little comfort or hope. Forget the power of technology and science. Forget the promise of progress and advancement. Forget any notion of common humanity or compassion.

There is no peace amongst the stars, for in the grim darkness of the far future, there is only war.

CONTENTS

A GHOST RETURN

I

They were walking by lamplight, finding their way by the criss-crossing beams of their lamp packs. They were deep underground, so of course it was going to be dark.

Except it seemed unnecessarily, *extravagantly* dark. Lightless. As though some kind of anti-light, an un-light, had been poured into the gloom to thicken it.

Every few seconds, and to no particular rhythm, the earth shook.

Ibram Gaunt could feel it through his boots. He swapped his lamp pack to his right hand, and placed his left palm against the tunnel wall. He felt the rough surface transmit the vibrations. At every subterranean quiver, dirt trickled down from the ceiling, or spilled from loose sections of the old, decaying arches.

The men in the advance squad could feel the shaking too, and it was putting them on edge. Gaunt could tell that by the way the beams of their lamps jerked and shifted at every tremble. Gaunt knew someone should say something. That someone was him, a part of his duty.

'Shelling,' he said. 'The Warmaster has focused the artillery divisions on Sangrel Hive. It's just shelling.'

'Feels like the world's moving,' muttered one of the troopers.

Gaunt tilted his lamp to find the man's face. Picked out starkly by the lamp's beam, Trooper Gebbs shielded his eyes at the glare.

'It's just shelling,' Gaunt assured him. 'Concussion from the shelling.'

Gebbs shrugged.

The ground shook. Pebbles skittered.

'Why are we here?' asked another man. Gaunt's lamp beam moved to identify Trooper Ari Danks.

'You getting all philosophical now, Ari?' Gebbs asked with a chuckle made throaty by the dust in the air.

'I just wondered what the Throne we were supposed to be doing?' Danks replied. 'There's nothing out here. Just these endless, pitch-black bloody ruins...'

'So you'd rather be hacking your way through Charismites in the hive-stacks, would you?' asked Trooper Hiskol.

'At least it wouldn't be as black as up my–'

'Enough,' said Gaunt. He didn't have to raise his voice, and the troopers didn't have to turn their beams to see his face and read its expression. They ceased their chatter. Some of them had served long enough to remember when Gaunt had just been 'the Boy', Oktar's cadet, but none of them were about to forget what that young cadet had become. Gaunt was the commissar. He was discipline.

The ground shook again. Gaunt heard a little river of grit spill down the curve of the tunnel wall. He had to admit that Trooper Danks had a point. What *were* they doing here?

Gaunt understood the mission parameters clearly enough, and frankly, given the intensity of the hive-war, this advance detail was a blessed relief.

Even so, he'd calculated the journey time that morning, overestimating to allow for detours where the maps didn't match the navigable reality of the undersink, and they should have reached their destination two hours ago.

Gaunt told the men to wait, and used his lamp to pick his way along the unlit tunnel. The officer in charge of the detail was standing at the next bend, checking his charts.

Major Czytel glanced up at the lamplight bobbing towards him.

'That you, Gaunt?'

'Yes, sir.'

'We may have taken a wrong turn back there, Gaunt,' Czytel said. 'At that junction where the tunnel split.'

He turned and twitched his beam back the way they had come, partly as an indicator, partly to pick out Gaunt's face.

Gaunt nodded. He'd presumed as much. Galen Czytel was old school, and most definitely remembered the time when Gaunt had merely been 'the Boy'. Unlike the rank and file, he had never really got over the idea that Ibram Gaunt was an over-educated, over-privileged scholam boy with too much book-learning and not enough actual soldiering. Czytel liked what he called 'honest men'. He seemed to be allergic to anybody who had an air of the officer class or entitlement. Czytel had 'dragged himself' up through the Hyrkan ranks. He'd freely tell you that, possibly several times in the course of one regimental dinner.

In fact, when Gaunt received his full promotion at Oktar's death-bed on Gylatus Decimus, Czytel had been one of a group of officers who had formally requested that Gaunt be transferred out of the Hyrkan Eighth to another unit. They felt that it would 'undermine morale' because the men 'would not take seriously the authority of an individual who had previously been the regiment's mascot.'

General Caernavar had thrown the request out quickly. Ironic then, it was officers like Czytel, and not the regular troops, who had found such difficulty in accommodating Gaunt's maturity.

Gaunt, for his part, had learned that it was best not to correct Czytel unless absolutely necessary. An officer's mistake could be carefully smoothed over by a diligent commissar. An open argument between an officer and a commissar had potentially devastating effects on discipline.

'We'll go back,' Gaunt said. 'It's not far. Or we could go on to the next intersection, and move east.'

'The next intersection?' asked Czytel.

In the lamplight, Gaunt could see that Czytel was looking at him with a sort of sneer. 'You haven't got your chart out. You just *remember* that, do you?'

'I reviewed the route this morning,' Gaunt replied. 'I don't have my chart out because—'

He stopped. He had been about to say 'because you, as officer in charge, were leading the route.'

'I will double-check,' Gaunt said. 'I could be wrong.' He reached for the data-slate pouch attached to his webbing, but Czytel just handed over his own slate. It looked like impatience, that Czytel didn't want to wait while Gaunt produced his data-slate and woke it up. But it was actually a small concession, one which allowed for the idea that Czytel might have made a navigational error. The major wanted to keep the peace too.

Gaunt reviewed the screen.

'Yes, you see, sir? The next intersection seems to allow access to this sinkway here. That should lead us directly to the shrine.'

'If it is a shrine,' said Czytel.

Which is the point of us being here, Gaunt thought, but did not say it. He just nodded.

Czytek turned the squad.

'Pick it up! Let's go!' he called into the darkness.

II

The Crusade had finally begun.
The Crusade.

The top brass had been talking about it for years, and received wisdom was that the region known as the Sabbat Worlds was past saving. It was a vast territory at the rimward edge of the Segmentum Pacificus, a major Imperial holding that had, in the course of two bloody centuries been overrun by the marauding armies of the Sanguinary Worlds. Some worlds had fallen to the Eternal Archenemy. Others, like Formal Prime, had struggled on, surrounded by the barbarous foe, fighting to maintain their Imperial identities. The Sabbat Worlds deserved the protection of the Throne, their seneschals and governors pleaded for it, but liberation was a monumental task. Few thought that High Command would ever sanction the massive expenditure that a crusade war would require.

Until Slaydo. Lord Militant Slaydo was a persuasive beast, and with the victories of the Khulan Wars on his honour roll, he had been declared Warmaster and allowed to prosecute the Sabbat Worlds Crusade.

It was the biggest Imperial mobilisation in the segmentum for three centuries. The Departmento Tacticae Imperialis estimated it would take a century to successfully complete the campaign.

Ibram Gaunt had no real interest in looking that far ahead. The fighting to retake Formal Prime's ancient and crumbling hives had been some of the most brutal and intense he'd experienced, and his career with the Hyrkans had not been lacking in bloodshed. Eight years since he'd joined the Imperial Guard as a Commissariat cadet, and he'd seen plenty of action, but nothing like this.

Sangrel Hive, the world's most massive hab centre, was the stronghold of an enemy 'magister' or warlord, a monster called Shebol Red-Hand. His cult followers, the Charismites, held their ground with a zealous rage that was quite intimidating. The previous week, Gaunt had seen more men die in one hour than he thought possible.

So this, this lamplight detour mission into the rambling, pitch-black undersinks seventy kilometres beyond the recognised limits of Sangrel Hive, this could be seen as something of a perk. It got a squad of men out of the front line for a few days. It had the personal sanction of the Warmaster. The surroundings might be dismal – the unnerving darkness, the steady seep of tarry ground-water, the smell of rot and mildew, the vermin, the unsafe sections of tunnel – but the Hyrkan soldiers were out of the front-line action, and there were no screaming waves of spear-wielding Charismites rushing their formation every few minutes.

The ground shook. Dirt trickled. Gaunt noted the agitation of the men once again, the flickering beams. He realised there was a chilly lick of sweat between his own shoulder blades. Sangrel Hive was a long way away. If they could feel the earth-shock of the artillery bombardment at this distance, what kind of hell had the main front turned into?

The assault of Formal Prime was part of Operation Redrake, the War-master's opening move. Named after the famous predatory serpent, Redrake was intended to be a lightning strike against multiple targets: four significant worlds at the trailing edge of the Sabbat group: Formal Prime, Long Halent, Onscard and Indrid. Slaydo had chosen to lead the Formal Prime assault personally. It was the keystone world.

If Redrake failed, then the Crusade was as good as botched before it had even got going. The High Lords of Terra would recall Slaydo. Tactics would be reconsidered. The Sabbat Worlds might be left to rot for another thousand years. Another ten thousand.

Gaunt tried not to think about it. He was an ambitious young man. He had achieved his status in the Hyrkans through sheer hard work and perseverance. He had welcomed the possibility of a major new campaign because it was an opportunity for an ambitious young man to prove himself and make a name.

The reality was bitter and exhausting. War was not a glorious thing, no matter what memories or reputations resulted from it. War was about suffering and loss, about struggle and sacrifice. It was about blood. Just a few weeks into the opening engagements of the conflict, Ibram Gaunt no longer thought about it in terms of proving himself, or building a reputation.

He had realised that the Sabbat Worlds Crusade was something he was going to have to endure. It was something a man simply had to survive.

Gaunt wondered what kind of strength that feat was going to require. He wasn't sure he had it. He wasn't sure he'd ever had it. He was just an over-educated, over-privileged scholam boy with too much book-learning and–

The ground shook.

'Here,' said Gaunt. 'Sir?'

Czytel turned. Gaunt shone his lamp down a side passage that was partly obscured by architectural debris.

'This is the junction?' the major asked.

'Yes, sir,' said Gaunt.

Czytel shrugged, and clambered through. The men followed, lasguns across their chests. Gaunt wanted to assign them a covering pattern, to send some men ahead to recon. However, the Hyrkans, excellent, well-drilled battlefield soldiers though they were, generally lacked an aptitude for scouting and recon.

Besides, it was not Gaunt's place to issue commands. That was the officer's job. Gaunt was merely the commissar.

III

The sinkway ran for about eighty metres, then opened out into a series of large, irregular caverns. It was part of the old arcology that had once formed the massive underhive realm of Sangrel, when the hive had been in its prime. Using his lamp, Gaunt could see rusted threads of technological out-ports and power cables embedded in the crumbling walls, and the remains of cross-arch roof supports and rockcrete pillaring. But the space was old, and had not been maintained at all in the century or more since the hive had shrunk and its outer quarters had been abandoned.

Like the undersink they had trekked through, it was derelict. The ceiling had collapsed in places, littering the ground with rubble and twisted metal rebar. Pools of oily water had accumulated in the darkness. Gaunt could hear the scratch of vermin. He could see the partial remains of an old, tiled floor, the relic of grander days.

There was light ahead. It seemed strange, out of place. Glow-globes and lumen units had been strung from the exposed girders or threaded up on wire supports to hook pins that had been power-sunk into the rock. They could hear the low, background throb of a generator.

Gaunt sniffed. He could smell rock dust, the fine dry powder kicked out by an excavator's drill.

Czytel flashed a few gestures, and the advance sharpened up. Lasrifles swung up ready, covering style, as the men fanned out and prowled forward. Zennet, the squad's sniper, unsleeved his long-las and popped the cover on the scope. He and Breccia, the squad's sweeper, had been lugging the charge panniers, so Zennet took up a spot nearby, allowing him to both scope the area and stay close enough to guard the payload. Breccia began to unpack and assemble his sweeper broom. His lascarbine lay ready on the ground beside him.

Czytel had drawn his laspistol. With his left hand, he flashed some more fingers, indicating numbers and groupings. The advance scurried forward, switching off their lamp packs and adjusting their eyes to the light of the strung lamps.

Gaunt took out his bolt pistol. It felt far too heavy.

Danks and Hiskol were beside him. Gaunt nodded, and they moved ahead into the lit cavern.

Right in front of them was a woman in work overalls, carrying a tray of potshards.

She saw them and yelped, dropping the tray as though it was red-hot. The contents smashed on the ancient tiles.

'Calm. Calm!' Gaunt told her. He reached for her and pulled her down into cover.

'Don't shout,' he said firmly.

'You're Guard?' she asked, breathless, looking up at him.

'Yes.'

'The Guard detail we sent for?'

'Yes. You're with the dig team?'

She nodded.

'You scared the living shit out of me,' she said.

'Kallie? Kallie? Are you all right?'

A man's voice echoed through the cavern. He appeared at the far end, bracing an autorifle.

'Kallie? I heard you cry out. Kallie?'

'Put it down,' Danks told him, aiming his lasrifle from the cheek.

'Do as he says,' Hiskol emphasised, closing from the other side, lasrifle aimed, one eye closed.

'Throne!' the man said, and lowered his rifle to the floor, terrified.

'Don't let them hurt him!' the woman told Gaunt.

Gaunt rose.

'Stand down,' he said. He approached the man, who was on his knees. Danks had kicked the autorifle away.

'Imperial Guard,' Gaunt said. 'Hyrkan Eighth. Are you a member of the survey team?'

'Yes,' said the man. 'Yes.'

'We came in response to your message,' Gaunt said. 'I'll need to see some identification.'

The man immediately reached for his pocket. Gaunt's aim with the bolt pistol was unwavering.

'Do it gently,' he advised.

The man produced an ident slate and proffered it to Gaunt.

'Wal Desruisseaux,' he said. 'Survey Advance. You scared me.'

'Yeah, we're supposed to do that,' said Danks, his aim still steady.

Gaunt suppressed a smile. He studied the slate.

'This survey was undertaken with the authority of the Warmaster,' Desruisseaux said. 'His personal authority–'

'I understand,' said Gaunt.

'No, he really–'

Gaunt looked at the kneeling archaeologist.

'I understand, sir. Warmaster Slaydo is particularly concerned that the Crusade recovers, authenticates and preserves all traces of the Saint

Beati Sabbat, especially her votive shrines. It is an underlying standing order. It explains why so many archaeological and survey teams
have been allowed prominence in the vanguard. It explains your presence here, and why we have responded so directly to your call for help.
Believe me, I understand, sir.'

He tossed the slate back to the archaeologist. Desruisseaux caught
it and got to his feet.

'Are you the officer in charge of–' Desruisseaux began.

'Throne, no,' replied Gaunt. 'You'll meet him shortly. How many of
you are there?'

'Eight,' said the archaeologist.

'Get them to come out right now. Into the open. My men are tight
on their triggers. Let's not have an incident.'

'I thought you said they weren't your men?' said Desruisseaux.

'Get them out front,' said Gaunt.

IV

They herded the eight archaeologists into the globe-lit inner cavern
space. Czytel's squad surrounded them and kept watch.

Desruisseaux was in charge. The girl that Gaunt had grabbed, the
survey team's second, was his wife.

'Explain what you have found,' Czytel said, lighting a lho-stick. 'Come
on, now, professor, we've come a long way through the dark.'

Desruisseaux glowered at him.

'So have we, sir,' he replied.

'We've spent our lives documenting and determining the history of
the Sabbat Beati,' said Kallie. 'This crusade provides us with an unpar-
alleled opportunity to physically investigate her–'

Czytel blew a raspberry.

'You're an encumbrance is what you are. Throne-damned academ-
ics, worming away where war is happening. We're dying, don't you
know, a Throne-awful lot as it is, without having to risk our lives protecting the likes of you.'

'The Beati–' Desruisseaux began.

'Shut it,' said Czytel.

'But this shrine–' the woman said.

'What have you found?' asked Gaunt.

V

It was a huge rockcrete plug, filling what might have once been the mouth
of a tunnel or a cavern in the rock. The walls around were covered in votive

offerings and the calcified drip of wax from a million candles. Though this undersink had been deserted for over a century, people had continued to come here and place offerings at the wall. This was sacred ground.

And it shook. The distant artillery bombardment made the cavern throb.

'This is your shrine?' asked Czytel.

'Sir, yes. It is obviously so,' Desruisseaux replied. 'See the layers of votive wax here, and the number of offerings. Even in modern times, during the cruel reign of Shebol, hivers have flocked here through the dark to make observance.'

'I don't really know what I'm looking at,' Czytel said, stepping back and frowning.

'As I understand it,' said Gaunt, 'the shrine lies in the cavern beyond. This rockcrete plug is sealing the entrance.'

'Exactly,' said Kallie. 'So, I take it you've brought the explosives?'

VI

Breccia and Zennet had been carrying the charge panniers. Cold-packed fyceline gel in ten-mil cases. Enough to bring down a curtain wall.

'Drill them in,' Czytel ordered.

Breccia nodded and hurried to oblige.

'Sir,' said Gaunt, taking him to one side, 'is that wise? We have no idea what we're–'

Czytel turned to look at him.

'Gaunt, they've called us in to blow up that rockcrete plug. Behind it, most probably, is a shrine to the Beati. If there is, the Warmaster will praise us. If there isn't, then he will approve our efforts to confirm or deny. Whichever way it turns out, we are going to blow that plug out.'

Gaunt stepped back and took a moment to look at the cavern. The idea of revealing a genuine shrine to the saint thrilled him, but there was something unnerving about the tilt and balance of the light in the space, something that gave him pause.

VII

'There was some inscription here,' Gaunt said.

'Yes,' said Kallie, following him along the wall beside the plug. 'It collapsed. It crumbled.'

Nearby, Breccia was drilling charge holes into the plug. He was fitting the explosives into position a stick at a time. Gaunt knew there was about an hour before they'd have to withdraw to a safe distance. Breccia was good at his job.

He reached down into the stone litter at the foot of the wall and picked up a shard on which there was a scrap of inscribed script.

'You never thought to piece this inscription together?' he asked.

'There's been too much work to do,' she replied. 'Why?'

'It looks significant,' Gaunt said. 'And it looks as if it's been cut away deliberately. As if the surface had been chipped or blasted away.'

'No, it just collapsed. It crumbled,' she insisted. 'It was very old.'

'Exactly. But you didn't think it was an imperative to reconstruct it?'

She looked at him.

'You're a soldier. What does it matter?'

'I'm an over-educated, over-privileged scholam boy,' Gaunt replied. 'That's why.'

VIII

Gaunt drew Czytel aside quietly and told him he thought they should stop placing the charges.

'Stop?' Czytel frowned.

'I believe we need to know more about this site, major. We–'

'For Throne's sake, Gaunt,' Czytel began. 'That's why we're going to blow it open. To find out. To prove it is a shrine. This is a fool's errand and a waste of time. I want it resolved one way or another.'

'I have a gut feeling that detonating the charges would be a bad idea, sir,' said Gaunt.

Czytel sniffed.

Gaunt's gut feelings were all too real and all too unreliable. He'd almost been split in two by Dercius's chainsword two years earlier. The sight of the scar across his belly made even veterans shiver.

Czytel looked at the young commissar.

'We're going to blow this open, Gaunt,' he said. 'We're going to find this shrine, and we're going to go back to the line and report a duty completed. The Warmaster will smile upon us, and we will all be warmed by that smile.'

Gaunt wanted to speak, but he hesitated.

'Yes, sir,' he said.

IX

The ground shook.

Breccia was working diligently. Gaunt watched for a while, then wandered along the outer wall of the alleged shrine. To either side of the rockcrete plug, the tunnel walls were thick with wax from the candles pilgrims had brought to light. The wax had set around old, dry flowers, coins, medals and other votive offerings fixed to the wall. Though they had been on site for a good while, the survey team had made no attempt to clear the wax and examine the wall. Gaunt was still puzzled by their disinclination to recover the inscription. The only real effort they seemed to have made was in futile drilling to unseal the plug.

The ground shook.

'Vedic?' Gaunt called. The squad's flame trooper hurried over from where he been waiting, chatting to fellow members of the advance.

'Sir?'

'Get a low heat on this section of wax,' Gaunt told him.

Vedic frowned, but made no comment. He tightened the flamer's light and washed a little fire over the wall. Old wax bobbled and streamed. Flowers crisped. Coins, loosened and heated, dropped onto the ground.

Gaunt had been hoping for more inscriptions, inscriptions that had been covered up by the wax. But the exposed wall was bare. The only inscription around the shrine entrance had been the one that had mysteriously crumbled.

He noticed that Breccia had stopped work.

'What's the matter?' Gaunt asked, crossing to him before Czytel noticed. He walked up the stone ramp to where Breccia stood by the plug.

'Something odd,' Breccia said, looking a little worried. He didn't want the commissar to think he was slacking.

He'd been using his sweeper unit to scan the plug and choose the best places to drill his charge holes.

'When I got closer to this side,' Breccia told Gaunt, 'I started to get a ghost return. It's not coming from the plug, but it's strong. I'd say a lump of metal or something, buried in the wall this side of the plug.'

'How deep?' Gaunt asked.

'Not deep at all.'

'How big?'

'The size of a munitions crate perhaps?'

'What was the survey team doing if they didn't detect this?' Gaunt asked.

'Beg your pardon, sir?' asked Breccia.

'Nothing,' Gaunt said. 'Keep placing the charges, or Czytel will get grumpy. Leave this with me.'

Gaunt unfastened his entrenching tool from his pack, locked the folding blade in place, and started to dig away at the wall. It wasn't as tough as rockcrete, but it took some effort to chip the surface away.

'What the Throne are you doing?' Desruisseaux called out.

'Something you should have done,' Gaunt replied. He nodded to the men to keep Desruisseaux and his team back. Stone chips and dust began to spatter out of the hole he was making.

'Gaunt?' Czytel asked, approaching.

'One moment.'

'Gaunt, in the name of the Throne–'

'Just give me one moment, major,' Gaunt said more firmly, working hard and not looking at the other officer.

'I'm not in the mood for this, Gaunt,' Czytel growled.

'Just wait!' Gaunt snapped. He'd made a hole, and exposed what appeared to be a small cavity or sealed alcove. He cut some more away, grabbed his lamp, and peered inside.

'Throne!' he gasped.

'What is it?' Czytel asked, crowding in behind him. 'What can you see?'

Gaunt reached in with both hands and gently, reverently, lifted out the object inside the cavity.

It was old, covered in dust. It had evidently been damaged.

It was a helmet from a suit of Adeptus Astartes armour.

'Glory!' said Czytel.

Gaunt set it down, and wiped some of the dust away.

'Iron Snakes,' Gaunt said.

'How do you know?' asked Czytel.

'I studied at scholam,' Gaunt said. 'The Chapters of the Adeptus Astartes were a particular draw for me. This emblem is of the Iron Snakes of Ithaka.'

'Why was it buried in the wall?' asked Breccia.

Czytel looked at Gaunt.

'The Adeptus Astartes would only leave something this precious here if the place were significant,' Gaunt said.

'Exactly. A shrine,' replied Czytel.

'Or a warning,' said Gaunt. He looked over at the vox officer.

'Transmit to Assault Command,' he said. 'My security code. Ask them for instruction. Tell them I want to talk to someone in Tactical. Someone with archive access. Tell them we will wait and hold position here until the bombardment is over, if necessary.'

'Gaunt!' Czytel barked.

Gaunt turned to look at the advance's commanding officer. He couldn't remember ever seeing the major this angry before.

Czytel beckoned Gaunt over to him, away from the men.

'Throne damn you, Gaunt,' Czytel hissed, as soon as Gaunt was close enough. 'I've had enough of this. You're out of line. I'll be speaking to the general about your performance. You don't give orders. You do not have command here. You have gravely overstepped your remit, and–'

'Then start giving some orders that make sense,' Gaunt replied, his voice equally low. 'With *respect*, sir, you seem to be ignoring basic evidence. There are questions here, too many questions. They should be resolved before we continue.'

'Oh, such as?'

Gaunt hesitated. He thought of the serpent symbol etched on the Corvus-pattern helm, and how he had immediately connected it to the snake the operation was named after. Foolish. Such connections could be made wherever you looked in the galaxy. They meant nothing. Just another example of his oh-so-unreliable gut instinct. Except it didn't feel unreliable.

He couldn't explain it. He knew Czytel would ignore him if he tried, but he also remembered what Oktar had taught him: 'In war, Ibram, the instincts that really count are the ones that feel so strong and sharp, you can't put them into words.'

'I think this is a mistake,' he said.

'What are you saying, Gaunt?'

'I'm saying... your command decisions are questionable right now. You may disparage my education, sir, but I've always admired your inherent wit and intelligence, neither of which you seem to be employing at the moment. I'm asking for good judgement.'

Czytel's face flushed red in the cheeks and jowls. He began, in a no longer suppressed tone, to tell Gaunt exactly what he thought of him. Gaunt let it come. He stepped back, not even listening. His mind was settled. He began rehearsing in his mind the precise wording of Commissariat Article 297. *By the authority of my rank, and by the terms agreed in Article 297 of the code, I have to inform you your actions in command have been found unsound, and therefore you are hereby removed from command until further notice.*

As a commissar, Gaunt had never had to resort to command level censure before. It was a serious step. As soon as Czytel stopped ranting, he would look him square in the eye and recite those words.

He hoped the evidence would uphold such a drastic action. If it didn't, it would be the end of Gaunt's career.

'Sir!'

They both looked around. The vox-officer had approached them. He looked very uncomfortable.

'Sir, I sent your message, as instructed,' he said. 'I told them quite specifically we would wait until the bombardment had stopped if necessary.'

'And?' asked Gaunt.

'The bombardment ended about three hours ago, sir,' said the voxman.

No one spoke. Gaunt looked at Czytel, and saw a new emotion cross-ing the major's face. The ground shook, and a little patter of dirt spilled down from the tunnel wall.

Gaunt turned, got back up on the ramp, and walked to the rockcrete plug. He took off his glove and pressed his hand against the plug's outer surface.

He felt the vibration. He felt something heaving and shaking deep underground, behind the massive plug.

Something trying to get out.

He looked back at Czytel.

'We stop,' he said. 'Right now.'

There was a sudden blast of gunfire from behind them.

Everyone scattered, desperate for cover. Las-rounds zipped through the chamber. Gaunt ducked behind a support beam, and saw that Wal Desruisseaux had snatched a lasrifle from Trooper Gebbs and opened fire. Gebbs was dead. Another two men had been dropped, dead or badly hit. Blood decorated the ancient tiled floor.

Desruisseaux was retreating back up the cavern, firing from the hip on auto. In the confined space, it was enough to keep everybody ducking.

'Get him! Shoot him!' Czytel yelled, then grunted as a las-round hit his left elbow and spun him onto the ground. Head down, Gaunt dashed across the space to the major's side.

'I'm all right! I'm all right!' Czytel growled, clutching his arm. 'Just get the bastard!'

Gaunt nodded. He had already drawn his bolt pistol. He started yell-ing orders to the men pinned around him.

Desruisseaux had reached decent cover in the rear part of the cham-ber. He had excellent angles on any assault that came at him. That smacked of military training. It would be suicide to move until the maniac had run out of ammunition.

Gaunt realised they didn't have that long. Desruisseaux was concen-trating his fire on the area of the plug and the ramp. He was trying to hit the panniers of charges that Breccia had left there.

He was trying to set them off.

Gaunt winced as a las-round banged off the edge of one of the steel containers. The gel charges could take quite a lot of rough treatment before they'd detonate, but a square-on hit from a las-bolt was not a healthy idea.

'Zennet!' Gaunt yelled. The squad's marksman was in cover on the other side of the chamber. He had lined up behind a pile of stone blocks, his long-las cradled. He had no clear angle.

'I'm going to try to buy you one clean opening,' Gaunt yelled over the gunfire. 'Don't waste it!'

Zennet nodded, and took aim.

Gaunt took a deep breath and then popped up fast, firing his bolt pistol in a two-handed grip. The bolt pistol was a powerful piece. Neither it, nor any of the lasweapons carried by the advance, had enough penetrative power to get through the cover Desruisseaux was using, but the bolt pistol's mass-reactive rounds exploded on impact. Unlike the las-fire that Czytel's men had been able to throw at Desruisseaux, which had chipped and dented and sparked off his cover, the bolt-round produced a withering cluster of explosions that sent debris spitting and flying in all directions.

It was enough to make Desruisseaux start and react. He moved sideways, towards the cover of a nearby pillar.

He was open for a second.

Zennet took the shot and the long-las howled.

X

They looked at the body. Gaunt tore open the front of Desruisseaux's worksuit, and they saw the old tattoo on his chest. It wasn't something you'd want to look at for long.

'A cultist,' murmured Czytel. He was looking on as Danks bandaged his elbow.

'A Charismite, I suspect,' said Gaunt. He got up. 'Check the other members of the survey team,' he told Hiskol. 'Have them strip down and check them for marks. He might have been working alone, infiltrating a genuine survey team, but I doubt it.'

Hiskol nodded.

'So,' mused Czytel, 'the Ruinous Powers wanted us to do their dirty work for them.'

'There's something behind that plug,' said Gaunt. 'Something they wanted to let out. No doubt it would have caused great disruption to the invasion of Formal Prime. Maybe stopped the whole crusade in its tracks.'

He glanced back at the plug.

'This cult evidently didn't have access to the explosives they needed, so they bluffed us into doing it.'

'What do you suggest we report?' Czytel asked.

'That we found a shrine. It just wasn't one of ours.'

Gaunt paused.

'Although, it was. The Iron Snakes closed this off a long time ago, and left a warning. I think the offerings here were offerings of respect to them and their efforts, not to whatever lies behind that plug. That's our shrine, the wall outside. The years of devotion.'

Gaunt holstered his bolt pistol.

'We inform the Inquisition and let them deal with it. The area will probably be interdicted. Some things are better left buried. For the good of the Imperium.'

He looked at the battered helm.

'Though we should see if we can have this sent back to Ithaka. With honours.'

The ground shook.

'Gaunt?' said Czytel quietly. 'What about... about our altercation? I want to–'

Gaunt shook his head.

'It was a difficult situation. We both did what we thought best. My report will say so.'

'But–'

'For the good of the Imperium, remember?' said Gaunt. 'For the Hyrkan regiment, at least. Some things are better left buried.'

The ground shook again.

'I think we should pull back from this area,' said Czytel.

Gaunt nodded.

'Look, I appreciate your attitude, Gaunt,' Czytel said. 'I showed you disrespect and I'm sorry. I think you've got a fine career ahead of you, no thanks to old bastards like me. Maybe one day you'll end up serving alongside a major who'll show you the proper respect, eh?'

Czytel tried to make a jolly laugh.

'I'm sure I will, sir,' said Ibram Gaunt.

FIRST AND ONLY

'The High Lords of Terra, lauding the great Warmaster Slaydo's efforts on Khulen, tasked him with raising a crusade force to liberate the Sabbat Worlds, a cluster of nearly one hundred inhabited systems along the edge of the Segmentum Pacificus. From a massive fleet deployment, nearly a billion Imperial Guard advanced into the Sabbat Worlds, supported by forces of the Adeptus Astartes and the Adeptus Mechanicus, with whom Slaydo had formed cooperative pacts.

'After ten hard-fought years of dogged advance, Slaydo's great victory came at Balhaut, where he opened the way to drive a wedge into the heart of the Sabbat Worlds.

'But there Slaydo fell. Bickering and rivalry then beset his officers as they vied to take his place. Lord High Militant General Hechtor Dravere was an obvious successor, but Slaydo himself had chosen the younger commander, Macaroth.

'With Macaroth as warmaster, the Crusade force pushed on, into its second decade, and deeper into the Sabbat Worlds, facing theatres of war that began to make Balhaut seem like a mere opening skirmish...'

— from *A History of the Later Imperial Crusades*

PART ONE

NUBILA REACH

The two Faustus-class Interceptors swept in low over a thousand slowly spinning tonnes of jade asteroid and decelerated to coasting velocity. Striated blurs of shift-speed light flickered off their gunmetal hulls. The saffron haze of the nebula called the Nubila Reach hung as a spread backdrop for them, a thousand light years wide, a hazy curtain which enfolded the edges of the Sabbat Worlds.

Each of these patrol Interceptors was an elegant barb about one hundred paces from jutting nose to raked tail. The Faustus were lean, powerful warships that looked like serrated cathedral spires with splayed flying buttresses at the rear to house the main thrusters. Their armoured flanks bore the Imperial eagle, together with the green markings and insignia of the Segmentum Pacificus Fleet.

Locked in the hydraulic arrestor struts of the command seat in the lead ship, Wing Captain Torten LaHain forced down his heart rate as the ship decelerated. Synchronous mind-impulse links bequeathed by the Adeptus Mechanicus hooked his meta-bolism to the ship's ancient systems, and he lived and breathed every nuance of its motion, power-output and response.

LaHain was a twenty-year veteran. He'd piloted Faustus Interceptors for so long, they seemed an extension of his body. He glanced down into the flight annex directly below and behind the command seat, where his observation officer was at work at the navigation station.

'Well?' he asked over the intercom.

The observer checked off his calculations against several glowing runes on the board. 'Steer five points starboard. The astropath's instructions are to sweep down the edge of the gas clouds for a final look, and then it's back to the fleet.'

Behind him, there was a murmur. The astropath, hunched in his small

31

throne-cradle, stirred. Hundreds of filament leads linked the astropath's socket-encrusted skull to the massive sensory apparatus in the Faustus's belly. Each one was marked with a small, yellowing parchment label, inscribed with words LaHain didn't want to have to read. There was the cloying smell of incense and unguents.

'What did he say?' LaHain asked.

The observer shrugged. 'Who knows? Who wants to?' he said.

The astropath's brain was constantly surveying and processing the vast wave of astronomical data which the ship's sensors pumped into it, and psychically probing the warp beyond. Small patrol ships like this, with their astropathic cargo, were the early warning arm of the fleet. The work was hard on the psyker's mind, and the odd moan or grimace was commonplace. There had been worse. They'd gone through a nickel-rich asteroid field the previous week and the psyker had gone into spasms.

'Flight check,' LaHain said into the intercom.

'Tail turret, aye!' crackled back the servitor at the rear of the ship.

'Flight engineer ready, by the Emperor!' fuzzed the voice of the engine chamber.

LaHain signalled his wingman. 'Moselle... you run forward and begin the sweep. We'll lag a way behind you as a double-check. Then we'll pull for home.'

'Mark that,' the pilot of the other ship replied and his craft gunned forward, a sudden blur that left twinkling pearls in its wake.

LaHain was about to kick in behind when the voice of the astropath came over the link. It was rare for the man to speak to the rest of the crew.

'Captain... move to the following co-ordinates and hold. I am receiving a signal. A message... source unknown.'

LaHain did as he was instructed and the ship banked around, motors flaring in quick, white bursts. The observer swung all the sensor arrays to bear.

'What is this?' LaHain asked, impatient. Unscheduled manoeuvres off a carefully set patrol sweep did not sit comfortably with him.

The astropath took a moment to respond, clearing his throat. 'It is an astropathic communiqué, struggling to get through the warp. It is coming from extreme long range. I must gather it and relay it to Fleet Command.'

'Why?' LaHain asked. This was all too irregular.

'I sense it is secret. It is primary level intelligence. It is Vermilion level.'

There was a long pause, a silence aboard the small, slim craft broken only by the hum of the drive, the chatter of the displays and the whirr of the air-scrubbers.

'Vermilion...' LaHain breathed.

Vermilion was the highest clearance level used by the Crusade's cryptographers. It was unheard of, mythical. Even main battle schemes usually only warranted a Magenta. He felt an icy tightness in his wrists, a tremor in his heart.

Sympathetically, the Interceptor's reactor fibrillated. LaHain swallowed.

A routine day had just become very un-routine. He knew he had to commit everything to the correct and efficient recovery of this data.

'How long do you need?' he asked over the link.

Another pause. 'The ritual will take a few moments. Do not disturb me as I concentrate. I need as long as possible,' the astropath said. There was a phlegmy, strained edge to his voice. In a moment, that voice was murmuring a prayer. The air temperature in the cabin dropped perceptibly. Something, somewhere, sighed.

LaHain flexed his grip on the rudder stick, his skin turning to gooseflesh. He hated the witchcraft of the psykers. He could taste it in his mouth, bitter, sharp. Cold sweat beaded under his flight-mask. Hurry up! he thought... It was taking too long, they were idling and vulnerable; and he wanted his skin to stop crawling.

The astropath's murmured prayer continued. LaHain looked out of the canopy at the swathe of pinkish mist that folded away from him into the heart of the nebula a billion kilometres away. The cold, stabbing light of ancient suns slanted and shafted through it like dawn light on gossamer. Dark-bellied clouds swirled in slow, silent blossoms.

'Contacts!' the observer yelled suddenly. 'Three! No, four! Fast as hell and coming straight in!'

LaHain snapped to attention. 'Angle and lead time?'

The observer rattled out a set of co-ordinates and LaHain steered the nose towards them. 'They're coming in fast!' the observer repeated. 'Throne of Earth, but they're moving!'

LaHain looked across his over-sweep board and saw the runic cursors flashing as they edged into the tactical grid.

'Defence system activated! Weapons to ready!' he barked. Drum autoloaders chattered in the chin turret forward of him as he armed the autocannons, and energy reservoirs whined as they powered up the main forward-firing plasma guns.

'Wing Two to Wing One!' Moselle's voice rasped over the long-range vox-caster. 'They're all over me! Break and run! Break and run in the name of the Emperor!'

The other Interceptor was coming at him at close to full thrust. LaHain's enhanced optics, amplified and linked via the canopy's systems, saw Moselle's ship while it was still a thousand kilometres away.

Behind it, lazy and slow, came the vampiric shapes, the predatory ships of Chaos. Fire patterns winked in the russet darkness. Yellow traceries of venomous death.

Moselle's scream, abruptly ended, tore through the vox-cast.

The racing Interceptor disappeared in a rapidly expanding, superheated fireball. The three attackers thundered on through the fire wash.

'They're coming for us! Bring her about!' LaHain yelled and threw the Faustus round, gunning the engines. 'How much longer?' he bellowed at the astropath.

'The communiqué is received. I am now... relaying...' the astropath gasped, at the edge of his limits.

'Fast as you can! We have no time!' LaHain said.

The sleek fighting ship blinked forward, thrust-drive roaring blue heat. LaHain rejoiced at the singing of the engine in his blood. He was pushing the threshold tolerances of the ship. Amber alert sigils were lighting his display. LaHain was slowly being crushed into the cracked, ancient leather of his command chair.

In the tail turret, the gunner servitor traversed the twin auto-cannons, hunting for a target. He didn't see the attackers, but he saw their absence – the flickering darkness against the stars.

The turret guns screamed into life, blitzing out a scarlet-tinged, boiling stream of hypervelocity fire.

Indicators screamed shrill warnings in the cockpit. The enemy had obtained multiple target lock. Down below, the observer was bawling up at LaHain, demanding evasion procedures. Over the link, Flight Engineer Manus was yelling something about a stress-injection leak.

LaHain was serene. 'Is it done?' he asked the astropath calmly.

There was another long pause. The astropath was lolling weakly in his cradle. Near to death, his brain ruined by the trauma of the act, he murmured, 'It is finished.'

LaHain wrenched the Interceptor in a savage loop and presented himself to the pursuers with the massive forward plasma array and the nose guns blasting. He couldn't outrun them or outfight them, but by the Emperor he'd take at least one with him before he went.

The chin turret spat a thousand heavy bolter rounds a second. The plasma guns howled phosphorescent death into the void. One of the shadow-shapes exploded in a bright blister of flame, its shredded fuselage and mainframe splitting out, carried along by the burning, incandescent bow-wave of igniting propellant.

LaHain scored a second kill too. He ripped open the belly of another attacker, spilling its pressurised guts into the void. It burst like a swollen balloon, spinning round under the shuddering impact and spewing its contents in a fire trail behind itself.

A second later, a rain of toxic and corrosive warheads, each a sliver of metal like a dirty needle, raked the Faustus end to end. They detonated the astropath's head and explosively atomised the observer out through the punctured hull. Another killed the flight engineer outright and destroyed the reactor interlock.

Two billiseconds after that, stress fractures shattered the Faustus class Interceptor like a glass bottle. A super-dense explosion boiled out from the core, vaporising the ship and LaHain with it.

The corona of the blast rippled out for eighty kilometres until it vanished in the nebula's haze.

A MEMORY

DARENDARA,
TWENTY YEARS EARLIER

The winter palace was besieged. In the woods on the north shore of the frozen lake, the field guns of the Imperial Guard thumped and rumbled. Snow fluttered down on them, and each shuddering retort brought heavier falls slumping down from the tree limbs. Brass shell-cases clanked as they spun out of the returning breeches and fell, smoking, into snow cover that was quickly becoming trampled slush.

Over the lake, the palace crumbled. One wing was now ablaze, and shell holes were appearing in the high walls or impacting in the vast arches of the steep roofs beyond them. Each blast threw up tiles and fragments of beams, and puffs of snow like icing sugar. Some shots fell short, bursting the ice skin of the lake and sending up cold geysers of water, mud, and sharp chunks that looked like broken glass.

Commissar-General Delane Oktar, chief political officer of the Hyrkan Regiments, stood in the back of his winter-camouflage painted halftrack and watched the demolition through his field scope. When Fleet Command had sent the Hyrkans in to quell the uprising on Darendara, he had known it would come to this. A bloody, bitter end. How many opportunities had they given the Secessionists to surrender?

Too many, according to that rat-turd Colonel Dravere, who commanded the armoured brigades in support of the Hyrkan infantry. That would be a matter Dravere would gleefully report in his despatches, Oktar knew. Dravere was a career soldier with the pedigree of noble blood who was gripping the ladder of advancement so tightly with both hands that his feet were free to kick out at those on lower rungs.

Oktar didn't care. The victory mattered, not the glory. As a commissar-general, his authority was well liked, and no one doubted his loyalty to the Imperium, his resolute adherence to the primary dictates, or the rousing fury of his speeches to the men. But he believed war was a simple thing, where caution and restraint could win far more for less cost.

He had seen the reverse too many times before. The command echelons generally believed in the theory of attrition when it came to the Imperial Guard. Any foe could be ground into pulp if you threw enough at them, and the Guard was, to them, a limitless supply of cannon fodder for just such a purpose.

That was not Oktar's way. He had schooled the officer cadre of the Hyrkans to believe it too. He had taught General Caernavar and his staff to value every man, and knew the majority of the six thousand Hyrkans, many by name. Oktar had been with them from the start, from the First Founding on the high plateaux of Hyrkan, those vast, gale-wracked industrial deserts of granite and grassland. Six regiments they had founded there, six proud regiments, and just the first of what Oktar hoped would be a long line of Hyrkan soldiers, who would set the name of their planet high on the honour roll of the Imperial Guard, from Founding to Founding.

They were brave boys. He would not waste them, and he would not have the officers waste them. He glanced down from his half-track into the tree-lines where the gun teams serviced their thumping limbers. The Hyrkan were a strong breed, drawn and pale, with almost colourless hair which they preferred to wear short and severe. They wore dark grey battledress with beige webbing and short-billed forage caps of the same pale hue. In this cold theatre, they also had woven gloves and long greatcoats. Those labouring at the guns, though, were stripped down to their beige undershirts, their webbing hanging loosely around their hips as they bent and carried shells, and braced for firing in the close heat of the concussions. It looked odd, in these snowy wastes, with breath steaming the air, to see men moving through gunsmoke in thin shirts, hot and ruddy with sweat.

He knew their strengths and weaknesses to a man, knew exactly who best to send forward to reconnoitre, to snipe, to lead a charge offensive, to scout for mines, to cut wire, to interrogate prisoners. He valued each and every man for his abilities in the field of war. He would not waste them. He and General Caernavar would use them, each one in his particular way, and they would win and win and win again, a hundred times more than any who used his regiments like bullet-soaks in the bloody frontline.

Men like Dravere. Oktar dreaded to think what that beast might do when finally given field command of an action like this. Let the little piping runt in his starched collar sound off to the high brass about him. Let him make a fool of himself. This wasn't his victory to win.

Oktar jumped down from the vehicle's flatbed and handed his scope to his sergeant. 'Where's the Boy?' he asked, in his soft, penetrating tones.

The sergeant smiled to himself, knowing the Boy hated to be known as 'The Boy'.

'Supervising the batteries on the rise, commissar-general,' he said in a faultless Low Gothic, flavoured with the clipped, guttural intonations of the Hyrkan home world accent.

'Send him to me,' Oktar said, rubbing his hands gently to encourage circulation. 'I think it's time he got a chance to advance himself.'

The sergeant turned to go, then paused. 'Advance himself, commissar – or advance, himself?'

Oktar grinned like a wolf. 'Both, naturally.'

The Hyrkan sergeant bounded up the ridge to the field guns at the top, where the trees had been stripped a week before by a Secessionist airstrike. The splintered trunks were denuded back to their pale bark, and the ground under the snow was thick with wood pulp, twigs and uncountable fragrant needles.

There would be no more airstrikes, of course. Not now. The Secessionist airforce had been operating out of two airstrips south of the winter palace which had been rendered useless by Colonel Dravere's armoured units. Not that they'd had much to begin with – maybe sixty ancient-pattern slamjets with cycling cannons in the armpits of the wings and struts on the wingtips for the few bombs they could muster.

The sergeant had cherished a sneaking admiration for the Secessionist fliers, though. They'd tried damn hard, taking huge risks to drop their payloads where it counted, and without the advantage of good air-to-ground instrumentation. He would never forget the slamjet which took out their communication bunker in the snow lines of the mountain a fortnight before. It had passed low twice to get a fix, bouncing through the frag-bursts which the anti-air batteries threw up all around it. He could still see the faces of the pilot and the gunner as they passed, plainly visible because the canopy was hauled back so they could get a target by sight alone.

Brave... desperate. Not a whole lot of difference in the sergeant's book. Determined, too – that was the commissar-general's view. They knew they were going to lose this war before it even started, but still they tried to break loose from the Imperium. The sergeant knew that Oktar admired them; and, in turn, he admired the way Oktar had urged the chief of staff to give the rebels every chance to surrender. What was the point of killing for no purpose?

Still, the sergeant had shuddered when the three thousand pounder had fishtailed down into the communications bunker and flattened it. Just as he had cheered when the thumping, traversing quad-barrels of the Hydra anti-air batteries had pegged the slamjet as it pulled away. It looked like it had been kicked from behind, jerking up at the tail and then tumbling, end over end, as it exploded and burned in a long, dying fall into the distant trees.

The sergeant reached the hilltop and caught sight of the Boy. He was standing amidst the batteries, hefting fresh shells into the arms of the gunners from the stockpiles half-buried under blast curtains. Tall, pale, lean and powerful, the Boy intimidated the sergeant. Unless death claimed him first, the Boy would one day become a commissar in his own right. Until then, he enjoyed the rank of cadet commissar, and served his tutor Oktar with enthusiasm and boundless energy. Like the commissar-general, the Boy wasn't Hyrkan. The sergeant thought then, for the first time, that he didn't even know where the Boy was from – and the Boy probably didn't know either.

'The commissar-general wants you,' he told the Boy as he reached him.

The Boy grabbed another shell from the pile and swung it round to the waiting gunner.

'Did you hear me?' the sergeant asked.

'I heard,' said Cadet Commissar Ibram Gaunt.

He knew he was being tested. He knew that this was responsibility and that he'd better not mess it up. Gaunt also knew that it was his moment to prove to his mentor Oktar that he had the makings of a commissar.

There was no set duration for the training of a cadet. After education at the Schola Progenium and Guard basic training, a cadet received the rest of his training in the field, and the promotion to full commissarial level was a judgement matter for his commanding officer. Oktar, and Oktar alone, could make him or break him. His career as an Imperial commissar, to dispense discipline, inspiration and the love of the God-Emperor of Terra to the greatest fighting force in creation, hinged upon his performance.

Gaunt was an intense, quiet young man, and a commissarial post had been his dearest ambition since his earliest days in the Schola Progenium. But he trusted Oktar to be fair. The commissar-general had personally selected him for service from the cadet honour class, and had become in the last eighteen months almost a father to Gaunt. A stern, ruthless father, perhaps. The father he had never really known.

'See that burning wing?' Oktar had said. 'That's a way in. The Secessionists must be falling back into their inner chambers by now. General Caernavar and I propose putting a few squads in through that hole and cutting out their centre. Are you up to it?'

Gaunt had paused, his heart in his throat. 'Sir... you want me to...'

'Lead them in. Yes. Don't look so shocked, Ibram. You're always asking me for a chance to prove your leadership. Who do you want?'

'My choice?'

'Your choice.'

'Men from the fourth brigade. Tanhause is a good squad leader and his men are specialists in room to room fighting. Give me them, and Rychlind's heavy weapons team.'

'Good choices, Ibram. Prove me right.'

They moved past the fire and into long halls decorated with tapestries where the wind moaned and light fell slantwise from the high windows. Cadet Gaunt led the men personally, as Oktar would have done, the lasgun held tightly in his hands, his blue-trimmed cadet commissar uniform perfectly turned out.

In the fifth hallway, the Secessionists began their last-ditch counterattack.

Las-fire cracked and blasted at them. Cadet Gaunt ducked behind an antique sofa that swiftly became a pile of antique matchwood. Tanhause moved up behind him.

'What now?' the lean, corded Hyrkan major asked.

'Give me grenades,' Gaunt said.

They were provided. Gaunt took the webbing belt and set the timers on all twenty grenades. 'Call up Walthem,' he told Tanhause.

Trooper Walthem moved up. Gaunt knew he was famous in the regiment for the power of his throw. He'd been a javelin champion back home on Hyrkan.

'Put this where it counts,' Gaunt said.

Walthem hefted the belt of grenades with a tiny grunt. Sixty paces down, the corridor disintegrated.

They moved in, through the drifting smoke and masonry dust. The spirit had left the Secessionist defence. They found Degredd, the rebel leader, lying dead with his mouth fused around the barrel of his lasgun.

Gaunt signalled to General Caernavar and Commissar-General Oktar that the fight was over. He marshalled the prisoners out with their hands on their heads as Hyrkan troops set about disabling gun emplacements and munitions stores.

* * *

'What do we do with her?' Tanhause asked him.

Gaunt turned from the assault cannon he had been stripping of its firing pin.

The girl was lovely, white-skinned and black haired, as was the pedigree of the Darendarans. She clawed at the clenching hands of the Hyrkan troops hustling her and other prisoners down the draughty hallway.

When she saw Gaunt, she stopped dead. He expected vitriol, anger, the verbal abuse so common in the defeated and imprisoned whose beliefs and cause had been crushed. But what he saw in her face froze him in surprise. Her eyes were glassy, deep, like polished marble. There was a look in her face as she stared back at him. Gaunt shivered when he realised the look was recognition.

'There will be seven,' she said suddenly, speaking surprisingly perfect High Gothic with no trace of the local accent. The voice didn't seem to be her own. It was guttural, and its words did not match the movement of her lips. 'Seven stones of power. Cut them and you will be free. Do not kill them. But first you must find your ghosts.'

'Enough of your madness!' Tanhause snapped, then ordered the men to take her away. The girl was vacant-eyed by now and froth dribbled down her chin. She was plainly sliding into the throes of a trance. The men were wary of her, and pushed her along at arm's length, scared of her magic. The temperature in the hallway itself seemed to drop. At once, the breaths of all of the men steamed the air. It smelled heavy, burnt and metallic, the way it did before a storm. Gaunt felt the hairs on the back of his neck rise. He could not take his eyes off the murmuring girl as the men bustled her away gingerly.

'The Inquisition will deal with her,' Tanhause shivered. 'Another untrained psyker witch working for the enemy.'

'Wait!' Gaunt said and strode over to her. He tensed, scared of the supernaturally-touched being he confronted. 'What do you mean? "Seven stones"? "Ghosts"?'

Her eyes rolled back, pupilless. The cracked old voice bubbled out of her quivering lips. 'The warp knows you, Ibram.'

He stepped back as if he had been stung. 'How did you know my name?'

She didn't answer. Not coherently, anyway. She began to thrash, gibber and spit. Nonsense words and animal sounds issued from her shuddering throat.

'Take her away!' Tanhause barked.

One man stepped in, then spun to his knees, flailing, blood streaming from his nose. She had done nothing but glance at him. Snarling oaths and protective charms, the others laid in with the butts of their lasguns.

Gaunt watched the corridor for five full minutes after the girl had been dragged away. The air remained cold long after she had disappeared. He looked around at the drawn, anxious face of Tanhause.

'Pay it no heed,' the Hyrkan veteran said, trying to sound confident. He could see the cadet was spooked. Just inexperience, he was sure. Once the Boy had seen a few years, a few campaigns, he'd learn to shut out the mad ravings of the foe and their tainted, insane rants. It was the only way to sleep at night.

Gaunt was still tense. 'What was that about?' he asked, as if he hoped that Tanhause could explain the girl's words.

'Rubbish is what. Forget it, sir.'

'Right. Forget it. Right.'

But Gaunt never did.

PART TWO

FORTIS BINARY
FORGE-WORLD

ONE

The night sky was matt and dark, like the material of the fatigues they wore, day after day. The dawn stabbed in, as silent and sudden as a knife-wound, welling up a dull redness through the black cloth of the sky.

Eventually the sun rose, casting raw amber light down over the trench lines. The star was big, heavy and red, like a rotten, roasted fruit. Dawn lightning crackled a thousand kilometres away.

Colm Corbec woke, acknowledged briefly the thousand aches and snarls in his limbs and frame, and rolled out of his billet in the trench dugout. His great, booted feet kissed into the grey slime of the trench floor where the duckboards didn't meet.

Corbec was a large man on the wrong side of forty, built like an ox and going to fat. His broad and hairy forearms were decorated with blue spiral tattoos and his beard was thick and shaggy. He wore the black webbing and fatigues of the Tanith and also the ubiquitous camo-cloak which had become their trademark. He also shared the pale complexion, black hair and blue eyes of his people. He was the colonel of the Tanith First and Only, the so-called Gaunt's Ghosts.

He yawned. Down the trench, under the frag-sack and gabion breastwork and the spools of rusting razor wire, the Ghosts awoke too. There were coughs, gasps, soft yelps as nightmares became real in the light of waking. Matches struck under the low bevel of the parapet; firearms were un-swaddled and the damp cleaned off. Firing mechanisms were slammed in and out. Food parcels were unhooked from their vermin-proof positions up on the billet roofs.

Shuffling in the ooze, Corbec stretched and cast an eye down the long, zigzag traverses of the trench to see where the picket sentries were returning, pale and weary, asleep on their feet. The twinkling

lights of the vast communication up-link masts flashed eleven kilometres behind them, rising between the rusting, shell-pocked roofs
of the gargantuan shipyard silos and the vast Titan fabrication bunkers and foundry sheds of the Adeptus Mechanicus tech-priesthood.

The dark stealth capes of the picket sentries, the distinctive uniform
of the Tanith First and Only, were lank and stiff with dried mud. Their
replacements at the picket, bleary eyed and puffy, slapped them on the
arms as they passed, exchanging jokes and cigarettes. The night sentries, though, were too weary to be forthcoming.

They were ghosts, returning to their graves, Corbec thought. As are
we all.

In a hollow under the trench wall, Mad Larkin, the first squad's
wiry sniper, was cooking up something that approximated caffeine in
a battered tin tray over a fusion burner. The acrid stink hooked Corbec by the nostrils.

'Give me some of that, Larks,' the colonel said, squelching across
the trench.

Larkin was a skinny, stringy, unhealthily pale man in his fifties with
three silver hoops through his left ear and a purple-blue spiral-wyrm
tattoo on his sunken right cheek. He offered up a misshapen metal cup.
There was a fragile look, of fatigue and fear, in his wrinkled eyes. 'This
morning, do you reckon? This morning?'

Corbec pursed his lips, enjoying the warmth of the cup in his hefty
paw. 'Who knows...' His voice trailed off.

High in the orange troposphere, a matched pair of Imperial fighters
shrieked over, curved around the lines and plumed away north. Fire
smoke lifted from Adeptus Mechanicus work-temples on the horizon,
great cathedrals of industry, now burning from within. A second later,
the dry wind brought the *crump* of detonations.

Corbec watched the fighters go and sipped his drink. It was almost
unbearably disgusting. 'Good stuff,' he muttered to Larkin.

A kilometre off, down the etched zigzag of the trench line, Trooper Fulke
was busily going crazy. Major Rawne, the regiment's second officer, was
woken by the sound of a lasgun firing at close range, the phosphorescent impacts ringing into frag-sacks and mud.

Rawne spun out of his cramped billet as his adjutant, Feygor,
stumbled up nearby. There were shouts and oaths from the men
around them. Fulke had seen vermin, the ever-present vermin, attacking his rations, chewing into the plastic seals with their snapping lizard
mouths. As Rawne blundered down the trench, the animals skittered
away past him, lopping on their big, rabbit-legs, their lice-ridden pelts

smeared flat with ooze. Fulke was firing his lasgun on full auto into his sleeping cavity under the bulwark, screaming obscenities at the top of his fractured voice.

Feygor got there first, wrestling the weapon from the bawling trooper. Fulke turned his fists on the adjutant, mashing his nose, splashing up grey mud-water with his scrambling boots.

Rawne slid in past Feygor, and put Fulke out with a hook to the jaw. There was a crack of bone and the trooper went down, whimpering, in the drainage gully.

'Assemble a firing squad detail,' Rawne spat at the bloody Feygor unceremoniously and stalked back to his dugout.

Trooper Bragg wove back to his bunk. A huge man, unarguably the largest of the Ghosts, he was a peaceable, simple soul. They called him 'Try Again' Bragg because of his terrible aim. He'd been on picket all night and now his bed was singing a lullaby he couldn't resist. He slammed into young Trooper Caffran at a turn in the dugout and almost knocked the smaller man flat. Bragg hauled him up, his weariness clamming his apologies in his mouth.

'No harm done, Try,' Caffran said. 'Get to your billet.'

Bragg blundered on. Two paces more and he'd even forgotten what he'd done. He simply had an afterimage memory of an apology he should have made to a good friend. Fatigue was total.

Caffran ducked down into the crevice of the command dugout, just off the third communication trench. There was a thick polyfibre shield over the door, and layers of anti-gas curtaining. He knocked twice and then pulled back the heavy drapes and dropped into the deep cavity.

TWO

The officer's dugout was deep, accessed only by an aluminium ladder lashed to the wall. Inside, the light was a frosty white from the sodium burners. The floor was well-made of duckboards and there were even such marks of civilisation as shelves, books, charts and an aroma of decent caffeine.

Sliding down into the command burrow, Caffran noticed first Brin Milo, the sixteen year-old mascot the Ghosts had acquired at their Founding. Word was, Milo had been rescued personally from the fires of their homeworld by the commissar himself, and this bond had led him to his status of regimental musician and adjutant to their senior officer. Caffran didn't like to be around the boy much. There was something about his youth and his brightness of eye that reminded him of the world they had lost. It was ironic – back on Tanith with only a year or two between them, they like as not would have been friends.

Milo was setting out breakfast on a small camp table. The smell was delicious: cooking eggs and ham and some toasted bread. Caffran envied the commissar, his position and his luxuries.

'Has the commissar slept well?' Caffran asked.

'He hasn't slept at all,' Milo replied. 'He's been up through the night reviewing reconnaissance transmissions from the orbital watch.'

Caffran hesitated in the entranceway to the burrow, clutching his sealed purse of communiqués. He was a small man, for a Tanith, and young, with shaved black hair and a blue dragon tattoo on his temple.

'Come in, sit yourself down.' At first, Caffran thought Milo had spoken, but it was the commissar himself. Ibram Gaunt emerged from the rear chamber of the dugout looking pale and drawn. He was dressed in his uniform trousers and a white singlet with regimental braces strapped tight in place. He gestured Caffran to the seat opposite him at the small camp table and then swung down onto the other stool.

Caffran hesitated again and then sat at the place indicated.

Gaunt was a tall, hard man in his forties, and his lean face utterly matched his name. Trooper Caffran admired the commissar enormously and had studied his previous actions at Balhaut, at Formal Prime, his service with the Hyrkan Eighth, even his majestic command of the disaster that was Tanith.

Gaunt seemed more tired than Caffran had ever seen, but he trusted this man to bring them through. If anyone could redeem the Ghosts it would be Ibram Gaunt. He was a rare beast, a political officer who had been granted full regimental command and the brevet rank of colonel.

'I'm sorry to interrupt your breakfast, commissar,' Caffran said, sitting uneasily at the camp table, fussing with the purse of communiqués.

'Not at all, Caffran. In fact, you're just in time to join me.' Caffran hesitated once more, not knowing if this was a joke.

'I'm serious,' Gaunt said. 'You look as hungry as I feel. And I'm sure Brin has cooked up more than enough for two.'

As if on cue, the boy produced two ceramic plates of food – mashed eggs and grilled ham with tough, toasted chunks of wheatbread. Caffran looked at the plate in front of him for a moment as Gaunt tucked into his with relish.

'Go on, eat up. It's not every day you get a chance to taste officers' rations,' Gaunt said, wolfing down a forkful of eggs.

Caffran nervously picked up his own fork and began to eat. It was the best meal he'd had in sixty days. It reminded him of his days as an apprentice engineer in the wood mills of lost Tanith, back before the

Founding and the Loss, of the wholesome suppers served on the long tables of the refectory after last shift. Before long, he was consuming the breakfast with as much gusto as the commissar, who smiled at him appreciatively.

The boy Milo then produced a steaming pot of thick caffeine, and it was time to talk business.

'So, what do the dispatches tell us this morning?' Gaunt started.

'I don't know, sir,' Caffran said, pulling out the communiqué purse and dropping it onto the tabletop in front of him. 'I just carry these things. I never ask what's in them.'

Gaunt paused for a moment, chewing a mouthful of eggs and ham. He took a long sip of his steaming drink and then reached out for the purse.

Caffran thought to look away as Gaunt unsealed the plastic envelope and read the print-out strips contained within.

'I've been up all night at that thing,' Gaunt said, gesturing over his shoulder to the green glow of the tactical communication artificer, built into the muddy wall of the command burrow. 'And it's told me nothing.'

Gaunt reviewed the dispatches that spilled out of Caffran's purse. 'I bet you and the men are wondering how long we'll be dug into this hell-hole,' Gaunt said. 'The truth is, I can't tell you. This is a war of attrition. We could be here for months.'

Caffran was by now feeling so warm and satisfied by the good meal he had just eaten that the commissar could have told him his mother had been murdered by orks and he wouldn't have worried much.

'Sir?' Milo's voice was a sudden intruder into the gentle calm.

Gaunt looked up. 'What is it, Brin?' he said.

'I think... that is... I think there's an attack coming.'

Caffran chuckled. 'How could you know–' he began but the commissar cut him off.

'Somehow, Milo's sensed each attack so far before it's come. Each one. Seems he has a gift for anticipating shell-fall. Perhaps it's his young ears.' Gaunt crooked a wry grin at Caffran. 'Do you want to argue, eh?'

Caffran was about to answer when the first wail of shells howled in.

THREE

Gaunt leapt to his feet, knocking the camp table over. It was the sudden motion rather than the scream of incoming shells which made Caffran leap up in shock. Gaunt was scrabbling for his side-arm, hanging in its holster on a hook by the steps. He grabbed the speech-horn of the vox-caster set, slung under the racks that held his books.

'Gaunt to all units! To arms! To arms! Prepare for maximum resistance!'

Caffran didn't wait for any further instruction. He was already up the steps and banging through the gas curtains as volleys of shells assaulted their trenches. Huge plumes of vaporised mud spat up from the trench head behind him and the narrow gully was full of the yells of suddenly animated guardsmen.

A shell whinnied down low across his position and dug a hole the size of a drop-ship behind the rear breastwork of the trench. Liquid mud drizzled down on him. Caffran pulled his lasgun from its sling and slithered up towards the top of the trench firestep. There was chaos, panic, troopers hurrying in every direction, screaming and shouting.

Was this it? Was this the final moment in the long, drawn-out conflict they had found themselves in? Caffran tried to slide up the side of the trench far enough to get a sight over the lip, across no-man's-land to the enemies' emplacements which they had been locked into for the last six months. All he could see was a mist of smoke and mud.

There was a crackle of lasweapons and several screams. More shells fell. One of them found the centre of a nearby communications trench. Then the screaming became real and immediate. The drizzle that fell on him was no longer water and mud. There were body parts in it.

Caffran cursed and wiped the sight-lens of his lasgun clean of filth. Behind him he heard a shout, a powerful voice that echoed along the traverses of the trench and seemed to shake the duckboards. He looked back to see Commissar Gaunt emerging from his dugout.

Gaunt was dressed now in his full dress uniform and cap, the camo-cloak of his adopted regiment swirling about his shoulders, his face a mask of bellowing rage. In one hand he held his bolt pistol and in the other his chainsword, which whined and sang in the early morning air.

'In the name of Tanith! Now they are on us we must fight! Hold the line and hold your fire until they come over the mud wall!'

Caffran felt a rejoicing in his soul. The commissar was with them and they would succeed, no matter the odds. Then something closed down his world with a vibratory shock that blew mud up into the air and seemed to separate his spirit from his body.

The section of trench had taken a direct hit. Dozens of men were dead. Caffran lay stunned in the broken line of duckboards and splattered mud. A hand grabbed him by the shoulder and hauled him up. Blinking, he looked up to see the face of Gaunt. Gaunt looked at him with a solemn, yet inspiring gaze.

'Sleeping after a good breakfast?' the commissar enquired of the bewildered trooper.

'No sir... I... I...'

The crack of lasguns and needle lasers began to whip around them from the armoured loopholes on the trench head. Gaunt wrenched Caffran back to his feet.

'I think the time has come,' Gaunt said, 'and I'd like all of my brave men to be in the line with me when we advance.'

Spitting out grey mud, Caffran laughed. 'I'm with you, sir,' he said, 'from Tanith to wherever we end up.'

Caffran heard the whine of Gaunt's chainsword as the commissar leapt up the scaling ladder nailed into the trench wall above the fire-step and yelled to his men.

'Men of Tanith! Do you want to live forever?'

Their reply, loud and raucous, was lost in the barrage of shells. But Ibram Gaunt knew what they had said.

Weapons blazing, Gaunt's Ghosts went over the top and blasted their way towards glory, death or whatever else awaited them in the smoke.

FOUR

There was a sizzling thicket of las-fire a hundred paces deep and twenty kilometres long where the advancing legions of the enemy met the Imperial Guard regiments head on. It looked for all the world like squirming nests of colonial insects bursting forth from their mounds and meeting in a chaotic mess of seething forms, lit by the incessant and incandescent sparking crossfire of their weapons.

Lord High Militant General Hechtor Dravere turned away from his tripod-mounted scope. He smoothed the faultless breast of his tunic with well-manicured hands and sighed.

'Who would that be dying down there?' he asked in his disturbingly thin, reedy voice.

Colonel Flense, field commander of the Jantine Patricians, one of the oldest and most venerated Guard regiments, got off his couch and stood smartly to attention. Flense was a tall, powerful man, the tissue of his left cheek disfigured long ago by a splash of tyranid bio-acid.

'General?'

'Those... those ants down there...' Dravere gestured idly over his shoulder. 'I wondered who they were.'

Flense strode across the veranda to the chart table where a flat glass plate was illuminated from beneath with glowing indication runes. He traced a finger across the glass, assessing the four hundred kilometres of battlefield frontline which represented the focus of the war here on Fortis Binary, a vast and ragged pattern of opposing trench systems, facing each other across a mangled deadland of cratered mud and shattered factories.

'The western trenches,' he began. 'They are held by the Tanith First Regiment. You know them, sir – Gaunt's mob, what some of the men call "The Ghosts", I believe.'

Dravere wandered across to an ornate refreshment cart and poured himself a tiny cup of rich black caffeine from the gilt samovar. He sipped and for a moment sloshed the heavy fluid between his teeth.

Flense cringed. Colonel Draker Flense had seen things in his time that would have burned through the souls of most ordinary men. He had watched legions die on the wire, he had seen men eat their comrades in a frenzy of Chaos-induced madness, he had seen planets, whole planets, collapse and die and rot. There was something about General Dravere that touched him more deeply and more repugnantly than any of that. It was a pleasure to serve him.

Dravere swallowed at last and set aside his cup. 'So Gaunt's Ghosts get the wake-up call this morning,' he said.

Hechtor Dravere was a squat, bullish man in his sixties, balding and yet insistent upon lacquering the few remaining strands of hair across his scalp as if to prove a point. He was fleshy and ruddy, and his uniform seemed to require an entire regimental ration of starch and whitening to prepare each morning. There were medals on his chest which stuck out on a stiff brass pin. He always wore them. Flense was not entirely sure what they all represented. He had never asked. He knew that Dravere had seen at least as much as him and had taken every ounce of glory for it that he could. Sometimes Flense resented the fact that the lord general always wore his decorations. He supposed it was because the lord general had them and he did not. That was what it meant to be a lord general.

The ducal palace on whose veranda they now stood was miraculously intact after six months of serial bombardment and overlooked the wide rift valley of Diemos, once the hydro-electric industrial heartland of Fortis Binary, now the axis on which the war revolved. In all directions, as far as the eye could see, sprawled the gross architecture of the manufacturing zone: the towers and hangars, the vaults and bunkers, the storage tanks and chimney stacks. A great ziggurat rose to the north, the brilliant gold icon of the Adeptus Mechanicus displayed on its flank. It rivalled, perhaps even surpassed, the Temple of the Ecclesiarchy, dedicated to the God-Emperor. But then, the Tech-Priests of Mars would argue this entire world was a shrine to the God-Machine Incarnate.

The ziggurat had been the administrative heart of the tech-priests' industry on Fortis, from where they directed a workforce of nineteen billion in the production of armour and heavy weaponry for the Imperial war machine. It was a burned-out shell now. It had been the uprising's first target.

In the far hills of the valley, in fortified factories, worker habitats and material store yards, the enemy was dug in – a billion strong, a vast massed legion of daemonic cultists. Fortis Binary was a primary Imperial forge-world, muscular and energetic in its industrial production.

No one knew how the Ruinous Powers had come to corrupt it, or how a huge section of the massive labour force had been infected with the taint of the Fallen Gods. But it had happened. Eight months before, almost overnight, the vast manufactory arks and furnace-plants of the Adeptus Mechanicus had been overthrown by the Chaos-corrupted workforce, once bonded to serve the machine cult. Only a scarce few of the tech-priests had escaped the sudden onslaught and evacuated off-world.

Now the massed legions of the Imperial Guard were here to liberate this world, and the action was very much determined by the location. The master-factories and tech-plants of Fortis Binary were too valuable to be stamped flat by an orbital bombardment.

Whatever the cost, for the good of the Imperium, this world had to be retaken a pace at a time, by men on the ground: fighting men, Imperial Guard, soldiers who would, by the sweat of their backs, root out and destroy every last scrap of Chaos and leave the precious industries of the forge-world ready and waiting for re-population.

'Every few days they try us again, pushing at another line of our trenches, trying to find a weak link.' The lord general looked back into his scope at the carnage fifteen kilometres away.

'The Tanith First are strong fighters, general, so I have heard.' Flense approached Dravere and stood with his hands behind his back. The scar-tissue of his cheek pinched and twitched slightly, as it often did when he was tense. 'They have acquitted themselves well on a number of campaigns and Gaunt is said to be a resourceful leader.'

'You know him?' the general looked up from his eye-piece, questioningly.

Flense paused. 'I know *of* him, sir. In the main by reputation,' he said, swallowing many truths, 'but I have met him in passing. His philosophy of leadership is not in tune with mine.'

'You don't like him, do you, Flense?' Dravere asked pertinently. He could read Flense like a book, and could see some deep resentment lay in the colonel's heart when it came to the subject of the infamous and heroic Commissar Gaunt. He knew what it was. He'd read the reports. He also knew Flense would never actually mention it.

'Frankly? No, sir. He is a commissar. A political officer. But by a turn of fate, he has achieved a regimental command. Warmaster Slaydo granted him the command of the Tanith on his deathbed. I understand the role of commissars in this army, but I despise his officer status. He is sympathetic where he should be inspiring, inspirational where he should be dogmatic. But... still and all, he is a commander we can probably trust.'

Dravere smiled. Flense's outburst had been from the heart, and honest, but it still diplomatically skirted the real truth. 'I trust no other commander than myself, Flense,' the general said flatly. 'If I cannot see the victory, I will not trust it to other hands. Your Patricians are held in reserve, am I correct?'

'They are barracked in the work habitats to the west, ready to support a push on either flank.'

'Go to them and bring them to readiness,' the lord general said. He crossed to the chart table again and used a stylus to mark out several long sweeps of light on the glassy top. 'We have been held here long enough. I grow impatient. This war should have been over and done months ago. How many brigades have we committed to break the deadlock?'

Flense wasn't sure. Dravere was famously extravagant with manpower. It was his proud boast that he could choke even the Eye of Terror if he had enough bodies to march into it. Certainly in the last few weeks, Dravere had become increasingly frustrated at the lack of advance. Flense guessed that Dravere was anxious to please Warmaster Macaroth, the new overall commander of the Sabbat Worlds Crusade. Dravere and Macaroth had been rivals for Slaydo's succession. Having lost to Macaroth, Dravere probably had a lot to prove. Like his loyalty to the new warmaster.

Flense had also heard rumours that Inquisitor Heldane, one of Dravere's most trusted associates, had come to Fortis a week before to conduct private talks with the lord general. Now it was as if Dravere yearned to move on, to be somewhere, to achieve something even grander than the conquest of a world, even a world as vital as Fortis Binary.

Dravere was talking again. 'The Shriven have shown their hand this morning, in greater force than before, and it will take them eight or nine hours to withdraw and regroup from whatever advances they make now. Bring your regiments in from the east and cut them off. Use these Ghosts as a buffer and slice a hole into the heart of their main defences. With the will of the beloved Emperor, we may at last break this matter and press a victory.' The lord general tapped the screen with the point of the stylus as if to emphasise the non-negotiable quality of his instruction.

Flense was eager to comply. It was his determined ambition that his regiments should be fundamental in achieving the victory on Fortis Binary. The notion that Gaunt could somehow take that glory from him sickened him, made him think of–

He shook off the thought, and basked in the idea that Gaunt and his low-born scum would be used, expended, sacrificed on the enemy guns to affect his own glory. Still, Flense wavered for a second, about to leave. There was no harm in creating a little insurance. He crossed back to the chart table and pointed a leather-gloved finger at a curve of the contours on the map. 'There is a wide area to cover, sir,' he said, 'and if Gaunt's men were to... well, break with cowardice, my Patricians would be left vulnerable to both the dug-in forces of the Shriven and to the retreating elements.'

Dravere mused on this for a moment. Cowardice: what a loaded word for Flense to use in respect to Gaunt. Then he clapped his chubby hands together as gleefully as a young child at a birthday party. 'Signals! Signals officer in here now!'

The inner door of the lounge room opened and a weary soldier hurried in, snapping his worn, but clean and polished boots together as he saluted the two officers. Dravere was busy scribing orders onto a message slate. He reviewed them once and then handed them to the soldier.

'We will bring the Vitrian Dragoons in to support the Ghosts in the hope that they will drive the Shriven host back into the flood plains. In this way, we should ensure that the fighting is held along the western flank for as long as it takes your Patricians to engage the enemy. Signal to this effect, and signal also the Tanith commander, Gaunt. Instruct him to push on. His duty today is not merely to repel. It is to press on and use this opportunity to take the Shriven frontline trenches. Ensure that this instruction is clearly an order directly from me. There will be no faltering, tell him. No retreat. They will achieve or they will die.'

Flense allowed himself an inward smile of triumph. His own back was now comfortably covered, and Gaunt had been forced into a push that would have him dead by nightfall. The soldier saluted again and made to exit.

'One last thing,' Dravere said.

The soldier skidded to a halt and turned, nervously.

Dravere tapped the samovar with a chunky signet ring. 'Ask them to send in some fresh caffeine. This is stale.' The soldier nodded and exited. From the clunk of the ring it was clear that the big, gilt vessel was still nearly full. A regiment could drink for several days on what the general clearly intended to throw away. He managed to wait until

he was out of the double doors before he spat a silent curse at the man
who was orchestrating this bloodbath.

Flense saluted too and walked towards the door. He picked up his
peaked cap from the sideboard and carefully set it upon his head, the
back of the brim first.

'Praise the Emperor, lord general,' he said.

'What? Oh, yes. Indeed,' Dravere said absently, as he sat back on his
chaise and lit a cigar.

FIVE

Major Rawne threw himself flat into a foxhole and almost drowned in
the milky water which had accumulated in its depths. Spluttering, he
pulled himself up to the lip of the crater and took aim with his lasgun.
The air all around was thick with smoke and the flashing streams of
gunfire. Before he had time to fire, several more bodies crashed into
the makeshift cover by his side: Trooper Neff and the platoon adjutant,
Feygor, beside them Troopers Caffran, Varl and Lonegin.

There was Trooper Klay as well, but he was dead. The fierce crossfire had cauterised his face before he could reach cover. None of them
looked twice at Klay's body in the water behind them. They had seen
that sort of thing a thousand times too often.

Rawne used his scope to check over the rim of the foxhole. Somewhere out there the Shriven were using some heavy weapon to support
their infantry. The thick and explosive fire was cutting a wedge out of
the Ghosts as they advanced. Neff was fiddling with his weapon and
Rawne glanced down at him.

'What's the matter, trooper?' he asked.

'There's mud in my firing mechanism, sir. I can't free it.'

Feygor snatched the lasgun from the younger man, ejected the magazine and slung back the oiled cover of the ignition chamber, so that it
was open and the focus rings exposed.

Feygor spat into the open chamber and then slammed it shut with
a clack. Then he shook it vigorously and jammed the energy magazine back into its slot. Neff watched as Feygor swung round again and
lifted the gun above his head, firing it wholesale into the smoke beyond
the foxhole.

Feygor tossed the weapon back to the trooper. 'See? It's working now.'

Neff clutched the returned weapon and wriggled up to the lip of
the hole.

'We'll be dead before we go another metre,' Lonegin said from below
them.

'For feth's sake!' Trooper Varl spat. 'We'll just get them ducking then.' He unhooked a clutch of grenades from his webbing and tossed them out to the other soldiers, sharing them like a schoolboy shares stolen fruit. A click of the thumb primed each weapon and Rawne smiled to his men as he prepared to heave his into the air.

'Varl's assessment is correct,' Rawne said. 'Let's blind them.'

They hefted the bombs into the sky. They were frag grenades, designed to deafen, blind and pepper those in range with needles of shrapnel.

There was the multiple *crump* of detonation.

'That's got them ducking at least,' Caffran said, then realised that the others were already scrambling up out of the foxhole to charge. He followed quickly.

Screaming, the Ghosts charged over a short stretch of grey ooze and then slithered down into a revetment, screened from them by the smoke. The blackened impacts of the grenades were all around them, as were the twisted bodies of several of their dead foe.

Rawne slammed onto his feet at the bottom of the slide and looked around. For the first time in six months on Fortis Binary, he saw the enemy face to face. The Shriven, the ground forces of the enemy he had been sent here to fight.

They were surprisingly human, but twisted and malformed. They wore combat armour cleverly adapted from the worksuits that they had used in the forges of the planet, the protective masks and gauntlets actually woven into their wasted, pallid flesh. Rawne tried not to linger on the dead. It made him think too much about those legions he had still to kill. In the smoke he found two more of the Shriven, crippled by the grenade blasts. He finished them quickly.

He found Caffran close behind him. The young trooper was shocked by what he saw.

'They have lasguns,' Caffran said, aghast, 'and body armour.'

Beside him, Neff turned one of the corpses over, with his toe. 'And look… they have grenades and munitions.' Neff and Caffran looked at the major.

Rawne shrugged. 'So they're tough bastards. What did you expect? They've held the Imperium off for six months.' Lonegin, Varl and Feygor hurried along to join them. Rawne waved them along, further into the enemy dugout. The space widened in front of them and they saw the metal-beamed, stone barns of an industrial silo.

Rawne quickly gestured them into cover. Almost at once las-fire started to sear down the trench towards them. Varl was hit and his shoulder vanished in a puff of red mist. He went down hard on his backside and then flopped over clutching with the one arm that would still work. The pain was so momentous he couldn't even scream.

'Feth!' spat Rawne. 'See to him, Neff!'

Neff was the squad medic. He pulled open his thigh pouch of field dressings as Feygor and Caffran tried to drag the whimpering Varl into cover. Gleaming lines of las-fire stitched the trench line and tried to pin them all. Neff quickly bound Varl's ghastly injury. 'We have to get him back, sir!' he shouted down the grey channel to Rawne.

Rawne was pushing himself into the cover of the defile, the grey ooze matting his hair as the las-bursts burned the air around him. 'Not now,' he said.

SIX

Ibram Gaunt leapt down into the trench and broke the neck of the first Shriven he met with his descending boots. The chainsword screamed in his fist and as he reached the duckboards of the enemy emplacement he swung it left and right to cut two more apart in drizzles of blood. Another charged him, a great curved blade in his hand. Gaunt raised his bolt pistol and blew the masked head into vapour.

This was the thickest fighting Gaunt and his men had encountered on Fortis, caught in the frenzied narrows of the enemy trenches, sweeping this way and that to meet the incessant advance of the Shriven. Pinned behind the commissar, Brin Milo fired his own weapon, a compact automatic handgun that the commissar had given him some months before. He killed one – a bullet between the eyes – then another, winging him first and then putting a bullet into his upturned chin as he flailed backwards. Milo shivered. This was the horror of war that he had always dreamt of, yet never wished to see. Passionate men caught against each other in a dug out hole three metres wide and six deep. The Shriven were monsters, almost elephantine with the long, nozzled gas masks sewn into the flesh of their faces. Their body armour was a dull industrial green and rubberised. They had taken the protective garb of their workspace and made it their battledress, daubing everything with eye-aching symbols.

Slammed against the trench wall by a falling body, Milo looked down at the corpses which gathered around them. He saw for the first time, in detail, the nature of his foe... the twisted, corrupted human forms of the Chaos host, incised with twisted runes and sigils painted on the dull green rubber of their armour or carved into their raw flesh.

One of the Shriven ploughed in past Gaunt's shrieking sword and dove at Milo. The boy dropped and the cultist smashed into the trench wall. Scrabbling in the muddy wetness of the trench bed, Milo retrieved one of the lasguns that had fallen from the dying grasp of one of Gaunt's previous victims. The Shriven was on him as he hefted the weapon up and fired, point blank. The flaming round punched through his opponent's torso and the dead cultist fell across him, forcing him down by sheer weight into the sucking ooze of the trench floor. Foul water surged into his mouth, and mud and blood. A second later he was heaved, coughing, to his feet by Trooper Bragg, the most massive of the men of Tanith, who was somehow always there to watch over him.

'Get down,' Bragg said as he hoisted a rocket launcher onto his shoulder. Milo knelt and covered his ears, tight. Hopefully muttering the Litany of True Striking to himself, Bragg fired his huge weapon off down the companionway of the trench. A fountain of mud and other unnameable things were blown into fragments. He often missed what he was aiming at, but under these conditions that wasn't an option.

To their right, Gaunt was scything his way into the close-packed enemy. He began to laugh, coated with the rain of blood that he was loosing with his shrieking chainsword. Every now and then he would fire his pistol and explode another of the Shriven.

He was filled with fury. The signal from Lord General Dravere had been draconian and cruel. Gaunt would have wanted to take the enemy trenches if he could, but to be ordered to do so with no other option except death was, in his opinion, the decision of a flawed, brutal mind. He'd never liked Dravere, not at any time since their first meeting twenty years before, when Dravere had still been an ambitious armour colonel. Back on Darendara, back with Oktar and the Hyrkans...

Gaunt had kept the nature of the orders from his men. Unlike Dravere, he understood the mechanisms of morale and inspiration. Now they were taking the damned trenches, almost in spite of Dravere's orders rather than because of them. His laughter was the laughter of fury and resentment, and pride in his men for doing the impossible regardless.

Nearby, Milo stumbled to his feet, holding the lasgun.

We're there, Gaunt thought, we've broken them!

Ten metres down the line, Sergeant Blane leapt in with his platoon and sealed the event, blasting left and right with his lasgun as his men charged, bayonets first. There was a frenzy of las-fire and a flash of silver Tanith blades.

Milo was still holding the lasgun when Gaunt snatched it from him and threw it down onto the duckboards. 'Do you think you're a soldier, boy?'

'Yes, sir!'

'Really?'

'You know I am.'

Gaunt looked down at the sixteen year-old boy and smiled sadly.

'Maybe you are, but for now play up. Play a tune that will sing us to glory!'

Milo pulled his Tanith pipes from his pack and breathed into the chanter. For a moment it screamed like a dying man. Then he began playing. It was Waltrab's Wilde, an old tune that had always inspired the men in the taverns of Tanith to drink and cheer and make merry.

Sergeant Blane heard the tune and with a grimace he laid into the enemy. By his side, his adjutant, vox-officer Symber, started to sing along as he blasted with his lasgun. Trooper Bragg simply chuckled and loaded another rocket into the huge launcher that he carried. A moment later, another section of trench dissolved in a deluge of fire.

Trooper Caffran heard the music, a distant plaintive wail across the battlefield. It cheered him for a moment as he moved with the men under Major Rawne's direction up over the bodies of the Shriven, side by side with Neff, Lonegin, Larkin and the rest. Even now, poor Varl was being stretchered back to their lines, screaming as the drugs wore off.

That was the moment the bombardment started. Caffran found himself flying, lifted by a wall of air issued from a bomb blast that created a crater twelve metres wide. A huge slew of mud was thrown up in the sky with him.

He landed hard, broken, and his mind frayed. He lay for a while in the mud, strangely peaceful. As far as he knew, Neff, Major Rawne, Feygor, Larkin, Lonegin, all the rest, were dead and vaporised.

As shells continued to fall, Caffran sank his head into the slime and silently begged for release from his nightmare.

A long way off, Lord High Militant General Dravere heard the vast emplacements of the Shriven artillery begin their onslaught. He realised that it would not be today, after all. Sighing angrily, he poured himself another cup from the freshly refilled samovar.

SEVEN

Colonel Corbec had three platoons with him and moved them forward into the traversed network of the enemy trenches. The bombardment had been howling over their heads for two hours now, obliterating the front edge of the Shriven emplacements and annihilating all those of the Guard who had not made it into the comparative cover of enemy positions. The tunnels and channels they moved through were empty and abandoned. Clearly the Shriven had pulled out as the bombardment began. The trenches were well-made and engineered, but at every turn or bend there was a blasphemous shrine to the Dark Powers that the enemy worshipped.

Corbec had Trooper Skulane turn his flamer on each shrine they found and burn it away before any of his men could fully appreciate the grim nature of the offerings laid before it.

By Curral's estimation, after consulting the tightly-scrolled fibre-light charts, they were advancing into support trenches behind the Shriven main line. Corbec felt cut off – not just by the savage bombardment that shook their very bones every other second, and he fervently prayed no shell would fall short into the midst of them – but more, he felt cut off from the rest of the regiment. The electro-magnetic aftershock of the ceaseless barrage was scrambling their communications, both the micro-bead intercoms that all the officers wore and the long range vox-caster radio sets. No orders were getting through, no urgings to regroup, to rendezvous with other units, to press forward for an objective, or even to retreat.

In such circumstances, the rulebook of Imperial Guard warfare was clear: if in doubt, move forward.

Corbec sent scouts ahead, men he knew were fast and able: Baru, Colmar and Scout-Sergeant Mkoll. They pulled their Tanith stealth cloaks around them and slipped away into the dusty darkness. Walls of smoke and powder were drifting back over the trench lines and visibility was dropping. Sergeant Blane gestured silently up at the billowing smoke banks that were descending.

Corbec knew his intent, and knew that he didn't wish to voice it for fear of spooking the unit. The Shriven had no qualms about the use of poison agents, foul airborne gases that would boil the blood and fester the lungs. Corbec pulled out a whistle and blew three short blasts. The men behind him put guns at ease and pulled respirators from their webbing. Colonel Corbec buckled his own respirator mask around his face. He hated the loss of visibility, the claustrophobia of the thick lensed gas hoods, the shortness of breath that the tight rubber mouthpiece provoked. But poison clouds were not the half of it. The sea of mud that the bombardment was agitating and casting up into the wind as vapour droplets was full of other venoms – the airborne spores of disease incubated in the decaying bodies out there in the dead zone: typhus, gangrene, livestock anthrax bred in the corrupting husks of pack animals and cavalry steeds, and the vicious mycotoxins that hungrily devoured all organic matter, transforming it into a black, insidious mould.

As first officer to the Tanith First, Corbec had been privy to the dispatches circulated from the general staff. He knew that nearly eighty per cent of the fatalities amongst the Imperial Guard since the invasion began had been down to gas, disease and secondary infection. A Shriven soldier could face you point-blank with a charged lasgun and still your chances of survival would be better than if you took a stroll in no-man's-land.

Muffled and blinkered by the mask, Corbec edged his unit on. They reached a bifurcation in the support trenches and Corbec called up Sergeant Grell, officer of the fifth platoon, instructing him to take three fire-teams to the left and cleanse whatever they found. The men moved off and Corbec became aware of his increasing frustration. Nothing had come back from the scouts. He was moving as blind as he had been before he sent them out.

Advancing now at double-time, the colonel led his remaining hundred or so men along a wide communication trench. Two of his sharper-eyed vanguard moved in front, using magnetically sensitive wands attached to heavy backpacks to sweep for explosives and booby traps. It seemed that the Shriven had pulled back too rapidly to leave any surprises, but every few metres, the column stopped as one of the sweepers found something hot: a tin cup, a piece of armour, a canteen tray. Sometimes it was a strange idol made of smelt ore from the forge furnaces that the corrupted workers had carved into some bestial form. Corbec personally put his laspistol to each one and blew it into fragments.

The third time he did this, the wretched thing he was destroying blew up in sharp fragments as his round tore it open along some fault. Trooper Drayl, cowering a few paces away, was hit in the collarbone by a shard, which dug into the flesh. He winced and sat back in the mud, hard. Sergeant Curral called up the medic, who put on a field dressing.

Corbec cursed his own stupidity. He was so anxious to erase any trace of the Shriven cult he had hurt one of his own.

'It's nothing, sir,' Drayl said through his gas mask as Corbec helped him to his feet. 'At Voltis Watergate I took a bayonet in the thigh.'

'And back home on Tanith he got a broken bottle end in his cheek in a bar fight!' laughed Trooper Coll behind them. 'He's had worse.'

The men around them laughed, ugly, sucking sounds through their respirators. Corbec nodded to show he was in tune with them. Drayl was a handsome, popular soldier whose songs and good humour kept his platoon in decent spirits. Corbec also knew that Drayl's roguish exploits were a matter of regimental legend.

'My mistake, Drayl,' Corbec said, 'I owe you a drink.'

'At the very least, colonel,' Drayl said and deftly armed his lasgun to show he was ready to continue.

EIGHT

They moved on. They reached a section of trench where a monumental shell had fallen short and blown the thin cavity open in a huge crater wound nearly thirty metres across. Already, brackish ground water was welling up in its bowl. With only the sweepers ahead of him, Corbec waded in first to lead them across into the cover where the trench recommenced. The water came up to his mid-thigh and was acidic. He could feel it burning the flesh of his legs through his fatigues and there was a faint swirl of mist around the cloth of his uniform as the fabric began to burn. He ordered the men behind him back and scrambled up on the far side to join the sweepers. The three of them looked down at their legs, horrified by the way the water had already begun to eat into the tunic cloth. Corbec felt lesions forming on his thighs and shins.

He turned back to Sergeant Curral at the head of the column across the crater.

'Move the men up and round!' he cried. 'And bring the medic over in the first party.' Afraid by the exposure of moving around the lip of the crater against the sky, the men traversed quickly and timidly. Corbec had Curral regroup them on the far side in fire-team lines along each side of the trench. The medic came to him and the sweepers, and sprayed their legs with antiseptic mist from a flask. The pain eased and the fabric was damped so that it no longer smouldered.

Corbec was picking up his gun when Sergeant Grell called to him. He moved forward down the lines of waiting men and saw what Grell had found.

It was Colmar, one of the scouts he had sent forward. He was dead, hanging pendulously from the trench wall on a great, rusty iron spike which impaled his chest. It was the sort of spike that the workers of the forge world would have used to wedge and manipulate the hoppers of molten ore in the Adeptus Mechanicus furnace works. His hands and feet were missing.

Corbec gazed at him for a minute and then looked away. Though they had met no serious resistance, it was sickeningly clear that they weren't alone in these trenches. Whatever the number of the Shriven still here, be it stragglers left behind or guerrilla units deliberately set to thwart them, a malicious presence was shadowing them in the gullies and channels of the support trenches.

Corbec took hold of the spike and pulled Colmar down. He took out the ground sheet from his own bedroll and rolled the pitiful corpse in it so that no one would see. He could not bring himself to incinerate the soldier, as he had done with the shrines.

'Move on,' he instructed and Grell led the men forward behind the sweepers.

Corbec suddenly stopped dead as if an insect had stung him. There was a rasping in his ear. He realised it was his micro-bead link. He registered an overwhelming sense of relief that the radio link should be live at all even as he realised it was a short range broadcast from Mkoll, sergeant of the scouting unit.

'Can you hear it, sir?' came Mkoll's voice.

'Feth! Hear what?' Corbec asked. All he could hear was the ceaseless thunder of the enemy guns and the shaking tremors of the falling shells.

'Drums,' Scout-Sergeant Mkoll said, 'I can hear drums.'

NINE

Brin Milo heard the drums before Gaunt did. Gaunt valued his musician's almost preternaturally sharp senses, but they sometimes disturbed him nonetheless. The insight reminded him of someone. The girl perhaps, years ago. The one with the sight. The one who had haunted his dreams for so many years afterwards.

'Drums!' the boy hissed – and a moment later Gaunt caught the sound too.

They were moving through the silos and shelled-out structures of the rising industrial manufactories just behind the Shriven lines, sooty shells of melted stone, rusted metal girderwork and fractured ceramite. Gargoyles, built to protect the buildings against contamination, had been defaced or toppled completely. Gaunt was exceptionally cautious. The action of the day had played out unexpectedly. They had advanced far further than he had anticipated from the starting point of a simple repulse of an enemy attack, thanks both to good fortune and Dravere's harsh directive. Reaching the front of the enemy lines they had found them generally abandoned after the initial fighting, as if the majority of the Shriven had withdrawn in haste. Though a curtain of enemy bombardment cut off their lines of retreat, Gaunt felt that the Shriven had made a great mistake and pulled back too far in their urgency to avoid both the Guard attack and their own answering artillery. Either that or they were planning something.

Gaunt didn't like that notion much. He had two hundred and thirty men with him in a long spearhead column, but he knew that if the Shriven counterattacked now he might as well be on his own.

As they progressed, they swept each blackened factory bunker, storehouse and forge-tower for signs of the enemy, moving beneath flapping, torn banners, crunching broken stained glass underfoot. Machinery had been stripped out and removed, or simply vandalised. There was nothing whole left here – apart from the Chaos shrines which the Shriven had erected at regular intervals. Like Colonel Corbec, the commissar had a flamer brought up to expunge any trace of these outrages. However, ironically, he was moving in exactly the opposite direction along the trench lines to Corbec's advance. Communication was lost and the breakthrough elements of the Tanith First and Only were wandering blind and undirected through what was by any estimation enemy territory.

The sound of the drums rolled in. Gaunt called up his vox-caster operator, Trooper Rafflan, and tersely barked into the speech-horn of the heavy backpack set, demanding to know if there was anyone out there.

The drums rolled.

There was a return across the radio link, an incomprehensible squawk of garbled words. At first, Gaunt thought the transmission was scrambled, but then he realised that it was another language. He repeated his demand and after a long painful silence a coherent message returned to him in clipped Low Gothic.

'This is Colonel Zoren of the Vitrian Dragoons. We are moving in to support you. Hold your fire.'

Gaunt acknowledged and then spread his men across the silo concourse in cover, watching and waiting. Ahead of them something flashed in the dull light and then Gaunt saw soldiers moving down towards them. They didn't see the Ghosts until the very last minute. With their tenacious ability to hide in anything, and their obscuring cloaks, Gaunt's Ghosts were masters of stealth camouflage.

The Dragoons approached in a long and carefully arranged formation of at least three hundred men. Gaunt could see that they were well-drilled, slim but powerful men in some kind of chain-armour that was strangely sheened and which caught the light like unpolished metal.

Gaunt shrugged off the Tanith stealth cloak that had been a habitual addition to his garb since he joined the First and Only, and moved out of concealment, signalling them openly as he rose to his feet from cover. He advanced to meet the commanding officer.

Close to, the Vitrians were impressive soldiers. Their unusual body armour was made from a toothed metallic mail which covered them in form-fitting sections. It glinted like obsidian. Their helmets were full face and grim with narrow eye slits, glazed with dark glass. Their weapons were polished and clean.

'Commissar Gaunt of the Tanith First and Only,' Gaunt said as he saluted a greeting.

'Zoren of the Vitrian Dragoons,' came the reply. 'Good to see that there are some of you left out here. We feared we were being called in to support a regiment already slaughtered.'

'The drums? Are they yours?'

Zoren slid back the visor of his helmet to reveal a handsome, dark-skinned face. He caught Gaunt with a quizzical stare. 'They are not... we were just wondering what in the name of the Emperor it was ourselves.'

Gaunt looked away into the smoke and the fractured buildings around them. The noise had grown. Now it sounded like hundreds of drums... thousands... from all around. For each drum, a drummer. They were surrounded and completely outnumbered.

TEN

Caffran dragged himself across the mud and slid into a crater. Around him the bombardment showed no signs of easing. He had lost his las-gun and most of his kit, but he still had his silver knife and an autopistol that had come his way as a trophy at some time or other.

Wriggling to the lip of the crater he caught sight of figures far away, soldiers who seemed to be dressed in glass. There was a full unit of them, caught in the crossfire of the serial bombardment. They were being slaughtered.

Shells fell close again and Caffran slid down to cover his head with his arms.

This was hell and there was no way out of it. Curse this, in the name of feth!

He looked up and grabbed his pistol as something fell into the shell-hole next to him. It was one of the glass-clad soldiers he had seen from a distance, presumably one who had fled in search of cover. The man held up his hands to avoid Caffran's potential wrath.

'Guard! I'm Guard, like you!' the man said hastily, pulling off his dark-lensed full-face helmet to reveal an attractive face with skin that was almost as dark and glossy as polished ebonwood. 'Trooper Zogat of the Vitrian Regiment. We were called in to support you and half our number were in the open when the artillery cranked up.'

'My sympathies,' Trooper Caffran said humourlessly, holstering his pistol. He held out a pale hand to shake and was aware of the way the man in the articulated metallic armour regarded the blue dragon tattoo over his right eye with disdain.

'Trooper Caffran, Tanith First,' he said. After a moment the Vitrian shook his hand.

A shell fell close and showered them in mud. Getting up from their knees they turned and looked out at the apocalyptic vista all around.

'Well, friend,' Caffran said, 'I think we're here for the duration.'

ELEVEN

To the west, the Jantine Patricians moved in under the command of Colonel Flense. They rode on Chimera personnel carriers that lurched and reeled across the slick and miry landscape. The Patricians were noble soldiers, tall men in deep purple uniforms dressed with chrome. Flense had been honoured when, six years before, he had become their commanding officer. They were haughty and resolute, and had won for him a great deal of praise. They had a regimental history that dated back fifteen generations to their first Founding in the castellated garrisons of Jant Normanidus Prime, generations of notable triumphs, and associations with illustrious generals and campaigns. There was just the one blemish on their honour roll, just the one, and it nagged at Flense day and night. He would rectify that. Here, on Fortis Binary.

He took his scope and looked at the battlefield ahead. He had two columns of vehicles with upwards of ten thousand men scissoring in to cut into the flank of the Shriven as the Tanith and the Vitrians drove them back. Both those regiments were fully deployed into the Shriven lines. But Flense had not counted on this bombardment from the Shriven artillery in the hills.

Two kilometres ahead the ground was volcanic with the pounding of the macro-shells and a drizzle of mud fogged back to splatter their vehicles. There was no way of going round and Flense didn't even wish to consider the chances of driving his column through the barrage. Lord General Dravere believed in acceptable losses, and had demonstrated this practicality on a fair few number of occasions without compunction, but Flense wasn't about to commit suicide. His scar twitched. He cursed. For all his manoeuvring with Dravere, this wasn't the way it was meant to go. He had been cheated of his victory.

'Pull back!' he ordered into the vox handset and felt the gears of his vehicle grind into reverse as the carrier pulled around.

His second officer, a big, older man called Brochuss, glared at him under the low brim of his helmet. 'We are to pull out, colonel?' he asked, as if obliteration by artillery shell was something he craved.

'Shut up!' spat Flense and repeated the order into the vox-caster.

'What about Gaunt?' Brochuss asked.

'What do you think?' Flense sneered, gesturing out of the Chimera's vision slit at the inferno that raged along the deadland. 'We may not get glory today, but at least we can content ourselves in the knowledge that the bastard is dead.'

Brochuss nodded, and a slow smile of consolation spread across his grizzled features. None of the veterans had forgotten Khedd 1173.

The Patrician armoured convoy snaked back on itself and thundered home towards friendly lines before the Shriven emplacements could range them. Victory would have to wait a while longer. The Tanith First and Only and the Vitrian support regiments were on their own. If there were indeed any of them left alive.

A MEMORY

Oktar died slowly. It took eight days.

The commander had once joked – on Darendara, or was it Folion? Gaunt forgot. But he remembered the joke: 'It won't be war that slays me, it'll be these damn victory celebrations!'

They had been in a smoke-filled hall, surrounded by cheering citizens and waving banners. Most of the Hyrkan officers were drunk on their feet. Sergeant Gurst had stripped to his underwear and climbed the statue of the two-headed Imperial eagle in the courtyard to string the Hyrkan colours from the crest. The streets were full of bellowing crowds, static, honking traffic and wild firecrackers.

Folion. Definitely Folion.

Cadet Gaunt had smiled. Laughed, probably.

But Oktar had a way of being right all the time, and he had been right about this. The Instrumentality of the Gylatus World Flock had been delivered from the savage ork threat after ten months of sustained killing on the Gylatan moons. Oktar, Gaunt with him, had led the final assault on the ork war bunkers at Tropis Crater Nine, punching through the last stand resistance of the brutal huzkarl retinue of Warboss Elgoz. Oktar had personally planted the spike of the Imperial Standard into the soft grey soil of the crater bottom, through Elgoz's exploded skull.

Then here, in the Gylatan hive-city capital on Decimus, the victory parades, the hosts of jubilant citizenry, the endless festivities, the medal ceremonies, the drinking, the–

The poison.

Canny, for orks. As if realising their untenable position, the orks had tainted the food and drink reserves in the last few days of their occupation. Taster servitors had sniffed most of it out, but that one stray bottle. That one stray bottle.

Adjutant Broph had found the rack of antique wines on the second night of the liberation festivities, hidden in a longbox in the palace rooms which Oktar had commandeered as a playground for his officer cadre. No one had even thought–

Eight were dead, including Broph, by the time anyone realised. Dead in seconds, collapsed in convulsive wracks, frothing and gurgling. Oktar had only just sipped from his glass when someone sounded the alarm.

One sip. That, and Oktar's iron constitution, kept him alive for eight days.

Gaunt had been off in the barracks behind the hive central palace, settling a drunken brawl, when Tanhause summoned him. Nothing could be done.

By the eighth day, Oktar was a skeletal husk of his old, robust self. The medics emerged from his chamber, shaking hopeless heads. The smell of decay and corruption was almost overpowering. Gaunt waited in the anteroom. Some of the men, some of the toughest Hyrkans he had come to know, were weeping openly.

'He wants the Boy,' one of the doctors said as he came out, trying not to retch.

Gaunt entered the warm, sickly atmosphere of the chamber. Locked in a life-prolonging suspension field, surrounded by glowing fire-lamps and burning bowls of incense, Oktar was plainly minutes from death.

'Ibram...' The voice was like a whisper, a thing of no substance, smoke.

'Commissar-general.'

'It is past time for this. Well past time. I should never have left it to a finality like this. I've kept you waiting too long.'

'Waiting?'

'Truth of it is, I couldn't bear to lose you... not you, Ibram... far too good a soldier to hand away to the ladder of promotion. Who are you?'

Gaunt shrugged. The stench was gagging his throat.

'Cadet Ibram Gaunt, sir.'

'No... from now you are Commissar Ibram Gaunt, appointed in the extremis of the field to the commissarial office, to watch over the Hyrkan regiments. Fetch a clerk. We must record my authority in this matter, and your oath.'

Oktar willed himself to live for seventeen minutes more, as an Administratum clerk was found and the proper oath ceremony observed. He died clutching Commissar Gaunt's hands in his bony, sweat-oiled claws.

Ibram Gaunt was stunned, empty. Something had been torn out of his insides, torn out and flung away. When he wandered out into the anteroom, he didn't even notice the soldiers saluting him.

PART THREE

ONE

It wasn't the drums that Corbec really detested, it was the rhythm. There was no sense to it. Though the notes were a regular drum sound, the beats came sporadically like a fluctuating heart, overlapping and syncopated. The bombardment was still ever-present but now, as they closed on the source of the beating, the drumming overrode even the roar of the explosions beyond the front trenches.

Corbec knew his men were spooked even before Sergeant Curral said it. Down the channel ahead, Scout-Sergeant Mkoll was returning towards them. He had missed the signal to put on his respirator and his face was pinched, tinged with green. As soon as he saw the masked men of his company, he anxiously pulled on his own gas-hood.

'Report!' Corbec demanded quickly.

'It opens up ahead,' Mkoll said through his mask, breathing hard. 'There are wide manufactory areas ahead of us. We've broken right through their lines into the heart of this section of the industrial belt. I saw no one. But I heard the drums. It sounds like there are... well, thousands of them out there. They're bound to attack soon. But what are they waiting for?'

Corbec nodded and moved forward, ushering his men on behind him. They hugged the walls of the trench and assumed fire pattern formation, crouching low and aiming in a sweep above the head of the man in front.

The trench opened out from its zigzag into a wide, stone-walled basin which overlooked a slope leading down into colossal factory sheds.

The thump of the drums, the incessant and irregular beat, was now all-pervading.

Corbec waved two fire-teams forward on either flank, Drayl taking the right and Lukas taking the left. He led the front prong himself. The

71

slope was steep and watery-slick. By necessity, they became more concerned with keeping upright and descending than with raising their weapons defensively.

The concourse around the sheds was open and empty. Feeling exposed, Corbec beckoned his men on, the front prong of the attack spearheading out into a wide phalanx as men slipped down the slope and joined them. Drayl's team was now established to his right covering them, and soon Lukas's was also in position.

The drums now throbbed so loudly they vibrated the hard plastic lenses in their respirator masks and thudded against their chest walls.

Corbec scurried across the open space with eight men accompanying him and covering every quarter. Sergeant Grell moved another dozen in behind them as Corbec reached the first of the sheds. He looked back and saw the men were keeping the line well, although he was concerned to see Drayl lift his respirator for a moment to wipe his face with the back of his cuff. He knew the man was ill at ease following that unhappy injury, but he still disliked undisciplined activity.

'Get that fething mask in place!' he shouted at Trooper Drayl and then, with seven lasguns covering the angles, he entered the shed.

The gabled building throbbed with the sound of drums. Corbec could scarcely believe what he saw. Thousands of makeshift mechanisms had been set up in here, rotary engines and little spinning turbines, all in one way or another driving levers that beat drumsticks onto cylinders of every shape and size, all stretched with skin. Corbec didn't even want to think where that skin had come from. All that he was aware of was the syncopated and irregular thudding of the drum machines that the Shriven had left here. There was no pattern to their beat. Worse still, Corbec was more afraid that there was a pattern, and he was too sane to understand it.

A further sweep showed that the building was vacant, and scouting further they realised all of the sheds were filled with the makeshift drum machines... ten thousand drums, twenty thousand, of every size and shape, beating away like malformed, failing hearts.

Corbec's men closed in around the sheds to hold them and assumed close defensive file, but Corbec knew they were all scared and the rhythms throbbing through the air were more than most could stand.

He called up Skulane, his heavy flamer stinking of oil and dripping petroleum. He pointed to the first of the sheds. 'Sergeant Grell will block you with a fire-team,' he told the flame-thrower. 'You don't have to watch your back. Just burn each of these hell-holes in turn.'

Skulane nodded and paused to tighten a gasket on his fire-blackened weapon. He moved forward into the first doorway as Grell ordered up a tight company of men to guard him. Skulane raised his flamer, his finger whitening under the tin guard of the rubberised trigger.

There was a beat. A single beat. For one incredible moment all of the eccentric rhythms of the mechanical drums struck as one.

Skulane's head exploded. He dropped like a sack of vegetables onto the ground, the impact of his body and the spasm of his nervous system clenching the trigger on his flamer. The spike of fierce flame stabbed around in an unforgiving arc, burning first the portico of the blockhouse and then whipping back to incinerate three of the troopers guarding him. They shrieked and flailed as they were engulfed.

Panic hit the men and they spread out in scurrying bewildered patterns. Corbec howled a curse. Somehow, at the point of death, Skulane's finger had locked the trigger of the flamer and the weapon, slack on its cable beneath his dead form, whipped back and forth like a fire-breathing serpent. Two more soldiers were caught in its breath, three more. It scorched great conical scars across the muddy concrete of the concourse.

Corbec threw himself flat against the side wall of the shed as the flames ripped past him. His mind raced and thoughts formed slower than actions. A grenade was in his hand, armed with a flick of his thumb.

He leapt from cover, and screamed to any who could hear him to get down even as he flung the grenade at Skulane's corpse and the twisting flamer. The explosion was catastrophic, igniting the tanks on the back of the corpse. Fire, white hot, vomited up from the door of the shed and blew the front of the roof out. Sections of splintered stone collapsed down across the vestigial remains of Trooper Skulane.

Corbec, like many others, was knocked flat by the hot shockwave of the blast. Cowering in a ditch nearby, Scout-Sergeant Mkoll had avoided the worst of the blast. He had noticed something that Corbec had not, though with the continual beat of the drums, now irregular and unformed again, it was so difficult to concentrate. But he knew what he had seen.

Skulane had been hit from behind by a las-blast to the head. Cradling his own rifle, he scrambled around to try and detect the source of the attack. A sniper, he thought, one of the Shriven guerrillas lurking in this disputed territory.

All the men were on their bellies and covering their heads with their hands, all except Trooper Drayl, who stood with his lasgun held loosely and a smile on his face.

'Drayl!' Mkoll yelled, scrambling up from the trench. Drayl turned to face him across the concourse with a milky nothingness in his eyes. He raised his gun and fired.

* * *

TWO

Mkoll threw himself flat, but the first shot seared down the length of his back and broke his belt. Slumping into the ditch, he felt dull pain from the bubbled flesh along his shoulder blade. There was no blood. Las-fire cauterised whatever it hit.

There was shouting and panic, more panic than before. Whooping in a strange and chilling tone, Drayl turned and killed the two Ghosts nearest to him with point blank shots to the back of the head. As others scrambled to get out of his way, he turned his gun to full auto and blazed at them, killing five more, six, seven.

Corbec leapt to his feet, horrified at what he saw. He swung his lasgun into his shoulder, took careful aim and shot Drayl in the middle of the chest. Drayl barked out a cough and flew backwards with his feet and hands pointing out, almost comically.

There was a pause. Corbec edged forward, as did Mkoll and most of the men, those that didn't stop to try and help those that Drayl had blasted who were still alive.

'For feth's sake...' Corbec breathed as he walked forward towards the corpse of the dead guardsman. 'What the hell is going on?'

Mkoll didn't answer. He crossed the concourse in several fierce bounds and slammed into Corbec to bring him crashing to the ground.

Drayl wasn't dead. Something insidious and appalling was blistering and seething inside the sack of his skin. He rose, first from the hips and then to his feet. By the time he was standing, he was twice human size, his uniform and skin splitting to accommodate the twisting, enlarging skeletal structure that was transmuting within him.

Corbec didn't want to look. He didn't want to see the bony thing which was erupting from Drayl's flesh. Watery blood and fluid spat from Drayl as the Chaos infection grew something within him, something that burst out and stepped free of the shredded carcass that it had once inhabited.

Drayl, or the thing that had once been Drayl, faced them across the yard. It stood four metres high, a vast and grotesque skeletal form whose bones seemed as if they had been welded from tarnished sections of steel. The head was huge, topped by polished horns that twisted irregularly. Oil and blood and other unnameable fluids dripped from its structure. It looked like it was smiling. It turned its head from left to right, as if anticipating the carnage to come.

Corbec saw that, despite the fact that all fabric and flesh of Drayl had been shed away, the obscenity still wore his dog-tags.

The beast reached up with great metallic claws and screamed at the sky.

'Get into cover!' Corbec screamed to his terrified men and they fled into every shadow and crevice they could find. Corbec and Mkoll dropped into a culvert; the scout was shaking. Along the damp drainage channel, Corbec could see Trooper Melyr, who carried the company's rocket launcher. The man was too terrified to move. Corbec slithered down to him through the foetid soup and tried to pull the rocket launcher from his shoulder. Melyr was too limp and too scared to let it go easily.

'Mkoll! Help me, for feth's sake!' Corbec shouted as he wrestled with the weapon.

It came free. He had it in his hands, the unruly weight of the heavy weapon unfamiliar to his shoulders. A quick check told him it was primed and armed. A shadow fell across him.

The beast that was no longer Drayl stood over him and hissed with glee through its blunt, equine teeth.

Corbec fell on his back and tried to aim the rocket launcher, but it was wet and slippery in his hands and he slid in the mud of the culvert. He began to mutter: 'Holy Emperor, deliver us from the Darkness of the Void, guide my weapon in your service... Holy Emperor, deliver us from the Darkness of the Void...' He squeezed the trigger. Nothing happened. Damp was choking the baffles of the firing mechanism.

The thing reached down towards him and hooked him by the tunic with its metal fingers. Corbec was lifted up out of the channel, dangling at arm's length from the abomination. But the baffles were now clear. He squeezed the trigger mechanism again and the blast took the beast's head off at point blank range.

The explosion somersaulted Corbec back twenty paces and dumped him on his back in a pile of mud and slag. The rocket launcher skittered clear.

Headless, the obscenity teetered for a moment and then collapsed into the culvert. Sergeant Grell was right behind with a dozen men that he had roused out of their panic with oathing taunts. They stood around the lip of the culvert and fired their lasguns down at the twitching skeleton. In a few moments, the sculptural, metallic form of the beast was reduced to shrapnel and slag.

Corbec looked on a moment longer, then flopped back and lay prostrate.

Now he had seen everything. He couldn't quite get over the idea that it had been his fault all along. Drayl had been contaminated by that fragment from the damned statuette. Get a grip, he hissed to himself. The men need you. His teeth chattered. Rebels, bandits, even the foul orks he could manage, but this...

The bombardment continued over and behind them. Close at hand the drum machines continued to patter out their staccato message. For the first time since the fall of Tanith, weary beyond measure, Corbec felt tears in his eyes.

THREE

Evening fell. The Shriven bombardment continued as the light faded, a roaring forest of flames and mud-plumes three hundred kilometres wide. Gaunt believed he understood the enemy tactic. It was a double-headed win-win manoeuvre.

They had launched their offensive at dawn in the hope of breaking the Imperial frontline, but expecting stiff opposition which Gaunt and his men had provided. Failing to break the line, the Shriven had then countered by falling back far further than necessary, enticing the Imperial Guard forward to occupy the Shriven frontline... and place themselves in range of the Shriven's artillery batteries in the hills.

Lord Militant General Dravere had assured Gaunt and the other commanders that three weeks of carpet bombing from orbit by the Navy had pounded the enemy artillery positions into scrap metal, thus ensuring comparative safety for an infantry advance. True enough, the mobile field batteries used by the Shriven to harry the Imperial lines had taken a pasting. But they clearly had much longer range fixed batteries higher in the hills, dug in to bunker emplacements impervious even to orbital bombardment.

The weapons that were throwing the shells their way were leviathans, and Gaunt was not surprised. This was a forge-world after all, and though insane with the doctrines of Chaos, the Shriven were not stupid. They had been spawned among the engineers and artisans of Fortis Binary, trained and schooled by the Tech-Priests of Mars. They could make all the weapons they wanted and they had had months to prepare.

So here it was, a finely executed battlefield trap, drawing the Tanith First, the Vitrian Dragoons and Emperor knew who else across no-man's-land into abandoned trench lines and fortifications where a creeping curtain of shell-fire would slowly pull back, a metre at a time, and obliterate them all.

Already, the frontline of the Shriven's old emplacements had been destroyed. Only hours before, Gaunt and his men had fought hand to hand down those trenches to get into the Shriven lines. Now the futility of that fighting seemed bitter indeed.

The Ghosts with Gaunt, and the company of Vitrian Dragoons with whom they had joined up, were sheltering in some ruined manufactory spaces, a kilometre or so from the creeping barrage that was coming their way. They had no contact with any other Vitrian or Tanith unit. For all they knew, they were the only men to have made it this far. Certainly there was no sign or hope of a supporting manoeuvre from the main Imperial positions. Gaunt had hoped the wretched Jantine Patricians or perhaps even some of Dravere's elite storm troops might have been sent in to flank them, but the bombardment had put paid to that possibility.

The electro-magnetic and radio interference of the huge bombardment was also cutting their comm-lines. There was no possible contact with headquarters or their own frontline units, and even short range vox-cast traffic was chopped and distorted. Colonel Zoren was urging his communications officer to try to patch an uplink to any listening ship in orbit, in the hope that they might relay their location and plight. But the upper atmosphere of a world where war had raged for half a year was a thick blanket of petrochemical smog, ash, electrical anomalies and worse. Nothing was getting through.

The only sounds from the world around them were the concussive rumble of the shelling – and the background rhythm of the incessant drums.

Gaunt wandered through the dank shed where the men were holed up. They sat huddled in small groups, camo-cloaks pulled around them against the chilly night air. Gaunt had forbidden the use of stoves or heaters in case the enemy rangefinders were watching with heat-sensitive eyes. As it was, the plasteel-reinforced concrete of the manufactory would mask the slight traces of their body heat.

There were almost a hundred more Vitrian Dragoons than there were Ghosts, and they kept themselves pretty much to themselves, occupying the other end of the factory barn. Some slight interchange was taking place between the two regiments where their troops were in closer proximity, but it was a stilted exchange of greetings and questions. The Vitrians were a well-drilled and austere unit, and Gaunt had heard much praise heaped upon their stoic demeanour and approach to war.

He wondered himself if this clinical attitude, as clean and sharp-edged as the famous glass-filament mesh armour they wore, might perhaps be lacking in the essential fire and soul that made a truly great fighting unit. With the shellfire falling ever closer, he doubted he would ever find out.

Colonel Zoren gave up on his radio efforts and walked between his men to confront Gaunt. In the shadows of the shed, his dark-skinned face was hollow and resigned.

'What do we do, commissar-colonel?' he asked, deferring to Gaunt's braid. 'Do we sit here and wait for death to claim us like old men?'

Gaunt's breath fogged the air as he surveyed the gloomy shed. He shook his head. 'If we're to die,' he said, 'then let us die usefully at least. We have nearly four hundred men between us, colonel. Our direction has been chosen for us.'

Zoren frowned as if perplexed. 'How so?'

'To go back walks us into the bombardment, to go either left or right along the line of the fortification will take us no further from that curtain of death. There is only one way to go: deeper into their lines, forcing ourselves back to their new front line and maybe doing whatever harm we can once we get there.'

Zoren was silent for a moment, then a grin split his face. Even white teeth glinted in the darkness. Clearly the idea appealed to him. It had a simple logic and an element of honourable glory that Gaunt had hoped would please the Vitrian mindset.

'When shall we begin to move?' Zoren asked, buckling his mesh gauntlets back in place.

'The Shriven's creeping bombardment will have obliterated this area in the next hour or two. Any time before then would probably be smart. As soon as we can, in fact.'

Gaunt and Zoren exchanged nods and quickly went to rouse their officers and form the men up.

In less than ten minutes, the fighting unit was ready to move. The Tanith had all put fresh power clips in their lasguns, checked and replaced where necessary their focusing barrels, and adjusted their charge settings to half power as per Gaunt's instruction. The silver blades of the Tanith war knives attached to the bayonet lugs of their weapons were blackened with soil to stop them flashing. Camo-cloaks were pulled in tight and the Ghosts divided into small units of around a dozen men, each containing at least one heavy weapons trooper.

Gaunt observed the preparations of the Vitrians. They were drilled into larger fighting units of about twenty men each, and had fewer heavy weapons. Where heavy weapons appeared, they seemed to prefer the plasma gun. None of them had meltaguns or flamers as far as Gaunt could see. The Ghosts would take point, he decided.

The Vitrians attached spike-bladed bayonets to their lasguns, ran a synchronised weapons check with almost choreographed grace, and adjusted the charge settings of their weapons to maximum. Then, again in unison, they altered a small control on the waistband of their armour. With a slight shimmer in the darkness, the finely meshed glass of their body suits flipped and closed, so that the interlocking teeth were no longer the shiny ablative surface, but showed instead the dark, matt reverse side. Gaunt was impressed. Their functional armour had an efficient stealth mode for movement after dark.

The bombardment still shuddered and roared behind them, and it had become such a permanent feature they were almost oblivious to it. Gaunt conferred with Zoren as they both adjusted their micro-bead intercoms.

'Use channel Kappa,' said Gaunt, 'with channel Sigma in reserve. I'll take point with the Ghosts. Don't lag too far behind.'

Zoren nodded that he understood.

'I see you have instructed your men to set charge at maximum,' Gaunt said as an afterthought.

'It is written in the *Vitrian Art of War*: "Make your first blow sure enough to kill and there will be no need for a second."'

Gaunt thought about this for a moment. Then he turned to lead the convoy off.

FOUR

There were just two realities: the blackness of the foxhole below and the brilliant inferno of the bombardment above.

Trooper Caffran and the Vitrian cowered in the darkness and the mud at the bottom of the shell-hole as the fury raged overhead, like a firestorm on the face of the sun.

'Sacred Feth! I don't think we'll be getting out of here alive...' Caffran said darkly.

The Vitrian didn't cast him a glance. 'Life is a means towards death, and our own death may be welcomed as much as that of our foe.'

Caffran thought about this for a moment and shook his head sadly. 'What are you, a philosopher?'

The Vitrian trooper, Zogat, turned and looked at Caffran disdainfully. He had the visor of his helmet pulled up and Caffran could see little warmth in his eyes.

'The Byhata, the *Vitrian Art of War*. It is our codex, the guiding philosophy of our warrior caste. I do not expect you to understand.'

Caffran shrugged, 'I'm not stupid. Go on... how is war an art?'

The Vitrian seemed unsure if he was being mocked, but the language they had in common, Low Gothic, was not the native tongue of either of them, and Caffran's grasp of it was better than Zogat's. Culturally, their worlds could not have been more different.

'The Byhata contains the practice and philosophy of warriorhood. All Vitrians study it and learn its principles, which then direct us in the arena of war. Its wisdom informs our tactics, its strength reinforces our arms, its clarity focuses our minds and its honour determines our victory.'

'It must be quite a book,' Caffran said, sardonically.

'It is,' Zogat replied with a dismissive shrug.

'So do you commit it to memory or carry it with you?'

The Vitrian unbuttoned his flak armour tunic and showed Caffran the top of a thin, grey pouch that was laced into its lining. 'It is carried over the heart, a work of eight million characters transcribed and encoded onto mono-filament paper.'

Caffran was almost impressed. 'Can I see it?' he asked.

Zogat shook his head and buttoned up his tunic again. 'The filament paper is gene-coded to the touch of the trooper it is issued to so that no one else may open it. It is also written in Vitrian, which I am certain you cannot read. And even if you could, it is a capital offence for a non-Vitrian to gain access to the great text.'

Caffran sat back. He was silent for a moment. 'We Tanith... we've got nothing like that. No grand art of war.'

The Vitrian looked round at him. 'Do you have no code? No philosophy of combat?'

'We do what we do...' Caffran began. 'We live by the principle, "Fight hard if you have to fight and don't let them see you coming." That's not much, I suppose.'

The Vitrian considered this. 'It certainly... lacks the subtle subtext and deeper doctrinal significances of the Vitrian Art of War,' he said at last.

There was a long pause.

Caffran sniggered. Then they both erupted in almost uncontrollable laughter.

It took some minutes for their hilarity to die down, easing the morbid tension that had built up through the horrors of the day.

Even with the bombardment thundering overhead and the constant expectation that a shell would fall into their shelter and vaporise them, the fear in them seemed to relax.

The Vitrian opened his canteen, took a swig and offered it to Caffran. 'You men of Tanith... there are very few of you, I understand?'

Caffran nodded. 'Barely two thousand, all that Commissar-Colonel Gaunt could salvage from our home world on the day of our Founding as a regiment. The day our home world died.'

'But you have quite a reputation,' the Vitrian said.

'Have we? Yes, the sort of reputation that gets us picked for all the stealth and dirty commando work going, the sort of reputation that gets us sent into enemy-held hives and death worlds that no one else has managed to crack. I often wonder who'll be left to do the dirty jobs when they use the last of us up.'

'I often dream of my home world,' Zogat said thoughtfully, 'I dream of the cities of glass, the crystal pavilions. Though I am sure I will never see it again, it heartens me that it is always there in my mind. It must be hard to have no home left.'

Caffran shrugged. 'How hard is anything? Harder than storming an enemy position? Harder than dying? Everything about life in the Emperor's army is hard. In some ways, not having a home is an asset.'

Zogat shot him a questioning look.

'I've nothing left to lose, nothing I can be threatened with, nothing that can be held over me to force my hand or make me submit. There's just me, Imperial Guardsman Dermon Caffran, servant of the Emperor, may he hold the Throne for ever.'

'So then you see, you do have a philosophy after all,' Zogat said.

There was a long break in their conversation as they both listened to the guns. 'How... how did your world die, man of Tanith?' the Vitrian asked.

Caffran closed his eyes and thought hard for a moment, as if he was dredging up from a deep part of his mind something he had deliberately discarded or blocked. At last he sighed. 'It was the day of our Founding...' he began.

FIVE

They couldn't stay put, not there. Even if it hadn't been for the shelling that slowly advanced towards them, the thing with Drayl had left them all sick and shaking, and eager to get out.

Corbec ordered Sergeants Curral and Grell to mine the factory sheds and silence the infernal drumming. They would move on into the enemy lines and do as much damage as they could until they were stopped or relieved.

As the company – less than a hundred and twenty men since Drayl's corruption – prepared to move out, the scout Baru, one of the trio Corbec had sent ahead as they first moved in the area, returned at last, and he was not alone. He'd been pinned by enemy fire for a good half an hour in a zigzag of trenches to the east, and then the shelling had taken out his most direct line of return. For a good while, Baru had been certain he'd never reunite with his company. Edging through the wire festoons and stake posts along the weaving trench, he had encountered to his surprise five more Tanith: Feygor, Larkin, Neff, Lonegin and Major Rawne. They'd made it to the trenches as the bombardment had begun and were now wandering like lost livestock looking for a plan.

Corbec was as glad to see them as they were to see the company. Larkin was the best marksman in the regiment, and would be invaluable for the kind of insidious advance that lay ahead of them. Feygor, too, was a fine shot and a good stealther. Lonegin was good with explosives, so Corbec sent him immediately to assist Curral and Grell's demolition detail. Neff was a medic, and they could use all the medical help they could get. Rawne's tactical brilliance was not in question, and Corbec swiftly put a portion of the men under his direct command.

In the flicker of the shellfire against the night, which flashed and burst in a crazy syncopation against the beat of the drums, Grell returned to Corbec and reported the charges were ready; fifteen-minute settings.

Corbec advanced the company down the main communication way of the factory space away from the mined sheds at double-time, in a paired column with a floating spearhead fire-team of six: Sergeant Grell, the sniper Larkin, Mkoll and Baru the scouts, Melyr with the rocket launcher and Domor with a sweeper set. Their job was to pull ahead of the fast moving column and secure the path, carrying enough mobile firepower to do more than just warn the main company.

The sheds they had mined began to explode behind them. Incandescent mushrooms of green and yellow flame punched up into the blackness, shredding the dark shapes of the buildings and silencing the nearest drums.

Other, more distant rhythms made themselves heard as the roar died back. The drum contraptions closest to them had masked the fact that others lay further away. The beating ripple tapped at them. Corbec spat sourly. The drums were grating at him, making his temper rise. It reminded him of nights back home in the nalwood forests of Tanith. Stamp on a chirruping cricket near your watchfire and a hundred more would take up the call beyond the firelight.

'Come on,' he growled at his men. 'We'll find them all. We'll stamp 'em all out. Every fething one of 'em.'

There was a heartfelt murmur of agreement from his company. They moved forward.

Milo grabbed Gaunt's sleeve and pulled him around just a heartbeat before greenish explosions lit the sky about six kilometres to their west.

'Closer shelling?' Milo asked. The commissar pulled his scope round and the milled edge of the automatic dial whirred and spun as he played the field of view over the distant buildings.

'What was that?' Zoren's voice rasped over the short range intercom. 'That was not shellfire.'

'Agreed,' Gaunt replied. He ordered his men to halt and hold the area they had reached, a damp and waterlogged section of low-lying storage bays. Then he dropped back with Milo and a couple of troopers to meet with Zoren who led his men up to meet them.

'Someone else is back here with us, on the wrong side of hell,' he told the Vitrian leader. 'Those buildings were taken out with krak charges, standard issue demolitions.'

Zoren nodded his agreement. 'I... I am afraid...' he began respectfully, '...that I doubt it is any of mine. Vitrian discipline is tight. Unless driven by some necessity unknown to us, Vitrian troops would not ignite explosions like that. It might as well act as a marker fire for the enemy guns. They'll soon be shelling that section, knowing someone was there.'

Gaunt scratched his chin. He had been pretty sure it was a Tanith action too: Rawne, Feygor, Curral... maybe even Corbec himself. All of them had a reputation of acting without thinking from time to time.

As they watched, another series of explosions went off. More sheds destroyed.

'At this rate,' Gaunt snapped, 'they might as well vox their position to the enemy!'

Zoren called his communications officer to join them and Gaunt wound the channel selector on the vox-set frantically as he repeated his call sign into the wire-framed microphone. The range was close. There was a chance.

They had just set and flattened the third series of drum-sheds and were moving into girder-framed tunnels and walkways when Lukas called over to Colonel Corbec. There was a signal.

Corbec hurried over across the wet concrete, ordering Curral to take his demolition squad to the next row of thumping, clattering drum-mills. He took the headphones and listened. A tinny voice was repeating a call sign, chopped and fuzzed by the atrocious radio conditions. There was no mistaking it – it was the Tanith regimental command call sign.

At his urgings, Lukas cranked the brass dial for boost and Corbec yelled his call sign hoarsely into the set.

'Corbec!... olonel!... peat is that you?... mining... peat s... ive away p...'

'Say again! Commissar, I'm losing your signal! Say again!'

Zoren's communications officer looked up from the set and shook his head. 'Nothing, commissar. Just white noise.'

Gaunt told him to try again. Here was a chance, so close, to increase the size of their expeditionary force and move forward in strength – if

Corbec could be dissuaded from his suicidal actions in the face of the guns.

'Corbec! This is Gaunt! Desist your demolition and move sharp east at double time! Corbec, acknowledge!'

'Ready to blow,' Curral called, but stopped short as Corbec held up his hand for quiet. By the set, Lukas craned to hear past the roar of the shelling and the thunder of the drumming.

'W-we're to stop... he's ordering us to stop and move east double-time... w-we're...'

Lukas looked up at the colonel with suddenly anxious eyes.

'He says we're going to draw the enemy guns down on us.'

Corbec turned slowly and looked up into the night, where the shells streaking from the distant heavy emplacements tore whistling furrows of light out of the ruddy blackness.

'Sacred Feth!' he breathed as he realised the foolhardy course his anger had made them follow.

'Move! Move!' he yelled, and the men scrambled up in confusion. At a run, he led them around, sending a signal ahead to pull his vanguard back around in their wake. He knew he had scarce seconds to get his men clear of the target zone they had lit with their mines, an arrow of green fire virtually pointing to their advance.

He had to pull them east. East was what Gaunt had said. How close was the commissar's company? A kilometre? Two? How close was the enemy shelling? Were they already swinging three tonne deuterium macro-shells filled with oxy-phosphor gel into the gaping breeches of the vast Shriven guns, as range finders calibrated brass sights and the sweating thews of gunners cranked round the vast greasy gears that lowered the huge barrels a fractional amount?

Corbec led his men hard. There was barely time for running cover. He put his faith in the fact that the Shriven had pulled back and left the area.

The Vitrian communications officer played back the last signal they had received, and made adjustments to his set to try to wash the static out. Gaunt and Zoren watched intently.

'A response signal, I think,' the officer said. 'An acknowledgement.'

Gaunt nodded. 'Take up position here. We'll hold this area until we can form up with Corbec.'

At that moment, the area to their west where Corbec's mines had lit up the night, and the area around it, began to erupt. Lazily blossoming fountains of fire, ripple after ripple, annihilated the zone. Explosion overlaid explosion as the shells fell together. The Shriven had pulled a section of their overall barrage back by about three kilometres to target the signs of life they had seen.

Gaunt could do nothing but watch.

Colonel Flense was a man who'd modelled his career on the principle of opportunity. That was what he seized now, and he could taste victory.

Since the abortive Jantine advance in the late afternoon, he had withdrawn to the Imperium command post to consider an alternative. Nothing was possible while the enemy barrage was curtaining off the entire front. But Flense wanted to be ready to move the moment it stopped or the moment it faltered. The land out there after such a bombardment would be ash-waste and mud, as hard for the Shriven to hold as it was for the Imperials. The perfect opportunity for a surgical armoured strike.

By six that evening, as the light began to fail, Flense had a strike force ready in the splintered streets below a bend in the river. Eight Leman Russ siege tanks, the beloved Demolishers with their distinctive short thick barrels, four standard Phaethon-pattern Leman Russ battle tanks, three Griffon Armoured Weapons Carriers, and nineteen Chimeras carrying almost two hundred Jantine Patricians in full battledress.

He was at the ducal palace, discussing operational procedures with Dravere and several other senior officers, who were also trying to assess the losses in terms of Tanith and Vitrians sustained that day, when the vox-caster operator from the watchroom entered with a sheaf of transparencies that the cogitators of the orbital Navy had processed and sent down.

They were orbital shots of the barrage. The others studied them with passing interest, but Flense seized on them at once. One shot showed a series of explosions going off at least a kilometre inside the bombardment line.

Flense showed it to Dravere, taking the general to one side.

'Short fall shells,' was the general's comment.

'No sir, these are a chain of fires... the blast areas of set explosions. Someone's inside there.'

Dravere shrugged. 'So someone survived.'

Flense was stern. 'I have dedicated myself and my Patricians to taking this section of the front, and therein taking the world itself. I will not stand by and watch as vagabond survivors run interference behind the lines and ruin our strategies.'

'You take it so personally, Flense...' Dravere smiled.

Flense knew he did, but he also recognised an opportunity. 'General, if a break appears in the bombardment, do I have your signal permission to advance? I have an armoured force ready.'

Bemused, the lord general consented. It was dinner time and he was preoccupied. Even so, the prospect of victory charmed him. 'If you win this for me, Flense, I'll not forget it. There are great possibilities in my future, if I am not tied here. I would share them with you.'

'Your will be done, Lord Militant General.'

Flense's keen opportunistic mind had seen the possibility – that the Shriven might retarget their bombardment, or better still a section of it, to flatten the activity behind their old lines. And that would give him an opening.

Taking his lead from the navigation signals transmitted from the fleet to an astropath in his lead tank, Flense rumbled his column out of the west, along the river road and then out across a pontoon bridge-head as far as he dared into the wasteland. The Shriven bombardment dropped like fury before his vehicles.

Flense almost missed his opportunity. He had barely got his vehicles into position when the break appeared. A half-kilometre stretch of the bombardment curtain abruptly ceased and then reappeared several kilometres further on, targeting the section that the orbital shots had shown.

There was a doorway through the destruction, a way in to get at the Shriven.

Flense ordered his vehicles on. At maximum thrust they tore and bounced and slithered over the mud and into the Shriven heartland.

SIX

The voice of Trooper Caffran floated out of the fox-hole darkness, just audible over the shelling.

'Tanith was a glorious place, Zogat. A forest world, evergreen, dense and mysterious. The forests themselves were almost spiritual. There was a peace there... and they were strange too. What they call motile treegrowth, so I'm told. Basically, the trees, a kind we called nalwood, well... moved, replanted, repositioned themselves, following the sun, the rains, whatever tides and urges ran in their sap. I don't pretend to understand it. It was just the way things were.

'Essentially, the point is, there was no frame of reference for location on Tanith. A track or a pathway through the nal-forest might change or vanish or open anew overnight. So, over the generations, the people of Tanith got an instinct for direction. For tracking and scouting. We're good at it. I guess we can thank those moving forests of our homeworld for the reputation this regiment has for recon and stealth.'

'The great cities of Tanith were splendid. Our industries were agrarian, and our off-world trade was mainly fine, seasoned timbers and wood carving. The work of the Tanith craftsmen was something to behold. The cities were great, stone bastions that rose up out of the forest. You say you have glass palaces back home. This was nothing so fancy. Just simple stone, grey like the sea, raised up high and strong.'

Zogat said nothing. Caffran eased his position in the dark mud-hole to be more comfortable. Despite the bitterness in his voice and his soul, he felt a mournful sense of loss he had not experienced for a long while.

'Word came that Tanith was to raise three regiments for the Imperial Guard. It was the first time our world had been asked to perform such a duty, but we had a large number of able fighting men trained in the municipal militias. The process of the Founding took eight months, and the assembled troops were waiting on wide, cleared plains when the transport ships arrived in orbit. We were told we were to join the Imperial Forces engaged in the Sabbat Worlds campaign, driving out the forces of Chaos. We were also told we would probably never see our world again, for once a man had joined the service he tended to go on wherever the war took him until death claimed him or he was mustered out to start a new life wherever he had ended up. I'm sure they told you the same thing.'

Zogat nodded, his noble profile a sad motion of agreement in the wet dark of the crater. Explosions rippled above them in a long, wide series. The ground shook.

'So we were waiting there,' Caffran continued, 'thousands of us, itchy in our stiff new fatigues, watching the troop ships roll in and out. We were eager to be going, sad to be saying goodbye to Tanith. But the idea that it was always there, and would always be there, kept our spirits up. On that last morning we learned that Commissar Gaunt had been appointed to our regiment, to knock us into shape.' Caffran sighed, trying to resolve his darker feelings towards the loss of his world. He cleared his throat. 'Gaunt had a certain reputation, and a long and impressive history with the veteran Hyrkan regiments. We were new, of course, inexperienced and certainly full of rough edges. High Command clearly believed it would take an officer of Gaunt's mettle to make a fighting force out of us.'

Caffran paused. He lost the track of his voice for a moment as anger welled inside him. Anger – and the sense of absence. He realised with a twinge that this was the first time since the Loss that he had recounted the story aloud. His heart closed convulsively around threads of memory, and he felt his bitterness sharpen. 'It all went wrong on that very last night. Embarkation had already begun. Most of the troops were either aboard transports waiting for takeoff or were heading up into orbit already. The Navy's picket duty had not done its job, and a significantly-sized Chaos fleet, a splinter of a larger fleet running scared since the last defeat the Imperial Navy had inflicted, slipped into the Tanith system past the blockades. There was very little warning. The forces of Darkness attacked my home world and erased it from the galactic records in the space of one night.'

Caffran paused again and cleared his throat. Zogat was looking at him in fierce wonder. 'Gaunt had a simple choice to deploy the troops at his disposal for a brave last stand, or to take all those he could save and get clear. He chose the latter. None of us liked that decision. We all wanted to give our lives fighting for our home world. I suppose if we'd stayed on Tanith, we would have achieved nothing except maybe a valiant footnote in history. Gaunt saved us. He took us from a destruction we would have been proud to be a part of so that we could enjoy a more significant destruction elsewhere.'

Zogat's eyes were bright in the darkness. 'You hate him.'

'No! Well, yes, I do, as I would hate anyone who had supervised the death of my home, anyone who had sacrificed it to some greater good.'

'Is this a greater good?'

'I've fought with the Ghosts on a dozen warfronts. I haven't seen a greater good yet.'

'You do hate him.'

'I admire him. I will follow him anywhere. That's all there is to say. I left my home world the night it died, and I've been fighting for its memory ever since. We Tanith are a dying breed. There are only about twenty hundred of us left. Gaunt only got away with enough for one regiment. The Tanith First. The First and Only. That's what makes us "ghosts", you see. The last few unquiet souls of a dead world. And I suppose we'll keep going until we're all done.'

Caffran fell silent and in the dimness of the shell-hole there was no sound except the fall of the bombardment outside. Zogat was silent for a long while, then he looked up at the paling sky. 'It will be dawn in two hours,' he said softly. 'Maybe we'll see our way out of this when it gets light.'

'You could be right,' Caffran replied, stretching his aching, mud-caked limbs. 'The bombardment does seem to be moving away. Who knows, we might live through this after all. Feth, I've lived through worse.'

* * *

SEVEN

Daylight rolled in with a wet stain of cloud, underlit by the continued bombardment. The lightening sky was streaked and cross-hatched by contrails, shell-wakes and arcs of fire from the massive Shriven emplacements in the distant shrouded hills. Lower, in the wide valley and the trench lines, the accumulated smoke of the onslaught, which had now been going on for just about twenty-one hours, dropping two or three shells a second, curdled like fog, thick, creamy and repellent with the stink of cordite and fyceline.

Gaunt brought his assembled company to a halt in a silo bay that had once held furnaces and bell kilns. They pulled off their rebreather masks. The floor, the air itself, was permeated with a greenish microdust that tasted of iron or blood. Shattered plastic crating was scattered all over the place. They were five kilometres from the bombardment line now, and the noise of the drum-mills, chattering away in barns and manufactories all around them, was even louder than the shells.

Corbec had got his men away from the fire zone just about intact, although everyone had been felled by the shockwave and eighteen had been deafened permanently by the air-burst. The Imperial Guard infirmaries over the lines would patch ruptured ear drums with plastene diaphragms or implant acoustic enhancers in a matter of moments. But that was over the lines. Out here, eighteen deaf men were a liability. When they formed up to move, Gaunt would station them in the midst of his column, where they could take maximum guidance and warning from the men around them. There were other injuries too, a number of broken arms, ribs and collarbones. However, everyone was walking and that was a mercy.

Gaunt took Corbec to one side. Gaunt knew a good soldier instinctively, and it worried him when confidence was misplaced. He'd chosen Corbec to offset Rawne. Both men commanded respect from the Tanith First and Only, one because he was liked and the other because he was feared.

'Not like you to make a tactical error of that magnitude...' Gaunt began.

Corbec started to say something and then cut himself short. The idea of making excuses to the commissar stuck in his throat.

Gaunt made them for him. 'I understand we're all in a tight spot. This circumstance is extreme, and your lot had suffered particularly. I heard about Drayl. I also think these drum-mills, which you decided to target with an almost suicidal determination, are meant to disorientate.

Meant to make us act irrationally. Let's face it, they're insane. They are as much a weapon as the guns. They are meant to wear us down.'

Corbec nodded. The war had pooled bitterness in his great, hoary form. There was a touch of weariness to his look and manner.

'What's our plan? Do we wait for the barrage to stop and retreat?'

Gaunt shook his head. 'I think we've come in so deep, we can do some good. We'll wait for the scouts to return.'

The recon units returned to the shelter within half an hour. The scouts, some Vitrian, mostly Tanith, combined the data from their sweeps and built a picture of the area in a two kilometre radius for Gaunt and Zoren.

What interested Gaunt most was a structure to the west.

They moved through a wide section of drainage pipelines, through rain-washed concrete underpasses stained with oil and dust.

The cordite fog drifted back over their positions. To the west rose the great hill line, to the immediate north the shadowy bulk of habitat spires, immense conical towers for the workforce that rose out of the ground fog, their hundred thousand windows all blown out by shelling and air-shock. There were fewer drum-mills in this range of the enemy territory, but still no sign of a solitary living thing, not even vermin.

They began passing blast-proofed bunkers of great size, all empty except for scattered support cradles and stacking pallets of grey fibre-plast. A crowd of battered, yellow, heavy-lift trolleys were abandoned on the concourses before the bunkers.

'Munitions stores?' Zoren suggested to Gaunt as they advanced. 'They must have stockpiled a vast amount of shells for this bombardment and they've already emptied these sheds.'

Gaunt thought this a good guess. They edged on, cautious, marching half-time and with weapons ready. The structure the reconnaissance had reported was ahead now, a cargo loading bay of tubular steel and riveted blast-board. The bay was mounted with hydraulic cranes and derricks on the surface, poised to lower cargo into a cavity below ground.

The guardsmen descended on the metal grilled stairway onto a raised platform that lay alongside a wide, well-lit tunnel that ran off out of sight into the impacted earth. The tunnel was modular, circular in cross section, with a raised spine running along the lowest part. Feygor and Grell examined the tunnel and the armoured control post overlooking it.

'Maglev line,' said Feygor, who had done all he could to augment his basic engineering knowledge with off-world mechanisms. 'Still active. They cart the shells from the munitions dump and lower them into the bay, then load them onto bomb trains for fast delivery to the emplacements in the hills.'

He showed Gaunt an indicator board in the control position. The flat-plate glowed green, showing a flickering runic depiction of a track network. 'There's a whole transit system down here, purpose-built to link all the forge factories and allow for rapid transportation of material.'

'And this spur has been abandoned because they've exhausted the munitions stores in this area.' Gaunt was thoughtful. He took out his data-slate and made a working sketch of the network map.

The commissar ordered a ten-minute rest, then sat on the edge of the platform and compared his sketch with area maps of the old factory complexes from the slate's tactical archives. The Shriven had modified a lot of the details, but the basic elements were still the same.

Colonel Zoren joined him. 'Something's on your mind,' he began.

Gaunt gestured to the tunnel. 'It's a way in. A way right into the central emplacements of the Shriven. They won't have blocked it because they need these maglev lines active and clear to keep the bomb trains moving to feed their guns.'

'There's something odd, though, don't you think?' Zoren eased back the visor of his helmet.

'Odd?'

'Last night, I thought your assessment of their tactics was correct. They'd tried a frontal assault to pierce our lines, but when it failed they pulled back to an extreme extent to lure us in and then set the bombardment to flatten any Imperial forces they'd drawn out.'

'That makes sense of the available facts,' Gaunt said.

'Even now? They must know they could only have caught a few thousand of us with that trick, and logic says most of us would be dead by now. So why are they still shelling? Who are they firing at? It's exhausting their shell stocks, it must be. They've been at it for over a day. And they've abandoned such a huge area of their lines.'

Gaunt nodded. 'That was on my mind too when dawn broke. I think it began as an effort to wipe out any forces they had trapped. But now? You're right. They've sacrificed a lot of land and the continued bombardments make no sense.'

'Unless they're trying to keep us out,' a voice said from behind them. Rawne had joined them.

'Let's have your thoughts, major,' Gaunt said.

Rawne shrugged and spat heavily on to the floor. His black eyes narrowed to a frowning squint. 'We know the spawn of Chaos don't fight wars with any tactics we'd recognise. We've been held on this front for months. I think yesterday was a last attempt to break us with a conventional offensive. Now they've put up a wall of fire to keep us out while they switch to something else. Maybe something that's taken them months to prepare.'

'Something like what?' Zoren asked uncomfortably.

'Something. I don't know. Something using their Chaos power. Something ceremonial. Those drum-mills... maybe they aren't psychological warfare... maybe they're part of some vast... ritual.'

The three men were silent for a moment. Then Zoren laughed, a mocking snarl. 'Ritual magic?'

'Don't mock what you don't understand!' Gaunt warned. 'Rawne could be right. Emperor knows, we've seen enough of their madness.' Zoren didn't reply. He'd seen things too, perhaps things his mind wanted to deny or scrub out as impossible.

Gaunt got up and pointed down the tunnel. 'Then this is a way in. And we'd better take it – because if Rawne's right, we're the only units in a position to do a damn thing about it.'

EIGHT

It was possible to advance down the maglev tunnel four abreast, with two men on each side of the central rider spine. It was well lit by recessed blue-glow lighting in the tunnel walls, but Gaunt sent Domor and the other sweepers in the vanguard to check for booby traps.

An unopposed advance down the stuffy tunnels took them two kilometres east, passing another abandoned cargo bay and forks with two other maglev spurs. The air was dry and charged with static from the still-powered electromagnetic rail, and hot gusts of wind breathed on them periodically as if heralding a train that never came.

At the third spur, Gaunt turned the column into a new tunnel, following his map. They'd gone about twenty metres when Milo whispered to the commissar.

'I think we need to go back to the spur fork,' he said.

Gaunt didn't query. He trusted Brin's instincts like his own, and knew they stretched further. He retreated the whole company to the junction they had just passed. Within a minute, a hot breeze blew at them, the tunnel hummed and a maglev train whirred past along the spur they had been about to join. It was an automated train of sixty open carts, painted khaki with black and yellow flashing. Each cart was laden with shells and munitions, hundreds of tonnes of ordnance from distant bunkers destined for the main batteries. As the train rolled past on the magnetic-levitation rail, slick and inertia free, many of the men gawked openly at it. Some made signs of warding off and protection.

Gaunt consulted his sketch map. It was difficult to determine how far it was to the next station or junction, and without knowing the frequency of the bomb trains, he couldn't guarantee they'd be out of the tunnel before the next one rumbled through.

Gaunt cursed. He didn't want to turn back now. His mind raced as he reviewed his troop files, scrabbling to recall personal details.

'Domor!' he called, and the trooper hurried over.

'Back on Tanith, you and Grell were engineers, right?'

The young trooper nodded. 'I was apprenticed to a timber haulier in Tanith Attica. I worked with heavy machines.'

'Given the resources at hand, could you stop one of these trains?'

'Sir?'

'And then start it again?'

Domor scratched his neck as he thought. 'Short of blowing the mag-rail itself... You'd need to block or short out the power that drives the train. As I understand it, the trains move on the rails, sucking up a power source from them. It's a conductive electrical exchange, as I've seen on batteries and flux-units. We'd need some non-conductive material, fine enough to lay across the rider-spine without actually derailing the train. What do you have in mind, sir?'

'Stopping or slowing the next train that passes, jumping a ride and starting it again.'

Domor grinned. 'And riding it all the way to the enemy?' He chuckled and looked around. Then he set off towards Colonel Zoren, who was conversing with some of his men as they rested. Gaunt followed.

'Excuse me, sir,' Domor began with a tight salute, 'may I examine your body armour?'

Zoren looked at the Tanith trooper with confusion and some contempt but Gaunt soothed him with a quiet nod. Zoren peeled off a gauntlet and handed it to Domor. The young Tanith examined it with keen eyes.

'It's beautiful work. Is this surface tooth made of glass bead?'

'Yes, mica. Glass, as you say. Scale segments woven onto a base fabric of thermal insulation.'

'Non-conductive,' Domor said, showing the glove to Gaunt. 'I'd need a decent-sized piece. Maybe a jacket – and it may not come back in one piece.'

Gaunt was about to explain, hoping Zoren would ask for a volunteer from among his men. But the colonel got to his feet, took off his helmet and handed it to his subaltern before stripping off his own jacket.

Standing in his sleeveless undervest, his squat, powerful frame, shaven black hair and black skin revealed for the first time, Zoren paused only to remove a slim, grey-sleeved book from a pouch in his jacket before handing it to Domor. Zoren carefully tucked the book into his belt.

'I take it this is part of a plan?' Zoren asked as Domor hurried away, calling to Grell and others to assist him.

'You'll love it,' Gaunt said.

A warm gust of air announced the approach of the next train, some seventeen minutes or so after the first they had seen. Domor had wrapped the Vitrian major's jacket over the rider-rail just beyond the spur and tied a length of material cut from his own camo-cloak to it.

The train rolled into view. Every one of them watched with bated breath. The front cart passed over the jacket without any problem, suspended as it was just a few centimetres above the smooth rail by the electromagnetic repulsion so that the whole vehicle ran friction-free along the spine. Gaunt frowned. For a moment he was sure it hadn't worked.

But as soon as the front cart had passed beyond the non-conductive layer, the electromagnetic current was broken, and the train decelerated fast as the propelling force went dead. Forward momentum carried the train forward for a while – by the track-side, Domor prayed it would not carry the entire train beyond the circuit break, or it would simply start again – but it went dead at last and came to a halt, rocking gently on the suspension field.

There was a cheer.

'Mount up! Quick as you can!' Gaunt ordered, leading the company forward. Vitrians and Tanith alike clambered up onto the bomb-laden carriages, finding foot and handholds where they could, stowing weapons and holding out hands to pull comrades aboard. Gaunt, Zoren, Milo, Bragg and six Vitrians mounted the front cart alongside Mkoll, Curral and Domor, who still clutched the end of the cloth rope.

'Good work, trooper,' Gaunt said to the smiling Domor and held a hand up as he watched down the train to make sure all had boarded and were secure. In short order, the entire company was in place, and relays of acknowledgements ran down the train to Gaunt.

Gaunt dropped his hand. Domor yanked hard on the cloth cord. It went taut, fought him and then flew free, pulling Zoren's jacket up and out from under the cart like a large flatfish on a line.

In a moment, as the circuit was restored, the train lurched and silently began to move again, quickly picking up speed. The tunnel lights began to strobe-flash as they flicked past them.

Clinging on carefully, Domor untied his makeshift cord and handed the jacket back to Zoren. Parts of the glass fabric had been dulled and fused by contact with the rail, but it was intact. The Vitrian pulled it back on with a solemn nod.

Gaunt turned to face the tunnel they were hurtling into. He opened his belt pouch and pulled out a fresh drum-pattern magazine for his bolt pistol. The sixty round capacity clip was marked with a blue cross to indicate the inferno rounds it held. He clicked it into place and then thumbed his wire headset.

'Ready, weapons ready. Word is given. We're riding into the mouth of hell and we could be among them any minute. Prepare for sudden engagement. Emperor be with you all.'

Along the train, lasguns whined as they powered up, launchers clicked to armed, plasma packs hummed into seething readiness and the ignitors on flamer units were lit.

NINE

'Come on,' Caffran said, wriggling up the side of the stinking shell-hole that had been home for the best part of a day. Zogat followed. They blinked up into the dawn light. The barrage was still thundering away, and smoke-wash fog licked down across no-man's-land.

'Which way?' Zogat asked, disorientated by the smoke and the light.

'Home.' Caffran said. 'Away from the face of hell while we have the chance.'

They trudged into the mud, struggling over wire and twisted shards of concrete.

'Do you think we may be the only two left?' the Vitrian asked, glancing back at the vast barrage.

'We may be, we may be indeed. And that makes me the last of the Tanith.'

The Jantine armoured unit stabbed into the Shriven positions behind the barrage, but in two kilometres or more of advancing they had met nothing. The old factory areas were lifeless and deserted.

Flense called a halt and rose out of the top hatch to scan the way ahead through his scope. The ruined and empty buildings stood around in the fog like phantoms. There was a relentless drumming sound that bit into his nerves.

'Head for the hill line,' he told his driver as he dropped back inside. 'If we do no more than silence their batteries, we will have entered the chapters of glory.'

* * *

Four kilometres, five, passing empty stations and unlit cargo bays. A spur to the left, then to the left again, and then an anxious pause of three minutes, waiting while another bomb train passed ahead of them from another siding. Then they were moving again.

The tension wrapped Gaunt like a straitjacket. All of the passing tunnel looked constant and familiar, there were no markers to forewarn or alert. Any moment.

The bomb train slid into a vast cargo bay on a spur siding, coming to rest alongside two other trains that were being offloaded by cranes and servitor lifters. An empty train was just leaving on a loop that would take it back to the munitions dumps.

The chamber was lofty and dark, lit by thousands of lanterns and the ruddy glare of work-lamps. It was hot and smelled bitter, like a furnace room. The walls, as they could see them, were inscribed with vast sigils of Chaos, and draped with filthy banners. The symbols made the guardsmen's eyes weep if they glanced at them and made their heads pound if they looked for longer. Unclean symbols, symbols of pestilence and decay.

There were upwards of two hundred Shriven in the dim, gantried chamber, working the lifters or sliding bomb trolleys. None of them seemed to notice the new train's extra cargo for a moment.

Gaunt's company dismounted from the train, opening fire as they went, laying down a hail of las-fire that cracked like electricity in the air. There was the whine of the Tanith guns on the lower setting and the stinging punch of the full-force Vitrian shots. Gaunt had forbidden the use of meltas, rockets and flamers until they were clear of the munitions bay. None of the shells were fused or set, but there was no sense cooking or exploding them.

Dozens of the Shriven fell where they stood. Two half-laden shell trolleys spilled over as nerveless hands released levers. Warheads rolled and chinked on the platform. A trolley of shells veered into a wall as its driver was shot, and overturned. A crane assembly exploded and collapsed.

The guardsmen surged onwards. The Vitrian Dragoons fanned out in a perfect formation, taking point of cover after point of cover and scything down the fleeing Shriven. A few had found weapons and were returning fire, but their efforts were dealt with mercilessly.

Gaunt advanced up the main loading causeway with the Tanith, blasting Shriven with his bolt pistol. Nearby, Mad Larkin and a trio of other Tanith snipers with the needle-pattern lasguns were ducked in cover and picking off Shriven on the overhead catwalks.

Trooper Bragg had an assault cannon which he had liberated from a pintle mount some weeks before. Gaunt had never seen a man fire one without the aid of a power armour's recoil compensators or lift capacity before. Bragg grimaced and strained with the effort of steadying the howling weapon with its six cycling barrels, and his aim was its usual miserable standard. He killed dozens of the enemy anyway. Not to mention a maglev train.

The Ghosts led the fight up out of the cargo bay and onto loading ramps which extended up through great caverns cut into the hillside. A layer of blue smoke rose up under the flickering pendulum lighting rigs.

Clear of the munitions deck, Gaunt ordered up his meltas, flamers and rocket launchers, and began to scour a path, blackening the concrete strips of the ramps and fusing Shriven bone into syrupy pools.

At the head of the ramps, at the great elevator assemblies which raised the bomb loads into the battery magazines high above them in the hillside, they met the first determined resistance. A massed force of Shriven troops rushed down at them, blasting with lasguns and autorifles. Rawne commanded a fire-team up the left flank and cut into them from the edge, matched by Corbec's platoons from the right, creating a crossfire that punished them terribly.

In the centre of the Shriven retaliation, Gaunt saw the first of the Chaos Space Marines, a huge horned beast, centuries old and bearing the twisted markings of the Iron Warriors Chapter. The monstrosity exhorted his mutated troops to victory with great howls from his augmented larynx. His ancient, ornate boltgun spat death into the Tanith ranks. Sergeant Grell was vaporised by one of the first hits, two of his fire-team a moment later.

'Target him!' Gaunt yelled at Bragg, and the giant turned his huge firepower in the general direction with no particular success. The Chaos Marine proceeded to punch butchering fire into the Vitrian front line. Then he exploded. Headless, armless, his legs and torso rocked for a moment and then fell.

Gaunt nodded his grim thanks to Trooper Melyr and his missile launcher. Las-fire and screaming autogun rounds wailed down from the Shriven units at the elevator assembly. Gaunt ducked behind some freight pallets and found himself sharing the cover with two Vitrians who were busy changing the power cells of their lasguns.

'How much ammo have you left?' Gaunt asked briskly as he swapped the empty drum of his bolt pistol with a fresh sickle-pattern clip of Kraken penetrators.

'Half gone already,' responded one, a Vitrian corporal.

Gaunt thumbed his micro-bead headset. 'Gaunt to Zoren!'

'I hear you, commissar-colonel.'

'Instruct your men to alter their settings to half-power.'

'Why, commissar?'

'Because they're exhausting their ammo! I admire your ethic, colonel, but it doesn't take a full power shot to kill one of the Shriven and your men are going to be out of clips twice as fast as mine!'

There was a crackling pause over the comm-line before Gaunt heard Zoren give the order.

Gaunt looked across at the two troopers who were adjusting their charge settings.

'It'll last longer, and you'll send more to glory. No point in overkill,' he said with a smile. 'What are you called?'

'Zapol,' said one.

'Zeezo,' said the other, the corporal.

'Are you with me, boys?' Gaunt asked with a wolfish grin as he hefted up his pistol and thumbed his chainsword to maximum revs. They nodded back, lasrifles held in strong, ready hands.

Gaunt and the two dragoons burst from cover firing. They were more than halfway up the loading ramp to the elevators. Rawne's crossfire manoeuvre had fenced the Shriven in around the hazard-striped blast doors, which were now fretted and punctured with las-impacts and fusing burns.

As he charged, Gaunt felt the wash of fire behind him as his own units covered and supported.

He could hear the whine of the long-pattern sniper guns, the crack of the regular lasweapons, the rattle of Bragg's cannons.

'Keep your aim up, Try Again...' Gaunt hissed as he and the two dragoons reached the makeshift defences around the enemy.

Zeezo went down, clipped by a las-round. Gaunt and Zapol bounded up to the debris cover and cut into the now-panicked Shriven. Gaunt emptied his boltgun and ditched it, scything with his chainsword. Zapol laid in with his bayonet, stabbing into bodies and firing point blank to emphasise each kill.

It took two minutes. They seemed like a lifetime to Gaunt, each bloody, frenzied second playing out like a year. Then he and Zapol were through to the elevator itself and the Shriven were piled around them. Five or six more Vitrians were close behind.

Zapol turned to smile at the commissar.

The smile was premature.

The elevator doors ahead of them parted and a second Iron Warrior Chaos Marine lunged out at them. It was loftier than the tallest guardsman, and clad entirely in an almost insect-like carapace of ancient power armour dotted with insane runes in dedication to its deathless masters. It was preceded by a bow-wave of the most foetid stench, exhaled from its grilled mask, and accompanied by a howl that grazed Gaunt's hearing and sounded like consumptive lungs exploding under deep pressure.

The beast's chainfist, squealing like an enraged beast, pulped Zapol with a careless downwards flick. The Vitrian was crushed and liquefied. The creature began to blast wildly, killing at least four more of the supporting Vitrians.

Gaunt was right in the thing's face. He could do nothing but lunge with his chainsword, driving the shrieking blade deep into the Chaos Marine's armoured torso. The toothed blade screamed and protested, and then whined and smoked as the serrated, whirling cutting edge meshed and glued as it ate into the monster's viscous and toughened innards.

The Iron Warrior stumbled back, bellowing in pain and rage. The chainsword, smoking and shorting as it finally jammed, impaled its chest. Reeking ichor and tissue sprayed across the commissar and the elevator doorway.

Gaunt knew he could do no more. He dropped to the floor as the stricken creature rose again, hoping against hope.

His prayers were answered. The rearing thing was struck once, twice... four or five times by carefully placed las-shots which tore into it and spun it around. Gaunt somehow knew it was the sniper Larkin who had provided these marksman blasts.

On one knee, the creature rose and raged again, most of its upper armour punctured or shredded, smoke rising and black fluid spilling from the grisly wounds to its face, neck and chest.

A final, powerful las-blast, close range and full-power, took its head off.

Gaunt looked round to see the wounded Corporal Zeezo standing on the barricade.

The Vitrian grinned, despite the pain from his wound. 'I went against orders, I'm afraid,' he began. 'I reset my gun for full charge.'

'Noted... and excused. Good work!'

Gaunt got to his feet, wet and wretched with blood and fouler stuff. His Ghosts, and Zoren's Vitrians, were moving up the ramp to secure the position. Above them, at the top of the elevator shaft, were maybe a million Shriven, secure in their battery bunkers. Gaunt's expeditionary force was inside, right in the heart of the enemy stronghold.

Ibram Gaunt smiled.

TEN

It took another precious half hour to regroup and secure the bomb deck. Gaunt's scouts located all the entranceways and blocked them, checking even ventilation access and drainage gullies.

Gaunt paced, tense. The clock was ticking and it wouldn't take long for the massive forces above them to start wondering why the shell supply from below had dried up, and come looking for a reason.

There was the place itself too: the gloom, the taste of the air, the blasphemous iconography scrawled on the walls. It was as if they were inside some sacred place, sacred but unholy. Everyone was bathed in cold sweat and there was fear in everyone's eyes.

The comm-link chimed and Gaunt responded, hurrying through to the control room of the bomb bays. Zoren, Rawne and others were waiting for him. Someone had managed to raise the shutters on the vast window ports.

'What in the name of the Emperor is that?' Colonel Zoren asked.

'I think that's what we've come to stop,' Gaunt said, turning away from the stained glass viewing ports.

Far below them, in the depths of the newly-revealed hollowed cavern, stood a vast megalith, a menhir stone maybe fifty metres tall that smoked with building Chaos energy. Its essence filled the bay and made all the humans present edgy and distracted. None could look at it comfortably. It seemed to be bedded in a pile of... blackened bodies. Or body parts.

Major Rawne scowled and flicked a thumb upwards.

'It won't take them long to notice the bomb levels aren't supplying them with shells any more. Then we can expect serious deployment against us.'

Gaunt nodded but said nothing. He crossed to the control suite where Feygor and a Vitrian sergeant named Zolex were attempting to access data. Gaunt didn't like Feygor. The tall, thin Tanith was Rawne's adjutant and shared the major's bitter outlook. But Gaunt knew how to use him and his skills, particularly in the area of cogitators and other thinking machines.

'Plot it for me,' he told the adjutant. 'I have a feeling there may be more of these stone things.'

Feygor touched several rune keys on the glass and brass machined device.

'We're there...' Feygor said, pointing at the glowing map sigils. 'And here's a larger scale map. You were right. That menhir down there is part of a system buried in these hills. Seven all told, in a star pattern. Seven fething abominations! I don't know what they mean to do with them, but they're all charging with power right now.'

'How many?' Gaunt asked too quickly.

'Seven,' Feygor repeated. 'Why?'

Ibram Gaunt felt light-headed. 'Seven stones of power...' he murmured.

A voice from years ago lilted in his mind. The girl. The girl back on Darendara. He could never remember her name, try as hard as he could. But he could see her face in the interrogation room, and hear her words.

When her words about the Ghosts had come true, two years earlier, he had been chilled and had spent several sleepless nights remembering her prophecies. He'd taken command of the worldless wretches of Tanith and then one of the troop, Mad Larkin, it was asserted, had dubbed them Gaunt's Ghosts. He'd tried to put that down to coincidence, but ever since, he'd watched for other fragments of the Night of Truths to emerge.

Cut them and you will be free, she had said. *Do not kill them.*

'What do we do?' asked Rawne.

'We have mines and grenades a plenty,' Zoren said. 'Let's blow it.'

Do not kill them.

Gaunt shook his head. 'No! This is what the Shriven have been preparing, some vast ritual using the stones, some industrial magic. That's what has preoccupied them, that's what they've tried to distract us from. Blowing part of their ceremonial ring would be a mistake. There's no telling what foul power we might unleash. No, we have to break the link...'

Cut them and you will be free.

Gaunt got to his feet and pulled on his cap again. 'Major Rawne, load as many hand carts as you can find with Shriven warheads, prime them for short fuse and prepare to send them up on the elevator on my cue. We'll choke the emplacements upstairs with their own weapons. Colonel Zoren, I want as many of your men as you can spare – or more specifically, their armour.'

The major and the colonel looked at him blankly.

'Now!' he added sharply. They leapt to their feet.

Gaunt led the way up the ramp towards the menhir. It smoked with energy and his skin prickled uncomfortably. Chaos energy smelt that way, like a tangy stench of cooked blood and electricity. None of them dared look down at the twisted, solidified mound below them.

'What are we doing?' Zoren asked by his side, clearly distressed about being this close to the unutterable.

'We're breaking the chain. We want to disrupt the circle without blowing it.'

'How do you know?'

'Inside information,' Gaunt said, trying hard to grin. 'Trust me. Let's short this out.'

The Vitrians by his side moved forward at a nod from their commander.

Tentatively, they approached the huge stone and started to lash their jackets around the smooth surface. Zoren had collected the mica armoured jackets of more than fifty of his men. Now he fused them together as neat as a surgeon with a melta on the lowest setting. Gingerly the Vitrians wrapped the makeshift mica cloak around the stone, using meltas borrowed from the Tanith like industrial staplers to lock it into place over the stone.

'It's not working,' Zoren said.

It wasn't. After a few moments more, the glass beads of the Vitrian armour began to sweat and run, melting off the stone, leaving the fabric base layers until they too ignited and burned.

Gaunt turned away, his disheartened mind churning.

'What now?' Zoren asked, dispiritedly.

Cut them and you will be free.

Gaunt snapped his fingers. 'We don't blow them! We realign them. That's how we cut the circle.'

Gaunt called up Tolus, Lukas and Bragg. 'Get charges set in the supporting mound. Don't target the stone itself. Blow it so it falls away or drops.'

'The mound...' Lukas stammered.

'Yes, trooper, the mound,' Gaunt repeated. 'The dead can't hurt you. Do it!'

Reluctantly, the Ghosts went to work.

Gaunt tapped his micro-bead intercom. 'Rawne, send those warheads up.'

'Acknowledged.'

A 'sir' wouldn't kill him, Gaunt thought.

At the elevator head, the troops under Rawne's command thundered trolleys of warheads into the car.

'Shush!' a Vitrian said suddenly. They stopped. A pause – then they all heard the clanking, the distant tinny thumps. Rawne swung up his lasgun and moved into the elevator assembly. He pulled the lever that opened the upper inspection hatch.

Above him, the great lift shaft yawned like a beast's throat.

He stared up into the darkness, trying to resolve the detail.

The darkness was moving. Shriven were descending, clawing like bat-things down the sheer sides of the shaftway.

Terror punched Rawne's heart. He slammed the hatch and screamed out, 'They're coming!'

The intercom lines went wild with reports as sentries reported hammerings at the sealed hatches and entranceways all around. Hundreds of fists, thousands of fists.

Gaunt cursed, feeling the panic rising in his men. Trapped, entombed, the infernal enemy seeping in from all sides. Speakers mounted on walls and consoles all around squawked into life, and a rasping voice, echoing and overlaying itself from a hundred places, spat inhuman gibberish into the chambers.

'Shut that off!' Gaunt yelled at Feygor.

Feygor scrabbled desperately at the controls. 'I can't!' he cried.

A hatchway to the east exploded inwards with a shower of sparks. Men screamed. Las-fire began to chatter. A little to the north, another doorway blew inwards in a flaming gout and more Shriven began to battle their way inwards.

Gaunt turned to Corbec. The man was pale. Gaunt tried to think, but the rasping, reverberating snarls of the speakers clogged his mind. With a bark, he raised his pistol and blasted the nearest speaker set off the wall.

He turned to Corbec. 'Start the retreat. As many as we dare to keep the covering fire.'

Corbec nodded and hurried off. Gaunt opened his intercom to wide band. 'Gaunt to all units! Commence withdrawal, maximum retreating resistance!' He sprinted down through the mayhem into the megalith chamber, knocked back for a second by the noxious stench of the place. Lukas, Tolus and Bragg were just emerging, their arms, chests and knees caked with black, tarry goo. They were all ashen and hollow-eyed.

'It's done,' Tolus said.

'Then blow it! Move out!' Gaunt cried, pushing and shoving his stumbling men out of the cavern. 'Rawne!'

'Almost there!' Rawne replied from over at the elevator. He and the Ghost next to him looked up sharply as they heard a thump from the liftcar roof above them. Cursing, Rawne pushed the final trolley of shells into the elevator bay.

'Back! Back!' Rawne shouted to his men. He hit the riser stud of the elevator and it began to lift up the shaft towards the Shriven emplacements high above. They heard impacts and shrieks as it pulverised the Shriven coming down the shaft.

The Ghosts and Vitrians with Rawne were running for their lives. Somewhere far above, their payload arrived – and detonated hard enough to shake the ground and sprinkle earth and rock chips down from the cavern roof. Lamp arrays swung like pendulums.

Gaunt felt it all going off above them, and it strengthened his resolve. He was moving towards the maglev tunnel in the middle of a tumble of guardsmen, almost pushing the dazed Bragg by force of will. Shriven fire burned their way. A Ghost dropped, mid-flight. Others turned, knelt, returned fire. Las-fire glittered back and forth.

Behind them all, in the megalith chamber, the charges planted by Domor's team exploded. Its support blown away, the great crackling stone teetered and then slumped down into the pit. The speakers went silent.

Total silence. The Shriven firing had stopped. Those that had penetrated the chamber were prostrate, whimpering.

The only sound was the thumping footfalls and gasping breaths of the fleeing guardsmen.

Then a rumbling started. Incandescent green fire flashed and rippled out of the monolith chamber. Without warning the stained glass view ports of the control room exploded inwards. The ground rippled, ruptured; concrete churned like an angry sea.

'Get out! Get out now!' bellowed Ibram Gaunt.

ELEVEN

The shelling faltered, then stopped. Caffran and Zogat paused as they trudged back across the deadscape and looked back.

'Feth take me!' Caffran said. 'They've finally–'

The hills beyond the Shriven lines exploded. The vast shockwave threw them both to the ground. The hills splintered and puffed up dust and fire, swelling for a moment before collapsing into themselves.

'Emperor's throne!' Zogat said as he helped the young Tanith trooper up. They looked back at the mushroom cloud lifting from the sunken hills.

'Hah!' Caffran said. 'Someone just won something!'

In the villa, Lord High Militant General Dravere put down his cup and watched with faint curiosity as it rattled on the cart. He walked stiffly to the veranda rail and looked through the scope, though he hardly needed it. A bell-shaped cloud of ochre smoke boiled up over the horizon where the Shriven stronghold had once been. Lightning flared in the sky. The vox-caster speaker in the corner of the room wailed and then went dead. Secondary explosions, munitions probably, began to explode along the Shriven lines, blasting the heart out of everything they held.

Dravere coughed, straightened and turned to his adjutant. 'Prepare my transport for embarkation. It seems we're done here.'

A firestorm of shockwave and flame passed over the armoured vehicles of Colonel Flense's convoy. Once it had blown itself out, Flense scrambled out of the top hatch, looking towards the hills ahead of him, hills that were sliding down into themselves as secondary explosions went off.

'No...' he breathed, looking wide-eyed at the carnage.

'No!'

They had been knocked flat by the shockwave, losing many in the flare of green flame that followed them up the tunnel. Then they were blundering through darkness and dust. There were moans, prayers, coughs.

In the end it took almost five hours for them all to claw their way up and out of the darkness. Gaunt led the way up the tunnel himself. Finally the surviving Tanith and Vitrian units emerged, blinking, into the dying light of another day. Most flopped down, or staggered into the mud, sprawling, crying, laughing. Fatigue washed over them all.

Gaunt sat down on a curl of mud and took off his cap. He started to laugh, months of tension sloughing off him in one easy tide. It was over. Whatever else, whatever the mopping up, Fortis was won.

That girl, damn whatever her name was, had been right.

A MEMORY

'What...' The voice paused for a moment, in deep confusion. 'What are you doing?'

Scholar Blenner looked up from the draughty tiles of the long cloister where he was kneeling. There was another boy standing nearby, looking down at him in quizzical fascination. Blenner didn't recognise him, though he was also wearing the sober black-twill uniform of the schola progenium.

A new boy, Blenner presumed.

'What do you think I'm doing?' he asked tersely. 'What does it look like I'm doing?'

The boy was silent for a moment. He was tall and lean, and Blenner guessed him to be about twelve years old, no more than a year or two less than his own age. But there was something terribly old and horribly piercing about the gaze of those dark eyes.

'It looks,' the new boy said, 'as if you're polishing the spaces between the floor tiles in this cloister using only a buckle brush.'

Blenner smirked humourlessly up at the boy and flourished the tiny brush in his grimy hand. It was a soft-bristle tool designed for buffing uniform buttons and fastenings. 'Then I think you'll find that you've answered your own question.' He dipped the tiny brush back into the bowl of chilly water at his side and began to scrub again. 'Now if you don't mind, I have three sides of the quadrangle still to do.'

The boy was silent for several minutes, but he didn't leave. Blenner scrubbed at the tiles and could feel the stare burning into his neck. He looked up again. 'Was there something else?'

The boy nodded. 'Why?'

Blenner dropped the brush into the bowl and sat back on his knees, rubbing his numb hands. 'I was reckless enough to use live rounds in the weapons training silos and somewhat – not to say completely – destroyed a target simulator. Deputy Master Flavius was not impressed.'

'So this is punishment?'

'This is punishment,' Blenner agreed.

'I'd better let you get on with it,' the boy said thoughtfully. 'I imagine I'm not even supposed to be talking to you.'

He crossed to the open side of the cloister and looked out. The inner quadrangle of the ancient missionary school was paved with a stone mosaic of the two-headed Imperial eagle. The air was full of thin rain, cast down by the cold wind which whined down the stone colonnades. Above the cloister roofs rose the ornate halls and towers of the ancient building, its carved guttering and gargoyles worn almost featureless by a thousand years of erosion. Beyond the precinct of the Schola stood the skyline of the city itself, the capital of the mighty Cardinal World, Ignatius. Dominating the western horizon was the black bulk of the Ecclesiarch Palace, its slab-like towers over two kilometres tall, their up-link masts stabbing high into the cold, cyan sky.

It seemed a damp, dark, cold place to live. Ibram Gaunt had been stung by its bone-deep chill from the moment he had stepped out of the shuttle which had conveyed him down to the landing fields from the frigate ship that had brought him here. From this cold world, the Ministorum ruled a segment of the galaxy with the iron hand of the Imperial faith. He had been told that it was a great honour for him to be enrolled in a schola progenium on Ignatius. Ibram had been taught to love the Emperor by his father, but somehow this honour didn't feel like much compensation.

Even with his back turned, Ibram knew that the older, thicker-set boy scrubbing the tiles was now staring at him.

'Do you now have a question?' he asked without turning.

'The usual,' the punished boy said. 'How did they die?'

'Who?'

'Your mother, your father. They must be dead. You wouldn't be here in the orphanage if they weren't gone to glory.'

'It's the schola progenium, not an orphanage.'

'Whatever. This hallowed establishment is a missionary school. Those who are sent here for education are the offspring of Imperial servants who have given their lives for the Golden Throne.

'So how did they die?'

Ibram Gaunt turned. 'My mother died when I was born. My father was a colonel in the Imperial Guard. He was lost last autumn in an action against the orks on Kentaur.'

Blenner stopped scrubbing and got up to join the other boy. 'Sounds juicy!' he began.

'Juicy?'

'Guard heroics and all that. So what happened?'

Ibram Gaunt turned to regard him and Blenner flinched at the depth of the gaze. 'Why are you so interested? How did your parents die to bring you here?'

Blenner backed off a step. 'My father was a Space Marine. He died killing a thousand daemons on Futhark. You'll have heard of that noble victory, no doubt. My mother, when she knew he was dead, took her own life out of love.'

'I see,' Gaunt said slowly.

'So?' Blenner urged.

'So what?'

'How did he die? Your father?'

'I don't know. They won't tell me.'

Blenner paused. 'Won't tell you?'

'Apparently it's... classified.'

The two boys said nothing for a moment, staring out at the rain which jagged down across the stone eagle.

'Oh. My name's Blenner, Vaynom Blenner,' the older boy said, turning and sticking out a hand.

Gaunt shook it. 'Ibram Gaunt,' he replied. 'Maybe you should get back to your–'

'Scholar Blenner! Are you shirking?' a voice boomed down the cloister. Blenner dived back to his knees, scooping the buckle brush out of the bowl and scrubbing feverishly.

A tall figure in flowing robes strode down the tiles towards them. He came to a halt over Blenner and stood looking down at him. 'Every centimetre, scholar, every tile, every line of junction.'

'Yes, deputy master.'

Deputy Master Flavius turned to face Gaunt. 'You are scholar-elect Gaunt.' It wasn't a question. 'Come with me, boy.'

Ibram Gaunt followed the tall master as he paced away over the tiles. He turned back for a moment. Blenner was looking up, miming a throat-cut with his finger and sticking his tongue out in a choking gag.

Young Ibram Gaunt laughed for the first time in a year.

The high master's chamber was a cylinder of books, a veritable hive-city of racks lined with shelf after shelf of ancient tomes and data-slates. There was a curious cog trackway that spiralled up the inner walls of the chamber from the floor, a toothed brass mechanism whose purpose utterly baffled Ibram Gaunt.

He stood in the centre of the room for four long minutes until High Master Boniface arrived.

The high master was a powerfully-set man in his fifties – or at least he had been until the loss of his legs, left arm and half of his face. He sailed into the room on a wheeled brass chair that supported a suspension field generated by the three field-buoys built into the chair's framework. His mutilated body moved, inertia-less, in the shimmering globe of power.

'You are Ibram Gaunt?' The voice was harsh, electronic.

'I am, master,' Gaunt said, snapping to attention as his uncle had trained him.

'You are also lucky, boy,' Boniface rasped, his voice curling out of a larynx enhancer. 'The Schola Progenium Prime of Ignatius doesn't take just anyone.'

'I am aware of the honour, high master. General Dercius made it known to me when he proposed my admission.'

The high master referred to a data-slate held upright in his suspension field, keying the device with his whirring, skeletal, artificial arm. 'Dercius. Commander of the Jantine regiments. Your father's immediate superior. I see. His recommendations for your placement here are on record.'

'Uncle... I mean, General Dercius said you would look after me, now my father has gone.'

Boniface froze, before swinging around to face Gaunt. His harshness had gone suddenly, and there was a look of – was it affection? – in his single eye.

'Of course we will, Ibram,' he said.

Boniface rolled his wheelchair into the side of the room and engaged the lateral cogs with the toothed trackway which spiralled up around the shelves. He turned a small handle and his chair started to lift up along the track, raising him up in widening curves over the boy.

Boniface stopped at the third shelf up and took out a book. 'The strength of the Emperor...? Finish it.'

'Is Humanity, and the strength of Humanity is the Emperor. The sermons of Sebastian Thor, volume twenty-three, chapter sixty-two.'

Boniface wound his chair up higher on the spiral and selected another book.

'The meaning of war?'

'Is victory!' Gaunt replied eagerly. 'Lord Militant Gresh, *Memoirs*, chapter nine.'

'How may I ask the Emperor what he owes of me?'

'When all I owe is to the Golden Throne and by duty I will repay,' Gaunt returned. '*The Spheres of Longing* by Inquisitor Ravenor, volume... three?'

Boniface wound his chair down to the carpet again and swung round to face Gaunt. 'Volume two, actually.'

He stared at the boy. Gaunt tried not to shrink from the exposed gristle and tissue of the half-made face.

'Do you have any questions?'

'How did my father die? No one's told me, not even Un– I mean, General Dercius.'

'Why would you want to know, lad?'

'I met a boy in the cloisters. Blenner. He knew the passing of his parents. His father died fighting the Enemy at Futhark, and his mother killed herself for the love of him.'

'Is that what he said?'

'Yes, master.'

'Scholar Blenner's family were killed when their world was virus bombed during a genestealer insurrection. Blenner was off-planet, visiting a relative. An aunt, I believe. His father was an Administratum clerk. Scholar Blenner always has had a fertile imagination.'

'His use of live rounds? In training? The cause of his punishment?'

'Scholar Blenner was discovered painting rude remarks about the deputy high master on the walls of the latrine. That is the cause of his punishment duty. You're smiling, Gaunt. Why?'

'No real reason, high master.'

There was a long silence, broken only by the crackle and fizz of the high master's suspension field.

'How did my father die, high master?' Ibram Gaunt asked.

Boniface clenched the data-slate shut with an audible snap. 'That's classified.'

PART FOUR

CRACIA CITY,
PYRITES

ONE

The Imperial Needle was quite a piece of work, Colonel Colm Corbec decided. It towered over Cracia, the largest and oldest city on Pyrites, a three thousand metre ironwork tower, raised four hundred years before, partly to honour the Emperor but mostly to celebrate the engineering skill of the Pyriteans. It was taller than the jagged turrets of the Arbites Precinct, and it dwarfed even the great twin towers of the Ecclesiarch Palace. On cloudless days, the city became a giant sundial, with the spire as the gnomon. City dwellers could tell precisely the time of day by which streets of the city were in shadow.

Today was not a cloudless day. It was winter season in Cracia and the sky was a dull, unreflective white like an untuned vista-caster screen. Snow fluttered down out of the leaden sky to ice the gothic rooftops and towers of the old, grey city, edging the ornate decorations, the wrought-iron guttering and brass eaves, the skeletal fire-escapes and the sills of lancet windows.

But it was warm down here on the streets. Under the stained glass-beaded ironwork awnings which edged every thoroughfare, the walk-ways and concourses were heated. Kilometres below the city, ancient turbines pumped warm air up to the hypocaust beneath the pavements, which circulated under the awning levels. A low-power energy sheath broadcast at first floor height stopped rain or snow from ever reaching the pedestrian levels, for the most part.

At a terrace cafe, Corbec, the jacket of his Tanith colonel's uniform open and unbuckled, sipped his beer and rocked back on his black, ironwork chair. They liked black ironwork here on Pyrites. They made everything out of it. Even the beer, judging by the taste.

Corbec felt relaxation flood into his limbs for the first time in months. The hellhole of Fortis Binary was behind him at last: the mud, the vermin, the barrage.

It still flickered across his dreams at night and he often woke to the thump of imagined artillery. But this – a beer, a chair, a warm and friendly street – this was living again.

A shadow apparently bigger than the Imperial Needle blotted out the daylight. 'Are we set?' Trooper Bragg asked.

Corbec squinted up at the huge, placid-faced trooper, by some way the biggest man under his command. 'It's still early. They say this town has quite a nightlife, but it won't get going until after dark.'

'Seems dead. No fun,' Bragg said drearily.

'Hey, lucky we got Pyrites rather than Guspedin. By all accounts that's just dust and slag and endless hives.'

The lighting standards down each thoroughfare and under the awnings were beginning to glow into life as the automated cycle took over, though it was still daylight.

'We've been talking–' Bragg began.

'Who's we?' Corbec said.

'Uh, Larks and me... and Varl. And Blane.' Bragg shuffled a little. 'We heard about this little wagering joint. It might be fun.'

'Fine.'

'Cept it's, uh–'

'What?' Corbec said, knowing full well what the 'uh' would be.

'It's in a cold zone,' Bragg said.

Corbec got up and dropped a few coins of the local currency on the glass-topped table next to his empty beer glass. 'Trooper, you know the cold zones are off limits,' he said smoothly. 'The regiments have been given four days' recreation in this city, but that recreation is contingent on several things. Reasonable levels of behaviour, so as not to offend or disrupt the citizens of this most ancient and civilised burg. Restrictions as to the use of prescribed bars, clubs, wager-halls and brothels. And a total ban on Imperial Guard personnel leaving the heated areas of the city. The cold zones are lawless.'

Bragg nodded. 'Yeah... but there are five hundred thousand guardsmen on leave in Cracia, clogging up the star ports and the tram depots. Each one has been to fething hell and back in the last few months. Do you honestly think they're going to behave themselves?'

Corbec pursed his lips and sighed. 'No, Bragg. I suppose I do not. Tell me where this place is. The one you're talking about. I've an errand or two to run. I'll meet you there later. Just stay out of trouble.'

* * *

TWO

In the mirror-walled, smoke-wreathed bar of the Polar Imperial, one of the better hotels in uptown Cracia, right by the Administratum complex, Commissar Vaynom Blenner was describing the destruction of the enemy battleship, *Eradicus*. It was a complex, colourful evocation, involving the skilled use of a lit cigar, smoke rings, expressive gestures and throaty sound effects. Around the table, there were appreciative hoots and laughs.

Ibram Gaunt, however, watched and said nothing. He was often silent. It disarmed people.

Blenner had always been a tale-spinner, even back in their days at the schola progenium. Gaunt always looked forward to their reunions. Blenner was about as close as he came to having an old friend, and it strangely reassured him to see Blenner's face, constant through the years when so many faces perished and disappeared.

But Blenner was also a terrible boast, and he had become weak and complacent, enjoying a little too much of the good life. For the last decade, he'd served with the Greygorian Third. The Greys were efficient, hard working and few regiments were as unswervingly loyal to the Emperor. They had spoiled Blenner.

Blenner hailed the waiter and ordered another tray of drinks for the officers at his table. Gaunt's eyes wandered across the crowded salon, where the officer classes of the Imperial Guard relaxed and mixed.

On the far side of the room, under a vast, glorious gilt-framed oil painting of Imperial Titans striding to war, he caught sight of officers in the chrome and purple dress uniform of the Jantine Patricians, the so-called 'Emperor's Chosen'. Amidst them was a tall, thickset figure with an acid-scarred face that Gaunt knew all too well – Colonel Draker Flense.

Their gaze met for a few seconds. The exchange was as warm and friendly as a pair of automated range finders getting a mutual target lock. Gaunt cursed silently to himself. If he'd known the Jantine officer cadre was using this hotel, he would have avoided it. The last thing he wanted was a confrontation.

'Commissar Gaunt?'

Gaunt looked up. A uniformed hotel porter stood by his armchair, his head tilted to a position that was both obsequious and superior. Snooty ass, thought Gaunt; loves the Guard all the while we're saving the universe for him, but let us in his precious hotel bar to relax and he's afraid we'll scuff the furniture.

'There is a boy, sir,' the porter said disdainfully. 'A boy in reception who wishes to speak with you.'

'Boy?' Gaunt asked.

'He said to give you this,' the porter continued. He held out a silver Tanith ear hoop suspiciously between velveted finger and thumb.

Gaunt nodded, got to his feet and followed him out.

Across the room, Flense watched him go. He beckoned over his aide, Ebzan, with a surly curl of his finger. 'Go and find Major Brochuss and some of his clique. I have a matter I wish to settle.'

Gaunt followed the strutting porter out into the marble foyer. His distaste for the place grew with each second. Pyrites was soft, pampered, so far away from the harsh warfronts. They paid their tithes to the Emperor and in return ignored completely the darker truths of life beyond their civilised domain. Even the Imperium troops stationed here as a permanent garrison seemed to have gone soft.

Gaunt broke from his reverie and saw Brin Milo hunched under a potted ouroboros tree. The boy was wearing his Ghost uniform and looked most unhappy.

'Milo? I thought you were going with the others. Corbec said he'd take you with the Tanith. What are you doing in a stuffy place like this?'

Milo fetched a small data-slate out of his thigh pocket and presented it. 'This came through the vox-cast after you'd gone, sir. Executive Officer Kreff thought it best it was brought straight to you. And as I'm supposed to be your adjutant... well, they gave the job to me.'

Gaunt almost grinned at the boy's weary tone. He took the slate and keyed it open. 'What is it?' he asked.

'All I know, sir, is that it's a personal communiqué delivered on an encrypted channel for your attention forty-' He paused to consult his timepiece. 'Forty-seven minutes ago.'

Gaunt studied the gibberish on the slate. Then the identifying touch of his thumbprint on the decoding icon unscrambled it. For his eyes only indeed.

'Ibram. You only friend in area close enough to assist. Go to 1034 Needleshadow Boulevard. Use our old identifier. Treasure to be had. Vermilion treasure. Fereyd.'

Gaunt looked up suddenly and snapped the slate shut as if caught red-handed. His heart pounded for a second. Throne of Earth, how many years had it been since his heart had pounded with that feeling – was it really fear? Fereyd? His old, old friend, bound together in blood since–

Milo was looking at him curiously. 'Trouble?' the boy asked innocuously.

'A task to perform...' Gaunt murmured. He opened the data-slate again and pressed the 'Wipe' rune to expunge the message.

'Can you drive?' he asked Milo.

'Can I?' the boy said excitedly.

Gaunt calmed his bright-eyed enthusiasm with a flat patting motion with his hands. 'Go down to the motor-pool and scare us up some transport. A staff car. Tell them I sent you.'

Milo hurried off. Gaunt stood for a moment in silence. He took two deep breaths – then a hearty slap on the back almost felled him.

'Bram! You dog! You're missing the party!' Blenner growled.

'Vay, I've got a bit of business to take care–'

'No no no!' the tipsy, red-faced commissar said, smoothing the creases in his leather greatcoat. 'How many times do we get together to talk of old times, eh? How many? Once every damn decade it seems like! I'm not letting you out of my sight! You'll never come back, I know you!'

'Vay... really, it's just tedious regimental stuff...'

'I'll come with you then! Get it done in half the time! Two commissars, eh? Put the fear of the Throne itself into them, I tell you!'

'Really, you'd be bored... it's a very boring task...'

'All the more reason I come! To make it less boring! Eh? Eh?' Blenner exclaimed. He edged the vintage brandy bottle that he had commandeered out of his coat pocket so that Gaunt could see it. So could everyone else in the foyer.

Any more of this, thought Gaunt, and I might as well announce my activities over the tannoy. He grabbed Blenner by the arm and led him out of the bar.

'You can come,' he hissed, 'just... behave! And be quiet!'

THREE

The girl gyrating on the apron stage to the sounds of the tambour band was quite lovely and almost completely undressed, but Major Rawne was not looking at her.

He stared across the table in the low, smoky light as Vulnor Habshept kal Geel filled two shot glasses with oily, clear liquor.

Even as a skeleton, Geel would have been a huge man. But upholstered as he was in more than three hundred kilos of chunky flesh he made even Bragg look undernourished.

Major Rawne knew full well it would take over three times his own body-mass to match the opulently dressed racketeer. Rawne was also totally unafraid.

'We drink, soldier boy,' Geel said in his thick Pyritean accent, lifting one shot glass with a gargantuan hand.

'We drink,' Rawne agreed, picking up his own glass. 'Though I would prefer you address me as "Major Rawne"... racketeer boy.'

There was a dead pause. The crowded cold zone bar was silent in an instant. The girl stopped gyrating.

Geel laughed.

'Good! Good! Very amusing, such pluck! Ha ha ha!' He chuckled and knocked his drink back in one. The bar resumed talk and motion, relieved.

Rawne slowly and extravagantly gulped his drink. Then he lifted the decanter and drained the other litre of liquor without even blinking. He knew that it was a rye-based alcohol with a chemical structure similar to that used in Chimera and Rhino anti-freeze. He also knew that he had taken four anti-intoxicant tablets before coming in. Four tabs that had cost a fortune from a black market trader, but it was worth it. It was like drinking spring water.

Geel forgot to close his mouth for a moment and then recovered his composure.

'Major Rawne can drink like Pyritean!' he said with a complimentary tone.

'So the Pyriteans would like to think...' Rawne said. 'Now let's to business.'

'Come this way,' Geel said and lumbered to his feet. Rawne fell into step behind him and Geel's four huge bodyguards moved in behind.

Everyone in the bar watched them leave by the back door.

On stage, the girl had just shed her final, tiny garment and was in the process of twirling it around one finger prior to hurling it into the crowd. When she realised no one was watching, she stomped off in a huff.

In a snowy alley behind the club, a grey, beetle-nosed six-wheeled truck was waiting.

'Hocwheat liquor. Smokes. Text-slates with dirty pictures. Everything you asked for,' Geel said expansively.

'You're a man of your word,' Rawne said.

'Now, to the money. Two thousand Imperial credits. Don't waste my time with local rubbish. Two thousand Imperial.'

Rawne nodded and clicked his fingers. Trooper Feygor stepped out of the shadows carrying a bulging rucksack.

'My associate, Mr Feygor,' Rawne said. 'Show him the stuff, Feygor.'

Feygor stood the rucksack down in the snow and opened it. He reached in and pulled out a laspistol.

The first two shots hit Geel in the face and chest, smashing him back down the alley.

With practiced ease, Feygor grinned as he put an explosive blast through the skulls of each outraged bodyguard.

Rawne dashed over to the truck and climbed up into the cab.

'Let's go!' he roared to Feygor who scrambled up onto the side even as Rawne threw it into gear and roared it out of the alley.

As they screamed away under the archway at the head of the alley, a big dark shape dropped down into the truck, landing on the tarpaulin-wrapped contraband in the flatbed. Feygor, hanging on tight and monkeying up the restraints onto the cargo bed, saw the stowaway and lashed out at him. A powerful jab laid him out cold in the canvas folds of the tarpaulin.

At the wheel, Rawne saw Feygor fall in the rear-view scope and panicked as the attacker swung into the cab beside him.

'Major,' Corbec said.

'Corbec!' Rawne exploded. 'You! Here?'

'I'd keep your eyes on the road if I were you,' Corbec said glancing back, 'I think Geel's men are after a word with you.'

The truck raced on down the snowy street. Behind it came four angry limousines.

'Feth!' Major Rawne said.

FOUR

The big, black staff-track roared down the boulevard under the glowing lamps in their ironwork frames. Smoothly and deftly it slipped around the light evening traffic, changing lanes.

Drivers seemed more than willing to give way to the big, sinister machine with its throaty engine note and its gleaming double-headed eagle crest.

Behind armoured glass in the tracked passenger section, Gaunt leaned forward in the studded leather seats and pressed the speaker switch. Beside him, Blenner poured two large snifters of brandy and chuckled.

'Milo,' Gaunt said into the speaker, 'not so fast. I'd like to draw as little attention to ourselves as possible, and it doesn't help with you going for some new speed record.'

'Understood, sir,' Milo said over the speaker.

Sitting forward astride the powerful nose section, Milo flexed his hands on the handlebar grips and grinned. The speed dropped. A little.

Gaunt ignored the glass Blenner was offering him and flipped open a data-slate map of the city's street-plan.

Then he thumbed the speaker again. 'Next left, Milo, then follow the underpass to Zorn Square.'

'That... that takes us into the cold zones, commissar,' Milo replied over the link.

'You have your orders, adjutant,' Gaunt said simply and snapped off the intercom.

'This isn't Guard business at all, is it, old man?' Blenner said wryly.

'Don't ask questions and you won't have to lie later, Vay. In fact, keep out of sight and pretend you're not here. I'll get you back to the bar in an hour or so.'

I hope, Gaunt added under his breath.

Rawne threw the truck around a steep bend. The six chunky wheels slid alarmingly on the wet snow. Behind it, the heavy pursuit vehicles thrashed and slipped.

'This is the wrong way!' Rawne said. 'We're going deeper into the damn cold zone!'

'We didn't have much choice,' Corbec replied. 'They're boxing us in. Didn't you plan your escape route?'

Rawne said nothing and concentrated on his driving. They were flung around another treacherous turn.

'What are you doing here?' he asked Corbec at last.

'Just asking myself the same thing,' Corbec reflected lightly. 'Well, truth is, I thought I'd do what any good regimental colonel does for his men on a shore leave rotation after a nightmare tour of duty in a hell-pit like Fortis, and take a trip into the downtown districts to rustle up a little black market drink and the like. The men always appreciate a colonel who looks after them.'

Rawne scowled, fighting the wheel.

'Then I happened to see you and your sidekick, and I realised that you were doing what any good sneaking low-life weasel would do on shore leave rotation. To wit, scamming some local out of contraband so he can sell it to his comrades. So I thought to myself – I'll join forces. Rawne's got exactly what I'm after and without my help, he'll be dead and floating down the River Cracia by dawn.'

'Your help?' Rawne spat. The glass at the rear of the cab shattered suddenly as bullets smacked into it. Both men ducked.

'Yeah,' Corbec said, pulling an autopistol out of his coat. 'I'm a better shot than that feth-wipe Feygor.'

Corbec wound his door window down and leaned out, firing back a quick burst of heavy fire from the speeding truck.

The front screen of one of the black vehicles exploded and it skidded sharply, clipping one of its companions before slamming into a wall and spinning nose to tail three times before coming to rest in a spray of glass and debris.

'I rest my case,' Corbec said.

'There are still three of them out there!' Rawne said.

'True,' Corbec said, loading a fresh clip, 'but, canny chap that I am, I thought of bringing spare ammo.'

Gaunt made Milo park the staff-track around the corner from Needle-shadow Boulevard. He climbed out into the cold night. 'Stay here,' he told Blenner, who waved back jovially from the cabin. 'And you,' Gaunt told Milo, who was moving as if to follow him.

'Are you armed, sir?' the boy asked.

Gaunt realised he wasn't. He shook his head.

Milo drew his silver Tanith dagger and passed it to the commissar. 'You can never be sure,' he said simply.

Gaunt nodded his thanks and moved off.

The cold zones like this were a grim reminder that society in a vast city like Cracia was deeply stratified. At the heart were the great palace of the Ecclesiarch and the Needle itself. Around that, the city centre and the opulent, wealthy residential areas were patrolled, guarded, heated and screened, safe little microcosms of security and comfort. There, every benefit of Imperial citizenship was enjoyed.

But beyond, the bulk of the city was devoid of such luxuries. League after league of crumbling, decaying city blocks, buildings and tenements a thousand years old, rotted on unlit, unheated, uncared for streets. Crime was rife here, and there were no Arbites. Their control ran out at the inner city limits.

It was a human zoo, an urban wilderness that surrounded civilisation. In some ways it almost reminded Gaunt of the Imperium itself – the opulent, luxurious heart surrounded by a terrible reality it knew precious little about. Or cared to know.

Light snow, too wet to settle, drifted down. The air was cold and moist.

Gaunt strode down the littered pavement. 1034 Needleshadow Boulevard was a dark, haunted relic. A single, dim light glowed on the sixth floor.

Gaunt crept in. The foyer smelled of damp carpet and mildew. There were no lights, but he found the stairwell lit by hundreds of candles stuck in assorted bottles. The light was yellow and smoky.

By the time he reached the third floor, he could hear the music. Some kind of old dancehall ballad by the sound of it. The old recording crackled. It sounded like a ghost.

Sixth floor, the top flat. Shattered plaster littered the worn hall carpet.

Somewhere in the shadows, vermin squeaked. The music was louder, murmuring from the room he was approaching on an old audio-caster. The apartment door was ajar, and light, brighter than the hall candles, shone out, the violet glow of a self-powered portable field lamp.

His fingers around the hilt of the knife in his greatcoat pocket, Gaunt entered.

FIVE

The room was bare to the floorboards and the peeling paper. The audio-caster was perched on top of a stack of old books, warbling softly. The lamp was in the corner, casting its spectral violet glow all around the room.

'Is there anyone here?' Gaunt asked, surprised at the sound of his own voice.

A shadow moved in an adjoining bathroom.

'What's the word?' it said.

'What?'

'I haven't got time to humour you. The word.'

'Eagleshard,' Gaunt said, using the code word he and Fereyd had shared years before on Pashen Nine-Sixty.

The figure seemed to relax. A shabby, elderly man in a dirty civilian suit entered the room so that Gaunt could see him. He was lowering a small, snub-nosed pistol of a type Gaunt wasn't familiar with.

Gaunt's heart sank. It wasn't Fereyd.

'Who are you?' Gaunt asked.

The man arched his eyebrows in reply. 'Names are really quite inappropriate under these circumstances.'

'If you say so,' Gaunt said.

The man crossed to the audio-caster and keyed in a new track. Another old-fashioned tune, a jaunty love song full of promises and regrets, started up with a flurry of strings and pipes.

'I am a facilitator, a courier and also very probably a dead man,' the stranger told Gaunt. 'Have you any idea of the scale and depth of this business?'

Gaunt shrugged. 'No. I'm not even sure what business you refer to. But I trust my old friend, Fereyd. That is enough for me. By his word, I have no illusions as to the seriousness of this matter, but as to the depth, the complexity...'

The man studied him. 'The Navy's intelligence network has established a web of spy systems throughout the Sabbat Worlds to watch over the Crusade.'

'Indeed.'

'I'm a part of that cobweb. So are you, if you but knew it. The truth we are uncovering is frightening. There is a grievous power struggle under way in the command echelon of this mighty Crusade, my friend.'

Gaunt felt impatience rising in him. He hadn't come all this way to listen to arch speculation. 'Why should I care? I'm not part of High Command. Let them squabble and backstab and–'

'Would you throw it all away? A decade of liberation warfare? All of Warmaster Slaydo's victories?'

'No,' Gaunt admitted darkly.

'The intrigue threatens everything. How can a Crusade force this vast continue when its commanders are at each other's throats? And if we're fighting each other, how can we fight the foe?'

'Why am I here?' Gaunt cut in flatly.

'He said you would be cautious.'

'Who said? Fereyd?'

The man paused, but didn't reply directly. 'Two nights ago, associates of mine here in Cracia intercepted a signal sent via an astropath from a scout ship in the Nubila Reach. It was destined for Lord High Militant General Dravere's fleet headquarters. Its clearance level was Vermilion.'

Gaunt blinked. *Vermilion level.*

The man took a small crystal from his coat pocket and held it up so that it winked in the violet light.

'The data is stored on this crystal. It took the lives of two psykers to capture the signal and transfer it to this. Dravere must not get his hands on it.'

He held it out to Gaunt.

Gaunt shrugged. 'You're giving it to me?'

The man pursed his lips. 'Since my network here on Cracia intercepted this, we've been taken apart. Dravere's own counter-spy network is after us, desperate to retrieve the data. I have no one left to safeguard this. I contacted my off-world superior, and he told me to await a trusted ally. Whoever you are, friend, you are held in high regard. You are trusted. In this secret war, that means a lot.'

Gaunt took the crystal from the man's trembling fingers. He didn't quite know what to say. He didn't want this vile, vital thing anywhere near himself, but he was beginning to realise what might be at stake.

The older man smiled at Gaunt. He began to say something.

The wall behind him exploded in a firestorm of light and vaporising bricks. Two fierce blue beams of las-fire punched into the room and sliced the man into three distinct sections before he could move.

* * *

SIX

Gaunt dived for cover in the apartment doorway. He drew Milo's blade, for all the good that would do.

Feet were thundering up the stairs.

From his vantage point at the door he watched as two armoured troopers swung in through the exploded wall. They were big, clad in black, insignia-less combat armour, carrying compact, cut-down las-rifles. Adhesion clamps on their knees and forearms showed how they had scaled the outside walls to blow their way in with a directional limpet mine. They surveyed the room, sweeping their green laser tagger beams. One spotted Gaunt prone in the doorway and opened fire. The blast punched through the doorframe, kicking up splinters and began stitching along the plasterboard wall.

Gaunt dived headlong. He was dead! Dead, unless–

The old man's pistol lay on the worn carpet under his nose. It must have skittered there when he was cut down. Gaunt grabbed it, thumbed off the safety and rolled over to fire.

The gun was small, but the odd design clearly marked it as an ancient and priceless specialised weapon. It had a kick like a mule and a roar like a Basilisk.

The first shot surprised Gaunt as much as the two stealth troops and it blew a hatch-sized hole in the wall. The second shot exploded one of the attackers.

A little rune on the grip of the pistol had changed from 'V' to 'III'. Gaunt sighed. This thing clearly wasn't over-blessed with a capacious magazine.

The footfalls on the stairway got louder and three more stealth troopers stumbled up, wafting the candle flames as they ran.

Gaunt dropped to a kneeling pose and blew the head off the first. But the other two opened fire up the well with their lasguns and then the remaining trooper in the apartment behind him began firing too. The cross-blast of three lasguns on rapid-burst tore the top hallway to pieces. Gaunt dropped flat so hard he smashed his hand on the boards and the gun pattered away down the top steps.

After a moment or two, the firing stopped and the attackers began to edge forward to inspect their kill. Dust and smoke drifted in the half-light. Some of the shots had punched up through the floor and carpet a whisker from Gaunt's nose, leaving smoky, dimpled holes. But Gaunt was intact.

When the trooper from the apartment poked his head round the door, a cubit of hard-flung Tanith silver impaled his skull and dropped him to the floor, jerking and spasming. Gaunt leapt up. A second, two seconds, and he would have the fallen man's lasgun in his hands, ready to blast down the stairs.

But the other two from below were in line of sight. There was a flash and he realised their green laser taggers had swept over his face and dotted on his heart. There was a quick and frantic burst of lasgun fire and a billow of noxious burning fumes washed up the stairs over Gaunt.

Blenner climbed the stairs into view, carefully stepping over the smouldering bodies, a smoking laspistol in his hand.

'Got tired of waiting,' the commissar sighed. 'Looks like you needed a hand anyway, eh, Bram?'

SEVEN

The grey truck, with its single remaining pursuer, slammed into high gear as it went over the rise in the snowy road, leaving the ground for a stomach-shaking moment.

'What's that?' Rawne said wildly, a moment after they landed again and the thrashing wheels re-engaged the slippery roadway.

'It's called a roadblock, I believe,' Corbec said.

Ahead, the cold zone street was closed by a row of oilcan fires, concrete poles and wire. Several armed shapes were waiting for them.

'Off the road! Get off the road!' Corbec bawled. He leaned over and wrenched at the crescent steering wheel.

The truck slewed sideways in the slush and barrelled beetle-nose-first through the sheet-wood doors of an old, apparently abandoned warehouse. There, in the dripping darkness, it grumbled to a halt, its firing note choking away to a dull cough.

'Now what?' Rawne hissed.

'Well, there's you, me and Feygor...' Corbec began. Already the trooper was beginning to pull himself groggily up in the back. 'Three of Gaunt's Ghosts, the best damn fighting regiment in the Guard. We excel at stealth work and look, we're here in a dark warehouse!'

Corbec readied his automatic. Rawne pulled his laspistol and did the same. He grinned.

'Let's do it,' he said.

Years later, in the speakeasies and clubs of the Cracian cold zones, the story of the shoot-out at the old Vinchy Warehouse would do the rounds. Thousands of shots were heard, they say, mostly the bass chatter of the autogun sidearms carried by twenty armed men, mob overbaron Vulnor Habshept kal Geel's feared enforcers, who went in to smoke out the off-world gangsters.

All twenty died. Twenty further shots, some from laspistols, some from a big-bore autogun, were heard. No more, no less.

No one ever saw the off-world gangsters again, or found the truck laden with stolen contraband that had sparked off the whole affair.

The staff-track whipped along down the cold zone street, heading back to the safety of the city core. In the back, Blenner poured another two measures of his expensive brandy. This time, Gaunt took the one offered and knocked it back.

'You don't have to tell me what's going on, Bram. Not if you don't want to.'

Gaunt sighed. 'If I had to, would you listen?'

Blenner chuckled. 'I'm loyal to the Emperor, Gaunt, and doubly loyal to my old friends. What else do you need to know?'

Gaunt smiled and held his glass out as Blenner refilled it.

'Nothing, I suppose.'

Blenner leaned forward, earnest for the first time in years. 'Look, Bram... I may seem like an old fogey to you, grown fat on the luxuries of having a damn near perfect regiment... but I haven't forgotten what the fire feels like. I haven't forgotten the reason I'm here. You can trust me to hell and back, and I'll be there for you.'

'And the Emperor,' Gaunt reminded him with a grin.

'And the bloody Emperor,' Blenner said and they clinked glasses.

'I say,' Blenner said a moment later, 'why is your boy slowing down?'

Milo pulled up, wary. The two tracked vehicles blocking the road ahead had their headlamps on full beam, but Milo could see they were painted in the colours of the Jantine Patricians. Large, shaven-headed figures armed with batons and entrenching tools were climbing out to meet them.

Gaunt climbed out of the cabin as Milo brought them to a halt. Snow drifted down. He squinted at the men beyond the lights.

'Brochuss,' he hissed.

'Colonel-Commissar Gaunt,' replied Major Brochuss of the Jantine Patricians, stepping forward. He was stripped to his vest and oiled like a prize fighter. The wooden spoke in his hands slapped into a meaty palm.

'A reckoning, I think,' he said. 'You and your scum-boys cheated us of a victory on Fortis. You bastards. Playing at soldiers when the real thing was ready to take the day. You and your pathetic Ghosts should have died on the wire where you belong.'

Gaunt sighed. 'That's not the real reason, is it, Brochuss? Oh, you're still smarting over the stolen glory of Fortis, but that's not it. After all, why were you so unhappy we won the day back there? It's the old honour thing, isn't it? The old debt you and Flense still think has to be paid. You're fools. There's no honour in this, in back-street murder out here, in the cold zones, where our bodies won't be reported for months.'

'I don't believe you're in a position to argue,' said Brochuss. 'We of Jant will take our repayment in blood where it presents itself. Here is as good a place as any other.'

'So you'd act with dishonour, to avenge a slight to honour? Brochuss, you ass – if you could only see the irony! There was no dishonour to begin with. I only corrected what was already at fault. You know where the real fault lies. All I did was expose the cowardice in the Jantine action.'

'Bram!' Blenner hissed in Gaunt's ear. 'You never were a diplomat! These men want blood! Insulting them isn't going to help their mood.'

'I'm dealing with this, Vay,' Gaunt said archly.

'No you're not, I am...' Blenner pushed Gaunt back and faced the Jantine mob. 'Major... if it's a fight you want I won't disappoint you. A moment? Please?' Blenner said holding up a finger. He turned to Milo and whispered, 'Boy, just how fast can you drive this buggy?'

'Fast enough,' Milo whispered, 'and I know exactly where to go...'

Blenner turned back to the Patrician heavies in the lamplight and smiled. 'After due consultation with my colleagues, Major Brochuss, I can now safely say... burn in hell, you shit-eating dog!'

He leapt back aboard, pushing Gaunt into the cabin ahead of him. Milo had the staff-track gunned and slewed around in a moment, even as the enraged troopers rushed them.

Another three seconds and Gaunt's ride was roaring off down the snowy street at a dangerous velocity, the engines raging. Squabbling and cursing, Brochuss and his men leapt into their own machines and gave chase.

'So glad I left that to you, Vay,' Gaunt grinned. 'I don't think I would've have been that diplomatic.'

EIGHT

Trooper Bragg kissed his lucky dice and let all three of them fly. A cheer went up across the wagering room and piles of chips were pushed his way.

'Go on, Bragg!' Mad Larkin chuckled at his side. 'Do it again, you fething old drunk!'

Bragg chuckled and scooped up the dice.

This was the life, he thought. Far away from the warzone of Fortis, the mayhem and the death, here in a smoke-filled dome in the cold zone back-end of an ancient city, him and his few true friends, a good number of pretty girls and wager tables open all night.

Varl was suddenly at his side. His intended friendly slap was hard and stinging – Varl had still to get used to the cybernetic implant shoulder joint the medics had fitted him with on Fortis.

'The game can wait, Bragg. We've got business.'

Bragg and Larkin kissed their painted lady-friends goodbye and followed Varl out through the rear exit of the gaming club onto the boarding ramp. Suth was there: Melyr, Meryn, Caffran, Curral, Coll, Baru, Mkoll, Raglon... almost twenty of the Ghosts.

'What's going on?' Bragg asked.

Melyr jerked his thumb down to where Corbec, Rawne and Feygor were unloading booze and smokes from a battered six wheeler.

'Colonel's got us some tasty stuff to share, bless his Tanith heart.'

'Very nice,' Bragg said, licking his lips, not entirely sure why Rawne and Feygor looked so annoyed. Corbec smiled up at them all.

'Get everyone out here! We're having a party, boys! For Tanith! For us!'

There was cheering and clapping. Varl leapt down into the bay and opened a box with his Tanith knife. He threw bottles up to those clustered around.

'Hey!' Raglon said suddenly, pointing out into the snowy darkness beyond the club's bay. 'Incoming!'

The staff track slid into the bay behind Corbec's truck and Gaunt leapt out. A cheer went up and somebody tossed him a bottle. Gaunt tore off the stopper and took a deep swig, before pointing back out into the darkness.

'Lads! I could do with a hand...' he began.

Major Brochuss leaned forward in the cab of his speeding staff-track and looked through the screen where the wiper was slapping snow away.

'Now we have him! He's stopped at that place ahead!'

Brochuss flexed his hand and struck it with his baton.

Then he saw the crowds of jeering Ghosts around the drive-in bay. A hundred... two hundred.

'Oh balls,' he managed.

The bar was almost empty and it was nearly dawn. Ibram Gaunt sipped the last of his drink and eyed Vaynom Blenner who was asleep face-down on the bar beside him.

Gaunt took out the crystal from the inside pocket where he had secreted it and tossed it up in his hand once, twice.

Corbec was suddenly beside him.

'A long night, eh, commissar?'

Gaunt looked at him, catching the crystal in a tight fist.

'Maybe the longest so far, Colm. I hear you had some fun.'

'Aye, and at Rawne's expense, you'll no doubt be pleased to hear. Do you want to tell me about what's going on?'

Gaunt smiled. 'I'd rather buy you a drink,' he said, motioning to the weary barkeep. 'And yes, I'd love to tell you. And I will, when the time comes. Are you loyal, Colm Corbec?'

Corbec looked faintly hurt. 'To the Emperor, I'd give my life,' he said, without hesitating.

Gaunt nodded. 'Me too. The path ahead may be truly hard. As long as I can count on you.'

Corbec said nothing but held out his glass. Gaunt touched it with his own. There was a tiny chime.

'First and Last,' Corbec said.

Gaunt smiled softly. 'First and Only,' he replied.

A MEMORY

They had a house on the summit of Mount Resyde, with long colon-nades that overlooked the cataracts. The sky was golden, until sunset, when it caught fire. Light-bugs, heavy with pollenfibres, ambled through the warm air in the atrium each evening. Ibram imagined they were navigators, charting secret paths through the empyrean, between the hidden torments of the warp.

He played on the sundecks overlooking the mists of the deep cata-ract falls that thundered down into the eight kilometre chasms of the Northern Rift. Sometimes from there, you could see fighting ships and Imperium cutters lifting or making planetfall at the great landing silos at Lanatre Fields. From this distance they looked just like light-bugs in the dark evening sky.

Ibram would always point, and declare his father was on one.

His nurse, and the old tutor Benthlay, always corrected him. They had no imagination. Benthlay didn't even have any arms. He would point to the lights with his buzzing prosthetic limbs and patiently explain that if Ibram's father had been coming home, they would have had word in advance.

But Oric, the cook from the kitchen block, had a broader mind. He would lift the boy in his meaty arms and point his nose to the sky to catch a glimpse of every ship and every shuttle. Ibram had a toy Dreadnought that his Uncle Dercius had carved for him from a hunk of plastene. Ibram would swoop it around in his hands as he hung from Oric's arms, dog-fighting the lights in the sky.

Oric had a huge lightning flash tattoo on his left forearm that fasci-nated Ibram. 'Imperial Guard,' he would say, in answer to the child's questions. 'Jantine Third for eight years. Mark of honour.'

He never said much else. Every time he put the boy down and

131

returned to the kitchens, Ibram wondered about the buzzing noise
that came from under his long chef's overalls. It sounded just like the
noise his tutor's arms made when they gestured.

The night Uncle Dercius visited, it was without advance word of his
coming.

Oric had been playing with him on the sundecks, and had carved
him a new frigate out of wood. When they heard Uncle Dercius's voice,
Ibram had leapt down and run into the parlour.

He hit against Dercius's uniformed legs like a meteor and hugged
tight.

'Ibram, Ibram! Such a strong grip! Are you pleased to see your uncle,
eh?'

Dercius looked a thousand metres tall in his mauve Jantine uniform.
He smiled down at the boy, but there was something sad in his eyes.

Oric entered the room behind them, making apologies. 'I must get
back to the kitchen,' he averred.

Uncle Dercius did a strange thing; he crossed directly to Oric and
embraced him. 'Good to see you, old friend.'

'And you, sir. Been a long time.'

'Have you brought me a toy, uncle?' Ibram interrupted, shaking off
the hand of his concerned-looking nurse.

Dercius crossed back to him.

'Would I let you down?' he chuckled. He pulled a signet ring off
his left little finger and hugged Ibram to his side. 'Know what this is?'

'A ring!'

'Smart boy! But it's more.' Dercius carefully turned the milled edge
of the ring setting and it popped open. A thin, truncated beam of laser
light stabbed out. 'Do you know what this is?'

Ibram shook his head.

'It's a key. Officers like me need a way to open certain secret dispatches. Secret orders. You know what they are?'

'My father told me! There are different codes... it's called "security
clearance".'

Dercius and the others laughed at the precocity of the little boy. But
there was a false note in it.

'You're right! Codes like Panther, Esculis, Cryptox, or the old
colour-code levels: cyan, scarlet, it goes up, magenta, obsidian and
vermilion,' Dercius said, taking the ring off. 'Generals like me are given
these signet rings to open and decode them.

'Does my father have one, uncle?'

A pause. 'Of course.'

'Is my father coming home? Is he with you?'

'Listen to me, Ibram, there's–'

Ibram took the ring and studied it. 'Can I really have this, Uncle Dercius? Is it for me?'

Ibram looked up suddenly from the ring in his hands and found that everyone was staring at him intently.

'I didn't steal it!' he announced.

'Of course you can have it. It's yours…' Dercius said, hunkering down by his side, looking as if he was preoccupied by something.

'Listen, Ibram, there's something I have to tell you… About your father.'

PART FIVE

THE EMPYREAN

ONE

Gaunt had been talking to Fereyd. They had sat by a fuel-drum fire in the splintered shadows of a residence in the demilitarised zone of Pashen Nine-Sixty's largest city. Fereyd was disguised as a farm boss, in the thick, red-wool robes common to many on Pashen, and he was talking obliquely about spy work, just the sort of half-complete, enticing remarks he liked to tease his commissar friend with. An unlikely pair, the commissar and the Imperial spy: one tall, lean and blond, the other compact and dark. Thrown together by the circumstances of combat, they were bonded and loyal despite the differences of their backgrounds and duties.

Fereyd's intelligence unit, working the city-farms of Pashen in deep cover, had revealed the foul Chaos cult – and the heretic Navy officers in their thrall. A disastrous fleet action, brought in too hastily in response to Fereyd's discovery, had led to open war on the planet itself and the deployment of the Guard. Chance had led Gaunt's Hyrkans to the raid which had rescued Fereyd from the hands of the Pashen traitors. Together, Gaunt and Fereyd had unveiled and executed the traitor Baron Sylag.

They were talking about loyalty and treachery, and Fereyd was saying how the vigilance of the Emperor's spy networks was the only thing that kept the private ambitions of various senior officers in check. But it was difficult for Gaunt to follow Fereyd's words because his face kept changing. Sometimes he was Oktar, and then, in the flame-light, his face would become that of Dercius or Gaunt's father.

With a grunt, Gaunt realised he was dreaming, bade his friend goodbye and, dissatisfied, he awoke.

The air was unpleasantly stuffy and stale. His room was small, with a low, curved ceiling and inset lighting plates that he had turned down to their lowest setting before retiring. He got up and pulled on his clothes, scattered where he had left them: breeches, dress shirt, boots, a short leather field-jacket with a high collar embossed with interlocked Imperial eagles. Firearm-screening fields meant there was no bolt pistol in his holster on the door hook, but he took his Tanith knife.

He opened the door-hatch and stepped out into the long, dark space of the companionway. The air here was hot and stifling too, but it moved, wafted by the circulation systems under the black metal grille of the floor.

A walk would do him good.

It was night cycle, and the deck lamps were low. There was the ever-present murmur of the vast power plants and the resulting micro-vibration in every metal surface, even the air itself.

Gaunt walked for fifteen minutes or more in the silent passageways of the great structure, meeting no one. At a confluence of passageways, he entered the main spinal lift and keyed his pass-code into the rune-pad on the wall. There was an electronic moan as cycles set, and a three-second chant sung by non-human throats to signal the start of the lift. The indicator light flicked slowly up twenty bas-relief glass runes on the polished brass board.

Another burst of that soft artificial choir. The doors opened.

Gaunt stepped out into the Glass Bay. A dome of transparent, hyper-dense silica a hundred metres in radius, it was the most serene place the structure offered. Beyond the glass, a magnificent, troubling vista swirled, filtered by special dampening fields. Darkness, striated light, blistering strands and filaments of colours he wasn't sure he could put a name to, bands of light and dark shifting past at an inhuman rate.

The empyrean. Warp space. The dimension beyond reality through which this structure, the Mass Cargo Conveyance *Absalom*, now moved.

He had first seen the *Absalom* through the thick, tinted ports of the shuttle that had brought him up to meet it in orbit. He was in awe of it. One of the ancient transport-ships of the Adeptus Mechanicus, a veteran vessel. The Tech-Lords of Mars had sent a massive retinue to aid the disaster at Fortis, and now in gratitude for the liberation they subordinated their vessels to the Imperial Guard. It was an honour to travel on the *Absalom*, Gaunt well knew. To be conveyed by the mysterious, secret carriers of the God-Machine cult.

From the shuttle, he'd seen sixteen solid kilometres of grey architecture, like a raked, streamlined cathedral, with the tiny lights of the troop transports flickering in and out of its open belly-mouth. The crenellated surfaces and towers of the mighty Mechanicus ship were rich with bas-relief gargoyles, out of whose wide, fanged mouths the turrets of the sentry guns traversed and swung. Green interior light shone from the thousands of slit windows. The pilot tug, obese and blackened with the scorch marks of its multiple attitude thrusters, bellied in the slow solar tides ahead of the transport vessel.

Gaunt's flagship, the great frigate *Navarre*, had been seconded for picket duties to the Nubila Reach so Gaunt had chosen to travel with his men on the *Absalom*. He missed the long, sleek, waspish lines of the *Navarre*, and he missed the crew, especially Executive Officer Kreff, who had tried so hard to accommodate the commissar and his unruly men.

The *Absalom* was a different breed of beast, a behemoth. Its echoing bulk capacity allowed it to carry nine full regiments, including the Tanith, four divisions of the Jantine Patricians, and at least three mechanised battalions, including their many tanks and armoured transport vehicles.

Fat lift-ships had hefted the numerous war machines up into the hold from the depots on Pyrites.

Now they were en route – a six-day jump to a cluster of war-worlds called the Menazoid Clasp, the next defined line of battle in the Sabbat Worlds campaign. Gaunt hoped for deployment with the Ghosts into the main assault on Menazoid Sigma, the capital planet, where a large force of Chaos was holding the line against a heavy Imperial advance.

But there was also Menazoid Epsilon, the remote, dark death world at the edge of the Clasp. Gaunt knew that Warmaster Macaroth's planning staff were assessing the impact of that world. He knew some regimental units would be deployed to take it.

No one wanted Epsilon. No one wanted to die.

He looked up into the festering, fluctuating light of the empyrean beyond the glass and uttered a silent prayer to the Most Blessed Emperor: spare us from Epsilon.

Other, even gloomier thoughts clouded his mind. Like the infernal, invaluable crystal that had come into his hands on Pyrites. Its very presence, its unlockable secret, burned in the back of his mind like a meltagun wound. No further word had come from Fereyd, no signal, not even a hint of what was expected of him. Was he to be a courier – if so, for how long? How would he know who to trust the precious jewel to when the time came? Was something else wanted from him? Had some further, vital instruction failed to reach him? Their long friendship aside, Gaunt cursed the memory of Fereyd. This kind of complication was unwelcome on top of the demands of his commissarial duties.

He resolved to guard the crystal. Carry it, until Fereyd told him otherwise. But still, he fretted that the matter was of the highest importance, and time was somehow slipping away.

He crossed to the knurled rail at the edge of the bay and leaned heavily on it. The enormity of the warp shuffled and spasmed in front of him, milky tendrils of proto-matter licking like ribbons of fluid mist against the outside of the glass. The Glass Bay was one of three imma-terium observatories on the *Absalom*, allowing the navigators and the clerics of the Astrographicus Division visual access to the void. In the centre of the bay's deck, on a vast platform mechanism of oiled cogs and toothed gears, giant sensorium scopes, aura-imagifiers and lumi-nosity evaluators cycled and turned, regarding the maelstrom: charting, cogitating, assessing and transmitting the assembled data via chattering relays and humming crystal stacks to the main bridge eight kilometres away at the top of the *Absalom's* tallest command spire.

The observatories were not forbidden areas, but their spaces were not recommended for those new to space crossings. It was said that if the glass wasn't shielded, the view could derange and twist the minds of even hardened astrographers. The elevator's choral chime had been intended to warn Gaunt of this. But he had seen the empyrean before, countless times on his voyages. It no longer scared him. Filtered in this way, he found the fluctuations of the warp somehow easeful, as if its cataclysmic turmoil allowed his own mind to rest. He could think here.

Around the edge of the dome, the names of militant commanders, lord-generals and master admirals were etched into the polished iron-work of the sill in a roll of honour. Under each name was a short legend indicating the theatres of their victories. Some names he knew, from the history texts and the required reading at the schola back on Ignatius. Some, their inscriptions old and faded, were unknown, ten centuries dead. He worked his way around the edge of the dome, reading the plaques. It took him almost half a circuit before he found the name of the one he had actually known personally: Warmaster Slaydo, Mac-aroth's predecessor, dead at the infamous triumph of Balhaut in the tenth year of this crusade through the Sabbat Worlds.

Gaunt glanced around from his study. The elevator doors at the top of the transit shaft hissed open and he caught once more a snatch of the chanted warning chime. A figure stepped onto the deck; a Navy rating, carrying a small instrument kit. The rating looked across at the lone figure by the rail for a moment and then turned away and disap-peared from view behind the lift assembly. An inspection patrol, Gaunt decided absently.

He turned back to the inscriptions and read Slaydo's plaque again. He remembered Balhaut, the firestorms that swept the night away and took the forces of Chaos with it. He and his beloved Hyrkans had been at the centre of it, in the mudlakes, struggling through the brimstone atmosphere under the weight of their heavy rebreathers. Slaydo had taken credit for that famous win, rightly enough as warmaster, but in sweat and blood it had been Gaunt's. His finest hour, and he had Slaydo's deathbed decoration to prove it.

He could hear the grind of the enemy assault carriers even now, striding on their long, hydraulic legs through the mud, peppering the air with sharp needle blasts of blood-red light, washing death and fire towards his men. A physical memory of the tension and fatigue ran down his spine, the superhuman effort with which he and his best fire-teams had stormed the Oligarchy Gate ahead of even the glorious forces of the Adeptus Astartes, driving a wedge of las-fire and grenade bursts through the overlapping plates of the enemy's buttress screens.

He saw Tanhause making his lucky shot, still talked about in the barracks of the Hyrkan: a single las-bolt that penetrated a foul, demented Chaos Dreadnought through the visor-slit, detonating the power systems within. He saw Veitch taking six of the foe with his bayonet when his last powercell ran dry.

He saw the Tower of the Plutocrat combust and fall under the sustained Hyrkan fire.

He saw the faces of the unnumbered dead, rising from the mud, from the flames.

He opened his eyes and the visions fled. The empyrean lashed and blossomed in front of him, unknowable. He was about to turn and return to his quarters.

But there was a blade at his throat.

TWO

There was no sense of anyone behind him – no shadow, no heat, no sound or smell of breath. It was as if the cold sharpness under his chin had arrived there unaccompanied. He knew at once he was at the mercy of a formidable opponent.

But that alone gave him a flicker of confidence. If the blade's owner had simply wanted him dead, then he would already be dead and none the wiser. There was something that made him more useful alive. He was fairly certain what that was.

'What do you want?' he asked calmly.

'No games,' a voice said from behind him. The tone was low and even, not a whisper but of a level that was somehow softer and lower still. The pressure of the cold blade increased against the skin of his neck fractionally. 'You are reckoned to be an intelligent man. Dispense with the delaying tactics.'

Gaunt nodded carefully. If he was going to live even a minute more, he had to play this precisely right.

'This isn't the way to solve this, Brochuss,' he said carefully.

There was a pause. 'What?'

'Now who's playing games? I know what this is about. I'm sorry you and your Patrician comrades lost face on Pyrites. Lost a few teeth too, I'll bet. But this won't help.'

'Don't be a fool! You've got this wrong! This isn't about some stupid regimental rivalry!'

'It isn't?'

'Think hard, fool! Think why this might really be happening! I want you to understand why you are about to die!' The weight of the blade against his throat shifted slightly. It didn't lessen its pressure, but there was a momentary alteration in the angle. Gaunt knew his comments had misdirected his adversary for a heartbeat.

His only chance. He struck backwards hard with his right elbow, simultaneously pulling back from the blade and raising his left hand to fend it off. The knife cut through his cuff, but he pulled clear as his assailant reeled from the elbow jab.

Gaunt had barely turned when the other countered, striking high. They fell together, limbs twisting to gain a positive hold. The wayward blade ripped Gaunt's jacket open down the seam of the left sleeve.

Gaunt forced the centre of balance over and threw a sideways punch with his right fist that knocked his assailant off him. A moment later the commissar was on his feet, drawing the silver Tanith blade from his belt.

He saw his opponent for the first time. The Navy rating, a short, lean man of indeterminate age. There was something strange about him. The way his mouth was set in a determined grimace while his wide eyes seemed to be... pleading? The rating flipped up onto his feet with a scissor of his back and legs, and coiled around in a hunched, offensive posture, the knife held blade-uppermost in his right hand.

How could a deck rating know moves like that? Gaunt worried. The practised movements, the perfect balance, the silent resolve – all betrayed a specialist killer, an adept in the arts of stealth and assassination. But close up, Gaunt saw the man was just an engineer, his naval uniform a little tight around a belly going to fat. Was it just a disguise? The rank pins, insignia and the coded identity seal mandatory for all crew personnel all seemed real.

The blade was short and leaf-shaped, shorter than the rubberised grip it protruded from. There was a series of geometric holes in the body of the blade itself, reducing the overall weight whilst retaining the structural strength. It plainly wasn't metal; it was matte blue, ceramic, invisible to the ship's weapon-scan fields.

Gaunt stared into the other's unblinking eyes, searching for recognition or contact. The gaze which met him was a desperate, piteous look, as if from something trapped inside the menacing body.

They circled, slowly. Gaunt kept his body angled and low as he had learned in bayonet drill with the Hyrkans. But he held the Tanith blade loosely in his right hand with the blade descending from the fist and tilted in towards his body. He'd watched the odd style the Ghosts had used in knife drill with interest, and one long week in transit aboard the *Navarre*, he had got Corbec to train him in the nuances. The method made good use of the weight and length of the Tanith war-knife. He kept his left hand up to block, not with a warding open palm as the Hyrkans had practised – and as his opponent now adopted – but in a fist, knuckles outward. 'Better to stop a blade with your hand than your throat,' Tanhause had told him, years before. 'Better the blade cracks off your knuckles than opens a smile in your palm,' Corbec had finessed more recently.

'You want me dead?' Gaunt hissed.

'That was not my primary objective. Where is the crystal?' Gaunt started as the man replied. Though the mouth moved, the voice was not coming from it. The lip movements barely synched with the words. He'd seen that before somewhere, years ago. It looked like... possession. Gaunt bristled as fear ran down his back. More than the fear of mortal combat. The fear of witchcraft. Of psykers.

'A commissar-colonel won't be easily missed,' Gaunt managed.

The rating shrugged stiffly as if to indicate the infinite raging vastness beyond the glass dome. 'No one is so important he won't be missed out here. Not even the warmaster himself.'

They had circled three times now. 'Where is the crystal?' the rating asked again.

'What crystal?'

'The one you acquired in Cracia City,' returned the killer in that floating, unmatched voice. 'Give it up now, and we can forget this meeting ever took place.'

'Who sent you?'

'Nothing in the known systems would make me answer that question.'

'I have no crystal. I don't know what you're talking about.'

'A lie.'

'Even if it was, would I be so foolish to carry anything with me?'

'I've searched your quarters twice. It's not there. You must have it. Did you swallow it? Dissection is not beyond me.'

Gaunt was about to reply when the rating suddenly stamped forward, circling his blade in a sweep that missed the commissar's shoulder by a hair's breadth. Gaunt was about to feint and counter when the blade swept back in a reverse of the slice. The touch of a stud on the grip had caused the ceramic blade to retract with a pneumatic hiss and re-extend through the flat pommel of the grip, reversing the angle. The tip sheared through his blocking left forearm and sprayed blood across the deck.

Gaunt leapt backwards with an angry curse, but the rating followed through relentlessly, reversing his blade again so it poked up forward of his punching fist. Gaunt blocked it with an improvised turn of his knife and kicked out at the attacker, catching his left knee with his boot tip.

The man backed off but the circling did not recommence. This was unlike the sparring in bayonet training, the endless measuring and dancing, the occasional clash and jab. The man rallied immediately after each feint, each deflection, and struck in once more, clicking his blade up and down out of the grip to wrong-foot Gaunt, sometimes striking with an upwards blow on the first stroke and thumbing the blade downwards to rake on the return.

Gaunt survived eight, nine, ten potentially lethal passes, thanks only to his speed and the attacker's unfamiliarity with the curious Tanith blade technique.

They clashed again, and this time Gaunt jabbed not with his knife but with his warding left hand, directly at the man's weapon. The blade cut a stinging gash in his knuckles, but he slipped in under the knife and grabbed the man by the right wrist. They clenched, Gaunt driving forwards with his superior size and height. The man's left hand found his throat and clamped it in an iron grip. Gaunt gagged, choking, his vision swimming as his neck muscles fought against the tightening grip.

Desperately, he slammed the man backwards into the guard rail. The rating thumbed his blade catch again and the reversing tongue of ceramic stabbed down into Gaunt's wrist. In return he plunged his own knife hard through the tricep of the arm holding his throat.

They broke, reeling away from each other, blood spurting from the stab wounds in their arms and hands. Gaunt was panting and short of breath from the pain, but the man made no sound. As if he felt no pain, or as if pain was no hindrance to him.

The rating came at him again, and Gaunt swung low to block, but at the last moment, the man tossed the ceramic blade from his right hand to his left, the blade reversing itself through the grip in mid air so that what had started as an upwards strike from the right turned into a downward stab from the left. The blade dug into the meat of Gaunt's right shoulder, deadened only by the padding and leather of his jacket. White-hot pain lanced down his right side, crushing his ribs and the breath inside them.

The blade slid free cleanly and blood drizzled after it. The hot warmth was coursing down the inside of his sleeve and slickening his grip on the knife handle. It dripped off his knuckles and the silver blade. If he kept bleeding at that rate, even if he could hold off his assailant, he knew he would not survive much longer.

The rating crossed his guard again, switching hands like a juggler, to the right and then back to the left, reversing the blade direction with each return. He feinted, sliced in low at Gaunt's belly with a left-hand pass and then pushed himself at the commissar.

Gaunt stabbed in to meet the low cut, and caught the point of his silver blade through one of the perforations in the ceramic blade.

Instinctively, he wrenched his blade back and levered at the point of contact. A second later, the ceramic tech-knife whirled away across the Glass Bay and skittered out of sight over the cold floor. Suddenly disarmed, the rating hesitated for a heartbeat and Gaunt rammed his Tanith knife up and in, puncturing the man's torso and cracking his sternum.

The rating reeled away sharply, sucking for air as his lungs failed. The silver knife was stuck fast in his chest. Thin blood jetted from the wound and gurgled from his slack mouth. He hit the deck, knees first, then fell flat in his face, his torso propped up like a tent on the hard metal prong of the knife.

Gaunt stumbled back against the rail, gasping hoarsely, his body shaking and burning pain jeering at him. He wiped a bloody hand across his clammy, ashen face and gazed down at the rating's body as it lay on the floor in a pool of scarlet fluid.

He sank to the deck, trembling and weak. A laugh, half chuckle, half sob broke from him. When next he saw Colm Corbec, he would buy him the biggest–

The rating got up again.

The man wriggled back on his knees, rippling the pool of blood around him, and then swung his body up straight, arms swaying limp at his sides. Kneeling, he slowly turned his head to face the prone, dismayed Gaunt. His face was blank, and his eyes were no longer pleading and trapped. They were gone, in fact. A fierce green light raged inside his skull, making his eyes pupilless slits of lime fire. His mouth lolled open and a similar glow shone out, back-lighting his teeth. With one simple, direct motion, he pulled the Tanith knife out of his chest. There was no more blood, just a shaft of bright green light poking from the wound.

With a sigh of finality, Gaunt knew that the psychic puppetry was continuing. The man, who had been a helpless thrall of the psyker magic when he first attacked, was now reanimated by abominable sorcery.

It would function long enough to win the fight.

It would kill him.

Gaunt battled with his senses to keep awake, to get up, to run. He was blacking out.

The rating swayed towards him, like a *zumbay* from the old myths of the non-dead, eyes shining, expression blank, the Tanith blade that had killed him clutched in his claw of a hand.

The dead thing raised the knife to strike.

THREE

Two las-shots slammed it sideways. Another tight pair broke it open along the rib cage, venting an incandescent halo of bright psychic energy. A fifth shot to the head dropped the thing like it had been struck in the ear with a sledgehammer.

Colm Corbec, the laspistol in his hand, stalked across the deck of the Glass Bay and stood looking down at the charred and smouldering shape on the floor, a shape that had self-ignited and was spilling vaporous green energies as it ate itself up.

Somewhere, the weapons interdiction alarm started wailing.

Using the rail for support, Gaunt was almost on his feet again by the time Corbec reached him.

'Easy there, commissar...'

Gaunt waved him off, aware of the way his blood was still freely dribbling onto the deck.

'Your timing...' he grunted, 'is perfect... colonel.'

Corbec grimly gestured over his shoulder. Gaunt turned to look where he pointed. Brin Milo stood by the elevator assembly, looking flushed and fierce.

'The lad had a dream,' Corbec said, refusing to be ignored and looping his arm under his commander's shoulder. 'Came to me at once when he couldn't find you in your quarters.'

Milo crossed to them. 'The wounds need attention,' he said.

'We'll get him to the apothecarion,' Corbec began.

'No,' Milo said firmly and, despite the pain, Gaunt almost laughed at the sudden authority his junior aide directed at the shaggy brute who was the company commander. 'Back to our barrack decks. Use our own medics. I don't think the commissar wants this incident to become a matter for official inquiry.'

Corbec looked at the boy curiously but Gaunt nodded. In his experience, there was no point fighting the boy's gift for judgement.

Milo never intruded into the commissar's privacy, but he seemed to understand instinctively Gaunt's intentions and wishes. Gaunt could not keep secrets from the boy, but he trusted him – and valued his insight beyond measure.

Gaunt looked at Corbec. 'Brin's right. There's more to this... I'll explain later, but I want the ship hierarchy kept out of it until we know who to trust.'

The weapons alarm continued to sound.

'In that case, we better get out of here–' Corbec began.

He was cut off by the elevator shutters gliding open with a breathy hiss and a choral exhalation. Six Imperial Navy troopers in fibre-weave shipboard armour and low-brimmed helmets exited in a pack and dropped to their knees, covering the trio with compact stub-guns. One barked curt orders into his helmet vox-link. An officer emerged from the elevator in their wake. Like them, his uniform was emerald with silver piping, the colours of the Segmentum Pacificus Fleet, but he was not armoured like his detail. He was tall, a little overweight and his puffy flesh was unhealthily pale.

A career spacer, thought Corbec. Probably hasn't stood on real soil in decades.

The officer stared at them: the shaggy Guard miscreant with his unauthorised laspistol; the injured, bloody man leaning against him and bleeding on the deck; the rangy, strange-eyed boy.

He pursed his lips, spoke quietly into his own vox-link and then touched a stud on the facilitator wand he carried, waving it absently into the air around him. The alarm shut off mid-whine.

'I am Warrant Officer Lekulanzi. It is my responsibility to oversee the security of this vessel on behalf of Lord Captain Grasticus. I take a dim view of illicit weapons on this holy craft, though I always expect Imperial Guard scum to try something. I look with even greater displeasure on the use of said weapons.'

'Now, this is not how it loo–' Corbec began, moving forward with a reassuring smile. Six stub-gun muzzles swung their attention directly at him. The detail's weapons were short-line, pump-action models designed for shipboard use.

The glass shards and wire twists wadded into each shell would roar out in a tightly packed cone of micro-shrapnel, entirely capable of shredding a man at close range. But unlike a lasgun or a bolter, there was no danger of them puncturing the outer hull.

'No hasty movements. No eager explanations.' Lekulanzi stared at them. 'Questions will be answered in due time, under the formal process of your interrogation. You are aware that the firing of a prohibited weapon on a transport vessel of the Adeptus Mechanicus is an offence punishable by court martial. Surrender your weapon.'

Corbec handed his laspistol to the trooper who rose smartly to take it from him.

'This is stupid,' Gaunt said abruptly. The guns turned their attention to him. 'Do you know who I am, Lekulanzi?'

The warrant officer tensed as his name was used without formal title. He narrowed his flesh-hooded eyes.

Gaunt hauled himself forward and stood free of Corbec's support. 'I am Commissar-Colonel Ibram Gaunt.'

Warrant Officer Lekulanzi froze. Without the coat, the cap, the badges of authority, Gaunt looked like any low-born Guard officer.

'Come here,' Gaunt told him. The man hesitated, then crossed to Gaunt, whispering a low order into his vox-link. The guard detail immediately rose from their knees, snapped to attention and slung their weapons.

'That's better...' Corbec smiled.

Gaunt placed a hand on Lekulanzi's shoulder, and the officer stiffened with outrage. Gaunt was pointing to something on the deck, a charred, greenish slick or stain, oily and lumpy. 'Do you know what that is?'

Lekulanzi shook his head.

'It's the remains of an assassin who set upon me here. The weapon's discharge was my First Officer saving my life. I will formally caution him for concealing a firearm aboard, strictly against standing orders.'

Gaunt smiled to see a tiny bead of nervous perspiration begin to streak Lekulanzi's pallid brow.

'He was one of yours, Lekulanzi. A rating. But he was in the sway of others, dark forces that beguiled and drove him like a toy. You don't like illicit weapons on your ship, eh? How about illicit psykers?'

Some of the security troopers muttered and made warding gestures. Lekulanzi stammered. 'But who... who would want to kill you, sir?'

'I am a soldier. A successful soldier,' Gaunt smiled coldly. 'I make enemies all the time.'

He gestured down at the remains. 'Have this analysed. Then have it purged. Make sure no foul, unholy taint has touched this precious ship. Report any findings directly to me, no matter how insignificant. Once my wounds have been treated, I will report to Lord Captain Grasticus personally and submit a full account.'

Lekulanzi was lost for words.

With Corbec supporting him, Gaunt left the Glass Bay. At the elevator doors, Lekulanzi caught the hard look in the boy's eyes. He shuddered.

In the elevator, Milo turned to Gaunt. 'His eyes were like a snake's. He is not trustworthy.'

Gaunt nodded. He had changed his mind. Just minutes before, he had reconciled himself to acting as Fereyd's courier, guardian to the crystal. But now things had changed. He wouldn't sit by idly waiting. He would act with purpose. He would enter the game, and find out the rules and learn how to win.

That would mean learning the contents of the crystal.

FOUR

'Best I can do,' murmured Dorden, the Ghosts' chief medic, making a half-hearted gesture around him that implicated the whole of the regimental infirmary. The Ghosts' infirmary was a suite of three low, corbel-vaulted rooms set as an annex to the barrack deck where the Tanith First were berthed. Its walls and roof were washed with a greenish off-white paint and the hard floors had been lined with scrubbed red stone tiles. On dull steel shelves in bays around the rooms were ranked fat, glass-stoppered bottles with yellowing paper labels, mostly full of treacly fluids, surgical pastes, dried powders and preparations, or organic field-swabs in clear, gluey suspensions. Racks of polished instruments sat in pull-out drawers and plastic waste bags, stale bedding and bandage rolls were packed into low, lidded boxes around the walls that doubled as seats. There was a murky autoclave on a brass trolley, two resuscitrex units with shiny iron paddles, and a side table with an apothecary's scales, a diagnostic probe and a blood cleanser set on it. The air was musty and rank, and there were dark stains on the flooring.

'We're not over-equipped, as you can see,' Dorden added breezily. He'd patched the commissar's wounds with supplies from his own field kit, which sat open on one of the bench lockers. He hadn't trusted the freshness or sterility of any of the materials provided by the infirmary.

Gaunt sat, stripped to the waist, on one of the low brass gurneys which lined the centre of the main chamber, its wheels locked into restraining lugs in the tiled floor. The gurney's springs squeaked and moaned as Gaunt shifted his weight on the stained, stinking mattress.

Dorden had patched the wound in the commissar's shoulder with sterile dressings, washed the whole limb in pungent blue sterilising gel and then pinched the mouth of the wound shut with bakelite suture clamps that looked like the heads of biting insects. Gaunt tried to flex his arm.

'Don't do that,' Dorden said quickly. 'I'd wrap it in false-flesh if I could find any, but besides, the wound should breathe. Honestly, you'd be better off in the main hospital ward.'

Gaunt shook his head. 'You've done a fine job,' he said. Dorden smiled. He didn't want to press the commissar on the issue. Corbec had muttered something about keeping this private.

Dorden was a small man, older than most of the Ghosts, with a grey beard and warm eyes. He'd been a doctor on Tanith, running an extended practice through the farms and settlements of Beldane and the forest wilds of County Pryze.

He'd been drafted at the Founding to fulfil the Administratum's requirements for regimental medical personnel. His wife had died a year before the Founding and his only son was a trooper in the ninth platoon. His one daughter, her husband and their first born had perished in the flames of Tanith. He had left nothing behind in the embers of his home world except the memory of years of community service, a duty he now carried on for the good of the last men of Tanith.

He refused to carry a weapon, and thus was the only Ghost that Gaunt couldn't rely on to fight... but Gaunt hardly cared. He had sixty or seventy men in his command who wouldn't still be there but for Dorden.

'I've checked for venom taint or fibre toxin. You're lucky. The blade was clean. Cleaner than mine!' Dorden chuckled and it made Gaunt smile. 'Unusual...' Dorden added and fell silent.

Gaunt raised an eyebrow. 'How so?'

'I understood assassins liked to toxify their blades as insurance.' Dorden said simply.

'I never said it was an assassin.'

'You didn't have to. I may be a non-combatant. Feth, I may be an old fool, but I didn't come down in the last barrage.'

'Don't trouble yourself with it, Dorden,' Gaunt said, flexing his arm again against the medic's advice. It stung, ached, throbbed. 'You've worked your usual magic. Stay impartial. Don't get drawn in.'

Dorden was scrubbing his suture clamp and wound probes in a bowl of filmy antiseptic oil. 'Impartial? Do you know something, Ibram Gaunt?'

Gaunt blinked as if slapped. No one had spoken to him with such paternal authority since the last time he had been in the company of his Uncle Dercius. No... not the last time...

Dorden turned back, wiping the tools on sheets of white lint. 'Forgive me, commissar. I– I'm speaking out of turn.'

'Speak anyway, friend.'

Dorden jerked a lean thumb to indicate out beyond the archway into the barrack deck. 'These are all I've got. The last pitiful scraps of Tanith genestock, my only link to the past and to the green, green world I loved. I'll keep patching and mending and binding and sewing them back together until they're all gone, or I'm gone, or the horizons of all known space have withered and died. And while you may not be Tanith, I know many of the men now treat you as such. Me, I'm not sure. Too much of the chulan about you, I'd say.'

'Koolun?'

'Chulan. Forgive me, slipping in to the old tongue. Outsider. Unknown. It doesn't translate directly.'

'I'm sure it doesn't.'

'It wasn't an insult. You may not be Tanith-breed, but you're for us every way. I think you care, Gaunt. Care about your Ghosts. I think you'll do all in your power to see us right, to take us to glory, to take us to peace. That's what I believe, every night when I lay down to rest, and every time a bombardment starts, or the drop-ships fall, or the boys go over the wire. That matters.'

Gaunt shrugged – and wished he hadn't. 'Does it?'

'I've spoken to medics with other regiments. At the field hospital on Fortis, for instance. So many of them say their commissars don't care a jot about their men. They see them as fodder for the guns. Is that how you see us?'

'No.'

'No, I thought not. So, that makes you rare indeed. Something worth hanging on to, for the good of these poor Ghosts. Feth, you may not be Tanith, but if assassins are starting to hunger for your blood, I start to care. For the Ghosts, I care.'

He fell silent.

'Then I'll remember not to leave you uninformed,' Gaunt said, reaching for his undershirt.

'I thank you for that. For a *chulan*, you're a good man, Ibram Gaunt. Like the *anroth* back home.'

Gaunt froze. 'What did you say?'

Dorden looked round at him sharply. 'Anroth. I said anroth. It wasn't an insult either.'

'What does it mean?'

Dorden hesitated uneasily, unsettled by Gaunt's hard gaze. 'The anroth... well, household spirits. It's a cradle-tale from Tanith. They used to say that the anroth were spirits from other worlds, beautiful worlds of order, who came to Tanith to watch over our families. It's nothing. Just an old memory. A forest saying.'

'Why does it matter, commissar?' said a new voice.

Gaunt and Dorden looked around to see Milo sat on a bench seat near the door, watching them intently.

'How long have you been there?' Gaunt asked sharply, surprising himself with his anger.

'A few minutes only. The anroth are part of Tanith lore. Like the *drud-fellad* who ward the trees, and the *nyrsis* who watch over the streams and waters. Why would it alarm you so?'

'I've heard the word before. Somewhere,' Gaunt said, getting to his feet. 'Who knows, a word like it? It doesn't matter.'

He went to pull on his undershirt but realised it was ripped and bloody, and cast it aside. 'Milo. Get me another from my quarters,' he snapped.

Milo rose and handed Gaunt a fresh undershirt from his canvas pack. Dorden covered a grin. Gaunt faltered, nodded his thanks, and took the shirt.

Both Milo and the medical officer had noticed the multitude of scars which laced Gaunt's broad, muscled torso, and had made no comment. How many theatres, how many fronts, how many life-or-death combats had it taken to accumulate so many marks of pain?

But as Gaunt stood, Dorden noticed the scar across Gaunt's belly for the first time and gasped. The wound line was long and ancient, a grotesque braid of buckled scar-tissue.

'Sacred Feth!' Dorden said too loudly. 'Where–'

Gaunt shook him off. 'It's old. Very old.'

Gaunt slipped on his undershirt and the wound was hidden. He pulled up his braces and reached for his tunic.

'But how did you get such a–'

Gaunt looked at him sharply. 'Enough.'

Gaunt buttoned his tunic and then put on the long leather coat which Milo was already holding for him. He set his cap on his head.

'Are the officers ready?' he asked.

Milo nodded. 'As you ordered.'

With a nod to Dorden, Gaunt marched out of the infirmary.

FIVE

It had crossed his mind to wonder who to trust. A few minutes' thought had brought him to the realisation that he could trust them all, every one of the Ghosts from Colonel Corbec down to the lowliest of the troopers. His only qualm lay with the malcontent Rawne and his immediate group of cronies in the third platoon, men like Feygor.

Gaunt left the infirmary and walked down the short companionway into the barrack deck proper. Corbec was waiting.

Colm Corbec had been waiting for almost an hour. Alone in the antechamber of the infirmary, he had enjoyed plenty of time to fret about the things he hated most in the universe. First and last of them was space travel.

Corbec was the son of a machinesmith who had worked his living at a forge beneath a gable-barn on the first wide bend of the River Pryze. Most of his father's work had come from log-handling machines: rasp-saws, timber-derricks, trak-sleds. Many times, as a boy, he'd shimmied down into the oily service trenches to hold the inspection lamp so his father could examine the knotted, dripping axles and stricken synchromesh of a twenty-wheeled flatbed, ailing under its cargo of young, wet wood from the mills up at Beldane or Sottress.

Growing up, he'd worked the reaper mills in Sottress and seen men lose fingers, hands and knees to the screaming bandsaws and circular razors. His lungs had clogged with saw mist and he had developed a hacking cough that lingered even now. Then he'd joined the militia of Tanith Magna on a dare and on top of a broken heart, and patrolled the sacred stretches of the Pryze County nalwood groves for poachers and smugglers.

It had been a right enough life. The loamy earth below, the trees above and the far starlight beyond the leaves. He'd come to understand the ways of the twisting forests, and the shifting nal-groves and clearings. He'd learned the knife, the stealth patterns and the joy of the hunt. He'd been happy. So long as the stars had been up there and the ground underfoot.

Now the ground was gone. Gone forever. The damp, piney scents of the forest soil, the rich sweetness of the leaf-mould, the soft depth of the nal-spores as they drifted and accumulated. He'd sung songs up to the stars, taken their silent blessing, even cursed them. All so long as they were far away. He never thought he would travel in their midst.

Corbec was afraid of the crossings, as he knew many of his company were afraid, even now after so many of them. To leave soil, to leave land, sea and sky behind, to part the stars and crusade through the immaterium. That was truly terrifying.

He knew the *Absalom* was a sturdy ship. He'd seen its vast bulk from the viewspaces of the dock-ship that had brought him aboard. But he had also seen the great timber barges of the mills founder, shudder and splinter in the hard water courses of the Beldane rapids. Ships sailed their ways, he knew, until the ways got too strong for them and gave them up.

He hated it all. The smell of the air, the coldness of the walls, the inconstancy of the artificial gravity, the perpetual constancy of the vibrating empyrean drives. All of it. Only his concern for the commissar's welfare had got him past his phobias onto the nightmare of the Glass Bay Observatory. Even then, he'd focussed his attention on Gaunt, the troopers, that idiot warrant officer – anything at all but the cavorting insanity beyond the glass.

He longed for soil underfoot. For real air. For breeze and rain and the hush of nodding branches.

'Corbec?'

He snapped to attention as Gaunt approached. Milo was a little way behind the commissar.

'Sir?'

'Remember what I was telling you in the bar on Pyrites?'

'Not precisely, sir... I... I was pretty far gone.'

Gaunt grinned. 'Good. Then it will all come as a surprise to you too. Are the officers ready?'

Corbec nodded perfunctorily. 'Except Major Rawne, as you ordered.'

Gaunt lifted his cap, smoothed his cropped hair back with his hands and replaced it squarely again.

'A moment, and I'll join you in the staff room.'

Gaunt marched away down the deck and entered the main billet of the barracks.

The Ghosts had been given barrack deck three, a vast honeycomb of long, dark vaults in which bunks were strung from chains in a herring-bone pattern. Adjoining these sleeping vaults was a desolate recreation hall and a trio of padded exercise chambers. All forty surviving platoons, a little over two thousand Ghosts, were billeted here.

The smell of sweat, smoke and body heat rose from the bunk vaults. Rawne, Feygor and the rest of the third platoon were waiting for him on the slip-ramp. They had been training in the exercise chambers, and each one carried one of the shock-poles provided for combat practice. These neural stunners were the only weapons allowed to them during a crossing. They could fence with them, spar with them and even set them to long range discharge and target-shoot against the squeaking, moving, metal decoys in the badly-oiled automatic range.

Gaunt saluted Rawne. The men snapped to attention.

'How do you read the barrack deck, major?'

Rawne faltered. 'Commissar?'

'Is it secure?'

'There are eight deployment shafts and two to the drop-ship hangar, plus a number of serviceways.'

'Take your men, spread out and guard them all. No one must get in or out of this barrack deck without my knowledge.'

Rawne looked faintly perplexed. 'How do we hold any intruders off, commissar, given our lack of weapons?'

Gaunt took a shock-pole from Trooper Neff and then laid him out on the deck with a jolt to the belly.

'Use these,' Gaunt suggested. 'Report to me every half hour. Report to me directly with the name of anyone who attempts access.' Pausing for a moment to study Rawne's face and make sure his instructions were clearly understood, Gaunt turned and walked back up the ramp.

'What's he up to?' Feygor asked the major when Gaunt was out of earshot. Rawne shook his head. He would find out. Until he did, he had a sentry duty to organise.

SIX

The staff room was an old briefing theatre next to the infirmary annex. Steps led down into a circular room, with three tiers of varnished wooden seats around the circumference and a lacquered black console in the centre on a dais. The console, squat and rounded like a polished mushroom, was an old tactical display unit, with a mirrored screen in its top which had once broadcast luminous three-dimensional hololithic forms into the air above it during strategy counsels. But it was old and broken; Gaunt used it as a seat.

The officers filed in: Corbec, Dorden, and then the platoon leaders, Meryn, Mkoll, Curral, Lerod, Hasker, Blane, Folore... thirty-nine men, all told. Last in was Varl, recently promoted. Milo closed the shutter hatch and perched at the back. The men sat in a semi-circle, facing their commander.

'What's going on, sir?' Varl asked. Gaunt smiled slightly. As a newcomer to officer-level briefings, Varl was eager and forthright, and oblivious to the usually reserved protocols of staff discussions. I should have promoted him earlier, Gaunt thought wryly.

'This is totally unofficial. Ghost business, but unofficial. I want to advise you of a situation so that you can be aware of it and act accordingly if the need arises. But it does not go beyond this chamber. Tell your men as much as they need to know to facilitate matters, but spare them the details.'

He had their attention now.

'I won't dress this up. As far as I know – and believe me, that's no further than I could throw Bragg – there's a power struggle going on. One that threatens to tear this whole Crusade to tatters.

'You've all heard how much infighting went on after Warmaster Slaydo's death. How many of the Lord High Militants wanted to take his place.'

'And that weasel Macaroth got it,' Corbec said with a rueful grin.

'That's Warmaster Weasel Macaroth, colonel,' Gaunt corrected. He let the men chuckle. Good humour would make this easier. 'Like him or not, he's in charge now. And that makes it simple for us. Like me, you are all loyal to the Emperor, and therefore to Warmaster Macaroth. Slaydo chose him to be successor. Macaroth's word is the word of the Golden Throne itself. He speaks with Imperium authority.'

Gaunt paused. The men watched him quizzically, as if they had missed the point of some joke.

'But someone's not happy about that, are they?' Milo said dourly, from the back. The officers snapped around to stare at him and then turned back equally sharply as they heard the commissar laugh.

'Indeed. There are probably many who resent his promotion over them. And one in particular we all know, if only by name. Lord Militant General Dravere. The very man who commands our section of the Crusade force.'

'What are you saying, sir?' Lerod asked with aghast disbelief. Lerod was a large, shaven-headed sergeant with an Imperial eagle tattoo on his temple. He had commanded the militia unit in Tanith Ultima, the Imperial shrine-city on the Ghost's lost home world, and as a result he, along with the other troopers from Ultima, were the most devoted and resolute Imperial servants in the Tanith First. Gaunt knew that Lerod would be perhaps the most difficult to convince. 'Are you suggesting that Lord General Dravere has renegade tendencies? That he is... disloyal? But he's your direct superior, sir!'

'Which is why this discussion is being held in private. If I'm right, who can we turn to?'

The men greeted this with uncomfortable silence.

Gaunt went on. 'Dravere has never hidden the fact that he felt Slaydo snubbed him by appointing the younger Macaroth. It must rankle deeply to serve under an upstart who has been promoted past you. I am pretty certain that Dravere plans to usurp the warmaster.'

'Let them fight for it!' Varl spat, and others concurred. 'What's another dead officer – begging your pardon, sir.'

Gaunt smiled. 'You echo my initial thoughts on the matter, sergeant. But think it through. If Dravere moves his own forces against Macaroth, it will weaken this entire endeavour. Weaken it at the very moment we should be consolidating for the push into new, more hostile territories. What good are we against the forces of the enemy if we're battling with ourselves? If it came to it, we'd be wide open, weak... and ripe for slaughter. Dravere's plans threaten the entire future of us all.'

Another heavy silence. Gaunt rubbed his lean chin. 'If Dravere goes through with this, we could throw everything away. Everything we've won in the Sabbat Worlds these last ten years.'

Gaunt leaned forward. 'There's more. If I was going to usurp the warmaster, I'd want a whole lot more than a few loyal regiments with me. I'd want an edge.'

'Is that what this is about?' Lerod asked, now hanging on Gaunt's words.

'Of course it is. Dravere is after something. Something big. Something so big it will actually place him on an equal footing with the warmaster. Or even make him stronger. And that is where we pitiful few come into the picture.'

He paused for a moment. 'When I was on Pyrites, I came into possession of this...'

Gaunt held up the crystal.

'The information encrypted onto this crystal holds the key to it all. Dravere's spy network was transmitting it back to him and it was intercepted.'

'By who?' Lerod asked.

'By Macaroth's loyal spy network, Imperial intelligence, working to undermine Dravere's conspiracy. They are covert, vulnerable, few, but they are the only things working against the mechanism of Dravere's ascendancy.'

'Why you?' Dorden asked quietly.

Gaunt paused. Even now, he could not tell them the real reason. That it was foretold. 'I was there, and I was trusted. I don't understand it all. An old friend of mine is part of the intelligence hub, and he contacted me to caretake this precious cargo. It seemed there was no one else on Pyrites close enough or trusted enough to do it.'

Varl shifted in his seat, scratching his shoulder implant. 'So? What's on it?'

'I have no idea,' Gaunt said. 'It's encoded.'

Lerod started to say something else, but Gaunt added, 'It's Vermilion level.'

There was a long pause, accompanied only by Blane's long, impressed whistle.

'Now do you see?' Gaunt asked.

'What do we do?' Varl said dully.

'We find out what's on it. Then we decide.'

'But how–' Meryn began, but Gaunt held up a calming hand.

'That's my job, and I think I can do it. Easily, in fact. After that... well, that's why I wanted you all in on this. Already, Dravere's covert network has attempted to kill me and retrieve the crystal. Twice. Once on Pyrites and now here again on the ship. I need you with me, to guard this priceless thing, to keep the Lord Militant General's spies from it. To cover me until I can see the way clear to the action we should take.'

Silence reigned in the staff room.

'Are you with me?' Gaunt asked.

The silence beat on, almost stifling. The officers exchanged furtive glances.

In the end, it was Lerod who spoke for them. Gaunt was particularly glad it was Lerod.

'Do you have to ask, commissar?' he said simply.

Gaunt smiled his thanks. He got up from the display unit and stepped off the dais as the men rose. 'Let's get to it. Rawne's already setting patrols to keep this barrack deck secure. Support and bolster that effort. I want to feel confident that the area of this ship given over to us is safe ground. Keep intruders out, or escort them directly to me. If the men question the precautions, tell them we think that those damn Patricians might try something to ease their grudge against us. Terra knows, that's true enough, and there are over four times our number of Patricians aboard this vessel on the other barrack decks. And the Patricians are undoubtedly in Dravere's pocket.

'I also want the entire deck searched for hidden vox-relays and vista-lines. Hasker, Varl... use any men you know with technical aptitude to perform the sweep. They may be trying all manner of ways of spying on us. From this moment on, trust no one outside our regiment. No one. There is no way of telling who might be part of the conspiracy around us.'

The officers seemed eager but unsettled. Gaunt knew that this was strange work for regular soldiers. They filed out, faces grave.

Gaunt looked at the crystal in his hand. What are you hiding? he wondered.

SEVEN

Gaunt returned to his quarters with the silent Milo in tow. Corbec had set two Ghosts to guard the commissar's private room. Gaunt sat at the cogitator set into a wall alcove, and began to explore the shipboard information he could access through the terminal. Lines of gently flickering amber text scrolled across the dark vista-plate. He was hoping for a personnel manifest, searching for names that might hint at the identity of those that opposed him. But the details were jumbled and incomplete. It wasn't even clear which other regiments were actually aboard. The Patricians were listed, and a complement of mechanised units from the Bovanian Ninth. But Gaunt knew there must be at least two other regimental strengths aboard, and the listing was blank. He also tried to view the particulars of the *Absalom's* officer cadre, and any other senior Imperial servants making the crossing with them, but those levels of data were locked by naval cipher veils, and Gaunt did not have the authority to penetrate them.

Technology, such as it was, was a sandbagged barricade keeping him out. He sat back in his chair and sighed. His shoulder was sore. The crystal lay on the console near his hand. It was time to try it. Time to try his guess. He'd been putting it off, in case it didn't work really. He got up.

Milo had begun to snooze on a seat by the door and the sudden movement startled him.

'Sir?'

Gaunt was on his feet, carelessly pulling his kitbag and luggage trunks from the wall locker.

'Let's hope the old man wasn't lying!' was all Gaunt said.

Which old man, Milo had no idea.

Gaunt rifled through his baggage. A silk-swathed dress uniform ended up on the floor. Books and data-slates spewed from pulled-open pouches.

Milo was fascinated for a moment. The commissar always packed his own effects, and Milo had never seen the few possessions Gaunt valued enough to carry with him. The boy glimpsed a bar of medals wound in tunic cloth; a larger, grand silver starburst rosette that fell from its velvet-lined case; a faded forage cap with Hyrkan insignia; a glass box of painkiller tablets; a dozen large, yellow slab-like teeth – ork teeth – drilled and threaded onto a cord; an antique scope in a wooden case; a worn buckle brush and a tin of silver polish; a tarot gaming deck which spilled out of its ivory box. The cards were stiff pasteboard, decorated with commemorative images of a liberation festival on somewhere called Gylatus Decimus. Milo bent to collect them up before Gaunt trampled them. They were clean and new, never used; the lid of the box was inscribed with the letters D. O.

Unheeding, Gaunt pulled handfuls of clothes out of his kitbag and flung them aside.

Milo grinned. He felt somehow privileged to see this stuff, as if the commissar had let him into his mind for a while.

Then something else bounced off the accumulating clutter on the deck and Milo paused. It was a toy battleship, rudely carved from a hunk of plastene. Enamel paint was flaking away, and some of the towers and gun turrets had broken off. Milo turned away. There was something painful about the toy, something that let him glimpse further into Ibram Gaunt's private realm of loss than he wanted to go.

The feeling surprised him. He retreated a little, dropping some of the cards he had been shuffling back into their ivory box, and was glad of the excuse to busy himself picking them up.

Gaunt suddenly turned from the mess, a look of triumph in his eyes. He held up an old, tarnished signet ring between his fingers.

'What you were looking for, commissar?' Milo asked brightly, feeling a comment was expected.

'Oh yes. Dear old Uncle Dercius, that bastard. Gave it me as a distraction that night–' Gaunt stopped suddenly, thoughts clouding his face.

He sat down on the bunk next to Milo, glancing over and chuckling sadly as he saw the deck the boy was sorting. 'Souvenirs. Hnh. Emperor knows why I keep them. Never glance at them for years and then they only dredge up black memories.'

He took the cards and rifled through them, holding up some to show Milo, laughing sourly as he did so, as if the Tanith youth could understand the reason for humour. One card showed a Hyrkan flag flying from some tower or other, another showed a heraldic design with an ork's skull, another a moon struck by lightning from the beak of an Imperial eagle.

'Seventy-two reasons to forget our noble victory in the Gylatus World Flock,' he said mockingly.

'And the ring?' Milo asked.

Gaunt put the cards aside. He turned the milling on the signet mount and a short beam of light stabbed out of the ring. 'Feth! Still power in the cell, after all this time!'

Milo smiled, uncertain.

'It's a decryption ring. Officer level. A key to let senior staff access private or veiled data. A general's plaything. They used to be quite popular. This was issued to the commander-in-chief of the noble Jantine regiments, a lord of the very highest standing. And that old bastard gave it to a little boy on Manzipor.'

Gaunt dug the crystal out of his tunic pocket and held it over the ring's beam. He glanced at Milo for a second. There was a surprisingly impish, youthful glee in Gaunt's eyes that made Milo snort with laughter.

'Here goes,' Gaunt said. He slipped the base of the crystal onto the ring mount. It fitted perfectly and engaged with a tiny whirr. Locked in place, as if the stone was now set on the ring band like an outrageously showy gem, it was illuminated by the beam of light. The crystal glowed.

'Come on, come on...' Gaunt said.

Something started to form in the air a few centimetres above the ring, a pict-form, neon bright and lambent in the dimness of the cabin.

The tight, small holographic runes hanging in the air read: 'Authority denied. This document may only be opened by Vermilion level decryption as set by order of Senthis, Administratum Elector, Pacificus calendar 403457.M41. Any attempts to tamper with this data-receptacle will result in memory wipe.'

Gaunt cursed and slipped the crystal off the mount, cancelling the ring's beam. 'Too old, too damn old! Feth, I thought I had it!'

'I don't understand, sir.'

'The clearance levels remain the same, but they revise the codes required to read them at regular intervals. Dercius's ring would certainly have opened a Vermilion text thirty years ago, but the sequences have been overwritten since then. I should have expected Dravere to have set his own confidence codes. Damn!'

Gaunt looked like he was going to continue cursing, but there was a sharp knock at the door of his quarters. Gaunt pocketed the crystal smartly and opened the door. Trooper Uan, one of the corridor sentries, looked in at him.

'Sergeant Blane has brought visitors to you, sir. We've checked them for weapons, and they're clean. Will you see them?'

Gaunt nodded, pulling on his cap and longcoat. He stepped out into the corridor. When he saw the identity of the visitors, Gaunt waved his men back and walked down to greet them.

It was Colonel Zoren, the Vitrian commander, and three of his officers.

'Well met, commissar,' Zoren said curtly. He and his men were dressed in ochre fatigues and soft caps.

'I didn't realise you Vitrians were aboard,' Gaunt said.

'Last minute change. We were bound for the *Japhet* but there was a problem with the boarding tubes. They re-routed us here. The regiments scheduled for the *Absalom* took our places on the *Japhet* once the technical problems were solved. My platoons have been given the barrack decks aft of here.'

'It's good to see you, colonel.'

Zoren nodded, but there was something he was holding back, Gaunt sensed. 'When I learned we were sharing the same transport as the Tanith, I thought perhaps an interaction would be appropriate. We have a mutual victory to celebrate. But-'

'But?'

Zoren dropped his voice. 'I was attacked in my quarters this morning. A man dressed in unmarked Navy overalls was searching my belongings. He rounded on me when I came in. There was a struggle. He escaped.'

Gaunt felt his anger return. 'Go on.'

'He was looking for something. Something he thought I might have, something he had failed to find elsewhere. I thought I should tell you directly.'

Milo, Uan and everyone in the corridor, including Zoren himself, was surprised when Gaunt grabbed the Vitrian colonel by the front of his tunic and dragged him into his quarters.

Gaunt slammed the door shut after them.

Alone in the room, Gaunt turned on Zoren, who looked hurt but somehow not surprised.

'That was a terribly well-informed statement, colonel.'

'Naturally.'

'Start making sense, Zoren, or I'll forget our friendship.'

'No need for unpleasantness, Gaunt. I know more than you imagine and, I assure you, I am a friend.'

'Of whom?'

'Of you, of the Throne of Terra, and of a mutual acquaintance. I know him as Bel Torthute. You know him as Fereyd.'

EIGHT

'It's...' Colonel Draker Flense began. 'It's a lot to think about.'

He was answered by a snigger that did nothing to calm his nerves. The snigger came from a tall, hooded shape at the rear of the room, a figure silhouetted against a window of stained glass imagery which was lit by the flashes and glints of the immaterium.

'You're a soldier, Flense. I don't believe thinking is part of the job description.'

Flense bit back on a sharp answer. He was afraid, terribly afraid of the man in the multi-coloured shadows of the window. He shifted uneasily, dying for a breath of fresh air, his throat parched. The chamber was thick with the smoke from the obscura water-pipe on its slate plinth by the steps to the window. The nectar-sweet opiate smoke swirled around him and stole all humidity from the air. His mind was slack and torpid from breathing it in.

Warrant Officer Lekulanzi stood by the door, and the three shrouded astropaths grouped in a huddle in the shadows to his left didn't seem to mind. The astropaths were a law unto themselves, and Flense had recognised the pallor of an obscura addict in Lekulanzi's face the moment the warrant officer had arrived at his quarters to summon him. Flense had led an assault into an addict-hive on Poscol years before. He had never forgotten the sweet stench, nor the pallor of the half-hearted resistance.

The figure at the window stepped slowly down to face him. Flense, two metres tall without his jackboots, found himself looking up into the darkness of the cowl.

'Well, colonel?' whispered the voice inside the hood.

'I– I don't really understand what is expected of me, my lord.'

Inquisitor Golesh Constantine Pheppos Heldane sniggered again. He reached up with his ring-heavy fingers and turned back his cowl. Flense blinked. Heldane's face was high and long, like some equine beast. His wet, sneering mouth was full of blunt teeth and his eyes were round and dark. Fluid tubes and fibre-wires laced his long, sloped skull like hair braids. His huge skull was hairless, but Flense could see the matted fur that coated his neck and throat. He was human, but his features had been surgically altered to inspire terror and obedience in those he… studied. At least, Flense hoped it was a surgical alteration.

'You seem uneasy, colonel. Is it the circumstance, or my words?'

Flense found himself floundering for speech again. 'I've never been admitted to a sacrosanctorium before, my lord,' he began.

Heldane extended his arms wide – too wide for anything but a skeletal giant like Heldane, Flense shuddered – to encompass the chamber. Those present were standing in one of the *Absalom's* astropath sanctums, a chamber screened from all intrusion. The walls were null field dead spaces designed to shut out both the material world and the screaming void of the immaterium. Sound-proofed, psyker-proofed, wire-proofed, these inviolable cocoons were dedicated and reserved for the astropathic retinue alone. They were prohibited by Imperial law. Only a direct invitation could admit a blunt human such as Flense.

Blunt. Flense didn't like the word, and hadn't been aware of it until Lekulanzi had used it.

Blunt. A psyker's word for the non-psychic. Blunt. Flense wished by the Ray of Hope he could be elsewhere. Any elsewhere.

'You are discomforting my cousins,' Heldane said to Flense, indicating the three astropaths, who were fidgeting and murmuring. 'They sense your reluctance to be here. They sense their stigma.'

'I have no prejudices, inquisitor.'

'Yes, you have. I can taste them. You detest mind scers. You despise the gift of the astropath. You are a blunt, Flense. A sense-dead moron. Shall I show you what you are missing?'

Flense shook. 'No need, inquisitor!'

'Just a touch? Be a sport.' Heldane sniggered, droplets of spittle flecking off his thick teeth.

Flense shuddered. Heldane turned his gaze away slowly and then snapped back suddenly. Impossible light flooded into Flense's skull. For one second, he saw eternity. He saw the angles of space, the way they intersected with time. He saw the tides of the empyrean, and the wasted fringes of the immaterium, the fluid spasms of the warp. He

saw his mother, his sister, both long dead. He saw light and darkness
and nothingness. He saw colours without name. He saw the birth torments of the genestealer whose blood would scar his face. He saw
himself on the drill-field of the Schola on Primagenitor. He saw an
explosion of blood. Familiar blood. He started to cry. He saw bones
buried in rich, black mud. He realised they, too, were his own. He
looked into the sockets. He saw maggots. He screamed. He vomited.
He saw a red-dark sky and an impossible number of suns. He saw a
star overload and collapse. He saw–

Too much.

Draker Flense fell to the floor of the sacrosanctorium, soiled himself and started to whimper.

'I'm glad we've got that straight,' Inquisitor Heldane said. He raised
his cowl again. 'Let me start over. I serve Dravere, as you do. For him,
I will bend the stars. For him, I will torch planets. For him, I will master the unmasterable.'

Flense moaned.

'Get up. And listen to me. The most priceless artefact in space
awaits our lord in the Menazoid Clasp. Its description and circumstance lies with Commissar Gaunt. We will obtain that secret. I have
already expended precious energies trying to reach it. This Gaunt is...
resourceful. You will allow yourself to be used in this matter. You and
the Patricians. You already have a feud with them.'

'Not this... not this...' Flense rasped from the floor.

'Dravere spoke highly of you. Do you remember what he said?'

'N– no...'

Heldane's voice changed and became a perfect copy of Dravere's. 'If
you win this for me, Flense, I'll not forget it. There are great possibilities in my future, if I am not tied here. I would share them with you.'

'Now is the time, Flense,' Heldane said in his own voice once more.
'Share in the possibilities. Help me to acquire what my Lord Dravere
demands. There will be a place for you, a place in glory. A place at the
side of the new warmaster.'

'Please!' Flense cried. He could hear the astropaths laughing at him.

'Are you still undecided?' Heldane asked. He stepped towards the
curled, foetal colonel. 'Another look?' he suggested.

Flense began to shriek.

NINE

'They're excluding us,' Feygor said out of the silence.

Rawne snapped an angry glance round at his adjutant, but he knew what the lean man meant. It had been four hours since the rest of the officers had been called into their meeting with Gaunt. How convenient that he and his platoon had been excluded. Of course, if what Corbec said was true and there was trouble aboard, a good picket was essential. But in the natural order of things, it should have been Folore's platoon, the sixteenth, who took first shift.

Rawne grunted a response and led his team of five men down to the junction with the next corridor. They'd swept this area six times since they had begun. Just draughty hull-spaces, dark corners, empty stores, dusty floors and locked hatches. He checked the time. A radio message from Lerod twenty minutes earlier had informed him that the shift change would take place on the next hour. He ached. He knew the men with him were tired and cold and in need of stove-warmth, caffeine and relaxation. By extension, all of his platoon, all fifty of them spread out patrolling the perimeter of the Ghosts' barrack deck in squads of five, would be demoralised and hungry too.

Rawne thought, as he often did, of Gaunt. Of Gaunt's motives. From the start, back at the bloody hour of the Founding itself, he had shown no loyalty to the commissar. It had astonished him when Gaunt had raised him to major and given him the tertiary command of the regiment. He'd laughed at it at first, then qualified that laughter by imagining Gaunt had recognised his leadership qualities. Sometime later, Feygor, the only man in the regiment he thought of as a friend, and then only barely, had reminded him of the old saying: 'Keep your friends close and your enemies closer.'

There was no escape from the Guard, so Rawne had got on with making the best of his job. But he always wondered at Gaunt. If he'd been the colonel-commissar, with a danger like himself at his heels, he'd have called up a firing squad long since.

Ahead, Trooper Lonegin was checking the locks on a storage bin. Rawne scanned the length of the corridor they had just advanced through.

Feygor watched his commander slyly. Rawne had been good to him – and they had worked together in the militia of Tanith Attica before the Founding. Quite a tasty racket they had running there until the fething Imperium rolled up and ruined it. Feygor was the bastard son of a black marketeer, and only his sharp mind and formidable physical ability had got him a place in the militia, and then the Imperial Guard. Rawne's background had been select. He didn't talk about it much, but Feygor knew enough to know that Rawne's family had been rich merchants, local politicians, local lords. Rawne had always had money, stipends from his father's empire of timber mills. But as the third son, he was never going to be the one to inherit the fortune. The militia service – and the opportunities for self advancement – had been the best option.

Feygor didn't trust Rawne. Feygor didn't trust anyone. But he never thought of the major as evil. Just... bitter. Bitterness was what had ruined him, bitterness was what had scalded his nature early on.

Like Feygor, the men of Rawne's platoon were the misfits and trouble-makers of the surviving Tanith. They gravitated towards Rawne, seeing him as a natural leader, the man who would make the best chances for them. During the draft process, Rawne had selected most of them for his own squads.

One day, Feygor thought, one day Rawne will kill Gaunt and take his place. Gaunt, Corbec, any who opposed. Rawne will kill Gaunt. Or Gaunt will kill Rawne. Whatever, there will be a reckoning. Some said Rawne had already tried.

Feygor was about to suggest they double back into the storerooms to the left when Trooper Lonegin cried out and spun across the deck, hit by something from behind. He curled, convulsing, on the grill-walkway and Feygor could clearly see the short boot-knife jutting from the man's ribs where it had impacted.

Rawne was already yelling when the attackers emerged around them from all sides. Ten men, dressed in the work uniforms of the Purpure Patricians. They had knives, stakes, clubs made from bunk-legs. A frenzy of close-quarter brutality exploded in the narrow confines of the hallway.

Trooper Colhn was smashed into a wall by a blow to the head and sank without a murmur before he could even turn. Trooper Freul struck one attacker hard with his shock-pole and knocked him over in a cas-cade of sparks before three knife jabs from as many assailants ripped into him and dropped him in a bloody mass. Feygor could see two of the Patricians clubbing the wounded, helpless Lonegin repeatedly.

Feygor hurled his shock-pole at the nearest Patrician, blasting him backwards and burning through the belly of his uniform with the dis-charge, and then pulled out his silver Tanith blade. He screamed an obscenity and hurled forward, ripping open a throat with his first attack. With a savage turn, using the moves that had won him respect in the backstreets of Tanith Attica, he wheeled, kicked the legs out from under another and took a knife-wielding hand off at the wrist.

'Rawne! Rawne!' he bellowed, fumbling for his radio bead. He was hit from behind. Stunned, he took two more strikes and dropped, roll-ing. Feet kicked into him. Something that felt white hot dug into his chest. He bellowed with pain and rage. The sound was diffused by the gout of blood in his mouth.

Rawne struck down one with his pole, wheeling and blocking. He cursed them with every oath in his vocabulary. A blade ripped open his tunic and spilled blood from a long, raw scratch. A heavy blow struck his temple and he went over, vision fogging.

The major tried to move but his body wouldn't respond. The cold grille of the deck pushed into his cheek and his slack mouth. Wet warmth ran down his neck. His unfocussed eyes looked up at the bulky Patrician who stood over him, a long-armed wrench raised ready to pulp his skull.

'Stay your hand, Brochuss!' a voice said. The wrench lowered, reluctantly.

Immobile, Rawne wished he could see more. Another figure replaced the shape of his wrench-swinging attacker. Rawne's eyes were dim and filmy. He wished he could see clearly. The man who stooped by him looked like an officer.

Colonel Flense hunkered down beside Rawne, looking sadly at the blood matting the hair and the twisted spread of the limbs.

'See the badge, Brochuss?' Flense said. 'He's the major, Rawne. Don't kill him. Not yet, at least.'

TEN

'How do you know him?' Gaunt demanded.

Colonel Zoren made a slight, shrugging gesture, the typically unemphatic body language of the Vitrians. 'Likely the same way you do. A chance encounter, a carefully established measure of trust, an informal working relationship during a crisis.'

Gaunt rubbed his angular chin and shook his head. 'If this conversation is going to get us anywhere, you'll have to be more specific. If you honestly do appreciate the critical nature of this situation, you'll understand why I need to be sure and certain of those around me.'

Zoren nodded. He turned, as if to survey the room, but the close confines of Gaunt's quarters allowed for little contemplation. 'It was during the Famine Wars on Idolwilde, perhaps three standard years ago. My Dragoons were sent in as a peacekeeping presence in the main city-state, Kenadie. That was just before the food riots began in earnest and before the fall of the local government. The man you know as Fereyd was masquerading as a local grain broker called Bel Torthute, a trade-banker with a place on the Idolwilde Senate. His cover was perfect. I had no idea he was an off-world operative. No idea he wasn't a native. He had the language, the customs, the gestures–'

'I know how Fereyd works. Observational perfection is his speciality, and that mimicry thing.'

'Then you'll know his modus operandi too. To work with what he calls the "trustworthy salt" of the Imperium.'

Gaunt nodded, a half-smile curving his mouth.

'To work in such environments, so alone, so vulnerable, our mutual friend needs to nurture the support of those elements of the Imperium he deems uncorrupted. Rooting out corruption and taint in Imperium-sponsored bureaucracies, he can't trust the Administratum, the Ministorum, or any ranking officials who might be part of the conspiratorial infrastructure. He told me that he always found his best allies in the Guard in those circumstances, in men drafted into crisis flash-points, plain soldiery who like as not were newcomers to any such event, and thus not part of the problem. That is what he found in me and some of my officer cadre. It took him a long time and much careful investigation to trust me, and just as long to win my trust back. Eventually, in the midst of the food riots, we Vitrians were the only elements he could count on. The Famine Wars had been orchestrated by a government faction with ties into the Departmento Munitorium. They were able to field two regiments of Imperial Guard turned to their purpose. We defeated them.'

'The Battle of Altatha. I have read some of the details. I had no idea Imperial corruption was behind the Famine Wars.'

Zoren smiled sadly. 'Such information is often suppressed. For the good of morale. We parted company as allies. I never thought to meet him again.'

Gaunt sat down on his cot. He leaned his elbows onto his knees, deep in thought. 'And now you have?'

'I received a message, encrypted, during my disembarkation from shore leave on Pyrites. Shortly after that, a meeting.'

'In person?'

Zoren shook his head. 'An intermediary.'

'And how did you know to trust this intermediary?'

'He used certain identifiers. Code words Bel Torthute and I had developed and used on Idolwilde. Cipher syllables from Vitrian combat-cant that only he would have known the significance of. Torthute made a point of studying the cultural heritage of the Vitrian Byhata, our Art of War. Only he could have sent the message and couched it so.'

'That's Fereyd. So you are my ally? I have a feeling you know more about this situation than me, Zoren.'

Zoren watched the tall, powerful man as he sat on the cot, his chin resting on his hands. He'd come to admire him during the Fortis action, and Fereyd's message had contained details specific to Gaunt. It was clear the Imperial covert agent trusted Commissar-Colonel Ibram

Gaunt more than almost anyone in the sector. More than myself, Zoren thought.

'I know this much, Gaunt. A group of high-ranking conspirators in the Sabbat Worlds Crusade High Command is hunting for something precious. Something so vital they may be prepared to twist the overall purpose of the crusade to achieve it. The key that unlocks that something has been deflected out of their waiting hands and diverted to you for safekeeping, as you were the only one of Fereyd's operatives in range to deal with it.'

Gaunt rose angrily. 'I'm no one's operative!' he snarled.

Zoren waved him back with a deft apologetic gesture to the mouth that indicated a misprision with language. Gaunt reminded himself that Low Gothic was not the colonel's first tongue. 'A trusted partner,' he corrected. 'Fereyd has been careful to establish a wide, remote circle of friends on whom he can call at times like this. You were the only one able to intercept and safeguard the key on Pyrites. After some further manipulation, he made sure I was on the same transport as you to assist. How else do you think we Vitrians ended up on the *Absalom* so conveniently? I imagine Fereyd and his agents in the warmaster's command staff risked great exposure arranging for us to be diverted to this ship. It would be about as overt an action as a covert dared.'

'Did he tell you anything else, this intermediary?' Gaunt said.

'That I was to offer you all assistance, up to and beyond counter-manding the direct orders of my superiors.'

There was a long quiet space as the enormity of this sunk in. 'And then?' Gaunt asked.

'The instructions said that you would make the right choice. That Fereyd, unable to directly intercede here, would trust you to carry this forward until his network was able to involve itself again. That you would assess the situation and act accordingly.'

Gaunt laughed humourlessly. 'But I know nothing! I don't know what this is about, or where it's going! This shadowplay isn't what I'm good at!'

'Because you're a soldier?'

'What?'

Zoren repeated it. 'Because you're a soldier? Like me, you deal in orders and commands and direct action. This doesn't sit easy with any of us that Fereyd employs. Us "Imperial salt" may be trustworthy and able to be recruited to his cause, but we lack the sophistication to understand the war. This isn't something we solve with flamers and fire-teams.'

Gaunt cursed Fereyd's name. Zoren echoed him, and they both began to laugh.

'Unless you can,' Zoren said, suddenly serious.

'Why?'

'Why? Because he trusts you. Because you're a colonel second and a commissar first, a political officer. And this war is all politics. Intrigue. We were both on Pyrites, Gaunt. Why did he divert the key to you and not me? Why am I here to help you, and not the other way around?'

Gaunt cursed Fereyd's name again, but this time it was low and bitter.

He was about to speak again when there was a fierce hammering at the door to the quarters. Gaunt swept to his feet and pulled the door open. Corbec stood outside, his face flushed and fierce.

'What?' managed Gaunt.

'You'd better come, sir. We've got three dead and another critical. The Jantine are playing for keeps.'

ELEVEN

Corbec led Gaunt, Zoren and a gaggle of others into the Infirmary annex where Dorden awaited them.

'Colhn, Freul, Lonegin...' Dorden said, gesturing to three shapes under sheets on the floor. 'Feygor's over there.'

Gaunt looked across at Rawne's adjutant, who lay, sucking breath through a transparent pipe, on a gurney in the corner.

'Puncture wound. Knife. Lungs are failing. Another hour unless I can get fresh equipment.'

'Rawne?' Gaunt asked.

Corbec edged forward. 'Like I said, sir, no sign. It was hit and run. They must have taken him with them. But they left this to let us know.'

Corbec showed the commissar the Jantine cap badge. 'Pinned it to Colhn's forehead,' he said with loathing.

Zoren was puzzled. 'Why such an outward show of force?'

'The Jantine are a part of all of this. But they also have a declared rivalry with the Ghosts. This comes to light, it'll look like inter-regiment feuding. There'll be reprimands, but it will cloud the true matter. They want to take credit... under cover of an open feud they can do anything they like.'

Gaunt realised they were all looking at him. His mind was racing. 'So we do the same. Colm, maintain the perimeter patrols on this deck, double strength. But also organise a raid on the Jantine. Lead it yourself. Kill some for me.'

A great smile crossed Corbec's face.

'Let's play along with their game and use it to our own ends. Doctor,' he gestured to Dorden, 'you're going to get medical supplies with my authority now you have a critical case.'

'What are you going to do?' Dorden asked, wiping his hands on a gauze towel.

Gaunt was thinking hard. He needed a plan now, a second option now that Dercius's ring had failed. He cursed his over-confidence in it. Now they had to start from scratch, both to safeguard themselves and to learn the crystal's secrets. But Gaunt was determined now. He would see this through. He would take the fight to the enemy.

'I need access to the bridge. To the captain himself. Colonel Zoren?'

'Yes?' Colonel Zoren moved up close to join Gaunt. He was entirely unprepared for the punch that laid him out, lip split and already bloody.

'Report that,' Gaunt said. His plan began to fall into place.

TWELVE

Chief Medical Officer Galen Gartell of the Jantine Patricians turned slowly from his patient in the bright, clean medical bay of the Jantine barrack deck. He had been tending the man since he had been brought in: a lout, a barbarian. One of the Tanith, the stretcher bearers had told him.

The patient was a slim, powerful man with hard, angular good looks and a blue starburst tattoo over one eye. Currently the lean, handsome temple was disfigured by a bloody impact wound. 'Keep him alive!' Major Brochuss had hissed as he had helped to carry the man in.

Such damage... such a barbarian... Gartell had mused as he had begun work, cleaning and healing. He disliked using his skill on animals like this, but clearly his noble regiment had shown mercy to some raiding rival scum and were going to heal his wounds and send him off as a gesture of their benign superiority to the deck rats they were bunked with. The voice that made him turn was that of Colonel Flense. 'Is he alive, doctor?'

'Just. I don't know why I should be saving a wretch like this, wasting valuable medical commodities.'

Flense hushed him and moved into the infirmary. A tall hooded figure followed him.

Gartell took a step back. The figure was well over two metres tall and there was a suggestion of smoke around him that fluctuated and masked his presence.

Who is this? Gartell wondered. The shadow-cloak – only a formidable scion of the Imperium would have such a device.

'What do you need?' Flense asked, addressing the figure. It hovered forward, past Gartell and looked down at the patient.

'Cranial clamps, a neural probe, perhaps some long, single-edged scalpels,' it said in a hollow voice.

'What?' Gartell stammered. 'What in the name of the Emperor are you about to do?'

'Teach this thing. Teach it well,' the figure replied, reaching out a huge, twisted hand to stroke the Ghost's brow. The fingernails were hooked and brown, like claws.

Gartell felt anger rise. 'I am chief medical officer here! No one performs any procedure in this infirmary without my–'

The hooded figure flicked its arm.

Galen Gartell suddenly found himself staring at his booted toes. It took the rest of his life for him to realise that something was wrong. Only when his headless body fell onto the deck next to him did he realise that... his head... cut... bastard... no.

'Flense? Clear that up, would you?' Inquisitor Heldane asked, gesturing to the corpse at his feet with a swish of the blood-wet, long-bladed scalpel in his hands. He turned back to the patient.

'Hello, Major Rawne,' he crooned softly. 'Let me show you your heart's desire.'

THIRTEEN

Reclining in his leather upholstered command throne, Lord Captain Itumade Grasticus, commander of the Adeptus Mechanicus Mass Conveyance *Absalom*, raised his facilitator wand in a huge, baby-fat hand and gestured gently at one of the many hololithic plates which hovered around him on suspensor fields, bobbing gently like a cluster of buoys in an ebb-tide.

The matt, dark surface of the chosen plate blinked, and a slow swirl of amber runes played across it. Grasticus carefully noted the current warp displacement of his vast ship, and then selected another plate to appraise himself of the engine tolerances.

Through reinforced metal cables that grew from the deck plates under his throne and clung like thick growths of creeper to the back of his chair, Grasticus felt his ship. The data-cables, many of them tagged with paper labels bearing codes or prayers, spilled over the headrest of his throne and entered his cranium, neck, spine and puffy cheeks through sutured bio-sockets. They fed him the sum total of the ship's being, the structural integrity, the atmospheric levels, the very mood of the great spacecraft. Through them, he experienced the actions of every linked crewman and servitor aboard, and the distant rhythm of the engines set the pace of his own pulse.

Grasticus was immense. Three hundred kilos of loose meat hung from his great frame. He seldom left his throne, seldom ventured outside the quiet peace of his private strategium, an armoured dome at the heart of the busy bridge vault, set high on the command spire at the rear of the *Absalom*.

One hundred and thirty standard years before, when he had inherited this vessel from the late Lord Captain Ulbenid, he had been a tall, lean man. Indolence, and the addictive sympathy with the ship, had made him throne-bound. His body, as if sensing he was now one with such a vast machine, had slowed his metabolism and increased his mass, as if it wanted him to echo the swollen bulk of the *Absalom*. The conveyance vessels of the Adeptus Mechanicus were not like ships of the Imperial Navy. Immeasurably older and often much larger, they had been made to carry the engines of war from Mars to wherever they were needed. Their captains were more like the Princeps of great walking Titans, hard-wired into the living machines through mind-impulse links. They were living ships.

Grasticus wanded another screen which allowed him direct observation of his beloved navigators, husks of men wired into their shrine, set in an alcove a few marble steps down from the main bridge. Their chanting voices sang him the immaterium coordinates and their progress, forming them into a data-plainsong which resonated a pale harmony through his mind. He listened, understood, was reassured.

There was a slight course adjustment which he relayed to the senior helm officers. The Menazoid Clasp was now just two day-cycles away. The ether showed no signs of storm fronts or warp pools, and the signal from the Astronomican beacon, whose psychic light guided all ships through the empyrean, was clear and clean. Blessed are the songs of the Navis Nobilite, murmured Grasticus in his thick voice, pronouncing part of the Navis Blessing Creed, for from them shines the Ray of Hope that lights our Golden Path.

Grasticus frowned suddenly. There was an uproar outside his hard-wired womb. Human voices raised in urgent conference. His flesh-heavy brow furrowed like sand-dunes slipping, and he wanded his throne to revolve to face the arched opening to the strategium.

'Warrant Officer Lekulanzi,' he said into his intercom horn, hanging on taut brass wires from the vaulted roof, 'enter and explain this disturbance.'

He dropped the storm shield guarding the entry arch with a flick of his wand and Lekulanzi hurried in, looking alarmed. The warrant officer gazed up at the obese bulk in the hammock-like throne above him and toyed with compulsive agitation at the hem of his uniform and his own facilitator wand. He seldom saw the captain face to face.

'Lord captain, a senior officer of the Imperial Guard petitions for audience with you. He wishes to make a formal complaint.'

'An item of cargo wishes to complain?' Grasticus said with slow wonder.

'A passenger,' Lekulanzi said, shuddering at the direct sound of the captain's seldom-heard voice.

Grasticus brushed the correction aside as he always did. He wasn't used to carrying humans. Compared to the beloved God-Machines it was his given task to convey, they seemed insignificant. But the humans had liberated Fortis Binary, and the tech-priests had sent him and his ship to assist them. It was a kind of gratitude, he supposed.

Grasticus disliked Lekulanzi. The whelp had been transferred to his command three months earlier on the orders of the Adeptus after Grasticus's acting warrant officer was killed during a warp storm. He doubted the man's ability. He loathed his spare, fragile build.

'Admit him,' Grasticus said, diverted by the unusual event. It would make a change to speak to people. To use his mouth. To see a body and smell its warm, fleshy breath.

Colonel Zoren entered the strategium flanked by two Navy troopers with shotguns. The man's face was marked by a bruise and a dressed cut.

'Speak,' said Grasticus.

'Lord captain,' the soldier began, uttering in the delicious accent-tones of a far-worlder. Grasticus hooded his eyes and smiled. The noise delighted him.

'Colonel Zoren, Vitrian Dragoons. We have the privilege of transport on your great vessel. However, I wish to complain strongly about the lack of inter-barrack security. Feuding has begun with those uncouth barbarians, the Tanith. Their commanding officer struck me when I approached him to complain about several brawling incidents.'

Through his data-conduits, Grasticus felt the waft of the psychic truth-fields that layered and screened his strategium. The man was speaking honestly; the Tanith commander – a... Gaunt? – had indeed struck him. There were lower levels of inconsistency and falsehood registered by the fields, but Grasticus put that down to the man's nervousness about approaching him directly.

'This is a matter for my security aide, the warrant officer here. Shipboard manners and protocol are his domain. Do not trouble me with such irrelevancies.'

Zoren cast a look at the agitated Lekulanzi, who dearly wished to be elsewhere.

Before either could speak, a new figure marched directly into the strategium, a tall man in the long coat and cap of an Imperial commissar. The troopers turned their weapons on him reflexively but he did not even blink.

'Lekulanzi is a fop. He is unable to perform his duties, let alone command peace on this ship. You must deal with it.'

The newcomer was astonishingly bold and direct. No formal address, no humble approach. Grasticus was impressed – and wrong-footed.

'I am Gaunt,' the newcomer said. 'My Tanith barracks have been raided and attempts have been made on my own life. Three of my men are dead, another critical and another missing. I mistook Zoren and his men as the culprits, hence my assault on him. The guilty party is in fact the Jantine Regiment. I ask you now, directly, to confine them and put their commanding officers on report.'

Again, Grasticus felt a hint of deceit in the flow of the astropathic truth-fields, but once more he put this down to the disarming awe of being in his presence. Essentially, this Gaunt was reading as utterly truthful and shamelessly direct.

'You have men dead?' Grasticus asked, almost alarmed.

'Three. More urgently, I require your authorisation to admit my medical officer to the stores of the Munitorium to obtain medical commodities to save my injured soldier.'

This insect is shaming me! In my own strategium! Grasticus thought with sudden revulsion.

His mind whirled and he shut out sixty percent of the data-flow entering his skull so he could concentrate. This was the first time in a dozen years he had to deal with a problem involving his cargo. Passengers! Passengers, that was what Lekulanzi had called them. Grasticus writhed gently in his throne. This was unseemly. This was insulting. This matter should have been contained long before now, before cargo was damaged, died, before complaints were brought to his feet.

He raised his facilitator wand and flicked it at a hovering plate. He would not lose face before these walking flesh-worms. He would show he was the captain, the lord captain, and that they all owed their safety and lives to him.

'I have given your medical officer authority. He has my formal mark to expedite his access to the stores.'

Gaunt smiled 'That's a start. Now confine the Jantine and punish their officers.'

Grasticus was amazed. He raised himself up on his ham-like elbows to study Gaunt, hefting his upper body free of the leather for the first time in fifteen months. There was a squeak of sweat-wet leather and a scent of stale filth wafted into the air of the strategium.

'I will not brook such insubordination,' Grasticus hissed, his cotton-soft words spitting from the loose folds of spare flesh that surrounded his small, glistening mouth like curtains on a proscenium arch. 'No one demands of me.'

'That's not good enough. Don't belabour us with threats. We require action!' This from Zoren now, stood side by side with the hawk-faced Gaunt. Grasticus reacted in surprise. He had thought the Vitrian more subdued, more deferential, but now he too challenged directly. 'Contain the Jantine and curtail their feuding or you'll have an uprising on your hands! Thousands of trained troopers, hungry for blood! More than your trooper details can handle!' Zoren cast a contemptuous glance at the Navy escort.

'Do you threaten me?' Grasticus almost gasped. The very thought of it. 'I will see you in chains for such a remark!'

'Is that how you deal with things you don't want to hear?' Gaunt snapped, pushing aside a trooper to approach Grasticus's throne. The trooper grappled with the larger commissar but Gaunt sent him sprawling with a deft swing of his arm.

'Are you the commander of this vessel, or a weak, fat nothing who hides at its heart?'

Lekulanzi fell back against the wall of the strategium, aghast and hyperventilating. No one spoke to the lord captain like that! No one–

Grasticus writhed ever-upwards from his bed-throne, sweeping the hovering plates aside with his hands so that they parted and cowered at the edges of the chamber behind him. He glared down at the Guard officers, rage rippling through his vast mass.

'Well?' Gaunt said.

Grasticus began to bellow, raising his thick, swollen voice for the first time in years.

Zoren cast a nervous glance at Gaunt. Weren't they pushing the lord captain too hard? Something in Gaunt's calm reassured him. He remembered the elements of their plan and started to send his own jibes at the captain in tune with Gaunt's.

Gaunt grinned inwardly. Now they had Grasticus's entire attention.

Outside the strategium, on the lower levels of the high-roofed, cool-aired bridge vault, the senior helm officers looked up from their dark, oiled gears and levers, and exchanged wondering glances. The basso after-echo of their captain rolled out of the armoured dome. The lord captain was clearly so angry he had diverted his attention from most of the systems temporarily. This was unheard of, unprecedented.

A detachment of ship troopers milled cautiously outside the door-arch of the strategium. 'Do we enter?' rasped one through his helmet intercom. None of them felt like confronting the lord captain's wrath.

They pitied the idiot Guard officers who had created this commotion.

Gaunt did not care. This was exactly what he had been after.

FOURTEEN

Chief Medic Dorden led his party in through the armoured hatchway of the Munitorium depot deck. Flanking him, Caffran, Brin Milo and Bragg formed a motley honour guard of uneven height for the elderly medico.

They entered a wide bay that smelled of antiseptic and ionisation filters. The grey deck was dusted with clean sand. Dorden consulted his chronometer.

'Cometh the hour...' he said.

'Come who?' Bragg asked.

'What I mean is, it's now or never. We've given the commissar long enough. He should be with the captain now,' Dorden said.

'I still don't get any of this,' Bragg said, scratching his lantern jaw. 'How's this meant to work? What's the old Ghostmaker trying to do?'

'It's called a diversion,' Milo said quietly. 'Don't worry about the details, just play along and act dumb.'

'Not a problem!' Bragg announced, baffled by Caffran's subsequent smirk.

Beyond metal cage doors at the end of the bay, three robed officials of the Munitorium were at work at low-set consoles. There were at least seven Navy troopers on watch around the place.

Dorden marched forward and rapped on the metal grille. 'I need supplies!' he called. 'Hurry now; a man is dying!'

One of the Munitorium men got up from his console, leaving his cloak draped over the seat back. He was a short, bulky man with physical power under his khaki Munitorium tunic. Glossy, chrome servitor implants were stapled into his cheek, temple and throat. He disconnected a cable from his neck socket as he approached them.

Dorden thrust his data-slate under the man's nose. 'Requisition of medical supplies,' he snapped.

The man viewed the slate. As he scrolled down the slate file, the troopers suddenly came to attention and grouped in the centre of the bay. Milo could hear the muffled back and forth of their helmet vox-casters. One of them turned to the Munitorium staff.

'Trouble on the bridge!' he said through his speaker, his voice tinny. 'Bloody Guard are feuding again. We've been detailed down to the barrack decks to act as patrol.'

The Munitorium officer waved them off with his hand. 'Whatever.' The troopers exited, leaving just one watching the grille entry.

The Munitorium officer slid back the cage grille and let the four Ghosts inside. He eyed the slate before directing them down an aisle to the left. 'Lord Captain Grasticus has issued you with clearance. Down there, chamber eleven. Get what you need. Just what you need. I'll be checking the inventory on the way out. No analgesics without a signed chit from the warrant officer, no purloining.'

'Feth you,' Dorden said, snatching back the slate and beckoning the others after him. 'We've got a life to save! Do you think we'd waste time trying to rustle some booty?'

The official turned away, disinterested. Dorden led the trio down the dark aisle, between racks of air-tanks, amphorae of wine and food crates stacked up to the high roof. They entered a junction bay in the dark depths of the storage holds, and through several hatches ahead saw the vast commodity stockpiles of the huge ship.

'Medical supplies down there,' Caffran said, noting the white marker tags on one of the hatch frames.

'There's a console,' Milo said, pointing down another of the aisles into a dark hold. They could see the dull, distant green glow of a Munitorium artificer. Dorden glanced at his chronometer again. 'Right, as we planned. Five minutes! Go!'

With Bragg at his heels, Dorden strode into the medical supply vault and started pulling bundles of sterile gauze, jars of counter-septic wash and packs of clean surgical tools off the black metal shelves. Bragg requisitioned a wheeled cargo trolley from an alcove near the door and followed him.

Milo and Caffran slunk down into the darker chamber, and the boy swung onto the low bench-seat in front of the console. He fumbled in his pocket and produced the memory tile that Gaunt had give him, gingerly fitting it into the slot on the desk-edge of the machine. Two teal-coloured lights winked and flashed as the artificer recognised the blank tile. His hands trembled. He tried to remember what the commissar had told him.

'Will this work?' Caffran asked, pulling out his blade and watching the door anxiously.

The Munitorium data banks were slaved directly to the ship's main cogitator. Remembering Gaunt's instructions piece by piece, Milo entered key search words via the ivory-toothed keyboard. The banks had full access to the ship's information stockpile, including the security clearance Gaunt's artificer lacked.

'Hurry up, boy!' Caffran snapped, edgy.

Milo ignored him, but that 'boy' nagged him and made him unhappy. His trembling fingers conducted his way across the worn keys into new levels of instruction that glowed in runic cursors on the flat plate of the console, just as the commissar had laid it out.

'Here!' Milo said suddenly, 'I think...' He awkwardly touched a rune-inscribed command key and the console hummed. Data began to download onto the blank tile. Gaunt would be proud. Milo had listened to his arcane ramblings about the use of machines well.

In the medical store, Dorden looked up from the cargo trolley he was filling and glanced once more at his chronometer. Bragg watched him, cautiously.

'This is taking too fething long!' Dorden said irritably.

'I can go back–' Bragg suggested.

'No, we've not got everything yet,' Dorden said, searching the racks for jars of pneumeno-thorax resin.

Milo's fingers hovered over the keys. 'We've got it!' he exclaimed.

Caffran didn't answer. Milo turned and saw Caffran frozen, the blunt nose of a deck-shotgun pressed to his temple. The Imperial Navy trooper said nothing, but nodded his helmet-clad head at Milo, indicating he should get up from the bench rapidly.

Milo rose, his hands where the trooper could see them.

'That's good,' the trooper said through the dull resonator of his headset. He pointed the muzzle of his gun at where he wanted Milo to stand.

Caffran slammed back, jabbing his elbow at the trooper's sternum, aiming for the solar plexus in one desperate move. The fibre-weave armour of the trooper's uniform stopped the blow and he swung around, smashing Caffran into the wall-racks with an open hand.

Milo tried to move.

The shotgun fired, a wide burst of incandescent fury in the darkness.

FIFTEEN

As they waited in the shadows, they noted that the Jantine had been issued with the finest barrack decks on the ship. The approach colonnade was a spacious embarkation hall, wide enough for the bulkiest of equipment. The glittering wall burners cast long purple shadows across the tiles.

Two Jantine Patricians in full dress armour, training shock-poles held ready, patrolled the far end. They were exchanging inconsequential remarks when Larkin appeared down the colonnade, bumbling along as if he'd missed his way. They snapped round in disbelief and Larkin froze, a look of horror on his leathery, narrow face. With an oath, he turned and began to run back the way he had come.

The two guards thundered after him with baying blood-cries. They'd gone ten metres before the shadows behind them unfolded and Ghosts emerged, dropping stealth cloaks and seizing them from behind. Mkoll, Baru, Varl and Corbec fell on the two Jantine, struck with shock-poles and Tanith blades, and dragged the fallen men into the darkness off the main hall.

'Why am I always the fething bait?' the returning Larkin asked, stopping by Corbec, who was wiping a trace of blood from the floor with the hem of his cape.

'You've got that kind of face,' Varl said, and Corbec smiled.

'Look here!' Baru called in a hiss from the end of the hall. They moved to join him and he grinned as he pulled his find from the corner of the archway the Jantine sentries had been watching. Guns! A battered old exotic bolt-action rifle with a long muzzle and ornately decorated stock, and a worn but serviceable pump stub-gun with a bandolier strap of shells. Neither were regular issue Guard pieces, and both were much lower tech than Guard standard-pattern gear. Corbec knew what they were.

'Souvenirs, spoils of war,' he murmured, his hands running a check on the stub-gun. All soldiers collected trophies like these, stuck them away in their kits to sell on, keep as mementoes, or simply use in a clinch. Corbec knew many of the Ghosts had their own... but they had dutifully handed them in with their issued weapons when they'd come aboard. He was not the least surprised that the Jantine had kept hold of their unrecorded weapons. The sentries had left them here as back up in case of an assault their shock-poles couldn't handle.

Varl handed the rifle to Larkin. There was no question who should carry it.

The weight of a gun in his hands again seemed to calm the old sniper. He licked his almost lip-less mouth, which cut the leather of his face like a knife-slash. He'd been complaining incessantly since they had set out, unwilling to be part of a vendetta strike.

'If they catch us, we'll be for the firing squad! This ain't right!'

Corbec had been firm, fully aware of how daring the mission was. 'We're in a regimental feud, Larks,' he had said simply, 'an honour thing. They killed Lonegin, Freul and Colhn. You think what they did to Feygor, and what they might be doing to the major. The commissar's asked us to avenge the blood-wrong, and I for one am happy to oblige.'

Corbec hadn't mentioned that he'd only selected Larkin because of his fine stealth abilities, nor had he made clear Gaunt's real reason for the raid: distraction, misdirection – and, like the Jantine, to promote the notion that what was really happening aboard the *Absalom* was a mindless soldier's feud.

Now, checking the long gun, Larkin seemed to relax. His only eloquence was with a firearm. If he was going to break ship-law, then best do it full-measure, with a gun in his hands; and they all knew he was the best shot in the regiment.

They edged on into the Jantine barrack area. From down one long cross-hallway came the sounds of singing and carousing, from another, the clash of shock-poles in a training vault.

'How far do we go with this?' Mkoll whispered.

Corbec shrugged. 'They killed three, wounded two. We should match that at least.'

He also had an urge to discover Rawne's fate, and rescue him if they could. But he suspected the major was already long dead.

Mkoll, the commander of the scout platoon, was the best stealther they had.

With Baru at his side, the pair melted into the hall shadows and swept ahead.

The other three waited. There seemed to be something sporadic and ill-at-ease in the distant rhythm of the ship's engines as they vibrated the deck. I hope we're not running into some fething warp-madness, Corbec mused, then lightened up as he realised that it may be Gaunt's work. He'd said he was going to distract and upset the captain.

Baru came back to them. 'We've hit lucky, really lucky,' he hissed. 'You'd better see.'

Mkoll was waiting in cover in an archway around the next bend. Ahead was a lighted hatchway.

'Infirmary,' he whispered. 'I went up close to the door. They've got Rawne in there.'

'How many Jantine?'

'Two troopers, an officer – a colonel – and someone else. Robed. I don't like the look of him at all...'

A scream suddenly cut the air, sobbing down into a whimper. The five Ghosts stiffened. It had been Rawne's voice.

SIXTEEN

The Navy trooper kicked Caffran's fallen body hard and then swung his shotgun round to finish him. Weapon violation sirens were sounding shrilly in the close air of the Munitorium store. The trooper pumped the loader-grip and then was smashed sideways into the packing cartons to his left by a massive fist.

Bragg lifted the crumpled form of the dazed trooper and threw him ten metres down the vault-way. He landed hard, broken.

'Brinny! Brinny boy!' Bragg called anxiously over the siren. Milo raised himself up from under the artificer. The shot had exploded the vista-plate, just missing him. 'I'm okay,' he said.

Bragg got the dazed Caffran to his feet as Brin slid the tile from the artificer slot.

'Go!' he said, 'Go!'

In under a minute, they had rejoined Dorden, helping him to push his laden trolley back out of the vault. By then, Munitorium officials and Navy troopers were rushing in through the cage.

Dorden was a master of nerve. 'Thank feth you're here!' he bellowed, his voice cracking. 'There are Jantine in there, madmen! They attacked us! Your man engaged them, but I think they got him. Quickly! Quickly now!'

Most of the detail moved past at a run, racking weapons. One stayed, eyeing the Ghost party cautiously.

'You'll have to wait. We're going to check this.'

Dorden strode forward, steely-calm now and held up his data-slate to show the man.

'Does this mean anything to you? A direct authorisation from your captain? I've got a man dying back in my infirmary! I need these supplies! Do you want a death on your hands, because by feth you're–'

The trooper waved them on, and hurried after his comrades.

'I thought this place was meant to be secure,' Dorden spat at the Munitorium official as they pushed past him towards the exit.

They slammed the cart into a lift and slumped back against the walls as it began to rise.

'Did you get it?' Dorden asked, after a few deep breaths.

Milo nodded. 'Think so.'

Caffran looked at the elderly doctor with a wide-eyed grin. '"There are Jantine in there, madmen! They attacked us! Your man engaged them, but I think they got him. Quickly!" What the feth was that all about?'

'Inspired, I'd say,' Bragg said.

'Back home, I was a doctor... and also secretary of the County Pryze Citizens' Players. My Prince Teygoth was highly regarded.'

Their relieved laughter began to fill the lift.

* * *

SEVENTEEN

Corbec's revenge squad was about to move when the deck vox-casters started to relay the scream of a weapons violation alert. The dull choral wails echoed down the hallway and 'Alert' runes began to blink above all of the archways.

The colonel pulled his men into cover as figures strode out of the infirmary, looking around. Squads of Jantine guards came up from both sides, milling around as vox-checks tried to ascertain the nature of the incident.

Corbec saw Flense and Brochuss, the Jantine senior officers, and another man, a hugely tall and grotesque figure in shimmering, smoke-like robes who filled him with dread.

'Weapons discharge on the Munitorium deck!' a Jantine trooper with a vox-caster on his back reported. 'The Navy details are closing to contain it... Sir, the channels are alive with cross-reports. They're blaming it on the Jantine! They say we conducted a feud strike on Tanith-scum in the supply vaults!'

Flense cursed. 'Gaunt! The devil's trying to match our game!' He turned to his men. 'Brochuss! Secure the deck! Security detail with me!'

'I'll stay and finish my work,' the robed figure said in a deep, liquid tone that quite chilled Corbec. As the various men moved off to comply with orders, the robed figure stopped Flense with a hand to his shoulder. Or rather, what seemed more like a long-fingered claw than a hand, Corbec noticed with a shudder.

'This isn't good, Flense,' the figure breathed at the suddenly trembling colonel. 'Use violence against a soldier like Gaunt and you can be assured he will use it back. And you seem to have underestimated his political abilities. I fear he has outplayed you. And if he has, you should fear for yourself.'

Flense shook himself free and hurried away. 'I'll deal with it!' he snarled defensively over his shoulder. The robed figure watched him leave and then withdrew into the infirmary.

'What do we do?' Varl hissed.

'Tell me we go back now,' Larkin whispered urgently.

Another scream issued from the chamber beyond.

'What do you think?' Corbec asked.

EIGHTEEN

Sirens wailed in the normally tranquil strategium. Grasticus shifted in his cot-throne, wanding screens to him and cursing at the information he was reading.

Gaunt and Zoren exchanged glances.

I hope this confusion is the confusion we planned, Gaunt thought.

Grasticus rose up on his elbows and bawled at the quaking Leku-lanzi. 'Weapons fire on the Munitorium deck! My data says it's Jantine feuders!'

'Are any of mine hurt?' Gaunt asked, pushing forward, urgent. 'I told you the Jantine were out for blood–'

'Shut up, commissar,' the captain said with a suddenly sour look. His day had been disrupted enough. 'The reports are unconfirmed. Get down there and see to it, warrant officer!'

Lekulanzi scurried out of the chamber. Grasticus turned back to the two Imperial Guard colonels.

'This matter needs my undivided attention. I will summon you when we can speak further.'

Zoren and Gaunt nodded and backed out of the strategium smartly. Side by side they crossed the nave of the bridge, through the hubbub of bridge crew, and entered the lifts.

'Is it working?' Zoren asked as the doors closed and the choral chime sang out.

'Pray by the Throne that it is,' Gaunt said.

NINETEEN

They took the infirmary in a textbook move.

The room was wide, long and low. The robed figure was bent over Rawne, who was strapped, screaming, to a gurney. A pair of Jantine troopers stood guard at the door. Corbec came in between them, ignoring them both as he dived into a roll, his shotgun raised up to fire. The robed figure turned, as if sensing the sudden intrusion. The shotgun blast blew him backwards into a stack of wheezing resuscitrex units.

The guards began to turn when Mkoll and Baru launched in on Corbec's heels and knifed them both. Corbec rolled up onto his feet, slung his shotgun by the strap and grabbed Rawne.

'Sacred Feth...' he murmured, as he saw the head wound, and the insidious pattern of scalpel cuts across the major's face, neck and stripped body. Rawne was slipping in and out of consciousness.

'Come on, Rawne, come on!' Corbec snapped, hauling the major up over his shoulder.

'We have to move now!' Mkoll bellowed, as secondary weapons violation sirens began to shrill. Corbec threw the shotgun over to him.

'Take point! We shoot our way out if we have to!'

'Colonel!' Baru yelled. Weighed down by Rawne, Corbec couldn't turn in time. The robed figure was clawing its way back onto its feet behind him. Its hood was thrown back, and they gasped to see the equine extension and bared teeth of the head. Fury boiled in the eyes of the man-monster, and violet-dark energy crackled around him.

Corbec felt the room temperature drop. Fething magic, was all he had time to think – before a shot took the man-monster's throat clean away.

Larkin stood in the doorway, the old rifle raised in his hands. 'Now we're leaving, right?' he said.

TWENTY

Gaunt took the tile Milo held out for him. Then he shut the door of his quarters on the faces of the men crowded outside. Inside, Corbec, Zoren and Milo watched him carefully.

'This had better be worth all that damn effort,' Corbec said eventually, voicing what they all thought.

Gaunt nodded. The gamble had been immense. But for the Jantine's bloodthirsty and brutal methods of pursuing their intrigue, they would never have got this far. The ship was still full of commotion. Adeptus Mechanicus security details clogged every corridor, conducting barrack searches. Rumour, accusation and threat rebounded from counter-rumour, counter-accusation and promise.

Gaunt knew his hands weren't spotless in this, and he would make no attempt to hide that his men fought back against the Jantine in a feud. There would be reprimands, punishment details, rounds of questioning that would lead to nothing conclusive. But, like him, the Jantine would not take the matter beyond a simple regimental feud. Only he and those secret elements pitched against him would know precisely what had been at stake.

He slotted the tile into his artificer, and then set the crystal in the read-slot. He touched a few keys.

There was a pause.

'It isn't working,' Zoren began.

It wasn't. As far as Gaunt could tell, Milo had indeed downloaded the latest clearance ciphers via the Munitorium artificer, but still they would not open the crystal. In fact, he couldn't even open the ciphers and set them to work.

Gaunt cursed.

'What about the ring?' Milo asked.

Gaunt paused, then fished Dercius's ring from his pocket. He fitted that into the read-slot beside the one that held the crystal and activated it.

Old and too out of date to open the dedicated ciphers of the crystal, the ring was nevertheless standardised in its cryptography enough to authorise use of the downloaded codes. The vista-plate scrolled nonsense for a moment, as runic engram languages translated each other and overlaid data, transcribing and interpreting, rereading and re-setting. The crystal opened, spilling its contents up in a hololithic display which projected up off the vista-plate.

'Oh feth... what's this mean?' Corbec murmured, instantly overwhelmed by the magnitude of what he saw.

Milo and Gaunt were silent, as they read on for detail.

'Schematics,' Zoren said simply, an awed note in his voice.

Gaunt nodded. 'By the Golden Throne, I don't pretend to understand much of this, but from what I do... now I see why they were so keen to get it.'

Milo pointed to a side bar of the display. 'A chart. A location. Where is that?'

Gaunt looked and nodded again, slowly. Things now made sense. Like why Fereyd had chosen him to be the bearer of the crystal. Things had just become a great deal harder than even he had feared.

'Menazoid Epsilon,' he breathed.

A MEMORY

KHEDD 1173,
SIXTEEN YEARS EARLIER

The Kheddite had not expected them to move in winter, but the High Lords of Terra's Imperial Guard, whose forces dwelt in seasonless ship holds plying the ever-cold of space, made no such distinction between campaigning months and resting months. They burned two clan-towns at the mouth of the River Heort, where the deep fjord inlets opened to the icy sea and the archipelago, and then moved into the glacial uplands to prosecute the nomads who had spent the summer harrying the main Imperial outposts with guerrilla strikes.

Up here, the air was clear like glass, and the sky was a deep, burnished turquoise. Their column of Chimera troop transports, ski-nosed half-traks commandeered locally, Hellhounds and Leman Russ tanks with big bulldozer blades, made fast going over the sculptural ice desert, snorting exhaust smoke and ice-spumes in their wake. The khaki body-camouflage from their last campaign in the dust-thick heatlands of Providence Lenticula had been painted over with leopard-pelt speckles of grey and blue on white. Only the silver Imperial eagles and the purple insignia of the Jantine Patricians remained on the flanks of the rushing, bouncing, roaring vehicles.

The Sentinel scouts, stalking as swift outriders to the main advance, had located a nomad heluka three kilometres away over a startlingly vivid glacier of green ice. General Aldo Dercius swung the column to a stop and sat on the turret top of his command tank, pulling off his fur mittens so he could sort through the sheaf of flimsy vista-prints the sentinels had brought back.

The heluka seemed of normal pattern – a stockade of stripped fir-stems surrounding eighteen bulbous habitat tents of tanned mahish hide supported on umbrella domes of the animals' treated rib-bones. There was a corral adjacent to the stockade, holding at least sixty anahig,

185

the noxious, hunch-backed, flightless bird-mounts that the Kheddite favoured. Damn things – ungainly and comical in appearance, but the biped steeds could run faster than an unladen Chimera across loose snow, turn much faster, and the scales under their oily, matted down-fur could shrug off las-fire while their toothed beaks sliced a man in two like toffee.

Dercius slid his flare goggles up for a better look at the vista-prints, and winced at the glare of the open snow. Down on the prow of the Leman Russ, his crew were taking time to stretch their limbs and relax. A stove boiled water for treacly caffeine and Dercius's two adjutants/ bodyguards were applying mahish fat to their snow-burned cheeks and noses out of small, round tins they had bartered from the local population. Dercius smiled to himself at this little thing. His Patricians had a reputation for aristo snobbery, but they were resourceful men – and certainly not too proud to follow the local wisdom and smear their faces with cetacean blubber to block the unforgiving winter suns.

His face caked in the pungent white grease, Adjutant Brochuss slid his tin away in the pocket of his fur-trimmed, purple-and-chrome Patrician battledress and took a wire-handled can of caffeine up to the turret.

Dercius accepted it gratefully. Brochuss, a young and powerfully built trooper, nodded down at the prints spread out on the turret canopy.

'A target? Or just another collection of *thlak* hunters?'

'I'm trying to decide,' Dercius said.

Since they had left the mouth of the Heort eight days before, they had made one early, lucky strike at a camp of nomad guerrilla Kheddite, and then wasted four afternoons assaulting helukas that had sheltered nothing more than herders and hunters in ragged family groups. Dercius was eager for another success. The Imperial Guard had strength, technology and firepower in their corner, but the nomad rebels had patriotic determination, a fanatical mindset and the harsh environment in theirs.

Dercius knew that many campaigns had faltered when the initially victorious forces had driven the natives back onto the advantage of inhospitable home turf. The last thing he wanted was a war of attrition that locked him here in a police action against elusive guerrillas for years. The Kheddite knew and used this beautiful, cruel environment well, and Dercius knew they could be hunting them for months, all the while suffering a slow erosion of strength to lightning strikes by the fast-moving foe. If they only had a base, a static HQ, a city that could be assaulted. But the Kheddite culture out here was fierce and nomadic. This was their realm, and they would be masters of it until he could catch them.

Still, he reassured himself that Warmaster Slaydo had promised him three more Guard units to help his Jantine Fourth and Eleventh in their hunt. Just a day or two more...

He looked back at the prints, and saw something. 'This is promising,' he told Brochuss, sipping his caffeine. 'It's a large settlement. Large by comparison with the herder/hunter helukas we've seen. Sixty plus animals. Those anahig are big; they look like war-mounts to me.'

'Veritable destrier!' Brochuss laughed, referring to the beautiful, sixteen-hand beasts traditionally bred in the stud-farms of the baronies on Jant Normanidus Prime.

Dercius enjoyed the joke. It was the sort of quip his old major, Gaunt, would have made; a pressure-release for the slow-building tension bubble of a difficult campaign. He rubbed the memory away. That was done, left behind on Kentaur.

'Look here,' he said, tapping a particular print. Brochuss leaned closer.

'What does that look like to you?' Dercius asked.

'The main habitat tent? Where your finger is? I don't know – a smoke flue? An airspace?'

'Maybe,' Dercius said and lifted the print so that his adjutant could get a closer look. 'There's certainly smoke issuing from it, but we all know how easy smoke is to make. That wink of light... there.'

Brochuss chuckled, nodding. 'Throne! An up-link spine. No doubt. They've got a vox-vista set in that place, with the mast extending up out of the opening. You've got sharp eyes, general.'

'That's why I'm the general, Trooper Brochuss!' Dercius snorted with ample good humour. 'So what does that give us? A larger than normal heluka, sixty head of war-mount in the pen...'

'And since when did thlak herders need an intercontinental up-link unit?' finished the adjutant.

'I think the Emperor has smiled on our fortune. Have Major Saulus circle the tanks into a crescent formation around the edge of the glacier. Bring the Hellhounds forward, and hold the troops back for final clearing. We will engulf them.'

Brochuss nodded and jumped back off the track bed of the Leman Russ, running to shout his orders.

Dercius poured the last dregs of his caffeine away over the side of the turret. It melted and stained the snow beside the tank's treads.

Just before sunset, with the first sun a frosty pink semi-circle dipping below the horizon and the second a hot apricot glow in the wispy clouds of the blackening sky, the heluka was a dark stain too.

The Kheddite had fought ferociously... as ferociously as any fur-clad ice-soldier whose tented encampment had been pounded by tank shells and hosed by infernos unleashed from the trundling Hellhounds. Most of the dead and the debris were fused into thick curls of the rapidly refreezing ice-cover: twisted, broken, blackened shapes around which the suddenly liquid ice had abruptly solidified and set.

Some twenty or so had made it to their anahig mount and staged a countercharge along the north flank. A few of his infantry had been torn apart by the clacking beaks or churned under the heavy, three-toed feet. Dercius had pulled the troops back and sent in the tanks with their relentless dozer blades.

The sunset was lovely on Khedd. Dercius pulled his vehicle up from the glacier slope until he overlooked the ocean. It was vibrant red in the failing light, alive with the flashing bioluminescence of the micro-growth and krill which prospered in the winter seas. Every now and then, the dying light caught the slow glitter of a mahish as it surfaced its great bulk to harvest the surface. Dercius watched the flopping thick-red water for the sudden breaks of twenty-metre flukes and dorsal spines and the sonorous sub-bass creaks of deep-water voices.

The vox-caster set in the lit turret below him was alive with back-chat, but he started as he heard a signal cut through: a low, even message couched in simple Jantine combat-cant.

'Who knows that... who's broadcasting?' he murmured, dropping into the turret and adjusting the dial of the set.

He smiled at first. Slaydo's promised reinforcements were coming in. The Hyrkan Fifth and Sixth. The message was from the Hyrkan commissar, little Ibram Gaunt.

Fog lights lit the glacier crest as the armoured column of the Hyrkan hove in to view, kicking up snow-dust from their tracks as they bounced down towards the Jantine column.

It will be good to see Ibram, Dercius thought. What's it been... thirteen, fourteen years? He's grown up since I last saw him, grown up like his father. Served with the Hyrkan, made commissar.

Dercius had kept up with the long-range reports of Ibram's career. Not just an officer, as his father intended, a commissar no less. Commissar Gaunt. Well, well, well. It would be good to see the boy again.

Despite everything.

Gaunt's half-trak slewed up in the snow next to the general's Leman Russ. Dercius was descending to meet it, putting his cap on, adjusting his regimental chainsword in its decorative sheath.

He hardly recognised the man who stepped out to meet him.

Gaunt was grown. Tall, powerful, thin of face, his eyes as steady and penetrating as targeting lasers. The black uniform storm-coat and cap of an Imperial commissar suited him.

'Ibram...' Dercius said with a slow smile. 'How long has it been?'

'Years,' the commissar said flatly, face expressionless. 'Space is wide and too broad to be spanned. I have looked forward to this. For too long. I always hoped circumstance would draw us together again, face to face.'

'Ah... so did I, Ibram! It's a joy to see you.' Dercius held his arms out wide.

'Because I am, as my father raised me, a fair man, I will tell you this, Uncle Dercius,' Gaunt said, his voice curiously low. 'Four years ago on Darendara, I experienced a revelation. A series of revelations. I was given information. Some of it was nonsense, or was not then applicable. Some of it was salutary. It told me a truth. I have been waiting to encounter you ever since.'

Dercius stiffened. 'Ibram... my boy... what are you saying?'

Gaunt unsheathed his chainsword. It murmured waspishly in the cold air. 'I know what happened on Kentaur. I know that, for fear of your own career, my father died.'

Dercius's adjutant was suddenly between them. 'That's enough!' Brochuss spat. 'Back off!'

Major Tanhause and Sergeant Kleff of the Hyrkan stood ready to second Gaunt.

'You're speaking to an Imperial commissar, friend,' Gaunt said. 'Think hard about your objections.' Brochuss took a pace back, uncertainty warring with duty.

'Now I am a commissar,' Gaunt continued, addressing Dercius, 'I am empowered to deliver justice wherever I see it lacking. I am empowered to punish cowardice. I am granted the gift of total authority to judge, in the name of the Emperor, on the field of combat.'

Suddenly realising the implications behind Gaunt's words, Dercius pulled his own chainsword and flew at the commissar. Gaunt swung his own blade up to block, his grip firm.

Madness and fear filled the Jantine commander... how had the little bastard found out? Who could have known to tell him? The calm confidence, which had filled his mind since the Khedd campaign began, washed away as fast as the dying light was dulling the ice-glare around them. Little Ibram knew. He knew! After all this time, all his care, the boy had found out! It was the one thing he always dreaded, always promised himself would never happen.

The scything chainswords struck and shrieked, throwing sparks into the cold night, grinding as the tooth belts churned and repelled each other. Broken sawteeth spun away like shrapnel. Dercius had been tutored in the duelling schools of the Jant Normanidus Military Academy. He had the ceremonial honour scars on his cheek and forearms to bear it out. A chain-blade was a different thing, of course; ten times as heavy and slow as a coup-epee, and the clash-torsion of the chewing teeth was an often random factor. But Dercius had retrained his swordsmanship in the nuances of the chainsword on admission to the Patricians. A duel, chainsword to chainsword, was rare these days, but not unheard of. The secrets were wrist strength, momentum and the calculated use of reversal in chain direction to deflect the opponent and open a space.

There was no feinting with a weapon as heavy as a chainsword. Only swing and re-address. They turned, clashed, broke, circled, clashed again. The men were calling out, others running to see. No one dared step in. From the frank determination of the officers, it was clear this was an honour bout.

Dercius hooked in low, cycling the action of his blade to a fast reversal and threw Gaunt's weapon aside with a shriek of tortured metal.

An opening. He sliced, and the sweep took Gaunt across the gut. His commissar's coat and tunic split open, and blood exploded from a massive cut across his lower belly.

Gaunt almost fell. The pain was immense, and he knew the ripped, torn wound was terrible. He had failed. Failed his honour and his father. Dercius was too big, too formidable a presence in his mind to be defeated. Uncle Dercius, the huge man, the laughing, scolding, charismatic giant who had strode into his life from time to time on Manzipor, full of tales and jokes and wonderful gifts. Dercius, who had carved toy frigates for him, told him the names of the stars, sat him on his knee and presented him with ork tooth souvenirs.

Dercius, who, with the aid of awning rods, had taught him to fence on the sundecks over the cataracts. Gaunt remembered the little twist-thrust that always left him sitting on his backside, rubbing a bruised shoulder. Deft with an épée, impossible with a chainsword.

Or perhaps not. Trailing blood and tattered clothes and flesh, Gaunt twisted, light as a child, and thrust with a weapon not designed to be thrust.

There was a look of almost unbearable surprise on Dercius's face as Gaunt's chainsword stabbed into his sternum and dug with a convulsive scream through bone, flesh, tissue and organs until it protruded from between the man's shoulder blades, meat flicking from the whirring teeth. Dercius dropped in a bloody quaking mess, his corpse vibrating with the rhythm of the still-active weapon impaling it.

Gaunt fell to his knees, clutching his belly together as warm blood spurted through the messy gut-wound. He was blacking out as Tanhause got to him.

'You are avenged, father,' Ibram Gaunt tried to say to the evening sky, before unconsciousness took him.

PART SIX

MENAZOID EPSILON

ONE

No one wanted Epsilon. No one wanted to die.

Colonel-Commissar Gaunt recalled his own deliberations in the Glass Bay of the *Absalom* with a rueful grin. He remembered how he had prayed his Ghosts would be selected for the main offensive on the main planet, Menazoid Sigma. How things change, he laughed to himself. How he would have scoffed back then in the Glass Bay if he had been told he would deliberately choose this action.

Well, choose was perhaps too strong a word. Luck, and invisible hands, had been at work. When the *Absalom* had put in at one of the huge beachhead hexathedrals strung out like beads across the Menazoid Clasp, there had been a bewildering mass of regiments and armoured units assembling to deploy at the Menazoid target zones. Most of the regimental officers had been petitioning for the glory of advancing on Sigma, and Warmaster Macaroth's tactical counsel had been inundated with proposals and counter-proposals as to the disposition of the Imperial armies. Gaunt had thought of the way that Fereyd, the unseen Fereyd and his network of operatives, had arranged for the Vitrians to support him on the *Absalom*. With no direct means of communication, he trusted that they would observe him again and where possible facilitate his needs, tacitly understanding them to be part of the mutual scheme.

So he had sent signals to the tactical division announcing that he believed his Ghosts, with their well-recognised stealth and scout attributes, would be appropriate for the Epsilon assault.

Perhaps it was chance. Perhaps it was because no other regiment had volunteered. Perhaps it was that Fereyd and his network had noted the request and manipulated silently behind the scenes to ensure that it happened. Perhaps it was that the conspiring enemy faction, rebuffed in their attempts to extract the secrets of the crystal from him, had decided the only way to reveal the truth was to let him have his way and follow him. Perhaps he was leading them to the trophy they so desired.

It mattered little. After a week and a half of levy organisation, resupply and tactical processing at the hexathedrals, the Ghosts had been selected to participate in the assault on Menazoid Epsilon, advancing before an armoured host of forty thousand vehicles from the Lattarii Gundogs, Ketzok 17th, Samothrace 4th, 5th and 15th, Borkellid Hellhounds, Cadian Armoured 3rd and Sarpoy Mechanised Cavalry. With the Tanith First in the field would be eight Mordian and four Pragar regiments, the Afghali Ravagers 1st and 3rd, six battalions of Oudinot Irregulars – and the Vitrian Dragoons.

The inclusion of the Vitrians gave Gaunt confidence that deployment decisions had been influenced by friendly minds.

The fact that the Jantine Patricians were also part of the first wave, and that Lord General Dravere was in overall charge of the Epsilon theatre, made him think otherwise.

How much of it was engineered by Fereyd's hand; how much by the opposing cartel? How much was sheer happenstance? Only time would tell. Time... and slaughter.

The lord general's strategists had planned out six dispersal sites for the main landing along a hundred and twenty kilometre belt of lowlands adjacent to a hill range designated Shrine Target Primaris on all field charts and signals. Four more dispersal sites were spread across a massive salt basin below Shrine Target Secundus, a line of steeple-cliffs fifteen hundred kilometres to the west, and three more were placed to assault Shrine Target Tertius on a wide oceanic peninsula two thousand kilometres to the south.

The waves of landing ships came in under cover of pre-dawn light, tinting the dark undersides of the clouds red with their burners and attitude thrusters. As the sun came up, pale and weak, the lightening sky was thick with ships... the heavyweight troop carriers, glossy like beetles, the smaller munitions and supply lifters moving in pairs and trios, the quick, cross-cutting threads of fighter escort and ground cover. Some orbital bombardment – jagging fire-ripples of orbit-to-surface missiles and the occasional careful stamp of a massive beam weapon – softened the empty highlands above the seething dispersal fields.

Down in the turmoil, men and machines marshalled out of black ships into the dawn light. Troops components formed columns or waiting groups, and armour units ground forward, making their own roads along the lowlands, assembling into packs and advance lines on the churned, rolling grasses. The air was thick with exhaust fumes, the growl of tank engines, the roar of ship-thrusters and the crackle of vox-chatter. Platoon strength retinues set dispersal camps, lit fires, or were seconded to help erect the blast-tents of the field hospitals and communication centres. Engineer units dug fortifications and defence baffles. Munitorium supply details broke out the crates from the material ships, and distributed assault equipment to collection parties from each assembling platoon. Amid the hue and cry, the Ministorum priesthood moved solemnly through their flock, chanting, blessing, swinging incense burners and singing unceasing hymns of valour and protection.

Gaunt came down the bow-ramp of his drop-ship into the early morning air and onto a wide mud-plain of track-chewed earth. The noise, the vibration, the petrochemical smell, was intense and fierce. Lights flashed all around, from campfires and hooded lanterns, from vehicle headlights, from the winking hazard lamps of landing ships or the flicking torch-poles of dispersal officers directing disembarking troop columns or packs of off-loading vehicles.

He looked up at the highland slopes beyond: wide, rising hills thick with dry, ochre bracken. Beyond them was the suggestion of crags and steeper summits: the Target Primaris. There, if the Vermilion-level data was honest, lay the hopes and dreams of Lord High Militant General Dravere and his lackeys – the destiny of Ibram Gaunt and his Ghosts too.

Further down the field, Devourer drop-ships slackened their metal jaws and disgorged the infantry. The Ghosts came out blinking, in platoon formation, gazing out at the rolling ochre-clad hills and the low, puffy cloud cover. Gaunt moved them up and out, under direction of the marshals, onto the rise that was their first staging post. Clearing the exhaust smog which choked the dispersal site, they got their first taste of Menazoid Epsilon. It was dry and cool, with a cutting wind and a permeating scent of honeysuckle. At first, the sweet, cold smell was pleasing and strange, but after a few breaths it became cloying and nauseating.

Gaunt signalled his disposition and quickly received the command to advance as per the sealed battle orders. The Ghosts moved forward, rising up through the bracken, leaving countless trodden trails in their wake. The growth was hip-high and fragile as ash, and the troopers were encumbered by tripping roots and wiry sedge weeds.

Gaunt led them to the crest of the hill and then turned the regiment west, as he had been ordered. Two kilometres back below them, on the busy dispersal field, burners flared and several of the massive drop-ships rose, swinging low above the hillside, shuddering the air and billowing up a storm of bracken fibres as they lifted almost impossibly into the cloudy sky.

Three kilometres distant, Gaunt could see through his scope two regiments of Mordian Iron Guard forming up as they advanced from their landing points. Another two kilometres beyond them, the Vitrian Dragoons were advancing from their first staging. The rolling hilly landscape was alive with troops, clusters of black dots marching up from the blasted acres of the dispersal site, forward through the scrub.

By mid-morning, the parallel-advancing regiments of Imperial Guard armour and infantry were pushing like fingers through the bracken and scree-marked slopes of the highlands. At the dispersal sites now left far behind, ships were still ferrying components of the vast assault down from orbit. Thruster-roar rolled like faraway thunder around the sleeve of hills.

They began to see the towers: forty-metre tall, irregular piles of jagged rock rising out of the bracken every five hundred metres or so. Gaunt quickly passed the news on to command, and heard similar reports on the vox-caster's cross-channel traffic. There were lines of these towers all across the highland landscape. They looked like they had been piled from flat slabs, wide at the base, narrowing as they rose and then wider and flat again at the top. They were all crumbling, mossy, haphazard, and in places time had tumbled some of their number over in wide spreads of broken stone, half-hidden amidst the bracken.

Gaunt wasn't sure if they were natural outcrops, their spacing and linear form seemed to suggest otherwise. He was disheartened as he remembered the singular lack of data on Epsilon that had been available at the orbital preparatory briefings.

'Possibly a shrineworld' had been the best the Intelligence cadre had had to offer. 'The surface of the planet is covered in inexplicable stone structures, arranged in lines that converge on the main areas of ruins – the targets Primaris, Secundus and Tertius.'

Gaunt sent Mkoll's scouting platoon ahead, around the breast of the hill through a line of mouldering towers and into the valley beyond. He flipped out the data-slate which he had secreted in his storm-coat pocket for two days and consulted the crystal's data.

Calling up Trooper Rafflan, he took the speaker-horn from the field-caster on his back and relayed further orders. His units would scout ahead and the Mordians, advancing in their wake, would lay behind until he signalled. It was now local noon.

Turning back to his men, Gaunt saw Major Rawne nearby, standing in a grim hunch, his lasgun hanging limply in his hands.

Gaunt had all but refused to allow Rawne to join them, but the hexathedral medics had pronounced him fit. He was a shadow of his former self since the torture by the Jantine and that mysterious robed monster

which Larkin had shot. Gaunt missed the waspish, barbed attitude that
had made Rawne a dangerous ally – and a good squad leader.

Feygor, his adjutant, was here too, his life owed to Dorden. Feygor
was a loose cannon now, an angry man with an axe to grind. He'd railed
against the Jantine in the barracks and cursed that they were sharing
this expedition. Gaunt feared what might happen if the Ghosts and the
Jantine crossed on Epsilon, particularly without Rawne sharp enough
to keep his adjutant in line.

What will happen will happen, Gaunt decided, hearing Fereyd's
counsel in his head. He checked his boltgun for luck and was about
to turn and tell Milo to play up when the shivering notes of a march
spilled from the chanters of the Tanith pipes and echoed across the
curl of the valley.

They were here. Now they would do this.

TWO

Lord General Dravere's Command Leviathan, a vast armoured, trundling fortress the size of a small city, crawled forward across the loamy
soil of the lowland slope overlooking one of the main dispersal sites
for the Primaris target.

At its heart, Dravere swung around in his leather command
g-hammock. He was in a good mood. Thanks to his urgent requests,
Warmaster Macaroth had personally instructed him to the command of
the Epsilon offensive. The fool! Here lay the secret that the freak-beast
Heldane had told him of on Fortis Binary. The reward. The prize that
would win him everything.

Dravere had spent two days reviewing the available data on Menazoid Epsilon before the drop. Little more than a moon compared to
its vast partner Sigma, it was reckoned to be a shrine world to the
Dark Powers. Vast, mouldering structures of inexplicable ancient
design dominated the northern uplands, arranged in patterns that
could only be appreciated from high orbit. The vast bulk of the Chaos
legions arrayed against them had dug in to defend their cities on
the primary world, but intelligence reports had picked up hints of
an unknown mass of defence established here. It was clear that,
though there was no obvious wealth or value to the moon-world,
the foe regarded it as significant. Why else would they have risked
splitting their forces?

Dravere had heard talk of simply obliterating Epsilon from orbit,
but had fiercely vetoed the Navy plan. He wanted Epsilon taken on
the ground, so that they might capture and examine whatever it was

the enemy held in such regard. That was the authorised explanation for this assault.

Dravere knew more. He knew that the fact the rebellious Gaunt had requested this theatre alone made it significant. Dravere readied himself. He knew how to use manpower. He had based his career upon it. He would use Gaunt now. The commissar had not given up the priceless data, so they would instead use Gaunt to lead them to it.

Dravere pulled on a lever to rotate his command hammock, speed-reading the deposition reports from the repeater plates that hung around his station. He linked in with the command globes of Marshal Sendak and Marshal Tarantine, who were overseeing the assaults on target locations Secundus and Tertius respectively. They reported their dispersal complete and their forces in advance. No contact with any enemy thus far.

The afternoon was half gone, and the first day with it. Dravere was unhappy that fighting had not yet begun at any of the three battlefronts, but he was gratified in the knowledge that he had supervised the landing of an expeditionary force of this size, divided between three targets, in less than a single day. He knew of few Imperial Guard commanders who could have done the same in treble that time.

He selected other plates and surveyed the disposition of the army under his direct command, the Primaris invasion. The infantry regiments were down and advancing strongly from the dispersal sites, and the motorised armour were disembarking from their landing craft into the lower valleys. He was pushing on three prongs to encircle the ancient mountainside structures of Shrine Target Primaris, fanning his armour out to support three infantry advances, led by the Mordian to the west, the Lattarii to the east and the Tanith to the south. So far there had been no sign of an enemy to engage. No sign at all, in fact, that there were anything other than Imperium forces alive on Epsilon.

Dravere took up a stylus and inscribed a short message on a data-slate to Colonel Flense of the Jantine. Flense would be his eyes and ears on the ground, tailing the Tanith Ghosts and standing ready to intercede. Gaunt's advance was the only one he was interested in.

Dravere coded the message in Jantine combat-cant and broadcast it to the Patricians on a stammered vox-burst. Flense would not fail him.

He sat back in his harness and allowed a smile to cross his thin lips. He knew this gambit would cost him, but he had lives enough to pay. The lives of the fifty thousand infantry under his command here on Epsilon. He considered them a down-payment on his apotheosis.

He decided to take the opportunity to rest and meditate.

* * *

The second day was dawning when he returned to his command-hammock, and overviewed the intelligence from the night. All of his units had advanced as expected until dark and then established watch-camps and stagings. At first light, they were moving again. The night had brought no sign of the foe, nor had Dravere expected such news. His staff would have roused him immediately at the first shot fired.

Chatter and industry filled the command globe beyond the circular guard rail surrounding his hammock-pit. Navy officers and Munitorium aides mixed with Guard tactical officials and members of his own staff, manning the artificers and codifiers, processing, analysing and charting movement on the huge hololithic deployment map, a three-dimensional light-shape projecting down from the domed roof.

A sudden call rang through the deck: 'Marshal Tarantine reports his Cadian and Afghali units have engaged. Heavy fighting now at Shrine Target Tertius!'

First blood, Dravere thought, at last. Red indicator runes flashed on the continental deployment map. Stains of tell tale brown and crimson shone out to delineate firefight spread and range at the Tertius location. Enemy positions flashed into life as they were assessed, appearing as aggressive little yellow stars.

He issued more orders, bringing the heavy artillery and tanks around to begin bombardment to cover Tarantine's line. Two more heavy fighting zones erupted on the map, as the Secundus push suddenly ground hard into hidden enemy emplacements. A counter-bombardment opened up from the enemy forces. More stains, more yellow stars. Dravere kept one eye fixed on the jinking signals that flagged the swift Tanith advance, with Mordian, Jantine and Vitrian columns at its heels. The Primaris assault was unopposed so far.

'It begins, lord,' a voice said to his left. Dravere looked up into the face of Imperial Tactician Wheyland. Wheyland was a grizzled, bald man with a commanding frame and piercing eyes. He wore the black and red-braid uniform of Macaroth's tactical advisors, but Dravere had known who the man really was when he first met him. A spy, a watcher, an observer, sent by Macaroth to supervise Dravere's efforts.

'Your assessment, Wheyland?' Dravere said smoothly.

The tactician scrutinised the deployment map. 'We expected fierce resistance. I anticipate they have more than this up their sleeves.'

'Nothing yet here at Primaris. We expected this to be the worst, didn't we?'

'Indeed.' Wheyland seemed oblivious to Dravere's sarcasm. 'Not yet, but it will come. If this is the shrineworld we fear it to be, their defence will be more indomitable and fanatical than we can imagine. Do not advance your forces too swiftly, lord general, or you will render them vulnerable and over-extended.'

Dravere wished he could tell the tactician exactly what he thought of his advice, but Wheyland was part of Macaroth's military aristocracy and an insult would be counter-productive. He wanted to shout: I've dispersed this invasion faster and more efficiently than any commander in the fleet and you dare advise me to slow? But he simply nodded, biting his tongue for now.

Wheyland sat on the guard rail and sighed reflectively. 'It's been a long time for us, eh, Hechtor?'

Dravere looked at him crossly. 'Long time? What do you mean?'

Wheyland smiled at him. 'The heat of combat? We were both footsloggers once. Last action I saw was against the accursed eldar on Ondermanx, twenty years past. Now we're data-slate watchers, plate-pushers. Command is an honourable venture, but sometimes I miss the sweat and toil of combat.'

Dravere licked his lips at the delicious thought which had just come to him. 'I can use any able-bodied, willing fighting man, Wheyland. Do you want to get out there?'

Wheyland looked startled for a moment, then grinned suddenly, getting up. 'I never refuse such an opportunity. The combat technique of this much-celebrated Tanith regiment fascinates me. I'm sure the tactical counsel could incorporate many new ideas from close observation of their stealth methods. With your permission, I'd gladly join them.'

You're so damn transparent, Dravere thought sullenly. You want to see for yourself, don't you? But he also knew he couldn't argue. To deny an Imperial tactician now might risk compromising his plan. I can deal with you later, he decided.

'Would you care to deploy in the field as an observer? I could always use an eye on the ground.'

'With your permission,' Wheyland said, making to leave. 'I'll take a Chimera from the reserve and move up the line. I have a detail of bodyguards who can act as a fire-team squad. Naturally, I'll report all findings to you.'

'Naturally,' Dravere agreed humourlessly. 'I'll enter your identifier on the chart. Your battle code will be what?'

Wheyland seemed to think for a moment. 'How about my old unit call sign? Eagleshard.'

Dravere noted it and passed the details to his aide.

'Good hunting... tactician,' he said as the man left the command dome.

* * *

THREE

Gaunt looked up from the inscription that Communications Officer Rafflan had made of the intercepted vox-burst.

'Mean anything to you, sir?' he asked. 'I logged it yesterday afternoon.'

Gaunt nodded. It was a message in Jantine combat-cant. Watchful of Macaroth's agencies, he had instructed Rafflan to keep his vox-cast unit open to listen for all battlefield traffic. The message was from Dravere to Flense – a direct order to shadow the Ghosts. Gaunt rubbed his chin. Slowly, the enemies were showing their hand.

He looked ahead, up the high mountain pass, choked with bracken, and its lines of slumping towers. He was tempted to send Rawne back down the slope to mine the way in advance of the Jantine at their heels, but when all was said and done, they were on the same side. Word had come that the fighting had opened at the other two target sites, heavy and bloody.

There was no telling what they would encounter up ahead in the thin altitude. He dared not drive back the units which might be the only forces to support the Tanith in a direct action.

Gaunt pulled a notepad from the pocket of his storm-coat and consulted several pages that Colonel Zoren had written. Carefully, with uncertainty, he composed a message in the Vitrian battlefield language, using the code-words Zoren had told him. Then he had Rafflan send it.

'Speaking in tongues, sir?' the vox-officer laughed, ironically using the Tanith's own war-dialect that Gaunt had made sure he had learned early on. Many of the regiments used their own languages or codes for internal messages. On the battlefield, secrecy was imperative in vox-commands, and Dravere couldn't know Gaunt had a working knowledge of Jantine combat-cant.

Gaunt called up Sergeant Blane. 'Take the seventh platoon and function as a rearguard,' he told Blane directly.

'You're expecting a hindquarters strike, then?' asked Blane, puzzled. 'Mkoll's scouts have covered the hill line. The enemy won't be sneaking round on us.'

'Not the given enemy,' Gaunt said. 'I want you watching for the Jantine who are following us up. Our code word will be "Ghostmaker". Given from me to you, or you back to me, it will indicate the Jantine have made a move. I don't want to be fighting our own... but it may come to that. When you hear the word, do not shrink from the deed. If you signal me, I will send everything back to support you. As far as I am concerned, the Jantine are as much our foe as the things that dwell up here.'

'Understood,' Blane said, looking darkly at his commander. Corbec had briefed the senior men well after Gaunt's unlocking of the crystal. They knew what was at stake, and were keeping the thought both paramount and away from their men, who had enough to concern them. Gaunt had a particular respect for the gruff, workmanlike Blane. He was as gifted and loyal an officer as Corbec, Mkoll or Lerod, but he was also dependable and solid. Almost despite himself, Gaunt found himself offering Blane his hand.

They shook. Blane realised the weight of the duty, the potentially terrible demands.

'Emperor go with you, sir,' he said, as he broke the grip and turned to retreat down the bracken slope.

'And may He watch over you,' Gaunt returned.

Nearby, Milo saw the quiet exchange. He shook spit from the chanters of his Tanith pipes and prepared to play again. This is it, he thought. The commissar expects the worst.

Sergeant Mkoll's scouts were returning from the higher ground. Gaunt joined them to hear their report.

'I think it's best if you see it yourself,' Mkoll said simply and gestured back at the heights.

Gaunt spread the fire-teams of three platoons along the width of the valley slope and then moved forward with Mkoll's scout unit. By now, all of the Ghosts had rubbed the absorbent fabric of their stealth cloaks with handfuls of ochre bracken and dusted them so that they blended into the ground cover. Gaunt smiled as Mkoll scolded the commissar's less than Tanith-like abilities, and scrupulously damped down the colour of Gaunt's cloak with a scrub of ashy bracken. Gaunt removed his cap and edged forward, trying to hang the cloak around him as deftly as the Tanith scout. Behind them, there were two thousand Ghosts on the bracken-thick mountainside, but their commanding officer could see none of them.

He reached the rise, and borrowed Mkoll's scope as they bellied down in the fern and the dust.

He hardly needed the scope. The rise they were ascending dropped away and a cliff face rose vertically ahead of them, looking like it was ten thousand metres tall. The milky-blue granite face was carved into steps like a ziggurat, a vast steepled formation of weather-worn storeys, rows of archways and slumped blocks. Gaunt knew that this was his first look at Shrine Target Primaris. Other than that, he had no idea what it was. A burial place, a temple, a dead hive? It simply smacked of evil, of the darkness. A vile corruption seeped up from every pore of the rock face, every dark alcove and pillared recess.

'I don't like the look of it,' Mkoll said flatly.

Gaunt smiled grimly and consulted his own data-slate. 'Neither do I. We don't want to approach it directly. We need to sweep around to the left and follow the valley line.' Gaunt scoped down to the left. The carved granite structure extended away beyond the curve of the vale and several of the stalking lines of towers marched up the bracken slopes to meet it, as if they were feelers spread out from the immense shrine itself. Beyond and higher, he could now see towers of blue granite in the clouds: spires, steeples and buttresses. This was just the outskirts of an ancient necropolis, a city long dead that had been raised by inhuman hands before the start of recorded time.

The honeysuckle scent in the air was becoming a stench. Vox-level chatter over the micro-bead in his ear told him that his men were starting to succumb to a vague, indefinable nausea.

'You want to go left?' Mkoll asked. 'But that's not in accord with the order of battle.'

'I know.'

'The lord general will be furious if we divert from the given advance.'

'I have my own orders,' Gaunt said, tapping his data-slate.

'And the Emperor love you for your loyalty!' Mkoll shook his head. 'Sir, we were told to assault this... this place directly.'

'And we will, Mkoll – just not here.'

Mkoll nodded. 'How far down?'

'A kilometre or two. The crystal spoke of a dome. Find it for me.'

'Gladly,' Mkoll said. 'You know that if we alter our advance it will give the Jantine dogs more reason to come for us.'

'I know,' Gaunt said. More than ever he appreciated the way his senior officers had accommodated the truth of their endeavour. They knew what was at stake and what the real dangers were.

Mkoll and Corporal Baru led the advancing Ghosts along the top of the valley, just under the crest, and past the threatening, tower-haunted steppes of the graven hillside.

Scout Trooper Thark was the first to spot it. He voxed back to the command group: a dome, a massive, bulbous dome swelling from the living rock of the cliff face, impossibly carved from granite.

Gaunt moved up to see it for himself. It was like some vast stone onion, a thousand metres in diameter, sunk into the stepped rock wall around it, the surface inscribed with billions of obscure sigils and marks.

Thark was also the first to die. A storm of autocannon rounds whipped up the slope, exploding bracken into dust, spitting up soil and punching him into four or five bloody parts. At the cue, other weapon placements in the steppe alcoves of the facing cliff opened fire, raining las-fire, bullets and curls of plasma down at the Ghosts.

The answering fire laced a spider's web of las-light, tracer lines and fire wash between the sides of the valley.

The dying began.

FOUR

Marshal Gohl Sendak, the so-called Ravager of Genestock Gamma, had abandoned his Command Leviathan to lead his forces from the front. He rode a Leman Russ battle tank of the Borkellid regiments, heading a fast-moving armoured phalanx that was smashing its way across the rocky escarpments below the weathered stone structures of Shrine Target Secundus.

Laying down a ceaseless barrage, they broke through two lines of crumbling curtain walls and into the lower perimeters of the shrine structure itself. Wide, rubble-strewn slopes faced them, dotted with the lines of those infernal towers. Sendak voxed to the Oudinot infantry at his tail and urged them to follow him in. Fire as heavy as he had ever known blazed down from the archways and alcoves facing them

Sendak felt a dry stinging in his nose, and snorted it away. That damn honeysuckle odour, it was beginning to get to him like it was getting to his men.

He felt a wetness heavy his moustache and wiped it. Fresh blood smeared his grey-cloth sleeve. There was more in his mouth and he spat, his ears throbbing. Looking around in the green-lit interior of the tank, he saw all the crew were suffering spontaneous nose-bleeds, or were retching and hacking blood.

There was a vibration singing in the air: low, lazy, ugly.

Sendak swung the tank's periscope around to scan the scene outside. Something was happening to the lines of towers which flanked them on either side. They were glowing, fulminating with rich curls of vivid damask energy. Mist was columnating around the old stones.

'Blood of the Emperor!' Sendak growled, his teeth and lips stained red with his own dark blood.

Outside, in the space of a human heartbeat, two things happened. The lines of towers, just ragged rows of stone spines a moment before, exploded into life and became a fence, a raging energy field forty metres tall. Lashing and fizzling lines of force whipped and crackled from tower to tower like giant, supernatural barbed wire. Each tower connected blue and white brambles of curling energy with its neighbour. Any man or machine caught in the line between towers was, in two heartbeats, burned or exploded or ripped into pieces. The rest were penned between the sudden barriers, hemmed in and unable to turn or flank.

As the energy wires ignited between the previously dormant stone stacks, something else happened on the flat tops of each tower. In puffs of pinkish, coloured gas, figures appeared on each tower platform.

Teleported into place by sciences too dark and heretical for a sane mind to understand, these squads of soldiers instantly deployed heavy weapons on tripods and laid down fire on the penned aggressors beneath them. The Chaos forces were thin, wasted beings in translucent shrouds and scowling masks made of bone. They manned tripod-mounted las-cannons, meltaguns and other more arcane field weapons with hands bandaged in soiled strips of plastic. Amongst them were their corrupt commanders, quasi-mechanical Chaos Marines, Obliterators.

Sendak screamed orders, trying to turn his advance in the chaos. Two tanks to his right swung blindly round into the nearest energy fence and were obliterated, exploding in huge clouds of flame as their munitions went off. Another tank was riddled with fire from the tops of the two nearest towers.

Sendak suddenly found the enemy had heavy weapon emplacements stretching back along the tower-lines around, between and behind his entire column.

He almost admired the tactic, but the technology was beyond him, and his eyes were so clouded and swimming with the blood-pain in his sinuses he could barely think.

He grabbed the vox-caster horn and fumbled for the command channel. 'It's worse than we feared! They are luring us in and using unholy science to bracket us and cut us to pieces! Inform all assault forces! The towers are death! The towers are death!'

A cannon round punched through the turret and exploded Sendak and his gunner. The severed vox-horn clattered across the deck, still clutched by the marshal's severed hand. A second later, the tank flipped over as a frag-rocket blew out its starboard track, skirt and wheelbase. As it landed, turret-down, in the mud, it detonated from within, blowing apart the Leman Russ next to it.

Behind the decimated tanks, the Oudinot were fleeing.

But there was nowhere to flee to.

FIVE

Every opening in the stepped structure which rose above the Tanith Ghosts along the far side of the cliff around that gross, inscribed dome seemed to be spitting fire. Las-fire, bolter rounds, the heavier sparks of cannon fire, and other exotic bursts, odd bullets that buzzed like insects and flew slowly and lazily.

Corbec ran the line of the platoons which had reached the crest, his great rich voice bawling them into cover and return-fire stances.

There was little natural cover up here except the natural curl of the hill brow, and odd arrangements of ancient stones which poked like rotten, discoloured teeth from the bracken.

'Dash! Down! Crawl! Look!' Corbec bellowed, repeating the training chant they had first heard on the Founding Fields of lost Tanith. 'Take your sight and aim! Spraying and praying is not good enough!'

Down the crest, near Lerod's command position, Bragg opened up with the rocket launcher, swiftly followed by Melyr and several other heavy weapons troopers. Tank-busting missiles whooped across the gully into the crumbling stone facade of the tumbled structure, blowing gouts of stone and masonry out in belches of flame.

On hands and knees, Gaunt regrouped with Corbec under the lip of the hill. The barrage of shots whistled over their heads and the honeysuckle stench was augmented by the choking scent of ignited bracken.

'We have to get across!' Gaunt yelled to Corbec over the firing of ten thousand sidearms and the scream of rockets.

'Love to oblige!' returned Corbec ruefully, gesturing at the scene. Gaunt showed him the data-slate and they compared it to the edifice beyond, gingerly keeping low for fear of the whinnying shot.

'It isn't going to happen,' Corbec said. 'We'll never get inside against a frontal opposition like this!'

Gaunt knew he was right. He turned back to the slate. The data they had downloaded from the crystal was complex and in many places completely impenetrable. It had been written, or at least translated, from old code notations, and there was as much obscure about it as there was comprehensible. Some more of it made sense now – now Gaunt had the chance to compare the information with the actual location. One whole part seemed particularly clear.

'Hold things here,' he ordered Corbec curtly and rolled back from the lip, gaining his feet in the steep bracken and hurrying down the slope they had advanced up.

He found the tower quickly enough, one of the jagged, mouldering stone formations, a little way down the slope. He pulled bracken away from the base and uncovered the top of an old, decaying shaft he hoped – knew – would be there. He crouched at the mouth and gazed down into the inky depths of the drop beneath.

Gaunt tapped his micro-bead to open the line, and then ordered up personnel to withdraw to his position: Mkoll, Baru, Larkin, Bragg, Rawne, Dorden, Domor, Caffran.

They assembled quickly, eyeing the black shaft suspiciously.

'Our back door,' Gaunt told them. 'According to the old data, this sink leads down some way and then into the catacombs beneath the shrine structure. We'll need ropes, pins, a hammer.'

'Who'll be going in there?' Rawne asked curtly.

'All of us... me first,' Gaunt told him.

Gaunt beaded to Corbec and instructed him to marshal the main Tanith levies and sustain fire against the facade of the structure.

He stripped off his storm-coat and cloak, and slung his chainsword over his back. Mkoll had tapped plasteel rooter pins into the stone-work at the top of the shaft and played a length of cable around them and down into the darkness.

Gaunt racked the slide of his bolt pistol and holstered it again. 'Let's go,' he said, wrapping the cord around his waist and sliding into the hole.

Mkoll grabbed his arm to stop him as Trooper Vench hurried down the slope from the combat-ridge, calling out. Gaunt slid back out of the cavity and took the data-slate from Vench as he stumbled up to them.

'Message from Sergeant Blane,' Vench gasped. 'There's a Chimera coming up the low pass, sending signals that it desires to join with us.'

Gaunt frowned. It made no sense. He studied the slate's transcript. 'Sergeant Blane wants to know if he should let them through,' Vench added. 'They're identifying themselves as a detail of tactical observers from the warmaster's counsel. They use the code-name "Eagleshard".'

Gaunt froze as if he had been shot. 'Sacred Feth!' he spat.

The men murmured and eyed each other. It was a pretty pass when the commissar used a Tanith oath.

'Stay here,' Gaunt told the insurgence party and unlashed the rope, heading downhill at the double. 'Tell Rafflan to signal Blane!' he yelled back at Vench. 'Let them through!'

SIX

The Chimera, its hull armour matt-green and showing no other mark-ings than the Imperial crest, rumbled up the slope from Blane's picket and slewed sidelong on a shelf of hillside, chewing bracken under its treads. Gaunt scrambled down to meet it, warier than he had ever been in his life.

The side hatch opened with a metallic clunk and three troopers leapt out, lasguns held ready. They wore combat armour in the red and black

liveries of the Imperial Crusade staff, elite bodyguard troops for the
officer cadre. Reflective visor masks hid their faces. A taller, heftier
figure in identical battledress joined them and stood, hands on hips,
surveying the scene as Gaunt approached.

The figure slid back his visor and then pulled the helmet off. Gaunt
didn't recognise him... until he factored in a few years, some added
muscle and the shaven head.

'Eagleshard,' Gaunt said.

'Eagleshard,' responded the figure. 'Ibram!'

Gaunt shook his old friend's hand. 'What do I call you?'

'I'm Imperial Tactician Wheyland here, but my boys are trustworthy,'
the big man said, gesturing to the troopers, who now relaxed their
spread. 'You can call me by the name you know.'

'Fereyd...'

'So, Ibram... bring me up to speed.'

'I can do better. I can take you to the prize.'

The stone chimney was deep and narrow. Gaunt half-climbed,
half-rappelled down the flue, his toes and hands seeking purchase in
the mouldering stonework. He tried to imagine what this place had
been at the time of its construction; perhaps a city, a living place built
into and around the cliff. This flue was probably the remains of an
air-duct or ventilator, dropping down to Emperor-knew-what beneath.

Gaunt's feet found the rock floor at the base, and he straightened
up, loosening the ropes so that the others could join him. It smelled of
sweaty damp down here, and the tunnel he was in was low and jagged.

'Lasgun!' came a call from above. The weapon dropped down the
flue and Gaunt caught it neatly, immediately igniting the lamp pack
which Dorden had webbed to the top of the barrel with surgical tape.
He played the light over the dirty, low walls, his finger on the trigger.
Above him came the sounds of others scrambling down the ragged
chimney.

It took thirty minutes for the rest to join him. They all held lasguns
with webbed-on lamps, except Dorden, who was unarmed but carried a torch, and Bragg, who hefted a massive autocannon. Bragg had
enjoyed the hardest descent; bulky and uncoordinated, he had struggled in the flue and begun to panic.

Larkin was moaning about death and claustrophobia, young Caffran
was clearly alarmed, Dorden was sour and defeatist, Baru was scornful
of them all and Rawne was silent and surly. Gaunt smiled to himself. He
had selected them well. They were all exhibiting their angst and worries
up front. Nothing would linger to come out later. But between them,

they encompassed the best stealth, marksmanship, firepower, medical ability and bravery the Tanith First and Only had to offer.

All of them seemed wary of the Imperial tactician and his trooper bodyguard which the commissar had suddenly decided to invite along. The troopers were tough, silent types who had scaled the chimney with professional ease. They stuck close to their leader, limpet-like, guns ready.

The party moved down the passage, stooping under outcrops and sags of rock and twisted stone. Their lamps cut obscure shadows and light from the uneven surfaces.

After two hundred careful steps and another twenty minutes, they emerged into a dripping, glistening cavern where the ancient rock walls were calcified and sheened with mineral moisture. Ahead of them, their lamps picked out an archway of perfectly fitted, dressed stone.

Gaunt raised his weapon and flicked the lamp as an indicator.

'After me,' he said.

SEVEN

'He wants to see you, sir,' the aide said.

Lord General Dravere didn't want to hear. He was still staring at the repeater plates which hung in front of him, showing the total, desperate carnage that had befallen Marshal Sendak's advance on Target Secundus. Even now, plates were fizzing out to blankness or growing dim and fading. He had never expected this. It was... It was not possible.

'Sir?' the aide said again.

'Can you not see this is a crisis moment, you idiot?' Dravere raged, swinging around and buffeting some of the floating plates out of his way. 'We're being murdered on the second front! I need time to counter-plan! I need the tactical staff here now!'

'I will assemble them at once,' the aide said, speaking slowly, as if he was scared of a thing far greater than the raging commander. 'However, the inquisitor insists.'

Dravere hesitated, and then released the toggle of his harness and slid out of the hammock. He didn't like fear, but fear was what now burned in his chest. He crossed the command globe to the exit shutter and turned briefly to order his second-in-command to take over and assemble the advice of the tactical staff as it came in.

'Signal whatever remains of Sendak's force to withdraw to staging ground A11-23. Alert the other forces to the danger of the towers. I want assessments and counter-strategies by the time I return.'

A brass ladder led down into the isolation sphere buried in the belly of the command globe.

Dravere entered the dimly-lit chamber. It smelled of incense and disinfectant. There was a pulse tone from the medical diagnosticators, and pale steam rose from the plastic sheeting tented over the cot in the centre of the room. Medical staff in cowled red scrubs left silently as soon as he appeared.

'You wanted to see me, Inquisitor Heldane?' Dravere began.

Heldane moved under the loose semi-transparent flaps of the tent. Dravere got a glimpse of tubes and pipes, draining fluid from the ghastly rent in the man's neck, and of the ragged wound in the side of his head, which was encased in a swaddling package of bandage, plastic wrap and metal braces.

'It is before us, my Lord Hechtor,' Heldane said, his voice a rasping whisper from vox-relays at his bedside. 'The prize is close. I sense it through my pawn.'

'What do we do?'

'We move with all stamina. Advance the Jantine. I will guide them in after Gaunt. This is no time for weakness or subtlety. We must strike.'

EIGHT

Death flurried down over the Tanith ranks from the stepped arches of the necropolis. A blizzard of las-shot showered down, along with the arcing stings of arcane electrical weapons. The air hummed, too, with the whine of the slower metal projectile-casters the enemy were using. Barb-like bullets, slow-moving enough to be seen, buzzed down at them like glittering hornets. Where they hit flesh, they did untold explosive damage. Corbec saw men rupture and come apart as the barbed rounds hit. Others were maimed by shrapnel as the vile shells hit stone or metal beside them and shattered.

A barbed round dug into the turf near Corbec's foxhole cover and became inert.

The colonel flicked it out with his knife-point and studied it – a bulb of dull metal with forward-pointing, overlaid leaves of razor-sharp alloy. The blackened, fused remains of a glass cartridge at the base showed its method of propulsion. Shot from simple tube-launchers, Corbec decided, the propellant igniting as the firing pin shattered the glass capsule. He turned it over in one hand, protected by the edge of his stealth cape. Evil and ingenious, the barb's leaves were scored to ease impact-shatter – either against a hard surface to produce a cloud of shrapnel, or against bone as it chewed through tissue to effect the worst wounds possible. The leaves were slightly spiralled too, suggesting that the launcher's rifling set them spinning as they fired. Corbec decided he had never seen a more savage, calculated, more grotesque instrument of death and pain.

He sighed as the firestorm raged above him. Still no word had come from the commissar's infiltration team, and only Corbec's knowledge of Gaunt's secret agenda allayed his fears at the high-risk tactic.

Corbec contacted his platoon leaders and had them edge the men forward along the facing lip, winning any inch they could. He had close on two thousand lasguns and heavier weapons raking the front of the pile, and the alcove-lined facade was shattering, slumping and collapsing under the fusillade. But the return fire was as intense as ever.

Trooper Mahan, communications officer for Corbec's own platoon command, crouched in the foxhole beside him, talking constantly into the voice-horn of his heavy vox-set, relaying and processing battle-reports from all the units. Mahan suddenly leaned back, grabbed the colonel by a cuff and dragged him close, pushing the headset against his ear.

'...are death! The towers are death!' Corbec heard.

He shot a stare at Mahan, who was encoding the information on his data-slate.

'Target Secundus is routed,' Mahan said grimly, scribing as he spoke and relaying the data in stuttered code-bursts through the handset of the vox-caster. 'Sendak is dead... Feth, it sounds like they're all dead. Dravere is signalling a total withdrawal. The towers-'

Corbec grabbed the slate and studied the scrolling text Mahan was direct-receiving from High Command. There were flickering, indistinct images captured from Sendak's last transmission. He saw the towers erupt into life, laying down their destructive fences, saw the forces of the enemy manifest on the tower tops.

Instinctively, he looked up at the towers nearest them. If it happened here, they would suffer a similar fate.

Even as he formed the thought, a ragged flurry of frenzied reports flooded the comm-lines. The towers had ignited at Target Tertius too. Marshal Tarantine had received enough warning from the Secundus advance to protect the advance of his forces, but still he was suffering heavy losses. They were generally intact, but their assault was stymied.

'Sacred Feth!' Corbec hissed, heating the air with his curse. He keyed his micro-bead to open traffic and bellowed an order.

'Any Ghosts within twenty metres of a tower! Use any and all available munitions to destroy those towers! Do it, for the love of us all!'

Answering links jabbered back at him and he had to shout to be heard. 'Now, you fething idiots!' he bawled.

Two hundred metres away, a little way down a slope in the hill,

Sergeant Varl's platoon reacted fastest, turning their rocket launchers on the nearest two towers and toppling them in earthy *crumps* of
dirt and flame. Folore and Lerod's platoons quickly followed suit to
the left of Corbec's position. Seven or more of the towers were demolished in the near vicinity. Sergeant Curral's platoon, guarding the rear
of the main defence, set to blasting towers further down the slope with
their missile launchers. Stone dust and burnt bracken fibres drifted in
the scorched air.

There was a report from Sergeant Hasker, whose platoon had lost all
of its heavy weapon troops in the first exchange. Hasker was sending
men up close to the towers in his sector to mine them with grenade
strings and tube bombs.

By Corbec's side, Mahan was about to say something, but stopped
short in surprise, suddenly wiping fresh blood from his upper lip. Corbec felt the hot dribble in his own nose too, and sensed the sickly tingle
in the air.

'Oh–' he began.

Mahan shook his head, trying to clear it, blood streaming from
his nose. Suddenly he convulsed as catastrophic static noise blasted
through his headset to burst his eardrums. He winced up in pain, crying out and tearing at his ear pieces.

He rose too far. A barbed round found him as he exposed his head
and shoulders over the cover, and tore everything above his waist into
bloody spatters. The comms unit on his back exploded. Corbec was
drenched in bloody matter and took a sidelong deflection of shrapnel
in the ribs, a piece of the barbed round that had fractured on impact
with Mahan's sternum.

Corbec slumped, gasping. The pain was hideous. The broken leaf of
metal had gone deep between his ribs and he knew it had ruptured
something inside him. Blood pooled in the bracken roots beneath him.

Fighting the agony, he looked up. The air-sting and the nosebleeds
could only mean one thing – and Corbec had fought through enough
theatres against Chaos to know the cursed signs.

The Primaris target had activated its towers.

Almost doubled up, clutching his side with bloodstained fingers,
Corbec looked down the length of the assault line. His warning had
come just in time. The Ghosts had demolished enough of the towers
to break the chains. Foetid white energy billowed out of the necropolis, swirling in grasping tendrils that whipped forward to find the relay
towers that were no longer there. Corbec's orders had cut the insidious counter-defences of the enemy.

Unable to link with the tower relays, the abysmal energy launched from the necropolis wavered and then boiled backwards into the city. In an instant, the enemy's own thwarted weapons did more damage to the city façade than Corbec's regiment could have managed in a month of sustained fire. Entire plateaux of stone work exploded and collapsed as the untrained energy snapped back into the dead city. Granite shards blasted outwards in choking fireballs, and sections of the edifice slipped away like collapsing ice-shelves, baring tunnelled rock faces beneath.

Down the Tanith line, Hasker's platoon had not been so lucky. Their mining efforts were only partially complete when the defence grid activated. The better part of fifty men, Dorain Hasker with them, were caught in the searing energy-fence and burned.

But Hasker had his revenge at the last, as the tower's energy set off his munitions. The whole slope shuddered at the simultaneous report. Crackling towers dissolved in sheets of flame and great explosions of earth and stone. The feedback there was far greater. The flickering, blazing fence wound back on itself as the towers collapsed, lashing back into the necropolis and scourging a new ravine out of the mountainside.

As if stunned, or mortally crippled, the enemy gunfire trailed away and died.

Corbec rolled in the belly of the foxhole, awash with his own blood, and Mahan's. He pulled a compress from his field kit and slapped it over the wound in his side, and then gulped down a handful of fat counter-pain tablets from his medical pouch with three swigs from his water flask while reciting a portion of the Litany for Merciful Healing.

More than the recommended dose, he knew. His vision swam, and then he felt a strength return as the pain dulled. His ribs and his chest throbbed, but he felt almost alive again. Alive enough to function, though at the back of his mind he knew it was no more than a bravura curtain call.

There were eight tablets left in his kit. He put them in his pocket for easy access. A week's worth of dose, and he'd use it in an hour if he had to. He would fight until pain and death clawed through the analgesic barriers and stopped him.

He hefted himself up, recovered his lasgun and keyed his micro-bead.

'Corbec to all the Ghosts of Tanith... now we advance!'

NINE

Over the vale beyond them, Colonel Draker Flense and his Patrician units saw the flicker of explosions that backlit the hills and underlit the clouds. Night was falling. The concussion of distant explosions, too loud and large for any Guard ground-based weaponry, stung the air around them.

Trooper Defraytes, Flense's vox-officer, stood to attention by him and held out the handset plate on which the assimilated data of Command flickered like an endless litany.

Flense read it, standing quite still in the dusk, amid the bracken and the soft flutter of evening moths.

The Tanith had met fierce opposition, but thanks to the warnings from the other target sites, they had broken the Chaos defence grid and blasted the opposition. Those thunderclaps still rolling off the far hills were the sounds of their victory.

'Sir?' Defraytes said, holding out his data-slate. A battle-coded relay from Dravere was forming itself across the matt screen in dull runes.

Flense took it, pressing his signet ring against the reader plate so that it would decode. The knurled face of the ring turned and stabbed a stream of light into the slate's code-socket. Magenta clearance, for his eyes only.

The message was remarkably direct and certain.

Flense allowed himself a moment to smile. He turned to his men, all six thousand of them spread in double file swirls down the scarp.

Nearby, Major Brochuss stared at his commander under hooded lids. Flense keyed his micro-bead.

'Warriors of Jant Normanidus Prime, the order has come. Evidence has now proved to our esteemed commander Lord General Dravere that the Colonel-Commissar Gaunt is infected with the taint of Chaos, as are his so-called Ghosts. They, and they alone, have passed through the defences of Chaos which have halted Marshal Sendak and Marshal Tarantine. They are marked with the badge of evil. Lord General Dravere has granted us the privilege of punishing them.'

There was a murmur in the ranks, and an edgy eagerness.

Flense cleared his throat. 'We will take the scarp and fall upon the Tanith from behind. No longer think of them as allies, or even human. They are stained with the foul blackness of our eternal foe. We will engage them – and we will exterminate them.'

Flense cut his link and turned to face the top of the scarp. He flicked his hand to order the advance and knew without question that they would follow.

TEN

The light died.

Gaunt tore the lamp pack off the muzzle of his lasgun and tossed it away. Dorden was at his side, handing him another.

'Eight left,' the elderly medic said, holding out a roll of surgical tape to help Gaunt wrap the lamp in place.

Neither of them wanted to talk about the darkness down here. A Guard issue lamp-pack was meant to last six hundred hours. In less than two, they had exhausted the best part of twenty between them. It was as if the dark down in the underworld of the necropolis ate up the light. Gaunt shuddered. If this place could leach power from energetic sources like lamp packs, he dared not think what it might be doing to their human frames.

They still edged forward: first the scouts, Mkoll and Baru, silent and almost invisible in the directionless dark, then Larkin and Gaunt. Gaunt noticed that Larkin was sporting some ancient firing piece instead of his lasgun, a long-limber rifle of exotic design. He had been told this was the weapon Larkin had used to take down the Inquisitor Heldane, and so it was now his lucky weapon. There was no time to chastise the man for superstitious foolishness. Gaunt knew Larkin's mental balance hung by a thread as it was. He simply hoped that, come a firefight, the strange weapon would have a cycle rate commensurate to the lasgun.

Behind them came Rawne, Domor and Caffran, all with lamp pack equipped lasguns at the ready. Domor had his sweeper set slung on his shoulder too, if the need came to scan for mines. Dorden followed, unarmed, and then Bragg with his massive autocannon. Behind them came Fereyd, with his anonymous, still visored troops as their rearguard.

Gaunt called a halt while the scouts took fresh bearings and inspected the tunnels ahead. Fereyd moved over to him.

'Been a long time, Bram,' he said in a smooth voice that was almost a whisper.

He doesn't want the men to hear, thought Gaunt. He doesn't know how much I've told them. He doesn't even know what I know.

'Aye, a long time,' Gaunt replied, tugging the straps of his rifle sling tighter and casting a glance in the low lamplight at Fereyd's unreadable face. 'And now barely time for a greeting and we're in it again.'

'Like Pashen.'

'Like Pashen,' Gaunt nodded with a phantom smile. 'We do always seem to make things up as we go along.'

Fereyd shook his head. 'Not this time. This is too big. It makes Pashen Nine-Sixty look like a blank-round exercise. Truth is, Bram, we've been working together on this for months, had you but realised it.'

'Without direct word from you, it was hard to know anything. First I knew was Pyrites, when you volunteered me as custodian for the damn crystal.'

'You objected?'

'No,' Gaunt said, tight and mean. 'I'd never shirk from service to the Throne, not even dirty clandestine shadowplay like this. But that was quite a task you dropped in my lap.'

Fereyd smiled. 'I knew you were up to it. I needed someone I could trust. Someone there...'

'Someone who was part of the intricate web of friends and confidantes you have nurtured wherever you go?'

'Hard words, Ibram. I thought we were friends.'

'We are. You know your friends, Fereyd. You made them yourself.'

There was a silence.

'So tell me... from the beginning.' Gaunt raised a questioning eyebrow.

Fereyd shrugged. 'You know it all, don't you?'

'I've had gobbets of it, piecemeal... bits and scraps, educated guesses, intuitions. I'd like to hear it clean.'

Fereyd put down his lasgun, drew off his gloves and flexed his knuckles. The gesture made Gaunt smile. There was nothing about this man, this Tactician Wheyland, that remotely resembled the Fereyd he'd known on the city farms of Pashen Nine-Sixty, such was the spy's mastery of disguise. But now that little gesture, an idiosyncrasy even careful disguise couldn't mask. It reassured the commissar.

'It is standard Imperial practice for a warmaster to establish a covert network to observe all of his command. Macaroth is cautious, a son of the Emperor in instinct. And glory knows, he's got a lot of shadows to fear. Slaydo's choice wasn't popular. Many resent him, Dravere most of all. Power corrupts, and the temptation of power corrupts even more. Men are just men, and they are fallible. I've been part of the network assigned by Macaroth to keep watch and check on his Crusade's officers. Dravere is a proud man, Bram, he will not suffer this slight.'

'You've said as much before. Hell, I've even paraphrased you to my men.'

'You've told your men?' Fereyd asked quickly, with a sharp look.

'My officers. Just enough to make sure they are with me, just enough to give them an edge if it matters. Fact is, I've probably told them all I know, which is precious little. The prize, the Vermilion trophy... that's what has changed everything, isn't it?'

'Of course. Even with regiments loyal to him, Dravere could never hope to turn on our beloved warmaster. But if he had something else, some great advantage, something Macaroth didn't have...'

'Like a weapon.'

'Like a great, great weapon. Eight months ago, part of my network on Talsicant first got a hint that Dravere's own covert agencies had stumbled upon a rumour of some great prize. We don't know how, or where... we can only imagine the efforts and sacrifices made by his operatives to locate and recover the data. But they did. A priceless nugget of ancient, Vermilion level secrets snatched from some distant, abominable reach of space and conveyed from psyker to psyker, agent to agent, back to the Lord High Militant General. It couldn't be sent openly, of course, or Macaroth would have intercepted it. Nor was it possible to send it directly, as it was being carried out of hostile space, far from Imperial control. On the last leg of its journey, transmitted from the Nubila Reach to Pyrites, we managed to track it and intercept it, diverting it from Dravere's agents. That was when it fell into your hands.'

'And the general's minions have been desperate to retrieve it ever since.'

Fereyd nodded. 'In anticipation of its acquisition, Dravere has set great wheels in motion. He knew its import, and the location it referred to. With it now in our hands – just – we couldn't allow it to fall back into Dravere's grasp. But we were not positioned strongly or closely enough to recover it. It was decided – I decided, in fact – that our best choice was to let you run with it, in the hope that you would get to it for us before the Lord General and his coterie of allies.'

'You have terrifying faith in my abilities, Fereyd. I'm just a footslogger, a commander of infantry.'

'You know you're more than that. A loyal hero of unimpeachable character, resourceful, ruthless... one of Warmaster Slaydo's chosen few, a man on whom the limelight of fame fell full enough to make it difficult for Dravere to move against you directly.'

Gaunt laughed. 'If the attempts to kill me and my men recently weren't direct, I hate to think what direct means!'

Fereyd caught his old friend with a piercing look. 'But you did it! You made it this far! You're on top of the situation, close to the prize, just as I knew you would be! We did everything we could behind the scenes, to facilitate your positioning and give you assistance. The deployment of the Tanith in the frontline here was no accident. And I'm just thankful I was able to manipulate my own cover as part of the Tactical Counsel to get close enough to join you now.'

'Well, we're here now, right enough, and the prize is in our grasp...' Gaunt began, hefting up his rifle again and preparing to move.

'May I see the crystal, Bram? Maybe it's time I read its contents too... if we're to work together on this.'

Gaunt swung round and gazed at Fereyd in slow realisation. 'You don't know, do you?'

'Know?'

'You don't know what it is we're here risking our lives for?'

'You thought I did? Even Macaroth and his allies don't know for sure. All any of us are certain of is that it is something that could make Dravere the man to overthrow the Crusade's High Command. As far as I know, you're the only person who's decoded it. Only you know – you and the men you've chosen to share it with.'

Gaunt began to laugh. The laughter rolled along the low stone tunnel and made all the men look round in surprise.

'I'll tell you then, Fereyd, and it's as bad as you fear–'

Mkoll's hard whistle rang down the space and cut them all silent.

Gaunt spun around, raising his rifle and looked ahead into the blackness, his fresh lamp pack already dimmer. Something moved ahead of him in the darkness. A scrabbling sound.

A barbed round hummed lazily out of nowhere, missing the flinching Larkin by a whisker and exploding against the stone wall of the corridor. Domor started screaming as Caffran held him. Shrapnel had taken his eyes and his face was a mask of flowing blood.

Gaunt seared five shots off into the darkness, and heard the chatter of Bragg's autocannon starting up behind him. The party took up firing positions along the rough-hewn walls of the tunnel.

Now the endgame, Gaunt thought.

ELEVEN

The medics, trailing their long red scrubs like priests' robes, their faces masked by gauze, moved silently around the isolation sphere in the belly of the Leviathan. They reset diagnosticators and other gently pulsing machines, muttering low intonations of healing invocations.

Heldane knew they were the best medics in the Segmentum Pacificus fleet. Dravere had transferred a dozen of his private medical staff to Heldane when he learned of the inquisitor's injury. It mattered little, Heldane knew as a certainty. He was dying. The rifle round, fired at such close range, had destroyed his neck, left shoulder and collarbone, left cheek and throat. Without the supporting web of the medical bay and the Emperor's grace, he would already be cold.

He eased back in his long-frame cot, as far as the tubes and regulator pipes piercing his neck and chest would allow. Beyond the plastic sheeting of his sterile tent, he could see the winking, pumping mechanisms on their brass trolleys and racks that were keeping him alive. He could see the dark fluids of his own body cycling in and out of centrifuge scrubs, squirting down ridged plastic tubes supported by aluminium frames.

Every twenty seconds, a delicate silvered scorpion-form device screwed into the bones of his face bathed his open wound with a mist of disinfectant spray from its hooked tail. Soothing smoke rose from incense burners around the bed.

He looked up through the plastic veil at the ceiling of the sphere, lucidly examining the zigzag, black and white inlay of the roof-pattern. With his mind, the wonderful mind that could pace out the measures of unreal space and stay sane in the full light of the immaterium, he considered the overlaid pattern, the interlocking chevrons of ivory and obsidian. The nature of eternity lay in their pattern. He unlocked it, psychically striding beyond his ruined physicality, penetrating the abstract realms of light and dark, the governing switches on which all reality was triggered.

Light interlocked with dark. It pleased him. He knew, as he had always known, that his place lay somehow in the slivered cracks of shadow between the contrasting white and black. He entered this space between, and it embraced him. He understood, as he was sure the Emperor himself did not understand, the miraculous division between the Light of mankind and the Darkness of the foe. It was a distinction so obvious and yet so overlooked. Like any true son of the Imperium of Man, he would fight with all his soul and vigour against the blackness, but he would not do so standing in the harshness of the pure white. There was a shadow between them, a greyness, that was his to inhabit. The Emperor, and his heir Macaroth, were oblivious to the distinction and that was what made them weak. Dravere saw it, and that is why Heldane bent his entire force of will to support the lord general. What did he care if the weapon they hunted for was made by, or polluted by, Chaos? It would still work against the Darkness.

If man was to survive, he must adjust his aspect and enter the shadow. Ninety years as an inquisitor had shown Heldane that much at least. The political and governing instincts of mankind had to shift away from the stale Throne of Earth. The blackness without was too deep, too negative for such complacency.

Despite his weakness, Heldane lazily read the blunt minds of the medics around him, as a man might flick through the pages of open books. He knew they feared him, knew that some found his inhuman form repulsive. One, a medic called Guylat, dared to regard him as an animal, a beast to be treated with caution. Heldane had been happy to work on Guylat's prejudices, and from time to time he would slide into the man's mind anonymously, fire a few of the synapses he found, and send the medic racing to the latrine rooms beyond the sphere with a loose bowel or a choking desire to vomit.

Usable minds. They were Heldane's favourite tools.

He scanned out again, thumbing through blunt intelligences that frankly alarmed him with their simple limits. Two medics were talking softly by the door – out of earshot, they thought, from the patient in the bed. One supposed Heldane to be insane, such was the damage to his brain. The other concurred.

They were afraid of him. How delightful, Heldane chuckled.

He had exercised his mind enough. It was free and working. He could perform his task. He knitted his raking brow and summoned one of the medics. The medic came at once, unsure as to why he was lifting the edge of the plastic tent and approaching Heldane.

'A mirror. I require a mirror,' Heldane said through the larynx augmenters. The man nodded, swept back out of the tent, and returned in a moment with a round surgical mirror.

Heldane took hold of it with his right hand, the only limb that would still function. He dismissed the blunt with a curt thought and the medic went back to his work.

Heldane raised the mirror and looked into it, glimpsing the steepled line of his own skull, the grinning mouth, the bloody wound edges and medical instrumentation. He looked into the mirror.

Creating a pawn was not easy. It involved a complex focusing of pain and a training of response, so that the pawn-mind became as a lock shaped to fit Heldane's psychic key. The process could be done rudely with the mind, but was better effected through surgery and the exquisite use of blades.

Heldane enjoyed his work. Through the correct application of pain and the subtle adjustment of mind response, he could fashion any man into a slave, a psychic puppet through whose ears and eyes he could sense – and through whose limbs he could act.

Heldane used the mirror to summon his pawn. He focused until the face appeared in the mirror, filmy and hazed. The pawn would do his bidding. The pawn would perform. Through the pawn, he would see everything. It was as good as being there himself. As he had promised Dravere, his pawn was with Gaunt now. He sensed everything the pawn could: the wet rock, the swallowing darkness, the exchange of fire.

He could see Gaunt, without his cap and storm-coat, dressed in a short leather jacket, blasting at the foe with his lasgun.

Gaunt.

Heldane reached out and took control of his pawn, enjoyed the rich seam of hatred for Ibram Gaunt that layered through his chosen pawn's mind. That made things so much easier. Before he submitted to death,

Heldane told himself, he would use his pawn to win the day. To win everything.

TWELVE

Rawne threw himself flat as laser fire and barb-shells winnowed down the corridor. He raised his lasgun, hunting for a target. A flat pain, like a migraine headache, darted through his head, disturbing memories of sharp physical pain. In his mind, Rawne saw the beast, the arch-manipulator, the inquisitor, with his hooked blades and micro-surgery drills, leaning over him.

Heldane. The bastard's name had been Heldane. His blades had opened Rawne's body and unshackled his mind. Heldane's venomous, obscene mind had swept into the breach...

He shook his head and felt droplets of sweat flick away. Heldane be damned. He fired off a trio of shots into the darkness of the vault and silently thanked the mad sniper, Larkin, and his shot that had blasted Heldane apart. He had never thanked Larkin personally, of course. A man like him verbally acknowledge a peasant like Mad Larkin?

The infiltration team had all made cover, except for Baru who had lost a knee to a las-round and was fallen in the open, crawling and gasping.

Gaunt bellowed a command down the narrow tunnel and Bragg swept out of cover, thumping sizzling shots from his autocannon in a wide covering spread, which gave Gaunt and Mkoll time to drag Baru into shelter. Domor was still screaming, even as Caffran tried to bind his face wounds from the field kit.

Las-fire whickered along the passage around them, but Rawne feared the barbs more. Even missing or deflecting or ricocheting, they could do more damage. He squeezed off two hopeful shots, breathless for a target. Unease coiled in his mind, a faint, stained darkness that had been there since his torture at the hands of the lean giant, Heldane. He fought it off, but it refused to go away.

Gaunt slid across to Domor, taking the shuddering man's bloody hands in his own.

'Easy, trooper! Easy, friend! It's me, the commissar... I've come all the way from Tanith with you, and I won't leave you to die!'

Domor stopped whimpering, biting on his lip. Gaunt saw that his face was an utter mess. His eyes were ruined and the flesh of his right check hung shredded and loose. Gaunt took the ribbons of bandage from Caffran and strapped the trooper's head back together, winding the tape around his eyes in a tight blindfold. He hissed to Dorden, who was just finishing field-dressing Baru's knee. The medical officer wriggled over under the sporadic fire. Gaunt had stripped Domor's sleeve away from his forearm with a jerking cut of his blade and Dorden quickly sunk a dose of painkiller into the man's bulging wrist veins.

Gaunt had seen death wounds before, and knew that Domor would not live long outside of a properly-equipped infirmary. The eye wounds were too deep, and already rusty smears of blood were seeping through the pale white bindings. Dorden shook his head sadly at Gaunt, and the commissar was glad Domor couldn't see the unspoken verdict.

'You'll make it,' Gaunt told him, 'if I have to carry you myself!'

'Leave me...' Domor moaned.

'Leave the trooper who hijacked the maglev train and led us to our victory battle on Fortis? We won a world with your help, Domor. I'd rather hack off an arm and leave that behind!'

'You're a good man,' Domor said huskily, his breathing shallow, 'for an anroth.'

Gaunt allowed himself a thin smile.

Behind him, Larkin sighted the ancient weapon he had adopted and dropped a faint figure in the darkness with a clean shot.

Fereyd's troopers, supported by Rawne and Mkoll, fired las-rounds in a pulsing rhythm that battered into the unseen foe.

Then it fell suddenly quiet.

Together with one of Fereyd's men, Mkoll, a shadow under his stealth cloak, edged forward. After a moment, he shouted back: 'Clear!'

The party moved on, Caffran supporting the weakening Domor and Dorden helping the limping Baru. At a turn in the corridor, they picked their way between the fallen foe: eight dead humans, emaciated and covered in sores, dressed in transparent plastic body gloves, their faces hidden by snarling bone masks. They were inscribed with symbols: symbols that made their minds hurt; symbols of plague and invention. Gaunt made sure that the dead were stripped of all plasma ammo packs. Rawne slung his lasgun over his shoulder and lifted one of the barb-guns – a long, lance-tube weapon with a skate-like bayonet fixed underneath. He pulled a satchel of barb-rounds off the slack arm of one of the corpses.

Gaunt didn't comment. Right now, anything they could muster to their side was an advantage.

THIRTEEN

The citadel had fallen silent. Smoke, some thin and pale, some boiling and black, vented from the jagged stone facade.

Breathlessly light-headed on painkillers, Colonel Colm Corbec led the first advance down into the steep, rubble-strewn ditch and up into the cliff face of buildings. Silent, almost invisible waves of Tanith warriors crept down after him, picking their way into the ruins, lasguns ready.

Corbec had not sent any signals back to Command. This advance would be as unknown as he could manage. This would be the Ghosts alone, taking what ground they could before crying for help.

They edged through stone, shattered and fused into black bubbles, crushing the ashen remains of the foe underfoot. The feedback of the fence weapons had done greater damage than Corbec could have imagined. He called up Varl's platoon and sent them forward as scouts, using double the number of sweepers.

Corbec turned suddenly, to find Milo standing next to him.

'No tunes now, I'd guess, sir,' the boy said, his Tanith pipes slung safely under his arm.

'Not yet,' Corbec smiled thinly.

'Are you all right, colonel?'

Corbec nodded, noticing for the first time there was the iron tang of blood in his mouth. He swallowed.

'I'm fine...' he said.

FOURTEEN

'What do you make of that, sir?' Trooper Laynem asked, passing the scope to his platoon sergeant, Blane. The seventh platoon of the Ghosts were, as per Gaunt's instructions, hanging back to guard the back slopes of the rise over which the main force were advancing. Blane knew why; the commissar had made it plain. But he hadn't found the right way to tell his men.

He squinted through the scope. Down the valley, massed formations of the Jantine Patricians were advancing up towards them, in fire-teams formed up in box-drill units. It was an attack dispersal. There could be no mistake.

Blane swung back into his bracken-edged foxhole and beckoned his comms officer, Symber. Blane's face was drawn.

'They... they look like they mean to attack us, sergeant,' Laynem said in disbelief. 'Have they got their orders scrambled?'

Blane shook his head. Gaunt had been over this and had seemed quite certain, but still Blane had fought to believe it. Guard assaulting Guard? It was... not something to even think about. He had obeyed the commissar's directive, of course – it had been so quietly passionate and direct – but he still had not understood the enormity of the command. The Jantine were going to attack them. He took the speakerhorn Symber offered.

'Ghosts of the Seventh,' he said simply, 'form into defensive file along the slope and regard the Jantine advance. If they fire upon us, it is not a mistake. It is real. Know that the commissar himself warned me of this. Do not hesitate. I count on you all.'

As if on cue, the first blistering ripple of las-fire raked up over their heads from the Jantine lines.

Blane ordered his men to hold fire. They would wait for range. He swallowed. It was hard to believe. An entire regiment of elite Jantine heavy infantry against his fifty men?

Las-fire cracked close to him. He took the speakerhorn and made Symber select the commissar's own channel.

He paused. The word hung like a cold, heavy marble in his dry mouth until he made himself say it.

'Ghostmaker,' he breathed.

FIFTEEN

Dank, clammy darkness dripped down around them. Gaunt moved his team along through the echoing chambers and caves of wet stone. Caffran led Domor by the hand and one of Fereyd's elite and anonymous troopers assisted the limping Baru.

The place was lifeless except for the cockroaches which swarmed all around them. At first, there had been just one or two of the black-bodied vermin bugs, then hundreds, then thousands. Larkin had taken to stamping on them but gave up when they became too numerous. Now they were everywhere. The darkness all around the infiltration team murmured and shifted with beetles, coating the walls, the floor, the roof. The insistent chattering of the insects susurrated in the gloom, a low, crackling slithering from the shifting blanket of bodies instead of distinct, individual sounds.

Shuddering, the Tanith moved on, finally leaving the mass of beetles behind and heading into galleries that were octagonal in cross section, the walls made of glass blocks fused together. The glass, its surface a dark, crazed patina where the slow passage of time had abraded it, cast back strange translucent phantoms from their failing lights; sometimes sharp reflections, sometimes wispy glows and embers.

Mkoll's sharp eyes saw shapes in the glass, indistinct relics of semi-molten bone set in the vitreous wall like flecks of grit in pearls… or the tan-flies he used to find set in hard, amber nodes of sap while scouting the nalwood forests back home.

Mkoll, a youthful-looking fifty year-old with a wiry frame and a salting of grey in his hair and beard, remembered the forests keenly for a moment. He remembered his wife, dead of canth-fever for twelve years now, and his sons who had timbered on the rivers rather than follow his profession and become woodsmen.

There was something about this place, this place he could never in all his life have imagined himself in all those years ago when his Eiloni still lived, that reminded him of the nal-forests.

Sometime after the First Founding, when the commissar had noted his background from the files and appointed him sergeant of the scouting platoon with Corbec's blessing, he had sat and talked of the nalwood to Gaunt. Commissar Gaunt had remarked to him that the unique shifting forests of Tanith had taught the Ghosts a valuable lesson in navigation. He conjectured that was what made them so sure and able when it came to reconnaissance and covert insertion.

Mkoll had never thought about it much before then, but the suggestion rang true. It had been second nature to him, an instinct thing, to find his way through the shifting trees, locating paths and tracks which came and went as the fibrous evergreens stalked the sun. It had been his life to track the cuchlain herds for pelts and horn, no matter how they used the nal to obscure themselves.

Mkoll was a hunter, utterly attuned to the facts of his environs, utterly aware of how to read solid truth from ephemerally-shifting inconsequence. Since Gaunt had first remarked upon this natural skill, a skill shared by all Tanith but distilled in him and the men of his platoon, he'd prided himself in never failing the task.

Yes, now he considered, there was something down here that reminded him very strongly of lost Tanith.

He signalled a halt. The crusade staff trooper whom Tactician Wheyland – or Fereyd, as the commissar called him – had sent forward to accompany him glanced around. Probably asking an unvoiced question, but any expression was hidden by the reflective visor of his red and black armour. Mkoll inherently mistrusted the tactician and his men. There was just something about them. He disliked any man who hid his face and even when Wheyland had revealed himself, Mkoll had found little to trust there. In his imagination he heard Eiloni tut-tutting, scolding him for being a loner, slow to trust.

He blinked the memory of his wife away. He knew he was right. These elite bodyguard troops were certainly skilled; the trooper had moved along with him as silently and assuredly as the best in his platoon. But there was just something, like there was something about this place.

Gaunt moved up to join the head of the advance.

'Mkoll?' he asked, ignoring Wheyland's trooper, who was standing stiffly to attention nearby.

'Something's wrong here,' Mkoll said. He pointed left and right with a gesture. 'The topography is, well, unreliable.'

Gaunt frowned. 'Explain?'

Mkoll shrugged. Gaunt had made him privy to the unlocked data back on the *Absalom*, and Mkoll had studied and restudied the schematics carefully. He had felt privileged to be taken that close to the commissar's private burden.

'It's all wrong, sir. We're still on the right tack, and I'll be fethed if I don't get you there – but this is different.'

'To the map I showed you?'

'Yes... And worse, to the way it was five minutes ago. The structure is static enough,' Mkoll slapped the glass-brick wall as emphasis, 'but it's like direction is altering indistinctly. Something is affecting the left and right, the up and down...'

'I've noticed nothing,' Wheyland's trooper interrupted bluntly. 'We should proceed. There is nothing wrong.'

Gaunt and Mkoll both shot him a flat look.

'Perhaps it's time I saw your map,' a voice said from behind. Tactician Wheyland had approached, smiling gently. 'And your data. We were... interrupted before.'

Gaunt felt a sudden hesitation. It was peculiar. He would trust Fereyd to the Eye of Terror and back, and he had shown the data to chosen men like Mkoll. But something was making him hold back.

'Ibram? We're in this together, aren't we?' Fereyd asked.

'Of course,' Gaunt said, pulling out the slate and drawing Fereyd aside. What in the Emperor's name was he thinking? This was Fereyd. Fereyd! Mkoll was right; there was something down here, something that was even affecting his judgement.

Mkoll stood back, waiting. He eyed the Crusade trooper at his side. 'I don't even know your name,' he said at last. 'I'm called Mkoll.'

'Cluthe, sergeant, Tactical Counsel war staff.'

They nodded to each other. Can't show me your fething face even now, Mkoll thought.

Back down the gallery, Domor was whimpering gently and Dorden was inspecting his eyes again. Larkin hunted the shadows with his gun-muzzle.

Rawne was staring into the glass blocks of the wall with a hard-set face. 'Those are bones in there,' he said. 'Feth, what manner of carnage melted bones into glass so it could be made into slabs for this place?'

'What manner and how long ago?' Dorden returned, rewinding Domor's gauze.

'Bones?' Bragg asked, looking closer at what Rawne had indicated. He shuddered. 'Feth this place for a bundle of nal-sticks!'

Behind them, Caffran hissed for quiet. He had been carrying the team's compact vox-set ever since Domor had been injured, and had plugged the wire of his micro-bead earpiece into it to monitor the traffic. The set was nothing like as powerful as the heavy vox-casters carried by platoon comm-officers like Raglon and Mkann, and its limited range was stunted further by the depth of the rock they were under. But there was a signal: intermittent and on a repeating automatic vox-burst. The identifier was Tanith, and the platoon series code that of the Seventh. Blane's men.

'What is it, Caff?' Larkin asked, his eyes sharp.

'Trooper Caffran?' Major Rawne questioned.

Caffran pushed past them both and hurried up the tunnel to where Gaunt stood with the Imperial tactician.

As he approached, he saw Wheyland gazing at the lit displays of Gaunt's data-slate, his eyes wide.

'This is... unbelievable!' Fereyd breathed. 'Everything we hoped for!'

Gaunt shot a sharp glance at him. 'Hoped for?'

'You know what I mean, Bram. Throne! That something like this could still exist... that it could be so close. We were right to chase this without hesitation. Dravere cannot be allowed to gain control of... of this.'

Fereyd paused, reviewing the data again, and looked back at the commissar. 'This makes all the work, all the loss, all the effort... worthwhile. To know there really was a prize here worth fighting for. This proves we're not wasting our time or jumping at ghosts – no offence to the present company.' He said this with a diplomatic smile at Caffran as the trooper edged up closer.

Watching the tactical officer, Mkoll stiffened. Was it the fething place again, screwing with his mind? Or was there something about this grand Imperial tactician that even Gaunt hadn't noticed?

'Caffran?' Gaunt said, turning to his make-do vox-officer.

Caffran handed him the foil from the field-caster that he had just printed out. 'A signal from Sergeant Blane, sir. Very indistinct, very chopped. Took me a while to get it.'

'It says "Ghostmaker", sir.'

Gaunt screwed his eyes shut for a moment.

'Bram?'

'It's nothing, Fereyd,' Gaunt said to his old friend. 'Just what I was expecting and hoped wouldn't come to pass. Dravere is making his counter-move.'

Gaunt turned to Caffran. 'Can we get a signal out?' he asked, nodding to the voxer on its canvas sling over Caffran's shoulder.

'We can try fething hard and repeatedly,' responded Caffran, and Gaunt and Mkoll both grinned. Caffran had borrowed the line from comms-officer Raglon, who had always used that retort when the channels were particularly bad.

Gaunt handed Caffran a pre-prepared message foil. A glance showed Caffran it wasn't in Tanith battle-tongue, or Imperial Guard Central Cipher either.

He couldn't read it, but he knew it was coded in Vitrian combat-cant.

Caffran fed the foil into the vox-set, let the machine read it and assemble it and then flicked the 'send' switch, marked by a glowing rune at the edge of the set's compact fascia.

'It's gone.'

'Repeat every three minutes, Caffran. And watch for an acknowledgement.'

Gaunt turned back to Fereyd. He took the data-slate map back from him smartly.

'We advance,' he told the Imperial tactician. 'Tell your men,' he nodded at the Crusade troopers, 'to follow every instruction my scout gives, without question.'

With Mkoll in the front, the raiding party moved on.

A long way behind, back down the team, Major Rawne shuddered. The image of the monster Heldane had just flickered across his mind again. He felt the seeping blackness of Heldane's touch and felt his surly consciousness wince.

Get out! His thoughts shrilled in his head. Get out!

SIXTEEN

It was, Sergeant Blane decided, ironic.

The defence was as epic as any hallowed story of the Guard. Fifty men gainsaying the massed assault of almost a thousand. But no one would ever know. This story, of Guard against Guard, was too unpalatable for stories. The greatest act of the Tanith First and Only would be a record hushed up and unspoken of, even by High Command.

The Jantine units, supported by light artillery and heavy weapons in the valley depths, swung up around the rise Blane's men commanded in a double curl, like the arms of a throat-torc, extending overlapping fans of las-fire in disciplined, double-burst shots. The rain of shots, nearly fifteen hundred every twenty seconds, spat over the Ghosts' heads or thumped into the sloping soil, puffing up clods of smoky dust and igniting numerous brush fires through the cloaking bracken.

Sergeant Blane watched them from cover through his scope, his flesh prickling as he saw the horribly assured way they covered the ground and made advance. The warrior-caste of Jant were heavy troops, their silver and purple combat armour made for assault, rather than speed or stealth. They were storm troopers, not skirmishers; the Tanith were the light, agile, stealthy ones. But for all that, the drilled brilliance of the Jantine was frightening. They used every ounce of skill and every stitch of cover to bring the long claw of their attack up and around to throttle the Ghosts' seventh platoon.

Blane had fought the temptation to return fire when the Jantine first addressed them. They had nothing to match the range of the Jantine heavy weapons and Blane told himself that the las-fire fusillade was as much a psychological threat as anything.

His fifty men were deployed along the ridge line in a straggled stitch of natural foxholes that the Ghosts had augmented with entrenching tools and sacking made of stealth cloaks and sleeping rolls, lashed into bags and filled with dust and soil. Blane made his command instructions clear: fix blades, set weapons to single shot, hold fire and wait for his signal.

For the first ten minutes, their line was silent as las-fire crackled up at them and the air sifted with white smoke plumes and drifting dust. Light calibre field shells fluttered down, along with a few rocket-propelled grenades, most falling way short and creating new foxholes on the slope. Blane first thought they were aiming astray until he saw the pattern. The field guns were digging cover-holes and craters in the flank of the hillside for the Jantine infantry to advance into. Already, to his west, Jantine squads had crossed from their advance and dug in to a line of fresh shell-holes a hundred metres short of the Ghosts' line. Immediately, the field guns adjusted their range and began digging the next line for advance.

Blane cursed the Jantine perfection. Commissar Gaunt had always said there were two foes most to be feared, the utterly feral and the utterly intelligent, and of the pair, the second were the worst. The Jantine were schooled and educated men who excelled at the intricacies of war. They were justly feared. Blane had, in fact, heard stories of the Jantine Patricians even before he had entered the Guard. He could hear them singing now, the long, languid, low hymn of victory, harmonised by nearly a thousand rich male voices, beautiful, oppressive... demoralising. He shuddered.

'That damn singing,' Trooper Coline hissed beside him.

Blane agreed but said nothing. The first las-rounds were now crossing overhead and if the Jantine guns were reaching them it meant one reassuring fact: the Jantine were in range.

Blane tapped his microbead link, selecting the open command channel. He spoke in Tanith battle-cant: 'Select targets carefully. Not a wasted shot now. Fire at will.'

The Ghosts opened fire. Streams of single-shot cover fire whipped down from their hidden positions into the advancing fans of the Jantine. In the first salvo alone, Blane saw ten or more of the Jantine jerk and fall. Their rate of fire increased. The wave punctured the Jantine ranks in three dozen places and made the incoming rain of fire hesitate and stutter.

The infantry duel began: two lines of dug-in troopers answering each other volley for volley up and down a steeply angled and thickly covered slope. The very air became warm and electric-dry with the ozone stench of las-fire. It was evenly pitched, with the Tanith enjoying the greater angle of coverage and the greater protection the hill afforded. But, unlike the Jantine, they were not resupplied every minute by lines of reinforcement.

Even firing off a well-placed round every six seconds, and scoring a kill one out of four shots, Blane felt they were helpless. They could not retreat, neither could they advance in a charge to use the ground to their advantage. Defeat one way, overwhelming death the other; the Ghosts could do nothing but hold their line and fight to the last.

The Jantine had more options, but the one they decided to use amazed Blane. After a full thirty minutes of fire exchange, the Patricians charged. En masse. Close on a thousand heavy troopers, bayonets fixed to muzzle-clips, rose as one from the bracken-choked foxholes and stormed up the slope towards his platoon.

It was an astonishing decision. Blane gasped and his first thought was that madness had gripped the Jantine command. A sort of madness had, but one that would surely win the day. The fifty guns of the Ghosts had more targets then they could pick. Dozens, hundreds of Jantine never made it up the slope, their twitching thrashing or limp bodies collapsing brokenly into the ochre undergrowth. But there was no way Blane's men could cut them all down before they reached the hill line.

'Blood of the Emperor!' spat Blane as he understood the tactic: superior numbers, total loyalty and an unquenchable thirst for victory. The Jantine commander had deployed his troops as expendable, using their sheer weight to soak up the Ghosts' fire and overwhelm them.

Three hundred Jantine Patricians were dead before the charge made it into Tanith lines. Dead to the Tanith guns, the slope of the hill, the angles of death. But that still left close on seven hundred of them to meet head on in screaming waves at the ditch line of the slit-trenches.

* * *

Singing the ancient war-hymn of Jant Normanidus, the Alto Credo, Major Brochuss led the assault over the Tanith Ghosts' paltry defence line. A las-round punched through his cloth-armoured sleeve and scorched the flesh of one arm. He swung around, double-blasting the Ghost before him as teams of his soldiery came in behind him.

The Ghosts were nothing... and to tear into them like this was a joy that exorcised Brochuss's own ghosts, ghosts which had been with him one way or another since the humiliation on Khedd, and which had been further reinforced on Fortis Binary and Pyrites. Anger, battle-joy, lust, rage – they thrilled through the powerful body of the Jantine Patrician.

The tempered steel of his bayonet slashed left and right, impaling and killing. Twice he had to fire his rifle point-blank to loosen a corpse stuck on his blade.

The nobility of his upbringing made him recognise the courage and fighting skill of the spidery black-clad men they crushed in this trench. They fought to the last, and with great skill. But they were light troops, dressed in thin fabrics, utterly unmatching the physical strength and resilience of his hard-armoured Jantine. His men had the discipline of the military academies of Jant in their blood, the fierce will to win. That was what made them Patricians, what made them as feared by others of the Imperial Guard as the Guards feared the Adeptus Astartes.

If Brochuss thought of the cost, which had earned them the route to the top of the hill, it was only in terms of the victory hymns they would sing at the mass funerals. If it cost one or a thousand, victory was still victory – and a punishment victory over traitor scum like this was the most cherished of all. The Ghosts were vermin to be exterminated. Colonel Flense had been right to give the order to charge, even though he had seemed strangely pale and horrified when he had given it.

Victory was theirs.

Sergeant Blane caught the first Jantine over the lip of the ditch in the belly with his bayonet and threw him over his head as he rolled. The man screamed as he died. A second bayoneted Blane's left thigh as he followed in and the sergeant bellowed in pain, swinging his las-gun so that the blade cut open the man's throat under the armour of the helmet. Then Blane fired a single shot point-blank into the writhing man's face.

Coline shot two Jantine on the lip of the line and then fell under a hammer-blow of fixed blades. Fighting was now thick, face to face, close-quarter. Symber shot three of Coline's killers before a loose las-shot took the top of his head off and dropped his twitching body into a narrow ditch already blocked by a dozen dead.

Killing another Jantine with a combination of bayonet thrust and rifle butt swipe, Blane saw the vox-caster spin from Symber's dying grasp, and wished he had the time to grab it and send a signal to Gaunt or Corbec. But the top of the ridge was a seething mass of men, stabbing, striking, firing, dying, and there was no pace to give and no moment to spare. This was the heat of battle, white heat, hate heat, as it is often spoken of by soldiers but seldom seen.

Blane shot another Patrician dead through the chest at a range of two metres and then swung his blade around into the chin of another that lunged at him. Something hot and hard nudged him from behind. He looked down and saw the point of a Jantine bayonet pushing out through his chest, blood gouting around its steel sheen.

Snarling with glee, Major Brochuss fired his lasgun and let the shot blow the stumbling Ghost off his blade. Sergeant Blane fell on his face without a murmur.

SEVENTEEN

It was as hot as Milo had ever known it.

The main column of the Ghosts was slowly advancing through the tumbled stones of the necropolis, and had emerged into a long valley of ancient colonnades which rose on either hand in sun-blocking shadows. The valley, a natural rift in the mountain on either side of which the primitive architects had built towering formations of alcoves, was nearly eight kilometres long, and its floor, half a kilometre wide, was treacherous with the slumped stonework and rockfalls cast down from the high structures by slow time.

The energetic feedback of the defence grid had exploded ruinously in here as well and the fallen rocks, tarry-black and primeval, had soaked it up and were now radiating it out again. It was past sixty degrees down here, and dry-hot. Sweat streaked every Tanith man as he crept forward. Their black fatigues were heavy with damp and none except the scouts still wore cloaks.

Trooper Desta, advancing alongside Milo, hawked and spat at the gritty black flank of a nearby slab and tutted as his spittle fizzled and fried into evaporated nothingness.

Milo looked up. The gash of sky above the rift sides was pale and blue, and bespoke a fair summer's day. Down here, the long shadows and rocky depth suggested a cool shelter. But the heat was overwhelming, worse than the jungle miasma of the tropical calderas on Caligula, worse than the humid reaches of Voltis, worse than anything he had ever known, even the parching hot-season of high summer at Tanith Magna.

The radiating rocks glowed in his mind, aching their way into his drying bones and sinuses. He longed for moisture. He teased himself with memories of Pyrites, where the stabbing wet-cold of the outer city reaches had seemed so painful. Would he was there now. He took out his water flask and sucked down a long slug of stale, blood-warm water.

A half-shadow fell across him. Colonel Corbec stayed his hand.

'Not so fast. We need to ration in this heat and if you take it down too fast you'll cramp and vomit. And sweat it out all the faster.'

Milo nodded, clasping his bottle. He could see how pale and drawn Corbec had become, his flesh pallid and wet in the deep shadows of the rift's belly.

But there was more. More than the others were suffering. Pain.

'You're wounded, aren't you, sir?'

Corbec glanced at Milo and shook his head.

'I'm fine and bluff, lad. Yes, fine and bluff.' Corbec laughed, but there was no strength in his voice. Milo clearly saw the puncture rip in the side of Corbec's tunic which the colonel tried to hide.

Black fabric showed little, but Milo was sure that the wet patches on Corbec's fatigues were not sweat, unlike the patches on the other men.

A cry came back down the rift from the scout units and a moment later something creaked on the wind.

Corbec howled an order and the Ghosts fanned out between the sweltering rock, rock that afforded them cover but which they dare not touch. The enemy was counter-attacking.

They came at them down the valley, some on foot, most in the air. Dozens of small, missile-shaped airships, garish and fiercely-bright in colour and adorned with the grotesque symbols of Chaos, powered down the rift towards them, propellers thumping in their diesel-smoking nacelles, their belly-slung baskets, gondolas and platforms filled with armed warriors of Chaos. The swarm of airships drifted down across the Ghosts, raking the ground with fire.

Now it was all or nothing.

EIGHTEEN

Dravere, his face angry and hollow-eyed, pushed aside the medics in the isolation sphere and yanked apart the plastic drapes veiling Inquisitor Heldane's cot. The inquisitor gazed up at him with fathomlessly calm eyes from beneath the clamped medical support devices covering him.

'Hechtor?'

Dravere flung a data-slate on the cot. The inquisitor's one good hand carefully put down the small mirror he had been holding and took up the slate, keying the data-flow with his long-nailed thumb.

'Madness!' Dravere spat. 'The Jantine have taken the rise and exterminated Gaunt's rearguard, but Flense reports that the main Tanith unit has actually advanced into Target Primaris. What by the Throne do we do now? We're losing more men to our own than to the foe, and I still require victory here! I'll not face Macaroth for this!'

Heldane studied the slate's information. 'Other regiments are moving in. The Mordian here, the Vitrians... they're close too. Let Gaunt's Ghosts lead the assault on the Target as they have begun. Sacrifice them to open a wedge. Move the Patricians in behind to consolidate this and finish off the Ghosts. Your main forces should be ready to advance after them by then.'

Dravere took a deep breath. Tactically, the advice was sound. There was still a good opportunity to silence the Ghosts without witnesses and still effect a victory. 'What of Gaunt?'

Heldane took up his mirror again and gazed into it. 'He progresses well. My pawn is still at his side, primed to strike when I command it. Patience, Hechtor. We play games within games, and all are subservient to the intricate processes of war.'

He fell silent, resolving images in the distances of the mirror invisible to the lord general.

Dravere turned away. The inquisitor was still useful to him, but as soon as that usefulness ended he would not hesitate to remove him.

Gazing into the mirror, Heldane absently recognised the malicious thought in Dravere's blunt intellect. Dravere utterly misunderstood his place in the drama. He thought himself a leader, a manipulator, a commander. But in truth, he was nothing more than another pawn – and just as expendable.

NINETEEN

Colonel Flense led the Jantine Patricians down the great outer ditch and into the outskirts of the necropolis ruins, passing through the exploded steatite fragments and blackened corpses left by Corbec's assault. Distantly, through the archways and stone channels they could hear gunfire. The Ghosts had plainly met more opposition inside.

The afternoon was lengthening, the paling sky striated with lingering bands of smoke from the fighting. Flense had six hundred and twelve men left, forty of that number so seriously injured they had been retreated to the field hospitals far back at the deployment fields. Fifty Tanith, fighting to the last, had taken over a third of his regiment.

He felt bitterness so great that it all but consumed him. His hatred of Ibram Gaunt, and the rivalry with the Tanith First that it had bred, had been a burning frustration. Now when they actually had the chance to face them on the field, the Tanith skirmishers had fought above their weight and scored a huge victory, even in defeat.

He cared little now what happened. The other Ghosts could live or die. All he wanted was one thing: Gaunt. He sent a Magenta level communiqué to Dravere, expressing his simple wish.

The reply surprised and delighted him. Dravere instructed Flense to place his main force under Brochuss's direct command to continue the advance into the Target Primaris. The battle orders were to neutralise the Ghosts and then prosecute a direct assault on the enemy itself. With luck, the Tanith would be crushed between the Jantine and the forces of Chaos.

But for Flense there was a separate order. Dravere had learned from the Inquisitor Heldane that Gaunt was personally leading an insertion team into the city from below. The entry point, a shaft beneath an outcrop of stones on the hillside, was identified and a route outlined. On Dravere's personal orders, Flense was to lead a fire-team in after the commissar and destroy him.

Flense quietly conveyed the directive to Brochuss as they stood watching the men advance in three file-lines up into the vast ancient necropolis. Brochuss was swollen with pride at this command opportunity. The big man turned to face his colonel with a battle-light firing his eyes. He drew off his glove and held out his hand to Flense. The colonel removed his own gauntlet and they shook, the thumb-clasping grip of brotherhood learned in the honour schools of Jant Normanidus.

'Advance with hope, fight with luck, win with honour, Brochuss,' Flense said.

'Sheath your blade well, colonel,' his second replied.

Flense turned, pulling his glove back on and tapping his micro-bead. 'Troopers Herek, Stigand, Unjou, Avranche and Ebzan report to the colonel. Bring climbing rope.'

Flense took a lasrifle from one of the dead, blessed it silently to assuage the soul of its previous owner, and checked the ammo clips. Brochuss had two of his platoon gather spare lamp packs from the passing men. The rearguard platoon watched over Flense and his team as they made ready and descended into the shaft under the stones.

In the isolation sphere of the command globe, Heldane sensed this manoeuvre. He hadn't been inside the fool Flense's mind for long enough to turn him, but he had left his mark there, and through that psychic window he could sense and feel so much already. Above all, he could feel Flense's bitter hatred.

So, Dravere was trying a ploy of his own, playing his own man Flense into the intrigue, anxious to secure his own leverage. Aching with dull pain, Heldane knew he should be angry with the lord general. But there was no time, and he hadn't the willpower to spare for such luxuries. He would accommodate Dravere's counter-ploy, and appropriate what elements of it he could use for his own devices. For mankind, for the grand scheme at hand, he would serve and manipulate and win the Vermilion treasure hidden beneath Target Primaris. Then, and only then, he would allow himself to die.

He swallowed his pain, blanked out the soft embrace of death. The pain was useful in one sense; just as it allowed him to co-opt the minds of blunt tools, so it gave his own mind focus. He could dwell upon his own deep agony and drive it on like a psychic scalpel to slit open the reserve of his pawn and make him function more ably.

He looked at the mirror again, the life-support machines around him thumping and wheezing. He saw how his hand trembled, and killed the shake with a stab of concentration.

He saw into the small mind of his pawn again, sensed the close, cold, airless space of the tunnels he moved through, far beneath the tumbling steatite of the necropolis. He branched out with his thoughts, seeing and feeling his way into the spaces ahead of his pawn. There was warmth there, intellect, pulsing blood.

Heldane tensed, and sent a jolt of warning to his pawn: ambush ahead!

TWENTY

They had reached a long, low cistern of rock, pale-blue and glassy, which branched off ahead in four directions. Oily black water trickled and pooled down the centre of the sloping floor-space.

Rawne felt himself tense and falter. He reached out a hand to support himself against the gritty wall as a stabbing pain entered his head and clung like a great arachnid, biting into the bones of his face. His vision doubled, then swirled.

It was like a warning... warning him that something ahead was...

The major screeched an inarticulate sound that made the others turn or drop in surprise. The noise had barely begun to echo back down the cistern when Wheyland was firing, raking the darkness ahead with his lasgun, bellowing deployment orders.

A volley of barbs and las-blasts spat back at them.

Gaunt dropped against a slumped rock as gunfire cracked and fizzed against the glassy walls over him. They almost walked into that! If it hadn't been for Rawne's warning and Fereyd's rapid reaction... But how had Rawne known? He was well back in the file. How could he have seen anything that Mkoll's sharp eyes, right at the front, had missed?

Fereyd was calling the shots at the moment but Gaunt didn't resent the abuse of command. He trusted his friend's tactical instinct and Fereyd was in a better position and line of sight to direct the tunnel fight. Gaunt clicked off his lamp pack to stop himself becoming a target and then swung his lasrifle up to sight and fire. Mkoll, Caffran, Baru and the tactician's troopers were sustaining fire from their own weapons, and Larkin was using his exotic rifle to cover Bragg while he moved the hefty auto-cannon up into a position to fire. Dorden cowered with Domor.

Rawne bellied forward and fitted a barbed round to his stolen weapon. He rose, fingers feeling their way around the unfamiliar trigger grip, and blasted a buzzing barb up the throat of the passage. There was a *crump* and a scream. Rawne quickly reloaded and fired again, his shot snaking like a slow, heavy bee between the darting light-jags of the other men's lasguns.

Larkin's rifle fired repeatedly with its curious clap-blast double sound. Then Bragg opened up, shuddering the entire chamber with his heavy, rapid blasts. The close air was suddenly thick with cordite smoke and spent fycelene.

'Cease fire! Cease!' Gaunt yelled with a downward snap of his hand. Silence fell.

Heartbeats pounded for ten seconds, twenty, almost a minute, and then the charge came. The enemy swarmed down into the chamber, flooding out of two of the tunnel forks ahead.

Gaunt's men waited, disciplined to know without order how long to pause. Then they opened up again: Rawne's barb-gun, Bragg's auto-cannon, Larkin's carbine, the lasguns of Gaunt, Fereyd, Mkoll, Baru, Caffran, and the three Crusade bodyguards. The cistern boxed the target for them. In ten seconds there were almost thirty dead foe bunched and crumpled in the narrow chamber, their bodies impeding the advance of those behind, making them easier targets.

Gaunt knelt in concealment, firing his lasgun over a steatite block with the drilled track-sight fire readdress pattern which he had trained into his men. He expected it of them and knew they expected no less in return. They were slaughtering the enemy, every carefully placed shot exploding through plastic body suits and masked visors. But there was no slowing of the tide. Gaunt began to wonder what would run

out first: the flow of enemy, his team's ammo or airspace in the cistern
not filled with dead flesh.

TWENTY-ONE

They emerged from the stifling shadows of the necropolis arches and
into a vast interior valley of baking heat and warmth-radiating rock.
Brochuss and his men blinked in the light, eyes watering at the intense
heat. The major snapped orders left and right, bringing his men up and
thinning the file, extending in a wide front between the jumbled mon-
oliths and splintered boulders. He kept as many of his soldiers in the
sweeping overhanging shadows of the valley sides as he could.

Ahead, no more than two kilometres away, a great combat was taking place. Brochuss could see the las-fire flashing over and between
the rocky outcrops of the valley basin, and the boiling smoke plumes
of a pitched infantry battle were rising up into the pale light above the
valley. He could hear laser blasts, the rasp of meltas, the occasional
fizz of rockets, and knew that Colonel Corbec's despicable Ghosts had
engaged ahead. There were other sounds too: the whirr of motors, the
buzz of barbs, the chatter of exotic repeater cannons, and bellows and
screams of men, a long, backwash of noise that ululated up and down
the sound-box of the valley.

Brochuss tapped his micro-bead link. 'A tricky play, my brave boys.
We come upon the Tanith from the rear to crush them. But defend
against the vermin they are engaging. Kill the Ghosts so we get to face
the enemy ourselves. Face them and carry back the glory of victory to
the ancestral towers of Jant Prime! Normanidus excelsius!'

Six hundred voices answered in a ripple of approval, uttering the
syllables of the devotional creed, and the war hymn began spontaneously, echoing like the sonorous swell of an Ecclesiarchy litany from
the rock faces around and above them, as if from the polished basalt
of a great cathedral.

Most of the Patricians had raised their blast-cowls because of the
heat, but now they snapped the visors back down in place, covering
their faces with the diamond eye-slit visages of war. Their battle hymn
moved to the channels of their micro-beads, resounding in the ears of
every man present.

Brochuss slid down his own blast-cowl so that the hymn swam in
his earpiece and around the close, hot-metal confines of his battledress helmet. He turned to Trooper Pharant at his side and unslung his
lasgun. Wordlessly, Pharant exchanged his heavy stubber and ammunition webbing for his commander's rifle. He nodded solemnly at the

honour; the commander would carry his heavy weapon into combat at the head of the Patricians, the Emperor's Chosen.

Brochuss arranged the heavy webbing around his waist and shoulders with deft assistance from Pharant, settling the weighty pouches with their drum-ammo feeders against his back and thighs. Then he braced the huge stubber in his gloved fists, right hand around the trigger grip, the skeleton stock under his right armpit, his left hand holding the lateral brace so that he could sweep the barrel freely. His right thumb hit the switch that cycled the ammo-advance. The belt feed chattered fat, ugly cartridges into place and the water-cooled barrel began to steam and hiss gently.

Brochuss had advanced to the head of his phalanx when one of his rearguard voxed directly to him. 'Troop units! Inbound to our rear!'

Brochuss turned. At first he saw nothing, then he detected faint movement against the milky-blue and charred blocks of the archway curtain behind them. Soldiers were coming through in their wake. Hundreds of them, almost invisible in the treacherous side-light of the valley. The body-armour they wore was reflective and shimmering. The Vitrians.

Brochuss smiled under his blast-cowl and prepared to signal the Vitrian commander. With the support of the Vitrian Dragoons, they could–

Las-fire erupted along the rear line of his regiment.

Colonel Zoren led his men directly down onto the exposed and straggling line of the Jantine Patricians. They were upwards of six hundred in number and the Vitrians only four hundred, but he had them on the turn.

Gaunt's message had been as per their agreement, though it was still the worst, most devastating message he had received in sixteen years as a fighting man. Their mutual enemies had shown their hands and now the success of the venture depended upon his loyalty. To Colonel-Commissar Gaunt. To the man called Fereyd, among other things. To the Emperor.

It went against all his schooling as an Imperial Guardsman, all his nature. It went against the intricate teachings of the Byhata. But still, the Byhata said there was honour in friendship, and friendship in valour. Loyalty and honour, the twinned fundamental aspects of the *Vitrian Art of War*.

Let Dravere have him shot, him and all four hundred of his men. This was not insubordination, nor was it insurrection. Gaunt had shown the colonel what was at stake. He had shown him the greater levels of loyalty and honour at stake on Menazoid Epsilon. He had been truer

to the Emperor and truer to the teachings of the Byhata than Dravere
could ever have been.

In a triple arrowhead formation, almost invisible in their glass armour,
the Vitrian Dragoons punched into the hindquarters of Brochuss's
extended advance line; a tight, dense triple wedge where the Patricians were loose and extended. The Jantine had formed a lateral file to
embrace the enemy, utterly useless for countering a rearguard sweep.
So it said in the Byhata: book six, segment thirty-one, page four hundred and six.

The Patricians had greater strength, but their line was convex where
it should have been concave. Zoren's men tore them apart. Zoren had
ordered his men to set lasweapons for maximum discharge. He hoped
Colonel-Commissar Gaunt would forgive the extravagance, but the Jantine heavy troops wore notoriously thick armour.

The First Regiment of the Jantine Patricians, the so-called Emperor's
Chosen, the Imperial Guard elite, was destroyed that late afternoon
in the valley inside the necropolis of the Target Primaris. The noble
forces of the Vitrian Dragoon's Third, years later to be decorated and
celebrated as one of the foremost Guard armies, took on their superior numbers and vanquished them in a pitched battle that lasted
twenty-eight minutes and relied for the most part on tactical discretion.

Major Brochuss denied the Vitrians for as long as he was able. Screaming in outrage and despair, he smashed back through his own ranks to
confront the Vitrians with Pharant's massive autocannon. It was in no
way the death he had foreseen for himself, nor the death of his celebrated company.

He bellowed at his men, admonishing them for dying, kicking at
corpses as they fell around him in a raging despair to get them to stand
up again. In the end, Brochuss was overwhelmed by a stinging wash
of anger that having come so far, fought so hard, he and his Patricians
would be cheated.

Cheated of everything they deserved. Cheated of glory by this inglo-
rious end. Cheated of life by lesser, weaker men who nevertheless had
the resolve to fight courageously for what they believed in.

He was amongst the last to die, as the last few shells clattered out
of his ammo drums, raining into the Vitrian advance as he squeezed
the trigger of the smoking, hissing stubber on full rapid. Brochuss personally killed forty-four Vitrian Dragoons in the course of the Jantine
First's last stand. His autocannon was close to overheating when he
was killed by a Vitrian sergeant called Zogat.

His armoured torso pulverised by Zogat's marksmanship, Brochuss toppled into the flecked mica sand of the valley floor, and his name, bearing, manner and being was utterly extinguished from the Imperial Record.

TWENTY-TWO

Then Baru died. The filthy barbed round smelted into the rock-face behind him and ribboned him with its lethal backwash of shrapnel. He didn't even have time to scream.

From his cover, seeing the death and regretting it desperately, Gaunt slid around and set his lasgun to full auto, bombarding the torrent of foe with a vivid cascade of phosphorescent bolts. He heard Rawne scream something unintelligible.

Baru, one of his finest, as good a scout and stealther as Mkoll, pride of the Tanith. Pulling back into cover to exchange ammo clips, Gaunt glanced back at the wet ruin that had been his favoured scout. Claws of misery dug into him. For the first time since Khedd, the commissar tasted the acrid futility of war. A soldier dies, and it is the responsibility of his commander to rise above the loss and focus. But Baru: sharp, witty Baru, a favourite of the men, the clown and joker, the invisible stealther, the truest of true. Gaunt found he could not look at the corpse, at the torn mess that had once been a man he called friend and whom he trusted beyond simple trust.

Around him, and he was oblivious to it, the other Guard soldiers blasted into the ranks of the enemy. Abruptly, as if turned off like a tap, the flow of charging cultists faltered and stopped. Larkin continued to pop away with his long-snouted carbine, and Rawne sent round after round of barb-heads into the dark. Then silence, darkness, except for the fizzle of ignited clothing and the seep of blood.

Fereyd's voice lifted over them, urgent and strong, 'They're done! Advance!'

He's too eager, thought Gaunt, too eager... and I'm the commander here. He rose from cover, seeing the other troopers scrambling up to follow Fereyd. 'Hold!' he barked.

They all turned to face him, Fereyd blinking in confusion.

'We do this my way or not at all,' Gaunt said sternly, crossing to Baru's remains. He knelt over them, plucking the Tanith silver icon up and over his shirt collar, dangling it on the neck chain. In low words, echoed by Dorden, Larkin and Mkoll, he pronounced the funeral rites of the Tanith, one of the first things Milo had taught him. Rawne, Bragg and Caffran lowered their heads. Domor slumped in uneasy silence.

Gaunt stood from the corpse and tucked the chain-hooked charm away. He looked at Fereyd. The Imperial tactician had marshalled his men in a solemn honour guard, heads steepled low, behind the Tanith.

'A good man, Bram; a true loss,' Fereyd said with import.

'You'll never know,' Gaunt said, snatching up his lasgun in a sudden turn and advancing into the thicket of enemy dead.

He turned. 'Mkoll! With me! We'll advance together!'

Mkoll hustled up to join him.

'Fereyd, have your men watch our backs,' Gaunt said.

Fereyd nodded his agreement and pulled his troopers back into the van of the advance. Now it went Gaunt and Mkoll, Bragg, Rawne and Larkin, Dorden with Domor, Caffran, Fereyd and his bodyguard.

They trod carefully over and between the fallen bodies of the foe and found the tunnel dipped steeply into a wider place. Light, like it was being emitted from the belly of a glowing insect, shone from the gloom ahead, outlining an arched doorway. They advanced, weapons ready, until they stood in its shadows.

'We're there,' Mkoll said with finality.

Gaunt slipped his data-slate out of his pocket and thought to consult his portable geo-compass, but Mkoll's instinct was far more reliable than the little purring dial. The commissar looked at the slate, winding the decoded information across the little plate with a touch of the thumb wheel.

'The map calls this the Edicule – a shrine, a resting place. It's the focus of the entire necropolis.'

'And it's where we'll find this... thing?' Mkoll asked darkly.

Gaunt nodded, and took a step into the lit archway. Beyond the crumbling black granite of the arch, a great vault stretched away, floor, walls and roof all fashioned from opalescent stone lit up by some unearthly green glow. Gaunt blinked, accustoming his eyes to the lambent sheen. Mkoll edged in behind him, then Rawne. Gaunt noticed how their breaths were steaming in the air. It was many degrees colder in the vault, the atmosphere damp and heavy. Gaunt clicked off his now redundant lamp pack.

'It looks empty,' Major Rawne said, looking about them. They all heard how small and muffled his voice sounded, distorted by the strange atmospherics of the room. Gaunt gestured at the far end wall, sixty metres away, where the thin scribing of a doorway was marked on the stone wall. A great rectangular door or doors, maybe fifteen metres high, set flush into the wall itself.

'This is the outer approach chamber. The Edicule itself is beyond those doors.'

Rawne took a pace forward, but pulled up in surprise as Sergeant Mkoll placed an arresting hand on his arm.

'Not so fast, eh?' Mkoll nodded at the floor ahead of them. 'These vaults have been teeming with the enemy, but the dust on that floor hasn't been disturbed for decades, at least. And you see the patterning in the dust?'

Both Rawne and Gaunt stooped their heads to get an angle to see what Mkoll described. Catching the light right they could see almost invisible spirals and circles in the thick dust, like droplet ripples frozen in ash.

'Your data said something about wards and prohibitions on the entrance to the Edicule. This area hasn't been traversed in a long while, and I'd guess those patterns are imprints in the dust made by energies or force screens. Like a storm shield, maybe. We know the enemy here has some serious crap at their disposal.'

Gaunt scratched his cheek, thinking. Mkoll was right, and had been sharp-witted to remember the data notes at a moment where Gaunt was all for rushing ahead, so close was the prize. Somehow, Gaunt had expected gun emplacements, chain-fences, wire-strands – conventional wards and prohibitions. He caught Rawne's eye, and saw the resentment burning there. Gaunt had still managed to exclude the major from the details he had shared with the other officers, and Rawne remained in the dark as to the nature of this insertion, if not its importance. Gaunt had only brought him along because of his ruthless expertise in tunnel fighting.

Because, after the business on the *Absalom*, he wanted to keep Rawne where he could see him. And, of course, there was...

Gaunt blinked off the thoughts. 'Get me Domor's sweeper set. I'll sweep the room myself.'

'I'll do it, sir,' a voice said from behind them. The others had edged into the chamber behind them, with Fereyd's men watching the arch, though even they were clearly more interested in what lay ahead. Domor himself had spoken. He was standing by himself now, a little shaky but upright. Dorden's high-dose painkillers had given him a brief respite from pain and a temporary renewal of strength.

'It should be me,' Gaunt said softly, and Domor angled his blind face slightly to direct himself at the sound of the voice.

'Oh no, sir, begging your pardon.' Domor smiled below the swathe of eye-bandage. He tapped the sweeper set slung from his shoulder. 'You know I'm the best sweeper in the unit... and it's all a matter of listening to the pulse in the headset. I don't need to see. This is my job.'

There was a long silence in which the dense air of the ancient vault seemed to buzz in their ears. Gaunt knew Domor was right about his skills, and moreover, he knew what Domor was really saying: I'm a ghost, sir, expendable.

Gaunt made his decision, not based on any notion of expendability. Here was a task Domor could do better than any of them, and if Gaunt could still make the man feel a useful part of the team, he would not crush the pride of a soldier already dying.

'Do it. Maximum coverage, maximum caution. I'll guide you by voice and we'll string a line to you so we can pull you back.'

The look on what was left of Domor's face was worth more than anything they could find beyond those doors, Gaunt thought.

Caffran stepped forward to attach a rope to Domor as Mkoll checked the test-settings on the sweeper set, and adjusted the headphones around Domor's ears.

'Gaunt, you're joking!' Fereyd snapped, pushing forward. His voice dropped to a hiss. 'Are you seriously going to waste time with this charade? This is the most important thing any of us are ever going to do! Let one of my men do the sweep! Hell, I'll do the sweep–'

'Domor is sweeper officer. He'll do it.'

'But–'

'He'll do it, Fereyd.'

Domor began his crossing, moving in a straight line across the ancient floor, one step at a time. He stopped after each footfall to retune the clicking, pulsing sweeper, listening with experience-attuned ears to every hiss and murmur of the set. Caffran played out the line behind him. After a few yards, he edged to the right, then a little further on, jinked left again. His erratic path was perfectly recorded in the dust.

'There are... cones of energy radiating from the floor at irregular intervals,' Domor whispered over the micro-bead intercom. 'Who knows what and for why, but I'm betting it wouldn't be a good idea to interrupt one.'

Time wound on, achingly slow. Domor slowly, indirectly, approached the far side of the chamber.

'Gaunt! The line! The fething line!' Dorden said abruptly, pointing.

Gaunt immediately saw what the doctor was referring to. Domor was safely negotiating the invisible obstacles, but his safety line was trailing behind him in a far more economical course between the sweeper and his team. Any moment, and its dragging weight might intersect with an unseen energy cone.

'Domor! Freeze!' Gaunt snarled into the intercom. On the far side of the vault, Domor stopped dead. 'Untie your safety line and let it drop,' the commissar instructed him. Wordless, Domor complied, fumbling blindly to undo the slip-knot Caffran had tied. It would not come free. Domor tried to gather some slack from the line to ease the knot, and in jiggling it, shook the strap of the sweeper set off his shoulder. The rope came free and dropped, but the heavy sweeper slipped down his arm and his arm spasmed to hook it on his elbow. Domor caught the set, but the motion had pulled on the cord of his headset and plucked it off. The headset clattered onto the dusty floor about a metre from his feet.

Everyone on Gaunt's side of the chamber flinched but nothing happened. Domor struggled with the set for a moment and returned it to his shoulder. 'The headset? Where did it go?' he asked over the micro-bead.

'Don't move. Stay still.' Gaunt threw his lasgun to Rawne and as quickly as he dared followed Domor's route in the dust across the chamber. He came up behind the frozen blind man, spoke low and reassuringly so as not to make Domor turn suddenly, then reached past him, crouching low, to scoop up the headset. He plugged the jack back into its socket and placed the ear-pieces back around Domor's head.

'Let's finish this,' Gaunt said.

They moved on, close together, Gaunt letting Domor set the pace and direction. It took another four minutes to reach the doorway.

Gaunt signalled back at his team and instructed them to follow the pair of them over on the path Domor had made. He noticed that Fereyd was first in line, his face set with an urgent, impatient scowl.

As they came, Gaunt turned his attention back to the door. It was visible only by its seams in the rock, a marvellously smooth piece of precision engineering. Gaunt did what the data crystal had told him he should; he placed an open palm against the right hand edge of the door and exerted gentle pressure.

Silently, the twin, fifteen metre tall blocks of stone rolled back and opened. Beyond lay a huge chamber so brightly lit and gleaming it made Gaunt close his eyes and wince.

'What? What do you see?' Domor asked by his side.

'I don't know,' Gaunt said, blinking, 'but it's the most incredible thing I've ever seen.'

The others closed in behind them, looking up in astonishment, crossing the threshold of the Edicule behind Gaunt and the eager Fereyd. Rawne was the last inside.

TWENTY-THREE

Inquisitor Heldane allowed himself a gentle shudder of relief. His pawn was now inside the sacred Edicule of the Menazoid necropolis, and with him went Heldane's senses and intellect. After all this time, all this effort, he was right there, channelled through blunt mortal instruments until his mind was engaging first hand with the most precious artefact in space.

The most precious, the most dangerous, the most limitless of possibilities. A means at last, with all confidence, to overthrow Macaroth and the stagnating Imperial rule he espoused. It would make Dravere warmaster, and Dravere would in turn be his instrument. All the while mankind fought the dark with light, he was doomed to eventual defeat. The grey, thought Heldane, the secret weapons of the grey, those things that the hard-liners of the Imperium were too afraid to use, the devices and possibilities that lay in the blurred moral fogs beyond the simple and the just. That is how he would lead mankind out of the dark and into true ascendancy, crushing the perverse alien menaces of the galaxy and all those loyal to the old ways alike.

Of course, if Dravere used this weapon and seized control of the Crusade, used it to push the campaign on to undreamed-of victory, then the High Lords of Terra would be bound to castigate him and declare him treasonous. But they wouldn't know until it was done; and then, in the light of those victories, how could they gainsay his decision?

Some of the orderlies in the isolation bay began to notice the irregularities registering in the inquisitor's bio-monitors and started forward to investigate. He sent them scurrying out of sight with a lash of his psyche.

Heldane took up the hand mirror again and gazed into it until his mind loosed once more and he was able to psychically dive into its reflective skin like a swimmer into a still pool.

Invisible, he surfaced amongst Gaunt's wondering team in the Edicule. He turned the eyes of his pawn to take it all in: a cylindrical chamber a thousand metres high and five hundred in diameter, the walls fibrous and knotted with pipes and flutes and tubes of silver and chromium. Brilliant white light shafted down from far above. The floor underfoot was chased with silver, richly inscribed with impossibly complex algorithmic paradoxes, a thousand to a square metre. Heldane expanded his mind in a heartbeat and read them all... solved them all.

Bounding eagerly beyond this trifle, he looked around and focused on the great structure which dominated the centre of the chamber. A machine, a vast device made of brilliant white ceramics, silver piping, chromium chambers.

A Standard Template Constructor. Intact.

The secrets of originating technology had been lost to mankind for so long. Since the Dark Ages, the Imperium, even the Adeptus Mechanicus could only manufacture things they had learned by recovering the processes of the ancient STC systems. From scraps and remnants of shattered STC systems on a thousand dead worlds, the Imperium had slowly relearned the secrets of construction, of tanks and machines and laser weapons. Every last fragment was priceless.

To find a dedicated Constructor intact was a find made once a generation, a find from which the entire Imperium benefited.

But to find one like this intact was surely without precedent. All of the speculation had been correct. Long ago, thousands of years before Chaos had overwhelmed it, Menazoid Epsilon had been an arsenal world, manufacturing the ultimate weapon known to those lost ages. The secrets of its process and purpose were contained within those million and a half algorithms etched into the wide floor.

The Men of Iron. A rumour so old it was a myth, a myth from the oldest times, before the Age of Strife, from the Dark Age of Technology, when mankind had reached a state of glory as the masters of a techno-automatic Empire, the race that had perfected the standard template construct. They created the Men of Iron, mechanical beings of power and sentience but no human soul. Heretical devices in the eyes of the Imperium. War with the self-aware Men of Iron had led to the fall of that distant Empire and, if the old, deeply arcane records Heldane had been privy to were correct, that was why the Imperium had outlawed any soulless mechanical intelligence. But as servants, implacable warriors – what could not be achieved with Men of Iron at your side?

Here, at the untouched heart of the ancient arsenal world, was the STC system to make such Men of Iron.

There was more! Heldane broadened his focus and took in the walls of the chamber for the first time. At floor level, all around, were alcoves screened by metal grilles. Behind them, as still and silent as terracotta statues guarding a royal tomb, stood phalanxes Men of Iron. Hundreds, hundreds of hundreds, ranked back in symmetrical rows into the shadows of the alcove. Each stood far taller than a man, with faces like sightless skulls of burnished steel, the sinews and arteries of their bodies formed from cable and wire encased in anatomical plate-sections of lustreless alloy. They slept, waiting the command to awaken, waiting to receive orders, waiting to ignite the great device once more and multiply their forces again.

Heldane breathed hard to quell his excitement. He wound his senses back into his pawn and surveyed the gathered men.

Gaunt gazed in solemn wonder; the Ghosts were transfixed with awe and bafflement, the Crusade staff alert and eager to investigate. Gaunt turned to Dorden and ordered him to take Domor aside and let him rest. He told the other Ghosts to stand down and relax. Then he crossed to Fereyd, who was standing before the vast STC device, his helmet dangling by its chin-strap from his hand.

'The prize, old friend,' Fereyd said, without turning.

'The prize. I hope it was worth it.'

Now Fereyd turned to look. 'Do you have any idea what this is?'

'Ever since I unlocked that crystal, you know that I have. I don't pretend to understand the technology, but I know that's an intact standard template weapons maker. And I know that's as unheard of as a well-manicured ork.'

Fereyd laughed. 'Sixty years ago on Geyluss Auspix, a rat-water world a long way from nothing in Pleigo Sutarnus, a team of Imperial scouts found an intact STC in the ruins of a pyramid city in a jungle basin. Intact. You know what it made? It was the standard template constructor for a type of steel blade, an alloy of folded steel composite that was sharper and lighter and tougher than anything we've had before. Thirty whole Chapters of the great Astartes are now using blades of the new pattern. The scouts became heroes. I believe each was given a world of his own. It was regarded as the greatest technological advance of the century, the greatest discovery, the most perfect and valuable STC recovery in living memory.'

'That made knives, Bram... knives, daggers, bayonets, swords. It made blades and it was the greatest discovery in memory. Compared to this... it's less than nothing. Take one of those wonderful new blades and face me with the weapon this thing can make.'

'I read the crystal before you did, Fereyd. I know what it can do. Men of Iron: the old myth, one of the tales of the Great Old Wars.'

Fereyd grinned. 'Then breathe in this moment, my friend. We've found the impossible here. A device to guarantee the ascendancy of man. What's a stronger, lighter, sharper, better blade when you can overrun the home world of the man wielding it with a legion of deathless warriors? This is history, you know, alive in the air around us. This makes us the greatest of men. Don't you feel it?'

Gaunt and Fereyd both turned slowly, surveying the silent ranks of metal beings waiting behind the grilles.

Gaunt hesitated. 'I feel... only horror. To have fought and killed and sacrificed just to win a device that will do more of the same a thousandfold. This isn't a prize, Fereyd. It is a curse.'

'But you came looking for it? You knew what it was.'

'I know my responsibilities, Fereyd. I dedicate my life to the service of the Imperium, and if a device like this exists then it's my duty to secure it in the name of our beloved Emperor. And you gave me the job of finding it, after all.'

Fereyd set his helmet on the silver floor and began to unlace his gloves, shaking his head. 'I love you like a brother, old friend, but sometimes you worry me. We share a discovery like this and you trot out some feeble moral line about lives? That's called hypocrisy, you know. You're a killer, slaved to the greatest killing engine in the known galaxy. That's your work, your life, to end others. To destroy. And you do it with relish. Now we find something that will do it a billion times better than you, and you start to have qualms? What is it? Professional jealousy?'

Gaunt scratched his cheek, thoughtful. 'You know me better. Don't mock me. I'm surprised at your glee. I've known the Princeps of Imperial Titans who delight in their bloodshed, and who nevertheless regard the vast power at their disposal with caution. Give any man the power of a god, and you better hope he's got the wisdom and morals of a god to match. There's nothing feeble about my moral line. I value life. That is why I fight to protect it. I mourn every man I lose and every sacrifice I make. One life or a billion, they're all lives.'

'One life or a billion?' Fereyd echoed. 'It's just a matter of proportion, of scale. Why slog in the mud with your men for months to win a world I can take with Men of Iron... and not spill a drop of blood?'

'Not a drop? Not ours, maybe. There is no greater heresy than the thinking machines of the Iron Age. Would you unleash such a heresy again? Would you trust these... things not to turn on us as they did before? It is the oldest of laws. Mankind must never again place his fate in the hands of his creations, no matter how clever. I trust flesh and blood, not iron.'

Gaunt found himself almost hypnotised by the row of dark eye-sockets behind the grille. These things were the future? He didn't think so. The past, perhaps, a past better forgotten and denied.

How could any one wake them? How could anyone even think of making more and unleashing them against...

Against who? The enemy? Warmaster Macaroth and his retinue? This was how Dravere planned to usurp control of the Crusade? This was what it had all been about?

'You've really taken your poor orphan Ghosts into your heart, haven't you, Bram? The concern doesn't suit you.'

'Maybe I sympathise. Orphans stick with orphans.'

Fereyd walked away a few paces. 'You're not the man I knew, Ibram Gaunt. The Ghosts have softened you with their wailing and melancholy. You're blind to the truly momentous possibilities here.'

'You're not, obviously. You said "I".'

Fereyd stopped in his tracks and turned around. 'What?'

'"A world I can take without spilling a drop of blood." Your words. You would use this, wouldn't you? You'd use them.' He gestured to the sleeping iron figures.

'Better I than no one.'

'Better no one. That's why I came here. It's why I thought you had come here too, or why you'd sent me.'

Fereyd's face turned dark and ugly. 'What are you blathering about?'

'I'm here to destroy this thing so that no one can use it,' said Colonel-Commissar Ibram Gaunt.

He turned away from Fereyd's frozen face and called to Caffran and Mkoll. 'Unpack the tube charges,' he instructed. 'Put them where they count. Rawne knows demolition better than any. That's why I brought him along. Get him to supervise. And signal Corbec, or whoever's left up top. Tell them to pull out of the necropolis right now. I dare not imagine what will happen when we do this.'

In the isolation sphere, Heldane froze and clenched the mirror so tightly that it cracked. Thin blood oozed out from under his hooked thumb. He had entirely underestimated this Gaunt, this blunt fool. Such power, such scope; if only he had been given the chance to work on Gaunt and make him the pawn.

Heldane swallowed. There was no time to waste now. The prize was in his grasp. No Imperial Guard nobody would thwart him now. Discretion and subterfuge went to the winds. He lanced his mind down into the blunt skull of his pawn, urging him to act and throw off the deceit. To kill them all, before this madman Gaunt could damage the holy relic and kill the Men of Iron.

Sitting at the edge of the Edicule chamber, checking his barb-lance with his back resting against the silver wall, Rawne shuddered and blood seeped down out of his nose, thick in his mouth. He felt the touch of the bastard monster Heldane more strongly than ever now, clawing at his skull, digging in his eyes like scorpion claws. His guts churned and trembling filled his limbs.

Major Rawne stumbled to his feet, sliding a barb-round into the lance-launcher and swinging it to bear.

TWENTY-FOUR

With the sudden reinforcement of Zoren's Vitrians, Corbec's platoons pushed the Chaos elements back into the ruins of the necropolis, slaughtering as they went. The misshapen forces of madness were in rout.

Leaning on a boulder and wheezing at the pain flooding through his ribs, Corbec thought to order up a vox-caster and signal command that the victory was theirs, but Milo was suddenly at his side, holding a foil-print out from a vox-caster.

'It's the commissar,' he said, 'We have to get clear of the Target Primaris. Well clear.'

Corbec studied the film slip. 'Feth! We spend all day getting in here...'

He waved Raglon over and pulled the speakerhorn from the caster set on the man's back.

'This is Corbec of the Tanith First and Only to all Tanith and Vitrian officers. Word from Gaunt: pull back and out! I repeat, clear the necropolis area!'

Colonel Zoren's voice floated across the speaker channel. 'Has he done it, Corbec? Has he achieved the goal?'

'He didn't say, colonel,' Corbec snapped in reply. 'We've done this much on his word, let's do the rest. Withdrawal plan five-ninety! We'll cover and support your Dragoons in a layered fall back.'

'Acknowledged.'

Replacing the horn, Corbec shuddered. The pain was almost more than he could bear and he had taken his last painkiller tab an hour before.

He returned to his men.

TWENTY-FIVE

Bragg cried out in sudden shock, his voice dwarfed by the vastness of the Edicule. Gaunt, walking towards Dorden and Domor by the doorway, spun around in surprise, to find Fereyd and his bodyguard raising their lasrifles to bear on the Ghosts.

For a split second, as Fereyd swung his gun to aim, Gaunt locked eyes with him. He saw nothing in those deep, black irises he recognised of old. Only hate and murder.

In a heartbeat...

Gaunt flung himself down as Fereyd's first las-bolt cut through the air where his head had been.

Fereyd's elite troopers began firing, winging Bragg and scattering the other Ghosts. Dorden threw himself flat over Domor's yelling body.

Rawne sighted and fired the barb-lance.

The buzzing, horribly slow round crossed the bright space of the Edicule and hit Fereyd's face on the bridge of the nose. Everything of

Imperial Tactician Wheyland above the sternum explosively evaporated in a mist of blood and bone chips.

Larkin howled as he fell, shot through the forearm by a las-round
from one of the elite troopers flanking the tactician.

Caffran and Mkoll, both sprawling, whipped around to return fire
with their lasguns, toppling one of the bodyguards with a double hit
neither could truly claim.

Gaunt rolled as he dived, pulling out his laspistol and bellowing
curses as he swung and fired. Another of Fereyd's troopers fell, blasted
backwards by a trio of shots to his chest. He jerked back, arms and legs
extended, and died.

Gaunt squeezed the trigger again, but his lasgun just retched and
fizzed. The energy draining effect of the catacombs, which had sapped
their lamp packs, had wasted ammo charges too. His weapon was spent.

The remaining bodyguard lurched forward to blast Gaunt, helpless
on the floor – and dropped with a laser-blasted hole burned clean
through his skull. His body smashed back hard against the side of the
STC machine and slid down, leaving a streak of blood down the chased
silver facing. Gaunt scrambled around to look.

Clutching the bawling Domor to him, Dorden sat half-raised with
Domor's laspistol in his hand.

'Needs must,' the doctor said quietly, suddenly tossing the weapon
aside like it was an insect which had stung him.

'Great shot, doc,' Larkin said, getting up, clutching his seared arm.

'Only said I wouldn't shoot, not that I couldn't,' Dorden said.

The Ghosts got back to their feet. Dorden hurried to treat the wounds
Bragg and Larkin had received.

'What's that sound?' Domor asked sharply. They all froze.

Gaunt looked at the great machine. Amber lights were flicking to life
on a panel on its flank. In death, the last Crusader had been blown back
against the main activation grid. Old technologies were grinding into
life. Smoke, steam perhaps, vented from cowlings near the floor. Processes moved and turned and murmured in the device.

There was another noise too. A shuffling.

Gaunt turned slowly. Behind the dark grilles in the alcoves, metal
limbs were beginning to flex and uncurl. As he watched, eyes lit up in
dead sockets. Blue. Their light was blue, cold, eternal. Somehow, it was
the most appalling colour Gaunt had ever seen. They were waking. As
their creator awoke, they awoke too.

Gaunt stared at them for a long, breathless moment, his heart pounding. He looked at them until he had lost count of the igniting blue eyes.
Some began to jerk forward and slam against the grilles, rattling and

shaking them. Metal hands clawed at metal bars. There were voices now too. Chattering, just at the edge of hearing. Codes and protocols and streams of binary numbers. The Men of Iron hummed as they woke.

Gaunt looked back at the STC. 'Rawne!'

'Sir?'

'Destroy it! Now!'

Rawne looked at him, wiping the blood from his lip.

'With respect, colonel-commissar... is this right? I mean – this thing could change the course of everything.'

Gaunt turned to look at Major Rawne, his eyes fiercely dark, his brow furrowed. 'Do you want to see another world die, Rawne?'

The major shook his head.

'Neither do I. This is the right thing to do. I... I have my reasons. And are you blind? Do you want to greet these sleepers as they awake?'

Rawne looked round. The cold blue stares seemed to stab into him too. He shuddered.

'I'm on it!' he said with sudden decisiveness and moved off, calling to Mkoll and Caffran to bring up the explosives.

Gaunt yelled after him. 'These things are heresies, Rawne! Foul heresies! And if that wasn't enough, they've been sleeping here on a Chaos-polluted world for thousands of years! Do any of us really want to find out how that's altered their thinking?'

'Feth!' Dorden said, from nearby. 'You mean this whole thing could be corrupted?'

'You'd have to be the blindest fool in creation to want to find out, wouldn't you?' Gaunt replied.

He stared down at the remains of his friend Fereyd. 'It wasn't me who changed, was it?' he murmured.

TWENTY-SIX

Heldane was totally unprepared for the death of his pawn. It had been such a victory to identify and capture Macaroth's little spy, and then such a privilege to work on him. It had taken a long time to turn Fereyd, a long time and a lot of painful cutting. But the conceit had been so delicious: to take the greatest of the warmaster's agents and turn him into a tool. Heldane had learned so much more through Fereyd than he would have through a lesser being. Duplicity, deceit, motive. To use one of the men the warmaster had been channelling to undermine him? It had been beautiful, perfect, daring.

In his final moments, Heldane wished he could have had time to finish with Rawne. *There* had been a likely mind, however blunt. But the Ghosts Corbec and Larkin had cheated him of that, and left Rawne merely aware of his influence rather than controlled by it.

It mattered little. Heldane had miscalculated. Impending death had slackened his judgement. He had put too much of himself into his pawn. The backlash when the pawn died was too much. He should have shielded his mind to the possible onrush of death-trauma. He had not.

Fereyd had suffered the most painful, hideous death imaginable. All of it crackled down the psychic link to Heldane. He felt every moment of Fereyd's death. In it, he felt his own.

Heldane spasmed, burst asunder. Untameable psychic energies erupted out of his dead form, lashing outwards indiscriminately. Impact resounded on impact. Above in his command seat, Hechtor Dravere noticed the shuddering of the deck, and began to look around for the cause.

In a mushroom of light, the unleashed psychic energies of the dying inquisitor blew the entire Leviathan apart, atom from atom.

TWENTY-SEVEN

'We're clear!' Rawne yelled as he sprinted across the chamber with Caffran next to him. Gaunt had marshalled the others at the doorway. By now, the huge machine was rumbling and the gas-venting was continuous.

'Mkoll! Come on!' Gaunt shouted.

On the far side of the chamber, a section of the ancient grille finally gave way. Men of Iron stumbled forward out of their alcove, their metal feet crunching over the fallen grille sheet. All around, their companions rattled and shook at their pens, eyes burning like the blue-hot backwash of missile tubes, murmuring their sonorous hum.

The metal skeletons spilling out of the cage began to advance across the chamber, bleary and undirected. Mkoll, fixing the last set of charges to the side of the vibrating STC, looked round in horror at their jerking advance.

There was a sudden rush of noise beside him and a hatch aperture slid open in the side of the STC, voiding a great gout of steam. Caught in it, Mkoll fell to his knees, choking and gagging.

'Mkoll!'

Kneeling with his back turned to the hot steam, the coughing Mkoll couldn't see what was looming out of the swirling gas behind him.

A newborn Man of Iron. The first to be produced by the STC after its long slumber. As soon as it appeared, the others, those loosed and those still caged, began keening, in a long, continuous, piteous wail that was at once a human shriek and a rapid broadcast of machine code sequences.

There was something wrong with the newborn. It was malformed, grotesque compared to the perfect anatomical symmetry of the other Men of Iron. A good head taller, it was hunched, blackened, one arm far longer than the other, draped and massive, the other hideously vestigial and twisted. Corrupt horns sprouted from its over-long skull and its eyes shone a deadened yellow. Oil like stringy pus wept from the eye sockets. It shambled, unsteady. Its exposed teeth and jaws clacked and mashed idiotically.

Dorden howled out something about Gaunt being right, but Gaunt was already moving and not listening. He dived across the chamber at full stretch and tackled the coughing Mkoll onto the floor a second before the newborn's larger arm sliced through the space the stealther had previously occupied.

The respite was brief. Rolling off Mkoll and trying to pull him up, Gaunt saw the newborn turn to address them again, its jaw champing mindlessly. Behind it, in the reeking smoke of the hatchway, a second newborn was already emerging.

Two las-rounds punched into the newborn and made it stagger backwards. Caffran was trying his best, but the dully reflective carapace of the newborn shrugged off all but the kinetic force of the shots.

It struck at Gaunt and Mkoll again, but the commissar managed to roll himself and the scout out of the way. Its great metal claw sparked against the algorithm-inscribed floor, incising an alteration to the calculations that was permanent and insane.

Gaunt struggled to drag Mkoll away from the shambling metal thing, cursing out loud. In a second, Dorden and Bragg were with him, easing his efforts, pulling Mkoll upright.

The unexpected blow smashed Gaunt off his feet. The newborn had reached out a glancing blow and taken a chunk of cloth and flesh out of his back. How could it

Gaunt rolled and looked up. The newborn's massive forelimb had grown, articulating out on extending metallic callipers, forming new pistons and extruded pulleys as it morphed its mechanical structure.

The monstrous thing struck at him again. The commissar flopped left to dodge and then right to dodge again. The metal claw cracked into the floor on either side of him.

Rawne, Larkin and Caffran sprang in. Caffran tried to shoot at close range but Larkin got in his way, capering and shouting to distract the machine. A second later, Larkin was also sent flying by a backhanded swipe.

Rawne hadn't had time to load another barbed round into his lance, so he used it like an axe, swinging the bayonet blade so that it reverberated against the creature's iron skull. Cable-sinews sheared and the newborn's head was knocked crooked.

The machine-being swung round with its massive fighting limb and smacked Rawne away, extending its reach to at least five metres. Gaunt dived across the floor and came up holding Rawne's barb-lance. He scythed down with it and smashed the Man of Iron's limb off at the second elbow, cutting through the increasingly diminished girth of the extending limb. Then Gaunt plunged the weapon, point first, into the newborn's face. The blade came free in an explosion of oil and ichor-like milky fluid.

The monstrosity fell back, cold and stiff, the light dying in its eyes.

By then, six new demented newborns had spilled from the STC's hatch. Behind them, forty or more of the Men of Iron had burst from their cages and were thumping forward. The others rattled their pens and began to howl.

'Now! Now we're fething leaving!' Gaunt yelled.

TWENTY-EIGHT

It had taken them close on four hours to find and fight their way in; four hours from the bottom of the chimney shaft on the hillside to the doors of the Edicule. Now they had closed the doors on the shuffling blue-eyed metal nightmares and were ready to run. But even with the simple confidence of retracing their steps, Gaunt knew he had to factor in more time, so in the end he had Rawne set the tube-charge relays for four and three-quarter standard hours.

Already their progress back to the surface was flagging. Domor was getting weaker with each step, and though able-bodied, both Bragg and Larkin were slowing with the dull pain of their wounds from the firefight. Most of their weapons had been dumped, as the powercells were now dead. There was no point carrying the excess weight. Rawne's barb-lance was still functioning and he led the way with Mkoll, whose lasrifle had about a dozen gradually dissipating shots left in its dying clip.

Dorden, Domor, and Larkin were unarmed except for blades. Larkin's carbine, still functioning thanks to its mechanical function, was of no use to him with his wounded arm, so Gaunt had turned it over to Caffran to guard the rear. Bragg insisted on keeping his autocannon, but there was barely a drum left to it, and Gaunt wasn't sure how well the injured trooper would manage it if it came to a fight.

Then there was the darkness of the tunnels, which Gaunt cursed himself for forgetting. All of their lamp packs were now dead, and as they moved away from the Edicule chambers into the darker sections of the labyrinth, they had to halt while Mkoll and Caffran scouted ahead to salvage cloth and wood from the bodies of the dead foe in the cistern approach. They fashioned two dozen makeshift torches, with cloth wadded around wooden staves and lance-poles, moistened with the pungent contents of Bragg's last precious bottle of sacra liquor. Lit by the flickering flames, they moved on, passing gingerly through the cistern and beyond.

As they lumbered through the stinking mass of enemy corpses choking the cistern, Gaunt thought to search them for other weapons, mechanical weapons that were unaffected by the energy-drain. But the scent of meat had brought the insect swarms down the passage, and the twisted bodies were now a writhing, revolting mass of carrion.

There was no time. They pressed on. Gaunt tried not to think what wretchedness Mkoll and Caffran had suffered to scavenge the material for the torches.

The torches themselves burned quickly, and illuminated little but the immediate environs of the bearer. Gaunt felt fatigue growing in his limbs, realising now more than ever that the energy-leaching affected more than lamp packs and lasgun charges. If he was weary, he dreaded to think what Domor was like. Twice the commissar had to call a halt and regroup as Mkoll and Rawne got too far ahead of the struggling party.

How long had it been? His timepiece was dead. Gaunt began to wonder if the charges would even fire. Would their detonator circuits fizzle and die before they clicked over?

They reached a jagged turn in the ancient, sagging tunnels. They must have been moving now for close on three hours, he guessed. There was no sign of Mkoll and Rawne ahead. He lit another torch and looked back as Larkin and Bragg moved up together past him, sharing a torch.

'Go on,' he urged them, hoping this way was the right way. Without Mkoll's sharp senses, he felt lost. Which turn was it? Larkin and Bragg, gifted with that uncanny Tanith sixth sense of direction themselves, seemed in no doubt. 'Just move on and out. If you find Sergeant Mkoll or Major Rawne, tell them to keep moving too.'

The huge shadow of Bragg and his wiry companion nodded silently to him and soon their guttering light was lost in the tunnel ahead.

Gaunt waited. Where the feth were the others?

Minutes passed, lingering, creeping.

A light appeared. Caffran moved into sight, squinting out into the dark with Larkin's carbine held ready.

'Sir?'

'Where are Domor and the doctor?' Gaunt asked.

Caffran looked puzzled. 'I haven't passed–'

'You were the rearguard, trooper!'

'I haven't passed them, sir!' Caffran barked.

Gaunt bunched a fist and rapped his own forehead with it. 'Keep going. I'll go back.'

'I'll go back with you, sir–' Caffran began.

'Go on!' Gaunt snapped. 'That's an order, trooper! I'll go back and look.'

Caffran hesitated. In the dim fire-flicker, Gaunt saw distress in the young man's eyes.

'You've done all I could have asked of you, Caffran. You and the others. First and Only, best of warriors. If I die in this pit, I'll die happy knowing I got as many of you out as possible.'

He made to shake the man's hand. But Caffran seemed overwhelmed by the gesture and moved away.

'I'll see you on the surface, commissar,' Caffran said firmly.

Gaunt headed back down the funnel of rock. Caffran's light remained stationary behind him, watching him until he was out of sight.

The rocky tunnel was damp and stifling. There was no sign of Dorden or the wounded Domor. Gaunt opened his mouth to call out and then silenced himself. The blackness around him was too deep and dark for a voice. By now, the awakened Men of Iron could be lumbering down the tunnels, alert to any sound.

The passage veered to the left. Gaunt fought a feeling of panic. He didn't seem to be retracing his steps at all. He must have lost a turn somewhere. Lost, a voice hissed in his mind. Fereyd's voice? Dercius's? Macaroth's? You're lost, you witless, compassionate fool!

His last torch sputtered and died. Darkness engulfed him. His eyes adjusted and he saw a pale glow far ahead. Gaunt moved towards it.

The tunnel, now crumbling underfoot even as it sloped away, led into a deep cavern, natural and rocky, lit by a greenish biolumines-cent growth throbbing from fungus and lichens caking the ceiling and walls. It was a vast cavern full of shattered rock and dark pools. His foot slipped on loose pebbles and he struggled to catch himself. Almost invisible in the darkness, a bottomless abyss yawned to his right. A few steps on and he fumbled his way around the lip of another chasm. Black, oily fluid bubbled and popped in crater holes. Grotesque blind insects with dangling legs and huge fibrous wings whirred around in the semi-dark.

Domor lay on his side on a shelf of cool rock, still and silent. Gaunt crawled over to him. The trooper had been hit on the back of the head with a blunt instrument. He was alive, just, the blow adding immeasurably to the damage he had already suffered. A burned-out torch lay nearby, and there was a spilled medical kit, lying half-open, with rolls of bandages and flasks of disinfectant scattered around it.

'Doctor?' Gaunt called.

Dark shapes leapt down on him from either side. Fierce hands grappled him. He caught a glimpse of Jantine uniform as he fought back. The ambush was so sudden, it almost overwhelmed him, but he was tensed and ready for anything thanks to the warning signs of Domor and the medi-kit. He kicked out hard, breaking something within his assailant's body, and then rolled free, slashing with his silver Tanith blade. A man yelped – and then screamed deeper and more fully as his staggering form mis-footed and tumbled into a chasm. But the others had him, striking and pummelling him hard. Three sets of hands, three men.

'Enough! Ebzan, enough! He's mine!'

Dazed, Gaunt was dragged upright by the three Patricians. Through fogged eyes, across the cavern, he saw Flense advancing, pushing Dorden before him, a lasgun to the pale old medic's temple.

'Gaunt.'

'Flense! You fething madman! This isn't the time!'

'On the contrary, colonel-commissar, this is the time. At last the time... for you, for me. A reckoning.'

The three Jantine soldiers muscled Gaunt up to face Flense and his captive.

'If it's the prize you want, Flense, you're too late. It'll be gone by the time you get there,' Gaunt hissed.

'Prize? Prize?' Flense smiled, his scar-tissue twitching. 'I don't care for that. Let Dravere care, or that monster Heldane. I spit upon their prize! You are all I have come for!'

'I'm touched,' Gaunt said and one of the men smacked him hard around the back of the head.

'That's enough, Avranche!' Flense snapped. 'Release him!'

Reluctantly, the three Jantine Patricians set him free and stood back. Head spinning, Gaunt straightened up to face Flense and Dorden.

'Now we settle this matter of honour,' Flense said.

Gaunt grinned disarmingly at Flense, without humour. 'Matter of honour? Are we still on this? The Tanith-Jantine feud? You're a perfect idiot, Flense, you know that?'

Flense grimaced, pushing the pistol tighter into the wincing forehead of Dorden. 'Do you so mock the old debt? Do you want me to shoot this man before your very eyes?'

'Mock on,' Dorden murmured. 'Better he shoot me than I listen to any more of his garbage.'

'Don't pretend you don't know the depth of the old wound, the old treachery,' Flense said spitefully.

Gaunt sighed. 'Dercius. You mean Dercius! Sacred Feth, but isn't that done with? I know the Jantine have never liked admitting they had a coward on their spotless honour role, but this is taking things too far! Dercius, General Dercius, Emperor rot his filthy soul, left my father and his unit to die on Kentaur. He ran away and left them. When I executed Dercius on Khedd all those years ago, it was a battlefield punishment, as is my right to administer as an Imperial commissar!

'He deserted his men, Flense! Throne of Earth, there's not a regiment in the Guard that doesn't have a black sheep, a wayward son! Dercius was the Jantine's disgrace! That's no reason to prolong a rivalry with me and my Ghosts! This mindless feuding has cost the lives of good men, on both sides! So what if we beat you to the punch on Fortis? So what of Pyrites and aboard the *Absalom*? You jackass Jantine don't know when to stop, do you? You don't know where honour ends and discipline begins!'

Flense shot Dorden in the side of the head and the medic's body crumpled. Gaunt made to leap forward, incandescent with rage, but Flense raised the pistol to block him.

'It's an honour thing, all right,' Flense spat, 'but forget the Jantine and the Tanith. It's an honour thing between you and me.'

'What are you saying, Flense?' growled Gaunt through his fury.

'Your father, my father. I was the son of a dynasty on Jant Normanidus. The heir to a province and a wide estate. You sent my father to hell in disgrace and all my lands and titles were stripped from me. Even my family name. That went too. I was forced to battle my way up and into the service as a footslogger. Prove my worth, make my own name. My life has been one long, hellish struggle against infamy thanks to you.'

'Your father?' Gaunt echoed.

'My father. Aldo Dercius.'

The truth of it resonated in Ibram Gaunt's mind. He saw, truly understood now, how this could end no other way. He launched himself at Flense.

The pistol fired. Gaunt felt a stinging heat across his chest as he barrelled into the Patrician colonel. They rolled over on the rocks, sharp angles cutting into their flesh. Flense smashed the pistol butt into the side of Gaunt's head.

Gaunt mashed his elbow sideways and felt ribs break. Flense yowled and clawed at the commissar, wrenching him over his head in a cart-wheel flip. Gaunt landed on his back hard, struggled to rise and met Flense's kick in the face. He slammed back over the rocks and loose pebbles, skittering stone fragments out from under him.

Flense leapt again, encountering Gaunt's up-swinging boot as he dived forward, smashing the wind out of his chest. Flense fell on Gaunt; the Patrician's hands clawed into his throat. Gaunt was aware of the chanting voices of the three Jantine soldiers watching, echoing Flense's name.

As Flense tightened his grip and Gaunt choked, the chant changed from 'Flense!' to that family name that had been stripped from the colonel at the disgrace.

'Dercius! Dercius! Dercius!'

Dercius. Uncle Dercius. Uncle fething Dercius...

Gaunt's punch lifted Flense off him in a reeling spray of mouth blood. He rolled and ploughed into the Patrician colonel, throwing three, four, five well-met punches.

Flense recovered, kicked Gaunt headlong, and the commissar lay sprawled and helpless for a moment. Flense towered over him, a chunk of rock raised high in both hands to crush Gaunt's head.

'For my father!' screamed Flense.

'For mine!' hissed Gaunt. His Tanith war-knife bit through the air and pinned the Patrician's skull to the blackness for a second. With a mouthful of blood bubbling his scream, Flense teetered away backwards and fell with a slapping splash into a pool of black fluid.

His body shattered and aching, Gaunt lay back on the rock shelf. His men, he thought, they'll...

There was the serial crack of an exotic carbine, a lasrifle and a barb-lance. Gaunt struggled up. Caffran, Rawne, Mkoll, Larkin and Bragg stalked into the cavern. The three Jantine lay dead in the gloom.

'The surface... we've got to... ' Gaunt coughed.

'We're going,' Rawne said, as Bragg lifted the helpless form of Domor.

Gaunt stumbled across to Dorden. The medic was still alive. Drained of power by the cavern, Flense's pistol had only grazed him, as it had only grazed Gaunt's chest when he had thrown himself at Flense. Gaunt lifted Dorden in his arms. Caffran and Mkoll moved to help him, but Gaunt shrugged them off.

'We haven't got much time now. Let's get out of here.'

TWENTY-NINE

The subsurface explosion ruptured most of the Target Primaris on Menazoid Epsilon and set it burning incandescently. Imperial forces

pulled away from the vanquished moon and returned to their support
ships in high orbit.

Gaunt received a communiqué from Warmaster Macaroth, thank-
ing him for his efforts and applauding his success.

Gaunt screwed the foil up and threw it away. Bandaged and aching,
he moved through the medical wing of the frigate *Navarre*, checking
on his wounded... Domor, Dorden, Corbec, Larkin, Bragg, a hundred
more...

As he passed Corbec's cot, the grizzled colonel called him over in a
hoarse, weak whisper.

'Rawne told me you found the thing. Blew it up. How did you know?'

'Corbec?'

'How did you know what to do? Back on Pyrites, you told me the path
would be hard. Even when we found out what we were looking for, you
never said what you'd do when you found it. How did you decide?'

Gaunt smiled.

'Because it was wrong. You don't know what I saw down there, Colm.
Men do insane things. Feth, if I'd been insane enough to try and harness
what I found... if I'd succeeded... I could have made myself warmaster.
Who knows, even emperor...'

'Emperor Gaunt. Heh. Got a ring to it. Bit fething sacrilegious, though.'

Gaunt smiled. The feeling was unfamiliar. 'The Vermilion secret of
Epsilon was heretical and tainted by Chaos. Bad, whichever way you
care to gloss it. But that's not what really made me destroy it.'

Corbec hunkered up onto his elbows. 'Kidding me? Why then?'

Ibram Gaunt put his head in his hands and sighed the sigh of someone released from a great burden. 'Someone told me what to do,
colonel. It was a long time ago...'

A MEMORY

Four Hyrkan troopers were splitting fruit in the snowy courtyard, lit by a ring of braziers. They had found some barrels in an undercroft and opened them to discover the great round globe-fruit from a summer crop stored in spiced oil. They were joking and laughing as they set them on a mounting block and hacked them into segments with their bayonets. One had stolen a big gilt serving platter from the kitchens, and they were piling it with slices, ready to carry it through to the main hall where the body of men were carousing and drinking to their victory.

Night was stealing in across the shattered roofs of the Winter Palace, and stars were coming out, frosty points in the cold darkness.

The Boy, the cadet commissar, wandered out across the courtyard, taking in the stillness. Distant voices, laughing and singing, filtered across the stone space. Gaunt smiled. He could make out a barrack-room victory song, harmonised badly by forty or more Hyrkan voices. Someone had substituted his name in the lyric in place of the hero. It didn't scan, but they sang it anyway, rousingly when it came to the bawdy parts.

Gaunt's shoulder blades still throbbed from the countless congratulatory slaps he had taken in the last few hours. Maybe they would stop calling him 'The Boy' now.

He looked up, catching sight of the landing lights of a dozen troop ships ferrying fresh occupation forces down from orbit, their bulks invisible against the darkness of the night. The landing lights reminded him of constellations. He had never been able to make sense of the stars. People drew figures in them: warriors, bulls, serpents, crowns; arbitrary shapes, it seemed to him, imperfect sense made of stellar positions.

Back on Manzipor, back home years ago, the cook Oric would sit him

263

on his knee at nightfall and teach him the names of the star groups. Years ago. He really had been a boy then. Oric knew the names, drew the shapes, linked stars until they made a ram or a lion. Gaunt had never been able to see the shapes without the lines linking the stars.

Here, now, he knew the lines of lights represented drop-ships, but he couldn't imagine their shapes. Just lights. Stars and lights, lights and stars, signifying meanings and purposes he couldn't yet see.

Like the stars, the sweeping ship-lights occasionally went dim as they passed beyond the wreathes of smoke that were streaming, black against the black sky, from the parts of the Winter Palace that still smouldered.

Buttoning his storm-coat, Gaunt crossed the wide expanse of flag-stones, his boots slipping in the slush. He passed a great stack of Secessionist helmets, piled in a trophy mound. There was a stink of stale sweat and defeat about them. Someone had painted a crude version of the Hyrkan regimental griffon on each and every one.

The men at the braziers looked up as his figure loomed out of the darkness.

'It's the Boy!' one cried. Gaunt winced and smirked at the same time.

'The Victor of Darendara!' another said with a drunken glee that entirely lacked irony.

'Come and join the feast, sir!' the first said, wiping his juice-stained hands on the front of his tunic. 'The men would like to raise a glass or two with you.'

'Or three!'

'Or five or ten or a hundred!'

Gaunt nodded his appreciation. 'I'll be in shortly. Open a cask for me.'

They jibed and cackled back, returning to their work. As Gaunt moved past, one of them turned and held out a dripping half-moon of fruit.

'Take this at least! Freshest thing we've had in weeks!'

Gaunt took the segment, scooping the cluster of seeds and pith out of its core with a finger. In its smile of husky, oil-wet rind, the fruit was salmon-pink, ripe and heavy with water and juice. He bit into it as he strode away, waving his thanks to the men.

It was sweet. Cool. The fruit flesh disintegrated in his hungry mouth and flooded his throat with rich, sugary fluid. Juice dribbled down his chin. He laughed, like a boy again. It was the sweetest thing he'd tasted on Darendara.

No, not the sweetest.

The sweetest thing he had tasted here was his first triumph. His first victorious command. His first chance to serve the Emperor and the Imperium and the service he had been raised to obey and love.

In a lit doorway ahead, a figure appeared. Gaunt recognised the bulky silhouette immediately. He fumbled with the fruit segment, about to salute.

'At ease, Ibram,' Oktar said. 'Carry on munching. That stuff looks good. Might just have to get myself a piece too.

'Walk with me.'

Gnawing the sweet flesh back to the rind, Gaunt fell in beside Oktar. They passed the men at the brazier again, and Oktar caught a whole fruit as it was tossed to him, splitting it open with his huge thumbs. The pair walked on wordlessly towards the Palace chapel grounds, through a herb-scented garden cast in blue darkness. Both ate, slobbering and spitting pips. Oktar handed a portion of his fruit to Gaunt and they finished it off.

Standing under the stained glass oriel of the chapel, they cast the rinds aside and stood for a long while, swallowing and licking juice from their dripping fingers.

'Tastes good,' Oktar said at last.

'Will it always taste this fine?' Gaunt asked.

'Always, I promise you. Triumph is the endgame we all chase and desire. When you get it, hang on to it and relish every second.' Oktar wiped his chin, his face a shadow in the gloom.

'But remember this, Ibram. It's not always as obvious as it seems. Winning is everything, but the trick is to know where the winning really is. Hell, killing the enemy is the job of the regular trooper. The task of a commissar is more subtle.'

'Finding how to win?'

'Or what to win. Or what kind of win will really count in the long term. You have to use everything you have, every insight, every angle. Never, ever be a slave to simple tactical directives. The officer cadre are about as sharp as an ork's arse sometimes. We're political animals, Ibram. Through us, if we do our job properly, the black and white of war is tempered. We are the interpreters of combat, the translators We give meaning to war, subtlety, purpose even. Killing is the most abhorrent, mindless profession known to man. Our role is to fashion the killing machine of the human species into a positive force. For the Emperor's sake. For the sake of our own consciences.'

They paused in reflection for a while. Oktar lit one of his luxuriously fat cigars and kissed big white smoke rings up into the night breeze.

'Before I forget,' he suddenly added, 'there is one last task I have for you before you retire. Retire! What am I saying? Before you join the men in the hall and drink yourself stupid!'

Gaunt laughed.

'There is an interrogation. Inquisitor Defay has arrived to question the captives. You know the usual witch-hunting post mortem High Command insists on. But he's a sound man, known him for years. I spoke to him just now and apparently he wants your help.'

'Me?'

'Specifically you. Asked for you by name. One of his prisoners refuses to speak to anyone else.'

Gaunt blinked. He was confused, but he also knew who the commissar-general was talking about.

'Cut along to see him before you go raising hell with the boys. Okay?'

Gaunt nodded.

Oktar smacked him on the arm. 'You did well today, Ibram. Your father would be proud.'

'I know he is, sir.'

Oktar may have smiled, but it was impossible to tell in the darkness of the chapel garden.

Gaunt turned to go.

'One thing, sir,' he said, turning back.

'Ask it, Gaunt.'

'Could you try and encourage the men to stop referring to me as "The Boy"?'

Gaunt left Oktar laughing raucously in the darkness.

Gaunt's hands were sticky with drying juice. He strode down a long, lamp-lit hallway, straightening his coat and setting his cadet's cap squarely on his head.

Under an archway ahead, Hyrkans in full battledress stood guard, weapons hanging loosely from shoulder slings. There were others, too: robed, hooded beings skulking in candle-shadows, muttering, exchanging data-slates and sealed testimony recordings.

Incense hung in the air. Somewhere, someone was whimpering.

Major Tanhause, supervising the Hyrkan presence, waved him through with a wink and directed him down to the left.

There was a boy in the passage to the left, standing outside a closed door. No older than me, mused Gaunt as he approached. The boy looked up. He was pale and thin, taller than Gaunt, wearing long russet robes, and his eyes were fierce. Lank black hair flopped down one side of his pale face.

'You can't come in here,' he said sullenly.

'I'm Gaunt. Cadet-Commissar Gaunt.'

The lad frowned. He turned, knocked at the door and then opened it slightly as a voice answered. There was an exchange Gaunt could not hear before a large figure emerged from the room, closing the door behind him.

'That will be all for now, Gravier,' the figure told the boy, who retreated into the shadows. The figure was tall and powerful, bigger even than Oktar. He wore intricate armour draped with a long purple cloak. His face was totally hidden behind a blank cloth hood that terrified Gaunt. Bright eyes glared at him through the hood's eye slits for a moment, appraising him. Then the man peeled the hood off.

His face was handsome and aquiline. Gaunt was surprised to find compassion there, pain, fatigue, understanding. The face was cold white, the flesh pale, but somehow there was a warmth and a light.

'I am Defay,' the inquisitor said in a low, resonating voice. 'You are Cadet Gaunt, I presume.'

'Yes, sir. What would you have me do?'

Defay approached the cadet and placed a hand on his shoulder, turning him before he spoke. 'A girl. You know her.'

It was not a question.

'I know the girl. I... saw her.'

'She is the key, Gaunt. In her mind lie the secrets of whatever turned this world to disorder. It's tiresome, I know, but my task is to unlock such secrets.'

'We all serve the Emperor, my lord.'

'We certainly do, Gaunt. Now look. She says she knows you. A nonsense, I'm sure. But she says you are the only one she will answer to. Gaunt, I've performed my ministry long enough to recognise an opening. I could... extricate the secrets I seek in any number of ways, but the most painless – to me and her both – would be to use you. Are you up to it?'

Gaunt looked round at Defay. His stern yet avuncular manner reminded him of someone. Oktar – no, Uncle Dercius.

'What do you want me to do?'

'Go in there and talk to her. Nothing more. There are no wires to record you, no vista-grams to watch you. I just want you to talk to her. If she says what she wants to say to you, it may provide an opening I can use.'

Gaunt entered the room and the door shut behind him. The small chamber was bare except for a table with a stool on either side. The girl sat on one. A sodium lamp fluttered on the wall.

Gaunt sat down on the other stool, facing her.

Her eyes were as black as her hair. Her dress was as white as her skin. She was beautiful.

'Ibram! At last! There are so many things I need to tell you!' Her voice was soft yet firm, her High Gothic perfect. Gaunt backed away from her direct stare.

She leaned across the table urgently, gazing into his eyes.

'Don't be afraid, Ibram Gaunt.'

'I'm not.'

'Oh, you are. I don't have to be a mind reader to see that. Though, of course, I am a mind reader.'

Gaunt breathed deeply. 'Then tell me what I want to know.'

'Clever, clever,' she chuckled, sitting back.

Gaunt leaned forward, insistent. 'Look, I don't want to be here either. Let's get this over with. You're a psyker – astound me with your visions or shut the hell up. I have other things I would rather be doing.'

'Drinking with your men. Fruit.'

'What?'

'You crave more of the sweet fruit. You long for it. Sweet, juicy fruit...'

Gaunt shuddered. 'How did you know?'

She grinned impishly. 'The juice is all down your chin and the front of your coat.'

Gaunt couldn't hide his smile. 'Now who's being clever? That was no psyker trick. That was observation.'

'But true enough, wasn't it? Is there a whole lot of difference?'

Gaunt nodded. 'Yes... yes there is. What you said to me earlier. It made no sense, but it had nothing to do with the stains on my coat either. Why did you ask for me?'

She sighed, lowering her head. There was a long pause.

The voice that finally replied to him wasn't hers any more. It was a scratchy, wispy thing that made him start backwards. By the Emperor, but it was suddenly so cold in here!

He saw his own breath steam and realised it wasn't his imagination.

The whisper-dry voice said: 'I don't want to see things, Ibram, but still I do. In my head. Sometimes wonderful things. Sometimes awful things. I see what people show me. Minds are like books.'

Gaunt stammered, sliding back on his seat. 'I... I... like books.'

'I know you do. I read that. You liked Boniface's books. He had so many of them.'

Gaunt froze, tremors of worry plucking at his spine. He felt an ice cold droplet of sweat chase down his brow from his hairline. He felt trapped.

'How could you know about that?'

'You know how.'

The temperature in the room had dropped to freezing. Gaunt saw the ice crystals form across the table top, crackling and causing the wood to creak. Gooseflesh pimpled his body.

He leapt up and backed to the door. 'That's enough! This interview is over!'

He tried the door, making to leave. It was locked. Or at least, it would not open for him. Something held it shut. Gaunt hammered on it. 'Inquisitor! Inquisitor Defay! Let me out!'

His voice sounded blunt and hollow in the tiny confines of the freezing room. He was more terrified than he had ever been in his life.

He looked round. The girl was crawling across the floor towards him, her eyes blank and filmed. Spittle welled out of her lolling mouth. She smiled. It was the most dreadful thing young Ibram Gaunt had ever seen.

When she spoke, her voice did not match her mouth. The utterances came from some other, horrid place. Her lips were just keeping bad time with them.

Cowering in a corner, watching her slow, animalistic approach across the icy floor, Gaunt managed to whisper: 'What do you want from me? What?'

'Your life.' A feathery, inhuman voice.

'Get away from me!' Gaunt murmured, struggling with the door handle, to no avail.

'What do you want to know?' the horror asked, suddenly, calculatingly.

His mind raced. Maybe if he kept it talking, he could slow it down, figure a way out... 'Will I make commissar?' he snapped, hammering on the door, not really caring about his question.

'Of course.'

The lock was straining, starting to give. A few moments more. Keep it talking! 'Tell me the rest,' he urged, hoping she would cease her crawl towards him.

She was silent for a few seconds as she thought. Her eyes went blacker. The tremulous, thin voice spoke again. 'What I told you before. There will be seven. Seven stones of power. Cut them and you will be free. Do not kill them. But first you must find your ghosts.'

Gaunt shrugged, fighting with the lock, still not really listening. 'What the feth does that mean?'

'What does "feth" mean?' she replied plainly.

Gaunt hesitated. He had no idea what the word meant or why he had used it.

'Your future impinges on you, Ibram. Ghosts, ghosts, ghosts.'

Gaunt turned. He'd fight if he had to. The door wasn't giving and the slack-mouthed freak was getting too close. 'In my profession I make plenty of those. Tell me something useful.'

'You're an anroth.'

'A what?'

She hissed and stared up at him. 'I haven't the faintest idea what it means, but I know you are one. Anroth. Anroth. That's you.'

Gaunt scrabbled across the room to the far wall to put more space between them.

She crawled around slowly.

'This is all madness! I'm leaving,' he said.

'So leave. But one thing before you go.'

He looked back and she smiled terrifyingly at him under her veil of loose black hair.

'The warp knows you, Ibram Gaunt.'

'To hell with the warp!' he barked.

'Ibram, there will come a day... far off, far away, when something coloured in vermilion will be the most valuable thing you have ever known. Chase it. Find it. Others will seek it, and you will defend it in blood. The blood of your ghosts.'

'Enough with this!'

She shuffled forward on her knees like an animal. Spit from her mouth splashed the floor.

'Remember this! Ibram! Ibram! Please! So many will die if you don't! So many, so very many!'

'If I don't what?' he snapped, trying to find a way out of this hell.

'Destroy it. You must destroy it. The vermilion thing. Destroy it. It makes iron without souls.'

'You're insane!'

'Iron without souls!'

She clawed at his legs, scratching and pulling at the ice-rimed cloth.

'Get off me!'

'Worlds will die! A warmaster will die! Don't let any of them have it! Any of them! It is not a matter of the wrong hands! All will be wrong hands! No one has the right to use it! Destroy it! Ibram! Please!'

He threw her off and she fell away from him, sprawling on the frozen floor, crying.

He reached the door, his hand on the latch. It was suddenly unlocked. He turned back to her. She rose from the floor, her dark eyes wet with tears. Her voice was her own again now.

'Don't let them, Ibram. Destroy it.'

'I've never heard such rubbish,' Gaunt said diffidently. He took a deep breath. 'If you're truly gifted, why don't you tell me something real? Something I might actually want to know. Like... like how did my father die?'

She pulled herself up onto the stool. The room went cold again. Fiercely cold. She looked deep into his eyes and Gaunt felt the stare pressing into his brain.

Despite himself, he sat down again on the stool. He looked at her dark eyes. Something told him what was coming.

In her own voice, she began. 'Your father... you were his first and his only son. First and only...'

She fell silent again for a second, then she continued: 'Kentaur. It was on Kentaur. Dercius was commanding the main force and your father was leading the elite strike...'

OF THEIR LIVES
IN THE RUINS
OF THEIR CITIES

It feels like the afterlife, and none of them are entirely convinced that it isn't.

They have pitched up in a cold and rain-lashed stretch of lowland country, on the morning after somebody else's triumph, with a bunch of half-arsed orders, a dislocating sense that the war is elsewhere and carrying on without them, and very little unit cohesion. They have a couple of actions under their belts, just enough to lift their chins, but nothing like enough to bind them together or take the deeper pain away and, besides, other men have collected the medals. They're out in the middle of nowhere, marching further and further away from anything that matters any more, because nothing matters any more.

They are just barely the Tanith First and Only. They are not Gaunt's Ghosts.

They are never going to be Gaunt's Ghosts.

Silent lightning strobes in the distance. His back turned towards it and the rain, the young Tanith infantryman watches Ibram Gaunt at work from the entrance of the war tent. The colonel-commissar is seated at the far end of a long table around which, an hour earlier, two dozen Guard officers and adjutants were gathered for a briefing. Now Gaunt is alone.

The infantryman has been allowed to stand at ease, but he is on call. He has been selected to act as runner for the day. It's his job to attend the commander, to pick up any notes or message satchels at a moment's notice, and deliver them as per orders. Foot couriers are necessary because the vox is down. It's been down a lot, this past week. It'd been patchy and unreliable around Voltis City. Out in the lowlands, it's useless, like audio soup. You can hear voices, now and then. Someone said maybe the distant, soundless lightning is to blame.

Munitorum-issue chem lamps, those tin-plate models that unscrew and then snap out for ignition, have been strung along the roof line, and there is a decent rechargeable glow-globe on the table beside Gaunt's elbow. The lamps along the roof line are swaying and rocking in the wind that's finding its way into the long tent. The lamps add a golden warmth to the tent's shadowy interior, a marked contrast to the raw, wet blow driving up the valley outside. There is rain in the air, sticky clay underfoot, a whitewashed sky overhead, and a line of dirty hills in the middle distance that look like a lip of rock that someone has scraped their boots against. Somewhere beyond the hills, the corpse of a city lies in a shallow grave.

Gaunt is studying reports that have been printed out on paper flimsies. He has weighed them down on the surface of the folding table with cartons of bolter-rounds so they won't blow away. The wind is really getting in under the tent's skirt. He's writing careful notes with a stylus. The infantryman can only imagine the importance of those jottings. Tactical formulations, perhaps? Attack orders?

Gaunt is not well liked, but the infantryman finds him interesting. Watching him work at least takes the infantryman's mind off the fact that he's standing in the mouth of a tent with his arse out in the rain.

No indeed, Colonel-Commissar Ibram Gaunt is not well liked. A reputation for genocide will do that to a man's character. He is intriguing, though. For a career soldier, he seems surprisingly reflective, a man of thought not action. There is a promise of wisdom in his narrow features. The infantryman wonders if this was a mistake of ethnicity, a misreading brought about by cultural differences. Gaunt and the infantryman were born on opposite sides of the sector.

The infantryman finds it amusing to imagine Gaunt grown very elderly. Then he might look, the infantryman thinks, like one of those wizened old savants, the kind that know everything about fething everything.

However, the infantryman also has good reason to predict that Gaunt will never live long enough to grow old. Gaunt's profession mitigates against it, as does the cosmos he has been born into, and the specific nature of his situation.

If the Archenemy of Mankind does not kill Ibram Gaunt, the infantryman thinks, then Gaunt's own men will do the job.

A better tent.

Gaunt writes the words at the top of his list. He knows he'll have to look up the correct Munitorum code number, though he thinks it's 1NX1G1xA. Sym will know and–

Sym *would have* known, but Sym is dead. Gaunt exhales. He really has to train himself to stop doing that. Sym had been his adjutant and Gaunt had come to rely on him; it still seems perfectly normal to turn and expect to find Sym there, waiting, ready and resourceful. Sym had known how to procure a dress coat in the middle of the night, or a pot of collar starch, or a bottle of decent amasec, or a copy of the embarkation transcripts before they were published. He'd have known the Munitorum serial code for a *tent/temperate winter*. The structure Gaunt is sitting in is not a *tent/temperate winter*. It's an old tropical shelter left over from another theatre. It's waxed against rain, but there are canvas vents low down along the base hem designed to keep air circulating on balmy, humid days. This particular part of Voltemand seldom sees balmy humid days. The east wind, its cheeks full of rain, is pushing the vents open and invading the tent like a polar gale.

Under *A better tent* he writes: *A portable heater*.

He hardly cares for his own comfort, but he'd noted the officers and their junior aides around the table that morning, backs hunched, moods foul, teeth gritted against the cold, every single one of them in a hurry to get the meeting over so they could head back to their billets and their own camp stoves.

Men who are uncomfortable and in a hurry do not make good decisions. They rush things. They are not thorough. They often make general noises of consent just to get briefings over with, and that morning they'd all done it: the Tanith officers, the Ketzok tankers, the Litus B.R.U., all of them.

Gaunt knows it's all payback, though. The whole situation is payback. He is being punished for making that Blueblood general look like an idiot, even though Gaunt had had the moral high ground. He had been avenging Tanith blood, because there isn't enough of that left for anyone to go around wasting it.

He thinks about the letter in his pocket, and then lets the thought go again.

When he'd been assigned to the Tanith, Gaunt had relished the prospect as it was presented on paper: a first founding from a small, agrarian world that was impeccable in its upkeep of tithes and devotions. Tanith had no real black marks in the Administratum's eyes, and no longstanding martial traditions to get tangled up in. There had been the opportunity to build something worthwhile, three regiments of light infantry to begin with, though Gaunt's plans had been significantly more ambitious than that: a major infantry force, fast and mobile, well-drilled and disciplined. The Munitorum's recruitment agents reported that the Tanith seemed to have a natural knack for tracking and covert work, and Gaunt had hoped to add that speciality to the regiment's portfolio. From the moment he'd reviewed the Tanith dossier, Gaunt had begun to see the sense of Slaydo's deathbed bequest to him.

The plans and dreams have come apart, though. The Archenemy, still stinging from Balhaut, burned worlds in the name of vengeance, and one of those worlds was Tanith. Gaunt got out with his life, just barely, and with him he'd dragged a few of the mustered Tanith men, enough for one regiment. Not enough men to ever be anything more than a minor infantry support force, to die as trench fodder in some Throne-forgotten ocean of mud, but just enough men to hate his living guts for the rest of forever for not letting them die with their planet.

Ibram Gaunt has been trained as a political officer, and he is a very good one, though the promotion Slaydo gave him was designed to spare him from the slow death of a political career. His political talents, however, can usually find a positive expression for even the worst scenarios.

In the cold lowlands of Voltemand, an upbeat interpretation is stubbornly eluding him.

He has stepped away from a glittering career with the Hyrkans, cut his political ties with all the men of status and influence who could assist him or advance him, and ended up in a low-value theatre on a third-tier warfront, in command of a salvaged, broken regiment of unmotivated men who hate him. There is still the letter in his pocket, of course.

He looks down at his list, and writes:

Spin this shit into gold, or get yourself a transfer to somewhere with a desk and a driver.

He looks at this for a minute, and then scratches it out. He puts the stylus down.

'Trooper,' he calls to the infantryman in the mouth of the tent. He knows the young man's name is Caffran. He is generally good with names, and he makes an effort to learn them quickly, but he is also sparing when it comes to using them. Show a common lasman you know his name too early, and it'll seem like you're trying far too hard to be his new best friend, especially if you just let his home and family burn.

It'll seem like you're weak.

The infantryman snaps to attention sharply.

'Step inside,' Gaunt calls, beckoning with two hooked fingers. 'Is it still raining?'

'Sir,' says Caffran non-committally as he approaches the table.

'I want you to locate Corbec for me. I think he's touring the west picket.'

'Sir.'

'You've got that?'

'Find Colonel Corbec, sir.'

Gaunt nods. He picks up his stylus and folds one of the flimsies in half, ready to write on the back of it. 'Tell him to ready up three squads and meet me by the north post in thirty minutes. You need me to write that down for you?'

'No, sir.'

'Three squads, north post, thirty minutes,' says Gaunt. He writes it down anyway, and then embosses it with his biometric signet ring to transfer his authority code. He hands the note to the trooper. 'Thirty minutes,' he repeats. 'Time for me to get some breakfast. Is the mess tent still cooking?'

'Sir,' Caffran replies, this time flavouring it with a tiny, sullen shrug.

Gaunt looks him in the eye for a moment. Caffran manages to return about a second of insolent resentment, and then looks away into space over Gaunt's shoulder.

'What was her name?' Gaunt asks.

'What?'

'I took something from every single Tanith man,' says Gaunt, pushing back his chair and standing up. 'Apart from the obvious, of course. I was wondering what I'd taken from you in particular. What was her name?'

'How do you–'

'A man as young as you, it's bound to be a girl. And that tattoo indicates a family betrothal.'

'You know about Tanith marks?' Caffran can't hide his surprise.

'I studied up, trooper. I wanted to know what sort of men my reputation was going to depend upon.'

There is a pause. Rain beats against the outer skin of the tent like drumming fingertips.

'Laria,' Caffran says quietly. 'Her name was Laria.'

'I'm sorry for your loss,' says Gaunt.

Caffran looks at him again. He sneers slightly. 'Aren't you going to tell me it will be all right? Aren't you going to assure me that I'll find another girl somewhere?'

'If it makes you feel better,' says Gaunt. He sighs and turns back to look at Caffran. 'It's unlikely, but I'll say it if it makes you feel better.' Gaunt puts on a fake, jaunty smile. 'Somewhere, somehow, in one of the warzones we march into, you'll find the girl you're supposed to be with, and you'll live happily ever after. There. Better?'

Caffran's mouth tightens and he mutters something under his breath.

'If you're going to call me a bastard, do it out loud,' says Gaunt. 'I don't know why you're so pissed off. You were walking out on this Laria anyway.'

'We were betrothed!'

'You'd signed up for the Imperial Guard, trooper. First Founding. You were never going to see Tanith again. I don't know why you had the nerve to get hitched to the poor cow in the first place.'

'Of course I was coming back to her–'

'You sign up, you leave. Warp transfers, long rotations, tours along the rim. You never go back. You never go home, not once the Guard has you. Years go by, decades. You forget where you came from in the end.'

'But the recruiting officer said–'

'He lied to you, trooper. Do you think any bastard would sign up if the recruiters told the truth?'

Caffran sags. 'He lied?'

'Yes. But I won't. That's the one thing you can count on with me. Now go and get Corbec.'

Caffran snaps off a poor salute, turns and heads out of the tent.

Gaunt sits down again. He begins to collect up the flimsies, and packs away the bolter shell cartons holding them down. He thinks about the letter in his pocket again.

On his list, he writes:

Appoint a new adjutant.

Under that, he writes:

Find a new adjutant.

Finally, under that, he writes:

Start telling a few lies?

He pulls his storm coat on as he leaves the tent, partly to fend off the rain, and partly to cover his jacket. It's his number one staff-issue field jacket, but it's become too soiled with clay from the trek out of Voltis City to wear with any dignity. He has a grubby, old number two issue that he keeps in his kit as a spare, but it still has Hyrkan patches on the collar, the shoulders and the cuffs, and that's embarrassing. Sym would have patched the skull-and-crossed-knives of the Tanith onto it by now. He'd have got out his sewing kit and made sure both of Gaunt's field uniforms were code perfect, the way he kept the rest of Gaunt's day-to-day life neat and sewn up tight.

Steamy smoke is rising from the cowled chimneys of the cook-tents, and he can smell the greasy blocks of processed nutrition fibre being fried. His stomach rumbles. He sets off towards the kitchens. Beyond the row of mess tents lies the canvas city of the Tanith position, and to the north-east of that, the batteries of the Ketzok.

Beyond that, the edge of the skyline flicks on and off with the unnervingly quiet lightning, far away, like a malfunctioning lamp filament that refuses to stay lit.

Slab is pretty gruesome stuff. Pressure-treated down from any and all available nutritional sources by the Munitorum, it has no discernible flavour apart from a faint, mucusy aftertaste, and it looks like grey-white putty. In fact, years before at Schola Progenium on Ignatius Cardinal, an acquaintance of Gaunt's had once kneaded some of it into a form that authentically resembled a brick of plastic explosive, complete with fuses, and then carried out a practical joke on the Master of the Scholam Arsenal that was notable for both the magnificent extent of the disruption it caused, and the stunning severity of the subsequent punishment. Slab, as it's known to every common Guard lasman, comes canned and it comes freeze-dried, it comes in packets and it comes in boxes, it comes in individual heated tins and it comes in catering blocks. Company cooks slice, dice and mince it, and use it as the bulk base of any meal when local provision sources are unavailable. They flavour it with whatever they have to hand, usually foil sachets of powder with names like *groxtail* and *vegetable (root)* and *sausage (assorted)*. Ibram Gaunt has lived on it for a great deal of his adult and sub-adult life. He is so used to the stuff, he actually misses it when it isn't around.

Men have gathered around the cook tents, huddled against the weather under their camo-cloaks. Gaunt still hasn't got used to wearing his, even though he'd promised the Tanith colonel he would, as a show of unity. It doesn't hang right around him, and in the Voltemand wind, it tugs and tangles like a devil.

The Tanith don't seem to have the same trouble. They half-watch him approach, shrouded, hooded, some supping from mess cans. They watch him approach. There is a shadow in their eyes. They are a wild lot. Beads of rainwater glint in their tangled dark hair, though occasionally the glints are studs or nose rings, piercings in lips or eyebrows. They like their ink, the Tanith, and they wear the complex, traditional patterns of blue and green on their pale skins with pride. Cheeks, throats, forearms and the backs of hands display spirals and loops, leaves and branches, sigils and whorls. They also like their edges. The Tanith weapon is a long knife with a straight, silver blade that has evolved from a hunting tool. They could hunt with it well enough, silently, like phantoms.

Gaunt's Ghosts. Someone had come up with that within a few days of their first deployment on Blackshard. It had been the sociopath with the long-las, as Gaunt recalled it, a man known to him as 'Mad'. A more withering and scornful nickname, Gaunt can't imagine.

* * *

Rawne says, 'Here comes the fether now.'

He takes a sip from his water bottle, which does not contain water, and turns as if to say something to Murt Feygor.

'But I paid you that back!' Feygor exclaims, managing to make his voice sound wounded and plaintive, the wronged party.

Rawne makes a retort and steps back, in time to affect a blind collision with Gaunt as he makes his way into the cook tent. The impact is hard enough to rock Gaunt off his feet.

'Easy there, sir!' cries Varl, hooking a hand under Gaunt's armpit to keep him off the ground. He hoists Gaunt up.

'Thank you,' Gaunt says.

'Varl, sir,' replies the trooper. He grins a big, shit-eating grin. 'Infantryman first class Ceglan Varl, sir. Wouldn't want you taking a tumble now, would I, sir? Wouldn't want you to go falling over and getting yourself all dirty.'

'I'm sure you wouldn't, trooper,' says Gaunt. 'Carry on.'

He looks back at Rawne and Feygor.

'That was all me, sir,' says Feygor, hands up. 'The major and I were having a little dispute, and I distracted him.'

It sounds convincing. Gaunt doesn't know much about the trooper called Feygor, but he's met his type before, a conniving son of a bitch who has been blessed with the silken vocal talent to sell any story to anyone.

Gaunt doesn't even bother looking at him. He stares at Rawne.

Major Rawne stares right back. His handsome face betrays no emotion whatsoever. Gaunt is a tall man, but Rawne is one of the Tanith he doesn't tower over, and he only has a few pounds on the major.

'I know what you're thinking,' Rawne says.

'Do you, Rawne? Is that an admission of unholy gifts? Should I call for emissaries of the Ordos to examine you?'

'Ha ha,' says Rawne in a laughless voice. He just says the sounds. 'Look, that there was a genuine slip, sir. A genuine bump. But we have a little history, sir, you and I, so you're bound to ascribe more motive to it than that.'

A little history. In the Blackshard deadzones, Rawne had used the opportunity of a quiet moment alone with Gaunt to express his dissatisfaction with Gaunt's leadership in the strongest possible terms. Gaunt had disarmed him and carried Rawne's unconscious body clear of the fighting area. It's hard to say what part of that *history* yanks Rawne most: the fact that he had failed to murder Gaunt, or the fact that Gaunt had saved him.

'Wow,' says Gaunt.

'What?'

'You used the word *ascribe*,' says Gaunt, and turns to go into the cook tent. Over his shoulder, he calls out, 'If you say it was a bump, then it was a bump, major. We need to trust each other.'

Gaunt turns and looks back.

'Starting in about twenty minutes. After breakfast, I'm going to take an advance out to get a look at Kosdorf. You'll be in charge.'

They watch him pick up a mess tin from the pile and head towards the slab vat where the cook is waiting with a ladle and an apologetic expression.

He sits down with his tin at one of the mess benches. The slab seems to have been refried and then stewed along with something that was either string or mechanically recovered gristle.

'I don't know how you can eat that.'

Gaunt looks up. It's the boy, the civilian boy. The boy sits down facing him.

'Sit down, if you like,' Gaunt says.

Milo looks pinched with cold, and he has his arms wrapped around his body.

'That stuff,' he says, jutting his chin suspiciously in the direction of Gaunt's tin. 'It's not proper food. I thought Imperial Guardsmen were supposed to get proper food. I thought that was the Compact of Service between the Munitorum and the Guardsmen: three square meals a day.'

'This is proper food.'

The boy shakes his head. He is only about seventeen, but he's going to be big when he fills out. There's a blue fish inked over his right eye.

'It's not proper food,' he insists.

'Well, you're not a proper Guardsman, so you're not entitled to a proper opinion.'

The boy looks hurt. Gaunt doesn't want to be mean. He owes Brin Milo a great deal. Two people had gone beyond the call to help Ibram Gaunt get off Tanith alive. Sym had been one, and the man had died making the effort. Milo had been the other. The boy was just a servant, a piper appointed by the Elector of Tanith Magna to wait on Gaunt during his stay. Gaunt understands why the boy has stuck with the regiment since the Tanith disaster. The regiment is all Milo has left, all he has left of his people, and he feels he has nowhere else to go, but Gaunt wishes Milo would disappear. There are camps and shelters, there are Munitorum refugee programmes. Civilians didn't belong at the frontline. They remind troopers of what they've left behind or, in the Tanith case, lost forever. They erode morale. Gaunt has suggested several times that Milo might be better off at a camp at Voltis City. He even has enough pull left to get Milo sent to a Schola Progenium or an orphanage for the officer class.

Milo refuses to leave. It's as if he's waiting for something to happen, for someone to arrive or something to be revealed. It's as if he's waiting for Gaunt to make good on a promise.

'Did you want something?' Gaunt asks.

'I want to come.'

'Come where?'

'You're going to scout the approach to Kosdorf this morning. I want to come.'

Gaunt feels a little flush of anger. 'Rawne tell you that?'

'No one told me.'

'Caffran, then. Damn, I thought Caffran might be trustworthy.'

'No one told me,' says Milo. 'I mean it. I just had a feeling, a feeling you'd go out this morning. This whole taskforce was sent to clear Kosdorf, wasn't it?'

'This whole taskforce was intended to be an instrument of petty and spiteful vengeance,' Gaunt replies.

'By whom?' asks Milo.

Gaunt finishes the last of his slab. He drops the fork into the empty tin. Not the best he'd ever had. Throne knows, not the worst, either.

'That general,' Gaunt says.

'General Sturm?'

'That's the one,' Gaunt nods. 'General Noches Sturm of the 50th Volpone. He was trying to use the Tanith First, and we made him look like a prize scrotum by taking Voltis when his oh-so-mighty Bluebloods couldn't manage the trick. Throne, he even let us ship back to the transport fleet before deciding we should stay another month or so to help clean up. He's done it all to inconvenience us. Pack, unpack. Ship to orbit, return to surface. March out into the backwaters of a defeated world to check the ruins of a dead city.'

'Make you eat crap instead of fresh rations?' asks Milo, looking at the mess tin.

'That too, probably,' says Gaunt.

'Probably shouldn't have pissed him off, then,' says Milo.

'I really probably shouldn't,' Gaunt agrees. 'Never mind, I heard he's getting retasked. If the Emperor shows me any providence, I'll never have to see Sturm again.'

'He'll get his just desserts,' says Milo.

'What does that mean?' asks Gaunt.

Milo shrugs. 'I dunno. It just feels that way to me. People get what they deserve, sooner or later. The universe always gets payback. One day, somebody will stick it to Sturm just like he's sticking it to you.'

'Well, that thought's cheered me up,' says Gaunt, 'except the part about getting what you deserve. What does the universe have in store for me, do you suppose, after what happened to Tanith?'

'You only need to worry about that if you think you did anything wrong,' says Milo. 'If your conscience is clear, the universe will know.'

'You talk to it much?'

'What?'

'The universe? You're on first name terms?'

Milo pulls a face.

'Things could be worse, anyway,' Milo says.

'How?'

'Well, you're in charge. You're in charge of this whole task force.'

'For my sins.'

Gaunt gets to his feet. A Munitorum skivvy comes by and collects his tin.

'So?' asks Milo. 'Can I come?'

'No,' says Gaunt.

He's walked a few yards from the mess tents when Milo calls out after him. With a resigned weariness, Gaunt turns back to look at the boy.

'What?' he asks. 'I said no.'

'Take your cape,' says Milo.

'What?'

'Take your cape with you.'

'Why?'

Milo looks startled for a moment, as if he doesn't want to give the answer, or it hadn't occurred to him that anyone would need one. He dithers for a second, and seems to be making something up.

'Because Colonel Corbec likes it when you wear it,' he says. 'He thinks it shows respect.'

Gaunt nods. Good enough.

The advance is waiting for him at the north post, the end marker of the camp area. There are two batteries of Ketzok Hydras there, barrels elevated at a murky sky that occasionally blinks with silent light. Gunners sit dripping under oilskin coats on the lee side of their gun-carriages. Tracks are sunk deep in oozing grey clay. Rain hisses.

'Nice day for it,' says Colm Corbec.

'I arranged the weather especially, colonel,' replies Gaunt as he walks up. The clay is wretchedly sticky underfoot. It sucks at their boots. The men in the three squads look entirely underwhelmed at the prospect of the morning's mission. The only ones amongst them who aren't standing slope-shouldered and dejected are the three scout specialists that Corbec has chosen to round out the advance. One is the leader of the scout unit, Mkoll. Gaunt has already begun to admire Mkoll's abilities, but he has no read on the man himself. Mkoll is sort of nondescript, of medium build and modest appearance, and seems a little weather-beaten and older than the rank and file. He chooses to say very little.

Gaunt hasn't yet learned the names of the two scouts with Mkoll. One, he believes, he has overheard someone refer to as 'lucky'. The other one, the taller, thinner one, has a silent, faraway look about him that's oddly menacing.

'It may just have been me,' says Corbec, 'but didn't we spend an hour or so in the tent this morning agreeing not to do this?'

Gaunt nods.

'I thought,' says Corbec, 'we were to stay put until the Ketzok had been resupplied?'

They were. The purpose of the expedition is to evaluate and secure Kosdorf, Voltemand's second city, which had been effectively taken out in the early stages of the liberation. Orbit watch reports it as ruined, a city grave, but the emergency government and the Administratum want it locked down. The whole thing is a colossal waste of time. Voltis City, which had been the stronghold for the charismatic but now dead Archenemy demagogue Chanthar, was the key to Voltemand. The Kosdorf securement is the sort of mission that could have been handled by PDF or a third-tier Guard strength.

General Sturm is playing games, of course, getting his own back, and doing it in such a way as to make it look like he is being magnanimous. As his last act before passing control of the Voltemand theatre to a successor, Sturm appointed Gaunt to lead the expedition to Kosdorf, a command of twenty thousand men including his own Tanith, a regiment of Litus Battlefield Regimental Units, and a decent support spread of Ketzok armour.

Everyone, including the Litus and the Ketzok, have seen it for what it is, so they've started making heavy going of it, dragging their heels. At this last encampment, supposedly the final staging point before a proper run into Kosdorf, the Ketzok have complained that their ammo trains have fallen behind, and demanded a delay of thirty-six hours until they can be sure of their supplies.

The Ketzok are a decent lot. Despite a bad incident during the Voltis attack, Gaunt has developed a good working relationship with the armoured brigade, but Sturm's edict has taken the warmth out of it.

The Ketzok aren't being difficult with him, they're being difficult with the situation.

'The Ketzok can stay put,' says Gaunt. 'There's no harm getting some exercise though, is there?'

'I suppose not,' Corbec agrees.

'In this muck?' someone in the ranks calls out from behind him.

'That's enough, Larks,' Corbec says without turning. Corbec is a big fellow, tall and broad, and heavy. He raises a large hand, scoops the heavy crop of slightly greying hair out of his face, and flops it over his scalp before tying it back. Raindrops twinkle like diamonds in his beard. Despite the bullying wind, Gaunt can smell a faint odour of cigars on him.

Gaunt wonders how he's going to begin to enforce uniform code when the company colonel looks like a matted and tangled old man of the woods.

'This is just going to be a visit to size the place up,' says Gaunt, looking at Mkoll. 'I intend for us to be back before nightfall.'

Mkoll just nods.

'So what you're saying is you were getting a little bored sitting in your tent,' says Corbec.

Gaunt looks at him.

'That's all right,' Corbec smiles. 'I was getting pretty bored sitting in mine. A walk is nice, isn't it, lads?'

No one actually answers.

Gaunt walks the line with Corbec at his side, inspecting munition supplies. They're going to be moving light, but every other man's got an extra musette bag of clips, and two troopers are carrying boxes of RPGs for the launcher. Nobody makes eye contact with Gaunt as he passes.

Gaunt comes to Caffran in the line.

'What are you doing here?' Gaunt asks.

'Step forward, trooper,' says Corbec.

'I thought I was supposed to stay with you all day,' Caffran replies, stepping forward. 'I thought those were my orders.'

'Sir,' says Corbec.

'Sir,' says Caffran.

'I suppose they are,' says Gaunt and nods Caffran back into the file. *A march in the mud and rain is the least you deserve for talking out of turn*, Gaunt thinks, *especially to a civilian.*

There's a muttering somewhere. They're amused by Caffran's insolence. Gaunt gets the feeling that Corbec doesn't like it, though Corbec does little to show it. The colonel's position is difficult. If he reinforces Gaunt's authority, he risks losing all the respect the men have for him. He risks being despised and resented too.

'Let's get moving,' says Gaunt.

'Advance company!' Corbec shouts, holding one hand above his head and rotating it with the index finger upright. 'Sergeant Blane, if you please!'

'Yes, sir!' Blane calls out from the front of the formation. He leads off.

The force begins to move down the track into the rain behind the sergeant. Mkoll and his scouts, moving at a more energetic pace, take point and begin to pull away.

Gaunt waits as the infantrymen file past, their boots glopping in the mire. Not one of them so much as glances at him. They have their heads down.

He jogs to catch up with Corbec. He had hoped that getting out and doing something active might chase away his unhappiness. It isn't working so far.

He still has that letter in his pocket.

'Back again?' asks Dorden, the medicae.

The boy hovers in the doorway of the medical tent like a spectre that needs to be invited in out of the dark. The rain has picked up, and it's pattering a loud tattoo off the overhead sheets.

'I don't feel right,' says Milo.

Dorden tilts his chair back to upright and takes his feet down off the side of a cot. He folds over the corner of a page to mark his place, and sets his book aside.

'Come in, Milo,' he says.

In the back of the long tent behind Dorden, the medicae orderlies are at work checking supplies and cleaning instruments. The morning has brought the usual round of complaints generated by an army on the move: foot problems, gum problems, and gut problems, along with longer term conditions like venereal infections and wounds healing after the Voltis fight. The orderlies are chattering back and forth. Chayker and Foskin are play-fencing with forceps as they gather up instruments for cleaning. Lesp, the other orderly, is bantering with them as he prepares his needles. He's got a sideline as the company inksman. His work is generally held as the best. The ink stains his fingertips permanent blue-black, the dirtiest-looking fingers Dorden's ever seen on a medical orderly.

'How don't you feel right?' Dorden asks as Milo comes in. The boy pulls the tent flap shut behind him and shrugs.

'I just don't,' he says. 'I feel light-headed.'

'Light-headed? Faint, you mean?'

'Things seem familiar. Do you know what I mean?'

Dorden shakes his head gently, frowning.

'Like I'm seeing things again for the first time,' says the boy.

Dorden points to a folding stool, which Milo sits down on obediently, and reaches for his pressure cuff.

'You realise this is the third day you've come in here saying you don't feel right?' asks Dorden.

Milo nods.

'You know what I think it is?' asks Dorden.

'What?'

'I think you're hungry,' says Dorden. 'I know you hate the ration stuff they cook up. I don't blame you. It's swill. But you've got to eat, Brin. That's why you're light-headed and weak.'

'It's not that,' says Milo.

'It might be. You don't like the food.'

'No, I don't like the food. I admit it. But it's not that.'

'What then?'

Milo stares at him.

'I've got this feeling. I think I had a bad dream. I've got this feeling that–'

'What?'

Milo looks at the ground.

'Listen to me,' says Dorden. 'I know you want to stay with us. This man Gaunt is letting you stay. You know he should have sent you away by now. If you get sick on him, if you get sick by refusing to eat properly, he'll have the excuse he needs. He'll be able to tell himself he's sending you away for your own good. And that'll be it.'

Milo nods.

'So let's do you a favour,' says Dorden. 'Let's go to the mess tent and get you something to eat. Humour me. Eat it. If you still feel you're not right, well, then we can have another conversation.'

The lightning leads them. The rain persists. They come up over the wet hills and see the city grave.

Kosdorf is a great expanse of ruins, most of it pale, like sugar icing. As they approach it, coming in from the south-east, the slumped and toppled hab blocks remind Gaunt more than anything of great, multi-tiered cakes, fancy and celebratory, that have been shoved over so that all the frosted levels have crashed down and overlapped one another, breaking and cracking, and shedding palls of dust that have become mire in the rain. A shroud of vapour hangs over the city, the foggy aftermath of destruction.

Overhead, black clouds mark the sky like ink on pale skin. Shafts of

lightning, painfully bright, shoot down from the clouds into the dripping ruins, straight down, without a sound. The bars underlight the
belly of the clouds, and set off brief, white flashes in amongst the ruins
where they hit, like flares. Though the lightning strikes crackle with secondary sparks, like capillaries adjoining a main blood vessel, they are
remarkably straight.

The regular strobing makes the daylight seem strange and imperma-
nent. Everything is pinched and blue, caught in a twilight.

'Why can't we hear it?' one of the men grumbles.

Gaunt has called a stop on a deep embankment so he can check
his chart. Tilting, teetering building shells overhang them. Water gurgles out of them.

'Because we can't, Larks,' Corbec says.

Gaunt looks up from his chart, and sees Larkin, the marksman
assigned to the advance. The famous Mad Larkin. Gaunt is still learning names to go with faces, but Larkin has stood out from early on. The
man can shoot. He's also, it seems to Gaunt, one of the least stable indi-
viduals ever to pass recruitment screening. Gaunt presumes the former
fact had a significant bearing on the latter.

Larkin is a skinny, unhappy-looking soul with a dragon-spiral inked
onto his cheek. His long-las rifle is propped over his shoulder in its
weather case.

'Altitude,' Gaunt says to him.

'Come again, sir?' Larkin replies.

Gaunt gestures up at the sky behind the bent, blackened girders of
the corpse-buildings above them. Larkin looks where he's pointing,
up into the rain.

'The electrical discharge is firing from cloud to cloud up there, and
it can reach an intensity of four hundred thousand amps. But we can't
hear the thunder, because it's so high up.'

'Oh,' says Larkin. Some of the other men murmur.

'You think I'd march anyone into a dead zone without getting a full
orbital sweep first?' Gaunt asks.

Larkin looks like he's going to reply. He looks like he's about to say
something he shouldn't, something his brain won't allow his mouth
to police.

But he shakes his head instead and smiles.

'Is that so?' he says. 'Too high for us to hear. Well, well.'

They move off down the embankment, and then follow the seam of
an old river sluice that hugs the route of a highway into the city. There's
a fast stream running down the bed of the drain, dirty rainwater that's
washed down through the city ruin, blackened with ash, and then is

running off. It splashes and froths around their toecaps. Its babbling sounds like voices, muttering.

There's the noise of the falling rain all around, the sound of dripping. Things creak. Tiles and facings and pieces of roof and guttering hang from shredded bulks, and move as the inclination of gravity or the wind takes them. They squeak like crane hoists, like gibbets. Things fall, and flutter softly or land hard, or skitter and bounce like loose rocks in a ravine.

The scouts vanish ahead of the advance, but Mkoll reappears after half an hour, and describes the route ahead to Corbec. Gaunt stands with them, but there is subtle body language, suggesting that the report is meant for Corbec's benefit, and Gaunt is merely being allowed to listen in. If things turn bad, Mkoll is trusting Corbec to look after the best interests of the men.

'Firestorms have swept through this borough,' he says. 'There's not much of anything left. I suggest we swing east.'

Corbec nods.

'There's something here,' Mkoll adds.

'A friendly something?' Corbec asks.

Mkoll shrugs.

'Hard to say. It won't let us get a look at it. Could be civilian survivors. They would have learned to stay well out of sight.'

'I would have expected any citizens to flee the city,' says Gaunt.

Mkoll and Corbec look at him.

'Flight is not always the solution,' says Mkoll.

'Sometimes, you know, people are traumatised,' says Corbec. 'They go back to a place, even when they shouldn't. Even when it's not safe.'

Mkoll shrugs again.

'It's all I'm saying,' says Corbec.

'I haven't seen bodies,' replies Gaunt. 'When you consider the size of this place, the population it must have had. In fact, I haven't seen any bodies.'

Corbec purses his lips thoughtfully.

'True enough. That *is* curious.' Corbec looks at Mkoll for confirmation.

'I haven't seen any,' says Mkoll. 'But hungry vermin can disintegrate remains inside a week.'

They turn to the east, as per Mkoll's suggestion, and leave the comparative cover of the rockcrete drainage ditch. Buildings have sagged into each other, or fallen into the street in great splashes of rubble and ejecta. Some habs lean on their neighbours for support. All glass has been broken, and the joists and beams and roofs, robbed of tiles or slates, have been turned into dark, barred windows through which to watch the lightning.

The fire has been very great. It has scorched the paving stones of the streets and squares, and the rain has turned the ash into a black paste that sticks to everything, except the heat-transmuted metals and glass from windows and doors. These molten ingots, now solid again, have been washed clean by the rain and lie scattered like iridescent fish on the tarry ground.

Gaunt has seen towns and cities without survivors before. Before Khulan, before the Crusade even began, he'd been with the Hyrkans on Sorsarah. A town there, he forgets the name, an agri-berg, had been under attack, and the town elders had ordered the entire population to shelter in the precincts of the basilica. In doing so, they had become one target.

When Gaunt had come in with the Hyrkans, whole swathes of the town were untouched, intact, preserved, as though the inhabitants would be back at any moment.

The precincts of the basilica formed a crater half a kilometre across.

They stop to rest at the edge of a broad concourse where the wind of Voltemand, brisk and unfriendly, is absent. The rain is relentless still, but the vapour hangs here, a mist that pools around the dismal ruins and broken walls.

They are drawing closer to the grounding lightning. It leaves a bloody stink in their nostrils, like hot wire, and whenever it hits the streets and ruins nearby, it makes a soft but jarring click, part overpressure, part discharge.

An explosive device of considerable magnitude has struck the corner of the concourse and detonated, unseating all the heavy paving slabs with the rippling force of a major earthquake. Gravity has relaid the slabs after the shockwave, but they have come back down to earth misaligned and overlapping, like the scales of a lizard, rather than the seamless, edge-to-edge fit the city fathers had once commissioned.

Larkin sits down on a tumbled block, takes off one boot, and begins to massage his foot. He complains to the men around him in a loud voice. The core of his complaint seems to be the stiff and unyielding quality of the newly-issued Tanith kit.

'Foot sore?' Gaunt asks him.

'These boots don't give. We've walked too far. My toes hurt.'

'Get the medicae to treat your foot when we get back. I don't want any infections.'

Larkin grins up at him.

'I wouldn't want to make my foot worse. Maybe you should carry me.'

'You'll manage,' Gaunt tells him.

'But an infection? That sounds nasty. It can get in your blood. You can die of it.'

'You're right,' Gaunt says. 'The only way to be properly sure is to amputate the extremity before infection can spread.'

He puts his hand on the pommel of his chainsword.

'Is that what you want me to do, Larkin?'

'I'll be happy to live out me born days without that ever happening, colonel-commissar,' Larkin chuckles.

'Get your boot back on.'

Gaunt wanders over to Corbec. The colonel has produced a short, black cigar and clamped it in his mouth, though he hasn't lit it. He takes another out of his pocket and offers it to Gaunt, perhaps hoping that if Gaunt accepts it, it'll give him the latitude to break field statutes and light up. Gaunt refuses the offer.

'Is Larkin taunting me?' Gaunt asks him quietly.

Corbec shakes his head.

'He's nervous,' Corbec replies. 'Larks gets spooked very easily, so this is him dealing with that. Trust me. I've known him since we were in the Tanith Magna Militia together.'

Gaunt throws a half shrug, looking around.

'He's spooked? I'm spooked,' he says.

Corbec smiles so broadly he takes the cigar out of his mouth.

'Good to know,' he says.

'Maybe we should head back,' Gaunt says. 'Push back in tomorrow with some proper armour support.'

'Best plan you've had so far,' says Corbec, 'if I may say so.'

The Tanith scout, the tall, thin man with the menacing air, appears suddenly at the top of a ridge of rubble and signals before dropping out of sight.

'What the hell?' Gaunt begins to say. He glances around to have the signal explained by Corbec or one of the men.

He is alone on the concourse. The Tanith have vanished.

What the feth is he doing, Caffran wonders? He's just standing there. He's just standing there out in the open, when Mkvenner clearly signalled...

He hears a sound like a bundle of sticks being broken, slowly, steadily.

Not sticks, las-shots; the sound echoes around the concourse area. He sees a couple of bolts in the air like luminous birds or lost fragments of lightning.

With a sigh, Caffran launches himself from under the cover of his camo-cloak, and tackles Colonel-Commissar Gaunt to the ground. Further shots fly over them.

'What are you playing at?' Caffran snaps. They struggle to find some cover.

'Where did everyone go?' Gaunt demands, ducking lower as a zipping las-round scorches the edge of his cap.

'Into cover, you feth-wipe!' Caffran replies. 'Get your cloak over you! Come on!'

The ingrained, starch-stiff commissar inside Gaunt wants to reprimand the infantryman for his language and his disrespect, but tone of address is hardly the point in the heat of a contact. Perhaps afterwards. Perhaps a few words afterwards.

Gaunt fumbles out his camo-cloak, still folded up and rolled over the top of his belt pouch. He realises the Tanith haven't vanished at all. At the scout's signal, they have all simply dropped and concealed themselves with their cloaks. They are still all around him. They have simply become part of the landscape.

He, on the other hand, nonplussed for a second, had remained standing; the lone figure of an Imperial Guard commissar against a bleak, empty background.

The behaviour of a novice. A fool. A... what was it? *Feth-wipe*? Indeed.

Corbec looks over at him, his face framed between the gunsight of his rifle and the fringe of his cape.

'How many?' Gaunt hisses.

'Ven said seven, maybe eight,' Corbec calls back.

Gaunt pulls out his bolt pistol and racks it.

'Return fire,' he orders.

Corbec relays the order, and the advance company begins to shoot. Volleys of las-shots whip across the concourse.

The gunfire coming their way stops.

'Cease fire!' Gaunt commands.

He gets up, and scurries forwards over the rubble, keeping low. Corbec calls after him in protest, but nobody shoots at Gaunt. You didn't have to be a graduate of a fancy military academy, Corbec reflects, to appreciate that was a good sign. He sighs, gets up, and goes after Gaunt. They move forwards together, heads down.

'Look here,' says Corbec.

Two bodies lie on the rubble. They are wearing the armoured uniform of the local PDF, caked with black mud. Their cheeks are sunken, as if neither of them have eaten a decent plate of anything in a month.

'Damn,' says Gaunt, 'was that a mistaken exchange? Have we hit some friendlies? These are planetary defence force.'

'I think you're right,' says Corbec.

'I am right. Look at the insignia.'

'Poor fething bastards,' says Corbec. 'Maybe they've been holed up here for so long, they thought we were–'

'No,' says Mkoll.

Gaunt hasn't seen the scout standing there. Even Corbec seems to start slightly, though Gaunt wonders if this is for comic effect. Corbec is unfailingly cheerful.

The chief scout has manifested even more mysteriously than the Tanith had vanished a few minutes ago.

'There was a group of them,' he says, 'a patrol. Mkvenner and I had contact. We challenged them, making the same assumption you just did, that they were PDF. There was no mistake.'

'What do you mean?' asks Gaunt.

'I thought maybe they were scared,' says Mkoll, 'scared of everything. Survivors in the rubble, afraid that anything they bumped into might be the Archenemy. But this wasn't scared.'

'How do you know?' asks Gaunt.

'He knows,' says Corbec.

'I'd like him to explain,' says Gaunt.

'You know the difference between scared and crazy, sir?' Mkoll asks him.

'I think so,' says Gaunt.

'These men were crazy. There were speaking in strange tongues. They were ranting. They were using language I've never heard before, a language I never much want to hear again.'

'So you think there are Archenemy strengths here in Kosdorf, and they're using PDF arms and uniforms?'

Mkoll nods. 'I heard the tribal forces often use captured Guard kit.'

'That's true enough,' says Gaunt.

'Where did the others go?' asks Corbec, looking down at the corpses glumly.

'They ran when your first couple of volleys brought these two over,' says Mkoll.

'Let's circle up and head back,' says Corbec.

There's a sudden noise, a voice, gunfire. One of the other scouts has reappeared. He is hurrying back across the fish-scale slabs of the square towards them, firing off bursts from the hip. A rain of las-fire answers him. It cracks paving stones, pings pebbles, and spits up plumes of muck.

'Find cover!' the scout yells as he comes towards them. 'Find cover!'

They have jammed a stick into the ruins of Kosdorf, and wiggled it around until the nest underneath the city has been thoroughly disturbed.

Hostiles in PDF kit, caked in dirt, looking feral and thin, are assaulting the concourse area through the ruins of an old Ecclesiarchy temple and, to the west of that, the bones of a pauper's hospital.

They look like ghosts.

They come surging forwards, out of the dripping shadows, through the mist, into the strobing twilight. In their captured kit, they look to Gaunt like war-shocked survivors trying to defend what's left of their world.

'Fall back!' Corbec yells.

'I don't want to fight them,' Gaunt says to him as they run for better cover. 'Not if they're our own!'

'Mkoll was pretty sure they weren't!'

'He could have been wrong. These could be our people, come through hell. I don't want to fight them unless I have to.'

'I don't think they're going to give us a choice!' Corbec yells back.

The Tanith are returning fire, snapping shots from their corner of the open space. The air fills with a laced crossfire of energy bolts. The mist seems to thicken as the crossfire stirs the air. Gaunt sees a couple of the men in Kosdorfer uniforms crumple and fall.

'In the name of the Emperor, cease your firing,' he hollers out across the square. 'For Throne's sake, we serve the same master!'

The Kosdorf PDFers shout back. The words are unintelligible, hard to make out over their sustained gunfire.

'I said in the name of the Emperor, hold your fire,' Gaunt bellows. 'Hold your fire. I command you! We're here to help you!'

A PDFer comes at him from the left, running out of the shadows of the hospital ruins. The man has a hard-round rifle equipped with a sword bayonet. His eyes are swollen in their sockets, and one pupil has blown.

He tries to ram the bayonet into Gaunt's gut. The blade is rusty, but the thrust is strong and practiced. Gaunt leaps backwards.

'For the Emperor!' Gaunt yells.

The man replies with a jabbering stream of obscenity. The words are broken, and have been purloined from an alien language, and he is only able to pronounce the parts of them that fit a human mouth and voice-box. Blood leaks out of his gums and dribbles over his cracked lips.

He lunges again. The tip of the sword bayonet goes through Gaunt's storm coat and snags the hip pocket of his field jacket underneath.

Gaunt shoots the man in the face with his bolt pistol.

The corpse goes over backwards, hard. Bloody back-spatter over-paints the dirt filming Gaunt's face and clothes.

'Fire, fire! Fire at will!' Gaunt yells. He's seen enough. 'Men of Tanith, pick your targets and fire at will!'

Another PDFer charges in at him through an archway, backlit for a second by a pulse of lightning. He fires a shot from his rifle that hits the wall behind Gaunt and adds to the wet haze fuming the air. Gaunt fires back and knocks the man out of the archway, tumbling into two of his brethren.

The Tanith advance has been rotated out of line by the sudden attack, and Gaunt has been pushed to the eastern end of the formation. He has lost sight of Corbec. It is hard to issue any useful commands, because he has little proper overview on which to base command choices.

Gaunt tries to reposition himself. He hugs the shadows, keeping the crumbling pillars to his back. The firefight has lit up the entire concourse. He listens to the echoes, to the significant sound values coming off the Tanith positions. Gaunt can hear the hard clatter of full auto and, in places along the rubble line, see the jumping petals of muzzle flashes. The Tanith are eager, but inexperienced. The lasrifles they have been issued with at the Founding are good, new weapons, fresh-stamped and shipped in from forge worlds. Many of the Tanith recruits will never have had an automatic setting on a weapon before; most will have been used to single shot or even hard-round weapons. Finding themselves in a troop-fight ambush, they are unleashing maximum firepower, which is great for shock and noise but not necessarily the most effective tactic, under any circumstances.

'Corbec!' Gaunt yells. 'Colonel Corbec! Tell the men to select single f–'

He ducks back as his voice draws enemy fire. Plumes of mire and slime spurt up from the slabs he is using as cover. Impacts spit out stinging particles of stone. He tries shouting again, but the concentration of fire gets worse. The vapour billowing off the shot marks gets in his mouth and makes him retch and spit. Two or three of the PDFers have advanced on his position, and are keeping a heavy fire rate sustained. He can half see them through the veiling mist, calmly standing and taking shots at him. He can't see them well enough to get a decent shot back.

Gaunt scrambles backwards, dropping down about a metre between one rucked level of paving slabs and another, an ugly seismic fracture in the street. Loose shots are whining over his head, smacking into the plaster facade of a reclining guild house and covering it with black pockmarks. He clambers in through a staring window.

A Tanith trooper inside switches aim at him and nearly shoots him.

'Sacred Feth. Sorry, sir!' the trooper exclaims.

Gaunt shakes his head.

'I snuck up on you,' he replies.

There are four Tanith men in the ground floor of the guild house. They are using the buckled window apertures to lay fire across the concourse from the east. They'd been on the eastern end of the advance force when it turned unexpectedly, and thus have been effectively cut off. Gaunt can't chastise them. Oddities of terrain and the dynamic flow of a combat situation do that sometimes. Sometimes you just get stuck in a tight corner.

For similar reasons, he's got stuck there with them.

'What's your name?' he asks the man who'd almost shot him, even though he knows it perfectly well.

'Domor,' the man replies.

'I don't think we want to spend too much more time in here, do we, Domor?' Gaunt says. Enemy fire is pattering off the outside walls with increasing fury. It is causing the building to vibrate, and spills of earth, like sand in a time-glass, are sifting down from the bulging roof. There's a stink of sewage, of broken drains. If enemy fire doesn't finish them, it will finish the building, which will die on their heads.

'I'd certainly like to get out of here if I can, sir,' Domor replies. He has a sharp, intelligent face, with quick eyes that suggest wit and honesty.

'Well, we'll see what we can do,' Gaunt says.

One of the other men groans suddenly.

'What's up, Piet?' Domor calls. 'You hit?'

The trooper is down at one of the windows, pinking rounds off into the concourse outside.

'I'm fine,' he answers, 'but do you hear that?'

Gaunt and Domor clamber up to the sill alongside him. For a moment, Gaunt can't hear anything except the snap and whine of las-fire, and the brittle rattle of masonry debris falling from the roof above.

Then he hears it, a deeper noise, a throaty rasp.

'Someone's got a burner,' says the trooper in a depressed tone. 'Someone out there's got a burner.'

Domor looks at Gaunt.

'Gutes is right, isn't he?' he asks. 'That's a flamer, isn't it? That's the noise a flamer makes?'

Gaunt nods.

'Yes,' he says.

None of the Munitorum skivvies has the nerve to argue when Feygor helps himself to one of the full pots of caffeine on the mess tent stove.

Feygor carries the pot over to where Rawne is sitting at a mess table with the usual repeat offenders. Meryn, young and eager to impress, has brought a tray of tin cups. Brostin is smoking a lho-stick and flicking his brass igniter open and shut. Raess is cleaning his scope. Caober is putting an edge on his blade. Costin has produced his flask, and is pouring a jigger of sacra into each mug 'to keep the rain out.'

Feygor dishes out the brew from the pot.

'Come on, then,' says Rawne.

Varl grins, and slides the letter out of his inside pocket. He holds it gently by the bottom corners and sniffs it, as though it is a perfumed billet-doux. Then he licks the tip of his right index finger to lift the envelope's flap.

He starts to read to himself.

'Oh my!' he says.

'What?' asks Meryn.

'Listen to this... *My darling Ibram, how I long for your strong, manly touch...*' Varl begins, as if reading aloud.

'Don't be a feth-head, Varl,' warns Rawne. 'What does it actually say?'

'It's from somebody called Blenner,' says Varl, scanning the sheet. 'It goes on a bit. Umm, I think they knew each other years back. And from the date on this, he's been carrying it around for a while. This Blenner says he's writing because he can't believe that Gaunt got passed over after "all he did at Balhaut". He's asking Gaunt if he chose to go with "that bunch of no-hope backwoodsmen", which I think would be us.'

'It would,' says Rawne.

Varl sniffs. 'Anyway, this charming fellow Blenner says he can't believe Gaunt would have taken the field promotion willingly. Listen to this, he says, "what was Slaydo thinking? Surely the Old Man had made provision for you to be part of the command structure that succeeded him. Throne's sake, Ibram! You know he was grooming! How did you let this slight happen to you? Slaydo's legacy would have protected you for years if you'd let it".'

Varl looks up at the Tanith men around the table. 'Wasn't Slaydo the name of the Warmaster?' he asks. 'The big honking bastard commander?'

'Yup,' says Feygor.

'Well, this can't mean the same Slaydo, can it?' asks Costin.

'Of course it can't,' says Caober. 'It must be another Slaydo.'

'Well, of course,' says Varl, 'because otherwise it would mean that the feth-wipe commanding us is a more important feth-wipe than we ever imagined.'

'It doesn't mean that,' says Rawne. 'Costin's right. It's a different Slaydo, or this Blenner doesn't know what he's talking about. Go on. What else is there?'

Varl works down the sheet.

'Blenner finishes by saying that he's stationed on Hisk with a regiment called the Greygorians. He says he's got pull with a Lord General called Cybon, and that Cybon's promised him, that is Gaunt, a staff position. Blenner begs Gaunt to reconsider his "ill-advised" move and get reassigned.'

'That's it?' asks Rawne.

Varl nods.

'So he's thinking about ditching us,' murmurs Rawne.

'This letter's old, mind you,' says Varl.

'But he kept it,' says Feygor. 'It matters to him.'

'Murt's right,' says Rawne. 'This means his heart's not in it. We can exert a little pressure, and get rid of this fether without any of us having to face a firing squad.'

'Having fun?'

They all turn. Dorden is standing nearby, watching them. The boy Milo is behind him, looking pale and nervous.

'We're fine, Doc,' says Feygor. 'How are you?'

'Looks for all the world like a meeting of plotters,' says Dorden. He takes a step forwards and comes in amongst them. He's twice as old as any of them, like their grandfather. He's no fighter either. Every one of them is a young man, strong enough to break him and kill him with ease. He pours himself a mug of caffeine from their tray.

Costin makes a hasty but abortive attempt to stop him.

'There's a little–' Costin begins, in alarm.

'Sacra in it?' asks Dorden, sipping. 'I should hope so, cold day like this.'

He looks across at Varl.

'What's that you've got, Varl?'

'A letter, Doc.'

'Does it belong to you?'

'Uh, not completely.'

'Did you borrow it?'

'It fell out of someone's pocket, Doc.'

'Do you think it had better fall back in?' asks Dorden.

'I think that would be a good idea,' says Varl.

'We were just having a conversation, doctor,' says Rawne. 'No plots, no conspiracies.'

'I believe you,' Dorden replies. 'Just like I believe that no lies would ever, ever come out of your mouth, major.'

'With respect, doctor,' says Rawne, 'I'm having a private conversation with some good comrades, and the substance of it is of no consequence to you.'

Dorden nods.

'Of course, major,' he replies. 'Just as I'm here to find a plate of food for this boy and minding my own business.'

He turns to talk to the cooks about finding something other than slab in the ration crates.

Then he looks back at Rawne.

'Consider this, though. They say it's always best to know your enemy. If you succeed in ousting Colonel-Commissar Gaunt, who might you be making room for?'

'Where's the chief?' Corbec asks, ducking in.

'Frankly, I've been too busy to keep tabs on that gigantic fether,' Larkin replies.

'Oh, Larks,' murmurs Corbec over the drumming of infantry weapons, 'that lip of yours is going to get you dead before too long unless you curb it. Disrespecting a superior, it's called.'

Larkin sneers at his old friend.

'Right,' he says. 'You'd write me up.'

He is adjusting the replacement barrel of his long-las, hunkered down behind the cyclopean plinth of a heap of rubble that had once been a piece of civic statuary.

'Of course I would,' says Corbec. 'I'd have to.'

Corbec has got down on one knee on the other side of a narrow gap between the plinth and a retaining wall that is leaning at a forty-five degree angle. Solid-round fire from the enemy is travelling up the gap between them, channelled by the actual physical shape, like steel pinballs coursing along a chute. The shots scrape and squeal as they whistle past.

Corbec clacks in a fresh clip and leans out gingerly to snap some discouraging las-rounds back up the gap.

'Why?' Larkin asks. 'Why would you have to?'

Larkin laughs, mirthlessly. Corbec can almost smell the rank adrenaline sweat coming out of the wiry marksman's pores. The stress of a combat situation has pushed Larkin towards his own, personal edge, and he is barely in control.

'Because I'm the fething colonel, and I can't have you bad-mouthing the company commander,' Corbec replies.

'Yeah, but you're not really, are you?' says Larkin. 'I mean, you're not really my superior, are you?'

'What?'

'Gaunt just picked you and Rawne. It was random. It doesn't mean anything. There's no point you carrying on like there's suddenly any difference between us.'

Corbec gazes across at Larkin, watching him screw the barrel in, nattering away, stray rounds tumbling past them like seed cases in a gale.

'I mean, it's not like your shit suddenly smells better than mine, is it?' says Larkin. He looks up at last and sees Corbec's face.

'What?' he asks. 'What's the matter with you?'

Corbec glares at him.

'I am the colonel, Larks,' he snarls. 'That's the point. I'm not your friend any more. This is either real or there's no point to it at all.'

Larkin just looks at him.

'Oh, for feth's sake!' says Corbec. 'Stop looking at me with those stupid hang-dog eyes! Hold this position. That's an order, trooper! Mkoll!'

The chief scout comes scurrying over from the other corner of the plinth, head down. He drops in behind Larkin and looks across the gap at Corbec.

'Sergeant Blane's got the top end of the line firm. I'm going back down that way,' Corbec says, jerking a thumb over his shoulder. 'We seem to have lost Gaunt.'

'It's tragic,' says Larkin.

'Keep this section in place,' Corbec continues.

Mkoll nods. Corbec sets off.

'What's got into him?' Larkin mutters.

'Probably something you said,' says Mkoll.

'I don't say anything we're not all thinking,' Larkin replies.

Outside, the flamer makes its sucking roar again.

All four of the Tanith men with Gaunt express their unhappiness in strong terms. Gutes and Domor are cursing.

'We're done for,' says another of them, a man called Guheen.

'They'll just torch us out like larisel in a burrow,' says the fourth.

'Maybe–' Gaunt begins.

'No maybe about it!' Gutes spits.

'No, I was trying to say, maybe this gives us a chance we didn't have before,' Gaunt tells them.

He ducks down beside Gutes again, and peers out into the mist and rain, craning for a better view. There is still no sign of the flamer, but he can certainly hear it clearly now, retching like some volcanic hog clearing its throat. He can smell promethium smoke too, the soot-black stench of Imperial cleansing.

He looks up at the ominously low ceiling bellying down at them.

'What's upstairs?' he asks.

'Another floor,' says Guheen.

'Presuming it's not all crushed in on itself,' adds Domor.

'Yes, presuming it's not,' Gaunt agrees. 'Which of you is the best shot?'

'He is,' Domor says, pointing to the fourth man. Guheen and Gutes both nod assent.

'Merrt, isn't it?' Gaunt asks. The fourth man nods.

'Merrt, you're with me. You three, sustained fire pattern here, through these windows. Just keep it steady.'

Gaunt clambers over the scree of rubble and broken furniture to the back of the chamber. A great deal of debris has poured down what had once been the staircase, blocking it. Wires and cabling hang from ruptured ceiling panels like intestinal loops. Water drips. Broken glass flickers when the lightning scores the sky outside.

Merrt comes up behind Gaunt and touches his arm. He points to the remains of a heat exchanger vent that is crushed into the rear wall of the guild house like a metal plug. They put their shoulders against it and manage to push it out of its setting.

Light shines in. The hole, now more of a slot thanks to the deformation of the building, looks directly out on to rubble at eye level. They hoist themselves up and out, on to the smashed residue of a neighbouring building that has been annihilated, and has flooded its remains down and around the guild house, packing in around its slumped form like a lava flow sweeping an object up.

Gaunt and Merrt pick their way up the slope, and re-enter the guild house through a first-floor window. The floor is sagging and insecure. A few fibres of waterlogged carpet seem to be all that's holding the joists in place.

'You're a decent shot, then?' Gaunt murmurs.

'Not bad.'

'Pull this off, I'll recommend you for a marksman lanyard.'

Merrt grins and flashes his eyebrows.

'Should've got one anyway,' he says. 'The last one went to Larkin. After his psyche evaluation, marksman status was the only special dispensation Corbec could pull to get his old mate a place in the company.'

'Is that true?' Gaunt asks.

'You ought to know. I thought you were in charge?'

Gaunt stares at him.

'I'm really looking forward to meeting a Tanith who isn't insolent or cocksure,' says Gaunt.

'Good luck with that,' says Merrt.

Gaunt shakes his head.

'I've got a smart mouth, I know,' says Merrt. 'I said a few things about Larkin getting my lanyard, earned some dark looks from the Munitorum chiefs. My mouth'll get me in trouble, one day, I reckon.'

'I think you're already in trouble,' says Gaunt. He gestures out of the window. 'I think this qualifies.'

'Feels like it.'

'So you reckon you're good?'

'Better than Larkin,' says Merrt.

They settle in by the window. The mist shrouding the concourse and the surrounding ruins has grown thicker, as though the discharge of weapons has caused some chemical reaction, and it's disguising the enemy approach.

Below, about fifteen metres shy of them, they can see the blasts of the approaching flamer, like a sun behind cloud.

'Nasty weapon, the flamer,' says Gaunt.

'I can well imagine.'

'Then again, it is essentially a can or two of extremely flammable material.'

'You going to be my shot caller?' Merrt asks.

'We have to let it get a little closer,' says Gaunt. 'You see where it burps like that?'

Another gout of amber radiance backlights the fog in the square below.

Merrt nods, raising the lasrifle to his shoulder.

'Watch which way the glow moves. It's moving out from the flamer broom.'

'Got it.'

'So the point of origin is going to be behind it, and the tank or tanks another, what, half a metre behind that?'

The flamer roars again. A long, curling rush of fire, like the leaf of a giant fern, emerges from the mist and brushes the front of the guild house. Gaunt hears Domor curse loudly.

'He's widened the aperture,' Gaunt tells Merrt. 'He's seen buildings ahead, and he's put a bit of reach on the flame, so he can scour the ruins out.'

Merrt grunts.

'We've got to do this if we're going to,' says Gaunt.

There is another popping cough and then another roar. This time, the curling arc of fire comes up high, like the jet of a pressurised hose.

Gaunt grabs Merrt, and pulls him back as the fire blisters the first-storey windows. It spills in through the window spaces, roasting the frames and sizzling the wet black filth, and plays in across the ceiling like a catch of golden fish, coiling and squirming in a mass, landed on the deck of a boat.

The flames suck out again, leaving the windows scorched around their upper frames and the ceiling blackened above the windows. All the air seems to have gone out of the room. Gaunt and Merrt gasp as if they too have just been landed out of a sea net.

Gaunt recovers the lasrifle and checks it for damage. Merrt picks himself up.

'Come on!' Gaunt hisses.

As Merrt settles into position again, Gaunt peers down into the swirl.

'There! There!' he cries, as the flames jet through the mist and rain again.

Merrt fires.

Nothing happens.

'Feth!' Merrt whispers.

'When the flame lights up, aim closer to the source,' Gaunt says.

The flamer gusts again, ripping fire at the front of the guild house.

Merrt fires again.

The tanks go up with a pressurised squeal. A huge doughnut of fire rips through the mist, rolling and coiling, yellow-hot and furious. Several broken metal objects soar into the air on streamers of flame, shrieking like parts of an exploding kettle.

Gaunt raises his head cautiously and looks down. He can see burning figures stumbling around in the fog, PDF troopers caught in the blast. They sizzle loudly in the rain.

'Let's get out of here,' he says to Merrt.

Gaunt calls to the three Tanith men below, and all five leave the guild house together and work their way back along the edge of the concourse to the advance main force, skirting the open spaces.

'I've been looking for you,' says Corbec matter-of-factly when Gaunt appears.

'Not hard enough, I'd say,' Gaunt replies.

Corbec tuts, half entertained.

'You set something off over there?' he asks.

'Just a little parlour trick to keep them occupied while we got out of their way.'

'"A little parlour trick"...' Corbec chuckles. 'You're a very amusing man, you know that?'

'Wait till you get to know me,' says Gaunt.

Corbec looks at him sadly and says nothing.

'What shape are we in, colonel?' Gaunt asks.

'Fair,' Corbec replies.

'No losses so far?'

'Couple of scratches. But look, their numbers are increasing all the time. Another hour or so, we could start losing friends fast.'

'Can we vox in for support?'

'The vox is still dead as dead,' says Corbec.

'Recommendation?'

'We pull back before the situation becomes untenable. Then we rustle up some proper strength, come back in, finish the job.'

Gaunt nods.

'There are problems with that,' he says.

'Do tell.'

'For a start, I'm still not sure who we're fighting.'

'It's tribal Archenemy,' says Corbec, 'like Mkoll says. They've just ran-sacked the city arsenal.'

Gaunt touches his arm and draws him out of earshot.

'You never left Tanith before, did you, Corbec?'

'No, sir.'

'Never fought on a foreign front?'

'I've been taught about the barbaric nature of the Archenemy, if that's what you're worried about. All their cults and their ritual ways–'

'Corbec, you don't know the half of it.'

Corbec looks at him.

'I think they *are* Kosdorfers,' Gaunt says. 'I think they were, anyway. I think the Ruinous Powers, may they stand accursed, have salvaged more than kit and equipment. I think they've salvaged men too.'

'Feth,' Corbec breathes. Rain drips off his beard.

'I know,' says Gaunt.

'The very thought of it.'

'I need you to keep that to yourself. Don't say anything to the men.'

'Of course.'

'None of them, colonel.'

'Yes. Yes, all right.'

Corbec's taken one of his cigars out again and stuck it in his mouth, unlit.

'Just light the damn thing,' says Gaunt.

Corbec obeys. His hands shake as he strikes the lucifer.

'You want one?'

'No,' says Gaunt.

Corbec puffs.

'All right,' he says. He looks at Gaunt.

'All right,' says Gaunt, 'if we give ground here and try to fall back, we leave ourselves open. If they take us out on the way home, they'll be all over our main force without warning. But if we can manage to keep their attention here while we relay a message back...'

Corbec frowns. 'That's a feth of a lot to ask, by any standards.'

'What, the message run or the action?' asks Gaunt.

'Both,' says Corbec.

'You entirely comfortable with the alternative, Corbec?'

Corbec shrugs. 'You know I'm not.'

'Then strengthen our position here, colonel,' Gaunt says. 'We can afford to drop back a little if necessary. Given the visibility issues, the concourse isn't helping us much.'

'What do you suggest?' asks Corbec.

'I suggest you ask Mkoll and his scouts. I suggest we make the best of that resource.'

'Yes, sir.'

Corbec turns to go.

'Corbec – another thing. Tell the men to select single shot. Mandatory, please. Full auto is wasting munitions.'

'Yes, sir.'

Corbec stubs out his cigar and moves away. Keeping his head down, Gaunt moves along the shooting line of jumbled pavers and column bases in the opposite direction.

'Trooper!'

Caffran looks up from his firing position.

'Yes, sir?'

'It's your lucky day,' says Gaunt.

He gets down beside Caffran and reaches into his jacket pockets for his stylus and a clean message wafer.

His hip pocket is torn open and flapping. It's empty. He checks all the pockets of his jacket and the pockets of his storm coat, but his stylus and the wafer pad have gone.

'Do you have the despatch bag, Caffran?'

Caffran nods, and pulls the loop of the small message satchel off over his head. Gaunt opens it, and sees it is in order: fresh message wafers, a stylus, and a couple of signal flares. Caffran has taken his duty seriously.

Gaunt begins writing on one of the wafers rapidly. He uses a gridded sheet to draw up a simple expression of their route and the layout of the city's south-eastern zone, copying from his waterproof chart. Rain taps on the sheet.

'I need you to take this back to Major Rawne,' he says as he writes. 'Understand that we need to warn him of the enemy presence here and summon his support.'

Gaunt finishes writing and presses the setting of his signet ring against the code seal of the wafer, authorising it.

'Caffran, do you understand?'

Caffran nods. Gaunt puts the wafer back into the message satchel.

'Am I to go on my own?' Caffran asks.

'I can't spare more than one man for this, Caffran,' says Gaunt.

The young man looks at him, considers it. Gaunt is a man who quite bloodlessly orders the death of people to achieve his goals. This is what's happening now. Caffran understands that. Caffran understands he is being used as an instrument, and that if he fails and dies, it'll be no more to Gaunt than a shovel breaking in a ditch or a button coming off a shirt. Gaunt has no actual interest in Caffran's life or the manner of its ending.

Caffran purses his lips and then nods again. He hands his lasrifle and the munition spares he was carrying to Gaunt.

'That'll just weigh me down. Somebody else better have them.'

The young trooper gets up, takes a last look at Gaunt, and then begins to pick his way down through the ruined street behind the advance position, keeping his head down.

Gaunt watches him until he's out of sight.

Under Mkoll's instruction, the advance gives ground.

Working as spotters out on the flanks, Mkoll's scouts, Bonin and Mkvenner, have pushed the estimate of enemy numbers beyond eight hundred. Gaunt doesn't want to show that he is already regretting his decision not to pull out while the going was good.

Against lengthening, lousy odds, he's committed his small force to the worst kind of combat, the grinding city fight, where mid-range weapons and tactics become compressed into viciously barbaric struggles that depend on reaction time, perception and, worst of all, luck.

The Tanith disengage from the edge of the concourse, which has become entirely clouded in a rising white fog of vapour lifted by the sustained firefight, and drop back into the city block at the south-west corner. Here there are two particularly large habitat structures, which have slumped upon themselves like settling pastry, a long manufactory whose chimneys have toppled like felled trees, and a data library.

The scouts lead them into the warren of ruined halls and broken floors. It is raining inside many of the chambers. Roofs are missing, or water is simply descending through ruptured layers of building fabric. The Tanith melt from view into the shadows. They cover their cloaks with the black dirt from the concourse, and it helps them to merge with the dripping shadows. Gaunt does as they do. He smears the dirt onto his coat and pulls the cloak on over the top, aware that he is looking less and less like a respectable Imperial officer. Damn it, his storm coat is torn and his jacket is ruined anyway.

They work into the habs. Gunfire cracks and echoes along the forlorn walkways and corridors. Broken water pipes, weeping and foul, protrude from walls and floors like tree stumps. The tiled floor, what little of it survives, is covered with broken glass and pot shards from crockery that has been fragmented by the concussion of war.

Gaunt has kept hold of Caffran's rifle. He's holstered his pistol and got the infantry weapon cinched across his torso, ready to fire. It's a long time since he's seen combat with a rifle in his hands.

Mkoll looms out of the filmy mist that fills the air. He is directing the Tanith forward. He looks at Gaunt and then takes Gaunt's cap off his head.

'Excuse me?' says Gaunt.

Mkoll wipes his index finger along a wall, begrimes it, and then rubs the tip over the silver aquila badge on Gaunt's cap.

He hands it back.

'It's catching the light,' says Mkoll.

'I see. And it's not advisable to wear a target on my head.'

'I just don't want you drawing fire down on our unit.'

'Of course you don't,' says Gaunt.

Every few minutes the gunfire dies away. A period of silence follows as the enemy closes in tighter, listening for movement. The only sound is the downpour. The entire environment is a source of noise: debris and rubble can be dislodged, kicked, disturbed, larger items of wreckage can be knocked over or banged into. Damaged floors groan and creak. Windows and doors protest any attempt to move them. When a weapon is discharged, the echoes set up inside the ruined buildings are a great way of locating the point of origin.

The Tanith are supremely good at this. Gaunt witnesses several occasions when a trooper makes a rattle out of a stone in an old tin cup or pot and sets up a noise to tempt a shot from the demented Kosdorfers. As soon as the shot comes, another Tanith trooper gauges the source of the bouncing echo and returns fire with a lethal volley.

The enemy becomes wise to the tricks, and starts acting more circumspectly. Unable to out-stalk the Tanith, the Kosdorfers begin to call out to them from the darkness.

It is unnerving. The voices are distant and pleading. Little sense can be made of them in terms of meaning, but the tone is clear. It is misery. They are the voices of the damned.

'Ignore them,' Gaunt orders.

They have to stick tight. The enemy has a numerical advantage. By getting out of the open, the Tanith has forced its own spatial advantage.

Gaunt wonders if it will be enough.

The ruins still feel like a grave site, a waste of mouldering funereal rot. He wonders if this place will mark the end of his life and soldiering career; a well-thought-of officer who wound up dying in some strategically worthless location because he didn't make the right choices, or shake the right hand, or whisper in the right ear, or dine with the right cliques. He's seen men make high rank that way, through the persuasive power of the officers' club and the staff coterie. They were politicians, politicians who got to execute their decisions in the most literal way. Some were very capable, most were not. Gaunt believes that there is no substitute at all for practical apprenticeship, for field learning to properly supplement the study of military texts and the codices of combat. Slaydo had believed that too, as had Oktar, Gaunt's first mentor.

The vast mechanism of the Imperial Guard, as a rule, did not. Slaydo had once said that he believed he could, through proper reform of the Guard, improve its efficiency by fifty or sixty per cent. Soberly, he had added that mankind was probably too busy fighting wars to ever initiate such reforms.

There is truth in that. Gaunt knows for a fact that Slaydo had a reform bill in mind to take to the Munitorum after the Gorikan Suppression, and again after Khulan. Every time, a new campaign beckoned, a new theatre loomed to occupy the attentions of military planners and commanders. The Sabbat Worlds, now it was the Sabbat Worlds. Slaydo had committed to it mainly, Gaunt knew, for personal reasons. After Khulan, the High Lords had tempted Slaydo with many offers: he'd had the pick of campaigns. He had turned them down, hoping to pursue a more executive office in the latter part of his life and work to the fundamental improvement of the Imperial Guard, which he believed had the capacity to be the finest fighting force in known space.

However, the High Lords had outplayed him. They had discovered his old and passionate fondness for the piety of Saint Sabbat Beati and the territories she had touched, and they had exploited it. The Sabbat Worlds had long since been thought of as unrecoverable, lost to the predations of the Ruinous Powers spreading from the so-called Sanguinary Worlds. No commander wanted to embrace such a career-destroying challenge. The High Lords wanted a leader who would stage the offensive with conviction. They sweetened the offer with the rank of Warmaster, sensing that Slaydo would be unable to resist the opportunity to liberate a significant territory of the Imperium that he felt had been woefully neglected and left to over-run, and at the same to acquire a status that allowed him much greater political firepower to achieve his reforms.

Instead, Balhaut had killed him. All he accomplished was the commencement of a military campaign that was likely to last generations and cost trillions of lives.

Thus are dreams dashed and good intentions lost. Everything returns to the dust, and everything is reduced to blind fighting in the shadowed ruins of cities against men who were brothers until madness claimed their minds.

Everything returns to the dirt, and the dirt becomes your camou-flage, and hides your face and your cap badge in the dark, when death comes, growling, to find you out.

Faced alone, out of sight of the other men, the ruination of Kosdorf brings tears into his eyes.

Caffran understands the urgency of his mission, but he's also smart enough not to run. Headlong running, as the chief scout has pointed out so often, just propels a man into the open, into open spaces he hasn't checked first, across hidden objects that might be pressure-sensitive, through invisible wires, into the line of predatory gunsights.

Caffran is fit, as physically fit as any of the younger men who've been salvaged from Tanith. That's one of the reasons he's been selected as a courier.

The advance came into the grave city as a unit, testing its way and proceeding with recon. Now he's exiting alone, a solitary trooper, pro-tected by his wits and training. There's no doubt in his mind that the enemy will have spread strengths out through the dead boroughs sur-rounding the fighting zone to catch any stragglers.

Kosdorf reminds him of Tanith Magna. Architecturally, it's nothing like it, of course. Tanith Magna was a smaller burg, high-walled, a gathering of predominantly dark stone towers and spires rising from the emer-ald canopy of Tanith like a monolith. It had nothing of Kosdorf's dank, white, mausoleum quality. It's simply the mortality of Kosdorf that has stabbed him in the heart. Caffran knows that Tanith Magna doesn't even persist as a ruin any more, but Voltemand's second city, in death, inevita-bly makes him think of it, and the ruins become a substitute for his loss.

More than once, he feels quite sure he knows a street, or a particu-lar corner. Memories superimpose themselves over alien habs and thoroughfares, and nostalgia, fletched with unbearable melancholy, spears him. He thinks he recognises one flattened frontage as the pub-lic house where he used to meet his friends, another shell as the mill shop where he had been apprenticed, and a broken walkway as the nar-row street that had always taken him to the diocese temple. A patch of burned wasteland and twisted wire is most certainly the street market where he sometimes bought vegetables and meat for his ageing mother.

This terrace, this terrace with its cracked and broken flagstones, is definitely the square beside the Elector's Gardens, where he used to meet Laria. He can smell nalwood–

He can smell wet ash. Lightning jags silently.

He wipes a knuckle across his cheekbone, knowing that humiliating tears are mixing with the rain on his face.

He takes a deep breath. He isn't concentrating. He isn't paying enough attention. He stops to get his bearings, trusting the innate wiring of the Tanith mind to sense direction.

If the God-Emperor, who Caffran dutifully worshipped all his life at the little diocese temple, has seen fit to take everything away from him except this single duty, then Caffran is fething well determined to do it properly. He–

He feels the hairs prick up on the back of his neck.

The las-shot misses his face by about a palm's length. Just the slightest tremor of a trigger finger was the difference between a miss and a solid headshot. The light and noise of it rock him, the heat sears him, flash-drying the dirty tears and rain on his cheek into a crust.

Caffran throws himself down, and rolls into cover. He scrabbles in behind the foundation stones of a levelled building. Two more rounds pass over him, and then a hard round hits the block to his left. Caffran hears the distinctly different sound quality of the impact.

He thanks the God-Emperor with a nod. The enemy has just provided information. A minimum of two shooters, not one.

Caffran gets lower still. With his face almost pressing into the ooze, he repositions himself, and risks a look around the stone blocks.

Another shot whines past him, but it is speculative. The shooter hasn't seen him. A filthy PDFer is hopping across the rubble towards his position, clutching an old autorifle. He looks like a hobbled beggar. The puttee around one of his calves is loose and trailing, and his breeches are torn. His face is concealed by an old gas mask. The air pipe swings like a proboscis, unattached to any air tank. One of the glass eye discs is missing.

Behind him, a distance back, a second PDFer stands on the top of a sloping section of roof that is lying across a street. He has a lascarbine raised to his shoulder and sighted. As the PDFer in the gas mask approaches, the other one clips off in Caffran's general direction.

Caffran draws his only weapon, the long Tanith knife.

He stays low, hearing the crunch of the approaching enemy trooper. He can smell him too, a stench like putrefaction.

Another las-shot sings overhead. Caffran tries to slow his breathing. The footsteps get closer. He can hear the man's breath rasping inside the mask.

Caffran turns the knife around in his hand until he is holding the blade, and then very gently taps the pommel against the stone block, using the knife like a drum stick.

Chink! Chink! Chink!

He hears the enemy trooper's respiration rate change, his breath sounds alter as he turns to face a different direction. His footsteps clatter loose stone chips and crunch slime. He is right there. He is coming around the other side of the stone block.

The moment he appears, Caffran goes for him. He tries to make full body contact so he can bring the man over before he can aim his rifle. Caffran tries to force the muzzle of the rifle in under one of his arms rather than point it against his torso.

Locked together, they tumble down behind the block. The autorifle discharges.

From his vantage on the fallen roof slope, the other trooper hesitates, watching. He lowers his lasrifle, then raises it to sight again.

A shape pops back into view over the stone slab, a filthy shape, with a grimed gas-masked face. The watching trooper hesitates from firing.

The figure with the gas mask brings up an autorifle in a clean, fluid swing and fires a burst that hits the hesitating PDFer in the throat and chest, and tumbles him down the roof slope, scattering tiles.

Caffran drops the autorifle and wrenches off the gas mask as he falls to his knees. He gags and then vomits violently. The stench inside the borrowed mask, the *residue*, has been foul, even worse than he could have imagined. The mask's previous owner lies on his back beside him, beads of bright red blood spattering his mud-caked chest. Caffran slides the warknife out and wipes the blade.

Then he throws up again.

He can hear activity in the ruins behind him. It's time to move. He stares at the autorifle, and tries to weigh up the encumbrance against the usefulness of a ranged weapon. He reaches over and searches the large canvas musette pouches his would-be killer has strapped to the front of his webbing. One is full of odd junk: meaningless pieces of stone and brick, shards of pottery and glass, a pair of broken spectacles and a tin of boot polish. The other holds three spare clips for the rifle, and a battered old short-pattern autopistol, a poor quality, mass-stamped weapon with limited range.

It will have to do. He puts it into his pocket.

It's really time to move.

It's getting dark. Night doesn't drop like a lid on Voltemand like it did on Tanith. It fills the sky up slowly, billowing like ink in water.

The rain's still hammering the Imperial camp, but the dark rim of the sky makes the silent lightning more pronounced. The white spears are firing every twenty or thirty seconds, like an automatic beacon set to alarm.

The boy's asleep, legs and arms loosely arranged like a dog flopped by a grate. Dorden hates to abuse his medicae privileges, but he believes that the God-Emperor of Mankind will forgive him for crushing up a few capsules of tranquiliser and mixing them into the boy's broth. He'll do penance if he has to. They had plenty of temple chapels back in the city, and a popular local saint, a woman. She looked like the forgiving sort.

The boy's on a cot at the end of the ward. Dorden brews a leaf infusion over the small burner and turns the page of his book, open on the instrument rest. It's a work called *The Spheres of Longing*. He's yet to meet another man in the Imperial Guard who's ever heard of it, let alone read it. He doubts he will. The Imperial Guard is not a sophisticated institution.

Nearby, Lesp is cleaning his needles in a pot of water. He's done two or three family marks tonight at the end of his shift, a busy set. His eyes are tired, but he keeps going long enough to make sure the needles are sterile for the next job. Lesp is always eager to work. It's as if he's anxious to get down all the Tanith marks before he forgets them. Dorden sometimes wonders where Lesp will ink his marks when he runs out of Tanith skin to make them on.

The boy kicks as a dream trembles through him. Dorden watches him to make sure he's all right.

The doorway flap of the tent opens and Rawne steps in out of the lengthening light and the rain. Drops of it hang in his hair and on his cloak like diamonds. Dorden gets to his feet. Lesp gathers his things and makes himself scarce.

'Major.'

'Doctor.'

'Can I help you?'

'Just doing the rounds. Is everything as it should be here?'

Dorden nods.

'Nothing untoward.'

'Good,' says Rawne.

'It's getting dark,' Dorden says, as Rawne moves to leave.

'It is.'

'Doesn't that mean the advance unit is overdue?'

Rawne shrugs. 'A little.'

'Doesn't that concern you?' asks Dorden.

Rawne smiles.

'No,' he says.

'At what point will it concern you?' Dorden asks.

'When it's actually dark and they're officially missing.'

'That could be hours yet. And at that point it will be too late to mobilise any kind of force to go looking for them,' says Dorden.

'Well, we'd absolutely have to wait for morning at least,' says Rawne.

Dorden looks at him, and rubs his hand across his face.

'What do you think's happened to them?' he asks.

'I can't imagine,' says Rawne.

'What do you hope's happened to them?' Dorden asks.

'You know what I hope,' says Rawne. He's smiling still, but it's just teeth. There's no warmth. It's like lightning without thunder.

Dorden sips his drink.

'I'd ask you to consider,' he says, 'the effect it would have on the Tanith Regiment if it lost both of its senior commanding officers.'

'Please, doctor,' says Rawne, 'this isn't an emergency. It's just a thing. They've probably just got held up somewhere.'

'And if not?'

Rawne shrugged.

'It'll be a terrible loss, like you said. But we'd just have to get over it. We've had practice at that, haven't we?'

The emaciated ghosts of Kosdorf come at them through the skeletal ruins. They have become desperate. Their need, their hunger has overwhelmed their caution. They loom through useless doors and peer through empty windows. They clamber out of sour drains and emerge from cover behind spills of rubble. They fire their weapons and call out in pleading, raw voices.

The rain has thickened the dying light. Muzzle flashes flutter dark orange, like old flame.

The Tanith knot tight, and fend them off with precision. They fall back through the manufactory into the data library.

It's there they lose their first life. A Tanith infantryman is caught by autogun fire. He staggers suddenly, as if winded. Then he simply goes limp and falls. His hands don't even come up to break his impact against the tiled floor. Men rush to him, and drag him into cover, but Gaunt knows he's gone by the way his heels are kicking out. Blood soaks the man's tunic, and smears the floor in a great curl like black glass when they drag him. First blood.

Gaunt doesn't know the dead man's name. It's one of the names he hasn't learned yet. He hates himself for realising, just for a second, that it's one less he'll have to bother with.

Gaunt keeps the nalwood stock of Caffran's lasrifle tight against his shoulder and looses single shots. The temptation to switch to auto is almost unbearable.

The lobby of the data library is a big space, which once had a glass roof, now fallen in. Rain pours in, every single moving drop of it catching the light. Kosdorfer ghosts get up on the lobby's gallery, and angle fire down at the Tanith below. The top of the desk once used by the venerable clerk of records stipples and splinters, and the row of ornate brass kiosks where scholars and gnostics once filled out their data requests dent and quiver. Floor tiles crack. The delicate etched metal facings of the wall pit and dimple.

Corbec looks out at Gaunt from behind a chipped marble column.

'This won't do,' he shouts.

Gaunt nods back.

'Support!' Corbec yells.

They've been sparing with their heavy weapon all day. They're only a light advance team, and they weren't packing much to begin with.

The big man comes up level with Corbec, head down. He's carrying the lascarbine he's been fighting with, but he's got a long canvas sleeve across his back. He unclasps it to slide out the rocket tube.

The big man's name is Bragg. He really is big. He's not much taller than Corbec, but he's got breadth across the shoulders. There's a younger Tanith with him, one of the kids, a boy called Beltayn. He's carrying the leather box with the eight anti-tank rockets in it, and he gets one out while Bragg snaps up the tube's mechanical range-finder.

'Any time you like, Try!' Larkin yells out from behind an archway that is becoming riddled with shots.

'Shut your noise,' Bragg replies genially. He glances at Gaunt abruptly.

'Sorry, colonel-commissar, sir!' he says.

'Get on with it, please!' Gaunt shouts. It's not so much the heavy fire they're taking, it's the voices. It's probably his imagination, but the pleading, moaning voices of the Kosdorfers calling out to them are starting to make sense to him.

Beltayn goes to offer up the rocket to Bragg's launcher, and a las-bolt fells him. Gaunt's eyes widen as the rocket tumbles out of the hands of the falling boy and drops towards the tiled floor.

It hits, bounces, a tail-fin dents slightly.

It doesn't detonate.

Gaunt dashes forward. Corbec has reached Bragg too. Bragg has picked up the rocket. He taps it cheerfully against his head.

'No fear,' he says. 'Arming pin's still in.'

Gaunt snatches the rocket, and stoops to the box to swap it for an undamaged one.

'See to the boy!' he says to Corbec.

'Just a flesh wound!' Corbec replies, hunched over Beltayn. 'Just his arm.'

'Get him back to the archway!'

'I can't leave–'

'Get his arse back to the archway, colonel! I'll do this!'

'Yes sir!'

Corbec starts dragging the boy back towards the main archway. Men come out of cover to help him. Gaunt gets a clean rocket out of the box. He rolls it in his hands to check it by eye. It's been a long time since he loaded, a long time since he learned basic skills. A long time since he was the boy, the Hyrkan boy, apprenticed to war, born into it as if it was a family business.

'Set?' he asks the big man.

'Yes, sir!' says Bragg.

Gaunt fits the rocket and removes the arming pin. Bragg hoists the top-heavy tube onto the shelf of his shoulder and takes aim at the lobby gallery. Gaunt slaps him twice on the shoulder.

'Ease!' he yells.

'Ease!' Bragg yells back. The word opens the mouth and stops the eardrums bursting.

Bragg pulls the bare metal trigger. The ignition thumps the air, and blow-back spits from the back of the tube and throws up dust. The rocket howls off in the other direction, on a trail of flame. It hits the gallery just under the rail, and detonates volcanically. The entire gallery lifts for a second, and then comes down like an avalanche, spilling rubble, stonework, grit, glass and men. It collapses with a drawn-out roar, a death rattle of noise and disintegration.

Gaunt looks at Bragg. Bragg grins. Their ears are ringing.

Gaunt signals *back to the archway*.

They run in through the archway, through the smoke blowing from the lobby. They get down. Corbec has signalled a pause while they wait to hear how the enemy redeploys.

It gets quieter. The building settles. Rubble clatters as it falls now and then. Glass tinkles.

Gaunt sinks down next to Bragg, his back to a wall.

'First time that time,' says Larkin from a corner nearby.

'I know,' says Bragg. He looks at Gaunt. He's proud of himself.

'Sometimes I miss,' he explains.

'I know,' says Gaunt. The big man's nickname is *Try Again* because he's always messing up the first shot.

Gaunt sits quiet for a minute or two. He wipes the sweat off his face. He thinks about trying again, and second chances. Sometimes there just isn't the opportunity or the willingness to make things better. Sometimes you can't simply have another go. You make a choice, and it's a bad one, and you're left with it. No amount of trying again will fix it.

Don't expect anyone to feel sorry for you, to cut you slack; you made a mistake you'll have to live with.

It was like failing to play the glittering game when he had the chance as one of Slaydo's brightest; like leaving the Hyrkans; like trying to salvage anything from the Tanith disaster; like thinking he could win broken, grieving men over; like coming out with a small advance force into a city grave, just because he was bored of sitting in his tent.

He takes his cap off, leans the crown of his head back against the damp wall and closes his eyes. He opens them again. It's dark above him, the roof-space of the library. Beads of rainwater and flakes of plaster are dripping and spattering down towards him, catching the intermittent lightning, like snow, like the slow traffic of stars through the aching loneliness of space.

He remembers something, one little thing. He puts his hand in his pocket, just to touch the letter, just to put his fingers on the letter his old friend Blenner sent him: Blenner, his friend from Schola Progenium, manufacturer of fake plastic explosives and practical jokes.

Blenner, manufacturer of empty promises, too, no doubt. The letter's old. The offer may not still stand, if it ever did. Vaynom Blenner was not the most reliable man, and his mouth had a habit of making offers the rest of him couldn't keep.

But it's a small hope, a sustaining thing, the possibility of trying again.

The letter is gone.

Suddenly alert, torn from his reverie, Gaunt begins to search his pockets. It's really gone. The pocket he thought he'd put it in is hanging off, thanks to the thrust of a rusty sword bayonet. All the pockets of his field jacket and storm coat are empty.

The letter's lost. It's outside somewhere in this grave of a city, disintegrating in the rain.

'What's the matter?' asks Bragg, noticing Gaunt's activity.

'Nothing,' says Gaunt.

'You sure?'

Gaunt nods.

'Good,' says Bragg, sitting back again. 'I thought you might have the torments on you.'

'The torments?'

'Everyone gets them,' says Bragg. 'Everyone has their own. Bad dreams. Bad memories. Most of us, it's about where we come from. Tanith, you know.'

'I know,' says Gaunt.

'We miss it,' says Bragg, like this idea might, somehow, not be clear to anyone. 'It's hard to bear. It's hard to think about what happened to it, sometimes. It gets us inside. You know Gutes?'

Bragg points across at Piet Gutes, one of the men who was in the guild house with Domor. Like all the Tanith, Gutes is resting for a moment, sitting against a wall, feet pulled in, gun across his knees, listening.

'Yeah,' says Gaunt.

'Friend of mine,' says Bragg. 'He had a daughter called Finra, and she had a daughter called Foona. Feth, but he misses them. Not being away from them, you understand. Just them not being there to return to. And Mkendrick?'

Bragg points to another infantryman. His voice is low.

'He left a brother in Tanith Steeple. I think he had family in Attica too, an uncle–'

'Why are you telling me this, trooper?' Gaunt asks. 'I know what happened. I know what I did. Do you want me to suffer? I can't make amends. I can't do that.'

Bragg frowns.

'I thought,' he starts to say.

'What?' asks Gaunt.

'I thought that's what you were trying to do,' says Bragg. 'With us. I thought you were trying to make something good out of what was left of Tanith.'

'With respect, trooper, you're the only man in the regiment who thinks that. Also, with respect to the fighting merits of the Tanith, I'm an Imperial Guard commander, not a miracle worker. I've got a few men, a handful in the great scheme of things. We're never going to accomplish much. We're going to be a line of code in the middle of a Munitorum levy report, if that.'

'Oh, you never know,' says Bragg. 'Anyway, it doesn't matter if we don't. All that matters is you do right by the men.'

'I do right by them?'

'That's all we want,' says Bragg with a smile. 'We're Tanith. We're used to knowing where we're going. We're used to finding our way. We're lost now. All we want from you is for you to find a path for us and set us on it.'

Someone nearby says something. Corbec holds up a hand, makes a gesture. Pattering rain. Otherwise, silence. Everyone's listening.

Gaunt pats the big man on the arm and goes over to join Corbec.

'What is it?' he asks.

'Beltayn says he heard something,' Corbec replies. The boy is settled in beside Corbec, the wounded arm packed and taped. He looks at Gaunt.

He says, 'Something's awry.'

'What's that supposed to mean?' asks Gaunt.

Corbec indicates he should listen. Gaunt cranes his neck.

The Kosdorfers are moving. They're talking again. Their whispers are breathing out of the ruins to reach the Tanith position.

Gaunt looks sharply at Corbec.

'I think I can understand the words,' he says.

'Me too,' Corbec nods.

Gaunt swallows hard. He's got a sick feeling, and he's not sure where it's coming from. The feeling is telling him that he's not suddenly comprehending the Kosdorfers because they are speaking Low Gothic.

He's understanding them because he's learned their language.

The boy wakes up with a start.

'Go back to sleep,' Dorden tells him. 'You need your sleep.'

Dorden's standing in the doorway of the tent, watching the evening coming in.

Milo gets up.

'Are they back yet?' he asks.

Dorden shakes his head.

'Someone needs to go and look for them,' the boy says flatly. 'I had another dream. A really unpleasant one. Someone needs to go and look for them.'

'Just go back to sleep,' Dorden insists. The boy slumps a little, and turns back to his cot.

'You dreamed they were in trouble, did you?' Dorden asks, trying to humour the boy.

'No,' replies the boy, sitting down on the cot and looking back at the medicae. 'That's not why I have the feeling they're in trouble. I didn't dream it, that's just common sense. They're overdue. My bad dream, it was just a dream about numbers. Like last night and the night before.'

'Numbers?' asks Dorden.

Milo nods. 'Just some numbers. In my dream, I'm trying to write these numbers down, over and over, but my stylus won't work, and for some reason that's not a pleasant dream to have.'

Dorden looks at the boy. He asks, 'So what are the numbers, Brin?', still humouring him.

The boy reels the numbers off.

'When did he tell you that?' Dorden asks.

'Who?'

'Gaunt.'

'He didn't tell me anything,' says the boy. 'He certainly didn't tell me those numbers. I just told you, they were in my dream. I dreamed about them.'

'Are you lying to me, Brin?'

'No, sir.'

Dorden keeps staring at the boy a minute more, as if a lie will suddenly give itself away, like the moon coming out from behind a cloud.

'Why do those numbers matter?' the boy asks.

'They're Gaunt's command code,' says Dorden.

'Explain yourself,' the voice demands. It comes out like an echo, from the ruins, the ghost of a voice. 'Explain yourself. We don't understand why.'

The voice tunes in and out, like a vox that's getting interference.

'We're hungry,' it adds.

Corbec looks at Gaunt. He wants to reply, Gaunt can see it on his face. Gaunt shakes his head.

'You left us here,' the voice says. It's two or three voices now, all speaking at once, like two or three vox sets tuned to the same signal, their speakers slightly out of sync. 'Why did you leave us here? We don't understand why you left us behind.'

'Feth's sake is that?' Corbec mutters to Gaunt. All good humour has gone from him. He's looking pinched and scared.

'You left us behind, and we're hungry,' the voices plead.

'I don't know,' says Gaunt. 'A trick.'

He says it, but he doesn't believe it. It's an uglier thing than that. The voices don't really sound like voices when you listen hard, or vox transmits either. They sound like... like other noises that have been carefully mixed up and glued together to make voice sounds. All the noises of the dead city have been harvested: the scatter of pebbles, the slump of masonry, the splinter and smash of glass, the creak of rebar, the crack of tiles, the spatter of rain. All those things and millions more besides, blended into a sound mosaic that almost perfectly imitates the sound of human speech.

Almost, but not quite.

Almost human, but not human enough.

'You left us behind, and we're hungry. Explain yourself. We don't understand why you left us. We don't understand why you didn't come.'

The Tanith are all up, all disturbed. Knuckles are white where hands grip weapons. Everyone's soaking wet. Everyone's watching the dripping shadows. Gaunt needs them to keep it together. He knows they can all hear it. The inhuman *imperfection* in the voices.

'I know what that is,' says Larkin.

'Steady, Larks,' growls Corbec.

'I know what that is. I know, I know what that is,' the marksman says. 'I know it. It's Tanith.'

DAN ABNETT

'Shut up, Larks.'

'It's Tanith. It's dead Tanith calling to us! It's Tanith calling to us, calling us back!'

'Shut up please, Larks!'

'Larkin, shut your mouth!' Gaunt barks.

Larkin makes a sound, a mewling sob. Fear's inside him, deep as a bayonet.

The voices are out there in the dark and the rain. The words seem to move from one speaker to the next. Dead speakers. Broken throats.

'We don't understand why you didn't come. We don't understand. We don't know who we are any more. We don't know where we belong.'

Gaunt looks at Corbec.

'We getting out?' he asks.

'Through the back way?'

'Whatever way we can find.'

'What happened to holding this place until reinforcements arrive?' asks Corbec.

'No one's coming this way that we want to meet,' says Gaunt.

Corbec turns to the advance force.

'Get ready to move,' he orders.

The voice pleads, 'Where do we belong? We don't know where we belong.'

'It's Tanith!' Larkin cries out. 'It's the old place calling out to us!'

Gaunt grabs him, and pushes him against a wall.

'Listen to me,' he says. 'Larkin? Larkin? Listen to me! Get yourself under control! Something worse than death happened here, something much worse!'

'What?' Larkin whines, wanting to know and not wanting to know.

'Something Tanith was spared, do you understand me?'

Larkin makes the sobbing sound again. Gaunt lets him go, lets him sag against the wall. He turns, and the men are all around him. Mkoll's right there, Mkvenner too, looking as if they're going to step in and pull Gaunt and Larkin apart. The Tanith men are all staring at him. No one's looking away.

'Do you understand?' Gaunt asks them. 'All of you? Any of you?'

'We understand what you did,' one of them says.

'Oh, this isn't helping anything, lads!' Corbec rumbles.

Gaunt ignores Corbec and laughs a brutal laugh. 'I'm a destroyer of worlds, am I? You credit me with too much power. Indecent amounts of it. And anyway, I don't much care what you think of me.'

'Let's go! Let's go now,' says Corbec.

'There's only one thing I want you to understand,' Gaunt says.

'What's that?' asks Larkin, his mouth trembling.

'The worst thing you can imagine,' says Gaunt, 'is not the worst thing. Not by a long way.'

In the open, the rain is heavy, like a curtain. Caffran knows he's never going to make it. The straggly figures hunting him are closing in, and they've been calling to him for the last ten minutes, using the voices of people he used to know, twisted by bad vox reception.

'We don't know why you left us,' the voices plead. 'Where do we belong? We don't know where we belong.'

Caffran's feet are sore. He's got the pistol in his hand. Its clip is empty. He's killed three more men on his way out of the ruins.

The voices call out, 'We've forgotten what we're supposed to be.'

He's reached the ramparts of the hills, with the city grave at his back. He kneels down. The Imperial camp is somewhere ahead, below and far away. He can't see it, because rain and night shadows are filling the valley, but he knows it must be there. Too far, too far.

There are signal flares in his message satchel. He's pulling them out as the heavy raindrops bounce off his shoulders and his scalp. Does he need to find higher ground? There'll be obs positions looking this way, won't there? Spotters and look-outs?

The voices call to him.

He stands and fires a flare. It makes a hollow bang and soars up into the wet air, a white phosphor star with a gauzy tail, like a drawing of a comet in an old manuscript. It maxes altitude, and then starts to descend, slow, trembling, drifting.

Caffran's watching it, the other flare in his hand ready to fire. He knows there's no point.

The flare looks too much like the silent lightning.

There are figures on the hillside around him. They come towards him. They call out to him.

Bonin locates the remains of a depository entrance in the south-western corner of the data library, and they exit, via the basement stacks. They make their break out from there.

The basement is flooded, up to their hips. They have to cannibalise an RPG shell to make a charge to blow the hatch open. Then they're out into the street, into the rain, and they're drawing heavy fire right from the start.

Gaunt orders bounding cover, and they push along a street from position to position. They stay in good formation, despite the level of fire coming at them. No one switches back to full auto, despite the temptation.

Even so, the advance is pushing the limits of the ammo supplies it's packing.

They begin to string out into a longer and longer line. They make it to the circus where two dead boulevards cross, and pick their way through the underwalks of the crippled tramway shelters to achieve the far side. Volleys of shots rain off the crumpled metal roofs of the shelters. The objective is the arterial route that joins the eastern boulevard. Gaunt and Corbec tell Blane to push ahead and edge back to bring the rear of the line up.

The advance is halfway across the circus when it's rushed by enemy ambushers. The ambushers come out of one of the underwalks that looked like it was choked with rubble. They're armed like trench raiders with clubs and mauls and butcher hooks. They hit the Tanith advance in the midsection of its bounding spread. They rush Gaunt as he's trying to direct the force forwards.

Gaunt goes down and his head strikes something. He's too stunned to know what's happened. A raider swings a hook to split his head and finish him.

Mkoll intercepts the raider, and guts him with his silver warknife. He meets the next one head-on, somehow evades a wide swing from a spiked mace, and rams the knife up through the throat so the point exits the apex of the skull.

Corbec's also been caught in the initial rush. He takes his attacker over with him, and breaks his neck using body weight and a wrestling hold he'd learned watching his old dad compete at the County Pryze fair.

He looks up in time to see Mkoll pull the knife out. Blood ribbons up in a semicircle, like a red streamer in the rain, and the raider curves backwards in the opposite direction. Through the sheeting rain, Corbec can see more raiders coming out of the underwalk at Mkoll. Corbec's lasrifle is wedged under the corpse of the man he just killed. He yells Mkoll's name. He yells *idiot* and *feth* too, for good measure. Mkoll's las is strapped over his shoulder. He's facing three men with just his knife.

There's the whine of a small but powerful fusion motor, the unmistakable whir of a chainsword firing up. Gaunt comes in beside the scout. Gaunt's got blood down the side of his face and his cap's gone missing. The three raiders are too close to Mkoll for Gaunt to risk a shot with his rifle or his bolter.

He takes a head clean off with his chainsword. The neck parts in a bloodmist venting from the blade's moving edge. Corbec can see from Gaunt's stance and the way he presents that he's been trained in sword work to the highest degree. Covered in dust and blood, on a slope of rubble, fighting feral ghouls, he still looks like a duelling master.

Gaunt lunges and puts the chainsword through the torso of a second raider, freeing Mkoll enough to tackle the last of the group in quick order. More are running in from the underwalk. Gaunt rotates, extending, and slices the chainsword around in a wide, straight-armed arc that neatly removes the top of a skull like a lid.

Corbec's on his feet. He pulls his lasrifle in against his gut and flips the toggle over. Then he rakes the mouth of the underwalk. Full auto flash lights up the rubble. Figures twist and jerk. He exhausts a power clip, and then lobs his last grenade down the underwalk to take care of any stragglers.

Gaunt looks around for his cap.

'Why didn't you do that?' he asks Mkoll.

'You wanted to conserve ammo,' says Mkoll.

'In all fairness, he probably could have taken them all with his knife,' says Corbec.

From up ahead, towards the east boulevard, they hear lasrifles starting to cut loose on full auto. The chatter is unmistakable.

'Ah. I've set a bad example,' says Corbec.

Gaunt moves forward, shouting orders. He heads towards the front of the advance force, trying to restore firing discipline. Right away, he realises how badly broken their formation is. The ambush to the midsection of the spread has almost cut the advance in two. It's the beginning of the end. The enemy is exploiting their flaws, breaking them down, cutting them into manageable parts, reducing them. He knows the signs. It's exactly what he'd do.

It'll be over in minutes.

The back of the party is lagging too far behind. Gaunt tries to get the forward section to drop back and rejoin it, or at least hold position and not extend the break. It's still pushing ahead to try to reach the arterial route. Corbec's hollering at men, calling them by their first names, names Gaunt's never heard, let alone learned. Full auto fire is clattering away up ahead. Some PDFers loom over the rubble line, and Gaunt drops them with support fire from Domor and Guheen.

'Single shots! Single shot fire!' he's yelling.

He sees the Tanith fanning towards him, firing on full auto. At least one of his orders has got through, he thinks. At least they've swung back to keep the unit whole.

Then he's eyes-on, properly. These Tanith aren't members of the advance.

Rawne rakes a couple of bursts into the rubble line, and then approaches Gaunt as reinforcements pour in behind him.

'Major?'

'Sir.'

'Surprised to see you.'

'We ran into Caffran,' Rawne says.

'You ran into him?'

'We saw his flare. He was heading home, but we were already on our way out.'

'Why is that, major?' Gaunt asks.

'Concern was expressed to me by the medical chief that the advance was overdue. A support mission seemed prudent, before it got dark and out of the question.'

'It's appreciated, Rawne. As you can see, things are a little lively.'

Rawne keeps looking at his timepiece.

'Let's keep falling back apace,' he says. 'Let's not outstay our welcome.'

Gaunt nods. 'Lead the way.'

Rawne turns and yells out to the men running his flanking units. Varl and Feygor get their fireteams to interlock firing patterns. They lay down a kill zone of las-fire that moves with the Tanith like a shadow. It burns through ammo, but it covers the retreat off the east boulevard and onto the main arterial route. They leave spent munition clips behind them, and the pathetic corpses of the enemy.

Adare and Meryn distribute ammo to Blane and the forward portion of the advance. Gaunt sees Caffran with Varl's squad. He tosses his rifle and his musette bag back to him. Caffran catches them and nods.

Rawne's still glancing at his timepiece.

'Let's go! Let's go!' he shouts. It's really getting dark. The fluttering, stammering barrage of the gun battle is lighting up the whole city block.

'We're going as fast as we can,' Gaunt says to Rawne.

Rawne looks at him, and sucks in a breath between clenched teeth that suggests that there's no such thing as too fast.

Gaunt hears a noise, a swift, loud, rushing hiss, the sound of a descent, of a plunge, of an angelic fall from grace. It ends in a noise shock that quakes the ground and nearly knocks him down. It feels like the lightning has found its voice at last.

Then it happens again and again.

Light blinds them. Bright detonations rip through the eastern boroughs of Kosdorf, some as close as a block or two away from their position. Blast overlaps blast, detonation touches detonation. It's precision wrath. It's bespoke annihilation.

'The Ketzok,' yells Rawne to Gaunt. 'A little early,' he admits.

Gaunt watches the heavy shelling for a moment, hand half-shielding his eyes from the flash. Then he turns the Tanith out of the zone with a simple hand signal.

It's too loud for voices any more.

Dorden cleans his head wound.

'It's going to mend nicely,' he says, dropping the small forceps into an instrument bath. Threads of blood billow through the cleaning solution like ink in water.

Gaunt picks up a steel bowl and uses it as a mirror to examine the sutures.

'That's neat work,' he says. Dorden shrugs.

Outside, in the morning light, the Ketzok artillery is still pounding relentlessly, like the slow, steady movement of a giant clock. Munitions resupply is an hour away, the bombardiers report. A huge pall of smoke is moving north across the sky over the hills.

'Rawne says you were instrumental in urging him to mount a reinforcement,' Gaunt says.

Dorden smiles.

'I'm sure Major Rawne was simply following standard operational practices,' he says.

Gaunt leaves the medicae tent. There's still rain in the air, though now it's spiced with the stink of fyceline from the sustained bombardment. The camp is active. They'll be striking soon. Directives have come through, order bags from command. The Tanith are being routed to another front line.

He's got things to think about. A week spent getting the regiment embarked and on the lift ships will give him time.

'Sir.'

He turns, and sees Corbec.

'Caligula, I hear,' says Corbec.

'That's the next stop,' Gaunt agrees. They fall into step.

'I don't know much about Caligula,' says Corbec.

'Then request a briefing summary from the Munitorum, Corbec,' says Gaunt. 'We have libraries of data about the Sabbat Worlds. It would pay the regiment dividends if the officers knew a little bit about the local conditions before they arrived in a fighting area.'

'I can do that, can I?' asks Corbec.

'You're a regimental colonel,' says Gaunt. 'Of course you can.'

Corbec nods.

'I'll get on it,' he says.

He grins, flops back his camo-cape, and produces one of his cigars and a couple of lucifers from his breast pocket.

'Thought you might enjoy this now we're outside field discipline conditions,' he says.

Gaunt takes the gift with a nod. Corbec knocks him a little salute and walks away.

Gaunt goes into his quarters tent to spend an hour packing his kit. The rain is tapping on the roof skin.

His spare field jacket is hanging on the back of the folding chair. Someone's sponged it clean and brushed up the nap. They've taken off the Hyrkan badges and sewn Tanith ones on in their place.

There is no clue at all as to who has done this.

Gaunt takes off the muddy coat and jacket he's been wearing all night and slips the spare on, not even sure it's his. He strokes it down, adjusts the cuffs and puts his hands in the pockets.

The letter's in the right-hand hip pocket.

He slides it out and unfolds it. He'd been so certain it was in his number one field jacket. So certain.

He reads it, and re-reads it, and smiles, hearing the words in Blenner's voice.

Then he strikes one of the lucifers Corbec gave him, and holds the letter by the lower left-hand corner as he lights the lower right. It burns quickly, with a yellow flame. He holds on to it until the flames approach his fingertips, and then shakes it into the ash box beside his desk.

Then he goes out to find some breakfast.

GHOSTMAKER

'Inheriting command of the Sabbat Worlds Crusade force from the late and lauded Warmaster Slaydo, Warmaster Macaroth renewed the Imperial offensive to liberate the Sabbat Worlds, a cluster of nearly one hundred inhabited systems along the edge of the Segmentum Pacificus.

'Many legendary actions distinguished that twenty year campaign, and many legends were made: the last stand of the Latarii Gundogs at Lamicia, the Iron Snakes' victories at Presarius, Ambold Eleven and Fornax Aleph, and the dogged prosecution of the enemy by the so-called Ghosts of Tanith on Canemara, Spurtis Elipse, Menezoid Epsilon and Monthax. Of these, perhaps Monthax presents the most intriguing question for Imperial historians. Ostensibly a head-on confrontation with the forces of Chaos, this action is clouded in mystery and the details are still sequestered in the archives of Imperial High Command. Only speculation remains as to what truly occurred on the tangled shores of that hideous battle site.'

— from *A History of the Later Imperial Crusades*

It was summer here, apparently.

Intermittent but heavy rain sluiced the Imperium lines from a sky wrinkled with grey cloud cover. Barbed, twisted root-plants with florid, heavy leaves groped their way out of every inch of muddy land and poked from the shimmering waterbeds too. As land went, most of it had gone. Lagoons and long pools of sheened water forked through the groves of undergrowth, home to billowing micro-flies and unseen, chirruping insects.

There was a smell in the air, a smell like rank sweat. The smell didn't surprise Colonel-Commissar Ibram Gaunt. What did surprise him was that it wasn't coming from his men. It was exuding from the water, the plants, the mud. Monthax reeked of corruption and rot.

There was no digging-in on Monthax. Trenches were raised abutments of imported flak-board and locally cut timber. Levees and sand-bagged walls had been dug out and raised by the Ghosts. For three days, since the drop-ships landed them, there had been no other sound except the squelch of entrenching tools as work parties filled plastic sacks. No other sound except the chirrup of a billion insects.

Seeping sweat into his freshly-donned tunic from the moment he had it on, Gaunt emerged from his command shed, a three chamber modular habitat staked up on girder poles out of the soupy water. He put his commissar's cap squarely on his head, knowing full well that it would make sweat run into his eyes. He wore high boots, breeches and a tunic shirt, carrying his weatherproof overcoat over his shoulders. It was too hot to wear it, too wet to go without.

Ibram Gaunt stepped down off the shed steps and his feet settled in satin-skinned water twenty centimetres deep. He paused. The oily ripples ebbed away and he looked down at himself. A reflected Gaunt lay horizontal in the rank water at his feet. Tall, lean, with a sculpted, high-cheeked face that ironically mocked his name.

He looked away, up, through the fleshy leaves of the thickets and the coiled low cover of the plant growth. On the horizon, partly screened by sweating mist, firepower roared back and forth as Imperial gunnery duelled with the heavy artillery of Chaos.

He strode forward through the slushy water, up through the dry land of an islet thick with tendrils and overhanging flowers, and along a duck-board walkway towards the lines.

Behind a long, meandering, S-shaped embankment levee three kilometres long, the Tanith First-and-Only stood ready. They had raised this dyke themselves, armouring it with rapidly decaying planks of flak-board. Artificial mounds had been dug behind the defence to keep ammo piles out of the water. His men stood ready in fire-teams, fifteen hundred strong, dressed in the black capes and dull body-armour uniform that was their signature. Some stood at eyeholes in the dyke, guns fixed. Others manned heavy weapon nests. Others stood and smoked and chatted and speculated. All stood in at least fifteen centimetres of murky slime.

The bivouacs, also raised on girder legs out of the swamp, were set back from the dyke line by about thirty metres. Little sanctuaries of dryness lifted out of the ooze.

Gaunt wandered along the dyke to the first group of men, who were digging up a footstep by the dyke wall from mud spaded out of the waterline.

Whooping birds swung overhead, large-winged and stark-white with folded, gangly pink legs. The insects chirruped.

Sweat made half moons in the underarms of his tunic in less than a dozen paces. Flies stung him. All thoughts of future glory, of the bitter action to come, left Ibram Gaunt's mind. Instead, the echoes came. The memories.

Gaunt cursed quietly, wiped his brow. It was days like this, in the slow, loaded hours while they waited for combat, that the memories flooded back at their most intense. Of the past, of lost comrades and missed friends, of glories and defeats long gone, of ends.

And of beginnings...

ONE

GHOSTMAKER

Fire, like a flower. Blossoming. Pale, greenish fire, scuttling like it was alive. Eating the world, the whole world...

Opening his eyes, Ibram Gaunt, Imperial commissar, gazed into his own lean, pale face.

Trees, as dark green as an ocean at night, rushed past behind his eyes.

'We're making the final approach now, sir.'

Gaunt looked round, away from his reflection in the small, thick port of the orbital cutter, and saw his adjutant, Sym. Sym was an efficient man of middle years, his slightly puffy flesh marked across the throat and cheek by a livid, ancient burn.

'I said, we're making the final approach,' Sym repeated.

'I heard you,' Gaunt nodded gently. 'Remind me again of the schedule.'

Sym sat back in his padded leather G-chair and perused a data-slate. 'Official greeting ceremony. Formal introductions to the Elector of Tanith and the government assembly. Review of the Founding regiments. And a formal dinner tonight.'

Gaunt's gaze drifted back to the vast forests that flew by under the window. He hated the trappings of pomp and protocol, and Sym knew it.

'Tomorrow, sir, the transfer shifts begin. We'll have all the regiments aboard and ready to embark before the end of the week,' the man said, trying to put a more positive spin on things.

Gaunt didn't look round but said, 'See if you can get the transfers to begin directly after the review. Why waste the rest of today and tonight?'

Sym nodded, thoughtful. 'That should be possible.'

A soft chime signalled imminent landfall, and they both felt the sudden pull of deceleration G-forces. The other passengers in the craft's long cabin: an astropath, silent in his robes, and officials of the Adeptus Ministorum and the Departmento Munitorum, began to buckle their harnesses and settle back for landing. Sym found himself looking out of the port, watching the endless forests that so intrigued Gaunt.

'Strange place this, this Tanith. So they say.' He rubbed his chin. 'They say the forests move. Change. The trees apparently... uhm... shift. According to the pilot, you can get lost in the woods in a matter of minutes.'

Sym's voice dropped to a whisper. 'They say it's a touch of Chaos! Can you believe that? They say Tanith has a touch of Chaos, being this close to the Edge, you see.'

Gaunt did not reply.

The spires and towers of Tanith Magna rose to meet the small barbed shape of the cutter. The city, set here amid the endless oceans of evergreen trees, looked from the air like a complex circle of standing stones, dark grey slabs raised in a clearing in defiance of the forest around. Banners and brazier smoke fluttered from the higher fortress walls, and outside the city perimeter, Gaunt could see a vast plain cut from the forest. Row upon row of tents stood there, thousands of them, each with its own cookfire. The Founding Fields.

Beyond the tent-town, the huge black shadows of the bulk transports, whale-mouths and belly ramps open, squatting in fire-blackened craters of earth, ready to eat up the men and the machines of the new regiments of Tanith. His regiments, he reminded himself, the first Imperial Guard regiments to be founded on this enigmatic, sparsely populated frontier world.

For eight years, Gaunt had served as political officer with the Hyrkan 8th, a brave regiment that he had been with from its founding on the windy hills of Hyrkan to the ferocious victory of Balhaut. But so many had fallen, and another founding would fill familiar uniforms with unfamiliar faces. It was time to move on, and Gaunt had felt grateful to be reassigned. His seniority, his experience... his very notoriety made him an ideal choice to whip the virgin units of Tanith into shape. Part of him, a young, eager but small part deep inside, relished the prospect of building a fresh name for the Guard's roll of honour. But the rest of him was dull, set rigid, empty. More than anything, he felt he was simply going through the motions.

He had felt that way since Slaydo's death. The old commander would have wanted him here, wanted him to carry on to glory... after all, wasn't that why he'd made his gift? Promoting him there, on the firefields of Balhaut, to colonel-commissar... making him one of the few political officers in the Guard capable of commanding a regiment. Such trust, such faith. But Gaunt was so tired. It didn't seem much like a reward now.

The cutter dipped. Great brass shutters atop one of the city's largest towers hinged open like an orchid's petals to receive it.

On the Founding Fields, the men looked up as the approaching cutter purred overhead, banked against the slow cloud and settled like a beetle over the city wall towards the landing tower.

'Someone important,' noted Larkin, squinting up at the sky. He spat on the wirecloth in his hand and resumed polishing his webbing buckles.

'Just more traffic. More pompous off-worlders.' Rawne lay back and turned his face to the sun.

Corbec, stood by his tent, shielded his eyes against the glare and nodded. 'I think Larkin's right. Someone important. There was a big Guard crest on the flank of that flier. Someone come for the Founding Review. Maybe this colonel-commissar himself.'

He dropped his gaze and looked about. On either side of him, the rows of three-man tents stretched away in ordered files, and Guardsmen in brand new uniforms sat around, cleaning kit, stripping guns, eating, dicing, smoking, sleeping.

Six thousand men, all told, mostly infantry but some artillery and armoured crews, three whole regiments and men of Tanith all.

Corbec sat down by his own cook stove and rubbed his hands. His new, black-cloth uniform chafed at the edges of his big frame. It would be the very devil to wear in. He looked across at his tent-mates, Larkin and Rawne. Larkin was a slender, whipcord man with a dagger face. Like all the Tanith, he was pale-skinned and black-haired. Larkin had dangerous eyes like blue fire, a left ear studded with three silver hoops, and a blue spiral-wyrm tattoo on his right cheek. Corbec had known him for a good while: they had served together in the same unit of the Tanith Magna militia before the Founding. He knew Larkin's strengths – a marksman's eyes and a brave heart – and his weaknesses – an unstable character, easily rattled.

Rawne he did not know as well. Rawne was a handsome devil, his clean, sleek features decorated by a tattoo starburst over one eye. He had been a junior officer in the militia of Tanith Attica, or one of the other southern cities, but he didn't talk about it much. Corbec had a bad feeling there was a murderous, ruthless streak under Rawne's oily charm.

Bragg – huge, hulking, genial Bragg – shuffled over from his tent, a

DAN ABNETT

flask of hot sacra in his hands. 'Need warming up?' he asked and Corbec nodded a smile to the giant man. Bragg poured four cups, and passed one to Larkin, who barely looked up but muttered thanks, and one to Rawne, who said nothing as he knocked it back.

'You reckon that was our commissar, then?' Bragg said at last, asking the question Corbec knew he had been dying to get out since overhearing Corbec's remark.

Corbec sipped and nodded. 'Gaunt? Yeah, most like.'

'I heard stuff, from the Munitorum blokes at the transports. They say he's hard as nails. Got medals too. A real killer, they say.'

Rawne sniffed. 'Why can't we be led by our own, is what I want to know. A good militia commander's all we need.'

'I could offer,' Corbec joked softly.

'He said a good one, dog!' Larkin snapped, returning to his obsessive polishing.

Corbec winked across at Bragg and they sipped some more.

'It seems funny to be going though, dunnit?' Bragg said after a spell. 'I mean, for good. Might never be coming back.'

'Most like,' Corbec said. 'That's the job. To serve the Emperor in his wars, over the stars and far away. Best get used to the idea.'

'Eyes up!' Forgal called from a tent nearby. 'Here comes big Garth with a face on!'

They looked around. Major Garth, their unit commander, was thumping down the tent line issuing quick orders left and right. Garth was a barrel-chested buttress of a man, whose sloping bulk and heavy, lined features seemed to suggest that gravity pulled on him harder than most. He drew up to them.

'Pack it up, boys. Time to ship,' he said.

Corbec raised an eyebrow. 'I thought that was tomorrow?' he began.

'So did I, so did Colonel Torth, so did the Departmento Munitorum, but it looks like our new colonel-commissar is an impatient man, so he wants us to start lifting to the troop-ships right after the Review.'

Garth passed on, shouting more instructions.

'Well,' Colm Corbec said to no one in particular, 'I guess this is where it all starts.'

Gaunt's head ached. He wasn't sure if it was the interminable introductions to Tanith dignitaries and politicos, the endless small talk, the achingly slow review of the troops out on the marshalling yard in front of the Tanith Assembly, or simply the bloody pipe music that seemed to be playing in every damn chamber, street and courtyard of the city that he walked into.

And the troops hadn't been that impressive either. Pale, dark-haired, undernourished-looking somehow, haggard in plain black fatigues, each with a piebald camo-cloak swept over the shoulder opposite the one to which their lasgun was slung. Not to mention the damn earstuds and hoops, the facial tattoos, the unkempt hair, the lilting, sing-song accents.

The 'glorious 1st, 2nd and 3rd of Tanith', the new regiments: a scrawny, scruffy mob of soft-voiced woodsmen indeed, and nothing to write home about.

The Elector of Tanith, the local planetary lord, himself sporting a cheek tattoo of a snake, had assured Gaunt of the fighting mettle of the Tanith militia.

'They are resolute and cunning,' the Elector had said as they stood on the terrace overlooking the massed ranks. 'Tanith breeds indefatigable men. And our particular strengths are in scouting and stealth. As you might expect on a world whose moving forests blur the topography with bewildering speed, the Tanith have an unerring sense of place and direction. They do not get lost. They perceive what others miss.'

'In the main, I need fighters, not guides,' Gaunt had said, trying not to sound too snide.

The Elector had merely smiled. 'Oh, we fight too. And now for the first time we are honoured to be adding our fighting spirit to that of the Imperium. The regiments of Tanith will serve you well, colonel-commissar.'

Gaunt had nodded politely.

Now Gaunt sat in private in an anteroom of the Assembly. He'd slung his greatcoat and his cap on a hardwood chest nearby and Sym had laid out his dress jacket for the dinner that would commence in thirty minutes. If only he could rid himself of his headache and of the bad taste in his throat that he had landed a weak command.

And the music! The damn pipe music, invading his head even here in the private rooms!

He got to his feet and strode to the sloping windows. Out beyond the cityscape and the Founding Fields, orange fire thumped into the twilight as the heavy transports departed and returned, ferrying the regimental components to the vast troop carriers in high orbit.

That music still!

Gaunt walked to a set of dark green velvet drapes and swept them aside. The music stopped.

The boy with the small set of pipes looked at his raging eyes in astonishment.

'What are you doing?' Gaunt asked, as threatening as a drawn knife.

'Playing, sir,' the boy said. He was about seventeen, not yet a man, but tall and well-made. His face, a blue fish tattoo over the left eye, was strong and handsome. His be-ringed fingers clutched a Tanith pipe, a spidery clutch of reeds attached to a small bellows bag that was rhythmically squeezed under the arm.

'Was this your idea?' Gaunt asked.

The boy shook his head. 'It's tradition. For every visitor, the pipes of Tanith will play, wherever they go, to lead them back through the forest safely.'

'I'm not in the forest, so shut up!' Gaunt paused. He turned back to the boy. 'I respect the traditions and customs of the Tanith, but I... I have a headache.'

'I'll stop then,' the boy said. 'I– I'll wait outside. The Elector told me to attend on you and pipe you while you were here. I'll be outside if you need me.'

Gaunt nodded. On his way out of the door, the boy collided with Sym, who was on the way in.

'I know, I know...' Gaunt began. 'If I don't hurry, I'll be late for the dinner and– What? Sym? What is it?'

The look on Sym's face immediately told Gaunt that something was very, very wrong.

Gaunt gathered his senior staff in a small, wood-panelled lobby off the main banqueting hall. Most were dressed for the formal function, stiff in gilt collars and cuffs. Junior Munitorum staff watched the doors, politely barring the entry of any Tanith dignitaries.

'I don't understand!' said a senior Departmento Munitorum staffer. 'The nearest edge of the warzone is meant to be eighty days from here! How can this be?'

Gaunt was pacing, reviewing a data-slate with fierce intensity. 'We broke them at Balhaut, but they splintered. Deep intelligence and the scout squadrons suggested they were running scared, but it was always possible that some of their larger components would scatter inwards, looping towards us, rather than running for the back end of the Sabbat Worlds and away.'

Gaunt wheeled on them and cursed out loud. 'In the name of Solan! On his damn deathbed, Slaydo was quite precise about this! Picket fleets were meant to guard all the warpgates towards territories like Tanith, particularly when we're still at founding and vulnerable like this! What does Macaroth think he's playing at?'

Sym looked up from a flatplan-chart he had unfurled on a desk. 'The lord high militant commander has deployed most of the Crusade Forces in the liberation push. It is clear he is intent on pressing the advantage won by his predecessor.'

'Balhaut was a significant win...' began one of the Ecclesiarchy.

'It will only stay a victory if we police the won territories correctly. Macaroth has broken the new front by racing to pursue the foe. And that's let the foe through, in behind our main army. It's textbook stupidity! The enemy may even have lured us on!'

'It leaves us wide open,' another Ecclesiarch agreed flatly.

Gaunt nodded. 'An hour ago, our ships in orbit detected a massive enemy armada coming in-system. It is no exaggeration to say that Tanith has just hours of life left to it.'

'We could fight–' someone ventured bravely.

'We have just three regiments. Untried, unproven. We have no defensive position and no prepared emplacements. Half of our force is already stowed in the troop carriers upstairs and the other half is penned in transit. We couldn't turn them around and get them unlimbered and dug in in under two full days. Either way, they are cannon fodder.'

'What do we do?' Sym asked. Some of the others nodded as if urging the same question.

'Our astropaths must send word immediately to the main crusade command, to Macaroth, and tell him of the insurgency. If nothing else, they need to turn and guard their flank and back. The rest of you: the carrier ships will leave orbit in one hour or at the point of attack, whichever comes first. Get as much of the remaining disembarked men and equipment aboard as you can before then. Whatever's left gets left behind.'

'We're abandoning Tanith?' a Munitorum aide said, disbelief in his thin voice.

'Tanith is already dead. We can die with it, or we can salvage as many fighting men as we can and re-deploy them somewhere they will actually do some good. In the Emperor's name.'

They all looked at him, incredulous, the enormity of his decision sinking in.

'DO IT!' he bawled.

The night sky above Tanith Magna caught fire and fell on the world. The orbital bombardment blew white-hot holes out of the ancient forests, melted the high walls, splintered the towers, and shattered the paved yards.

Dark shapes moved through the smoke-choked corridors of the Assembly, dark shapes that gibbered and hissed, clutching chattering, whining implements of death in their stinking paws.

With a brutal cry, Gaunt kicked his way through a burning set of doors and fired his bolt pistol.

He was a tall, powerful shape in the swirling smoke, a striding figure with a long coat sweeping like a cloak from his broad shoulders. His bright eyes tightened in his lean, grim face and he wheeled and fired again into the gloom. In the smoke-shadows nearby, red-eyed shapes shrieked and burst, spraying fluid across the stonework.

Las fire cut the air near him. He turned and fired, and then took the staircase at a run, vaulting over the bodies of the fallen. There was a struggling group up ahead, on the main landing. Two bloodied fighting men of the Tanith militia, wrestling with Sym at the doors to the launch silos.

'Let us through, you bastard!' Gaunt could hear one of them crying, 'You'd leave us here to die! Let us through!'

Gaunt saw the autopistol in the hand of the other too late. It fired the moment before he ploughed into them.

Raging, he broke one's jaw with the butt of his bolter, knocking the man backwards to the head of the stairs. He picked up the other and threw him over the stair rail into the smoke below.

Sym lay in a pool of blood.

'I– I've signalled... the carrier fleet, as you ordered... for the final withdrawal... Leave me and get aboard the cutter or–' Sym began.

'Shut up!' Gaunt snapped, trying to lift him, his hand slick with the man's blood. 'We're both going!'

'T-there's no time, not for me... just for you! Go, sir!' Sym rasped, his voice high with pain. From the bay beyond, Gaunt heard the scream of the cutter's thrusters rising to take-off readiness.

'Damn it, Sym!' Gaunt said. The aide seemed to reach for him, clawing at his tunic. For a second, Gaunt though Sym was trying to pull himself up so that Gaunt could carry him.

Then Sym's torso exploded in a red mist and Gaunt was thrown back off his feet.

At the head of the stairs, the grotesque shock troops of Chaos bayed and advanced. Sym had seen them over Gaunt's shoulder, had pulled himself up and round to shield Gaunt with his own body.

Gaunt got to his feet. His first shot burst the horned skull of the nearest beast. His second and third tore apart the body of another. His fourth, fifth and sixth gutted two more and sent them spinning back into their comrades behind on the steps.

His seventh was a dull clack of dry metal.

Hurling the spent bolter aside, Gaunt backed away towards the silo bay doors. He could smell the rancid scents of Chaos over the smoke now, and hear the buzz of the maggot-flies. In a second they would be on him.

Autocannon fire blasted into the heathen nightmares, sustained heavy fire from an angle nearby. Gaunt turned, and saw the boy, the piper with the fish tattoo. He was laying down an arc of covering fire from the portico of the silo bay with a sentry's autocannon that he had rested across the stonework. 'Get in! The last cutter's waiting for you!' cried the boy.

Gaunt threw himself through the bay doors into the fierce whirlwind of the cutter's engine backwash. The side hatch was just closing and he scrambled through, losing the tails of his coat to the biting hinge.

Enemy weapons fire resounded off the hull.

Gaunt was face down on the cabin floor, drenched in blood, looking up at the terrified faces of the Munitorum officials who made up this last evacuation flight to the fleet.

'Open the door again!' he yelled. 'Open it again!'

None of them moved to do so. Gaunt hauled himself up and heaved on the hatch lever. The door thumped open and the boy scrambled inside.

Gaunt dragged him clear of the hatch and yanked it shut. 'Now!' he bellowed down the cabin to the pilot's bay. 'Go now if you're going!'

The cutter rose from the tower bay hard and fast, lifter jets screaming as they were jammed into overdrive. Aerial laser fire exploded the brass orchid-shutters around them and clipped a landing stanchion. Hovering, the cutter wobbled. Below it, Tanith Magna was a blazing inferno.

Forgetting fuel tolerances, flight discipline, even his own mother's name, the pilot hammered the main thrusters to maximum and the cutter fired itself up through the black smoke like a bullet.

Left to die, the forests burned.

Gaunt fell against a bulkhead and clawed his way to a porthole. Just like in his dreams – fire, like a flower. Blossoming. Pale, greenish fire, scuttling like it was alive. Eating the world, the whole world.

Ibram Gaunt gazed into his reflection, his own lean, pale, bloody face. Trees, blazing like the heart of a star, rushed past behind his eyes.

High over the cold, mauve, marbled world of Nameth, Gaunt's ships hung like creatures of the deep marine places. Three great troop carriers, their ash-grey, crenellated hulls vaulted like monstrous cathedrals, and the long, muscular escort frigate Navarre, spined and blistered with lance weapons and turrets, hooked and angular like a woodwasp, two kilometres long.

In his stateroom on the *Navarre*, Gaunt reviewed the latest survey intelligence. Tanith was lost, part of a conquered wedge of six planet systems that fell to the Chaos armada pincer which Macaroth had allowed to slip behind his over-eager warfront. Now Crusade forces were doubling back and re-engaging the surprise enemy. Sporadic reports had come in of a thirty-six hour deep-space engagement of capital ships near the Circudus. The Imperial Crusaders now faced a war on two fronts.

Gaunt's ruthless retreat had salvaged three and a half thousand fighting men, just over half of the Tanith regiments, and most of their equipment. The cruellest, most cynical view could call it a victory of sorts.

Gaunt slid a data-slate out from under a pile of other documents on his desk and eyed it. It was the transcript of the communiqué from Macaroth himself, applauding Gaunt's survival instinct and his great feat in salvaging for the crusade a significant force of men. Macaroth had not seen fit to mention the loss of a planet and its population. He spoke of 'Colonel-Commissar Gaunt's correct choice, and frank evaluation of an impossible situation', and ordered him to a holding position at Nameth to await deployment.

It made Gaunt queasy. He tossed the slate aside.

The shutter opened and Kreff entered. Kreff was the frigate's executive officer, a hard-faced, shaven-headed man in the emerald, tailored uniform of the Segmentum Pacificus Fleet. He saluted, a pointless over-formality given that he had been covering as Gaunt's adjutant in Sym's place, and had been in and out of the room ten times an hour since Gaunt came aboard.

'Anything?' Gaunt asked.

'The astropaths tell us that something may be coming soon. Perhaps our orders. There is a current, a feeling. And also, uhm...' Kreff was obviously uncomfortable. He didn't know Gaunt and vice versa. It had taken Sym four years to get used to the commissar.

Sym...

'What is it?' Gaunt asked.

'I wondered if you would care to discuss our more immediate concern? The morale of the men.'

Gaunt got up. 'Okay, Kreff. Speak your mind.'

Kreff hesitated. 'I didn't mean with me. There is a deputation from the troop-ships–'

Gaunt turned hard at this. 'A what?'

'A deputation of Tanith. They want to speak to you. They came aboard thirty minutes ago.'

Gaunt took his bolt pistol out of the holster slung over his chair back and checked the magazine. 'Is this your discreet way of announcing a mutiny, Kreff?'

Kreff shook his head and laughed humourlessly. He seemed relieved when Gaunt reholstered his weapon.

'How many?'

'Fifteen. Mostly enlisted men. Few of the officers came out alive.'

'Send three of them in. Just three. They can choose who.'

Gaunt sat down behind his desk again. He thought about putting his cap on, his jacket. He looked across the cabin and saw his own reflection in the vast bay port. Two metres twenty of solid bone and sinew, the narrow, dangerous face that so well matched his name, the cropped blond hair. He wore his high-waisted dress breeches with their leather braces, a sleeveless undershirt and jack boots. His jacket and cap gave him command and authority. Bare-armed, he gave himself physical power.

The shutter clanked and three men entered. Gaunt viewed them without comment. One was tall, taller and older than Gaunt and built heavily, if a little paunchy. His arms were like hams and were decorated with blue spirals. His beard was shaggy, and his eyes might once have twinkled. The second was slim and dark, with sinister good looks that were almost reptilian. He had a blue star tattooed across his right eye. The third was the boy, the piper.

'Let's know you,' Gaunt said simply.

'I'm Corbec,' said the big man. 'This is Rawne.'

The snake nodded.

'And you know the boy,' Corbec said.

'Not his name.'

'Milo,' the boy said clearly. 'Brin Milo.'

'I imagine you're here to tell me that the men of Tanith want me dead,' said Gaunt simply.

'Perfectly true,' Rawne said. Gaunt was impressed. None of them even bothered to acknowledge his rank and seniority. Not a 'sir', not a 'commissar'.

'Do you know why I did what I did?' Gaunt asked. 'Do you know why I ordered the regiments off Tanith and left it to die? Do you know why I refused all your pleas to let you turn and fight?'

'It was our right–' Rawne began.

'Our world died, Colonel-Commissar Gaunt,' Corbec said, the title bringing Gaunt's head up sharp. 'We saw it flame out from the windows of our transports. You should have let us stand and fight. We would have died for Tanith.'

'You still can, just somewhere else.' Gaunt got to his feet. 'You're not men of Tanith any more. You weren't when you were camped out on the Founding Fields. You're Imperial Guard, servants of the Emperor first and nothing else second.'

He turned to face the window port, his back to them. 'I mourn the loss of any world, any life. I did not want to see Tanith die, nor did I want to abandon it. But my duty is to the Emperor, and the Sabbat Worlds Crusade must be fought and won for the good of the entire Imperium. The only thing you could have done if I had left you on Tanith was die. If that's what you want, I can provide you with many opportunities. What I need is soldiers, not corpses.'

Gaunt gazed out into space. 'Use your loss, don't be crippled by it. Put the pain into your fighting spirit. Think hard! Most men who join the Guard never see their homes again. You are no different.'

'But most have a home to return to!' Corbec spat.

'Most can look forward to living through a campaign and mustering to settle on some world their leader has conquered and won. Slaydo made me a gift after Balhaut. He gave me the military rank of colonel and granted me settlement rights to the first planet I win. Help me by doing your job, and I'll help you by sharing that with you.'

'Is that a bribe?' Rawne asked.

Gaunt shook his head. 'Just a promise. We need each other. I need an able, motivated army, you need something to take the pain away, something to fight for, something to look forward to.'

Gaunt saw something in the reflection on the glass. He didn't turn his head. 'Is that a laspistol, Rawne? Would you have come here and murdered me?'

Rawne grinned. 'What makes you put that in the past tense, commissar?'

Gaunt turned. 'What do I have here then? A regiment or a mutiny?'

Corbec met his gaze. 'The men will need convincing. You've made ghosts of them, hollow echoes. We'll take word back to the troop-ships of why you did what you did and what the future might hold. Then it's up to them.'

'They need to rally around their officers.'

Rawne laughed. 'There are none! Our command staff were all on the Founding Fields trying to embark the men when the bombardment started. None of them made it off Tanith alive.'

Gaunt nodded. 'But the men elected you to lead the deputation? You're leaders.'

'Or simply bold and dumb enough to be the ones to front you,' Corbec said.

'It's the same thing,' Gaunt said. 'Colonel Corbec. Major Rawne. You can appoint your own juniors and unit chiefs and report back to me in six hours with an assessment of morale. I should have our deployment by then.'

They glanced at each other, taken aback.

'Dismissed,' prompted Gaunt.

The trio turned away confused.

'Milo? Wait, please,' Gaunt said. The boy stopped as the shutter closed after the two men.

'I owe you,' Gaunt told him baldly.

'And you paid me back. I'm not militia or Guard. I only got off Tanith alive because you brought me.'

'Because of your service to me.'

Milo paused. 'The Elector himself ordered me to stay with you, to see to your needs. I was just doing my duty.'

'Those two brought you along because they thought the sight of you might mollify me, didn't they?'

'They're not stupid,' noted Milo.

Gaunt sat back at his desk. 'Neither are you. I have need of an adjutant, a personal aide. It's dogsbody, gopher work mostly, and the harder stuff you can learn. It would help me to have a Tanith in the post if my working relationship with them is going to continue.'

Before Milo could answer, the shutter slammed open again and Kreff entered, a slate in his hand. He saluted again. 'We've got our orders, sir,' he said.

Distant, rumbling explosions seemed a constant feature of the deadzone on Blackshard. The persistent crump of heavy gunnery drummed the low, leaden sky over the ridgeline. An earthwork had been built up along the ridge's spine and, under hardened bunkers, a detachment of Imperial Guard – six units of the 10th Royal Sloka – were readying to mobilise.

Colonel Thoren walked the line. The men looked like world-killers in their ornate battledress: crested, enamelled scarlet and silver warsuits built by the artisans of Sloka to inspire terror in the enemy.

But perhaps not this enemy. General Hadrak's orders had been precise, but Thoren's heart was heavy. He had no relish for the approaching push. He had no doubt at all it would cost him dearly.

To push blind, unsupported, into treacherous unknown territory in the hope of finding a wormhole into the enemy positions that might not even be there. The prospect made him feel sick.

Thoren's subaltern drew his attention suddenly to the double file of sixty men moving down the covered transit trench towards them. Scrawny ruffians, dressed in black, camo-cloaks draped over them, plastered to their bodies by the rain.

'Who in the name of Balor's blood...?' Thorne began.

Halting his column, the leader, a huge blackguard with a mess of tangled beard and a tattoo – a tattoo! – marched up to Thoren and saluted.

'Colonel Corbec, First Tanith. First-and-Only. General Hadrak has ordered us forward to assist you.'

'Tanith? Where the hell is that?' asked Thoren.

'It isn't,' replied the big man genially. 'The general said you were set to advance on the enemy positions over the deadzone. Suggested you might need a covert scouting force seeing as how your boys' scarlet armour stands out like a baboon's arse.'

Thoren felt his face flush. 'Now listen to me, you piece–'

A shadow fell across them. 'Colonel Thoren, I presume?'

Gaunt dropped down into the dugout from the trench boarding. 'My regiment arrived here on Blackshard yesterday night, with orders to reinforce General Hadrak's efforts to seize the Chaos stronghold. That presupposes co-operative efforts between our units.'

Thoren nodded. This was Gaunt, the upstart colonel-commissar, it had to be. He'd heard stories.

'Appraise me, please,' said Gaunt.

Thoren waved up an aide who flipped up a map-projector, and displayed a fuzzy image of the deadzone. 'The foe are dug in deep in the old citadel ruins. The citadel had a sizeable standing defence force, so they're well equipped. Chaos cultists, mostly, about seventeen thousand able fighting men. We also...' he paused.

Gaunt raised a questioning eyebrow.

'We believe there may be other abominations in there. Chaos spawn.' Thoren breathed heavily. 'Most of the main fighting is contained in this area here, while artillery duels blight the other fronts.'

Gaunt nodded. 'Most of my strength is deployed along the front line. But General Hadrak also directed us to this second front.'

Thoren indicated the map again. 'The foe are up to more than simply holding us out. They know sooner or later we'll break through, so they must be up to something – trying to complete something, perhaps. Recon showed that this flank of the city might be vulnerable to a smaller force. There are channels and ducts leading in under the old walls, a rat-maze, really.'

'My boys specialise in rat-mazes,' Gaunt said.

'You want to go in first?' Thoren asked.

'It's mud and tunnels. The Tanith are light infantry, you're armoured and heavy. Let us lead through and then follow us in support when we've secured a beachhead. Bring up some support weapons.'

Thoren nodded. 'Very well, colonel-commissar.'

Gaunt and Corbec withdrew to their men.

'This will be the first blooding for this regiment, for the Tanith First-and-Only,' began Gaunt.

'For Gaunt's Ghosts,' someone murmured. Mad Larkin, Corbec was sure.

Gaunt smiled. 'Gaunt's Ghosts. Don't disappoint me.'

They needed no other instructions. At Corbec's gesture, they hurried forward in pairs, slipping their camo-cloaks down as shrouds around them, lasguns held loose and ready. The hybrid weave of the hooded cloaks blurred to match the dark grey mud of the ridgeway, and each man stooped to smear his cheeks and brow with wet mud before slipping over the earthwork.

Thoren watched the last one disappear and then span the trench macro-periscope around. He looked out, but of the sixty plus men who had just passed his position, there was no sign.

'Where in the name of Solan did they go?' he breathed.

Gaunt was amazed. He'd seen them practise and train in the belly holds of the big carrier ships, but now here, in the wild of a real deadzone, their skills startled him. They were all but invisible in the stinking mire, just tiny blurs of movement edging between stacks of debris and over mounds of wreckage towards the slumped but massive curtain walls of the citadel.

He pulled his own Tanith camo-cloak around him. It had been part of his deal with Corbec: he insisted on leading them in to assure loyalty, they insisted he didn't give their position away.

The micro-bead in his ear tickled. It was Corbec. 'First units at the tunnels now. Move up close in pairs.'

Gaunt touched his throat mike. 'Hostiles?' he asked.

'A little light knife work,' crackled the reply.

A few moment later he was entering the dripping, dark mouth of the rubble tunnel. Five Chaos-bred warriors in the orange robes of their cult lay dead. Before him, the Tanith were forming up. Corbec was wiping blood from the blade of his long, silver knife.

'Let's go,' said Gaunt.

The Elector of Tanith, may his soul rest, had not lied about anything, Gaunt decided. The Ghosts had proved their cunning stealth crossing the open waste of the deadzone, and he had no clue as to how they threaded their way through the crazy lightless warren of the tunnels so surely. 'They do not get lost,' the Elector had boasted, and it was true. Gaunt suspected that the foe had assumed nothing bigger than a cockroach would ever find its way through those half-collapsed, death-trap tunnels.

But Corbec's men had, effortlessly, in scant minutes. Rising from the tunnels' ends inside the curtain wall of the city, and taking long, silver Tanith knives to pallid, blotchy throats, they had burned their way in through the enemy's hindquarters. Now the Tanith First-and-Only were proving they could fight. Just like the Elector had said.

From behind a shattered pillar, Gaunt blasted with his bolter, blowing two cultists apart and destroying a doorway. Around him, the advancing Tanith lacerated the air with precise shots from five dozen lasguns.

Near to Gaunt, a sharp-faced, older Tanith Gaunt had heard the men call Larkin was sniping cultists off the top of the nearest balconies. His eye was tremendous. A little further on, a huge man, a gentle giant called Bragg, was shouldering the heavy bolter and taking down walls and columns. The big weapon had originally been pintle-mounted on a sled, but Bragg had torn it off its mount and slung it up like a rifle. Gaunt had never seen a heavy bolter carried by an unarmoured man before. The Tanith called Bragg 'Try Again' Bragg. He was a terrible shot, admittedly, but with firepower like that he could afford to be sloppy.

Just ahead, a six man fire-team led by Corbec gained the entrance to a temple building complex, grenaded the doorway and went in with lasguns, paired off to give bounding cover.

'Heavy fire in my section!' Corbec radioed to Gaunt. 'Some kind of church or temple. Could be a primary target.'

Gaunt acknowledged. He would move more teams up.

Creeping down the aisle of the massive temple, Corbec edged through rubble and heavy crossfire. He nodded a pair past him – Rawne and Suth – and then the next. His own cover partner, Forgal, bellied up close in the mica dust of the temple floor and unslung his lasgun.

'Down there,' he hissed, his eyes as sharp as ever. 'There's a lower storey down behind the altar. They've got a lot of defence around that doorway. The big arch under the stained-glass.'

It was true.

'You smell that?' Rawne asked over the radio.

Corbec did. Decay, stale sweat, dead blood. Rank and harsh, oozing from the crypt.

Forgal began to crawl forward. A lucky shot vaporised the top of his head.

'Sacred Feth!' Corbec howled and opened up in rage, bringing the entire stained glass window down in a sheet onto the altar.

Rawne and Suth took advantage of the confusion to grab a few more metres. Rawne unwrapped a tube-charge and hurled it over-arm into the archway.

The blast was deafening.

Gaunt heard Corbec's call in his ear-piece. 'Get in here!' He scrambled into the smoky interior of the temple. At the door, he paused. 'Larkin! Bragg! Orcha! Varl! With me! You three, cordon the door! Cluggan, take two teams down the flank of the building and scout!'

Gaunt entered the chapel, mashing broken glass under foot. He could smell the stink.

Corbec and Rawne were waiting for him, their other men stood around, watching with lasguns ready.

'Something down here,' Rawne said and led Gaunt on down the littered steps. Gaunt slammed fresh rounds home into his boltgun, then holstered it and picked up Forgal's fallen lasgun.

Beneath the chapel was an undercroft. Dead cultists were strewn like rag dolls around the smouldering floor. In the centre of the chamber stood a rusty, metallic box, two metres square, its lid etched with twisted sigils of Chaos.

Gaunt reached out. The metal was warm. It pulsed.

He snatched his hand back.

'What is it?' asked Corbec.

'I don't think any of us want to know,' Gaunt said. 'Some relic of the enemy, some unholy object, an icon… Whatever, it's something valuable to these monsters, something they're defending to the last.'

'That Sloka colonel was sure there was a reason they were holding on,' Corbec said. 'Maybe they're hoping support will arrive in time to save this.'

'Let's spoil those chances. I want a systematic withdrawal from this point, back out under the wall. Each man is to leave his tube-charges here. Rawne, collect them and rig them – you seem to be good with explosives.'

Within minutes, the Ghosts had withdrawn. Rawne crouched and connected the firing pins of the small but potent anti-personnel charges. Gaunt watched him and the door.

'Pick it up, Rawne. We haven't much time. The enemy aren't going to leave this area open for long.'

'Nearly done,' Rawne said. 'Check the door again, sir. I thought I heard something.'

The 'sir' should have warned him. As Gaunt turned, Rawne rose and clubbed him around the back of the head with his fist. Gaunt dropped, stunned, and Rawne rolled him over next to the charges.

'A fitting place for scum like you to die, ghost maker!' he murmured. 'Down here amongst the vermin and the filth. It's so tragic that the brave commissar didn't make it out, but the cultists were all over us.' Rawne drew his laspistol and lowered it towards Gaunt's head.

Gaunt kicked out and brought Rawne down. He rolled and slammed into him, punching him once, twice. Blood marked Rawne's mouth.

He tried to hit again but Gaunt was so much bigger. He struck Rawne so hard he was afraid he'd broken his neck. The Tanith lolled in the dust.

Gaunt got up, and eyed the timer setting. It was just dropping under two minutes. Time to leave.

Gaunt turned. But in the doorway of the room, the warriors of Chaos moved towards him.

The blast sent a column of dirt and fire up into the sky that could be seen from the Guard trenches across the deadzone. Six minutes later, the defenders' big guns stopped and fell silent. Then all firing ceased completely from the enemy lines.

Guard units moved in, cautiously at first. They found the cultists dead at their positions. Each one had, in unison, taken his own life, as if in response to some great loss. In the conclusion of his report on the victory at Blackshard, General Hadrak surmised that the destruction of the Chaos relic, which had given meaning to the cult defence, robbed them of the will or need to continue. Hadrak also noted the significant role in the victory played by the newly founded Tanith 1st, which had supplemented his own forces. Though as C-in-C of the Blackshard action, he took overall credit for the victory, he was magnanimous in acknowledging the work of 'Gaunt's Ghosts', and particularly recommended their stealth and scouting abilities.

Colonel-Commissar Gaunt, wounded in the stomach and shoulder, emerged alive from the deadzone twenty minutes after the blast and was treated by medical teams before returning to his frigate. He might have made his way out of the enemy lines faster, had he not carried the unconscious body of one of his officers, a Major Rawne, back to safety.

Stiff with drug-dulled pain, Gaunt walked down the companion way of the troop carrier and into the holding bay. Nearly nine hundred of the Tanith were billeted here. They looked up from their weapons drills and Gaunt felt the silence on him.

'First blood to you,' he said to them. 'First blood to Tanith. The first wound of vengeance. Savour it.'

By his side, Corbec began to clap. The men picked it up, more and more, until the hold shook with applause.

Gaunt eyed the crowd. Maybe there was a future here, after all. A regiment worth the leading, a prize worth chasing all the way to glory.

His eyes found Major Rawne in the crowd. Their eyes fixed. Rawne was not applauding.

That made Gaunt laugh. He turned to Milo and gestured to the Tanith pipes cradled in his aide's hands.

'*Now* you can play something,' he told him.

Gaunt walked the line through the early morning, the stink of the Monthax jungle swards filling and sickening his senses. Tanith, working stripped to the waists, digging the wet ooze with entrenching tools to fill sacking, paused to nod at his greetings, exchange a few words with him, or ask cautious questions about the fight to come.

Gaunt answered as best he could. As a commissar, a political officer, charged with morale and propaganda, he could turn a good, pompous phrase. But as a colonel, he felt a duty of truth to his men.

And the truth was, he knew little of what to expect. It would be bitter, he knew that much, though the commissar part of him spared the men that thought. Gaunt spoke of courage and glory in general, uplifting terms, talking softly and firmly as his mentor, Commissar-General Oktar, had taught him all those years ago when he was just a raw cadet with the Hyrkans. 'Save the yelling and screaming for battle, Ibram. Before that comes, build their morale with gentle encouragement. Make it look like you haven't a care in the world.'

Gaunt prided himself on knowing not only the names of all his men, but a little about each of them too. A private joke here, a common interest there. Oktar's way, tried and tested, Emperor rest his soul these long years. Gaunt tried to memorise each muddy, smiling face as he passed along. He knew his soul would be damned the day he was told Trooper so-and-so had fallen and he couldn't bring the man's face to mind. 'The dead will always haunt you,' Oktar had told him, 'so make certain the ghosts are friendly.' If only Oktar had known the literal truth of that advice.

Gaunt paused at the edge of a dispersal gully and smiled to himself at the memory. Beyond, some troopers were kicking a balled sack of mud around in an impromptu off-watch game. The 'ball' came his way, and he hoisted it back to them on the point of his boot. Let them have their fun while it lasts. How many would be alive to play the game again tomorrow?

How many indeed? There were losses and losses. Some worthy, some dreadful, and some plain unnecessary. Still the memories dogged his mind in these crawling hours of waiting. Praise be the Emperor that Gaunt's losses of brave, common troopers would never be as great, as wholesale or as senseless as that day on Voltemand, a year before...

TWO

A BLOODING

They were a good two hours into the dark, black-trunked forests of the Voltemand Mirewoods, tracks churning the filthy ooze and the roar of their engines resonating from the sickly canopy of leaves above, when Colonel Ortiz saw death.

It wore red, and stood in the trees to the right of the track, in plain sight, unmoving, watching his column of Basilisks as they passed along the trackway. It was the lack of movement that chilled Ortiz. He did a double take, first seeing the figure as they passed it before realising what it was.

Almost twice a man's height, frighteningly broad, armour the colour of rusty blood, crested by recurve brass antlers. The face was a graven death's head. Daemon. Chaos Warrior. *World Eater.*

Ortiz snapped his gaze back to it and felt his blood drain away. He fumbled for his radio link.

'Alarm! Alarm! Ambush to the right!' he yelled into the set. Gears slammed and whined, and hundreds of tons of mechanised steel shuddered, foundered and slithered on the muddy track, penned, trapped, too cumbersome to react quickly.

By then the Chaos Space Marine had begun to move. So had its six comrades, each emerging from the woods around them.

Panic seized Ortiz's convoy cluster: the ten-vehicle forward portion of a heavy column of eighty flame-and-feather painted Basilisk tanks of the 'Serpents', the Ketzok 17th Armoured Regiment, sent in to support the frontal push of the Royal Volpone 50th, the so-called 'Bluebloods'. The Ketzok had the firepower to flatten a city, but caught on a strangled trackway, in a thick woodland, with no room to turn or traverse, and with monstrous enemies at close quarters, far too close to bring the main guns to bear, they were all but helpless. Panic alarms spread

357

backwards down the straggled column, from convoy portion to portion. Ortiz heard tree trunks shatter as some commanders tried to haul their machines off the track.

The World Eaters started baying as they advanced, wrenching out of their augmented throats deep, inhuman calls that whooped across the trackway and shivered the metal of the tank armour. They howled the name of the bloody abomination they worshipped.

'Small arms!' Ortiz ordered. 'Use the pintle mounts!' As he spoke, he cranked round the autocannon mounted on his vehicle's rear and angled it at the nearest monster.

The killing started. The rasping belch of flamers reached his ears and he heard the screams of men cooking inside their superheated tank hulls. The Chaos Marine he had first spotted reached the Basilisk ahead of his and began to chop its shell like firewood with a chain-axe. Sparks blew up from punctured metal. Sparks, flames, metal shards, meat.

Screaming, Ortiz trained his mounted gun on the World Eater and fired. He shot long at first, but corrected before the monster could turn. The creature didn't seem to feel the first hits. Ortiz clenched the trigger and streamed the heavy tracer fire at the red spectre. At last the figure shuddered, convulsed and then blew apart.

Ortiz cursed. The World Eaters soaked up the sort of punishment that would kill a Leman Russ. He realised his ammo drum was almost empty. He was snapping it free and shouting to his bombardier for a fresh one when the shadow fell on him.

Ortiz turned.

Another Chaos Marine stood on the rear of the Basilisk behind him, a giant blocking out the pale sunlight. It stooped, and howled its victory shout into his face, assaulting him with concussive sonic force and wretched odour. Ortiz recoiled as if he had been hit by a macro shell. He could not move. The World Eater chuckled, a macabre, deep growl from behind the visor, a seismic rumble. The chainsword in its fist whined and swung up...

The blow didn't fall. The monster rocked, two or three times, swayed for a moment. And exploded.

Smeared with grease and ichor, Ortiz scrambled up out of his hatch. He was suddenly aware of a whole new layer of gunfire – sustained lasgun blasts, the chatter of support weapons, the crump of grenades. Another force was moving out of the woods, crushing the Chaos Marine ambush hard against the steel flanks of his artillery machines.

As Ortiz watched, the remaining World Eaters died. One was punctured dozens of times by lasgun fire and fell face down into the mire. Another was flamed repeatedly as he ripped apart the wreck of a

Basilisk with his steel hands. The flames touched off the tank's magazine and the marine was incinerated with his victims. His hideous roar
lingered long after the white-hot flames had consumed him.

The column's saviours emerged from the forest around them. Imperial
Guards: tall, dark-haired, pale-skinned men in black fatigues, a scruffy,
straggle-haired mob almost invisible in their patterned camo-cloaks.
Ortiz heard strange, disturbing pipe music strike up a banshee wail in
the close forest, and a victory yelp erupted from the men. It was met
by cheers and whoops from his own crews.

Ortiz leapt down into the mud and approached the Imperial Guardsmen through the drifting smoke.

'I'm Colonel Ortiz. You boys have my earnest thanks,' he said. 'Who
are you?'

The nearest man, a giant with unruly black hair, a tangled, braided
beard and thick, bare arms decorated with blue spiral tattoos, smiled
jauntily and saluted, bringing up his lasgun. 'Colonel Corbec, Tanith
First-and-Only. Our pleasure, I'm sure.'

Ortiz nodded back. He found he was still shaking. He could barely
bring himself to look down at the dead Chaos Marine, sprawled in the
mud nearby. 'Takes discipline to ambush an ambush. Your men certainly know stealth. Why is–'

He got no further. The bearded giant, Corbec, suddenly froze, a look
of dismay on his face. Then he was leaping forward with a cry, tackling
Ortiz down into the blue-black mud.

The 'dead' World Eater lifted his horned skull out of the muck and
half-raised his bolter. But that was all. Then a shrieking chainsword
decapitated him.

The heavy, dead parts flopped back into the mud. One of them rolled.

Ibram Gaunt brandished with his keening chain sword like a duel-
list and then thumbed it to 'idle'. He turned to Corbec and Ortiz as they
got up, caked in black filth. Ortiz stared at the tall, powerful man in the
long dark coat and cap of an Imperial Commissar. His face was blade
thin, his eyes as dark as space. He looked like he could rip a world
asunder with his hands.

'Meet the boss,' Corbec chuckled at Ortiz's side. 'Colonel-Commissar
Gaunt.'

Ortiz nodded, wiping his face. 'So, you're Gaunt's Ghosts.'

Major Gilbear poured himself a brandy from the decanter on the teak
stand. 'Just who the hell are these awful barbarian scum?' he asked,
sipping from the huge crystal balloon.

At his desk, General Noches Sturm put down his pen and sat back.

'Oh, please, help yourself to my brandy, Gilbear,' he muttered, though the sarcasm was lost on his massive aide.

Gilbear reclined on a chaise beside the flickering amber displays of the message-caster, and gazed at his commander. 'Ghosts? That's what they call them, isn't it?'

Sturm nodded, observing his senior adjutant. Gilbear – Gizhaum Danver De Banzi Haight Gilbear, to give him his full name – was the second son of the Haight Gilbears of Solenhofen, the royal house of Volpone. He was nearly two and a half metres tall and arrogantly powerful, with the big, blunt, bland features and languid, hooded eyes of the aristocracy. Gilbear wore the grey and gold uniform of the Royal Volpone 50th, the so-called Bluebloods, who believed they were the noblest regiment in the Imperial Guard.

Sturm sat back in his chair. 'They are indeed called Ghosts. Gaunt's Ghosts. And they're here because I requested them.'

Gilbear cocked a disdainful eyebrow. 'You requested them?'

'We've had nigh on six weeks, and we can't shake the enemy from Voltis City. They command everything west of the Bokore Valley. Warmaster Macaroth is not pleased. All the while they hold Voltemand, they have a road into the heart of the Sabbat Worlds. So you see I need a lever. I need to introduce a new element to break our deadlock.'

'That rabble?' Gilbear sneered. 'I watched them as they mustered after the drop-ships landed them. Hairy, illiterate primitives, with tattoos and nose rings.'

Sturm lifted a data-slate from his desktop and shook it at Gilbear. 'Have you read the reports General Hadrak filed after the Sloka took Blackshard? He credits Gaunt's mob with the decisive incursion. It seems they excel at stealth raids.'

Sturm got to his feet and adjusted the sit of his resplendent Blueblood staff uniform. The study was bathed in yellow sunlight that streamed in through the conservatory doors at the end, softened by net drapes. He rested his hand on the antique globe of Voltemand in its mahogany stand by the desk and span it idly, gazing out across the grounds of Vortimor House. This place had been the country seat of one of Voltemand's most honoured noble families, a vast, grey manse, fringed with mauve climbing plants, situated in ornamental parkland thirty kilometres south of Voltis City. It had been an ideal location to establish his Supreme Headquarters.

Outside, on the lawn, a squad of Blueblood elite in full battle dress were executing a precision synchronised drill with chainswords. Metal flashed and whirled, perfect and poised. Beyond them, a garden of trellises and arbours led down to a boating lake, calm and smoky in the afternoon light. Navigation lights flashed slowly on the barbed masts of the communications array in the herbarium. Somewhere in the stable block, strutting gaudcocks whooped and called.

You wouldn't think there was a war on, mused Sturm. He wondered where the previous owners of the manse were now. Did they make it off-world before the first assault? Are they huddled and starving in the belly hold of a refugee ship, reduced overnight to a level with their former vassals? Or are they bone-ash in the ruins of Kosdorf, or on the burning Metis Road? Or did they die screaming and melting at the orbital port when the legions of Chaos first fell on their world, vaporised with the very ships they struggled to escape in?

Who cares? thought Sturm. The war is all that matters. The glory, the crusade, the Emperor. He would only care for the fallen when the bloody head of Chanthar, demagogue of the Chaos army that held Voltis Citadel, was served up to him on a carving dish. And even then, he wouldn't care much.

Gilbear was on his feet, refilling his glass. 'This Gaunt, he's quite a fellow, isn't he? Wasn't he with the Hyrkan Eighth?'

Sturm cleared his throat. 'Led them to victory at Balhaut. One of old Slaydo's chosen favourites. Made him a colonel-commissar, no less. It was decided he had the prestige to hammer a new regiment or two into shape, so they sent him to the planet Tanith to supervise the Founding there. A Chaos space fleet hit the world that very night, and he got out with just a few thousand men.'

Gilbear nodded. 'That's what I heard. Skin of his teeth. But that's his career in tatters, stuck with an under-strength rabble like that. Macaroth won't transfer him, will he?'

Sturm managed a small smile. 'Our beloved overlord does not look kindly on the favourites of his predecessor. Especially as Slaydo granted Gaunt and a handful of others the settlement rights of the first world they conquered. He and his Tanith rabble are an embarrassment to the new regime. But that serves us well. They will fight hard because they have everything to prove, and everything to win.'

'I say,' said Gilbear suddenly, lowering his glass. 'What if they do win? I mean, if they're as useful as you say?'

'They will facilitate our victory,' Sturm said, pouring himself a drink. 'They will not achieve anything else. We will serve Lord Macaroth two-fold, by taking this world for him, and ridding him of Gaunt and his damn Ghosts.'

'You were expecting us?' Gaunt asked, riding on the top of Ortiz's Basilisk as the convoy moved on.

Colonel Ortiz nodded, leaning back against the raised top-hatch cover. 'We were ordered up the line last night to dig in at the north end of the Bokore Valley and pound the enemy fortifications on the western side. Soften them up, I suppose. En route, I got coded orders sent, telling us to meet your regiment at Pavis Crossroads and transport you as we advanced.'

Gaunt removed his cap and ran a hand through his short fair hair. 'We were ordered across country to the crossroads, all right,' he responded. 'Told to meet transport there for the next leg. But my scouts picked up the World Eaters' stench, so we doubled back and met you early.'

Ortiz shuddered. 'Good thing for us.'

Gaunt gazed along the line of the convoy as they moved on, taking in the massive bulk of the Basilisks as they ground up the snaking mud-track through the sickly, dim forest. His men were riding on the flanks of the great war machines, a dozen or more per vehicle, joking with the Serpent crews, exchanging drinks and smokes, some cleaning weapons or even snoozing as the lurch of the metal beasts allowed.

'So Sturm's sending you in?' Ortiz asked presently.

'Right down the river's floodplain to the gates of Voltis. He thinks we can take the city where fifty thousand of his Bluebloods have failed.'

'Can you?'

'We'll see,' Gaunt said, without the flicker of a smile. 'The Ghosts are new, unproven but for a skirmish on Blackshard. But they have certain... strengths.' He fell silent, and seemed to be admiring the gold and turquoise lines of the feather serpent design painted on the barrel of the Basilisk's main weapon. Its open beak was the muzzle. All the Ketzok machines were rich with similar decorations.

Ortiz whistled low to himself. 'Down the Bokore Valley into the mouth of hell. I don't envy you.'

Now Gaunt smiled. 'Just you keep pounding the western hills and keep them busy. In fact, blow them all away to kingdom come before we get there.'

'Deal,' laughed Ortiz.

'And don't drop your damn aim!' Gaunt added with a threatening chuckle. 'Remember you have friends in the valley!'

Two vehicles back, Corbec nodded his thanks as he took the dark thin cigar his Basilisk commander offered.

'Doranz,' the Serpent said, introducing himself.

'Charmed,' Corbec said. The cigar tasted of licorice, but he smoked it anyway.

Lower down the hull of the tank, by Corbec's sprawled feet, the boy

Milo was cleaning out the chanters of his Tanith pipe. It wheezed and squealed hoarsely.

Doranz blanched. 'I'll tell you this: when I heard that boy's piping today, that hell-note, it almost scared me more than the damn blood cries of the enemy.'

Corbec chuckled. 'The pipe has its uses. It rallies us, it spooks the foe. Back home, the forests move and change. The pipes were a way to follow and not get lost.'

'Where is home?' Doranz asked.

'Nowhere now,' Corbec said and returned to his smoke.

On the back armour of another Basilisk, hulking Bragg, the biggest of the Ghosts, and small, wiry Larkin, were dicing with two of the tank's gun crew.

Larkin had already won a gold signet ring set with a turquoise skull. Bragg had lost all his smokes, and two bottles of sacra. Every now and then, the lurch of the tank beneath them would flip the dice, or slide them under an exhaust baffle, prompting groans and accusations of fixing and cheating.

Up by the top hatch with the vehicle's commander, Major Rawne watched the game without amusement. The Basilisk commander felt uneasy about his passenger. Rawne was slender, dark and somehow dangerous. A starburst tattoo covered one eye. He was not... likeable or open like the other Ghosts seemed to be.

'So, major... what's your commissar like?' the commander began, by way of easing the silence.

'Gaunt?' Rawne asked, turning slowly to face the Serpent. 'He's a despicable bastard who left my world to die and one day I will slay him with my own hands.'

'Oh,' said the commander and found something rather more important to do down below.

Ortiz passed Gaunt his flask. The afternoon was going and they were losing the light. Ortiz consulted a map-slate, angling it to show Gaunt. 'Navigation puts us about two kilometres or so short of Pavis Crossroads. We've made good time. We'll be on it before dark. I'm glad, I didn't want to have to turn on the floods and running lights to continue.'

'What do we know about Pavis?' Gaunt asked.

'Last reports were it was held by a battalion of Bluebloods. That was at oh-five-hundred this morning.'

'Wouldn't hurt to check,' Gaunt mused. 'There are worse things than rolling into an ambush position at twilight, but not many. Cluggan!'

He called down the hull to a big, grey-haired Ghost sat with others playing cards.

'Sir!' Cluggan said, scrambling back up the rocking Basilisk.

'Sergeant, take six men, jump down and scout ahead of the column. We're two kilometres short of this crossroads,' Gaunt showed Cluggan the map. 'Should be clear, but after our tangle with the damn World Eaters we'd best be sure.'

Cluggan saluted and slid back to his men. In a few moments they had gathered up their kits and weapons and swung down off the skirt armour onto the track. A moment more and they had vanished like smoke into the woods.

'That is impressive,' Ortiz said.

At Pavis Crossroads, the serpents spoke. Stretching their great painted beaks towards the night sky, they began their vast barrage.

Brin Milo cowered in the shadow of a medical Chimera, pressing his hands to his ears. He'd seen two battles up close: the fall of Tanith Magna and the storming of the citadel on Blackshard, but this was the first time he had ever encountered the sheer numbing wrath of armoured artillery.

The Ketzok Basilisks were dug in along the ridge in a straggled line about half a kilometre long. They were hull-down into the grey earth, main weapons swung high, hurling death at the western hills across the valley nine kilometres away. They were firing at will, a sustained barrage that could, Corbec had assured him, go on all night. Every second at least one gun was sounding, lighting the darkness with its fierce muzzle flash, shaking the ground with its firing and recoil.

Pavis Crossroads was a stone obelisk marking the junction of the Metis Road that ran up the valley from Voltis City, and the Mirewood track that carried on towards the east. The Serpents' armour had rolled in at nightfall, ousting the encamped Bluebloods who held the junction, and deploying around the ridge-line, looking west. As the first stars began to shine, Ortiz's men began their onslaught.

Milo kept his eyes sharp for the commissar, and when he saw Gaunt striding towards a tented dugout beside the orbital communication stack, accompanied by his senior officers, Milo ran to join them.

'My scope!' requested Gaunt over the barrage. Milo pulled the commissar's brass-capped nightscope from his pack and Gaunt stepped up onto the parapet, scanning out of the dugout.

Corbec leaned up close by him, a thin black tube protruding from his beard.

Gaunt glanced round. 'What is that thing?' he asked.

Corbec took it out and displayed it proudly. 'Cigar. Liquorice, no less. Won a box off my gun-crate's C.O. and I think I'm getting a taste for them.

'See much?' he added.

'I can see the lights of Voltis. Watch fires and shrine-lights mostly. Not so inviting.'

Gaunt flipped his scope shut and jumped down from the parapet, handing the device back to Milo. The boy had already set up the field-map, a glass plate in a metal frame mounted like an easel on a brass tripod. Gaunt cranked the knurled lever on the side and the glass slowly lit with bluish light. He dropped in a ceramic slide engraved with the local geography and then angled the screen to show the assembled men: Corbec, Rawne, Cluggan, Orcha and the other officers.

'Bokore Valley,' Gaunt said, tapping the glass viewer with the tip of his long, silver Tanith war-knife. As if for emphasis, the nearest Basilisk outside fired and the dugout shook. The field map wobbled and soil trickled in from the roof.

'Four kilometres wide, twelve long, flanked to the west by steep hills where the enemy is well established. At the far end, Voltis City, the old Capital of Voltemand. Thirty-metre curtain walls of basalt. Built as a fortress three hundred years ago, when they knew the art. The invading Chaos Host from off-planet seized it at day one as their main stronghold. The Volpone 50th have spent six weeks trying to crack it, but the bastards we met today show the kind of force they've been up against. We'll have a go tonight.'

He looked up, oblivious to the constant thunder outside. 'Major Rawne?'

Rawne stepped forward, almost reluctant to be anywhere near Gaunt. No one knew what had passed between them when they had been alone together on Blackshard, but everyone had seen Gaunt carry Rawne to safety on his shoulder, despite his own injuries. Surely that sort of action bonded men, not deepened their enmity?

Rawne adjusted a dial on the field-map's edge so that the plate displayed a different section of the chart-slide. 'The approach is straightforward. The Bokore River runs along the wide valley floor. It is broad and slow-moving, especially at this time of year. Most of the way is choked with bulrushes and waterweed. We can move down the river channel undetected.'

'You've scouted this?' Gaunt asked.

'My squad returned not half an hour ago,' Rawne said smoothly. 'The Bluebloods had tried it a number of times, but they are semi-armoured and the mud was too great an impediment. We are lighter – and we are good.'

Gaunt nodded. 'Corbec?'

The big man sucked on his cigar. His genial eyes twinkled and it made Milo smile. 'We move by dark, of course. In the next half-hour. Staggered squads of thirty men to spread out our traces.' He tapped the map-screen at another place. 'Primary point of entry is the old city watergate. Heavily defended of course. Secondary squads under Sergeant Cluggan will attempt to storm the wall at the western sanitation outfalls. I won't pretend either way will be a picnic.'

'Objective,' Gaunt said, 'get inside and open the city. We'll move in squads. One man in every ten will be carrying as much high explosive as he can. Squad leaders should select any man with demol experience. We provide cover for these demolition specialists to allow them to set charges that will take out sections of wall or gates. Anything that splits the city open.

'I've spoken to the Blueblood colonel. He has seven thousand men in motorised units ready to advance and take advantage of any opening we can make. They will be monitoring on channel eighty. The signal will be "Thunderhead".'

There was silence, silence except for the relentless hammering of the Basilisk guns.

'Form up and move out,' Gaunt said.

Outside, Ortiz stood talking to several of his senior officers, one of them Doranz. They saw the Ghost officers emerge from the dugout and orders being given.

Across the emplacement, Ortiz caught Gaunt's eye. It was too loud for words, so he clenched his fist and rapped it twice against his heart, an old gesture for luck.

Gaunt nodded.

'Scary men,' Doranz said. 'I almost feel sorry for the enemy.'

Ortiz glanced round at him.

'I'm joking, of course,' Doranz added, but Ortiz wasn't sure he was.

Midnight had seen them waist deep in the stinking black water of the Bokore River reed beds, assailed by clouds of biting flies. Three hours' hard trudge through the oily shallows of the old river, and now the sheer walls of Voltis rose before them, lit by cressets and braziers high up. Behind them, like a distant argument, the Basilisks spat death up into the heavens, a distant, rolling roar and a series of orange flashes on the skyline.

Gaunt adjusted his nightscope and panned it round, seeing features in the darkness as a green negative. The watergate was thirty metres across and forty tall, the mouth of a great chute and adjoining system

that returned water to the Bokore once it had driven the mills inside
the city. Gaunt knew that somewhere sluices must have been lowered,
and the flow staunched, closing off the chute's operation. Sandbagged
emplacements could be made out up in the shadows behind the gate's
breastwork.

He adjusted his micro-bead link. 'Corbec?'

Colm Corbec heard his commander in the darkness and acknowledged. He waded forward through the reeds to Bragg, who had
hunkered down behind a rotting jetty.

'When you're ready...' Corbec invited.

Bragg grinned, teeth bright in the starlight. He dragged the canvas
cover off one of the two huge weapons he had lugged on his shoulders
from Pavis Crossroads. The polished metal of the missile launcher had
been dulled down with smears of Mirewood mud.

'Try Again' Bragg was a spectacularly lousy shot. But the watergate
was a big target, and the missile rack held four melta-missiles.

The night exploded. Three missiles went straight up the throat of the
chute. The force of the heat-blast sent stone debris, metal shards, water
vapour and body parts out in a radius of fifty metres. The fourth vaporised a chunk of wall, and brought down a small avalanche of basalt
chunks. For a moment the heat was so intense that Gaunt's night-
scope read nothing but emerald glare. Then it showed him the chiselled
mouth of the watergate had become a bubbling, blazing wound in the
huge wall, a ragged, slumping incision in the sheer basalt. He could
hear agonised screaming from within the chute. Beyond the city wall,
alarm bells and sirens rose in pandemonium.

The Ghosts charged the watergate. Orcha led the first squad up the
sloping drain-away under the molten arch of ruptured stone. He and
three of his men swung flamers in wide arcs, scorching and scouring
up into the darkness of the echoing chute.

Behind them, Corbec brought in fire teams with lasguns who darted
down into the side passages and cisterns of the watergate, butchering
the cultists who had limped or crawled into cover after the first attack.

The third wave went in, under Major Rawne. In the front rank was
Bragg, his empty launcher discarded in favour of the heavy bolter that
he had liberated from its mounting back on Blackshard and now lugged
around like a smaller man might heft a heavy rifle.

Gaunt leapt forward too, bolt pistol in one hand, chainsword in the
other. He bellowed after his attacking men, all of them racing silhou-
ettes backlit against the glittering water by fire.

Milo sprang up, fumbling with the Tanith pipes under his arm.

'Now would be a good time, Brin,' Gaunt said.

Milo found the mouthpiece, inflated the bag and began to keen an old battle lament of Tanith, 'The Dark Path of the Forest'.

Up in the chute, Orcha and his squad heard the shrill wail of the pipes outside. Damp darkness was before them.

'Close up,' Orcha snapped into his micro-bead.

'Aye.'

'To your left,' Brith yelled suddenly.

An assault cannon raged out of the darkness of a side chute. Brith, Orcha and two others disintegrated instantly into red mist and flesh pulp.

Troopers Gades and Caffran ducked back behind the buttress work of the huge vault.

'Enemy fire!' Caffran yelled into his bead. 'They have the chute covered in a killing sweep.'

Corbec cursed. He might have expected this.

'Stay down!' he ordered the young Ghost over the mike as he beckoned his first two squads up the lower chute, black water swilling around their knees.

'Hell of a foul place for a firefight,' mourned Mad Larkin, scoping with his lasgun.

'Stow it, Larks,' Corbec growled. Ahead they heard the nightmare chatter of the cannon, and the added rhythm of drums and guttural chants. Corbec knew Larkin was right. A tight, confined, unyielding stone tunnel was no place for a serious fight. This was a two-way massacre in the making.

'They're just trying to psyche us out,' he told his Ghosts smoothly as they edged forward.

'What d'you know? It's working!' Varl said.

The drums and chanting got louder, but suddenly the cannon shut off.

'It's stopped,' Caffran reported over the link.

Corbec looked round into Larkin's crazed eyes. 'What do you think? A trick to lure us out?'

Larkin sniffed the thick air. 'Smell that? Burning ceramite. I'd wager they've got an overheat jam.'

Corbec didn't answer. He cinched his bayonet onto his lasgun and charged up the slope of the chute, screaming louder and shriller than Milo's pipes. In uproar, the Ghost squads followed him.

Caffran and Gades joined the charge, bellowing, weapons held low as they splashed out from behind the buttress into the main vault.

Corbec leapt clear a sandbag line damming one gully and disembowelled the two cultists who were struggling to unjam the assault cannon.

Larkin dropped down on one knee in the brackish soup and popped the cover on his lasgun's darkscope. Carefully selecting his expert long shots, he blasted four cultists further down the chute.

Las and bolt fire slammed back at the Ghosts, dropping several of them. The charging Guardsmen met the cultist force head on in a tight, tall sub-chute, no wider than two men abreast. Bodies exploded, blasted at close range. Bayonets and blades sliced and jabbed. Corbec was in the thick of it. Already a chainsword had gashed his left hand and cost him a finger, and blood blurted from a slash to his shoulder. He speared a man, but lost his gun when the corpse's weight on the bayonet tore it out of his hands. He ripped out his fallback weapons, a laspistol and his Tanith knife of sheer silver. Around him in the frenzy, men killed or died in a confined press that was packed in close like a busy work transit, crowded at rush hour. Already the water level was rising because of the depth of bodies and body parts in the gully.

Corbec shot a cultist through the head as he was charged, and then lashed sideways with the silver blade, opening a throat.

'For Tanith! First and Last and Only!' he screamed.

Advancing up the tunnel fifty paces back, Gaunt could hear the sheer tumult of the nightmarish close-quarters fight in the chute. He looked down and saw that the trickle of Bokore River water that ran down over his boots was thick and red.

Ten metres further, he found Trooper Gades, part of Orcha's original squad. The boy had lost his legs to a chainsword and the water had carried his twitching form back down the smooth slope of the channel.

'Medic! Dorden! To me!' Gaunt bellow, cradling the coughing, gagging Gades in his arms.

Gades looked up at his commissar. 'A real close fight, so it is,' he said with remarkable clarity, 'packed in like fish in a can. The Ghosts will make ghosts tonight.'

Then he coughed again. Bloody matter vomited from his mouth and he was gone.

Gaunt stood.

Milo had faltered, looking down at Gades's stricken, miserable death.

'Play up!' urged Gaunt, and turned to shout down the chute to the Ghost main force in the bulrushes. 'Advance! Narrow file! For the Emperor and the glory of Tanith!'

With a deafening bellow, Gaunt's Ghosts charged forward en masse, breaking down into files of three, surging into the throttling entrance to hell.

Up ahead, in the dark, close, smoky killing zone, Rawne slumped against a buttress, splashed in gore, and panted. By his side, Larkin squatted and fired shot after shot into the darkness.

Corbec suddenly loomed out of the smoke, a terrible apparition drenched in blood.

'Back!' he hissed. 'Back down the chute! Sound the retreat!'

'What is it?' Rawne said.

'What's that rumbling?' Larkin asked, distracted, pressing his ear to the stone work. 'Whole tunnel is vibrating!'

'Water,' Corbec said grimly. 'They've opened the sluices. They're going to wash us out!'

The cultists were everywhere.

Sergeant Cluggan's secondary expedition force poured in through the stinking crypts of the western sanitation outfalls, and the enemy rose to meet them all around. It was hand to hand, each step of the way won by strength and keen blades. The dark, tight confines of the drainage tunnels were lit by the flashes of las-fire, and shots ricocheted from the roof and walls.

'What the hell is that smell?' Forbin wailed, blasting away down an airless cavity with his lasgun.

'What do you think? This is the main sewage drain,' Brodd snapped, a one-eyed man in his fifties. 'Notice how the others get the nice clean watergate.'

'Keep it together!' Cluggan snarled, firing in a wide sweep and cutting down a trio of attacking cultists. 'Forget the smell. It's always been a dirty job.'

More, heavy fire came their way. Forbin lost his left arm and then the side of his head.

Cluggan, Brodd and the others returned fire in the close channel. Cluggan eyed the cultist troops they cut through: bloated, twisted men in robes that had been white silk before they had been dyed in vats of blood. They had come from off-world, part of the vast host of Chaos cultists that had descended like locusts onto Voltemand and destroyed its people. The sigils and runes of the blasphemy Khorne were cut into the flesh of their brows and cheeks. They were well equipped, with bolters and lasguns, and armoured. Cluggan hoped to the sweet, dead gods of Tanith that his commissar was faring better.

The Ghosts staggered and stumbled back from the spewing watergate, through the reed beds, towards the comparative cover of the riverbank. Enemy fire from the walls high above killed dozens, their bodies joining the hundreds swept out, swirling and turning, by the torrent of brown water roaring from the watergate.

Micro-bead traffic was frantic with cross-chatter and desperately confused calls. Despite their discipline, the madness of the flight from the water had broken Gaunt's main force into a ragged jumble, scrambling for their lives.

Soaked through, furious, Gaunt found himself sheltering by some willows in a scummy river bend eighty metres from the watergate. With him were Caffran, Varl, a corporal called Meryn and two others.

Gaunt cursed. Cultists he could fight... World Eaters, daemons... anything. He'd set square with any beast in the cosmos. But seventy million litres of water pressured down through a stone conduit...

'May have lost as many as forty to the flood,' Varl said. He'd dragged Caffran by the tunic from the water and the young man could only retch and cough.

'Get a confirmed figure from the squad leaders! I don't want rumours!' Gaunt snarled, then keyed his own radio link and spoke into his bead. 'Squad leaders! Discipline the radio traffic. I want regroup status! Corbec! Rawne!'

The channels crackled and a more ordered litany of units and casualties reeled in.

'Corbec?' Gaunt asked.

'I'm west of you, sir. On the banks. Got about ninety men with me.' Corbec's voice hissed back.

'Assessment?'

'Tactical? You can forget the watergate, sir. Once they realised they couldn't hold us out in a straight fight, they blew the sluices. It could run at flood for hours. By then they'll have the chute exits on the city side sewn up with emplacements, maybe even mines.'

Gaunt cursed again. He wiped a wet hand across his face. They'd been so close and now it was all lost. Voltis would not be his.

'Sir?' Meryn called to him. The corporal was listening to other frequencies on his bead. 'Channel eighty. The word has just been given.'

Gaunt crossed to him, adjusting his own setting. 'What?'

'The word. "Thunderhead",' Meryn said, confused.

'Source that signal!' Gaunt snapped, 'If someone thinks that's a joke, I'll–'

He got no further.

The blast was so loud, it almost went beyond sound. The shockwave mashed into them, chopping the water like a white squall.

A kilometre away, a hundred metre section of the curtain wall blew out, ripping a vast wound in the city's flank, burning, raw, exposed.

The channels went mad with frenzied calls and whoops.

Gaunt looked on in disbelief. Corbec's voice cut through, person to person on the link.

'It's Cluggan, sir! The old bastard got his boys into the sanitation out-falls and they managed to dump all of their high-ex into a treatment cistern under the walls. Blew the crap out of the cultists.'

'So I saw, colonel,' Gaunt said wryly.

'I mean it literally, sir,' Corbec crackled innocuously. 'It was Clug-gan sent the signal. We may have lost the fight to take the watergate, but Cluggan has won us the battle!'

Gaunt slumped back against a tree bole, up to his waist in the stink-ing river. Around him the men were laughing and cheering.

Exhaustion swept over him. And then he too began to laugh.

General Sturm took breakfast at nine. The stewards served him toasted black bread, sausage and coffee. He read a stack of data-slates as he ate, and the message-caster on the sideboard behind him chattered and dealt out a stream of orbital deployment updates.

'Good news,' said Gilbear, entering with a coffee and a message slate in hand. 'The best, in fact. Seems your gamble paid off. These Ghost fellows have taken Voltis. Broken it wide out. Our attack units followed them in en masse. Colonel Maglin says the city will be cleansed by nightfall.'

Sturm dabbed his mouth with a serviette. 'Send transmissions of congratulation and encouragement to Maglin and to Gaunt's mob. Where are they now?'

Gilbear eyed his slate and helped himself to a sausage from the dish. 'Seems they've pulled out, moving back to Pavis Crossroads along the eastern side of the Bokore Valley.'

Sturm set down his silver cutlery and started to type into his memo-slate. 'The greater half of our work here is accomplished, thanks to Gaunt,' he told the intrigued Gilbear. 'Now we thank him. Send these orders under extreme encryption to the C.O. of the Ketzok Basilisks at Pavis. Without delay, Gilbear.'

Gilbear took the slate. 'I *say*...' he began.

Sturm fixed him with a stare. 'There are dangerous cultist units fleeing along the eastern side of the valley, aren't there, Gilbear? Why, you've just read me the intelligence reports that confirm it.'

Gilbear began to grin. 'So I did, sir.'

Colonel Ortiz snatched the radio from his com-officer and yelled 'This is Ortiz! Yes! I know, but I expressly query the last orders we received.

I realise that, but– I don't care! No, I– Listen to me! Oh, general! Yes, I... I see. I see, sir. No, sir. Not for a moment. Of course for the glory of the Emperor. Sir. Ortiz out.'

He sank back against the metal flank of his Basilisk.

'Make the guns ready,' he told his officers. 'In the name of the Emperor, make them ready.'

The guns had been silent for ten hours. Ortiz hoped he would never hear them blaze again. Dawn frosted the horizon with light. Down in the valley, and in the Blueblood emplacements, victory celebrations continued with abandon.

Dorentz ran over to Ortiz and shook him. 'Look, sir!' he babbled. 'Look!'

Men were coming up the Metis Road out of the valley towards them, tired men, weary men, filthy men, walking slowly, carrying their dead and wounded. They were a straggled column that disappeared back into the morning mist.

'In the name of mercy...' Ortiz stammered. All around, shocked, silent Basilisk crew were leaping down from their machines and going to meet the battered men, supporting them, helping them, or simply staring in appalled disbelief.

Ortiz walked over to meet the arrival. He saw the tall figure in the long coat, now ragged, striding wearily out of the mist. Ibram Gaunt was half-carrying a young Ghost whose head was a bloody mess of bandages.

He stopped in front of Ortiz and let medics take the wounded Ghost from him.

'I want–' Ortiz began.

Gaunt's fist silenced him.

'He's here,' Gilbear said with an insouciant smirk. Sturm got to his feet and straightened his jacket. 'Bring him in,' he said.

Colonel-Commissar Ibram Gaunt marched into the study. He stood, glowering at Sturm and his adjutant.

'Gaunt!' Sturm said. 'You opened the way for the Royal Volpone. Good show! I hear Chanthar turned a melta on himself.' He paused and absently tapped at a data-slate on his desk. 'But then this business with what's-his-name...?'

'Ortega, sir,' Gilbear said helpfully.

'Ortiz,' Gaunt corrected.

'The Ketzok fellow. Striking a fellow officer. That's a shooting offence, and you know it, Gaunt. Won't have it, not in this army. No, sir.'

Gaunt breathed deeply. 'Despite knowing our position, and line of retreat, the artillery unit pounded the eastern flanks of the Bokore Valley for six hours straight. They call the phenomenon "friendly fire", but I can tell you when you're in the target zone with nothing but twigs and dust for cover, it's nothing like friendly. I lost nearly three hundred men, another two hundred injured. Amongst the dead was Sergeant Cluggan, who had led the second prong of my assault and whose actions had actually won us the city.'

'Bad show indeed,' Sturm admitted. 'but you must learn to expect this kind of loss, Gaunt. This is war.' He tossed the data-slate aside. 'Now this hitting business. Chain of command and all that. My hands are tied. It's to be a court martial.'

Gaunt was level and unblinking. 'If you're going to shoot me for it, get on with it. I struck Ortiz in the heat of the moment. In hindsight, I realise he was probably following orders. Some damn fool orders from HQ.'

'Now look, you jumped up–' Gilbear began, stepping forward.

'Would you like me to demonstrate what I did to Ortiz?' Gaunt asked the bigger man acidly.

'Silence, both of you!' snarled Sturm. 'Commissar Gaunt... *Colonel*-commissar... I take my duty seriously, and that duty is to enforce the discipline and rule of Warmaster Macaroth, and through him the beloved Emperor himself, strictly and absolutely. The Imperial Guard is based upon the towering principles of respect, authority, unswerving loyalty and total obedience. Any aberration, even from a officer of your stature, is to be– *What the hell is that noise?'*

He crossed to the window. What he saw made him gawp speechlessly. The Basilisk tank thundering up the drive was dragging part of the main gate after it and scattering gaudcocks and drilling Bluebloods indiscriminately in its path. It slewed to a halt on the front lawn, demolishing an ornamental fountain in a spray of water and stone.

A powerful man in the uniform of a Serpent colonel leapt down and strode for the main entrance to the house. His face was set and mean, swollen with bruises down the left side. A door slammed. There was some shouting, some running footsteps. Another slamming door.

Some moments later, an aide edged into the study, holding out a data-slate for Sturm. 'Colonel Ortiz has just filed an incident report. He suggested you saw it at once, sir.'

Gilbear snatched it and read it hastily. 'It seems that Major Ortiz wishes to make it clear he was injured by his own weapon's recoil during the recent bombardment.' Gilbear looked up at Sturm with a nervous laugh. 'That means–'

'I know what it means!' Sturm snapped. The general glared at Gaunt, and Gaunt glared right back, unblinking.

'I think you should know,' Gaunt said, low and deadly, 'it seems that callous murder can be committed out here in the lawless warzones, and the fact of it can be hidden by the confusion of war. You should bear that in mind, general, sir.'

Sturm was lost for words for a moment. By the time he had remembered to dismiss Gaunt, the commissar had already gone.

'Oh, for Feth's sake, play something more cheerful,' Corbec said from his troop-ship bunk, flexing his bandaged hand. He was haunted by the ghost of his missing finger. Appropriate, he thought.

In the bunk below him, Milo squeezed the bladder of his pipes and made them let out a moan, a shrill, sad sigh. It echoed around the vast troop bay of the huge, ancient starship, where a thousand Tanith Ghosts were billeted in bunks. The dull rhythm of the warp engines seemed to beat in time to the wailing pipes.

'How about... "Euan Fairlow's March"?' Milo asked.

Above him, Corbec smiled, remembering the old jig, and the nights he heard it played in the taverns of Tanith Magna.

'That would be very fine,' he said.

The energetic skip of the jig began and quickly snaked out across the iron mesh of the deck, between the aisles of bunks, around stacks of kits and camo-cloaks, through the smoky groups where men played cards or drank, over bunks where others slept or secretly gazed at portraits of women and children who were forever lost, and tried to hide their tears.

Enjoying the tune, Corbec looked up from his bunk when he heard footsteps approach down the deck-plates. He jumped up when he saw it was Gaunt. The commissar was dressed as he had first met him, fifty days before, in high-waisted dress breeches with leather braces, a sleeveless undershirt and jack boots.

'Sir!' Corbec said, surprised. The tune faltered, but Gaunt smiled and waved Milo on. 'Keep playing, lad. It does us good to hear your merrier tunes.'

Gaunt sat on the edge of Milo's bunk and looked up at Corbec.

'Voltemand is credited as a victory for the Volpone Bluebloods,' he told his number two frankly. 'Because they seized the city. Sturm mentions our participation with commendations in his report. But this one won't win us our world.'

'Feth take 'em!' spat Corbec.

'There will be other battles. Count on it.'

'I'm afraid I do, sir,' Corbec smiled.

Gaunt bent down and opened the kit-bag he was carrying. He produced half a dozen bottles of sacra.

'In the name of all that's good and holy!' Corbec said, jumping down from his bunk. 'Where–'

'I'm an Imperial commissar,' Gaunt said. 'I have pull. Do you have glasses?'

Chuckling, Corbec pulled a stack of old shot glasses from his kit.

'Call Bragg over, I know he likes this stuff,' Gaunt said. 'And Varl and Meryn. Mad Larkin. Suth. Young Caffran... hell's teeth, why not Major Rawne too? And one for the boy. There's enough to share. Enough for everyone.' He nodded down the companion way to the three bewildered naval officers who were approaching with a trolley laden with wooden crates.

'What do we drink to?' Corbec asked.

'To Sergeant Cluggan and his boys. To victory. And to the victories we are yet to have.'

'Drink to revenge, too,' Milo said quietly from his bunk, setting down his pipes.

Gaunt grinned. 'Yes, that too.'

'You know, I've got just the treat to go with this fine brew,' Corbec announced, searching his pockets. 'Cigars, liquorice flavour...'

He broke off. What he had pulled from his coat pocket had ceased to be cigars a good while before. There were a matted, frayed, water-logged mess.

Corbec shrugged and grinned, his eyes twinkling as Gaunt and the others laughed.

'Ah, well,' he sighed philosophically, 'Some you win...'

Heavy, spoon-billed wading birds flew west across the lines, white against the encroaching dark. In the thickets, the daytime chirruping insects gave up their pitches to the night beetles, the nocturnal crickets, the tick-flies, creatures that spiralled and swam in the light of the stove fires and filled the long hot darkness with their percussion. Other cries rolled in the sweaty air: the whoops and gurgles of unseen climbers and grazers in the swamp. The distant artillery had fallen silent.

Gaunt returned to the command shed just as the grille-shaded watch lights came on, casting their greenish glow downwards into the slush, bull's-eye covers damping their out-flung light in any direction other than down. No sense in making a long range target of the base. Furry, winged insects the size of chubby hands flew in at once to bounce persistently off the lit grilles with a dull, intermittent thok thok thok.

Gaunt took one last look around the base site, now distinguished only by the points of light: the cook-fires, stoves, watch lights and moving torches. He sighed and went inside.

The command centre was long and low, with a roof of galvanised corrugate and walls of double ply flak-board. The floor was fresh-cut local wood sawn into planks and treated with vile-smelling lacquer. Blast shutters on the windows stood half-open and the wire screens inside them were already thick with a fuzzy, quivering residue – the mangled bodies of moths and night-bugs which had thrown themselves at the mesh.

Gaunt's command equipment and his duffel bags of personal effects were set off the floor on blocks of wood. They'd been sat directly on the floor for the first two days until it was discovered that where damp didn't seep up, burrowing worms did.

He draped his coat on a wire hanger and hung it from a nail on the overhead rafter, then pulled up a camp chair and sat down heavily. Before him, block-mounted, sat a cogitator, a vox-uplink and a flat-screen mimeograph. A tech-priest had spent over an hour diligently intoning prayers of function as he made the sacred machines ready. They were still propped in their half-open wrought-iron casings to protect against the damp, and thick power feeds snaked off from them and ran from clip supports on the rafters, out of a socket-shutter and off to the distant generator. Lights and light images shimmered and flickered on glass plates glossed by condensation. Setting dials throbbed a dull orange. The vox-link made a low-level serpent hiss as it rose and fell through frequencies.

Gaunt leaned forward and idly surveyed the latest information and tactical data coming through from the orbital fleet and other units. A skein of coded runes crossed and blinked on the dark glass.

Quiet as nightfall, Milo entered from the ante-room. He offered a pewter beaker to his commissar. Gaunt took it with a nod, delighting at the beaded coolness of the metal.

'The tech-priests got the cooling units working again just now,' Milo muttered by way of explanation. 'For a few minutes. It's only water, but it's cold.'

Gaunt nodded his appreciation and sipped. The water was metallic and sharp, but it was deliciously cool.

There was a thump on the outside step, then a quiet knock at the door. Gaunt smiled. The thump had been deliberate, a reassuring advance warning from a man who made no sound if he did not wish to.

'Come in, Mkoll,' Gaunt said.

Mkoll entered, his lined face a little quizzical as if surprised at being recognised in advance.

'Patrol report, sir,' he said, standing stiffly in the doorway.

Gaunt gestured him to a seat. Mkoll's battledress and cloak were drenched in wet mud. Everything including his face was splattered – everything except his lasgun, miraculously clean.

'Let's have it.'

'Their positions are still far back,' Mkoll began, 'beyond the offensive line coded alpha pink. A few forward patrols.'

'Trouble?'

The powerful, wiry man grimaced noncommittally. 'Nothing we couldn't handle.'

'I've always admired your modesty,' Gaunt said, 'but I need to know.'

Mkoll screwed up his mouth and nose. 'We took six of them in the western swamps. No losses on our side.'

Gaunt nodded approval. He liked Mkoll, the Tanith's finest scout.

Even in a regiment of stealthers and covert warriors, Mkoll was exceptional. A woodsman back home on lost Tanith, he had reconnaissance skills that had proved themselves time and again to the Ghosts. A ghost amongst ghosts, and modest with it. He never bragged, and it was certain he had more to brag about than most.

Gaunt offered his beaker to the man.

'Thank you, sir, no.' Mkoll looked down at his hands.

'It's cold,' Gaunt assured him.

'I can tell. But no. I'd rather go without something I could get used to.'

Gaunt shrugged and sipped again. 'So they're not moving?'

'Not yet. We sighted a... I'm not sure what it was, an old ruin of some kind.' Mkoll rose and pointed to a position on the wall chart. 'Around here, far as I can tell. Could be nothing, but I'd like to follow it through with a survey in the morning.'

'An enemy position?'

'No, sir. Something... that was already here.'

'You're right: deserves a look. In the morning then,' Gaunt agreed.

'If that'll be all, sir?'

'Dismissed, Mkoll.'

'I'll never get the measure of him,' Gaunt said to Milo after Mkoll had left. 'Quietest man I've ever known.'

'That's what he does, isn't it, sir?' Milo said.

'What?'

'*Quiet.*'

THREE

SOUND AND FURY

All around there was a hushing sound, as if the whole world wanted to silence him.

Mkoll bellied in low amid the forest of ferns, trying to pick through the oceanic rushing sound they made as the wind stirred them.

The fern growth in that part of Ramillies 268-43, flourishing on the thin, ashy soils of the long-cold volcanic slopes, was feathery and fibrous, mottled stalks rough as cane rising three man-heights into swaying multi-part fronds as white as water-ice.

They reminded him of the nalwood forests back home, when there was still a back home, the nalwoods in winter, when he'd gone out logging and hunting. Frost had crusted the evergreen needles on the sighing trees then until they had tinkled like wind chimes.

Here, now, there was only the sigh, the motion of the dry ferns and the clogging dust that got into every pore and rasped the soft tissue at the back of the throat. The sunlight was bright and harsh, stabbing down through the pale, spare air out of a sky translucent blue. It made a striated web out of the ground cover under the ferns – stark sun-splashes and jagged shadows of blackness.

He crept forward twenty metres into a break of skeleton brush. His lower legs were already double-wrapped with chain-cloth to protect against the shredding thorns. He had his lasgun held to his chest on a tightly cinched strap to keep it clear of the dust but, every ten minutes or so, he checked its moving parts and cleared the dust, fern-fibres, twig-shreds and burrs that accumulated constantly.

Several cracks made him turn and freeze, sliding his gun into a firing grip between smooth, dry palms. Something was moving through the thicket to his left, cracking the occasional spent thorn underfoot.

To be fair, they were moving with extreme and trained stealth, but still their progress sounded like a careless march to Mkoll's acute hearing.

Mkoll drew his knife, its long silver blade deliberately dulled with ash. He backed into a thorn stalk and moulded his body to the kinking plant. Two steps, one.

He swung out, only pulling back his blade at the last moment.

Trooper Dewr cried out and fell backwards, splintering dry stalks as he dropped. Mkoll was on top of him in a second, pinning his arms and pushing the blade against his neck.

'Sacred Feth! You could've killed me!' Dewr barked agitatedly.

'Yes, I could,' said Mkoll, a whisper.

He relaxed his grip, rolled off and let the man rise.

'So could anything else out here, noise you were making.'

'I...' Dewr dropped his voice suddenly. 'Are we alone?'

Mkoll didn't answer. Chances were, if anything else was out here, it would have heard Dewr's fall too.

'I didn't mean anything,' Dewr began hoarsely, wincing as he plucked out the thorns he had fallen on.

Mkoll was scanning around, his gun ready. 'What the feth did they teach you during basic?' he whispered. 'You're meant to be a scout!'

Dewr didn't reply. All the scouts knew Mkoll's exacting standards, and knew just as well how they all failed to meet them. Dewr felt angry, in fact. During basic training, before that as a hunter in the southern gameland of Tanith Attica, he'd been reckoned as a good tracker. That was why they had selected him for the scout unit when the regiment mustered, for feth's sake! And this old bastard made him feel like a fool, a clumsy fool!

Wordlessly, ignoring the stare he knew Dewr was boring into the back of his head, Mkoll signalled an advance, heading down the slope into the fern-choked vale.

The Tanith had arrived on Ramillies two weeks before, just in time to miss the main action. The Adeptus Astartes had cleaned out and secured the four enemy strongholds, banishing Chaos from the world. The Ghosts had assembled on the low plains near one burning fortress, seeing Space Marines, threatening bulks in the smoky distance like the giants of myth, piling the ragged corpses of slain cultists onto pyres. The air had been thick with filthy char.

It seemed some small components of the enemy had fled the defeat, making into the fern forests in the north, too small and insignificant for the glorious Space Marines to waste time upon. The commissar was charged with a search and destroy detail. The Ghosts had advanced into the low hills and the dense forestation, to smoke out the last of the foe.

There were a few early successes: enclaves of cultists, some well-armed, dug into bolt-holes and lodges, making a last stand. Then, after a week, as they reached the colder, higher plateaux and the real thickness of the fern-cover, a working pattern developed. Mkoll would plan recon sweeps each day, deploying a couple of dozen scouts in a wide fan into the thickets. They would quarter each area and report back, signalling in the main Ghost forces if contact was made.

Perhaps they had become lazy, complacent. Major Rawne averred that they had silenced the last of the enemy and were now wasting their time and patience cutting deeper and deeper into the lonely territories of the hinterland. The commissar himself seemed devoted to discharging the task properly, but even he had doubled the reach and range of the scout sweeps. Another few days and they would quit, he had told Mkoll.

This day, this high cold windy day, with the ever present whisper of the ferns, the scouts had gone deeper and wider into the hills. There had been no contact with anything for two whole sweeps. Mkoll sensed that less dedicated troopers like Dewr were getting slack with the routine.

But he himself had seen things that kept him sharp and made him determined to press on. Things he had reported to Gaunt to convince him to work the forests a little longer: broken paths in the vegetation; trampled areas; torn, apparently random trails in the underbrush. There was something still out here.

They crossed the valley floor and came up the shaded side, where the ferns listed restlessly, like shadow-fans. Every dozen or so steps, Dewr's feet cracked a thorn or a seed case, or chinked a rock, no matter how delicately he walked. He cursed every sound. He was determined to prove his ability to Mkoll. And he had no clue how Mkoll moved so silently, like he was floating.

The ferns hissed in the wind.

Mkoll stopped to check his compact chart and referred his eyes to sun and compass. Within a quarter of an hour their circuit should bring them into contact with Rafel and Waed, on a mirror sweep towards them.

Mkoll suddenly held up a hand and Dewr stopped sharp. The scout sergeant fanned his fingers twice to indicate Dewr should cover, and the other slid in low beside a thick fern stem, knelt and raised his lasgun. There was dust on the exchanger and he wiped it off. Dust in his eyes too, and he wiped them. He braced and then took aim, rolling it left and right as Mkoll advanced.

Mkoll dropped down another few metres and found another torn trail in the fern. As wide as three men walking abreast, ferns uprooted or snapped and trampled. Mkoll gingerly touched one sappy, broken twist of stalk. It was as thick as his thigh, and the bark was tough as iron. He could not have severed it this clean even with a wood axe. He checked the ground. Trample marks, deep and wide, like giant footsteps. The trail snaked away both ahead and behind as far as he could see, uneven, weaving. Mkoll raised three fingers and circled them. Dewr advanced to join him.

The younger man looked at the trail, questions in his mouth, but the look in Mkoll's eyes told him not to ask them. Not to say anything. There was no sound at all except the hissing of the fronds. Dewr knelt and looked at the trail for himself. Something... someone... big, moving blindly. His fingers touched something buried in the ashy soil and he plucked it out. A chunk of blackened metal, part of the rim of something, large as a cupped hand. He held it out to Mkoll. The sergeant took it with genuine interest, studied it, and tucked it into his thigh pouch. He nodded a firm acknowledgement to Dewr for his sharp eyes. Dewr felt greater pride in that fleeting moment than he had ever done in his life before. Or would again.

They moved on, down the trail line, following the bent-forward fronds which indicated the direction of motion. After sixty metres, the trail veered uphill. Mkoll stopped and wiped his weapon again.

A scream cut the air, as bright and sharp as a Tanith blade. They both started. It shut off abruptly, but while it lasted it had been unmistakably human. Mkoll was moving in an instant, following the source of the sound. Dewr went after him, trying to keep his hurried steps silent. They moved off the trail into the thickets. Ahead, the foliage changed. Under the crest of the slope, thicker, spined cacti grew in clusters; fibrous, gourd-like growths lined with long needles were arrayed down each seam of the plant sac. There were hundreds of the plants, some knee high, some higher and fatter than a man, a forest of needle-studded bulbs.

Another, weaker scream came, as from a man waking from a nightmare and abruptly dying away as he realised it was but a dream. And another sound, close on the heels of the scream. A hollow, plosive, spitting sound, like someone retching fruit pits from his throat.

They found Rafel crumpled amid the gourd-bulbs. A trail of blood, bright spatters on the ashy ground, showed where he had dropped and how he had crawled. Over a dozen needles, some more than a foot long, impaled him. One went through his eye into his brain. Dewr, in horror, was about to speak, but Mkoll whirled and clamped his hand over the younger man's mouth. Mkoll pointed to the nearest of the large cactus growths, indicating where a line of spines were absent, leaving only a line of sap-drooling orifices.

'I say again, Trooper Rafel! What is your position?' The voice crackled out of the corpse's intercom. Mkoll drove himself into Dewr, knocking him aside, away from Rafel as the three bulbs nearest the body shuddered and spat spines. A salvo of those hollow spitting coughs again. Needles stabbed into Rafel's corpse like arrows and bounced off the ground around them.

One went through Dewr's shin. He wanted to scream but managed to master it. The pain was sharp, then dull. His leg went cold. Mkoll rolled off him. Dewr pointed feebly at his leg, but the sergeant seemed to ignore it. He made a quick adjustment to the intercom at his collar and then reached down to Dewr's, switching it off.

Only then did he turn to the wound. He took out his knife and cut the cloth away from Dewr's shin, slicing the straps holding the chain-cloth bandages in place. The needle had passed right through the chain, directly through the eye of some links and severing others. Mkoll turned the knife round and forced the hilt into Dewr's mouth. Instinctively, Dewr bit down and Mkoll yanked the needle free.

There was very little blood. That was bad. The blood was clotting and turning yellow fast and the sticky residue on the spine suggested venom. But the needle had only punctured flesh, which was good. The force of it could have shattered the shin bone.

Dewr bit hard on the hilt a while longer. As the pain ebbed, he slackened his mouth and the knife slid out down his cheek onto the ground. Mkoll rose. He would get Rafel's field dressings and bind the wound. Rafel wouldn't need them now. He turned. His foot cracked a thorn on the ground. A moment of carelessness, triggered by his concern for Dewr. A bulb shuddered at the crack and spat a needle. It passed through the stock of Mkoll's lasgun and the point stopped an inch from his belly.

He unfroze and breathed, then pulled it out. Mkoll crossed to Rafel and freed his field dressing pouch, pinned to his waist by another needle through the strap. He returned to Dewr and bound the wound.

Dewr's head began to spin. It was an easy, fluid feeling, like his cares were ebbing away. There was a gnawing feeling in his leg and hip, but it was somehow pleasant.

Mkoll saw the vacant glaze coming over Dewr's eyes. Unceremoniously, he took another length of gauze dressing and jammed it into Dewr's mouth, taping the gag tightly in place. A delirious man may not realise the sound he is making.

He was about to lift Dewr onto his shoulder when another sound came. A ripping and crashing, distant at first, accompanied by the relentless retching spit of the bulbs as the tearing sound set them off.

Something was coming, something drawn by Rafel's last scream. Something gigantic.

As it burst into the clearing, all of the cacti around them spontaneously shed their needles in a blitz of venomous barbs. The fusillade rattled off the metal carapace and legs. Mkoll threw himself over Dewr and they lay there, silent and still under the storm of darts.

The Chaos Dreadnought came to a halt on its great hydraulic feet, sighing and hissing. There was a stench of heat and a throb of electro-magnetic power that prickled the hairs on Mkoll's neck. It was four metres tall, wider than three men, blackened and scorched as if it had walked through hell and back. All signs of paint or insignia had been burnt off, to bare metal in some places. A malign presence oozed from it, filling the atmosphere. Such a great machine was terrifying enough in itself, but the malevolent feeling of it... Mkoll felt his gorge rise and clamped his jaws. Dewr seemed unconscious.

The Dreadnought took a step forward, almost tentative and dainty though the great steel hoof shook the earth as it fell and triggered another volley of spines. Its body rotated as if scanning, and it took another step. Another plank-plank of rebounding spines.

It was blind. Mkoll could see that at a glance. The wounds of the Adeptus Astartes were deep and fearful across its visor. Its optical units had been blown away in some great act. Mkoll knew the semi-circle of burnt metal Dewr had found was from the recess socket of one of its eyes. It had been blundering around the fern forests for days, hunting by sound alone.

Another step. Another hiss of pistons and a growl of motivator. Another thump of footfall, and other rain of darts. It was only three metres from them now, still cranking its body around, listening.

Dewr started and woke up. He saw the Dreadnought – and his filmy, poisoned eyes made even greater nightmares out of the existing one. He convulsed and screamed. Despite the gauze gag, the scream was fierce and high pitched, strangulated and horrible through the choke.

Mkoll knew he had an instant to react, even as Dewr stirred. He dived aside.

The Dreadnought swung and targeted the source of the scream as rapidly as the plants around them did. Poison needles spat into a body that had, mere microseconds before, been incinerated by a belching plasma gun.

Needles rattled off the Dreadnought again.

Mkoll moved low, sliding round the bulk of the bulbs, trying to keep the listening death machine in sight. His heart was thumping. He cursed it for being so loud.

Behind the next break of growth, he slid in low and checked his weapon. There were fern fronds caught in the trigger. He thought at once to pull them free and then stopped. It would make a sound, and what was the use? What good would a lasgun be against that?

He moved again, his foot skittering a stone. Needles spat ineffectually. The Dreadnought began to move, following the sound, walking through rains of needles that convulsed and flew at each footfall.

Mkoll thought to run. It was blind, the plants were blind. If he could only stay silent – and that was his gift – he could slip away and take the information to Gaunt. But would they find it again? Out here, in such a wilderness? It could take weeks to relocate the Dreadnought, the lives of many to neutralise it. If he could only...

No. Madness. Suicide.

Then he heard the voice. Distant. It was Waed, calling for Rafel. He was beyond the needle bulbs, searching, querying why Rafel had stopped transmitting. In moments, surely, he would be triggering needles.

Or summoning the Dreadnought. Already, the blind beast had turned and begun to stride through the thicket, crushing the spitting cacti into ochre mash.

Mkoll had seconds to think. He would not lose another of his scout cadre, not like this.

He took out a grenade, primed it and threw it left. The crump took out a cluster of bulbs in a spray of fire and matted fibres, and caused a flurry of spines to shoot. Mkoll then headed directly for the blast site. He slid in with his back to one of the bulbs that had triggered at the sound of the explosion. Its needle apertures were spent. He could use it as cover safely now it was unarmed.

The Dreadnought was thumping his way, drawn by the sound of the grenade. Waed had fallen silent.

Mkoll adjusted his gun and set it on the ground. Then he spoke.

'Over here, you bastard!'

It sounded impossibly loud. A final taunt to follow the grenade. Bulbs popped around him. But none had spines left on the sides facing him.

The Dreadnought crunched into the clearing. Its left foot clinked against something in the dust. It bent to retrieve it.

Mkoll's lasgun.

The Dreadnought raised it in its bionic claws, holding the gun up to its already ruptured frontal armour as if to sniff or taste it.

Mkoll started to run.

By his estimation, there were five seconds before the lasgun magazine overloaded as he had set it.

He threw himself flat as it went off.

Hundreds of cacti loosed needles at the roar.

Then silence.

With Waed, silently, Mkoll re-entered the thicket. They found the Dread-nought broken open in the blackened clearing. The overload had not killed it, but it had split its armour as the towering machine had strode forward. Poison darts had done the rest, puncturing and killing the now-vulnerable once-man inside. Mkoll could see where the mad-dened Chaos beast-machine had strode arrogantly on for a few heavy steps after the puny laser blast. Then it had toppled, poisoned, dead.

They headed back onto the trail.

'You're a fething hero!' Waed said finally.

'How is that?'

'A fething Dreadnought, Mkoll! You killed a Dreadnought!'

Mkoll turned and faced Waed with a look that brooked no denial.

'We'll tell the commissar that the area is cleared. Understood? I don't want any stupid glory. Is that clear?'

Waed nodded and followed his sergeant. 'But you killed it...' he ventured softly.

'No, I didn't. I listened and waited and was silent... and when I made the opening, Ramillies did the rest.'

Colm Corbec was sat outside his habitat unit. As regimental second officer, he was given a bivouac like Gaunt's, but the commissar knew that he preferred to sleep in the open.

As Gaunt approached, he saw that Corbec was whittling a piece of bark with his Tanith knife. Gaunt slowed and watched the thick-set man. If he himself died, Gaunt mused, could Corbec hold them together? Could he lead the Ghosts with Gaunt gone?

Corbec would say 'no', Gaunt knew, but he was confident of Corbec's abilities. Even though he had chosen his second in command on a decision that was as simple as a flick of a coin.

'Quiet night,' Corbec said as Gaunt crouched next to him and his fire.

'So far,' Gaunt replied. He watched the big man's hands play the blade over the pale wood. He knew Corbec hated the role of command, would do almost anything to distract himself. Gaunt also knew that Corbec hated ordering men to their deaths or glories. But he did it well. And he took charge when it was needed. Never more so, than on Caligula...

FOUR

THE HOLLOWS OF HELL

He would be sick. Very soon, very violently. Of this sole fact, Brin Milo was absolutely sure.

His stomach somersaulted as the troop-ship plunged out of the sky, and every bone in his body shook as the impossibly steep descent vibrated the sixty-tonne vessel like a child's rattle.

Count...

...think happy thoughts...

...distract yourself...

...counselled a part of his mind in desperation. It won't look good if the commissar's aide, the regimental piper, wonderboy and all round lucky bloody charm hurls his reconstituted freeze-dried ready-pulped food rations all over the deck.

And whatever you do, don't think about how pulpy and slimy those food rations were... advised another, urgent part of his brain.

Deck? What deck? wailed another. Chuck now and it'll wobble out in free fall and–

Shut up! Brin Milo ordered his seething imagination.

For a moment, he was calm. He breathed deeply to loosen and relax, to centre himself, as Trooper Larkin had taught him during marksman training.

Then a tiny little black-hearted voice in his head piped up: Don't worry about puking. You'll be incinerated in a hypervelocity crash-landing any second now.

Like pepper falling from a mill, thought Executive Officer Kreff, gazing down out of the vast observation blister below the prow of the escort frigate, *Navarre*.

Behind him, on the raised bridge, there was a murmur as the systems

391

operators and servitors softly relayed data back and forth. Control systems hummed. The air was cool. Occasionally, the low, reverential voices of the senior helm officers would announce another order from the ship's captain, who lurked alone, inscrutable, in his private strategium, an armoured dome at the heart of the bridge.

The frigate's bridge was Kreff's favourite place in the universe. It was hushed like a chapel and always serene, even though it controlled a starship capable of crossing parsecs in a blink, a starship with the firepower to roast cities.

He returned to his study of the vast bright bulk of Caligula below him, plump and puffy like an orange, speckled with white-green blotches of mould.

Imperial starships hung in the blackness between it and him: some vast, grey and vaulted like cathedrals twenty kilometres long, some bloated like oceanic titans; others long, lean and angular like his own frigate. They floated in the sea of space and tiny black dots, thousands upon thousands of dots, tumbled out of them, fluttering down towards the ripe planet.

Kreff knew the dots were troop-ships: each speck was a two-hundred tonne dropcraft loaded with combat-ready troops. But they looked just like pepper ground from a mill. As if the Imperial fleet had come by to politely season Caligula.

Kreff wondered which of the pepper grains contained Commissar Gaunt. Things had certainly livened up since Gaunt had arrived: Ibram Gaunt, the notorious, decorated war hero, and the rag-tag regiment known as the Ghosts that he had salvaged from the murdered planet Tanith.

Kreff smoothed the emerald trim of his Segmentum Pacificus Fleet uniform and sighed. When he had first heard the *Navarre* had been assigned to Gaunt's mob, he had been dismayed. But true to his track record, Gaunt had shaped the so-called Ghosts up and taken them through several courageous actions.

It had been an education having him aboard. As executive officer, the official representative of the captain in all shipboard organisational matters, he'd had to mix with the Ghosts more than other Navy personnel. He'd got to know them: as well as anyone could know a band of black-haired, raucous, tattooed soldiers, the last survivors from a planet that Chaos had destroyed. He'd been almost afraid of them at first, alarmed by their fierce physicality. Kreff knew war as a silent, detached, long-distance discipline, a chess-game measured in thousands of kilometres and degrees of orbit. They knew war as a bloody, wearying, frenzied, close-up blur.

He'd been invited to several dinners in the Guard mess, and spent

one strange, only partially-remembered evening in the company of
Corbec, the regiment's colonel, a hirsute giant of a man who had, on
closer inspection, a noble soul. Or so it had seemed after several bottles and hours of loose, earnest talk. They had debated the tactics of
war, comparing their own schools and methods. Kreff had been dismissive of Corbec's brutal, primitive ethos, boasting of the high art that
was Navy fleet warfare.

Corbec had not been insulted. He'd grinned and promised Kreff
would get to fight a real war one day.

The thought made Kreff smile. His eyes went back to the dots falling
towards the planet and the smile faded.

Now he doubted he would see either Gaunt or Corbec again.

Far away, below, he could see the scorching flashes of anti-orbit
guns, barking up at the fluttering pepper grains. That was a dog's life,
going down there into the mouth of hell. All that noise and death and
mayhem.

Kreff sighed again, and felt suddenly grateful for the tranquil bridge
around him. This was the only way to fight wars, he decided.

Milo opened his eyes, but it hadn't gone away. The world was still convulsing. He glanced about, down the hold of the troop-ship where
another twenty-five Guardsmen sat rigid, clamped in place by the
yellow-striped restraint rigs, their equipment shuddering in mesh packs
under every seat. The air was sweet with incense, and the ship was shaking so hard that he could not read the inspirational inscriptions etched
on the cabin walls. Milo heard the roaring of the outer hull, white-hot
from the steep dive. What he couldn't hear was the booming cough of
the anti-orbit batteries down below, welcoming them.

He glanced around for a friendly face. Hulking Bragg was gripping
his restraints tight, his eyes closed. Young Trooper Caffran, only three
years older than Milo, was gazing at the roof, muttering a charm or
prayer. Across from him, Milo found the hard eyes of Major Rawne.

Rawne smiled and nodded his head encouragingly.

Milo took a breath. Being encouraged by Major Rawne in these circumstances was like being patted on the back by the Devil at the gates
of Hell.

Milo shut his eyes again.

In the rear of the slender cockpit, strapped in his G-chair, Commissar
Gaunt craned his neck round to see past the pilots and the astropath
and look through the narrow front ports. Chart displays flickered across
the thick glass and the ship was bucking wildly, but Gaunt could see

the target coming up: the hive city called Nero, poking up out of the ochre soil through a caldera ninety kilometres wide, like an encrusted lump of coal set in a plump navel.

'Sixty seconds to landfall,' the pilot said calmly. His voice was electronically tonal as it rasped via the intercom.

Gaunt pulled out his bolt pistol and cocked it. He started counting down.

High above the sunken city of Nero, the troop-ships came down like bullets, scorching in out of the cloud banks. Anti-air batteries thumped the sky.

Then the cotton-white clouds began to singe. The fluffy corners scorched and wilted. A dark purple stain leached into the sky, billowing through the cumulus like blood through water. Lightning fizzed and lashed.

Leagues above, Kreff paused and stared. Something was discolouring the atmosphere far below.

'What the–' he began.

'Weather formation!' the co-pilot yelped, frantically making adjustments. 'We're hitting hail and lightning.'

Gaunt was about to query further but the shaking had increased. He glanced round at the astropath, suddenly aware that the man was uttering a low, monotone growl.

He was just in time to see the astropath's head explode. Blood and tissue painted the pilot, co-pilot, Gaunt and the entire cabin interior.

The pilot was screaming a question.

It was a psychic storm, Gaunt was horribly sure. Far below them, something of unimaginable daemonic power was trying to keep them out, trying to ward off the assault with a boiling tempest of Chaos.

The ship was shaking so hard now Gaunt could no longer focus. Multiple warning runes flashed up in series across the main control display, blurring into scarlet streaks before his rattling eyes.

Something, somewhere exploded.

The vibration and the shrieking didn't stop, but they changed. Milo suddenly knew that they were no longer crash-diving into attack.

They were simply crash-diving.

He wasn't feeling sick any more. But the wicked incinerated-in-a-hypervelocity-crashlanding-voice started to crow: *I told you so.*

* * *

There was impact...

...so huge, it felt like every one of his joints had dislocated.

There was sliding...

...sudden, shuddering, terrifying.

And finally...

...there was roaring fire.

And, as if as an afterthought...

...complete excruciating blackness.

Hundreds of Imperial troop-ships were already well below the cloud-bank when the psychic typhoon exploded into life, and so escaped the worst of its effects. Levelling out, they descended on the massive citadel of Nero Hive like a plague of locusts. The air was thick with them, ringing with the roar of their thrusters as they banked in and settled on the wasteland outskirts of the towering black city-hive. Traceries of laser and plasma fire divided the sky in a thousand places, making it look for all the world like some insanely complex set of blueprints. Some struck landing ships which flared, fluttered and died. Flak shells sent loud, black flowers up into the air. Marauder air-support shrieked in at intervals, moving in close, low formations like meteorites hunting as a pack, strafing the ground with stitching firestorms.

Above it all, the purple sky boiled and thrashed and spat electric ribbons.

At ground level, Colonel Colm Corbec of the Tanith First-and-Only led his squad down the ramp of the troop-ship and into the firezone. To either side, he could see lines of ships disgorging their troops into the field, a tide of men ten thousand strong.

They reached the first line of cover – a punctured length of pipeline running along rusted pylons – and dropped down.

Corbec took a look each way and keyed in his micro-bead comm link. 'Corbec to squad. Sound off.'

Voices chatted back along the link, responding.

By Corbec's side, Trooper Larkin was cradling his lasgun and looking up at the sky with trembling fear.

'Oh, this is bad,' he murmured. 'Psyker madness, very bad. We may think we had it hard at Voltis Watergate or Blackshard deadzone, but they'll seem like a stroll round the garden next to *this*...'

'Larks!' Corbec hissed. 'For Feth's sake, shut up! Haven't you ever heard of morale?'

Larkin turned his bony, weasel face to his senior officer and old friend in genuine surprise. 'It's okay, colonel!' he insisted. 'I didn't have me comm link turned on! Nobody heard!'

Corbec grimaced. 'I heard, and you're scaring the crap out of me.'

They all ducked down as a swathe of autocannon fire chewed across the lines. Someone a few hundred metres away started screaming. They could hear the piercing shrieks over the roar of the storm and the landing troop-ships and the bombardment.

Just.

'Where's the commissar?' Corbec growled. 'He insisted he was going to lead us in.'

'If he ain't landed, he ain't coming,' Larkin said, looking up at the sky. 'We were the last few to make it through before that happened.'

Next to Larkin, Trooper Raglon, the squad's communications officer, looked up from the powerful voxcaster set. 'No contact from the commissar's dropcraft, sir. I've been scanning the orbital traffic and the Navy band, colonel. This filthy psyker storm took out a whole heap of troop-ships. They're still counting the crash fires. We was lucky we got down before it really started.'

Corbec shivered. He didn't feel lucky.

Raglon went on: 'Our psykers upstairs are trying to break the storm, but...'

'But what?'

'It looks pretty certain the commissar's troop-ship was one of those vaporised in the storm.'

Corbec growled something indistinct. He felt cold, and could see the look on the faces of his men as the word spread down the line.

Corbec lifted his lasgun and keyed up his micro-bead. He had to rally them fast, get them moving. 'What are you waiting for?' he bawled. 'Diamond formation fire-team spread! Double time! Fire at will! Advance! For the memory of Tanith! Advance!'

Brin Milo woke up.

He was upside down, blind, suspended painfully from his restraint rig, his ribs bruised blue and a taste of blood in his mouth. But – unless someone was about to play a really nasty trick on him – he was alive.

He could hear... very little. The trickle and patter of falling water. A creaking. Someone moaning softly.

There was a loud bang and light flared into his dark-accustomed eyes. He smelled thermite and realised someone had just ejected the emergency hull-plates using the explosive bolts. Daylight – thin, green, wet daylight – streamed in.

Bragg's huge face swam up in front of Milo's, upside down.

'Hang on, Brinny-boy,' Bragg said softly. 'Soon have you down.' He started rattling the restraints and slamming the lock handle back and forth.

The restraints abruptly stopped restraining and Milo uttered a little yelp as he dropped two and a half metres onto the sloping roof of the troop-ship.

'Sorry,' Bragg said, helping him up. 'You hurt, lad?'

Milo shook his head. 'Where are we?' he asked.

Bragg paused as if he was thinking about this carefully, Then, with deliberation, he said 'We're earlobe deep in doo-doo.'

The troop-ship, now just a crumpled sleeve of metal, had impacted at a steep angle on its roof.

Milo climbed down and gazed back up at the mangled wreck. What amazed him only slightly less than the fact he was still alive, was that they had come down in what appeared to be a jungle. Enormous pinkish trees that looked like swollen, magnified root vegetables, formed a dense forest of flaccid trunks around them. The huge growths were strung with thick ropey vines, creepers and flowering tendrils, and thorny fern and horsetail covered the moist, steaming ground. Everything was green, as all light – except for a single clear shaft which slanted down through the trees where the troop-ship had burst through – was filtered by the dense canopy of foliage above their heads. It was humid, and sticky, and sappy water dripped from the trees. There was a sweet stink of fungoid flowers.

Bragg clambered down from the wreck, and joined the boy. A dozen other Ghosts had clambered out and were sat down or leaning against trees, waiting for spinning heads and ringing ears to clear. All had minor cuts and scrapes, except Trooper Obel who lay on a makeshift stretcher, his chest bloody and torn. Corporal Meryn had taken charge. He and Caffran were trying to open other emergency hatches to look for more survivors.

Milo saw Rawne had survived. The major stood to one side with a tall, pale Ghost called Feygor, who served as his aide.

'I didn't know there were any jungles on this world,' Milo said.

'Me neither,' Bragg answered. He was catching and piling equipment packs Meryn was tossing down from the side of the wreck. 'Actually, I didn't even know what this world was called.'

Milo found Rawne by his side.

'We're in a forest hollow,' Rawne said. 'The surface of Caligula is barren pumice, but it's punctured in many places by deep rift basins, many of them old craters or volcanic sinks. The cities are built down into the largest of them, but others sustain microclimates wet enough for these forests. I think some of them were actually farmed... before the fething enemy came in.'

'So... where are we?' Feygor asked.

Rawne rubbed his throat, thoughtful. 'We've come down a good way off target. I think there were some forest calderas north of Nero. On the wrong side of the lines.'

Feygor swore.

'I think the major is correct,' said a voice.

Gaunt appeared, sliding down from a side vent in the punctured hull. He was tattered and bruised, with blood soaking the shoulder and side of his tunic under his coat. Meryn hurried over to him to assist.

'Not me,' Gaunt said, waving him off. 'The co-pilot's alive and he needs to be cut free.'

'It's a miracle anyone got out of that front end,' Meryn said with a whistle.

Gaunt crossed to Milo, Rawne and the others.

'Report, major,' he said.

'Unless we find anyone else alive in there, we've got twelve able-bodied men, plus yourself, the boy Milo and the co-pilot. Minor injuries all round, though Trooper Grogan has a broken arm. But he can walk. Obel has chest injuries. Pretty bad. Brennan is inside. He's a real mess and pinned, but he's alive. The rest are pulp.'

Rawne looked up at the wreck. 'Lucky shot got us, I guess. Missile–'

'Psykers!' Gaunt growled. 'They threw some freakshow storm up. Smashed us out of the sky.'

Everyone fell silent at the thought. Fear prickled them. Some looked away, uneasy and shaken.

Gaunt crossed to the pile of equipment packs Bragg and Caffran were offloading and opened a compact carry-box. Out of this he slid a topolabe from its cushioned slot and held it up by the knurled handgrip. The small brass machine whirred and the concentric dials span and clicked as the gravimetric gyros turned in the glass bubble of inert gas.

After a moment, the machine chimed and published a read-out on a back-lit blue display.

'We're in a forest caldera called K7-75, about forty kilometres north north-east of the Nero city perimeter. Your assessment was good, major. We're on the wrong side of the lines and in pretty damn inhospitable country. There's dense forest for at least eight kilometres in any direction, and this sinkhole's about a kilometre deep. We'd better get ready to move.'

'Move?' Feygor asked. 'Commissar... we can get the crash beacon up and running...'

'No we can't,' Meryn said. He showed them the molten resdue of the beacon unit.

'And even if we could, Feygor?' Gaunt shook his head sadly. 'About fifty kilometres south of us, the Imperial Guard is engaged in a massive assault. Thousands are dying. Every ship, and craft and man is committed to the attack. There will be nothing to spare to come looking – across enemy lines, mark you – for a few lost souls like us. They'll have already written us off. Besides, there's a psyker-bred storm raging up there, remember? No one could get to us even if they wanted to.'

Rawne spat and cursed. 'So what do we do?'

Gaunt grinned, but without humour. 'We see how far we can get. Better that than just wait here to die.'

In fifteen minutes, the survivors were assembled and injuries tended. Salvageable equipment and weapons were divided up. Both Milo and the dazed co-pilot were given a laspistol and a few spare power cells. Obel and the now-freed Brennan lay unconscious on stretcher pallets.

Rawne looked grimly at Gaunt. He nodded his head at the two injured men. 'We should... be merciful.'

Gaunt frowned. 'We're taking them with us.'

Rawne shook his head. 'With respect, they'll probably both be dead in an hour. Taking them will tie up four able-bodied soldiers as stretcher bearers.'

'We're taking them,' Gaunt repeated.

'If you lashed 'em both to a frame,' Bragg put in thoughtfully, 'I could drag 'em along. Better me than four other boys.'

Meryn and Feygor raised the two stretcher cases onto an A-frame of wood and Bragg took the weight of the point on his shoulder. Caffran had used his silver Tanith knife to cut lengths of waxy creeper and bound them on for a grip.

'I won't be fast, mind,' Bragg noted. But with the party clearing the way, he could pull them along on the sling-bed efficiently enough.

The commissar checked the topolabe again, scanning for closer detail.

'Interesting,' he murmured. 'About four kilometres east there's some kind of structure. Maybe an old farming complex or something. Might provide us with some shelter. Let's see.' Gaunt had armed himself with a lasgun from one of the dead. He handed his chainsword to Rawne. 'Take point please, major,' he said.

Rawne moved to the head of the column and started to slice his way through the dense, wet forest.

* * *

The Tanith Ghosts advanced through the outer complexes of the hive city, surging down an embankment and across the blasted ferrocrete of a six-lane arterial highway.

Broken vehicles littered the lanes, and great pools of motor oil blazed up curtains of fire. Corbec urged the Ghosts forward, under traffic control boards that still flashed and winked speed limits and direction pointers. Guns blazing, they began to assault a vast block of worker residences on the far side.

As the battle group swept into the shattered hallways of the old worker residences, where peeling placards exhorted the citizen workers to meet production targets and praise the Emperor at all times, fighting became a close-quarter business with the enemy forces, now seen face to face for the first time. Humans, corrupted by Chaos, cult worshippers whose physical forms had become twisted and warped. Most wore the black, vulcanised work suits of the hive workforce, daubed now with Chaos patterns, their heads protected with tight grey hoods and industrial glare visors. They were well armed, too.

Bodies littered the concourses and galleries of the residences, shattered glass and twisted plastic covered the ground. Intense fires blazed through some areas, and the air was full of drifting cinders, like incandescent snow.

And flies: dark, fat-bodied flies.

Blasting as he advanced, Corbec fired to left and right, through doorways and thin plastic-board walls, cutting down or exploding the foe all around.

Flanked in a fire-team, Larkin, Suth, Varl, Mallor, Durcan and Billad worked in immediate support. Larkin snatched off the occasional shot, his aim as fine as usual, though Corbec knew that thanks to the storm, he was closer to snapping than ever. Suth had the squad's melta, and seared them a path.

Bolt fire and las-shot cut their way. Billad jerked as he was hit repeatedly, sprawling back against a wall and sliding down.

Corbec sent a steady stream of shot into the smoke haze.

The flies buzzed.

Radio chatter was almost as deafening as the firefight. Guard forces had begun to pincer the city. A combined force of Royal Volpone 50th and Raymian 13th and 16th had driven a steel fist into the ore-smelter heartland of the hive, meeting the enemy's main motorised units in an armoured battle in the vast, echoing barns of the starship yards and dry-docks. Rumours were a battalion of Lakkarii Gundogs and some Raven Guard Space Marines had punched through into the upper levels, into the Administratum tower itself.

But an overall victory seemed so far away, especially given the psychic storm, which effectively shut off any further reinforcements. Or anything else.

'Any joy with the air-cover?' Corbec asked over the crackle of laser fire.

Trooper Raglon answered on the bead-link. 'Marauder flights are all out of action, sir. Fleet Command recalled them because of the storm. The Chaos effects are screwing their guidance.'

Corbec glanced up at the corrosive purple turbulence that passed for sky. Forget the aircraft, that nightmare was screwing with his guidance. This close to a manifestation of Chaos, his senses were whirling. His balance was shot and he felt nauseous, with a throbbing pain in his temple. Terror dimpled his skin and ached in his marrow. He dared not think about what was out there, waiting for him.

And he knew his men were the same. There had been a dozen spontaneous nosebleeds already, and several men had convulsed, vomiting.

Still, they were making headway, clawing through the grim habitat towers and the workforce residence blocks where things came down to knife and pistol, room to room, in the old, dirty tenements where the lowest level of worker had dwelt.

The commissar would have been proud, Corbec thought. The Ghosts had done the job. He spat out a fly and listened carefully to the flow of radio traffic again for a moment. The Fleet Command channel repeated its overriding directive: unless the enemy psykers could be neutralised, the Fleet couldn't land any more reinforcements, any more of the five million Imperial Guard troops still waiting in troop-ships in orbit. Or deploy air-cover. The fate of the entire battle teetered in the balance.

Corbec brushed off another fly. The air was thick with them now, choked with flies and cinders and ash. The smell was unbearable. Colm Corbec took a deep, shuddering breath. He knew the signs: they were close to something, something bad. Something of Chaos.

'Watch yourselves!' he warned his group over the link. 'We're getting into a real nest of Hell here!'

Through the swarming clouds of buzzing flies, the fire-team edged along a corridor littered with clear plastic shards and torn paper. Out in the concourse below, a fierce hand-to-hand battle was ending in screams and sporadic pistol fire. Something blew up a kilometre or so away, shaking the ground.

Corbec reached the turn in the hall and waved his men back.

Just in time, his fire-team sheltered in doorways as heavy stub gun fire raked up and down the old back-stairway, disintegrating the steps and tearing down the stained wall tiles.

Corbec looked round at Larkin, who was murmuring some Imperial prayer under his breath, waving off the flies. It was probably the oath of allegiance to the Emperor they'd all been taught at school back home on Tanith.

Home...

This had once been someone's home, thought Corbec, snapping back to the hard facts of real time. A dingy old hallway in a dingy old high rise, where humble, hardworking people came back from the shift-work at the fabrication plants in the hive and cooked meagre meals for their tired children.

'Larks!' He gestured up the stairwell. 'A little Mad Magic on that stubber!'

Larkin wiped his mouth and shook out his neck like a pianist about to play. He took out his nightscope, a little heat-sensitive spotter he'd used back home poaching larisel out in the woods at night. He trained it up the hall, found a hub of heat emanating from the wall.

Most would have aimed for that, thinking it the body heat of the gunner. Larkin knew better. The source was the muzzle heat of the big cannon. That put the gunner about sixty centimetres behind it, to the left.

'A bottle of sacra says it's a head shot,' whispered Corbec as he saw Larkin snuggle down and aim his lasgun.

'Done,' Varl said.

Larkin punched a single shot up the stairwell and through the wall.

They moved forward, cautious at first, but there was no further firing.

Covering each other, they moved up the smashed staircase, past the landing where the cult soldier lay dead across his stub gun, head half gone. Corbec smiled and Varl sighed.

Then they entered a further landing and fanned out. There was a smell of burning flesh here, and the flies were thicker than ever.

Larkin edged along one wall, looking at the trash and broken possessions that had been dropped in the rubble. Along the wall, under a series of Chaos markings rendered in dark paint, someone had nailed up a series of dolls and other childrens' toys. Something in Larkin's heart broke as he gazed on the crucified dolls, remembering a world of family and friends and children forever lost to him.

Then he realised that not all of the dolls were dolls.

Larkin fell to his knees, retching.

On the far side of the gallery, Corbec, Durcan and Suth burst into a long concrete chamber that had once been a central meeting hall for the tenement block. It was dark inside. Several thousand eyes blinked in their direction.

They all belonged to the same... thing.

Something immeasurably vast began to coil up out of the darkness, extending the flaccid, blue-white mass of its bloated body, toxic spittle drooling from its befanged mouths. Jellied things quivered in the dark spaces of its translucent skin and flies billowed around it like a cloak.

Corbec's nose spurted blood and soaked his beard as he backed away, his mind seized in horror. Suth dropped the melta with a clatter and started to retch, sliding down the wall, unable to stand. Durcan seemed unable to move. He began to cry, wailing as he fumbled to raise his lasgun. Limpid, greasy coils lashed out of the dark chamber and encircled him, embraced him, and then crushed him so hard and so suddenly he burst like a tomato.

Mallor and Varl turned and saw the horror slithering up from the chamber, saw Suth helpless and Corbec frozen, saw the pulpy red slick that had been Durcan.

'Daemon! Daemon!' Varl screamed down the comm link. 'DAEMON!'

Gaunt held up a hand and announced a ten minute rest. The group eased back and took the weight off their feet, leaning on tree trunks, hunkering down.

Meryn took the medi-pack back to Bragg and helped him lower the stretcher-bed.

'Oh, feth!' Milo heard him say.

Milo crossed over as Gaunt himself approached.

Meryn looked up, treating the ugly wounds of the two unconscious men. 'It's this place,' he explained, 'hot, wet... spores in the air... insects. Their wounds get re-infected as fast as I clean them. Obel's fading fast. Some kind of fungus necrotizing the raw flesh. Maggots too.' He shook his head and continued with his work.

Milo moved away. The smell rising from the wounded men was not pleasant.

Nearby stood the co-pilot. He'd pulled his flight helmet off, and was staring nervously into the green darkness around them, clutching his laspistol. Milo thought he looked young, no older than him. The flesh around his cranial implants looked raw and fresh. He probably feels just like me, Milo decided. In over his head.

He had just considered approaching the navy cadet and speaking to him when the low whine of gunfire sang through the trees. Everyone ducked for cover, and there was a staccato series of safety locks disengaging and power-cells humming to life.

Near to Milo, Gaunt crawled forward, tapping his micro-bead.

'Rawne? Answer!' he hissed. The major, with Feygor, Caffran and a trooper called Kalen, had scouted ahead towards the mysterious structure.

'Firefight!' came Rawne's response, Milo picking it up via his own comm-bead. 'We're pinned! Daagh! Throne of God! There's–'

The link went dead.

'Damn!' Gaunt hissed. He clambered to his feet. 'Meryn! Bragg! Guard the wounded! You, Navy boy! Stay with them! The rest with me, fire-team spread!'

The Ghosts moved forward and Milo moved with them, checking his pistol was cleared to fire. Despite the fear, he felt pride. The commissar had needed all the men he could muster. He had not thought twice about including Milo.

Corbec was sure his life was over when Larkin started shooting. Driven over the edge by what he had seen nailed along the wall, Larkin just went crazy; mindless, oblivious to the otherwise transfixing image of Chaos in that old tenement. Larkin simply opened fire and kept firing.

'Larkin! Larkin!' Corbec hissed.

The little man's howl was drying away into a hoarse whisper. A repetitive clicking came from the lasgun in his hands, the power cell exhausted.

The lashing tentacles of the vast thing in the hallway had been driven back by the hammerblow of relentless laser fire.

They had a moment of grace, time to retreat.

Corbec led his scrambling fire-team back down the tenement hall, half-carrying Larkin.

'Oh feth! Oh feth! Oh feth!' Larkin repeated, over and over.

'Shut up, Larks!' warned Corbec. 'Contact Fleet Command!' he yelled to Raglon over his bead. 'Tell them what we've found!'

In the cover of a slumped tree-stump, Trooper Caffran sighted his lasgun to his shoulder and loosed a burst of laser shot that sliced explosively through the foliage ahead. Bolter fire returned, smacking into the wood around him, blasting sprays of splinters and gouts of sap.

'Major Rawne?' Caffran yelled. 'Comm link's dead!'

'I know!' spat Rawne, dropped down against a tree nearby as metal shot exploded the bark behind him. He threw down Gaunt's chainsword and swung his own lasgun up to fire.

Feygor took up a prone position, blasting with his own weapon, Kalen to his side. The four Ghost lasguns blasted an arc of fire into the dense trees, the dim grove flickering with the muzzle flashes.

Rawne span, his gun lowered, but dropped his aim with a curse as he saw Gaunt moving in behind them, the men in fire-team line.

'Report!' hissed Gaunt.

'We just walked into heavy bolter fire. Enemy positions ahead, unseen. Feels like an ambush, but who knew we were coming?'

'Comm link?'

'Dead... jammed.'

'Would help if we could see what we were shooting at,' Gaunt remarked. He waved a 'come here' to Trooper Brostin, who hurried over, cradling the single flamer they'd pulled intact from the troop-ship.

'Positions!' Gaunt yelled, and fanned his men out so that all could take a clear shot once the target was revealed. 'Brostin?'

The trooper triggered the flame cannon and a volcanic spear of liquid fire spat into the dense undergrowth. Maintaining the spurt, like a horizontal fountain of fire, Brostin swept it left and right.

The trees, horsetails and giant ferns ahead flared and blazed, some of them igniting as if their sap was petrol, some wilting and withering like dust. In twenty seconds, a wall of jungle had been scorched aside and they had a clear view sixty metres into an artificially cleared area.

Silence. Not even the bolter fire which had got them ducking.

'Scope!' called Gaunt, and took the instrument as Milo offered it up.

'Looks like we have...' Gaunt paused as the self-focus dials on his scope whirred and spun. 'An Imperial installation. Three armoured, modular cabins, two larger hardened shelters... they've all had the insignia spray-painted out. Communicator-array and up-link mast for a voxcaster, that's probably what's jamming us... perimeter defence net... slaved servitors mounted into autoloader bolt cannons. You must have tripped a sensor as you came in, major. Triggered them off. I think we've fried a couple of them.'

'What is this place?' Caffran murmured.

'A way out... a chance we never thought we had. If we can get in there alive, that is.' Gaunt fell silent

'But what's it doing out here in the middle of this jungle?' Milo found himself asking.

Gaunt looked round at him. 'Good question.'

The word wasn't good. All ground forces were stretched to breaking point maintaining the gains they had made. There was no one to move in to support the Ghosts.

'How can we fight that kind of stuff?' stammered Suth.

Corbec shook his head. He'd pulled the entire battle group back to the embankment overlooking the highway and the tenements beyond.

Tenements that held the most abominable thing he'd ever seen.

'But it has to die!' Larkin whispered. 'Don't you see? It's causing the storm. Unless it dies, we're all stuck here!'

'You can't know that, Larks!' Varl sneered.

Corbec wasn't so sure. Larkin's gut instincts had always been good bets. 'Emperor save us all!' Corbec said, exasperated. He thought hard. There had to be something... something... what would Gaunt have done? Something arrogant, no doubt. Pulled rank, broken the rules, thrown the strategy books out of the window and used the resources he knew he could count on...

'Hey, Raglon! Over here, lad!' he yelled to his comm-officer. 'Patch me a link to the *Navarre*!'

Executive Officer Kreff cleared his throat, took a deep breath and stepped into the Strategium, the captain's armoured inner sanctum at the centre of the *Navarre*'s bridge.

Captain Wysmark sat in dark, contemplative silence on a reclined throne, quietly assessing the flickering overlays of runic and schematic data that flowed across the smoothly curved walls and roof of the room.

He turned in his chair slightly. 'Kreff?'

'I have, um, this is unorthodox, sir, but–'

'Out with it, man.'

'I've just spoken with Colonel Corbec, the acting chief of the Tanith First. His battle group is assaulting the western edge of the Nero Hive. He requests we... activate the main batteries and present on a target he has acquired.'

Wysmark sneered, the glow of the readouts flickering across his face in the gloom.

'Doesn't this idiot know anything about Naval tactics?' he chuckled. 'Fleet weapons will only engage a surface target from orbit before troop deployment. Once the ground forces are in, air-strikes are the responsibility of the attack squadrons.'

Kreff nodded. 'Which are grounded due to the psychic storm, sir. The colonel is aware it is counter to usual tactics, as orbital bombardment is not known for its... um... finesse. However, he claims this is a critical situation... and he can supply us with pinpoint co-ordinates.'

Wysmark frowned, thoughtful. 'Your assessment, Kreff? You've spent more time with these footsloggers since they've been aboard than anyone. Is this man mad, or should I grant his request?'

Kreff dared a little smile. 'Yes... and yes, sir.'

Wysmark grinned back, very slightly. He rotated his chair to face Kreff. 'Let's see those co-ordinates.'

Kreff jumped forward and handed him the data-slate.

Wysmark keyed his micro-bead intercom. 'Communications: patch me to Fleet Command. I wish to advise them of our next action. Fire control, energise the main batteries... I have a firing solution here. All stations, this is the captain... rig for main weapon firing.'

All so very neat and civil, Kreff smiled. This really was the only way to fight a war.

There was a blink of light, an astonishing shockwave that knocked them all down, and then a deafening roar that hammered across them.

Corbec rose, coughing dust and picked Raglon up.

'Right on the button,' he remarked jovially to his astonished men.

They scrambled up to the top of the slope and looked over the balustrade. Below them, the ruinous expanse of a ten-lane highway stretched into the dark industrial high rises of the hive. Across the highway, a vast blazing crater stood where the tenements had been.

'Holy Throne of Earth!' Varl stammered.

'Friends in high places,' sniggered Corbec. He glanced down the slope at the hundreds of waiting troops below, troops who could already sense the change in the air. There was smoke, and fumes and cordite – but the stink of Chaos was retreating. The storm was blowing itself out.

'Let's go!' he yelled into his bead.

The comms officer saluted Kreff as he crossed the polished deck of the serene bridge.

'Signal from the surface, sir.'

Kreff nodded.

'Standard Guard voxcaster encryption, data and time as now, orbit lag adjusted. Message reads: "Ghostly gratitude to the *Navarre*. Kreff, you bastard, we knew you had it in you." Message ends. Sorry about the vulgarity, sir.'

The comms officer looked up from the slate.

'I'll take that,' Kreff said, trying to hide his grin as he sauntered away.

Gaunt moved in close to the cabins, bolt pistol in hand. Behind him came Feygor and Caffran, edging slowly.

There was a low whirr and one of the servitors nearby detected the movement and swung around, bringing its automated weapon to bear.

Gaunt blasted it apart with three quick shots. Diving forward, he slammed in through the doorway, rolling up in the blue, cold, artificial light of the interior, hunting for a target.

There was nothing but darkness. And dead stillness. Gaunt moved into the low habitat, mindful of the gloom. Ahead, a dull phosphorescence shone. There was a dark bunkroom full of over-thrown furniture and scattered papers. Gaunt took a look at one leaf and knew he would have to have them all burnt.

Rawne and Feygor slid in behind him.

'What is this?' Rawne asked.

'We'll see...' murmured Gaunt.

They moved through the habitat into a greenhouse where the air was humid.

There were things growing in the hydroponics vats that Gaunt didn't want to look at. Fibrous, swollen, bulging things, pulsing with hideous life.

'What is this place?' asked Feygor, horrified.

'The start of it... the beginning of Caligula's fall,' Gaunt said. 'One of the industrialists of this world, hot-housing something he could not understand. The competition for better crops is fierce here. This poor fool didn't realise what he was growing.'

Or at least, Gaunt thought, I hope he didn't. If this had been done with foreknowledge, deliberately... He shook the idea away.

'Burn it. Burn it all,' he told his men.

'Not all,' Kalen said, entering behind them. 'I scouted around the perimeter. Whoever owned this place has a shuttle bedded in a silo out back.'

Gaunt smiled. The Emperor will always provide.

'So he didn't die?' mused Corbec, sat on his bunk in the troop bay. Bragg shook his head and swigged from the bottle of sacra. 'Don't think nothing's gonna kill old Gaunt. He said he was gonna get us all out, and he did. Even Obel and Brennan.'

Corbec thought about this. 'Actually,' he said finally, 'I meant Rawne.'

They both looked across the quiet bay to where Rawne and Feygor sat in quiet conversation.

'Oh, him. No, worse luck.' Bragg passed the bottle back to Corbec. 'So, I hear you had some fun of your own?'

A forward post, looking out into the water-choked thickness of the Monthax jungles. The flies were thick out here, like sparkling dust in the air. Amphibians gurgled and chugged in the mudbanks.

The sappers had raised the spit-post out beyond the broad levees of the main embankment, one of six that allowed the Tanith snipers greater reach into the front line. They were long, zagged and lined with frag-sacking and a double layer of overlapped flak-boards.

Gaunt edged along the spit, keeping low, passing the sentries at the heavy-bolter post at the halfway point. The mud, unmoving and stagnant in the dug-away bed, stank like liquescent death.

The sagging cable of a land-line voxcaster ran down the length of the sacking, held above the water by iron loop-pins.

Gaunt knew it ended at a vox-set at the sniper post. In the event of attack, he would want the earliest warning from his keen-eyed forwards, and one that could be conveyed by good old, reliable, un-scrambleable cable.

Larkin was his usual edgy self. At the loop hole at the end of the spit-post, he was sat on a nest of sacking, meticulously polishing his weapon.

A compulsive, Gaunt thought. The commissar stepped up to him. Larkin looked around, tense.

'You always look like you're afraid of me,' Gaunt said.

'Oh no, sir. Not you, sir.'

'I'd hate to think so. I count on men like you, Larkin. Men with particular skills.'

'I'm gratified, commissar.'

Larkin's weapon was sparkling, yet still the man worked the cloth to it.

'Carry on,' said Gaunt.

But for how much longer, he wondered?

FIVE

THE ANGEL OF BUCEPHALON

Larkin thought about death. He thought he might well have begged for it long ago, had he not been so scared of it. He had never figured out, though he had spent whole nights wondering it, whether he was more afraid of death itself or the fear of death. Worse, there had been so many times when he had expected to find out. So many moments caught in Death's frosty gaze, snapped at by Death's steel incisors. The question had been nearly answered so many times.

Now perhaps, he would find out. Here. Death, or the fear of death.

If the Angel knew, she was saying nothing. Her stern face was turned down, demure, eyes closed as if sleeping, praying hands clasped at her breast.

Outside, below them, the war to take Bucephalon raged. The stained glass in the huge lancet window, what remained of it, shook and twinkled with reflections of tracer sprays, salvos of blazing rockets, bright air-bursts.

Larkin sat back against the cold stone pillar and rubbed a dirty hand around his lean jaw. His breathing was slowing now at last, his pulse dropping, the anxiety attack that had seen him wailing and gasping five minutes ago was passing like a cyclone. Or maybe he was just in the eye of that storm.

The ground shook. He felt it through the pillar. His pulse leapt for a moment. He forced himself to breathe deeply through his mouth, slow, deep inhalations of the sort he used to steady himself before taking a shot.

'You were telling me how you came to be here.'

Larkin looked round at the Angel. Though her head was still angled down, now she was gazing at him, smiling grimly. Larkin licked his lips and gestured idly around with one dirt-caked hand.

'War. Fighting. Fate.'

'I meant specifically,' said the Angel.

'Orders. The will of the Emperor.'

The Angel seemed to shrug her robed shoulders slightly. 'You are very defensive. You hide yourself and the truth behind words.'

Larkin blinked. For a moment, sickle-shaped moons of bright white light and fuzzy oblongs of red blackness lurched across his vision. A tiny moment of nausea. He knew the signs. He'd known them since childhood. The visual disturbances, the nausea, the taste of tin in his mouth. Then, the anxiety, the tunnel vision. After that, if he was lucky, a white hot migraine pain that would burst inside his skull and leave him dazed and helpless for hours. If he was unlucky: fits, spasms, blackouts and an awakening hours later, bruised and bloodied from the thrashing seizures; empty, miserable, destroyed inside.

'What's the matter?' asked the Angel.

Larkin tapped his forehead gently with his index finger. 'I'm... not right. Never have been, not in all my life. The fits used to scare my mother, but not half as much as they did me. They come on me from time to time.'

'Times like now? Under pressure? In the presence of danger?'

'That doesn't help. But it's just another trigger. You know what a ploin is?'

'No.'

'Round fruit. Soft, green-skinned, juicy. Lots of black pips in pink flesh. They used to grow in my uncle's orchard on Tanith. Divine things, but even the smell of them would trigger an attack.'

'Is there no medicine you can take?'

'I had tablets. But I forget to take them.' He took a little wooden pill-box from his jacket, opened the lid and showed her it was empty. 'Or I forget when I run out.'

'What do they call you?' asked the Angel.

'They call me Mad Larkin.'

'That is cruel.'

'But true. I'm not right in my mind. Mad.'

'Why do you think you are mad?'

'I'm talking to a statue of the Imperium, aren't I?'

She laughed and smoothed the folds of the white robes over her kneeling legs. There was a low and perfect radiance to her. Larkin blinked and saw glowing moons and oblongs in after-image again.

Outside, a hail of gunfire lit the evening and a ripple of explosions crackled the air. Larkin got to his feet and crossed to the nearest window. He looked out through interlocking pieces of coloured glass at the city below. Steepled, tall, rising within a curtain of walls eighty metres high, the capital city-state of Bucephalon clung to the ridge of the mountains. Smoke obscured the sky. Las-fire filled the air like bright sleet. Two or more kilometres away, he saw the pair of enormous storming ramps that the sappers of the Imperial Guard had raised against the walls. Huge embankments of piled earth and concrete rubble almost a kilometre long, rising high and broad enough to deliver armoured vehicles to the top of the wall. Heavy fighting within blooms of flame lit the ramps.

Below, nearer, the men on the ground looked like insect dots. Thousands, churning in trenches, spilling out across the chewed and cratered mess of the battlefront to assault the forbidding walls.

Larkin's vantage point was high and good. This shelled, ruined fortress was part of a stone complex which straddled and guarded the main aqueduct into the city, a huge structure that had defied the most earnest attempts of the enemy to fell with mines. Though heavily defended, it had seemed to Commissar Gaunt a good way in for a stealth team. Not the first time the commissar had been wrong.

Gaunt had told them that, before the clutch of Chaos fell upon it, the city-state had been ruled by thirty-two noble families, the descendants of merchant dynasties that had established the settlement. Their brilliant banners, the heraldic displays of thirty-two royal houses, were displayed on the walls, tatters of rich cloth draped from massive timber awnings. Those mighty awnings were now additionally decorated with the crucified bodies of the leaders of those noble families.

It had been Nokad's first act. Nokad the Blighted, Nokad the Smiling, the charismatic cult leader whose malign forces had risen to conquer Bucephalon from within, and win one of the most honourable of the Sabbat Worlds. In his great liberation address at the start of the crusade, Warmaster Slaydo himself had listed proud Bucephalon as one of the worlds he was most eager to save.

Shells burst outside the windows and Larkin ducked back into cover. Glass pattered and tinkled onto the stone floor. The flashes behind his eyes were getting worse and he could taste the tang of metal in his saliva. There was a moaning, too, a dull aching groan in his inner ear. That was a particularly bad sign. He had only got that a time or two before, just prior to the very worst madnesses. His vision was not entirely stable. Everything in the chapel around him seemed elongated and stretched, like in the mirror tent at the Attica carnival. In places his vision belled and warped, objects shimmering in and out of focus, drifting near and then away again.

He shuddered, deep in his bones.

The Angel was lighting tapers at the wrought iron offertory. Her movements were slow and lovely, pure grace.

She asked, 'Why don't you believe in angels?'

'Oh, I do.' Larkin sighed. 'Not just now, before. A friend of mine, Cluggan, a sergeant, he was a bit of a military historian. He said that at the Battle of Sarolo, angels appeared over the lines just before dawn and inspired the Imperial forces to victory.'

'Were they visions, do you think? Mass hallucinations brought on by fatigue and fear?'

'Who am I to say?' Larkin replied, as the Angel finished her taper-lighting and blew the long flame-reed out. 'I'm mad. Visions and phantoms appear to me on a daily basis, most of them conjured by the malfunctions of my mind. I'm not in a position to say what is real and what is not.'

'Your opinion is no less valid than any other. Did they see angels at Sarolo?'

'I...'

'Say what you think.'

'I think so.'

'And what were those angels?'

'Manifestations of the Emperor's will, come to vitalise his loyal forces.'

'Is that what you think?'

'It's what I'd like to think.'

'And the alternative?'

'Hnh! Group madness! The meddling of psykers! Lies constructed by relieved men after the fact! What you said... mass hallucinations.'

'And if it was any or all of those things, does that make it any less important? Whatever they saw or thought they saw, it inspired them to victory at Sarolo. If an angel isn't really an angel but has the inspirational effect of one, does that make it worthless?'

Larkin shook his head and smiled.

'Why should I even listen to you? A hallucination asking me about hallucinations!'

She took his hands in hers. The feeling shocked him and he started, but there was something infinitely calm and soothing in her touch. Warmth wriggled into his fingers, palms, forearms, heart.

He sighed again, more deeply and looked up into her shadowy face.

'Am I real, Hlaine Larkin?'

'I'd say so. But then... I'm mad.'

They laughed together, hands clasped, his dirty, ragged fingers wrapped in her smooth white palms. Face to face they laughed, his wheezing rattle tying itself into her soft, musical humours.

'Why did you abandon your men?' she asked.

He shivered and pulled his hands out of her grip, struggling away from her. 'Don't say that!'

'Larkin... why did you do it?'

'Don't ask me! Don't!'

'Do you deny it?'

He bumped against a pillar across the debris-littered aisle and turned back to her with ferocious eyes. His vision was pulsing now, lights and alterations dancing and flexing across his line of sight. She seemed far away, then huge and upon him. His guts churned biliously.

'Deny? I... I never left them... I...'

The Angel stood and turned away from him. He could see the way her silver-gold tresses fell to waist length between the powerful furled wings which emerged from slits in her samite gown. Her head was bowed. She spoke again after a long pause.

'Commissar Gaunt sent his fire-team into the aqueduct, on an insurgency mission to enter Bucephalon. The primary target was Nokad himself. Why was that?'

'K-kill the head and the body dies! Gaunt said we'd never take this place in a year unless Nokad's charismatic leadership was broken! The whole city-state has become his Doctrinopolis, the wellspring of his cult, to seed and spread the deceitful charm of his sensibilities to the other city-states on this world and beyond!'

'And what did you do?'

'W-we entered the aqueduct channels. Rawne's company led the way to draw fire and break the defence. Corbec's slid in behind to leapfrog the fighting as Rawne met it and enter the city through the canal trenches.'

'Wouldn't you drown?'

'The canals have been dry for six months. They were mined and wired but we had sweepers.'

'You were with Corbec's company?'

'Yes. I didn't want to go... Feth! I hated the idea of taking a suicide run like that, but I'm Corbec's sniper... and his friend. He insisted.'

'Why?'

'Because I'm Corbec's sniper and his friend!'

'Why?'

'I don't know!'

'Might it have been because you are the best shot in the entire regiment? That if anyone could get a shot at Nokad, it was you? Might Corbec, your friend, have been reluctant to take you? Might he have been afraid you could snap if the going got too hard?'

'I don't know!'

'Think about it! Might he have decided to take you in the end because, no matter what the risk and no matter how fragile your mind, you are still the best shot in the regiment? Might he have valued that in you? Might he have needed that asset despite the risk?'

'Shut up!'

'Might you have let him down?'

Larkin screamed and pressed his face into the stone floor. His wiry body began to twitch as the storm of madness, the tidal wave of anxiety, rose and crested in his thundering mind. He saw nothing but colours now: his vision was a neon kaleidoscope blur.

'And what did you do? That firefight in the canal. Close quarters. Lopra dead, head blown off; Castin disembowelled; Hech, Grosd, the others, the screaming, the misty smoke of burning blood. Corbec bellowing for reinforcements, daggers of light cutting the air. And what did you do?'

'Nothing!'

'Not nothing. You ran. You ran away. You scrambled and ran and ran and ran and ended up here. Sobbing, vomiting, soiling yourself.'

'No...' Larkin breathed, spread face down on the cold floor. He felt he was in a vacuum now. There was no sound, no vision, no pain. Just her voice.

'You deserted them. That makes you a deserter.'

Larkin looked up sharply. The Angel stood by the reliquary, lifting the studded wooden lid. She took something out and placed it upon her head, smoothing her silver-gold hair under the brim. It was a cap. A commissar's regimental cap. Gaunt's cap.

She reached into the holy box and lifted out something else, wrapped in dusty, mouldering cloth. Her perfect hands unwound it. A bolt pistol. With incongruous sureness, her slender hands slammed a sickle-pattern magazine into the slot, racked the slide and thumbed off the safety. She turned.

Her face, below the commissar's cap, was lean and angular. Larkin hadn't realised how chiselled and thin her cheeks and chin were before. Cut out of stone, firm and fierce, like Ibram Gaunt. She raised the bolt pistol in her right hand and pointed it at Larkin. Her wings opened and spread, twenty metres wide, a vast arch of perfect white eagle feathers.

'Do you know what we do to deserters, Larkin?' she asked grimly.

'Yes.'

'We are created to inspire and uplift, to carry the spirit of battle forward, to maintain the sense of glory in the hearts of the Imperial warrior. But if that spirit falters, we are also here to punish.'

'Y-you sound like Gaunt...'

'Ibram Gaunt and I have much in common. A common purpose, a common function. Inspiration and punishment.'

It seemed as if the world outside the chapel had fallen silent. As if the war had stopped.

'Did you desert, Larkin?'

He stared at her, at the gun, at the terrible wingspan. Slowly, he got to his knees and then his feet.

'No.'

'Prove it.'

Every joint in his body ached, every nerve sang. His head was clear and yet racing and strange. He walked with measured care over to his fallen pack.

'Prove it, Larkin! The Emperor needs you with him at this hour! Muster your strength!'

He looked back at her. The gun and the gaze had not faltered.

'How did you know my name?'

'You told me.'

'My forename. Hlaine. I don't use that any more. How did you know?'

'I know everything.'

He laughed. Loud and hard, his thin chest shaking as he stripped open his pack. 'Feth take you! I'm no deserter!'

'Tell me why.'

'See this?' Larkin slid his sniper rifle from the sling across the back of his pack. He held it up and freed the firing mechanism with a deft twist of his hand.

'A gun.'

'A lasgun. Workhorse of the Guard. Solid, dependable, tough. You can knock it, drop it, club with it, submerge it and it just keeps on going.'

The Angel took a step forward, looking at the gun he held out to her. 'It's not standard. Not a standard M-G pattern. Where's the integral optics, the charge-setting slide? That barrel: It's too long, too thin. And that flash suppressor?'

Larkin grinned and reached into his pack. 'It's the sniper variant. Same body, but stripped down. I did some of the work myself. I took out the integral optics because I use this.' He held up a bulky tube to show her for a moment, then slotted it into a bracket on the side of the gun case. He flipped covers off both ends of the tube and the device spread a faint red glow ahead of the gun.

'Night spotter. My own. I tooled the bracket to fit. I used to use it to spot for larisel in the woods back home.'

'Larisel?'

'Small rodents with a fine pelt. Made a good income hunting them before the Founding.'

He slid his hands down the gun and tapped the barrel. 'XC 52/3 strengthened barrel. Longer, and thinner than the standard. Good for about twenty shots.' He kicked the pack at his feet, which clinked. 'I always carry two or three spares. They twist and pull out. You can switch them in about a minute if you know what you're doing.'

'Why the strengthened barrel?'

'Increased range for a start, tighter accuracy, and because I use these...' Larkin pulled a power pack from his kit and slammed it into place. 'We call them "hotshots". Overpowered energy clips, liquid metal batteries juiced to the limit. Bigger hits but fewer. Perfect for marksman work. And that's why there's no charge setting slider on my piece. One size fits all.'

'The stock is made of wood.'

'Nalwood, Tanith grown. I like what I know.'

'And that long flash suppressor?'

'I'm a sniper, Angel. I don't want to be seen.'

'Are you a sniper, Hlaine Larkin? I was sure you were a deserter.' The gloomy voice echoed around the chapel.

Larkin turned away from her, expecting a bolt round in the back of the head. His own head was clear, clearer than it had been in months.

'Think what you like. I'll tell you what I know.'

He crossed to the arched doorway of the chapel and settled down in a crouch, the lasgun resting on a finial of stonework. It afforded him a wide view down onto the half-ruined canal on the upper level of the great aqueduct.

Larkin settled himself, shook out his neck, flexed his arms. He took a sight through the eyepiece of his scope.

'My company's primary mission was to take Nokad. He's a charismatic. He leads by personality and that means he stays at the fore. This aqueduct has been recognised by both sides as the primary weakness of Bucephalon. We've attacked it. Hard. Nokad will want to defend it just as hard. And that means inspiring his troops along the length of it. And that, in turn, means he'll be here in person.'

'And if he's not?' asked the Angel.

'Then I'm just another nameless wooden marker in the cemetery.' He was no longer looking at her, no longer caring about her terrible presence. She could be holding that boltgun to his temple for all he cared.

'You trust that scope to make the shot?' she whispered.

'I calibrated it myself. And yes, I trust the scope. Funny thing, but whatever goes on around me, whatever madness...' – and at that Larkin dared a glance round at the hovering presence at his shoulder – 'I always see the truth through my scope. It shows me the world as it really is. Truth, not what my fethed-up mind tells me is there.'

A long pause.

'Maybe I should look through the scope at you some time?' he ventured.

'Haven't you got a job to do, Hlaine?'

'Yes. My job.' He turned back to the scope and shut his eyes.

'Your eyes are closed. What are you doing?'

'Shhh! To take a shot, your breathing must be controlled. More than that, your weapon must be pointing naturally at the target.' He opened his eyes again and fiddled with the lasgun as it lay in the lip of stone.

'What's the matter?'

'I need to baffle the barrel against the stone. I need cloth to wrap around it.' He began to pull at his cloak, trying to tear a strip off it. There was a shredding noise behind him. A perfect hand passed him a long strip of glowing white cloth, light and warm to the touch.

'Use this, Hlaine.'

Larkin smiled. He wrapped the silky material around the muzzle of his rifle and then nested it back into the stony over hang. It rested better now, bandaged with angelic satin, neatly snuggled into the turn of the hard buttress.

'Thanks,' he said, resuming his position.

'What are you doing now?'

Larkin flexed, as if fidgeting. 'I must have a stable firing position. If the gun wobbles even slightly, the shots can go wild. I need a firm grip, but not too tight. I want it to point naturally at the target. If I have to apply pressure to keep it aimed, then it's going to miss. See, here's the trick...'

He closed his eyes.

'Take aim and then close your eyes. Open them again. Chances are your aim will have wandered. Realign your body and repeat.'

'How many times?'

'As many as is necessary.' Larkin closed his eyes again, opened them, shuffled, closed his eyes.

'Eventually, when you open your eyes, the gun will be pointing precisely, naturally, exactly where your body falls and directs it.'

'You're breathing slowly,' said the Angel, a whisper in his ear. 'Why?'

Larkin smiled, but ever so slightly as to not disrupt the perfect pattern of his firing position. 'Once you're in position, breathe slow, a regular rhythm. Keep it going, nice and relaxed. When you get the shot, take a couple of deep breaths, pause, breathe out just a tad, and then hold. Then fire. Then breathe out fully.'

DAN ABNETT

'How long will this take?' the Angel asked behind him.
'As long as it takes to get a target.'

Nokad the Smiling sang to his brethren as they advanced down the upper canal of the aqueduct. An echelon of things that had been men, now trailing long tattered robes sewn from the hides of those they had defeated. They brandished weapons, slapping them in dull time to the chant. They passed over the butchered and exploded remains of the foe who had assaulted their one weak link that afternoon.

Nokad the Smiling was well over two metres tall, his frame heavy set and powerful. Piercings studded his naked torso and arms: loops, rings, chains and spikes armouring his sheened skin and glittering as brightly as his perfect teeth.

'Make trophies of them!' Nokad grinned as he passed the corpses. Imperial Guard, weak, puny things, draped in dull fatigues and anonymous cloaks. There was fighting ahead, the barking returns of lasguns at close range.

Corbec was in the canal gully with three remaining men and Rawne yelling through the intercom.

'It's no good! They've got it sealed tight! We have to withdraw!'
'Feth you, Rawne! This is the only way! We move in! Bring your men forward!'
'It's suicide, Corbec, you fool! We'll all be dead in a moment!'
'Are you deserting me, major? Is that what you're doing? There's a price for that!'
'Feth you, you insane moron! You'd have to be utterly mad to go in there!'

Nokad advanced. His men loved him. They sang together, jubilant as they forced the invaders back.

On the canal lip, Nokad howled his inspirational verses to his men, arms uplifted, chainsword whirring.

There was a crack, a stab of light – and Nokad's head vanished in a film of blood.

Larkin fell back in the doorway, frothing and convulsing, spasms snapping his body as the brain fever took hold once more.

'Larks? Larks?' Corbec's voice was soft.
Larkin lay in a foetal ball, messed by his own fluids, in the doorway

of the shattered chapel. As he came around he felt his mind was clear, violently clear, like it had been purged with light.

'Colm...'

'You son of a bitch, Larks!' Corbec pulled him upright, unsteady on his legs.

Larkin's lasgun lay on the floor, its barrel broken, burned and spent.

'You got him! You got him, you old bastard! You smoked him good!'

'I did?'

'Listen to that!' Corbec crowed, pulling Larkin around towards the doorway. There was a cheering and chanting noise rising from below the aqueduct. 'They've surrendered! We've taken Bucephalon! Nokad is fried!'

'Shit...' Larkin sank to his knees.

'And I thought you'd run on us! Honestly! I thought you'd fething deserted!'

'Me?' Larkin said, looking up.

'I shouldn't have doubted you, should I?' Corbec asked, bear-hugging the wiry little sniper.

'Where's the angel gone?' Larkin said quietly.

'Angel? There's no angel here except her!' Corbec pointed to the damaged statue of the angel above the chapel font, a beautiful winged woman knelt in the attitude of prayer. Her perfect hands were clasped. Her head was bowed demurely. The inscription on the plinth rejoiced that she was a symbol of the God-Emperor, a personification of the Golden Throne who had come to the elders of Bucephalon in the first days of the colony and watched over them as they conquered the land.

An old myth. A hunk of stone.

'But–' Larkin started as Corbec dragged him to his feet.

'But nothing!' Corbec laughed.

Larkin began to laugh too. He convulsed and gagged with the force of laughter inside him.

Corbec dragged him from the chapel, both laughing still.

The very last thing Larkin saw before Corbec wrenched him away was his fallen lasgun, with the peerless, scorched white cloth still wrapped around the barrel.

A sudden barrage of enemy guns, distant, impatient, came on just before the middle of the night over Monthax, and stippled the belly of the low brown sky with reflected flashes of fire and light. Wet, hollow rumbles barked and growled through the swamps and ground mist like starving hounds. Leagues away, some brutal night-combat was underway.

Gaunt woke instinctively at the sound of the guns and took a walk out of the command shed. The sound was coming from the east and he had a sergeant circle around to check on the sentry lines. The artillery sounded like someone flapping and cracking a large, sweat-damp sheet in the hot, heavy air.

He crossed a gurgling creek via a duck-board bridge and made it into the tree line just as the humidity broke and cold drooling rain began to fall through air suddenly stirred by chill breezes. It was almost a relief, but the rain was sticky and sappy and stung his eyes.

Gaunt found himself on the embanked approach to one of the main sentry towers and pulled himself up the ladder. The towers, set at hundred metre intervals along the main defile, rose some ten metres out of the surface filth. They were fashioned from groups of tree-trunks, shored together and stoutly buttressed with riveted beams, and supported large flak-board gun-nests mounted on the top.

Up in the dark nest, Trooper Bragg tended a cradle-mounted pair of twinned heavy bolters, drums of shells piled around his huge feet. A flak-board cover kept the rain off and the nest was shrouded by netting.

'Sir!' Bragg saluted, his big face cracking into a broad, embarrassed grin. He was making fortified caffeine over a little burner, his huge paws dwarfing the pot and cup. He tried to hide the flask of sacra behind the stove, but the scent of the liquor was pungent in the close air of the nest.

Gaunt nodded the salute. 'I'll have one myself,' he said. 'A stiff one.'

Bragg seemed to relax. He sloshed a generous measure of sacra into a second battered cup and fussed over the boiling pot. Gaunt was amused, as always, by the combination of brutal strength and timidity in this giant of a man. Bragg's hands were big and strong enough to crush skulls, but he moved almost meekly, as if afraid of his own strength – or afraid of what others might think him capable of.

He handed the commissar a hot cup and Gaunt sat on a pile of shell-drums, gesturing out across the jungle to the east. The nest's raised vantage point afforded a better view of the distant fighting. Flares and tracers showed above the trees, and as the rain dissipated the mist, there were ruddy ground fires to be seen amid the trunks.

'Someone's having fun,' he remarked.

Bragg nodded, sipping his own cup. 'I make four or maybe five enemy positions, infantry support teams. They've advanced and dug in, because the fire-patterns are static, but they've found something to shoot at.'

'If they move this way, we'll need to take action.'

Bragg patted his heavy weapons. 'Let 'em come.'

Gaunt grinned. Bragg was a good heavy weapons technician, but his aim had scarcely improved since the Founding. Still, with guns with that sort of cycle rate and that much ammo, he should hit something.

'Oh, while I remember,' Gaunt said, 'the western embankments are collapsing again. I told Major Rawne that you'd help the detail re-dig tomorrow. They need some heavy lifting.'

Bragg nodded without question. His great physical strength was an asset to the Ghosts, and was matched by his geniality and willingness to help. He reminded Gaunt of some great blunt weapon, like a club: deadly when delivered properly, but difficult to wield or aim.

Bragg batted a moth away from his face. 'Precious little place we've found here,' he remarked.

'Monthax is... short on charm,' Gaunt admitted, studying the hulking trooper quizzically. Bragg was a strange man. Gaunt had decided that long ago. He'd never met a human so physically powerful, yet mentally restrained, as if he was somehow afraid of the terrible power he could unleash. Others took it for stupidity and regarded big old Bragg as dumb. But the man patently wasn't stupid. In his own, quiet, mountainous way, he was the most formidable and dangerous Ghost of all. So preoccupied by his physical power, others always underestimated the mind behind it.

And the mind, Gaunt knew, was the strongest thing of all.

SIX

THAT HIDEOUS STRENGTH

Caligula, after the Imperial liberation. Nights as bright as day, lit by the burning hive cities; days as dark as night, choked by the petrochemical smoke. Soot, like fat, black snowflakes, fluttered down everywhere. Even out here, in the deadlands.

Steepled canyons of coral-bright rock. Wisps of fluorescent dust licking the high places and the rims of the calderas. Cracked, dry basins of hard, russet cake-earth. Wide, slumping ridges of glass-sand. And death, bleached and baked white, like bones that had been out in the sun for years.

Eighteen cargo transports, thirty-wheel monsters, coughing blue exhaust from their vertical pipe-stacks, ground down the red-rock pass in low gear. The tractor units at the front of each payload wagon were monsters, armoured cabs of scorched metal rattling on top of a huge engine unit, glaring forward through multiple fog-lamp eyes and grinning fly-flecked smiles of fender bars, radiator grilles and spiked running boards. Flanking the massive transports were the outriders, rushing through the dust on track-bikes and in armoured cars.

Palapr Tuvant, transport driver, Caligula born and bred, wrestled with the half-moon wheel of the convoy's lead freighter and glanced around at his co-driver. Tlewn Milloom was looking out of the cab window, occasionally regarding his chronometer.

They were both wringing with sweat, entombed by the heat from the roaring engine under their feet. Milloom had dropped the window armour panels and opened the metal vents in the hope of washing them with cool breeze from outside. But the surface temperature out in the deadlands was pushing forty degrees, and they baked. Occasionally, sprays of hot engine oil spurted back from the leaky head gasket and spattered in at them through the forward grille-screen.

Milloom sat back in his ripped leather seat and looked up at the cab's ceiling hatch. 'He's still up there?'

Tuvant nodded, wrenching the wheel. Both of them were all too used to the juddering, shaking motion of the vehicle. 'Probably sticking his head out of the turret like a dog, enjoying the rush of air.'

Milloom chuckled. 'Kec, but he's a dumb-ass, right? Never stood in line for brains.'

Tuvant nodded. 'Typical Guard, all muscle and no head. Where the kec were they when the hives fell? Huh? Answer me that?'

'In a troop-ship in transit,' Trooper Bragg answered plainly, his huge bulk clambering down the rungs from the top hatch to join them. He stood at the back of the cab, holding onto a roll-bar for support as the tractor lurched over uneven ground. 'Colonel-Commissar Gaunt said we got here as fast as we could.' He smiled sheepishly at the two-man driving team.

'I'm sure he did,' Tuvant murmured.

Bragg edged forward, using handholds to stop himself from falling. 'We're making good time, aren't we?'

'Brilliant time,' Milloom replied, turning away from the big Ghost. 'Calphernia Station will rejoice when we arrive.'

'I'm sure it will,' Bragg smiled, sinking into the bench seat behind the driver's position. 'That'll be good. When the colonel-commissar ordered me to command this convoy detail, I said to him I will get it through on time, trust me, colonel-commissar. I will. And we are, aren't we?'

'Yes, we are. Right on time,' Tuvant said.

'Good. That's good. The colonel-commissar will be pleased.'

Milloom muttered something unflattering about the high and mighty colonel-commissar.

'What did you say?' Bragg asked sharply.

Milloom stiffened. He looked across at Tuvant. They'd been in the company of this huge Guardsman for maybe three hours all told, and had so far reckoned him to be dim-witted and slow. Of course, his sheer bulk was impressive, but they had felt confident about laughing at him behind his back. Now Milloom tensed, feeling perhaps he'd gone too far, feeling the giant behind them might suddenly unleash his undoubted physical power in a mindless tantrum.

'I... I didn't say anything.'

'You did. You said something about my colonel-commissar. Something bad.'

Milloom turned slowly to face the huge Tanith. 'I didn't mean anything. I was just joking.'

'So it was a bad thing. An insult.'

'Yes, but just a joke.' Milloom tensed, expecting the worst, reaching his left hand down beside his seat for the axle-bar he kept stowed there.

'That's okay,' Bragg said lightly, turning to look out of a window. 'Everyone is entitled to their opinion. The colonel-commissar told us that.'

Milloom sat back and exchanged knowing grins with the driver. A total dummy, they agreed wordlessly.

'So,' Tuvant asked, teasing, looking at Bragg in the rear-view mirror, 'you do everything this colonel-commissar tells you?'

'Of course!' the giant replied brightly. 'He's the colonel. And the commissar. We're his men. We're Imperial Guard. Tanith First-and-Only. We're loyal to the Emperor and we do everything the colonel-commissar tells us.'

'What if he told you to jump off a cliff?' Milloom laughed, conspiratorially sharing the baiting with Tuvant.

'Then we'd jump off the cliff. Was that a trick question?'

The convoy rolled on into the deadlands. It had assembled that morning on a stained curtain road outside the half-burned ruin of the Aurelian Hive City, where a second front of Imperial Guard had seized control after the main assault on Nero Hive. The mammoth Imperium victory was in no doubt, but still pockets of enemy soldiers held out, fighting a lingering war of wastage and attrition to wear out the lines of supply.

The Imperial Guard closed in en masse to root out and eradicate all remnants of resistance, and the work to rebuild Caligula began. What resources were available – and despite everything Aurelian Hive was rich in storehouses – had to be redistributed. The convoy marked the first attempt to convey relief supplies to the stricken Hive Calphernia. That meant a two hundred kilometre crossing of the battlewaste recently dubbed 'the deadlands.'

Six convoys had departed Aurelian Hive that dawn. Four were headed to Nero Hive, one to Tiberius and one to Calphernia. Gaunt's Ghosts, the Tanith First, were given the protection duty. It was agreed that the run to Calphernia was the most dangerous, as it crossed the territories of bandits – ex-hive workers who had fled the war and set themselves up as feudal warlords in the waste. Not a single relief vehicle had made it through in the last six weeks and the rumours told of thousands of rebels, stockpiling weapons. Some even whispered that Chaos powers were involved.

Everyone, including Bragg himself, was amazed when Gaunt chose Bragg to command the defence of the Calphernia convoy. Gaunt had ignored all the protests and taken the bemused Bragg into his command bunker to brief him.

Caober, Rawne, Larkin and the other Ghosts decided that Gaunt's choice simply represented an acceptance that the Calphernia convoy wouldn't get through. It was a write-off and Gaunt wasn't going to waste any decent commander to such long odds.

'And so our caring commissar shows his true colours!' Rawne had hissed, playing with the hilt of his silver Tanith dagger. Others fidgetted nervously, unhappy with what seemed to be going on but unwilling to question Gaunt's authority directly.

Bragg simply grinned at the honour bestowed upon him. It seemed he missed the irony. He was oblivious to the fact that he was already given up as dead. Rawne spat in the dust.

At the behest of the men, Corbec had approached Gaunt fiercely, demanding to know why Gaunt had been so callous as to deem Bragg expendable. 'Sir, with me or Hasker or Lerod at the helm, we might get a chance to drive that convoy through. Don't throw it away, don't waste Bragg–'

'I know what I'm doing,' Gaunt had replied curtly, sending the proud Bragg and seventy other Ghosts off on the detail from which everyone was sure no one would come back.

The convoy rumbled down a wide-bottomed crevasse and began to cross a cracked, red dust-plain of baked earth. Heat shimmered up, distorting the horizons. Outrider one roared ahead of the convoy, a track-bike driven by Corporal Meryn with Trooper Caffran manning the pintle-mounted twin autocannons in the rear. Both had their stealth cloaks wrapped up around their mouths against the heat and dust, and wore filmed, heat-crazed goggles.

Meryn heaved the cycle to a halt on a rise, the convoy a kilometre behind them, and pulled down his swaddling dust-veils to spit and cough.

'You feel that?' he called back to Caffran. 'Eyes watching us from all around?'

'Just your imagination,' Caffran returned, cranking the guns round all the same.

Caffran felt a pulse in his temple that wasn't simply the heat. He'd seen the expression on Colonel Corbec's face when Gaunt had given the convoy command to Bragg. They were dead out here, as good as written off. The hundred burned and crucified bodies they had passed on the roadside an hour before had nothing to do with imagination. Caffran shuddered.

Other outriders whirred forward in hazes of dust. Trooper Kelve drove one cycle with Merrt, one of Corbec's favoured sharpshooters, in the rear cradle. Merrt had his sniper gun wrapped in oil-cloth in the foot-well below him, ready to switch to it when the autocannon rig ran dry. Kelve pulled them up to a revving halt on a sand-rise.

To their left, engine idling, was Ochrin and his gunner Hellat. To their right, five hundred metres distant, Mkendrick and his gunner Beris. A signal, waved from bike to bike, then they all flew forward into the dusty basin beyond, racing parallel to the track left by Meryn and Caffran. The huge convoy thundered in after them.

Tailing it, and flanking the rear, came three more outriders: Fulke with Logris gunning, Mktea with Laymon at the weapons, and Tan-hak with Grummed manning the cannons. Behind them, an Imperial Guard half-track driven by Wheln, with Abat and Brostin at the weap-ons stations, and another with long, double-tracks driven by Mkteeg with Rahan and Nehn crewing a missile launcher platform.

Bragg clambered up into the gun-turret over the cab of his tractor, half-hearing the whispered slanging of the Caligulan drivers, Milloom and Tuvant. Heat and dust assaulted his big face. The sun was a tor-rential heat. His nostrils immediately clogged with ash-dust and he had to hawk and spit to clear his head. As an afterthought, he wrapped his stealth cloak around his mouth and nose, pulling out the goggles he had been issued and also remembering to wipe zinc paste over his exposed skin.

The paste, clagging and damp in a small circular tin, smelled bad, but the colonel-commissar had told them all to use it. Bragg lifted his micro-bead comms-set and slid the plug into his ear.

'Bragg to all Ghosts, remember to use your sun-paint. The zinc stuff. Like the colonel-commissar told us. Over.'

Over the vox-link came a round of curses and protests.

'I mean it,' Bragg said. 'Wipe it on, Tanith. There's burning and there's burning, the colonel-commissar said, and our fair skins won't last a minute out in this.'

Sliding his bike to a halt, Ochrin pulled out his tin and grudgingly applied paste to his brow and nose. He held the tin out, straight armed, to Hellat in the back.

There was soft, distant ping, a hollow, empty sound.

Hellat took the tin from Ochrin's outstretched hand just as he real-ised Ochrin no longer had a face. Ochrin's corpse flopped stiffly back off the saddle.

Hellat cried out in alarm, gripping the yokes of his pintle weapon and raining metal fury on the distant dunes.

'Ochrin's down! We are attacked!' he screamed as he fired.

A second later a missile lifted his cycle into the air and blew Hellat and Ochrin's corpses into pieces of cooked meat each no larger than a clenched fist.

Vox-traffic suddenly tumbled in confusion over the static. Murmuring the litany of protection the Ecclesiarch had taught him back on Tanith, at the Primer Educatory, Mkteeg drew his half-track hull-down behind a salty dune and his weapon crew spat a rack of missiles into the cliff edges.

Meryn drove his cycle around in a wide arc, pulling to rejoin, puffing up a wide skim of dust. Caffran rattled round the gun mount and flickered off a curving row of tracer shells into the position marked by Hellat's last assault. Ochrin and Hellat's vehicle lay in a burning heap on a crisped sand-rise.

The main convoy slowed as the attack made itself known. The enemy fire whickered into them from the right hand side like rain – a few shots at first, then faster and more furious.

Mkendrick raced his bouncing bike in, screaming a Tanith warcry, and only when his gunner didn't begin firing did he turn to find Beris hanging dead over the pintle mount, sunlight shining through a vast hole in his torso. Mkendrick braked, leapt out of the driver's position and tossed Beris's corpse aside, maniacally training and firing the guns from a stationary position.

As his cycle raced into the firefight, Merrt knew he had a good angle, pumping round after round from the big calibre guns into the distant dust dunes. He screamed to his driver to go faster and to overrun the enemy. Kelve was about to reply, or was half-way through saying something, when a salvo of stub rounds tore the vehicle to pieces and overturned them.

Merrt pulled himself out of the dust and looked round to see Kelve trapped under the wreckage, shrieking in pain. The control column had impaled him, ripping him open and pinning him into the sand under three tonnes of twisted, smouldering metal.

Merrt ran to him, trying to raise the wreck, trying to tip it over. Kelve bayed at him, begging, pleading.

When Merrt realised how heavy the wreck was and how grievous Kelve's wound, he did as his driver instructed him. He took out his laspistol and shot Kelve through the head, point blank. Kelve's body spasmed and died, gratefully.

Merrt dived flat as further fire found his position. He located his swaddled sniper gun, thrown clear out from the wreck. There was no time to check for damage. He pulled off the cloth, lay low, and sighted, snuggling a fresh power cell into the receiver. His long sight brought the enemy into view, magnified, hazy, distant figures milling around trying to reload a khaki-painted missile launcher.

He made his first shot. It went long. He adjusted his scope, as Larkin had taught him, breathed out, and made the second shot a clean kill. The enemy were turning in confusion when he made the next three shots in calm, cold series.

Three clean hits. Sniper Master Larkin would be proud.

Atop the main tractor, Bragg yelled into his micro-bead, ordering the convoy to form a defensive circle. Various counter-demands whipped into his ears over the link and he shouted them down, gripping the gun-yokes with both of his huge hands and sending tight bursts of hammer-fire into the starboard hills.

The convoy vehicles reluctantly obliged, following Bragg's orders, circling round and forming a defensive position that the remaining out-riders circled. Vehicles two and four in the convoy took heavy hits, and vehicle six exploded outright as a rocket torched into its tractor unit. The side-panelling of the cargo-unit rippled off as internal explosions blistered out through the metal skin, shredding it. Scraps of metal hull span away from the boiling black-smoked fireball, puffing hundreds of individual ripples in the ashy sand all around.

Relieved at the turret guns by Trooper Cavo, Bragg dropped down into the cab to find Milloom and Tuvant sheltering under window level, the grid-shields and hatches pulled up.

'This is madness, you stupid kec!' Tuvant bellowed. 'They'll pin us down and murder us all!'

'I don't think these bandits are really so tough,' Bragg began.

Tuvant turned on him. 'You kec-head! They're all over us! God-Emperor, but there are thousands of bandits out here, more than enough to kill us all! We should have kept moving! Stopping like this, we'll give them all a chance to congregate for the kill!'

Bragg shambled across to the Caligulan drivers. There was a dull look in his eye Tuvant didn't like. With one meaty, hairy-knuckled paw, Bragg lifted Tuvant off the cabin deck by his throat.

'I'm in charge here,' he growled, his voice as deep and solid as his build, reverberative. 'The colonel-commissar said so. If we have to fight our way through to Calphernia a micron at a time, we will. And we will all fight. Clear?'

'C-clear!' gasped Tuvant, going blue.

'Now, can you make yourself useful?'

'How?' snarled Milloom acidly from behind. Bragg dropped Tuvant, who sprawled, retching, and turned to face the other driver. Milloom had his greasy axle-bar in his hands. 'You don't scare me, Ghost.'

'Then you must be very stupid,' Bragg muttered, turning aside without interest. Milloom launched forward to crush the big man's skull with five kilos of cold-stamped metal. Bragg broke stride lightly, impossibly lightly it seemed for such a great bulk. He caught the descending bar in one palm. There was an audible slap. Milloom gasped as the bar was pulled out of his hands. Bragg tossed it aside.

'You can start by not attacking me. You fething non-combatants really wind me up. Where the feth would you be if we hadn't come to pull your arses out of the Chaos pit?'

'Safe and sound in Aurelian Hive, probably!' Milloom jeered. 'Not out in the deadlands, surrounded by terrorist infantry!'

Bragg shrugged. 'Probably. With the other cowards. Are you a coward, Driver Milloom?

'Kec you!'

'Just asking. The colonel-commissar told me to watch out for cowards. Told me to shoot them on sight, as they were treasonous dogs who didn't deserve the salvation of the Golden Throne. I wouldn't shoot them, not me.'

There was a pause.

Bragg smiled. 'I'd just hit them. Has a similar result. Do you want me to hit you, Milloom?'

'N... no.'

'Then don't assault me again. You can help even if you don't know the business end of a weapon from your own arse. Get on the vox-caster. Recite the Ecclesiarchy's Oath of Obedience. You know that?'

'Of course I know that! Then what?'

'Then recite it again. Make it clear and proud. Recite it again, then again and then again. If you get bored, insert the Emperor's Daily Prayer for variation. Maybe the Imperial Litany of Deliverance for good measure. Fill the vox-channels with soothing, inspiring words. Can you do that?'

Milloom nodded and crossed to the vox-caster built into the tractor's dash.

'Good man,' Bragg said. Milloom started to speak into the caster horn, remembering the verses he had learned as a child.

Outside, laser and stub fire whined into the circled convoy. The outriders were laying in hard. Meryn drew his bike in so that Caffran could do real damage to the slowly encircling bandits.

Fulke, Mktea and Tanhak ran the line. From the back of Fulke's machine, Logris excelled and scored four kills. Mktea's gunner Laymon made one of his own before the upper part of his head was scythed off by a las-shot at the mouth. Tanhak and Grummed made six, maybe seven, good kills before a short-range missile ended their lives and their glory. Debris and body parts flew out from a searing typhoon of ignited bike fuel.

'Bragg! Bragg! We have to retreat!' Wheln yelled from the half-track, Abat dead behind him and Brostin blazing with his flamer.

In the cab of his freighter, Bragg was calmly unwrapping his auto-cannons from a felt shroud. Behind him, Milloom was steadily reciting into the vox-horn. Bragg paused, fingering his micro-bead to open the vox-line.

'No, Wheln. No retreat. No retreat.' he said simply.

Rubbing his sore throat, Tuvant scrambled up from the floor, about to argue with the huge Ghost, but he stopped dead as he saw the weapon that the Tanith hulk was preparing. Not one but two autocannons, the like of which were usually fixed to tripod or pintle mounts. Bragg had them lashed together, with a makeshift trigger array made out of a bent ration-pack fork so he could fire them as a pair. Long belt loops of ammunition played out from the gun-slots, leading back to a par-cel of round-boxes.

Bragg punched out the perspex window section from the rear of the cab and laid his twin muzzles across the sill. He looked back at Tuvant.

'You wanted something?'

'No,' Tuvant replied, ducking suddenly as stub-fire perforated the cab and showered them with metal shards and soot.

'I can fire this on my own if I have to, but it would be easier if I had someone to feed.'

Tuvant blinked. Then he scrambled forward and grabbed the ammo-belts, easing them around so they would pull unobstructed from the boxes.

'Thanks,' smiled Bragg quickly, then turned to hunch and squint out of the window port. He squeezed the trigger assembly. The twin guns barked deafeningly in the confines of the cab. Milloom paused in his recitation, and covered his ears with a grimace. Tuvant shuddered, but kept working dutifully to play the ammo-belts out clear and clean. Shell cases billowed through the air like chaff.

Bragg's first devastating salvo had gone wide, passing over the top of the nearby cliffs. He grinned at himself and adjusted his aim.

'Try again...' he murmured.

'What?' asked Tuvant.

'Nothing.'

Bragg opened fire again, the barking chatter of the paired guns fill-ing the cab again. Now his shots were stitching along the valley wall and crossing the far dunes. Something he touched exploded in a vio-lent plume of red fire. Bragg played his guns around that area again for a minute or so.

Out on the dunes, with the convoy circled behind him, Merrt crawled forward, re-adjusting his aim. He could hear the anxious but determined voice reciting the Emperor's Prayer over his ear-plug and it filled him with a sense of right and dignity. He blinked dust out of his eyes. He'd ditched his sand-goggles the moment he'd hit the ground. Larkin had told him that nothing should get between a sniper's scope and his naked eye. You only saw the truth of the world when your eye was clear and you were looking down your scope, Larkin had said in training. Merrt smiled at the memory. He remembered how Larkin would often carry his scope around in his thigh-pouch and take it out to look at people through it. 'To tell if they're lying,' he always said.

Merrt's scope wasn't lying now. He could see over three dozen bandits advancing over the dunes under cover of the foggy dust kicked up by the firefight. They were running low, heads down, hugging the contours of the ground. Merrt took aim at the nearest one. He sighed and fired, timing his finger to the moment of respiratory emptiness so nothing in his torso would jerk the aim. The laser burst punched through the top of the bandit's bowl-helmet, presented as it was by his head-down approach. The shot probably passed down through his skull, his neck and his torso, following the line of his spinal column, Merrt thought, as the figure dropped stone dead in a crumpled pile.

He adjusted his aim and took another bandit in the face when he looked up to take a bearing. A slight swing to the left, and another came into his sight, scurrying forward to gain new cover. A sigh. A squeeze. A slight recoil. The figure flipped back and fell still.

Merrt readjusted and was about to target a small group of infantry when their position dissolved in a haze of heat and outflung debris. Missile hit, he thought.

Rahan and Nehn were keeping the aim of the missile turret low, sliding off single shots that hugged the ground cover and buried themselves in the foe. Mkteeg edged the half-track along the lip of the folded dunes, skirting the enemy as best he could. His weapon crew had almost expended their missiles, so he set the drive in idle and clambered back into the turret bed to set up the stub-gun folded away in a deck-locker.

He had it up and lashed in to the armoured side panel of the track as Rahan volleyed off five missiles high into the air. They looked like burning javelins as they arched over the desert and flew down onto unseen targets below the dune.

Mktea fired the autocannon mount Laymon had been manning until the feeder belt jammed and the gun glowed red. With a curse, he snatched up his lasrifle and dived over the side. Enemy las-fire reached his vehicle a moment later and blew it up in a shower of metal debris that pattered around him as he crawled through the sand. Mktea felt a sharp and painful impact in his ankle. Looking back, prone on his belly, he realised his combat trousers were smouldering from the wash of cinders and a thick piece of metal debris had pierced his foot.

He beat down the fire then rolled over to yank the debris from his ankle. It was the shattered handle of his vehicle's autogun return, he realised. The pain was immense. He pulled at it and passed out momentarily. Coming to, he realised that the shrapnel wasn't going to come free from the bones of his foot without a surgeon. He chewed down a handful of painkillers, and as the heady high smacked into his brain, he rolled over and began firing his lasgun into the dune crest behind him.

Wheln blasted away from his vehicle's turret next to Brostin, who had ditched his flamer for a lasrifle. Bandits were running at them from a scoop of low-lying desert, and they shot everything that moved.

Mkendrik realised his guns were out as the last of the belt-feed whickered through the slot and the weapons coughed dry. Bandit troops were all over him, charging up to take his machine. He pulled out his laspistol and shot the first one through the head, gutting the second and blowing a knee off the third. Then he took a glancing wound in the left shoulder that turned him sideways and knocked him to the deck.

There was a roaring sound.

Meryn's bike came over the rise in a puff of dust, landing hard, Caffran hammering the enemy with his guns. Meryn slewed to the left as Caffran played the cannons around, exploding most of the enemy who were in eye-shot. The others scrambled for cover.

'Come aboard!' Meryn shouted over the roar of his engine and Mkendrik leapt onto the flat-bed next to Caffran. Meryn gunned the engine and they hammered straight at the enemy lines.

Firing from the back of his vehicle, Logris, one of Mkoll's elite scout brigade, realised his driver was losing it. Fulke was crying out, screaming, resisting the hammer of weaponsfire. He slewed the bike around, away from the action.

'Pull us back around! The war's over there!' Logris bellowed. Fulke said something absurd and gunned the motor of the outrider towards the comparative safety of the convoy circle. Logris climbed forward over the ammo boxes and feeder-cables strewn across the back-platform of the bike. He came upon the whimpering Fulke from behind and slammed his head sideways into the armour panel of the pilot's door. The bike shuddered to a sidelong halt as Fulke went limp.

Logris spat on the driver. 'Coward,' he said, then turned back. Enemy troops were scurrying across the cracked dust-land towards him. He took out his lasgun and armed it.

'Let's go,' he said to them, though they couldn't hear.

Bragg pulled back from the window and released his finger on the trigger assembly.

'What?' Tuvant asked.

'Get out,' Bragg said suddenly. 'You and Milloom, get out of the cab and back onto the trailer.'

'Why?'

'Fire-patterns...'

'What?'

Bragg turned and cursed at the Caligulan driver. 'Fire-patterns! Fire-patterns! They're concentrating their fire on the tractor units. It's the freight they want! If you want to be safe, get into the sections they don't dare shoot at!'

Tuvant and Milloom hurried back through the communicating door into the freight section. Bragg wiped his brow. His hand was rich with sweat and soot. Over the vox-link, he ordered all his crews to do the same. The bandits want this cargo... and so, Throne help me, they'll be less sure of shooting at us when we're part of it.

He yanked his autocannons off the sill and dragged them and the ammo boxes out onto the top of the freight unit.

'We're gonna die here!' Tuvant said, looking out from the top of the freight unit at the hundreds of bandit troopers who were advancing on their circle of machines.

'No, we're not,' Bragg told him.

'You're mad!' spat Tuvant. 'We're surrounded by them! Thousands of them! They'll pick us off, every last man!'

Bragg sighed and closed his eyes.

The Maurader bombers came low over the ridge, annihilating the enemy with their belly-slung payloads.

'There are bandits... hiding out there in the deadlands, impossible to target.' Bragg smiled, repeating what Gaunt had told him. 'Unless there is something to draw them out and unify them. Something like... this convoy.'

Tuvant looked at the huge ghost in disbelief. 'We were bait?'

'Yes.'

'Kec you for using us!'

'I'm sorry. It was the colonel-commmissar's idea.'

Tuvant sagged down onto the freighter-top walkway.

Bragg hunkered next to him. Around them, sheets of incendiary bombs and phosphor fire scorched the hills. The Imperial fighter-bombers shattered the air as they went supersonic and crossed the low hills to pull around for another massacre run.

'Tuvant?'

Tuvant looked round at the giant.

'We were bait, but we still have a purpose. We'll get this convoy through. Calphernia will rejoice, just like I said. It's just the colonel-commissar–'

Tuvant turned, eyes red. 'I'm getting kec tired of hearing that title!'

'His name's Gaunt. A good man. General Thoth ordered him to supervise the relief work here on your world. He knew that couldn't happen all the while the terrorists and bandit-clans were out here. So he set a lure. A lure of fat, tasty freight trucks bound for Calphernia.'

'Great.'

'We got them all in one place so that the Navy air-wing could dispose of them. Be happy, man! We've won a great victory here!'

Tuvant looked up at him. His face was pale. 'All I know is I've been used as bait by your colonel-commissar. You knew that all along.'

Bragg sat back against the guard rail, smelling the acid-rich reek of the burning napalm. 'Yes. The bandits aren't working blind, you know. Hive workers in Aurelian are tipping them off as to the movement of supply convoys. Why else do you think the colonel-commissar put me in charge of this run?'

Tuvant blinked at him, uncertain.

Bragg patted his vast chest with huge hands. 'I'm big... I must be stupid. No brain. The sort of – what was it again? – "kec" who would drive the convoy into trouble and then circle it in a defence position for easy pickings. The sort of idiot who was likely to deliver the convoy right into the hands of the bandits.'

'Are you telling me you were part of the lure too?'

'The sweet part, the part they couldn't resist. The part the workers on the inside would vox to their bandit friends about. Convoy's coming, boys and there's an idiot in charge. Right, Milloom?'

Milloom glared back at them from his place against the rail.

'Kec you!'

Bragg shook his great head. He held up a data-slate. 'Friend of mine, Trooper Raglon... Comms-Officer Raglon, was monitoring your cipher traffic. I've got you here, tipping off your bandit friends as to the time, schedule, make-up and strength of this convoy. Colonel-Commissar Gaunt told me to do it.'

'Milloom?' Tuvant stammered.

A compact auto-pistol was suddenly in Milloom's hand as he leapt up. 'Kec you, Guard filth!'

Bragg was up in an instant, shielding Tuvant and swinging a massive fist at Milloom.

The gun went off. There was a sickening gristle-crack of impact. The
shot went wild.

His face mashed beyond recognition, Tlewn Milloom tumbled off
the walkway of the freight unit and was dead before his body snapped
on the hard-packed desert twenty metres below.

Bragg turned back to Tuvant and helped him up. There was blood on
his bulky knuckles. Behind them, the sky was washed with heat-wash
and cinder-smog from the bombing runs.

'He was a traitor. And a coward,' Bragg explained to Tuvant.

'Colonel-Commmissar Gaunt told you that, right?'

'No, I worked that out all by myself. Now, I believe we have a date
with Calphernia Hive.'

A rusty dawn split the sky over Monthax. The air reminded Gaunt of the tall windows at the Schola Progenium back on Ignatius Cardinal where he had been reared and trained years ago, after his father's death. Smoky, like glass, fading through scattered panels of reds and ochres to the frostier tones of mauve and purple high above where the stars still twinkled. All it lacked was the lead-edged figure of some champion of the Imperium, some holy saint frozen in an attitude of victory over the piled heads of the slain.

For a moment, he thought he heard the plainsong of the Schola choir, singing the dawn celebrant as the star Ignatius rose. But he shook himself. He was mistaken. Across the long daybreak shadows that laced the stinking, muddy trench lines, he heard men singing a rougher, more brutal Guard anthem as they set their cooking fires and made breakfast. Milo was amongst them, edging the throaty music of the men's husky, dreamy voices with silvery notes from a slender reed-pipe.

Just as much an offering, just as celebrational for the providence of a new day, safe-delivered from night, Emperor be thanked. Beyond the lines, the unyielding jungles steamed as the heat of the rising sun boiled the damp out of them. Mist coated the dark trees. In that darkness of foliage and water and mud and flies, what miseries awaited the Imperial Guard?

Near to him, one man wasn't singing. Major Rawne sat back on a folded bedroll set by the fire before his tent. He was shaving, using a bowl of hot water, a broken mirrored tile and the razor edge of his silver Tanith knife. He had lathered with a tiny hunk of soap and Gaunt could hear the scratch of the blade against the bristles of his cheek and throat.

The commissar found himself almost hypnotised by the practiced, meticulous motions; the way Rawne held the skin of his cheek taut with his free hand as he looked sidelong into the propped mirror, drew the knife in a short scrape and then rattled it clean in the shallow bowl.

A knife against a knife, Gaunt thought. He always saw Rawne's face as a thin dagger, sleek and handsome. A dagger... or a snake, perhaps.

Both would be appropriate. Gaunt admired Rawne's abilities, and indeed even his ruthlessness. But there was no love lost. He wondered how many throats had been opened by the knife Rawne now stroked delicately across his own vulnerable flesh.

Watching him shave, without so much as a nick, it emphasised the dangerous control of the tall, slender man. Precise, perfect, the tiny difference between a clean shave and killing stroke.

And with *that* knife in particular...

Rawne looked up and caught Gaunt's eye. He made no other sign of recognition and continued with his work. But Gaunt knew how dearly Rawne would love to rattle that blade clean of soap-foam and bristles, and plunge it into his heart.

Or turn into a serpent and bite him.

Gaunt turned away. He would always have to watch his back against Rawne. Always, *forever*. It was the way of things. Ibram Gaunt had a billion enemies out there, but the bitterest was at his side, amongst his own, waiting for the moment to come where he could make a ghost of Gaunt.

SEVEN

PERMAFROST

There is a valley on Typhon Eight where frozen screams saw at the air, day and night, through eternity. The valley is a glacial cleft, its sheer sides nine kilometres deep. Where the starlight catches the top flanks, the ancient ice is so white, the eye can only take it briefly. Deeper, as it plunges, the ice becomes translucent blue, mauve, then crimson. Algae forms, frozen billions of years before into the rock-ice, stain it with their dyes and fluids.

It is the wind that screams, shredded and sliced by the razor-edged outcrops of ice along the valley crest, twisted and amplified by the gorge. Typhon Eight is an ice moon, its surface a crust of frozen water sometimes a hundred kilometres deep. Below that, boiling oceans of hydrocarbons pulse with the tidal rhythms of the planetoid's living core.

The screaming loud in his ears, Rawne rolled and slipped down a slope of scarlet ice at the bottom of the valley. The piercing wind raked at him, trying to steal his camo-cloak. Despite the cloak and his gloves and the insulation of his cold-weather fatigues, he was numb and leaden. The feeling – or the lack of feeling – replaced the rawness of an hour before and was no more welcome. He lay still, fumbling with his lasgun. Ice crystals formed on the metal of the weapon. He could barely hold it.

More shots came his way. Rawne had become used to the peculiar sound the impacts made in this place: a wet popping and a sizzle as superheated rounds punched into ice which melted around them and refroze. Blackened wounds, perfect circles, dotted the red ice sheet around him. He slithered into a deeper depression in the icescape and held himself low. More shots, low and desperate, one buzzing a hand's breadth over his head.

Then silence, or as close to silence as the perpetual screaming would allow. He rolled onto his back and, with his chin on his chest, looked back along the valley the way he had come. There was no sign of anyone or anything, except a crumpled black shape one hundred metres behind him that he knew was Trooper Nylat.

Dead. They were all dead, and he was the last.

He wriggled up and took a sight. The lens of the lasgun spotter was cracked and filmed with ice, ice which had formed from the moisture of his own eye. He pulled back, cursing. A day before, Trooper Malhoon had frozen his eyeball to his sight while spotting for targets on the ice floes. He could still hear the man's screams as they had separated him from his weapon.

He fired a triple salvo blind, wayward, into the dark of the gorge. In answer, a dozen guns opened up on him, and blew up an artificial blizzard in the ice-dust.

Caves: low, arched, steepled defiles in the ice-cliff wall carved by the slow shift of the crust. Short of breath and with a shrapnel wound stinging his thigh, Rawne half-fell into the nearest and lay on his face until the cold ache of the ice made him roll over. It abruptly seemed breathlessly hot in the cave. Rawne realised that it was because he was suddenly shielded from the slicing wind. Though only a few degrees above zero in the ice cave, out of the wind it felt almost tropical in there. He pulled off his cloak and his gloves and, after a moment, his insulated vest too. He shuddered, damp and too hot, sweat built up under his insulating garments trickling like sauna moisture off his back.

He checked his leg. There was a hole in his fatigues at mid-thigh and it looked like he had been burnt by a melta. Then he realised the blood had not clotted on the flesh wound. It had frozen. He snapped the black ice off his flesh and, wincing as the action pinched, looked at the oozing wet gash in his leg.

Not for the first time in his military career and certainly not for the last, he cursed the name of Ibram Gaunt.

Rawne reached for his medi-pouch and pulled it open. He took the flesh clamps out and worked with them as the medic, Dorden, had instructed them all during Foundation Training. But the wire clamps were frozen and his numb fingers managed little more than to ping them off across the floor instead of opening them.

It took him an age to extract a needle from the sterile paper packets. He dropped four or five before he grasped one, and then set it between his teeth as he tried to find the loose end of the surgical thread.

Finally, it was pinched between unfeeling fingers. He took the needle and tried to thread it. He'd have had more chance making a bull's-eye on a target ten kilometres away with a wrong-sighted lasgun. After twenty attempts, he put the needle back between his teeth and tried to twist together the now frayed ends of the thread.

Something hit him hard from behind, smashing him head first into the snow floor.

He lay on his face, fazed, slowly becoming aware of the snorting and sniffling behind him. His tongue hurt and his mouth was full of blood which drooled out and frosted down into the ice. A big shape was moving behind him.

He turned his head slowly and dared to take a look. Circumspect, sidelong, as one might do into a mirror whilst shaving.

The ork was nearly three metres tall and almost as wide. Impossibly large muscles corded its shoulders and arms and stinking furs swaddled its bulk. Its head was huge, twice the size of a human's, thrust forward and seated on the vast lower jaw. Blackened teeth stuck like chisel blades out of the rotten gums. He couldn't see the eyes. He could smell the reeking breath, the corrosive saliva that spattered and dripped from the half-open mouth.

Playing dead, he watched as it toyed with his medi-pouch, rooting through the contents with hands big enough to break a human throat like a twig. It took out a roll of gauze and bit it, munching and then spitting out.

It's hungry, thought Rawne, and his guts iced and tightened at the idea.

Suddenly, it moved to him, pulling him up by the hair and jerking him back like a puppet, rummaging in his clothing with the other hand for food pouches, rations, munitions.

Blood spilled out of Rawne's jerked-open mouth, spattering down his chest. He tried to remain limp, but his left hand crept down towards the knife sheathed at his waist. The huge ork jerked and twisted him like a sack of bones, sniffing and gurgling behind his ear, hot breath on Rawne's neck, rancid smell in his nose.

Rawne found his knife and slid it out. He must have tensed doing so because the ork froze and then muttered something in its arcane tongue. Rawne moved to swing his knife, but the ork's huge paw was suddenly around his blade-hand, crushing it and slamming it into the icy wall beside them. Two slams and Rawne's hand gave up. The Tanith dagger whipped away.

The ork roared, a guttural bellow that deafened Rawne and shook his diaphragm. Holding him from behind, it bear-hugged, pulling its arms apart, determined to rip his torso in two. Rawne screamed, fighting futilely at the greater strength, tearing his arms free. He was dead, he knew that. Death was a moment away.

Pain made him reach into his mouth, to pull at whatever throbbed in his tongue. He found the end of the surgical needle, protruding from the flesh of his tongue. He yanked it out. A shockingly long spurt of blood followed it. Then he stabbed back behind his head with the little sliver of metal.

The ork screamed and dropped him. Rawne landed, spitting and coughing blood from his pulsing tongue. The ork was flailing around the cave wildly, holding one eye that dribbled with clear fluid and stained ichor. The noise of its rage was deafening in the ice-hole.

Rawne scrambled for a weapon, but the ork turned and sent him flying across the cave with a flat backhand. Rawne hit the ice wall hard with his shoulders, upside down and horizontal. His shoulder blade cracked and he dropped to the floor.

The ork charged him, one eye half-closed and oozing around the stub-eye of the surgical needle impaling it. Rawne rolled. His lasgun was on the far side of the cave, but his knife was in reach.

His knife. How many fights had he won with that? How many throats had he cut, how many hearts had he burst, how many stomachs had he opened?

He reached it, grasped it, turned in a low crouch to meet the attacker, a gleeful look on his face.

The ork faced him, its back to the cave mouth, a huge, crude bolt-pistol in its ichor-spattered fist.

The ork spoke, slow, rumbling, alien. Rawne didn't know what it said, but he knew what it meant.

There was a blinding flash and the roar of a weapon loosed in the confines of the cave.

Rawne had always wondered what it would feel like to take the killing hit. To be shot mortally. To die. But there was no feeling. No sense. In the blink of an eye, he saw the ork explode, its mid-section disintegrating in a burst of light.

It fell, almost in two parts. Its body fluids froze as it flopped to the ground.

There was a tall figure in the care entrance, blocking the light.

'Major Rawne?'

Ibram Gaunt entered the cave and holstered his bolt pistol.

It seemed that the commissar had fared no better than him. The ork warband had decided to take advantage of the chaos of the crusade's push to seize Typhon as part of its attempt to build a raiding foothold into the Sabbat Worlds. Charged with destroying the menace, the Ghosts had deployed into the long gorges and ice-floes of the moon and come undone. As Rawne's platoon had been cut down along the eastern edge of the screaming valley, so Gaunt's had to the west. In retreat, the greenskins had proved the more determined adversaries.

The commissar and the major crouched down in the ice cave together. Rawne had made no sign of gratitude. In many ways he knew he would rather be dead than remain beholden to the off-worlder.

'How's your tongue?' Gaunt asked, getting a fire lit with chemical blocks.

'Why?'

'You're not saying much.'

Rawne spat. 'It's fine. A clean wound with a sharp instrument.' Truth was, his swollen tongue felt like a bedroll in his mouth, but he would not let the commissar have the satisfaction of knowing his discomfort. But he could not disguise the pain his leg gave him.

'Let me see to that,' Gaunt said.

Rawne shook his head.

'That was an order,' Gaunt sighed.

He moved over, pulling his own medi-pouch open. His clips were frozen too, but he warmed them over the chemical flame and then pinched the lips of Rawne's thigh wound shut. He sprayed the area with antiseptic from the one-use flask. Rawne felt his limb go dead.

Then Gaunt warmed his numb fingers and threaded surgical cord into a fresh needle. He handed Rawne his dagger. 'Bite the hilt.'

Rawne did so and stayed silent as Gaunt sewed the torn flesh together. Gaunt bit off the cord and tied it, wrapping a dressing over the wound. Rawne spat the dagger out.

Gaunt packed the kit away and then settled a kettle pan over the flames, dropping a scoop of ice into it.

'Seems to me Typhon has levelled us, major,' he said after a while.

'How so?'

'The high-born commissar, with all his airs and graces and rank, his schola training and his expertise; the low-life Tanith gangster with his wiles and tricks and diversions – it's put us on a level. Equals. Both fighting the same hostility with the same chances.'

Rawne didn't manage his retort. His tongue was too swollen and sore. He managed to spit again.

Gaunt smiled and watched the ice-water boil in the pan.

'Good. Maybe not. If you can still spit at me and hold me in contempt, we're not equal. I can lower myself down towards your level to help you... Feth, save you. But the day we're both on a level, your level, I'll kill myself.'

'Is that a promise?' Rawne asked.

Gaunt laughed. He dropped some dehydrated food cubes into the bubbling pan and stirred them. Dry-powdered bean soup puffed and formed. He was still laughing as he poured the soup into two tin cups.

The wind rose as night fell. It howled outside the mouth of the cave, raising the volume and intensity of the screaming. They sat together in the dark, watching the fire. There were only four fuel-blocks left to feed the blaze and Gaunt was being careful.

'You want to know some other differences between us, Rawne?'

Rawne wanted to say 'No', but his tongue was now too swollen and useless. He spat at Gaunt again instead.

Gaunt smiled and nodded down at the spittle freezing on the ice.

'There's one: this place might be a ball of frozen moisture, but you won't see me going around losing body moisture like that. The wind will freeze you dry in a few hours. Conserve your body water. Stop spitting at me and you might live.'

He held out a bowl of tepid water to Rawne and after a moment, the major took it and drank.

'Here's another. It's warm in here. Warmer than outside. But it's still close to zero. You're half-stripped and you're shivering.'

Gaunt was still dressed in his full uniform and his cloak was pulled around him. Rawne realised how numb he had become and began to pull his vest and cloak around him again.

'Why?' the major asked thickly.

'Why? Because I know... I've fought through cold zones before.'

'Not that... why? Why would you want to keep me alive?'

Gaunt was silent for a while.

'Good question...' he said at last. 'Given that you'd like nothing better than to see me dead. But I'm a commissar of the Imperial Guard, charged by the Emperor to keep his fighting legions able and intact in the face of battle. I won't let you die. That's my job. That's why I saved you here, that's why I saved the Tanith from the destruction of their world.'

There was a long silence, broken only by the crackling chemical bricks of the fire.

'You know I'll never see it that way,' Rawne said, his voice cold and small. 'You left Tanith to die. You didn't let us stand and fight. I will never forgive you that.'

Gaunt nodded. 'I know.' Then, after a moment, 'I wish it wasn't so.'

Rawne rolled himself up into a cleft of the ice cave and pulled the cloak around him. He felt only one thing. Hate.

* * *

Somehow, somewhen, dawn had come up. Thin, frail light poked into the cave.

Gaunt was asleep, huddled down under his cloak, covered in frost. Rawne slowly got to his feet, fighting the ache in his bones and the almighty cold. The fire had long since gone out.

He edged around the cave, staring down at Gaunt. Pain ebbed through his sewn leg, his shoulders, his mouth. The pain cleared the fuzziness of his head and made him sharp. He picked up his Tanith knife, wiped the frost from it, and knelt to place its blade against Gaunt's throat.

No one would know. No one would ever find the body. And even if they did...

Gaunt shuddered in his sleep. He spoke the name of Tanith twice as his eyelids rolled and flicked. Then he spoke, curling up on himself: 'Won't let them die! No, not all of them! In the name of the Emperor, Sym!'

Then his voice died away into mumbling. Rawne's hand tensed on the knife. He hesitated.

Gaunt spoke again, his dreaming voice a low monotone. 'No, no, no, no... it's burning... burning... I would never... I would never....'

'Never what?' Rawne hissed, about to pull the dagger up in a quick killing slice.

'Tanith... In the name of the Emperor...'

Rawne twisted where he crouched. He pulled the dagger up, not in a killing slice but in an arc that threw it across at the mouth of the cave and impaled the throat of the ork creeping inside towards them.

As it fell back, gurgling, Rawne heard raucous baying from outside. He kicked Gaunt in the ribs to rouse him and swung up his lasgun, firing wildly at the cave mouth.

'They're on us, Gaunt, you bastard!' he screamed. 'They're on us!'

Eight fierce, wordless minutes, weapons spitting and cracking in their hands. Gaunt roused from deep, troubled sleep to combat readiness with the speed of long experience. Six orks had come right up to the mouth of the cave, and without cover could do little but shoot and die. Caught in the mouth of the cave, the two Imperial soldiers had better cover and the advantage of the slope. Huge carcasses fell and slid, smoking down the crimson ice.

Rawne dropped the last of them and turned to find Gaunt scanning the valley floor with his scope.

'We can't stay here,' the commissar said. 'That exchange will bring them from all around.

'We have cover here,' Rawne argued.

Gaunt kicked the ice at the cave mouth. 'All we have is a tomb. Get enough of them around to pen us in and they'll bring the ice-cliff down and bury us. We have to move. And fast.'

They ditched bed rolls and anything else it would take too long to repack. Gaunt prioritised ammo, food, Rawne's small satchel of tube-charges, their cold weather gear. In less than a minute they were fleeing down the slope outside, cloaks flying, into the dawn chill.

Twelve kilometres away, the steep angles of the rising sun lit the far wall of the valley, but they were in twilight here, a frosty darkness in which the scarlet ice around them glowed and shone like marble. Or meat in a butcher's shop. Distantly, the crump of weapons fire. They hugged the valley wall, using ice rocks as cover as the wind wailed and agonised around them.

A kilometre or so from the cave, they rested, sweating in their insulated fabrics, crouched down in the cover of a block splinter fallen from high above.

Rawne wiped the ork blood off his knife and cut a hank of cloth from the edge of his stealth cape. He'd lost a glove somewhere, and his hand was aching and raw with the cold. He bound the cloth around his hand, tying it tight like a mitten.

Gaunt touched his shoulder and pointed back the way they had come. Lights, big gleaming lamps, bobbed and bounced along the valley floor: vehicles. The wind was too loud to make out engine notes.

'Come on,' said Gaunt.

From shelter, a scoop cut in the ice floor, they watched the vehicles pass five hundred metres away. Four big ork machines, black and pumping blacker smoke from crude combustion engines. Thick-treaded tyres with chains gave the front end of the machines traction, and the rear sections were carried on sled runners or tracks. Each vehicle carried at least two other warriors beside the driver, and hefty weapons on pintle or turret mounts. They howled past, spraying up sheets of ice particles, close enough for the men to see the tribal markings on the battered flanks of the machines and smell the stink of their burning oil.

Once they had passed, Gaunt made to continue, but Rawne pulled him back.

'They know how fast we can run,' he said. Sure enough, a roar reached them over the howling wind a minute or so later and the vehicles sped back past they way they had come, searching back over the ground to see what they had missed. One pulled away west and two more raced onwards. The fourth curved around in a spray of ice and moved towards them to search along the wall of the valley.

They were trapped. They could not run because there was nowhere to run to without exposing themselves to the orks if they rose from the scoop. Huddled low, they watched.

The ork half-sled slowed and one of the burly warriors jumped down, running alongside the vehicle, firing into caves along the valley wall. The other warrior traversed the heavy weapon of the trundling vehicle from side to side. Closer...

Gaunt turned to Rawne and nodded to his lasgun. 'More range, better sight. Take the weapon's operator.'

'Not the driver?'

'If his gunner's dead, all he can do is drive. If he dies, the gunner can still fire. Target the gunner... and when you've got him, re-aim on the foot soldier.'

Rawne nodded and breathed hard on his sight to warm the lens. He clicked in a fresh energy clip as quietly as he could. Though the wind was screaming, the hard metal clack would carry like a shot.

He saw Gaunt carefully doing the same with the sickle-pattern magazine of his bolt-pistol.

The motor sled turned their way, its harsh lights catching the lip of their ice scoop, making the scarlet ice translucent and all the more like fresh meat. Rawne took his aim. He knew he was no marksman like Larkin or Elgith, but he was passable. Even so, he let the sled slip closer in before he felt confident of a shot. His only target, the silhouette of the vehicle behind the lights. Closer... almost on them.

Rawne fired.

His blazing shot hit the black shape behind the lights. There was a double flash and then a series of loud, fierce explosions, like gunshots. The sled veered sideways, bumping to a halt. Rawne realised they had been gunshots. He had hit the gunner squarely, but his shot had passed through the weapon mount on the way, exploding the heavy bolter and igniting the ammo drum. The gunner's smoking corpse hung from the burning weapon and, even as they watched, stray rounds super-heated and went off like fireworks. The driver was also dead, the back of his skull and neck riddled with shrapnel from the exploding ammo.

Gaunt and Rawne leaped up out of the scoop and ran towards the motorised sled. The ork left on foot was running their way, firing from the hip. Bolt rounds whizzed and sang around them, fizzling into the ice. Yelling as he charged the advancing ork, Rawne fired on full auto, his lasgun bucking as he carried it low against his side. Two laser shots spun the monstrous ork off his feet and dropped him on the ice, where he lay twitching.

Gaunt reached the sled, screwing up his nose at the smell of burning flesh. The gun and the gunner were still burning, but fire had not spread to the rest of the machine. He stepped forward, but darted back as another round went up. Then it was quiet.

He leaped up onto the tail-boards and put a point-blank round through the gunner's back, though he was sure the ork was dead. He had heard too many tales of the greenskin resilience to injury. Gaunt pitched the cadaver off the platform onto the ice, then grabbed hold of the smouldering, ruined weapon. There was a handle release to free the gun and its drums from the mount. He heaved on it, his hands slipping in thick grease. No human strength had tightened this latch. He put his weight behind it, cursing and grunting, expecting another round to explode in his face at any moment.

The latch gave. With a gasp, and an effort that tore ligaments in his back and arms, he hefted the entire gun and ammo carriage off the metal bars of the mount frame and tipped it over off the vehicle. As it landed, three more rounds went off, one scudding across the surface of the ice in slithering jags like a phosphorescent sprite.

Gaunt's gloves had caught fire from the red-hot metal and he jerked them off, throwing them aside. He clambered forward onto the driver's position and tried to pull the driver's body out of the cockpit. Nearly four hundred kilos of dead weight refused to budge.

He looked back at Rawne, in time to see him finishing the fallen footsoldier with his blade. Gaunt yelled him over, his voice lost in the keening wind.

Together they pried the driver's corpse free and flopped it into the ice. It had already begun to freeze and fell like a sack of rocks. Gaunt got into the cockpit, felt the space roomy and too big for a human operator. It stank of sweat and blood in the enclosed cabin. He tested the handlebar grips and found the foot pedals. His first tries at control revved the engine to a scream and then braked the sled in a jolt that threw the cursing Rawne onto his back in the troop bay behind him. Then he had the measure of it. It was a crude version of the landcars he had driven with his father back home, years ago. There was a foot throttle and also a foot brake, though that did little but dig a massive spike down from the underside into the ice to retard motion. The anchor would only work in conjunction with de-throttling. With the engine racing, the spike would shatter and pull the guts out from under the motor sled. The gears, three of them, were set by a twist on the left handlebar grip. There were gauges on the crude dash calibrated in greenskin script which he couldn't read or understand, but he began to measure the way the juddering needles spiked and dipped.

'Hold on, major!' he warned and raced them off towards the distant end of the valley. Rawne, in the back, clung on tight, the wind whipping his face and neck.

Gaunt focussed all his will into control. The massive machine bucked and jinked on every irregularity in the ice, but Gaunt quickly came to judge the way ahead, and knew what conditions would skid them round, or slide them, or make them spin treads. There was no power assist to the steering, and he fought it. It was beyond his strength to keep the steering true and he realised that he would never be able to drive the machine as fast as the stronger orks could. It fought too much and his strength was human, not inhuman.

They rocked and bumped and jolted. More than once, they spun out as he failed to keep the drive wheels true and the back end came around in a flurry of ice shards. After the last such lapse, the raging engine stalled and refused to restart. There was a starter switch under the steering column, but it flopped slackly.

Gaunt peered down and found the kick start stirrup to the left of the brake. He bent and flopped it down, trying it with his boot.

'Gaunt!'

He looked up. Rawne was standing on the flatbed, pointing back. A kilometre away, three dark shapes were kicking up ice-smoke as they raced after them. The orks, with their superior strength and experience of the snow machines, were making better speed in their pursuit.

Gaunt kicked viciously at the starter bar time and again until the engine yowled alive, and then hastily adjusted the protesting throttle.

They spun again, fishtailed, then chugged away. Gaunt pushed the machine as fast as he thought he could control it. Another misread flaw in the ice, another spin out, another stall, and they would be overrun. Or overturned, necks snapped under the rolling tonnage of the motor sled.

They came out of the night shadows of the valley onto the wide expanse of the ice floe. Sunlight seared them and Gaunt and Rawne were blind for a moment, even after they pulled their glare goggles down.

Ahead was the ice sea. White, scarlet, purple, green in patches, the ice was scalloped and curled like foam. Thousands of kilometres of open, frozen sea, spread out to a horizon where it met the blackness of space. The sunlight was a hostile white menace.

The sea and all its waves had frozen as if in mid-ebb, and now the sled bounced and flew, rose and fell, across the dimpled peaks of breakers that had frozen a millennium before. The motor sled over-revved each time it left the ground and kicked ice chunks each time it landed. Gaunt could barely control the machine as the drive wheels and slithering skids kissed ice again. Rawne had thought about firing back at the ork machines closing on them, but the bumpy ride had thrown him to the greasy deck and it was all he could do to cling on and lie flat. Face to the metal deck-boarding, he saw the punctures for the first time. Shrapnel holes, from the exploding bolter drums. There was a stink of oil rising from them. He crawled, hand over hand, to the tail gate as the sled jumped and crashed, and saw a staining line of brown marking their wake.

He turned and yelled. 'We're bleeding fuel! The tank is punctured!'

Gaunt cursed. Now he understood what one of the gauges – the one with the rapidly dipping needle – really meant.

The ork pursuit was closing. Heavy bolter-rounds and other explosive munitions rained down around them, blowing geysers of ice and steam up from the frozen sea.

Gaunt realised his naked, glove-less hands were beginning to freeze solid around the steering grips. The pain brought tears to his eyes, tears which froze behind his goggles and blurred his vision, biting his cheeks.

Two over-shot projectiles from the orks brought bigger explosions to the left of them. Sprays of glutinous, boiling liquid erupted far into the air from their impacts. Gaunt saw that the rushing landscape ahead of them was duller blue, more like frosted glass, cracked and crazed.

They made the next rise. Then the engine coughed, spluttered, died. They slid sideways in a long, wide deceleration, ice gouged up by Gaunt's desperate use of the anchor. He kicked the starter. The engine flared once, then died forever in a cough of stinking oil smoke. Dry rotors and cylinders burst and ground.

The ork machines were a hundred metres behind them. They could hear them whooping in victory. For the first time, Rawne realised that the wind was no longer screaming now they were out of the valley.

Gaunt clambered out of the cockpit. 'Tube-charges, Rawne!' he bawled.

'What?'

Gaunt pointed to where other wide shots from their pursuers dug steaming vents from the glassy ice.

'The ice is thin here. We're riding over a thin skin. The living ocean is right below us.'

Another shot whinnied down and exploded the steering section of the sled where Gaunt had just been sitting.

'Now!'

Rawne understood the commissar's idea just as suddenly as he recognised the insanity of it. But the orks were only fifty paces away. Rawne realised the desperation too.

He had twelve stick mines in his satchel and he pulled them all out, handing half to Gaunt. He kicked the glass off one of the vehicle's lamps and used the white-hot filament to light the fuses. The two humans took three in each hand and hurled them as far and as hard as they could, scattering them wide.

Twelve huge explosions, each big enough to kill a tank. They split the world apart. But more particularly, they burst and shattered the ice. The steaming hydrocarbon sea, so close beneath, rushed up to plume and boil and froth in the air.

One ork machine cartwheeled, an explosion taking it over. It tore itself and its occupants into fragments as it landed on ice that was beginning to separate and fracture in huge bobbing sections. Another dodged the rain of blasts and flew straight off the edge of an ice chunk into the sea, where it vaporised and burned. The last stopped short, the riders bellowing, just missing a gap in the ice. Then the ice chunk it sat on collapsed and they all dropped shrieking into the frothing, flaming liquid.

The ice was coming apart, fracturing into chunks that burned and steamed as the rising ocean, locked in for so many thousands of years, welled up and conquered the surface. On the back of their dead machine, Gaunt and Rawne leapt and yelled in triumph until they realised the ice collapse was spreading their way fast.

The ocean fizzed and thrashed up around their sled runners and the motor-sled dipped suddenly. Gaunt jumped clear onto a nearby iceberg, newly formed and sizzling in the hideous liquid.

He held out his hand. Rawne jumped after him, grabbing Gaunt's hand, allowing himself to be pulled clear as their ruined machine slid backwards into the liquid and exploded.

'We can't stay here,' Gaunt began. It was true. Their iceberg was rocking and dissolving like an ice cube in hot water. They leapt off it to the next, and then the next, hoping that the fractured sections of ice would remain intact long enough for them to reach some kind of shore. Vapours gasped and billowed around them.

On the fourth, Rawne slipped and Gaunt caught him just centimetres from the frothing water.

They made the next floe and Rawne moved ahead. He heard a cry behind him and turned to see the ice plate upending and Gaunt sliding backwards on his belly, clawing the surface as he slipped down towards the seething ocean of hydrocarbons.

He could let him die. Rawne knew that. No one would know. No one would ever find the body. And even if they did... Besides, he couldn't reach him.

Rawne pulled out his knife and hurled it. It stuck fast, blade down, in the tilting ice just above Gaunt's hand and gave the commissar a grip. Gaunt pulled himself up on the dagger and then got his foot braced on it until he could reach up and take Rawne's hand. The major hauled him up high enough for the pair to make a safe jump to the next berg. This was larger, more solid. They clung to it, side by side, panting and out of strength.

The ice chunk behind them fell back into the ocean, taking Rawne's silver dagger with it.

They sat together on top of the iceberg for six hours. Around them, the ocean refroze and its seething hiss died away. But they could go nowhere. The reforming ice skin was but a few centimetres thick – thick enough to enclose the lethal liquid but not so hard as to bear weight. The distress beacon from Gaunt's pack blinked and sighed behind them on the top of the ice chunk.

'I owe you,' Gaunt said at last.

Rawne shook his head. 'I don't want that.'

'You pulled me up there. Saved me. I owe you for that. And frankly, I'm surprised. I know you'd like to see me dead and this was an opportunity that spared your hands from blood.'

Rawne turned to look at Gaunt, his face half-lit by the dwindling starlight. His cheeks and chin seemed to catch the light more like a dagger now than ever before. And his eyes were hooded like a snake's.

'One day, I will kill you, Gaunt,' he said simply. 'I owe it to Tanith. To myself. But I'm no murderer and I respect honour. You saved me from that greenskin in the cave and so I owed you.'

'I would do as much for any man in my command.'

'Precisely. You may think I'm a malcontent, but I stay loyal to the Emperor and the Guard always. I owed you and, though I hate myself for it, I repaid. Now we're even.'

'Even,' Gaunt murmured, measuring the word softly in his mouth. 'Or level, perhaps.'

Rawne smiled. 'The day will come, Ibram Gaunt. But it will be on equal terms. *Level* terms, as you put it. I will kill you, and I will rejoice in it. But now is not the time.'

'Thank you for being so forthright, Rawne.' Gaunt pulled out his Tanith knife, the knife given to him by Corbec when they first mustered for war.

Rawne tensed, jerking back. But Gaunt held it out to him, hilt first.

'You lost yours. I know any Tanith would be incomplete without a long blade at his hip.'

Rawne took the knife. He held it in his hands for a second, spun it with deft fingers, and then slid it into his empty belt sheath.

'Do with it as you see fit,' Gaunt said, turning his back on Rawne.

'I will... one of these days,' replied Major Elim Rawne.

The Infirmary lay well back from the main embankment defence here on Monthax. Like Gaunt's modular hut, it was raised out of the soupy ground on stacks. Long, swoop-roofed, the Infirmary's wall planking was washed an arsenic green, while the roof was black with bitumen. Grey blast-curtains protected the doors and window hatches, and bunches of pipes and cables carried in air from the scrubbers and power from the chattering turbine behind the place. Symbols of the Imperium, and of the medical corps, were stencilled on the walls, for all that Chaos would notice them if they stormed over the bulwark. Gaunt climbed up a metal ladder next to the rush-ramp for stretcher parties, and pushed inside through the screens and heavy curtaining.

Inside he found a paradise and a surprise. It was by far the coolest and most fragrant place in the camp, probably the coolest, most fragrant place on Monthax itself. Sweet odours of sap rose from the fresh timber of the floor and the clean rush matting. There was a scent of antiseptic fluids, rubbing alcohol and some purifying incense that burned in a bowl next to the small shrine set near the western end. The forty beds were made up and empty. Pale, artificial light shone from gauze hooded lamps.

Gaunt wandered the length of the ward and let himself through a screen door at the end. There, access led off into storerooms, latrines, a small operating theatre, and the Chief Medical Officer's quarters. Dorden wasn't in his little, tidy office, but Gaunt saw his distinctive handiwork in the careful arrangement of medical texts, chart folders, and the labels-front regimentation of the flasks and bottles in the locked dispensary cabinet.

The medic was in the operating theatre, polishing the stainless-steel surface and blood drains of the theatre table. Gleaming surgical tools, an autoclave and a resussitrex unit sat in corners.

'Commissar Gaunt!' Dorden looked up in surprise. 'Can I help you?'

'As you were. Just a routine walkabout. Anything to report, any problems?'

Dorden stood up straight, balling the polishing cloth in his hands and dropping it into a ceramic bowl of disinfectant. 'Not one, sir. Come to inspect the place?'

'Certainly an improvement on the last few facilities you've had to work with.'

Dorden smiled. He was a small, elderly man with a trimmed grey beard and genial eyes that had seen more pain than they deserved. 'It's empty yet.'

'I admit that surprised me when I came in. So used to seeing your places overflowing with wounded, Emperor spare us.'

'Give it time,' Dorden said, ominously. 'It unnerves me, I have to say. Seeing all those empty beds. I praise the Golden Throne I'm idle, but idleness doesn't suit me. Must've polished and swept the place a dozen times already.'

'If that's the worst work you have here on Monthax, we may all give thanks.'

'May we all indeed. Can I offer a cup of caffeine? I was about to light the stove.'

'Perhaps later, when I come back this way. I have to inspect the magazines. There are stirrings beyond us.'

'So I heard last night. Later then, sir.'

Gaunt nodded and left. He doubted he'd have time to stop by later, and he doubted too that this little paradise would remain unsullied much longer.

Dorden watched the commissar leave, and stood for a while longer surveying the clean ward with its empty cots. Like Gaunt, he had no illusions as to the horror-hole this place would become. It was inevitable.

He closed his eyes, and for a moment he could see the floor matting drenched in black blood; the soiled sheets; the moaning, screaming faces. And the silent ones.

His nostrils seemed to detect blood and burned flesh for a second, but it was just the incense.

Just the incense.

EIGHT

BLOOD OATH

The fallen men, scattered on the roadway and across the low, muddy fields of Nacedon, looked like they were wearing black mail armour. But they weren't. The meat-flies were busy. They covered the flesh like seething black links of armour. They glittered furiously, moving like a single thing.

'Medic!'

Tolin Dorden looked away from the flies. The afternoon sky lay wide and misty over the low, flat fens. Trackways and field boundaries were marked with dykes and hedge ways, all of them ruined and overrun with razor-posts, concertina wire and churned tank paths. The mist smelled of thermite powder.

'Medic!' The call again. Sharp and insistent, from down the roadway. Slowly, Dorden turned and trudged from the gutter of the road where, for a hundred metres, more corpses lay twisted and crumpled and coated in flies.

He advanced towards the buildings. Feth, but he'd seen enough of this war now, no matter what the world. He was tired and he was spent. Sixty years old, older by twenty years than any of the other Ghosts. He was weary: weary of the death, the fighting, weary of the young bodies he had to patch back together. Weary, too, of being regarded as a father by so many men who had lost their own at the fall of Tanith.

Smoke clogged the late afternoon sky across the low fields. He approached the old red-brick buildings with their blown-out windows and crumpled walls. It had been a farm complex once, before the invasion. A feudal estate with a main house, outbuildings and barns. Agricultural machinery lay rusting and broken in waterlogged swine pens. A wide trench gully and a double fence of seared flak-boards topped with more spools of wire enclosed the complex in a horseshoe, with the northern side, the one that faced away from the frontline, open. Ghosts stood point all around, weapons ready. Trooper Brostin nodded him inside.

Dorden passed a sandbagged gunnery post from which the weapon had been hastily removed and entered the first of the buildings, the main house, through a doorway that had been shot out of the brick by sustained las-fire. More flies, billowing in clouds in the afternoon sunlight. The smell of death he was so, so used to. And other smells: antiseptic, blood, waste.

Dorden stepped across a tiled floor. Half the tiles were broken, littered with glass and pools of oil that shimmered rainbow colours. Corbec loomed out of the shadows nearby, shaking his weary head. 'Doc,' he acknowledged.

'Colonel.'

'Field hospital...' Corbec said, gesturing around himself. Dorden already knew as much.

'Anyone alive?'

'That's why I called for you.'

Corbec led him through to a vaulted hallway. The various stenches were stronger in here. Perhaps five dozen men lay on pallet beds in the chamber, half-lit by pallid yellow sunlight that streaked down through shattered lights in the sloping roof. Dorden walked the length of the room and then back.

'Why have they been left here?' he asked.

Corbec shot him a questioning look. 'Why do you think? We're all retreating. Too much to carry. Can you... sort them?'

Dorden cursed quietly. 'These men are what?'

'Bluebloods. Volpone 50th. You remember those devils from Volte-mand? Their command units pulled out this morning, as per orders.'

'And they left the wounded here?'

Corbec shrugged. 'Seems so, Doc.'

'What kind of animal leaves his sick and wounded behind to die?' Dorden spat, moving to change the dressings on the nearest man.

'The human kind?' Corbec asked.

Dorden looked round sharply. 'This isn't funny, Corbec. It's not even whimsical. Most of these men will live with the proper attention. We're not leaving them.'

Corbec groaned softly. He rubbed the top of his scalp, folding the thick black hair between his big, swarthy fingers. 'We can't stay here, Doc. Commissar's orders...'

Dorden turned and looked at the colonel with fierce, old eyes. 'I'm not leaving them,' he stated plainly. Corbec seemed to start to say something, then hesitated and decided better of it. 'See what you can do for them,' he said, and left Dorden to his work.

Dorden was treating a leg wound when he heard the crunch of gravel on the roadway outside and the rumble of a troop carrier. He looked up to locate the source of the sound only after he had finished what he was doing.

'Thank you, sir,' said the young man whose leg he had treated. The boy was pale and sallow, too weak to rise from his pallet bed.

'What's your name?' Dorden asked.

'Culcis, sir. Trooper, Blueblood.' Dorden was sure that Culcis would have wanted to punctuate that statement with an exclamation mark, but he was too weak to manage it.

'I'm Dorden. Medic. Tanith. You need me, Trooper Culcis, you call my name.'

The boy nodded. Dorden went outside, approaching the Chimera parked below the leaning walls. Corbec was speaking to the tall figure perched on top.

The figure moved, dropped down to the soil, began to march towards him: Gaunt, his cap on, his face a shadow, his long coat flying.

'Sir!' Dorden said.

'Dorden – Corbec says you won't move.'

'Sixty-eight wounded here, sir. Can't leave them; won't leave them.'

Gaunt took Dorden's arm and led him across the muddy yard to the side wall that looked out across trampled farmland and vacant swine pens towards the setting suns beyond.

'You must, Dorden. Enemy forces are half a day behind us. General Muller has called us all to retreat. We can't carry them with us. I'm sorry.'

Dorden shook off the commissar's grip. 'So am I,' he said.

Gaunt turned away. For a moment, Dorden thought the commissar might round on him and discipline him with a fist. But he didn't. Instead, the man sighed. On reflection, Dorden knew violence wasn't Gaunt's first or chosen way of command. The endless war and his experience of other officer cadres in the field had soured Dorden's expectation, something he wasn't proud of.

Gaunt looked back at the medic. 'Corbec told me you'd say as much. Look, the counter-push for Nacedon is scheduled for tomorrow night. Then, and only then, Emperor willing, we'll retake this land and drive the enemy back.'

'Few of them will last the night and day unattended. And none if they are found and attended by the Chaos filth!'

Gaunt took off his cap and smoothed his cropped blond hair. The dying suns-light silhouetted his angular profile, but kept his internal thoughts in shadow. 'You have my respect, medic. You've always had it, since the Founding Fields even. The only Ghost who refuses to bear arms, the only man who can keep us alive. The Ghosts owe you, many of them owe you their lives. I owe you for that. I'd hate to have to give you an order.'

'Then don't, commissar. You know I'll refuse it. I'm a medic first and a Ghost second. Back on Tanith, as a community practitioner, I worked for thirty years ministering to the sick, the infirm, the new-born and the weak in the Beldane District and County Pryze. I did it because I took an oath at the Medical College in Tanith Magna. You understand allegiances and oaths, commissar. Understand mine.'

'I understand the weight of the medical oath well enough.'

'And you've honoured it! Never asked me to break my vow on confidentiality over men with private problems... drink, pox, mind-troubles... you've always let me do as my oath bids. Let me now.'

Gaunt replaced his cap. 'I can't leave you here to die.'

'But you'd leave these men to die?'

'They're not the Ghosts' chief medic!' Gaunt spat the answer and then fell silent.

'A doctor is vowed to serve any injured. Oh, I swore to the Emperor, on the Founding Fields, to serve him and you and the Imperial Guard. But I'd already sworn to the Emperor to uphold life. Don't make me break that vow.'

Gaunt tried logic. 'Our illustrious forces were routed on the delta at Lohenich. We are fleeing before a massed Chaos army that thunders at our heels, barely half a day away. You're a non-combatant. How could you hold this place?'

'With words, if I have to. With volunteers, if any will stay and you'll allow it. After all, it's only until tomorrow night. Until your counter-push retakes this place. Or was that a lie? Propaganda?'

Gaunt said nothing for a while, tilting his tall bulk into the evening suns, adjusting his muddy coat. Then he turned back to the old medic.

'No lie. We will retake this land, and beyond. We will drive them back as they come to us. But to leave you out here, even for a night...'

'Don't think of me. Think of the Volpone wounded in there.'

Gaunt did. It didn't change his mind much. 'They would have had us butchered–'

'Don't go to that place!' Dorden warned. 'Hate has no place between allies. These are men, Troopers, valuable soldiers. They could live to fight again, to turn another conflict for the better. Leave me to care for them, with whoever you can spare. Leave me, and come back for us all.'

Gaunt cursed. 'I'll give you a squad. I can spare no more. Ten men, volunteers. If it doesn't come to ten, tough. Muller will have my head for leaving any in the field as it is.'

'I'll take whatever I can get,' Dorden said. 'Thank you.'

Gaunt strode away abruptly, then turned, came back and took Dorden's hand tightly in his own.

'You're a brave man. Don't let them take you alive... and don't make me regret allowing you to be too brave.'

Gaunt and the retreating lines of Ghosts passed on and then they were alone. Dorden was working in the long hall, and only noticed the passing of time as the sunshine through the skylights faded to blue and dusk fell. He lit lamps on crates placed between the wounded and went outside into the yard. Overhead, alien stars were coming out in the mauve sky.

He saw three Ghosts at first: Lesp, Chayker and Foskin, who acted as his orderlies and were skilled field medics. They were sorting through the medical supplies Gaunt had left for them. Dorden had half-expected them to volunteer and stay, hoped for it, but to see his three staffers working as usual was refreshing and uplifting. He crossed to them, meaning to carry on as normal and ask about the supply level, but all he found in his throat was thanks. Each one smiled, took his hand as he offered it, grunted an acknowledgement of duty. Dorden was proud of them.

He started to give them dispersal instructions, and began to run through the needs of the sick in priority order, when other Ghosts stepped into view: Mkoll, the chief scout and Dorden's closest friend in the unit, accompanied by Troopers Brostin, Claig, Caffran and Gutes. They had just finished a patrol sweep of the horseshoe boundary and were preparing to dig in for the night.

Dorden greeted Mkoll. 'You needn't have stayed.'

'And leave you alone here?' Mkoll laughed. 'I'll not have the records say "Medic Dorden died and where was his friend, the warrior Mkoll?" The commissar asked for volunteers and so we volunteered.'

'I'll not forget this, however short my life,' Dorden replied.

'We have the flank guarded well,' Mkoll told Dorden, indicating the double fence. 'All ten of us.'

'Ten?'

'That's what the colonel-commissar allowed. Us five, your three, and the other two. All of the Ghosts were arguing over who could stay, did you know? Everyone volunteered for the duty.'

'Everyone? Not Major Rawne, I'd bet!'

Mkoll grinned ruefully, 'All right, not everyone. But there was a scramble for places. Gaunt finally decided on first come, first served. So you got your three, me, Brostin, Claig, Caffran and Gutes. Plus Tremard, on watch at the gates. And...'

'And?'

Dorden whipped round, sensing someone was suddenly behind him. He looked up into the smiling bearded face of Colm Corbec.

'And me. So, Doc, you're in charge. How do we play this?'

Night fell. The air cleared. Distantly, carrion-dogs howled. Three or more moons rose and set, duelling with each others' orbits. The darkness was clear and cold and smelled of death. Far away, on the southern horizon, amber clouds thumped and boiled, a storm approaching. A mighty land army was moving towards them. That, and a real storm. Lightning shuddered the sky in hazes of white-flash. The air became heavy and sweet.

Inside the farmhouse, one of the Bluebloods spasmed and died. Dorden was fighting for that life, his apron-smock slick with spurting blood. There was nothing he or Lesp could do.

Dorden stepped back from the cooling corpse and handed bloodied instruments to Lesp. 'Record time and manner of death, and the name and number from the tags,' he said darkly. 'Emperor willing, we can pass it to the Volpone adjutant's office and they can adjust their records.'

Lesp snorted. 'The Bluebloods have doubtless marked all these as dead already.'

Lesp was a tall, thin man from Tanith Longshore, with cold blue eyes and an Adam's apple that looked like a knee in his slender neck. He'd been a fisherman back on the Lost Place, part of a sea-fishing family which plied the ocean currents beyond the archipelago. He owned a fierce skill with a sail-cloth and net needle, and an almost surgical knack with a blade learned from gutting fish back in those days. Dorden had put those skills to use in the name of healing when he had co-opted Lesp as an orderly. Lesp had taken to it well, and enjoyed his work alongside the chief medic.

Dorden took all the willing, able help he could get. Most of the trained medics who had founded with the Ghosts on Tanith had never made it off-world. Originally, the only fully qualified medics had been Dorden, Gherran and Mtane, with twenty other troopers trained as field medics. Dorden had interviewed and studied all of the surviving men to recruit for the badly needed medical staff. Without devoted, constantly learning amateurs like Lesp, Foskin and Chayker, the health of the regiment would have failed long ago.

Mtane and Gherran had moved on with Gaunt's main force, though both had wanted to stay. Losing all three trained medics in one rash act was more than Gaunt would tolerate.

Dorden stepped out into the muddy yard and, as if on cue, the heavens opened and sheeting rain hammered down on him, washing another's blood out of his tunic. He stood there, dripping, as the downpour eased a little.

'You'll get wet out there,' came a voice from nearby.

Dorden swung round to face Corbec, who was smoking a cigar in the cover of the slumping side-roof. All Dorden could see was the shape and the red coal of the light.

Dorden crossed to him. Corbec offered up a waxy box of smokes. 'Liquorice. Got the taste of them on Voltemand and it's taken me an age to get some on the black market. Take one for now and one for later.'

Dorden took two, slid one behind his ear unlit and lit up the other from Corbec's half-smoked stick.

They looked out into the night.

'It's going to be rough,' remarked Corbec softly.

He was looking at the flash and howl of the storm, but Dorden knew what he meant.

'Yet you stayed.'

Corbec took a deep drag and white smoke plumed out of his hairy shadow. 'I'm a sucker for good deeds.'

'Or lost causes.'

'The Emperor will provide. And aren't we all just one big lost cause? The First and Last and Lost? You don't see me giving up on that.'

Dorden smiled. The cigar was strong and the flavour hellish, but he was enjoying it. It had been twenty years since he'd smoked. His wife had never approved, said it didn't set a good example to the patients Dorden tended to.

Then the kids came along, Mikal and Clara, and he'd kicked the habit, so–

Dorden shut off the thoughts. Tanith had taken his wife with it, and Clara and her husband and their baby too. All he had was Mikal, Trooper Mikal Dorden, vox-caster operator in Sergeant Hasker's platoon.

'You're thinking about home,' Corbec muttered.

Dorden broke his sad reverie. 'What?'

'I know that look.'

'It's dark, colonel!'

'I know that... feeling, then. The set of a man's shoulders. Comes on us all, time to time.'

'I'd guess the commissar has told you to stamp it out where ever you see it? Bad for morale.'

'Not in my book. Tanith still lives while we all carry it here...' Corbec tapped his forehead. 'And we don't know where we're going if we don't know where we came from.'

'Where are we going, do you suppose?'

Corbec flicked his butt onto the mud and let it sputter dead. 'On a bad day, to hell. On a good day, I'd say we were bound for that trophy world Gaunt's promised us. Slaydo's gift: the first world we truly win we can take and claim and settle as our own.'

Dorden gazed at the storm. 'New Tanith, huh? Like the men talk of when they're drunk or dying? Do you believe that? Might we ever take a world ourselves, get the credit clean and true? We're less than two thousand. Every theatre we enter, we do so alongside other regiments, and that muddies victory claims and credit. I'm not a pessimist, colonel, but I doubt any of us will ever find that New Tanith, except in drink or death.'

Corbec smiled, his white teeth shining in the gloom. 'Then lucky me. One way or another, I'll see more of it than most.'

A door banged to their left. Chayker, shrouded in his cape, emerged from the hospital and carried a tin drum over to the well. A few moments' cranking, and he struggled with it back to the buildings. Dorden and Corbec could already smell the broth Chayker and Foskin were brewing for all the company.

'Something smells good,' Corbec said.

'Foskin found tubers and grain in a field beyond the ditch walls, and we turned up dried pulses and salt meat in an old pantry. Should be the best supper any of us have had in a while. But first rations go to any of the patients who can take it.'

'Of course. They need it more than us. I've got a flask of sacra and a box of these smokes. Should keep me going awhile.'

'Come in when you're ready for proper nourishment,' Dorden instructed, as if issuing a prescription. 'Thanks for the cigars.' He headed back to the ward.

A circuit of the wounded took another hour and a half. Lesp and the other orderlies had done well, and many had eaten or at least taken fluid. There were twelve who were too far gone to remain conscious, and Dorden carefully rationed out his supply of drugs to prioritise them. The boy, Culcis, along with a few others, were now sitting up, chatting, grateful. All of them, Volpone aristo-blood, were disdainful of the Tanith, but civil nevertheless. Being cut adrift by their regiment, and spared from death only by a barbarian unit, would seem to have altered many of their deeper prejudices and snobberies. For that at least, Dorden felt pleased.

He saw Trooper Caffran, coming in soaked from a patrol circuit, taking his bowl of broth to sit with Culcis. They were about the same age, Dorden reckoned. The same age as Mikal. He heard them share a joke.

Lesp took his arm. One of the critical cases was showing signs of fading. With Chayker's help, they carried the man out into what had once been the household kitchen, and now served as a surgical theatre. A refectory table sat there, long enough for a man, and they heaved him onto it.

The Blueblood, a Corporal Regara by his tags, had lost a leg below the knee and taken shrapnel in the chest. His blood was far from blue. The refectory table became slick and blood drooled off onto the flagstones. Chayker almost slipped and Dorden ordered him to fetch a mop and more wadding.

'There are no mops,' Chayker shrugged.

'Then find something *like* a mop.'

Dorden had to take off more of the ruined leg from the shrieking Regara with his handsaw before he could staunch and tie the haemorrhage. He directed Lesp's sure fingers in to suture the breach with fine, sail-maker's stitches. By then, Chayker had returned. Dorden found he was mopping the floor with shredded strips from his cape tied to an old rake handle. For a Ghost to tear up his treasured stealth cloak to mop blood... Dorden's admiration for his volunteers' devotion to duty grew.

They carried the softly moaning Regara back to his bed. With luck, and a fever-breaking shot of mascetamine, he might yet live. But Dorden was called away almost at once to a seizure that Foskin couldn't cope with, and then to a man who had woken from near-coma, only to begin violently retching blood.

The ward fell quiet towards midnight, as other dramas came and passed. Dorden was scrubbing his chrome rib-spreaders in a bucket of scalding water when Mkoll came in, shaking the water from his cape. The storm was still booming outside and thunder rattled the casements and roofing. Every now and then, loose glass in a window somewhere fell in, or tiles slipped off and shattered. The storm had continued all that evening, but until then, Dorden had blanked it out.

He watched Mkoll sit and clean his gun, the first thing he always did before seeing to other duties like food or warmth. Dorden took him a bowl of broth.

'Anything out there?'

Mkoll shook his head. 'If we're lucky, the storm is slowing their advance.'

'And if we're not?'

'They conjured the storm.'

Mkoll looked up at the rafters and the high roof. 'This must have been quite a place. A good homestead, worth the working. The soil is healthy and they had plenty of livestock.'

'A family home,' Dorden pondered, who hadn't thought about it before. The thought of another home and family lost to the war now bit at him. He felt weary again. Old.

Mkoll spooned his broth quietly. 'There's an old chapel at the rear of the house. Blown in, of course, but you can still see the painted reredos commemorating the Emperor. The Volpone used it as a privy. Whoever lived here were devout servants of the Imperium, working the land, raising their kin.'

'Until this.'

Dorden fell silent. Chaos had taken this world, Nacedon, two months gone, as part of their counter-punch to thwart Macaroth's crusade. It hadn't been occupied, or even corrupted from within. Nacedon, an agricultural world with three million Imperial colonists, had been violated and invaded in the space of three nights.

What kind of universe was it, Dorden wondered, where humans could struggle and break their backs and love their families and worship the Emperor and build for years, only to lose it all in a few hours? His universe, he concluded, the same one that had taken Tanith away.

A late moon was up, a lonely sentry in a sky suddenly clear of storm. The rain had stopped and silver clouds scudded across the purple openness of the heaven.

Counterpart to the moon, a lone sentry stood at the gate of the station. Trooper Tremard, sitting his second shift at the gate in the sandbag emplacement, watched the tree lines, black fuzzes of darkness edging the flats of the equally black fields and fens. He was tired, and he wished that the fething Volpone had left their heavy gun in the emplacement.

Mist rose across the fenland, drifting sideways like smoke. Something twinkled in the dark.

Tremard started up, grabbing his scope from the sandbags. He fumbled with the focus ring, pulling the green-on-green night vision view into true. Mist – and other things in it. The twinkle he had seen. Moonlight flashing back from the staring reflective retina of hunting eyes.

He triggered his micro-bead link. 'Gate to Ghosts! Can you hear me, colonel? To arms! To arms! Movement to the south!'

Corbec rose abruptly from his cot, like a dead man lifting from a grave, making Dorden start. The colonel had been catching forty winks on a spare bed in the ward as the medic sorted pills into paper twists.

'What is it?'

Corbec was on his feet. 'Three guesses, Doc.'

Dorden was up too. He looked around at the fragile hall, the vulnerable, half-dead men, as Corbec readied his lasgun and voxed-in with the other troopers. Dorden felt suddenly stupid. He knew what a full-on assault of Chaos was like. They'd all be shattered like an egg-shell. He'd been stupid to insist on staying. Now he had them all dead – the Blue-bloods, the Ghosts… valuable, peerless Ghosts like Corbec and Mkoll. He'd wasted them all, over some foolish pride in an old oath. An old medical oath, taken in safer times, in a nice community practice where the worst injury was a laceration at the sawmill.

Feth me for a fool! Feth me for my pride!

'We'll front them as long as we can. The boys know some tricks,' Corbec told him. 'I'll need Chayker and Foskin… Lesp can stay with you. If we lose the first attack, you need to be ready to get as many of the wounded out into the back rooms. They're ruins I know, but it'll put more walls between you and the fighting.'

Dorden swallowed, thinking of the work it would take him and Lesp to carry sixty-seven men out into the rear of the dwelling on stretchers. He heard the distant wail of las-fire and realised it wouldn't be half the effort Corbec and his soldiers were about to make. So he simply nodded, beckoning Lesp to him.

'Emperor be with you and watch over you, Colm Corbec,' he said.

'And you, Doc.'

Tremard held the gate. Dark shapes moved across the fields and through the dim hedgerows towards him, crackling out green pulses of laser fire and white-hot bolt rounds. The treacherous moon showed movement and the occasional glint of armour, and he picked his targets well, barking orange slices of laser into the open fenland beyond the farm.

Ducking the incoming sprays of fire, a figure dropped into the position beside him. It was Colonel Corbec. Corbec grinned at Tremard, made some obscene remark as to the maternal origins of the enemy that had Tremard cackling at its vulgarity, and leaned up over the bags to loose a volley of shots from his lasgun down the lane into the fens.

Along the ditch walls, the other Ghosts opened up. Eight lasguns against the encroaching dark, eight lasguns picking their targets through scope and skill, matching the hundreds of fire-points blasting back at them from the fens.

'Where's Brostin?' Corbec barked into his micro-bead, over the howl of gunplay, sustaining a regular fire-pattern.

A second later, his query was lost in a withering assault which blasted down the lane and onto his position. A hundred or more warriors of Chaos were forcing their approach at the main gate, charging them, weapons blazing. Corbec and Tremard could see nothing but the light-blur of their guns.

Corbec ducked under the intense volley. He didn't even curse. It was over, he knew. The end of Colm Corbec. By his side, Tremard, a second too late in ducking, flew backwards, his left arm gone in a shredded waste of flesh below the shoulder. He fell on his back, screaming and writhing. His lasgun, with his left hand still holding the grip, sat miraculously on the parapet where he had rested it.

Corbec scrambled to him, under the hideous rain of bolt and las-fire, grabbing the struggling man and holding him close. He had to calm him and make him still before he could tie up that awful stump. *If he lived that long.*

Tremard screamed and screamed, fighting like a scalded cat, drenching Corbec and himself with the pumping arterial spray of his stump. Corbec glanced up to see black forms in quilted armour, faces covered by gas-hoods, scrambling over the lip of the sandbags towards him. He could smell their rank animal scent, and the badges of the Dark Gods blazoned on their armour burned in his mind even at a glimpse and turned his stomach.

There was a double click, dry and solid, and then a whoosh of heat as the night lit up. Corbec winced. Trooper Brostin stood over him, raking the tops of the sandbags and the lane beyond with his flamer. The hurricane force of the flame gout cut the enemy away like dry grass.

'I was wondering where you'd got to,' Corbec said to Brostin. Then he tapped his micro-bead. 'Medic! Medic!'

Dorden and Lesp were halfway through transporting the injured into the rear of the house when the call came through. Stray shots were punching through the ward hall, exploding rafters and shattering wall-plaster and brick.

Dorden fumbled with his micro-bead, trying to steady the stretcher he was sharing with the backing Lesp.

'Dorden! What?'

'Tremard's down bad. Get out here!' Any more of Corbec's message was lost in crackling static, drowned by the gunfire.

'Set it down! I'll drag it!' Lesp cried to Dorden as a las-round punched a hole in the plaster near his head.

Dorden did so and Lesp hauled the stretcher through the archway, its wooden handles screeching on the floor. 'Just like a fish box back home!' Lesp yelled over the onslaught as he disappeared.

Dorden grabbed his kit. 'Corbec! I'm coming out, but you need to send someone in to help Lesp move the wounded!'

'Feth that! We're all engaged out here! Can't spare a man!'

'Don't give me that!' Dorden returned, scuttling under the puncture level of the las-range as the hall fell apart around him. 'Lesp needs help! These men need help!'

A hand took his shoulder. He looked round. It was the Blueblood Culcis. Several more of the less seriously injured Volpone were with him. 'I can't manage a stretcher with my leg, but I can man a fire-point, doctor. I'll take any lasgun free if it means able bodies can help you here!'

Dorden smiled at the young man's bravery. Pain was slashed into the Blueblood's thin face.

He nodded them forward to the door and they looked out into the rain of fire.

'Caffran!' Dorden called on the link. 'I'm sending a Blueblood over to you. Give him your weapon and then return!'

He didn't wait for an answer.

Using Chayker's mop as a crutch, Culcis scurried out into the yard and made the inner wall, where Caffran was blasting through a fire-slot. A nod, and Caffran gave up his gun and position to the Blueblood. Culcis settled in, leaning against the flak-boards, and resumed blasting. Caffran ran back to the farmhouse door where Dorden was waiting.

'Help Lesp! Go! Go!'

In three minutes, Dorden had substituted three more Volpones on the defence line, men with leg wounds or head wounds, but able-bodied. In return, he got Claig, Gutes and Foskin.

Dorden told Foskin the drill, and Foskin supervised the five able-bodied Ghosts into a slick pattern of removing the wounded into the rear sections of the house.

Shaken by the onslaught which lit up the feeble night, Dorden reached the gatepost, running in a stoop. Brostin and Corbec were blasting away. Brostin was now using Tremard's lasgun, switching to the big flamer every time the assault became too great.

Dorden knelt by Tremard, assessed his injury and set to work. 'I need a stretcher for him!' Dorden yelled at Corbec.

'Help him, Brostin,' Corbec snapped. As Dorden and Brostin carried Tremard back to the farmhouse, Corbec held the gate. Dorden's last view of him was clear: the huge Tanith warrior, his hair loose and flowing in the night wind as the storm came down again, crackling and flashing, flamer in one hand, lasgun in the other, dealing death to anything that moved.

The enemy assault had pivoted to the western side of the horseshoe, and heavy fire slammed against the flakboarding, throwing some sheets up out of the muck and shattering them. Mkoll felt more than saw the change in emphasis and rushed from his position at the east end to support Chayker and a Blueblood called Vengo who had substituted for Gutes. Chaos soldiers were pushing through the holes in the outer flak-board wall and the three Guardsmen, firing single, aimed shots to preserve power on Corbec's orders, dropped dozens into the slime pit of the ditch. Soon bodies blocked the fence holes as well as the missing boards had done.

Well enough when they come at us with boltguns and las-weapons, Mkoll thought to himself darkly. But what do we do when they bring up flamers, meltas, grenades... or worse?

The cacophony of the assault was ear-splitting and a double echo rolled back to them from the wide fens like thunder, almost as loud as the real thing. The storm or the storming shook the earth, and Mkoll wasn't sure which.

Vengo, bandaged up with a gut wound, found his strength failing and his vision swimming. The majesty and fury of the open assault, the desperation and the frantic effort, had quite numbed him to the dull pain of his injuries, but they were telling on him none the less. Drenched by the downpour, he tried to reposition himself, changing spent clip for fresh with cold, wet hands. The fresh power clip slipped away and dropped into the mud under his feet. He stooped.

A soldier of Chaos, cut down and presumed dead in the ditch, had crawled forward, and now loomed over the inner fence above the scrabbling Volpone. His chest had been blasted open, and blood and tissue dribbled from exposed ribs. His gas-hood was also gone, revealing the fanged snout and grey hide of his corrupted face. He swung up a rusty entrenching tool.

Chayker, dazzled by the volleys of las-light and the strobe effect of the lightning, saw his assailant in a flash of white, frozen mid-swing. He wrenched his lasgun out of the fire-slot and blasted down the gully, blowing the attacker out over the fence. Rising with the recovered clip, deafened by the sensory overload of the storm and fighting, Vengo had no idea how he had been spared or how close he had been to death.

Bolt rounds drummed into the flak-boards around Mkoll's slot, and nailed wooden splinters into his cheek and neck. He cried out and dropped back for a second. Rubbing at the bloody grazes in his face, he moved back to the slot, re-aiming. Other dark shapes were stirring in the filth at the bottom of the ditch. Vengo's close call had been a warning. Even killing shots didn't seem to finish all of these abominations. Many of those that they had cut down were far from dead, and now were crawling and clambering up to attack the inner fence.

'Brace!' he yelled over the comm-link to Chayker and Vengo. He had a few tube-charges left, and he hefted three over the inner fence into the ditch with its half-seen stirrings.

The triple blast rocked them and pelted the inner flak-boards with liquid mud and liquefied organics.

'Keep checking the ditch!' Mkoll voxed. 'They don't die easy.'

Vengo caught the hint at once, and lowered his aim to pick off two more of the supposed dead who were writhing through the mire towards him. Others clustered around the breaches in the outer fence, cut down by the trap as fast as they gathered and pressed in.

How many of them are there out there, Chayker wondered? The force of the assault seemed to be increasing with every moment.

On the eastern turn of the horseshoe, Culcis held the line with his other two Volpone substitutes, Drado and Speers. Brostin had returned from his stretcher run to the house and fell in beside Culcis, hefting a misfiring Volpone heavy stubber he'd found leaning against the wall in the long hall. It had a drum of sixty rounds left in it, and he'd resolved to use them all before switching to his laspistol. His flamer was in Corbec's meaty hands at the gate.

All they could hear or see from the gate area, at the southern point of the horseshoe, were belches of flame and las-chatter and Corbec's increasingly colourful exclamations over the vox-link.

Brostin settled in, getting to know the unfamiliar stubber. Its cyclic rate was poor and it jammed frequently, but when it fired, the thump and blast was satisfying. He shredded half a dozen shapes that loomed beyond the outer fence. At the eastern side, the tree-line and woods were closer than at the west, which looked out over fenland interrupted only by hedges and dykes. Here, the enemy was on them with little warning, rushing out of the trees to assault the double fence and the ditch.

Brostin found himself admiring the shooting skills of the Blueblood Culcis. Arrogantly, against Corbec's orders, he had adjusted the power setting to full and was firing off searing orange blasts. But each one counted.

His eye's as good as Mad Larkin's, thought the heavy-set Ghost, and that's a real compliment.

Drado and Speers were doing their part too, but Drado's aim was off. Though able-bodied, the man had a head wound and one eye bandaged. The lack of binocular range-finding was ruining his shot. Brostin hunkered down and moved along the fence to him.

'Aim left!' he yelled over the barrage and the thunder. 'You're shooting wide!'

Drado turned on him, his noble, half-bandaged face curled into a haughty sneer. 'No low-life gutter-dog tells a Volpone how to fight!'

Brostin smacked him hard with the side of his fist and slammed the Blueblood into the mud.

'Get up!' Brostin said fiercely, fist raised. 'This is a last stand of the Tanith First-and-Only. We're only here because of you and your kinsmen! Fight like a Ghost or stand aside and let someone else do it!'

Drado hauled himself up and spat at Brostin. 'You'll pay...' he began.

Firing his stubber out at the enemy, Brostin laughed. 'Pay? Of course I'll pay! But not to you! If we live through this, my Blueblood friend, you can hammer me to hell, and get your oh-so-noble brothers to help! See me care! If we don't die here, tonight, guarding the line to protect your precious wounded, then I'll go laughing into any retribution you care to dish out! What could be worse than this?'

Drado didn't answer. He set to firing again, and Brostin noted with approval that he was compensating now and favouring the left side. He made hits.

'Much better, you feth-wit,' he muttered.

Inside the manor house, Dorden checked the state of the wounded they had moved. With the help of Lesp, Gutes, Caffran, Foskin and Claig, he had transferred the patients back, one at a time, through to the rear chambers and then down in the long undercroft. This low, vaulted cellar space was made of thick stone. The best protection they could afford. They might survive the attack here – or be buried like rats.

With Foskin's help, he treated Tremard's wound and got him stable. Then he ordered all the Ghosts back out to the defence, all except Lesp, whom he needed. Another comatose Volpone had woken during the rough relocation and was convulsing.

Caffran, Foskin, Gutes and Claig made their way up the cellar steps, taking their pick of the broken Volpone weapons stacked in the stable-block on their way to rejoin the defence.

The convulsing Volpone died. Though he showed no outward signs of injuring except severe bruising, Dorden knew his innards had been turned to jelly by artillery concussion. Lesp helped him haul the corpse back up the undercroft stairs and dump it in the hall.

They went back down. The undercroft was damp and pungent, lit by hissing chemical lamps the Ghosts had set up hurriedly. The injured moaned and sighed. Some slept like they were dead. The earth around them all shook and trickles of liquid mud spurted down from the roof every now and then as the onslaught rattled the foundations of the house.

'We're all going to die here, aren't we, sir?' Lesp asked, his voice clear and certain.

Dorden stammered for a moment, lost for words. He thought, desperately, what Gaunt might say in such circumstances. What would a trained political officer do here, trying to raise the spirits of men looking death in he face? He couldn't do it. It wasn't in him. He couldn't compose any deft line about 'the greater good of the Imperial Guard' or the 'lifeblood of the Emperor'. Instead, all he could manage was something entirely personal.

'I'm not,' he told Lesp. 'When I die, my wife and daughter and grand-daughter die too, their memories lost with me. For them, I'll not die here, Lesp.'

Lesp nodded, his big Adam's apple gulping in his narrow throat. He thought of the memories he carried: mother, father, brothers, crew mates on the archipelago trawler.

'Neither will I, then,' he managed.

Dorden turned towards the stairs.

'Where are you going?' Lesp asked.

'You manage things here. I'm going to take a look up top. From the sound of things, they may need a medic.'

Lesp pulled out his laspistol and offered it, butt-first, to the chief medic.

Dorden shook his head. 'I can't start that now,' he said.

Upstairs, the old ruin was quiet. It seemed as if the storm and the assault had abated together for the moment. Dorden edged into the vacated long hall and tried his micro-bead but it was dead. The ceiling lamps swung and loose debris fluttered down. Free of bodies, the stinking cots looked pitiful and sadly spoiled. Dorden stepped over pools of blood and shreds of discarded clothing.

He strode into the outer kitchen, looking once at the stained table where he had excised a part of Regara's leg. He saw the old fireplace for the first time. Black iron, just like the one he had sat before at home on Tanith. He and his wife, at the end of a long night, with a book and a glass of something warming, before the grate-light.

Along the mantle, small blocks of what looked like chalk sat in a row.

He moved over and took one in his hand. A tusk. The small, shed tusk of a pig. The inhabitants of this manor, whoever they were, had raised swine, cared for them enough to treasure the trophies of their growth and development. Pig teeth, each marked in a delicate hand with a name... *Emperor, Sire, His Lordship...* and dates.

This touch of frugal humanity, the day-to-day chronicle of a farmstead, affected him deeply. It wasn't mawkish, it mattered somehow. Why pigs? Who had lived here, raised the swine, toiled in the fens, brought up a family?

A sound from the long hall brought him up to the surface of his thoughts. He moved back to meet a gaggle of men as they limped and blundered in through the hall doors from the outside. The Volpone substitutes and the Ghosts, all except Corbec. They were shell-shocked and dazed, weary on their feet.

Dorden found Mkoll at the rear of the group.

'They've fallen back,' Mkoll said. 'It's dead quiet out there. That can mean only one thing...'

'I'm a medic, not a soldier, Mkoll! What does it mean?'

Mkoll sighed as Dorden attended to the splinter wounds in his face. 'They've failed with a physical assault. They're drawing back so they can bring up artillery.'

Dorden nodded. 'Get below, into the undercroft, all of you. Foskin – Lesp will help you cook up some food for all. Do it! Artillery or not, I want everyone sustained.'

The men filed away towards the steps into the cellar. Dorden was alone again in the hall.

Corbec entered, covered in blood and fire-soot. He dropped Brostin's empty flamer onto one cot and threw Tamard's spent lasgun the other way.

'Time's trickling away, Doc,' he said. 'We held them – feth but we held them! – but they're gonna hammer us now. I scoped movement over the fens, big guns being wheeled into place. An hour, if we're lucky, and then they'll level us from a distance.'

'Colm... I thank you for all you and the men have done tonight. I hope it was worth it.'

'It's always worth it, Doc.'

'So what do we do now? Bury ourselves in the cellar?'

Corbec shrugged. 'That won't save us from their shells. Don't know about you, but I'm going to do the only thing I can think of at a time like this?'

'Which is?'

'Pray to the Emperor. Mkoll said there was an old shrine out back of this place. Prayers are all we have left.'

* * *

Together, Corbec and Dorden pulled their way through a litter of rubble and debris and broken furniture into the little room at the back of the farmhouse. It had lost its roof and the stars twinkled above them.

Corbec had brought a lamp. He played its light over the rear walls, picking up the flaking painted image on the ornamental screen Mkoll had mentioned. It showed the Divine Emperor subduing the Heretics, and smaller figures of a man, a woman, and three small children, shown in obeisance to the central figure of the God-Emperor of Man.

'There's an inscription here,' Dorden said, scraping the dirt away from the wall with his cuff pulled up over the ball of his hand.

'A pig! What is this?'

Corbec raised the lamp and read off the inscription. 'Here's irony for you, Doc: this was a trophy world. A New Tanith. The master of this hall was a Farens Cloker, of the Imperial Guard, Hogskull Regiment. The Hogskulls won this world during the first advance into the Sabbat one hundred and ninety years ago. Winning it, they were awarded settlement rights. Cloker was a corporal in the Guard, and he took his rights gladly. Settled here, made a family, raised swine in honour of the mascot beast of his old regiment. His kin have honoured that ever since.'

Corbec faltered, something like sadness in his eyes. 'Feth! To get there, to win it, to take the trophy world... and still it comes down to this?'

'Not for all. How many trophy worlds are there out there where the soldiers of the Guard have retired and lived out their days?'

'I don't know. This is all too real. To fight for your lifetime, get the prize you wanted, and then this?'

Corbec and Dorden sank down together in the debris-strewn chapel.

'You asked me why I stayed with you, Doc. I'll tell you now as we're dead and we have nothing to live for.' With that last remark, Corbec flung his hand towards the reredos' inscription.

'Well?'

'You were the doctor for Pryze County for twenty years.'

'Twenty-seven. And Beldane.'

Corbec nodded. 'I was raised in Pryze. My family were wood workers there. I was born out of wedlock and so I took my father's name, when I knew him. My mother now... I was a difficult birth.'

Dorden stiffened, knowing somehow what must come next.

'She'd have died in labour, had it not been for the young medic who charged out in the night and saw to her. Landa Meroc. Remember her?'

'She would have died if I hadn't–'

'Thank you, Doctor Dorden.'

Dorden looked round at Corbec in wonder. 'I delivered you? Feth! Fething feth! Am I that old?!'

They laughed together until they were choking. And until the thump of artillery began, blasting the quiet of the night away.

The Imperial Guard drove the enemy back with their shelling and Gaunt was on the foremost half-track as they ploughed back into the fenlands in the early light of dawn. They caught the enemy almost unawares, and were blasting the Chaos artillery and infantry even as the enemy wheeled their own blasphemous guns around into position in the dark.

The farmhouse, and its shattered defence of horseshoe fences, was almost unrecognisable. Mud, burnt flak-board and shattered corpses lay piled amidst the devastated ruins. He ordered the vehicle to stop, and it spun wheels on the fenland muck as it slid to a halt.

Trooper Lesp was on duty at the gateway. He saluted the colonel-commissar as he passed in. Dorden and Corbec were waiting for him in the littered yard.

'Medical evac is coming,' Gaunt told them. 'We'll get the Volpone wounded out of here.'

'And our own too?' Dorden asked, thinking of Tremard, and Mkoll's lacerated face.

'All of the wounded. So, you've had an adventure out here, it seems?'

'Nothing to speak of, sir,' Corbec said.

Gaunt nodded and moved off into the manor house ruin.

Corbec turned to Dorden and showed him the pig's tooth he had clutched in his hand. 'I won't forget this,' he said. 'It may not have worked here on Nacedon for this Guardsman, but by this tooth, I'll trust it will work for us Ghosts. A trophy world, brighter and better than you can imagine.'

Dorden's hand held a pig-tooth too, marked 'The Emperor'.

'I trust you to do that, Colm. Do it. Doctor's orders.'

Swing, address, stab, return... swing, address, stab, return...

In the shade of the cycads at the edge of the Tanith encampment on Monthax, Trooper Caffran was practising bayonet discipline. Stripped to the waist, his powerful young shoulders glistening with sweat, he whirled his lasgun in time to his rhythmic chant, snapping it round, clutching it horizontally, lunging forward and killing the bole of one of the trees over and again. After each strike, he tugged it free with effort, and repeated the drill. The trunk was slashed and puckered, oozing orange sap from the wounds left by his nimble work.

'Good skill,' Gaunt said from behind him. Caffran snapped around, realising he was being watched. He shook sweat from his brow and began a salute.

'At ease,' Gaunt said. 'I'm just walking the lines. Everything alright with you? The men in your platoon?'

Caffran felt tongue-tied, as he always did when Gaunt addressed him directly. He still, after all this time, had mixed feelings about the commissar who had both saved them and made them Ghosts in the same action.

'We're all waiting for the word,' he said at last. 'Itching for action. This waiting...'

'It's the worst part, I know.' Gaunt sat down on a nearby log. 'Until the killing starts and you realise the waiting wasn't all that bad after all.'

Caffran caught the smile in Gaunt's eyes and grinned as well, unable to stop himself.

Gaunt was pleased. He was very aware of the stiffness Caffran always manifested around him. A good soldier, one of the youngest, but so very nearly one of Rawne's malcontents.

'Go again,' Gaunt suggested.

Self-consciously, Caffran turned and repeated his drill. Swing, address, stab, return... It took a moment to pull his blade free from the thick bark.

'Slide it,' Gaunt said. 'It'll come out easier if you slide it laterally before pulling.'

Caffran did so. It was true.

Gaunt got up, moving on with his circuit. 'Not long now, Caffran,' Gaunt said as he moved away.

Caffran sighed. No, not long. Not long before the frenzy and the madness would start.

Swing, address, stab, slide, return... Swing, address, stab, slide, return...

NINE

A SIMPLE PLAN

Engines screaming, the Imperial troop carriers fell upon the ocean world, Sapiencia.

Like swarms of fat, black beetles shrilling in over the edges of a pond, they assaulted the Bay of Belano. Their combined down-draughts boiled the choppy surface water into foam mist, an embankment of steam three kilometres long and two hundred metres high that stormed forward across the beach rocks and blinded the island's outer defences.

It entirely hid the merciless wall of solid water driven up under the spray by the concussive force, and this tidal wave exploded across the western sea-fall emplacements of Oskray Island twenty seconds after the steam cloud choked them. Rock and metal and flesh were pulverised, blasted into the air, then sucked back into the basin of the bay as pressures equalised and hydraulic action righted itself. A spume haze hung over the island, clogging the beaches and masking the final, slow approach of the gargantuan troop-ships.

The heavy emplacements higher on the cliffs of Oskray spat fierce salvos down into the mist, or up into the striated clouds where further formations of troop ships were beginning their final approaches to the island shore. The fire from the batteries, blue and flickering, danced like luminous damsel flies amongst the beetle-like ships. Some craft burst as they were touched, and burned; some dropped, bleeding smoke and trailing lines of debris.

The twenty kilometres of Oskray Island was only partly rock. It was, in point of fact, a cluster of islets, linked as one by the massive industrial fortification built up upon the shoulders of submarine mountains. Behind ocean-blocking walls of stone a hundred metres thick, pump structures, drill towers, flame-belching waste stacks and pylons rose against the sky. The primary target, the great refinery hive of Oskray Island One.

Red hazard lights flashed and hooters started their deafening cater-waul as the jaw-hatch locks of troop-ship *Lambda* disengaged with a massive leaden thump. Dim light began to pour in from outside as the jaw-sections hinged open. Caffran, tensed tight and ready, knew they were assaulting a sea-bound target, and that the way in for the infantry was up the beach. That was the plan. But as the troop-hatch opened, he believed for a moment they had come in too low and it was trans-lucent torrents of water that were spurting into the dispersal deck. He gulped in his breath, held it, but it was only steam and pale light that rushed over him.

The yells of men, of boots racing on metal decking, and of the hooters, were overwhelming. With fifty others, lasguns raised, he charged out of the hatch mouth. For a second, on the ramp, the dispersal deck noises were swamped by the greater volume of the thundering drop-ships all around. Caffran could see nothing beyond the men closest to him and the solid atmosphere of mist and smoke. He could smell salt and ozone, oil and thermite.

Then nothing. Rushing silence, roaring dullness, a coldness all over him, enveloping him, dark grey blurs in his eyes.

He was underwater, floundering in the chilly, muffled dark of the sea, writhing black bodies struggling and flailing around him, each one bejewelled with trapped baubles of silver air.

The troop-ship had come up short of the beach slope, and all the men dropping blind off the ramp were falling into thirty metres of ocean where the island shelved steeply away.

Caffran couldn't swim. He'd been born and raised in a forest a thou-sand kilometres from any open water. He'd never seen the ocean, any ocean, though he'd heard others, like the medic-fisherman Lesp, speak of it. He was going to do the last thing he had ever expected to do: drown.

Momentarily, he realised he had not yet released the deep breath he had instinctively sealed into his lungs when he thought the dispersal deck was going to flood, and he almost laughed, almost releasing the air.

Instead, he held on to it, felt it burning and exhausting inside him as he rose slowly to what seemed the surface. It saved his life, where others had gone screaming and exhaling off the ramp.

Sinking, blundering, black shapes thrashed around him: Tanith com-bat dress, dark as dry blood, faces pale like phantoms or ghouls. A body sank beside him, arms frozen in claws, mouth open to emit a dribble of bubbles, eyes glazed. Caffran kicked upwards again.

Something struck him stunningly hard on the back of the neck and he lost his precious saved breath in a blurt of silvery air pebbles. Men were still coming off the ramp-end above, falling on those Ghosts now coming up from below. A boot had hit him. The man it belonged to was inverted in the water behind him, panicking, dying. Caffran kicked away, trying to rise and not breathe in to ease his emptied, screaming lungs. He saw men explode into the grey, dreamy world from above, fighting the water as they hit and sank. But that at least told him the surface was only a few metres away.

The man who had kicked him on his way down had become entangled with another by the slings of their lasguns. One of them fired his lasgun in desperation, twice, three times. The water boiled around each slicing minnow of orange light. Caffran's ears throbbed as they heard the fizzing report of the underwater shots. One of the las-rounds punctured a drifting corpse nearby; another punched through the leg of a desperate swimmer next to Caffran. Blood fogged the water. Caffran heard the distant voices of his ancestors in his ears, muffled by pressure and fluid and distance and time.

He surfaced in a gasping explosion, retching, treading water, blood streaming from his nose. He looked around to see Ghosts surfacing all around, kicking towards the shore or just panicking. Some were floating in the surge, lifeless, already lost. Noise rushed back to him, the momentous noise of combat now unfiltered by the deadness of the sea. Screaming, the whicker of lasguns, the roar of troop-ship downwash. He could smell blood, water and smoke, but was thankful, because that meant he was breathing. Behind him, las-rounds punched up out of the water into the fog as other unfortunates lost their grip on everything but their triggers as they drowned.

Caffran paddled forward, hacking up each and every slop of sea-water he accidentally swallowed. The pall of smoke and fog cut visibility at the surface to ten metres. For a moment, he heard the voices of his ancestors again – then realised that wasn't what he'd heard at all. It was his micro-bead intercom, crackling with staccato traffic, screeching into his ear-plug. Underwater, it had been the tinny whisper of ghosts.

Caffran felt gravel or sand under his boots, a slope. He felt weight and momentum return to him as he churned up through shallower and still shallower water, falling twice and choking. Bolt rounds and las-fire whipped and stitched the breakers around him, cutting down the Ghost beaching next to him. The man fell face-down, his body lifted and pulled back, lifted and pulled back again by the choppy waves.

Caffran fell again as a las-round scorched across the top of his left shoulder, dropping him to his knees. His shins scraped on the stony gravel, shredding his fatigue pants from the knee down. He felt his lasgun grow heavier and flop away. The shot had cut his gun-strap across the shoulder.

Hands pulled him up as he grabbed hold of his weapon.

'Caffran!'

It was Domor, the squad's sweeper. He was laden down with the heavy backpack of the sweeper unit and its long handled sensor-broom. Domor had lost his eyes – and almost his life – in that final push on Menazoid Epsilon six months before. They had been there together for that fatal time, in the thick of it as they were here. Domor's metal-irised artificial implants shuttered and whined as they adjusted to look down at Caffran. The sweeper's cybernetic implants looked like truncated binocular scopes crudely sutured into the scar tissue of his eye-sockets.

'We can make the beach!' Domor yelled, pulling the young trooper to his feet. They ran, blundering through the breakers. Others charged or staggered in with them, a ragged line of Ghosts making landfall on the fog-washed shore, some falling over submerged barricade crosses or entangling themselves on rolls of rusting razor-wire. The fire-storm fell amongst them and some dropped silently, or screaming, or in minced pieces.

Now, the flinty shingle slope of the beach. They crashed up it, pebbles flying from each footfall. Twenty metres up, they ducked below the lichen-fronded line of an old wooden groyne, black as tar. Las-fire slammed into its weighty bulk.

'What's the plan? What have we got?' Caffran yelled.

'Nothing! Visibility is low! Heavy resistance from up there!' Domor pointed up into the spray-fog at something only his augmented vision could resolve, and then only barely.

Two more bodies flung themselves down next to them, then a third. Trooper Mkendrik with his flamer; Trooper Chilam, missing an ear and yowling like a cat as he dabbed his salty hand at the bloody hunk of cartilage on the side of his head. And then, Sergeant Varl.

Varl was a popular officer amongst the Ghosts; young, field-promoted from the rank of trooper, a wise-cracking, hard-nosed bastard refreshingly lacking all the airs and graces of the officer class. He'd lost his shoulder on Fortis Binary, and his black tunic bulged over the cybernetic joint the medics had given him. It was clear to Caffran that the sergeant was in some pain. Varl cursed and struggled with his artificial shoulder.

Sea-water had soaked into the shoulder joint, shorting out servos and fusing linkages. His arm was dead and useless, but still the raw neural connections transmitted flickers of shorting electrical failure to his brain. Domor had been lucky. His ocular units had been sealed into his skull enough to prevent such damage... though Caffran wondered how long it would take the insidious touch of sea-water corrosion to blind the man.

With Mkendrik's help, Caffran stripped off Varl's tunic and unscrewed the bolts on the small inspection plate in Varl's metal shoulder blade. With the point of his Tanith dagger, Mkendrik prised out the flat battery cells revealed there, cutting the electrical relay which governed the limb. Varl sighed as his arm went dead and Caffran strapped it up, tight against the sergeant's body. It was a desperate gesture. Without the booster relay of the cells, not only all neural control, but all life support would be cut from the organic parts of Varl's repaired arm. He needed proper help, or within an hour or two his now-lifeless arm would begin to decay and perish.

For now, though, the sergeant was grateful. He scrambled over, supporting himself on his one good hand, and took a look over the cover-line. Along the beach, under the downpour of fire, men were coming ashore. Most were dying; some were making it to cover.

'Where in Feth's name is the armour?' Varl wailed. 'They should have led the assault and opened this beach up!'

Caffran scoped around, and saw heavy Basilisk tanks half-submerged, struggling up the beach a hundred metres away. They were in too deep, drowning like beached whales, squirming and coughing exhaust smoke as their engines flooded and died.

'The troop-ships dropped us short,' he said to Varl.

Varl looked where Caffran pointed. 'They've drowned the front end of this fething assault!' he bellowed.

'They were blind... This spray–' Caffran began

'Feth them for not doing their job!' Varl spat.

A whinnying bolt round ricocheted off the top of the groyne's solid woodwork and took Chilam straight in the face, exploding his head. He flew back onto the shingle, full length.

'We have to advance! We have to!' Varl yelled. Micro-bead chatter, discordant and contradictory, rasped in their ears.

'There's no going forward,' Domor said quietly.

The spume of the spray-mist was receding, and now they could see what he saw. The vast white curtain wall of Oskray Island's sea-defences rose ahead of them, almost a kilometre high. Apart from some stray scorch marks, it was unblemished.

The Basilisks had been meant to flatten it and break through for the infantry. But the wall still stood, impassive, cold, like a denial of any possible future.

Varl cursed.

Caffran heard the protesting wail first. He looked back out to sea, then grabbed Domor and Varl and threw them flat into the painful jumble of the shingle. Mkendrik dived down too.

A troop-ship, one of the great fat beetles, on fire from end to end, was coming in low, half-sidelong, nose down, spilling burning fuel and shreds of fuselage. It was huge, blocking out the sky, six hundred tonnes of dying metal keening in towards the beach over their heads. Its jaw-hatches were still closed.

Men are cooking in there, Caffran thought, wondering which regiment, and then, as it came down on top of his head, his thoughts guttered out like a candle flame in a hurricane.

Mkendrik shook him awake. Caffran stirred, and woke up into the roar of the assault. 'How long have I been out?'

'Less than a minute,' Mkendrik said.

Caffran struggled up out of the shingle. It had felt like hours, like all his fatigue and pain had overwhelmed him and sent him to sleep. 'What happened?' he gasped. 'I thought for Feth we were dead then.'

Mkendrik pointed. At first there was little to see. The white steam and mist had become fouled with black smoke, and the ashy curls of it, thick with glowing cinders, enveloped the beach. Then, Caffran made out more. The stricken troop-ship had slammed over them, coming to rest at the head of the beach where the last few seconds of its crash-flight had been broken by the fortified seawall of Oskray Island. The impact had blown the wall in. For six hundred metres, its immeasurably old and solid stone was fused and fractured. A blackened chasm had opened into the heart of the refinery. The men aboard that troop-ship had bought a way into the target with their lives as surely as if they had fought their way up the beach.

Caffran gathered scattered items which had spilt from his burst pack, and recovered his fallen lasgun. Mkendrik was changing las-cells. A short way off, Varl and Domor were making ready, and small groups of Ghosts in foxholes along the beach were also preparing to make use of this new way in.

Enemy fire still strafed down from the wall, though it was thinner now such a chunk of the wall had gone. The incoming troop-ships, still roaring and settling over the tide-line behind them, were jockeying into this blind spot to avoid the tracking fire from the main batteries on the cliffs. Caffran heard thunder, and turned to see four Basilisks hoving up the beach, properly delivered, moving past them into the breach and tracking to fire. They sizzled up wet stone flecks as they rolled, cranking their huge, decorated bulks up and over the groynes. Caffran recognised the markings. Ketzoks, the 17th Armoured Regiment, the so-called Serpents who had been gulled into slaughtering them back on Voltemand.

With Varl, Domor, Mkendrik and several others, Caffran moved in towards the breach, running over stone litter and smouldering fragments of blackened mechanicals, the last remnants of the troop-ship. Stray las-shots winged down at them and stubber rounds rattled with a curious clack-clack sound off the stone facings to their left.

Entering the chasm in the wall, Caffran passed into deep shadow. Ahead, one hundred metres down the V-shaped channel blasted by the crash, a dimness loomed. He felt a sense of pride. They would be the first – the Ghosts would be the first to break through the stalwart defences of the target.

He was close to the far end now, stumbling with the others through the shadow, picking his way around mangled hull fragments. Ahead, the dimness was becoming a forest of steel and iron. The refinery itself.

Gaunt had been precise in his briefing. The fleet could have vaporised Oskray Island from orbit, but it was too valuable. That meant a land assault to retake it from the legions of Chaos. The vile host here called themselves the Kith, some hive-fermented sub-cult of Khorne... Caffran had blanked on some of the briefing's complexities, partly because it was alien gibberish to him, and partly because the gibberish made him feel ill. He didn't want to listen to the details concerning the filth they were going up against. The Kith: that was all he focussed on. The Kith were the sub-human vermin he was here to eradicate. Their leader was a monster called Sholen Skara. Fragments of the Chaos armada stopped at Balhaut had run to Sapiencia for shelter, and their leaders had conjoined with a Chaos cult already thriving in the underclass of the vast hive to overthrow Imperial rule and seize the fuel-oil and promethium wells.

Colonel-Commissar Gaunt had spoken long and passionately about the Kith in his briefing. Caffran knew Gaunt had been part of the great Balhaut victory, back when he was still a political officer with the Hyrkan Eighth. Gaunt loathed all Chaos, but loathed especially the tendrils of it which had escaped destruction at Balhaut only to twist and pollute other worlds, thanks, as he saw it, to the tactical miscalculations of Warmaster Macaroth. Gaunt had spoken of Sholen Skara, renegade of the Balhaut murder-camps, as if he had known him personally. That was why the colonel-commissar had volunteered his Ghosts for the Oskray assault. He had made it plain to them all.

And that, mused Caffran, was why they had been drowned and blasted and torn apart on the razor-wire.

Caffran often thought about Gaunt. Ibram Gaunt. He rolled the name in his mind, a name he would never dare voice aloud. The colonel, the commissar. A strange man, and Caffran's feelings for him were strange too. He was the best, most caring, most charismatic leader Caffran could imagine. Caffran had seen, time and again, the way Gaunt looked after the Ghosts. Caffran had also seen enough of other regiments and their commanders and politicos to know how rare a thing that was. Many, like beloved Colonel Corbec, regarded Gaunt as a saviour, a friend, a brother, and Caffran could not deny he admired Gaunt and would follow him to the ends of any earth.

But Caffran knew Feygor, Rawne and the other malcontents well, and in bitter moments he shared their contempt for the colonel-commissar. For all his fatherly love, like their own private Emperor, Gaunt had left Tanith to die. From time to time, Caffran had been tempted to throw aside his reservations about Gaunt and worship him as so many others did. But always, that creeping resentment in his heart had stopped him from total devotion. Gaunt was ruthless, calculating, direct. He would never stint from sending men to their deaths, for his duty was to the Emperor and the rule of Terra long before it was to the lost souls of Tanith.

Caffran saw the boy Milo, the so-called adjutant, as a constant reminder of the lost youth of his homeworld. Milo was only a year or two younger than Caffran, but a gulf divided them. He never spoke to the boy. Gaunt, in his oh-so generous wisdom, had saved Milo from the fires of Tanith Magna. Saved one – but no one else.

Caffran thought, at such times, of Laria. How he had loved her. How very much. All Caffran knew for sure was that Laria was dead now. How she had died he had no idea, and frankly, he was thankful for that. But Laria haunted him. Laria embodied everything he had lost. Tanith itself, his friends, his life, his family. For Laria's sake, Caffran knew he would always remain one of those Ghosts in the middle way, one who would follow Gaunt to hell devoutly, but would never forgive him when they arrived.

Here, in the wall gully of Oskray, it was easy to hate Gaunt. The stink of death and fire filled the place. Caffran slid in low against a fallen tower of stone blocks as he approached the opening into the island proper. Varl, Mkendrik and Trooper Vulliam dropped in beside him.

Behind them, down the crash-chasm at the mouth of the breach, Caffran could hear shouts and grinding tracks.

He looked at Varl questioningly.

'The fething Basilisks!' the sergeant said. 'They want to storm in ahead of the infantry, but they can't get their fat arses into the gap.'

'Then we still have point,' Caffran smiled. 'Feth the armour!'

Varl chortled. 'Feth them indeed. Did us no favours on Voltemand, doing us no favours now.'

Varl signalled the advance beyond the breach gap, and fifty-nine Ghosts rose from cover and moved forward. Vulliam, two metres ahead of Caffran, was one of the first to break into the open. Stub rounds broke him messily into four.

Six more Ghosts died as they broke cover. Though hammered, the Kith had their side of the chasm in the wall soundly covered. Caffran fell back with the others as las-rounds and bolts and stub charges peppered the exit of the breach.

In cover, they lay trembling as the deadly rain continued to drum the opening ahead.

'Blocked as surely as we were before,' Domor said, scratching at his eye-sutures.

'You all right?' Mkendrik asked.

'Vision's a little foggy. Got water in there. Hope...' Domor said no more, but Caffran knew what he was thinking. The seawater had ruined Varl's arm, and now it seemed to be starting its slow work on Domor's eyes.

'Might as well have left this fething wall standing for all the good it's going to do us!' Trooper Callun said.

Varl nodded, nursing his strapped arm.

His laspistol, the only weapon he could handle now, lay in his lap.

'What about missiles? Munitions?' Mkendrik wondered. 'We could blow them out and–'

'What do we aim at?' Varl asked sourly. 'Do you even see them?

Mkendrik settled back with no answer. Ahead of them was nothing but a sliced mouth cut in the wall. Beyond, the steeple girders and scaffolds of the refinery, thirty storeys high. The enemy gunners could be anywhere.

Silence fell. Sand flies billowed around the dead, and oceanic carrion swooped in to peck at the cindered flesh with hooked, pink beaks. The birds mobbed the chasm, squawking and shrilling. Trooper Tokar drove them off with a scatter burst of las-fire.

There was movement and voices behind them. Caffran and the others turned to see several Ketzok gunnery troopers creeping their way, pausing to exchange words with each group of Ghosts.

One hurried over to them, bent double, and saluted Varl's sergeant patch as he crouched next to them.

'Corporal Fuega, Ketzok 17th Serpents.'

'Varl, sergeant, Ghost. And your purpose is?'

Fuega scratched his ear for a moment, unmanned by Varl's attitude. 'Our Basilisks can't manage this breach, so we're going to split it wider with shelling. My commander asks you to fall back out of the fire-zone.'

'Wish he'd given us such a warning on Voltemand,' Domor said icily.

Fuega stepped back. 'That black day is forever in our shame, Tanith. If we could give anything, even our lives, to change it, we would.'

'I'm sure you would,' Varl sneered. He got up to face the Ketzok corporal. 'What's the plan?'

Fuega coughed. 'Orders from General Kline. You pull out, we shell, then we advance with heavy infantry.'

'Heavy infantry?'

'The Volpone have just beached in legion strength. They have heavy armour and weapons. We will clear the way for their advance.' Fuega turned away. 'You have fifteen minutes to withdraw.'

The Ghosts sat in a stupefied gaggle. 'All this, all we lost, for nothing?' Domor sighed.

Varl was angry. 'Feth those Volpone, and the Ketzok too! We die in the wire to open the beach and then they march in and follow the tanks to glory!'

'I don't know about you, sergeant, but I don't want to be sitting here still, complaining about life, when those Basilisks open up.'

Varl spat and sighed. 'Me neither. Okay! By platoon team, call the retreat.'

The Ghosts all around scrambled up and prepared to fall back. Domor, looking up, caught Caffran by the arm.

'What?'

'Up there – do you see it?'

Domor pointed and Caffran looked up. The broken wall rose like a cliff above them, scabbed with slumping masonry and broken reinforcement girders. Fifty metres up, just above a severed end of pipe work, Caffran saw the door. 'Feth, but your eyes are sharp!'

'There were tunnels in the wall, troop tunnels buried deep. This hole has cut through one of them and exposed it.'

Caffran called Varl over, and a group of Ghosts gathered to look up. 'We could get a fire-team inside the wall… follow the tunnel to where ever it led us.'

'Hell?' supposed Trooper Flaven.

'It's high up…' Varl began.

'But the cliff is ragged and full of good handholds. The first man up could secure a line. Sergeant, it's a plan…'

Varl looked round at Caffran. 'I'd never make it, with one arm dead. Who'd lead?'

'I could,' said Sergeant Gorley of Five platoon. He was a tall, barrel-chested man with a boxer's nose. 'You get the wounded back onto the beach. I'll take a squad and see what we can do.'

Varl nodded. He began to round up the walking wounded, and sec-
onded several able bodies to help him with the more seriously injured.
Gorley selected his commando squad: Caffran, Domor, Mkendrik,
Flaven, Tokar, Bude, Adare, Mkallun, Caill.

Mkendrik, raised in the mountains of Tanith Steeple, led off, clambering up the splintered wall, hand over hand. He left his flamer and
its tanks with Gorley, to raise them later on a line.

By the time the ascent was made, and ropes secured, their leeway
was almost up, and the ten Ghosts were alone in the chasm. Within
moments, the Basilisks at the throat of the breach would start their
bombardment.

The men went up quickly, following the ropes. Gorley was last, securing a line around the flamer unit and other heavy supplies. The team at
the top, crowded into the splintered doorway, hauled them up.

Gorley was halfway up the ascent when the bombardment began. The
nine Ghosts above cowered into the shelter of the concrete passageway they had climbed into and covered their ears at the concussion.

A shell hit the wall and vapourised Gorley, as if he had never been
there.

Realising he was gone, Caffran urged the party to collect their equipment and move inwards. Soon this entire wall section would be brought
down.

The Ghost squad crept up the unlit passageway. Though generally
intact, the tunnel had slumped a little following the massive shockwave
from the troop-ship crash. The ground was split in places, exposing
crumbling rock. Pipes and cables dangled from the cracked roof; dust
trickled down from deep fissures. In places, the shock-impact had sec-
tioned the wall, cutting the originally straight and horizontal tunnel into
a series of cleanly stepped slabs. The Tanith clambered on, probing the
dusty darkness with the cold green glare of assault lamps.

Behind them, the stonework of the great sea wall began to shake.
The Ketzok had redoubled their furious work. Caffran found himself
leading, as if there had been an unspoken vote electing him in Gorley's
place. He presumed it was because he had suggested this incursion in
the first place. The Ghosts picked up their speed and moved deeper
into the tunnel system that threaded the marrow of the wall.

They reached a vertical communications shaft, down the centre of
which ran a great wrought-iron spiral staircase. The air was damp and
smelled of wet brick and the sea. Shock damage was evident here too,
and the bolts securing the metal stairway and its adjoining walkways to
the shaft-sides had sheared off or snapped. The entire metal structure,

hundreds of tonnes of it filling the shaft, creaked uneasily with each
shuddering impact from the guns of the distant Basilisks.

The Ghosts stepped across the metal landing of the stair-coil to where
the tunnel resumed beyond. It squealed and yelped with every step,
sometimes threatening to tilt or fall.

Caill and Flaven were last across. A metal bolt-end the size of a man's
forearm rang off the gantry, just missing Caill. It had come loose far
above.

'Move!' yelled Caffran.

With a protesting, non-vocal scream, the staircase collapsed, tearing itself apart and rattling away down into the black depths of the
bottomless shaft. Where larger parts of the structure remained intact –
a few turns of steps laced together, a long section of handrail, a series
of stanchion poles – they fell with heavy fury, raking sparks and hideous shrieks from the shaft walls.

Empty, the stairs fallen away, the brick shaft seemed immense,
uncrossable.

Domor looked back at the tunnel they had come along, out of reach
now across the gulf. 'No going back now...' he muttered.

'Good thing that's not the way we're going,' Caffran replied, pointing
into the darkness to come with the barrel of his lasgun.

Wide cisterns opened up around them. The cement floors were painted
with glossy green paint and the wall bricks matt white. The walls tapered
upwards so that the ceiling was narrower than the floor, and the whole
tunnel turned a few degrees to the left. The entire passageway was following both the line and the profile of the wall it ran through. Grilled
lighting panels, glowing phosphorescent white, hung at intervals from
the roof. They looked like a giant stream of tracer rounds, arcing off
down the line of the tunnel, frozen in time.

Caffran's Ghosts – and indeed now they were 'his' Ghosts, bonding
to him as leader now that they were cut off from outside without asking or deciding – haunted the long passageways, hugging the walls in
the fierce white glow of the lights.

Every sixty metres, tunnels bisected the main route on the inland
side: deep, wide throats of brick and concrete that sloped downwards.
Mkendrik thought they might be drainage channels, but if that was true,
the size alarmed Caffran. They were big enough to take a man walking
upright and just as broad. If that kind of liquid quantity flooded these
tunnels from time to time...

Domor believed the channels to be for personnel movement, or for
running carts of ammo and supplies up to the emplacements buried

in the sides and along the top of the great sea wall. But they'd seen no vertical cargo shafts for munitions lifting, and Caffran doubted sheer manpower could roll enough shells up the sloping channels without mechanical assistance.

And they had met no one, not a trace of the Kith soldiery, not even a corpse.

'They're all fully engaged, deploying on the defences,' Caill suggested.

Caffran thought it a fair bet. 'We wanted to get inside, I figure we might get further than we expected.' They had just reached the latest of the mysterious sloping shafts. Caffran nodded to it. 'It leads into the heart of the island itself. Let's try it.'

'And then what?' Bude asked.

'Then?'

'I mean, what's your plan, Caff?'

Caffran paused. Getting in, that had been everything. Now... 'We're inside,' he began, 'no one's got this far.'

Bude and others nodded. 'But what then?' Flaven asked.

Again, Caffran was lost for words. 'We... we... we see how far we can get. Inside.'

None demurred. Lighting in the sloped tunnel was built into the wall and hidden behind transparent baffles. The concrete floor had a mesh grill set into it, providing greater purchase for walking.

They moved in formation. Half a kilometre, by Domor's gyro-compass. A kilometre. The air became damp-cold. The tunnel began to level out. The distant thump and shudder of the sea-wall assault dimmed behind them.

They heard the humming before they saw the end of the tunnel. A low, ululating throb that bristled the air. It reminded Caffran of the heavy fruit-wasps in the nal-forests of Tanith, crossing glades on iridescent wings to bury their long ovipositors into soft bark in search of nal-grubs to use as living kindergartens.

Adare, at the head of the pack with Mkalluи, called out. The tunnel was sealed fifty metres ahead by a vast metal hatchway. A thick iron-work seal surrounded a man-sized hatch closed with lever-latches and greased hydraulic hinges. The door and its frame were painted matt green with rust-proof paint, all except the clean steel inner rods of the extended hydraulics, which glittered with filmy brown oils.

The throbbing was coming from the far side of the hatch.

Adare checked the hatch seals, but they were wound tightly shut and locked, it seemed, from the other side. Caffran shouldered his way forward and reached out a hand to the metal barrier. It was wet-cold but it tingled, vibrating gently with the reverberations behind it.

'How do we get through?' Caffran murmured.

'Do we want to get through?' Bude returned.

Domor knelt down and started to open the clasps of his sweeper pack. Caffran noticed with some concern that Domor was regularly pausing to fidget and scratch at his eyes now, as if irritated by persistent flies. Domor pulled the head of the sweeper broom out of the pack, removed the soft cloth bag it was wrapped in, and carried it to the wall with his set unit and his headphones. He plugged the headphones and the sweeper head into the unit and switched it on, listening patiently to the clicking returns in his ear-pieces as he moved the flat pad of the sweeper head across the metal door surround. Three or four times he stopped, went back to check, and then marked the green-painted metal with a graphite cross, using a stick he kept in his bicep pocket.

Domor turned back to Caffran, pulling his headphones back down around his neck. 'The main internal lock for the hatch is buried inside the frame. Those crosses mark the threads of the gears.'

Caffran let Tokar do the honours. He put a point-blank las-round through each of the crosses, leaving round puncture holes with sharp metal edges.

The latches and locks spun free easily now their mechanisms were ruined. Adare and Flaven hauled the green hatch open and the Ghosts crept forward into a blue, gloomy realm of smoke.

Caffran knew they were emerging on the land side of the great sea wall, deep in the refinery complex of Oskray Island. They were exiting onto a lattice walkway of scrubbed iron that jutted out of the fastness wall and crossed a gulf whose depths he had no way of judging. Above, below and around, everything was smoke.

The walkway was five metres wide, with a low handrail, and reached across forty metres to a tower that rose skeletally out of the haze.

The air smelled of cordite and salt. It was cold and clammy suddenly.

Caffran scanned around. Behind them, the way they had come, he was just able to make out the back of the vast sea wall rising up, lost in the fog. The throbbing and pulsing was much louder now and Caffran knew it must be coming from the fuel-mills, the promethium pumps and the other working systems of the vast refinery.

Domor was next to him, prying into the smoke with his prosthetic eyes. The focus rings were buzzing now, and he strained with them. Thick, discoloured tears trickled down his stubbled cheeks. The salt water had really done its devious work.

'This smoke is backwash from the enemy guns along the wall top,' Domor said. 'The sea air and the downdraft of our ships is blowing it back over the wall and it's pooling here in the inner basin of the refinery.'

All the better for them to move unseen, thought Caffran, but... to where? Adrenaline had brought them so far. Where was the plan?

They were nearly at the tower, a vast red-painted skeletal needle of girders with dull flashing lamps at the corners. Other walkways stretched away from it into the soupy air. Caffran was beginning to make sense of the place, and picked out other catwalks and walkways above, below and parallel to the one the Ghosts used, through the billowing smoke.

Laser fire peppered down at them suddenly, rebounding from the iron walkway or punching through it. Bude stumbled as a round hit him in the top of the left shoulder and exited through his right hip. Caffran knew he was dead, but he tried desperately to get to him nevertheless. Bude leaned on the rail for a moment, upright, then pitched over and fell away into the smoke below silently.

There were dark shapes on a catwalk forty metres above and to the left of them. More zinging fire spat down through the clouds. The Ghosts opened up in return, pasting shots up into the roof of the smoke. A body fell past them. Mkendrik swivelled his flamer and vomited huge curls of fire up at the enemy position. The catwalk above them collapsed and spilled four fire-streaming comets down into the chasm: burning, screaming, flailing human forms.

Caffran led the way to the tower at a run and entered a grilled-off section that faced an open-sided elevator car. Caill and Mkallun joined him first, the others close on their heels. A steep stairwell of open-backed mesh steps led both down and up the tower alongside the open elevator shaft.

More las-fire, and stub rounds, started spanking off the ironwork and tinging around the metal cage of the tower.

'Which way?' bellowed Caill.

'Up!' Caffran decided.

'Where's the sense in that? We'll be trapped like rats at the top of the tower with nowhere to run!'

'No,' Caffran countered, trying desperately to think.

He was trying to bring back the briefing. The commissar had shown them aerial views of the Oskray facility, concentrating on the sea wall area they were meant to assault. He tried to picture the other, inner derrick areas he had glimpsed. Towers, dozens of them, just like the one on which they stood, bridging to each other at various levels, including some higher than the sea wall. If that was true – if the memory was true – they could cross to other towers higher up as well as lower down.

'Trust me,' Caffran said and started up the stairs, blasting las-rounds over the side at distant walkways where muzzles flashed in their direction.

They ascended.

Caffran fought the panic in his mind. The way in, the chance to sneak inside, had seemed a good plan, a brave plan, but now they were here, eight men alone in a city of the enemy, he had no idea what they had even expected to be able to achieve. There was no plan, not even the raw materials for a plan. He dreaded any of the others asking him to explain their purpose here.

Fire from below; three or four storeys down, squads of Kith soldiery were moving up the tower, blasting upwards. Las-rounds popped and thumped through the mesh steps around them. Mkallun lost the front of his foot and toppled, screaming in pain. Adare, just a few steps below him, arrested his fall and hauled the whimpering man up with him. The others blasted downwards and an odd vertical firefight began, laser salvos spitting up and down the tower structure. Mkendrik, last of the ascending Ghosts, hosed the stairs below them with his flamer and belching clouds of fire drizzled down through the open metal edifice and torched the closest of the pursuers.

Six more flights up, a bridging walkway opened to their left, crossing the smoky chasm to another tower. There seemed to be no one on the other structure, and Caffran gestured the men across, stopping to help Adare with Mkallun. Adare grabbed Caffran's shoulder and pointed to the swiftly ascending elevator in the tower they were leaving. It was packed with enemy troopers, climbing far faster than those on the stairs. Caffran sent Adare hobbling onwards with Mkallun, then pulled a pair of tube-charges from his pack. He set short fuses and rolled them along the bridge onto the tower deck, then ran to join the others.

The blast tore through the tower assembly, blowing out stanchions and main-supports all around. With a deafening howl, the tower crumpled and collapsed, hundreds of metres of steeple section from above sliding down with almost comical slowness, splintering the body of the tower below. The packed elevator car fell like a stone. Power servos tore out and exploded. Secondary explosions rippled out into the gloom.

The collapse tore away the bridge they had just crossed by, and ripped the bridge supports out of their side of the crossing, shearing metal and girders around them, shaking the other tower. Heavier impacts shook them as bridges higher up tore loose with the descending tumult and came slamming or dragging down the length of their tower.

From below, as the tower mass crashed to the ground, other explosions fluttered out as fuel stores and pumps detonated under the impact. Plumes of fire gusted around them.

'What the feth have you done?' bellowed Flaven.

Caffran wasn't sure. In desperation, he hadn't really thought through the consequences of mining the tower. One simple thing occurred to him.

'I've bought us some time,' he whispered.

Now they moved downwards, partly because down seemed to make sense, and partly because none of them trusted the stability of the tower now that its neighbour had been torn so brutally away. They descended into thicker, blacker smoke. Bright cinders floated on the wind and there was a deep, rank smell of burning fuel and spilt promethium. Even from here, they knew the collapsing tower had done vast damage to the plant.

Down, thought Caffran. Still he had no plan he could speak of, but down seemed to be instinctively right. What could they do here except perhaps some small, specific act? Like... take out the Kith's command cadre.

He laughed to himself as he thought the words. Bold, ridiculous words. As if they could even find Sholen Skara and his seniors in an island-hive this size. But it was a notion worth hanging on to.

A few hundred metres from the ground, he instructed his men to work stealthily, to do what the Ghosts did best. They blackened their skin with soot from the handrails, and pulled down their camo-cloaks, melting into the darkness of the smoke and the blackened tower-scaffold.

Below them, around the base of the tower, twisted, burning wreckage lay scattered five hundred metres in every direction. Flames leapt from small lakes of petroleum and mineral gels. The debris from the fallen tower, some of it great chunks of tower-section intact and twisted on the concrete, crushed beneath it smaller buildings and storage blocks, cranes and other rig service vehicles. Charred bodies lay crumpled or burst here and there. They passed at least one section of walkway dangling from their tower like a loose flap, clanking as it swung back and forth against the girders. Reedy klaxons barked through the smoke like the sound of yapping guard dogs.

They strode out from the base of the tower into the wreckage in fire-team formation, Caffran and Tokar at point. Domor supported the hopping Mkallun; Caffran wasn't going to leave him behind.

Spools of chain, frayed wire hawsers, splashes of oil and metal litter covered the concourse. Caffran skirted around a pair of Kith corpses, men who had clung together as they fell and been mangled into one hideous ruin by the ground.

Sending Mkendrik ahead in his place, Caffran dropped back to check on Domor and Mkallun. A hefty shot of analgesic had left Mkallun vacant, lolling and useless. Domor was blind. The iris shutters

on his bionic implants had finally failed and shut tight. Filmy fluid
leaked around the focussing rings and wept down his face. It hurt
Caffran to see his friend like this. It was like Menazoid Epsilon all
over again, when Domor had lost his eyes and still fought on without them, playing his part with a valour and tenacity even Gaunt
had been awed by.

'Leave us,' Domor told him. Caffran shook his head. He wiped away
the sweat that beaded his brow and trickled down the blue dragon
tattoo on his temple. Caffran opened Mkallun's pack and took out a
one-shot plastic injector of adrenaline, stamping it into Mkallun's bare
forearm. The injured trooper roared as he came out of his stupor. Caffran slapped him.

'Domor will be your legs – you have to be his eyes.'

Mkallun growled and then spat and nodded as he understood. The
adrenaline rush was killing all his pain and refortifying his limbs.

'I can do it, I can do it...' he said, clutching hold of Domor hard.

They moved on. Beyond the area of debris, the hive complex was
a warren of drum silos and loading docks, red-washed girder towers marked with the Imperial eagle and then defaced with sickening
runes of Chaos.

In one open concourse there was a row of fifty cargo trucks, flatbeds,
smashed and burned out. Along one wide access ramp, millions of
sections of broken pipe and hose, scattered in small random mounds.
Inside one damaged silo, countless pathetic bodies were piled and
jumbled: a mass grave of those Oskray workers who would not join
Skara's cause.

So Flaven suggested. 'Perhaps not,' Caffran said, covering his mouth
and nose with the edge of his cloak as he looked in. 'Enemy insignia
there, and armour. These aren't long dead.'

'When have they found time to gather and pile their dead? There's
an assault going on!'

Caffran agreed with Flaven's incredulity, but the signs were there.
What purpose... what peculiar intent lay behind this charnel heap?

They heard shots, a ripple of las-fire from beyond the silo and swung
in close, moving with the shadows. More shots, another almost simultaneous volley. Perhaps... a hundred guns, thought Caffran? He ordered
them to stay down and crept forward with Adare.

What they saw beyond the next bunker shocked them.

There was a wide concourse, almost a kilometre square, at the heart
of this part of the island complex. From the markings on the ground,
this had been a landing pad for the cargo lighters. Across the centre,
a thousand Kith soldiers stood in ranks of one hundred. Facing them

was a messy litter of bodies which tractors with fork shovels and dozer blades were heaping into freight trucks.

Caffran and Adare watched. The front rank of the Kith took twenty steps forward and turned to face the other rows. At a signal from a nearby officer, what was now the front rank raised their weapons and cut the file of a hundred men down in an uneven burst of gunfire. As the tractors pushed the bodies aside, the rank that had fired stepped forward and marched to where their targets had been. They turned, waited. Another order. Another ripple of fire.

Caffran wasn't sure what sickened him most: the scale of the mass firing squads or the willing, uncomplaining way each rank slew the last and then stepped forward and waited to be cut down.

'What the Feth are they doing?' Adare gasped.

Caffran thought for a moment, reaching into his memory to recover the parts of the briefing he had blanked. The parts where Gaunt had spoken about Sholen Skara.

It came back to him, out of the darker reaches of his mind, recollections rising like marsh-gas bubbles out of the mire of forgetfulness. Suddenly, Gaunt's voice was in his ear, Gaunt's image before him. The briefing auditorium of the mighty troop-ship *Persistence*, Gaunt, in his long storm coat and cap, striding onto the dais under the stone lintel of the staging, glancing up at the gilt spread-eagle with its double heads on the velvet drop behind him. Gaunt, removing his coat and dropping it on the black leather chair, standing there in his dress jacket, taking off his cap once to smooth his cropped hair as the men came to order.

Gaunt, speaking of the abominations and filthy concepts Caffran had blanked from his mind.

'Sholen Skara is a monster. He worships death. He believes it to be the ultimate expression of the Chaotic will. On Balhaut, before we came in, he ran murder-camps. There, he ritually slaughtered nearly a billion Balhauteans. His methods were inventive and '

Even now, Caffran could not bring himself to think of Gaunt's descriptions. The names of the foul species of Chaos that Sholen Skara had commanded, the symbolic meaning of their crimes. Now though, he understood why Ibram Gaunt, champion of human life and soldier of the divine Emperor, would so personally loathe the likes of the monster called Skara.

'He kills to serve Chaos. Any death serves him. Here, we can be sure, he will have butchered any Imperially-loyal hive workers en masse. We can also be sure that if he believes defeat is close, he will begin a systematic purge of any living things, including his own troops. Mass suicide, to honour Chaos. To honour the blasphemy they call Khorne.'

Gaunt coughed at the word as if his gorge was rising, and a murmur of revulsion passed through the assembled Ghosts.

'That is a way we have of winning. We can defeat him – and we can convince him he will be defeated and thus save us the bother of killing them all. If he thinks he is losing, he will begin to slaughter his own as a final hymn of defiance and worship.'

Caffran's mind swam round to the present. Adare was speaking.

'–fething more of them, Caff! Look!'

Kith soldiers, in their hundreds, were marching out onto the concourse to fall in behind the rows already slaughtered.

Not slaughtered, thought Caffran: harvested. It reminded him of the rows of corn stooks back on the meadows of Tanith, as the mechanical threshers came in reaping row after row.

Despite the sickness in his stomach, a sickness that pinched and viced with each echo of gunfire, Caffran smiled.

'What?' Adare asked.

'Nothing...'

'So what do we do now? What's the plan?'

Caffran grinned again. He realised he did have a plan, after all. And he'd already executed it. When he'd brought that tower crashing down, he'd made Sholen Skara believe a significant enemy force was inside Oskray Hive. Made him believe that defeat loomed.

As a result, Skara was ordering the Kith to kill themselves, one hundred at a time. One hundred every thirty seconds.

Caffran sat back. His aching body throbbed. There was a las-burn across his thigh he hadn't even noticed before.

'You're laughing!' said Adare, perplexed.

Caffran realised he was.

'Here's the plan,' he said at last. 'We wait.'

Afternoon squalls from the ocean were clearing the smoke from Oskray Hive, but even the wind and rain couldn't pry the stink of death from the great refinery. Formations of Imperial gunships shrieked overhead, pummelling the rain clouds with their fire-wash.

Gaunt found Caffran asleep amongst several hundred other Ghosts under a tower piling. The young trooper snapped to attention as soon as he realised who had woken him.

'I want you with me,' Gaunt said.

They crossed the great concourse of the refinery city, passing squads of Ghosts, Volpone and Abberloy Guardsmen detailed at

building-to-building clearance. Shouts and whistles rang commands
through the air as the Imperial forces took charge of the island hive
and marshalled ranks of dead-eyed prisoners away.

'I never thought you to be a tactical man, Caffran,' Gaunt began as
they walked together.

Caffran shrugged. 'I have to say I made it up as I went along, sir.'

Gaunt stopped and turned to smile at the young Ghost. 'Don't tell
Corbec that, for Feth's sake, he'll get ideas.'

Caffran laughed. He followed Gaunt into a blockhouse of thick stone
where oil-drum stacks had been packed aside to open a wide space.
Sodium lamps burned from the roof.

A ring of Imperial Guardsmen edged the open area; Volpone mostly,
but there were some Ghosts, including Rawne and other officers.

In the centre of the open area, a figure kneeled, shackled. He was
a tall, shaven-headed man in black, tight-fitting robes. Powerful, Caffran presumed, had he been allowed to stand. His eyes were sunken
and dark, and glittered out at Gaunt and Caffran as they approached
from the edge of the guarding circle.

'The little juicy maggot of the Imperial–' the figure began, in a soft,
sugar-sweet tone. Gaunt smacked him to the ground with the back of
his fist to silence him.

'Sholen Skara,' Gaunt said to Caffran, pointing down at the sprawled
figure who was trying to rise, despite his fetters, blood spurting from
his smashed mouth.

Caffran's eyes opened wide. He gazed down.

Gaunt pulled out his bolt pistol, checked it, cocked it and offered it
to Caffran. 'I thought you might like the honour. There's no court here.
None's needed. I think you deserve the duty.'

Caffran took the proffered gun and looked down at Skara. The monster had pulled himself up onto his knees and grinned up at Caffran,
his teeth pink with blood.

'Sir–' Caffran began.

'He dies here, today. Now. By the Emperor's will,' Gaunt said curtly.
'A duty I would dearly liked to have saved for myself. But this is your
glory, Caffran. You wrought this.'

'It's... an honour, commissar.'

'Do it... Do it, little Ghost-boy... What are you waiting for?' Skara's
sick-sweet tones were clammy and insistent. Caffran tried not to look
down into the sunken, glittering eyes.

He raised the gun.

'He wants death, sir.'

'Indeed he does! It is the least we can do!' Gaunt snapped.

Caffran lowered the gun and looked at Gaunt, aware that every eye in the chamber was on him.

'No, sir, he wants death. Like you told us. Death is the ultimate victory for him. He craves it. We've won here on Sapiencia. I won't soil that victory by handing the enemy what he wants.' Caffran passed the gun back to Gaunt, grip first.

'Caffran?'

'You really want to punish him, commissar? Let him live.'

Gaunt thought for a moment. He smiled.

'Take him away,' he said to the honour guard as it closed ranks around Skara.

'I may have to promote you someday,' Gaunt told Caffran as he led him away.

Behind them, Skara screamed and begged and pleaded and shrieked. And lived to do so, again and again.

Brin Milo, Gaunt's young adjutant, brought the commissar a tin cup of caffeine brew and the data-slates he hadn't requested – though he had been about to. Gaunt was sat on a camp chair on the deck outside his command shelter, gazing out at the Tanith lines and the emerald glades of Monthax beyond them. Milo gave the data-slates to the commissar and then paused as he turned away, guilty as he realised what he had done.

Gaunt eyed the slates, scrolling the charts on the lit fascia of the top one. 'Mkoll's surveys of the western swamps... and the orbital scans of Monthax. Thank you.'

The boy tried to cover his mistake. 'I thought you'd want to look them over,' he began. 'When you attack today, you'll–'

'Who said I'd attack today?'

Milo was silent. He shrugged. 'A guess. After last night's action, so close, I thought...'

Gaunt got up and looked the boy squarely in the eyes. 'Enough of your guesses. You know the trouble they might cause. For me. For you. For all the Ghosts.'

Milo sighed and leaned against the rail of the command shed's stoop where he attended the commissar. Mid-morning light lit the marshy groves beyond, lighting the tops of the tree cover an impossibly vivid green. Armoured vehicles rumbled through the mire somewhere, kilometres away. There was the distant thump of guns.

'Is there some crime...' he ventured at last, 'in anticipation? Sir. Isn't that what a good adjutant is supposed to do? Anticipate his officer's needs and requirements ahead of time? Have the right thing to hand?'

'No crime in that, Brin,' Gaunt replied, sitting back down. 'That's what makes a good adjutant, and you're making a fine job of being one. But... you anticipate too well sometimes. Some times it spooks me, and I know you. Others might view it another way. I don't need to tell you that.'

'No...'

'You know what happened in orbit last week. That was too close.'

'It was a conspiracy. I was set up.'

Gaunt wiped the sweat from his temple. 'You were. But it was easy to do. You'd be an easy victim for a determined manipulator. And if it came to that again, I'm not sure I could protect you.'

'About that... I have a request, sir. You do protect me... you have since Tanith.'

'I owe you. But for your intervention, I would have died with your world.'

'And from that you know I can handle myself in a combat situation. I want to be issued with a gun. I want to fight with the Tanith in the next push. I don't care what squad you put me in.'

'You've seen your share of fighting, Brin,' Gaunt said, shaking his head. 'But I won't make a soldier out of you. You're too young.'

'I was eighteen three days ago,' the boy said flatly.

Gaunt frowned. He hadn't realised. He flapped away a persistent fly and sipped his cup. 'Not a lot I can say to counter that,' he admitted.

He sat back down. 'What if we make a deal?'

Milo looked back at him with bright eyes and a cautious smile. 'Like what?'

'I give you a brevet field rank, a gun, and stick you next to Corbec. In return, you stop anticipating – completely.'

'Completely?'

'That's right. Well, I don't mean stop doing your job. Just stop doing things that people could take the wrong way. What do you say?'

'I'd like that. Thank you. A deal.'

Gaunt flashed him a rare smile. 'Now go and find me Corbec and Mkoll. I need to run through some details with them.'

Milo paused and Gaunt turned, looking down off the stoop to see the colonel and the scout sergeant standing side by side, looking up at him expectantly.

'Milo suggested that we should stop by. When we had a chance,' Corbec said. 'Is now a good time?'

Gaunt turned back to find Milo but the boy, probably on the basis of another wise anticipation, had made himself scarce.

TEN

WITCH HUNT

Varl lifted the Tanith camo-cloak off the censer on the floor like a magician about to perform a conjuring trick. There was a hushed silence around the ship's hold as the veil came away.

The game was simple and enticing and completely fixed, and Sergeant Varl and the boy mascot made a good team. They had a jar of fat, jumping lice scooped from the troop-ship's grain silos and that beaten old censer borrowed from the Ecclesiarch chapel. The censer was a hollow ball of rusty metal whose hemispheres hinged open so that incense could be crumbled into the holder inside and lit. The ball's surface was dotted with star-shaped holes.

'The game is simple,' Varl began, holding up the jar and jiggling it so all could see the half dozen, thumb-sized bugs inside. He held it in his mechanical hand, and the servos hummed and whirred as he agitated the glass.

'It's a guessing game. A game of chance. No trickery, no guile.'

Varl was something of a showman, and Milo liked him very much. He was one of what Milo regarded as the inner circle of Ghosts, a close friend of Corbec and Larkin, one of a gaggle of tight-knit friends and comrades mustered together from the militia of Tanith Magna at the Founding. Varl's sharp tongue and speak-your-mind attitude had retarded his promotion chances early on, but then he had lost his arm on Fortis Binary during the heroic reconquest of the forge world and by the time of the now-legendary actions of Menazoid Epsilon he had been made a squad sergeant. Many thought it was well past time. Next to the ruthless command styles of Rawne and Feygor, and the intense military mindset of the likes of Mkoll and the commissar himself, Varl, like the beloved Colonel Corbec, injected a note of humanity and genial compassion into the Ghosts' command structure. The men liked him:

he told jokes as often as Corbec, and they were for the most part funnier and cruder; his prosthetic arm proved he was not shy of close fighting; and he could, in his own, informal, garrulous way, spin a fine, inspiring speech to rouse his squad if the need called for it.

Just now, though, in one of the troop-ship's echoing holds with an audience of off-duty Guardsmen roused from their cots and stoves all around, he was turning his charismatic tongue to something far more important. The pitch.

'Here's the deal, my friends, my brave fellow Guardsmen, praise be the Golden Throne, here's the deal.'

He spoke clearly, slowly, so that his sing-song Tanith accent wouldn't confuse the other Guard soldiers here. Three other regiments were sharing this transport with the Ghosts: big, blond, square-jawed brutes from the Royal Volpone 50th, the so-called Bluebloods; sallow-skinned, idle-looking compact men from the 5th Slamabadden; and tall, tanned, long-haired types from the 2nd Roane Deepers. Worlds and accents, separated by a common tongue. Varl worked his crowd with care and precision, making sure nothing he said was lost or misunderstood.

He handed the censer to Milo, who opened it. 'See now, a metal ball, with surface holes. The grain-lice go in the ball...' He tipped a couple from his jar out into the censer as Milo held it ready. 'And my young friend here closes it up. Notice how I've scratched a number next to all the holes. Thirty-three holes, a number next to each. No tricks, no guile... you can examine the ball if you like.'

Varl took the rusty ball from Milo and set it on the floor where all could see. A large washer welded to the censer's base stopped it from rolling. 'Now, see, I sets it down. The lice want the light, right? So sooner or later, they'll hop out... through one of the holes. There's the game. We wager on the number.'

'And we lose our money,' said a Deeper near the front, his voice twanged with that odd, rounded Roane accent.

'We'll all make a bet, friend,' Varl said. 'I will, you will, anyone else. If you guess the right number or get closest, you win the pot. No tricks, no guile.'

As if on cue, a bug emerged from one of the star-shaped holes and lit off onto the deck, where a Blueblood crunched it sourly underfoot.

'No matter!' Varl cried. 'Plenty more where he came from... and if you've seen the grain silos, you'll know what I mean!'

That brought general laughter and keen sense of suffering comradeship. Milo smiled. He loved the way Varl could play a crowd.

'What if we don't trust you, Ghost?' asked a Blueblood, the big ox who had mashed the bug. He wore his grey and gold twill breeches and black boots, but was stripped down to his undershirt. His body was a mass of well-nourished muscles and he stood two heads taller than Varl. Arrogance oozed from him.

Milo tensed. He knew that some rivalry existed between the Ghosts and the Bluebloods, ever since Voltemand. No one had ever said, but the rumour was that the Blueblood's own commanders, steering the invasion force, had ordered the barrage on the Voltis riverbed where so many Ghosts had died. The Bluebloods, so high and Emperor-damned mighty, seemed to despise the 'common born' Ghosts, but then they despised everyone. This aristocratic giant, with his hooded eyes and bullying manner, had at least six friends in the crowd, and all were as big as him. What the feth do they feed them on back home to raise such giants? Milo wondered.

Varl, unconcerned, got down off the crates he had been using as a stage and approached the giant. He held out his hand. It whirred. 'Ceglan Varl, Sergeant, Tanith First-and-Only. I admire a man who can express his doubts... sergeant?'

'Major Gizhaum Danver De Banzi Haight Gilbear, Royal Volpone 50th.' The giant didn't offer to take the outstretched hand.

'Well, major, seems you've no reason to trust a low-life like me, but it's all a game, see? No tricks, no guile. We all make a bet, we all have a laugh, we all pass the voyage a little quicker.'

Major Gilbear did not seem convinced.

'You've rigged it. I'm not interested if you place a bet.' He swung his look past Varl and took in Milo. 'Let your *boy* do it.'

'Oh. Now, that's just silly!' Varl cried. 'He's just a kid... he knows nothing about the fine and graceful art of gamesmanship. You want to play this with gamblers!'

'No,' Gilbear said simply. Others in the crowd agreed, and not just Bluebloods. Some seemed in danger of walking away, disinterested.

'Very well, very well!' Varl said, as if it was breaking his heart. 'The boy can play in my stead.'

'I don't want to, sir!' Milo squeaked. He prayed his outburst had the right mix of reluctance and concern, and that it didn't sound too much on cue.

'Now then, lad,' Varl said, turning to him and putting a heavy bionic arm around his shoulders paternally. 'Be good now and play along so that the nice gentlemen here can enjoy a simple game.' Unseen to all others present, he winked at Milo. Milo fought the fiercest battle of his life not to laugh.

'O-okay,' he said.

'The boy will play in my place!' Varl said, turning back to the crowd and raising his arms. There was cheers and applause in reply.

They set to it. A larger crowd gathered. Paper markers were handed out and coin produced. Gilbear decided to play, as did two Roane Deepers and three of the Slammabadden. In the crowd, secondary bets were laid on winners and losers. Varl opened the censer and took up his jar.

Gilbear plucked it from his hand, opened it and dropped the lice out onto the deck, crunching them all underfoot. He held it out to one of his men. 'Raballe! Go fetch fresh lice from the silos!'

'Sir!'

'What is this?' Varl gasped, dropping to his knees and wiping away what seemed to Milo a real tear as he surveyed his crushed insects. 'Do you not even trust my lice, Major Gilbear, Blueblood, sir?'

'I don't trust anything I can crush with my boot,' Gilbear replied, looking down and apparently dangerously close to stamping on Varl too. A tidal change swept through the secondary betting, some of it in sympathy with the damaged Ghost and his crushed pets, some sensing trickery was routed and heaping money on the Blueblood major.

'You could have drugged them, overfed them – they seemed docile. You could place your money on the lower holes so that the sluggish things simply fell from the bottom as gravity pulled.' Gilbear smiled at his deduction and his men growled approval. So did several of the wily Slammabadden, and Milo was afraid the mood might turn ugly.

'I'll tell you what,' Varl said to the major as he got up. The Blueblood's second was returning with a jar packed full of agitated lice and semi-digested meal where he had scooped it from the dank silos. 'We'll use your pick of the bugs... and you can set the censer whichever way up you like.' Varl pulled a cargo hook from the crates behind him to use as a makeshift base. 'Happy?'

Gilbear nodded.

They made ready. The gamblers, Milo included, prepared to make their guess on the paper slips provided. Varl flexed his good shoulder, as if easing out an old hurt. A signal, the next cue.

'I'll play this too,' Caffran said, pushing forward through the huddle. He seemed to sway and he stank of sacra. Many gave him a wide berth.

'Cafy, no... you're not up to it...' Varl murmured.

Caffran was pulling out a weight of coins, rolls of thick, high-issue disks.

'Give me the paper... I like a bet,' Caffran mumbled, slurring.

'Let your Ghost play,' Gilbear growled with a smirk as Varl began to protest.

It looked to all present like the Tanith showman had lost control of his simple game, and if there had been any trickery in it, any guile, then all of it was ruined now.

The first lice went in. Gilbear spun the censer and set it down. Markers were overturned. A Slammabadden came closest, closest to guessing the exit by three holes. Milo was nowhere near and seemed to whimper.

Caffran raged as his money was scooped away. He produced more.

A Deeper won the next, the winner of the last round given the honour of placing the censer. He was no closer than five holes, but the others were grouped and very wrong. Milo begged Varl to let him stop but Varl shook him off, glancing sidelong at the glowering Gilbear.

Gilbear won the next by guessing within two. He collected a massive pile of coins and one of the Deepers dropped out in disgust. The level of the bets – and off-game bets – had risen considerably and now real money was at stake. Cash was changing hands all around. The Bluebloods were jubilant and so were others. Others still bemoaned their losses. Two more Slammabadden and another Deeper stepped up to play, their bets bolstered by whip-rounds amongst their friends. No Blueblood dared to play against Gilbear.

Flushed with success, Gilbear placed his won pot again, and doubled it. Some of the Guardsmen present, especially the Deepers and the watching Ghosts, had never seen so much ready cash in their lives. Caffran made a fuss and swigged from a bottle of sacra, imploring his friend Brostin for a sub which was eventually, reluctantly, given.

The next round. Gilbear and a Deeper, each three holes away from the winning aperture, split the now considerable pot.

The next round. Playing was Gilbear, three of the Slammabadden, two Deepers, Caffran (now subbing from a worried-looking Raglon, Brostin having exited in a convincing rage) and Milo. A huge pile of wagers.

Caffran came out two off the mark, a Slammabadden was one off. Gilbear was on the other side of the censer. Milo was spot on.

Howls, anger, jubilation, tumult.

'He was just lucky,' Varl said, collecting up the winnings. 'Are we done?'

'The boy got a fluke,' Gilbear said, ordering his subalterns to empty their pockets. Another big wager was assembled. The Deepers had dropped out, and so had Caffran, leaving the chamber with Raglon. The Slammabadden mustered their strengths into one wager.

Milo turned the censer and set it down.

Silence.

The bug ticked and bounced against the inside of the metal ball.

It emerged.

Milo had it again, spot on.

Pandemonium. It seemed like a riot would overturn the troop bay. Varl collected the winnings and the censer and pulled Milo out of the chamber by the scruff of his tunic. Men were shouting, milling around, and a fight had begun over the outcome of one of the side-bets.

In the companionway that led back to the Tanith troop deck, Varl and Milo rejoined Caffran, Raglon and Brostin. They were all laughing, and Caffran seemed suddenly sober. He would have to wash his tunic to get the stink of sacra out of it, of course.

Varl grinned at them and held up the bulky pouch containing their winnings. 'Spoils to be divided, my friends!' he announced to them, slapping Milo across the back with his bionic arm. He had never got used to its strength and Milo nearly fell.

Caffran uttered a warning. Dark shapes loomed down the companionway behind them. It was Gilbear and four of his men.

'You'll pay for that trickery, whore's-son,' Gilbear told Varl.

'It was a fair game,' began Varl, but realised at once that his silver tongue was useless now.

There were five on each side, but each of the Bluebloods towered over Brostin, the largest of the Tanith present. In a close-quarter brawl, the Ghosts might score, draw even perhaps, but it would be bloody.

'Is there a problem?' asked the sixth member of the Tanith scam team. Bragg pulled his vast bulk into the light behind his comrades, squinting in a relaxed way down at the five Bluebloods. He seemed to fill the corridor.

The Ghosts parted to let Bragg lumber through. He adopted the slow gait Varl had trained him in, to emphasise his power. 'Go away, little Bluebloods. Don't make me hurt you,' he said, repeating the cue Varl had also given him. It came out stilted and false, but the Bluebloods were too amazed at his size to notice.

They turned. With a final scowl, Gilbear followed them.

The Ghosts began to laugh so hard, they wept.

Below him, Monthax, green, impenetrable.

Gaunt gazed down through the arched viewports of the hexathedral *Sanctity*, studying the distant surface of the planet that, within a week, his forces would be assaulting. From time to time, he referred to a data-slate map in his hand, checking off geographical details. The dense jungle cover was the biggest problem they faced. They had no idea of the hidden enemy's strength.

Advance reports suggested a vast force of Chaos filth had retreated from a recent engagement at Piolitus and dug in here. Warmaster Macaroth was taking no chances. Around the huge bulk of the orbiting hexathedral, a colossal towered platform designed as a mustering point for the invasion forces, great legions massed. Over a dozen huge troop-ships were already docked around the crenellated rim of the hexathedral's skirt platform, like fat swine at the teats of their obese mother, and tugs were easing another in now to join them. More were due. Further away, Imperial battlecruisers and escort ships, including the frigate *Navarre* on which Gaunt and the Ghosts had been stationed for a while, sat at high orbit anchor, occasionally buzzing out clouds of attack squadrons heading off for surface runs or patrol sweeps.

Gaunt turned from the windows and stepped down a short flight into the cool, echoing vastness of one of the *Sanctity*'s main tactical chapels, the Orrery. A vast circular dial was set flush in the centre of the chamber's floor, thirty metres across and made of intricate, interlocking, moving parts of brass and gold, like a giant timepiece. As it whirred and cycled, the three-dimensional globe of coloured light it projected upwards altered and spun, advancing data, chart runes, bars of information across the luminous surface.

Trim uniformed Guard officers, robed members of the Ecclesiarch and the Munitorum, Navy commanders in their Segmentum Pacificus deck dress, and the hooded deaconal staff of the hexathedral itself, prowled the edges of the great Light Orrery, consulting the data and conferring in small groups. Skeletal servitors, emaciated, wired into the machine banks via cables from their eyes, spines, mouths and hands, hunkered in booth-cribs, murmuring and chattering. Around the sides of the great chamber, under cloistered roofing, great chart tables were arranged at intervals, each showing different sections of Monthax. Staff groups stood around every table, engaged in more specific and detailed planning sessions. The air chimed with announcements and updates, some of these overlapping and chattering with data noise. The Orrery turned, whirring, and new details and deployments appeared.

Gaunt walked a circuit of the chamber, nodding to those fellow officers he knew, saluting his seniors. The whole place had an exceptional, expectant hush, like a great hunting animal, breathless, coiled to pounce.

The commissar decided it was time he took a walk down to the Ghosts' troop-ship. The men would be restless, awaiting news of debarkation and deployment, and Gaunt knew well that trouble was always likely to brew when Guardsmen were cramped together in transportation, idle and nervous.

And bored. That was the worst of it. In any Guard regiment, disciplinary matters rose in number during such times, and he and the other commissars, the political enforcers of the Imperial Guard, would be busy. There would be brawls, thefts, feuds, drunkenness, even murder in some of the more barbaric regiments, and such disorder quickly spread without the proper control.

Across the chamber, Gaunt saw General Sturm, the commander of the Volpone 50th, and some of his senior aides. Sturm did not seem to see him, or chose not to acknowledge Gaunt if he did, and Gaunt made no effort to salute. The crime of Voltemand was still raw in his mind, despite the interval of months. When he learned that the Volpone Bluebloods and the Ghosts would encounter each other again at Monthax, for the first time since Voltemand, he had been apprehensive. The action on Menazoid Epsilon had shown him personally what a long-standing feud between regiments could do. But there was no chance of redeployment, and Gaunt comforted himself that it was only Sturm and his senior staff he had a problem with. The rank and file of the Ghosts and the Bluebloods had no reason for animosity. He would keep a careful watch, but he was sure they could billet side by side safely enough until the assault sent them their separate ways.

And, unlike on Voltemand, Sturm wasn't in charge here. The Monthax offensive was under the supreme command of Lord Militant General Bulledin.

Gaunt saw Commissar Volovoi, serving with the Roane Deepers, and stopped to talk with him. It was mostly inconsequential chat, though Volovoi had heard some word that Bulledin had consulted the Astropathicus. Rumours of psyker witchery on the planet below had started to spread. There was talk that auguries and the Tarot had been consulted to determine the truth of the situation.

'Last thing we need,' muttered Volovoi to Gaunt. 'Last thing I need. The Roane are the very devil to keep in line. Good fighters, yes, when they're roused to it, but damned idle for the most part. A few weeks of transportation confinement like this, and I'll have to kick each and every one of their arses to get them down the drop-ship ramp. Languid, lazy – and this makes it worse: they're superstitious, more than any band of men I've ever known. The rumours of witchcraft will get them spooked and that will make my work twice as hard.'

'I sympathise,' Gaunt said. He did. His old regiment, the Hyrkans, were tough as deck plate, but there had been times when the thought of psyker madness had balked them in their tracks.

'What of you, Gaunt?' Volovoi asked. 'I hear you're taken up with a low-tech rabble now. Don't you miss the Hyrkan discipline?'

Gaunt shook his head. 'The Tanith are sound, quietly disciplined in their way.'

'And you have actual command of them too, is that right? Unusual. For a commissar.'

'A gift of the late Slaydo, may the Emperor watch his rest. I resented it at first, but I've grown to like it.'

'You've done well with them, so I hear. I read the reports on that campaign in the Menazoid Clasp last year, and they say your men turned the key that opened the door at Bucephalon too.'

'We've had our moments.'

Gaunt realised Volovoi was studying something over Gaunt's shoulder.

'Don't turn, Gaunt,' Volovoi went on, without changing the timbre of volume of his talk. 'Are your ears burning? Someone's talking about you.'

'How so?'

'The Blueblood general. Sturm, is it? Arrogant piece of yak flop. One of his officers just came on deck and is bending his ear. And they're looking this way.'

Gaunt didn't turn. 'Let me guess: the newcomer is a big ox with hooded eyes?'

'Aren't they all?'

'This one's a piece of work even by the Volpone standards of breeding. A major.'

'That's what his rank pins say. You know him?'

'Not particularly, though even that is more than I'd care for. Name's Gilbear. He and I and Sturm had a... difference of opinion on Voltemand eighteen months ago.'

'What sort of difference?'

'They cost me several hundred men.'

Volovoi whistled. 'You'd think it would be you whispering about them!'

Gaunt smiled, though it was dark. 'We are, aren't we, Volovoi?'

Gaunt made to leave. Crossing the Orrery deck, he was afforded a better view of the Volpone staff. Gilbear was stood alone now, staring at Gaunt with a burning look that did not flinch. Sturm, escorted by his aides, was heading up the long flight of steps to the Lord Militant General's private chambers in the spire above.

Walking the troop decks with Gaunt, Corbec brought his commander up to speed.

'Quiet really. There was a fight over some rations, but it was nothing and I broke it up. Costin and two of his pals got falling down tipsy inhaling paint thinners in the armour shops and Costin then fell down for real, breaking his shin.'

'I've warned the armouries to lock that sort of material up...'

'They did, but Costin has a way with locks, sir, if you get me.'

'Put him and the others on report and punishment detail.'

'I'd say Costin's paid for his ill-gotten–' Corbec began.

'I won't stand for it. They've got rations of grog and sacra. I can't use men with fume-ruined heads.'

Corbec scratched his chin. 'Point there, sir. But the men get bored. And some of them use their sacra rations up in the first few days.'

Gaunt turned to his second, anger flickering in his eyes. 'Let it be known, Colm: the Emperor grants them recreational liquor and smokes. If they abuse that privilege, I'll take it away. From all of them. Understand?'

Corbec nodded. They stopped at the rail and looked down into the vast troop bay. The air was laced with smoke and rank sweat. Below them, bench cots by the hundred in rows, men by the hundred, sleeping, dicing, chatting, praying, some just staring into nothing. Priests walked the rows, dispensing solace and benediction where it was requested or simply needed.

'Is there something on your mind, sir?' Corbec asked.

'I think trouble's brewing,' Gaunt said. 'I'm not sure what yet, but I don't like it.'

There was someone moving in the outer room.

Gaunt awoke. It was night cycle on the troop-ship and the wall lamps had been doused by the automatic control. He had fallen asleep on his cot with a weight of data sheets and slates on his chest.

Movement from the ante-room beyond his bed quarter had roused him.

Gaunt rose silently, placing the data sheets on a wall shelf. His bolt-gun and chainsword were slung over a wooden stand in the outer room, but he pulled a compact laspistol from his foot locker and slid it into the back of his waistband. He was dressed in his boots, trousers, braces and an undershirt. He thought for a moment about re-donning his jacket and cap, but cast the idea aside.

The cot-room door was ajar. The light of a tight-beam flashlight stabbed the darkness beyond. Someone was going through his things.

He moved in an instant, kicking open the door and grabbing the intruder from behind, turning him, twisting his arms, and slamming him face first into the round observation port of the outer room. The man – robed, struggling – protested until the moment of impact. His nose broke against the glass and he lolled unconscious.

The lights went on. Gaunt sensed there were two others behind him. He heard the whine of charging las-packs.

He spun and threw his unconscious prey at the nearest, who tumbled under the weight. The other tried to take a bead with his gun, but Gaunt dropped, slid sideways, and broke his jaw with a heavy blow. Only then, a few seconds after the whole thing had begun, did he see the man he had dropped was a security trooper dressed in the brown armour of the hexathedral. His comrade, scrambling up from under the weight of the fallen robed man, lunged forward, and Gaunt turned, catching his probing hands, breaking an elbow with a deft twist and then flooring him with a straight punch to the bridge of the nose.

Gaunt pulled out his compact and covered the room. Two hexathedral troopers and a man in long robes lay at his feet, twitching and moaning.

The door opened.

'Many would look with disfavour at such violence, commissar,' the figure who entered the room announced softly.

Gaunt kept the gun trained at the intruder's throat. 'Many look on intrusion and burglary in a similar way. Identify yourself.'

The figure moved into the light. She was tall, dressed in a simple uniform of black: boots, breeches, jacket. Her ash-fair hair was pinned tight up around her skull. Her face was calm, angular, lean, beautiful.

'I am Lilith. Inquisitor Lilith.'

Gaunt lowered the pistol and set it down on the side-table.

'You have not requested my seal of office. You believe me then?'

'I know of you. Pardon, ma'am; there are few females holding your rank and duty.'

Lilith moved forward into the room and gently kicked one of the troopers. He moaned and roused. 'Get yourself out of here. These two as well.'

The bloodied trooper clambered to his feet and dragged the others out.

'I apologise, commissar,' Lilith said. 'I had been told you were in a planning session. I would not have sent my men in if I had known you were sleeping here.'

'You'd have had my rooms searched had I been absent?'

She turned to him and laughed. It was attractive, confident – and hard. 'Of course! I'm an inquisitor, commissar. That's what I do.'

'What, precisely, is it you're doing here?'

'The boy.' She pulled out a chair and sat back, leaning against the back rest with relaxed ease. 'I need to know about the boy. Your boy, commissar.'

Gaunt stayed where he was and fixed his gaze on her. 'I don't like your tone, or your methods,' he growled. 'If I continue not to like them, I can assure you the fact you are a woman won't–'

'Are you really threatening me, commissar?'

Gaunt breathed deeply. 'I believe I am. You saw what I did to your lackeys. I won't stand for this unless you show me good reason.'

Lilith sighed and steepled her long, pale fingers. Then she pointed the compact laspistol right at Gaunt.

He started, amazed. She had not moved, but now she held a gun which had been lying right across the room from her.

'How good a reason do I need?' she asked, smiling. Gaunt stepped back.

'That little demonstration would seem good enough...'

Lilith smiled and dropped the gun into her lap. She clasped her hands together again and set her head back.

'Good. We'll begin. By the proclamation of the Most High Emperor, governed as I am by His will, in totally, till the end of all days, as a servant of the Inquisition, I require you to furnish with me with answers of complete truth and veracity to your best knowledge. The penalties for deception are manifold and without limit. Do you understand?'

'Get on with it.'

She smiled again. 'I like you, commissar. "The very devil", they said. They were right.'

'Who's "they"?'

Lilith didn't answer. She rose, holding the pistol loose in her left hand. She circled Gaunt. He was unnerved by her masculine height and her unblinking stare.

'Skipping further formalities, as you suggest, why don't you tell me about the boy?'

'What boy?'

'So coy. His name is Brin Milo, a Tanith native, part of your cadre but a civilian.'

'What do you want to know, inquisitor?'

'Oh, everything, Ibram; everything.'

Gaunt cleared his throat. 'Milo is... here by chance. The regimental piper, mascot... my aide.'

'Why?'

'He's smart, sharp, eager. The men like him. He can do the jobs I ask of him quickly and efficiently.'

Lilith held up a finger. 'Start from the beginning. Why is he here?'

'When Chaos fell on Tanith, and consumed it, I elected to withdraw all the able bodied men I could from the world. My own exit was barred and the boy intervened, clearing my way. In gratitude, I took him with me. He's too young for infantry, so I made him my aide.'

'Because of his skills?'

'Yes. And because there was nothing other to be done with him.'

Lilith came close to Gaunt and stared into his eyes. 'What are his skills?'

'Efficiency, ability, keenness to–'

'Really, commissar. You can admit it. Taking a liking to a clean-limbed young cabin mate and–'

The slap resounded in the close air of the cabin. Lilith didn't flinch. She turned away, laughing.

'Very good. Very direct. So we can cut the crap, can we? I have notice that the boy is a witch. How do you respond?'

'He is not.' Gaunt swallowed. 'The poison of the warp turns my guts. You think I would have truck with it for a second?' He paused. 'Present company excepted, naturally.'

Lilith circled him. 'But he's useful. I've done my ground work, Gaunt. He predicts things, guesses them before they happen... attacks, incidents, what files the commissar needs. What the commissar wants for breakfast–'

'That's no witchcraft. He's smart. He anticipates.'

'There was a game... a scam... in the lower decks. He was a key part of it. He knew how to win it. He was perfect in his guesses. What do you say to that?'

'I say: who put you up to this?'

'Does it matter?'

'It was Sturm, wasn't it? And his pet ox, Gilbear. They have an agenda; how can you trust their word?'

She faced him and fixed him with her eyes. 'But of course. They cannot hide it from me. Sturm and Gilbear hate you and despise your Ghosts. They tried to obliterate you on Voltemand and failed. Now they seek to bring you down by whatever means they have.'

Gaunt was almost speechless. 'You know this and still you come here?'

'I'm an inquisitor, Ibram,' she replied with a smile. 'Sturm and his men are brutes. I have no interest in their internecine hatred for you and your men. But Lord Militant General Bulledin has brought me here to assess and sanction the dangers of witchcraft during the liberation of Monthax. Enemy witchcraft... and also that which lurks within like a cancer. The boy has been brought to my attention and I am duty bound to examine the evidence. They say he's a witch. I don't care why they say it or what they hope to earn from such accusations. But if they're right... That's why I'm here. Is Milo touched? Is he a psyker? Don't protect him, Gaunt. It will be so much the worse for you if you do.'

'He isn't. This is all political nonsense. The Bluebloods have seen a potential weakness they wish to exploit.'

'We'll see. I need to speak with this Milo. Now.'

* * *

To be summoned by his commissar during night cycle was not a new experience for Brin Milo; there were often out-of-hours errands to be run. But as soon as he arrived outside Gaunt's quarters, he realised something was wrong. Gaunt was in full dress uniform, with jacket and cap, and his face was grim. A tall woman in black with an oddly malevolent air about her waited to the side.

'This servant of the Emperor has some questions for you,' Gaunt explained. He refrained from using the loaded word 'inquisitor'. 'Answer her honestly and directly.'

Wordlessly, Lilith led them down the long deck hall and into the docking ring. They crossed over into the hexathedral itself. Milo was apprehensive. He had not set foot on the great docking craft before. The air smelled different, sacred and cool after the stuffy humidity of the troop transport, and the scale of the chambers they passed through startled him. The only people they met were deacons in robes, brown-armoured troopers and small groups of ranking officers. It was another world.

Lilith led the way on a route that took twenty minutes to walk and passed through several main chapels and chambers of the hexathedral, including the Orrery. Gaunt understood her tactics. The route was overlong and unnecessary, except it would disarm and over-awe the boy and make his psychological reserve weaker. She was clever to the point of cruel.

They reached an iris shutter at the end of a long corridor flanked by windows of stained glass. Lilith made a slight gesture with her hand and the hatch spiralled open. She waved the boy inside and turned on the threshold to speak with Gaunt.

'You may attend, but make no interruption. Gaunt, you're a valuable officer, and if this boy turns out to be tainted, I can make it so you suffer nothing more than a slight reprimand for being unaware of his status.'

'A generous suggestion. What are the conditions?'

Lilith smiled. 'We are complementary instruments, commissar, you and I. My duty is to worm out corruption, yours is to punish it. If Milo is corrupt, you will exonerate yourself by performing summary execution yourself. It will reflect your outrage and determination to clean house.'

Gaunt was silent. The possibility clawed at his mind.

'There would be no other way to salvage your reputation, command or career. Indeed your very life may be forfeit if it is thought you conspired to protect a pawn of the Darkness. Do you hear me, Gaunt?'

'I hear your threat to my life and its future. I deal with threats as a profession.'

'Then I'll be blunter. Sturm has initiated this process because he sees it as a way of bringing you and the Ghosts down. If Milo is corrupt and you do not distance yourself from him and act like a commissar, your life will be over – and Sturm will make sure the Ghosts are dismantled. He has already seeded the idea in Bulledin's mind that if one Ghost is a witch, so might others be. The Tanith First would be taken, to a man, by the Inquisition and they would all suffer extreme investigation. Most would die. The rest would be cast aside as no longer fit to serve the Imperial Guard. I am bound by duty to investigate Sturm's claim. I do not wish to be party to his vendetta against the Tanith, but I will become so if you do not act accommodatingly, willingly and honourably.'

'I see. Thank you for your candour.'

'Chaos is the greatest threat mankind faces, Gaunt. We cannot allow psychic power to exist within any untrained mind. If the boy is touched, he must be destroyed.'

'Not evaluated by the Black Ships... as you were?'

She looked at him with a sharp frown. 'Not this time. The political situation is too delicate. If Milo is a witch, he must be put to death to appease all parties.'

'I see.'

She nodded and stepped inside. Gaunt paused and found himself looking down at his holstered bolt pistol. Could he do it? The life of every Ghost might depend on the sacrifice of Milo, and to have struggled to bring them so far, to save them and give them purpose was not something Gaunt felt he could throw aside. He owed it to the Tanith to do all he could to safeguard them. But to execute Brin... the boy who had selflessly saved his life, selflessly served... it went so against his personal honour the thought crushed his chest.

Yet if the boy really was touched, really was tainted with the unbearable stain of Chaos...

His face grim and cold, he ducked inside, and the iris hatch whispered shut behind him.

The room was wide and high, lacking windows in its walls but sporting a great circular port in the roof. Stars gleamed down from above and their light was almost all there was, except for small, dim lamps set around the edges of the floor. There was a carpet on the floor, a thick, coloured weave that bore the Imperial eagle crest. Two seats, facing each other, sat in the centre of the carpet – a high-backed wooden throne with knurled armrests, and a smaller wooden stool. Lilith sat on the stool and motioned Milo to occupy the huge throne. Its wooden embrace seemed to swallow him up. Gaunt stood back, watching uneasily.

'Your name?'

'Brin Milo.'

'I am Lilith. I am an inquisitor.' That word now, finally, biting the air with its menace and threat. Milo's eyes were wide and fearful.

She asked him about Tanith, his past, his life there. He answered, halting at first, but as her questions flowed – innocent, innocuous questions about his memories – he spoke more confidently.

She asked him to recount his first meeting with Gaunt, his memories of the fall of Tanith, the choice he had made to fight for Gaunt there.

'Why? You were not a soldier. You are not a soldier now. Why did you defend this off-worlder you hardly knew?'

Milo glanced at Gaunt briefly. 'The Elector of Tanith, whose household I served as musician and attendant, ordered me to stay with the commissar and see to his needs. His needs at that point were mortal. He was being attacked and had little chance of survival. I was doing as I had been ordered.'

She sat back, drumming her fingers on her knees. 'It interests me, Milo, that you have not yet asked why this interrogation is happening. Most brought before me usually express outrage and protest innocence, wondering why this should be happening to them. But you do not. In my experience, the guilty always know why they're here and seldom ask. Do you know why you're here?'

'I can guess.'

Gaunt froze. *Wrong answer, Brin, wrong answer...*

'Guess out loud,' she invited. 'I hear you're remarkably good at guessing.'

Milo seemed to tremble. 'I am considered by many to be a misfit. Some of the Tanith don't like to have me around. I am not like them.'

Feth, Milo! I said answer honestly, but there's honest and there's this! Gaunt thought darkly. His heart raced.

'What do you mean? How are you not like them?'

'I... I'm different. It makes them uneasy.'

'How are you different?' she asked, almost eager.

Here it comes, thought Gaunt.

'I'm not a soldier.'

'You're... what?'

'They're all soldiers. That's why they're here, that's why they survived the fall of Tanith. They were all new-founded Guards, mustered to leave Tanith anyway, and the commissar only evacuated them because of their worth to the Emperor. But I'm not. I'm a civilian. I shouldn't be here. I shouldn't have survived. The Tanith see me and they think "Why did that boy survive? Why is he here? If he's here, why not my brother, my daughter, my father, my wife?" I represent a possibility of survival denied to them all.'

She was silent for a moment.

It was all Gaunt could do to stop himself smiling. Milo's answer had been perfect, as had the way he had allowed it to seem she was leading him into a trap. It made his response seem all the more honest.

Lilith got to her feet and crossed to Gaunt's side. He could see the fierce annoyance in her face. She whispered, 'Have you briefed the boy? Coached him in good answers for just such an event?'

Gaunt shook his head. 'No, and if I had, don't you suppose such an admission might make it look as if I knew Milo had something to hide?'

She hissed a curse and thought for a moment.

'Why this charade of questions?' Gaunt asked. 'Why not just probe his mind? You have the gift, don't you?'

She looked and him and nodded. 'You know I do. But a good psyker, a dangerous psyker, can hide his power. The questions are an effective method of opening up his guard and winkling out the truth. And if his mind is the seething furnace we fear, I have no wish to touch it directly.'

She turned back, pacing around Milo's throne. From behind him, she said. 'Tell me about the game.'

'Game?'

'The game you and your Tanith friends play in the troop decks.'

She paced round in front of him and held out her right hand, palm down, balled in a fist. She turned it over and opened it. A grain-louse sat in the palm, twitching and alive.

'This game.'

'Oh,' Milo said. 'It's a betting game. You bet on which hole the bug will come out.'

She put the bug on his knee and it made no effort to jump away. Milo looked down at it with fascination. Lilith crossed to the side of the room and took something from a wall cupboard. The object was covered in a velvet cloth. When she unveiled it, it was like a magician about to perform a conjuring trick. But not half as much as when Varl did it.

She gave the rusty censer ball to Milo. 'Open it. Put the bug inside.'

He obeyed.

'Now, Milo. This isn't a game, is it? It's a scam. It's a trick the Tanith use to win cash from the other Guardsmen. And if it's a scam, it needs a sting. It needs a foolproof method to make it a sure thing the Tanith will win. You're the sting, aren't you? On demand, you can guess right... because that's what you do, isn't it? Your mind does the trick and makes it a certainty.'

Milo shook his head. 'It's just a game...'

'I have it on good authority that it is not. If it's a game, why do you play it with unsuspecting troops from other regiments? By my own investigation, you and your friends have earned a small fortune from other men in these last few days. More than you would expect to win if it was just chance.'

'Lucky, I gu– I suppose.'

'You cannot run a scam on such wide odds. How do you really ensure the bug emerges from the right hole?'

Brin lifted the censer. The bug ticked inside. 'Okay... if it matters so much, I'll show you. Pick a hole.'

'Sixteen,' she said, sitting down on the stool facing him, apparently eager.

'I say nine.' He set it down. The bug emerged from hole twenty.

'You win. You were closer.'

She shrugged.

He opened the censer and put the bug back inside. 'That was round one. You're more confident now. You'll play again. Pick.'

'Seven.'

'Twenty-five,' said Milo. They waited, and then the bug wriggled out of hole six and hopped across the carpet.

'Again you win. You're feeling good now, aren't you? Two wins. On the troop deck, you might have a pile of coins now, and you might wager the lot. You put the bug in.'

She did so and handed the censer back to Milo.

'Pick?' he said.

'Nineteen. All my money and all the cash my comrades-in-arms have on nineteen.'

He smiled. 'One,' he said.

The bug squirmed out of hole one.

'And so I take my huge winnings, look you in your open-mouthed face and say good night.' Milo sat back.

'A beautiful demonstration... and one that may have just incriminated you. How could you do that, to order, at just the right moment, unless your mind knew in advance which way the bug was going?'

Milo tapped his head. 'You're so sure it's my mind, aren't you, ma'am? So sure it's the twisted workings I've got up here... You think I'm a *psyker*, don't you?'

Her expression was icy. 'Show me an alternative.'

He tapped his jacket pocket. 'It's not up there, it's down here.'

'Explain.'

'At the start of each game, we reach into our pockets for the next wager. I let you place the bug and so on, but I'm the last to handle the censer. The bugs love sugar dust. There's some in the seam of my pocket. I wipe my finger in it as I take out my money and then wipe that finger around the hole I want as I place the censer down. The dust's invisible on that rusty surface of course. But the scam is, I always know which hole it's going to come out of. I choose every time: the first few rounds to let you win, and then when you're confident you've got me on the ropes and start wagering everything, I play to win.'

Lilith got up smartly, crushing the bug underfoot with a deliberate heel. It left a brown stain on one beak of the Imperial crest. She turned to Gaunt.

'Get him out of here. I will report to Bulledin and Sturm. This matter is closed.'

Gaunt nodded and led Milo to the doorway.

'Commissar!' she called out after them. 'He might not be a witch, but if I were you I'd think twice about having a devious and underhand little cheat like him anywhere near me.'

'I'll take that under advisement, Inquisitor Lilith,' Gaunt replied and they left.

They walked back together through the hallways of the hexathedral. Night cycle was coming to an end, and dawn prayers and offerings were being made in the echoing chapels and chambers around. Incense and plainsong filled the air.

'Well done. I'm sorry you had to go through that.'

'You thought she'd get me, didn't you?' Milo asked.

'I've never doubted the goodness or honesty in you, Brin, but I've always been uneasy about your knack of anticipating things ahead of time. I always feared that someone would take exception to it and that you would land us all in trouble.'

'You'd have shot me though, right?'

Gaunt stopped in his tracks. 'Shot you?'

'If I'd let you down and landed the Ghosts in trouble. If I'd been... what she thought I was.'

'Oh.' They walked on. 'Yes, I would. I would have had to.'

Milo shrugged.

'That's what I thought you'd say,' he murmured.

ELEVEN

SOME DARK & SECRET PURPOSE

Gaunt woke, and remembered that he had been dreaming of Tanith. That wasn't unusual in itself; the visions of the fall of that world stalked his dreams regularly. But this time, for the first time, it seemed to him that he had been dreaming about the world as it had been: alive, flourishing, thriving.

The dream disquieted him, and he would have dwelt on it, had there been time. But then he realised that an urgent commotion had roused him. Outside, the pre-dawn gloom of Monthax was riven with shouts and alarms and the distant, eager sounds of warfare. Someone was hammering on the door of the command centre. Gaunt could hear Milo's insistent voice.

He pulled on his boots and went outside, the cool morning air stiffening the night-sweat soaking his tight undershirt and breeches. He blinked at the cold glare, batting aside a persistent insect, as he half-listened to Milo's hasty reports, half-read the vox-caster print-outs and data-slates the boy handed him. Gaunt's eyes looked westward. Pink and amber flashes underlit the low night clouds to the west, like a false dawn, every now and then punctured by the brief, trailing white star of a flare-charge, or the brighter, whiter flashes of some powerful energy support weapon.

Gaunt didn't need Milo or the printed communiqués to know that the major offensive had begun at last. The enemy was moving, in force.

He ordered the platoon leaders to ready their men – though most had begun to do so already – and summoned the senior officers for a tactical meeting in the command centre. He sent Milo away in search of his cap and jacket, and his weapons.

In under ten minutes, Corbec brought Rawne, Lerod, Mkoll, Varl and the other seniors to the centre, to find Gaunt, now dressed, spreading out the communiqués on the camp table. There were no preliminaries.

'Orbital reconnaissance and forward scouting has shown a massed, singular column of Chaos moving through the territory to the west.'

'Objective?' Corbec asked.

Gaunt shrugged. It was a disarming gesture from one usually so confident. 'Unclear, colonel. We've been expecting a major attack for days, but this doesn't seem to focus any strength on our positions at all. Early reports show the enemy have cut through – well, destroyed, in fact – a battalion-strength force of Kaylen Lancers. But I have a hunch that's only because the Lancers were in the way. It's as if our enemy has another objective, one they're determined to achieve. One we don't know about.'

Mkoll was eyeing the charts carefully. He'd scouted and mapped the area in question thoroughly during the previous week. His sharp tactical mind saw no obvious purpose to the assault either. He said as much.

'Could their intelligence be wrong?' Varl asked. 'Maybe they've made their play at positions they think we hold.'

'I doubt that,' Mkoll answered. 'They've seemed well informed up to now. Still, it's a possibility. They've committed a huge portion of their strength to a mistake if that's true.'

'If it's a mistake, we'll use it. If they have some dark and secret purpose, well, we'll do ourselves no favours by waiting to find out what it is.' Gaunt paused and scratched his chin thoughtfully.

'Besides,' he said, 'our orders are clear. General Thoth is sending us in, as soon as we're ready, on orders from Lord Militant General Bulledin himself. The Tanith will form one arm of a counter assault. Upwards of sixty thousand men from various regiments are to be deployed against the enemy. Because of the peculiar, not to say perplexing orientation of their advance, we'll catch them side on. The Ghosts will cover a salient about nine kilometres long.' Gaunt indicated their area of the new front on the chart, marking little runic symbols on the glass plate with his wax pencil. 'I don't want to sound over-confident, but if they've presented laterally to us by mistake, or if they're driving towards something else, we should be able to do a lot of damage to their flank. Thoth has demanded a main force assault, what the beloved and devout Chapterhouses like to call a meat-grinder. Rip into them along the flank and try, if nothing else, to break their column and isolate parts of it.'

'Begging your pardon, commissar,' Rawne's sibilant tones whispered through the centre's close humidity like a cold draught. 'The Tanith aren't heavy troops. Main force, without playing to our strengths? Feth, that'll get us all killed.'

'Correct, major.' Gaunt fixed the man with a tight stare. 'Thoth has given the regimental commanders some discretion. Let's remember the depth of ground cover and jungle out there. The Ghosts can still use their stealth and cunning to get close, get in amongst them if need be. I'll not send you in en masse. The Ghosts will deploy in platoon sections, small scattered units designed to approach the foe unseen through the glades. I think that way we will give as good an account of ourselves as any massed charged of armoured infantry.'

The briefing was over, save to agree platoon order and position. The officers filed out.

Gaunt stopped Mkoll. 'This notion they've made a mistake: you don't hold with it?'

'I gave my reasons, sir,' Mkoll said. 'It's true, these jungles are dense and confusing, and we can use that. But I don't believe they've made a mistake, no, sir. I think they're after something.'

'What?'

'I wouldn't like to guess,' Mkoll said, but he gestured down at the chart. Just off centre in the middle of the area mapped out as the new front, Gaunt saw what he was pointing to. A mark on the map representing the estimated position of the pre-human ruins Mkoll had found while scouting just a few days before.

'I never did get a look at that, first hand. I... couldn't find it again.'

'What? Say that again?'

Mkoll shrugged. 'I saw it from a distance on patrol – that's when I reported it to you. But since then, I've been unable to relocate it. The men think I'm slipping.'

'But you think...' Gaunt let the silence and Mkoll's expression finish the sentence.

Gaunt began to strap on his holster belt. 'When we get in there, prioritise getting a good assessment of that ruin. Find it again, priority. Keep this between us. Report it back to me directly.'

'Understood, colonel-commissar. To be frank, it's an honour thing now, I know I saw it.'

'I believe you,' Gaunt said. 'Feth, I trust your senses more than my own. Let's move. Let's go and do what they sent us here to do.'

The stone walls were lime quartz, smooth, perfectly finished, lambent. They enclosed the Inner Place like walls of water, like a section cut through the deepest ocean. As if some sublime power had cut the waters open and set aside a dry, dark place for him to walk in, unmolested by the contained pressure of the flood.

He was old, but not so old that such an idea couldn't touch him with the feeling of older myth. It warmed his dying bones somehow. Not a

528   DAN ABNETT

thrill as such, but a powerful reassurance. To be in tune with such an ancestral legend.

The Inner Place was silent, except for the distant chiming of a prayer bell. And beyond that, a muffled clamour, far away, like an eternally restless god, or the rumble of a deep, primeval star.

With long, fragile fingers, freed from the mesh-armoured glove which swung from his wrist-guard by its leather loop and the energy coupler, the Old One traced the gold symbols inscribed on the green stone of the lower walls. He closed his real eyes, dry rheumy lids shutting tight like walnut shells, and the auto-sensitive iris shutters of his helmet optics closed in synch.

Another old tale remembered itself to him. Back, before the stars were crossed, when his kind only knew one world, and knew the star and the kindred worlds that revolved around it only through the astronomical lenses they trained at the sky. Then, as the weight of years swung by, slow and heavy as the slide of continents, and their abilities grew, they slowly learned of other stars, other worlds, a galaxy. And they realised they were not one and alone but one amongst countless others. And those other lights beckoned and, as they were able to, they fled to them.

So it seemed now, an echo. The Old One had been alone for a long while, conscious only of the few lives that orbited his in the Inner Place, the lives of his devoted kin. Then, in the outer blackness, other lights began to emerge and reveal themselves to his mind. A few at first, then dozens, thousands, legions.

The Old One's mind was a fearfully powerful apparatus. As hundreds of thousands of life-lights slowly appeared and began to congregate on this place, it seemed to him as if whole constellations were forming and becoming real. And so many of those life-lights were dark and foul.

Time was against him and his kind. He despised the urgency, because haste was one thing his long, careful life had previously been free of. But now there was precious little time left. A heartbeat by his measuring. And he would have to use every last pulse of it to achieve his purpose.

Already his mind had set things in motion. Already, he had shaken out his dreams and let his rich imagination drape across the place like a cloak. Simple deceits, such as would normally beguile the lesser brains of other races, had already been set in motion.

They would not be enough.

The Old One sighed. It had come to this. A sacrifice, one that he knew would one day punctuate his long life. Perhaps it had been the very reason for his birth.

He was ready. At least it would, in its turn, make a new legend.

***

Under the thick, wet trees and creeper growth, Third platoon skirted the ditches and mud-banks of the glades, moving ever nearer to the thunder-war in the west. Dawn was now on them and light lanced down through the canopy in cold, stale beams.

Third platoon; Rawne's. They'd had Larkin seconded to them from Corbec's unit because Rawne's sniper was busy heaving his fever-ridden guts into a tin bucket in the infirmary. Blood-flies, and tiny biting insects that swirled like dust, had begun to spread disease and infection through the ranks. Dorden had been braced for wounded, but what he had got, suddenly in the last day and night, were the sick.

Milo was with Rawne's platoon too. The boy wasn't sure who hated his presence there most, Rawne or Milo himself. Just before deployment, Gaunt had taken Milo to one side and instructed him to accompany the major's advance.

'If anyone's going to benefit from your rousing pipes, it's going to be the Third,' the commissar had said. 'If any section is going to break, it's going to be them. I want you there to urge them on – or at least vox me if they falter.'

Milo would have refused but for the look in Gaunt's eyes. This was a trust thing, a subtle command responsibility. Gaunt was entrusting him to watch the Third from the inside. Besides, he had his lasgun now, and his shoulder pip, and Rawne's sniper wasn't the only man in the Third to fall sick.

'Keep up!' Feygor hissed to Milo as they crept through the weeds. Milo nodded, biting back a curse. He knew he was moving more swiftly and silently than many in Rawne's platoon. He knew too that he had fastened his webbing and applied his camo-paint better than any of them. Colm Corbec had taken time to teach him well.

But he also knew he wasn't an outsider any more, a boy piper, a mascot. He was a Ghost, and as such he would obey the letter of his superiors. Even if they were dangerous, treacherous men.

With Rawne's scout Logris in the vanguard, the ten men filed through the glades and thickets of the Monthax jungle. Milo found himself behind Caffran, the only trooper in the platoon who he liked. Or trusted.

Rawne paused them in a basin of weed and silt-muck which stank of ripe vegetation while Logris and Feygor edged ahead. Tiny flies swirled like dust over the soup.

Caffran, his face striped with camo-paint, turned to Milo and gently adjusted the straps of the lad's weapon, like a big brother looking after a younger sibling.

'You've seen action, though, haven't you?' Caffran whispered. 'This is nothing new.'

Milo shrugged. 'Yes, but not like this. Not as a trooper.'

Caffran smiled. 'You'll be fine.'

Across the silky water, Larkin watched them from his position curled into the root network of a mangrove. He knew that Caffran and the piper boy had never been friends before now. He had heard Caffran talk of it. Though little more than two years separated them, Caffran felt uneasy around the lad, because he reminded him too much of home. Now that seemed to be forgotten and Larkin was glad. It seemed having Milo in his company had given Caffran purpose. A novice, a little brother, someone junior to the youngest Ghost that Caffran could take care of.

Caffran felt it too. He no longer despised Brin Milo. Trooper Milo was one of them now. It was like… it was like they were back home. Caffran couldn't understand why he had shunned the boy so. They were all in this together. All Tanith, after all. And besides, if Gaunt had seen fit to protect Milo all this time, Caffran was damned if anything would happen to the boy.

Rawne waited at the ditch edge for Logris and Feygor. His eyes were fierce diamonds of white with hard, dark centres, flashing from the band of camo-paint across his face. There was something terribly familiar about their situation. He could feel it in his marrow. Soon there would be killing.

Spoonbills flapped by. Mkoll turned to Domor and slung his weapon.

'Sir?' Domor asked quietly.

'Take them forward, Domor,' Mkoll said.

'Me?'

'You're up to it?'

Domor shrugged a 'yes', the focussing rings of his bionic eyes whirring as they tried to manufacture the quizzical expression his real eyes would have wanted.

'I need to move ahead. Scout. I can only do that alone. You bring the Ninth up after me.'

'But–'

'Gaunt won't mind. I've spoken to him.' Mkoll tapped the ear-piece of his micro-bead intercom twice and softly told the rest of his platoon that Domor was now in charge. 'Follow him like you would me,' he urged them.

He looked back at Domor. 'This is important. It may be the life or death of us. Okay?'

Domor nodded. 'For Tanith.'

'For Tanith, like it's still alive.'

Mkoll was gone an instant later, vanishing into the brooding, puffy, waterlogged vegetation like a rumour.

'Form on me and renew advance,' Domor whispered into his bead, and Ninth platoon formed and renewed.

Under the shade of great, oil-sweet trees, Corbec's platoon, the Second, moved into the mire and the glades. The colonel missed Larkin, but his squad already had the crack-shot Merrt, so it would have been churlish to complain.

Feth, Corbec was thinking, all this time driven mad by Larks's babbling and scaremongering, and now I actually wish he was here.

Ahead, the glades widened into a lagoon. The still water was coated with russet weed, and black, rotten wood limbs and roots poked up out of it. Corbec motioned the Second on behind him, the thigh-deep water leaving a greasy film on his fatigues. He raised his gun higher.

'Up there!' Merrt breathed through the intercom. Along the far end of the lagoon, Corbec could see shapes: moving figures.

'Ours?' Merrt asked.

'Only Varl could be dumb enough to bring his platoon in front of ours, and he's on the eastern limit. No. Let's go.'

Corbec raised his gun to firing position, heard nine other safeties hum off. 'For Tanith! For the Emperor! For us!' he bellowed.

Las-fire volleyed across the water of the lagoon and figures at the far end fell. Some dropped into the water, face down; others knelt for cover in the tree roots of the bank and returned fire. Laser shots echoed and returned across the water course. The lowest bolts cut furrows as they flew across the water. Others steamed as they hit the liquid or exploded sodden, decomposing bark.

Others hit flesh, or cut through armour, and figures tumbled down the far bank, sliding into the water or being arrested by root systems. Merrt made three priceless head shots before a stray return took him in the mouth and he dropped, face down and gurgling, into the ooze of the lagoon.

Corbec bellowed into his vox-bead that contact had been made and that he was engaging. Then he set his lasgun for full auto-fire and ploughed into the water, his finger clenching the trigger.

One for Merrt. Two. Three. Four. Not enough. Not even *half* enough.

'Second platoon has engaged!' Comms-Officer Raglon reported quickly to Gaunt.

'Ahead now!' Gaunt ordered, urging the men of First forward through the shin-deep water along the glade bed. His chainsword was in his hand and purring. They could hear the close shooting, harsher and more immediate than the distant thunder of the mysterious war they were approaching: Corbec's platoon, fighting and firing. But the source was unspecified, remote. Gaunt damned the thickness and false echoes of the glades. Why was this place so impossibly confused?

Las-fire spat across the glades at the First platoon. Lowen fell, cut through and smouldering. Raglon went down too, a glancing burn to his cheek. Gaunt hauled the vox-caster man to his feet and threw him into cover behind a thick root branch.

'All right?'

'I'll live,' returned the comms-officer, dabbing the bloody, scorched weal along the side of his face with a medicine swab.

The enemy fire was too heavy to charge against. Gaunt fell his platoon into cover and they began to return fire with drilled, careful precision. They loosed their las-rounds down the funnel of the glade, and the salvos that came back at them were loose and unfocused. Gaunt could see the position of the enemy from their muzzle flashes. They were badly placed and poorly spaced.

He ordered his men up, searching for a rousing command. None came but for: '*First platoon... like you're the First and Only! Kill them!*'

It would do. *It would do.*

Third platoon froze, half at a hand gesture from Rawne, half at the sudden sounds of fighting from elsewhere in the glades. They settled in low, in the dark green shadows of the canopy, white eyes staring up from dark camo-paint at every ripple of sound. Feygor wiped a trickle of sweat off his cheek. Larkin tracked around with his custom rifle, hunting the trees around them with his night-scope. Wheln chewed at his lower lip, eyes darting. Caffran was poised like a statue, gun ready.

'To the left,' Rawne hissed, indicating with a finger. 'Fighting there. No further than two hundred metres.'

Just behind him, Milo jerked a thumb off to the right. 'And to the right, sir. A little further off.' His voice was a whisper.

Feygor was about to silence the impudence with a fist, but Rawne raised a hand and nodded, listening. 'Sharp ears, boy. He's right. The echoes are confusing, but there is a second engagement.'

'All around us, then... What about our turn?' Feygor breathed.

Rawne could feel Feygor's itching impatience. The waiting, the fething anticipation, was often harder than the fighting itself.

'We'll find our fight soon enough.' Rawne slid out his silver dagger – given to him by Gaunt, Emperor damn his soul! – the blade dulled with fire-soot, and clipped it into the lugs under his lasgun's muzzle. His men fixed their own knives as bayonets in response.

'Let's keep the quiet and the surprise as long as we have it,' Rawne told them, and raised them to move on.

There was the sound of water, drizzling. The spitting noise almost blocked out the muffled fighting elsewhere. But not the distant heavy bombardment of the duelling armour.

Mkoll followed a lip of rocks, slick with black lichen, around the edge of a pool in deep shadow. A skein of water fell from a mossy outcrop thirty metres above, frothing the plunge pool. It was as humid and dark as a summer night in this dim place.

Mkoll heard movement, a skittering of rocks high above at the top of the falls. Cover was scant, so without hesitation he slid off the lip of stone into the water, sinking down to his neck, his lasgun held up in one hand at ear level, just above the surface. With fluid precision, he glided under the shadow of the rock, moving behind the churning froth of the cataract.

Shadows moved along the top of the rock above him. Fifteen, perhaps twenty warriors. He caught their scent: the spicy, foul reek of something barely human. He heard low, clipped voices crackle back and forth via helmet intercoms, speaking a language that he was thankful he could not understand.

Mkoll felt his guts vice involuntarily. It wasn't fear of the enemy, or of death; it was fear of what the enemy was. Their nature. Their *abomination*.

The water seemed glass-cold around him. His limbs were deadening. But hot sweat leaked down his face. Then they were gone.

Mkoll waited a full two minutes until he was sure. Then he crawled up out of the water and padded off silently in the direction from which his enemy had come.

Seventh platoon came out of a deep grove into sudden sunlight and even more sudden gunfire. Three of Sergeant Lerod's men were down before he had time to order form and counter. Enemy fire stripped the trees all around, pulverising bark and foliage into sap mist and splinters. The enemy had at least two stub guns and a dozen las-weapons in cover on the far side of the narrow creek.

Lerod bellowed orders in the whistling flashes of the exchange, moving backwards and firing from the hip on auto. Two of his men had made good cover and were returning hard. Others fought for places with him. Targin, the vox-operator, was hit twice in the back and fell

sideways, his twitching corpse held upright, like a puppet, in a dra-
pery of moss-creepers.

A las-round stung Lerod's thigh. He knelt helplessly, then dropped
to his belly in desperation, blasting up into the trees. His wild fire hit
something – a weapon power-pack, perhaps – and a seething sheet of
flame rushed out of the far creek bank, stripping and felling trees and
tossing out two blackened bodies which cartwheeled in the air and fell
into the creek bed. Pin-pointing Lerod as the source of this little victory, the unseen stubbers traversed and sent stitching lines of firepower
down the earth trail where he sprawled.

He saw them in a split second: the twin lines of ferocious tracers
etching their way across the loam to slice him into the ground. There
was nothing he could do... no time. He closed his eyes.

Lerod opened them again. By some miracle, both lines of fire had
missed him, passing either side of his prone form.

He began to laugh at the craziness of it and rolled into the cover of
trees a few metres to the left, exhorting his surviving company with
renewed vigour to give back and give hard. He felt jubilant, like he had
on the Founding Fields below Tanith Magna, before the Loss. He had
never thought he would have that feeling again.

With bitter resentment, Corbec pulled the Second back from the lagoon
where they were stymied. They were outgunned and partly circled. The
Tanith fell back quickly and silently into the trees, leaving tripwires and
tube rounds in their wake.

A quick vox-exchange brought the Second round alongside the First
platoon and Gaunt himself, holding the line of a wide creek.

'Thick as flies!' Corbec yelled to Gaunt as his men reinforced the
First. 'Big numbers of them, determined too!'

Gaunt nodded, directing his men forward a metre at a time trying to
out-mark and topple the enemy possession of the far bank.

Explosions crackled through the trees in the direction of Corbec's
retreat as the advancing foe tripped the first of the mines. Gaunt cursed.
This terrain was meant to give the Ghosts the advantage with their stealth
skills, but the enemy was everywhere, as if milling and confused. And
though that meant they were not working to a cohesive plan, it also meant
the larger enemy force was splintered, unpredictable and all around them.

Raglon was firing from cover and Gaunt ducked in behind him, waving Corbec over. Corbec sprinted across the open ground, his tunic and
face splattered with pulverised leaf flecks and sap. He looked like the
Old Man of the Woods in the traditional Feast of Leaves, back home
on Tanith, whe–

Gaunt froze, startled and confused. *Back home on Tanith?* What tricks was his mind playing now? He'd never heard of any Feast of the Leaves, yet it had seemed to bob up from his memory as a truth. For a moment, he could even smell the sugared nal-fruit as they roasted in their charcoal ovens.

'What's up, sir?' Corbec asked, trying to squeeze his bulk into the scant cover as las-rounds whipped around them.

Gaunt shook his head. 'Nothing.' He pulled his data-slate from the pocket of his leather coat and plugged the short lead into the socket at the base of the vox-link on Raglon's back. Then he tapped his clearance into the small board of rune-marked keys, and main battle-data began to display on his slate, direct from General Thoth's Leviathan command base. Gaunt selected an overall tactical view so he and Corbec could take in the state of the battle.

The Tanith were shown as a thin, vulnerable line, static and held along the main watercourse. To either side of them, heavier regiments and armoured units were making greater headway, but these too were slow and foundering. The Volpone were pushing from the east, with massive artillery support, but the Trynai Sixth and Sixteenth were pinned down and slowly being slaughtered.

'Feth, but it's bad...' Corbec muttered. 'This whole push is grinding to a halt.'

'We'll have to see if we can improve matters,' Gaunt returned, solemn and occupied. He wound the dial to bring up a specific display of the Ghosts' struggling advance. All of the platoons were essentially halted and most engaged in heavy fire. Lerod's unit was taking the brunt of it. Rawne's, Gaunt noticed, had so far failed to engage.

'Have they got the luck?' Corbec asked.

'Or are they not trying?' Gaunt said aloud.

The Third edged on, passing a deep hidden pool with a glittering waterfall that fell from a crop of mossy rock. Rawne split his platoon and moved them up either side of the water.

Feygor stooped to pick up something and showed it to the major. It was a cell from a lasgun, but not Imperial issue.

'They've been through here.'

'And we've missed them!' Rawne cursed. 'Feth take this bastard jungle! We're in amongst them and we can't see them!'

On the far side of the pool, Milo paused and turned to Caffran. 'Smell that?' he whispered.

Caffran frowned. 'Mud? Filthy water? Pollen?'

'This jungle doesn't smell like it did before. I can almost smell... nal-wood.' Milo rubbed his own nose, as if he distrusted it.

Caffran was about to laugh, but then realised that he smelled it too. It was astonishing, almost overwhelming in its nostalgia. The air indeed smelt of the rich conifers of Tanith. Now he thought about it, the trees and foliage around them seemed darker, much more like the wet-land forests of his lost homeworld. Nothing like the stinking, seething jungle they had known since arriving on Monthax.

'This is crazy,' he said, reaching out and touching one of the familiar trees.

Milo nodded. It was crazy – and scary too.

From the cover of some low, flowering bushes, busy with insects, Mkoll could see a clearing ahead. There had been brief, heavy fighting there not more than two hours before. The earth was churned up, trees burned back and splintered. Bodies smouldered on the ground.

He crept forward to look. The dead were Chaos soldiery, heavily armed and armoured in quilted red fatigues and bare steel armoured sections. Their helmets were inscribed with such horrific symbols and figures he began to dry-heave until he looked away.

Others had fallen here too, but their bodies had been removed. No Imperial unit had got this far in. There was another force at play on Monthax. Mkoll looked at the wounds on the fallen. Here and there, a helmet or metal breast-plate had been punctured, not by an energy round or explosive shell, but by something sharp and clean which had punched right through composite metal. In a tree stump behind one corpse, Mkoll found a missile embedded, a wickedly sharp metal star with razor-edged points.

With a long, slow sigh that wheezed out of his helmet's mouthpiece, the Old One sat back on the stone seat at the centre of the Inner Place.

Like a spider at the heart of a complex web, he reached out mentally and tested the strands of his net of deceit, the cloak of confusion he had spread out around him, leagues in every direction. It was serving its purpose for now. He studied the minds caught in his net: so very many of them cruel and brutish and overflowing with the poison of Chaos. And the others, the brief human sparks. The Imperials had engaged too, he realised, coming in to try their strength against the forces of Chaos as they moved. He saw bloody fighting. He saw primitive courage.

Humans always surprised him that way. Such little life-spans, so furiously exhausted. Their valour would be almost admirable if it wasn't so futile.

Yet perhaps he could use that. To make allies was out of the question, but he could use all the time he could buy, and these determined Imperial humans, with their relentless urge to fight and win, could help him in that.

It was past time for him to play his last hand. He would work the humans, for what little good they could do, into that gambit. A final check now.

Muon Nol, Dire Avenger, master of the bodyguard, entered the Inner Place at the Old One's mental summons. He held his great white-crested helm under one arm, the red plume crest perfect and trim, and his opalescent blue armour glittered with flecks of gold, like the heart of a cooling star. The braided tassels of his cape hung down to his waist, shrouding the weapons cinched tight to his back. His noble, ancient eyes studied the Old One. There was fatigue in his long, solemn face.

'Muon Nol: how goes the work?'

'The Way is open, lord.'

'And it must be closed. How much longer?'

Muon Nol looked down at the smooth stone floor where the shimmer of his blue armoured form was reflected. 'All but the bodyguard have departed, lord. The Closing of the Way has now begun. It will be a little time yet before we are finished.'

'A little time for us, perhaps, Muon Nol. Not for the enemy. More than long enough for them, I fear. There is no time for proper closure now. We must sever.'

'Lord!'

The Old One held up his hand, the one that was bare of a glove. The sight of those ancient fingers, almost translucent with wasting age, silenced Muon Nol's protests.

'It is not the way we wished it, Muon Nol. But it is all we can do now. Dolthe must be protected. I will now do as I told you and commit my final reserves to the last delaying tactics.'

Muon Nol dropped to his knees before the seated figure and lowered his head. 'But that it should come to this, Lord Eon Kull!'

Eon Kull, the Old One, sat back with a half-smile. 'I am this Way, Muon Nol. It has been my charge and duty all these measures of time. It and I are as one. If it must be shut now forever – and it must – it is only right that the book of my life shuts with it. It is appropriate and necessary. I do not see it as a failure or a loss. Neither should you. Lord Eon Kull closes his Way for the last time, for all time. Lord Eon Kull will pass away with it.'

Muon Nol raised his head. Were those tears in his dark eyes? Eon Kull considered that perhaps tears from his most faithful warrior were not out of place.

'Leave me now. Tell your Guard to brace themselves for the mind-trauma. I will call you again when it is done, so that we may say farewell.'

The master of the bodyguard rose and began to turn.

'Muon Nol?'

'Lord?'

Eon Kull, the Old One, lifted his weapon from the rim of the stone seat. The dim light shone from the long, smooth barrel of the buanna, and twinkled on the inlay at the grip and shoulder guard. Uliowye, the Kiss of Sharp Stars. The weapon of a champion, precious and celebrated. In Eon Kull's hands, it had won fabulous victories for Dolthe.

'Take this. Stand your place when the time comes and use it well.'

'Uliowye... I cannot, lord! She has always been yours!'

'Then she is mine to *give*, Muon Nol! Uliowye will not be happy to sleep through this great passing. She must kiss the foe at least once more.'

Muon Nol took the old shrieker cannon reverently. 'She will not go silently, high lord. You do me a great honour.'

Eon Kull nodded and said no more, shushing Muon Nol away and out of the Inner Place. The Old One sat for a while longer, thinking of nothing but the silence to come. Then his mind woke again to the noisy hosts outside the walls, the minds milling and fighting and killing and dying in the deep jungle of Monthax around him.

Eon Kull rose and stepped down off the throne. He knelt on the cool floor of the Inner Place and unclasped the decorated purse at his belt. The contents clacked together. Eon Kull the warlock spilled them out onto the flagstones. Slivers of bone, each inscribed with a rune of power. Though this was a dim place, they shone like ice in the noon sun and he observed their pattern. Slowly, with his bare fingers, he slid them around, forming intricate conjunctions, pairing some slivers, placing other runes alone or in small piles. The arrangement was quite precise.

Eon Kull tensed as he felt the raw moaning of the warp. The psycho-reactive runes gave him access to the unbridled power of the warp-spaces, acting as keys to open the locks of his powerful mind to the warp outside.

He started to draw and channel the force of the warp through the rune keys. They began to glow more brilliantly now, humming with energy. His mind began to struggle. He had never attempted to channel such levels of power before.

No, that wasn't true. In his youth, as he began upon the Witch Path, he had performed great feats, and then with fewer runes. He had added to his knowledge and technique over the centuries, but he was not young any more. It took more out of him now to harness the power. In sympathy, the spirit stones inset on his rune-armour flickered, as did dozens of others ranged at the side of his throne. Waking from their eternal slumber at his bidding, the souls of other seers and warlocks, long flesh-dead, conjoined with him to guide him and strengthen his power.

A few of the older and more surly spirits chided him for attempting so great a deed. Others aided him unequivocally, and soothed the complaints of their fellow spirits. The cause was simple and pure: Dolthe. Dolthe must persist, and Eon Kull was right to try the limit of his powers to make it so.

A noise from behind almost distracted him. But it was Fuehain Falchior, tasting battle, twitching in her wraithbone rack.

'Be still, witchblade,' Eon Kull murmured and turned his full attention back to the deed.

Now the runes glowed more brightly still. Some quivered on the floor, rattling as if disturbed by seismic shaking. The spirit stones flickered and pulsed. Eon Kull looked into the warp and the warp poured into him. He germinated power, a racing, fecund rhythm.

His bare hand clasped like a claw. Veins stood out on his wrist. Now the pain welled inside him. Watery blood dribbled from his nose.

Despite the pain, he laughed to himself. No matter how strange, how bittersweet, there would be victory in this. Or at least, for Dolthe and his kind, he hoped that there would.

The sky over that section of the Monthax glade-wilderness buckled and exploded. Blinding forks of lightning blinked downwards in a hundred places out of a heaven that had previously been clear and sultry blue. Stands of trees exploded under the electrical hammerblows. Several armoured vehicles in the Imperial vanguard were struck and destroyed. A Volpone Hellhound, struck by ball-lightning, went up like a torch as its huge fuel reserves were touched off. At another place, on a creek bed, fourteen Basilisk self-propelled guns, their long barrels raised to the sky ready for bombardment, became lightning conductors. Electrocuted, the gun-crews danced and jerked, or melted onto the white-hot hulls for ten seconds before the combined munitions blew a square kilometre of the jungle into the sky in a column of superheated energy and debris.

The blast shook the hulking, hundred-metre-high Imperial command Leviathan stationed sixteen kilometres back and threw the bridge crew to the deck. General Thoth leapt up as his multiple screens and main holographic display fizzled and went out. He yelled frantic orders into the darkness.

Rain sheeted down on top of the lightning, walls of cold, unseasonable downpour which demolished the ripe foliage of the upper tree cover and the moss-vines, and shredded trunks back to the heartwood. Drenched, the Imperial forces fell back blind into watercourses suddenly swollen by rich, red tides of floodwater, the battle forgotten.

Varl's platoon fell into cover under rocks, praying and gasping in the icy rain. Vox-lines were broken and no one could see more than a metre in any direction.

Fear tightened its grip on the Imperium forces. The enemy were lost in the storm all along the war-front. Chaos artillery persisted in firing, but their blasts and recoils seemed pathetic next to the elemental commotion. Guardsmen spoke of a Chaos-summoned witch-storm.

Lerod's platoon, what was left of it, ran back through the drumming rain, blind and almost grateful for the chance to break the impasse.

Half of Domor's platoon were carried away down a flash-flooding waterway. Two drowned.

Then, amidst the rain, came hail like fists. This fell on the west, breaking bones and killing nineteen men outright in the Volpone phalanx. The hail was so hard it dented tank armour.

Suddenly up to their knees in rushing, liquid mud, First and Second platoons of the Tanith backed from the breaching lagoon, Gaunt leading the way, gripping saplings and vines to stay upright. Corbec chased the stragglers, half-carrying Trooper Melk who had lost a knee.

'What in the name of Feth is this?' Gaunt screamed into the rain.

No one had an answer. Witchery, they all thought.

Typhoon-force winds surged in along the edges of the storm. Imperial air-cover was pulled out and grounded, but not before two Marauders had been torn out of the air and smashed. One, its stabilisers gone and its thrusters screaming, managed to turn its death into a pyrrhic victory by taking out a line of Chaos tanks gummed down in a clearing which had abruptly become a lake. The vast, multiple explosions were lost in the roar of the storm.

Caught in a sudden flash flood, stunned by the force of the hail and rain, Mkoll clung on to a nearly uprooted mangrove to stop himself being carried off. Blinking water from his eyes, he saw his lasgun ride away in the leaf-choked froth. He felt the loss acutely. He had been so careful and protective of that simple, standard-issue gun. There was none better kept, better cared for, or cleaner in the Tanith regiment. Now it spun away from him, ruined, swamped. But he had his life still – for as long as the roots would hold.

Rawne pushed Third platoon forward through the deluge. Their hair and uniforms were plastered to their pale skins. Some edifice rose ahead, a structure of stone raised from fashioned blocks. To Rawne, it seemed almost familiar. His urgent commands were lost in the hurricane winds.

A snapped off branch whickered through the gale and the near-horizontal downpour and struck Trooper Logris in the throat. Milo tried to help him but it was too late. His neck was broken and his head lolled around the wrong way. Already, his crumpled body was being sucked down into the swelling mud by the hideous rain.

Caffran grabbed Milo and dragged him through the storm of wind and rain and flurrying leaves into the cover of the stone ruin. Rawne yanked them in to join the other members of his platoon: Feygor, Cown, Wheln, Mkendrik, Larkin, Cheffers. But Cheffers was dead. There was no sign of injury on him until Cown spotted the blood oozing from a slit in his throat. Something protruded from it. It was a leaf. Carried point-first by the stabbing wind, the stiff leaf had punctured Cheffers's throat and cut his windpipe.

Horrified, with the wind and rain wailing against the stone block at their backs, they saw how their tunics and cloaks had been torn and sliced by other such leaf missiles.

'What kind of storm is this?' Caffran howled over the roar.

'And where the feth did it come from so suddenly?' Feygor bawled.

Rawne didn't know. Everything had been going smoothly until then. The mustering on the Founding Fields. The preparation for disembarkment. And now a storm like nothing he'd seen before had fallen on Tanith Magna.

'Bet your lives it's the work of the enemy!' he yelled to his men. 'A surprise attack to take Tanith from us! Ready your weapons!'

Every one of them responded, checking their lasguns.

Except Milo. 'Major – *what* did you just say?'

Rawne looked down at the boy. 'I know it's your first taste of battle, worm, but try to think like a trooper! You have only just mustered here, wet behind the ears from the Magna province farms, but you're in for a fight!'

Milo blinked. The roar of the storm just outside the stone blocks sheltering them seemed to have left him concussed. Rawne and the others had gone mad. *This wasn't Tanith! They were acting like it was the homeworld and–*

He stopped. The stone wall in front of him was a solid section of Tanith basalt, mined from the quarries at Pryze Junction. The crest of the Elector was inscribed into it. He knew this place... a side corridor just off the main western fortification of the capital city. But–

For a moment, Milo faltered. He could remember something. A dying

world, a small brotherhood of survivors... ghosts... playing the pipes
to urge them on.

Just a dream. Just a bad dream, he realised. They were mustering at
the Foundation of the Tanith regiments and Chaos had attacked their
homeworld. They had no choice. Stand and fight, or die. And if they
died, Tanith would die with them.

The storm, a spinning electrical disk of clouded black fury sixty kilometres in diameter, held its position unerringly above the battle front.
Its power and force were so great, even the mighty cogitators of the
hexathedral *Sanctity*, high in orbit, couldn't compute its magnitude
or penetrate the dome of blistering interference it created. Any Imperial forces that still had a measure of mobility, those that had not been
swept away or mired, began to pull back to their lines, making what
headway they could in the appalling conditions. Many units, most of
them armour and heavy fighting vehicles, were cut off or swamped,
helpless and detached from the main retreat.

No one, not even General Thoth's chief tacticians, could begin to
guess the state, response or position of the foe they were meant to be
engaging. Had they broken too? Were they just as lost, or had all of them
been obliterated by the hurricane? Or was this their doing?

Many of the Imperial veterans and officers had seen psychic storms
before, a favoured terror-weapon of the Chaotic foe. But this was not
the same. There was no pestilential quality to it, no reek of unholy filth,
no heaviness in the air that made skin crawl and bowels churn and
minds spin into waking nightmares.

Just titanic fury. Almost pure, elemental power. A null. Yet, if they
could read it, the warp was there. The unmistakable flavour of the warp.

Inquisitor Lilith had no doubts at all. Her attuned senses had no trouble in detecting the cold psyker power galvanising the deluge. Indeed,
it was all she could do to shut it out and stop it howling and screaming through her mind. The rumours of psyker-witchery said to haunt
this world were true, but this witchery had a power and clarity like
none she had ever felt.

She strode through the downpour in a long cape of dripping black
leather, her cowl pulled up. She stared fixedly at the storm which boiled
in the sky two leagues or so from her position. Her honour guard escort
marched in her train. She could feel their nervousness and unwilling-
ness to proceed into an area all other right-minded Guard units were
fleeing from. But Lord Militant General Bulledin had appointed them
to serve Lilith as she prosecuted this event, and they feared the Lord
Militant and the inquisitor more than any storm.

The escort was thirty troopers from the Royal Volpone 50th, the Blue-bloods. They wore the grey and gold body armour and low-brimmed bowl helmets of the Volpone, with wet-weather oilskins draped lankly over their torsos. Their shoulders and arms were massive with seg-mented carapace armour, and they were each armed with a matt-black hellgun fresh from the weapon shops of Leipaldo. Each man had a bright indigo Imperial eagle stud pinned into his armaplas collar sec-tion, marking them all as from the Volpone Tenth Brigade, the elite veteran force. Only the best of the best for an Imperial inquisitor. With them came a shrouded astropath, one of Lilith's own staff. He jerked and staggered at every twitch of the storm, and was given a wide berth by the Volpone soldiers.

The detail commander, Major Gilbear, fell in step with the inquisitor. His face was set grimly, but he projected a sickening sense of pomp-ous pride at taking this duty. Lilith could barely shut that out either.

'Can you outline our purpose and approach, my lady inquisitor?' Gil-bear asked, using the formal aristocratic dialect of the highest Imperial courts. It was partly to impress her, Lilith knew, and partly to establish his own self-importance. The huge Volpone clearly wanted to show he believed himself to be more than a common soldier. As if they were... equals...

'I'll let you know when I decide, major,' she replied in the blunt and crude low-Gothic of the common soldiery. An insult, she knew, but one that might make him quit his airs and graces. She hadn't time to be bothered with him right now.

He nodded curtly, and she smiled at the throb of bitten-down anger he radiated.

They crossed a foaming waterbed, shallow, but fast running, where a dozen Chimeras of the Roane Deepers were struggling to dig them-selves out. Agitated, spooked troopers milled around, shouting, cursing and heaving on stripped tree trunks to lever out clogged track units. Fine drizzle from the edge of the storm whipped across them, creat-ing a billion impact ripples in the water.

On the far side, the inquisitor's party followed the bank in towards the edge of the storm. There was debris in the spraying water here: shreds of equipment, helmets, pieces of foliage, drowned bodies, all swirling downstream in the flood.

Inquisitor Lilith called a halt in a clearing where vast deciduous trees had been reduced to blackened columns by lightning strikes. A raft of wood pulp and leaves sloshed and ebbed over the swamped ground. She pulled out her data-slate and reviewed it. It showed the positions of all the Imperial forces, each individual unit, as last recorded before the storm came down. A complex data-mosaic of thousands of individual components, one that would take a trained tactician hours to assess. But she had already located the one element which interested her: the Third platoon of the First-and-Only Tanith.

Mkoll made it to higher ground, the rain and wind pelting him. The sky was black, and it was as dark as night, but his night-vision couldn't adjust because of the frequent blinding flashes of lightning which strobed across him. He was all but deaf with the near-constant thunder. In places, mud-slides had brought parts of the high ground slope down, and more than once he was almost carried off his feet as thick, slimy folds of mud came loose and oozed away down the incline. He glimpsed something in the next lightning flash that made him stop in his tracks, and he waited for the next searing discharge to confirm what he had seen.

The ruin. The ruin he had glimpsed on patrol before and had spent so long trying to find once more. He wouldn't lose it again. Mkoll stayed put and waited through the next three or four flashes, memorising the elements of the landscape, both near and far, as it was revealed to him in split-second snapshots.

In the last flash, he saw the movement too.

Enemy warriors, higher up the slope, stumbling across him in the deluge by chance. As the world went black again, they fired his way, cracking red lines in the darkness and the rain. Mkoll slid down onto his knees in the mud, trying to use the slope to give him as much cover as possible against the killers moving down the hill from above.

Another flash. They were closer. Six or more, most holding their weapons one-handed as they clung onto sagging saplings and outcrops of rock to keep themselves upright as they came down the incline. In the darkness, more red fire-bolts.

Mkoll pulled out his laspistol. He was blind, but the red flashes were a focus in the dark. He waited for more shots, then fired directly at the source of the blasts.

Then he scrambled to his left so they couldn't use the same trick on him.

His precaution was wise. The muddy ridge which had previously sheltered him was hit by four separate bursts of enemy fire. Boiled mud spattered up in lazy splashes. The tumultuous rain washed the steam away immediately.

More lightning. This brief gift of sight revealed to Mkoll the huge shape of a Chaos soldier almost on top of him. He'd either been trying to flank Mkoll's last position or been brought down the slick, treacherous slope faster than intended. They had almost collided.

Mkoll swung up his laspistol and shot him through the chest, point blank, before he could react. The enemy, a stinking dead-weight draped in loose chains and angular, rusty armour plates, slammed into Mkoll and flattened him back into the ooze. Locked under the corpse, Mkoll began to slide back down the mud-slope. He fought to get out from under the body and freed himself. Now he and the corpse slid down the hill more gently, head first, on their backs, side to side.

Mkoll swung over onto his knees, slipping down again twice before he properly righted himself. He was coated with mud and slime, though the slap of the rain washed it out of his eyes. He felt it had poured thickly into his ears too, because he was truly deaf now. Or had the detonations of the thunder finally burst his eardrums? Gunfire chased his way, hunting his last shot. He could see the red rips in the rain, but they were silent now. There was nothing but a low, constant grumble in his ears.

He got down next to the corpse. There was no sign of its main weapon, but an antique laspistol was hooked into its waistband. He pulled it out. It was longer, heavier and far more ornate than his simple, standard-pattern Guard pistol. The pear-shaped hand-grip was wrapped in fine chain and leather cord, and grotesque symbols were inlayed along the under-barrel furniture in pearl and silver. A yellow dot of light showed it was fully charged.

Blue light, harsh and electrical, shone over him. Phosphor flares, two first, then a third, trembled up into the sheeting rain over the hillside. Mkoll's eyes adjusted to the bright, flickering twilight. He could see the trees in stark black relief, the solid, blurring veil of the rain. He could see the enemy, nine or more, scrambling down the bank onto him, the closest twenty metres away.

And they could see him.

They opened fire. It was silent still, just that rumble like grinding teeth, but plumes of mud burst up from impacts around him, and scythed through the bole of a tree to his left, bringing the fifty metre tall trunk crashing down. Mkoll slid under it where the ground dipped, pulling himself through a gully full of rushing water. Emerging on the other side, with the fallen trunk as cover, he found sound had returned. The water had sluiced the sticky mud from his ears and the sides of his head. Noise rushed in at him: the thunder, the crack of shots, the clamouring voices like a baying pack of hounds.

Digging his heels into the soft ground for purchase, he swung up and leaned across the tree trunk, firing a pistol in each hand. The laser bolts from his regular gun were stark and white. Those from the captured weapon were dirty and red. He shot at the two attackers closest to him and dropped them straight off. One fell twisted, into a tangle of foliage. The other slid on his nose, spread-eagled, right down the slope and disappeared into the rushing water of the creek bed below.

Mkoll ducked down and crept along the length of the fallen trunk as return fire cremated and split the section he had been using for cover. Digging his feet in again, he popped up once more, and shot another enemy through the side of the head.

Two more were close on him, but a thick brake of trees baffled his aim. Shots tore at him. He blasted with his twin guns again, exploding the shoulder of an attacker flanking him to the left. A las-round exploded the trunk in front of him and he reeled back into shelter, sucking at the new splinters of wood slivered into his forearms and fingers.

Mkoll fought away the sharp, superficial pain. He began to crawl along under the block of the tree trunk again, but back towards his original position of cover to wrong-foot them. The next time he rose to bring his weapons to bear, three of the enemy soldiers had reached his last position and were clambering over the fallen log to blast down into the gully beyond. Firing down the length of the tree, Mkoll killed them all before they realised they were shooting at nothing. One toppled back and slid under the trunk, another fell across it and dropped into thick mud that sucked his corpse half-under. The third fell draped across the log.

The flares were dying and the strobe lighting of the storm was beginning to reassert itself.

Mkoll saw that dozens more of the enemy were advancing down the slope from above, and there were still four or five in his immediate field of fire.

He was running out of chances and options. He began to run, back down the length of the fallen log, then across the contour of the hill towards the ruin in the incline beyond. Shots chased him. He fell once – and it saved his life, as las-rounds cut the air that had, just a second before, been occupied by his head. He rolled down the bank, only partly voluntarily, then scrambled up again and ran on. More flares lit the sky. Silver light kissed the ground, the muddy slope and the curtain of rain. The trees became black fingers with multiple shadows.

Two enemy soldiers charged at him out of the spray, head on. One fired, his shots going wild. Mkoll's guns were still in his hands and he shot each one in the head as he ran between them. Behind the dead, three more. One managed to react fast enough to pull his trigger and Mkoll felt his neck recoil as something painfully hard and hot stung across his scalp. Blood streamed down his face. He wondered if he had been shot in the head, if his thoughts and motions were simply a nervous reaction carrying him forward past the point of death, his brain cooked backwards out of the exploded cup of his skull.

Whatever the truth, he wasn't going to stop. He shot the foe who had hit him with both pistols, then leapt the corpse, extending his guns out on either side to target the other pair. The leap was brave but foolish. Treacly mud took his feet away as he landed and his shots went wild. Tracking him as he leapt between them, the two soldiers of Chaos fired simultaneously and killed each other. Mkoll struggled up, laughing out loud at this little piece of Imperial justice. Then he stopped and holstered one of his guns, feeling his scalp with his freed hand. He fully expected to find a jagged edge of skull like a broken egg, but there was a just bloody gouge across the top of his head, and a section of his hair was crisped away. His cap had vanished. It had been a glancing wound. No doubt Rawne would have remarked upon the obstinate solidity of his skull.

He stumbled on towards the rise, needles of red light sweeping his trail. Outnumbered and outgunned, he realised it was time for the most drastic action.

Mkoll reached a tough-looking stump and lashed himself to it with his webbing. He took three tube-charges out of his thigh pouch, wound them tightly in a bunch with tape and hurled them back up the slope behind him.

Lightning broke at the same second the charges went off, washing out the flash and the roar. Then the entire hill-face squealed and fell away, a vast mud-slide that brought thousands of tonnes of liquid mud, rock and plants down, sweeping the enemy away with it into a soft tomb at the creek bed.

Waves of mud and liquid filth smashed into Mkoll; timbers carried down from higher up slammed into him. He choked and vomited on the fluid rush.

Then it was over. The storm blitzed on and the air was reeking with the pungent smell of freshly exposed soil. Mkoll was hanging from the tree stump by his webbing. The slide had washed away his footing and carried off several metres of topsoil, but the stump's deep roots had been more firmly bedded. It was one of the few things still standing proud of the smooth, sagging, crescent-shaped mud-slip.

Mkoll pulled off his webbing and dropped free. Nearby, the clawing hand of a buried foe warrior jerked and clawed up from the thick mud. Mkoll fired into the mud until the hand stopped twitching.

He made it to the next rise and looked down into the deep jungle cavity where the ruin sat, solemn and mysterious on a high mound. The second volley of flares were dying away now, but he knew what he saw.

The ruin was besieged by Chaos. Hundreds of thousands of enemy warriors, glistening and churning like beetles in the downpour, assaulted the great ruin from all sides.

They were relentless, ignoring the storm as if all that mattered was the jagged crown of stones at the top of the mound.

'What is that place?' Mkoll breathed aloud. 'What is it you want?'

Still shrieking and exploding overhead, the storm didn't answer him.

The sky spasmed above them, stricken with electrical convulsions. First platoon, with the remnants of Corbec's unit and the stragglers of Lerod's who had joined them by accident in the storm's chaos, struggled on as they beat the retreat.

Gaunt came upon Corbec, who was clambering in the lead through the rain and the undergrowth. Trooper Melk was now on a stretcher carried in the rear of the retreat.

'What?' Gaunt gasped to his colonel, water streaming off his lean face.

'A river!' Corbec spat, surprised. Ahead of them, a thunderous torrent roared through the trees, foamy and deep and dangerously fast. It hadn't been there when they had come in. Gaunt stood, pummelled by the rain, and tried to make sense of the landscape in the flickering dark. He ordered Trooper Mktea forward and took one of his tube-charges. Corbec watched in disbelief as Gaunt taped it to the base of a massive ginkgo trunk and primed the fuse.

'Back!' Gaunt shouted.

The explosion cut the tree above the root and dropped its sixty-metre mass across the boiling tide: a bridge of sorts.

One by one, the men crawled across. Corbec led them to prove it could be done, cursing as each handhold slipped and tore away from the sodden bark. Trooper Vowl lost his grip and dropped from the horizontal log. The flash-flood carried him away like a cork. A screaming cork.

On the far side, Corbec saw to the defence of the position, ordering each drenched man fresh from the crossing into place, lasgun aimed, creating a wide dispersal of ready soldiers in a fan to protect those still crossing the timber bridge.

Corbec moved forward himself, into the horsetail ferns and hyacinths, their fronded leaves lashed and shaken by the drumming rain. There was movement ahead. He reported it via his micro-bead but got nothing back. The storm was playing merry hell with the vox-links. Clammy, cold hands tightening on his lasgun, Corbec inched forward.

A hellgun fired to his right, wide, a piercing distinctive report. He started forward and fell into the grip of three large figures which slammed into him out of the pulsing darkness. He lost his lasgun. A fist hit him in the back of the neck and he dropped, then recovered and punched out. One of his assailants went down in the mud. Another kicked at him and Corbec kicked back, breaking something crucial.

He was wrestling with the biggest of his opponents now, blind in the rain and the mud spray. Corbec got a glimpse of gold and grey carapace armour, an Imperial eagle stud of precious blue. Underneath his rolling foe, he punched upwards into what should have been the face twice and then rolled his stunned aggressor over so that he was straddling him.

A flash of lightning. Corbec saw he was astride a Volpone Blueblood, a big man with a battered, bloodied face. A major. Corbec had his hands around the man's throat.

'What the feth?' he gasped. Hellgun muzzles were suddenly pressing to his head.

'You stinking bastard!' the major underneath him groaned venomously, trying to rise.

Corbec raised his hands in a gesture of surrender, wary of the guns around him. The major, released, threw Corbec back off him and rose, pulling out his hellpistol and aiming at Corbec's head.

'Don't,' said a voice, quiet yet more commanding than the thunder.

Gaunt stepped into the clearing, his bolt pistol aimed squarely at Major Gilbear's cranium. The Blueblood guns swung around to point at him but he didn't flinch.

'Now,' Gaunt added. His gun was unfaltering. Corbec looked up from the mud, lying on his back, conscious that the Blueblood major's gun was still pointed his way.

'Shoot him and I can assure you, Gilbear, you will be dead before any of your men can fire.' Gaunt's voice was low and threatening. Corbec knew that tone.

'Gaunt...' Gilbear murmured, not slackening his aim.

More Ghosts moved in around the commissar, guns aimed.

'Something of a stand-off,' Corbec muttered from the ground. Gilbear kicked him, his aim not leaving Corbec's head, his gaze not leaving Gaunt.

'Lower your weapon, Major Gilbear.' Inquisitor Lilith stepped into the glade, her cowl drawn up, a staccato roll of thunder eerily punctuating her words.

Gilbear wavered and then holstered his gun.

'Help Colonel Corbec to his feet,' Lilith added in the perfect, effete tones of the courtly dialect.

Gaunt's aim had not changed.

'And you, commissar. Put up your weapon.'

Gaunt lowered his bolt pistol.

'Inquisitor Lilith.'

'We meet again,' she said, turning away, a shrouded, sinister figure in the rain.

Gilbear held his hand down to Corbec and pulled him to his feet. Their eyes locked as Gilbear brought him up. Gilbear had the advantage of a few centimetres in height, and his broad shoulders, encased in the bulky carapace segments, eclipsed Corbec's shambling form, but the Tanith colonel had the benefit of sheer mass.

'No offence,' Gilbear hissed into Colm Corbec's face.

'None taken, Blueblood... until next time.'

Gaunt passed Gilbear as he approached Lilith, and the commissar and the major exchanged looks. Neither had forgotten Voltemand.

'Inquisitor Lilith,' Gaunt began, raising his voice over the cacophony of the storm, 'is this a chance encounter or have you sniffed me out with your psyker ways?'

She turned and looked at him, clear eyed. 'What do you think, Ibram?'

'What am I supposed to think, inquisitor?'

She half-smiled, rain pattering off her white skin. 'A psyker storm lights up the battle zone, aborting our assault against the foe.'

'You're not telling me anything I hadn't already noticed.'

'Where is your Third platoon?'

Gaunt shrugged. 'You tell me. Voxing has become impossible in this hell.'

She showed him the lit dial of her data-slate.

'They're right in there, as last reported. Tell me, don't you think it's significant?'

'What?'

'Milo... Oh, he answered my questions and wriggled out, but still, I wonder.'

'What do you wonder, inquisitor?'

'A boy suspected of psyker power, given rank by you, in the depth of this when it begins.'

'This is not Brin Milo's work.'

'Isn't it? How can you be sure?'

Gaunt was silent.

'What do you know of psykers, commissar? What do you know? Have you talked with them? Have you seen the way they blossom? A boy, a girl, barely in their teens, never having shown any spark of the craft, suddenly becoming all that we fear.'

Gaunt stayed quiet. He didn't like where this was going.

'I've seen it, Ibram. The sudden development of untrained powers, the sudden eruption of activity. You can't know for sure this isn't Milo's doing.'

'It isn't. I know it isn't.'

'We'll see. After all, that's what we are here to find out.'

* * *

Rawne stared down from a slit window in the thick stonework, night rain and high winds lashing the outside. There were fires outside, but no longer the reassuring lines of cook fires on the Founding Fields. The sky had fallen. Doom had come to Tanith. If there had been any doubt, Rawne had seen warning flares rise and fall above the tree line not three minutes past.

Rawne clutched his freshly-issued lasgun to his chest. At least he would get to use it before he died.

'What's happening, sir?' Trooper Caffran asked. Rawne bit back the urge to yell at him. The boy was a novice. First taste of battle. And Rawne was the only officer present.

'Planetary assault. The enemy have fallen on us while we were still mustering.'

Others in the squad moaned.

'We're finished,' Larkin howled and Feygor disciplined him with a blow to his kidneys.

'Enough of that talk!' Rawne snapped. 'They'll not take Tanith without a fight from us! And we can't be the only unit inside the Elector's palace! We have a duty to protect the life of the Elector.'

The rest murmured and nodded. It was a desperate course, but it seemed right. They all felt it.

Feygor checked his intercom again. 'Nothing. The lines are dead. Must be scrambling us.'

'Keep trying. We have to locate the Elector and form a cohesive defence.'

Brin Milo's head was spinning. It all seemed so unreal, but he cautioned himself that was just shock at the speed of events.

It had been stressful enough to prepare to leave Tanith for ever. All the men had been edgy these last few days. Now... this nightmare.

That was what it was like. A nightmare. A twisting of reality where some things seemed blurred and others bright and over-sharp.

There was no time to settle his nerves or soothe it away. Gunfire and a gout of flame rushed down the stone hallway from behind them. The enemy had gained access to the palace.

Rawne's squad took cover-places along the wall and returned fire.

'For Tanith!' Rawne yelled. 'While it yet lives!'

Eon Kull, the Old One, awoke with a start. He cried out, an animal bark of pain. He found himself lying on the polished stone floor of the Inner Place. For a moment, he did not remember who or what he was.

Then it trickled back, like sand through the waist of an hourpiece, a grain at a time. He had lost consciousness and lain here, undiscovered, in his delirium.

He could barely rise. His hands trembled; his limbs were as weak as a fildassai. Blood was clotting in his mouth and nose. He felt his beating organs and pumping lungs rustle and wheeze inside his ribs like dying birds in a cage.

He had to take stock. Had he been successful?

The spirit stones had all gone dark. Fuehain Falchior sat silent and still in her rack. The rune slivers were scattered across the floor as if someone had kicked over the arrangement. Some glowed red hot and smouldered like iron in a smelter. Others were wisps of curled ash.

Eon Kull Warlock gasped at the sight. He clawed at the runes, gathering up the fragments and the ash, burning his fingers. In the name of Vaul the Smithy-God, what had he wrought this day? What had he done? Attempted too much, that was certain. His age and his frailty had failed him, made him pass out and lose control, but surely for only a second or two. What had he unleashed? Sacred Asuryan, what had he done?

His exhausted mind sensed Muon Nol returning to the Inner Place. The warrior should not, would not see him like this. Eon Kull found strength from somewhere and hauled himself back into his throne, clasping the purse of ash and bone-cinders to his belt. Joints cracked like bolter shots and he felt blood rise in his gorge as his head span.

'Lord Eon Kull? Are you... well?'

'Fatigued, no more. How goes it?'

'Your... storm... it is a work of greatness. More fierce than I had imagined.'

Eon Kull frowned. What did Muon Nol mean? He couldn't show his ignorance to the warrior. He would have to reach out and see for himself. But his mind was so weak and spent.

'The Way must be closed now. The storm won't last forever.'

Muon Nol knelt on both knees and made the formal gesture of petition. 'Lord, I beseech you once more, for the last time, let us not abandon the Way here. Let me send to Dolthe for reinforcements. With exarchs, with the great Avatar itself, we can hold out and–'

Eon Kull bade him rise, shaking his helmeted head slowly. He was glad Muon Nol couldn't see the blood that tracked down his septum and over his dry lips. 'And I tell you, for the last time, it cannot be. Dolthe can spare no more for us. They are beset. Have you any idea of the scale of the foe here on Monthax?' Eon Kull leaned forward and touched Muon Nol's brow with his bared hand, sending a hesitant mental pulse that conveyed the unnumbered measure of the foe-host as he had sensed it. Muon Nol stiffened and shuddered. He looked away.

'Chaos must not take us. They must be denied access to the Webway. Our Way here must be closed now, as I have wished it.'

'I understand,' the warrior nodded.

'Go see to the final provisions. When all is ready, come and escort me to the High Place. That is where I will meet my end.'

Alone again, Eon Kull the Old One flexed his mind, trying to peer out beyond the Inner Place and sense the outside world. But he had no strength. Had he expended so much? What had Muon Nol meant when he remarked upon his storm?

Shuffling, unsteady, Eon Kull crossed the Inner Place and opened the lid of a quartz box set against the wall. It was full of charred dust and some empty silk bags. A rare few still held objects and he took one out now. The wraithbone wand slipped out of its protective bag into his hand. It was warm, pulsing; one of the last he had left. He shuffled back to the throne, sank onto the seat with a sigh and clutched the wand to his chest. He prayed that there was strength enough in it to channel and focus his dissipated powers. The embers of his power lit through the wand, and the spirit stones around him and set into his armour blinked back into a semblance of life. Most of them, at least. Some remained dull and dead. Many merely flickered with a dull luminosity.

His mind blinked, two or three times, flashing images of the outside which roared and wailed. Then it coalesced and he saw.

He saw the storm, the magnitude of the storm. He cursed himself. He should have realised that he had been too weak to control such a conjuration. He had intended a storm, of course, as a diversion to cover his more subtle, complex illusions. But the stress had robbed him of consciousness, and he had lost control.

He had unleashed a warp-storm, a catastrophic force that now raged entirely beyond his ability to command. Far from covering the humans and allow them in close enough for the illusions to work them to his cause, he had all but blasted them away.

His head lolled back. His final deed had been a failure. He had exhausted his entire power, burned his runes, extinguished some of his guide spirits, and all for this. Kaela Mensha Khaine! An elemental force of destruction that fell, unselective, upon all. It roared about him, like a war-hound he had spent months training, only to see it go feral.

There were a few faint spats of light, the traces of a handful of humans who had been close enough to become wrapped in his illusions. But far from enough.

Lord Eon Kull, Old One, warlock, wept. He had tried. And he had failed.

Mkoll had been stumbling through the torrential rain for fifteen or more minutes before he stopped dead in his tracks, shook himself in amazement, and then hurled himself into the cover of a dripping, exposed tree-root.

It was not possible. It was... some kind of madness.

He look up at the stormy sky, shuddered and hugged himself. All along, he had suspected the storm was not natural in origin. Now he knew it was playing with his mind.

This was Monthax, Monthax, he told himself, over and over. Not Tanith.

Then why had he spent the last twenty minutes making his way home to the farmstead he shared with his wife and sons in the nal-groves above Heban?

Shock pounded in his veins. It was like losing Eiloni all over again, though he knew she was dead of canth-fever these last ten, fifteen years. It was like losing Tanith again. Losing his sons.

He had been so convinced he was hurrying back through a summer storm from the high-pasturing cuchlain herds, so convinced he had a wife and a farm and a family and a livelihood to return to. But in fact he had been scrambling his way back towards the ruin and the massed forces of the enemy.

How had his mind been so robbed of truth? What witchcraft was at work?

He pulled himself to his feet and made off again, now in the opposite direction, towards what he prayed were friendly lines.

On Lilith's orders, a sizable force of men began pushing back into the storm-choked jungles. Her bodyguard formed around her, following a roughly equal number of Tanith Ghosts under Gaunt, the regrouped remnants of the First, Second and Seventh platoons. The wounded had been sent on to the lines.

Gilbear had protested, both at the advance and the co-operation of the Tanith, but Lilith had made no great efforts to disguise her contempt for him when she denied his objections. If her fears were realised, this was Gaunt's business as much as hers. Besides, the Ghosts had already been in there, and had a taste of what to expect. For all the vaunted veteran skills of the Volpone's elite Tenth Brigade, she wanted a serious fighting force, with enough numbers that losses wouldn't dent. Sixty men, or thereabouts, half dedicated heavy infantry, ordered to guard her by the general, half the best stealth fighters in the Guard, led by their own charismatic commissar.

A reasonable insurgency force, she reckoned. Still, she had had her astropath signal back for reinforcements. Thoth had been reluctant until she had pulled rank and suggested the magnitude of the threat.

Now five hundred Bluebloods under Marshal Ruas and three hundred Roane Deepers under Major Alef and Commissar Jaharn were moving up in their wake, an hour or so behind them. The astropath was now dead from the effort of sending and receiving through the storm. They left his body where it lay.

It seemed bloody-minded to push a unit back into the storm zone when all other Imperials had retreated out of it, and it seemed to compound that error by sending in fresh numbers after them. But Lilith knew that, storm or no storm, Chaos host or no Chaos host, the key to victory on Monthax lay in the heart of that zone. And the focus of her own, personal inquisition too, perhaps.

Lerod led the spearhead. He had volunteered, brimming with an enthusiasm that Gaunt found faintly alarming. Yael, one of Lerod's men from the Seventh, had told of Lerod's miraculous escape from the enemy gunners on the creek bank, and explained that Lerod now thought his life charmed.

Gaunt wondered for a moment. He'd seen that sort of luck-flare before, where a man thought himself invulnerable. The consequences could be appalling. But he'd rather have Lerod laying his 'luck' at the front than cursing them lower down the file.

Besides, Lerod was a fine soldier. One of the best, the most level-headed.

And more than that... All of the Ghosts, Corbec included, seemed somehow eager to get back into the deadly storm. It was as if something called to them. Gaunt had seldom seen them so highly motivated.

And then, in a pause, he realised that he, too, was more than willing to turn back into the fatal onslaught besetting the dense jungle and creeks. He couldn't account for it. It alarmed him.

Lilith's brigade slogged in through the creek-ways and water-runs, beaten by the rain and wind. The muddy ground became steep slopes, the low rises of upland rain forests above the flooded swamps.

Lilith sent pairs of men forward to secure lines. Corbec and a couple of Ghosts and Bluebloods clambered forward with Lerod up the muddy escarpments, playing out cables that they secured to trees and stumps along the way. Lightning berated them, exploding the tallest trees round about.

The brigade moved forward, following the twin lines of cable the advance had played out.

High on a slope, Corbec nailed the end of his cable line to a stump, and then set watch with his party as the main force struggled up behind. One of the Bluebloods looked at him, smiling.

'Culcis?'

'Colonel Corbec!'

Corbec slapped the younger man on the armoured shoulder, and the other Bluebloods eyed this camaraderie with suspicion.

'Where was it – Nacedon?'

'In the farm. I owe you my life, colonel.'

Corbec guffawed. 'I remember you fought as hard as the next that night, Culcis!'

The young man grinned. Rainwater dripping down his face from his helmet lip.

'So you made the Tenth, huh?' Corbec asked, settling in next to the Blueblood and taking aim into the blistering dark.

'Your medic wrote well of me, and your leader, Gaunt, mentioned me in dispatches. Then I got a lucky break on Vandamaar and won a medal.'

'So you're veteran now? One of the Blueblood elite? Best of the best, and all that?'

Culcis chuckled. 'We're all just soldiers, sir.'

The twin lines of advance progressed slowly up the slopes along the cable lines, weaving between the heavy trees and saturated foliage.

The ground was like watered honey, loose and fluid, coming up to their shins. At least there were no insects abroad in the onslaught.

They moved on in fire-team formation, following a deep valley into the jungle uplands and the heart of the roiling storm. Lilith called a halt, to get a fix on their position. She was just raising her data-slate when a searing light flashed and they were deafened.

Lightning had struck a tree twenty paces back, exploding it in a welter of wooden shrapnel. Two Bluebloods had been atomised by electrical arcs and another two, along with one of the Tanith, had been flayed alive by the wood chips.

Major Gilbear slammed into Lilith as he stumbled up the slope. 'We must retreat, inquisitor! This is madness!'

'This is necessary, major,' she corrected, and returned her gaze to the slate. Gaunt was by her side. They compared data, pelting rain pattering off the screens of their respective devices.

'There's your Third platoon,' she said.

'As you had it last fixed before the storm came down,' corrected Gaunt. 'They were in the eye of the storm then, but can you get a true fix on their location now? Or on ours?'

Lilith cursed silently. Gaunt was right. They were cut off from orbital locator signals, and the storm was playing merry hell with all their finders and codiciers. All they had to work on was a memory or location and terrain. And none of that seemed reliable.

Gaunt drew her to one side, out of Gilbear's earshot. 'My men are the best scouts in the Guard, but they're coming up blind. If this storm is psyker like you say, it's foxing us. I'm not sure we can find our way to the last recorded position of the Third.'

'And so you suggest?'

'I don't know,' Gaunt said, meeting her grim eyes. 'But if we move much further in, I'm not sure we'll be able to find our way back...'

'Sir! Commissar!' It was Raglon, the vox-officer. He scrambled back down the muddy slope to Gaunt and held out his headset.

'Third, sir! I've got them! Indistinct, broken, but it's Major Rawne and the others all right. I copy micro-bead traffic, trooper to trooper. Sounds like they're in a fight.'

Gaunt took the headset and listened. 'Can you get a fix?'

Raglon shook his head. 'The storm's fething everything, sir. I can't get the vox signals to jibe with anything. It's like... like they're nowhere and everywhere.'

'Nonsense!' Gilbear barked, snatching the headset from Gaunt and adjusting the dials on Raglon's caster set. After a moment, he gave up with a curse.

'Try sending to them,' Gaunt told Raglon. 'Repeat signal, wide-beam.'

'Message?' Raglon asked.

'Gaunt to Tanith Third platoon. Give status and position signal.'

Raglon dialled it in. 'Nothing sir, repeating... Wait! A response! Sir, it reads: "Position: Elector's Palace, Tanith Magna. Rearguard".'

'What?' Gaunt grabbed the headset again. 'Rawne! Rawne! Respond!'

The Third were holed up at a bend in the hallway, las-rounds blistering back and forth from a ferocious firefight. Over his micro-bead, Rawne could hear Gaunt's signal.

'Try them again,' he urged Wheln, who was fumbling with the dials on the vox-caster backpack.

Rawne hated this Gaunt already, this new commander brought from off-world to lead them. Where was he? What did he care for Tanith?

Wheln interrupted Rawne's thoughts. 'Gaunt signals, sir! He says to withdraw and pull out. Instructs us to rally with him at the following co-ordinates.'

Rawne eyed the print out and threw it aside. It made no sense. Gaunt was ordering them to abandon the palace and Tanith Magna itself.

'Give me that!' he shouted to Wheln, taking the headset.

'Sir?' Raglon held out his headset to Gaunt. 'I don't understand...'

Gaunt took it and listened.

'...won't give up now... won't let Tanith fall! Damn you, Gaunt, if you think we'll give up on the planet now!'

Gaunt lowered his hand, letting the headset droop.

'Crazy,' Gaunt murmured. 'He's crazy...'

Mkoll shouldered on through the rain. He focused his mind on reality and shut up the yearnings in his head. Home, the lines... he would make it...

Las-shots scorched at his heels, exploding trees. He glanced backwards and began to run.

An enemy warrior loomed ahead of him and Mkoll blasted with one of his pistols, taking the head clean off.

All around him, in the rain, Chaos warriors were closing.

He ducked into cover as laser blasts puffed up leaf-mould and weed. Two shots to the left. Two to the right. A hit, and body falling and twisting in the grime. Then Mkoll was up and running again.

A shot clipped his head and he went down, full length, into the mud. He tried to rise, but his body was slow and dazed. The mud sucked at him.

A powerful hand took him by the shoulder and yanked him over, the mud sucking as it kissed him goodbye.

Mkoll looked up into the face of Death, the raddled face of an enemy trooper. He shot him point blank and then rose, cutting the knees off the next foe who advanced with a double spit of las-fire from his guns.

Mkoll started shooting wholesale, picking off shadows that loomed between the trees through the storm, and fired on him.

Another shot kissed his flank and burned a scar that would never leave him. Mkoll dropped to one knee, firing with both pistols. He killed left and right. Maximum firepower. Then he realised his captured laspistol was coughing inert gas. He threw it aside.

As he went to reload his issue pistol, a huge form barrelled into him and knocked him down. The Chaos trooper had his bayonet raised to rip Mkoll's life out of his body.

They wrestled in the mud for a few moments, until Mkoll was able to use his trained skill to roll the other off him.

The sprawling warrior threw his bayonet and it impaled Mkoll's left knee with a clack of metal on bone and a ripping of tendons. Mkoll faltered and fell.

The enemy was back on him, hands outstretched and a murderous howl on his sutured lips.

They fell back, thrashing, fighting. Mkoll couldn't reach the Tanith blade in his waistband, but he found the enemy bayonet sticking out of his knee and wrenched it free.

Cursing his life and mourning Eiloni, Mkoll plunged the dagger two, three, four times into the side of his aggressor's neck, until the bestial warrior shuddered and died.

Mkoll pulled himself free of the corpse, blood jetting from his knee with a force too great for the downpour to diminish.

He stumbled on, armed only with the enemy knife now. He was getting weaker as he lost blood. The foot of his wounded leg was hot with blood, yet cool. His knee didn't work properly. More fire came his way, cutting the limbs of trees and bursting ripe fruit-flowers.

A deflecting laser round took him in the small of the back, and dropped him, face down, in the mire. Stunned, he writhed, no breath coming, mud sucking into his nose and mouth.

Something made him pull himself up. Something, some urge.

Eiloni. She stood over him, as pale and as beautiful as she had been at twenty.

'What are you doing down there? What will the boys do for supper? Husband?'

She was gone as quickly as she had appeared, but Mkoll was already on his feet when the first of the Chaos spawn closed in on him. On his feet and seared with passion.

Despite the burn, agonising, on his back, Mkoll took the first down with his hands, breaking his neck and ribs and crushing his skull.

Capturing the lasgun, he turned, setting it to full auto and cutting down a wave of Chaos infantry as they pressed in on his heels.

He was still shooting, blindly into the night, his lasgun's power cell almost exhausted and three dozen slain foe about him, when Corbec found him.

Gaunt established a picket perimeter in the sloping forest to guard them as the field medics treated Mkoll. The storm continued to lacerate the sky above and sway the trees with the sheering force of wind and nearly horizontal rain.

Lilith, Gilbear and Gaunt stood by as Trooper Lesp opened his field narthecium and dressed Mkoll's many cuts and las-burns. The scout's head was bandaged and his pierced knee had been strapped.

'He's a tough old dog,' Corbec murmured to Gaunt, sidling up to the commissar.

'He never ceases to impress me,' Gaunt whispered back.

Lilith looked over at them, a question in her face. Gaunt knew what it was: how had this man survived?

'We're wasting time,' Gilbear said abruptly. 'What are we doing?'

Gaunt turned on him, angry, but Lilith stepped between them.

'Major Gilbear. Are you still my bodyguard commander?'

'Yes, lady.'

'No new duties have fallen to you since you were given that task?'

'No, lady.'

'Then shut up and leave this to the commissar and myself, if you don't mind.'

Gilbear swung around and made off to check the pickets.

Corbec poked his tongue out at the major's back and made a vulgar noise. Gaunt was about to reprimand him when he saw Lilith was laughing.

'He's a pompous ass,' Lilith said.

'Indeed,' the commissar nodded.

'I meant no disrespect, inquisitor,' Corbec said hurriedly.

'Yes, you did,' Lilith smiled.

'Well, yes, but not really,' Corbec stammered.

'Check the picket, colonel, if you please,' Gaunt said quietly.

'But the major's gone to–'

'And you trust him to do a good job?' Gaunt asked.

'Not on his current form, no,' Corbec grinned, saluting Gaunt and making an over-lavish bow to the inquisitor before hurrying off.

'You'll have to excuse my second-in-command. His style of leadership is casual and spirited.'

'But it works?' asked Lilith.

'Yes, but... yes. Corbec is the soundest officer I've ever worked with. The men love him.'

'I can see why. He has charisma, courage. Just the right amount of healthy disrespect. Colm is a very attractive man.'

Gaunt paused and looked off into the night where Corbec had vanished.

'He is?'

'Oh yes. Trust me on that.' Lilith turned her attention back to Mkoll. 'So, we have your best scout, beaten and shot to hell, come to us out of the maelstrom?'

'Yes.' Gaunt cleared his throat. 'Mkoll's the best I have, all in all. Looks like he's been through fething hell and back.'

'Feth... nice word. Good weight. I'll be using that if you don't mind.'

Gaunt was puzzled. 'Mind? I–'

'What does it mean?'

Gaunt suddenly got a very clear and vivid mental picture of what it literally meant. He and Lilith were acting it out.

'I– I'm not sure...'

'Yes you are.'

Lightning struck a tree nearby, causing Bluebloods to run yelping for cover. The detonation was like a slap in the face for Gaunt. His mind cleared, sober.

'Don't play your mind tricks with me, inquisitor,' he snarled.

'I don't know what you mean.'

'Yes, you do. Twisting a feeling of jealousy in me against Corbec. And the images you were broadcasting. Feth is one of the Tanith tree-gods. Not some barbaric euphemism. I'll work with you, but not *for* you.'

Lilith smiled solemnly and held up her hands. 'Fair point. I'm sorry, Gaunt. I'm used to making allies where I can't find them, using my powers to twist wills to my purpose. I suppose it's strange for me to have a willing comrade.'

'Such is the way of the inquisitor. And I thought the commissar's path was lonely.'

She stared into his eyes and another smile lit her pale face. Gaunt wondered if this was another of her guiles, but it seemed genuine.

'We both need to find and conquer the source of this,' Gaunt told her, gesturing up at the storm. 'We both want victory here. You'll find me a much more able ally if I am in full command of my powers, rather than spellbound by you.'

She nodded. 'We both want victory here,' she said, repeating him. 'But that's not all I want,' she added, mysteriously.

Gaunt was about to pick her up on it when she shivered, pushing back her cowl and running a hand through her fine hair. The commissar-colonel realised how strained she looked.

'This storm... it's really hard for you, isn't it?'

'I'm at my limit, Ibram. The warp is all around me, tugging at my mind. I'm sorry about before. Desperation.'

Gaunt stepped towards her, ushering her towards Mkoll. 'You said you liked to make allies where you couldn't find them. Why so hard on Gilbear?'

She grinned. 'He loves it. Are you kidding? A powerful woman ordering him around. He wants me so bad he'd die for me.'

Now Gaunt grinned. 'You're a scary woman, Inquisitor Lilith.'

'I'll take that as a compliment.'

'Just promise you won't use such base tactics on me.'

'I promise,' she said. 'I don't think I need to.'

Gaunt suddenly became aware of how long he had been looking into her eyes. He broke the gaze. 'Let's talk to Mkoll.'

'Let me.'

'No,' he corrected. 'Let *us*.'

* * *

Gilbear walked the picket in the slicing rain. Invisible amphibians croaked and rattled in the wet gloom. By a fold of trees, watching the left flank, he found two Tanith Ghosts occupied in trying to light smokes from a damp tinder box.

Gilbear pounced at them, kicking one in the gut and punching the other over onto his back.

'What is this?' he seethed. 'Are you watching the flank? No? You're too busy lighting up and joking!'

One of the men protested and Gilbear kicked him again. In the face, the ribs, the kidneys as he went down. He kept kicking.

'There's a universe of hate out there, and you can't be bothered to watch for it!'

The other Ghost had risen to defend his fallen, balled-up comrade, and Gilbear turned on him, punching him out, then laying in with the boot.

A big hand caught the Blueblood major by the shoulder.

'There's a universe of hate waiting in here too,' Corbec said.

He dropped Gilbear with a headbutt that split the Blueblood's forehead. Then Corbec whaled in with two hard punches to the mouth and chest. The latter was deflected by the carapace segments.

Gilbear sprawled in the mud, pulling Corbec down on him in a threshing frenzy.

'You want me, Ghost? You got me!' he growled.

'Not before time,' Corbec agreed, snapping Gilbear's head backwards with his fist. 'It's been a long while coming. That was for Cluggan, rest his soul.'

Gilbear folded his legs up and propelled Corbec headlong over him with a kick. The big Ghost slammed down against a tree stump, upside down, the sharp stump-ends raking his back.

Now Gilbear was on his feet, fists balled. Corbec leapt up to meet him, throwing off his cape, fury in his eyes. They edged around the muddy clearing in the slanting rain, water washing off them and sluicing the blood from their wounds. Punch and counter-punch, followed by bellow and charge. The two beaten Ghosts were up on their feet, cheering and jeering. Others, Ghosts and Bluebloods both, congregated in a ring as the two officers battled by lightning flash.

Gilbear was a boxer, a heavyweight champion back on Volpone, with a stinging right hook and a terrifying capacity to take punishment. Corbec was a wrestler, Pryze County victor three years running, at the Logging Show. Gilbear bounced on spread legs, throwing humiliating punches. Corbec came in low, soaking them up, clawing his hands around Gilbear's throat.

With a roar, Corbec drove in under the whistling fists and slammed Gilbear backwards through a break of trees. They tumbled together down a short incline into a creek bed swollen with storm water. The Ghost and Volpone audience hovered at the rim of the creek, looking down and chanting.

Gilbear rose first, black with the muddy water, and swung a punch. It kissed air. Corbec exploded up out of the flood, greased jet-black with liquid mud, and doubled Gilbear with a low punch to the gut, then sent him over in a spray of silver droplets with an upper cut to the chin.

Gilbear wasn't done. He came back out of the water like a surfacing whale, as loud and vicious as the storm which quaked the sky above, and knocked Corbec back two, three steps with blow after blow. Corbec's mouth was split open and his nose broken, flooding his beard with blood.

Corbec ducked in low, throwing punches before he shoulder-charged Gilbear off his feet. Corbec lurched the massive Blueblood backwards on his shoulder, legs dangling, then twisted and threw him over himself in a perfect wrestling move, slamming Gilbear down into the creek on his back. Corbec kicked him for good measure.

Trooper Alhac, a Blueblood, was pounding his hands together wildly until he realised his side had lost. He was about to turn his venom on the cheering Tanith beside him when the undergrowth to his left flickered.

Alhac froze. So did the Ghost he was about to strike.

Something black and abominable grew out of the jumping lights in the thicket.

Alhac died, cut into streaks of evaporating flesh. The Ghost beside him perished the same way a second later. Then another Blueblood, skinned in an instant. The other Ghosts and Bluebloods who had been cheering the fight from the creek edge fled in panic.

'Oh feth!' Corbec said, dripping with ooze, looking up.

'What?' asked Gilbear, rising beside him.

'That!'

The creature was like a dog, if a dog could be the size of a horse, if a horse could move as fast as a humming bird. A red, arched-backed quadruped with long, triple-jointed limbs and a skinless, blistered pelt. Its skull was huge and short, blunt, with the lower jaw extending beyond the upper, and multiple rows of triangular saw-teeth in each. It had no eyes. A warp creature, loosed from the storm and hunting for Chaos.

'Oh feth!' Corbec spat.

'Great Vulpo!' barked Gilbear.

The dog-thing leapt down into the creek and began to pound towards them. Corbec and Gilbear turned and ran as fast as they could through the root-twisted waterway. It was right behind them, baying.

The thing leapt on Gilbear and dragged him down, ripping at his carapace armour with its tusks. Strips of armaplas shredded off his shoulder panels. Gilbear cried out, helpless.

Corbec leapt astride the warp-beast, pulling its head back by the mane and plunging his Tanith dagger into its throat. Foetid purple blood squirted from the wound and the thing opened its mouth to howl and squeal.

'Now, Blueblood! Now!' Corbec shouted, riding the beast, pulling its skull back.

Gilbear pulled a frag grenade from his belt and threw it straight into the beast's mouth, right down its gullet past the wincing pink larynx.

Gilbear threw himself down and Corbec propelled himself clear.

The dog-thing exploded from within, showering both them and the creek bed with stinking meat.

Corbec pulled himself up out of the fluid muck at the bottom of the watercourse. He looked across at Gilbear, sat with his back against the creek wall, eyes straining.

'You all right?' Corbec gurgled.

Gilbear nodded.

'About time we called a truce, eh?'

Gilbear nodded again. They both got up, unsteady and filmed with mud and flecks of putrid meat.

'A truce. Yes. A truce...' Gilbear was still stunned. 'For now.'

'The ruin, sir, the one I glimpsed before. I found it again.' Mkoll's voice was soft and brittle, his breath laboured. He sat on a fallen log, sipping alternately from a water canteen and a sacra flask that Bragg had manifested. He was bandaged and caked in mud. Gaunt crouched by him, listening carefully. Mkoll seemed a little spooked by Lilith, but she read this response quickly and held back so Gaunt could talk to his valued scout.

'What is it?' asked Gaunt.

Mkoll shrugged. 'No idea. Big, old, fortified. It's on top of a mound that I don't think is natural. Too regular. All I know is, the enemy are surrounding it thicker than sap-flies round a glucose trap.'

Gaunt felt a tingle of alarm. Not only did he know precisely what Mkoll meant, he had a brief, vivid mental flash of the long-bodied insects themselves, swarming around a beaker of glistening fluid on a woodsman's hut-stoop. Insects native to Tanith. Insects he had never seen.

'Numbers?' he pressed on.

'I didn't take a headcount,' Mkoll muttered dryly. 'I was a little busy. Tens of thousands is my guess. Maybe more, beyond my line of sight. The terrain was hilly, thick cover. There could have been hundreds of thousands up there.'

'What are they after?' Gaunt wondered out loud.

'I think we have to find out,' Lilith said quietly.

Gaunt rose and looked round at the inquisitor, her face in shadow from her cowl. 'Before we explore the insanity of sending sixty men up against a possible force of hundreds of thousands, may I remind you that we can't even find this place? Our locators and auspex are screwed, my scouts can't tell one direction from another. Feth, Mkoll's my best, and he admits he only found it again by accident.'

Lilith nodded. 'There is a deep level of misdirection and conceal-ment in this storm. I don't know the answer.'

'I could lead you there again,' Mkoll said darkly from behind them.

Gaunt turned to look at him. 'You could? You claimed it was elu-sive before.'

Mkoll rose shakily to his feet. 'That was then. I don't know... I just feel I could find it again now. Something in my bones. It would be like... like finding my way home again.'

Gaunt looked at Lilith. 'Let's try,' she said. 'Mkoll seems confident and I trust him like you do. If opposition gets too hot, we can pull out again.'

Gaunt nodded. He was about to call up Raglon and issue new orders to advance when the dull crump of a frag grenade rolled through the storm. A few moments later, lasguns and hellguns were firing, spo-radic, the distinctive crack of laser fire overlapping the higher shriek of hell-shots. Gaunt scrambled down the bank, pulling out his chainsword, shouting for reports.

Sergeant Lerod was directing the men in the east flank of the picket. 'Lerod?'

'Sir! There are things coming out of the storm, sir! Brutes! Creatures!'

Gaunt peered out into the dark jungle, and saw scuttling monstrosi-ties being born out of tendrils of lightning. There was a sickening whiff of Chaos. Blueblood and Tanith guns blew the things apart as they came close.

'Warp creatures,' Lilith hissed, appearing by his side. 'Manifestations of this unholy storm. Mindless, but lethal.'

Corbec staggered up, looking very much the worse for wear. He was ordering the west flank of the picket to loop back closer to the centre.

'What happened to you?' Gaunt asked sharply, seeing an equally bedraggled Gilbear moving in with a fire-team of Bluebloods.

'Bit of a fight,' Corbec said. 'Some fething thing came out of the dark.'

Gaunt didn't want to know any more. This was no time for fierce reprimands. He had to keep the whole unit tight and together. He keyed his micro-bead. 'Gaunt to brigade. We're advancing, double time. Spearhead formation. Tanith First platoon and half the Volpone unit at the point. Take your direction from Scout-Trooper Mkoll. Everyone else, watch the flanks and the rear. Inquisitor Lilith instructs that warp-spawn could appear around or among us at any time. Don't hesitate; shoot. Sergeant Lerod, take a six-man drill and guard the back of the formation. All commanders acknowledge understanding of these orders and signal readiness.'

A chatter of responses came back swiftly. Raglon, monitoring them with the vox-caster, nodded to Gaunt that all the brigade had signalled in.

Gaunt hadn't finished. The devoted Tanith had made his commissarial duties easy these last few years. But now they were in thick, spooked, and the company was mixed with troopers he didn't know or even trust. Morale, discipline – the watchwords of the commissariat. He thought back to his training at the Schola Progenium, to his field apprenticeship as a cadet under Oktar. He took the speaker horn of the vox-set from Raglon.

'I won't pretend this will be easy. But it is vital. Vital to Imperial success on this world, vital perhaps to the entire Crusade. The enemy and their ambitions will be denied, if it takes every spark of our lives and every drop of our blood. We fight for the Emperor today, fight as if we were standing at his side as his chosen bodyguard. Protect the men to your left and right as if they were the Emperor himself. Do not slacken, do not falter. Victory awaits you, and if not victory, then the glory of a brave death in service to the Golden Throne of Terra. The Emperor will provide, if you are true. His hand guides us, his eyes watch over us, and even in death he will bring us to him and we shall sit in splendour at his side beyond the Eternity Gate.

'For Lost Tanith, for Mighty Volpone, for Imperial Earth... advance!'

Like a single, lithe entity, the brigade swept up the escarpment, pushing onwards into the jagged hills as the storm shook the world around them. Blueblood and Ghost moved in perfect, trained order together, all animosities set aside. Gaunt smiled as he observed the tight drilled formation of his own, and was suitably impressed that it was matched by the bulky Volpone elite. Every now and then, las-shots sang out from the vanguard as warp-things were sighted and dispatched.

Lilith moved with him. She slid a plasma pistol out from under her cloak and charged it with a flick of her black-gloved hands. 'Good speech,' she grinned at him. 'Got them motivated. Oktar trained you well.'

'You've checked up on me. My background.'

'I'm an inquisitor, Gaunt. What do you expect? I enquire.'

'And what are you really inquiring about here on Monthax?' he asked curtly.

'What do you mean?'

'I'm no psyker, but I read people well enough. This is about more than victory here, more than the successful prosecution of psyker-deviants in our forces. You have an agenda.'

She flashed a smile at him. 'No mystery, Ibram. Back on the Sanctity, I told you. Bulledin had reported back to us because it was suspected some powerful psyker component might be at work here. We thought that it was the enemy itself, that we were in for a mind-war. But now, this ruin. The foe embark on an advance, ignoring us completely, and seem hell-bent on taking that place. You've got to wonder why. You've got to believe that there's something very valuable up there.'

'Something that caused this storm?'

She shrugged. 'Or something that made them cause this storm to cover their movement towards it. But I think your guess is probably more likely.'

'And that's what you want?'

'It's my duty, Ibram. And I don't think I need to explain that concept to one of the Imperium's best commissars.'

'Don't try distracting me with flattery. Give me some idea what you mean by "something valuable".'

'Think back to Menazoid Epsilon. I told you, I checked your background thoroughly. As an inquisitor, I got to look at some very classified reports. You know what was at stake there.'

Gaunt was wary. 'You're talking about technology? Artefacts?'

She nodded. 'It could be.'

'Ancient human? Alien?'

Lilith produced something from her pocket. 'Mkoll found this. He dug it out of a tree stump at a battle site just before the storm hit. You tell me what you think it means.'

She held up the metal star with the sharpened points. Gaunt stared at it with dark comprehension.

'Now you know as much as I do.'

The brigade moved down a deep defile into a tree sheltered vale that blocked the raging storm partially for the first time. Gaunt was becoming numb with the incessant wind and rain, and knew his men must be too. It was a blessed, temporary relief to move through the deep gorge with its almost cathedral-like arches of ancient cattails and clopeas, where rain arrested by the leaf canopy simply drooled down to the ground in long, slow, sappy streams. The storm raged, muffled, far above them.

Gaunt moved up to Mkoll at the point of the formation.

'Still on track?'

Mkoll nodded. 'Like I said, I couldn't lose the trail now if I wanted to.'

'Like coming home, you said,' Gaunt reminded him.

Mkoll closed his eyes and saw Eiloni just ahead, beckoning him back to the farmstead. She was whispering promises of a hot supper, and of rowdy boys ready for one of their father's fireside tales before bed.

'You have no idea, commissar.'

The advancing tide of Chaos warriors only stopped when the numbers of their dead choked the passageway.

Rawne ordered his platoon back and they hauled a set of double doors closed, barring them to seal the tunnel. Milo helped Wheln swing the doors shut, his fingers tracing the heraldic badge of the Tanith Elector inscribed on the heavy nal-wood panels. He blinked, and for a second saw taller, more slender doors of polished onyx, marked with alien runes he did not understand.

'What's up?' Wheln asked, panting.

Milo blinked again. The doors were arched nal-wood in the Tanith pattern again, the Elector's insignia clearly marked.

Feygor and Mkendrik dropped a long bar across the door loops to lock it tight. Beyond the thick barrier, they could hear muffled explosions and the rasp of flamers as the enemy tried to unblock the corpse-packed tunnel.

The eight Tanith men were exhausted. A day ago, at the Founding, none of them – with the possible exception of Rawne and Feygor – had ever fired a weapon in anger, let alone killed. Now they were truly baptised. There was no counting the dead they had piled up.

Cown sank to his heels against the wall, fighting for breath. 'Are we lost?' he asked. 'Is Tanith lost?'

Rawne turned to face him, fire in his eyes. 'Are we alive? Is Tanith living? Get up! Get up and move! Only that feckless off-worlder Gaunt seems to have given up on Tanith! Withdraw? Abandon? What kind of leadership is that? He'd make worldless ghosts of us!'

'Ghosts...' murmured Larkin, leaning slackly against the far wall, cheek and shoulder pressed against the cold stone. 'Gaunt's Ghosts...'

'What did you say?' Milo asked directly, blood racing in his ears. It was like a dream was breaking in his head.

'Ignore him!' Feygor ordered. 'Fething fool is weak in the head. But for his good eye, I'd have shot him as dead-weight before now.'

'No,' began Milo. 'This isn't right... it...'

'Of course it's not right!' Feygor snarled into Milo's face. Milo winced as spittle hit his cheek. 'The Imperium comes to Tanith when it needs men, but where is the Imperium now when Tanith needs it? They're leaving us to die!'

Caffran pulled Feygor back from Milo sharply. 'Then we'll die well, Feygor! We'll die fething well!' The young trooper's face was bright with passion. The thought of Laria burned in his mind. She was out there somewhere and he would fight and kill and kill again to save this place and be with her once more.

'Caff's right, Feygor,' Mkendrik said. Wheln and Cown both nodded in agreement. 'Let's die well so Tanith can live.'

'And feth any off-world commissar who says otherwise!' spat Cown.

Feygor, subdued, turned and nodded, deftly exchanging the power cell of his lasgun for a fresh one.

Rawne had been absent for a few moments and now strode back into view. 'I hear fighting down the hall, maybe three hundred spans away. Sounds like another group of our boys in defence. I say we move in to support.'

Mkendrik nodded. 'Bolster our numbers. Maybe they know where the Elector is sheltering.'

'If we could get him to the transport stables, we could maybe fly him to safety in a cutter,' Cown added.

Rawne nodded. 'Feygor, make the door a surprise.'

Feygor grinned and took out a brace of tube-charges from his pack. He strapped them with quick, practiced diligence to the door bar. Anything that broke in here now after them would snap the trigger wire and bring the hallway down on top of them.

'Let's go!' Rawne ordered.

Milo fell into step with the others as they hurried on down the long palace hallway, boot-steps resounding from the stone flags. He wished with all his heart and soul he could work out what was wrong with... with reality. There was no other word. Reality itself seemed wrong and dreamlike and it was making his stomach turn. It must be the Chaos daemons, Milo thought. Maybe Major Rawne knew wh–

Milo paused. *Major* Rawne? In the tents of the Founding Fields outside Tanith Magna, Rawne had bivouacked with the common soldiers. A trooper, nothing more. No rank, no seniority. Since when had he got the collar pins and the promotion?

Have I forgotten something? Milo wondered. Have I...

Another flicker in his mind. An image of... of a cramped cabin on a starship. Rawne, Corbec, Milo. A deputation. A tall, powerful, lean-faced man that could only have been Commissar-Colonel Ibram Gaunt, rising to meet them. How could he know what this Gaunt looked like? He'd never seen him. He could hear Gaunt speaking, making bold, confident field promotions: Colonel Corbec, Major Rawne.

Another dream?

There was no time to think about it. They were almost on the fighting. Gunshots. Screaming, just ahead.

That wasn't las-fire, Milo thought to himself as he and all the platoon checked stride and raised weapons. He'd heard enough lasgun exchanges in the last half an hour to know the distinctive snap. This was an eerie, singing shrill: a shrieking, a buzzing, like the saw-note of a wasp, amplified and broken into harsh, serried blasts.

What the feth was it?

'You hear that?' he gasped to Larkin beside him. Larkin was tuning the night-scope on his long gun, stabbing a slender target beam of porcelain blue light up at the roof.

'What? Lasguns on full auto? Yeah... someone's having a busy day.'

It's not a lasgun, thought Milo, it's *not...*

Third platoon rounded a corner in the hallway, moving in tight overlap formation, and broke into a wide audience hall of dark, volcanic stone. Shattered stained glass windows depicting anroth, the household and forest spirits of Tanith, lined one side of the vaulted chamber. Nal-wood pews, many shattered or overturned, filled the main body of the room. The banner of the Elector hung in smouldering tatters over an oriole window at the far end.

Three Tanith troopers, their backs to them, were in position behind the pews, blasting with lasguns down at an arched door under the oriole. Chaos spawn were battling to get in through the door, their dead sprawled all around the entrance. Five or more other Tanith troopers lay dead amid the wooden wreckage.

Without question or hesitation, the Third fell in beside their brethren and took up the fight, blasting at the doorway and cutting into the advancing enemy. The three Tanith holding the chamber glanced around in surprise at the newcomers. Milo didn't recognise any of them, though the colonel was an unforgettable giant with a mane of white hair riven with a red streak, a long noble face and the blue tattoo of a scythe on his cheek.

'For Tanith! For the Elector! For Terra!' Rawne yelled as he blasted.

The big colonel hesitated again, then returned his attention to the killing. 'As you say,' he boomed melodiously, his accent strange, 'for... Tanith!'

Muon Nol, of the Dire Avengers Aspect, had been holding the green onyx vault with a squad of his warriors, seeing them cut down one by one as Chaos forced their way into the chamber via the diamond-shaped prayer chute at the end, under the rosette of spirit stones set high in the wall beneath the wraith-silk standard of Dolthe.

The only cover was the tangled mess of psycho-plastic benches which had once lined the celebrant vault, benches that had been splintered or wilted by enemy fire. To the side of them, slender pointed windows paned with translucent wraithbone showed images of Asuryan, the Phoenix King, Khaine of the Bloody Hand, Vaul, the crippled smith-god, Morai-heg the fate-crone, and Lileath the Maiden, goddess of dream fortune, backlit by Farseer Eon Kull's warp-storm outside. It was Lileath who Muon Nol most worshipped, that beautiful diviner of futures and possibilities. He wore her rune on a thread around his neck, under his jade-blue aspect armour.

Muon Nol's white crested helmet was dinted with black las-scores, and the red plume crest was singed. Still Uliowye, Lord Eon Kull's holy buanna, spat whickering onslaughts of jagged, flickering star-rounds at the foe, slicing them to pieces, a thousand rounds in each tight burst. The stabilising gyros whirred as the great, ornate shrieker cannon bucked in his mesh-gloved hands. The accelerator field shimmered around the muzzle base. Uliowye, the Kiss of Sharp Stars. He had perhaps six rods of solid ammunition left; he would make them count. For Lileath, he would make them count. For Dolthe.

Suddenly, eight humans in drab, muddy uniforms fell in beside him, blasting their lasguns at the enemy. They were resilient and fierce, and seemed to show no shock or surprise at their surroundings or sudden, new-found comrades-in-arms.

Psychically, Muon Nol ordered his remaining men to accept them and fight on. This was undoubtedly Lord Eon Kull's work – and Lord Eon Kull's deceit.

And, Khaine, but these mon-keigh fought! Like they were fighting for their own homeworld it seemed, fighting for everything they loved!

In under five minutes the reinforcement of the human soldiers had driven the Chaos spawn back. They pushed forward together down the prayer chute and killed the last of the attackers, closing a great stone hatch shut to block the rest.

The Master of the Bodyguard turned to the slim, dark-haired human who appeared to be the newcomers' leader. He searched for his grasp of Low Gothic, as he had learned in the training symposiums of Dolthe craftworld.

'I am Muon Nol, of Dolthe, of this Way Place. Your Intervention and aid is greeted with welcome. Lord Farseer Eon Kull will thank you for it.'

'Colonel Munnol, from Tanith Dale. Good to see you boys, and no mistake. The Elector needs all the men he can get right now.'

The tall Tanith officer with the mane of white hair turned to the Third as the shutter hatch closed. The exploded carcasses of Chaos troops lay all around them.

Rawne nodded. 'Glad to help. I'm Rawne, Major, commanding... well, what's left of Third platoon. Place us where you want us, colonel.'

Munnol nodded, but he seemed bewildered somehow, Milo thought. Come to that, he'd never seen a Tanith man with anything but black hair. Not only were Munnol's white locks odd, but both his men, who seemed uneasy now he noticed, were white-haired too.

Colonel Munnol nodded to a doorway to the left. It was a strange gesture. And what kind of weapon was he holding? A lasgun... but long and extended, longer and thicker than Larkin's sniper gun. Milo felt something tugging anxiously at his mind.

'If you're willing, Rawne human, the western emplacements need support desperately,' Colonel Munnol was saying.

'Lead on!' barked Rawne, changing his energy cell and dropping the spent one to the floor. Munnol shrugged and nodded, beckoning them after him.

Rawne human? Had he misheard? Milo followed, unnerved. Human? The nightmare refused to slip away. He hated the terrible nauseous feeling of confusion.

At a fast pace, Munnol led the Third and his own men down a black granite corridor. Ahead of them, through an archway, they could see two dozen more Tanith troopers lining a battlement, firing lasguns down into the stormy night. Except that the noise was the shrieking chatter of something odd and otherworldly, not the reassuring snap-return of las-fire.

Rawne hurried beside the tall colonel, Feygor at his heels.

'Can you believe this luck?' he laughed. 'Chaos attacking us on the very day of our Founding?'

'No... indeed,' Munnol replied.

'I'll be honest with you, Munnol... I almost didn't sign up,' Rawne went on. 'What kind of life is it, fighting your way through the stars for the love of some fething uncaring Emperor, no hope of ever going home again?'

'Not an enticing prospect, Rawne human,' Munnol agreed.

'Feth, but I had a nice life back in Tanith Attica. A nice little business, if you understand me. Nothing too illegal, but, you know, on the wrong side...'

'I understand...'

'Feygor was with me back then. Weren't you, Feygor?' Rawne said, nodding at his comrade.

'Aye, Rawne, aye,'

'Nice work, good returns, didn't want to give it up... but, Feth take me for a chulan... I'm glad I did! Feth the Golden Throne... thank the anroth I'm armed and ready to stand for Tanith at this dread hour!'

'We all thank the anroth for that, Rawne human,' Munnol replied.

They were out on the battlements now, enemy fire ripping over them. Colonel Munnol called to his Tanith soldiers, who looked around from the loopholes and crenellations where they had been firing down at the foe. White hair, streaked with red, thought Milo with a shudder. They all have white hair.

He thought he was going to be sick.

'Men of Dolthe!' Munnol exclaimed.

Dolthe? Dolthe? Where was that? Milo wondered.

'Our Kin arrive to fight with us! Major Rawne and other humans! Treat them well, they are resolute and with us to the end!'

A rousing cheer greeted Colonel Munnol's words.

Rawne ordered the Third in alongside the Tanith already in place, taking position and firing down into the stormy dark over the jagged lip of laser-chewed stonework.

Milo was about to take his place when he saw Larkin was cowering behind them all, crouched in the corner of the battlement away from the fight, clutching his sniper rifle and shaking uncontrollably.

Milo crossed to him. 'Larkin? What is it?'

'T-took a look through my scope... B-brin... They're not human!'

'What?' Milo felt his guts clench, but he wasn't going to give in.

'I know what I saw! Through my... my scope. It never lies. This big bastard Munnol and the rest! They're not... not Tanith!'

Milo snatched the sniper gun out of Larkin's wavering hands, and sighted it at Munnol, looking through the scope. The bead of the blue light beam kissed Munnol's drab camo-cloak like a tiny spotlight. Milo looked through the scope viewer, seeing Munnol as a ghost of blues and shadows.

Munnol, as if sensing the beam on him, turned to look back at Milo. Through the scope, Milo saw Munnol as he swung slowly around, his eyes hooked and slanted in his cold pale face. A second more, and those eyes became the visor slits of a great sculpted helmet of gleaming white armour, backed by a towering crest of red feathers. Munnol's grey fatigues became a tight suit of blue armour that locked majestically about his huge, powerful frame. The lasgun in his hands became a long, fluted lance weapon with a ridged, coiled pipe, silver vents and a beautiful inlay of chased pearl and gold. Munnol became quite the most frightening thing Milo had ever seen.

'Oh my Emperor...' he breathed. 'They're *eldar*!'

Lilith's brigade broke from the gorge into a fan of lowlands where the jungle had vanished under sculptural folds of mud which had slid in vast curls down the slopes and obliterated everything in their path. The going was slower, the troops wading waist-deep in ochre slime in some places. Above the roar of the storm, the forward scouts could now pick up the sounds of massed combat from the valley beyond. Flashes of light backlit the hilltop, and it wasn't lightning.

Gaunt ordered battle readiness via an encrypted vox-burst, marshalling the Volpone heavyweights up the flank of the hill under Gilbear's lead and funnelling the Ghosts in two detachments led by Lerod and Corbec along the edge of the mud slip below. Gaunt and Lilith moved at the front of Corbec's band.

Mkoll had led them true. Round the curve of the hill, they got their first sight of the mound and its ruin – and the massed forces of the enemy surrounding it. Even prepared by Mkoll's description, Gaunt found the scale was immense. Thousands of enemy troops, some with heavy weapons, were swarming the mound's slopes and bombarding the great, dark edifice with a force stone had no right to resist. The entire scene was a flickering mess of fire-flashes and explosions. The wet air was pungent with blood and thermite.

The Guardsmen were engaging before they realised it. Gilbear's Bluebloods had come into the rear positions of enemy heavy weapons emplacements, and the crews were turning, startled, counter-attacking with close-quarter side arms. A moment later, and both detachments of Ghosts were hemmed in by Chaos units that peeled back from the main assault to face this surprise rear contact. Las-fire and bolt rounds seared a miserable light-streak criss-cross over the smooth mud flats.

Blasting with his bolt pistol, Gaunt saw a tiny opportunity: break and fall back now, or become locked irrevocably into the fighting.

He saw Gilbear's unit spill down the rise and fall upon the enemy weapon stations with a ferocious and admirable grace, overwhelming and slaughtering them in a matter of a minute or two. The powerful hellguns, supported by two grenade launchers and a plasma rifleman, ripped into the hindquarters of the guncrews' position and cut them down.

Gilbear haughtily voxed his success as his men took over control of the enemy weapons, turning missile launchers and field artillery on the ranks of the Chaos army beyond. The Volpone Tenth Elite were damn good, Gaunt had to admit. Rotation training on all combat disciplines meant that they could take a gun post and then man that gun as surely and deftly as if they were dedicated artillery troops.

Gaunt knew the moment had gone. To break now would have left the Volpone alone. His choice was made for him. Battle was truly joined and there would be no respite.

The twin prongs of the Ghosts punched into the rear of the besiegers. Gilbear, tactically astute, turned the aim of captured guns down the turn of the valley and covered the Ghost push, creating huge breaks in the enemy's makeshift flanking manoeuvre. Shells whistled down under Gilbear's direction, pin-point accurate, throwing ribbons of mud, strands of foliage and pieces of Chaos troopers into the air not twenty metres in front of the advancing Ghosts.

The fighting was close range and white hot. Incredibly, but for a few grazes and glancing burns, Gaunt found his men suffered no casualties.

Within five minutes of first contact, the Imperials had cut a wedge into the enemy rearguard, made up half a kilometre of ground and slaughtered upwards of two hundred enemy troops, at no mortal cost.

Gilbear held the line as long as he could, but there came a point, mutually agreed between him and Gaunt over the vox-link, when the separation of the two small Imperial advances would become too great.

When the signal was given, the Bluebloods mined the gun emplacements and pushed on, scything a double-time advance to swing themselves in behind the Ghosts. Timed explosions, staggered and staggering, set off the emplacement munitions and excavated a new valley where a small plateau had been.

Into the heat now, on the lower slopes of the mound, the Imperial expedition force slicing a break in the foe as a spearhead formation, Ghosts to the right, Volpone to the left, with Gaunt and Corbec at the tip.

Gaunt knew the Tanith fought well, but he had never seen them discharge themselves so determinedly, so brilliantly. In his heart, he couldn't believe that this was a simple response to his motivational speech. They were fighting for something, something deep in their hearts, something that would not be denied.

'For Tanith! For Tanith, bless her memory!' he heard Corbec yelling as he advanced.

The cry, as it was taken up by Ghosts all around him, prompted a deep, emotional response in Gaunt. It shocked him. They were indeed fighting for Tanith... not for some memory or for a sense of vengeance. They were fighting for the love of their homeworld, of the misty cities, the darkling woodlands, the majestic seas.

He knew this because he felt it too. He had spent all of a day on Tanith before the fall, and most of that inside the dim ante-rooms of the Elector's palace at Tanith Magna. But it felt as if it had been his home, something he had grown to love through years of upbringing, something that was still attainable...

With Corbec and two other Ghosts, he was the first to reach a defence ditch on the lower slopes of the mound where superior numbers of Chaos filth were turning from their assault of the ruin to repel the hind attack. Gaunt led with his chainsword, slicing the enemy apart. It seemed like he was las-proof. All opposing shots went wild. The joy of Tanith sang in his heart.

He dropped into the ditch, cutting the first aggressor before him open down the middle, then swung the whining blade left to decapitate another. In his other hand, his bolt pistol blasted down the ditch, blowing the legs off two charging ghouls with fixed bayonets. His bolter clacked empty. Corbec was beside him, bellowing, blasting with his lasgun at figures who fell and squirmed and fled down the narrow defile. To the other side, Troopers Yael and Mktea fought hand to hand with silver daggers, passionate, furious. Beyond them, Bragg, blasting with his autocannon over the ditch top.

Gaunt threw his bolter and his sword aside and grabbed the firing handles of an enemy storm-bolter with a belt feed set into the lip of the ditch. The massive gun was set on flak-board, with wire tie-downs to prevent the tripod from skating. Gaunt thumbed the trigger and swept the shuddering gun left and right, decimating the ranks of enemy advancing up the hill above him.

He felt a hand on his arm. Lilith was beside him, her face pale, her eyes full of tears.

'What?' he barked, continuing to fire.

'Can't you feel it? You're swept up in the storm-magic too!'

He released his hands and the drum belt rattled round on auto-feed. 'Magic?'

'The web of deceit I spoke of... it's enflamed all your men, the Blue-bloods too. It's tearing at my mind! Gaunt...!'

Involuntarily, he held her. She pushed him off after a second. 'I'm all right! All right!'

'Lilith!'

'Whatever... whoever... it is up there in the ruin, they're preying on our emotions.'

'What do you mean?'

'I... I think they want all the help they can get, Gaunt! They've woven a psychic spell through the storm that makes us... makes us respond by touching our deepest desires! For your Ghosts, this is Tanith... a Tanith where it's still possible to win and save the world! For the Bluebloods, it's Ignix Majeure, where they lost after a desperate fight! But Ibram... it's *killing me*! So strong, so powerful!'

Gaunt fought to catch his breath. 'W-why me? Why Tanith?'

'What?' she asked, wiping her puffy eyes.

'I'm not Tanith, but the will inside me responded that way. Why aren't I fighting for some great cause in my own life? Why have I been living and breathing Tanith in my waking dreams all this while?'

She smiled, simply and painfully, her perfect face lit by the fire-flashes around them. 'Don't you know it, Ibram? Tanith is your cause, no matter if you were born there or not. You've devoted your service and life to these men, to the memory of their world.

'The fate of Tanith consumes you, as it does them, and though you're not a true son of the forests, this magic plays on your deepest urges! You're a Ghost, Ibram Gaunt, whether you know it or not! You're not just their master, you're one of them!'

Gaunt pulled off his cap and wiped brow-sweat back into his cropped hair. He was panting, painfully high on adrenaline. 'This is all false?' he began.

'We're being used. Manipulated. Driven to fight by something that touches our deepest causes.'

'Then... in the Emperor's name, if it helps us kill the Chaos scum, let's not deny it! Let's use it!' Gaunt cued his micro-bead and opened a channel to his force. 'Sixty men against ten thousand! The stuff of legends! Push on! Push on, for Tanith and for Ignix Majeure! Take the slope and make for the ruin!'

At the head of his wave of Bluebloods, Gilbear heard the call and screamed into the night as he emptied yet another powerpack out through the glowing muzzle of his hellgun. The Volpone took the rise, scattering enemy before them.

Lerod, who now thought himself truly immortal, led his detachment up the mound, stampeding over the panicking, splintering waves of Chaos filth.

Corbec, with Bragg firing solid lines of destruction from his heavy weapon at his side, pushed the other Ghost band up between the prongs. To either side of the Imperial advance, a hundred thousand soldiers of the foe swarmed and regrouped. But the sixty or so Imperials cut a line up through them that wouldn't be denied.

Years later, painstakingly reconstructing the details of this assault from patchy data collected at the time, Imperial tacticians on Foridon would be utterly unable to account for the success of the action. Even given the surprise nature of the assault, from the rear, there was no sense to the data. Simple statistics should have had Gaunt's expeditionary force cut down to the last man, at most a half kilometre from the ruin. The tacticians would factor in charismatic leadership, tactical insight, luck... and still there was no mistake. Gaunt's men should have been entirely slaughtered long before they reached the ruin.

But that was not the case. Gaunt drew his forces, without the loss of a single man, up to the walls of the ruin perhaps thirty minutes after they had first engaged the back of the enemy positions. They had cut through a legion of the foe who outnumbered them ten thousand to one, and attained a target area the enemy had been trying to force its way into for hours. They slew, approximately, two-point-four thousand soldiers of the enemy.

Eventually, after a prolonged analytical study, the tacticians would decide that the only explanation could be that there were no enemy units on the field that day. It was all an illusion. Gaunt had mounted an assault through open, undefended ground. Only then did the computations and the statistics and the possibilities match up.

None of them could admit that this wasn't the case. And so, perhaps the greatest and most spectacular success of Macaroth's great Crusade, out-classed and out-numbered but still successful, was deleted from the Imperial Annals as a phantom engagement. Such is the fate of true heroism.

There was a door: a tall, pointed arch of stone faced with stone, in the side of the smooth flank of the ruin. Gaunt grouped his force around it as relentless firepower strafed up at them from the muddled but regrouping legions of the enemy.

Gilbear intended to mine the door in the hope of blowing it open, though, as Corbec pointed out, the scorch marks on the stone facing seemed to indicate that the enemy had tried that more than once and failed.

They were about to argue the point some more when the door opened. Brin Milo stood there, looking out at them, flanked by Caffran and a spectacularly grim eldar warrior with a red plume set behind his white helmet.

The storm flashed above, still furious and wild.

'You've come this far,' Milo said. 'Now let's finish this.'

* * *

Sealed inside the onyx walls of the Way-Place, Gaunt and his force heard the low wailing of eldar mourners, remorsefully singing the last songs of closure.

Muon Nol faced Gaunt for a long while, until Gaunt saluted and held out his hand.

'Ibram Gaunt.'

Nothing more need be said, Gaunt thought.

Muon Nol looked at the proffered hand, then slung Uliowye over his shoulder and clasped it.

He spoke, a bewildering slither of otherworldly language.

'You've just been formally worshipped as a fellow warrior,' Lilith said, stepping up. Muon Nol turned his huge gaze to look at her.

'I am Lilith, of the Imperial Inquisition,' she stated.

Muon Nol, a head taller than even Gilbear, paused and nodded slowly.

Gaunt looked round sharply at the inquisitor. 'We're not getting anywhere fast,' he hissed. 'Does anyone here speak eldar?'

'I do,' Lilith said, but Muon Nol spoke simultaneously.

'There is no need,' he said in melodiously accented Low Gothic. 'I understand. You must follow me now. The farseer-lord awaits.'

'Fine...' Gaunt began.

Muon Nol stepped back. 'No. Not you. The female.'

Lord Eon Kull felt the wash and burn of the Chaos hosts as they assaulted the ruin around him. Fuehain Falchior had begun to rattle in her rack again.

The door of the Inner Place slid open and Muon Nol entered, escorting a cowled human female, a hulking stormtrooper in grey and gold, and a human male in a long coat and cap.

Muon Nol bowed. Lilith did likewise. Gilbear and Gaunt remained upright.

Eon Kull spoke, perfectly using the clumsy Low Gothic he had once wasted a brief year mastering.

'I am Eon Kull Farseer. My enchantments have brought you into this. I make no apologies. The Way must be closed to the Dark and I will use all my powers to accomplish that.'

Muon Nol took a step forward, gesturing to indicate Lilith. 'My lord... this female is called Lilith, in the human tongue. Is that not a sign?'

'Of what?'

'Of purpose... lord?'

Eon Kull seemed about to answer, as if he too recognised the symbolic coincidence. But then he slumped against the side of his throne, blood leaking from under the seal of his helmet.

'My lord!'

Gaunt reached him first, pulling off the tall helm and cradling the pale skull of the worn-out, dying Eldar farseer in his gloved hands.

'I can send for medics... healers,' he began.

'No... n-no... no time. No purpose to it. I want to die, Gaunt human. The Way must be closed before Chaos can corrupt it.'

Holding Eon Kull, Gaunt looked up hopelessly at Lilith. She came and took his place, embracing the frail eldar's head and body.

'That's what the Chaos forces are here on Monthax for, isn't it, far-seer lord?'

'You speak truth. This Way has stood open for twenty-seven centuries. Now the enemy have found it and through it they will invade Dolthe craftworld. For the sake of Dolthe, for the living souls of the eldar, this Way must be closed. For this great purpose I have conjured you. For this great purpose, my aspect warriors have given their all and their last.'

'All of this... some trick of a stinking alien scumbag...' Gilbear growled.

Gaunt launched himself forward, bringing down Muon Nol before the enraged eldar could splinter Gilbear to pieces with his shrieker cannon.

Gaunt got up off the aspect warrior and strode across the onyx room to face Gilbear.

'What? What did I say that was so bad?' Gilbear asked, a second before Gaunt's fist laid him out unconscious on the flag stones.

'Ibram!' Gaunt turned as Lilith cried out. She was cradling Eon Kull in her arms. Gaunt rushed to her, with Muon Nol at his elbow, but there was no mistaking the signs.

Farseer Eon Kull, the Old One, was dead.

They placed his frail remains on the floor.

'We are lost, then,' Muon Nol said. 'Without the farseer, we can no longer conjure the pacts with the warp and close the Web. Dolthe will die as surely as Farseer Eon Kull.'

'Lilith can do it,' Gaunt said suddenly.

Muon Nol and Lilith looked at him.

'I know you can, and I know you want to. That is why you're here, Lilith.'

'What are you talking about, Ibram?' she said

'You're not the only one with pull, the only one who can chase records and dig out hushed files. I did my research on you as surely you did mine. Lilith Abfequarn... psyker, inquisitor, black notation rating.'

'God of Terra,' she smiled. 'You're good, Ibram.'

'You don't know how good. The Black Ships singled you out when they found you. Daughter of a planetary governess whose world edged the stamping grounds of the eldar. She died in one of their raids. You swore... first to destroy them and then, as you grew, to understand the strange species that had robbed you so. And that's why you wanted this mission: you craved a chance to contact your nemesis. You want this, Lilith.'

She sank and sat hard on the onyx floor beside Eon Kull's corpse.

Muon Nol lifted her up. 'You are Lileath. You can do what the farseer would have done. Close the gate, Lileath. Take us back to Dolthe forever.'

Lilith looked at Gaunt. Gaunt noticed for the last time how beautiful she was. 'Do it... That is why you came.'

She took his shoulders, hugged him briefly and then pulled away to look into his face.

'It would have been interesting, commissar.'

'Fascinating, inquisitor. Now do your job.'

They said goodbye. Mkoll said goodbye to Eiloni, Caffran said goodbye to Laria. The Ghosts said goodbye to Tanith and the Blueblood bade farewell to Ignix Majeure.

A cold light, hard as vacuum, bright as diamond, pierced the sky above the ruin, evaporating the storm in little more than a minute. Seventy-five per cent of the astropaths aboard the Imperial fleet elements in orbit suffered catastrophic seizures and died. The others passed out. The psychic backwash of the event was felt light years away.

The spell ended as the Way finally closed. The eldar left Monthax forever, and took Lilith back to Dolthe craftworld with them. She closed the Way, as she had, perhaps, been born to do. Once the Way was shut, closely-targeted orbital bombardments incinerated the massed forces of the enemy.

The jungles of Monthax burned.

Once the bombardment stopped, Gaunt led his Ghosts and the Volpone unit back towards the line. The storm was dead and pale sunlight fell on them. The world around them was a wasted desert of baked mud and burned vegetation.

The only man Gaunt had lost in the final assault had been Lerod, taken by a remarkably lucky glancing shot off the roof of the eldar temple.

Ibram Gaunt slept for a day and half in his command cabin. His fatigue was total. He woke when Raglon brought him directives from Lord Militant General Bulledin, orchestrating the Imperial withdrawal from Monthax.

He put on his full dress uniform, adjusted his cap and went out into the smoky sunlight to oversee the Tanith as they packed up and prepared for evacuation. The vast troop transports cast flickering shadows across the lines as they came in, droning down from high orbit.

Gaunt could sense the feeling of the men: weariness, aches, the joy of a great victory somehow dulled and strange.

He found Milo, sat alone on the side steps of the abandoned infirmary, cleaning his lasgun. Gaunt sat down next to him.

'Odd the way things work out, isn't it?' Milo said bluntly.

Gaunt nodded.

'I think it was a good thing, though.'

'What?'

'The eldar trick. Good for us. Good for the Ghosts.'

'Explain?' Gaunt asked.

'I know how I feel. I've heard the men talking too. This was Tanith again for us, for you too, I think. Deep down I think we all hate the fact we never got a chance to fight for Tanith. Some are blatant about it. Men like... like Major Rawne. Others can understand why we had to leave, why you ordered us out. But they don't like it.'

He looked around at Gaunt.

'Just a mind trick maybe, but for a few hours there forty or so of us got to fight for Tanith, got to fight for our world, got the chance to do what we'd always been cheated out of. It felt good. Even now I know it was a lie, it still feels good. It... exorcised a few ghosts.'

Gaunt smiled. The boy's pun was awful, but he was right. The Ghosts of Tanith had laid their own ghosts to rest here. They would be stronger for it.

And so would he, he realised. They were *his* ghosts after all.

Gaunt's Ghosts.

NECROPOLIS

'After the victories at Monthax and Lamacia, Warmaster Macaroth drove his forces swiftly along the trailing edge of the Sabbat Worlds cluster and turned inwards to assault the notorious enemy fortress-worlds in the Cabal system. Successful conquest of the Cabal system was a vital objective in the Imperial crusade to liberate the entire Sabbat Worlds group. To achieve this massive undertaking, the warmaster sent the line ships of his Segmentum Pacificus fleet forward in a pincer formation to begin the onslaught, while assembling and reforming his enormous Imperial Guard reserves ready for ground assault.

'It took close to eight months for the troop components to convene at Solypsis, thousands of mass-conveyance transports carrying many million Imperial Guardsmen. There were many delays, and many minor skirmishes to settle en route. The Pragar regiments were held up for six weeks engaging the remnants of a Chaos Legion on Nonimax, and a warp-storm forced the Samothrace and Sarpoy troop ships to remain at Antioch 148 for three whole months. However, it is the events that took place on the industrial hive-world of Verghast that are of particular interest to any student of Imperium military history...'

– from *A History of the Later Imperial Crusades*

ONE

ZOICA RISING

'The distinction between trade and warfare is seen only by those who have no experience of either.'
– Heironymo Sondar, House Sondar,
from his inaugural address

The klaxons began to wail, though it was still an hour or more to shift-rotation.

The people of the hive-city paused as one. Millions of eyes checked timepieces, faltered in their work, looked up at the noise. Conversations trailed off. Feeble jokes were cracked to hide unease. Young children began to cry. House soldiery on the Curtain Wall voxed in confirmation and clarification requests to the Main Spine command station. Line supervisors and labour-stewards in the plants and manufactories chivvied their personnel back into production, but they were uneasy too. It was a test, surely? Or a mistake. A few moments more and the alarms would shut down again.

But the klaxons did not desist.

After a minute or so, raid-sirens in the central district also began keening. The pattern was picked up by manufactory hooters and mill-whistles all through the lower hive, and in the docks and outer habs across the river too. Even the great ceremonial horns on the top of the Ecclesiarchy Basilica started to sound.

Vervunhive was screaming with every one of its voices.

Everywhere, hazard lamps began to spin and flash, and secondary storm shutters cycled down on automatic to block windows. All the public-address plates in the city went black, erasing the glowing lines of weather, temperature, exchange-rate data, the local news and the ongoing output figures. They fuzzed darkly for a few seconds and then the words 'Please stand by' scrolled across all of them in steady repeats.

In the firelit halls of Vervun Smeltery One – part of the primary ore processing district just west of the Spoil – rattling conveyers laden with unprocessed rock shuddered to a halt as automatic safeties locked down. Above the main smelter silo, Plant Supervisor Agun Soric got up from behind a file-covered desk and crossed to the stained-glass window of his bureau. He looked down at the vast, halted plant in disbelief, then pulled on his work-jacket and went out onto the catwalk, staring at the thousands of milling workers below. Vor, his junior, hurried along the walk, his heavily booted feet ringing on the metal grill, the sound lost in the cacophony of hooters and sirens.

'What is this, chief?' he gasped, coming close to Soric and pulling the tubes of his dust-filter from his mouth-clamp.

Soric shook his head. 'It's fifteen thousand cubits of lost production, that's what the gak it is! And counting!'

'What d'you reckon? A malfunction?'

'In every alert system in the hive at once? Use your brain! A malfunction?'

'Then what?'

Soric paused, trying to think. The ideas that were forming in his mind were things he didn't really want to entertain. 'I pray to the Emperor himself that this isn't...'

'What, chief?'

'Zoica... Zoica rising again.'

'What?'

Soric looked round at his junior with contempt. He wiped his fat, balding brow on the back of his gold-braided cuff. 'Don't you read the news-picts?'

Vor shrugged. 'Just the weather and the stadium results.'

'You're an idiot,' Soric told him. And too young to remember, he thought. Gak, he was too young himself, but his father's father had told him about the Trade War. What was it, ninety years back, standard? Surely not again? But the picts had been full of it these last few months: Zoica silent, Zoica ceasing to trade, Zoica raising its bulwarks and setting armaments up along its northern walls.

Those raid-sirens hadn't sounded since the Trade War. Soric knew that as a bare fact.

'Let's hope you're right, Vor,' he said. 'Let's hope it's a gakking malfunction.'

In the Commercia, the general mercantile district north of the Main Spine, in the shadow of the Shield Pylon, Guilder Amchanduste Worlin tried to calm the buyers in his barter-house, but the sirens drowned

him out. The retinues were leaving, gathering up servant trains and produce bearers, making frantic calls on their vox-links, leaving behind
nothing: not a form-contract, not a promissory note, not a business
slate and certainly none of their funds.

Worlin put his hands to his head and cursed. His embroidered,
sleet-silk gown felt suddenly hot and heavy .

He yelled for his bodyguards and they appeared: Menx and Troor,
bull-necked men in ivory-laced body-gloves with the crest of Guild
Worlin branded on their cheeks. They had unshrouded their laspistols
and the velvet shroud-cloths dangled limply from their cuffs.

'Consult the high guild data-vox and the Administratum links!' Worlin spat. 'Come back and tell me what this is, or don't come back at all!'

They nodded and went off, pushing through the packs of departing traders.

Worlin paced back into his private ante-room behind the auction hall,
cursing at the sirens to shut up. The very last thing he needed now was
an interruption to trade. He'd spent months and a great deal of Guild
Worlin funds securing mercantile bonds with Noble House Yetch and
four of the houses ordinary. All of that work would be for nothing if
trade – and income – went slack. The whole deal could collapse. His
kin would be aghast at such losses. They might even strip him of his
badge and remove his trading rights.

Worlin was shaking. He crossed to the decanter on the wrought-brass
stack table and was about to pour himself a hefty shot of ten-year-old
joiliq to calm his brittle mood. But he paused. He went to his desk,
unlocked a drawer with the geno-key that he kept around his wrist on
a thin chain and took out the compact needle pistol.

He checked it was primed and armed, then fetched the drink. He sat
back on his lifter throne, sipping his liquor and holding his badge of
credit – the mark of his rank – gazing at the Worlin crest and its bright
ornament. He waited, the weapon in his lap.

The klaxons continued to wail.

At carriage station C4/a, panic had begun. Workers and low-classers
who had ventured into the mercantile slopes for a day's resourcing
began to mob every brass-framed transit that trundled in along the
cogged, funicular trackway. Carriages were moving out towards the
Outer Habs and the Main Spine alike, overloaded, some doors only
half closed.

Crowds on the platforms, shivering at each yelp of the alarms, were
getting fractious as more and more fully laden transits clattered through
without stopping. A slate-seller's stall was overturned in the press.

Livy Kolea, hab-wife, was beginning to panic herself. A body-surge of the crowd had pushed her past the pillars of the station atrium. She'd kept a firm grip on the handles of the child-cart and Yoncy was safe, but she'd lost sight of Dalin.

'My son! Have you seen my son?' she asked, imploring the frenzied crowd that washed around her. 'He's only ten! A good boy! Blond, like his father!'

She grabbed a passing guilder by the sleeve. A rich, lavish sleeve of painted silk.

'My son–' she began.

The guilder's bodyguard, menacing in his rust-coloured mesh, pushed her aside. He jerked the satin shroud off the weapon in his left hand, just briefly, as a warning, escorting his master on. 'Take the hand off, gak-swine,' his vox-enhanced larynx blurted gruffly, without emotion.

'My son–' Livy repeated, trying to push the child-cart out of the flow of bodies.

Yoncy was laughing, oblivious in his woollen wrap. Livy bent down under the segmented hood of the cart to stroke him, whispering soft, motherly words.

But her mind was racing. People slammed into her, teetering the cart and she had to hold on to keep it upright. Why was this happening – to her – now? Why was it happening on the one day a month she carriaged into the lower Commercia to haggle for stuff? Gol had wanted a new pair of canvas mittens. His hands were so sore after a shift at the ore face.

It was such a simple thing. Now this! And she hadn't even got the mittens.

Livy felt tears burst hot onto her cheeks.

'Dalin!' she called.

'I'm here, mam,' said a little voice, half hidden by the klaxons.

Livy embraced her ten-year-old son with fury and conviction, like she would never let go.

'I found him by the west exit,' a new voice added.

Livy looked up, not breaking her hug. The girl was about sixteen, she reckoned, a slut from the outer habs, wearing the brands and piercings of a hab-ganger.

'He's all right though.'

Livy looked the boy over quickly, checking for any signs of hurt. 'Yes, yes he is... He's all right. You're all right, aren't you, Dalin? Mam's here.'

Livy looked up at the outhab girl. 'Thank you. Thank you for...'

The girl pushed a ringed hand through her bleached hair.

'It's fine.'

The girl made Livy uneasy. Those brands, that pierced nose. Gang marks.

'Yes, yes... I'm in your debt. Now I must be going. Hold on to my hand, Dalin.'

The girl stepped in front of the cart as Livy tried to turn it.

'Where are you going?' she asked.

'Don't try to stop me, outhab! I have a blade in my purse!'

The girl backed off, smiling. 'I'm sure you have. I was just asking. The transits are packed and the exit stairs are no place for a woman with a kid and a cart.'

'Oh.'

'Maybe I could help you get the cart clear of this press?'

And take my baby... take Yoncy for those things scum like you do down in the outer habs over the river!

'No! Thank you, but... No!' Livy barked and pushed the gang-girl aside with the cart. She dragged the boy after her, pushing into the thicket of panic.

'Only trying to help,' Tona Criid shrugged.

The river tides were ebbing and thick, ore-rich spumes were coursing down the waters of the Hass. Longshoreman Folik edged his dirty, juddering flatbed ferry, the *Magnificat*, out from the north shore and began the eight-minute crossing to the main wharves. The diesel motor coughed and spluttered. Folik eased the revs and coasted between garbage scows and derelicts, following the dredged channel. Grey estuary birds, with hooked pink beaks, rose from the scows in a raucous swirl. To the *Magnificat*'s port side, the stone stilts of the Hass Viaduct, two hundred metres tall, cast long, cold shadows across the water.

Those damn sirens! What was that about?

Mincer sat at the prow, watching the low-water for new impediments. He gestured and Folik inched the ferry to starboard, swishing in between the trash hulks and the river-sound buoys.

Folik could see the crowds on the jetty. Big crowds. He grinned to himself.

'We'll make a sweet bundle on this, Fol!' Mincer shouted, unlooping the tarred rope from the catheads.

'I think so,' Folik murmured. 'I just hope we have a chance to spend it...'

Merity Chass had been trying on long-gowns in the dressing suites of the gown-maker when the klaxons first began to sound. She froze, catching sight of her own pale, startled face in the dressing mirror. The klaxons were distant, almost plaintive, from up here in mid-Spine, but local alarms shortly joined in. Her handmaids came rushing in from the cloth-maker's vestibule and helped her lace up her own dress.

'They say Zoica goes to war!' said Maid Francer.

'Like in the old times, like in the Trade War!' Maid Wholt added, pulling on a bodice string.

'I have been educated by the best tutors in the hive. I know about the Trade War. It was the most bloody and production-costly event in hive history! Why do you giggle about it?'

The maids curtseyed and backed away from Merity.

'Soldiers!' Maid Wholt sniggered.

'Handsome and hungry, coming here!' squealed Maid Francer.

'Shut up, both of you!' Merity ordered. She pulled her muslin fichu around her shoulders and fastened the pin. Then she picked up her credit wand from the top of the rosewood credenza. Though the wand was a tool that gave her access to her personal expense account in the House Chass treasury, it was ornamental in design, a delicate lace fan which she flipped open and waved in front of her face as the built-in ioniser hummed.

The maids looked down, stifling enthusiastic giggles.

'Where is the gown maker?'

'Hiding in the next room, under his desk,' Francer said.

'I said you'd require transportation to be summoned, but he refuses to come out,' Wholt added.

'Then this establishment will no longer enjoy the custom of Noble House Chass. We will find our own transport,' Merity said. Head high, she led her giggling maids out of the thickly carpeted gown-hall, through drapes that drew back automatically at their approach and out into the perfumed elegance of the Promenade.

Gol Kolea put down his axe-rake and pulled off his head-lamp. His hands were bloody and sore. The air was black with rock-soot, like fog. Gol sucked a mouthful of electrolyte fluid from his drinking pipe and refastened it to his collar.

'What is that noise?' he asked Trug Vereas.

Trug shrugged. 'Sounds like an alarm, up there somewhere.' The work face of Number Seventeen Deep Working was way below the conduits and mine-head wheels of the mighty ore district. Gol and Trug were sixteen hundred metres underground.

Another work gang passed them, also looking up and speaking in low voices.

'Some kind of exercise?'

'Must be,' Trug said. He and Gol stepped aside as a laden string of ore-carts loaded with loose conglomerate rattled by along the greasy mono-track. Somewhere nearby, a rock-drill began to chatter.

'Okay...' Gol raised his tool and paused. 'I worry about Livy.'

'She'll be fine. Trust me. And we've got a quota to fill.'

Gol swung his axe-rake and dug in. He just wished the scrape and crack of his blade would drown out the distant sirens.

Captain Ban Daur paused to button his double-breasted uniform coat and pull the leather harness into place. He forced his mind to be calm. As an officer, he would have been informed of any drill and usually he got wind even of surprise practices. But this was real. He could feel it.

He picked up his gloves and his spiked helmet and left his quarters. The corridors of the Hass West wall-fort were bustling with troop details. All wore the blue cloth uniform and spiked helmets of the Vervun Primary, the city's standing army. Five hundred thousand troops all told, plus another 70,000 auxiliaries and armour crews, a mighty force that manned the Curtain Wall and the wall forts of Vervunhive. The regiment had a noble heritage and had proved itself in the Trade War, from which time they had been maintained as a permanent institution. When foundings were ordered for the Imperial Guard, Vervunhive raised them from its forty billion-plus population. The men of Vervun Primary were never touched or transferred. It was a life-duty, a career. But though their predecessors had fought bravely, none of the men currently composing the ranks of Vervun Primary had ever seen combat.

Daur barked out a few commands to calm the commotion in the hallway. He was young, only twenty-three, but tall and cleanly handsome, from a good mid-Spine family and the men liked him. They seemed to relax a little, seeing him so calm. Not that he felt calm.

'Alert duty stations,' Daur told them. 'You there! Where's your weapon?'

The trooper shrugged. 'Came running when I heard the– Forgot it... sir...'

'Go back and get it, you dumb gak! Three days' discipline duty – after this is over.'

The soldier ran off.

'Now!' cried Daur. 'Let's pretend we've actually been trained, shall we? Every man of you knows where he should be and what he should be doing, so go! In the hallowed name of the Emperor and in the service of the beloved hive!'

Daur headed uptower, pulling out his autopistol and checking its clip.

Corporal Bendace met him on the steps. Bendace had a data-slate in one hand and a pathetic moustache on his upper lip.

'Told you to shave that off,' Daur said, taking the slate and looking at it.

'I think it's... dashing,' Bendace said soulfully, stroking it.

Daur ignored him, reading the slate. They hurried up the tower as troopers double-timed down. On a landing, they passed a corporal tossing autoguns from a wall rack to a line of waiting men.

'So?' asked Bendace as they started up the final flight to the fort-top.

'You know those rumours you heard? About Zoica going for another Trade War?'

'That confirms it?'

Daur pushed the slate back into Bendace's hands with a sour look. 'No. It doesn't say anything. It's just a deployment order from House Command in the Spine. All units are to take position, protocol gamma sigma. Wall and fort weapons to be raised.'

'It says that?'

'No, I'm making it up. Yes, it says that. Weapons raised, but not armed, until further House Command notice.'

'This is bad, isn't it?'

Daur shrugged. 'Define "bad"?'

Bendace paused. 'I–'

'Bad is your facial growth. I don't know what this is.'

They stepped out onto the windy battlements. Gun crews were raising the trio of anti-air batteries into position, hydraulic pistons heaving the weapon mounts up from shuttered hardpoints in the tower top. Autoloader carriages were being wheeled out from the lift-heads. Other troops had taken up position in the netted stub-nests. Cries and commands flew back and forth.

Daur crossed to the ramparts and looked around. At his back, the vast, smoke-hazed shape of the Main Spine itself rose into the sombre sky like a granite peak, winking with a million lights. To his right lay the glitter of the River Hass and the grimy shapes of the docks and outer habs on the far bank. Below him, the sweeping curve of the vast adamantine Curtain Wall curved away east to the smoke pall of the ore smelteries and the dark mass of the Spoil hunkered twenty-five kilometres further round the circumference of the city skirts.

To the south, the slum-growths of the outer habs outside the wall, the dark wheel-heads and gantries of the vast mining district, and the marching viaducts of the main southern rail link extended far away. Beyond the extremities of the hive, the grasslands, a sullen, dingy green, reached to the horizon. Visibility was medium. Haze shimmered the distance. Daur cranked a tripod-mounted scope around, staring out. Nothing. A pale, green, unresolvable nothing.

He stood back and looked around the ramparts. One of the anti-air batteries on the wall-top below was only half raised and troopers were cursing and fighting to free the lift hydraulics. Other than that, everything and everyone was in place.

The captain took up the handset of the vox-unit carried by a waiting trooper.

'Daur to all Hass West area positions. Reel it off.'

The junior officers sang over the link with quick discipline. Daur felt genuine pride. Those in his command had executed gamma sigma in a little under twelve minutes. The fort and the western portion of the wall bristled with ready weapons and readier men.

He glanced down. The final, recalcitrant anti-aircraft battery rose into place. The crew gave a brief cheer that the wind stole away, then pushed the autoloader-cart in to mate with it.

Daur selected a new channel.

'Daur, Hass West, to House Command. We are deployed. We await your orders.'

In the vast Square of Marshals, just inside the Curtain Wall, adjacent to the Heironymo Sondar Gate, the air shook with the thunder of three hundred tank engines. Huge Leman Russ war-machines, painted in the blue livery of Vervun Primary, revved at idle in rows across the square. More vehicles clanked and ground their way in at the back of the square, from the marshalling sheds behind the South-Hive barracks.

General Vegolain of the First Primary Armoured, jumped down from his mount, buckling on his leather head-shield, and approached the commissar. Vegolain saluted, snapping his jack-booted heels together.

'Commissar Kowle!'

'General,' Kowle replied. He had just arrived in the square by staff limousine, a sinister black vehicle that was now pulling away behind its motorbike escorts. There were two other commissars with him: Langana and the cadet Fosker.

Kowle was a tall, lean man who looked as if he had been forced to wear the black cap and longcoat of an Imperial commissar. His skin was sallow and taut, and his eyes were a disturbing beige.

Unlike Langana and Fosker, Kowle was an off-worlder. The senior commissar was Imperial Guard, seconded to watch over the Vervunhive standing army as a concession to its continued maintenance. Kowle quietly despised his post. His promising career with the Fadayhin Fifth had foundered some years before and against his will he had been posted to wet-nurse this toy army. Now, at last, he tasted the possibility of acquiring some glory that might rejuvenate his lustreless career.

Langana and Fosker were hive-bred, both from aspiring houses. Their uniform showed their difference from Kowle. In place of his Imperial double-eagle pins, they wore the axe-rake symbol of the VPHC, the Vervun Primary Hive Commissariat, the disciplinary arm of the standing army. The Sondar nobility was keen on discipline. Some even said that the VPHC was almost a secret police force, acting beyond the reach of the Administratum, in the interests of the ruling house.

'We have orders, commissar?'

Kowle scratched his nose absently and nodded. He handed Vegolain a data-slate.

'We are to form up at company strength and head out into the grasslands. I have not been told why.'

'I presume it is Zoica, commissar. They wish to spar with us again and–'

'Are you privy to the inter-hive policies of Zoica?' Kowle snapped.

'No, comm–'

'Do you then believe that rumour and dissent is a tool of control?'

'No, I–'

'Until we are told it is Zoica, it is no one. Is that clear?'

'Commissar. Will… will you be accompanying us?'

Kowle didn't reply. He marched across to Vegolain's Leman Russ and clambered aboard.

Three minutes later, the Sondar Gate opened with a great shriek of hydraulic compressors and the armoured column poured out onto the main south highway in triple file.

'Who has ordered this alarm?' The question came from three mouths at once, dull, electronic, emotionless.

Marshal Gnide, strategic commander of Vervun Primary and chief military officer of Vervunhive, paused before replying. It was difficult to know which face to answer.

'Who?' the voices repeated.

Gnide stood in the softly lit, warm audience hall of the Imperial House Sondar, at the very summit of the Main Spine. He wished he'd taken off his blue, floor-length, braid-trimmed greatcoat before entering. His plumed cap was heavy and itched his brow.

'It is necessary, High One.'

The three servitors, limp and supported only by the wires and leads that descended from the ceiling trackways, circled him. One was a thin, androgynous boy with dye-stained skin. Another was a voluptuous girl, naked and branded with golden runes. The third was a chubby cherub, a toy harp in its pudgy hands, swan-wings sutured to its back. All of them lolled on their tubes and strings, blank-eyed.

Servos whined and the girl swung closer to Gnide, her limp feet trailing on the tiled floor.

'Are you my loyal marshal?' she asked, in that same flat monotone, that voice that wasn't hers.

Gnide ignored her, looking past the meat puppet – as he called it – to the ornamental iron tank in the far corner of the room. The metal of the tank was dark and tarnished with startlingly green rust. A single round porthole looked out like a cataract-glazed eye.

'You know I am, High One.'

'Then why this disobedience?' the youth asked, atrophied limbs trembling as the strings and leads swung him round.

'This is not disobedience, High One. This is duty. And I will not speak to your puppets. I asked for audience with House Ruler Salvador Sondar himself.'

The cherub swung abruptly round into Gnide's face. Sub-dermal tensors pulled its bloated mouth into a grin that was utterly unmatched by its dead eyes.

'They are me and I am them! You will address me through them!'

Gnide pushed the dangling cherub aside, flinching at the touch of its pallid flesh on his hand. He stalked up the low steps to the iron tank and stared into the lens port.

'Zoica mobilises against us, High One! A new Trade War is upon us! Orbital scans show this to be true!'

'It is not called Zoica,' the girl said from behind him. 'Use its name.'

Gnide sighed. 'Ferrozoica Hive Manufactory,' he said.

'At last, some respect,' rattled the cherub, bobbing around Gnide. 'Our old foes, now our most worthy trading partners. They are our brethren, our fellow trade-hive. We do not raise arms against them.'

'With respect!' snapped Gnide. 'Zoica has always been our foe, our rival. There were times last century they bettered us in output.'

'That was before House Sondar took the High Place here. Vervunhive is the greatest of all, now and ever after.' The youth-puppet began to drool slackly as it spoke.

'All Vervunhive rejoices that House Sondar has led us to domination. But the Legislature of the Noble houses has voted this hour that we should prepare for war. That is why the alarms were sounded.'

'Without me?' the girl hissed, flatly.

'As it is written, according to the customs, we signalled you. You did not reply. Mandate 347gf, as ratified by your illustrious predecessor, Heironymo, gives us authority to act.'

'You would use old laws to unseat me?' asked the cherub, clattering round on its strings to stare into Gnide's face with dead eyes.

'This is not usurpation, High One. Vervunhive is in danger. Look!' Gnide reached forward and pressed a data-slate against the lens of the tank.

'See what the orbitals tell us! Months of silence from Zoica, signs of them preparing for war! Rumours, hearsay – why weren't we told the truth? Why does this spring down on us so late in the day? Didn't you know? You, all-seeing, all-knowing High One? Or did you just decide not to tell us?'

The puppets began to thrash and jiggle, knocking into Gnide. He pushed them off.

'I have been in constant dialogue with my counterpart in Ferrozoica Hive Manufactory. We have come to enjoy the link, the companionship. His Highness Clatch of House Clatch is a dear friend. He would not deceive me. The musterings along the Ferrozoica ramparts were made because of the crusade. Warmaster Slaydo leads his legions into our spatial territories; the foul enemy is resisting. It is a precaution.'

'Slaydo is dead, High One. Five years cold on Balhaut. Macaroth is the leader of the crusade now. The beloved Guard legions are sweeping the Sabbat Worlds clean of Chaos scum. We rejoice daily that our world, beloved Verghast, was not touched.'

'Slaydo is dead?' the three voices asked as one.

'Yes, High One. Now, with respect, I ask that we may test-start the Shield. If Zoica is massing to conquer us, we must be ready.'

'No! You undermine me! The Shield cannot be raised without my permission! Zoica does not threaten! Clatch is our friend! Slaydo is not dead!'

The three voices rose in a shrill chorus, the meat puppets quivering with unknowable rage.

'You would not have treated Heironymo with such disrespect!'

'Your brother, great one as he was, did not hide in an Awareness Tank and talk through dead servitors... High One.'

'I forbid it!'

Gnide pulled a glittering ducal seal from his coat. 'The Legislature expected this. I am empowered by the houses of Vervunhive, in expediency, to revoke your powers as per the Act of Entitlement, 45jk. The Legislature commends your leadership, but humbly entreats you that it is now taking executive action.' Gnide pushed the puppets aside and crossed to a brass console in the far wall. He pressed the centre of the seal and data-limbs extended like callipers from the rosette with a machined click. Gnide set it in the lock and turned it.

The console flashed into life, chattering runes and sigils scrolling down the glass plate.

'No!' screeched the three voices. 'This is insubordination! I am Vervunhive! I am Vervunhive!'

'You are dethroned for the good of the city,' Gnide snapped. He pressed the switches in series, activating the power generators deep beneath the hive. He entered the sequences that would engage the main transmission pylon and bring the Shield online.

The cherub flew at him. He batted it away and it upturned, tangling in its cords. Gnide punched in the last sequence and reached for the activation lever.

He gasped and fell back, reaching behind him. The girl puppet jerked away, a long blade wedged in her dead hands. The blade was dark with blood.

Gnide tried to close the gouting wound in his lower back. His knees gave and he fell. The girl swung in again and stuck the blade through his throat.

He fell, face down, soaking the carpet with his pumping blood.

'I am Vervunhive,' the girl said. The cherub and youth repeated it, dull and toneless.

Inside the iron tank, bathed in warm ichor and floating free, every organ and vessel connected by tubes to the life-bank, Salvador Sondar, High Master of Vervunhive... dreamed.

The salt grasses were ablaze. All along the scarp rise, Vervun Primary tanks were buckled and broken amid the rippling, grey grass, fire spilling out of them. The air was toxic with smoke.

Commissar Kowle dropped clear of the command tank as flames within consumed the shrieking Vegolain and his crew. Kowle's coat was on fire. He shed it.

Enemy fire pummelled down out of the smoke-black air. A Vervun tank a hundred metres away exploded and sent shockwaves of whickering shrapnel in all directions.

One shard grazed Kowle's temple and dropped him.

He got up again. Crews were bailing from burning tanks, some on fire, some trying to help their blazing fellows. Others ran.

Kowle walked back through the line of decimated hive armour, smelling the salt grass as it burned, thick and rancid in his nose.

He pulled out his pistol.

'Where is your courage?' he asked a tank gunner as he put a round through his head.

'Where is your strength?' he inquired of two loaders fleeing up the slope, as he shot them both.

He put his muzzle to the head of a screaming, half-burned tank captain and blew out his brains. 'Where is your conviction?' Kowle asked.

He swung round and pointed his pistol at a group of tank crewmen who were stumbling up the grassy rise towards him from their exploded tank.

'Well?' he asked. 'What are you doing? This is war. Do you run from it?'

They hesitated. Kowle shot one through the head to show he meant business.

'Turn! Face the foe!'

The remaining crewmen turned and fled towards the enemy positions. A tank round took them all apart a second later.

Missiles strafed in from the low, cloudlike meteorites and sundered twenty more tanks along the Vervun formation. The explosions were impossibly loud. Kowle was thrown flat in the grass.

He heard the clanking as he rolled over. On the far rise, battletanks and gun platforms painted in the ochre livery of Zoica rolled down towards him.

A thousand or more.

Out of nowhere, just before nightfall, about a half-hour after the klaxons had stopped yelping, the first shells fell, unexpected, hurled by long-range guns beyond the horizon.

Two fell short on the southern outer habs, kicking up plumes of wreckage from the worker homes.

Another six dented the Curtain Wall.

At Hass West, Daur yelled to his men and cranked the guns around. *A target... give me a target...* he prayed.

Dug-in Zoica armour and artillery, hidden out in the burning grasslands, found their range. Shells began to drop into the hive itself.

A gigantic salvo hit the railhead at Veyveyr Gate and set it ablaze. Several more bracketed the Vervun Primary barracks and atomised over a thousand troopers waiting for deployment.

Another scatter pounded the northern habs along the river. Derricks and quays exploded and shattered into the water. In mid-stream, Folik's over-laden ferry was showered with burning debris. Folik tried to turn in the current, yelling for Mincer. Another shell fell in the water nearby, drenching the screaming passengers with stinking river water. The ferry wallowed in the blast-wake.

Two more dropped beyond the *Magnificat*, exploding and sinking the ferry *Inscrutable*, which was crossing back over the tideway. The *Inscrutable* went up in a shockwave that peppered the water with debris. Diesel slicks burned on the choppy surface.

Folik pulled his wheel around and steered out into mid-channel. Mincer was screaming something at him, but the wail of shells drowned him out.

A staggered salvo rippled through the mining district, flattening wheel heads and pulley towers.

Deep below the earth, Gol Kolea tried to dig Trug Vereas out of the rock fall that had cascaded down the main lift chute of Number Seventeen Deep Working. All around, miners were screaming and dying.

Trug was dead, his head mashed.

Gol pulled back, his hands slick with his friend's blood. Lift cables whipped back down the shaft as cages smashed and fell. The central access had collapsed in on them.

'Livy!' he screamed up into the abyss. '*Livy!*'

Vor was obliterated by the first shell that came through the roof of Vervun Smeltery One. Agun Soric was thrown flat and a chip of ore flying from the blistering shock took out his left eye forever.

Blood from cuts to the scalp streamed down his face. He rolled over in the wreckage and then was lifted off the floor by another impact that exploded the main conveyor. A piece of oily bracket, whizzing supersonically across the work-floor, decapitated one of the screaming workers nearby and embedded itself in the meat of Soric's thigh. He howled, but his cry was lost in the tumult and the klaxons as they started again.

Livy Kolea looked around as the glass roof of the transit station fell in explosively and she tried to shield Yoncy and Dalin.

Glass shrapnel ripped her to pieces, her and another sixty civilians. The aftershock of hot air crisped the rest. Dalin was behind a pillar and remained miraculously unscathed. He got up, crunching over the broken glass, calling for his mother.

When he found what was left of her, he fell silent, too stunned for noise.

Tona Criid took him up in her arms.

'S'okay, kid. S'okay.' She pulled over the upturned cart and saw the healthy, beaming face of the baby smiling back at her. Tona took up the infant under one arm and dragged the boy behind her.

They were twenty metres from the south atrium when further shells levelled carriage station C4/a.

Menx and Troor escorted Guilder Worlin through the chaos of the Commercia. Several barter-houses to their west were ablaze and smoke

clogged the marketways. The closest carriage station with links to the
Main Spine was C4/a, but there was a vast smoke plume in that direction. Menx redirected their route through the abandoned Guild Fayk
barter-house and headed instead for C7/d.

By the time they reached the funicular railway depot, Guilder Worlin was crying with rage. The bodyguard thought it was for fear of his
life, but Worlin was despairing for purely mercantile reasons. Guild
Worlin had no holdings in weaponshops, medical supplies, or food
sources. War was on them and they had no suitable holdings to exploit.

They entered the carriage station, but the place was deserted. A few
abandoned possessions – purse-bags, pict-slates and the like – were
scattered on the platform. The transit indicator plate overhead was
blank.

'I want,' Worlin hissed through clenched teeth, 'to return to the Main
Spine now. I want to be in the family house, to be inside the Spine
hull. Now!'

Troor looked down the monotrack and turned back. 'I see lights, sir.
A transit approaches.'

The carriage train pulled into the station and stopped on automatic
for a moment. The twin cars were packed full of Low- and Mid-Spine
citizens.

'Let me in!' Worlin banged on the nearest door-hatch. Terrified faces
looked out at him silently.

Shells walloped into the Commercia behind him. Worlin pulled out
his needle pistol and opened fire through the glass. The passengers,
trapped like rats in a cage, screamed as they were slaughtered.

After a brief hesitation, Worlin's bodyguard joined him, slaughtering
twenty or more with their unshrouded guns. Others fled the carriage,
screaming. Pulling out bodies, the guards hauled Worlin into the carriage, just as the automatic rest period finished and the transit resumed.
It engaged on the cog-track and slowly began to crank up into the hull
of the main Spine.

'House Sondar, deliver us from evil,' hissed Worlin, sitting down on
a gilt bench seat and rearranging his robes. Menx and Troor stood
nearby, uneasy and unnerved.

Worlin gazed out of the window of the rising transit, apparently not
seeing the smoke blooms and fireballs rising across the city below –
just as he didn't seem to see the pools of blood that washed around
his shoes.

Volleys of shells and long-range missiles pounded into the southern
face of the Main Spine. Despite the thick adamantine and ceramite

sheath, some even punctured the skin of the great structure. A glass-maker's showrooms on the Mid-Spine Promenade took a direct hit and blew out, filling the air with whizzing splinters of lead-crystal and cer-amite wall debris. Fifty house ordinary nobles and their retainers were shredded or burnt as they hurried in panic down the plush walkways.

Just a few steps beyond the glassmaker's, shielded from the out-blast by a row of pillars, Merity Chass continued to stride on, her weeping maids huddled behind her.

'This is not happening,' Merity Chass told herself. 'This is not happening.'

Multiple shell hits lit up the Curtain Wall around Hass West. An anti-aircraft post, the one that had been slow rising from its pit, was blown away and its ignited munitions tore a bite out of the wall.

Captain Daur traversed his guns and looked for an enemy. The grass-lands were blank. Long-range weapons were reaching them, utterly beyond their power to resist.

If they even had the authority.

'Captain Daur to Marshal Gnide! Give us permission to arm! Give the order! Marshal, I'm begging you!'

In the dull quiet of the audience chamber, Gnide's corpse was lifted away from the carpet by the slack puppets. The desperate voice of Daur and hundreds of other field commanders bayed unheard from his vox-plug.

Three shells hit Hass West Fort in series. The first ignited the battery muni-tions. The second vaporised Corporal Bendace and sixteen other troopers. The third, a crippling shockwave, splintered the tower top and caused a vast chunk of rampart to slump away in a torrent of stone, dust and fire. Captain Daur fell with it, caught in the avalanche of rockcrete and ceram-ite. He had still not received the order to arm from the House Command.

In the Iron Tank, Salvador Sondar, High Master of Vervunhive, drifted and dreamed. The satisfaction he had gained from asserting his mas-tery over that fool Gnide was ebbing. There was something akin to pain creeping into him across the mind-impulse links that hooked his cortex into the data-tides and production autoledgers of the hive. He rolled over in the warm suspension fluid and accessed the information cur-rents of the Legislature and the guilds. The hive was... under attack.

He retuned his link to confirm. Even when the information was veri-fied, it seemed wrong. There was a discrepancy that his mind could not resolve. Vervunhive was attacked. Yet this should not be.

He needed time to think.

Petulantly, he activated the Shield generators.

TWO

AN OCHRE WAVE

'Be it one man or one million, the enemy of the Imperium must be treated the same and denied with all diligence.'
– Pius Kowle, Imperial commissar,
from his public education leaflets

Dusk came early at the end of the first day. The darkening sky was stained darker still by the smoke plumes rising from the hive and its outer districts, and by the great ashen pall looming over the salt grass-lands to the south. Thick, fire-swollen, black smoke boiled up from the mining district and the heavy industrial suburbs south of the Curtain Wall, and a murky brown flare of burning fuel rose from ruptured tanks and silos on the Hass docks to the north of the river. Other threads of white, grey and mauve smoke rose from hundreds of smaller, individual fires.

The bombardment continued, even though the Shield had been raised. A vast, translucent umbrella of field-energy extended out from the great Shield Pylon in the central district and unfurled itself in a dome that reached down to anchor substations inside the Curtain Wall. Thousands of shells and missiles burst against it every minute, dimpling the cloudy energy and making it ripple and wobble like green gelatine. From inside the Shield, it looked as if the green sky was blossoming with fire.

Observers on the southern wall, most of them soldiers of Vervun Primary, trained their scopes and magnoculars through the rising smoke and fires in the outer habs and saw the distant grass horizon flickering with a wall of flame seventy kilometres wide. The grass smoke – ash-grey but streaked with black from individual infernos down below the sky-line – tarnished the southern sky in the dying light. Bright, brief flashes underlit the horizon smoke, hinting at the fierce armour battle taking

605

place just out of sight. No communications had been received from General Vegolain's armoured column for two hours.

Now that the Shield was up to cover the main hive, the outer habs, the heavy industry sectors and the mining district south of the wall were taking the worst of it. Unprotected, they were raked mercilessly by long-range artillery, siege mortars and incendiary rockets. As the light faded, the southern out-hive suburb became a dark, mangled mass, busy with thousands of fires, drizzled by fresh rains of explosives. From the Wall, it was possible to see the shock waves radiating from each major strike, gusting the existing fires.

The population of the southern outer habs was in the order of nine million, plus another six million workers who dwelt in the main hive but travelled out to work the industrial district and the mines. They had little shelter. Some hid in cellars or underground storage bays and many died entombed in these places. Penetrator shells dug them out explosively like rats, opening the makeshift shelters to the sky. Others were sealed forever under thousands of tonnes of collapsed masonry.

There were a few deep-seated, hardpoint shelters in the southern habs, reserved for suburban officials and minor area legislators. These shelters had been dug ninety years before during the Trade War and few were in decent working order. One group of hab officials spent two hours trying to find the correct rune-code to let them into their assigned shelter and they were incinerated by a rocket before they could get the vault door open. Another group, a few blocks north, found themselves fighting off a terrified mob that wanted to gain access to a shelter too. A VPHC officer, leading the group, opened fire with his handgun to drive the frantic citizens away while the ranking official, a mill-boss with guild connections, opened the vault.

They sealed themselves in, twenty-three rank-privileged citizens of authority level three or less, in a bunker emplacement designed to shelter two hundred. They all died of suffocation by the following dawn. The air systems, long in need of overhaul and regular maintenance, failed the moment they were switched on.

By nightfall, millions of refugees were clogging the main arterial routes into the hive, bottled up at Sondar Gate, at the Hass West road entry and the ore works cargo route. They were even trying to gain access via the rail-link tunnel at Veyveyr Gate, but the terminal inside had been turned into an inferno in the first wave of bombing and the gate was blocked.

Others still, in desperate, slowly moving lines, many laden with possessions or injured family members, dared the Spoil and the mud flats, and some made it in through the as-yet-undamaged railhead at Croe Gate.

The Hass West Fort was still burning and the top of it was cascading debris down both inside and outside the Wall. However, the Wall and the Hass Gate itself were still firm and streams of refugees made it into the hive via the Hass Road under supervision of Vervun Primary troopers manning the damaged emplacement. But access was still slow and a column of people, two kilometres long and growing, tailed back from the Hass Gate into the dark, vulnerable to the ceaseless onslaught pummelling the outer habs. Thousands died before they could pass into shelter, as shells landed in the thick queue. Just as many, perhaps eight or nine thousand, fled the traffic stream northwest and made progress into the river shores.

The last kinking stretch of shield wall north of Hass West Fort, known as the Dock Wall, reached out into the mid-waters and there was no way through. Some perished in the treacherous mud-flats; others tried to swim the Hass itself and were lost by the hundreds. Most cowered in the stinking slime under the dock wall, wailing plaintively up at the soldiers two hundred metres above them on the wall top, men who could do nothing to help them. Almost two thousand people remained penned in that filthy corner of the Wall through the first days of the conflict, too afraid to try the route back round the wall to Hass Gate. Starvation, disease and despair killed them all within four days.

The Sondar Gate was open and the main tide of refugees sought entry there. The Vervun Primary troops, focussed en masse to control the crowd, admitted the people as quickly as possible, but it was miserably slow going and the column of people stretched three kilometres back into the burning outer habs.

Many of the tail-enders, certain they would be dead before ever reaching the safety of the hive's Shield, turned around and headed out into the salt grasslands by the hundreds. None were ever seen alive again.

In the Square of Marshals, just inside the Heironymo Sondar Gate, the hive troopers struggled to manage the overwhelming influx of citizens. Forty per cent of the arrivals were injured.

Captain Letro Cargin had been given charge of the operation and inside an hour he was close to despair. He had first tried to contain the refugees in the vast ceremonial square itself, but it quickly became filled to overflowing. Some family groups were climbing the pedestals of the statues around the square to find somewhere to crouch. There was group singing: work anthems of the hive or Imperial hymns. The massed, frail voices – set against the constant thunder of the bombardment and the crackle of the Shield above – unnerved his men.

The Vervun Primary barracks north-west of the square, which had taken hits in the first stage of the attack, was still blazing but under control. Cargin voxed House Command repeatedly until he was granted special permission from the guilds to open the Anko Chemical Plant west of the square and the guild manufactories to the east, to house the overspill. Quickly, these new areas became overfilled too. The guilds had issued particular instructions as to how much of those areas could be used or even entered. Cargin's men reported fights breaking out as they tried to deny access to certain areas. Shots were fired over the heads of the crowd. Compared to the onslaught they had weathered outside, the small arms of the troops were insignificant and the House Guard found themselves pushed back deeper into the industrial areas, trying to accommodate the intake. Most troopers were profoundly unwilling to shoot at their own citizens. In one instance, an angry junior officer actually fired into the encroaching crowd, killing two. He and his six-man squad were torn apart by a pack of smoke-blackened textile workers.

Cargin voxed frantically for supplies and advice. By eight in the evening, new orders were being issued from House Command and the Legislature, designating refugee assembly areas, hastily arranged in the inner worker habs south of the Pylon and the Commercia. Asylum traffic from the Sondar Gate, Hass Gate and, to a lesser extent, the Croe Gate was now choking the southern sectors of the hive. Some of the House Legislature, meeting in extraordinary session in the Main Spine, argued that it was the hive's duty to house the outer hab population. Others were simply afraid that with the main southern arterials choked, they would never be able to mobilise their armies. Six noble houses also volunteered aid, which began to be shipped by carriage route down to the Square of Marshals and the main city landing field where the refugees from Hass Gate were also congregating.

It was a start, but not enough. Cargin began to wonder if the upper echelon of the hive really understood the scale of the problem. The Imperial mottoes, hive slogans and other messages of calming propaganda flashing up on the public-address plates did little to deaden the general panic. Cargin had angry, frightened citizens by the thousands, most stone-deaf from concussion shock, many burned naked by the blasts, many more dying and stretcher-bound. Short of closing the Gate itself, he had no way to stem the flow. His three thousand men were vastly outnumbered by the mass.

Cargin was voxed to the north corner of the square. There he found a field station had been set up by medics from some inner hab infirmary. Hundreds of the injured had been laid out on the stone paving. Doctors and orderlies dressed in crimson gowns and masks tended to them.

'Are you Cargin?'

Cargin looked round. A gowned and masked figure was addressing him. She pulled off her mask to reveal an appealing, heart-shaped face. The eyes, though, were hard and bewildered.

'Yes... doctor?'

'Surgeon Ana Curth, Inner Hab Collective Medical Hall 67/mv. I've been given authority here. We are trying to set up a triage station under the carriage stands over there, but the flow is too great.'

'I'm doing my best, surgeon,' he said flatly. He could see tractor units and trucks lining the barrack road, headlamps blazing and engines gunning, moving in to transport those in need of immediate surgery to the main infirmary facilities in the inner habs and Low Spine.

'Likewise,' said Curth without humour. The air smelled of blood and burned flesh and was full of piteous shrieking. 'The medical halls are already full of wounded from the inner city. There were huge casualties from the start of the raid, before the Shield was ignited.'

'I don't know what to say,' Cargin shrugged. 'I've followed my orders and allowed the incoming to flow out of the square into adjacent areas. There seems to be no end to them. My observers on the wall-top say the queue outside is still three kilometres long.'

The surgeon looked at the blood-spattered paving for a moment, her hands on her hips. 'I...' she began, then paused. 'Can you get me a vox link? I'll try sending to my superiors. The Commercia has been evacuated and there is vast floorspace inside it. I doubt they'll grant permission, but I'll do what I can.'

Cargin nodded. He called his vox-officer over and told him to attend the surgeon. 'Whatever you can do is better than nothing,' he told her.

The tank roared and bounced over the trampled grass hillocks, heading north at full throttle, its turret reversed to spit shells into the firefields behind it, into the invisible enemy at its heels.

The night sky was ablaze. Scorching trails of rockets and shrieking shells tore overhead, heading for the hive.

Commissar Kowle crouched in the turret of the running tank, shouting orders to fire to the gun-crew in the lit space below him. The vox-link was down. He couldn't reach House Command. He had forty-two tanks left out of the armoured column of more than four hundred and fifty that had left the Sondar Gate that afternoon. No ranking Vervun Primary armour officer was left alive. Cadet Fosker was also dead.

Kowle had command now. Using the VPHC Commissar Langana as his second officer, he had managed to regroup the shattered remnants of the tank force and swing it back towards the city. It felt like retreat, but Kowle knew it was a sound tactical decision. They were facing an ochre wave out there on the grass-flats, a stupendous Zoica armoured front, pushing in through three salients. Only in his days with the Imperial Guard, during major offensives like Balhaut and Cociaminus, had he seen anything like this scale of assault. And there were infantry regiments behind, thick like locusts, following the armour.

Kowle didn't even want to think about the size of the opposition just now. It was... unbelievable. It was impossible. An ochre wave – that's all he could see, the tide of ochre-painted machines rolling over his forces, crushing them.

He tried the vox again, but the enemy was jamming all bands. Shells rained down amongst the retreating Vervun tanks. At least two blew out as munitions ignited, sending tank hulls end-over-end in fireballs, spraying track segments out like shattered teeth.

The driver was calling him over the intercom. 'Ahead, sir!'

Kowle swivelled round. Vervunhive was in sight now, the great luminous blister of green energy flickering on the skyline like a giant mushroom cloud, glowing in the night. Kowle grabbed his scope and saw the blackened, burning mass of the outer habs fast approaching. A persistent rain of explosives was still dropping into them.

'Kowle to column!' he spat into his inter-tank vox. 'Form up and follow me in down the Southern Highway. We will re-enter the city through the Sondar Gate. Let none shirk, for I will find them wanting and find them!'

He smiled at his last words. Even now, under a storm of fire, he could still turn a good, disciplinarian phrase.

The high-ceilinged, gilt-ornamented Hall of the Legislature, high and secure in the upper sections of the Main Spine, was full of arguing voices.

Lord Heymlik Chass, noble patriarch of House Chass, sat back in his velvet-upholstered bench and glanced aside to his aides and chamberlains.

The Legislature was full tonight. All nine noble houses were in attendance, as well as the representatives of the other twenty-one houses ordinary, along with the drones of over three hundred guild associations and families in their flamboyant finery. And down in the commons pit, hundreds of habitat and work-clave representatives bayed for action.

As a scion of a noble house, Chass's bench was in the inner circle, just above the Legislator's dais. Vox/pict drones mumbled and hovered along the benches like bumblebees. The Legislature Choir, told to shut up some minutes before by Noble Croe, sat sullenly in their balcony, balling up pages of sheet music and throwing them down on the assembly beneath. Master Jehnik, of House Ordinary Jehnik, was on his feet in the middle circle, reading from a prepared slate and trying to get someone to listen to his fifty-five-point plan.

Chass pressed the geno-reader on the side of his hardwood stall and the plate slid open before him.

He keyed in his authority rating, touched the statement runes and wrote: *Master Legislator, are we going to debate or simply argue all night?*

The words flashed up on the central plate and six other noble houses, fifteen houses ordinary and the majority of the guild associations assented.

Silence fell.

The Master Legislator, Anophy, an ancient hunchback with a tricorn, ribboned hat, crawled to his feet from his dais throne and began the Litany of Enfranchisement. The assembly was quiet as it was intoned. Anophy stroked his long, silver moustache, smoothed the front of his opalescent robe and asked the assembly for points of order.

Around seventy holographic runes lit the plate display and glowed overhead via hovering repeater screens.

'Noble Anko has the floor.' There were moans from the commons pit.

Anko got up, or rather was helped up by his entourage. His raspy, vox-amplified voice rang around the hall.

'I deplore the attack on our city-hive by our erstwhile friends of Zoica. I press to vote we deny them and send them home, tails between their legs.'

No argument there, thought Chass. Typical Anko, going for the easy vote.

Anko went on. 'I wish the Legislature to back me on another matter. My plant is being overrun by indigents from the suburbs. House officers tell me that the plant is already overwhelmed and immediate production will be impossible. This hurts Vervunhive. I move that House Anko be allowed to eject the indigents from its premises.'

More squabbling and yelling from below.

'Noble Yetch?'

'Are we to disabuse our work population so, cousin Anko? You like them well enough when they raise your quotas. Do you hate them now they choke your factories?'

Commotion, louder than before. Several nobles and many guilders thumped their assent sirens vigorously. Anko sat down, his expression vile.

'Noble Chass?'

Chass rose. 'I fear my cousin Anko fails to read the larger story here. Ninety years have passed since we faced such a crisis. We face a Second Trade War. Reports are that the wave of enemy force is quite humbling to our own defences. We have all seen how the tumult today has wounded our hive. Why, my own dear daughter barely reached home alive.'

Sympathetic holograms flashed sycophantically from the tiers of some of the houses ordinary.

Chass continued. 'If this attack inconveniences our houses, I say: Let us be inconvenienced! We have a duty to the hive population and cousin Anko should put that bald fact before his production quota. I wish to frame more important questions to this Legislature. One: Why did this attack come as a surprise? Two: Should we signal the Imperium for assistance? Three: Where is the High Master, what did he know of this and why was the Shield ignited so late?'

Now the roaring grew. Assent sigils lit up all around. The Legislator screamed for order.

'Noble Chass,' a voice said, lilting through the huge hall. 'How would you wish me answer that?'

The place fell silent. Escorted by ten impassive, uniformed officers of the VPHC, High Master Salvador Sondar entered the Hall.

He was blind in one eye and limping badly. His flesh was blistered and charred, and his clothes were tattered. But he was still plant supervisor.

Using an axe-rake as a crutch, Agun Soric bellowed as best his crisped lungs could manage, as he brought over three hundred smeltery workers out through the northern processing ramps of Vervun Smeltery One. Most were as soot-black as he was, the only things showing against the grime being the glistening red of wounds or the white of fresh dressings.

That and the workers' white, fear-filled eyes.

They carried their injured with them, some on makeshift stretchers, some in carriers made of tied sacking, some pushed in ore-barrows.

Soric stomped around and looked back with his one good eye. Vervun Smeltery One and parts of the surrounding ore plants were burning furiously. Chimney stacks collapsed in the heat, sending up white cinders against the yellow flames. The Veyveyr Rail Terminal, to the west, was also torching out.

He heard shouting and disputes from the concourse below him and he hobbled down, pushing his way through the rows of men and women from his plant.

A dozen Vervun Primary soldiers were stopping the survivors' advance down transit channel 456/k into the inner habs. A VPHC officer was leading them.

'We need to get in there,' Soric said, stomping up to the Commissariat officer. Even with one eye, Soric could see the twitchy, frantic light in the young VPHCer's eyes.

'Orders from Main Spine, old man,' the commissar told him. 'Low hab is choked with refugees. No more may be admitted. You camp here. Supplies will come in time.'

'What's your name?' Soric asked.

'Commissar Bownome.'

Soric paused, leaned awkwardly on his crutch, and wiped the ash from his supervisor's badge with a hawk of spit.

He held it up so the uniformed man could see. 'Soric, plant supervisor, Smeltery One. We've just been bombed to gak and my workers need access to cover and treatment. Now, not in time.'

'There is no way through. Access is denied. Make your people comfortable here.' The troopers behind Bownome raised their weapons as punctuation.

'Here? In a stinking street with the works burning behind us? I don't think so. Boy, Smeltery One is the property of Noble House Gavunda. We are all Lord Gavunda's souls. If he hears of this–'

'I answer only to House Sondar. As should you. Don't threaten me.'

'Where's the gakking threat, you idiot?' Soric asked, looking round at his massing workers and getting a spirited laugh in answer. 'A one-eyed cripple like me? Let us through.'

'Aye, let us through!' bellowed a worker beside Soric. Ozmac, probably, but it was impossible to tell under the soot. Other workers jeered and agreed.

'Do you understand what a State of Emergency is, old man?' Bownome asked.

'Understand? I'm gakking living it!' Soric blurted. 'Stand aside!' He tried to push past the VPHC officer, but Bownome pushed back and Soric fell off his crutch onto the debris-littered paving.

There were shouts of disbelief and anger. Workers surged forward. Bownome backed away, pulled out his autopistol and fired into the approaching mass.

Ozmac fell dead and another collapsed wounded.

'That's it! Enough! Be warned!' yelled the commissar. 'You will all stay where–'

Soric's axe-rake crutch shattered Bownome's skull and felled him to the ground. Before any of the troopers could react, the workers were on them like a tidal wave. All of the troopers were killed in a few seconds.

DAN ABNETT

The smeltery workers gathered up their weapons. Worker Gannif handed the commissar's pistol to Soric.

'I'll see you right!' Soric barked. He waved for them to follow him down the transit channel. They cheered him and moved on, at his heels, into the city.

'Marshal Gnide is dead,' High Master Sondar told the Legislature. The hall had remained silent as the High Master's floating throne ascended to the main dais with its stone-faced VPHC vanguard. Sondar's throne had locked into place above the High Legislator's dais and the master of Vervunhive had spent a long moment looking out at the assembly before speaking. He was dressed in regal robes, his face masked with a turquoise ceramic janus.

'Dead,' Sondar repeated. 'Our hive faces a time of war – and you, noble houses, low houses, guilders, you decide it is time to usurp my position?'

Silence remained.

Sondar's masked visage turned to look around at the vast swoop of the tiered hall.

'We are one, or we are nothing.'

Still the nervous silence.

'I believe you think me weak. I am not weak. I believe you think me stupid. I am not that either. I believe that certain high houses see this as an opportunity to further their own destinies.'

The High Master allowed Noble Anko to rise with a wave of his hand.

'We never doubted you, High Lord. The Trade War fell upon us so suddenly.'

You witless weakling, Chass thought. Sondar has led us to this blind and you reconcile sweetly. Where is the fervour that had us vote to take executive action this afternoon?

'Zoica will be denied,' Sondar said. Chass watched the High Lord's movements and saw how jerky they were. It's not him, he thought. The wretch has sent another servitor puppet to represent him.

'We have sent word to the Northern Foundry Collectives and to Vannick Magna. They will bolster us with garrison troops. Our counterattack will begin in two days.'

There was delighted commotion from the commons pit and the guild tiers.

Chass rose and spoke. 'I believe it is in the interests of Verghast as a whole to send to the Imperium for assistance.'

'No,' responded Sondar quickly. 'We have beaten Zoica before; we will do it again. This is an internal matter.'

'No longer,' a voice said from below. The assembly looked down at the benches where the officials of the Administratum sat. Hooded and gowned, Intendant Banefail of the Imperial Administratum got to his feet. 'Astropathic messages have already been sent out, imploring Imperial assistance from Warmaster Macaroth. Vervunhive's production of ordnance and military vehicles is vital for the constant supply of the Sabbat Worlds Crusade. The warmaster will take our plight seriously. This is a greater matter than local planetary politics, High Lord Sondar.'

Sondar, or rather the being that represented him, seemed to quiver in his throne. Rage, Chass presumed. The balance between hive and Imperial authority had always been delicate in Vervunhive, indeed in all the nobilities of Verghast. It was rare for it to clash so profoundly and so visibly. Chass well knew the fundamental strategic import of Vervunhive and the other Verghast manufactory cities to the crusade, but still the magnitude of the intendant's actions amazed him. The Administratum was the bureaucratic right hand of the Emperor himself, but it usually bowed to the will of the local planetary governor.

Our plight must truly be serious, he realised, a sick feeling seeping into his heart.

Holding the infant and pulling the small boy by the hand, Tona Criid ran through the burning northern section of the Commercia. The boy was crying now. She couldn't help that. If they could make the docks, she could get them clear across the river and to safety. But the routes were packed. As fast as refugees came into the hive from the south, inhabitants were fleeing to the north.

'Where we going?' asked the boy, Dalin.

'Somewhere safe,' Tona told him.

'Who are you?'

'I'm your Aunt Tona.'

'I don't have an aunt.'

'You do now. And so does Yancy here.'

'Yoncy.'

'Yeah, whatever. Come on.' Tona tried to thread them through the massing crowds that filled the transit channels down to the docks, but they were jammed tight.

'Where are we going?' asked the kid again as they sheltered in a barter-house awning to avoid the press.

'Away. To the river.' That was the plan. But with the crowds this thick, she didn't know if it was going to be possible. Maybe they'd be safer in the city, under the Shield.

The baby began to cry.

* * *

He couldn't breathe. The weight and blackness upon him were colossal. Something oily was dripping into his eyes. He tried to move, but no movement was possible. No, that wasn't true. He could grind his toes in his army boots. His mouth was full of rockcrete dust. He started to cough and found his lungs had no room to move. He was squashed.

There was a rattling, chinking sound above him. He could hear voices, distant and muffled. He tried to cry out, but the dust choked him and he had no room to choke.

Light. A chink of light, just above as rubble was moved away. Rubble moved and some pieces slumped heavier on him, vicing his legs and pelvis.

There was a face in the gap above him.

'Who's down there?' it called. 'Are you alive?'

Hoarse and dry, he answered. 'My name is Ban Daur – and yes, I am alive.'

His family house was deserted. Guilder Worlin strode inside, leaving a sticky tread of blood in his footprints. His clan was at the Legislature, he was sure. Let them go and bow and scrape to the High Lord.

He crossed the draped room to the teak trolley by the ornamental window and poured himself a triple shot of joiliq. Menx and Troor waited in the anteroom, whispering nervously.

'Bodyguard! To me!' Worlin called as the fire of the drink warmed his body. He waved an actuator wand at the wall plate and saw nothing but cycling scrolls of Imperium propaganda. He snapped the plate off and dropped the wand.

His bodyguard approached. They had both shrouded their weapons again, as was the custom inside guild households.

Worlin sat back on the suspensor couch and sipped his drink, smiling. Outside the window, the sprawl of Vervunhive spread out, many parts of it ablaze. The green, Shield-tinted sky contorted with the constant shelling.

'You have served me well tonight,' Worlin told them.

The bodyguards paused, uncertain.

'Menx! Troor! My friends! Fetch yourselves a drink from the cart and relax! Your master is proud of you!'

They hesitated and then turned. Troor raised a decanter as Menx found glasses. As soon as they had their backs to him, Worlin pulled the needle pistol from his robes and fired.

The first shot blew Menx's spine out and he was flung face first into the cart, which broke under him and shattered. Troor turned and the decanter in his hand was shattered by the second shot. The third exploded his face and he dropped backwards onto the cart wreckage.

Worlin got up and, drink in hand, fired thirty more needles into the twisted corpses, just to be sure. Then he sat back, sipping his drink, watching Vervunhive burn.

'The road is blocked, sir!' the tank driver yelled through the intercom to Kowle. Chasing up the Southern Highway, through the wrecked outer habs, with shells still falling, Kowle's column had reached the rear of the queue of refugees tailing back from Sondar Gate.

Kowle sat up in the turret, looking ahead, taking in the sea of milling bodies before them.

Shells fell to the west and lit up the night.

Kowle dropped into the turret and said, 'Drive through.'

The driver looked back at him in amazement.

'But commissar–'

'Are you denying a direct order?' Kowle snapped.

'No, sir, commissar, sir, but–'

Kowle shot him through the throat and dragged his twitching body out of the driver's seat.

He settled into the blood-slick metal chair and keyed the intercom. 'Armour column. Follow me.'

Just outhab wretches... worthless, he decided, as he drove the tank down through the masses, crushing a path to the distant gates of Vervunhive.

THREE

A MIDNIGHT SUN

'After this, all battles will be easy, all victories simple, all glories hollow.'

– General Noches Sturm,
after his victory on Grimoyr

The bombardment continued, both day and night, for two and a half weeks. By the close of the twelfth day, day and night were barely distinguishable, so great was the atmospheric smoke-haze hanging around Vervunhive. The Shield held firm, but the southern outhabs and manufactories became a fire-blown wasteland, fifty kilometres square. Some shelling had also been deliberately ranged over the Shield, catastrophically wounding the unprotected northern districts and large sections of the Hass docklands.

On the afternoon of the sixth day, Marshal Edric Croe, the Legislature's appointed successor to Gnide, ordered the closing of the southern hive gates. The new marshal, brother of Lord Croe of that noble house, had been a serving major-colonel in Vervun Primary and his election was ratified by seven of the nine noble houses. Noble House Anko – who were sponsoring their own General, Heskith Anko, for the post – voted to deny. Noble House Chass abstained.

Marshal Croe was a pale, white-haired giant, well over two metres tall. His fierce black eyes and hard gaze were the subject of barrack legend, but he was personally calm, quiet and inspirational, judicious in leadership and popular with the men. The majority vote of the noble houses reflected their confidence in him – and the fact they felt he would remain answerable to them in all circumstances. Heskith Anko, a plump, swarthy brute who approached war politically rather than tactically, was appointed Croe's chief of staff to appease House Anko. The two did not get on and their furious arguments in House Command became notorious.

620

DAN ABNETT

Croe's decision to close the gates – at this stage there were still some half a million refugees streaming in from the southern districts seeking sanctuary at Hass West, Sondar and Croe Gates – surprised the houses and the Legislature as a whole. Many believed Croe had bowed to Anko's persistent pressure. House Chass, House Rodyin and seven houses ordinary raised a bill of disapproval and railed against the cruelty of the action. Half a million, left to die, the gates sealed against them. 'It defies humanity,' Lord Rodyin stated in the Hall of the Legislature.

In fact, Marshal Croe's decision had been far more deeply affected by the advice of Commissar Kowle, who had returned from the frontline with the tattered remnants of the tank divisions on the second night. Despite the losses suffered by Vegolain's forces, Kowle was hailed by many as a hero. He had single-handedly rallied more than thirty vehicles and crews and pulled them back, bringing first-hand details of the enemy home to the hive. The public-address plates spoke freely of his heroism and loyalty. His name was chanted in the refugee camps and in all gatherings of citizens and workers. The title 'People's Hero' was coined and stuck. It was popularly believed he would be decorated for his actions and many in the low classes saw him as a folk hero and a better choice for marshal than Croe. When, on the ninth day, food, water and energy rationing was imposed hive-wide by the Legislature, a speech by Kowle was published on the address plates, stating how he would not only be observing rationing strictly, but also rationing his rations. This astute piece of propaganda was Kowle's idea and the hive population almost universally embraced the restrictions, wishing to be 'true to the People's Hero and his selfless behaviour.'

Croe realised quickly that he should not underestimate Kowle's power as a popular figure. But that also meant he couldn't ignore Kowle's tactical suggestions out of hand.

Croe, Anko and the assembled officer elite spent most of the fifth day in conference. They filled the briefing hall of House Command in the Main Spine to capacity. An expectant hush fell on the assembled soldiers when Croe asked Kowle to give his assessment of the opposition. Kowle rose to his feet, the shrapnel wound in his forehead clearly and crudely sutured (another carefully judged move on Kowle's part).

'I cannot overstate the magnitude of the enemy,' Kowle said, his calm voice carried around the vast, domed hall by hovering drones. 'I have seldom seen a military force of such scale. Eighty or ninety thousand armoured vehicles, thousands of gun batteries and an infantry force behind them of several million.'

The hall was deadly quiet.

Marshal Croe asked the commissar to confirm what he had just said. During the Trade War, ninety years before, Vervunhive had faced a Zoican army of 900,000 and barely survived.

'Millions,' Kowle repeated simply. 'In all the confusion, I had little opportunity to make a head count, of course–'

General laughter welled from the officer cadre.

'But I am sure, by disposition alone, that at least five million troops were embarked in file behind the armour advance. And those were only the ones I could see.'

'Preposterous!' Vice Marshal Anko barked. 'Vervunhive supports over forty million inhabs and from that we raise half a million troops! Zoica is a third our size! How could they conceivably field five or more million troops?'

'I repeat only what I saw, general.' There was hubbub and murmuring in the officer ranks.

Croe had requested orbital pictures prior to the meeting, pictures he had hoped would confirm or deny these outlandish claims. But the smoke patterns from the continued bombardment were blanketing the continent and nothing was discernible. He had to trust Kowle's estimation, an estimation supported by many of the armour crews he had brought back with him.

Croe also had to consider the political and popular suicide of contradicting the People's Hero.

Croe cleared his throat and his dark eyes fixed the commissar across the central chart table. 'Your recommendations, commissar?'

'The south gates to the hive must be closed. Sooner or later, the bombardment will stop. Then the Zoican legions will descend on us in unprecedented force. Already they may be approaching, cloaked by the barrage, entering the southern districts. We must make ourselves secure.'

Croe was silent. His gate officers had brought him updates on the refugee intake, the miserable statistics of the dispossessed and wounded still pressing for entry after five days. But Kowle's assessment was inarguable.

'The southern gates will close tomorrow at nine.' Croe hoped he would not live to regret this callous act. As a matter of record, he would not.

While the magnitude of this decision soaked into the stunned officers, Colonel Modile requested that the Wall Artillery be raised and armed. At the first alarm, the rampart defences had been manned and raised, but more potent heavy guns, dormant since the Trade War, were still muzzled in deployment silos in the Curtain Wall itself. Vice Marshal

Anko reported that this work was already underway. The hive's main firepower would be ready in two more days and at last the city would have long range artillery to answer the bombardment.

'What of the reinforcements High Master Sondar promised?' asked an artillery officer on the front bench.

'Ten regiments of auxiliaries are moving south to us from the Northern Foundry Collectives as we speak. Vannick Hive has promised us nine regiments within a week.'

'And the request to the Imperium?' asked Commissar Tarrian, head of the VPHC.

Croe smiled. 'The will of the Emperor is with us. Warmaster Macaroth has already responded to our needs. Ordinarily, his forces would be months away, but luck is on our side. A troop convoy from Monthax, regrouping to reinforce the Warmaster's main crusade assault into the Cabal system, is just nine days away. It has been rerouted. Six regiments of Guard Infantry and three armour groups are moving to us directly.'

There was general noise and some cheers.

Croe rose and hushed them all. 'But that is still nine days away. We must be strong, we must be fast, we must be secure well before then. The south gates close at nine tomorrow.'

A pitiful semblance of dawn was ebbing through the smoke cover when the Heironymo Sondar Gate shut the next morning. Dozens of refugees scrambled through in the last few moments. Dozens more were crushed by the slamming hydraulics. At West Hass and Croe Gates, the story was repeated. Veyveyr Gate had been immobilised by the first night's shelling, although the railhead fires were now out. Vervun Primary battalions, supervised by the VPHC, erected blockades of metal wreckage to close the gate, the Commissariat officers ordering the troops to fire on any refugees still trying to gain access.

The piteous screaming and wailing of those shut outside was more than some Vervun Primary troopers could bear. Many wrote in letters or journals that it was the worst part of the whole campaign for them. Soldiers who had overseen the closing of the gates at the start of the sixth day, and who survived the entire ordeal, never forgot that moment. Years after, men woke in the night, or at grey daybreak, sweating and screaming, echoing the noises they heard from outside the walls. It was the most merciless act of the conflict so far and it would only be matched when the gates fell open again, over a month later.

The Vervunhive Wall Artillery began firing just before noon on the eighth day. The massive silos opened their ceramite shutters and volleyed shells back into the salt-grass hinterland where the enemy forces were massing. The salvoes were answered with redoubled bombardment from the still-unseen foe.

On the morning of the eleventh day, troop convoys began to thread down the motor routes north of the Hass. Twenty thousand men and nearly five thousand war machines sent out from the Northern Collectives to reinforce Vervunhive or, more particularly, the Hass crossing which protected them from the Zoican advance. Kicking dust, the troop carriers and tanks rumbled through the bombed outer habs and damaged manufactories, braving the bombardment that still fell across the river from far away. Thousands of citizens had fled across the river by ferry, some trying to reach their homes in the northern outer habs, many more seeking sanctuary in the Northern Collectives. In places, the mass of people on the roadways slowed the NorthCol advance, but VPHC details were sent across the river by Vice Marshal Anko to clear the way.

By the afternoon, the NorthCol regiments were moving freely down to the waiting ferries at the docks, all refugee columns driven into the roadside fields to allow the convoys to pass. Some three hundred refugees had been executed by the VPHC to force them to make way. The refugees jeered the NorthCol columns as they roared past. General Xance of the NorthCol 2nd Enforcers later wrote, 'This humiliating greeting did more to burn out the NorthCol morale than a month of bitter resistance at the Wall.'

Such was the size of the NorthCol deployment and such was the capacity of the ferries that estimates suggested it would take four days to cross them over the Hass into Vervunhive. When told of this, Marshal Croe ordered the Hass Viaduct reopened so that rail links could resume. The rail route had been closed at the start of the bombardment. Bypassing the ferry route, NorthCol got its forces into the hive in just under two days. Many tanks and armoured personnel carriers actually crossed the viaduct under their own power, trundling along the rail tracks. Two divisions of the NorthCol infantry also marched across the viaduct in a break between trains.

So far, nothing had been heard of the promised reinforcements from Vannick Hive, the great refinery collective three thousand kilometres away to the east. Vannick had undertaken to provide nine regiments, but thus far the only thing that had come from them was the continued fuel-oil supplies carried by the eastern pipeline. Many in Vervunhive wondered if the forces of Zoica had reached them too.

* * *

At dawn on the fourteenth day, lights were seen in the upper atmosphere. Flaring their braking jets, Imperial Guard dropships descended, diverted to the main lift-port at Kannak in the Northern Collective Hives. With the Shield erected, Vervunhive's central landing field could accept no ships.

The Imperial Guard disembarked at Kannak and then marched south on the tail of the NorthCol forces. The simple sight of their high-orbit adjustments and blazing descents lifted the morale of the battered hive. The Guard was coming.

The Royal Volpone 1st, 2nd and 4th deployed south from Kannak Port swiftly, using the rail link to bring themselves deep into the hive. Marshal Croe personally greeted General Noches Sturm, the decorated victor of Grimoyr, on the rockcrete platform of the North Spine Terminus. A large crowd of politically approved citizens cheered them, under the watchful eyes of the VPHC.

Dressed in shimmering blue gowns, daughters of the noble houses – Merity Chass, Alina Anko, Iona Gavunda and Murdith Croe amongst them – were sent forward to decorate Sturm and his second officers, Colonels Gilbear and Corday, with silk floral wreathes.

Sturm was also greeted by the famous Commissar Kowle. The image of their smiling handshake was repeated on a million public-address plates across the hive.

The 5th and 7th regiments of the Roane Deepers, under General Nash, arrived by rail later that afternoon, amid more pantomime celebrations. Vice Marshal Anko was there to greet Nash and brass bands pomped and trumpeted the arrival. Amid the jubilation, Nash was able to confirm that three full regiments of Narmenian Armour were off-loading from carriers at the Kannak Port landing fields and would be en route south by dawn. The crowd rose, cheering the news, hailing the honoured Guard arrivals like they had already won the war.

The Tanith First and Only arrived by road, almost unnoticed, two nights later.

More than eighty matt-black troop trucks rumbled down the North-Col highway through the northern outhabs of Vervunhive. The canvas tilts had been removed and around thirty Tanith troopers rode in each, crouched down with their weapons, webbing, haversacks, musette bags and bedrolls gathered to them. The bouncing trucks – six-wheelers with large, snarling front grills and pop-eye headlamps – bore the quadruple chevron cab-marks of NorthCol Utility Transport Division Three. Jerry cans and spare wheels were slung to their sides on sponson fittings.

A dozen outriders astride black-drab motorcycles ran along their flanks, and behind the main column came thirty more high-cabbed eight-wheelers laden with ammunition crates and regimental supplies, as well as the numerous cooks, armourers, mechanics, servitors and other attendant hangers-on that followed a Guard regiment on the move. These freighters were dull yellow, the livery of the Kannak Port Cargo Union, and netting was draped over their payloads. NorthCol soldiers in pale blue overalls and forage caps drove all the trucks, but the outriders were Tanith, in their distinctive dark battledress. Twelve kilometres short of Vervunhive, they paused to trickle through a checkpoint on the highway and they gained a vanguard of two dark-blue staff cars crewed by VPHC officers to lead them in.

All the headlamps in the convoy were blazing. Night had fallen sometime, unnoticed in the thick wallow of smoke. The only sights were the battered districts to either side, the fuzzy green glow of the hive itself – partly obscured by the smoke – and the occasional flash and flare of long-range shells falling into the outer habs they raced through.

Brin Milo, the youngest Ghost, rode with the rest of number one platoon in the lead truck. A slender, pale youth just now filling out with adult bulk, he had been the only non-soldier saved from the ruins of Tanith when their homeworld was overrun and destroyed four years earlier. The commissar himself had saved his life and dragged him from the fires that burned Tanith away.

For a long while, he had been 'the Boy,' the company mascot, the piper, a little piece of Tanith innocence saved from hell, a reminder to all of the men of the place they had lost. But six months before, during the battle for Monthax, he had finally become a soldier too. He was proud of his issued equipment and lasgun, and he kept his pack in better order than any of the seasoned Tanith troopers.

He sat huddled in the cramped rear-bay of the rattling truck and polished the regimental crest on his black beret with a rag of gun-cloth.

'Milo.'

Brin looked up at Trooper Larkin opposite him. A wiry, taut-skinned man in his early fifties, Larkin was as well-known for his neurotic personality as his skill as the regiment's most able sniper. The long, specialised shape of his marksman's lasgun was sheathed in a canvas roll at his feet. Larkin had produced his gun-scope and was training it like a spyglass out of the truck. Larkin had once told Milo that he didn't trust anything he hadn't seen first through his beloved scope.

'Larkin?'

Larkin grinned and looked back, handing the delicate brass instrument to the youth, gently. From the tiny runes glowing on the setting dial, Milo noticed it was fixed to heat-see.

'Take a look. That way.'

Milo squinted into the scope, resting the rubberised cup to his eye-socket. He saw radiance and bewildering crosshair markers of floating red.

'What am I looking at?'

'The hive, boy, the hive.'

Milo looked again. He realised the radiance was the yellow dome of the Shield, a vast energy field that enveloped the unseen city-hive ahead.

'Looks big enough and ugly enough to look after itself,' he suggested.

'The same is said for so many of us,' Colonel Corbec said, holding on to the truck's iron tilt-hoops as he edged down to Milo and Larkin. 'Velvethive is in a pretty fix, so they say.'

'That's Vervunhive, chief,' Trooper Burun said from nearby.

'Feth you, clever-ass!' Corbec tossed back at the grinning soldier. 'Feth knows I can barely remember me own name most days, let alone where I'm supposed to be!'

First Platoon laughed.

Milo held the scope up to Corbec, who waved it off with disinterest.

'I'll meet the place that'll kill me when I meet it. Don't need to look for it in advance.'

Milo gave the precious scope back to Larkin, who took a final look and then slid the instrument back into its drawstring bag.

'Seen enough, Larks?' Corbec asked, his vast arms gripping the overhead frame, his beard split by a toothy grin.

'Seen enough to know where to aim,' Larkin replied.

In the juddering load-bay of the truck three vehicles back, Third Platoon were all wagering on cards. Trooper Feygor, a dangerous, lean man with hooded eyes, had bartered a full tarot pack from some Administratum fellow on the troopship and he was running a game of Hearts and Titans.

Trooper Brostin, big, heavyset and saturnine, had lost so much already he was ready to wager his flamer, with the fuel tanks, as his next lay-down.

Feygor, a thick cigar clenched between his sharp teeth, laughed at Brostin's discomfiture and shuffled the pack again.

As he flicked the big pasteboard cards out into hands around the grilled deck, the men of the platoon produced coins, crumpled notes, rings and tobacco rations to add to the pot.

Trooper Caffran watched him deal. Short, young and determined, just a year older than Milo, Caffran had gained the respect of them all during the beach assault at Oskray about a year before. Caffran disliked cards, but in Rawne's platoon it paid to mix in.

Major Rawne sat at the end of the truck-bay, his back to the rear wall of the cab. The Tanith second officer, he was infamous for his anger, guile and pessimism. Corbec had likened him to a snake more than once, both physically and in character.

'Will you play, major?' Feygor asked, his hands hesitating on the deal. Rawne shook his head. He'd lost plenty to his adjutant in the last forty days of transit in the troopship.

Now he could smell war and idle gaming had lost its interest.

Feygor shrugged and finished the deal. Caffran picked up his hand and sighed. Brostin picked up his hand and sighed more deeply. He wondered if wool socks would count as a wager.

The outriders raced around the speeding trucks, gunning for the destination. Sergeant Mkoll, head of the scout platoon, crossed his bike in between two of the troop vehicles and rode down the edge-gully so he could take a look at the hive emerging out of the smoke before them. It was big, bigger than any city he'd ever seen, bigger than the bastion towns of Tanith certainly.

He roared ahead, passing the staff cars of the local Commissariat, until he was leading the column down the broken highway towards the docks.

A volley of shells fell into the outhabs to the east. Dorden, the grizzled, elderly chief medic of the Tanith Regiment, heaved himself up to see. Conflagrations, bright and bitter-lemon in colour, sizzled out from the distant detonations. The truck sashayed into a pothole and Dorden was dropped on his arse.

'Why bother?' Dragg asked.

'Say again?' asked the doctor.

Bragg shifted his position in the flat-bed uncomfortably. He was huge, bigger than any other two Ghosts put together. 'We'll get there sooner or later; die there sooner or later. Why bother craning for a view of our doom?'

Dorden looked across at the giant. 'Is the cup half-full or half-empty, Bragg?' he asked.

'What cup?'

'It's hypothetical. Half-full or half-empty?'

'Yeah, but what cup are we talking about?'

'An imaginary cup.'

'What's in it?'

'That doesn't matter.'

'Does to me, doc,' Bragg shrugged.

'I, well, okay... it's got sacra in it. Half-full or half-empty?'

'How much sacra?' Bragg asked.

Dorden opened his mouth once, twice, then sat back again. 'Doesn't matter.'

Bragg pulled out a canvas bottle-flask. 'There's sacra in this,' he announced.

'Thanks, not just yet...' Dorden said, raising his hands as if in surrender.

Bragg, sat opposite him in the shuddering truck, nodded and took a long swig.

Shells wailed down, half a kilometre from the road, close enough to be uncomfortable. Dorden reached out for the flask. 'Ah well, if it's there...'

Sergeant Varl, gripping the iron hand-loops of the truck's flatbed with his whirring mechanical limb, tried to rouse the spirits of his platoon by encouraging a song. A few of them joined unenthusiastically with a verse or two of 'Over the Sky and Far Away' but it soon faltered. When Varl tried another, he was told to shut up, to his face.

Sergeant Varl handled people better than most of the officers in the regiment and he knew when to reprimand and when to back off. He'd been a dog-soldier himself for long enough.

But the mood in his platoon was bad. And Varl knew why. No one wanted this. No one wanted to get in the middle of a hive-war.

The *Magnificat* was waiting at the northern docks as the column rolled in out of the firelit night. All the Hass ferries were working full-stretch to keep the river open and convoy after convoy of military supplies and ammunition were arriving each hour from the Northern Collectives. Troops from Vervun Primary – in blue greatcoats, grey webbing and the distinctive spiked helmets – along with VPHC men, servitors and a good few red-robed clerks and overseers from the Administratum were now controlling the river freight, much to the fury of the regular longshoremen of the Dockmaster Guild. Ecclesiarchy priests had also arrived on the third or fourth day, establishing a permanent prayer-vigil to protect the crossing and make the waterway and the viaduct safe. The hooded clergy were grouped around a brazier at a pier end, chanting and intoning. They were there each time Folik drew the

Magnificat back to the northshore wharves. It seemed they never slept, never rested. He got into the habit of nodding to them every time he slid the ferry in past them. They never responded.

On this night run, Folik expected to take on more supply vehicles and crates, but the house troopers running the dockside had drawn the NorthCol freight trucks aside so that troop transports could move round them and roll down the landing stages.

Folik nursed the ancient turbines into station-keeping as Mincer dropped the ramp.

The first two trucks growled and bounced aboard. Mincer directed them to their deck spaces with a pair of dagger-lamps.

A tall, long-coated figure dropped from the cab of the first truck. He approached longshoreman Folik.

Folik was almost hypnotised by the commissar badge on the peaked cap. An awed smile creased his oil-spattered face and he took off his wool cap out of respect.

'Sir, it's an honour to have you aboard!'

'The pleasure's mine. What's your name?'

'Folik, Imperial hero, sir!'

'I... I had no idea my reputation preceded me this far. Greetings, Folik.'

'It's a true honour, sir, to be able to transport your reinforcement column to Vervunhive.'

'I appreciate the honour, Folik. My first vehicles are aboard. Shall we proceed?'

Folik nodded and shuffled away to get Mincer to unlap the rope coils.

'Commissar Kowle himself uses our boat!' gasped Folik to his crew mate.

'Kowle? Are you sure? The People's Hero?'

'It's him, I tell you, in the flesh, bold as all bastardy, right here on our tub!'

At the rail, Colonel Commissar Ibram Gaunt gazed out from the deck of the *Magnificat* and smiled as he overheard the words.

The *Magnificat* was in mid-stream when the eastern sky lit up brightly. There was a sucking shudder, like a wind-rush over the water. The eastern horizon blazed with a midnight sun.

'What was that?' Mincer cried. A commotion rose from the troops.

Gaunt raised his hand to shield his eyes from the glare as a heat-wash rolled down the river. He knew the blast-effects of a nuclear detonation when he saw it.

'That was the beginning of the end,' he said.

FOUR

HIVE DEATH

'Insanity! Insanity! What kind of war are we fighting?'
— Marshal Edric Croe,
on hearing the news from Vannick

Kowle went directly to House Command when the news was voxed to him. He had been touring the South Curtain and it took him almost an hour to cross the hive back to the Main Spine.

The control auditorium was a chaotic mess. Munitorum clerks, regimental aides and other junior personnel hurried about, gabbling, panicking, relaying reports from the operators manning the main tactical cogitators banked around the lower level of the large, circular chamber. Many Vervun Primary officers and even some VPHC troops were clogging the place too, anxious to find out if the rumours were true.

Kowle pushed past the onlookers at the chamber door and sent many back to their stations with curt words. None argued. They saluted and backed off from him quickly. He crossed the wide floor and then hurried up the ironwork staircase onto the upper deck of the auditorium, where the chiefs of staff were gathered around the vast, luminous chart table. Junior aides and technicians, many bearing important vox reports, made way for him without question.

Marshal Croe presided over the group at the chart table. His eyes were blacker than ever and he had removed his cap, as if the weight of it was too much now. His personal bodyguard, Isak, dressed in an armoured maroon body glove and carrying a shrouded gun, hovered at his shoulder. Vice Marshal Anko, wearing a medal-heavy white ceremonial uniform, stood glowering nearby. He had been attending a formal dinner thrown by House Anko to welcome the Volpone. Sturm and his aides stood alongside him, clad in the impressive dress uniforms of the Volpone. Also present were Xance of NorthCol – looking tired and drawn, along with several of his senior staff – the Narmenian Grizmund and his tank brigadiers, Nash of the Roane Deepers and his adjutants, and a dozen more senior Vervun Primary officers, as well as Commissar Tarrian of the VPHC.

'Is it true?' Kowle asked, removing his cap but making no other formal salute.

Croe nodded, but remained silent.

Tarrian coughed. 'Vannick Hive was destroyed ninety minutes ago.'

'Destroyed?'

'I'm sure you're familiar with the concept, Kowle,' Croe said flatly. 'It's gone.'

'Zoica has levelled it. We have no idea how. They got inside the Shield somehow and used a nuclear device–'

Croe cut Anko off mid-sentence. 'How is not the real issue here, vice marshal! There are any number of "hows" we might debate! The real question is why.'

'I agree, marshal,' General Sturm said. 'We must consider this may not have been deliberate. I've known emplacements destroyed accidentally by the over-ambitious actions of those attacking. Perhaps Zoica meant to take the hive and struck... too hard.'

'Is there any other way of striking when you use atomics?' a calm voice asked from the head of the stairs. The group turned.

'Gaunt...' Colonel Gilbear of the Volpone hissed under his breath.

The tall newcomer wore a commissar's cap and a long, black leather coat. He stepped towards them. His clothing was still flecked with dust from his journey. He saluted Marshal Croe smartly.

'Colonel-Commissar Gaunt, of the Tanith First. We arrived to reinforce you just as the event occurred.'

'I welcome you, Gaunt. I wish I was happier to see you,' the white-haired giant replied respectfully. 'Are your men billeted?'

'They were proceeding to their stations when I left them. I came here as soon as I could.'

'The famous Gaunt,' Anko whispered to Tarrian.

'You mean "notorious," surely?' Tarrian murmured back.

Gaunt stepped up to the chart table, pulling off his gloves and studying the display. Then he looked up and nodded a frank greeting to Nash.

'Well met, general.'

'Good to see you, commissar,' Nash replied. Their forces had served alongside each other on Monthax and there was a genuine, mutual admiration.

Gaunt greeted the Narmenian officers too, then looked over at Sturm, Gilbear and the other Volpone, who stared icily at him.

'General Sturm. Always a pleasure. And Major Gilbear.'

Gilbear was about to blurt out something but Sturm stepped forward, offering his hand to Gaunt.

'Gilbear's bravery on Monthax has earned him a colonel's pips, Gaunt.'

'Well done, Gilbear,' Gaunt smiled broadly. He shook the general's hand firmly.

'Good to know we have more brave, reliable Guard forces here with us, Gaunt. Welcome.'

Gaunt smiled to himself. The last time he had met Sturm in person, back on Voltemand, the pompous ass had been threatening him with court martial. Gaunt had not forgotten that Sturm's callous leadership had resulted in heavy losses in the Ghost ranks from friendly artillery.

You're only putting on this show of comradeship so you can look good in the eyes of the local grandees, Gaunt thought, returning Sturm's gaze with unblinking directness. You are an unspeakable wretch and I regret this place has the likes of you to look after it.

But Gaunt was a political animal as well as a combat leader, and he knew how to play this game as well as any runt general. He said, 'I'm sure our worthy brothers of the Volpone could handle this alone.'

Sturm nodded as the handshake broke, clearly trying to work out if there had been some cloaked insult in Gaunt's compliment.

'From your opening remark, may we presume you believe the loss of Vannick Hive is deliberate?' Kowle stepped forward to face Gaunt. The Imperial commissars nodded a stiff greeting to each other.

'Commissar Kowle, the People's Hero. It's been a long time since Balhaut.'

'But the memories never fade,' Kowle replied.

Gaunt turned away from him. 'Kowle judges my words correctly. The enemy has destroyed Vannick Hive deliberately. Can there be any other explanation for a nuclear event?'

'Suicide,' Grizmund said. 'Overrun, overwhelmed, perhaps a last act of desperation in the face of a victorious foe. A detonation of the hive's power plant.'

Several Vervun officers expressed dismay.

'You are new to Verghast, general, so we will not think badly of your comment,' Tarrian said softly. 'But no Verghastite would be so craven as to self-destruct in the face of the enemy. The hives are everything, praise the Emperor. Through them and their output, we hallow and honour him. Vannick Hive would no more destroy itself than we would.'

Many around the chart table averred.

'Brave words,' Grizmund said. 'But if this hive was conquered, Emperor save us... Would you let it fall into the hands of the enemy?'

Various voices rose in anger, but Gaunt's words cut them to quiet. 'I'm sure the general here is not questioning any loyalties. And he may have a point, but I think it doubtful Vannick Hive succumbed to anything other than an invader's wrath.'

'But why?' barked Croe. 'Again it comes back to this question! Invasion, conquest... I can understand those things! But to destroy what you have fought to take? Where is the sense?'

'Marshal, we must face the darkest truth,' said Gaunt. 'I have studied the data sent to me concerning this theatre. It seems that Commissar Kowle here has reported millions of foe, an assessment that beggars belief, given the proportional mustering capacity of a hive the size of Ferrozoica. The answer is there. Vervunhive can raise half a million from a forty million population. Zoica can only be raising millions from a population a third the size... if the entire population itself is being used.'

'What?' Anko barked, laughing at the idea.

'Go on, commissar,' Croe said.

'This is not a war of conquest. This is not a hive-war, a commercial spat, a new "Trade War", as you refer to it. Zoica is not massing, arming and rising to conquer and control the hive production of this planet or to subjugate its old rival Vervunhive. They are rising to exterminate it.'

'A taint,' murmured General Nash, slowly understanding.

'Quite so,' Gaunt said. 'To turn not just your potential fighting men into an army but your workers and hab families too, that takes a zealot mindset: an infection of insanity, a corruption, a taint. The vile forces of Chaos control Zoica, there can be no doubt. The poison of the warp has overrun your noble neighbour and set every man, woman and child in it on a frenzied path to obliterate the rest of this world and everything on it.'

FIVE

CLOSE QUARTERS

'In war, best know what enemies are around you in your own camp, before you step out to face the foe and wonder why you do so alone.'

– Warmaster Slaydo,
from *A Treatise on the Nature of Warfare*

A party of local troops in blue greatcoats waited for them at the entrance to a dingy shed complex, under the stark-white light of sodium lamps. Their weapons were slung over their shoulders and they wore woollen caps, their spiked helmets dangling from their webbing. They flashed the convoy in through the chain-link gate with dagger-lamps.

Sergeant Mkoll was first into the compound, slewing up his motor-bike on the greasy rockcrete skirt and heeling down the kickstand. The heavy machine leaned to the left and rested, its throaty purr cutting off. Mkoll dismounted as the Tanith troop trucks thundered into the yard after him.

Mkoll looked at the manufactory sheds around them. This was a dismal place, but the Tanith had billeted in worse. Despite the thunder of engines and shouts, he sensed a presence behind him and spun before the other could utter a word.

'Steady!' said the figure approaching behind him. He was a tall, well-made man in his twenties, dressed in the local uniform. A captain, his collar pins said. His right arm was bound up tight to his chest in a padded sling, so he wore his greatcoat on one side only, draping it like a cape over the other. Mkoll thought he was lucky that empty sleeve was not a permanent feature.

Mkoll made a brief salute. 'Sorry, you caught me by surprise. Sergeant Mkoll, 5th Platoon, Tanith First and Only.'

The captain saluted back stiffly with his left hand. Mkoll noticed he was also limping and there were sallow bruises along his forehead, cheek and around his eyes. 'Captain Ban Daur, Vervun Primary. Welcome to Vervunhive.'

Mkoll grunted a curt laugh. He'd never been personally welcomed to a warzone before.

'Can you introduce me to your commanding officer?' Daur asked. 'I've been given the job of supervising your billet. Not much good for anything else.' He said this with a rueful chuckle and a glance down at his slinged arm.

Mkoll fell in step beside him and they moved through a commotion of men, trucks, diesel fumes and unloading work. They made small, intense, flickering shadows under the harsh lighting gantries overhead.

'You've seen action already?' asked Mkoll.

'Nothing to get me a medal,' Daur said. 'I was on the ramparts on the first day when the shelling began. Didn't so much as even see what to shoot at before they took my position down and buried me in rubble. Be a few weeks yet till I'm fit, but I wanted to be useful, so I volunteered for liaison work.'

'So you've not even seen the enemy yet?'

Daur shook his head. 'Except for People's Hero Kowle and a few others who made it back from the grasslands, no one has.'

Corbec was standing by his truck, smoking a cigar, gazing placidly around the place, oblivious to the frenzy of activity all about him. He turned slowly, taking in the sheer scale of the hive around him, beyond the glare of the sodium lamp rigs: the towering manufactories and smelteries, the steeples of the work habs beyond them, then the great crest of some Ecclesiarch basilica, and behind it all, the vast structure of the Main Spine, a mind-numbingly huge bulk illuminated by a million or more windows. Big as a fething mountain peak back home on...

On nowhere. He still forgot, sometimes.

His eyes were drawn to a vast pylon near the Main Spine which rose just as high as the hive-mountain. It seemed to mark the heart of the whole city-hub. Storms of crackling energy flared from its apex, spreading out to feed the flickering green shield that over-arched it all. Corbec had never seen a shield effect this big before. It was quite something. He gazed south and saw the rippling light flashes of shells falling across the Shield, deflecting and exploding harmlessly. Quite something indeed and it looked like it worked.

He took another drag on his cigar and the coal glowed red. The sheer size of this place was going to take a lot of getting used to. He had seen how most of his boys had been struck dumb as they entered the hive, gaping up at the monumental architecture. He knew he had to beat that awe out of them as quickly as possible, or they'd be too busy gazing dumbly to fight.

'Put that out!' a voice ordered crisply behind him.

Corbec turned and for a moment he thought it was Gaunt. But only for a moment. The commissar stalking towards him had nothing of Gaunt's presence. He had local insignia and his puffy face was pale and unhealthy. Corbec said nothing but simply took the cigar from his mouth and raised one eyebrow. He was a good twenty-five centimetres taller than the black-coated officer.

The man halted a few paces short, taking in the sheer size of Colm Corbec. 'Commissar Langana, VPHC. This is a secure area. Put that gakking light out!'

Corbec put the cigar back between his lips and, still silent, tapped the colonel's rank pins on his shoulder braid.

'I...' the man began. Then, thinking better of everything, turned and stalked away.

'Colonel?'

Mkoll was approaching with another local, thankfully regular army-issue rather than one of the tight-arsed political cadre.

'This is Captain Daur, our liaison officer.' Daur snapped his heels together as well as any man with a leg-wound could, and saluted with his left hand. He blinked in surprise when Corbec held out his own left hand without hesitation. Then he shook it. The grip was tight. Daur immediately warmed to this bearded, tattooed brute. He'd taken Daur's injury in at a glance and compensated without any comment.

'Welcome to Vervunhive, colonel,' Daur said.

'Can't say I'm glad to be here, captain, but a war's a war, and we go where the Emperor wills us. Did you arrange these billets?'

Daur glanced around at the mouldering sheds where the Tanith First were breaking out their kits and lighting lamps in neat platoon order.

'No, sir,' he replied sheepishly. 'I wanted better. But space is at a premium in the hive just now.'

Corbec chuckled. 'In a place this big?'

'We have been overrun with refugees and wounded from the south. All free areas such as the Commercia, the Landing Field and the manufactories have been opened to house them. I actually requested some superior space for your men in the lower Main Spine, but Vice Marshal Anko instructed that you should be barracked closer to the Curtain Wall. So this is it. Gavunda Chem Plant Storebarns/Southwest. For what it's worth.'

Corbec nodded. Lousy chem plant barns for the Tanith Ghosts. He was prepared to bet a month's pay the Volpone Bluebloods weren't bedding down in some sooty hangar this night.

'We've cleared seven thousand square metres in these sheds for you and I can annex more if you need room to stack supplies.'

'No need,' Corbec said. 'We're only one regiment. We won't take much space.'

Daur led them both into the main hangar space where most of the Ghosts were preparing their billets. Through an open shutter, Corbec could see into another wide shed where the rest were making camp.

'My men have dug latrines over there and there are a number of worker washrooms and facilities still operational in the sheds to the left.' Daur pointed these features out in turn. 'So far, the main water supplies are still on, so the showers work. But I took the liberty of setting up water and fuel bowsers in case the supplies go down.'

Corbec looked where Daur indicated and saw a row of tanker trucks with fuel clamps and standpipes grouped by the western fence.

'Sheds three, four and five are loaded with food and perishable supplies, and munitions orders will arrive by daybreak. House Command has requisitioned another barn over there from House Anko for use as your medical centre.'

Corbec gazed across at the rickety long-shed Daur pointed to. 'Get Dorden to check it out, Mkoll,' he said. Mkoll flagged down a passing trooper and sent him off to find the chief medic.

'I've also set up primary and secondary vox-links in the side offices here,' said Daur as he led them through a low door into what had once been the factory supervisor's suite. The rooms were thick with dust and cobwebs, but two deep-gain vox units were mounted on scrubbed benches along one wall, flickering and active, chattering with staccato dribbles of link-talk. There were even fresh paper rolls and lead-sticks laid out near the sets. The thoroughness made Corbec smile. Maybe it was the worker-mentality of the hive.

'I assumed you'd use this as your quarters,' Daur said. He showed Corbec a side office with a cot and a folding desk. Corbec glanced in, nodded and turned back to face the captain.

'I'd say you had made us welcome indeed, Daur, despite the facilities granted us by your hive-masters. Looks like you've thought of everything. I won't forget your trouble in a hurry.'

Daur nodded, pleased.

Corbec stepped out of the offices and raised his voice. 'Sergeant Varl!'

Varl stopped what he was doing and came across the hangar space double-time, threading between billeting Tanith. 'Colonel?'

'Rejoice. You've won the supplies duty. Those sheds there,' Corbec glanced at Daur for confirmation, 'are for storage. Raise a detail and get our stuff housed from the trucks.'

Varl nodded and strode off, calling up volunteers.

With Daur and Mkoll beside him, Corbec surveyed the activity in the billet. 'Looks like the Ghosts are making themselves at home,' he murmured to no one in particular.

'Ghosts? Why do you call them that? Where are you from?' Daur asked.

'Tanith,' Mkoll said.

Corbec smiled sadly and contradicted the sergeant. 'Nowhere, Captain Daur. We're from nowhere and that's why we're ghosts.'

'This is the only space available,' Commissar Langana said flatly.

'Not good enough,' Dorden said, looking around the dimly-lit hangar, taking in the shattered windows, the piles of refuse and the layers of dust. 'I can't make a field hospital in here. The filth will kill more of my regiment than the enemy.'

The VPHC officer looked round sourly at the doctor. 'The vice marshal's orders were quite specific. This area is designated for medical needs.'

'We could clean up,' Trooper Lesp suggested. A thin, hangdog man, Lesp was skulking to one side in the doorway with Chayker and Foskin. The three of them represented Dorden's medical orderlies, troopers who had been trained for field hospital work by the chief medic himself. Gherran and Mtane, the only other fully qualified medics in the unit, were looking around behind them.

'With what?' Dorden asked. 'By the time we've scoured this place clean, the war will be over.'

Lesp shrugged.

'You must make do. This is war,' Langana announced. 'War levels all stations and makes us work with the bravery in our limbs and the ingenuity in our minds.'

Dorden turned his grizzled face to look directly into the puffy visage of the political officer. 'Do you make that crap up yourself, or does someone write it down for you?'

The orderlies behind him tried to cover their sniggers. Gherran and Mtane laughed out loud.

'I could break you for such insolence!' Langana spat. Anger made his cheeks florid.

'Hmm?' Dorden replied, not seeming to hear. 'And deprive an Imperial Guard regiment of their chief medic? Your vice marshal wouldn't be too happy to hear about that, would he?'

Langana was about to retort when a strong, female voice echoed through the dirty space.

'I'm looking for the doctor! Hello?'

Dorden pushed past the seething commissar and went to the door. He was met by a short, slim, young woman in a form-fitting red uniform with embroidered cuffs. She carried a medical pack over one shoulder and was escorted by five more dressed like her: three men and two women.

'Dorden, chief medical officer, Tanith First.'

'Surgeon Ana Curth, Inner Hab Collective Medical Hall 67/mv,' she replied, nodding to him and glancing around the dingy hall. 'Captain Daur, your liaison officer, was troubled by the state of the facilities and called my hall for support.'

'As you can see, Ana, it is a long way short of adequate,' said Dorden with a gentle gesture that took in the decay.

She frowned at him briefly. His use of her forename surprised her. Such informalities were rare in the hive. It was discourteous, almost condescending. She'd worked for her status and position as hard as any other hiver.

'That's Surgeon Curth, medic.'

Dorden looked round at the woman, surprised, clearly hurt that he had offended her in any way. Behind Dorden, Langana smiled.

'My mistake. Surgeon Curth, indeed,' Dorden looked away. 'Well, as you can see, this is no place for wounded. Can you possibly... assist us?'

She looked him up and down, still bristling but calming a little. There was something in his tired, avuncular manner that made her almost regret her tone. This was not some bravo trooper trying to hit on her. This was an old man with slumping shoulders. There was a weariness in his manner that no amount of sleep could ease. His lined eyes had seen too much, she realised.

Ana Curth turned to Langana. 'I wouldn't treat cattle in a place like this. I'm issuing an M-notice on it at once.'

'You can't–' Langana began.

'Oh, yes I can, commissar! Fifth Bill of Rights, Amendment 457/ hj: "In event of conflict, surgeon staff may commandeer all available resources for the furtherance of competent medical work." I want scrub teams from the hive sanitation department here by morning, with pressure hoses and steam scourers. I want disinfectant sluices. I want sixty cots, bedding, four theatre tables with lights, screens and instruments, flak-board lagging for the walls and windows, proper light-power, water and heat-links recoupled, and patches made to the gakking roof! Got it?'

'I–'

'Do you understand me, Political Officer Langana?'

Langana hesitated. 'I will have to call House Command for these requirements.'

'Do so!' barked Curth.

Dorden looked on. He liked her already.

'Use my hive caste-code: 678/cu. Got it? That will give you the authority to process my request. And do it now, Langana!'

The commissar saluted briefly and then marched away out of the chamber. He had to push through the smirking Tanith orderlies to exit.

Dorden turned to the woman. 'My thanks, Surgeon Curth. The Tanith are in your debt.'

'Just do your job and we'll get on fine,' she replied bluntly. 'I have more wounded refugees in my hall now than I can deal with. I don't want your overspill submerging me when the fighting starts.'

'Of course you don't. I am grateful, surgeon.'

Dorden fixed her with an honest smile. She seemed about to soften and smile back, but she turned and led her team away out of the door. 'We'll return in two days to help you set up.'

'Surgeon?'

She stopped, turning back.

'How overrun are you? With the wounded, I mean?'

She sighed. 'To breaking point.'

'Could you use six more trained staff?' Dorden asked. He waved casually at his fellow medics and waiting orderlies. 'We have no wounded yet to treat, Emperor watch us. Until we have, we would be happy to assist.'

Curth glanced at her chief orderly. 'Thank you. Your offer is appreciated. Follow us, please.'

Varl supervised the store detail, carrying more than his share thanks to the power of his artificial arm. With a team of thirty, he ordered the stacking and layout of the Tanith supplies. There was plenty of stuff in the barn already, well marked and identified by the triplicate manifest data-slates, but there was still more than enough room for the supplies and munitions they had brought with them.

Another truck backed up to the doorway, lights winking, and Domor, Cocoer and Brostin helped to shift the crates of perishables to their appointed stacks. Varl allocated another area for the munitions he had been told would arrive later.

Caffran looked up as the sergeant called to him. 'Sweep the back,' Varl ordered. 'Make sure the rear of the barn is secure.'

Caffran nodded, pulling his jacket and camo-cape from a nearby crate-pile and putting them back on. He was still sweat-hot from the

DAN ABNETT

work. Lifting his lasgun, he paced round the rear of the supply stacks, moving through the darkness and shadows, checking the rotting rear wall of the hangar for holes.

Something scurried in the dark.

He swung his gun round. Rodents?

There was no further movement. Caffran edged forward and noticed the edge of a crate that had been chewed away. The plastic-wrapped packets of dried biscuit inside had been invaded. Definitely rodents. There was a trail of crumbs and shreds of plastic seal. They'd have to set traps – and poison too probably.

He paused. The hole in the crate's side was far too high to be the work of rodents. Unless they bred something the size of a hound in the sewers of this place. That wouldn't surprise him, given the giant scale of everything else here in Vervunhive.

He armed his lasgun and slid around the edge of the next stack.

Something scurried again.

He hastened forward, gun raised, looking for a target. Feth, maybe the local vermin would be good eating. They'd had precious little fresh meat in the last forty days.

There was a movement to his left and he dropped to one knee, taking aim. Beyond the supply stacks, there was a pale, green slice of light, a jagged hole in the back of the barn through which the glow of the Shield high above leaked in.

Caffran shuffled forward.

A noise to the right.

He spun around. Nothing. He saw how several more crates had been clawed into.

Something flickered past the slice of light, something moving through it quickly, blocking out the glow.

Caffran ran forward, pulling himself sideways through the gap in the rotten fibre-planks of the hangar's rear wall and out into the tangled waste of debris and rubble behind the storage barn.

He crawled out, got down, raised his gun...

And saw the boy. A small boy, eight or nine years old it seemed to Caffran, scampering up a mound of rubble with a wrap of biscuits in his hand.

The boy reached the summit and another figure loomed out of the dark. A girl, older, in her late teens, clad in vulgar rags and decorated with piercings. She took the wrap from the boy and hugged him tightly.

Caffran got up, lowering his gun. 'Hey!' he called.

The child and the girl looked round at him sharply, like animals caught in a huntsman's light.

Caffran saw for just a moment the strong, fierce, beautiful face of the girl before the children ducked out of sight and vanished into the wasteland.

He ran up the slope after them, but they were gone.

In a foxhole a hundred metres away from the back of the storage barns, Tona Criid hugged Dalin to her and willed him to be quiet.

'Good boy, good boy,' she murmured. She took out the biscuits and tore the wrap open so he could have one.

Dalin wolfed it down. He was hungry. They were all hungry out here.

Nutrient clouds pumped into the Iron Tank fed the dreaming High Master of Vervunhive. He rolled in his oily fluid womb, pulling at his link feeds, feet and hands twitching like a dreaming dog. He dreamed of the Trade War, before his birth. The images of his dream were informed by the pict-library he had studied in his youth. He dreamed of his illustrious predecessor, the great Heironymo, haughtily spurning the rivalry with Ferrozoica, arming for war. How wrong, how very foolish! Such a grossly physical stubbornness! And the hive held him in such esteem for his heroic leadership! Fools! Cattle! Unthinking chaff!

Commerce is always war. But the war of commerce may be fought in such subtle, exquisite ways. To raise arms, to mobilise bodies, to turn beautiful hive profits into war machines and guns, rations and ammunition...

What a pathetic mind, Heironymo! How blind of you to miss the real avenues of victory! House Clatch would have bowed to mercantile embargoes long before the brave boys of Vervun Primary had overturned the walls of Zoica! A concession here, a bargain there, a stifling of funds or supplies, a blockade...

Salvador Sondar floated upwards, his dreams now machine-language landscapes of autoledgers, contoured ziggurats of mounted interest values, rivers of exchange rates, terraces of production value outputs.

The mathematical vistas of mercantile triumph he adored more than any other place in the universe.

He twitched again in the warm soup, iridescent bubbles coating his shrunken limbs and fluttering to the roof of the Iron Tank. He was pleased now that he had killed the old man. Heironymo had ruled too long! A hundred and twenty years old, beloved by the stupid, vapid public, still unwilling to make way for his twenty year-old nephew and obvious successor! It had been a merciful act, Salvador dreamed to himself, though the guilt of it had plagued him for the last fifty years. His sleeping features winced.

Yes, it had been merciful... for the good of the hive and for the further prosperity of House Sondar, noble line! Had output not tripled during his reign? And now Gnide and Croe and Chass and the other weaklings told him that mercantile war was no longer an option! Fools!

Gnide...

Now... he was dead, wasn't he?

And Slaydo too? The great warmaster, dead of poison. No, that wasn't right. Stabbed on the carpet of the audience hall... no... no...

Why were his dreams so confused? It was the chatter. That was it. The chatter. He wished it would cease. It was a hindrance to reason. He was High Master of Vervunhive and he wanted his dream-mind clean and unpolluted so he could command his vast community to victory once more.

The Shield? What? What about the Shield?

The chatter was lisping something.

No! N-n–

Salvador Sondar's dreams were suddenly as suspended as the dreamer for a moment. Fugue state snarled his dream-mind. He floated in the tank as if dead.

Then the dreams resumed in a rush. To poison the servitor taster, that had been a stroke of genius! No one had ever suspected! And to use a neural toxin that left no trace. A stroke, they had said! A stroke had finally levelled old Heironymo! Salvador had been forced to inject his own tear glands with saline to make himself cry at the state funeral.

The weeping! The mass mourning! Fifty years ago, but still it gnawed at him! Why had the hivers loved the old bastard so dearly?

The chatter was there again, at the very boundary of his mind-impulse limit, like crows in a distant treeline at dawn, like insects in the grass-lands at dusk.

Chattering...

The Shield? What are you saying about the Shield?

I am Salvador Sondar. Get out of my mind and–

The wasted body twitched and spasmed in the Iron Tank.

Outside, the servitors jiggled and jerked in sympathy.

The vast railhead terminal at Veyveyr Gate was a dank, blackened mess. Clouds of steam rolled like fog off the cooling rubble and tangled metal where millions of litres of fluid retardant had been sprayed on the incendiary fires to get them under control.

Major Jun Racine of the Vervun Primary moved between the strug-gling work teams and tried to supervise the clearance work. Tried... it was a joke. He had two hundred bodies, mostly enlisted men, but some Administratum labourers, as well as trackwrights and rolling-stock stewards from the Rail Guild. It was barely enough even to make a dent in destruction of this scale.

Racine was no structural engineer. Even with fourteen heavy tractors fitted with dozer blades at his disposal, there was no way he was going to meet House Command's orders and get the railhead secure in three days. Great roof sections had slumped like collapsed egg-shell, and rockcrete pillars had crumpled and folded like soft candy-sticks. He was reluctant to instruct his men to dig out anything for fear of bringing more down. Already he had sent five men to the medical halls after a section of wall had toppled on them.

The air was wet and acrid, and water dripped down from every surface, pooling five centimetres deep on any open flooring.

Racine checked his data-slate again. The cold, basic schematics on its screen simply didn't match anything here in real life. He couldn't even locate the positions of the main power and gas-feed mains. Nearby, a rail tractor unit sat up-ended in a vast crater, its piston wheels dangling off its great black iron shape. What if fuel had leaked from it? Racine thought about leaked fuel, shorting electrics, spilling gas – even unexploded bombs – an awful lot. He did the maths and hated the answer he kept getting.

'Tough job, major,' said a voice from behind him.

Racine turned. The speaker was a short, bulky man in his fifties, black with grime and leaning on an axe-rack as a crutch. He had a serious eye-wound bandaged with a filthy strip of linen. But his clothes, as far as Racine could make out under the char and the dirt, were those of a smeltery gang boss.

'You shouldn't be here, friend,' Racine said with a patient smile.

'None of us should,' Agun Soric replied, stomping forward. He stood beside Racine and they both gazed dismally out over the tangled ruins of the railhead towards the vast, looming shape of the gate and the Curtain Wall. It was a sea of rubble and debris, and Racine's workforce moved like ants around the merest breakwaters of it.

'I didn't ask for this. I'm sure you didn't either,' Soric said.

'Gak, but that's right! You from the refuges?'

'Name's Soric, plant supervisor, Vervun Smeltery One.' Soric made a brief gesture over at the vast, ruined shell of the once-proud ore plant adjacent to the railhead. 'I was in there when the shells took it. Quite a show.'

'I'll bet. Get many out?'

Soric sucked air through his teeth and looked down, shaking his bullet-head. 'Not nearly enough. Three hundred, maybe. Got ourselves places in a refuge – eventually. It was all a bit confused.'

Racine looked round at him, taking in the set power and simmering anger inside the hive worker. 'What's it like? I hear the refuges are choked to capacity.'

'It's bad. Imagine this,' Soric pointed to the railhead destruction, 'but the ruins are human, not rockcrete and ceramite. Supplies are short: food, clean water, medical aid. They're doing their best, but you know – millions of homeless, most of them hurt, all of them scared.'

Racine shivered.

'I tried to get some aid for my workers, but they told me that all refugees were set on fourth-scale rations unless they were employed in the hive war effort. That might get them bumped up to third-scale, maybe even second.'

'Tough times...' Racine said and they fell silent.

'What if I could bring you close on three hundred eager workers? Willing types, I mean, workers who can haul and labour and who know a bit about shifting and managing loose debris?'

'To help out?'

'Gak, yes! My mob are sick of sitting on their arses in the refuge, doing nothing. We could help you make a job of this.'

Racine looked at him cautiously, trying to see if there was a trick. 'For the good of the hive?' he smiled, questioningly.

'Yeah, for the good of the hive. And for the good of my workers, before they go crazy and lose morale. And I figure if we help you, you could put in a word. Maybe get us a better ration scale.'

Racine hesitated. His vox link was beeping. It would be a call from House Command, he was sure, asking for a progress report.

'I need to get this cleared, or at least a path cleared through it. My regiment have the gate blocked temporarily, but if the enemy hits us there, we need to have a secure wall of defence dug in, with supply lines and troop access. You and your mob help me do that, I'll get your bloody ration scale for you.'

Soric smiled. He tucked the axe-rack crutch under his armpit so he could extend a dirty hand. Racine shook it.

'Vervun Smeltery One won't let you down, major.'

The chronometer's chime told him it was dawn, but even up here in the Mid Spine, there was little change in the light outside. The glow of the Shield and the smoke haze saw to that.

Amchanduste Worlin took breakfast in the observation bubble of his clan's palace. He had risen earlier than any of his kin, though junior

Guild Worlin clerics and servitors were already about, preparing the day's work protocols.

In orange-silk night robes, he sat in a suspensor chair at the round mahogany table and consumed the breakfast his servants had brought him on a lacquered tray. The taster servitor had pronounced it safe and been dismissed. Worlin's attention oscillated between the panoramic view of the city outside and the data-plate built into the table top where the morning news and situation bulletins threaded and interwove in clusters of glowing runes.

An egg soufflé, smoked fish, fresh fruit, toasted wheatcakes and a jug of caffeine. Not recommended emergency rations, Worlin knew, but what was the point of being a member of the privileged merchant elite if you couldn't draw on the stockpiles of your clan's resources once in a while?

He improved the caffeine with a shot of joiliq. Worlin felt a measure of contentment for the first time in days and it wasn't just the alcohol. There was one holding owned by House Worlin, one under his direct control, that gave them commercial leverage in this war: liquid fuel. He had quite forgotten it in his initial dismay and panic.

Last season, he had won the fuel concession from Guild Farnora, much to his clan's delight. Thirty per cent of the fuel imports from Vannick Hive, three whole pipelines, were under the direct control of Guild Worlin. He looked at the megalitre input figures on his data-slate, then made a few calculations as to how the market price per barrel would soar exponentially with each day of conflict. He'd done the sums several times already, but they pleased him.

'Guild sire?' His private clerk, Magnal, entered the bubble.

'What is it?'

'I was just preparing your itinerary for the day. You have a bond-meeting with the Guild Council at eleven.'

'I know.'

Magnal paused.

'Something else?'

'I... I brought you the directive from the Legislature last night. The one that ordered all fuel pipelines from Vannick closed off now our kin-hive has fallen. You... you do not seem to have authorised the closure, guild sire.'

'The closure...'

'All guilds controlling fuel are ordered to blow the pipes on the north shore and block any remaining stretches with rockcrete.' Magnal tried to show a data slate to Worlin, but the guilder shrugged it away diffidently. 'Our work crews are standing by...'

'How much fuel have we stockpiled in our East Hass Storage facility?' Worlin asked.

Magnal muttered a considerable figure.

'And how much more is still coming through the pipe?'

Another murmur, a figure of magnitude.

Worlin nodded. 'I deplore the loss of our Vannick cousins. But the fuel still comes through. It is the duty Guild Worlin owes to Vervunhive that we keep the pipes open for as long as there is a resource to be collected. I'll shut the pipes the moment they run dry.'

'But the directive, guild sire...'

'Let me worry about that, Magnal. The flow may only last another day, another few hours. But if I close now, can you imagine the lost profits? Not good business, my friend. Not good at all.'

Magnal looked uncomfortable.

'They say there is a security issue here, guild sire...'

Worlin put down his caffeine cup. It hit the saucer a little too hard, making Magnal jump, though the kindly smile never left Worlin's face. 'I am not a stupid man, clerk. I take my responsibilities seriously, to the hive, to my clan. If I close the lines now, I would be derelict in my duties to both. Let the soldiery gain glory with their bravado at the war front. History will relate my bravery here, fighting for Vervunhive as only a merchant can.'

'Your name will be remembered, guild sire,' Magnal said and left the room.

Worlin sat for a while, tapping his silver sugar tongs on the edge of his saucer. There was no doubt about it.

He would have to kill Magnal too.

At the very southernmost edge of the outer habs and industry sectors, the great hive was a sky-filling dome of green light, pale in the morning sun, hazed by shell smoke.

Captain Olin Fencer of Vervun Primary crawled from his dug-out and blinked into the cold morning air. That air was still thick with the mingled reeks of thermite and fycelene, burning fuel and burned flesh. But there was something different about this morning. He couldn't quite work out what it was.

Fencer's squad of fifty troopers had been stationed at Outhab Southwest when the whole thing began. Vox links had been lost in the first wave of shelling and they had been able to do nothing but dig in and ride it out, as day after day of systematic bombardment flattened and ruptured the industrial outer city behind them.

There was no chance to retreat back into the hive, though Fencer knew millions of habbers in the district had fled that way. He had a post to hold. He was stationed at it with the thirty-three men remaining to him when Vegolain's armoured column had rolled past down the Southern Highway, out into the grasslands. His squad had cheered them.

They'd been hiding in their bunkers, some weeping in rage or pain or dismay, that night when the broken remnants of the column had limped back in, heading for the city.

By then, he had twenty men left.

In the days that followed, Fencer had issued his own orders by necessity, as all links to House Command were broken. Indeed, he was sure no one in the hive believed there was anyone still alive out here. He had followed the edicts of the Vervun Primary emergency combat protocols to the letter, organising the digging of a series of trenches, supply lines and fortifications through the ruins of the outhabs, though the shelling still fell on them.

His first sergeant, Grosslyn, had mined the roadways and other teams had dug tank-traps and dead-snares. Despite the shelling, they had also raised a three hundred-metre bulwark of earth, filled an advance ditch with iron stakes and railing sections, and sandbagged three stubbers and two flamers into positions along the Highway.

All by the tenth day. By then, he had eighteen soldiers left.

Three more had died of wounds or disease by the fourteenth day, when the high-orbit flares of troopships told them Guard reinforcements were on their way planetside.

Now it was sunrise on the nineteenth day. Plastered in dust and blood, Fencer moved down the main trench position as his soldiers woke or took over guard duty from the weary night sentries.

But now he had sixty troops. Main Spine thought everything was levelled out here, everything dead, but they were wrong. Not everyone on the blasted outer habs had fled to the hive, though it must have seemed that way. Many stayed, too unwilling, too stubborn, or simply too frightened to move. As the days of bombardment continued, Fencer found men and women – and some children too – flocking to him from the ruins. He got the non-coms into any bunkers he had available and he set careful rationing. All able-bodied workers, of either sex, he recruited into his vanguard battalion.

They'd raised precious medical supplies from the infirmary unit of a bombed-out mine and they'd set up a field hospital in the ruins of a bakery, under the supervision of a teenage girl called Nessa who was a trainee nurse. They'd pilfered food supplies in the canteens of three ruined manufactories in the region. A VPHC Guard House on West

Transit 567/kl had provided them with a stock of lasguns and small arms for the new recruits, as well as explosives and one of the flamers.

Fencer's recruits had come from everywhere. He had under his command clerks who'd never held a weapon, loom workers with poor eyesight and shell-shocked habbers who were deaf and could only take orders visually.

The core of his recruits, the best of them, were twenty-one miners from Number Seventeen Deep Working, who had literally dug their way out of the ground after the main lift shaft of their facility had fallen.

Fencer bent low and hurried down the trench line, passing through blown-out house structures, under fallen derricks, along short communication tunnels the miners had dug to link his defences. Their expertise had been a godsend.

He reached the second stub emplacement at 567/kk and nodded to the crew. Corporal Gannen was making soup in his mess tin over a burner stove, while his crewmate, a loom-girl called Calie, scanned the horizon. They were a perfect example of the way necessity had made heroes of them all. Gannen was a trained stub-gunner, but better at ammo feeding than firing. The girl had proven to be a natural at handling the gun itself. So they swapped, the corporal conceding no pride that he now fed ammo to a loom-girl half his age.

Fencer moved on, passing two more guard points and found Gol Kolea in the corner nest, overlooking the highway. Kolea, the natural leader of the miners, was a big man, with great power in his upper body. He was sipping hot water from a battered tin cup, his lasgun at his side. Fencer intended to give him a brevet rank soon. The man had earned it. He had led his miners out of the dark, formed them into a cohesive work duty and done everything Fencer could have asked of them. And more besides. Kolea was driven by grim, intense fury against the Zoican foe. He had family in the hive, though he didn't speak of them. Fencer was sure it was the thought of them that had galvanised Kolea to such efforts.

'Captain,' Kolea nodded as Fencer ducked in.

'Something's wrong, Gol,' Fencer said. 'Something's different.'

The powerfully built miner grinned at him. 'You haven't noticed?' he asked.

'Noticed?'

'The shelling has stopped.'

Fencer was stunned. It had been so much a part of their daily life for the last fortnight or more, he hadn't realised it had gone. Indeed, his ears were still ringing with remembered shockwaves.

'Emperor save us!' he gasped. 'I'm so stupid.'

He'd been awake for upwards of twenty minutes and it took a miner to tell him that they were no longer under fire.

'See anything?' Fencer asked, crawling up to the vigil slot in the sandbags next to Kolea for a look.

'No. Dust, smoke, haze... nothing much.'

Fencer was about to reach for his scope when Zoica began its land offensive.

A wave of las-fire peppered the entire defence line of the outhabs, like the flashes of a billion firecrackers. The sheer scale of the salvos was bewildering. Nine of Fencer's troops died instantly. Three more, all workers, fled, utterly unprepared for the fury of a land assault.

Grenades and rockets dropped in around them, blowing out two communication dug-outs. Another hit the mess hall and torched their precious food supplies.

Fencer's people began their resistance.

He'd ordered them all to set weapons for single fire to preserve ammunition and power cells. Even the stubbers had been ordered only to fire if they had a target. In response to the Zoican assault, their return seemed meagre and frail.

Fencer got up to the nest top and raised his lasgun. Five hundred metres ahead, through the smoke and the rubble, he saw the first shapes of the enemy, troopers in heavy, ochre-coloured battledress, advancing in steady ranks.

Fencer began firing. Below, Kolea opened up too.

They took thirteen down between them in the first five minutes.

Zoican tanks, mottled ochre and growling like beasts, bellied up the road and fanned out into the ruins, using the available open roadways and other aisles in the rubble sea. Mines took two of them out in huge vomits of flame and armour pieces, and the burning hulks blocked the advance of six more.

Rockets flailed into the bulwark and blew a fifteen-metre section out. Corporal Tanik and three other troops were disintegrated.

Another Zoican tank, covered with mesh netting, rumbled through the ruins and diverted down a dead-snare. Blocked in by rockcrete walls to either side and ahead, it tried to reverse and swing its turret as one of the Vervun flamer positions washed it with incandescent gusts of blowtorch fire and cooked it apart.

Sergeant Grosslyn, with two Vervun Primary regulars and six enlisted habbers, cut a crossfire down at Zoican troops trying to scramble a staked ditch on the eastern end of the file. Between them, they killed fifty or more, many impaled on the railings and wire. When Jada, the female worker next to him, was hit in the chest and dropped, screaming,

Grosslyn turned to try and help her. A las-round from one of the dying Zoican assault troops impaled on the stakes took the back of his head off.

Gannen and Calie held the west transit for two hours, taking out dozens of the enemy and at least one armoured vehicle which ruptured and blew out as the loom-girl raked it with armour-piercing stub rounds.

Gannen was torn apart by shrapnel from a rocket when the enemy pushed around to the left.

Calie kept firing, feeding her own gun until a tank round blew her, her stub gun and twenty metres of the defence bulwark into the sky.

Overwhelmed, Fencer's force fell back into the ruins of the outhab. Some were crushed by the advancing armour. One enlisted clerk, dying of blood-loss from a boltwound, made a suicide run with a belt of grenades and took out a stationary tank. The explosion lit up the low clouds and scraps of tank metal rained down over the surrounding streets.

Others fought a last-ditch attempt as the sheer numbers of the advancing infantry overran them. There were insane pockets of close fighting, bayonet to bayonet, hand to hand. Not a metre of Vervunhive's outhab territory was given up without the most horrific effort.

Gol Kolea, his las weapon exhausted, met the enemy at the barricade and killed them one by one, to left and right, with savage swings of his axe-rake. He screamed his wife's name with every blow.

A las-round punctured Captain Olin Fencer's body at the hip and exited through his opposite shoulder. As he fell, weeping, he clicked his lasgun to autofire and sprayed his massing killers with laser rounds.

His hand was still squeezing the trigger when the pack ran out.

By then, he was already dead.

SIX

CHAINS OF COMMAND

'A war waged by committee is a war already lost.'
— Sebastian Thor, *Sermons*, vol. XV, ch. DIV

Gaunt felt the monumental bulk of the Curtain Wall around him actually vibrate. The shellfire falling against its outer skin was a dull roar.

Captain Daur and three other officers of the liaison staff led the oversight party up the stair-drum of a secondary tower in the wall just west of the massive Heironymo Sondar Gate. Gaunt had brought Rawne and Mkoll, with Trooper Milo as his adjutant. General Grizmund – with three of his senior Narmenians – and General Nash – with two of his regimental aides – made up the rest of the party, along with Tarrian of the VPHC. They had a bodyguard detail of thirty Vervun Primary troopers in full battledress.

The oversight party emerged onto the tower-top, where hot breezes, stifling with fycelene fumes, billowed over them. Three missile launchers were raised and ready here, their crews standing by, but additional awnings of flak-board had been erected in preparation for the visit of the dignitaries, and the launchers, with no safe room for their exhaust wash under this extra sholtor, had fallen silent. The crews saluted the visitors smartly.

'These are for our benefit?' Gaunt asked Tarrian, indicating the freshly raised awnings.

'Of course.'

'You muzzle an entire defence tower so we can get a safe peek over the Wall?'

Tarrian frowned. 'General Sturm has made it a standing requirement every time he visits the Wall. I presumed you and the other eminent generals here would expect the same.'

'We've come to fight, not hide. Take them down and get these crews operational.'

Tarrian looked round at Nash and Grizmund. The Narmenian nodded briefly. 'Gaunt speaks for us all,' said Nash dryly. 'We don't need any soft-soap.'

Tarrian turned from the group and began issuing orders to the launcher crews.

The rest of the oversight party approached the rampart and took up magnoculars or used the available viewscopes on their tripod stands. Milo handed Gaunt his own scope from its pouch and the commissar dialled the magnification as he raised it and gazed out.

Below them, the miserable wasteland of the southern outer habs lay exposed and broken. There was no discernible sign of life, but a hateful storm of enemy shelling and missiles pounded in across it at the hive. A fair amount fell short into the habs, but a good percentage struck the Curtain Wall itself. Gaunt craned over for a moment, training his scope down the gentle slope of the Wall. Its adamantine surface was peppered and scarred like the face of a moon, as far as he could see. Every few seconds, batteries to either side of them on the Wall fired out, or the great siege guns in the emplacements below in the thickness of the Wall recoiled and volleyed again.

The vibration of the Wall continued.

'No way of knowing numbers or scale–' began Nash.

Grizmund shook his head. 'Not so, sir,' he replied, pointing out to the very edge of the vast, outer-hab waste. 'As we have been told, this is no longer the work of their long-range artillery out in the grasslands. This is ground assault from closer range – armour moving in through the outer habitations and factories.'

'Are you certain?' asked Gaunt.

'You can see the flashes of tank cannons as they fire. Four, five kilometres out, in the very skirts of the outer habs. Their weapons are on full elevation for maximum range, so the muzzle-flashes are high and exposed. It is a simple matter of observing, counting, estimating.'

Gaunt watched for flashes through his scope. Like Nash, he was an infantry commander, and he always appreciated technical insight from experienced officers with expertise in other schools of warfare. Grizmund had a fine reputation as an armour commander. Gaunt fully trusted the Narmenian's judgement in this. As he looked, he began to discern the flickering display of brief light points out in the hinterland.

'Your estimate?' asked Nash, also studying the scene and, like Gaunt, willing to listen to an expert opinion.

Grizmund glanced to his attending officers, who all looked up from their scopes.

'Nachin?'

The brigadier answered directly, his voice rich with the taut vowel sounds of the Narmenian accent. 'At a first estimate, armour to the magnitude of twenty thousand pieces. Straight-form advance, with perhaps a forced salient to the east, near those tall cooling towers still standing. Innumerable rockets and mortars, harder to trace, but all mobile. Forty, maybe forty-five thousand.'

The other Narmenians concurred. Grizmund turned back to Gaunt and Nash as Tarrian rejoined the group. 'Nachin knows his stuff as well as me. You heard his numbers. A multiple regiment-strength assault. Grand-scale armour attack. Yet – if what Commissar Kowle says is correct – not even a fraction of their numbers.'

'We can presume other army strengths are moving round through the mining district, the mud flats, perhaps the eastern outer habs and the Hass East river junction too,' said Nash dourly.

'I can make no estimates of troop strength, however,' Grizmund added.

'With permission, sir,' Rawne said, and Gaunt nodded for him to continue.

Rawne indicated the scene below with precise gestures of his nimble hands, his killer's hands. 'If you watch the armour flashes as General Grizmund has suggested, they form a rough line, like a contour. Compare that to the fall of shells. The edge of the shortest falling shells – you can see that from the explosions and from the smoke fires – approximately matches that line, with a break of perhaps a kilometre and a half between armour and line of fire. That is the space we might expect the infantry, advancing before the armour, to occupy.'

Nash nodded, impressed by the junior Tanith's insight.

'We can't judge their tactics by our own,' Rawne went on, 'Feth, I've seen the forces of the Chaos-scum perform many tactical aberrations on the fields of war, but assuming they are not intent on slaughtering their own troops, and assuming the widest margin of error, that shows us a clear belt of infantry advance. Even single line abreast, I'd say we were welcoming over half a million down there. Double the line, double the figure, triple it–'

'We may be senior cadre, but we follow your maths, major,' said Gaunt and the others laughed darkly. 'A fine assessment. Thank you.'

'At least a million,' said Mkoll, suddenly.

They all looked round at him.

'Scout-sergeant?'

'Listen, sir,' said Mkoll and they all did, hearing nothing more than the persistent wail and wail-echoes of the shelling and the crumps of explosions.

'Behind the impacts, a higher note, like a creaking, like the wind.'

Gaunt fought hard to screen out the sounds of the assault bombing. He heard vague whispers of the sound Mkoll described.

'Lasguns, sir. So many lasguns firing over each other that their individual sounds have become one shrieking note. You'd need a... a feth of a lot of lasguns to make that sound.'

At the back of the group, Daur noticed that Gaunt's adjutant, Milo, had crossed to the western lip of the tower and was gazing out. The adjutant was no more than a youth, his pale skin marked by a strange blue tattoo as seemed to be the custom with so many of the Ghosts.

Daur crossed to him, limping. 'What do you see?' he asked.

'What's that?' asked Milo, pointing down to the east. Far away, round the curve of the massive Curtain Wall, past the Sondar and Veyveyr Gates and the ruin of the Ore Works, a great, black slope extended down out of the hive, two kilometres wide and five deep. It looked like a tide of tar. The Curtain Wall broke in a gap fourteen hundred metres wide to let it out.

'The Spoil,' Daur replied. 'It's a... a mountain of rock refuse and processed ore waste from the smelteries and mine workings. One of the landmarks of Vervunhive,' he laughed.

'The Wall is broken there.'

'The Spoil's been there longer than the Wall. The Wall was built around it.'

'But still, it's a break in the defence.'

'Don't worry, it's well protected. The fifth division of my Regiment, the "Spoilers," are dedicated to guarding that area: twenty thousand men. They take their work seriously. Besides, the Spoil itself is bloody treacherous: steep, unsafe, constantly slipping. It's probably harder to get past than the Curtain Wall itself. An enemy would waste thousands trying a foolish gambit like that!'

Daur smiled encouragingly at Milo and then turned away and rejoined the oversight tour.

Milo felt sorry for him. Daur had no experience of the enemy, no knowledge of the way they expended and used their troops wholesale to gain their objectives. The soldiers of Vervunhive and the tactics they had evolved were too deeply focused upon the experience of fighting sane enemies.

In the main group, Gaunt looked to his fellow regiment commanders. 'Assessments?'

'Way too much armour for an infantry-based counterjab just now, but I'd as soon not let those bastards reach the walls,' said Nash.

'I'd like to deploy my tank divisions to engage them out there,' Grizmund said. 'Supported by whatever the NorthCol armour units can supply. We're not overwhelmed yet. If we can stop them in the outer habs clear of the main hive, we can push an advance spearhead right down into the heart of them. For all their infamous numbers, they are extended over a massive area. That's how I'd go. Armoured counter-assault, direct and sudden, take the ground out from under them, if only a section, then open a way to turn and flank them, cutting into their reserve lines. And dig a path for the infantry too.'

Nash agreed vehemently. 'I'll happily support an organised push of that sort.'

'So will I,' Gaunt said. 'They've taken more than enough ground. We should stop them dead, even if only in this west sector.'

Grizmund nodded. 'The gates this side of the hive must be opened. I'll gladly fight these bastards, no matter how many there are, but I need room for my machines to mobilise and manoeuvre. I'd rather do that out there in the habs than wait until they're at the Wall.'

'Or inside it,' Rawne added.

'Something of a first,' Gaunt smiled at his colleagues. 'Three regimental officers agreed on a tactical approach.'

There was more general laughter, cut short by the first shrieks of the missile launchers on the tower reopening fire now the awnings were down.

'That assessment does not jibe with General Sturm's strategy,' Tarrian said from the side.

Gaunt looked round at him. 'I feel uneasy whenever a political officer uses a vague word like "jibe", Commissar Tarrian. What do you mean?'

'I understand General Sturm's tactical recommendations for the prosecution of this conflict are already drawn up and under examination by Marshal Croe, the House Command Strategy Committee and representatives of the noble houses. I hear they have the full support of Vice Marshal Anko and Commissar Kowle.'

'It sounds like they're as good as decided!' Nash snarled, his heavy chin with its bristle of grey stubble set hard.

'Are we wasting our time up here? What good is this oversight tour if they've already set on a course?' Grizmund asked.

'I have had past dealings with the general of the Volpone,' Gaunt remarked sourly. 'I have no doubt he feels himself to be the senior Guard officer in this theatre and the hive elders have lauded him as such. But he is not a man for personal confrontation. Better he gives us something to occupy our attentions while he makes his own decisions. Hence this... sight-seeing.'

Gaunt turned sharply to look at Tarrian. 'And you'd know what those decisions were, wouldn't you, Tarrian?'

'It is not my place to say, colonel-commissar,' Tarrian said flatly.

'To hold the Wall, to keep the gates sealed, to give up all territory out-side and to dig in for a sustained siege, trusting the Shield, the Curtain Wall and the army strengths within Vervunhive to hold the enemy off forever, or at least until the winter breaks them.'

They all looked round. As he finished speaking, Captain Daur shrugged, ignoring the murderous look the VPHC commander was giving him. 'The plans were circulated this morning, with a magenta clearance rating. I have no reason to assume that clearance excluded senior echelon Guard officers.'

'Thank you, Daur,' Gaunt said. He looked back at Tarrian. 'The generals and I wish to see Sturm and the marshal. Immediately.'

Quietly, the quintet of ochre-clad troops picked their way down the corridor of the bombed-out workshop, moving through the dust-filled air. Outside, a tank grated past down the river of debris that had once been Outhab Transit Street 287/fd.

The soldiers wore ochre battledress, shiny, black leather webbing straps, and polished, newly stamped lasguns. On their heads were full-face composite helmets with flared, sneering features like blurred skulls and the crest of Ferrozoica inlayed on the brow.

The squad checked each doorway and damage section they came to. Gol Kolea could hear the hollow crackle of their terse vox-signals barking back and forth.

He slid back into cover and made a hand gesture that his company could read. They moved back, swallowed by the shadows and the dust.

Gol let the five troopers advance down the corridor far enough until the last one was standing on the false flooring. Then he connected the bare end of the loose wire in his hand to the terminals of the battery pack.

The concussion mine tore out a length of the corridor and oblite-rated the last trooper where he stood, tearing the one directly in front of him into pieces with fragments of shrapnel and shards of bone from his exploded comrade.

The other three fell, then scrambled up, firing blind in the smoke. Bright, darting bars of las-fire pierced the smoke cover like reef fish scudding through cloudy water.

Gol smashed out his fake wall and came down on the first of them from the rear, swinging the hook-bill of his axe-rake down through helmet and skull.

Sergeant Haller dropped down from the ceiling joists where he had been crouching and felled another of them, killing him with point-blank shots from his autopistol as his bodyweight flattened the trooper.

The remaining Zoican bastard switched to full auto and swung wild. His withering close-range shots punched right through a flak-board wall partition and blew the guts and thighs out of Machinesmith Vidor, who had been waiting to spring out from behind it.

Nessa came out of cover under some loose sacking and slammed the rock-knife into the back of the Zoican's neck. She held on, screaming and yanking at the blood-slick knife-grip as the trooper bucked convulsively. By the time he dropped, his head was nearly sawn off.

Gol hurried forward, picking Nessa up and pulling her off the corpse. She handed the bloody rock knife to him, shaking.

'Keep it,' he mouthed. She nodded. Eardrums ruptured by a close shell on the seventh day, she would never hear again without expensive up-hive surgery and implants – which meant simply she would never hear again. She was a trainee medic from the outer habs. Not the lowest of the low, but way, way down in the hive class system.

'You did good,' Gol signed. She smiled, but the fear in her eyes and the blood on her face diffused the power of the expression and diluted the beauty of the young woman.

'Not so easy,' she signed back. She'd learned to sign her remarks early on. Captain Fencer, the Emperor save his soul, had trained her well and explained how she could not modulate the volume of her own voice now she was deaf.

Gol looked round. Haller and the other members of Gol's team had recovered four working lasguns, two laspistols and a bunch of ammunition webs from the dead by then.

'Go! Move!' Gol ordered, emphasising his words with expressive sign-gestures for the deaf. Of his company of nine, six were without hearing. He took a last look at Vidor's corpse and nodded a moment of respect. He had liked Vidor. He wished the brave machinesmith had found the chance to fight. Then he followed his company out.

They moved out of the workshop, circuiting back around through a side alley and into a burned-out Ecclesiarchy chapel. The bodies of the Ministorum brothers lay all around, venting swarms of flies. They had not abandoned their holy place, even when the shells began to fall.

Haller crossed to the altar, straightened the slightly skewed Imperial eagle and knelt in observance. Tears dripped down his face, but he still remembered to sign his anguish and his prayer to the Emperor rather than speak it. Gol noticed this, and was touched and impressed by the soldier's dual devotion to the Emperor and to their continued safety.

Gol got his company into the chapel, spreading them out to cover the openings and find the obvious escape routes.

The ground shook as tank rounds took out the workshop where they had sprung their trap.

In the cover of the explosions, he dared to speak, signing at the same time. 'Let's find the next ones to kill,' he said.

'A squad of six, moving in from the west,' hissed loom-girl Banda, setting down her lasgun and peering out of a half-broken lancet window.

'Drill form as before,' Gol Kolea signed to his company, 'Form on me. Let's set the next snare.'

Lord Heymlik Chass sent his servitors and bodyguard away. The chief of the guard, Rudrec, his weapon dutifully shrouded, tried to refuse, but Chass was not in the mood for argument.

Alone in the cool, gloomy family chapel of House Chass, high up in the Main Spine upper sectors, the lord prayed diligently to the soul of the undying Emperor. The ghosts of his ancestors welled up around him, immortalised in statuary. Heymlik Chass believed in ghosts.

They spoke to him.

He unlocked the casket by the high altar between the family stasis-crypts with a geno-key that had been in his family for generations. He raised the velvet-padded lid, hearing the moan of ancient suspensor fields, and lifted out Heironymo's Amulet.

'What are you doing, father?' Merity Chass asked. His daughter's voice startled him and almost made him drop the precious thing.

'Merity! You shouldn't be here!' he murmured.

'What are you doing?' she asked again, striding forward under the flaming sconces of the chapel, her green velvet dress whispering as she moved.

'Is that...' Her voice trailed away. She could not utter the words.

'Yes. Given to our house by Great Heironymo himself.'

'You're not thinking of using it! Father!'

He stared down into her pained, beautiful face.

'Go away, my daughter. This is not for your eyes.'

'No!' she barked. She so reminded him of her mother when she turned angry that way. 'I am grown, I am the heir, female though I may be. Tell me what you are doing!'

Chass sighed and let the weight of the amulet play in his hands. 'What I must, what is good for the hive. There was a reason Old Heironymo bequeathed this to my father. Salvadore Sondar is a maniac. He will kill us all.'

'You have raised me to be respectful of the High House, father,' she said, a slight smile escaping her frown. That was her mother again, Heymlik noticed.

'It amounts to treason,' his daughter whispered.

He nodded and his head sank. 'I know what it amounts to. But we are on the very brink now. Heironymo always foretold this moment.'

He hugged her. She felt the weight of the amulet in his hands against her back.

'You must do what you must, father,' Merity said.

Like a slow, pollen-gathering insect, a vox drone hummed lazily in the chapel and crossed to the embracing figures. It bleeped insistently. Chass pulled away from his daughter, savouring the sweet smell of her hair.

'A vote is being taken in the Upper Legislature. I must go.'

Bumbling like a moth, the drone hovered in front of the Noble Lord, leading him out of the chamber.

'Father?'

Heymlik looked back at his beloved child, hunched and frightened by the cold, marble familial crypt.

'I will support you in whatever you do, but you must tell me what you decide. Don't keep me in the dark.'

'I promise,' he said.

The Privy Council was a circular theatre set on the Spine-floor above the spectacular main hall of the Legislature, and it was reserved for the noble houses only. The domed roof was a painted frieze of the Emperor and the god-machines of Mars hovering in radiant clouds. Columns of warm, yellow light stabbed down from the edges of the circular ceiling and lit the velvet thrones of the high houses. Apart from Chass, they were all there: Gavunda, Yetch, Rodyn, Anko, Croe, Piidestro, Nompherenti and Vwik.

Marshal Croe stood by his brother, the old, wizened Lord Croe, in deep conference. Vice Marshal Anko, beaming and obsequious, was introducing General Sturm to his resplendently gowned cousin, Lord Anko. Commissar Kowle was diplomatically greeting Lords Gavunda and Nompherenti. Servants and house retainers thronged the place, running messages, fetching silver platters of refreshments, or simply guarding their noble masters with shrouded sidearms.

A gong sounded four strokes. The main gilt shutter at the east side of the room slid up into the ceiling with a hiss and Master Legislator Anophy limped into the chamber, his opalescent robes glinting in the yellow light, his beribboned tricorn nodding with each heavy shuffle he took across the embroidered carpet. He was using the long, golden sceptre of his office as a stick. Child pages held his train and carried his gem-encrusted vox/pict drone and Book of Hive-law before him on tasselled cushions.

Anophy reached his place. He adjusted the silver arm of the vox-phone and spoke. 'Noble houses, your careful attention.' All looked round and quickly took their places. Kowle, Sturm and the other military men withdrew to one side.

Noble Chass's seat was vacant.

Anophy thumbed through the data on a slate held up by one of his pages and he set a palsy-trembling finger to his moist lips.

'A matter to vote. In all precision, before these houses, the ratification of the defence plans our noble friend, General Noches Sturm, has drawn up. The matter need not be lengthened further by discourse. The Hive, Emperor grant it wealth and longevity, awaits.'

Six assent runes, fizzling holograms, lit the air above Anophy. Rodyn and Piidestro houses voted against with dark-tinged, threatening lights.

'Carried,' said Anophy simply. The Privy Council began chattering and moving again.

A shutter of herring-bone steel to the west side of the chamber slid open and Noble Chass, accompanied by his bodyguard, entered the chamber. An awkward hush fell. It remained in place as Chass descended the steps, crossed the chamber and took his appointed seat. Once they had folded his great, silk train over the throne back, his bodyguard and servants stood away.

Chass gazed around the circular hall. Several of his fellow nobles did not meet his gaze.

'You have voted. I was not present.'

'You were summoned,' Lord Anko said. 'If you miss the given time, your vote is forfeit.'

'You know the rules, noble lord,' wheezed Anophy.

'I know when I have been... excluded.'

'Come now!' Anophy said. 'There is no exclusion in the upper parliament of Vervunhive. Given the extraordinary circumstances of this situation, I will allow you to vote now.'

Chass looked around again, very conscious of the way Lord Croe would not look at him.

'I see the matter has been voted six to two. My vote, whichever way I meant to cast it, would be useless now.'

'Cast it anyway, brother lord,' gurgled Gavunda through the silver-inlaid, wire-box augmentor that covered his mouth like an ornate, crouching spider.

Chass shook his head. 'I spoil my vote. There is no point to it.'

A group of figures was entering through the east hatch. Commissar Tarrian was trying to delay them, but they pushed past. It was Gaunt, Grizmund, Nash and their senior officers.

'I can scarce believe your guile, Sturm,' Nash spat, facing the other general. Gilbear moved forward to confront the Roane commander, but Sturm held him back with a curt snap of his fingers.

Gaunt crossed directly to the Master Legislator's place and took the data-slate from the hands of the surprised page. He reviewed it.

'So, it's true,' he said, looking up at Sturm and Marshal Croe.

'General Sturm's strategic suggestions have been agreed and ratified by the Upper Council,' Vice Marshal Anko said smoothly. 'And I strongly suggest you, and the other off-world commanders with you, show some order of respect and courtesy to the workings and customs of this high parliament. We will not have our ancient traditions flouted by-'

'You're all fools,' Gaunt said carelessly, setting the slate down and turning away, 'if you care more for ceremonial traditions than life. You've made a serious error here.'

'You've killed this hive and all of us with it!' Nash snapped, bristling with fury. Gaunt took the big Roane general by the shoulder and moved him away from confrontation.

'I am surprised at you, marshal,' Grizmund said, his stiff anger just held in check, like an attack dog on a choke chain, as he looked at Croe. 'From our meetings, I'd believed your grasp of tactics was better than this.'

Marshal Croe got up. 'I'm sorry at your unhappiness, General Grizmund. But General Sturm's plan seems sound to me. I have the hive to think of. And Commissar Kowle, who has – let's be fair – actually encountered our foe, concurs.'

Grizmund shook his head sadly.

'What would *you* have done?' Lord Chass asked.

There was a lot of shouting and protesting, all of it directed at Chass.

'Lord Chass has a right to know!' Ibram Gaunt's clear, hard voice cut the shouting away. Gaunt turned to face the nobleman. 'After due observation, Generals Nash, Grizmund and I would have opened the south-west gates and launched armour to meet them, infantry behind. A flanking gesture to front them outside of the Wall rather than give up all we have.'

'Would that have worked?' Chass asked.

'We'll never know,' Gaunt replied. 'But we do know this: if we wait until they reach the Wall, where do we have to fall back to after that? 'Nowhere.'

Noble Chass wanted to question further, but the Privy Council dissolved in uproar and Gaunt marched out, closely followed by the furious Grizmund and Nash.

* * *

'Commissar? Commissar-colonel?' In the crowded promenade hall out-side the Privy Council, where parliamentary and house aides thronged back and forth with guilders and house ordinary delegates, Gaunt paused and turned. A tall, grim-looking man in ornate body armour was pushing through the crowds after him, a satin-cloth covering the weapon in his right hand. Gaunt sent his staff ahead with the other generals and turned to face the man. A household bodyguard, he was sure.

The man approached and made a dutiful salute. 'I am Rudrec, life-guard of his excellency Lord Chass of Noble House Chass. My lord requests a meeting with you at your earliest convenience.'

The man handed Gaunt a small token-seal, with the Imperial eagle on one side and the Chass coat-of-arms on the other.

'With this, you may be admitted to House Chass at all times. My lord will await.'

Gaunt looked at the crest as the lifeguard bowed and departed, swal-lowed by the crowd.

Now what, he wondered?

Salvador Sondar half-woke, a dream teetering on the edge of memory. The water around him was sweet and warm, and pink bio-luminescence glowed softly.

The chatter murmured at him, soft, soothing, compelling. It was there almost all the time now, asleep or awake.

Sondar listed in the water.

What? What is it? What do you want?

The southern outer habs were ablaze and ash-smog was being driven through the rubble-strewn streets by the cross-winds surging cyclon-ically from the hottest blazes.

Despite fierce pockets of guerrilla resistance, the Zoican forces pushed up through the ruins in spaced phalanxes of infantry and col-umns of armour – thousands of them – grinding ever north through the confusion.

The first of them were now just a kilometre from the Curtain Wall.

SEVEN

DEATH MACHINES

'Victory and Death are the twin sons of War.'

– Ancient proverb

The bombardment from the advancing Zoican land assault fell abruptly silent in the mid-morning of the twenty-fifth day. Hive observers had been carefully tracking the advance of the enemy legions through the outer habs, but by day twenty-two, the level of smoke and ash-clouds veiling the region made such a task impossible once again. Eerie silence now fell.

No one doubted that this cessation of shelling signalled an imminent storm-assault of the Curtain Wall and House Command ordered a swift redeployment to be made all along the southern defence sections. The Curtain Wall and gates were already fully manned by the Vervun Primary troops, and now significant portions of the Volpone, Roane and North-Col armies were brought in to reinforce them. The Tanith Ghosts were also deployed to the frontline from their chem plant billet where they had been killing the hours in fretful indolence and frustration. Gaunt kept some platoons in reserve at the billet, but five platoons under Major Rawne were sent to the Hass West Fortress, and another four under Colonel Corbec were moved to Veyveyr Gate in support of the three Vervun Primary and two NorthCol companies already stationed there.

Corbec saw the vulnerability of Veyveyr Gate the moment he and his men arrived by transit truck. Superhuman efforts had been made to clear sections of the ruined rail terminal and he and his troops rode in past pioneer teams still clearing rubble or shaping it into effective barricade lines. The gate itself, seventy metres wide and a hundred high, had been blockaded with wreckage, a lot of it burned-out rolling stock from the railhead. But there were no great blast doors to seal it like at the other main Wall gates.

Corbec met with Colonel Modile and Major Racine, the ranking Vervun officers in the sector, and with Colonel Bulwar of the NorthCol contingent. Modile was earnest and businesslike, though clearly very nervous about the prospect of seeing action for the first time in his career. Corbec didn't like the idea that the officer at the apex of the command pyramid at Veyveyr was a combat virgin. The major, Racine, was a more likeable fellow, but he was dead on his feet with fatigue. Corbec found out later that the Vervun Primary Officer had been awake for the best part of three days straight, supervising the preparation of the Veyveyr defence.

Bulwar at least was a combat veteran who had seen action during the years of rebellion wars in the NorthCol colonies on Verghast's main satellite moon. He was a thickset man who wore the same regular, evergreen flak-armour and fatigues as his men, though the braided cap and the crackling power claw marked him out instantly as a command officer. As the four officers met around the chart table in Modile's shelter, Corbec soon noticed the way Modile deferred to Bulwar's suggestions. Bulwar saw it too and in effect began to take command. All he had to do was hint and speculate, and Modile would quickly take up the ideas and turn them into tactical policy as if they were his own.

That's fine and good now, thought Corbec, but what happens when the shooting starts? Without direct, confident command, the defence would fall apart.

After the meeting, at which the Ghosts had been drawn to take position along the east flank, against the perimeter of the Ore Works and Smeltery ruins, Corbec took Bulwar to one side.

'With respect, Modile's a weak link.'

Bulwar nodded. 'Agreed. I think the same of most of the Vervun Primary units. No experience. At least my forces have had baptism enough in the moon war. But this is Vervunhive's show and their House Command has authority over us all, colonel.'

'We need a safeguard,' Corbec said flatly, scratching at his collar. There were damn lice in those chem barns. 'I'm not talking insubordination...'

'I know what you mean. My old call sign was "anvil." Let that be a signal to co-ordinate orders above Modile's head if it becomes necessary. I won't be hung out to dry by an inexperienced man. Even a well-meaning one like Modile.'

Corbec nodded. He liked Bulwar. He hoped it wouldn't come to that.

Another day passed, with only silence and smoke outside the Curtain Wall. Nerves began to fray. All the while the shelling had been going on, there had at least been the illusion that a war was being fought.

Waiting, the common fighting man's worst foe, began to take its toll. Anxious minds had time to worry, to fear, to anticipate. Nearly three quarters of a million fighting men were in position at the southern Curtain Wall of Vervunhive, with nothing to do but doze, fidget, gaze up at the spectral flashes and crackles of the Shield far above, and distress themselves with their own imaginations.

The VPHC was busy. Sixty-seven deserters or suspected derelicts were executed in a twenty-four hour period.

On the afternoon of the twenty-seventh day, troops on the Wall top began to detect ominous grinding and clanking noises emanating from the smoke cover below. Machine noises, vast servos, threshing gears, rattling transmissions, creaking metal. It seemed that at any moment, the storm would begin.

But the noises simply continued until after dark and more urgently through the night. They were alien and incomprehensible, like the calls of unseen creatures in some mechanical jungle.

The twenty-eighth day was silent. The machine noises ceased at dawn. By noon, the smoke had begun to clear, especially after a rising wind from the southwest brought rain squalls in from the coast. But still visibility was low and the light was poor. There was nothing to see but the grey blur of the mangled outhabs.

On the twenty-ninth day, spotters on the Wall near Sondar Gate sighted a small group of Zoican tanks moving along a transit track adjacent to the Southern Highway, two kilometres out. With hurried permission from House Command in the Main Spine, they addressed six missile batteries and a trio of earthshaker guns and opened fire. There was jubilation all along the defence line, for no greater reasons than the soldiers finally had a visible enemy to target and the fighting drought was broken. The engagement lasted twelve minutes. No fire was returned from the enemy. When the shell-smoke cleared, there was no sign of the tanks that had been fired upon – not even wreckage.

During the evening of that day, the machine noises from outside grumbled and clanked again, sporadically. Marshal Croe made a morale-boosting speech to the population and the troops over the public-address plates. It helped ease the tension, but Gaunt knew Croe should have been making such speeches daily for the last week. Croe had only spoken now on the advice of Commissar Kowle. Despite his dislike of the man, Gaunt saw that Kowle truly understood the political necessities of war. He was enormously capable. Kowle issued a directive that evening urging all commissarial officers, both the VPHC and the regular Guard, to tour the lines and raise the mood. Gaunt had been doing just that since his units went into position, shuttling between Hass West and Veyveyr. On these tours, he had been impressed by the resolve and discipline of the Vervun Primary troopers who manned the defences alongside his men. He prayed dearly to the beloved Emperor that combat wouldn't sour that determination.

On that evening, riding his staff car down the inner transits to check on Rawne's units at Hass West, Gaunt found the seal Lord Chass's bodyguard had given to him in his coat pocket. There had been no time thus far to pay the noble a visit. Gaunt turned the token over in his gloved hand as the car roared down a colonnaded avenue. Perhaps tonight, after his inspection of Hass West.

He never got the chance. Just before midnight, as Gaunt was still climbing the stairs of the fort's main tower, the first Zoican storm began.

Despite the military preparations, no one in the hive was really prepared for the onslaught. It fell so suddenly. Its herald was a simultaneous salvo from thousands of tanks and self-propelled guns prowling forward through the outer-hab wastes less than a kilometre from the Wall. The roar shook the hive and the explosive display lit the night sky. For the first time, the enemy was firing up at the Curtain Wall, point-blank in armour terms, hitting wall-top ramparts and fracturing them apart. Precision mortar bombardments were landing on the wall-top itself, finding the vulnerable slit between Wall and Shield. Other ferocious rains of explosive force hammered at the gates or chipped and flaked ceramite armour off the Wall's face.

The defenders reeled, stunned. Hundreds were already dead or seriously injured and the ramparts were significantly damaged in dozens of places. Officers rallied the dazed soldiery and the reply began. With its rocket towers, heavy guns, support-weapon emplacements, mortars and the thousands of individual troopers on the ramparts, that reply was monumental. Once they began to fight, a gleeful fury seized the men of Vervunhive. To address the enemy at last. To fire in anger. It felt good after all the waiting. It was absolving.

The Curtain Wall firepower decimated the Zoican forces now advancing towards the Wall-foot outside. Vervunhive laid down a killing field four hundred metres deep outside their Wall and obliterated tanks and men as they churned forward. It was later estimated that 40–50,000 Zoican troops and upwards of 6,000 fighting vehicles were lost to Vervunhive fire in the first hour of attack.

But the sheer numbers of the enemy were overwhelming, both

physically and psychologically. No matter how many hundreds were killed, thousands more moved forward relentlessly to take their place, marching over the corpses of the slain. They were mindless and without fear in the face of the mass slaughter. Observing this from his trench position just inside Veyveyr Gate, Brin Milo reflected that this was precisely what he had been afraid of: the insane tactics of Chaos that Vervunhive's war plans simply did not take into account.

'You could fire a lasgun on full auto from the wall-top,' wrote General Xance of the NorthCol forces later, 'and kill dozens, only to see the hole you'd made in their ranks close in the time it took to change power cells. If war is measured by the number of casualties inflicted, then even in that first night, we had won. Sadly, that is not the case.'

'So many, so many...' were the last words spoken into his vox-set by a mind-numb Vervun Primary officer at Sondar Gate just before one of the VPHC shot him and took control of his frazzled forces.

At Hass West, Gaunt arrived on the main rampart just after a mortar round had taken out a section of wall-lip and blown the head off Colonel Frader, the commander of the area section. Gaunt took command, calling up a Vervun Primary vox-officer and grabbing the handset from his pack. Gaunt was accompanied by Liaison Officer Daur, who confidently relayed vocal commands to the troops in earshot. Gaunt was glad of him. Daur knew the tower and knew the men from his time stationed here, and they responded better to an officer of their own. Many had seemed overawed by the Imperial commissar. Gaunt accepted that fear was a command tool, but he loathed what the iron rule of the VPHC had done to the resolve of the local troops.

Gaunt reached Rawne on the vox-link. The major had the Tanith strength spread out along the lower towers and wall-line below the main fort.

'No casualties here,' the major reported, his voice punctuated by cracks and pops of static. 'We're pouring it on, but there are so many!'

'Stay as you are! Keep up the address! We know they won't break like a normal army, but you and I have faced this enemy before, Rawne. You know how to win this!'

'Kill them all, colonel-commissar?'

'Kill them all, Major Rawne!' And for all he personally trusted the man no further than he could throw him, Gaunt knew that was exactly what Rawne would do.

'What's that?' bellowed Feygor, firing over the buttress.

Rawne ducked along to him. 'What?'

Feygor pointed down. An armoured machine, three times the size of

a main battle tank, was advancing towards the wall's skirt, a huge derrick of armour-plated scaffolding growing out of its top.

'Siege engine! For feth's sake! Get on the vox, tell Gaunt!'

Feygor nodded.

Rawne scrambled closer to the lip and the las-storm below. 'Bragg!
Bragg!'

The big trooper crawled over, hefting his missile launcher.

'Kill it!'

Bragg nodded and raised the launcher to his shoulder, then banged
off three rockets that curled down towards the vast engine on plumes
of blue smoke. They hit the superstructure and ignited, but no serious
damage was done.

'Reload! Again!'

The monstrous siege engine reached the foot of the Wall and there
was a shrieking sound as the metal tower scraped against the ceramite
and stone facings. Gas-fired anchor ropes were shot into the Curtain
Wall to hold the engine in place. Hydraulic feet extended beneath the
armour skirts of the engine to steady it on the broken ground. With a
wail of metal, the derrick tower began to telescope up, extending to
match the height of the wall. Segmented armour, badged with the Zoican crest and other, less human insignias that made Rawne sick to see
them, unfurled upwards to protect the rising throat of the siege tower.

At the same time, the base unit of the vast machine opened a
well-protected hatch in its rear and Zoican troops began to pour into it.

The tower-top rose above the wall's lip, forty metres from Rawne.
Hydraulic arms wheezed out and gripped the buttress, steel claws biting
into the ceramite. The tower-top was an armoured structure with heavy
flamer mounts positioned either side of a hatch opening.

'*Get down! Get down!*' Rawne bellowed.

The flamers drenched the top of the Wall with liquid fire, swivelling
to rake the defences back and forth. Forty Vervun Primary troopers
and nine Ghosts were incinerated as they fled back from the engine.

In addition to the shrieking flamers, automatic grenade launchers on
the tower-top whirred and began to lob explosives out like hail. Multiple detonations exploded along the scorched wall.

Rawne fell into cover behind a bulwark with Bragg, Feygor and several other Ghosts. Feygor was firing his lasgun at the tower, but his shots
were simply dinking off the armoured superstructure. Vervun troops,
some on fire, fled past them.

'Bragg!'

'Got a blockage,' replied the giant, fighting with his launcher.

'Load him!' Rawne ordered Trooper Gyrd.

Gyrd, a grizzled Ghost in his forties, swung in behind Bragg as the big man got the launcher settled on his shoulder. The older Ghost fed fresh rockets into the load-cylinders of the massive weapon.

'Clear!' bawled Bragg as he sent a missile directly at the tower head. It blew the left-hand flamer mount clean off and ignited a huge fireball of venting prometheum. But the armoured delivery section remained unscathed.

'Wait, wait...' hissed Rawne. The skin on the left-hand side of his face was blackened and scorched by the flamer wash. If he lived till morning, he'd have what the Guard called a 'flamer-tan.'

'For what?' barked Feygor. 'Another moment and that hatch'll open. Then the bastards will be all over us!'

'For half a moment, then. We can't make a dent on this thing, so we wait for that hatch.'

The remaining flamer point raked back and forth, its white-hot fires beginning to blister the stone. Then it cut off and drips of fluid fire pooled out of its blackened snout. The grenade throwers stopped whirring.

The storm hatch opened with a shriek. For a scant second, the wall defenders saw the first of the ochre-armoured Zoican troops waiting to deploy out into Vervunhive.

Bragg fired three missiles, one of which went wide. The remaining pair disappeared into the hatchway. The tower-top blew out from within. Secondary explosions rippled down the tower structure and ablaze from inside, it toppled and crumpled with a tearing, metallic wail.

The defenders cheered wildly.

'Move back in! Cover the wall!' urged Rawne.

Six more siege engines had crawled forward towards the Curtain Wall in the time it had taken Rawne to repel the first.

Relentless fire from missile batteries had taken one apart before it could deploy, just short of the Sondar Gate. Another reached the Curtain Wall intact but positioned itself in front of an Earthshaker heavy battery in the Wall side. The massive, long-range cannons blew it apart point-blank, though the crews were fried by the flaming backwash that rushed into their silos.

A third reached Sondar Gate and deployed successfully, rising and clamping to the gatehouse top and then torching everything and everyone on the emplacement before opening its hatch and disgorging wave after wave of Zoican heavy troopers. The Vervun Primary forces were annihilated by this assault, but Volpone units from the neighbouring ramparts, under the command of Colonel Corday, scissored in to meet the invasion. Some of the fiercest fighting of the First Storm took place then, with twenty units of Volpone Bluebloods, including a detachment of the elite 10th Brigade under Major Culcis, undertaking a near hand-to-hand battlement fight with thousands of Zoican storm troops. The regular Bluebloods wore the grey and gold body armour of their regiment, with the distinctive low-brimmed bowl helmets. The elite 10th had carapace armour, matt-black hellguns and bright indigo eagle studs pinned into their armaplas collar sections. Culcis, who had won himself a valour medal on Vandamaar, was young for a member of the tenth elite, but his superiors had rightly noticed his command qualities. Despite seventy per cent losses, he held Sondar Gate through nothing more than tactical surety and brute determination.

The top of Sondar Gate and the walls adjacent were thick with corpses. Culcis and his immediate inferior, Sergeant Mantes of the regular Volpone, tried to disable the siege engine with tank mines. Mantes died in the attempt, but the mines blew the support claws off the tower and it collapsed soon after under its own weight. Culcis, who had lost a hand in the detonation of the mines, reformed his forces and slaughtered all the remaining Zoicans who had made the wall-top. For the first of what would be three serious attempts, Sondar Gate resisted the enemy.

The fourth siege engine reached the Wall east of Sondar Gate, midway along the stretch that curved round to Veyveyr. Here Roane Deepers were in position, hard-nosed shock troops in tan fatigues and netted helmets. General Nash was in command in person and he mobilised the wall batteries to target the tower neck as it extended up towards them. The ripples of missiles didn't destroy it, but they damaged some internal mechanism and the tower jammed at half-mast, unable to reach the Wall top and engage. It raked upwards with its flamers and grenades spitefully, and Nash lost more than forty men. But it could not press its assault and remained hunched outside the Curtain Wall, broken and derelict, for the remainder of the war.

The other two siege engines assaulted Hass West Fort.

Gaunt saw then coming, slow and inexorable, and drew up his heavy weapons. He'd seen the system of assault through his scope watching Rawne's position, and he didn't want it duplicated here.

Under his voxed commands, the wall batteries strafed the nearest engine heavily and succeeded in blowing it apart. The upper section of the tower, beginning to telescope, snapped off to the left in a fireball, destroying the base unit as it collapsed.

But despite Gaunt's efforts, the second siege engine reached the western portions of the ramparts and engaged its clamps. The tower hoisted into position.

Gaunt ordered his men back from the surrounding area as the flamers retched and blasted and the grenades rained.

In cover next to him, Captain Daur pulled off his sling.

'Your arm?'

'Stuff that, commissar! Give me a gun!'

Gaunt handed the Vervun captain his bolt pistol and then cycled his chainsword. 'Prepare yourself, Daur. This is as bad as it ever gets.'

Zoican troops spilled out of the tower top, thousands of them. They were met by the Ghosts and the Vervun Primary. Another infamous episode of the First Storm began.

Just before Gaunt's positions destroyed the first of the two engines, other Zoican death machines clanked out of the outhab wastes and assaulted the walls: a half-dozen tank-like vehicles, quickly dubbed the 'flat-crabs' by the Vervun troopers because of their resemblance to the edible crustaceans farmed in the Hass Estuary. They were the size of four or five tanks together, covered in a shell-like carapace of overlapped armour like huge beetles or horseshoe molluscs. A single, super-heavy weapon extended up from their dorsal mounts and they drummed the Wall with fast-cycle fire that shattered masonry and adamantine blocks.

The flat-crabs were siege-crackers, massive weapons designed to break open even the strongest fortifications. Two of them, with dorsal mounts slung to face forward and armed with massive rams, assaulted the gates at Hass West and Sondar. As they advanced, regular tanks, tiny by comparison, moved in beside them. The tidal wave of ochre-clad troops was undiminished.

Then it was the turn of the spiders, the largest and most fearsome of the Zoican siege weapons. A hundred metres long from nose to tail and propelled by eight vast, clawed cartwheels set on cantilever arms extending from the main bodies of their armoured structures, the spiders ground out of the smoke and rumbled towards the Wall. Gun and rocket batteries on their backs blazed up at the defences of Vervunhive.

When they reached the Curtain Wall, the spiders didn't stop. The wheel claws dug into the ceramite and raised the death machines up the face of the defence, climbing like insects up the sheer face of the massive Wall. Of all the siege engines deployed at Vervunhive, the Zoican spiders came closer to taking the hive than anything else that night. There were five of them. One was destroyed by the Wall guns as it advanced. Another was immobilised by rocket fire twenty metres short of the Wall and then set on fire by further salvos.

The other three made it to the walls and hauled their immense bulks upwards, screeching into adamantium and ceramite as they dug with their wheeled claws. One was stopped by the VPHC Commissar Vokane, who got his troops to roll munitions from the launcher dumps to the Wall head and tip them over onto the rising beast, charges set for short fuse. The spider was blown off the wall and fell backwards, crushing hundreds of Zoican troops under it. It lay on its back and burned. Vokane and fifty-seven of his men didn't live to cheer. The explosive backwash of the spider's death engulfed them and burned them to bone scraps.

The second spider made it to Veyveyr Gate and began to claw at the barricades. Its mighty wheels sliced and crushed rail stock apart as it pulled itself in through the gate opening. Heavy artillery and North-Col armour units met it with a pugnacious blitz of fire as it pushed its head through the gateway and they blew it apart. It settled sideways on its exploded wheels, half-blocking the entrance.

The remaining spider clawed its way over the Curtain Wall west of Hass West Fort. General Grizmund was waiting for it. As it scattered and burned the Wall defenders to left and right, Grizmund's Narmenian tanks, assembled in the open places of the House Anko chem works, elevated and fired, blasting the vast thing backwards off the Curtain Wall. The force of the salvo took part of the inner wall down too, but it was considered worthwhile. The spider was destroyed.

At Hass West, Gaunt's men met the tide of Zoicans spilling from the engaged siege engine. In the narrow defiles of the ramparts, it became a match of determined close combat. Gaunt personally killed dozens with his chainsword and cut a flanking formation down towards the tower-top of the engine. Daur was with him, blasting with his borrowed boltgun, and so were a pack of more than sixty Ghosts and Vervun Primary troopers mixed together.

Squads under Varl and Mkoll joined them, and Gaunt was gratified that they seemed to be killing the storm troops as fast as the foes could stream out of the boarding tower.

Gaunt heard a yell through the confusion and looked up to see Commissar Kowle leading fifty or so Vervun Primary troops in an interception along the lower battlements.

Between them, Gaunt realised, they had the enemy pinned.

'I need explosives!' he hissed back to Daur. The captain called up a grenadier with fat pouches of tube mines and antipersonnel bombs.

'All of them!' spat Gaunt. 'Into the neck of that thing! Come with me!'

Gaunt advanced through the enemy waves, his chainsword biting blood, armour shards, hair and flesh from them. He cut a space to the tower head and then yelled for the grenadier to follow up. A las-shot tore through the grenadier's brow and he fell.

Gaunt caught him. 'Daur!'

Daur ran forward and helped the commissar. Together, they lifted the corpse, laden with its strings of explosives, and carried it to the open mouth of the tower. Gaunt pulled out a stick charge, set it, pushed it back into the corpse's webbing and together they flung the dead soldier down through the mouth of the siege tower.

The grenade went off a couple of seconds later. A bare millisecond after that, the rest of his munitions exploded as he fell, touched off by the first bomb.

The tower shuddered and broke, falling headlong into the sea of Zoicans milling at the foot of the Curtain Wall.

Kowle's forces moved in, killing the last of the Zoicans on the ramparts.

At two in the morning, just into the thirtieth day, the Zoican assault stopped and the Zoicans withdrew into the smouldering shadows of the outhabs. Flat-crabs wallowed backwards into the smoke, escorted by files of Zoican tanks and legions of ochre troops. An Imperial victory hymn was played at full volume from every broadcast speaker in the hive.

Vervunhive had lost 34,000 troops, twenty missile emplacements, fifty gun posts and ten heavy artillery silos. The Curtain Wall was scarred and wounded and, in several places, fractured to the point of weakness.

But the First Storm had been resisted.

EIGHT

HARM'S WAY

'The first trick a political officer of the Commissariat learns is: learn to lie. The second is: trust no one. The third: never get involved with local politics.'

– Commissar-General Delane Oktar,
from his *Epistles to the Hyrkans*

Processions of Ministorum priests, the high faithful of the Imperial Cult, moved through the stone vaults of Inner Hab Collective Medical Hall 67/mv. They carried tapers and smoking censers, and chanted litanies of salvation and blessing for the wounded and dying now engulfing the place. Long, frail strips of parchment inscribed with the speeches of the Emperor trailed behind them like sloughs of snakeskin, dangling from the prayer boxes they carried.

Surgeon Ana Curth nodded respectfully to the clerics each time she encountered them in the wards and hallways of the medical facility, but privately she cursed them. They were in the way and they terrified some of the weaker or more critically injured who saw them as soul-catchers come to draw them from this life. Spiritual deliverance was all very well, but there was a physical crisis at hand, one in which any able personnel would help more by tending the bodies rather than the spirits.

The Zoican assault had brought convoys of new casualties to all the inner hive medical halls, places already barely coping with the sick and injured refugees from the first phase of the conflict. Military field hospitals and medical stations were being set up to help, and the medical officers and staff that had arrived with the Imperial Guard forces were proving to be invaluable. Curth and her colleagues were community medics with vast experience in every walk of life – except combat injuries.

It was evening on the thirtieth day and Curth had been on duty for nearly twenty hours. After the nightmare of the storm assault the previous night, the fighting had slowed, with nothing more than random exchanges of shelling from both sides across the litter of Zoican dead outside the Wall.

Or so Curth had heard from passing soldiers and Administratum officials. She'd barely had time to raise her head above the endless work. She paused to scrub her hands in a water bath, partly to clean them but mainly to feel the refreshingly cold liquid on her fingers. She looked up to see groups of dirty Vervun Primary troopers wheeling a dozen or more of their wounded comrades down the hall on brass gurneys. Some of the wounded were whimpering.

'No! No!' she cried out. 'The west wards are full! Not that way!'

Several troopers protested.

'Weren't you briefed on admittance? Show me your paperwork.'

She checked the crumpled, mud- and blood-stained admission bills one trooper handed her.

'No, this is wrong,' she murmured, shaking her head as she read. 'They've filled out the wrong boxes. You'll have to go back to the main triage station.'

More protests. She took out her stylus and over-wrote the details of the bills, signing them and scorching her seal-mark on the paper with a brief flash of her signet ring.

'Back,' she told them with authority. 'Back that way and they'll look after you.'

The troopers retreated. Curth turned, now hearing raised voices in Ward 12/g nearby.

Ward 12/g had been filled with refugees from the outhabs, most of them fever-sick or undernourished. Days of careful feeding and anti-fever inoculations had improved things, and she was hoping to be able to discharge many of them back to the refugee camps in the next day or two. That would make some valuable space.

She entered the arch-ceilinged ward: a long, green-washed, stone chamber with seven hundred cots. Some were screened. Other cot spaces were crowded with the families of the patients who had refused to be separated from their kin. There was a warm, cloying smell of living bodies and dirt in the air.

The shouting was coming from a cot-space halfway down the ward. Two of her orderlies, distinct in their red gowns from the grimy patients, were trying to calm an outhab worker as gaggles of other outhabbers looked on. The worker was a large male with no obvious injuries but a wasted, pale complexion. He was yelling and making nervous, threatening gestures at the orderlies.

Curth sighed. This wasn't the first such incident. Like far too many of the impoverished underclass, the worker was an obscura addict, hooked on the sweet opiate as a relief from his miserable shift-life. Obscura was cheaper, hit for hit, than alcohol. He probably used a waterpipe or maybe an inhaler. When the invasion began, the workers had fled in-hive. Now many of them were regretting leaving their opiate stashes behind in their desperation. She'd had ninety or more admitted with what at first seemed like the symptoms of gastric fever. After a few days of support and food, this had turned out to be withdrawal cramps.

Strung out, some addicts demanded medicinal drugs to ease their agonies. Others got through the withdrawal phases. Still others became violent and unreasonable. For a few – the chronic, long-term users – she had been forced to prescribe ameliorating tranquillisers.

Curth stepped between her orderlies and faced the man, her hands raised in a gesture of calm.

'I'm chief surgeon,' she said softly. 'What's your name?'

The worker snarled something inarticulate, foam flecking his chin as his jaw worked. His eyes showed too much white.

'Your name? What's your name?'

'N-Norand.'

'How long have you been using obscura, Norand?'

Another squeal of not-words. A stammering.

'How long? It's important.'

'S-since I was a j-journeyman...'

Twenty years at least. A lifelong abuser. There could be no reasoning here. Curth doubted the worker would ever be able to kick the habit that was destroying his brain.

'I'll get something for you right now that will help you feel better, Norand. You just have to be calm. Can you do that?'

'D-drugs?' he muttered, chewing at his lips.

She nodded. 'Can you be calm now?'

The worker quivered his head and sat back on his cot, panting and raking the sheets with his fingers.

Curth turned to her orderlies. 'Get me two shots of lomitamol. Move it!' One of the orderlies hurried off. She sent the other away to encourage patients back to their cots.

There was a pause in the background noise of the ward, just for a second. Curth had her back to the worker and realised her oh-so-very-basic mistake. She turned in time to see him leaping at her, lips drawn back from his rotting teeth, a rusty clasp-knife in one hand.

Wondering stupidly how in the name of the Emperor he'd got

that weapon into the hall unchecked, she managed to sidestep. The worker half-slammed into her and she went over backwards, overturning a water cart. The bottles smashed on the tiles. The worker, making a high-pitched whining sound, stepped over the mess while trying to keep his balance. He stabbed the knife at her and she cried out, rolling aside and cutting her arm on the broken glass. She scrabbled to rise, expecting to feel him plant the blade in her back at any moment.

Turning, she saw him choking and gagging, held in a firm choke-hold from behind. Dorden, the Tanith medical officer, had his left arm braced around the addict's neck, his right hand holding the knife-wrist tightly at full length away from them both. The addict gurgled. Dorden was completely tranquil. His hold was an expert move, just a millimetre or two of pressure away from clamping the carotid arteries, just a centimetre away from dislocating the neck. Only a brilliant medic or an Imperial assassin could be that precise.

'Drop it,' Dorden said into the worker's ear.

'N-n-nggnnh!'

'Drop. It,' the Ghost repeated emphatically.

Dorden dug his thumb into a pressure point at the base of the man's palm and the addict dropped his knife anyway. The rusty weapon clattered to the floor and Curth kicked it aside.

Dorden increased his chokehold for a fraction of a second, enough for the man to black out, and then dropped him facedown onto an empty cot. Orderlies hurried up.

'Restrain him. Give him the lomitamol, but restrain him all the same.'

He turned to Curth. 'This is a war now, you know. You should have guards in here. Things get dangerous during wars, even behind the lines.'

She nodded. She was shaking. 'Thank you, Dorden.'

'Glad to help. I was coming to find you. Come on.' He picked up a clutch of data-slates and paper forms he had dropped in order to engage the man, and he led her by the arm down the length of the ward to the exit.

In the cool of the corridor outside, she paused and leaned against the stone wall, taking deep breaths.

'How long have you been working? You need rest,' Dorden said.

'Is that a medical opinion?'

'No, a friend's.'

She looked up at him. She had still to get the measure of this off-worlder, but she liked him. And he and his Tanith medics had been the backbone of the combat triage station.

'You've been up as long as me. I saw you working at midnight last night.'

'I nap.'

'You what?'

'I *nap*. Useful skill. I'd rate it slightly higher than suturing. I know all the excuses about there being no time for sleep. I've used them myself. Hell, I've been a doctor for a lot of years. So I learned to nap. Ten minutes here, five there, in any lull. Keeps you fresh.'

She shook her head and smiled.

'Where do you nap?' she asked.

He shrugged. 'I've found there's a particularly comfortable linen cupboard on the third floor. You should try it. You won't be disturbed. They never change the beds in this place anyway.'

That made her laugh. 'I... thank you for that.'

He shrugged again. 'Learn the lessons, Surgeon Curth. Make time to nap. Trust your friends. And never turn your back on an obscura addict with a rusty knife.'

'I'll remember,' she said over-solemnly.

They walked down the hallway together, passing two crash-teams racing critical cases to the theatre.

'You were coming to find me?'

'Hmm,' he said, reminded, sheafing through the documents he was carrying. 'It's nothing, really. You'll think it stupid, but I have a thing about details. Another lesson, if you're in the mood for more. Take care of the details, or they'll bite you on the bloody arse.'

He stopped, looked at her and coloured. 'My apologies. I've been in the company of foul-mouthed soldiers for too long.'

'Accepted. Tell me about this detail.'

'I was in Intensive Ward 471/k, reviewing the situation. They are mostly inhab citizens up there, injured in the first raid. We've got blast wounds, shrapnel-hits, burn-cases, crush-injuries – a world of bad stuff, actually. They were all in the Commercia district when the bombs fell. Specifically,' he consulted the slates, 'Carriage Station C4/a and the eastern barter houses.'

She took the slate from him. 'Well?'

'I was checking to see if any could be discharged or at least moved to a non-intensive ward to make room. There are maybe twelve who could be shifted to the common wards.'

'Well?' she repeated. 'Was that it? An administrative suggestion?'

'No, no!' he said and leafed to another sheet. 'I told you the sort of injuries we were getting up there: mostly from the shelling, a few from panic stampedes. But there were two others, both in comas, critical. I... I was wondering why they had gunshot wounds?'

'What?' She snatched the slates and studied them closely.

'Small calibre, maybe a needle gun. Easy to mistake it for shrapnel wounding.'

'It says "glass lacerations" here. The station canopies all blew out and–'

'I know a needle-gun wound when I see it. And I'm seeing over a dozen shared between the two of them. They were shot at close range. I checked the records. Twelve others were brought in from the same site with identical wounds. But they were all dead on arrival.'

'This is the Commercia?'

'A subtransit station: C7/d. Not actually hit by direct shelling, so the records state. But there were at least twenty bodies recovered there.'

She read the forms again and then looked up at him.

'You're thinking what I'm thinking, aren't you?' he smiled. 'Hundreds of thousands, dead and dying, all needing us and I'm worried about just two of them. I shouldn't care how they were hurt, just that they need me.'

She paused. 'Yes, I am thinking that... but...'

'Ah: "but". Useful word. Why were they shot? Who was opening fire on helpless citizens in the middle of a raid?'

Despite her hours on duty, Ana Curth was suddenly awake again. Dorden was right: this was small compared to the scale of the general human misery in Vervunhive. But it could not go unmarked. The Scholam Medicalis had trained her to value every single life individually.

'Vervunhive is being murdered,' she said. 'Most of the murderers are out there, wearing ochre armour. Some, I have to say, are sitting pretty around the chart tables in House Command. But there is another – and we will find him.'

Gaunt straightened his cap, smoothed the folds of a clean leather jacket and left his escort of six Tanith troops at the elevator assembly. The escort, led by Caffran, stood easy, gazing around themselves at the lofty, gleaming architecture of the upper Spine. None of them had ever expected to see the inside of a hive's noble level.

'Even the fething lift has a carpet!' Trooper Cocoer hissed.

Gaunt looked round. 'Stay here. Behave yourselves.'

The Ghosts nodded, then congregated around an ornamental fountain where foamy water bubbled from conches held by gilt nymphs into a lily-skinned, green pool. Some of the Ghost guard rested their lasguns against the marble lip. Gaunt smiled to see Caffran check that the seat of his pants was clean before sitting on the marble.

So out of place, he thought as he left them with a last look, six dirty dog-soldiers, fresh from battle, in the middle of the serene vaults of the worthy and powerful.

He paced down the length of the promenade, his shiny boots hushing into the blue carpeting. The air was perfumed and gentle plainsong echoed from hidden speakers. The vault above was glass, supported by thin traceries of iron. Trees, real trees, grew in the centre beds of the long hall and small, bright songbirds fluttered through the branches. This is the privilege of power, Gaunt thought.

The great doors, crafted from single pieces of some vast tree, stood before him, the crest of House Chass raised in varnished bas-relief on their front. Ivy traces clad the walls to either side and small, blue flowers budded from fruit trees in the avenue that led to the doorway. He took out the token-seal and fitted it into a knurled slot in the door lock.

The great doors swung inwards silently. There was a fanfare of choral voices. He stepped inside, entering a high vault that was lit blue by the light falling through stained-glass oriels high above. The walls were mosaics, depicting incidents and histories that were unknown to him. The Chass crest was repeated at intervals in the mosaic.

'Welcome, honoured visitor, to the enclave of House Chass. Your use of a token emblem signifies you to be an invited and worthy guest. Please wait in the anteroom and refreshments will be sent while his lordship is informed of your arrival.'

The servitor's voice was smooth and warm, and it issued from the air itself. The great doors hushed closed behind Gaunt. He removed his cap and gloves and set them on a teak side table.

A second later, the inner doors opened and three figures entered. Two were house guards dressed in body armour identical to that of the one who had accosted Gaunt outside the Privy Council. They had satin shrouds over their handweapons and nodded to him stiffly. The third, a female servitor, her enhancement implants and plugs made of inlaid gold, carried a tray of refreshments on long, silver, jointed arms which supplemented her natural limbs.

She stopped before Gaunt. 'Water, joiliq, berry wine, sweetmeats. Please help yourself, worthy guest. Or if nothing pleases you, tell me, and I will attend your special needs.'

'This is fine,' Gaunt said. 'A measure of that local liquor.'

Holding the salver with her extra arms, the female servitor gracefully poured Gaunt a shot of joiliq into a crystal glass and handed it to him.

He took it with a nod and the servitor withdrew to the side of the room. Gaunt sipped the drink thoughtfully. He was beginning to wonder why he had come. It was clear there was a universe of difference between himself and Chass. What could they have in common?

'To be here you must have been invited, but I do not know you.'

Gaunt turned and faced a young noblewoman who had entered from the far side of the anteroom. She wore a long gown of yellow silk, with a fur stole and an ornate headdress of silver wire and jewels. She was almost painfully beautiful and Gaunt saw cunning intelligence in her perfect face.

He nodded respectfully, with a click of his heels.

'I am Gaunt, lady.'

'The off-world commissar?'

'One of them. Several of my stripe arrived with the Guard.'

'But you're the famous one: Ibram Gaunt. They say the People's Hero Kowle was beside himself with rage when he heard the famous Gaunt was coming to Vervunhive.'

'Do they?'

The girl circled him. Gaunt remained facing the way he was.

'Indeed they do. War heroes Kowle can manage to stomach, so they report, but a commissar war hero? Famous for his actions on Balhaut, Fortis Binary, the Menazoid Clasp, Monthax? Too much for Kowle. You might eclipse him. Vervunhive is large, but there can be only one famous, dashing commissar hero, can't there?'

'Perhaps. I'm not interested in rivalry. So... you're versed in recent military history, lady?'

'No, but my maids are.' She smiled dangerously.

'Your maids have taken an interest in my record?'

'Deeply, you and your – what was it they said? Your "scruffy, courageous Ghost warriors". Apparently, they are so much more exciting than the starchy Volpone Bluebloods.'

'That I can vouch for,' he replied. Though she was lovely, he had already had enough of her superior manner and courtly flirting. Responding to such things could get a man shot.

'I've six scruffy, courageous Ghost warriors right outside if you'd like me to introduce them to your maids,' he smiled, 'or to you.'

She paused. Outrage tried to escape her composed expression. She contained it well. 'What do you want, Gaunt?' she asked instead, her tone harder.

'Lord Chass summoned me.'

'My father.'

'I thought so. That would make you...'

'Merity Chass, of House Chass.'

Gaunt bowed gently again. He took another sip of the drink.

'What do you know of my father?' she asked crisply, still circling like a gaud-cock in a mating ritual.

'Master of one of the nine noble houses of Vervunhive. One of the three who opposed General Sturm's tactical policy. One who took an interest in my counterproposals. An ally, I suppose.'

'Don't use him. Don't dare use him!' she said fiercely.

'Use him? Lady–'

'Don't play games! Chass is one of the most powerful noble houses and one of the oldest, but it is part of the minority. Croe and Anko hold power and opposition. Anko especially. My father is what they call a liberal. He has... lofty ideals and is a generous and honest man. But he is also guileless, vulnerable. A crafty political agent could use his honesty and betray him. It has happened before.'

'Lady Chass, I have no designs on your father's position. He summoned me here. I have no idea what he wants. I am a warmaker, a leader of soldiers. I'd rather cut off my right arm than get involved in house politics.'

She thought about this. 'Promise me, Gaunt. Promise me you won't use him. Lord Anko would love to see my noble house and its illustrious lineage overthrown.'

He studied her face. She was serious about this – guileless, to use her own word.

'I'm no intriguer. Leave that to Kowle. Simple, honest promises are something I can do. They are what soldiers live by. So I promise you, lady.'

'Swear it!'

'I swear it on the life of the beloved Emperor and the light of the Ray of Hope.'

She swallowed, looked away, and then said, 'Come with me.'

With her bodyguards trailing at a respectful distance, she led Gaunt out of the anteroom, along a hallway where soft, gauzy draperies billowed in a cool breeze and out onto a terrace.

The terrace projected from the outer wall of the Main Spine and was covered by a dedicated refractor shield. They were about a kilometre up. Below, the vast sprawl of Vervunhive spread out to the distant bulk of the Curtain Wall. Above them rose the peak of the Spine, glossed in ice, over-arched by the huge bowl of the crackling Shield.

The terrace was an ornamental cybernetic garden. Mechanical leaf-forms grew and sprouted in the ordered beds, and bionic vines self-replicated in zigzag patterns of branches to form a dwarf orchard. Metal bees and delicate paper-winged butterflies whirred through the silvery stems and iron branches. Oil-ripe fruit, black like sloes, swung from blossom-joints on the swaying mechanical-tree limbs.

Lord Heymlik Chass, dressed in a gardener's robes, slight marks of oil-sap on his cuffs and apron, moved down the rows of artificial plants, dead-heading brass-petalled flowerheads with a pair of laser secateurs and pruning back the sprays of aluminium roses.

He looked up as his daughter led the commissar over.

'I was hoping you would come,' Lord Chass said.

'I was delayed by events,' Gaunt said.

'Of course.' Chass nodded and gazed out at the south Curtain for a moment. 'A bad night. Your men... survived?'

'Most of them. War is war.'

'I was informed of your actions at Hass West. Vervunhive owes you already, commissar.'

Gaunt shrugged. He looked around the metal garden.

'I have never seen anything like this,' he said honestly.

'A private indulgence. House Chass built its success on servitors, cogitators and mechanical development. I make working machines for the Imperium. It pleases me to let them evolve in natural forms here, with no purpose other than their own life.'

Merity stood back from the pair. 'I'll leave you alone, then,' she said.

Chass nodded and the girl stalked away between the wire-vines and the tin blooms.

'You have a fine daughter, lord.'

'Yes, I have. My heir. No sons. She has a gift for mechanical structures that quite dazzles me. She will lead House Chass into the next century.'

He paused, snicked a rusting flowerhead off into his waist-slung sack and sighed. 'If there is a next century for Vervunhive.'

'This war will be won by the Imperial force, lord. I have no doubt.'

Chass smiled round at the commissar. 'Spoken like a true political animal, Commissar Gaunt.'

'It wasn't meant to be a platitude.'

'Nor did I take it as one. But you are a political animal, aren't you, Gaunt?'

'I am a colonel of the Imperial Guard. A warrior for the almighty Emperor, praise His name. My politics extend as far as raising troop morale, no further.'

Chass nodded. 'Walk with me,' he said.

They moved through a grove of platinum trees heavy with brass oranges. Frills of wire-lace creepers were soldered to the burnished trunks. Beyond the grove, crossing iron lawns that creaked under their footsteps, they walked down a row of bushes with broad, inlaid leaves of soft bronze.

'I suppose my daughter has been bending your ear with warnings about my liberal ways?'

'You are correct, lord.'

Chass laughed. 'She is hugely protective of me. She thinks I'm vulnerable.'

'She said as much.'

'Indeed. Let me show you this.' Chass led Gaunt into a maze of hedges. The hedgerows crackled with energised life, like veils of illusions.

'Fractal topiary,' Chass said proudly. 'Mathematical structures generated by the stem-forms of the cogitators planted here.'

'It is a wonder.'

Lord Chass looked around at Gaunt. 'It leaves you cold, doesn't it, Gaunt?'

'Cold is too strong a word. It leaves me... puzzled. Why am I here?'

'You are an unusual officer, Gaunt. I have studied your record files carefully.'

'So have the housemaids,' Gaunt said.

Chass snorted, taking a cropping wand from his belt. He began to use it to shape the glowing, fractal hedges nearby. 'For different reasons, I assure you. The maids want husbands. I want friends. Your record shows me that you are a surprisingly moral creature.'

'Does it?' Gaunt watched the noble trim the light-buds of the bush, disinclined to speak further.

'True to the Imperial cause, to the crusade, but not always true to your direct superiors when those motives clash. With Dravere on Menazoid Epsilon, for example. With our own General Sturm on Voltemand. You seek your own way, and like a true commissar you are never negligent in punishing those of your own side who counter the common good.'

Gaunt looked out across the vast hive below them. 'Another sentence or two and you'll be speaking treason, Lord Chass.'

'And who will hear me? A man who roots out treason professionally? If I speak treason, Gaunt, you can kill me here.'

'I hope we can avoid that, lord,' Gaunt said quietly.

'So do I. From the incident in the Privy Council the other day, I understand you do not agree with General Sturm's tactical plan?'

Gaunt's measured nod spoke for him.

'We have something in common then. I don't agree with House Sondar's leadership either. Sondar controls Croe and Anko is its lapdog. They will lead us to annihilation.'

'Such machinations are far above me, Lord Chass,' Gaunt pointed out diplomatically.

Chass wanded the hedge again. He was forming a perfect Imperial eagle from the blister-tendrils of light. 'But we are both affected. Bad policy and bad leadership will destroy this hive. You and I will suffer then.'

Gaunt cleared his throat. 'With respect, is there a point to this, Lord Chass?'

'Perhaps, perhaps not. I wanted to speak with you, Gaunt, get the measure of you. I wanted to understand your inner mind and see if there was any kindred flame there. I have a great responsibility to Vervunhive, greater than the leadership of this noble house. You wouldn't understand and I'm not about to explain it. Trust me.'

Gaunt said nothing.

'I will preserve the life of this hive to my dying breath – and beyond it if necessary. I need to know who I can count on. You may go now. I will send for you again in time. Perhaps.'

Gaunt nodded and turned away. The Imperial eagle in the fractal topiary was now complete.

'Gaunt?'

He turned back. Lord Chass reached into his waist-sack and pulled out a rose. It was perfect, made of steel, just budding and faintly edged with rust. The silver stem was stiff and aluminium thorns split out of it.

Chass held it out.

'Wear this for honour.'

Gaunt took the metal rose and hooked it into the lapel of his jacket, over his heart.

He nodded. 'For honour, I'll wear anything.'

Chass stood alone as Gaunt threaded his way out of the metal garden and departed. Chass remained stationary in thought for a long time.

'Father?' Merity appeared out of the brass-orange grove.

'What did you make of him?'

'An honourable man. Slightly stiff, but not shy. He has spirit and courage.'

'Undoubtedly.'

'Can we trust him?'

'What do you think?'

Merity paused, stroking the fractal blooms absently.

'It's your choice, master of our house.'

Heymlick Chass laughed. 'It is. But you like him? That's important. You asked me to keep you informed.'

'I like him. Yes.'

Chass nodded. He took the amulet from the waist sack where it had been all the time, buried in the garden scraps.

He turned it over in his hands. It writhed and clicked.

'We'll know soon enough,' he told his daughter.

Day thirty-one passed without major incident. Shelling whined back and forth between the wall defenders and the waiting Zoican army.

At dawn on the thirty-second day, the second Zoican assault began.

NINE

VEYVEYR GATE

'Do not ask how you may give your life for the Emperor. Ask instead how you may give your death.'
                                        – Warmaster Slaydo, on his deathbed

It was a dismal, hollow dawn. The early daylight was diffused by cliffs of grey cloud that prolonged the night. Rain began to fall: spots at first for a half hour, then heavier, sheeting across the vastness of the hive and the wastelands beyond. Visibility dropped to a few hundred metres. The torrential downpour made the Shield crackle and short in edgy, disturbing patterns.

At the Veyveyr position, in the first hour of light, Colm Corbec walked the Tanith line, the eastern positions of the ruined railhead. His pie-bald camo-cloak, the distinctive garb of the Tanith, was pulled around him like a shroud, and he had acquired a wide-brimmed bowl helmet from somewhere – the NorthCol troops most likely – which made more than a few of his Ghosts chuckle at the sight of it. It was cold, but at least the Shield high above was keeping the rain off.

Corbec had surveyed the Ghost positions a dozen times and liked them less each time he did. There was a group of engine sheds and cargo halls through which sidings ran, all of them bombed-out, and then a forest of rubble and exploded fuel tanks leading down to the vast main gate, the white stone of its great mouth scorched black. Beyond the rear extremity of the railyard's eastern border rose the burned-out smelteries. A regiment of Vervun Primary troops – called the Spoilers, Corbec had been told – held that position and watched the approach up the treacherous slag-mountain. Corbec had around two hundred Ghosts dug in through the engine sheds and the rubble beyond, with forward scout teams at the leading edge towards the gate.

Colonel Modile's Vervun Primary units, almost five thousand strong, manned the main trenches and rubble glacis in the central sector of the wide railyard. Bulwar's NorthCol troops, two thousand or more, were positioned along the west, towards proud and grimy rows of as yet undamaged manufactories. Fifty units of NorthCol armour waited at the north end of the railhead in access roads and marshalling yards, ready to drive forward in the event of a breakthrough.

Corbec crossed between fire-blackened, roofless engine sheds, his hefty boots crunching into the thick crust of ash and rubble that littered the place despite the pioneer teams' clearance work.

In the shed, twenty Ghosts were standing easy, all except their spotters at blast-holes and windows, looking south. The roof was bare ribs and tangles of reinforcing metal strands poked from broken rockcrete.

Corbec crossed to where Scout MkVenner and Trooper Mochran squatted on a makeshift firestep of oil drums, gazing out through holes in the brickwork.

'You've a good angle here, boys,' Corbec said, pulling himself up onto the rusty drums and taking a look.

'Good for dying, sir,' MkVenner muttered dryly. He was a scout in the true mould of Scout Sergeant Mkoll, dour and terse. Mkoll had trained most of them personally. MkVenner was a tall man in his thirties with a blue, half-moon tattoo under his right eye.

'How's that, MkVenner?'

MkVenner pointed out at the gates. 'We're square on if they make a frontal, us and the locals in the main yard.'

'And our angles have been cut and blinded since that thing fell in,' Mochran added in a tired voice.

The 'thing' he referred to was the gigantic wreck of the spider siege engine which the NorthCol batteries had brought down during the First Storm three days before. Its massive bulk, slumped across the gatemouth barricades, half blocked the entrance and had proved impossible to shift, despite the efforts of pioneer teams and sappers with dozers and heavy lifters.

Corbec saw the trooper was right. Enemy infantry could come worming in around the bulk and be inside before they were visible. The war machine gave the enemy a bridge right in through the tangled, rusting hulks of the gate barricade.

Corbec told them something reassuring and light that made them both laugh.

Afterwards, though he tried, he could not recall what it was.

He sauntered southwards, skirting through a trenchline and entered the rubble scarps closer to the gate. He had eleven heavy weapon teams tied in here at intervals behind flakboards and bagging. Six heavy stubbers on tripod mounts, two autoguns on bipods with ammo feeders sprawled on their bellies next to the gunners, and three missile launchers. Between the weapon positions, Tanith troopers were spread in lines along the embrasures. Walking amongst them, Corbec sensed their vulnerability. There was nothing to their rear and east flank but the ruined smelteries and the Spoil. They had to trust the abilities of the unseen 'Spoilers' to keep them from surprises.

Corbec opened his vox-link and called up three flamer-parties from the reserves behind the engine sheds. Now he was out here, with dawn upon them, he could see how raw and open the scene was, and he wanted it secured.

He found Larkin in a foxhole close to the gates. The wiry sniper was breaking down his specialised lasgun and cleaning it.

'Any movement, Larks?'

'Not a fething hint.' Larkin clacked a fresh, reinforced barrel into place and then stroked a film of gun-oil off the exchanger before sliding one of the hefty charge packs into its slot.

Corbec sat down beside Larkin and took a moment to check his own lasgun. Standard issue, with a skeleton metal stock, it was shorter and rougher than the sniper's gun and lacked the polished nalwood grips and shoulder block.

'Gotta get myself one of those one day,' said Corbec lightly, nodding at Larkin's precious gun.

Larkin snorted and clicked his scope gently into place on the top of the weapon. 'They only give sniper-pattern M-G's to men who can shoot. You wouldn't know how to use it.'

Corbec had a retort ready to go when his vox-link chirped.

'Modile to all sections. Observers on the Curtain Wall have detected movement in the rain. Could be nothing, but go to standby.'

Corbec acknowledged. He looked up at the huge wall and the towering top of the gatehouse. He often forgot that they had men and positions up there, thousands of them, a hundred metres up, blessed with oversight and a commanding position of fire.

He nodded across at Larkin, who slid the long flash-suppresser onto his muzzle with a hollow clack.

'Ready?'

'Never. But that's usual. Bring 'em on. I'm tired of waiting.'

'That's the spirit,' Corbec said.

That was what his mouth said, anyway. The sound was utterly stolen by a marrow-pulping impact of shells and las-fire that bracketed the gatehouse and shook the wall. Billows of flame belched in over the ruined death machine and the barricade and swirled up above the railyard. Parts of the barricade, sections of rolling stock, fifty tonnes apiece, shredded and blew inwards.

Corbec dropped. Billions of zinging shards of shrapnel, many white-hot, whickered down over the Tanith lines. Already, he could hear urgent calls over his link for medics coming from the Vervun Primary positions in the centre of the yard. He swung round and saw shells falling in the Spoil behind the Tanith position, blowing up fierce spumes of rock-waste. The Second Storm had started.

Ferrozoica changed tactics for its second assault. The First Storm had been an all-out, comprehensive attack along the southern Curtain Wall. This time they began a sustained bombardment of the wall length to keep Vervunhive reeling and they focussed their invasion to three point-assaults. One, an armoured formation led by two of the fearsome 'flat-crabs,' hit Sondar Gate and pummelled at it for over two hours before being driven back by the wall-guns. Another slid west along the eastern rail-lines and struck at Croe Gate and the railhead behind it with battalion-strength force. The fighting in that sector, fronted by Vervun Primary and Roane Deeper regiments, lasted until the early afternoon.

The third attack went straight in for the vulnerable Veyveyr Gate.

In the first ten minutes of the Second Storm, flat-crabs and other heavy artillery siege-crackers brought down the barricade and blasted apart the corpse of the spider. The first flat-crab rolled right in through the gate, squashing metal and splintering rubble, driving down into the Vervun Primary positions in the main yard. Further artillery obliterated all defences along the bastions of the gateway and the walls nearby, and Veyveyr found itself shorn of its precious raised gunnery positions.

There were a few, desperate minutes of confusion as Colonel Modile tried to rally his splintered ground forces in the main area of the yard. They were falling back in droves before the armour attack, stampeding down the trenchways to escape the insurmountable power of the Zoican death machine. A second flat-crab began to grind in behind the first, searing shells to the right into the Tanith positions.

Modile fabricated a clumsy counter-assault and withdrew his infantry in a V-shape, allowing the NorthCol armour to press forward to meet the siege engines. The railhead air was full of clanking tracks and whinnying shells as the formations moved in. NorthCol tanks were blown apart by the heavy dorsal cannons of the flat-crabs, and other tanks and Chimeras were crushed flat under the siege engine's tracks.

All the infantry, Ghosts included, could do little but cower in the face of this monumental clash. The noise level was physically painful and the ground trembled.

There was a vast detonation and a cheer went up all along the infantry lines. Sustained fire from three dozen NorthCol tanks had finally crippled the first flat-crab and blown it apart. The second, grinding through the gate, was blocked by the wreck.

Corbec scurried round in his cover and started to break towards the flank of the second crab.

Larkin caught him by the arm.

'What the feth are you doing, Colm?'

'We have to hit that thing! Maybe a man on foot can get close enough to st–'

A close shell blast threw them into the ash-cover.

'You're mad!' cried Larkin, getting up. He found the brim of the defence and trained his gun out.

'Let the fething armour worry about the crabs! Here's our problem!'

Corbec crawled up alongside him.

Zoican infantry, hundreds of them, were charging through the breach the flat-crabs had gouged, pouring through Veyveyr Gate itself.

Corbec began to fire. The thin crack of his lasgun was quickly joined by the heavier whine of Larkin's sniper weapon. The support weapons along the Tanith lines opened up behind them.

Missiles from the heavy weapon positions hissed above his head as Brin Milo bellied forward through the rubble and began to scope for enemy infantry. Colonel Corbec's hasty orders were crackling over the vox-link. Hell was erupting around them.

Milo saw a few ochre shapes clambering across the dead zone in the gate mouth and took aim. His first shot went wide, but he adjusted and dropped a Zoican with his second and his third.

Trooper Baffels and Trooper Yarch flung themselves down beside him and started firing too. Las-fire slashed back and forth across the railyard, flickering in multicoloured, searing lines. Someone a few metres away was screaming.

Milo tried to shut it out. He aimed his weapon as Larkin had taught him, kept his breathing slow, squeezed. A blurt of las-fire. An ochre warrior spun off his feet.

Yarch crawled up to the lip of the embrasure and primed a grenade. He tossed it and a crumping vortex of wind blew grit back onto them.

'If we–' Yarch began.

Milo and Baffels never found out what Yarch was planning. A las-round entered his skull though his nose-bone, blowing out the back of his head. As he rose weightlessly and jerked back, two more lasrounds hit him, one through the throat and the other through the eye. He tumbled down the rubble. Another lost man lost.

Baffels, a bearded man in his early forties with a barrel chest and a blue tattoo claw that lined his cheek, pulled Milo back into cover as tremendous las-fire exploded along their trench top.

Together, they crawled down into the trench bottom and found Fulch, MkFeyd and Dremmond trying to edge round south.

A light-storm of las-fire drummed around them. A ricochet hit Fulch in the buttock and dropped him to his knees. MkFeyd tried to rise to the fire step, but las-fire walked along its edge, exploding the fore-grip of his weapon and taking off the tops of two fingers of his left hand. He fell back, cursing his luck and jetting the others with bright, red blood.

Milo started to bind MkFeyd's fingers with strips of field bandage, keeping his head low. Baffels was trying to patch the oozing wound in Fulch's hindquarters and was calling for a medic over his vox-link.

Dremmond, who was bringing one of the flamers Corbec had requested forward, crawled up to the lip and sent withering blasts of incendiary death over the top. He was already boasting a flamer-tan from the First Storm, in which he had fought at Hass West.

More troopers battled along to join them. Some, led by Sergeant Fols, went ahead down the zag in the trench line to create an enfilade.

Milo looked up from his work with MkFeyd's hand, his face smeared and dripping with blood, as a trooper nearby was cut in two. Dremmond kept firing with his flamer and three more Ghosts joined him at the firestep, opening up with their lasguns.

'Best I can do!' Milo said to the injured man, then crawled up to take his place at the firestep too. MkFeyd was working on pure adrenaline now and he crawled up alongside the boy. He managed to brace his gun with his bandaged hand and began firing. The line of Ghost lasguns barked and flashed down the length of the eastern position.

MkVenner moved his team out of the engine shed just as shelling from the second flat-crab blew it out. Mochran was already dead, punctured apart by a series of stub-rounds that had perforated the shed wall.

MkVenner had ordered his unit to fix bayonets – the long silver daggers of the Tanith – at some point early in the assault, and now he was glad of it. Zoican infantry, their faces hidden by those sculpted ochre masks, were pouring into the Tanith trench lines from the south. With no more than fifteen men around him, MkVenner engaged them, stabbing and slicing, firing weapons point-blank. The Zoicans were overrunning them. There seemed to be no end to the numbers of ochre enemy. As fast as MkVenner could kill them, there were more. It was like fighting the ocean tide.

Major Racine, of the Vervun Primary, had been out inspecting the forward arrays of his Veyveyr positions when the storm came down. He had tried to control the retreat and he debated fiercely with Colonel Modile about how best to counter the Zoican push. After a few bitter returns over the vox-line, it had gone dead. Modile clearly didn't want to argue with his subaltern any more.

Racine had five hundred men behind a glacis of rubble in the main yard, facing the encroachment of the second flat-crab. He called up his bombardier and took three satchels full of mine charges and grenades.

Then he hauled himself over the lip and ran towards the siege engine.

A raging storm of las- and bolt-rounds whipped around him. Not one touched him. All that saw it regarded it as a miracle. Racine was ten metres from the vast supertank, with its grinding segmented armour, when a las-round went through his ear into his brain and killed him. He dropped.

There was a dreadful hiss of wronged valour and injustice from his watching troops. He had got so close.

The flat-crab ground forward, crushing Racine's corpse into the ash.

The pressure set off the charges looped around him.

The vast cannonade of explosions flipped the crab up and over on its rear end. Quick-thinking gunners in the NorthCol armour hit its exposed belly hard. One shell touched off its magazine and it vaporised in a colossal jet of fire that blew out the top of Veyveyr Gate itself.

The Vervun Primary troops, wilting and shattered in the aftershock, swore that Racine would be remembered.

The Zoican troops were all over them. Corbec edged down a gully that had once been a side street in the railyard, the walls still standing, scarred and crater-peppered, around him. He had sixteen men with him, including Larkin and Trooper Genx, who carried a bipod autocannon.

Corbec's first thought was to order his men to hug the walls, but the streets seemed to funnel and corral the enemy fire, and las- and bolt-rounds ricocheted along them. He'd already lost three men who had kept to the walls and been blown down by the fire sliding down them. It was safer to stand out in the middle of the street.

They pushed ahead and met a detachment of Zoican storm troops, at least fifty of them, pouring into the eastern positions. Fire walloped back at them and Corbec marvelled at the way the las-rounds kissed and followed the stone walls. Trooper Fanck dropped, his chest gone. Trooper Manik was hit in the groin and his screams echoed around them.

Genx opened fire and his heavy cannon made a distinctive 'whuk-whuk-whuk' in the closed space. An enemy round took off his hand at the wrist and Corbec scooped up the autocannon and fired it himself. Genx, his stump instantly cauterised by the las-fire, got up without comment and began to feed his colonel's weapon.

Larkin took his targets as they came, blowing off heads or blowing out chests with the powerful kick of his sniper gun. The las-fire of the normal weapons was superhot but lacked stopping power. Larkin blanched as men beside him hit enemy troops who kept going despite precise hits which had passed through them cleanly. Only Larkin's sniper gun and Corbec's autocannon were actually dropping the foe first time so they wouldn't get up again.

The NorthCol were almost overrun. Colonel Bulwar called to Colonel Modine, but the Vervun Primary officer had apparently shut his vox link down.

'Anvil!' Bulwar signalled to Corbec, the only officer in this hell-fight he trusted. 'Anvil!'

Morning itself was rising above it all, unnoticed. At Sondar Gate, after more than two hours of intense fighting, the Zoican attack was driven off. Grizmund's Narmenian tanks had assembled in the Square of Marshals just inside the gate ready to face any force that broke in. They stood in rumbling lines just like Vegolain's had done in the first hours of the war, over a month before.

When the push at Sondar was repulsed, House Command signalled Grizmund to pull out and deploy along the southern manufactory highway to reinforce Veyveyr Gate. Two regiments of Vervun Primary Mechanised and a Volpone battlegroup were also directed to support Veyveyr, but the orders, handed down by Vice Marshal Anko, were imprecise and the reinforcement elements became throttled in queues on the arterial routes. Grizmund, frustrated and unable to get clear direction from House Command, moved his armour column off the highway and tried to approach Veyveyr via stock yards behind the manufactories. Proper authorisation for this was impossible as the vox-links were jammed with chatter from the chaos at the railhead. Grizmund had gone about two kilometres, forcing his tanks through chainlink fences and razorwire barricades, when VPHC units bellowing curses and orders through loudhailers headed them off and demanded they return to the highway.

The confrontation grew ugly. Grizmund himself descended from his tank and approached the VPHC troops directly, arguing that his unorthodox route was necessary. Tempers flew and when one of the VPHC commissars drew a pistol, Grizmund knocked him down. There was a brief brawl and the astonished Grizmund found himself and four of his senior commanders arrested at gunpoint. The VPHC dragged them off to House Command, leaving the Narmenian tank force leaderless and stymied, under the close watch of a growing force of VPHC.

The lack of concerted direction from House Command caused other disasters that made a bad day worse. The Vervun Primary and Volpone reinforcements were stalled all along the southern access. One group of Vervun motor-troops riding half-tracks with Hydra batteries mounted on the flatbeds were trapped in a side transit rout. In their agitation, they mistook a unit of Volpone Chimeras advancing behind them for an enemy force. By that stage, with nothing coming over the vox-links but undisciplined terror and panic from Veyveyr Gate, there was a general impression that the Zoicans had forced entry into the Hive and were sacking the southern quarters. The Hydra batteries opened fire, briefly, until the mistake was discovered. By then, thirteen Volpone troops were dead.

The Second Storm was showing up a great weakness in the Vervun-hive command structure. Vervun Primary, House Command and the VHPC had communication protocols and designated channels which worked efficiently during peace time or practice drills, but which were incapable of handling the sudden spikes in vox-traffic that accompanied heavy fighting. Worse still, the House Command vox-system, modelled on Imperial standard, used the same channel bands as the Imperial Guard and the NorthCol. Within an hour of the assault starting, it was virtually impossible for any unit commander to talk long range to his troops or for any order signals from House Command to reach the ground. It was even impossible to vox House Command for clarification. Only short-range vox-links between troops and officers in the field ground were still functioning. Some commanders tried to switch channels, hoping their men would have the same idea, but there was little chance of officers and men guessing the same new channel simultaneously.

At Croe Gate, General Nash had a measure of success. He switched to a wideband his Roane Deepers had famously been forced to use once on Kroxis and his vox-staffers on the ground had the same idea. For most of the day, Nash was the only senior commander in the field to have a direct open link to his forces.

A Volpone force under Corday also managed to resume contact with its distant elements. Corday adroitly used his short-range micro-beads to relay the new channel setting from man to man through the field. Unfortunately, he had chosen a channel that was crippled by interference from the Shield harmonics.

At Veyveyr, matters were made worse by the fact that Modile had shut down the main channel to cut off the demands of his officers – men like the late Racine – who were now questioning Modile's orders. Corbec received Bulwar's 'Anvil' code over the short-range and was able to co-ordinate his resistance with the NorthCol commander, but they found their forces conflicting with Vervun Primary troops following Modile's increasingly knee-jerk commands.

Gaunt, who had been at Hass West when the storm began, immediately headed for Veyveyr with Daur and a platoon of Tanith. Their troop-truck convoy found the back end of the reinforcement columns jammed fast and they struggled to find a way around or through. Gaunt tried Raglon's vox-set frantically to get House Command to rectify the growing logistical disaster, but he found the lines as jammed as the other commanders had before him.

He handed the speaker horn back to Raglon and looked down at the pale-faced Daur. The rumble and roar of the nightmarish Veyveyr battle backlit the buildings and habs ahead of them.

'How far to Veyveyr from here?' Gaunt snapped.

'Four, maybe five kilometres,' replied the Vervun Primary liaison.

Gaunt eyed the solid wall of troops and troop carriers choking the highway ahead and cursed quietly. Establishing proper and workable vox-protocols would be his priority once this day was done. The Vervun Primary were brave men and the noble houses were honourable institutions, but in war they were rank amateurs.

'Dismount!' Gaunt yelled back down his force and leaped out of the lead truck. Daur joined him, prepping the lasrifle he had drawn from stores after the First Storm. His arm still hurt and wasn't mended, but it worked well enough for him to carry a weapon and he'd be damned if he was going to follow the commissar into action again and have to ask to borrow a gun. He gulped down a couple of painkiller tablets to soothe the ache.

The fifty Tanith Ghosts had assembled on the road beside the trucks.

Gaunt walked down the rank, speaking directly and briefly. 'We're advancing on foot. It's five or so kilometres and we need to move fast, so ditch any extra weight – just carry weapons and ammunition, bayonets. Get rid of anything that'll slow you down or wear you out by the time we get there. Daur will lead.'

He looked round at Daur. 'Captain? Find a way.'

Daur nodded, confidently. Though a hiver born and bred, he knew the vast complexities of the southern manufactory district no better than the off-worlders. He pulled a chart-plate out of a thigh-pouch and deftly cycled through the map-patterns until he found the area they were in. With a stylus, he worked out a possible route. He was determined not to fail the Ghosts – and, more particularly, Gaunt.

'Follow me,' he said and headed off the road at a trot, pushing through a flak-board fence and into the service yard of a machinesmithy.

Gaunt and the Ghosts hurried after him.

At Croe Gate, the Zoican push was hitting the adamantine gates so hard and so frequently that they were denting and starting to glow with heat. Nash brought what mechanised forces he had into place inside the gates, in case they fell.

Outside, a line of enemy tanks and armoured fighting vehicles perhaps five hundred strong, stretched out down the cuttings of the rail tracks and the rockcrete supports of the elevated express line. Some Zoican infantry strengths were visible too, but so far it was entirely a war of cannon, rocket, mortar and wall-gun against tank and artillery. If the Vervunhive forces could only keep them out and keep the mighty gates sealed tight, the battle might never descend to the level of infantry mayhem that was occurring at Veyveyr.

If two such infantry fronts opened – if Croe Gate broke – Nash knew it could signal the start of an inexorable defeat for Vervunhive. He prayed to the holy Emperor of Terra that the Zoicans had no more death machines left to unleash.

Veyveyr was truly a nightmare. The air across the vast yard was thick with las-fire and tracers, gouts from flamers, whooping rockets and dense palls of smoke. Despite the volatile highlights of his combat career, Corbec had seldom seen anything so fierce or intense. Ducking into cover and trying to clear a feed-jam in the autocannon with Genx crouched next to him, Corbec wondered if it was because the fight was so enclosed: the Curtain Wall on one side, the manufactories around, the Shield above. It was as if this hellish firefight was being conducted in a box that concentrated the fury and amplified the noise.

Bulwar signalled him again and Corbec had to strain to hear. The NorthCol Commander was driving forward in a wedge from the west, bringing his armour in as well as his ground troops and several units of Vervun Primary that he had been able to pry away from the useless Modile. He wanted Corbec to support with his Ghosts from the east.

Corbec acknowledged. He sent the word down, from man to man, trying to unify them into a co-ordinated effort. But the Zoicans were everywhere and Corbec knew at least three parts of his force were bottled in behind him and fighting for their lives.

He took a look eastwards at the dank slopes of the Spoil. Enemy shelling still whooshed down into it and he could see the sparks of las-fire exchanged up and down the ore-slag. The Spoilers were engaging hostiles coming up the Spoil. He hoped the Zoicans would continue their push up at the well-defended Spoilers. If they turned west, they would flow in on his meagre force from the rear and–

He shut off the thought.

'How much?' he shouted at Genx.

With his one good hand, Genx indicated they had about three thousand rounds left for the autocannon, in loops around his body or in the panniers of ammo-drums he had collected. About two minutes' sustained fire, Corbec thought.

He voxed his men to present and move west. They rose, then immediately ducked back as a heavy rake of las-fire swept in from the northwest.

Corbec screamed a curse. The fething Vervun Primary, effectively leaderless and alone in the mid-yard, were firing at anything that moved and had flanked the Ghosts as well as if they'd planned it.

Corbec tried to raise Modile on the vox. All he got was Modile's adjutant screaming obscenities down the link, demanding that the NorthCol and the Tanith regroup as per battle orders.

Modile's dead. Gonna kill him myself, Corbec decided.

He rose and set the autocannon chugging a blurt of fire down the rubble line at Zoican movement.

A bolt-round slammed into the stone beside him and glanced off, hitting him in the thigh.

Corbec tumbled down with the impact and tried to claw the smouldering shell-case fragments out of his tunic pants. The cloth was punctured and there was blood. He found the round had been spent on impact with the stone and just the case had spun off into him, peppering his leg with dozens of metal scraps. He flexed the limb. It hurt and was bleeding freely, but he could use it.

Modile was definitely going to die.

There was no going west, not directly. He pulled his units after him and headed towards the gate under cover of the eastern trenches and barricades. They might be able to break west further down, beyond the range of the hopeless Vervun Primary.

Shells roared overhead and there were a great many more rockets banging in through the gate mouth now.

Corbec's force had gone a hundred metres when they met a battle-group of Zoican shock troops head on.

Milo reached the end of a shattered stretch of wall and tossed a grenade around the corner. As soon as the blast thumped out, vibrating his chest and spilling brick dust and plaster from the wall-section, he raced across the gap and took up station at the next las-chewed corner, kneeling, sweeping his lasgun around in the grenade smoke to cover Baffels, who crossed behind him.

A few enemy shots rang over their heads, higher than the wall, cracking the air.

Neskon and Rhys came up after, darting across the gap as Baffels and Milo fired cover.

'Where's Dremmond?' shouted Neskon over the roar. He was plastered in blood, but it wasn't his own.

'Ahead, I think!' yelled Milo. He tried his micro-bead link, but it just ground out static.

The platoon had been advancing down the ditchlines between the buildings towards the gate, in support of Colonel Corbec's brave push and for a while Dremmond's flamer had been clearing the way. But a trio of rockets had slammed into the ditch and broken the advance, and now the forward section of the platoon format, with Dremmond and Sergeant Fols in it, had advanced out of sight in the smoke.

Milo, Baffels and Rhys pushed on down the side of the next bombed-out storeblock as Neskon covered the gap for the next group of Ghosts: Domor, Filain and Tokar, followed by the vox-officer, Wheln, and Troopers Caill and Venar. Neskon and Domor then advanced, leaving Filain and Tokar to cover the overlap for the three following.

At the front of the group, Milo, Baffels and Rhys pushed forward again, grenading a break in the wall and sprinting across it to lay cover for the parties behind.

There was ferocious fighting from a hundred metres ahead. Milo's micro-bead squawked and he heard flashes of Corbec's commanding voice.

Domor and Neskon moved up to them and Domor probed the smoke cover ahead with the optic implants he had acquired after an injury on Menazoid Epsilon.

The focus rings hummed and whirred around the blank lenses. 'I read heat – lots of it. A flamer, pouring it on.'

Milo nodded. He could smell prometheum.

'Dremmond,' Baffels suggested.

Encouraged that they might be closing on their forward element, the platoon rallied and pushed forward. Milo realised that they seemed to be following him, looking to him for leadership, with Sergeant Fols absent. It was mad – they all had more combat experience than him, and all were older.

It was as if the gloss of Gaunt was on him, as if he represented some kind of natural authority simply by association with the commissar.

The cover ahead broke into a series of low-dug ditches punctuated with shell-craters. Enemy fire was sheeting across it, making it impassable. Milo saw at least two dead Ghosts twisted and broken in the ditch-line.

'Round! We go round!' he urged and Baffels nodded. The men liked Baffels too, and he seemed to be readily adopting the role of second to Milo's lead, like Corbec to Gaunt. Milo marvelled at the way structures simply evolved organically in combat, without question or spoken decision. With focus, fear and adrenaline that high, right on the tightrope of life and death, men made simple, natural decisions.

Or a well-trained, motivated unit like the Ghosts did at any rate. Milo was sure the Vervun Primary troops were collapsing simply because they lacked that resolve and that organic spontaneity.

He took his fellows left, towards the edge of the Spoil, through a series of drumlike scrap stores where greasy rail bogeys and axle blocks were stacked. Venar had an autocannon and several cans of ammo still strapped to his load-bearing harness, so Milo gave him point to clear the way. The rattle of short cannon bursts echoed through the stores as Venar picked the way ahead clean.

The stores opened out into a hectare or so of stockyard that was miraculously unscathed. Flatbed wagons and pipe-trucks sat in linked trains along six parallel sidings. There was a burned-out diesel locomotive at one buffer-end.

The platoon edged forward, through and around the dormant wagons, sometimes sliding under or between trucks, or clambering over hook assemblies thick with sooty oil.

Las-shots began to hammer into the wagons near Milo. They blew out sections on the wooden sideboarding, and Baffels and Milo were showered with splinters.

The men dropped into cover, spread out through the wagon yard. Curt assessments as to the angle and position of the shooters flicked back and forth through the micro-bead link. Venar fired a few bursts of cannon under the wagon he was sheltering behind, and Milo heard shots ping and ricochet off the ironwork of the bogeys.

The enemy fire increased.

Milo moved them forward. He saw Filain scoot out from between wagons and then duck back into cover as las-fire scooped up the gravel and stone around him. One shot severed a piece of track and the metal section broke with an almost musical chime.

Domor and Neskon also tried to move forward. They skirted back a few trucks and came out around a high-sided freight wagon. Las-shots spanged off the thin metal sides of the wagon. Neskon dropped, but Domor dragged him up and they fell into cover along the next truck line. Neskon wasn't hit. He had simply stumbled.

Milo and Baffels, with Rhys and Tokar just behind them, were pinned. Milo tried to creep around the end of the nearest wagon, but more firing erupted and he hit the ground, winded.

'You're hit!' he heard Baffels call.

'No, I'm fine–' Milo said.

'You're fething hit!' Baffels repeated.

Milo reached around and felt a wet hole in the left shoulder of his tunic. It was sore, but there was no real pain. He had been hit. He hadn't even felt it.

Milo got to his feet and then paused, lowering himself again and carefully looking out under the wagons. When he had dropped, he'd glimpsed something that his mind was only just identifying.

Three trains away, under the trucks, he could see feet. Armoured, heavy booted feet in distinctive ochre armour.

He waved the others down to look.

A dozen, maybe more.

Zoicans.

The punishing fire that had pinned them slowed. The Zoicans were evidently moving too, pushing in and around the trucks just as the Ghosts were, but from the other side.

Milo counted off the men and sent them wide, using the conceal-ment of the trucks. Few in the Imperial Guard moved as stealthily as the Tanith.

There was a burst of cannon fire twenty metres south of Milo. Then two more, a few answering las-shots. Venar had engaged.

More firing, brief and fierce, came from the next lane of wagons. Over the link, he heard Wheln curse, then laugh.

Baffels crawled ahead of Milo, down the length of a flatbed wagon. The Ghosts were all grey with gravel dust now, and their hands and knees were thick with oil.

Milo heard a dull sound from the body of the truck.

He yelled a warning and swung upwards as the Zoican storm-trooper appeared over the lip of the wagonbed and fired down. Baffels had rolled instinctively in under the side of the truck and slammed against the wheels and the sleepers as the Zoican's fire exploded the grit where he had been crawling.

Milo fired a burst upwards, punching three las-rounds through the aluminium siding of the wagon and the Zoican behind. The ochre-armoured figure convulsed and toppled clumsily out of the wagon. He landed next to the cowering Baffels, who automatically turned and shot the corpse through the head, point-blank.

Neskon, Rhys and Tokar were firing out between wagons, scoping for Zoicans just the other side of the track. Zoican las-fire and hard rounds came back between and under the wagons and forced Tokar to scramble on his arse back behind a slumped fuel drum. Neskon used the heavy bogey assembly of a wagon as cover and shuddered as persistent fire whipped under the cart-body and slammed into the huge iron wheels against his back.

Rhys rose, a las-round just missing his head, and lobbed a grenade over the wagon so that it fell neatly on the Zoican side of the rolling stock and vaporised them. A cracked Zoican helmet, split across the sneering, emotionless sculpture of the face, tumbled through the air and bounced near to his feet. He thought about taking it as a trophy until he realised there was the best part of a head left in it.

Milo heard Wheln cry out. The man was down. He could hear him moaning just a few paces away on the other side of the wagon.

'My leg... my leg...'

'Shut up!' Milo yelled, then dove over the hook-lock between wagons to roll clear on the other side of the track. Wheln was sprawled in the open between siding tracks, his left leg below the knee a ruin of blood, bone and tattered cloth.

Milo ran low to him, grabbed him under the arms and began to drag him into cover. Shots stitched the gravel around them. Two Zoicans appeared on the top of the next wagon over and another two edged out from between trucks. A las-shot cracked past Milo's nose, and then two more ripped through the loose folds of his camo-cape.

There was a bark of cannon fire, and the two Zoicans on the truck top came apart and fell. The others dropped back into cover. Milo got Wheln into the shelter of the back end of the wagon, pulling him in between the tracks. There was a group of Zoicans at the other end of the same truck, firing around it. Some fired under, but the shots were deflected by the axles. Milo looked frantically to each side for help. He saw Baffels in position behind a cart on the adjacent train, the one Milo had just scrambled from to reach Wheln. Baffels was too pinned with fire to make a shot.

Milo looked up, trying to ignore Wheln's moaning, and studied the hook-clamp that linked the wagon they were using as cover to the one behind them. It took him a few moments to figure out how to disengage it, his hands slipping on the greased iron.

When it was free, Milo hooked a grenade over a brake cable and pulled the pin. Then he yanked Wheln out from behind the truck and they fell down a slope the other side, Wheln shrieking with pain.

The grenade detonated and the force cannoned the freed truck, all eighteen tonnes of it, down the trackway, crushing the Zoicans sheltering at the far end between it and the next wagon on the rail. The entire length of rolling stock slammed and rattled into itself.

Rhys, Neskon and Baffels crossed over to cover Milo as the boy struggled to tie off Wheln's ruined limb and stop him bleeding out.

Wheln wouldn't stop screaming. Milo wanted to call for a medic, but he knew the vox-lines were useless and besides, Wheln had smashed the voxcaster when he fell. That was even supposing there was a medic anywhere near.

Baffels led Venar and the others and proceeded to clear the rest of the yard. A few brief exchanges with retreating Zoicans left more ochre bodies lying on or between the rails.

Milo could hear something else now, over the shooting and Wheln's shrieking and the constant thunder of the main battle.

Voices. Chanting voices, low and slick and evil.

The ammo-can clacked dry and the autocannon was useless. Corbec threw it aside and pulled his lasrifle off his shoulder, opening up again. His unit was right at the gate now, embroiled in an entirely structureless fight with the main force of the Zoican shock-troops. The fight blasted through the ruined outbuildings of the gatehouse complex and across the rubble-thick ground in the gate-mouth itself.

There were Zoicans everywhere.

Corbec had ceased to be a commander. There was nothing to command. He was simply a man fighting with every iota of strength and stamina left in him. He fought to stay alive and to kill the ochre shapes that drove at him from all sides.

It was the same for all the Ghosts in that engagement. The only thing that slowed the tide of Zoican invasion was the width of the blasted gate. In an open field, the forty or so Ghosts with Corbec would have been overrun long since.

Corbec was bleeding from a dozen light wounds. Those enemies he didn't kill outright with las-fire he demolished with blows from his rifle-stock and stabs of his bayonet.

Dremmond was suddenly alongside him, swathing the enemy in a wide cone of flames. The flamer pack on his back stuttered. Corbec knew that sound. The tanks were almost dry.

He yelled at Dremmond to wash the gates. What little flame they had left could best be used burning the entrance out.

Dremmond swung around, his spurting fire twisting like a whip. A dozen Zoicans crumpled, armour burning and melting off them. Some became torches that stumbled a few paces before they fell.

Dremmond bought Corbec a moment to think.

Corbec crossed, firing still, towards the wound-peppered wall of an outbuilding, glad he had jammed all the energy clips he could find into his jacket pockets that dawn.

Genx was in cover by the wall. By now the pain was beginning to trickle through and Genx was pale with trauma. Without his hand, he couldn't handle a lasrifle, although there were several fallen nearby, dropped by dead Zoicans and Tanith alike.

Corbec handed Genx his laspistol and the lad – Genx was no more than twenty, though built like a ox – began to crack away at any target in sight.

Supported by a trio of men, Sergeant Fols covered the entrance to a stairwell in the gatehouse, its roof blown off by the advance of the first flat-crab earlier. The blackened corpses of Vervun Primary gunners from the upper ramparts lay all around, amid the twisted wreckage of their fallen guns and piles of ceramite chunks.

Fols looked up at the mighty gate that they fought to protect. It was almost painful to see it with the top blown away, just two great gate towers adjoining the splintered Curtain Wall. The fort on top had fallen in and its debris made up the ground they fought over.

Fols also noticed how the Shield above them was rough-edged and intermittent. The death of the flat-crab which had blown out the arch of the massive gate had also taken down a relay station, and the Shield canopy was fraying and sparking out over them.

Fols felt wet and realised it was rain. The torrential downpour outside was still hammering and now, with the Shield ripped back for a hundred metres or so, it was falling on them too.

The ground was turning to mush as the rain made gluey soup out of the ankle-deep ash.

The Ghost next to Fols dropped wordlessly, his jaw vaporised. Streams of rain ran down them all, colouring with blood and dirt.

Fols rounded his two remaining men into the staircase, firing across the gate. The rain and smoke was killing visibility.

Fols saw the bright blurt of Dremmond's flamer a little way off, saw how the rain made steam off the white-hot blasts and heated stones.

The man next to him yelled something and Fols realised there were Zoican shock troops spilling over the side walls behind them by the dozen.

He turned, killed three. A welter of las-shots cut his men apart and splashed the wall they had just been using for cover with their blood. Fols lost a knee, an eye, an elbow and a fourth shot tore through his belly.

He was still firing when a Zoican bayonet impaled him to the wall.

The chanting continued. The Zoican shock forces were pushing through Veyveyr Gate holding banner-poles aloft, the whipping flags marked with the symbol of Ferrozoica and with other emblems that stung the eyes and nauseated the gut: the runes and badges of the Chaos pestilence that had overwhelmed them.

Some of the Zoicans had loudhailers wired and bolted to their helmet fronts and were broadcasting abominable hymns of filth and whining prayers of destruction.

From his position, Corbec knew the Zoicans believed their victory was assured.

He wished he could deny it, but with the pitiful numbers left to him, he didn't stand a chance.

He changed clips again, throwing the dead one away into the rubble. Next to him, Genx and two other troopers reloaded.

They would kill as many as they could. In the name of the Emperor, there was no more they could do.

Data-pulses told him the fighting was intense, bestial. But it was so very far away. It came to him only as unemphatic bursts of information, unemotional cascades of facts.

Salvador Sondar drifted in his Iron Tank. He was becoming increasingly disinterested in the trials of the hive soldiers. What was happening at Croe Gate and, more vitally, at Veyveyr was an inconsequential dream to him.

All that really mattered now to the High Master of Vervunhive was the chatter.

A rocket cremated Trooper Feax and threw Larkin into the air. He came down hard amid the rubble and the bodies, ears dead, vision swimming and his beloved rifle nowhere in sight.

He clambered up. He had been with Corbec's unit at the gate. That was the last thing he remembered.

His hearing began to return. He heard the wretched chanting of the

Zoican advance as from underwater. He saw the las-fire and banner poles as dancing bright colours in the smoke.

A Zoican was right on top of him, glaring down out of that fearsome mask-visor, stabbing with his bayonet.

Larkin lurched aside and fell off a length of wall, two metres down to a bed of debris below. Ignoring his spasming back, he yanked out his silver Tanith knife and leapt at the Zoican the moment he reappeared over the gully-lip.

The Zoican bayonet cut through Larkin's sleeve. He slammed the brute back over into the rubble and pushed his blade in, trying to find a space between the ochre armour plating.

It went in, just below the neck seal of the battle-suit. Foul-smelling blood began to spurt out over Larkin's arm and hand, and it stung like acid.

The Zoican thrashed and spasmed. Larkin fought back, clawing, kicking and wrenching on his blade's grip.

He and the Zoican rolled twenty metres down the rubble slope. At the foot, Larkin's frantic efforts ripped the Zoican's helmet off.

He was the first person in Vervunhive to see the face of the enemy, square on, naked, shorn of armour or mask or visor.

Larkin screamed.

And then stabbed and stabbed and stabbed.

A torrent of las-fire cut across the gate from the west. Zoicans crumpled, falling on their banner poles, loudspeakers exploding as they died. Corbec and his men, amazed, pushed around to support, hammering into the halted storm force with renewed vigour.

Nine platoons of Vervun Primary troops funnelled in across the open gate from the west with Commissar Kowle at the head.

Kowle had headed for Veyveyr Gate from House Command the moment the action began at dawn and it had taken him until now – almost noon – to reach the front. Unable to reach Modile or any Vervun command group, he had grabbed Vervun troops by force of authority and personality alone and led them towards the gate flanked by Bulwar's men and armour.

Kowle was singing an Imperial hymn at the top of his lungs and firing with a storm bolter.

Bulwar's NorthCol units pressed in behind, and Bulwar had the sense to spread them east to reinforce the failing Tanith line.

Corbec couldn't believe his eyes. At last, a co-ordinated effort. He rallied his remaining men and scoured the eastern flank of the gate for signs of Zoicans. His support helped Kowle reach the gate itself, a gate that had been held by the Tanith alone for more than an hour.

The three prongs – Tanith, Vervun and NorthCol – pushed the Zoicans back out into the outer habs and the torrential rain. Kowle moved his units aside to allow Bulwar's armour to finish the job and block the gate, though not before the commissar had posed for propaganda shots that were quickly relayed across the entire public-address system of the hive: Kowle, victorious in the blasted mouth of Veyveyr; Kowle, blasting at the enemy; Kowle, holding the Vervun banner aloft on a heap of rubble as Vervun Primary troops mobbed to help him plant the flag-spike in the ground.

By early afternoon, the gate was held fast by fifty tanks of the North-Col armoured. Kowle was once more the People's Hero. The battle for Veyveyr Gate was over.

At Croe Gate, as news of the overturn reached the Zoican elements, the fighting diminished. Nash sighed in relief as the enemy withdrew from the smouldering gate-hatches. He ordered the wall guns to punish them anyway.

None of the victorious public-address messages mentioned the losses: 440 Vervun Primary and 200 Roane Deepers at Croe Gate, 500 Vervun 'Spoilers' along the Spoil, 3,500 Vervun Primary, 900 NorthCol and almost a hundred Tanith at Veyveyr.

They had a victory and a hero, and that was all that mattered.

Gaunt and his small reinforcement group reached Veyveyr just as the battle was ending. Gaunt was hot with anger and determination.

Daur led him down a trench to the Vervun Primary Command post where Colonel Modile was rallying men and directing vox-links.

Modile looked around as Gaunt strode into the culvert shelter, stony-faced.

'The battle is over. We have won. Vervunhive is victorious,' Modile said blankly into Gaunt's face.

'I've been listening to the vox. I know what occurred here. You balked, Modile. You lost control. You hid. You shut down the vox-channels when you didn't like what you heard.'

Modile shrugged vacuously at Gaunt. 'But we won...'

The Tanith troops stepped into the command post around Gaunt. Even Daur, grim-faced, had a weapon drawn.

'Round up all the officers and detain them. I want a transcript of all vox-traffic,' Gaunt ordered. The Ghosts fanned out to do so and the Vervun Primary staffers blinked in confusion as they were jostled around.

'What are you doing?' Modile asked haughtily. 'This is my gakking command area!'

DAN ABNETT

'And you've commanded what, exactly? A bloodbath. You dismay me, Modile. Men were shrieking for orders and support, and you ignored them. I heard it all.'

'It was a difficult incident,' Modile said.

'I have a reputation, Modile,' Gaunt said, 'a reputation as a fair, honest man who treats his soldiers well and supports them in the face of darkness. Potentially, that reputation makes me soft. It seems I understand failure and forgive it.

'Some, like Kowle, believe me to be a weak commissar, not prepared to take the action my rank demands. Not prepared to enforce field discipline where I see it failing.'

Gaunt removed his cap and handed it to Daur. He stared at Modile, who still wasn't sure what was going on.

'I am an Imperial commissar. I will enflame the weak, support the wavering, guide the lost. I will be all things to all men who need me. But I will also punish without hesitation the incompetent, the cowardly and the treasonous.'

'Gaunt, I–' Modile began.

'*Commissar* Gaunt. Do not speak further. You have cost lives this day.'

Modile backed away, suddenly, horribly realising what was happening.

Gaunt took his bolt pistol from his holster. 'For courtesy, choose: a firing squad of your own men or a summary execution.'

Modile stammered, lost control of his bowels and turned to run.

Gaunt shot him through the head.

'Have it your own way,' he said sadly.

TEN

CASUALTIES

*'There came a point, a few years into my career, when I knew
I had seen enough. Since then, I have seen a lot more, but I
have blocked it out. The soul stands only so much.'*

– Surgeon Master Goleca, after the
Exsanguination of Augustus IX

From the sound of it, there was a hell of a brawl going on at Veyveyr Gate.
The sky under the Shield blazed up at intervals with explosive light, and
sound drummed across the hive. It had been going on since daybreak.

The baby, Yoncy, was crying plaintively and making sobbing, sucking noises. It had been doing it all night. Tona wasn't sure what to do.
Dalin was sullen and quiet, and he slept in the back of the trash-cave
most of the time.

Tona crawled forward out of her dugout and looked across the
shell-ruined slopes. Below, half a kilometre away, lay the fenced and
razor-wired troop billet of Gavunda Chem Plant Storebarns/Southwest.

That was where the off-world soldiers lived, the pale-skinned,
dark-haired ones with their black costumes and blue tattoos. Tona
wondered if they came from a hiveworld too, if the blue tats were gang
badges or rank marks.

She dreamed of their food. There was a banquet fit for the Emperor
secured down there in the back sheds. She'd sent Dalin in to scrounge
and steal a few times, but it was getting dangerous.

Tona knew it was up to her now. The baby was weak and crying. She
needed milk powder and basic nutrient paste.

There were over a thousand other refugees hiding in the trash slopes
and crater-plains in the shell-flattened manufactories near to her, but
she never thought to ask any for help. Everyone in Vervunhive was on
their own now.

A particularly fierce airburst cracked the sky above Veyveyr, and Tona turned to look. She'd been to Veyveyr railhead a few times and had stood in the glass hall of the main station, now long gone, watching the snooty up-Spine travellers move to and fro from platforms. Her twice-uncle Rika had run a snack-stall there, and she'd also been a part of a pocket-prey team for a few months.

The Grand Terminus had awed her, even as she worked it. It had seemed to her a doorway to anywhere. If she'd had the credit, she'd have jumped a train south to the tropical hives, to the archipelago, maybe even to Verghast Badport where, so they said, it was possible to buy a route to anywhere, including off-world.

Veyveyr Gate had always seemed to her a way off this rock. A possible future. A promise.

Now it was dead and burned out, and callous, off-world soldiers dirtied it with brutal war.

The baby was squalling again. Tona edged out of her bunker and looked back at Dalin. 'Stay with him. I'll be back soon with food.'

Tona slid down the rubble stacks and moved towards the wire fence of the troop compound.

Tona crossed the ruinscape of the manufactories, industrial areas that had been levelled on that first day before the Shield lit up. Shattered rockcrete buildings flanked the lips of craters twenty metres across or more. Ruptured metal sheeting and snapped pipes poked from the brick dust. Unrecognisable pieces of burnt machinery scattered the ground.

Bodies lay where they had fallen and after a month these were nothing more than loose husks of shrivelled bone and ragged clothing. The rescue teams had taken away most of the wounded in the initial recovery and habbers had carried their own dead out. But still bodies remained, crumpled and half-buried in the wide ruin. Carrion-dogs, lean, diseased and mangy, haunted the rubble, scavenging what they could – like her, she supposed, though unlike the hounds, she drew the line at feeding off corpses. There was a stagnant, rotten smell to the place and sickness lingered. Thousands like her, mostly low-caste or the dispossessed from the outer habs, had made this place a temporary home when the main refuge camps had over-spilled. Tona Criid, like many of Vervunhive's base-level citizens, avoided the refuges, for though they offered food and medical rations, they also represented authority and prejudice. The VPHC controlled most refuges brutally.

She saw others prowling the ruins. Adults mostly, a few children, all thin and dark with filth, their clothes wretched and ragged. Some stared at her as she passed; some ignored her. None spoke.

She passed a store block where parts of the side windows were intact and she saw her own reflection. It shocked her. A straggly, pale thing with dirty clothes and sunken eyes looked back at her. She had expected to see the bright-eyed, cocky hab-girl with the flashy piercings and snarling smile.

Seeing the leanness of her own face, she realised how hungry she was. She'd been blocking the feeling. Her empty belly knotted and ached with such sudden fury that she dropped to the ground for a moment, sitting on a cinder block until the pain eased enough for her to stand without cramps or wooziness.

She took the flask from her belt and sipped a few, precious mouthfuls from the drink-spout. Half full, it was the last of a box of electrolyte fluid bottles she'd recovered from a mining store near Vervun Smeltery One. She was sure that the fluid-packs were the main reason she'd kept herself and the children alive for the last month.

She hooked the flask back onto her belt and then took out her blade. The back fence of the military compound was just a few metres away now. It seemed deserted. Maybe they were all fighting at the gate. It sounded like it.

Her brother Nake had given her the blade on her tenth year-day, just a few weeks before he was killed in a gangfight in Down-Reach under the Main Spine. Nake Criid had been a member of the Verves, one of the key undergangs, and the knife's handle was decorated with a carefully carved Verve crest: a laughing skull resting in the dip of a gothic V. Tona sported a few gang badges herself – an ear-stud, a buckle, a small snake-tat on her shoulder – but she'd never been properly blooded into any gang to speak of. She had run with a few gang crowds and known a boy or two who'd been gang-blooded. While she was with them, they'd each tried to induct her, but she'd resisted. The one thing Tona Criid had always known, ever since Nake had died of stab wounds in an unlit, Down-Reach sewer seven years ago, was that ganger life was dumb and pointless and short. She'd make her own way in life, be her own master, or get nowhere at all.

The blade was a compact chain-form: a thick, decorated grip with an extending blade of steel fifteen centimetres long. A flick of the rubberised stud on the index-finger ridge activated an internal power-cell that made the blade-edge vibrate so fast it looked still. But, gak, could it cut!

She touched the stud and the blade purred. She switched it off and crawled towards the flak-board fence.

The supply barn was dark and as stacked with supplies as she remembered it. She couldn't read many of the labels on the crate stacks, so it was a matter of cutting them open and sampling them. The first she tried was full of small flat boxes packed with bootlaces.

The second had cartons of stoppered metal tubes. Hoping they might be food-paste, she squeezed a coil of black matter out into her palm and licked it.

She spat, retching. If this is what the off-world fighters ate, they were truly from another world. She moved on, leaving the half-squeezed tube of camo-paint on the floor behind her.

Ear-pieces with wires and plugs. Powercells. Rolls of gauze in paper wraps that smelled of disinfectant.

In the next crate-stack, foil-packs of freeze-dried buckwheat porridge. Better. She dropped half a dozen into her bag, then added a handful more. She'd eat them dry if she couldn't find water. Then she found chemical blocks for firelighting and a pile went into her bag. Next, metal beakers. She prised one out of its packing, then another. Dalin would want his own.

In the next row, pay dirt: corn crackers in long, plastic tubes, soya bars in vacuum-packets. She pushed a dozen or more into her bag and bladed one open, cramming the soft, wet food into her mouth and gulping it down, brine dribbling down her chin and pattering on the floor.

Tona froze, mid-swallow, her cheeks bulging, her stomach gnawing at her with the sudden input of food. A noise, behind her, to the right, a noise her wolfish chewing had half-hidden. She ducked into cover.

A flashlight flickered between supply stacks, three rows away. She willed herself invisible and huddled behind a tower of mess-tin crates, the blade in her hand. The beam of light jiggled around and she heard a voice, uttering a snarl. The sudden crack and flash of a lasweapon made her jump out of her boots. A carrion-dog went racing past her, yelping and trailing a burned hind leg.

She relaxed a little. The voice said something in an accent she couldn't work out. The flashlight wavered, then moved off and away.

She darted across the aisle into the next bank of crates. A few slices of her knife, all the while listening to the darkness around her. Nutrient packs for first aid. Tins of soup that heated themselves when the foil strip was pulled out. Jars of air-dried vegetables in oil. Small, flat cans of preserved fish. Cartons of heat-treated milk.

She took a handful of them all. Her pack was heavy now and she was pushing her luck. Time to go.

Light jabbed down into her face, making her cry out, and a hand grabbed her shoulder.

Tona Criid had been taught to fight by her brothers, all of them gangers. Instinctively, she pivoted back into the grip and shoulder-threw the owner of the hand. The flashlight bounced away across the rockcrete barn floor and the heavy male form bounced after it, barking out an oath and most of its breath.

But it had her still, and even as it went over her, it twisted her round in combat-trained hands and threw her sideways into the crate stack.

The impact stunned her. She tried to rise, hearing the other moving too. A few more oaths, a harsh question she didn't understand.

She rose and delivered a spin-kick into the darkness. It would be the VPHC, she was sure. She braced for the las-shot, the bolt-round, the mind-set that would treat her no better than a carrion-dog.

Her spinning foot connected and the figure went down with a bone-crack. More rampant cursing.

Tona ran for the crack in the barn wall.

A much larger form tackled her from behind in the dark and brought her down on her belly on the rockcrete floor. She was frantic now, kicking and thrashing.

Her assailant had her pinned by way of superior strength and technique. His weight slumped on top of her and the flashlight winked on again, probing down at her wincing eyes.

'It's all right, it's all right,' said a hoarse voice in tunefully accented Low Gothic. 'Don't fight me.'

She looked up, fighting still. She saw the face of the off-world soldier, the young one, the man who had chased Dalin out of the barn weeks before.

The blade purred in her hand and she sliced it upwards.

Caffran saw the vibro-blade coming and threw himself aside, releasing his captive. It was the gang girl, the beautiful one he had glimpsed across the rubble when he had gone chasing the boy.

She was on her feet now, menacing with the buzzing blade, head down. Knife-combat stance, thought Caffran, good enough to be a Ghost.

'Put it down,' he said carefully. 'I can help you.'

She turned and ran, heading for the slit in the fibre-board back wall of the barn.

Caffran pulled out his laspistol, braced his aiming hand and fired three times, blowing a ring of holes in the back wall of the shed around her. Daylight streamed in through the punctures. She skidded to a halt, frozen, as if expecting the next one to let the light shine through her too.

Caffran got to his feet, gun raised. 'I can help you,' he repeated. 'I don't want to see you live like that. You've got children, right, a boy at least? What do you need?'

She turned slowly to face him and his light, blade in one hand, the other raised against the stabbing beam. Caffran lowered it so it wouldn't blind her.

'Trick,' she said.

'What?'

'This is a trick. Just shoot me, you gak.'

'No trick.' He stepped forward and holstered his pistol. 'No trick.'

She flew at him, blade slicing the air. He flinched and grabbed her arms, rolling backwards to deposit her flat on her own back. The impact knocked her out for a moment.

Caffran kicked the purring blade away.

He pulled her up. She was coughing and gasping. She felt so thin and fragile in his hands, though he knew she was mean and tough enough to hurt him.

'What's your name?' he asked.

Her jabbing fingers punched into his eyes and he bellowed, rolling back and clutching his face.

By the time he struggled up again, she was pushing through the back wall to freedom. Caffran noticed she had been mindful enough to recover her blade.

He ran after her.

'Feth you, stop! I want to help! Stop!'

She looked back at him, her eyes as wild and mad as an animal. Her bulging pack was caught on a fork of fibre-boards, preventing her from squeezing through the hole.

'Get away! Get away!' she shrilled.

He approached her, hands held wide and empty, trying to look unthreatening.

'I won't hurt you... please... my name is Caffran. My friends call me Caff. I'm a lost soul like you. Just a Ghost without a home. I didn't ask for this and I know you fething didn't. Please...'

He was a hand's reach away from her now, hating the fear in her face. She spat and howled, then jabbed her blade round and cut the strap of her pack. It dropped to the ground, but she was free. Abandoning it, she flew out of the barn and sprinted away across the rubble.

Caffran pushed out after her, straining to get his greater bulk through the slit.

He got a glimpse of her looking back and terrified, darting over the splintered mounds of wreckage before dropping out of sight.

Tona lay in cover for a few minutes, buried in the soot of a crater, stinking corpses around her. When it seemed the soldier was not following, she crawled out and ran a few metres to a slumped wall and hid behind it.

Then she heard a crunch of boots on rubble and froze.

Twenty metres away, looking in the wrong direction, the black-uniformed soldier was walking up through the ruins, her pack dangling from his hand.

'Hello?' he was calling. 'Hello? You need this. You really do. Hello?'

He stood for a long while, maybe ten minutes, looking around. Tona remained in hiding. Finally, the soldier put the pack down.

'It's here if you want it,' he said. A long pause.

Then he walked back down the ruin slope and clambered back into the barn.

Tona waited a full fifteen minutes more before she moved. She ran from cover, scooped up the pack and leapt away into the confused maze of the ruins.

The soldier didn't reappear or follow.

In a foxhole, she hunched and opened the pack, studying the contents. Everything she had taken was there, everything – as well as three flasks of sterilised water, a field-dressing kit, a pack of one-shot antibiotic jabs, some net-wrapped dry sausage... and a laspistol, the very laspistol she was sure he had fired after her in the barn. The charge pack was almost full.

She was dazed for a while, then she laughed. Gleeful, she took up the sack of trophies and ran back to her shelter, taking a wide route so she wouldn't be followed.

It was only later, after she and Dalin had eaten their first good meal in a month and Yoncy was sleeping and content on milk-broth, that she found the cap-pin at the bottom of the pack: silver, clean, an Imperial eagle with the double head and the inscription *Tanith First, by the Grace of the God-Emperor of Terra* on the scroll held in the clawed feet.

In the gloomy dugout, her belly full, her wards fed and content, Tona Criid sat back by the light of a fire kindled from Guard-issue chemical blocks and wondered where she would pin the crest. As gang-badges went, it was better than most.

Behind Veyveyr Gate, the dead dominated the streets and squares.

Teams of Vervun Primary, work militia and Munitorum labourers, their faces masked by breathers or strips of torn cloth, carried the dead from the battle away from the smouldering railhead and laid them out in the open places north of Veyveyr for identification and disposal.

Agun Soric had brought his workforce in from the Commercia Refuge

after the fighting had died down, and he had put them to work assist-
ing the morbid but necessary duty.

He wanted to fight. Gak, but that brave Vervun Primary officer –
what was his name? Racine! The one who'd given them the chance to
pull their weight preparing the defence. He'd given Soric the taste of it.
But for want of proper weapons, Soric and his people would have been
at the front that morning. Let Ferrozoica tremble to face the wrath of
smeltery workers from Vervun One with the blood up!

From what he'd been able to learn from those milling about him –
some off-world Guard, some NorthCol – Soric knew the ferocious
battle had ended with Zoica pushed out against all odds. He hoped
to see Racine soon and slap the man's back and hear how the pioneer
efforts his workers had put in had helped to win the day by building
defences the enemy couldn't overrun.

There was time enough. With smeltery workers Gannif, Fafenge and
Modj, Soric began loading corpses onto a handcart. It was filthy, bes-
tial work. They tried to wrap each body in a skein of linen and they'd
been told to take tags and mark the identity of each on a data-slate.
But some bodies didn't come up in one piece. Some were only parts.
Some parts didn't match up obviously with others.

Some were still alive.

The place was a charnel house. Bodycarts moved all around them,
medical and clearance personnel milled around and the wounded
shuffled in slow, weary lines away from the gate railhead, many
exhibiting awful injuries. Every now and then, they made way for a
truck or a trundling medical Chimera, speeding away to the medical halls.

Soric, his hip braced on his axe-rake crutch, leaned down and slid his
paper-gloved hands under the armpits of a blackened, legless corpse.

As he raised the cadaver, it groaned.

'Medic! Medic!' he cried out, pulling back from the ruined thing he
had been touching.

A thickset medical officer pushed through the milling crowd, a man
in his fifties with a silver beard and the look of an off-worlder about
him. Under his hall-issue crimson apron he wore black fatigues and
Guard-issue boots.

'Alive?' the medic asked Soric.

'Gak me, I suppose so. Tried to move him.'

The medic took out a flexible tube, put one end to his ear and the
other to the blackened torso.

'Dead. You must have squeezed air out of the lungs when you lifted
him.'

Soric nodded as the medic stood up, folding his scope-tube away into his shoulder-slung pack.

'You're off-world, right?' asked Soric.

'What?' asked the medic, distracted.

'Off-worlder?'

The medic nodded curtly. 'Tanith First. Chief medic.'

Soric stuck out a hand, then pulled the paper glove off it. 'Thank you,' he said.

The medic paused, surprised, then took the hand and shook it.

'Dorden, Gaunt's First and Only.'

'Soric. I used to run that place.' Soric gestured over his shoulder at the ruin of Vervun Smeltery One east of the railhead.

'This is a bad time for all of us,' Dorden said, studying the bullish, noble man who leaned on his crutch, black with ash.

Soric nodded.

'That eye wound... has it been treated?' asked Dorden, stepping forward.

Soric held up his hand. 'Old news, friend, weeks old. There are others more needy of your skills.'

As if on cue, VPHC troops wheeled past a cart carrying a screaming, blood-soaked NorthCol soldier.

Mtane and one of Curth's people hurried to it.

Dorden looked round at Soric. 'You thanked me. Why?'

Soric shrugged. 'I've been through this from the start. We were left to die. You didn't have to come here but you did and I thank you for it.'

Dorden shook his head. 'Warmaster Macaroth sends us where he wills. I'm glad to be able to help, however.'

'Without you off-worlders, Vervunhive would be dead. That's why I thank you.'

'I appreciate it. Mine is often a thankless task.'

'Have you seen Major Racine? Vervun Primary? He's a good man...'

Dorden shook his head and turned to where stretcher-bearers were beginning to bring the Tanith wounded out of the warzone. Troopers Milo and Baffels were carrying Manik, howling from the wound to his groin, blood dribbling over the edges of the stretcher.

Dorden moved in to deal with Manik. He was sure the young trooper was going to bleed out any moment.

He looked around at Baffels and Milo as he worked. 'Racine? You know what happened to him?'

Dorden's hands were already slippery with Manik's blood. The groin artery had burst and he couldn't tie it. It was pulling back into the body cavity and Dorden bellowed for Lesp to bring clean blades.

'Major Racine?' Milo said, standing back from Manik's stretcher, adjusting the dressing on his shoulder wound. 'He died. Under a flat-crab. He killed it, but he died.'

Soric listened to the off-world boy and shook his head sadly.

Lesp stumbled over the rubble and brought Dorden a scalpel. Dorden used it to try and open the screaming Manik's groin wide enough so he could push his fingers in and pull the severed artery down to clamp it. It was too late. Manik bled out through his body cavity and died with Dorden's hand still inside him.

'Let me take him,' Soric said and, with his men, he gently lifted Manik's body onto his wheel-cart. Dorden was almost shocked by the reverence.

'Every soul for the hive, and the hive for every soul,' Soric said over his shoulder to the blood-soaked Dorden as he wheeled the dead Ghost away.

Ana Curth moved her orderlies through the confusion of Veyveyr Gate. There were more dead to recover than living.

She checked each corpse in turn, pulled off the tags and then left them for the recovery units.

She hesitated slightly when she found the corpses of Tanith. These were all Dorden's friends. She took off their tags carefully and entered all the names in her data-slate.

In the gateway of Veyveyr, she paused. She checked the latest set of tags three times to be sure.

Tears welled in her eyes and she pushed the bloody tags into her apron-front.

The thirty-second day drew to a close. It was a day the citizens of Vervunhive would remember perhaps more keenly than anything that had taken place so far. Despite the success of driving back the First Storm three days before, this seemed much more of a victory. Scant hours after the battle, the defence of Veyveyr began to take on a mythical flavour. In the Spine, the habs and the refuges alike, Vervunhivers spoke of it as a turning point, as the start of deliverance.

Public-address plates across the hive broadcast triumphant slogans, sanitised accounts of the battle and pictures from the glorious front, mainly those showing the People's Hero raising the flag in the shattered gate-mouth, surrounded by jubilant Vervun Primary troopers. In the Basilica of the Ecclesiarchy, a victory mass was organised, featuring a choir of over ten thousand and long liturgical readings from the Codex Imperialis. Loudspeakers broadcast the worship across all the hive levels.

Spontaneous celebrations began in different areas and some revels – amongst Vervun Primary troops heady with relief – were broken up by the VPHC.

But the mood was impossible to suppress in the highest and lowest quarters of the hive. Oilcan fires were lit along the wharves and in the refuges, and drums, many homemade or improvised, thundered into the night. There were many reports of decadent banqueting in the High Spine, as merchants and house ordinary families abandoned the rationing restrictions and indulged in sumptuous private dinners of unstinting debauchery.

When Gaunt heard about them, he sighed. These were either gestures of ignorance or acts of denial against what must surely still await.

But let them have their delights, he decided. They may be their last.

In a grim mood, he'd stayed on at Veyveyr as the light failed, touring his men, noting those lost, restructuring squads around those losses. He gave Trooper Baffels a field promotion to sergeant and placed him in charge of Fols's unit. The stocky, bearded trooper was almost overcome with emotion as Neskon, Domor, Milo and the others cheered him. He shook Gaunt's hand and wiped away a tear that trickled down over his blue claw tattoo. There had been a brief rumour that Gaunt would award the sergeant pin to Milo, but that was absurd. He was barely a trooper and it wouldn't look right, though Milo's actions and improvised leadership at Veyveyr had won him a considerable respect that sat well with his reputation as the avatar of Gaunt.

Under Corbec's command, the Tanith units who had seen action at Veyveyr pulled out to a mustering yard north of the Spoil, and fresh units under Rawne, partnered with Volpone forces commanded by Colonel Corday, moved in to hold the gate position. Stonemasons, metalworkers and engineers from the hab workforce were called up to assist the sapper units in defending the gate. Using fallen stone from the gate top, the masons erected two well-finished dyke walls just outside the gate, and the incandescent glare of oxylene torches fizzled in the night rain as the metalwrights crafted pavises and hoardings from broken tank plates. Sections of rail – and there were kilometres of it scattered throughout the railhead – were broken up and welded into cross-frames to carry barbed wire and razorwire strings.

In an intensive twelve-hour period, with work continuing throughout the night under lamp-rigs, the workforce raised impressive concentric rings of well-built defences both inside and outside the broken gate. There were ramps along the eastern edge to allow forward access for the NorthCol tank files marshalled behind the troop lines. A forest of howitzers, barrels raised almost upright like slightly leaning trees, was established on the site of the main terminus, with a clear field of fire to bombard up and beyond the gate.

In the mustering yard, weary Tanith and NorthCol units from the front sprawled on rolled up jackets or on the hardpan itself, many falling asleep as soon as they got off their feet. Mess trucks with tureens of soup, baskets of bread and crates of weak beer arrived to tend them. It was estimated that they would be there until dawn, when the arterial routes would be finally clear enough for transports to carry them back to their billets.

In the gloomy rear section of a NorthCol Chimera, Corbec and Bulwar shared a bottle and dissected the day. The performance of the Vervun troops and of Modile especially was cursed frequently. The bottle was vintage sacra from Corbec's own stock and he broke the wax-foil stamp with relish. Bulwar had set his power-claw on a metal rack and, flexing fingers stiff from the glove, produced two shot glasses from a leather box, and a tin of fat smokes, the best brand the Northern Collective hives produced.

Bulwar had never tasted the Tanith liquor before, but he didn't flinch and Corbec wasn't surprised. Bulwar was as grizzled and hardened a soldier as any Corbec had met in his career. They clinked glasses again.

'Anvil,' Corbec toasted, letting blue smoke curl out of his mouth to wreath his face.

Bulwar nodded. 'Let's hope we don't need it again. But I have an ache in my leg that says there's a measure left before us.'

'Your leg?'

Bulwar tapped his right thigh. 'Metal hip. A stub round during the moon war. Hurts like buggery when it's damp – and worse when trouble's coming.'

'Weather's changing. More rain on the way.'

'That's not why it's aching.'

Corbec refilled their glasses.

'But for this moon war, you've never been off this place?'

'No,' replied Bulwar. 'Wanted to muster for the Guard at the last founding, but I was a major by then and my path was set. Planetary Defence, like my father and his before him.'

'It's a noble calling. I could have wished for it myself, commanding the garrison of a city back home.'

'Where is that again? Tanith?'

Corbec toyed with the tiny glass in his paw. He pursed his lips. 'Dead and gone. We're the last of it.'

'How?'

'We were founding, the first founding Tanith had made. Three regiments assembled to join the Warmaster's crusade. This was just after Balhaut, you understand. Gaunt had been sent to knock us into shape. There was a... a miscalculation. A Chaos fleet slipped through the interdiction set up by the advancing Segmentum Pacificus Navy and assaulted Tanith. Gaunt had a choice: Get out with those troop elements he could save, or stay and die with the planet.'

'And he chose the former...'

'Like any good commander would. I like old Ibram Gaunt, but he's a commissar at heart. Hardline, worships the Emperor above his own life, dedicated to discipline. He took us out, about two thousand of us, and Tanith burned as we left it behind. We've been paying back the enemy ever since.'

Bulwar nodded. 'That's why you're called Ghosts, I suppose?'

Corbec chuckled and poured some more sacra for them both.

Bulwar was silent for a while. 'I can't imagine what it's like to lose your homeworld.' Corbec didn't make the reply that flashed into his mind, but Bulwar saw the logic of his own words and spoke the unspoken anyway. 'I hope I don't find out.'

Corbec raised his glass. 'By the spirit of my lost world,' he said mischievously, glancing at the sacra, 'may we Ghosts ensure there are never any Verghast ghosts.'

They downed their drinks with heartfelt gulps. Bulwar got up and began to rummage in a footlocker bolted to the carrier's hull. He pulled out map-cases, ammo-cans and a sheaf of signal flags before finding what he was looking for: a tall-shouldered bottle of brown glass. 'We've toasted with your Tanith brew, which I commend for its fine qualities, but it's only fair we toast now with a Verghast vintage. Joiliq. Ten year old, cask-fermented.'

Corbec smiled. 'I'll try anything once.' He knocked it back, savoured it, smiled again. 'Or twice,' he said, proffering his glass.

By a roaring oil-drum fire, Baffels sat with Milo, Venar, Filain and Domor. Filain and Venar were snoring, propped against each other. Domor was spooning soup into his mouth with weary, almost mechanical motions.

'I want you with me,' Baffels said quietly to Milo.

'Sergeant?'

'Oh, stop it with that crap! These pins should have been yours.'

Milo laughed and Filain looked up at the noise for a moment before slumping and snoring again.

'I've been a trooper for all of ten seconds. And I'm the youngest Tanith in the regiment. Gaunt would never have been crazy enough to make me sergeant. You deserve it, Baffels. No one denies it should be yours.'

Baffels shrugged. 'You led us today. No one denied that either. You're trusted.'

'So are you and we worked as a team. If they followed me at all it's only because you did. They may think of me as some lucky fething charm, touched by the commissar himself, but it's you they respect.'

'We did okay though, didn't we?'

Milo nodded.

'Whatever you say, I want you at point, right up near me, okay?'

'You're the sergeant.'

'And I'm making a command decision. The men respect you, so if you're near me and with me, they'll follow me too.'

Milo looked into the fire. He could sense Baffels was scared by his new responsibilities. The man was a great soldier, but he'd never expected unit command. He didn't want to fail and Milo knew he wouldn't, just as Gaunt had known when he'd made the promotion. But if it helped Baffels's confidence, Milo would do as he was asked. Certainly, through that strange, organic process Milo had observed in the firefight that morning, soldiers chose their own leaders in extremis, and Baffels and Milo had been chosen.

'Where's Tanith, d'you think?'

Milo glanced round, initially assuming Baffels had asked a rhetorical question. But the older man was looking up at the sky.

'Tanith?'

'Which of those stars did we come from?'

Milo gazed up. The Shield was a glowing aura of green light, fizzing with rain that fell outside. But even so, they could just glimpse the star-fields pricking the blackness.

Milo chose one at random.

'That one,' he said.

'You sure?'

'Absolutely.'

It seemed to please Baffels and he stared at the winking light for a long time.

'D'you still have your pipes?'

Milo had been a musician back on Tanith and before he'd made trooper he'd played the pipes into battle.

'Yes,' he said. 'Never go anywhere without them.'

'Play up, eh?'

'Now?'

'My first order as sergeant.'

Milo pulled the tight roll of pipes and bellows from his knapsack. He cleared the mouth-spout and then puffed the bag alive, making it whine and wail quietly. The hum of conversation died down at fires all around at the first sound.

Pumping his arm, he got the bellows breathing and the drone began, rising up in a clear, keening note. 'What shall I play?' he asked, his fingers ready on the chanter.

'My Love Waits in the Nalwoods Green,' Domor said suddenly from beside him.

Milo nodded. The tune was the unofficial anthem of Tanith, more sprightly than the actual planetary anthem, yet melancholy and almost painful for any man of Tanith to hear.

He began to play. The tune rose above the yard, above the flurries of sparks rising from the oil drums. One by one, the men began to sing.

'What is that?' asked Bulwar hoarsely as Corbec sang softly. Across the yard, the NorthCol men were silent as the bitter, haunting melody filled the air.

'A song sung by ghosts,' Corbec said as he reached for the sacra.

The Main Spine rang with the sound of massed voices. In the halls of the Legislature and the grand regimental chapel of House Command, victory choirs thousands strong sang victory masses and hymns of deliverance.

Crossing a marble colonnade with Captain Daur and several officers on the approach to House Command, Gaunt paused on a balcony and looked down into the regimental chapel auditorium. He sent his contingent on ahead and stood watching the mass for a while. Twelve hundred singers in golden robes, red-bound hymnals raised to their chests, gave voice to the hymn 'Behold! The Triumph of Terra' in perfect harmony, and the air vibrated.

The auditorium's high, arched roof was adorned with company banners and house flags, and censer smoke billowed into the candlelit air. A procession of Ministorum clerics carrying gilt standards and reliquary boxes, their long ceremonial trains supported by child servitors, shuffled down the main aisle towards the Imperial Shrine, where Intendant Banefail and Master Legislator Anophy waited. There were hooded Administratum officials in the procession and three astropaths from the guild, their satin-wrapped bulks bulging with tubes and pipes and feed-links. The astropaths were carried on litters by adult servitors, and many of the tubes and pipes issuing from the folds of their cloaks were plugged to cogitator systems built into the silver-plated litter-pallets.

'It lifts the heart, does it not?' a voice from behind Gaunt asked.

Gaunt turned. It was Kowle.

'If it lifts the morale of Vervunhive, so be it. In truth, it is premature.'

'Indeed?' Kowle frowned, as if not convinced. 'I am going to House Command. Will you walk with me?'

Gaunt nodded and the two grim, black figures in peaked caps strode together down the marble colonnade under the flickering ball-lamps strung along the walls.

'This day has seen victory, yet you seem low in spirit.'

Gaunt grunted. 'We drove them off. Call it a victory. It was bought too costly and the cost was unnecessary.'

'May I ask on what you base that assessment, colonel-commissar?'

They strode under a high arch where banners flapped in the cool air. The choir echoed after them.

'Vervunhive's command and control systems are inadequate for a military endeavour of this magnitude. The system broke down. Deployment was crippled behind the front and devastated at the sharp end. There is much to be criticised in the command structure of the Vervun Primary itself.'

Kowle stopped short. 'I would take such criticisms personally. I am, after all, the chief disciplinary officer of this hive.'

Gaunt stopped as well and turned back to face Kowle. There was an immoderate darkness in the man's face. 'You seem to excel in your duties, Commissar Kowle. You understand, better than any man I have ever met, the uses of propaganda and persuasion. But I wonder if you hold the officer ranks in place by force of will and fear rather than sound tactical order. The commanders of Vervun Primary have no experience of war on this scale. They know what they know from texts and treatises. They must be made to acknowledge the experience of active field officers.'

'Such as yourself and the other Guard commanders like General Grizmund?'

'Just so. I trust I can count on your support in this when we meet with House Command. I want you with me, Kowle. We can't be pushing from different angles.'

'Of course. I am of one mind with you on this, colonel-commissar.'

They walked on. Gaunt could read Kowle's soothing tone – and he despised it. He was well aware of the two dozen requests for transfer back into the active Guard which Kowle had made in the past three years. A master politico, Kowle was clearly courting Gaunt's favour, assuming Gaunt could make a good report and effect him that transfer.

'I understand you executed Modile,' Kowle said matter-of-factly.

'A necessary measure. His negligence was criminal.'

'It was, as you described, his inexperience, that let him down. Was summary execution too harsh for a man who might yet learn?'

'I hope you would have done the same, Kowle. Modile caused many deaths by his inaction and fear. That cannot be conscienced. He ignored both pre-orders and direct commands from above.'

Kowle nodded. 'Where a seasoned Guard commander would have held fast to the chain of command.'

'Indeed.'

Kowle smiled. It was an alarming expression on such a cruel face. 'Actually, I applaud your action. Decisive, forceful, true to the spirit of the Commissariat. Many have feared the great Gaunt has grown soft now he has a command of his own, that his commissarial instinct might have been diluted. But you disabused that notion today with Modile.'

'I'm glad to hear it.'

They had arrived at a set of great doors ornate with golden bas-relief. Vervun Elite troops in dress uniforms crusted with brocade, with plumes sprouting from their helmet spikes, opened the doors to admit them.

Beyond the doors, the audience theatre of House Command was seething with voices and commotion.

General Nash was at the lectern, trying to speak, but the noble houses were shouting him down. Junior Vervun Primary officers were stamping in their tiered seats and jeering, and Roane Deeper adjutants were yelling back at them, urged on by officers from NorthCol, the Narmenians and the Volpone.

Vice Marshal Anko rose to his feet, slamming his white-gloved hand into the bench-head for silence.

'While I welcome the aid our off-world kin have rendered us, I find this an affront. General Nash condemns our military organisations and says we are ill-equipped to deal with this fight. An insult, no less, no more! Does his highness General Sturm share this view?'

Sturm rose. 'War, honoured gentlemen,' he began in soothing, mellow tones, 'is a confusion. Emotions run high. It is hard to say if a system is right or wrong until it is found wanting in the fire of battle. The Vervun Primary are exemplary soldiers, well-drilled and highly motivated. Their bravery is beyond question. That our command channels clashed during today's engagement is simply unfortunate. It is not the fault of Vervun officers. I have already issued standing orders to range the vox-channels so that there will be no further overlap. Any deaths that have resulted from this misfortune are greatly regretted. Such incidents will not recur.'

'What about discipline?' Gaunt's voice cut across the great hall and all the faces turned to look. Gaunt walked to the end of the chamber and stepped up to the lectern. Kowle took his place on the front bench next to Anko.

'Colonel-commissar?' Marshal Croe rose and looked down the vast hall into Gaunt's eyes. 'Is there another matter? General Nash has already been unkind enough to reprimand Vervunhive for its weakness in command. Do you share that view?'

'In part, marshal. The communication problems General Sturm has referred to were only a piece of the crisis we faced today. We were lucky to survive the Veyveyr assault.'

Anko jumped to his feet. 'And have we not our own hero, Commissar Kowle, to thank for turning that crisis around?'

The hall broke out in ripples of applause and cheers, mainly from the Vervun majority. Kowle accepted the applause with a gracious, modest nod. Gaunt knew better than to point out the cosmetic nature of Kowle's involvement.

'Commissar Kowle's actions are a matter of record. History will record the nature of his contribution to the Vervunhive war.' Gaunt couched his response carefully. 'But the line of command failed severely during Veyveyr. Field commanders of the Vervun Primary, whose bravery is beyond question, failed to relay strategic orders or were unable – or unwilling – to redirect their forces in the face of the assault.'

Jeers and boos thundered down at Gaunt.

'I understand you have already exacted discipline, colonel-commissar,' Anko said stiffly.

'And I will do so again,' Gaunt raised his voice above the background roar. 'But that simply punishes the symptoms of the problem. It does not address the heart of it.'

'That problem being a failure to obey direct orders?' Kowle asked, rising to his feet amid more cheers.

Gaunt nodded. 'Chain of command must be observed at all times. Any who break it must do so knowing they risk the highest penalty. Without such order and control, this war will be lost. I trust Vervun Primary will respect this philosophy from now on.'

'So all who transgress must be punished?' Kowle asked.

He wants his transfer badly, Gaunt thought. He's supporting me every step of the way.

'Of course. Without the threat of sanction, insubordination will continue.'

'Then you will support the punishment of General Grizmund?' asked Vice Marshal Anko.

'What?'

'General Grizmund – who broke orders this day and began his own deployment of the Narmenian armour?' Now the Narmenian staff booed and heckled.

Gaunt faltered. 'I... I was not aware of this. It must have been a mistake. General Grizmund has my complete confidence and–'

'So, one rule for the locals, another for the Guard?' sneered Anko.

'I didn't say that. I–'

'General Grizmund defied direct orders from House Command and redeployed his tanks through noble house territory. Forgetting the collateral damage he caused, is not his action worthy of the most severe censure?' Tarrian of the VPHC looked across at Gaunt. 'That was the philosophy you were advocating, wasn't it?'

Gaunt looked away from the hooded eyes of the VPHC commandant and found Kowle's face in the throng. Kowle smiled back at him, unblinking, soulless.

He knew. He had known about Grizmund even before they had reached the chamber. He had manoeuvred Gaunt right into this trap.

Gaunt realised in an instant he had underestimated Kowle's ambition. The man was after more than a simple transfer off Verghast. He was after glory and command.

'Well, colonel-commissar? What do we do with Grizmund?' asked Anko.

Gaunt stepped away from the lectern and strode down the hall to the exit, yells and cat-calls showering over him.

Outside, he grabbed one of the Vervun Elite minding the door by the brocade and slammed him into the wall.

'Grizmund! Where is he?'

'In the s-stockade, sir! Level S-sub-40!'

Gaunt released him and strode away.

The rousing hymns of the great choirs shivered the air around him. Their sentiments sounded all too hollow.

The sunrise was an hour away.

A file of Ghosts moved up from trucks parked on the eastern hab expressway and entered the manufactory depots that backed on to the Spoil.

Thirty men, the cream of the Tanith scout cadre. The Vervun troops occupying the location, soldiers of the so-called Spoilers unit, greeted them in the undercroft of an ore barn. The air was thick with rock-dust and the light was poor, issuing from a few hooded lamps nailed to the wall.

'Gak' Ormon, the major in command of the Spoilers, saluted as Mkoll led his men in. He was a big, bulky man with bloodshot eyes and a flamer-burned throat.

'I understand you have good snipers and stealthers,' Ormon said to
Mkoll as he walked over to a chart table with him.

Mkoll nodded. He surveyed the chart. The Spoil, a vast heap of slag,
was a real vulnerability for Vervunhive. They knew as much, otherwise
they wouldn't have formed a dedicated defence force, but the battle of
the day before had decimated the Spoiler unit.

'General Sturm has acknowledged the Tanith ability in such endeav-
ours. We're here to support you.'

'Gak' Ormon's great bulk was clad in the blue greatcoat and spiked helmet of the Vervun Primary. He looked down at the wiry off-worlder with
his faded black fatigues and curious piebald cape. He was not impressed.

All of the Spoilers present, including Ormon, carried long-barrelled
autoguns with scopes dedicated to sniping. Their faces were striped
with bars of black camo-paint. Several had fresh wounds bound tightly.

Sergeant Mkoll called up his men so they could all study the chart.
The Ghosts grouped around the table, making comments, pointing.

'Why don't you just give them orders?' Ormon asked disdainfully.

'Because I want them to know the situation and understand the terrain. How can they defend an area effectively otherwise? Don't you
do the same?'

Ormon said nothing.

Mkoll broke his men into work-teams and sent them away in different
directions, though not before checking they had set their micro-beads
to the same channel.

Ormon joined Mkoll as the sergeant led his group of MkVenner,
Domor, Larkin and Rilke up shattered internal stairways to the third
storey overlooking the slag heap. Nine Spoilers were stationed at the
shattered windows up here, using scopes to watch the sleek slopes of
the Spoil.

The Ghosts took position amongst them.

Larkin and Rilke, both armed with sniper-variant lasguns, set themselves up carefully. Rilke used a length of pipe to disguise the end of his
gun as it protruded from the wall. Larkin covered his own gun down
to the muzzle under loose sacks.

Domor took Mkoll's scope, set it up on a tripod stand in the shadow
of a window and linked his mechanical eyes to the sight. He could now
see further and clearer than anyone in the fortification.

Ormon was about to ask Mkoll a question when he realised he and
the Ghost called MkVenner had vanished.

Mkoll and MkVenner moved invisibly down the Spoil slope, their capes
spread over them. The coal-like ore-refuse was wet and slimy underfoot.

They were outside the protection of the Shield and the night rain fell around them, making puddles amongst the rock waste.

They raised their scopes. Beyond the Spoil, two kilometres away, they saw the open, flat land and the blasted habs beyond. The heavy rain was creating standing water on the flat soil and the water was rippling like dimpled tin with the rainfall. Visibility was down and cloud cover was descending.

There was a sound. MkVenner armed his lasgun and Mkoll crawled forward.

It was singing. Chanting. From out in the enemy positions, via loud-hailers and speakers, a foul hymn of Chaos was ringing out to answer the triumph hymns of the hive.

It grew louder.

Mkoll and MkVenner shuddered.

In the ore-works behind them, Ormon felt his bladder vice and hurried away.

At his position, Larkin tensed. He was weary from the day's nerve-shredding battle and had only been sent in with Mkoll's men because of his skills as a sniper.

Every time he closed his eyes, he saw the face, the face of the Zoican. Now, from below, down the length of the Spoil, he could hear them. The Zoican filth were singing a name over and over, in a canon repeat.

Heritor Asphodel... Heritor Asphodel...

ELEVEN

THE HERITOR

'Kill us! Kill us all! In the name of Terra, before he–'
– Transcript of last broadcast from Ryxus V,
the first 'inherited' world

Level Sub-40 was almost a kilometre underground, deep in the foundation structure of the Main Spine. An armoured lift cage with grilled sides transported Gaunt down the last three hundred metres, lowering him into an underworld of dark, damp stone, stale air and caged sodium lamps.

He entered an underground concourse where ground water dripped from the pipework roof onto the concrete floor and rusting chains dangled over piles of mildewed refuse. Along one side was a row of wooden posts with shackle-loops at wrist height. The wall behind the posts was stippled with bullet pocks and darkly stained.

Gaunt approached an adamantine shutter marked with yellow chevrons. Rockcrete bunkers stood on either side of the shutter, blank except for letterbox slits set high up.

As he moved forward, automatic spotlights mounted above the hatch snapped on and bathed him with blue-white light.

'Identify!' a voice crackled out of a vox-relay.

'Colonel-Commissar Ibram Gaunt,' Gaunt replied curtly, reeling off his serial number afterwards.

'Your business?'

'Just open the shutter.'

There was a brief pause, then the great metal hatch screeched open. Gaunt stepped through and found himself facing a second shutter. The one behind him slammed shut before the inner one would open.

Inside the stockade, a caged walkway led down into a dispatch area with an open-sided shower stall and low tables for searching through personal effects. The sodium lamps gave the foetid, recirculated air a frosty hue.

Guards moved out of side bunkers to meet him. They were all VPHC troopers dressed in black shirts, black, peaked caps, graphite-grey breeches and black boots. Each one wore orange arm-bands and wide, black, leather belts with riot-batons and cuffs dangling from them. Three carried pump-action shotguns.

'Grizmund,' Gaunt told them briefly. He allowed himself to be frisked and handed over his bolt pistol. Two of the guards then led him through a series of cage doors with remotely activated electric locks, down the austere, red-washed hallways of the cell-block. There was an astringent ammonia stink of open drains, with a mouldering aftertaste of deep rock and soil. Every sound rang out and echoed.

Grizmund and the four officers arrested with him were sharing a large communal holding tank. They still wore their mustard-brown Narmenian uniforms, but caps, belts, laces and all rank pins had been removed.

Grizmund met Gaunt at the cage door. The VPHC guards refused to open it, so they were forced to talk through the bars.

'I'm glad to see you,' Grizmund said. He was pale, and there was a dark look of anger in his eyes. 'Get us out of this.'

'Tell me what happened. In your own words,' Gaunt said.

Grizmund paused, then shrugged. 'We were ordered to Veyveyr. Thanks to the gross idiocy of House Command organisation, the routes were blocked. I took my column off the roadway and headed on to the gate through an industrial sector. Next thing I knew, the VPHC were heading me off.'

'Did you disobey any direct order?'

'I was ordered to Veyveyr,' the man repeated. 'I was told to take Arterial Route GH/7m. When I couldn't get through, I tried to achieve my primary order to reach the appointed frontline.'

'Did you strike a VPHC officer?'

'Yes. He drew a gun on me first, without provocation.'

Gaunt was quiet for a moment.

'You'd think these bastards didn't want us to fight for them,' growled Grizmund.

'Their pride is hurt. The inadequacies of their command systems were shown up clearly today. They're looking for others to blame.'

'Screw them if they try to pin anything on me! This is crazy! Won't Sturm back you up?'

'Sturm is too busy trying to please both sides. Don't worry. I won't let this continue a moment longer than it has to.'

Grizmund nodded. Loud footsteps, unpaced and overlapping, reverberated down the dank cell-block behind them. Gaunt turned to see Commissar Tarrian enter with an escort of VPHC troops.

'Commissar Gaunt. You shouldn't be here. The Narmenian insubordination is a matter for the VPHC Disciplinary Review. You will not interfere with Verghastian military justice. You will not confer with the prisoners. My men will escort you back to the elevator.'

Gaunt nodded to Grizmund and walked over to the VPHC group, facing Tarrian for a moment. 'You are making a mistake both you and your cadre will regret, Tarrian.'

'Is that some kind of threat, Gaunt?'

'You're a commissar, Tarrian, or at least you're supposed to be. You must know commissars never issue threats. Only facts.'

Gaunt allowed himself to be marched out of the stockade.

The thirty-third dawn was already on them, with heavy rain falling across the entire hive, the outer habs and the grasslands beyond. Marshal Croe was taking breakfast in his retiring chamber off the war-room when Gaunt entered.

The room was long, gloomy and wood-panelled with gilt-framed oil paintings of past marshals lining the walls. Croe sat at the head of a long, varnished mahogany table, picking at food laid out on a salver as he read through a pile of data-slates. Behind him, the end wall of the room was armoured glass and overlooked the Commercia and Shield Pylon. Backlit by the great window and the grey morning glare, Croe was a dark, brooding shape.

'Commissar.'

Gaunt saluted. 'Marshal. The charges against the Narmenian officers must be dropped at once.'

Croe looked up, his noble, white-haired head inclining towards Gaunt like an eagle considering a lamb. 'Because?'

'Because they are utterly foolish and counterproductive. Because we need officers of Grizmund's standing. Because any punishment will send a negative message to the Narmenian units and to all Guard units as a whole: that Vervunhive values the efforts of the off-world forces very little.'

'And what of the other view? You heard it yourself: one rule for Vervun, one for the Guard?'

'We both know that's not true. Grizmund's actions are hardly capital in nature, yet the VPHC seems hell-bent on prosecuting them to the extreme. I'm not even sure this so-called "insubordination" was even that. A tribunal would throw it out, but to even get to a tribunal would be damaging. Narmenian and Guard honour would be slighted, and the VPHC would be made to look stupid.' At the last minute, Gaunt managed to prevent himself from saying 'even more stupid.'

'Tarrian's staff is very thorough. They would not undertake a tribunal if they thought it would collapse.'

'I am familiar with such "courts", marshal. However, that will only happen if the VPHC are allowed to run the hearing themselves.'

'It is their purview. Military discipline. It's Tarrian's job.'

'I will not allow the VPHC to conduct any hearing.'

Croe put down his fork and stared at Gaunt as if he had just insulted Croe's own mother. He rose to his feet, dabbing his mouth with a napkin.

'You won't... allow it?'

Gaunt stood his ground. 'Imperial Commissariat edict 4378b states that any activity concerning the discipline of Imperial Guardsmen must be conducted by the Imperial Commissariat itself. Not by planetary bodies. It is not Tarrian's responsibility. It should not be a matter for the VPHC.'

'And you will enforce this ruling?'

'If I have to. I am the ranking Imperial commissar on Verghast.'

'The interpretation of law will be murderous. Any conflicts between Imperial and Planetary rules will be argued over and over. Do not pursue this, Gaunt.'

'I'm afraid I have to, marshal. I am not a stranger to martial hearings. I will personally resource and provide all the legal precedents I need to throw Tarrian, his thugs and his pitiful case to the wolves.'

A Vervun Primary adjutant hurried into the retiring room behind Gaunt.

'Not now!' barked Croe, but the man didn't withdraw. He held out a data-slate to the fuming marshal.

'You – you need to see this, sir,' he stammered.

Croe snatched the slate out of the man's hands and read it quickly. What he read arrested his attention, and he went back and re-read slowly, his eyes narrowing.

Croe thrust the slate to Gaunt. 'Read it yourself,' he said. 'Our observers along the South Curtain have been picking it up since daybreak.'

Gaunt looked through the transcripts recorded by the wall-guards as they scrolled across the glowing screen.

'Heritor Asphodel,' he murmured. He looked round at Croe. 'I suggest you release Grizmund now. We're going to need all the men we can get.'

Gaunt and Croe left the retiring room together and strode down the short hall into the great control auditorium of House Command. Both the lower level and the wrought-iron upper deck of the place were jostling with activity. Hololithic projections of the warfront glowed upwards into the air from crenellated lens-pits in the floor, and the air throbbed with vox-caster traffic, astropaths' chants and the clack of the cogitator banks.

A gaggle of Munitorum staffers, Vervun Primary aides and technical operators hastened forward around the marshal as he entered, but he waved them all away, crossing to the ironwork upperdeck, his boots clanging up the metal steps. Vice Marshal Anko, General Sturm, Commissar Kowle and General Xance of the NorthCol were already assembled by the great chart table. Silent servitors, encrusted with bionics, and poised regimental aides waited behind them. An occasional vox/pict drone bumbled across the command space. Gaunt hung back at the head of the stairs, observing.

'Kowle?' asked Croe, approaching the chart table.

'No confirmation. It is impossible to confirm, lord marshal.'

Croe held up the data-slate. 'But this is an accurate transcript of the enemy broadcasts? They're chanting this at the gates?'

'Since dawn,' replied Sturm. He looked bleary-eyed, and his grey and gold Volpone dress uniform was crumpled, as if he had been roused hurriedly. 'And not just chanting.'

He nodded and a servitor opened a vox-channel. A chatter of almost unintelligible noise rolled from the speaker.

'Vox-central has washed the signal clean. The name repeats on all bandwidths as a voice pattern and also as machine code, arithmetical sequence and compressed pict-representation.' Sturm fell silent. He reached for a cup of caffeine on the edge of the chart table, his hand trembling.

'A blanket broadcast. They certainly want us to know,' Gaunt said.

Kowle looked round at him. 'They want us to be scared,' he said snidely. 'Just hours ago, you complimented me on my ability to control information. We can presume the enemy are similarly efficient. This could be propaganda. Demoralising broadcasts. They may simply be using the name as a terror device.'

'Possibly... but we agreed it would take a force of great charisma to turn a hive the size of Ferrozoica. Heritor Asphodel is just such a force. His fate and whereabouts since Balhaut are unknown.'

Anko looked away from Gaunt deliberately and turned to Kowle. 'You were on Balhaut, Kowle. What is this creature?'

Kowle was about to speak when Gaunt cut across. 'Both Kowle and I served on Balhaut. I believe the commissar was deployed on the south-west continent, away from the main battle for the Oligarchy. I encountered the Heritor's forces personally.'

Kowle conceded. He could barely hide his bitterness at the memory. 'The colonel-commissar may... have more experience than me.'

Croe turned his hooded eyes back to Gaunt. 'Well?'

'The Heritor was one of Archon Nadzybar's foremost lieutenants, a warlord in his own right, personally commanding a force of over a million. He was one of the chief commanders Nadzybar gathered in his great retinue to form the vast enemy force which overran the Sabbat Worlds, Emperor damn him. Despite the notoriety of the other warlords – filth like Sholen Skara, Nokad the Blighted, Anakwanar Sek, Qux of the Eyeless – Heritor Asphodel remains the most notorious. His sworn aim, both before and after Archon Nadzybar co-opted him into the pact, was to "inherit" Imperium world after Imperium world and return them to what he saw as the "true state" of Chaos. His ruthlessness is immeasurable, his brutality staggering and the charismatic force of his personality as a leader cannot be underestimated. And with the possible exception of Sek, he is probably the most tactically brilliant of all Nadzybar's commanders.'

'It almost sounds like you admire the bastard,' sniffed Sturm.

'I do not underestimate him, general,' Gaunt said coldly. 'That is different.'

'And he could be here? It could be more than an enemy lie?' Anko asked, failing to disguise the wobble in his voice.

'The Heritor fled Balhaut along with all the surviving warlords after Warmaster Slaydo slew the Archon. This may be his first reappearance. The Zoican forces have encircled us well and swiftly, and they have used both waiting and surprise to great effect. Both are tactics I know the Heritor favours. Furthermore, he delights in war machines. With access to Ferrozoica hive's fabricating plants, the baroque war machines we have seen are precisely the sort of things I would expect him to send out at us.'

Croe said nothing as he took it in. 'Suggestions? Gaunt?'

Astutely, Gaunt deferred to Kowle, aware of how the commissar was bristling at what he would no doubt see as the colonel-commissar's grandstanding. 'I would invite Commissar Kowle's ideas on how to deal with this information.'

Kowle greedily accepted the scrap thrown to him. 'We can't shut out blanket broadcasts, so we must refute them. All military, municipal and guilder institutions in Vervunhive, along with select representatives of the citizenry and the Legislature, must be clearly and emphatically briefed that this is hollow propaganda. We should prepare statements for the public address plates to repeat denials of this. I also urge we counter with broadcasts of our own. Simple repeats of the statement "the Heritor is dead" should suffice for now.'

'Begin the work. I want regular updates.' Croe waited as Kowle saluted and left, then faced Sturm and Xance. 'Battle standby remains in force, but I want all military resources moved into position now. No reserves. We must meet the next thrust with absolute power.'

Both generals nodded.

'I trust the revisions you ordered to the communications net have been affected, General Sturm?'

'New channel settings and new codes have been issued to our forces. The confusions of the last storm should not recur.'

Gaunt hoped Sturm was correct. He had reviewed the general's revisions and they seemed sound, though they favoured the Volpone Bluebloods and the Vervun Primary with the most accessible bands.

'Have you yet considered my proposal to engage them outside the Wall?' asked Xance.

'Impractical, general,' replied Croe.

'We saw how the Vervun Mechanised were destroyed in the grass-lands,' Sturm added.

'But now they are dug in and restricted by the streets of the outer habs. The policy vouched by Nash, Grizmund and Gaunt early on would seem more attractive now. The NorthCol and Narmenian armour could sally out with infantry support and shake them from their forward line.'

Gaunt listened, fascinated. This was the first he had heard of Xance's plan. Clearly Sturm, Anko and Croe had made efforts to suppress it. It could not be coincidence that Xance was voicing it now in Gaunt's presence.

'No!' barked Sturm, anger getting the better of him for a moment. 'We will not dilute our resistance here by wasting manpower and machines in an external raid.'

Xance shook his head and left the upper auditorium without saluting.

Sturm looked over at Gaunt with a scowl. 'Don't even begin to think about supporting Xance, Gaunt. The Imperial Forces here at Vervunhive will not go on the offensive now or in the foreseeable future.'

Gaunt nodded, saluted and left. He knew when it was time to argue, and he'd been sticking his neck out more than enough in the last few days.

The Zoicans recommenced sporadic bombardment at dusk, throwing shells and rockets up at the Curtain Wall at a listless rate, more to annoy than to do any real damage. The Wall positions returned fire intermit-tently, whenever a target was designated by the spotters.

Zoican ground forces, edging closer to the Wall, fired las- and bolt rounds at the gates from foxhole cover and ditches. At Sondar Gate, Vervun Primary corps under Captain Cargin elevated the armoured domes of the electric rotating turrets and peppered the ground in range outside with torrents of heavy autofire.

The new defences at Veyveyr Gate took their first battering. There was the *punk! punk!* of mortars dropping shells close to the skirts of the stone siege walls and dirt clouds drifted back across the troops at the parapet.

Feygor swivelled his scope, hunting for a target in the hab waste beyond, and he quickly identified the rising tendrils of smoke from the concealed mortars.

He ordered Bragg up to the wall-line and spotted for him as Bragg loaded rocket grenades into his shoulder launcher. Then Feygor voxed to Rawne for permission to fire.

Rawne was crossing the inner trenches below the gate when he received the request and told Feygor to hold fire.

He hurried down a dugout towards the Volpone command section, a half-smashed rail carriage buried to the axles in ash and rubble and shielded along its length with flak-board, sandbags and piled stone. Rawne had been ordered to co-ordinate the defence with his Volpone opposite number, but despite Sturm's communication review – or because of it, Rawne grimly suspected – the inter-unit vox links seemed stilted and slow.

Two Bluebloods of the elite 10th Brigade stood guard at the gas-curtained entrance. They were giants in their carapace battledress, the grey and gold of their segmented armaplas and fatigues spotless and austere. Each carried a gleaming black hellgun with a sawn-off pump-gun attached to the bayonet lug under the main barrel.

They blocked his advance.

'Major Rawne, Tanith area commander,' he said briskly and they stood aside to let him enter.

Colonel Nikolaas Taschen DeHante Corday was a true Blueblood: massive, powerful and square-jawed with hooded eyes. He was sitting at his chart desk in the carriage as Rawne entered and he looked the Tanith over like he was something he'd found adhering to his boot.

Rawne nodded. 'I wish to commence discriminate return of fire. There are mortars trying to range my positions.'

Corday looked at his chart again and then nodded. 'Do you want support?'

'They're simply harrying, biding their time. But I'd rather not sit my men there while they find their true range.'

'Is it worth drawing up the artillery?'

Rawne shook his head. 'Not yet. Let me silence the mortars and see what they try next.'

'Very good.'

Rawne turned to leave.

'Major? Rawne, isn't it?'

Rawne turned back to see that Corday had risen to his feet. 'I am anxious that the Volpone and the Tanith can complement each other in this position,' he said.

'I share your hope.'

'There is not a good record between our regiments.'

Rawne was surprised by the frankness.

'No. No, there isn't. May I ask... do you know why?'

Corday sighed. 'Voltemand. I was not part of that action, but I have reviewed the records. A miscalculation on General Sturm's part caused artillery to injure your units in the field.'

Rawne coughed gently. It was a polite and rather inaccurate appraisal, but he didn't want to antagonise the Blueblood officer.

'I don't believe the Volpone have ever formally apologised to the Tanith for it. For what it's worth, I make that apology now.'

'Is there a reason?' Rawne asked guardedly.

'One of my men, Culcis, speaks highly of the Ghosts, of your Colonel Corbec in particular. He fought with them on Nacedon. Others have praised Gaunt's leadership on Monthax.' Corday smiled. The smile seemed genuine, despite the aristocratic languor of the face. Rawne thought it would not be impossible to like Corday.

'Sturm, Emperor honour him... Gilbear... many of the upper echelon will of course despise the Tanith for eternity!' They both laughed. 'But you'll find me a fair man, Rawne. We Bluebloods have prided ourselves on our superiority for a long time. It is time we learned from others and realised that the Imperial Guard has other fine regiments within it that we might be honoured and educated to serve alongside.'

Rawne was quietly astonished. Like all the Ghosts, he had come to loathe the Bluebloods, and for a damaged, hating soul like Rawne that loathing came easy. He could never have believed he would hear such comradeship from one of them, especially a senior officer.

'I appreciate your words, colonel. I will bear them in mind and circulate your thoughts amongst my own men. It's fair to say that unless we learn to fight together, we will die here. In the spirit of co-operation, may I note that our inter-unit vox-links are still unreliable?'

Corday nodded and made a note on his data-slate with a stylus. 'Select band pi as a working link, with band kappa as reserve. I think

I'll send one of my subalterns with a vox-set to work as liaison. I suggest you reciprocate.'

Rawne nodded, saluted and left the carriage.

Corday called his bodyguard in to join him. 'Send Graven to the Tanith position with a vox-set. Tell him to act as intermediary. I want these disgusting Ghost scum kept sweet, make that clear to him. We don't want them hanging our arses out to dry when the fighting starts.'

Returning down the trench, Rawne sent a confirmation to Feygor at the leading wall. Bragg's launcher thumped and the mortar position erupted in a sheet of flame and debris as its munitions were hit.

After a while, las-fire began to pepper back from the Zoican lines. The Ghosts kept their heads down and waited.

At Hass East Fort, overlooking the estuary inlet, it was deathly quiet. Hass East had been spared all the fighting so far, but the position was still vital, as it watched the Vannick Highway and guarded the Ontabi Gate entrance to the hive, the only one of the five great city gates not yet assaulted.

On the high top of the tower, Sergeant Varl gazed out across the dusk settling on the reed-beds and islets of the matt-grey river. Waders and flycatchers darted and warbled over the water and rushes, and the riverside air was crazy with billowing gnats. The great bulk of the Hiraldi road-bridge to the north was just a silhouette.

The rain had eased off. There was a smell of thunder in the air. Varl, with two platoons of Tanith, was sharing defence of the Fort with three platoons of Roane Deepers under Captain Willard, and three hundred Vervun Primary gunners and wall artillerymen answering to Major Rodyin, a junior member of one of the lesser noble houses.

Varl got on with Willard. The Roane was about twenty-five, tanned and shaggy blond, with penetrating, brown eyes and an earthy sense of humour. Like Varl, Willard had a metallic implant – in his case, the fingers and palm of his right hand. They joked together about their experiences of body automation.

Rodyin was rather more difficult. Although they all faced death here, Rodyin had a more personal stake because this was his home. He was pale, earnest and prematurely balding, though he was only in his early twenties. He seemed utterly mystified by the jokes and quips that rattled freely between his two fellow officers, and he would stare at them myopically though the half-moon glasses that were permanently perched on the bridge of his nose. Varl understood that House Rodyin was one of the liberal families in the hive, more humanitarian and forward-thinking than the old noble houses or the guilders. House Rodyin's fortunes were built on food sources and their harvester-machines grazed the great pastoral uplands north of the Hass, gathering grain for the vast granaries in the dock district.

Varl liked Rodyin, but he didn't seem much of a soldier.

The Tanith sergeant crossed the tower top, slapping gnats off his skin, and toured the emplacements as the daylight faded.

He heard laughter and saw Willard and some of his tan-uniformed troops joking by a rocket station. Rodyin stood a little apart, scoping the river and the road with a high-power set of magnoculars.

Willard greeted Varl. 'But for these bloody flies, Ghost, I'd say we've pulled the best duty here! None of that bloody fighting stuff up here at Hass East, eh?'

Varl had already seen fighting in Vervunhive and was actually glad of the calm and quiet up here on the far eastern side of the city. But still, waiting was sometimes the mind-killer. 'Wouldn't object to a few Zoicans to pop though,' he grinned.

'Hell, no! A few of those bloody yellows to keep my eye in, eh?'

More laughter. Varl saw how Rodyin shifted uncomfortably, unwilling to be drawn in. The major took his duties and his war seriously – too seriously in Varl's opinion – probably because he'd never been in one before.

'See anything?' Varl asked, joining Rodyin at the parapet.

'A little river traffic. Barges, ferries. Most of them are crossing from the north bank with munition hauls. House Command has embargoed all but vital supply runs.'

Varl took his own single-lens scope from his pack and scanned the area. To the north of their position, near the bridge, sat the bulky pro-methium tanks of the dockside fuel depot, the main facility serving Vervunhive. On stilt legs, pipelines tracked away to the north and east, as far into the distance as Varl could see. They'd once pumped the fuel in from Vannick Hive, before it was lost. Now the only liquid fuel sup-plies available to Vervunhive were coming from NorthCol.

'Looks quiet enough,' Varl said.

Behind them, Willard finished a particularly coarse joke and the laughter of his men echoed down the battlements into the deepen-ing gloom.

Guilder Worlin returned to his guild house at nightfall. He was grin-ning broadly and his face was shiny with the glow of too much joiliq. An extraordinary guild meeting conducted in an armoured bunker under the Commercia had left his personal resources three times the

size they had been that dawn. The considerable promethium reserves
he had to bargain with had been snapped up greedily in a bidding war
between five major guild cadres, and he'd also managed to draw up a
resourcing agreement with representatives of Vervun Primary. His pipeline was still drawing fuel into the massive steel bowsers in the Worlin
commercial estates on the river. Vannick Hive might be dead, but its
legacy lingered on and Worlin was amassing a trade fortune with every
drop of it. By the time the war was over, Worlin was assured of a place
in the high circle of the Commercia guilds. House Worlin would affect
a promotion to the senior echelon of hive trade institutions. Its stock
price alone had quadrupled since the First Storm.

He sat in his private office, at a teak-topped desk with built-in
pict-plates, and sipped an overfilled glass of joiliq as he reviewed the
messages his communicator had collected during the day.

One stopped him in his tracks. It was a notification of enquiry from
some nobody called Curth at Inner Hab Collective Medical Hall 67/
mv. It wanted to know his whereabouts on the first day of attack. Had
he been anywhere near Carriage Station C7/d? There were irregularities that demanded investigation and they were taking statements from
anybody who had been in the area at that time. Monitor viewers along
the access ramp had recorded him and two of his houseguard crossing
that way during the bombardment of the Commercia. The message was
signed 'Curth, A.' and copied to an off-worlder medic named Dorden,
one of the Imperial Guard.

Worlin realised his hand was shaking and he was slopping joiliq
out of the glass. He set it down and sucked the drops off the ball of
his thumb.

He checked his weapon was still in the drawer of the desk. This
annoyance would need to be dealt with quickly.

The chatter was now so persistent that there was no other sign or meaning to the world. Salvador Sondar spasmed gently in his fluid world,
gnawing at his lips. The voice of his worthy Ferrozoican cousin Clatch
had been whittled away until it simply repeated two words, over and
again. A name. A daemonic name.

Sondar was emaciated and weak with hunger. His feeder tubes
had long since run dry and he had not the presence of mind to
cycle the automated systems to refresh them. Even his meat puppets were forgotten and slowly rotting as they dangled lifelessly
from their strings.

A rich smell of decay filled the High Master's chambers.

He was oblivious.

He knew what the chatter wanted. The notion appealed to him, because the chatter made it so appealing.

He couldn't form a coherent thought. He simply listened. Perhaps he would do it... just to shut the chatter up. Any time now.

Larkin had been perfectly still for over an hour. His eye never left the scope-sight. The Spoil-head manufactory around him was quiet and dark, but he was aware of the Vervun sniper Lotin crouched behind rubble further down the second-storey room.

Ten minutes before, Larkin had sensed movement down on the Spoil. He'd watched for it again and now he saw it: a brief flash of moon-light on armour.

He retrained his aim. Breathed.

The Zoicans were advancing up the Spoil. They were well-drilled and as stealthy as any practiced insurgency team. It was clear they had either switched their distinctive ochre armour for dull, night-fighting kit or had covered the livid yellow with soot.

He signalled his intelligence to Mkoll over the vox link, using only half a dozen code words.

Mkoll ordered the Tanith snipers to address and fire when they had a target. A second later, Ormon delivered the same command to his own men.

Larkin saw movement again, clearly in the foggy, green glow of his scope.

He breathed, squared and fired.

The stinging red pulse whipped down the ore slope and a black-clad figure was thrown up and backwards.

Larkin immediately dipped under the edge of the rubble and took a new position. He was certain his muzzle flash had been discreet, but there was no sense in advertising. He made his new vantage and aimed again, his extended barrel hidden inside a broken drain-gutter.

Lotin, ten metres away, fired. His lasgun made a loud crack and even from where he was, Larkin saw the muzzle flash and cursed.

He heard Lotin complain over the vox-link. He'd missed.

Move, move and re-aim! Larkin willed silently.

Lotin fired again. His whoop of success was quickly cut short by a perfectly aimed las-round from the Spoil below. The Zoicans had been watching for a repeat flash.

Lotin toppled back and slumped into the rubble scree on the floor, his face gone.

So, thought Larkin, *they have capable and careful snipers too.*

This war just got interesting.

* * *

748   DAN ABNETT

The night was on them now and the moons, two large and cream and one tiny and livid red, climbed slowly into a purple sky. Rain clouds, black and woolly, chased along the eastern skyline. Distant thunder rolled out in the grasslands.

The air was sultry and unseasonable, and at Hass East Fort, Varl was sweating freely into his black fatigues. The discomfort was made worse by the static build-up generated by the vast Shield behind them, fizzing and crackling in the dark, a glowing hemisphere of energy.

The plating of his lasgun and his bionic arm tingled with electricity. Varl yearned for the threatening storm to break over them and clear the stifling air.

There was a brutal flash from the north-east and then an ear-splitting bang, followed by an impact that threw Varl off his feet. Voices were shouting in the night, alarms were ringing and someone was scream-ing in agony.

The sky lit up again. Explosions were rippling along the entire stretch of Curtain Wall between Ontabi Gate and the Hass.

Varl got up, blinking. There was no sign of shelling. That had been... mines.

He ran down the parapet, yelling into his vox-link as more explosions shook the wall. Detonating mines meant one thing only: the enemy was right on top of them, close enough to set charges.

Men were milling all around, confused. Equally useless barks of vox-traffic answered Varl. Varl grabbed the wall for support as another explosion went off close by, flame slicking upwards in a tight ball inside the Wall.

Inside the Wall?

'They've penetrated! They've penetrated!' he bellowed, not under-standing it but desperate to get the message out. Almost at once, he came under fire. Las-shots flicked the air around him, coming up from the nearest Wall access stair.

Varl returned fire, rallying the Vervun Primary troops nearest to him. Crackling autoguns began to support him. He saw Zoican storm-troops spreading out onto the battlements from the stair access, their ochre armour dulled by dark, tarry stains.

Varl shot down one or two before realising many more were storm-ing the battlement behind him too. How in the name of feth had they got inside?

A huge blast shook him to his knees. An entire section of Hass East collapsed with a roar and brick dust billowed into the sky, underlit by flame. Further detonations sliced through the top of the wall.

Varl saw gun emplacements ripped apart and exploded and he

watched as entire sections of wall-defences blew outwards as mines set off ammunition silos and autoloader hoppers.

Like the wrath of a ruthless god, the war had come to Hass East at last.

TWELVE

DARKNESS FALLS

'What is the strongest weapon of mankind? The god-machines of the Adeptus Mechanicus? No! The Astartes Legions? No! The tank? The lasgun? The fist? No to all! Courage and courage alone stands above them all!'

– Macharius, Lord Solar, from his writings

Distant thunder woke Ibram Gaunt from a dreamless sleep.

His bedroom, part of a small suite of rooms disposed to him, adjacent to House Command, was dark except for the dull amber glow of rune sigils on the small codifier by the desk.

He turned on the lamp and slid off the bed where he had lain down only a couple of hours before, fully clothed. Sleep had overtaken him in an instant.

By the light of the lamp, he crossed to the desk, where stacks of ribbon-bound papers and data-slates were piled up. He took a sip of last night's wine from a glass on a side table.

The thunder came again. Somewhere, deadened by the thick walls, an alarm was ringing.

He activated the call stud of the intercom set into the marble facing of the wall, blankly regarding the great framed portrait over the bare grate opposite. Its thick, time-darkened oils portrayed a pompous-looking man in the Vervun Primary uniform of an older age, bedraggled with braid, one foot raised to rest on a pile of human skulls, a scroll in one hand and a power-sword in the other.

When the intercom replied, Gaunt was idly wondering who the subject of the portrait was supposed to be and who the skulls had belonged to.

'Sir?'

'What's going on?'

751

'Reports of a raid at Ontabi Gate. We're waiting for confirmation.'

'Appraise me swiftly. I have men at Hass East.'

'Of course, sir. There is... a visitor for you.'

Gaunt checked the clock. It was nearly two in the morning. 'Who?'

'He bears the Imperial seal and says you requested him.'

Gaunt sighed and said, 'Allow him in.'

The suite's outer door slid open and Gaunt went into the sitting room to meet his visitor, activating the wall lamps.

A gnarled, elderly man in long, purple robes shuffled in, peering at Gaunt through thick-lensed spectacles. His hair, where it protruded from under his high-crested, red, felt cap, was grey and unruly, and he leaned on an ebony cane. Behind him came a tall, pale young man in grey cleric's coat, laden down with old tomes and sheaves of paper.

'Commissar... Gaunt?' the old man wheezed, studying the officer before him.

'Colonel-commissar, actually. You are?'

'Advocate Cornelius Pater of the Administratum Judiciary. Your request for legal assistance was received this night and Intendant Banefail directed me to attend you with all urgency.'

'I thank the intendant for his alacrity and you for your time.'

The advocate nodded and wheezed his way over to a leather couch, leaving his assistant in the doorway, swaying under the weight of the manuscripts and volumes he carried.

'Set them down on the table,' Gaunt told him. 'You are?'

The man seemed wary of speaking.

'My clerk, Bwelt,' Pater answered for him. 'He will not speak. He is training for junior advocacy and must perforce learn the protocols of question and address. Besides, he knows nothing.'

'How do we undertake this?' Gaunt asked the advocate.

Pater cleared his throat. 'You will review the matter for my benefit – excluding no detail – you will show me any pertinent transcripts and you will furnish me with a glass of fortified wine.'

Gaunt glanced round at Bwelt. 'There's a bottle on the side table in the bedroom. Fetch him a glass.'

Pater refused to speak further until the crystal glass was in his withered hand and the first sip in his mouth. The cane lay across his lap.

Gaunt began. 'An Imperial Guard general – Grizmund of the Narmenian Armour – and four of his staff officers are charged with insubordination. They're being held in the VPHC stockade, pending prosecution by a VPHC court. The charges are spurious. I want them freed and back to duty immediately. I think the matter founders on a formality – the VPHC cannot prosecute Imperial Guard personnel. If

there is a crime to answer, it is an Imperial Commissariat matter. I am
the highest representative of that authority on Verghast.'

Pater adjusted his spectacles and studied the data-slate Gaunt
handed him.

'Hmm... clear-cut enough, I suppose. You're citing Imperial Commissariat Edict 4368b. The VPHC won't like it. Tarrian, in particular,
will hate you for it.'

'There's no love lost between us.'

'Bwelt? What is it? You gurn like a fool or a man with chronic gas.'

'It's 4378b, Advocate. The edict is 4378b.' Bwelt's voice was almost
a whisper.

'Just so,' Pater said, brushing off the correction and returning his gaze
to the slate. 'It may come to court. Tarrian has a miserable record of
dragging cases through all the due processes, even if he is bound to
lose. To him, there's some satisfaction in prolonging the agony.'

'I want it thrown out before then. We can't be without Grizmund
any longer. In the next few days, Vervunhive's future may depend upon
skilled armour.'

'Tricky. But the edict is well-precedented. A brief hearing, perhaps at
dawn tomorrow, and we should be able to pull the rug out from under
the VPHC.' Pater looked up at Gaunt. 'I'll derive satisfaction from that.
The VPHC have deemed themselves above Imperial Law for many
years. It's been nigh on impossible to practise clean law in the hive.
With your prestige involved, we can win.'

'Good. At least we know the VPHC can't act before then. However
they argue it, they know an Imperial commissar must be present for a
tribunal to be conducted.'

'Indeed. Even if they press for a court of their own, we can stall them
as long as you refuse to participate. Then – Bwelt? Again, you screw up
your face! What now?'

Bwelt paused and seemed to choose every word with great care.
'The... tribunal is in session now, advocate. You told me to collate all
information relating to this case before we came here and that fact was
diarised in the judiciary case-roll.'

'What?'

'Th-they are proceeding... because they have an Imperial commissar present. Commissar Kowle has agreed to represent the Imperial
interests and–'

Gaunt's vicious curse shut Bwelt up and made the old man start.
Pulling on his jacket, cap and weapon belt, Gaunt reeled off a colourful and descriptive tirade outlining what he would do to Tarrian, Kowle
and the entire VPHC in four-letter words.

'Come with me! Now!' he told the advocate and his trembling clerk, then flew out of the room.

At the eastern edge of the hive, the sky was on fire. From the outer dark of the river bend, enemy shelling had begun to hammer at the damage done to the adamantine Curtain Wall and the ramparts of Hass East Fort by the mines.

Varl stumbled through the firestorm, trying to regroup his men and get them down into the deep-wall bunkers. Zoican assaulters were everywhere. The defenders couldn't fight this. Varl tried to vox House Command or Tanith control, but the energy flare of the bombardment had scrambled the communication bands.

He got maybe twenty men around him, mostly Ghosts but some Roane and Vervun Primary, and ran them down the tower steps into the bowels of the fort. The stone walls were sweating as the heat of the burning levels above leeched into them. Plaster facings shrivelled and wilted, and the air was oven-hot and hurt the soldiers' lungs. At one point, a shell-fall punched through the corridor twenty metres behind them and passed on through the opposite wall, slicing stone so it dribbled like heated butter. The superheated air that slammed down the hall from the impact flattened them. They met groups of Zoicans and Varl's men cut them apart.

Two levels down, they ran into a stream of nearly sixty Vervun Primary and Roane Deepers with Major Rodyin amongst them. Several had bad burns.

'Where's Willard?' screamed Varl over the klaxons and the explosive hurricane roar.

'Haven't seen him!' barked Rodyin. One lens of his spectacles was crazed and he had a cut on his cheek.

'We have to get the men down! Down lower!' Varl yelled and the two officers began routing the surviving troops down a back staircase as firestorms billowed down the hallways towards them.

'They mined the Curtain Wall! From inside!' Rodyin bellowed as he and Varl pushed man after man past them onto the stairs.

'I know, feth it! How the hell did they get in?'

Rodyin didn't answer.

On a section of wall below the mauled fort, Corporal Meryn was leading a straggle of panicking troops to cover. Two squads of Ghosts – Brostin, Logris, Nehn and Mkteeg amongst them – pushed forward past him, but there were twenty or more Vervun Primary soldiers stumbling in their wake. Meryn bawled at them, waving his arms, trying to be heard above the shriek of the shelling and the detonations all around. Flames from the fort were reaching a hundred metres into the sky and billows of soot and burning fabric squalled around them. The heat was overwhelming. Somewhere close, a loader full of ammo had caught fire and heated rounds were firing off wildly, spanking off the stonework and cutting zigzag tracer paths in the air.

A shot hit the Vervun Primary trooper nearest to Meryn and exploded his spiked helmet.

There was a flash and some vast cutting beam drawn up outside the Wall swept over them. Meryn saw it and threw himself flat as the inexorable beam raked the parapet at chest height, vaporising the hurrying line of Vervun troopers in a murderous sequence. They simply vanished in turn, obliterated, leaving nothing but clouds of steam and the occasional smouldering boot behind.

The beam swept right over the prone Tanith Corporal, searing the back of his breeches, jacket and head-hair right off. He winced at the low throb of superficial burns, but he was startled to be alive.

He got to his feet, his black fatigues shredded and falling off his body, and stumbled to the nearest stairhead.

Hundreds of men – Tanith, Roane and Vervun Primary – fled the Wall fortifications and Ontabi Gate and ran for cover in the streets and habs adjacent to the docks. Enemy shelling and beam-fire were punching clean through the Wall and the fort structure now and blasting into the edges of the worker habs. The Shield, ignited above them, mocked the scene. What good was an energy screen when the enemy was blasting through ceramite and adamantium?

Stretches of the habs were engulfed in flame and thousands of hab-dwellers filled the streets in panic, mingling with the fleeing soldiery, choking the access routes and transits in a panicked stampede. Hass East Fort convulsed and collapsed volcanically, the great hatches of Ontabi Gate melting like ice. A breach had been cut in the Curtain Wall of Vervunhive more terrible and more extensive than any damage done so far, even than at the brutalised Veyveyr Railhead.

At Croe Gate, the next main fortification down the Curtain Wall from Hass East, some ten kilometres south of Ontabi, the wall troops and observers watched in incredulous horror as beams of destruction and heavy shelling punished the riverside defences. A plume of fire underlit the storm clouds and blazed up into the sky like a rising sun.

General Nash was at Croe Gate still and he dismally voxed the situation to House Command. He urgently requested significant reinforcements to his position. In the wake of a major breach like this, ground forces couldn't be far behind.

As if on cue, one of his spotters reported movement on the Vannick Highway, twenty kilometres north-east. Nash used his magnoculars on heat-see and gazed out at the shimmering, green phantoms of tanks and armoured vehicles, thousands of them, roaming towards Ontabi in a spearhead formation.

'I have contacts! Repeat, I have contacts! At least a thousand mech-anised armour units advancing down the Vannick Highway and the surrounding hinterlands! They'll be on top of Hass East in under an hour! Reinforce my position now! I need armour! Lots of bloody armour! House Command! Do you respond? Do you bloody respond?'

An almost eerie silence fell across the main auditorium of House Com-mand. Only the desperate chatter of vox-traffic could be heard, reeling out reports of fearful destruction from a thousand different locations.

His face pinched and pale, Marshal Croe looked down at the chart table on the upper level. Hass East was gone. A mass armour force was approaching from the eastern levels. Artillery was beginning to pound Croe Gate and the eastern wall circuit. Zoican troops were assaulting the Spoil and the defences at Veyveyr. Heavy tanks and infantry col-umns were hitting Sondar Gate and the wall stretches towards Hass Gate and Hass West Fort. Hass West Fort itself was receiving ferocious ranged shelling.

An attack on all fronts. The defences of Vervunhive were already at full stretch and Croe knew this was only the beginning.

'What – what do we do?' stammered Anko, his face as white as his dress uniform. 'Marshal? Marshal Croe? What do we do, Croe? Speak, you bastard!'

Croe struck Anko across his fat mouth and sent him whimpering to the ironwork floor. Croe looked across at Sturm. 'Your thoughts, gen-eral?' There was venom and ice in equal parts in Croe's voice.

'I...' Sturm began. He faltered.

'Don't even begin to suggest an evacuation, Sturm, or I'll kill you where you stand. Evacuation is not an option. You were sent here to defend Vervunhive, and that's what you'll do.' He handed Sturm his ducal signet. 'Go to the stockade. Take troops with you. Release Grizmund and set him to command the armour before its strength is wasted. If that bastard Tarrian or any VPHC resists, deal with them. I expect you back at Veyveyr Gate to assume command there as soon as Grizmund is free. We have spent too much time arguing amongst our-selves. Vervunhive lives or dies tonight.'

Sturm nodded stiffly and took the ring. 'Where will you be, marshal?'

'I will take personal command of Sondar Gate. The hive will not die while I yet live.'

The shutter hatch of the stockade remained resolutely shut. Gaunt hammered on it with the butt of his bolt pistol, but there was no response. Gaunt, Pater and Bwelt stood pinioned by the floodlights, locked out in the damp cold of Level Sub-40. Captain Daur was with them, bleary and pale with sleep. Gaunt had dragged the liaison officer from his quarters on his way down to the stockade.

Gaunt turned to the advocate, who was wheezing for breath and leaning on his cane after the exertions of the frantic journey down into the bottom of the Spine. 'Don't you have an override, an authorisation?'

Pater held up his badge of office. 'Administratum pass level magenta... but the VPHC are a law to themselves. They have their own lock codes. Besides, colonel-commissar, do you see a keyhole?'

Gaunt pulled off his leather coat and threw it to Bwelt. 'Hold that,' he said bluntly and swung out his chainsword. The weapon whined as he cycled it up to full power.

He stabbed it at the armoured shutter. It rode aside, shrieking, leaving scratch marks and sending broken saw-teeth away in a flurry of sparks. He dug again and sliced into the metal, cutting a jagged slot a few centimetres across before the sword meshed and over-revved. With the sheer force of his upper arms and his shoulders, Gaunt heaved down, snarling a curse out at the top of his lungs, tearing down another few centimetres.

'Sir?' Daur said sharply behind him.

Gaunt spun around, raising the chainsword, in time to see the armoured lift cage descend and clank to rest. The grill-doors squealed open. General Sturm, flanked by Colonel Gilbear and ten Blueblood stormtroops, emerged from the lift car.

'Sturm, don't make this worse by–'

'Oh, shut up, you stupid fool, and put that weapon away,' snapped Sturm. He and his men approached and surrounded the quartet at the shutter. Gilbear was oozing a dreadfully superior smile at Gaunt.

'Get him out of my face, Sturm, or I'll practise what I'm doing to the door on him.'

Gilbear raised his hellgun, but Sturm slapped it aside. 'You know, Gaunt,' Sturm said, 'I almost respect you. I could do with a few men of your passion in my regiment. But still and all, you are a benighted fool and beneath the contempt of civilised men. You've spent too much time with those Tanith savages and – *what are you doing, you old fool?*'

This last remark was directed at Pater, who was carefully and quietly dictating material for Bwelt to set down on his slate.

'Transcribing your words, general, in case the colonel-commissar wishes to press a slander action against you later on.' The old advocate's voice was utterly empty of expression or nuance: a true lawyer. Gaunt laughed out loud.

Sturm looked away from the old man. He held up Croe's ducal signet. 'If you want to get inside, you need one of these.' He pressed it against the centre of the shutter. There was a dull thunk, a noise of servos churning and the shutter, with its chainsword tear, rose.

The group entered and Sturm opened the inner shutter. They passed on into the sodium-lit inner hall of the stockade.

'Marshal Croe has ordered me to release Grizmund. The world is going all to hell above our heads, Gaunt. Zoica assaults on all fronts. It is time to forget all petty bickering.'

Three VPHC troopers ran forward to confront them. One started to ask what they were doing in the stockade. Gilbear and his pointman cut them down with loose, brutal shots.

Gaunt pushed forward past the bodies and kicked open a set of wooden double doors to the left of the inner concourse.

There was a large circular chamber beyond, lit by bracketed wall-lamps with glass chimneys. Grizmund and his officers, hands tied behind their backs and hoods over their heads, stood on a raised dais under spotlights in the centre of the room. Kowle, Tarrian and nine senior VPHC officers sat on a tiered rank of wooden stalls before them, and a dozen VPHC troops with riot-guns lined the walls.

'What the gak is this?' Tarrian roared, getting to his feet.

Sturm held up the ducal signet. 'By order of the marshal himself, this court is overthrown. The prisoners will be freed.'

Kowle rose too. 'The meeting is in session and obeys the edicts of both planetary and Imperial law. We–'

'Shut your damn face, Kowle!' snapped Gaunt. 'The hive is dying above us and you waste your time persecuting good, honest men for the sake of some political point-scoring. You have no idea what real war is, do you, you bastard? You didn't on Balhaut and you don't here!'

Kowle's face went purple with rage, but the furious Tarrian pushed him aside. 'Interference with VPHC proceedings is a capital offence, Gaunt! Your maverick actions won't get you anywhere except to the sharp end of a firing squad detail!'

'Actually, that's not correct,' said Bwelt firmly. 'Imperial Edict 95674, sub-clause 45, states that an Imperial judicial officer, such as a full commissar, may interrupt and foreclose any planetary legal affair without restraint or penalty.'

'You tell him, boy!' cackled Pater.

Gaunt stared at Tarrian. 'Don't push them, Tarrian.'

'Who?'

'Gilbear and the other Bluebloods. Sturm can't control them and I sure as feth can't either. From me, you'll get tough honesty. From them, you'll get a hell-round between the eyes.' Even as he spat the words, Gaunt felt them all crossing an almost imperceptible line. The line between a precarious confrontation and total mayhem.

'Gak you, you wretched off-world scum!' bawled Tarrian as he pulled his autopistol from its holster. Gilbear dropped him with a shot to the chest. Tarrian's body exploded out through the back of the wooden seating.

The VPHC guards surged forward, racking riot-guns and firing. Gaunt saw a Blueblood fly backwards, hit in the shoulder. Sturm was cursing and blasting with his regimental service pistol. The Bluebloods opened up and sprayed the room.

Grizmund and his officers, blind under their hoods, dropped to the floor in terror. Gaunt wrestled the gasping advocate and his stunned clerk to the ground out of harm's way. Daur's laspistol cracked repeatedly.

Point-blank, in the tight confines of the court chamber, Volpone met VPHC head on, hellgun against riot-gun, filling the air with smoke, blood-mist and death.

Salvador Sondar slumped. A dribble of blood-bubbles fluttered from his ear towards the roof of the tank. He gave in. The chatter filled him, eating into his flesh, his blood, his marrow, his mind.

He did what it told him to do.

He deactivated the Shield.

THIRTEEN

THE HARROWING

'Never.'

> – Warmaster Slaydo, on being asked under what
> circumstances he would signal surrender

There was a loud, subsonic bang of pressure as the great Shield collapsed.

Windows blew out all across the hive. The ambient temperature dropped by six whole degrees as the insulation of the energy dome vanished and the cold of the Verghast night swept in. The vortex of collapsing air whisked up the vast smoke banks collected around the Curtain Wall and blew them into the hive itself like acrid fog. Disconnected energies crackled up out of the great pylon and the anchor stations and burned themselves out ferociously in the blackness.

A shuddering and terrifying noise drove in across Vervunhive. It was the unified howl of triumph from the millions of Zoicans outside.

Marshal Croe, majestic in his robes and armour, had just reached Sondar Gate with his staff retinue, and he stopped in his tracks, gazing up incredulously into the cold dark. His first thought was mechanical failure or even sabotage, but the Shield generators were the most securely guarded installations in the hive, and he had expressly ordered work-teams to inspect them every hour.

This was unthinkable. Inside the ceramite of his freshly donned war armour, Croe felt his heart grow as cold as the night around him. The ungifted powersword of Heironymo Sondar, most valued of all the hive's war-icons, felt heavy and useless in his hand. He caught himself and glanced around. The bannerpoles of his colour-sergeants drooped and fluttered dismally about him.

'Lord marshal?' whispered his adjutant, Major Otte.

'We...' Croe began, his mind racing, frantic but empty. He was torn.

He wanted to return to the Main Spine at once and cut to the root of this disaster, get the Shield back on. It was Sondar, he felt it in his blood. That bastard Salvador had finally gone over the edge.

But the immediate fight was here at the hive wall, in the face of the massing foe. His men had seen his arrival and if he turned around now, just as he had arrived, it would destroy their morale.

The silence that had followed the ghastly massed howl of the Zoicans outside, a silence that in truth could only have lasted a few seconds, was lost abruptly as the ear-splitting bombardment resumed. For leagues, the sky behind the towering shadow of the Curtain Wall that rose above him was lit yellow by the flare of colossal assault. Croe saw a section of turret to the west of the gate explode and collapse down into the Square of Marshals in a shower of sparks and rubble.

He took the tower steps two at a time at the head of his retinue, blazing the sacred sword into life, raging out orders to both the men around him and those unseen on the wall-top via his microbead link.

One of those orders, direct and succinct, coded in House Croe battle language, was for the ears of Izak, Croe's personal bodyguard. The big house warrior, clad in maroon body-armour, faltered at the foot of the tower steps and then turned back, curtly acknowledging his lord's command. He ran back across the square to the armoured staff-track that had brought Croe to Sondar Gate, and he steered it away at full throttle towards the Main Spine.

Alarms and klaxons began to whoop and wail once again. In the refuges and the camps of the Commercia and the other open spaces of the hive, the multitude seethed in panic. They'd seen the Shield fail. They'd fought their way to the security of the hive and now that too was gone.

Stampeding in places, two and a half million refugees began to surge north towards the river, the deluge of their bodies choking the streets. Their vast numbers were quickly swelled by inner hab citizens, worker families and low guilders, who had all, in a brief few seconds, seen their protection from Zoica disappear. In a matter of minutes, the hive was haemorrhaging people, rivers of panicking, screaming civilians, heading in hordes to a river they couldn't hope to cross.

Lord Heymlik Chass looked up from his scriptorium and gazed out of the ogee window. The stylus dropped from his trembling fingers and made a blot of violet ink on the pages of his journal. He got up, his ornamental chair tumbling over onto its back, and he stumbled across to the window, pressing his hands against the lead glass.

'Oh, Salvador,' he said, tears in his eyes, 'what have you done?'

His daughter burst into the room, still dressed in her nightgown, her terrified maids trying to wrap a velvet robe around her. Outside in the hall, House Chass lifeguards were shouting and running to and fro. Lord Chass turned and saw the look of jolted fear and bewilderment in his daughter's eyes.

He took her in his arms.

'The alarms woke me, father. What–'

'Hush. You will be all right, Merity.' He stroked her hair, holding her head tight to his chest.

'Handmaids?'

The women barely curtsied. They were terrified and half-dressed themselves.

'Take my daughter to Shelter aa/6. Do it now.'

'The chamberlain is preparing the house shelter, lord,' said Maid Wholt.

'Forget the house shelter! Escort her now to aa/6 in the sub-levels!'

'A municipal bunker, lord?' gasped Maid Francer.

'Are you both deaf and stupid? The sublevels! Now!'

The maids scurried around, pulling at Merity. She clung on to her father. She was crying so much she couldn't speak.

'Go, daughter of Chass. Go now. I will follow shortly. I beg you, go!'

The maids managed to drag the sobbing girl out of the chamber and away towards the Spine elevators.

'Rudrec!' At Lord Chass's shout, the chief lifeguard appeared in the doorway. He was still buttoning on his ornate body-armour. His weapon was armed and unshrouded. He bowed.

Lord Chass handed him a small, silk satchel. 'Go with my daughter. See she is brought safe to the municipal shelter. No other will do – no other is deep enough. Take this for her: a few private family items. Make sure she gets them.'

Rudrec tucked the satchel inside the body of his flak-mail hauberk. 'It is my duty to escort you too, lord, I–'

'You are a good man, Rudrec. You have served this house well. Serve it again by doing as I order.'

Rudrec paused, his eyes meeting his lord's directly for the first and last time in his life.

'Go!'

Alone now, the hall outside thundering with footsteps and voices, Chass put on his ceremonial robes, his bicorn hat, his shot-silk gloves. He was shaking, but most of that was rage. He put his ducal seal in his coat pocket, pushed the heavy code-signet ring onto his gloved finger, and slid a compact, single-shot bolt pistol with inlaid grips into his gown's inner sleeve. A handful of shells followed it.

Chass strode out into the corridor, stopping three of his lifeguards short. They saluted uncertainly.

'Come with me,' he told them.

Less than five minutes after the Shield vanished, the first Zoican shells began to wound the inner hive. It was as if their artillery, their Earth-shakers, their siege mortars, their missile positions had all been ranged ready, waiting.

Wave after wave of shrieking missiles screamed in over the Curtain Wall and hit the central district. Concussive ripples of explosions blew out along block after block, closing arterial routes with rubble, setting fires that blazed through dozens of high-rise habitat structures. Thousands of habbers, either sheltering in their homes or fleeing through the streets, were obliterated or left crippled and helpless.

Siege mortar shells wailed in across Sondar Gate and punctured the stone concourse of the Square of Marshals. Flagstone sections, whizzing like blades, were flung out, decapitating or mashing wall troopers from behind. The distinguished lines of statues edging the square were toppled by the blasts or disintegrated outright.

Mass shelling pounded the manufactories alongside Croe Gate. Swathes of machine shops and warehousing caught fire, and the flames established a firm hold, licking west into the worker habs. Similar shelling, supported by ground-to-ground rockets, began to systematically hammer the habs and manufactories behind Hass West, and the impacts of their fall crept north into the elite sector. Guild holdings and house ordinary estates were flattened and torn apart.

The shelling and the dreadful cutting beams searing Hass East scored a hole a hundred metres wide where the Curtain Wall and the Ontabi Gate had once stood, and as the beams redirected towards the inner habs and the upper stretches of the Curtain, the Zoican armoured column and massed infantry along the Vannick Highway pressed in through the breach. The Zoican land forces made their first entry into Vervunhive proper thirteen minutes after the Shield came down, though the insurgent forces encountered by Sergeant Varl were, by then, well inside the hive.

Long-range shells – some two thousand kilos apiece, launched from railcars drawn up on hasty, makeshift trackways out in the southern grasslands – whistled and whooped as they dropped on the Commercia and the mercantile suburbs. Barter-houses blew out, their rich canopies igniting in sheets of flame as hot as the heart of a star. Shockwaves crumpled others and the massive shells dug vast craters in the rockcrete footing of the hive. Hundreds of thousands of refugees were still pressing to leave the commercial spaces. Most died in the firestorms or were instantly obliterated by the shelling. Some of the craters were five hundred metres across.

Shelling and missile attacks began to hit the vast Main Spine itself. In hundreds of places, the adamantine skin of the city-peak ruptured and holed. Fires burned unchecked through nine or more levels. House Nompherenti, on Level 68, took a direct hit from a massive incendiary rocket and the entire noble lineage was immolated. They died frenzied, tortured deaths amid the furnace of tapestries, furniture and drapes in their exalted court. Lord Nompherenti himself, ablaze from head to foot, ran screaming for a hundred paces and toppled from the raised balcony of his banquet hall. His burning body, streaming a trail of fire like a comet, plunged fifteen hundred metres down onto the roofs of the central district.

General Xance, with a tattered vanguard of seven hundred North-Col troops, was pushing through the firestorm chaos west of Croe Gate when pinpoint shells began to rip along his straggle of trucks and Chimera troop carriers. Vehicle after vehicle exploded, showering the street with metal debris, ignited ammunition and plumes of gushing fuel. NorthCol troopers fled the convoy to either side, dying in further shell-strikes everywhere they turned. Xance's truck was overturned by a shell that struck the road alongside it. Blacked out for a few seconds, the general found himself lying twisted in a mangle of ruptured wreckage and the bloody remains of his command team. There was a fine, dark drizzle in the air which he realised was a vapour of blood droplets.

He tried to move, but pain gutted him. A transverse-gear rod had disembowelled him. He was half-buried in splintered body parts.

He moved aside a fragment of leg that lay across his chest, coughing blood. Then a limbless torso that still had the NorthCol insignia on its braids. Then a severed arm.

He gazed at it. It was his own.

Shells dropped all around, lighting the space with flashes so bright they burned out his optic nerves. They made no sound, not to him anyway. His eardrums had been punctured by the initial shell strike. Blind and deaf, he could only sense the carnage around by the quaking of the ground and the shockwaves that buffeted at him.

Xance was almost the last of his seven hundred-strong unit to die. He had bled to death, howling in rage, before yet another shell vaporised him.

In House Command, Vice Marshal Anko had fallen silent, his voice robbed to hoarse whispers by the screaming orders he had been issuing.

He slumped across the great chart table as the command staff hurried around, stunned and helpless.

The chart table made no sense any more. Runes and sigils flicked on and off, unable to keep up with the progress of the assault, wavering as contradictory data pummelled back and forth through the straining codifiers. After a while, it repeated nothing but default setting repeats of house crests.

Anko got up and backed away from the disingenuous table and its silence. He smoothed the front of his white dress uniform, adjusted the waist buckle under the girth of his belly and pulled out his autopistol.

He shot the table eight times for disobedience, then changed clips and shot two of the aides who ran screaming from him. He tried to yell, but his voice was nothing but a feeble rasp.

He ran to the ironwork rail and began to fire indiscriminately down into the lower deck, killing or wounding five more tactical officers and exploding a cogitator unit. VPHC Officer Langana and two servitors tried to wrestle him to the ground. Anko shot Langana through the left eye and emptied the rest of his third clip into the mouth of one of the servitors, blowing the upper part of its head away.

Anko threw off the other servitor and got to his feet. He turned to face the great observation window, fumbling for another clip as the staff fled in panic all around.

He saw the missile plainly. It seemed to him he could even see the checkerboard markings around its nose-cone, though he knew that was impossible, given the speed at which it must have been travelling.

Even the fluting of the exhaust ducts, the rivets in the seams.

The missile entered House Command through the great window, slamming a blizzard of lead-glass inwards with its supersonic bow-wave before striking the rear wall and detonating.

The storm of glass shards stripped Vice Marshal Anko's considerable flesh from his bones a millisecond before the blast destroyed House Command.

A brace of Earthshaker shells struck the great Basilica of the Ecclesiarchy east of the Commercia.

The two-thousand-year-old edifice – which had stood firm through the Settlement Wars, the Colonial Uprising, the Piidestro/Gavunda power struggle and countless bouts of civil unrest and rioting – shattered like glass. The roof was thrown outwards by the multiple blasts and millions of slate tiles showered the area for kilometres around, whizzing down like blades.

Stone walls, two metres thick, were levelled in the deluge of fire, flying buttresses sundering and bursting apart. Precious relics almost as old as the Imperium itself were consumed along with the priesthood. The streets outside were awash with rivers of molten lead from the roof and the windows. Many devotees of the Imperial cult, citizens and clerical brethren alike, who had survived the initial impact hurled themselves into the building's pyre, their faith utterly destroyed.

At Croe Gate, General Nash tried to reform his beleaguered units and direct them north to the Ontabi breach, even though fierce Zoican attacks battered the gate position.

House Command was offline and there was no coordination of repulse. Nash reckoned correctly he had 1,500 Roane Deepers and 3,500 Vervun Primary troops. He had been waiting for support from the NorthCol and Xance, but he had a sick feeling it wasn't coming. The hammering of the shells was overwhelming.

Nash had been in the infantry since he joined the Guard and he had seen the very worst dog-soldier work it had to offer. In those first few hours of the Great Assault, his command and leadership was unrivalled in Vervunhive. He set a condensing resistance around Croe Gate that shut the invaders out, and he countermarched two-thirds of his forces north to Ontabi and the main breach, which was nothing short of overrun.

Nash's Roane Deepers, never the most celebrated regiment of the Imperial Guard, proved their worth that night at the eastern extremities of Vervunhive's Curtain Wall. They met the Zoican infantry pouring into the hive with determined marksmanship and hand-to-hand brutality.

The Deepers, despite their reputation for laziness and an easygoing attitude, stopped the inrush at Ontabi dead for two and a half hours. A thousand Roane – supported by and inspiring the Vervun Primary residue – took down almost 4,500 Zoican troops and nearly a hundred armour elements.

Nash died in a work-hab ruin just before dawn, shot nineteen times as the Zoicans finally broke his last-ditch defence and swarmed into the hive. Falling back, the Roane and Vervun Primary survivors continued to defend, street by street, block by block, as the Zoican force rolled in on them.

At Sondar Gate, Zoican stormtroops raised ladders and siege towers to overrun the wall. Marshal Croe had lost count of the ochre-armoured soldiers he had slain by the time a massive death machine shaped much like a vast praying mantis thundered forward out of the night and hooked its huge arms around the towers of the Sondar Gate, ripping them apart. The great mantis-limbs locked and bridging plates extended between them, forming a huge ramp that allowed the Zoican troops to finally overrun the battlements.

Croe fell as the vast limbs destroyed the entire frontage of the gate battlement.

He was still alive in the rubble outside the collapsed gateway when advancing Zoican troops passed in, bayoneting any living bodies they kicked.

Marshal Croe died – broken, covered in dust and unrecognisable – with a Zoican bayonet through his heart.

FOURTEEN

THE IMPERIAL WAY

'True to the Throne and hard to kill!'
— The battle-pledge of the Volpone Bluebloods

'Enough!' Gaunt snarled. The gunfire which had been shaking the martial court died away fitfully. The air reeked of laser discharge, cartridge powder and blood. VPHC corpses littered the floor and the shattered wooden seating ranks. One or two Bluebloods lay amongst them.

The half-dozen or so surviving VPHC officers, some wounded, had been forced into a corner, and Gilbear and his men, high on adrenaline, were about to execute them.

'Hold fire!' Gaunt snapped, moving in front of Gilbear, who glowered with anger-bright eyes and refused to put up his smoking hellgun. 'Hold fire, I said! We came down to break up an illegal tribunal. Let's not make another wrong by taking the law into our own hands!'

'You can dispense it! You're a commissar!' Gilbear growled and his men agreed loudly.

'When there's time – not here. You men, find shackles. Cuff these bastards and lock them in the cells.'

'Do as he says, Gilbear,' Sturm said, approaching and holstering his pistol. The Blueblood troopers began to herd the prisoners roughly out of the room.

Gaunt looked around the chamber. Pater sat against the far wall, with Bwelt fanning his pallid face with a scribe-slate. Daur was releasing the Narmenian defendants.

The room was a ruin. Sturm's elite troops had slaughtered more than two thirds of the VPHCers present in a brutal action that had lasted two minutes and had cost them three Bluebloods. Tarrian was dead, his ribcage blasted open like a burned-out ship's hull.

Gaunt crossed to Kowle. The commissar was sat on one of the lower seating tiers, head bowed, clutching a hell-burn across his right bicep.

'It's the end for you, Kowle. You knew damn well what an abuse of the law this was. I'll personally oversee the avulsion of your career. A public disgrace... for the People's Hero.'

Kowle slowly looked up into Gaunt's dark eyes. He said nothing, as there was nothing left to say.

Gaunt turned away from the disturbing beige eyes. He remembered Balhaut in the early weeks of that campaign. Serving as part of Slaydo's command cadre, he had first encountered Kowle and his wretchedly vicious ways. Gaunt had thought he embodied the very worst aspects of the Commissariat. After one particularly unnecessary punishment detail, when Kowle had had a man flogged to death for wearing the wrong cap-badge, Gaunt had used his influence with the Warmaster to have Kowle transferred to duties on the south-west continent, away from the main front. That had been the start of Kowle's career decline, Gaunt realised now, a decline that had led him to the Vervunhive posting. Gaunt couldn't let it go. He turned back.

'You had a chance here, Pius. A chance to make good. You've the strength a commissar needs, you just have... no control. Too busy enjoying the power and prestige of being the chief Imperial commissar to the armies of Verghast.'

'Don't,' whispered Kowle. 'Don't lecture me. Don't use my name like you're my friend. You're frightened of me because I have a strength you lack. It was the same on Balhaut, when you were Slaydo's lap-dog. You thought I would eclipse you, so you used your position to have me sidelined.'

Gaunt opened his mouth in astonishment. Words failed him for a moment. 'Is that what you think? That I reported you to advance my own career?'

'It's what I know.' Kowle got to his feet slowly, wiping flecks of blood from his cheek. 'Actually, I'm almost glad its over for me. I can go to my damnation relishing the knowledge that you've lost here. Vervunhive won't survive now, not with the likes of you and Sturm in charge. You haven't got the balls.'

'Like you, you mean?' Gaunt laughed.

'I would have led this hive to victory. It's a matter of courage, of iron will, of making decisions that may be unpalatable but which serve the greater triumph.'

'I'm just glad that history will never get a chance to prove you wrong, Kowle. Surrender your weapon and rank pins.'

Kowle stood unmoving for a while, then tossed his pistol and insignia onto the floor. Gaunt looked down at them for a moment and then walked away.

'Appraise me of the situation upstairs,' Gaunt said to Sturm. 'When you arrived, you said the hive was under assault.'

'A storm on all fronts. It looked grim, Gaunt.' Sturm refused to make eye contact with the Tanith commissar. 'Marshal Croe was ordering a full deployment to repulse.'

'Sir?'

Gaunt and Sturm looked round. Captain Daur stood nearby, his face alarmingly pale. He held out a data-slate. 'I used the stockade's codifier link to access House Command. I thought you'd want an update and...'

His voice trailed off.

Gaunt took the slate and read it, thumbing the cursor rune to scroll the illuminated data. He could barely believe what he was seeing. The information was already a half-hour old. The Shield was down. Massive assaults and shelling had punished the hive. Zoican forces were already inside the Curtain Wall.

Gaunt looked across at Grizmund and his fellow Narmenians, flexing their freed limbs and sharing a flask of water. He'd come down here on a matter of individual justice and when his back was turned, hell had overtaken Vervunhive.

He almost doubted there'd be anything left to return to now at the surface.

Under the co-ordinated command of Major Rawne and Colonel Corday, the Tanith and Volpone units holding Veyveyr Gate staunchly resisted the massive Zoican push for six hours, hammered by extraordinary levels of shelling. There was no ebb in the heedless advance of Zoican foot troops and the waste ground immediately outside the gate was littered for hundreds of metres around with the enemy dead. Along the ore-work emplacements at the top of the Spoil, Mkoll's marksmen and Ormon's Spoilers held the slag slopes with relentless expertise.

Mkoll voxed Rawne when his ammunition supplies began to dwindle. Both had sent requests to House Command for immediate resupply, but the link was dead, and neither liked the look of the great firestorms seething out of the hive heartland behind them.

Larkin, holding a chimney stack with MkVenner and Domor, had personally taken thirty-nine kills. It was his all-time best in any theatre, but he had neither time nor compunction enough to celebrate. The more he killed, the more the memory of the Zoican's bared face burned in his racing mind.

At the brunt-end of the Veyveyr position, Bragg ran out of rockets for his launcher and discarded it. It was overheating anyway. His auto-gun jammed after a few shots, so he moved down the trench, keeping his hefty frame lower than the parapet as las-fire hammered in, and he took over a tripod-mounted stubber whose crew had been shot.

As he began to squeeze the brass trigger-pull of the thumping heavy weapon, he saw Feygor spin back and drop nearby. A las-round had hit him in the neck.

Lesp, the field medic attending the trench, scrambled over to Feygor, leaving a gut-shot Volpone who was beyond his help.

'Is he okay?' Bragg yelled.

Lesp fought with the struggling Feygor, clamping wet dressings around the scorched and melted flesh of his neck and trying to clear an airway.

'His trachea is fused! Feth! Help me hold him!'

Bragg fired a last burst or two and then dropped from the stub-nest and ran to Feygor and the slender medic. It took all of his gargantuan strength to hold Feygor down as Lesp worked. The las-hit had cauter-ised the wound, so there was precious little blood, but the heat had melted the larynx and the windpipe into a gristly knot and Feygor was suffocating.

His eyes were white with pain and fear, and his mouth clacked as he screamed silent curses.

'Feth!' Lesp threw the small, plastic-handled scalpel away in disgust and pulled out his long, silver Tanith knife. He stuck it into Feygor's throat under the blackened mass of the scorched wound and opened a slot in the windpipe big enough to feed a chest-tube down.

Feygor began breathing again, rattling and gurgling through the tube.

Lesp yelled something up at Bragg that a nearby shell-fall drowned out.

'What?'

'We have to get him clear!'

Bragg hoisted Feygor up in his arms without question and began to run with him, back down the lines.

The Tanith units that had held Veyveyr two nights before pushed south from their temporary mustering yard as soon as the Shield failed. Cor-bec led them and Sergeant Baffels's platoon was amongst them.

Lacking orders from House Command, Corbec had agreed to move west while Colonel Bulwar's NorthCol forces moved east, hoping to reinforce the Veyveyr and Croe positions.

In tight manufactory enclaves behind the once-proud Veyveyr rail terminal, Corbec's deployment encountered crossfire from the west.

Corbec realised in horror that while Veyveyr might be sound, the enemy were pouring in through Sondar Gate unstaunched. He set up a scari-fying resistance in a factory structure called Guild Githran Agricultural and he tried to vox his situation to Rawne or Corday.

Corday eventually responded. It took a while for Corbec to convince him that enemy forces, already in the inner hive, were in danger of encircling the solid Veyveyr defence.

They chose a window each, coughing in the dust that the bombard-ment was shaking up from the old floor boards.

Milo saw las-rounds punching through the fibre-board sidings of the broken building, and he heard the grunt-gasp of flamers. The enemy was right outside.

From the windows, under Baffels's direction, they fired at will. It was difficult to see what they were hitting. Filain and Tokar both yowled out victory whoops as they guessed they brought Zoicans down.

Rhys, one window down from Milo, stopped firing and sagged as if very tired.

Milo pulled round and called out to him, stopping short when he saw the bloodless las-hole in Rhys's forehead.

A falling shell blew out a silo nearby and the building shook.

Colonel Corbec's voice came over the microbead link, calm and stern. 'This is the one, boys. Do it right, or die here.'

Milo loaded a fresh cell and joined his platoon in blasting from the chewed window holes.

More than three hundred Tanith were still resting, off-guard, in their makeshift chem-plant billet when the Shield came down and the onslaught began. Sergeant Bray, the ranking officer, had them all dress and arm at once, and he voxed House Command for instructions.

House Command was dead. Bray found he couldn't reach Corbec, Rawne or Gaunt – or any military authorities. What vox-links were still live were awash with mindless panic or the insidious chatter broad-casts of the enemy.

Bray made a command decision, the biggest he'd ever made in his career. He pulled the Tanith under his charge back from the billets and had them dig in amongst the rubble wastelands behind, wastelands created in the first bombardment at the start of the war.

It was an informed, judicious command. Gaunt had taught tactics thoroughly and Bray had listened. A move forward, towards Sondar Gate and the Square of Marshals three kilometres south, would have been foolhardy given the lack of solid intelligence. Staying put would have left them in a wide, warehouse sector difficult to secure or defend.

The rubble wastes played directly to the Ghosts' strengths. Here they could dig in, cover themselves and form a solid front.

As if to confirm Bray's decision, mortar fire levelled the chem-plant billets twenty minutes after the Tanith had withdrawn. Advance storm-units of Zoican infantry crossed into the wasteland half an hour later and were cut down by the well-defended Ghosts. In the following hours, Bray's men engaged and held off over two thousand ochre-clad troops and began to form a line of resistance that stymied the Zoican push in from Sondar Gate.

Then Zoican tanks began to arrive, trundling up through the blasted arterial roads adjoining the Square of Marshals. They were light, fast machines built for infantry support, ochre-drab and covered with netting, with turrets set back on the main hull, mounting pairs of small-calibre cannons. Bray had thoughtfully removed all the rocket grenades and launchers from the billet stockpile, and his men began to hunt tanks in the jagged piles of the wasteland, leaving their las-rifles in foxholes so they could carry, aim and load the rocket tubes. In three hours of intense fighting, they destroyed twenty machines. The slipways off the arterials were ablaze with crackling tank hulls by the time heavier armour units – massive main battle-tanks and super-heavy self-propelled guns – began to roll and clank up into the chem-district.

Caffran braced against the kick of the rocket launcher and banged off a projectile grenade that he swore went directly down the fat barrel of an approaching siege tank, blowing the turret clean off. Dust and debris winnowed back over his position, and he scrambled around to reach another foxhole, Trooper Trygg running with him with the belt of rockets.

Caffran could hear Bray yelling commands nearby.

He slipped into a drain culvert and sloshed along through the ankle-deep muck. Trygg was saying something behind him, but Caffran wasn't really listening.

It was beginning to rain. With the Shield down, the inner habs were exposed to the downpour. The wasteland became a quagmire of oily mud in under a quarter of an hour. Caffran reached the ruins of a habitat and searched for a good firing point. A hundred metres away, Tanith launchers barked and spat rockets at the rumbling Zoican advance. Every few moments, there would be a plangent thump and another tank round would scream overhead.

Caffran was wet through. The rainfall was cutting visibility to thirty metres. He clambered up on the scorched wreck of an old armchair and hoisted himself up into an upper window space, from which he could get a good view of the rubble waste outside.

'Toss me a few live ones!' he called down to Trygg.

Trygg made a sound like a scalded cat and fell, severed at the waist. Ochre-armoured stormtroops flooded into the ruin below Caffran, firing wildly. A shot hit Trugg's belt of grenades and the blast threw Caffran clear of the building shell and onto the rubble outside.

Caffran clawed his way upright as Zoicans rushed him from three sides. Pulling out his Tanith dagger, he plunged it through the eyeslit of the nearest. He clubbed the next down with his rocket tube.

Another shot at him and missed.

Caffran rolled away, firing his loaded rocket launcher. The rocket hit the Zoican in the gut, lifted him twenty metres into the air and blew him apart.

There was a crack of las-fire and a Zoican that Caffran hadn't seen dropped dead behind him.

He glanced about.

Holding the laspistol Caffran had given her as a gift, Tona Criid crept out of cover. She turned once, killing another Zoican with a double shot.

Caffran grabbed her by the hand and they ran into the cover of a nearby hab as dozens more Zoican troopers advanced, firing as they came.

In the shadows of the hab ruin, Caffran looked at her, one soot-smeared face mirrored by the other.

'Caffran,' he said.

'Criid,' she replied.

The Zoicans were right outside, firing into the ruins.

'Good to know you,' he said.

The cage elevators carried them up as far as Level Sub-6 before the power in the Low Spine failed and the cars ground to a screeching halt. Soot and dust trickled and fluttered down the echoing shaft from above.

They exited the lifts on their bellies, crawling out through grille-doors that had half missed the next floor, and they found themselves in a poorly lit access corridor between water treatment plants.

Gaunt and Bwelt had to pull Pater bodily out of the lift car and onto the floor. The old man was panting and refused to go on.

Gilbear and his troops had fanned down the hallway, guns ready. Daur had guard of Kowle and Sturm was trying to light a shredded stub-end of cigar. Grizmund and his officers were taut and attentive, armed with shotguns they had taken from the VPHC dead.

'Where are we?' Gaunt asked Bwelt.

'Level Sub-6. An underhive section, actually.'

Gaunt nodded. 'We need a staircase access.'

Down the damp hallway, one of Gilbear's men cried out he'd found a stepwell.

'Stay with him and move him on when he's able,' Gaunt told Bwelt, indicating the ailing Pater.

He crossed to Grizmund. 'As soon as we reach the surface, I need you to rejoin your units.'

Grizmund nodded. 'I'll do my best. Once I've got to them, what channel should we use?'

'Ten ninety gamma,' Gaunt replied. It was the old Hyrkan wavelength. 'I'm heading up-Spine to try to get the Shield back on. Use that channel to co-ordinate. Code phrase is "Uncle Dercius".'

'Uncle Dercius?'

'Just remember it, okay?'

Grizmund nodded again. 'Sure. And I won't forget your efforts today, colonel-commissar.'

'Get out there and prove my belief in you,' Gaunt snarled. 'I need the Narmenian armour at full strength if I'm going to hold this place.'

General Grizmund and his men pushed on past and hurried up the stairs.

'Sounds like you've taken command, Gaunt,' Sturm said snidely.

Gaunt turned to him. 'In the absence of other command voices...'

Sturm's face lost its smile and its colour.

'I'm still ranking Guard commander here, Ibram Gaunt. Or had you forgotten?'

'It's been so long since you issued an order, Noches Sturm, I probably have.'

The two men faced each other in the low, musty basement corridor. Gaunt wasn't backing down now.

'We have no choice, my dear colonel-commissar: a full tactical retreat. Vervunhive is lost. These things happen. You get used to it.'

'Maybe you do. Maybe you've had more experience in running away than me.'

'You low-life swine!' Gilbear rasped, stomping forward.

Gaunt punched him in the face, dropping him to the floor.

'Get up and get used to me, Gilbear. We've got a fething heavy task ahead of us, and I need the best the Volpone can muster.'

The Volpone troops were massing around them and even Pater had got up onto his feet for a better view.

'The Shield must be turned back on. It's a priority. We've got to get up into the top of the hive and effect that. Don't fight me here. There'll be more than enough fighting to go around later.'

Gaunt reached down with his hand to pull Gilbear up. The big Blueblood hesitated and then accepted the grip.

Gaunt pulled Gilbear right up to his face, nose to nose.

'So let's go see what kind of soldier you are, colonel,' the Blueblood said.

They climbed the dim stairs as far as Level Low-2 and then found a set of cargo lifts still supplied with power. The massive Spine shuddered around them, pummelled from the outside by the enemy.

Crowded into a lift car, the Volpone checked weapons under Gilbear's supervision. Sturm stood aside, silent. Gaunt crossed to Daur and his prisoner.

'Ban?'

'Sir?'

'I need schematics of the upper Spine. Anything you can get.'

Ban Daur nodded and began to resource data via his slate.

'Salvador Sondar has total control of the Shield mechanism,' said Kowle suddenly. 'He exists on Level Top-700. His palace is protected by obsidian-grade security.'

Gaunt looked at Kowle bemused.

'It sounded for a moment there like you were trying to help, Pius.'

Kowle spat on the floor. 'I don't really want to die, Ibram. I know this hive. I know its workings. I'd be the callous bastard you think I am if I didn't offer my knowledge.'

'Go on,' said Gaunt cautiously.

'Salvador Sondar has been borderline mad since I first met him. He's a recluse, preferring to spend his time in an awareness tank in his chambers. Yet he has absolute control of the hive defences. They're hard-wired into his brain. If you intend to turn the Shield back on, you'll have to deal with the High Master himself.'

The lift cage lurched as a shockwave passed through the Spine. Gaunt looked out of the cage door as they ascended and he saw a flickering procession of empty halls, then some thick with screaming habbers beating on the cage bars. They rose past fire-black levels and ones where twisted skeletons, baked dry by the heat of incendiaries, clawed at the lift doors.

One level was ablaze and they flinched as they passed up by its flames.

Daur handed Gaunt the slate with a plan of the upper Spine loaded onto it.

Another four hundred levels, Gaunt thought, watching the lights on the lift's indicator panel, and the High Master and I will have ourselves a reckoning.

Lord Chass and his three bodyguards had reached Level Top-700 and forced their way in through the powerless blast doors.

Shots came their way the moment they emerged, killing one of the bodyguards outright with a head wound.

Chass pulled out his gun and fired it as his remaining bodyguards unshrouded their hand-cannons and blasted tracer strings down the plush, marble-walled atrium.

A las-round hit Lord Chass in the left knee and dropped him face down onto the carpet. The pain was extraordinary, but he didn't cry out. His bodyguards ran to him and were both cut down by sprays of las-fire.

His lifeblood was pumping away through his leg wound. Lord Chass knew he was going to die very soon.

He crawled forward, a few centimetres at a time, soaking the priceless carpet with his blood. He couldn't see who or what was firing at him. The atrium was made of green cipolin stone and decorated with House Sondar banners. Light globes hung on chains from the high roof. At the atrium's far end, a wide arch led through into the audience hall, the Sondar chapel and the private residence.

He flopped over behind a sandstone jardinière and loaded a fresh shell into his compact handgun. He thought about reaching for one of the fallen bodyguards' laspistols, but they were exposed in the open, and Sondar's unseen protectors were raking the carpeted floor with steady fire.

Then the firing stopped. Three meat puppets swung into view in the archway: a cloaked female, a naked youth covered in gold body-paint, and something rank and emaciated that was only vaguely human any more. All lolled wretchedly, eyes vacant, lasrifles wired into their hands. They came unsteadily down the atrium, wobbling on the feed-tubes and wires that played out from a recessed trackway in the ceiling. Though their eyes didn't move, they seemed to sense him. Chass knew they were guided by heat and motion systems wired into the palace walls. They fired again, blowing chunks off the jardiniere and hitting Chass in the foot and shin of his already wounded leg. He fired his single-shot piece and the heavy round took the youth's head off. It continued to advance and shoot.

A sudden burst of autogun fire licked down the atrium and tore the puppets to pieces, leaving nothing but a few shreds of flesh trailing from the wires.

Four men came down the hall from the main entrance. Chass knew their maroon body-glove armour made them guards from Croe's personal retinue. Their leader was Isak. He knelt by Lord Chass as his companions moved on to secure the archway. Isak bowed his respect to the nobleman, then reached into his harness pouches for field dressings.

'The marshal sent you?'

'I am instructed to take any action necessary to restore the Shield, lord. That includes the suppression of High Master Sondar and his forces.'

At last Croe is acting with the same purpose as me, thought Chass. He felt no pain from Isak's work on his wounds. He was cold and everything seemed distant. 'Help me up,' he told the bodyguard. 'You'll need the geno-print of a noble to activate the Shield systems.'

Isak nodded and hoisted Lord Chass up by the armpits, as if he was as light as a feather. From beyond the arch came the sounds of renewed gunfire.

In the colonnade beyond the atrium – a long cloister of wooden beams and inlaid upper balconies with a roof of stained glass – Isak's men had encountered more servitor puppets. Some were appearing in the balcony galleries, others moving down the open length of the cloister. The House Croe guardsmen were pinned near the archway.

Lord Chass, leaning heavily on Isak for support, noticed a smell, a spicy taint that stung his nostrils, sweeter and more subtle than the sharp pungency of the discharged weapons. 'What is that smell?' he whispered, half to himself.

'Chaos,' Ibram Gaunt said.

Chass and Isak looked round from the archway where they were sheltering and saw Gaunt leading the team of Blueblood elite down the atrium with silent precision. Daur, Kowle and Sturm were at the back of the line, Gilbear alongside the commissar. All weapons were drawn.

'It seems we share a mission,' Gaunt said dryly. He gestured to Gilbear and the Volpone moved three of his seven troopers round to cover the far side of the arch. In a moment, they were adding the considerable force of their hellguns to the dispute.

'Sic semper tyrannis,' Chass whispered and smiled at Gaunt. 'I knew you would serve Vervunhive with true valour...'

His voice was faint. Gaunt looked at the wounds that mauled the nobleman's leg. Isak had applied a tourniquet high up on the thigh, but his robes were soaked with blood.

Gaunt caught Isak's look. They both knew how close to death Chass was.

Chass knew it too. 'I'd like to see us victorious before my passing, colonel-commissar.'

Gaunt nodded. He shouted to the Volpone. 'Let's not waste any more time! Take the chamber now!'

Gilbear looked across and tapped the grenade launcher mounted under his hellgun's barrel with a predatory grin. 'Permission?'

'Given!' said Gaunt. 'Tell your men in there to duck and cover!' he told Isak and the bodyguard snarled through his microbead.

Gilbear and one of his point men bellowed the Volpone battle-pledge at the tops of their lungs as they launched grenade after grenade in through the arch. The launcher mechanisms thumped and clacked as they pumped them.

The blast, a series of explosions piled on top of one another, ripped back down the colonnade and blew out the galleries and the glass roof. Debris and ash washed back through the arch.

Before the smoke even began to clear, the Volpone stormed the room, yelling and firing. Whatever else he thought about them, Gaunt had to give the Bluebloods their due. They were finely trained, ruthlessly effective heavy troops. He'd seen their worth on Monthax. Now they were proving it again.

With his bolt pistol and chainsword drawn, Gaunt ploughed into the colonnade after them, followed by Isak and the Croe guards, with Daur and Sturm left to assist Chass. Kowle simply wandered along behind.

The place was a ruin. Dismembered or support-severed servitors littered the wooden wreckage. One puppet, which had been standing on a now-collapsed balcony, swung above their heads like a corpse in a gibbet.

The Bluebloods fanned out, moving down side halls, exchanging fire with lifeless defenders.

'Which way?' Gaunt asked Chass, but the wounded man was only semi-conscious.

'The audience hall is down to the left,' Isak said.

'What did you mean, the smell was Chaos?' asked Chass suddenly swimming awake.

'The filth that corrupted Ferrozoica is here. It's got inside House Sondar, permeating everything. Probably why the bastard turned the Shield off. Kowle said Sondar was wired directly into the hive's systems. I'd lay bets that's how it got to him, infecting him like a disease.'

'You mean the hive systems are corrupted too?'

'No – but Sondar has listened to lies that have come directly into his mind. The fact they say he was mad to begin with can't help.' He checked ahead and saw the large double-doors to the chamber. 'With me!' Gaunt yelled, his chainsword buzzing murderously. The Volpone fireteam formed up behind him and had to run to keep up.

Gaunt burst through the doors and clashed directly with more servitor puppets in the entrance lobby. His chainsword cut through support wires and flesh. He hacked clear of their murderous attentions as Gilbear and his men came in behind, finishing the rest.

The audience chamber was large and softly lit. The air was warm and now so much thicker with the taint-smell. Muslin wall drapes twitched in the ventilator breeze. On the far side of the room sat a large, iron tank – its shell rich with verdigris from its brass fittings – fashioned with a single, baleful porthole in the front.

'I see you. What are you?' asked an electronic voice that came from all around.

Gaunt walked towards the awareness tank. 'I am the agency of Imperial authority on this world.'

'I am the authority here,' said the voice. 'I am the High Master of Vervunhive. You are nothing. I see you and you are nothing. Begone.'

'Salvador Sondar – if you still answer to that name – your power is ended. In the name of the God-Emperor of Mankind and for the continued welfare of this subject planet, I order you to surrender yourself to the Imperial Guard.'

'Surrender?'

'Do it. You will not enjoy the alternative.'

'You have nothing that threatens me. Nothing to tempt me. Heritor Asphodel has promised me this world in totality. The chatter has told me this.'

'Asphodel is the spawn of the warp, and his promises are meaningless. I give you one last chance to comply.'

'And I give you this.'

The servitor came into the room through a doorway concealed by muslin drapes. Sondar's macabre fascination with his meat-toys was infamous in the noble houses, and many efforts had been made to curtail his surgical whims and clone-farming over the years.

This thing was far more than that, more even than the deluded creation of a mad flesh-engineer. The insanity of the warp was in it: eighteen hundred kilos of scarred meat and gristle, bigger than a Hyrkan antlerdon, a jigsaw of human parts fused into the carcass of a wild auroch from the grasslands. Limbs twisted and writhed around it, some human with grasping hands, some animal, some wet, glistening pseudopods like the muscular feet of giant molluscs. The massive head was an eyeless mouth full of needle teeth, that smacked slackly and gurgled. The donor auroch's vast horns swept outwards from the low skull crest. A multitude of cables, feeds and wires suspended it, but unlike the other meat puppets, this thing moved of its own volition, pawing and stamping the soft carpet, writhing and pulsing.

The smell was overwhelming.

Gilbear and the Volpone backed off a few paces in astonishment. Sturm cried out in horror and one of the House Croe bodyguards turned and ran.

The meat-beast came for them, moving with a speed and fluidity that seemed impossible for something so vast. It howled as it came, a piercing, sibilant shriek of rage. Gaunt leapt aside and was knocked over by a flailing pseudopod. The slime burned through his leather coat where it touched.

Gilbear fired twice, blowing open holes in the lower belly of the thing. These issued spurts of stagnant pus onto the carpet. Then the Blueblood colonel was flying through the air, tossed aside by a twist of the huge horns.

Backing frantically, the other Volpone fired wildly. Blubbery, wet punctures appeared in the creature's flank, some oozing filmy fluid, others erupting with sprays of tissue and watery blood. A cloned human arm was blown right off and lay twitching on the ground.

A screaming Volpone was hoisted into the air and shaken violently to death, impaled through the chest on one of the horns. Another was crushed under the meat-beast's bulk, leaving a trampled mess of blood, bone and broken armour pressed into the carpet. Grasping limbs and curling pseudopods caught hold of a third and began to pull him apart, slowly and inexorably. His agonised wailing drowned out the meat-beast's keening roar.

Gaunt scrambled up, dazed, and shot the clasped Volpone through the head to end his drawn-out death. He fired again and again, until the sickle clip of his boltgun was empty, the powerful close-range shots blowing chunks of raw meat and translucent fat out of the creature. Blood and ichor spurted from the wounds.

The monster wheeled round at Gaunt, wailing. Head down, it charged him and the horns, one still decorated with the limp corpse of the Volpone soldier, smashed into the chamber wall, gouging the ceramite facing. Gaunt dived aside, swinging his chainsword round with both hands. The purring blade sliced through the top of the skull and chopped one of the horns off. Then Gaunt was rolling away again, trying to stay out of reach of the biting maw that chased after him, drooling spittle. With its attention on Gaunt, the meat-beast had turned away from the remaining Volpone and they resumed firing, ripping into the thing's hindquarters but apparently doing nothing to slow it down.

Gaunt knew that daemonic force pulsed inside the beast, a life-energy that animated it beyond any considerations of physical function. If there was a brain or any vital organs at all, they would be useless as targets. The thing wasn't alive in any real sense. It couldn't be killed the way a human could be killed.

Daur was firing too now, as were the remaining House Croe guards, and Kowle had scooped up the weapon of a dead Volpone, adding his own shots to the fight. Chass was slumped limply in a corner, unconscious. There was no sign of Sturm.

Gaunt hacked into the thing again, ripping through ribs. His chainsword was matted and clogged with the beast's fluid and tissue, and steam was rising from the blade where it was being eaten away by the toxic deposits.

Gaunt cursed. Delane Oktar, his old mentor, now long dead, had given him that sword on Darendara, right at the start of his career, when he had still been green and eager. He had carried it ever since, all through his time with the Hyrkans until his service under Slaydo at Balhaut, and beyond to Tanith and every victory of his beloved Ghosts. Its destruction hurt him more than he could say. It took the past from him, took his memories and victories away.

He jammed the dying blade into the beast's shoulder, kicking out a wash of toxic blood and bone chips. Wedged fast, the sword disintegrated and the power unit in the grip exploded. Gaunt was thrown backwards.

The thing lunged down after him, biting at his kicking boots as he scrambled backwards on his backside. Isak and two of the Volpone surged forward, firing to cover him and draw the thing away. As it wheeled on them, Gaunt found himself dragged clear. It was Gilbear. Blood flecked the front of his armaplas chestplate and there was rage in his eyes. He hauled Gaunt back towards the green bulk of the iron tank.

Another Volpone was caught by the beast's clamping jaws and shredded by savage bites of its teeth. The walls and drapes of the audience hall were sprayed heavily with blood now.

The creature turned on Isak, snapping off his head and shoulders with one crushing bite. His body fell beneath its clawing, stamping legs.

'A gun!' Gaunt yelled to Gilbear.

'Lost mine!' replied the Blueblood colonel, referring to the hellgun that had been tossed aside with him. He had out his powerful sidearm, a long-barrelled autogun plated with chrome. He put shell after shell into the creature's neck.

Gaunt scrambled forward, retrieving his boltgun, and slammed a fresh clip into the receiver. He would kill this thing before he died. By the ghosts of Tanith, he would.

The meat-beast slew one of the remaining Croe guards and flew at Daur and Kowle, trailing meat and blood from its mouth. Both men stood their ground, exhibiting levels of bravery as high as any Gaunt had ever witnessed. They pumped relentless shots into the approaching nightmare. Nothing slowed it.

Hastily they both dived aside. Daur rolled into Chass's crumpled body and frantically tried to reload.

Kowle landed on a Volpone corpse. The creature headed for him.

'Get clear!' Gaunt bellowed. Kowle was apparently fumbling with the dead Blueblood's equipment belts. Gaunt and Gilbear fired again in a futile attempt to drop the thing.

At the final moment, Kowle turned and rose. He faced the rushing beast with his arms held out. He was clutching a canvas web of grenades. The meat-beast bit his arms off at the elbows and Kowle tumbled backwards, blood jetting from the stumps. He didn't make a sound.

The creature convulsed, retched and exploded from within. Its massive torso blew out in a rush of flame and body matter. A spinning section of rib, thrown out by the blast, stuck quivering into the wall near Gaunt like a spear. Flames gouted out of the huge mouth.

The beast collapsed onto the floor, pulling feed lines and wires out of the ceiling. The pool of stinking fluid spreading beneath it began to burn the carpet away.

With Gilbear behind him, Gaunt crossed to the carcass. 'We need a flamer. We need to burn this abomination as soon as possible.'

'Yes, colonel-commissar,' Gilbear answered, turning to the surviving Volpone.

Kowle, on his back in a widening circle of blood, was still alive. Gaunt knelt beside him, soaking his knees.

'Said... you... didn't have the balls,' Kowle said, his voice so weak it was barely audible.

Gaunt had no words for him.

'Envy you...'

'What?' Gaunt asked, bending closer.

'Balhaut... You were there at the victory, with the warmaster. I envy you. I would have given... everything to share in that...'

'Pius, you–'

'Shut up, Gaunt... not interested in... anything you have to say to me. You took my honour away, you... ruined me. I hope the Emperor... will forgive you for robbing Terra of a... great leader like me...'

Gaunt shook his head. He reached into his pocket and pulled out Kowle's rank studs and cap badge. Carefully and deferentially, he pinned them back in place. Kowle seemed to notice what Gaunt was doing, though his eyes were wide and dilated, and the blood was now merely trickling from his ghastly stumps.

'Goodbye, commissar. You gave your best.'

Gaunt saluted, a sharp, smart gesture he hadn't made in a long time. Kowle smiled, barely, then died.

Gaunt got up from the corpse of the People's Hero and crossed to the awareness tank. 'Get Lord Chass up. Get the Shield back on,' he said to Daur sourly.

Daur nodded and began to raise the feeble Verghast noble.

Gilbear joined Gaunt at the tank. They looked down at the thickly glazed porthole.

'Come up with a way for me to pay you back as soon as you can,' Gaunt said, not looking round at the Volpone.

'What?'

'You pulled me clear of the beast. I don't want to be in the debt of a high-caste bastard like you any longer than I have to be.'

Gilbear grinned. 'I think I may have underestimated you, Gaunt. I had no idea you were such an arrogant swine.'

Gaunt glanced round. It would take another Ibram Gaunt and a whole different universe for there to be any trust or comradeship between him and Gilbear. But for now, in the thick of this nightmare, Gaunt couldn't help respecting the soldier, for that was what he was: a devoted soldier of the God-Emperor, just like Gaunt. They didn't have to like each other to make it work. A measure of understanding and honour between them was enough.

Gaunt bent down to look through the port glass, and Gilbear did likewise at his side.

Through the fog of murky, phlogistic fluid, they could just make out a frail, naked body, withered and corrupted, drifting inside the tank, its skull linked to wires and cables that curled upwards to the roof.

'We can call it quits if you let me finish this,' said Gilbear.

'He's all yours,' said Gaunt.

Gilbear smirked, arming the hellgun he had just retrieved. 'What about your due process? What about taking the law into your own hands?' he asked sarcastically.

'I can dispense it. I'm a commissar. That's what you said, wasn't it?'

Gilbear nodded and fired two shots through the portal window. Filthy green water rushed out in torrents, flooding the floor. Steam rose from it.

Gilbear leaned down once the force of the outrush slackened, and he watched the twitching, spasming form of the High Master trembling in his draining tank. He fired a grenade in through the broken port and turned away.

A dull crump and the sheet of steam that billowed out of the window hole marked the end of Salvadore Sondar, High Master of Vervunhive.

Daur had carried Chass over to the brass console in the wall and he helped the enfeebled lord punch in the override settings. Chass mumbled the codes to Daur just in time. The noble was dead by the time Gaunt reached them.

The runic sigils on the console plate asked for a noble geno-print. Gaunt simply lifted one of Chass's limp hands and pressed it to the reader-slate.

'Sic semper tyrannis, Lord Chass,' Gaunt whispered.

'Did he see victory, sir?' asked Daur.

'He saw enough. We'll find out if this is a victory or not.'

Automated systems cycled and whirred. Deep in the bowels of Vervunhive, field batteries throbbed. The pylon crackled and the anchor stations that remained intact raised their masts.

With a resounding, fulminating crack and a reek of ozone, the Shield was reignited.

Ibram Gaunt left the audience hall of House Sondar and walked up onto an enclosed roof terrace that overlooked the entire hive. Fires burned below, thousands of them, and streaks of constant shelling lit the air. The Shield overhead glowed and crackled.

Now the Last Ditch had begun.

FIFTEEN

DAY THIRTY-FIVE

'Target and deny! By our deaths shall they know us!'
— General Coron Grizmund, at the start
of the Narmenian counterattack

Overnight, between the thirty-fourth and thirty-fifth days of the war, Vervunhive had come to the brink of destruction. Now, like a clenching muscle, the Imperial forces tightened and backed through the inner habs and elite sectors, resisting the encircling foe. For all their massive numbers, the Zoicans could only attack by land with the Shield reactivated. The dense streets, city blocks, habitats and thoroughfares favoured the defenders, who could dig in and hold the Zoican push.

Corday and Rawne dragged their forces back from Veyveyr into the worker habs a bare half hour before they could be encircled by enemy forces reaching upwards from Sondar Gate. NorthCol and Vervun Primary battalions pushed west to support the retreating Roane, still resisting street by street as they fell back from the Croe and Ontabi Gates. Colonel Bulwar had nominal command of that front.

Five thousand Vervun Primary troopers under Captain Cargin still held the Hass West Fort fast, though looping columns of Zoican infantry were beginning to bracket them through the chemical plant district.

Throughout the inner habs south of the Main Spine, Imperial units tried to stem the advance. Sergeant Bray directed the Tanith in the wastes north of the chem district. Volpone, NorthCol and Vervun Primary sections strung out to his east, where Corbec's remaining Tanith and a force of Roane Deepers under Major Relf had consolidated a wide area of manufactories.

The fighting there was thick, as thick as any in the hive. Guild Githran Agricultural had been held since the small hours of the morning. Corbec's platoons had precious little ammo left and no food. They had been fighting all-out for six hours straight. Enemy flamer-tanks holding the north-south arterial highway tightly were preventing the Tanith from obtaining munitions from the better-provided Roane, just half a kilometre away to the east. The Tanith were forced to scavenge for ammo, running out of cover in twos and threes to loot the fallen Zoicans. At least with the Shield reactivated, they were spared the worst of the shelling, though the enemy armour and field pieces now set up inside the Shield dome were unrelenting.

Baffels whistled a command, and Milo, Neskon and Cocoer dashed from the cover of a derelict abattoir and scurried towards a burning textile mill. Dremmond covered their run with spurts from his flamer. The three Tanith had bayonets fixed. They were all out of ammo, except Cocoer, who had only a handful of shots left.

Six Zoicans lay dead behind the rear wall of the mill. The trio descended on them and stripped them of las-cells. Each corpse had six or seven as well as musette bags filled with stick grenades.

Milo looked up. The air throbbed with las-fire and though the Shield had shut out the rain, the ground was slick and muddy. He pulled Neskon down into cover. Enemy fire chased down the mill wall, cracking holes in the plaster facing and puffing out brick dust.

A fireteam of Zoican stormtroopers was advancing through the ruins to the west of the mill. Cocoer now had a fresh clip in his Guard-issue weapon and he fired twice, missing his targets but causing the Zoicans to duck and cover.

'We're pinned!' Milo hissed into his microbead.

'Stay down,' the voice of Sergeant Baffels crackled back.

They did. Neskon poked his head up long enough to be shot at.

'Come on, Baffels!' Milo added urgently. They could hear the crunching footfalls of the Zoicans barely ten paces from their cover.

'Just another moment,' Baffels reassured his friend.

Loud las-shots cracked over the ruins, single shots, high-powered.

'You're clear! Go!' Baffels squawked.

Milo led the way, Neskon and Cocoer on his heels. He got a glimpse of the Zoicans behind him, sprawled dead from clean head-shots.

Milo smiled.

The trio slid into cover in the agricultural manufactory, safe behind a solid ceramite wall. Baffels and other Tanith crowded round them as they shared out the clip-cells and the stick-bombs.

Milo looked across the roofless factory-space and saw Larkin dug in high up near a vent hatch. The Tanith snipers, along with the Spoilers, had drawn back from the Spoil. Milo had known that the precision killing of the Zoicans had been the work of marksmen.

He flashed a grin up at Larkin. The weasely sniper winked back.

Milo handed a cell to Baffels. 'Your turn next time,' he joked.

'Of course,' said Baffels. Hours before he had ceased to recognise the humour in anything.

'Colm?'

Corbec looked up out of the loophole he was holding, his shaggy head coated in soot and grime. He shot a beaming grin when he saw Mkoll.

'About time you got here.'

'Came as fast as we could. The bastards have the Spoil now. We left it to them.'

Corbec got up and slapped Mkoll on the arm. 'You all make it through?'

'Yeah, Domor, Larkin, MkVenner – all the boys. I've spread them out through our lines.'

'Good work. We need good marksman coverage all along. Feth, but this is ugly work.'

They looked round, hearing angry voices down the burned-out hall. Vervun Primary troops with long-barrelled lasguns were moving in to join the defence.

'The Spoilers, so called,' Mkoll explained to his colonel. 'Dedicated to protecting the Spoil. Took a while to convince them that falling back was the smart choice. They'd have held the slag-slopes forever. It's a pride thing.'

'We understand pride, don't we?' grimaced Corbec.

Mkoll nodded. He pointed out the leader of the Spoilers, a bulky man with bloodshot eyes who was doing most of the shouting and cursing. 'That's "Gak" Ormon. Spoiler commander.'

Corbec sauntered over to the big Verghastite.

'Corbec, Tanith First and Only.'

'Major Ormon. I want to lodge a complaint, colonel. Your man Mkoll ordered our withdrawal from the Spoil, and–'

Corbec cut him short. 'We're fighting for our fething lives and you want to complain? Shut up. Get used to it. Mkoll made a good call. Another half an hour and you would have been surrounded and dead. You want a "spoil" to defend? Take a look!' He gestured out of a shattered window at the wasteland around. 'Start thinking like a soldier, and stop cussing and whining. There's more than unit pride at stake here.'

Ormon opened and closed his mouth a few times like a fish.

'I'm glad we understand each other,' Corbec said.

In the north-eastern corner of the hive, Sergeant Varl and Major Rodyin had command of one hundred and seventy or so men holding the burning docks. Half were Tanith; the rest, Vervun Primary and Roane. Zoican stormtroops were blasting in along the Hass East Causeway under the Hiraldi road-bridge, and the Imperial forces were being driven back through the hive's promethium depots. Several bulk capacity tanks were already ablaze and liquescent fire spurted from derricks and spout-vents.

Firing tight bursts, Varl crossed a depot freightway and dropped into cover beside Major Rodyin, who had paused to fiddle with the cracked lens of his spectacles.

'No sign of support. I've been trying the vox. We're on our own,' the Vervun officer remarked.

Varl nodded. 'We can do that. Just a few of us should be able to keep them busy in these industrial sectors.'

'Unless they move armour our way.'

Varl sighed. The hiver was pessimism personified.

'Did you see the way the Zoicans' armour was smeared with tar and oil?'

'I did,' said Varl, clipping off a few more shots. 'What of it?'

'I think that's how they got in, how they broke us open. They came through the pipeline from Vannick Hive.' Rodyin pointed out across the depot to the series of vast fuel-pipe routes that came in over the river on metal stilt legs from the northern hinterlands. 'The pipes come in right under the Curtain Wall.'

'Why the feth weren't they shut down?' snapped Varl.

Rodyin shrugged. 'They were meant to be. That's what I was told, anyway. The directive was circulated weeks ago, right after Vannick was obliterated. The guilds controlling the fuelways were ordered to blow the pipes on the far shore and fill the rest with rockcrete.'

'Someone didn't do their job properly,' Varl mused. Somehow the information aggravated him. It was way too fething late to find out how they had been breached.

The fight at hand took his mind off it. Persistent rocket grenades were tumbling onto them from a loading dock at the edge of the depot. Varl ordered a pack of Roane down to establish covering fire and then sent Brostin in with the flamer.

He edged the rest of his men along down the devastated depot roadway, sometimes using the litter of metal plating and broken girders as cover, sometimes having to negotiate ways over or around it. A fuel tank sixty metres away blew out with huge, bright fury.

Logris, Meryn and Nehn, working forward with a handful of Vervun Primary troopers, almost ran into a Zoican fireteam in a drain-away under one of the main derrick rigs. The Tanith laid in fearlessly with bayonets, but the Vervunhivers tried to find room to shoot and several were cut down.

Hearing the commotion over his microbead, Varl charged in with several other Tanith, spiking the first ochre-suited soldier he met with his silver bayonet. Another sliced at him with a boarding hatchet and Varl punched his head off with one blow from his metal arm.

Major Rodyin came in behind, shooting his autopistol frantically. He seemed pale and short of breath. Varl knew that Rodyin had never been in combat like this before. In truth, the man had never been in combat at all before that day.

Three desperate, bloody minutes of close fighting cleared the drain-away of Zoicans. Logris and Nehn set up solid fire positions down the gully, overlooking the dock causeway.

Rodyin took off his glasses and tried to adjust the earpieces with shaking hands. He looked like he was about to weep.

'You alright, major?' Varl asked. He knew full well Rodyin wasn't, but he suspected it had less to do with combat shock and more to do with the sight of his home city falling around him. Varl could certainly sympathise with that.

Rodyin nodded, replacing his spectacles. 'The more I kill, the better I feel.'

Nearby, Corporal Meryn laughed. 'The major sounds like Gaunt himself!'

The notion seemed to please Rodyin.

'What now? Left or right?' Meryn asked. He was wearing bulky fuel-worker's overalls in place of the Tanith kit which had been scorched off him. His seared scalp was caked with dried blood and matted tufts of scorched hair.

'Feth knows,' Varl answered.

'Right. We try to push down the river towards the bridge,' Rodyin said with great certainty.

Varl said nothing. He'd rather have stayed put or even fallen back a little to consolidate. The last thing they wanted was to overreach themselves, yet Rodyin was determined. Varl was uneasy following the major, even though the Verghastite had rank. But Willard was dead – Varl had seen his burning body fall from the Wall – and there was no one of authority to back him up.

So they moved east, daring the open firestorms of the docks, winning back Vervunhive a metre at a time.

General Grizmund walked down the steps of the Main Spine exit, adjusting his cap and powersword. Wind-carried ash washed back across the stone terrace of the Commercia where the Narmenian tanks were drawn up: one hundred and twenty-seven main battle tanks of the Leman Russ pattern, with twenty-seven Demolishers and forty-two light support tanks. Their engines revved, filling the air with blue exhaust smoke and thunder.

Brigadier Nachin saluted his general.

'Good to have you back, sir,' he said.

Grizmund nodded. He and the other officers liberated by Gaunt from the hands of the VPHC were more than ready to see action.

Grizmund pulled his command officers into a huddle and flipped out the hololithic display of a data-slate. A three-dimensional light-map of the Commercia and adjacent districts billowed into the sooty air. Grizmund began to explain to his commanders what he wanted them to do, how they would be deployed, what objectives they were to achieve.

His voice was relayed by vox/pict drones to all the Narmenian crews. His briefing turned into a speech, a rousing declamation of power and victory. At the end of it, the tank crews, more than a thousand men, cheered and yelled.

Grizmund walked down the line of growling tanks and clambered deftly up onto his flag-armour, *The Grace of the Throne*, a long-chassis Russ variant with a hundred and ten-centimetre main weapon. Like all the Narmenian vehicles, it was painted mustard-drab and bore the Imperial eagle crest and the spiked fist sigil of Narmenia.

It felt like coming home. Grizmund dropped down through the main turret's hatch, strapped himself into the command chair, and plugged the dangling lead of his headset into the vox-caster.

Grizmund tested the vox-link and made sure he had total coverage.

He pulled the recessed lever that clanged the top-hatch down, and he saw his driver, gunner and loader grinning up at him from the lower spaces of the tank hull.

'Let's give them hell,' Grizmund said to his crew and, via the vox, to all his men.

The Narmenian tank units roared down through the Commercia and back into the war.

House Command was a molten ruin full of scorched debris and a few fused corpses. The blast that had taken it out had also blown out the floor and disintegrated the Main Spine structure for three levels below. Gaunt viewed it from the shattered doorway for a minute or two.

Searching the adjacent areas, Gaunt appropriated a Ministorum baptistry on Level Mid-36 as a new command centre. Under Daur's supervision, workteams cleared the pews and consecration tables and brought in codifiers and vox-systems liberated from dozens of houses ordinary on that level. Gaunt himself hefted a sheet of flakboard onto the top of the richly decorated font to make a desk. He began to pile up his data-slates and printouts.

Ecclesiarch Immaculus and his brethren watched the Imperial soldiers overrun their baptistry. It was one of the few remaining shrines in the hive still intact. They had been singing laments for the basilica when Gaunt arrived.

Immaculus joined Gaunt at his makeshift desk.

'I suppose you're going to tell me this is sacrilege,' Gaunt said.

The old man in long, purple robes shook his head wearily. 'You fight for the Imperial cause, my son. In such manner, you worship the Emperor more truly than a hundred of my prayers. If our baptistry suits your needs, you are welcome to it.'

Gaunt inclined his head reverently and thanked the Ecclesiarch.

'Baptise this war in blood, colonel-commissar,' Immaculus said.

The cleric had been nothing but gracious and Gaunt was anxious to show his appreciation. 'I will feel happier if you and your brothers would hold vigil here for us, watching over this place as a surety against destruction.'

Immaculus nodded, leading his brethren up to the celebratory, from where their plainsong chants soon echoed.

Gaunt viewed the data-slates, seeing the depth of the destruction. He made note marks on a paper chart of the hive.

Daur brought him the latest reports. Xance was dead; Nash too. Sturm had vanished. As Gaunt surveyed the lists of the dead, Major Otte of the Vervun forces, the lord marshal's adjutant, arrived in the baptistry. He was wounded and shellshocked, one of the few men to make it clear of the fall of Sondar Gate.

He saluted Gaunt. 'Marshal Croe is slain,' he said simply.

Gaunt sighed.

'As ranking officer of Vervun Primary, I hand command to you, as ranking Imperial commander.'

Gaunt stood up and solemnly received the salute with one of his own. What he had suspected ever since he led the assault on Sondar's lair was now confirmed: he was the senior surviving Imperial officer in Vervunhive and so overall military authority was now his. All senior ranks, both local and off-world, were dead or missing. Only Grizmund held a rank higher than Gaunt and armour was always subservient to an infantry command.

Otte presented Gaunt with Croe's sword of office: the powerblade of Heironymo Sondar.

'I can't accept–'

'You must. Whoever leads Vervunhive to war must carry the sword of Heironymo. It is a custom and tradition we have no wish to break.'

Gaunt accepted, allowing Otte to formally buckle the carrying sash around him.

Intendant Banefail of the Administratum, surrounded by a procession of servitors and clerks, entered the baptistry as Otte was performing the ceremony. He nodded to Gaunt gravely and accepted his authority without question.

'My ministry is at your disposal, commander. I have mobilised labour teams to assist in fire control and damage clearance. We… are overwhelmed by the situation. Most of the population is trying to flee across the river, all militarised units request ammunition supply, the main–'

Gaunt raised his hand. 'I am confident the Administratum will provide whatever they can, whatever is in their means. I trust the astropaths have been maintaining contact with the Warmaster?'

'Of course.'

'I will not ask Macaroth for aid, but I want him to understand the situation here. If he deems it worthy of his notice, he will assist us.'

Horns sounded, a pathetic gesture of pomp, and Legislator Anophy shuffled into the baptistry with his retinue: a long train of child-slaves, servitors and guards, some carrying banner poles. The banners and the robes were singed and grubby in places, and the slaves looked wet-eyed and terrified. Representatives of the guilds and high houses flocked in behind the Legislator's procession, shouting and disputing.

Gaunt turned to Banefail. 'You can help me immediately by keeping these worthies out of my face. Listen to their petitions and notarise them. I will review later – if there is an opportunity.'

'It will be done,' Banefail said. 'May the Emperor of Mankind provide for you in this hour.'

As the Administratum staff swept away behind Banefail to head off the angry mob of dignitaries, Gaunt resumed his review of the battle data. The first of the vox-links had just been set up and Daur brought him a speaker set.

Gaunt selected a channel. 'Vervunhive Command to Grizmund. Signal "Uncle Dercius".'

'"Uncle Dercius" given and heard,' crackled the receiver.

'I need you to deny the approaches to Croe Gate and Ontabi Gate. From what I can see here, the main vehicular invasion is pouring in that way.'

'Agreed. But there are tank squadrons coming up through Sondar Gate too.'

'Noted. I'll deal with that. May the God-Emperor guide you, general.'

'And watch over you, colonel-commissar.'

Adjusting his channel setting, Gaunt raised the commander of North-Col armour groups milling in confusion south of the Commercia. He directed them down towards Sondar Gate. Then he began to systematically contact all the tattered sections of infantry and Guard.

He got through to Corbec at Guild Githran Agricultural.

'Feth, commissar! I thought you were dead!'

'I thought the same of you, Colm. How is it?'

'Bad as anything I've seen. We're holding, just barely, but they're pouring it on. I could really do with a pinch of armour.'

'It's coming your way as we speak. Colm, we need to do more than hold, we have to push them back. The Shield will only work for us if we can hunt them out from under it.'

'You don't ask for much, do you?'

'Never.'

'You'll owe me a planet of my own for this, you realise?'

'I owe you that already, Corbec. Think bigger.'

A servitor brought Gaunt more data feeds from the newly engaged codifiers set up in the baptistry. Gaunt looked through them, his gaze stopped by a report relayed in from Varl.

'Daur?'

'Sir!'

'I want a list of guilds controlling fuel supply and accredited proof from every damn one of them that they closed their pipelines down.'

'Yes, commander.'

Gaunt spent the next ten minutes voxing tactical instructions to dozens of individual troop units throughout the hive. He was unable to reach Varl or any unit north of the Main Spine. As he worked, servitors and staff officers tracked the substance and matter of his battle-plan on a hololithic chart of the city, overlaying it with any data they received from the ground.

For a short while, Gaunt toyed with the settings of the vox-unit, hunting through the bands to locate the low frequencies the Zoicans were using. He still hoped they might intercept and unscramble the Zoican transmissions and eavesdrop on their tactical command net. But it was futile. The Zoican channels were seething with transmissions, but all in that incomprehensible chatter, the chatter that defied translation even by linguistic cogitators, a constant, meaningless stream of corrupt machine noise that gave up no secrets. Either that, or the chanting repeats of the Heritor's name on the propaganda wavelengths. Gaunt had fought Chaos long enough to know not to call in human scholars or astropaths to try to decode the chatter. He couldn't allow that filth to taint any mind in Vervunhive.

A commotion at the door roused Gaunt from his work. A detail of Vervun Primary soldiers was escorting General Sturm into the baptistry.

'We found him trying to join a party of refugees boarding a ferry at the viaduct jetty, sir,' the squad's leader told Gaunt.

Gaunt looked Sturm up and down. 'Desertion?' he said softly.

Sturm straightened his cap, bristling. 'I am senior commander here, Gaunt! Not you! Vervunhive is lost! I have given the signal to retreat and evacuate! I could have you all shot for disobedience!'

'You... gave the signal to evacuate? Then why are all Imperial forces and planetary units still fighting? Even your own Volpone? You must have given the signal very quietly.'

'Don't talk that way to me, you jumped-up shit!' Sturm croaked. The room fell silent around them and all eyes turned to observe the confrontation. 'I am the senior general of the Royal Volpone! I am ranking officer here in Vervunhive! You will obey me! You will respect me!'

'What's to respect?' Gaunt walked around Sturm, looking out at the watching faces with interest. No one showed any sign of leaping to the general's defence. 'You fled the assault on House Sondar. You fled the Main Spine and headed for the river. You gave up on Vervunhive.'

'I am ranking officer!'

With a brutal tear, Gaunt ripped Sturm's rank pins of his jacket.

'Not any more. You're a disgrace. A coward – and a murderer. You know damn well it was your orders that killed five hundred of my Tanith on Voltemand. Killed them because they managed to win what your Bluebloods could not.' Gaunt stared into Sturm's blinking eyes.

'How you ever made general, I don't know.'

Sturm seemed to sag.

'A weapon...' he said weakly.

'What?'

Sturm looked up with blazing eyes. 'Give me a cursing weapon, colonel-commissar! I'll not be lectured at by a lowborn shit like you! Or punished! Give me a weapon and allow me the good grace of making my own peace!'

Gaunt shrugged. He pulled his bolt pistol from its holster and held it out butt-first to the general.

'Final request granted. Officers of the watch, so note General Sturm has volunteered to exact his own punishment.' He looked back at Sturm. 'I've never even slightly liked you, Noches. Give me a reason to speak of you well. Make it clean and simple.'

Sturm took the proffered gun.

'Officers of the watch, also note,' hissed Sturm, 'that Ibram Gaunt refuses to signal evacuation. He's condemned you all to death by fire. I'm glad to be out of it.'

He cocked the weapon and raised it to his mouth.

Gaunt turned his back.

There was a long pause.

'Gaunt!' Captain Daur screamed.

Gaunt swung around, the powersword of Heironymo Sondar already out and lit in his hand. It sliced through Sturm's wrist before the Volpone general could fire the boltgun – the boltgun that had been aimed at Gaunt's skull.

Sturm fell sidelong on the baptistry flagstones, shrieking out as blood pumped from his wrist stump. Nerves spasmed in his severed hand and the bolt pistol fired once, blowing a hole through the ornate prayer screen behind Gaunt.

Gaunt glared down at the general's writhing form for a moment. Then he stooped and retrieved his bolt pistol from the detached hand.

'Get him out of my sight,' he told the waiting troopers with a dismissive gesture at Sturm. 'I don't want to look at that treacherous bastard any longer than I have to.'

By early afternoon on that fateful thirty-fifth day, whatever co-ordinated resistance could be made was being made. Gaunt's command post in the Main Spine had contacted and tactically deployed almost two-thirds of the available fighting strength in the hive, a feat of determined efficiency that left both the Administratum and the surviving officers of the Vervun Primary Strategic Planning Cadre dumbfounded. What made it altogether more extraordinary was that Gaunt had driven the work almost single-handedly. After the incident with Sturm, he worked with an intense devotion that was almost terrifying. Latterly, as the cohesion of his plan became clear, he was able to delegate work to the eager tactical staffers, but the core of the resistance plan was his alone.

Ban Daur stepped out of the baptistry a little after midday to clear his head and find water. He stood for a while under a blackened arch at the end of the hallway, watching through glassless windows as flickering areas of warfare boiled through the dense streets below.

Captain Petro, one of the tacticians, emerged from the baptistry too and came to stand with Daur, an old friend from their academy days.

'He's frightening...' Petro said.

'Gaunt?'

Petro nodded. 'His mind, his focus... it's like a codifier. All drive, all purpose.'

Daur sipped his glass. 'Like Slaydo,' he said. Petro raised a quizzical eyebrow.

'Remember how we studied the Warmaster's career? The keynote was always Slaydo's singularity of purpose – that he could look at a theatre and plan it in his head, hold the whole situation in his mind. That was military brilliance. I think we're seeing its like again.'

'He served with Slaydo, didn't he?'

'Yes. His record speaks for itself.'

'But as an infantry officer.' Petro frowned. 'Gaunt's reputation's never been for overall battlefield command, not on this scale.'

'I don't think he's ever had the chance to show it before – a commissar, a troop commander, always following the lead of higher ranks. He's never had an opportunity like this before. Besides... I think it may be because he's got everything to prove.'

'What the gak do you mean, Ban?'

'The high commanders are dead... or, like Sturm, disgraced. Fate and his own actions have put Gaunt in command, and I think he's determined to prove he should have been there all along.'

At a crossroads designated fg/567, in the heart of the eastern central habs, Bulwar's infantry divisions were close to breaking. They had no anti-armour ordnance left and the Zoican tank thrust was burning a spearhead through from Croe Gate, laying waste to hectares of habitat structures.

Bulwar and his NorthCol battlegroup moved south around the crossroads, tackling Zoican troops in the rockcrete tangles that had once been labour-homes. Tank rounds screamed down over them, blowing out sections of wall and roadway, collapsing precarious spires of rubble and masonry.

In the shell of a funicular carriage station, between the ornate marble pillars and the old brass benches, they fought at close quarters with a phalanx of Zoicans. More were pouring in through the ticket booths at the far end or climbing up into the station through the shattered wreck of a carriage train that had made its last stop at the platform. Civilian dead lay all around.

Bulwar led the attack, breaking body armour with his power claw and shooting with his autogun. Men fell around him, too many to count. A las-round struck his shoulder and he was thrown backwards off his feet.

When he got up, things had changed. A fighting force had erupted into the station from the passenger exits and it was tearing into the Zoicans from the side. They weren't NorthCol or Vervun Primary or even Guard. They were workers, hive labourers, armed with captured guns, axe-rakes, or any other weapon they could find. Bulwar realised they were one of the many 'scratch companies' informally raised by willing habbers to support the defence. He'd heard of many emerging from the ruins to assist the Imperial forces, but not one of this size and organisation. Their vengeful fury was astonishing.

The frenzied fighting lasted about eight minutes. Between them, Bulwar's platoon and the workers killed every Zoican in the station precinct.

There was cheering and whooping, and NorthCol troopers hugged Vervunhivers like lost brothers.

A short, thick-set worker with one eye, bedraggled in muck and blood, limped over to Bulwar and saluted.

'Who are you?' asked Bulwar.

'Soric, commander of the Smeltery Irregulars, sir!'

Bulwar couldn't help smiling. The worker boss had a general's pins, fashioned out of bottle caps, sewn into his jacket.

'I thank the Emperor for you, General Soric.'

Soric paused and glanced bashfully at his insignia. 'Sorry, sir; just a joke to rally the men. I'm just a plant supervisor—'

'Who fights like a Warmaster. How many are you?'

'About seven hundred, sir – workers, habbers, anyone really. We've been trying to do our bit for the hive ever since the start, and when the Shield went down, it was run or fight.'

'You'd put us to shame.'

Soric frowned. 'If we won't fight for our own bloody hive, sir, I don't know who should.'

Standing orders required all unit commanders to inform Spine Command of the size and composition of any scratch companies encountered so that they could be designated a marker code and factored into the defence structure. Bulwar called up his vox-officer and called in the details of Soric's Irregulars. He looked to Soric. 'We need to co-ordinate, general. I thank the Emperor for the likes of you, but we'll only win this thing if the military forces and the civilian levies work as one. Get your men to spread the word. Scratch companies must try to make contact with Imperial forces and be accounted for. They'll have to take orders too.'

Soric nodded and called his 'officers' up to brief them.

'You can't be a general though, I'm afraid,' said Bulwar. Soric was already pulling his makeshift rank pins off.

'Take a brevet rank, Soric. State-of-emergency field promotion. You're a sergeant now and you'll answer to me. Designate one man in every twenty a corporal, and fix a chain of command. You choose them; you know them.'

Soric nodded again, lost for words with pride.

Explosions thundered across the station, throwing some of the men to the ground. One of Soric's freedom fighters was yelling out. 'Enemy tanks! Enemy tanks!'

Bulwar and Soric scrambled over to the station's east entrance to see. The huge shapes of Zoican storm-tanks, long-barrelled and heavily armoured, were scything in towards the station and the surrounding habs. Others, including fast-moving light assault tanks and squat, super-heavy flamer platforms, were pushing round onto the transit streets leading to the Commercia and the Shield Pylon.

'We have explosives, sir,' said Soric, saluting again for good measure. 'Mining charges we lifted from the stores behind the smelteries.'

'Static charges with no launchers... against tanks?'

'It's how we've been doing it so far, sir: a man takes a wrap of charges and runs with it, anchors it to the tank hull–'

'Suicide!'

Soric frowned. 'Duty, sir. What other way is there?'

'How many tanks have you taken out with that method?'

'Twenty-four, I think.'

'How many men has it cost you?'

Soric shrugged. 'Twenty-four, of course.'

Bulwar wiped his mouth on the back of his glove. Incredible. The devotion, the determination. The sacrifice. The workers of Vervunhive, who had built this place with their sweat, were now buying it back with their blood. It was an object lesson in loyalty and devotion that even the finest Imperial Guard regiment could admire.

The tanks were closing now, hammering the station, blowing sections of the overhead trackway down. Sheets of fire leapt through the terminus hall.

'Throne of Earth!' Soric gasped, pointing.

Mustard-drab battle tanks, moving at full power across the rubble scarps, some of them bursting through sections of wall, were thundering forward from the west. They were firing freely, with huge accuracy, maintaining a cycle rate of fire that the Zoican armour, turning to the flank to greet them, couldn't even begin to match.

Neither Bulwar nor Soric had ever seen a mass armour charge before, certainly not one undertaken by a crack Imperial tank brigade like the Narmenians. They opened their mouths in awe, and nothing but wild cheers came out.

Grizmund called it 'Operation Dercius.' He'd sent his sentinel recon units and foot-troop spotter units forward towards Croe Gate as he composed his tank brigade in the Commercia. The spotters couldn't fix the position of the moving Zoican armour, but they could assess its force and direction. Grizmund had compiled the data and sent his main columns first south into the habs and then turned them east at full speed, to catch the enemy's flank. Grizmund truly understood the power of armoured vehicles, not just the physical power, but the psychological strength. If a tank was a threatening thing then a tank moving fast, and firing accurately and repeatedly, was a nightmare. The tank strike was his forte and he only admitted into the Narmenian cadre drivers who could handle thirty-plus tonnes of armour at speed, and gunners and layers who could fire fast, repeatedly and make kills each time.

In the command chair of *The Grace of the Throne*, Grizmund watched the picts on his auspex slate wink and flash as they marked hits on the glowing target runes. The interior of the turret was a red-lit sweat-box, alive with the chatter of the vox and the efficient call and return of the gun team. Fresh brass-stamped shells clanked down into the greased loading rack from the magazine over the aft wheels, and the layer primed them and shunted them forward to the gunner, who was hunting through the glowing green viewer of his scope. Every few seconds, the layer eased the muzzle recoil brake and the main gun fired with a retort that shook the tank and welled smoke into the turret, smoke quickly sucked out through the louvres of the outlets.

Grizmund's driver, Wolsh, was one of the finest and he kept them moving even when firing. He had a master's eye for terrain and seemed to know exactly what to ram and what to steer around, what to drive over and what to avoid. The Narmenians joked that Wolsh could smell a mine a kilometre off.

Operation Dercius threw forty fast-moving Narmenian heavy tanks down through fg/567 and cut through the neck of the Zoican column spread. Grizmund's forces had killed or crippled seventy-two enemy vehicles by the time they doubled back, swinging around without breaking speed to re-engage the shattered Zoican armour from the other side. By then, the Zoican armour was milling and fracturing in confusion.

Now came the part that required true skill, a manoeuvre Grizmund had dubbed 'The Scissors'. As his tanks came around to re-engage, another fifty under Brigadier Nachin charged the enemy from the other side, from the direction of Grizmund's original strike. A textbook disaster in the hands of less able commanders, but at the turn, Grizmund's forces had begun to send identifying vox beacons to distinguish them from the enemy, and Nachin's forces did the same. The rule was anything caught between their charges that didn't broadcast the correct beacon was a target. Grizmund had used this tactic nine times before and never lost a tank to his own fire.

That fine record was maintained at Vervunhive. Like the jaws of some vast beast, the opposing Narmenian armour charges tore in towards each other, crushing and destroying everything between them. Grizmund and Nachin's speeding tanks passed through each other's ranks, some vehicles missing others at full speed by only a hull's span.

And they had just begun. In the course of the thirty-fifth afternoon, the Narmenian divisions executed three more precision scissor manouvres, looping back and forth onto each other, slowly chewing the head, neck and shoulders off the vast Zoican incursion.

By four o'clock, the Zoicans had lost nearly two hundred tanks and armoured battle-hulks. The Narmenians had lost only two.

By nightfall, the Narmenians had driven the Zoican armour back into the inner habs, less than ten kilometres from Croe Gate, and cut a slice down the spearhead from Ontabi. With the routes behind them clear of enemy armour, efforts to resupply the Imperial ground troops were now no longer suicidal. Labour forces of the Administratum, the cargo guilds and Vervun Primary spread out in convoys and brought fresh ammunition to the dug-in infantry forces. Many, like Bulwar's, now resupplied with rockets, launchers and grenades, followed the Narmenian thrust out towards the great eastern gates, killing every Zoican tank the Guard armour had missed.

Rising from his seat at the font-desk in the baptistry, Gaunt took the data-slate Petro held out to him and smiled a weary smile as he read the reports of Grizmund's sally. He felt... justified: justified in his faith in the general, justified in fighting for him in the stockade, and justified in his tactical plans to hold the hive.

Towards Sondar Gate and Veyveyr, the position was less heartening. The NorthCol armour lacked the genius of leadership or the combat-experienced skill that shone in the Narmenians. Major Clodel, commanding the NorthCol units, had done little more than grind his tanks into a slugfest with the Zoican armour penetrating the hive from the south. He had stopped them, though, halting them at the edge of the southern manufactories, and for that he would get Gaunt's commendation. But now a blistering, static tank-war raged through the southern skirts, and there was no possibility of driving the invaders back and out or of sealing the gates. North of Veyveyr, the NorthCol were losing as many tanks as they were destroying. Gaunt wished for another of Grizmund's ilk to lead them, but he couldn't spare any of the Narmenians from the eastern repulse. He would be content with what he had.

And what he had was a shattered hive spared from the brink of defeat at the eleventh hour. He wasn't winning, but he wasn't losing either. To the east, he was driving the foe out. To the south and west, he was holding them hard. There was still a chance that they could win out and deny Heritor Asphodel and his Zoican zealots.

The baptistry hummed with activity and Gaunt wandered away into the side chapel as tacticians filled in for him at the hololithic chart. Daur was orchestrating the command workforce. A good man, Gaunt thought, rising courageously to his moment in Imperial history.

Can the same be said about me, he wondered?

The side chapel – a sacristy, peculiarly calm and softly lit given the apocalypse currently unleashed outside the Spine walls – seemed to welcome him. He was dead on his feet with fatigue. He'd spent all day at a desk, with a data-slate in one hand and a vox-horn in the other, and yet he'd fought the greatest and most exhausting battle of his career so far. This was command, true high command, wretched with absolutes and finites. He pulled his newly bestowed powersword from its sheath and leaned it on the edge of the gilt altar rail so he could sit down. Above him, a great, golden statue of the Emperor glowered. The air was full of the continuing song of the Ecclesiarch.

He made no obeisance to the Emperor. He was too tired. He sat on a bench pew in the tiny chapel, removed his cap and buried his face in his hands.

Gaunt thought of Oktar, Dercius, Slaydo and his father, the men who had moulded his life and brought him to this, equipping him, each in their own way, with the skills he now used. He missed them all, missed their confidences and strength. Oktar had trained him, and Gaunt had been at the great commissar-general's side when he had passed, wracked with ork poison on Gylatus Decimus, over twenty years before. Slaydo, the peerless warmaster – Gaunt had been at his deathbed too, on Balhaut after the finest victory of all. Gaunt's father had died far away when he was still a child. And Dercius – bad, old Uncle Dercius; Gaunt had killed him.

But each, in their own way, had made him. Oktar had taught him command and discipline; Dercius: ruthlessness and confidence; Slaydo: the merits of command and the selflessness of Imperial service. And his father? What he had gleaned from his father was more difficult to identify. What a father leaves to his child is always the most indefinable quality.

'Lord commander?'

Gaunt looked up from his reverie. Merity Chass, dressed in a simple, black gown of mourning, stood behind him in the arch of the sacristy. She held something in her hands.

Gaunt got up. 'Lady Chass?'

'I need to speak with you,' she began, 'about my father.'

SIXTEEN

THE LEGACY

'That our beloved hive should be conquered, or should fall into the controlling hands of unwise or unfit masters, I greatly fear and sadly anticipate. For this reason, I entrust this ultimate sanction to you. Use it wisely.'

– Heironymo Sondar, to Lord Chass

'It has been in the trust of my family since the Trade War,' she explained, her voice broken and exhausted.

Gaunt took the amulet from her hands and felt it purr and whisper between his fingers.

'Sondar made this?'

'It was his provision for the future. It is – in its own way – treachery.'

'Explain it again. I cannot see how this is treachery.'

Merity Chass looked up into Gaunt's tired eyes fretfully.

'Vervunhive is a democratic legislative. The High Lord is voted in by his noble peers. It is written in the sacred acts of constitution that absolute power should never be allowed to rest with any one individual who could not be unseated by the Legislature should it become necessary.'

'Yet the hive has suffered under one individual: Salvadore.'

'Precisely the kind of evil Heironymo dreaded, commander. My father told me that after the Trade War, great Heironymo wished to vouchsafe the future security of Vervunhive. Above all else, he feared a loss of control. That an invader – or a ruler not fit for the role – would seize control of Vervunhive so entirely that nothing could unseat him. What usurper or tyrant observes the mechanisms of constitution and law?'

Gaunt began to understand the far-reaching political dilemma attached to the device in his gloved hand. 'So this was his failsafe: the ultimate sanction, so very undemocratic, to be used when democracy was overturned?'

'And so you understand why it had to be a secret. Heironymo knew that by constructing such a device he would lay himself open to accusations of tyranny and dictatorship.'

She gestured towards the amulet. 'He made that and entrusted it to House Chass, whom he considered the most humanitarian and neutral noble house. It was never made to fall into the hands of any ruler. It was the safeguard against totalitarian rule.'

'And if House Chass became the High House?'

'We were to entrust it to another, as surety against our misuse of power.'

'And you give it to me?'

'You are the future of Vervunhive now, Gaunt. Why do you think my father made such efforts to evaluate you? He needed to be certain such insurance would not be handed to one who might abuse it. He knew you were no tyrant in the making, and I see that too. You are a soldier, true and brave, with nothing but the survival of our hive in your dreams.'

'Your father died well, Merity Chass.'

'I am glad to hear it. Honour him and the duty borne by his house, Ibram Gaunt. Do not prove him wrong.'

Gaunt studied the amulet. It was a system-slayer and, from what the girl said, quite the most powerful and formidable example of its kind he had ever heard of. In the time of Heironymo, House Sondar had specialised in codifier systems and sentient cogitators, and they had enjoyed long-term trade partnerships and research pacts with the tech-mages of the Adeptus Mechanicus. This was the masterpiece: in the event of anyone achieving total technological mastery of Vervunhive, the activation of this amulet would annihilate the command and control systems, erase all data and function programs, corrupt all codifiers and lobotomise all cogitators. It would cripple Vervunhive and allow the device's wielders to free the hive from would-be conquerors now rendered helpless.

In its peculiar way, it was more potent than atomics or a Chapter of the Adeptus Astartes. It was an ultimate weapon, forged for arenas of battle far beyond the remit of a dog-soldier like Gaunt. It was war on a refined, decisive level, light years away from the mud and las-fire theatres that Gaunt regularly experienced.

Still, he understood it. But he didn't like it. Such ancient high technology was a fearful thing, like psyker witchcraft.

He set it down on the pew next to him. It gurgled and hummed, system patterns reconfiguring like sunlight on moving water across its smooth casing.

'We don't need it.'

Merity Chass stiffened and stared up at the stained-glass rosette of the sacristy.

'I was afraid you'd say that.'

She turned to face him. Her face was pale, and her eyes were angry and dark. Multi-coloured light from the window behind her created a halo around her slim form. 'My father agonised about using it. When I reached the shelters and found he had hidden it in my belongings, I agonised too. Even as I came here to find you, I realised we had left it too late. You have already unseated cursed Salvador. Our dire situation is no longer a matter of control.'

'We have control,' Gaunt agreed. 'The problem is now simply one of physical warfare. Though Vervunhive stands at the brink of doom, it is not the doom Heironymo feared or planned for with this.'

She sat down next to him, smouldering with rage. 'If only I had brought it sooner – or urged my father to do the same. We could have used it to overthrow Salvador–'

'Praise the Throne we did not!'

She glanced around at him sharply.

Gaunt shrugged. 'We'd have crippled ourselves, crippled the hive systems, left ourselves with nothing to use to regain control. A system-slayer is an absolute weapon, lady.'

'So, my soul-searching, my father's painstaking deliberations... were all pointless anyway?' She laughed a thin, scratchy laugh. 'How fitting! House Chass, so gakking intellectual and refined, agonising over nothings while the hive bleeds and burns!'

He pulled off his gloves and tossed them aside. 'Heironymo's legacy was never to be taken lightly. That we can't use it now does not reflect badly on the care and devotion with which House Chass held that trust.'

She reached out her hand and clasped his callused fingers. 'What happens now, Gaunt?'

Slowly, he looked round at her. 'We fight a simple war, men and machines, lasguns and shells. We fight and try to drive them out. If we win, we live. If we lose, we die.'

'It sounds so bleak.'

'It's all I know, the crude equation of battle. It's not so bad. It's simple at least. There's no deliberation involved.'

'How long?'

'How long what?'

Her eyes, more alive than anything Gaunt had ever seen, gazed into his. 'How long before we know?'

Ibram Gaunt exhaled deeply, shaking his head. 'Just hours now. Perhaps a day, perhaps two. Then it will be over, one way or another.'

She pulled him to her, her arms stretched tightly around his broad back. He could smell her hair and her perfume, faint and almost worn away but still tangible despite the odours of cold and damp and dirt she had been exposed to in the shelters.

Gaunt had long forgotten the simple consolation of another's body warmth. He held her gently, swimming with fatigue, as the low voices of the Ecclesiarch choir ebbed through the sacristy. Her mouth found his.

He pulled back. 'I don't think–' he began.

'A common soldier messing with a high-born lady?' She smiled. 'Even if that mattered once, it doesn't now. This war has made us all equals.'

They kissed again, neither resisting. For a while, their passion was all that mattered to either of them. Two human souls, intimate and wordless, shutting the apocalypse out.

Midnight was long past. Bray's Tanith units, after a day and night of tank-busting in the slag-reaches of the chem plant district, fell back through the battered central hab zone towards the Shield Pylon. All the Zoican southern efforts seemed to be directed at the pylon and Bray knew that its strategic importance was unmatched by anything in the hive. Bray had about two hundred and eighty Tanith left, augmented by four hundred more Vervun Primary, Volpone, Roane and NorthCol stragglers, plus around six hundred hivers. The hivers were mostly non-coms, who looked to the troops for protection, and Bray and his colleague officers found themselves managing more of a refugee exodus than a troop retreat.

But some of the hivers had consolidated into scratch units, adding about one hundred and seventy fighting bodies to Bray's forces.

More than half of the scratch companies were made up of women, and Bray was amazed. He'd never seen women fight. Back on Tanith war was a masculine profession. But he couldn't deny their determination. And he understood it. This was their fething home, after all.

Bray's immediate command chain was formed by Vervun Primary and NorthCol, but though some of them outranked him, they looked to him for leadership. Bray suspected this was because Gaunt was now field commander. Everyone deferred to the Tanith now the endgame had begun.

Shells from Zoican armour whooped over his head and Bray sprinted into a trench-stretch between a blown-out meat-curing plant and a guild estate mansion. In the trench, Sergeant Zweck of the NorthCol and Major Bunce of the Vervun Primary were directing the men around the curing plant to engage the enemy's forward push.

Las-fire zagged down at them. Most of the Imperial shooters fired from shallow foxholes at the ranks of Zoican assault troops advancing, bayonets fixed, across the rubble. Mortar shells rebounded off the rockcrete slag and exploded as airbursts, causing significantly more damage

Behind the toppling lines of Zoican infantry, tanks rumbled in, many carrying troops clinging to the hull netting like apes.

Bray fired his weapon over the trench lip. Beside him, Zweck was decapitated by air-burst splinters. Blood saturated the side of Bray's dark fatigues.

He reached for another clip.

'What are their names?' Caffran yelled over the pounding thunder of the tanks. He had Yoncy under one arm and was leading Dalin by the hand. Tona hurried after him.

Scratch companies to their west were holding the Zoican front back, and they were struggling to keep up with a straggle of civilian refugees fleeing into the northern sectors. Caffran yelled again.

Tona Criid was busy and didn't answer Caffran.

She was firing her laspistol at the Zoican assault troops crossing into the street behind her. But she was in trouble. There was no one to cover her.

'Hold tight to your brother and get down!' Caffran cried at Dalin, pressing the swaddled baby into the boy's arms. 'I'm going back for your mother!'

'She's not my mother. She's Auntie Tona,' said Dalin.

Caffran glanced back confused and then ran on as lasbursts flickered around him.

He fired his lasgun wildly and dropped into the shell-hole where Tona cowered.

'Fresh clip!' she called.

He tossed her one. Reloaded, both rose and sent a stinging waft of kill-fire down the street at the Zoicans. Ochre bodies crumpled.

'Good shots. You're scary, Tona.'

'I do what I do. Fresh clip!'

He tossed her another.

'So they aren't yours? I thought you looked too young.'

Tona swung round to him, her face hard. 'They're all I have! Gak you! You won't take them from me, and neither will these bastards!'

She swung up and fired her gun, killing one, two, three...

Savage fighting continued unabated on all fronts right through into the early hours of the thirty-sixth day. By then, two thirds of the hive's immense civilian population were packed into the north-eastern sectors and docks, making desperate efforts to flee to the north bank. The flow was far beyond the abilities of the river ferries to manage. Working through the night, with only brief pauses to refuel, boats like the *Magnificat* shuttled back and forth across the Hass. Over two million refugees were now in the outhabs of the north shore or clogging the Northern Collective Highway. The night was cold and wet, and many – wounded, shocked, or unfed – suffered with exposure and fever.

In the hive it was worse. Millions choked the approaches to the wharves or lined the river in ranks as thick as the crowds on the terraces of the stadium watching a big game. Brutal battles broke out as citizens fought to win places on the approaching boats. Thousands died, almost two hundred of them aboard a ferry that they overloaded and capsized in a panic rush to get aboard. Hundreds more were trampled or simply crushed in the press or were pushed into the river by the mounting weight of bodies behind them. Those that didn't drown immediately died slowly, floundering in the cold of the water, unable to find enough room on the docks to clamber back ashore. An entire pier stretch collapsed under the weight of the refugees, spilling hundreds into the Hass. Rioting and panic fighting spread like wildfire back through the crowds. Like a wounded, enraged animal, Vervunhive began to claw and tear at itself.

Every small boat or craft that could be found was stolen and put to the water, usually overfilled and often guided by men or women with no idea of watercraft. Hundreds of others elected to try to swim or paddle across, clinging to packing bales or other items of floating material. The Hass was almost three kilometres wide, icy cold and plagued with strong currents. No one who tried to swim made it more than halfway before perishing, except for a very few who were pulled out of the water by passing ferry crews.

Streams of evacuees made it up from the docks onto the great viaduct and crossed on foot. The density of foot traffic on the railbridge was so great that many were pushed off and fell screaming into the river far below. Just after midnight, Zoican rockets ranged down the dock basin from the invading forces at the Hiraldi Bridge end to the east. Some fell on the docks or hit the water. Four blew out the central spans of the viaduct, toppling three of the great brick pier supports and killing hundreds. The viaduct as an evacuation route was finished, and those pressed on to the southern spans who had survived the rocket strike were trapped, unable to retreat back into the hive and reach the docks because the pressure of bodies behind them was so great. One by one, they were pushed off the shattered end of the viaduct.

A little after the destruction of the railbridge, Folik, steering his ferry on a return run across the Hass, saw lights and movement on the north shore to the east. Zoican motorised brigades were sweeping in along the far shore from the pipelines and the Hiraldi road, pincering round to deny the escape route. The Zoicans clearly intended no one should survive the destruction of the hive. By dawn, the Zoican army groups were assaulting the tides of refugees on the north bank. The hordes who had been lucky enough to get across the river were now systematically massacred on the far side. Perhaps as many as half a million were slaughtered outright. Hundreds of thousands fled, their numbers dissipating into the inhospitable hinterlands or the ruined outhabs.

Now there was no way across. The ferries returned to the south docks, many under fire from Zoican forces on the north side, and tied up. They were as trapped as the hosts on the banks now. A fearful hush of realisation fell across the multitude when they saw flight was no longer an option. The Zoicans began to fire across the river into the tightly packed refugees. Despite the wholesale killing, it was a matter of hours before the civilian masses began to draw back into the hive. It took that long for the message to filter back through the press of humanity to adjust their tidal flow.

Folik sat with Mincer on the foredeck of the rocking *Magnificat*, sharing a bottle of joiliq. They had decided not to flee. There seemed little point, especially now they were both roaring drunk. Sporadic enemy fire from across the Hass stippled the waters around them and smacked off the hull. Parts of the docks were ablaze now. Folik expected a rocket or mortar to blow them out of the water at any moment. He fetched another bottle from the wheelhouse and a las-round punched straight through the cabin window and out the other side over his shoulder as he stooped to reach into the steerage locker. It made him laugh. He stumbled back to Mincer. They decided to see if they could finish the bottle before they were killed.

Hass West Fort was encircled by the enemy and under siege. By dawn, it was close to destruction. Shells and rockets rattled into it from outside the Curtain Wall, and enemy troops and light armour pounded it from the manufactories and habs within. Captain Cargin, badly wounded, held his men together, barely six hundred of the five thousand with which he had started the night. There were virtually no gunners or artillerymen left alive, but that hardly mattered because all the munitions for the Wall and fort gun emplacements and missile racks were spent. The Vervun Primary troopers and their lasguns were all that remained. The fort itself was rattled with damage and lower levels were blocked or ablaze.

Cargin adjusted his spiked helmet and limped down the gate battlement, urging his men with a voice hoarse from hours of shouting. The rockcrete deckways were littered with dead. One of his men, Corporal Anglon, called to him. Through the smoke and flame, he had sighted something approaching through the outer habs.

Cargin took a look. Through his scope, he saw a colossal shape crawling through the suburb ruins fifteen kilometres south of the fort. Another death machine, he thought instinctively.

But this was different – larger, slower. A huge pyramid structure, five hundred metres high at the apex, its mechanical sides painted Zoican ochre and decorated with vast, obscene symbols of Chaos. It moved, as far as he could see, on dozens of fat, wide-gauge caterpillar units that crushed everything in its path. A gouged trail half a kilometre wide scored through the habs in its wake. Its flanks bristled with weapon turrets and emplacements, and huge, brass speaker-horns on its summit, with Chaos banners fluttering from poles between them, boomed out the Heritor chant and crackled the inhuman chatter.

'What is it?' Anglon hissed.

Cargin shrugged. He was cold and weak from blood-loss and pain. Every word, movement, or thought was an effort of superhuman concentration. He unstrapped the handset of the vox-unit he had been carrying over his shoulder since his comm-officer had been killed some hours before.

'Cargin/Hass West to Baptistry Command. Marker code 454/gau.'

'Received and recognised, Hass West.'

'We've got something out here, approaching the walls. Massive mechanised structure, mobile, armed. I'm only guessing, but unless there's more than one of these things, I'd lay real money it's the enemy's command centre. I've never seen a mobile unit so big.'

'Understood, Hass West. Can you supply visuals?'

'Pict-links are down, Command. You'll just have to take my word for it.'

'What is your situation, Hass West? We are trying to direct troop forces to support you.'

Cargin sighed. He was about to tell Baptistry Command he had less than a thousand men left, most of them wounded, at the end of their ammo supplies, with no artillery support, and an ocean of enemy on all sides. He was about to estimate they could hold on another hour at the most.

The estimate would have been inaccurate by fifty-nine and a half minutes. Anglon grabbed Cargin's arm, shouting out as fierce lights blinked and fizzled in dark recesses down the centre of the pyramid side facing them. The vast Zoican vehicle shuddered and then retched huge, searing beams of plasma energy at Hass West Fort: cutting beams, like the ones that had dissected Ontabi Gate, but larger still and far more powerful, energy weapons of a scale usually seen in the fleet engagements of naval flagships. The roar was deafening, sending out a shockwave that was felt kilometres away.

Hass West Fort and the gate it protected were obliterated. Cargin, Anglon and all the remaining defenders were disintegrated in one blinding instant. As the cutting beams faded, rocket and gunnery platforms all across the pyramid opened fire and piled destruction on the ruins. The air stank with ozone and static and fycelene. For half a kilometre in each direction, the Curtain Wall collapsed.

The pyramid machine began to trundle forward again, inching towards the dying hive, blaring the Heritor's name over and again.

Gaunt woke with a start, his mind spinning. Sleep had taken away his immediate fatigue, but every atom of his body ached and throbbed. It took him a moment to remember where he was. How long had he been asleep?

He clambered to his feet. The sacristy was chilly and silent, the Ecclesiarch choir long since finished.

Merity Chass stood nearby, gazing at the friezes of the Imperial cult. She wore his long overcoat and nothing else. She looked round at him and smiled. 'You'd better get dressed. They probably need you.'

Gaunt recovered his shirt and boots and pulled them on. He could still taste her on his lips. He stared at her for a moment more. She was... beautiful. If he didn't have a reason to fight for Vervunhive before, he did now. He would not allow this girl to perish.

He sat down on the pew and laughed to himself dryly.

'What?' she asked.

Gaunt shook his head. Such thoughts! He had committed the cardinal sin of any good officer. He'd placed his emotions in the firing line. Even now, he could hear Oktar's dirty chuckle in his mind, scolding him for becoming attached to anyone or anything. Over the years they had spent campaigning together, Gaunt had seen Oktar leave many tearful women behind as he moved on to the next warzone.

'Don't get involved, Ibram, not with anything. If you don't care, you won't care, and that makes the hardest parts of this army life that much easier. Do what you must, take what you need and move on. Never look back, never regret and never remember.'

Gaunt buttoned his shirt. He realised, perhaps for the first time, that he had broken with Oktar's advice a long time since. When he had met the Tanith and had brought them as Ghosts from the deathfires of their world, he had started to care. He decided he didn't see it as a weakness. In that one thing, old Oktar had been wrong. Caring for the Ghosts, for the cause, for the fight, or for anyone, made him what he was. Without those reasons, without an emotional investment, he would have walked away or put a gun-muzzle in his mouth years before.

Gaunt got to his feet and found his cap, his gloves and his weapon belt. He was trying to remember the furious notions that had woken him. Ideas, whirling...

Daur burst into the sacristy. 'Commissar! Sir, we–' Daur saw the naked woman cloaked in the overcoat and stopped in his tracks. He turned away, flushing.

'A moment, captain.'

Gaunt crossed to Merity.

'I must go. When this is over–'

'We'll either be dead, or we'll be a noble lady and a soldier once again.'

'Then I thank the Emperor for this precious interlude of equality. Until the hour of my death, however far away that is, I will remember you.'

'I should hope so. And I hope that hour is a long time coming.'

He kissed her mouth, stroked his fingers down her cheek, and then followed Daur out of the sacristy, pulling on his jacket and weapon-harness. At the door, he put on his cap and adjusted the metal rose Lord Chass had given him for honour. It was drooping in his lapel and he straightened it.

'Sorry, sir,' Daur said as Gaunt followed him down the hall.

'Forget it, Ban. You should have woken me earlier.'

'I wanted to give you all the rest you could get, sir.'

'What's the situation now?'

'A holding pattern as before. Intense fighting on all fronts. The enemy has taken the north shore. And Hass West fell a few minutes ago.'

'Damn!' Gaunt growled. They strode into the bustle of the Baptistry Command Centre. Additional cogitators and vox-sets had been added over night. Over three hundred men and women from Vervun Primary, the Administratum and the guilds now crewed them, working in concert with dozens of servitors. Major Otte was occupying 'the Font,' as the command station was now known. Intendant Banefail and members of his elite staff assisted the major.

Many saluted as Gaunt entered the chamber. He acknowledged the greetings while taking in the details of the main hololithic display.

'Just before it fell, Hass West reported seeing a massive mobile structure moving in towards them. We're fairly sure it is their main command vehicle.'

Gaunt spotted the marker on the display. The thing was certainly huge, and now close to the western extremity of the Wall. 'The marker code... "spike"?'

Banefail joined them. The distinguished lord was almost dead on his feet with fatigue. 'My fault, commissar. I referred to it as a bloody great spike, and the word stuck.'

'It'll do. What do we know about it?'

'It's a massive weapon, but slow moving,' Major Otte said, crossing the floor to Gaunt. 'I guess we can assume it's well armoured too.'

'What makes you think it's the command element?'

'It's the only one we've sighted,' Daur said, 'and its size clearly indicates its importance.'

'More than that,' Banefail said, gesturing at a vox-set manned by a female Administratum cleric, two servitors and a withered astropath. 'It's the source of the chatter.'

Gaunt glanced at the woman operating the set. She dialled up the speaker and the air filled briefly with the coded, incessant growl of the enemy.

'The enemy vox-traffic unites them all,' lisped the pallid astropath thickly. Gaunt tried not to look at him and the festoon of data-plugs stapled into his translucent scalp. The astropath lifted a bionically augmented, wasted limb and pointed to data runes flashing across the instrumentation. 'We knew it was coming from outside the hive and we suspected the source was Zoica. But it's mobile now and audio scans confirm it is being emitted by that structure.'

Gaunt nodded to himself. 'Asphodel.'

Banefail glanced around at the name. 'He's there? So close?'

'It matches his recorded behaviour. The Heritor likes to be near to his triumphs, and he likes to maintain intense control. He commands by charisma, intendant. Where his legions march, we will not find him far behind.'

'Golden Throne...' Otte murmured, looking at the display with frightened eyes.

Gaunt forced himself to look at the astropath. The stink of the warp hung about the cadaverous wretch. 'Your opinion? This chatter: could it be the control signal of the Zoican forces? An addictive broadcast that maintains the Heritor's hold over his zealots?'

'It is certainly patterned and hypnotic. I find myself reluctant to listen to it for any length of time. It is a Chaos pulse. Though we can't – daren't – interpret its meaning, the flow of the enemy troops and armour seems to match its rhythmic fluctuations.'

Gaunt turned away, deep in thought. The idea that had woken him reformed in his mind.

'I have a notion,' he told Daur, Otte and Banefail. 'Send word to Major Rawne's units and to Sergeant Mkoll and his scout platoon.' He ordered other preparations to be made, and then told Daur to fetch him a fresh box of bolter shells.

'Where are you going? We need you here, sir!' stammered Otte.

'You have my full confidence, major,' Gaunt said. He gestured to the hololithic display. 'The defence strategies are set in motion. You and this staff are more than able to direct them. I'm a foot soldier. A warrior, not a warmaster. It's time I did my job, the job I'm best at. And with the grace of the Emperor shining on me, I may take this field yet.'

Gaunt took Heironymo's amulet from his pocket and felt it whisper and chuckle in his hand. The flickering light patterns on its carapace roiled like the twisting flashes of the Immaterium.

'In my absence, Otte and Daur have field command. If I fail to return, intendant, you should signal Warmaster Macaroth and plead for salvation. But I believe it won't come to that.'

The amulet gurgled and quivered.

This could work, thought Gaunt. *God-Emperor save us, this could fething work!*

SEVENTEEN

OPERATION HIERONYMO

'I believe this Gaunt fellow is singularly overrated.'
– General Noches Sturm to Major Gilbear,
during the assault on Voltemand

A scratch company met them at 281/kl to guide them in. The company was forty strong and had been conducting guerrilla work in the southern outer habs before the Shield fell. Their leader, a powerful, saturnine ex-miner called Gol Kolea, saluted Gaunt as he approached. Gaunt looked every centimetre a leader, though the braid of his cap had been rubbed with ash to dull its glint. He wore the powersword at his waist and his boltgun in a holster across his chest, under a short, black, leather jacket. On top of that, draped expertly as Colm Corbec had instructed him during the first days of the Ghost regiment's existence, was his Tanith stealth cape.

The roar of battle thundered down the ruined streets beside them, but this sector was clear and quiet. Cold, morning light filtered in through the crackling Shield. Gaunt signalled his units up to join Kolea's scratch company: thirty men, all Tanith, pale-skinned, dark-haired warriors in black fatigues and stealth capes, their skin decorated with various, blue tattoo symbols. They were the cream of Rawne's unit and the pride of Mkoll's stealth scouts. Amongst them, Bragg, Larkin, Domor, MkVenner, Dremmond, Genx, Neskon, Cocoer, the medic Gherran – most of the very best.

Gaunt was beginning to outline 'Operation Heironymo' to his waiting squad when Rawne heard movement down a side street. The Ghosts and scratches fanned out and made ready, arming weapons freshly supplied for the mission.

A fireteam of ten Volpone advanced down the side street, led by Colonel Gilbear. They were all Volpone elite troops from the 10th: massive, carapace-armoured and holding hellguns ready.

Gaunt walked out into the rubble-strewn open to meet Gilbear. They saluted each other.

'Not going in without the Bluebloods, I hope, colonel-commissar?' Gilbear said archly.

'I wouldn't dream of it, colonel,' Gaunt replied. 'I'm glad you got my message and gladder still you found your way here. Join us. We're about to move out.'

Gaunt crossed to Rawne and Kolea as the Volpone meshed into the column spread.

'I don't fething believe you invited them,' Rawne cursed.

'Keep your thoughts to yourself, major. The Bluebloods may be bastards, but I feel I have reached an understanding with them. Besides, we'll need their muscle when it comes to it.'

Rawne spat in the puddles and made no reply.

'I understand you're command now,' Kolea said bluntly to Gaunt. 'May I ask what the gak you're doing here? Gnide and Croe never got their hands dirty.'

'Their command ethic was different, Kolea. I hope you'll appreciate my method of doing things.'

'Can you sign?'

'What?'

'Most of my company are deaf. Can you sign your commands?'

'I can, sir,' Mkoll piped up.

Gaunt gestured to the scout sergeant. 'Mkoll can relay my instructions to your fighters. Good enough?'

Gol Kolea scratched his cheek. 'Perhaps.'

Gaunt could tell Kolea had been through hell in the last thirty-odd days. Courage and determination seemed to ooze out of him like sweat. He was not a man Gaunt wanted to be on the wrong side of.

They followed dingy, battle-worn streets out through the southern extremities of the hive, and they left the shattered Curtain Wall behind them. Mkoll's scouts led the way, directed by Kolea's troops. The bulky Volpone struggled to keep up with the swift, silent advance. Clear of the Shield, they were all exposed to the bitter rain.

'You know these quarters well, Kolea. I guess they were your home,' Gaunt remarked softly to the miner.

'Correct. Just half a kilometre from here, I could take you to the crater where my hab once stood.'

'You lost family?'

'A wife, two children. I don't know they're dead, but – gak! What are the chances?'

Gaunt shrugged.

'How many did you lose coming here?' Kolea asked.

'Troops?'

Kolea shook his head. 'Family.'

'I didn't have any to lose. I don't know which of us is luckier.'

Kolea smiled, but without any light or laughter in his face.

'Neither one, commissar. And that's the tragedy.'

'I don't know about the girls,' Larkin muttered as they moved through the scorched-out, rain-pelted ruins. Bragg, his missile launcher and autocannon slung over his shoulders, raised his eyebrows and made no reply. There were eight females in Kolea's scratch company, none older than twenty-five. Each held a captured Zoican lasgun or a Vervun Primary autorifle and carried an equipment pack over their ragged work fatigues. Most of them, like the men, wore salvaged military boots wadded with socks and wrapped tight with puttees made of cargo tape to keep them fast. The women moved as silently and as surely as their male comrades. A month of intense guerrilla war in the outhabs had trained them well. Those that had not learned had not made it.

'Women can fight,' Rilke murmured, holding his sniper rifle with the stock high in his armpit and the long barrel pointing downwards. 'My sister, Loril, used to hold her own against the rowdies when it got to chucking-out time in my father's tavern back home. Feth, but she could throw a punch!'

'That's not what I meant,' growled Larkin, rain dripping off his thin nose. 'It doesn't seem right, sending women in like this, all gussied up in combat gear and waving lasguns. I mean, they're just girls. This is gonna get nasty. No place for women.'

'Keep it down!' Dremmond hissed, lugging his flamer with its weighty, refilled tanks. 'They'll hear you, Larks!'

'You heard what that big, bastard miner said. They're all shell-deaf! I can speak my mind without insulting no one! They can't hear me!'

'But we can read lips, Tanith,' Banda said, moving past the chief sniper with a smirk. Some of the other scratches nearby laughed.

'I– I didn't mean nothing by it,' Larkin began, moving his mouth over-emphatically to make sure she could hear. Banda looked back at him, a mocking expression on her dirty face.

'And anyway, I'm not deaf. Neither's Muril. And neither are the Zoicans. So why don't you clamp it and do us all a favour?'

They moved on, the eighty-strong assault group splashing down a damp, debris-strewn side road.

'That told you,' Dremmond whispered to Larkin.

'Shut up,' Larkin replied.

MkVenner scouted ahead as part of Mkoll's recon deployment. In his immediate field of vision was Scout Bonin and the scratch company guides: a girl called Nessa and a Vervun Primary sergeant named Haller, who was second in command of Kolea's makeshift group. Haller was one of nine Vervun Primary survivors to have found their way into the scratch company, though with his dirty, patched uniform and the woollen cap he wore in place of his spiked helmet, he didn't look much like a Primary infantryman any more. He seemed content to be commanded by a miner rather than a military officer. MkVenner knew the members of the scratch company had weathered the very worst of the war, and he couldn't begin to understand their loyalties or the circumstances that had brought them together.

Nessa guided them through a series of torched manufactories, covering the ground quickly, keeping low and making curt, direct gestures they could read easily. They crossed an arterial highway where the rockcrete was crumpled by a series of shell-holes, and they skirted the wrecks of two Zoican battletanks and an infantry carrier that had been flipped over onto its back.

Across the highway, they fanned through textile mills where the constant rain trickled in through the holed roofs and rows of iron-framed looms stood silent and shattered. The loose ends from hundreds of bales of twine rippled in the breeze. MkVenner stopped in a doorway and scanned around. He watched with idle fascination as droplets of rainwater crept down taut feed-threads over one loom, glinting like diamonds and thickening before dripping off the hanging brass bobbin onto the weaving frames beneath.

MkVenner realised he'd lost sight of the woman. Haller appeared behind him.

'You have to watch her,' Haller mouthed, signing at the same time. He knew full well MkVenner could hear, but the practice was now instinctive.

Bonin joined them and they edged down the length of the mill, until they found Nessa in an open loading dock at the far end, crouched behind an overturned bale-lifter. Outside, in the bright, thin light of the cargo yard, a quintet of Zoican flamer tanks grumbled by, heading north. The foot soldiers could smell the coarse stench of the promethium lapping in the tanks' heavy bowsers.

Once the tanks had passed, Nessa made a punching motion in the air and the troops hurried on, across the open yard and into the razorwire-edged enclosure of a guild's freight haulage plant. The rusting bulks of overhead cranes and hoists creaked in the wind above them. Rainwater had formed wide, shallow lakes across the rockcrete apron. They moved past rows of plasteel cargo crates and produce hoppers flaking paint. Near the haulage site office, a small Imperial chapel built for the workers had been desecrated by the advancing Zoicans. They'd shot out the windows and soiled the walls with excrement. A dozen site workers had been crucified along the front porch on gibbets made from rail sleepers. The bodies were little more than ghastly, stringy carcasses now. They'd been nailed up three weeks before, and the steady rain and the carrion birds had done their best to erode the flesh.

Haller's boot clipped an empty bottle and the noise of it tinkling away across the ground startled the birds, who rose in cawing, raucous mobs, revealing the gristly horrors beneath. Some of the birds were fat, glossy-black scavengers, the others dirty-white seabirds from the estuary with clacking pincer-bills. Black and white, the birds made a brief checker pattern in the air before flocking west to the haulage barn roof and settling. The open ground was peppered and sticky with their droppings.

There was a break in the fence behind the chapel. MkVenner held position long enough to check, via microbead, that the main force was within range behind them. Gaunt and the column were just entering the haulage site.

The land south of the freight-holding was a mass of chalky rubble and sprouting weeds. There were dark driver holes in the ground at intervals and the area was littered with thousands of gleaming, brass shell cases. In an earlier stage of the war, massive Zoican field pieces had been braced here, trained at the Wall. MkVenner was about to move on, but Nessa stopped him.

He made the gesture for question, and she signed and mouthed back at him.

'In our experience, the Zoicans trap-wire their sites when they move on.'

MkVenner nodded. He signalled back and Gaunt sent Domor forward. Haller helped Domor lock his sweeper set together, and then the Ghost began to creep away from them, playing the head of the broom back and forth over the dirt. Domor liked to do this work by sound and MkVenner smiled to see him closing the shutters of his bionic ocular implants by hand. The time when Domor could simply close his eyelids was long passed, way back on Menazoid Epsilon.

Domor had a path cleared in under five minutes, playing out a fibre-cord to mark its zigzag path. By the time he had finished, the assault force had caught up with them and were waiting with MkVen-ner, Haller, Nessa and Bonin at the fence.

'He found nothing?' asked Haller, pointing over at Domor on the far side of the area.

'No, he found plenty, but we're not here to mine-lift. Follow the cord,' replied MkVenner.

Single file, the eighty soldiers crossed the ex-artillery emplacement and moved down along a reinforced walkway that crossed one of the hive's main drainage gullies. Swollen by the heavy rains, the gully was in full flood. It was partially dammed in places by slews of debris rub-bish and bundles of corpses.

Up the other side, they climbed the chute slope by a metal stair-way and hurried in small packs across another highway. The ruined remains of bodies littering the road stretched as far as the eye could see. Most tried not to look. Larkin stared in horrified fascination as he crossed the road. Nothing more than bundles of rags, the bodies were those of workers and habbers slaughtered as they had tried to flee inwards towards Vervunhive. They had fallen weeks before, and no one had touched or moved them, except the mashing tracks of Zoican war machines heading north towards their target.

Gaunt called a halt-period in the broken habitats on the far side of the highway. His motley brigade set up defence watches all around as he climbed to the third storey of a hab block with Kolea and Gilbear.

'I smell smoke,' Gilbear said suddenly. He moved ahead, down the dirty, dank hallway, his weapon raised, and kicked open the rotting door of a worker flat.

Gaunt and Kolea, weapons ready, moved in behind him. All three stopped short.

The flat was thick with trash and overrun with vermin. The smoke issued from a small fire set in a tar bucket over which swung a metal pot on a wire frame that had once been a clothes hanger. The five inhab-itants of the room, a mother with three children and a much older woman, cowered in the far corner. They were emaciated and filthy, just terrified skin and bone clad in dirty tatters. The old woman whined like a caged animal and two of the children cried silently. The mother, her eyes bright and fierce in her soot-black face, held out a shank of metal, sharpened to a point.

'Back off! Now!' Gaunt told Kolea and Gilbear, though Kolea needed no urging.

'It's all right... I'm sorry,' Gaunt told the mother, his hands raised, open. The shank remained pointing at him.

'Leave them,' Kolea said. He pulled a wad of ration cakes from his

NECROPOLIS   823

pack and went over, dropping them on the floor in front of the group
when the mother refused to take them.

They went back out into the hallway and Kolea pulled the door back
into place.

'Throne of Earth...' Gaunt hissed, shaking his head.

'Quite,' joined Gilbear. 'What a waste of rations.'

Gaunt looked round at him, began to speak, and then just shook his
head. Explaining the real nature of his horror to Gilbear might take a
lifetime.

And that time, however it could be measured, was all Gaunt had left
to do something far more important than drum compassion into an
aristocratic warrior like the Blueblood colonel.

Kolea had heard Gilbear's remark and he glowered at the man with
utter disdain. Kolea doubted even the colonel-commissar understood
what it was like to claw and scrape for survival in the shelled ruins
of your home, day after day. Gol Kolea had seen enough of that misery since the Zoicans came, enough to last a hundred lifetimes. There
were thousands of hab families out here still, slowly dying from starvation, disease and cold.

The trio of officers climbed out onto a fire escape at the eastern end
of the hab block, and Gaunt and Gilbear pulled out their scopes.

Five kilometres south, across the ruins, through the smoke and rain,
rose the bulk of the Spike. It was moving at a slow crawl, up towards
the main hive. Gaunt swung his scope around and looked back at the
vast, glinting dome of the Shield and the massive Spine and hab structures within.

Gaunt offered his scope to Kolea, but the man wasn't interested. Gilbear gestured, suddenly and sharply, to them both and pointed down
at the highway below, the one they had just crossed. A host of Zoican
troopers, escorted by a vanguard of carriers and light tanks, was advancing towards them. Chaos banners flopped lankly in the rain and the
light shone off the wet, ochre-coloured armour.

Gilbear raised his hellgun, about to turn, but Gaunt stopped him.
'We're not here to fight them. Our fight is elsewhere.'

The commissar keyed his microbead. 'Mass enemy formation
approaching along the highway outside. Stay low and stay silent.'

Rawne voxed back an acknowledgement.

It took half an hour for the Zoican column to go by. Gaunt estimated
there were a little over two thousand foot troops and sixty armoured
vehicles – reserves, advancing to bolster the assault. He wished to the
Emperor himself he had reserves of such numbers to call upon. Feth,
he wished he had such strengths in his active units!

Once the column was safely past and clear, the Operation Heironymo assault cadre left the habitats and moved on through rain-swilled
ruins, towards the Spike.

The closer they got, the bigger it grew, dwarfing all the building structures around. Larkin bit back deep unease – it was big, so fething big!
How in the name of feth were eighty souls going to take on a thing
that size?

They were cowering in rubble. Larkin raised his head and saw Banda
grinning back at him.

'Scared yet, Tanith?' she hissed.

Larkin shook his head and looked away.

Mkoll, MkVenner and Gaunt moved forward with Kolea, Rawne and
Haller in a line behind them. Now they could hear the throbbing grind
of the Spike's enormous track sections, the deep growl of its engines.
Gaunt noticed dust and ash trickling down the rubble around him in
sharp, rhythmic blurts. He realised the vast machine, still a kilometre
distant, was vibrating the earth itself with its weight and motivation.

The rain grew suddenly heavier. An incessant patter filled the air
around them, accompanied by a regular, tinking chime. It came from
a broken bottle wedged in a spill of bricks, sounding every time a rain-
drop hit its broken neck.

Gaunt wiped water droplets from the end of his scope and studied the Spike.

'How do we do this?' he asked Mkoll.

Mkoll frowned. 'From above. Let's get ahead and find a suitable habitat overlook – unless it changes course.'

Gaunt took the group across the wide, pulverised trail behind the
advancing Spike, a half-kilometre strip of soil and ash compressed by
the vehicle's weight into glinting carbon. The Spike didn't steer around
buildings. It flattened them, making its own path.

The Imperial strikeforce overtook the great war machine on the right
flank and pressed ahead, hugging the ruins and the rubble. Mkoll
indicated a pair of worker hab blocks ahead of them that promised to
intersect the Spike's course. Gaunt detailed his troopers into two units
and sent one ahead under Gilbear, leading the other himself.

Gaunt's troop was climbing up the stairwell of the nearer hab, five
hundred paces ahead of the crawling target, when the Spike fired again.
Its awesome spinal weapon, the cutting beams, howled vast energies
above and past them at some target in the main hive. The sound was
louder than their ears could manage. The hab shuddered thoroughly,
and a harsh light-flash penetrated every crevice and opening in the

stairwell for a moment. A second later there was a pop of pressure, a wall of dissipating heat and the stink of plasma.

Gaunt and his troop exchanged glances. It had been like standing too near a star for a millisecond. Their eyes ached and the energised stench burned their sinuses. Gaunt wiped a thread of blood from his lip.

There was no time to waste, however. Gaunt and Mkoll led the party up to the fifth floor, to the flats at the far end. The Spike was almost on them. Half a dozen ragged habbers fled past them, running like beaten dogs from their hideaways.

Gaunt got a signal from Gilbear in the other block. The second unit was in position. He looked out of the end window, glassless and burned, and saw how close the massive machine now was.

Its lower slopes swiped the edge of the hab block and tore it away, rubble cascading down under the tracks. Gaunt moved his soldiers back as the passing armour wall tore the end off the room they waited in. Then they moved.

In pairs and trios they leapt clear of the ripped-open building and dropped seven metres onto the sloping sides of the Spike. Most slid down the ochre-painted hull before managing to cling fast to mould-ing projections, rivets or weld-seams. Gaunt landed hard, slid for a moment, then braced against a row of cold-punched bolt-heads. He heard a cry from above and looked up to see Larkin slithering down the armoured slope, his hands clawing uselessly at the tarnished metal. Gaunt snagged the sniper by his stealth cape and arrested his slide, nearly throttling him with the taut fabric. Larkin found purchase and crawled up beside Gaunt.

'Saving my arse again, Ibram?' Larkin stammered in relief.

Gaunt grinned. At a time like this, he hardly minded Mad Larkin's informality.

'You're welcome. It's my job.'

Ten metres down the Spike's side, Haller also lost his grip. He slid, barking out a helpless curse and slammed into Dremmond, who was barely holding on himself. The two of them tore away and started to slide much more swiftly down the flank, thrashing for handholds.

Bragg drew his Tanith blade, punched it into the Spike's plating to provide a firm anchor point, and caught them as they tumbled past. He captured Dremmond by the harness of his flamer, and Dremmond held tight to Haller. By then, they had barrelled into Muril – one of the scratch company loom girls – too, and Haller held on to her. Secured by one meaty fist around the hilt of his knife, Bragg supported three dangling humans.

'Feth!' he grunted, his arm shaking under the weight. 'Get a grip! Get a grip! I can't hold on much longer!'

Muril swung around and grabbed the edge of an armour plate, digging her fingertips into the seam. As soon as she was secure, Haller let go and slid down beside her. Bragg heaved the kicking Dremmond up next to him by the man's flamer's straps.

'Good fething catch,' Dremmond gasped, gripping tightly, trying to slow his anxious breathing.

'I don't always miss,' replied Bragg. He didn't dare voice his relief. For a moment, he had been close to dropping them – or being pulled away with them.

Gaunt's unit, forty bodies, clung to the sloping side of the gigantic Zoican war machine and slowly began to climb up it. The Spike's pyramid form was punctuated by shelflike terraces, like some step-temples of antiquity Gaunt had once seen on Fychis Dolorous. The soldiers crawled up over the lip and made themselves fast on the nearest horizontal shelf.

The progressing Spike, oblivious to the human lice now adhering to its hide, moved on and slammed over and through the hab block where Gilbear's team was waiting. Gaunt watched in horror as the metal slopes demolished a large chunk of the hab's lower storeys.

Then he saw Gilbear and his team leaping down from a far higher level. They'd clearly moved up a floor or two when the impact of the Spike's course had become evident.

The troopers, led by Gilbear, dropped far further than Gaunt's unit had done. They impacted on the hull above the shelf Gaunt and the others occupied, and most slid down onto that safe landing. Some clung on where they found purchase on the slopes above. Two – a Volpone and the Tanith scout Bonin – bounced away like rocks down a mountainside and dropped past Gaunt, disappearing a hundred metres below under the lip of the hull. Gaunt looked away. If the sheer fall hadn't killed them outright, they were dead under the massive caterpillar carriage.

Gaunt signalled around and made contact with the remaining troopers. They were all rendezvousing on the shelf-lip. The Curtain Wall of Vervunhive was now only minutes away and their time was disappearing fast. Weapons ready, reaching out hands to steady themselves against the motion of the Spike, the strike team followed Gaunt down the shelf.

The difficult part remained: how to find a way inside this armoured monster.

The hull was solid. Domor pulled out the head of his sweeper kit and pressed it against the throbbing metal.

'Dense – no cavities,' he growled disappointedly.

Gaunt sighed. They could blast or cut the hull open if there was a chance of accessing a hollow space within, but Domor was positive. It stood to reason a machine like this would be thick-skinned.

Two of Gilbear's Volpone returned along the shelf from scouting the far end. Gilbear heard their reports and edged along to Gaunt.

'The main weapon ports along the forward face. They're open, ready for firing. It's that or nothing.'

'And if they fire while we're entering?'

'Then we're dead. You want to stay out here for the rest of the war?'

Gaunt barked out a laugh at Gilbear's attitude.

'No. I guess we won't know anything about it if they fire.'

'It'll be quick, certainly,' Gilbear agreed.

Gaunt notified the squad leaders and led the single-file team along the shelf.

They were about to make the turn onto the forward face when the beam weapons fired again. The light flash was even more brutal out in the open and the sucking roar monstrous. The whole Spike shook.

'How long since the last salvo?' Gaunt asked Larkin as soon as his ears stopped ringing.

'Eight minutes, just about, boss.'

'I'm working with the idea it takes a while for the batteries to recharge. We've got eight minutes to get inside.'

'It sounds so easy when you put it like that,' snarled Rawne.

'Shouldn't we be moving rather than debating?' Kolea asked, shaming them all.

Gaunt nodded. 'Yes. Now. Go!'

Always, always lead from the front. Never expect a man under your command to undertake an action you're not prepared to make yourself. It was one of Delane Oktar's primary rules, drummed into Gaunt during his years with the Hyrkans. He was not about to forget his mentor's advice now.

Gaunt led the way around the corner of the hull and hurried towards the huge, main-weapon recesses below him. Visor hatches the size of the Sondar Gates were pulled up from the ports like eyelids. The air was sweet and tangy with burnt plasma and fluorocarbons.

Gaunt reached the edge of the emplacement recess and grabbed hold of one of the shutter stanchions, a heavyweight hydraulic limb at full extension. His leather glove slid off the oiled, shining metal. He pulled the glove off and took hold with his bare hand, arming his bolt-gun in the other.

Gaunt leapt and let himself fall, swinging down and around like an ape by one hand. Using his body weight's pendulum momentum, he threw himself in through the weapon hatch, letting go of the hydraulic limb at the same moment.

He fell, rather than jumped, inside the hull, landing and stumbling on a grilled cageway that ran alongside the massive snouts of the beam cannons. Rolling, he saw two black-clad Zoican gunners leap up from their firing consoles, and he shot them down.

Three Zoican soldiers in full battledress charged up onto the cageway, blasting at him. Gaunt lost his footing and fell, the las-shots screaming over his head. The shots blew apart the torso of the Volpone leaping in behind him and threw his corpse back and outwards so it fell away down the slope of the hull. Recovering, Gaunt resumed firing, aiming precise head-shots at the Zoicans, exploding their full-face helmets with high-explosive rounds.

Then Gilbear, Mkoll and three other Tanith had made it inside behind him. Mkoll opened up with his lasrifle, supporting Gaunt's fire-pattern, and Gilbear turned back to pull others of the strike force in through the huge awning.

Gaunt and Mkoll advanced with Crothe and Rilke, partly to secure the weapon deck and partly to make room. The commissar and his three Tanith troopers scoured the gun-control position, blasting dozens of Zoican personnel.

Within moments, the Zoican troopers set up a flaying return of fire. Crothe was blasted off his feet and Mkoll took a hit in his hip. He slammed back into the wall and fell, but somehow maintained his fire rate.

Now Gilbear and three of his elite Blueblood were coming in behind, laying down a field of fire with their hellguns. Behind them on the cageway, Haller and Kolea were dragging the other squad members in through the hatch.

Gilbear's fire team advanced and secured the gunnery deck behind the colossal beam emitters, slaying everything that moved. The air in the chamber was dense and rich with gunsmoke. The grilled deck was strewn with Zoican dead.

Somewhere an alarm began to wail.

Inside four minutes, Gaunt's strike team had entered the Spike via the gunports, all seventy-eight of them. Three had died in the initial engagement. Gaunt checked on Mkoll. His wound was superficial and he was already back on his feet.

The strike force spread out to cover all the exitways on the gloomy gundeck.

He led the way to a main blast door that gave access to the Spike's inner cavities. It was locked fast.

'I can blow it,' said Kolea at his side.

Gaunt drew the powersword of Heironymo Sondar, activated it, and sliced the incandescent blade through the hatch. A further three sweeps and a kick left the hatchway open, the cut section of metal clanging as it fell on the deck outside.

'Move!' cried Gaunt. 'Move!'

The Spike's main weapon deck was linked to the primary command sections by a long, sloping accessway wide enough for a Leman Russ to drive along it. It was painted matt red, the colour of meat, and thick bulkhead frames stood at every twenty metres. The floor was a metal grille and in the underfloor cavity, pipes, tubing and feeder cables could be seen. Off to either side, just on the other side of the blast door, stood service elevators with metal cage frames, set in circular loading docks. The elevators were heavy-duty freight lifts designed to haul shells from the munition stockpiles deep in the belly of the Spike up to the artillery blisters on the upper slopes. The metal walls of the accessway were covered with intricate emblems, the curious, nauseating runes of Chaos. Gaunt realised they had been fashioned from bone that had been inlaid into the metal and then polished flat with the wall so they glowed and shone like pearl.

Human bone, he guessed. The Heritor would demand such details.

A team of Zoican heavy troopers in segmented ochre body armour greeted them in the accessway as they entered, firing up the sloping tunnel from cover at the far end. One of the scratches, a man whose name Gaunt would never know, was sliced apart by the initial shots. His blood sprayed the bone icons on the wall, and the symbols began to squirm and shift.

Larkin saw this and fell back in horror, his guts churning. The eldritch symbols were alive, excited by blood. He knew he was about to vomit with fear.

'Taking a breather?' Banda asked sourly as she pushed past him, firing down at the enemy position. The Imperials were hugging the walls and using the bulkheads for cover, edging down the accessway as far as the enemy fire would allow.

'A breather?' Larkin gulped. He was incredulous. No smirking girl from the hab looms would show him up.

Forgetting his fear, he knelt in cover, shook out his neck, raised his sniper-variant lasrifle and put a hot-shot between the eyes of a Zoican heavy twenty paces away.

'Nice work,' Banda growled from her position and blew Larkin a cocky kiss.

Larkin grinned and made another kill-shot. Either he was beginning to like this woman, or he'd kill her himself.

Another of the scratches fell, ripped open by the mauling heavy weapons the enemy had trained on them. They were caught too tightly between the hall and the entry point Gaunt had cut open. His men fanned round into the side loading docks, but they were packed in.

Rawne hurled a tube charge down the tunnel, but the Zoicans had enough cover to shelter from it.

'Dremmond!' Gaunt yelled.

The flamer-trooper was still trying to pull his bulky tanks through the narrow opening Gaunt's powersword had sliced. Las-rounds peppered the metal around him. A Ghost nearby, Lonner, collapsed with the back of his neck blown out.

Dremmond was clear. Gaunt and Kolea physically dragged the big Ghost to the front of the line and Dremmond braced his scorched flame-gun, ensuring the feed-pipe wasn't twisted and the igniter was sparking.

He squeezed the trigger grip and billows of white-hot flame sheeted down the tunnel, incinerating the Zoican heavies. The scourging flame bubbled the paint off the walls and the twitching bone-runes began to shriek.

He washed the hall with another gout to be sure, and then Rawne, Haller and Bragg led off to secure the hall. Bragg reached the position the enemy had been holding and he stepped over the black, fused corpses. There was another accessway to his left and he sprayed bursts of autogun fire through the door mouth.

Haller moved to the right and went over hard as a half-burned Zoican soldier threw himself at the scratch officer. The blackened thing, its ceramite armour part-melted into its flesh by Dremmond's flames, tore at him in a frenzy. Haller screamed out, frantic. Rawne grabbed the Zoican and threw it off Haller. It bounced off a wall and, before it could rise, Rawne had shot it four times with his lasgun.

'I owe you, Ghost,' said Haller, getting up.

'No, you don't, habber. I don't like it when any one owes me anything. Forget it.'

Haller paused, as if slapped in the face. He hadn't much liked the look of the Tanith major when they had all first assembled. Banda had whispered Rawne had 'toxic eyes.' It seemed true. Even the haughty Volpone seemed to be making more of an effort to be comradely than this Tanith bastard.

'Suit yourself,' Haller said.

'He always does,' mocked Bragg. The big Ghost knew it was neither the time nor the place to bring Haller up to speed on Rawne's history, the fact that Rawne hated Gaunt with an inhuman passion precisely because 'he owed him.'

'Shut it and get soldiering!' Rawne snorted to Bragg. Already there were noises from the side tunnels and fresh Zoican forces were firing on them.

The main strike force had moved up by then. Gilbear swung a party of Bluebloods to the right and cremated a side-tunnel with grenades from their under-barrel launchers. MkVenner hurried right with four Tanith and a number of scratches, moving to secure their advance from enemy prosecution. A las-round hit him in the arm and spun him to the deck. Domor, right behind him, knelt over the injured scout and sprayed las-fire down at the hidden shooter, calling for a medic. Beside him, Vinya, one of the loom-girls, rebounded off the wall as a brace of las-shots caught her in the belly. Several troopers pushed past Domor to hold the side-tunnel, flaying las-fire down into the dark.

Gherran joined Domor, running low, holding a las pistol in one hand, the other hand curled around the narthecium kit to stop it jolting.

'It's MkVenner–' Domor began. The medic dropped to his knees beside the scout. The las-shot had exploded MkVenner's left elbow and disintegrated his biceps. He was curled up, crying with pain, but he forced his voice to work.

'Her first – her!' he said, nodding over at Vinya.

'Let me look at it, MkVenner,' Gherran said.

'No! You know fething triage: serious cases first! She's gut-shot! See to her!'

'Give him this,' Gherran told Domor, handing him a gauze-packed inoculator full of high-dose painkillers. He scrambled over to the sprawled scratch soldier. She was twisted like a broken puppet, her chin forced into her chest where she lay with the back of her head against the wall. Blood oozed out of her in a wide pool. The wound itself had self-cauterised in charred, knotty lumps, but the damage had shredded her insides, and she was bleeding out rapidly.

'Oh, feth!' Gherran spat. 'Someone give me a hand here!'

Kolea was beside him. 'Tell me how.'

'Pressure: here and here. Hold it tight. No, tight like you mean it!'

They were both sodden with her blood. She stirred, moaning.

'Vinya... s'okay... Stay awake...' Kolea murmured to her, his hands clamping hard on her ruined organs.

He looked around at Gherran as he worked frantically.

'She's not going to make it, is she?'

'Major trauma,' Gherran explained as he worked. 'I can stabilise her, but no, it's just a matter of time.'

Kolea nodded. He let go and leaned down to whisper in her ear, 'You fought well, Vinya Terrigo of Hab 45/jad. Vervunhive will never forget your courage. The hive loves you for your devotion.'

Then he reached down with huge, gentle hands and snapped her neck.

'Oh, God-Emperor!' Gherran cried, recoiling in horror.

'There's a man you can save,' Kolea said, pointing at MkVenner with a bloody hand. 'I love my people, and I will fight for them with every last measure of my strength, but this would have uselessly wasted the time of a good medic when there are better causes. Her pain is over. She has found peace.'

Gherran wiped his mouth.

'I–' he began.

'If you were going to tell me you couldn't begin to understand what we habbers have gone through to get here, save it. I don't want your pity.'

'Actually, friend, I was going to tell you I do understand. And admire your courage, to boot. Our lives are all on the line fighting for your home. Me, I don't have a home anymore. So, feth you and that oh-so-noble crap.' Gherran gathered his kit-pack and moved over to MkVenner.

Kolea picked up his lasgun and strode past, rejoining the fight.

Cocoer, Neskon and Flinn had made it to the corner of the right hand side access, and they drove the gathering Zoicans backwards. Gaunt, with Genx and Maroy, crawled up behind them.

'Access?' asked Gaunt.

'Not a fething hope, sir!' sang out Cocoer. The air was flickering with las crossfire.

'Bloody bastard hell!' Neskon cried as his gun jammed. He shook it. Gaunt grabbed him and yanked him down into cover just as laser blasts pummelled the wall above his head.

'Never forget the drill, Neskon. Gun jams: duck and cover. Don't stand there playing with it.'

'No, colonel-commissar.'

'I like you better alive.'

'Me... me too, sir.'

Rilke, reckoned to be the best sniper in the Ghosts after Larkin, and the scratch woman Nessa moved up to flank them. Rilke wasted two shots trying to hit a Zoican in cover down the tunnel. Nessa, with her standard-issue lasgun, picked him off and the Zoican behind him.

'Where'd you learn to shoot like that?' Rilke protested, but she didn't hear him. She couldn't hear him.

Gaunt looked across at her, waiting until she saw his face. 'Good,' he said.

She grinned.

A ceiling panel ten metres back slammed open and Zoican stormtroops began to drop down out of it like grains of sand through the neck of an hourglass. They sprayed shots in both directions. Four Ghosts, two scratches and a Blueblood went down. Bragg wheeled and decimated the spilling Zoicans, his withering autocannon supported by Haller, Rawne, Genx and a dozen others.

The Zoican dead lay in a heap under the ceiling drop. Bragg raised his muzzle and began to fire up into the roof, his heavy rounds punching smooth-edged holes through the sheet metal. Blood began to drip down through some of them.

'We're bottled in!' Mkoll yelled at Gaunt.

Gaunt knew as much. Gilbear had blocked the left-hand access, but the right was still thick with Zoicans. And now they were coming down through the ceiling, for feth's sake! At this rate, his strike cadre would exhaust themselves simply maintaining a perimeter. If they were going to do anything of note, they had to focus.

'Mkoll?' Gaunt called.

Mkoll knew what was being asked of him. Gaunt had always valued the chief scout's unnerving ability to find the right way. It wasn't a gift, really. Somehow, sometime back in the shifting, drifting forest ways of Tanith, he had come to understand the logic of structure, the underlying sense of any environment.

Mkoll's gut said straight ahead and down.

'Through the blast shields, sir,' Mkoll announced.

That was good enough for Gaunt. He crawled back, under heavy fire, to the shields. 'Rawne! Tube charges here!'

'What are you doing?' bellowed Gilbear, moving up. 'That way will lead us off into the right-hand side of the structure!'

Gaunt looked at Gilbear, las-shots whizzing around them. 'After all we've seen, Gilbear, do you trust me?'

'Very probably, but–'

'If you were constructing this Spike, would you put the main command deck in the dead centre where anyone would expect it to be?'

Gilbear thought for a moment and shook his head.

'Then humour me. I've learned to go with Mkoll's instincts. If I'm wrong, I'll stand you a case of wine. You can choose the vintage.'

'If you're wrong, we'll be dead!'

'Why do you think I made the bet?'

Gilbear laughed out loud.

'Cover and clear!' yelled Rawne, hastening from the bundle of tube charges he had glued to the shield hatch.

The channelled blast tore the doors inwards like paper. Whatever else you could say about him, Rawne knew explosives. There was barely a shockwave on the Imperial side of the hatch.

'For Tanith!' yelled Gaunt, hurling himself through the opening.

'For Volpone!' bawled Gilbear, right beside him.

'For Vervunhive!' mouthed Nessa to herself, close on their heels.

Guild Githran Agricultural had fallen. Corbec drove his Tanith back towards the base of the Main Spine with all hell following. Milo and Baffels guided their survivor company out of the ruins, chased by Zoican tank groups. Bray's mixed units wilted in retreat as divisions of Zoican stormtroopers drove up into the inner habs.

The Shield Pylon shuddered as it took shell after shell.

At Croe Gate, Grizmund's valiant counteraction finally reached a stop. Flat crabs and spider death machines lumbered in at them, in strengths even the crusade's finest tank regiment could not withstand.

On the dock causeway, Varl and Rodyin began to pull their infantry back, facing an ochre host ten thousand strong.

Along the edge of the Commercia, where one of the war's bloodiest battles had been waged, Bulwar ordered his NorthCol and scratch companies to retreat. Overhead, the Shield flickered and waned. It would not last much longer. In the middle of a horrendous brawl in a side trench, Soric hammered his axe-rake into the foe. He was one of the last to heed Bulwar's retreat order.

Corday's Volpone unit was pincered by Zoican detachments. The Bluebloods were slaughtered by crossfire in the rubble wastes that had once been the inner-sector habs. Corday died with his men.

In a lost pocket in the wastelands, Caffran held Tona Criid tight, Yoncy and Dalin curled between them. The sky was on fire and shells fell all around. It was just a matter of time, Caffran knew. But until then, he would hold her and the children as tight as he could.

In the baptistry, Ban Daur set aside his headset and sat back in his seat. The workers and staff servitors were still milling around, trying to maintain some semblance of control.

It was over. Daur got up and crossed to Otte at the Font. Windows blew in down the hall and the Main Spine shuddered as shells struck it.

'We gave it our best,' Daur said.

'For Vervunhive,' Otte agreed, weeping quietly with fatigue.

Intendant Banefail joined them. 'High Legislator Anophy has just been carried out. A heart attack.'

'Then he's been spared,' Daur said callously.

Otte looked at him reprovingly, but Banefail seemed to agree. 'This is the end, my brave friends. The Emperor love you for your efforts, but this is the end of all things. Vervunhive is lost. Make your peace.'

Daur looked round at Immaculus. The minister stood nearby with his robed clergy.

'Begin the mass, sir,' Daur told him. 'The requiem. I want the last sound I hear to be a psalm of loss voiced by the Emperor's own.'

Immaculus nodded. He led his brethren into the celebratory and the soft dirge, a haunting melody, began to lift above the baptistry and the high stations of Vervunhive.

In the abandoned hall of her house, high in the Spine, Merity Chass heard the low plainsong welling through the walls. She had put on a long, formal gown and her father's ducal chain and signet ring, which Daur had brought to her.

She had spent an hour putting the House Chass ledgers in order and encrypting all the family documents onto storage crystals. At the sound of the mass, she frowned.

'Not yet... not yet...' she murmured. 'He won't fail us...'

EIGHTEEN

THE LAIR OF ASPHODEL

'A friend of death, a brother of luck and a son of a bitch.'
— Major Rawne, of his commander

Its sounds amplified by the thick, metal walls around, carnage exploded into the Spike's command level. Savage fighting boiled through the dark, mesh-floored chambers. The strikeforce were engaging crew now as well as troops. The crew members wore loose flak-tunics and work-fatigues, and their heads were generally exposed. Gaunt's troopers could see for themselves the horror that had disturbed Larkin so at Veyveyr Gate. It wasn't the implants fused and sutured into their eyes, ears and scalps, linking their senses and brain patterns to the insidious chatter. It was the fact that they were men and women of all ages: hab workers, parents, guilders, older children, the elderly. The entirety of Zoica's population had mobilised for war, just as Gaunt had assessed. The bald proof was overwhelmingly tragic. With blank expressions, somehow even more lifeless than Sondar's servitor puppets, the people of Ferrozoica threw themselves at the attackers.

Gaunt hacked through a pair of Zoican troopers with his powersword, fighting to cut a route down onto the main bridge area. Through the seething press, the smoke and the flashes of las-fire, he could make out a wide, open platform of polished chrome, surrounded by black towers of control instrumentation. In the centre of the platform, the glowing, pinkish ball of a coherent light field, ten metres in diameter, coalesced up from an emitter ring in the floor. He fought his way to it, channelling his deepest reserves of aggression and determination.

Suddenly, he was on the platform itself, virtually alone, lit by the pink radiance. His last frenzied efforts to break through had been almost too successful. He'd effectively separated himself from the rest of his party, still locked into the mayhem in the adjacent bridge areas.

Gaunt was breathing hard and shaking. He'd lost his cap somewhere, his jacket was torn and he was splattered with blood. An almost painful adrenaline high fizzled through him like electricity glowing through fuse-wire. He had never been pushed to such an extremity of raw fury before in his life. His mind was locked out in a paroxysm of battle-rage. Everything had become distant and incomprehensible. For a moment, he couldn't remember what he was supposed to be doing.

Something flickered behind him and he wheeled, his blade flashing as it made contact. A tall, black figure lurched backwards. It was thin but powerful and much taller than him, dressed in form-fitting, glossy-black armour and a hooded cape of chainmail. The visage under the hood-lip was feral and non-human, like the snarling skull of a great wolf-hound with the skin scraped off. It clutched a sabre-bladed power-sword in its metal-gloved hands.

Gaunt had seen its like before, on Balhaut. He'd glimpsed its kind distantly on the fields of war, during the final stage of the battle, and then seen several corpses closer to after the victory. It was one of the Darkwatch, the elite retinue of Chaos champions who had been gifted to the warlord, Asphodel, as his personal bodyguard. The thing flickered again, employing its monstrous, innate control of the warp to shift its location around him. Gaunt yelled and blocked the incoming blade of the repositioned horror. The cold blue energies of Hcironymo's powersword clashed against the sparking, blood-red fires of the Darkwatcher's weapon.

It flicker-shifted again, just a few paces to the left, and sliced its sword around at him. Gaunt evaded, stumbling in his haste, rolling and then springing up in time to block the downward swing of the Chaos-tainted blade.

But this was not the same weapon. This was longer, straighter, incandescent with smoking green fire. A second Darkwatcher, shifting in to assist the first.

Without looking, Gaunt threw himself sideways, knowing the original fury was now behind him. Red energy sliced a gouge in the gleaming chrome deck.

He backed as they came at him together, both flickering in and out of reality. One was suddenly to his left, but Gaunt threw all his force behind a blocking strike that bounced the blade away. The other sliced in at him and caught Gaunt's right shoulder.

There was no pain. A cold, nauseating numbness ached into his wounded limb.

Gaunt hurled himself forward in a tuck roll, avoiding two more slashes. He knew he had never been this outmatched before, not even

face to face with howling World Eater Chaos Marines in the underworld
of Fortis Binary or surrounded by the Iron Men in the crypts of Menazoid Epsilon. He should be dead already.

But something kept him alive. Partly his elevated battle-edge, partly
his determination, but also, he was sure, Heironymo's sword. It seemed
to smell the shifting creatures and forewarn him – by a tingle – of their
impossible movements.

Their shifting was localised, as if they were moving in and out of
corporeal reality. Every time they became solid to strike, the sword
twitched in his grip, moving him to block.

He ducked a scything arc of green energy and stabbed upwards,
shearing one Darkwatcher's head off in a flurry of blue sparks. Lambent, frosty smoke jetted out of its tall form as it collapsed in upon
itself, flickering and fading. A inhuman scream rang around the bridge.

The other lunged at him, flickering into being right in his face, and
though the powersword pulled at him, he wasn't quick enough to avoid
the deep gouge the red blade sliced in his left thigh.

Gaunt fell.

A spray of autocannon split the air above him. Bragg had made it to
the edge of the platform and was blasting at the Darkwatcher on full
auto. The thing shuddered under the impacts, flickering in and out
of real-space, its chain cloak whipping as it turned to face the new
attack. Kolea and Mkoll were there too, heaving up onto the edge of
the chrome level, opening fire at the beast. A second later, Neskon,
Haller, Flinn, Banda and a Volpone called Tonsk had also reached the
edge of the platform. Sustained fire from all of them drove the raging
Chaos-thing backwards – and targeted the other two that had manifested in the last few moments. Bragg's unrelenting fire-cone gradually
disintegrated the red-bladed Darkwatcher, which advanced on him,
despite the colossal wash of bullets, before finally exploding a few
flicker-steps from him.

One of the others, wielding a pike-axe which smoked with orange
lightning, chopped Tonsk in two and severed Neskon's left leg at the
knee with one stroke. Haller snatched up the Blueblood's fallen hellgun, pumped the under-barrel launcher and blew the thing's head off
with a rocket-grenade.

The others, supported by more of the strike force just making it to the
platform, caught the remaining Darkwatcher in a crossfire. The thing
shrieked and flickered, twisting in the las-hail.

Behind them, the remaining elements of Gaunt's brigade fought a
desperate rearguard at the Zoicans pouring into the command area
from all around.

Gaunt clawed at one of the instrumentation towers at the edge of
the platform and pulled himself to his feet. Hololithic screens projecting from the domed roof above showed fuzzy, amber-tinted views
of the onslaught outside. The Spike, with its supporting armoured
legions, had exploded in through the Curtain Wall just east of Sondar
Gate, and the war machine's vast batteries, presumably recrewed after
Gaunt's entry assault, targeted and demolished the Shield Pylon in a
blaze of fire.

Sections of the huge structure crashed down across the Commercia, like a titanic tree being felled, wreathed in great washes of flame
instead of foliage. Rather than being deactivated as before, the Shield
collapsed, its massive energies unsecured and arcing out. The energy
flare, designed to protect the city of Vervunhive, ripped the top ten
levels off the Main Spine, and all the anchor stations around the city
perimeter exploded.

The powersword loose in his hand, Gaunt searched the instrumentation around him for some system he could recognise. It had been built
by the tech-wrights of Ferrozoica, so its essential patterns were Imperial, but the markings and format were wretched and alien.

Gaunt staggered across to the next tower and resumed his search.
He found what appeared to be a vox-terminal and a pict-link displayer.
But nothing else he could understand.

Behind him, the last Darkwatcher exploded, taking Trooper Flinn
with it.

The third tower. Halfway down, what could only be a data-slate reader
with a universal hub: standard Imperial fitting.

Gaunt felt himself sag, his leg wound pulling at him. Blood from his
shoulder wound soaked his sleeve and dripped off his hand.

'Gaunt!' yelled Kolea, at his side, supporting him. Mkoll was there
too, and Genx, Gherran and Domor.

'Let me see to your wounds!' Gherran was yelling.

'No t-time!'

'Let him help you, Gaunt!' Kolea growled, trying to keep the struggling commissar upright. 'Let me–'

'No!' Gaunt shook the big miner off. If this was the final act, it would
be his.

He pulled the ticking, chuckling amulet from his pocket and fitted
its link ports to the reader's hub.

It engaged, purred and turned twice like a kodoc beetle burying its
abdomen in the sand.

The lighting and instrument power in the command section shorted
on and off two, three, four times. A mechanical wailing of tortured,

over-raced turbines welled up from the vast machine pits below them. The chatter cut short.

Then the lights went out altogether.

Sudden, total darkness; sudden quiet. In the stillness, the groans of the dying and wounded; the bright, brief crackle and fizz of torn cables. A flash of las-fire.

Gaunt's eyes grew accustomed to the gloom. The heart of the Spike was dead. Smoke wafted, full of the rich, animal smells of war. Men stirred, blinking.

The force field in the centre of the platform had vanished.

A huge form, dark like a shadow, crouched where the field had been. It rose, unfurled, grew larger. In the half-light, Gaunt saw the richly embroidered silk of a vast cape spilling away from the figure as it stood. He saw an immense, metal-gloved hand reach out and beckon to him. He saw the shivering flame-light throw into relief a long, smooth armour-cowl split by narrow eye-slits. The cowl fanned up and out into massive, hooked steeples of polished horn.

Heritor Asphodel, Chaos warlord, daemon-thing, fuelled by his dark gods in the warp, standing fully six metres tall, lunged at the human worms who strove to defeat him. He made no sound. Darkness, which he seemed to wear and pull around him like a great cloak, sucked through the air as it moved with him.

Kolea buried his axe-rake in the Heritor's flank. A second later, he was flying sideways across the platform, most of his ribs shattered.

Firing and making two hits, Mkoll was knocked sideways, his shoulder broken.

Domor's lasgun exploded in his hands, blowing him up, back and off the platform.

Gherran was lacerated by an ebbing fold of darkness, sharp as a billion blades. His blood made a mist that drenched Gaunt.

Genx was pulverised by the concussive force of the daemon's fist as he tried to reload his weapon and fire.

Gaunt met Asphodel head on. He slammed the blazing blue spike of the powersword into and through the monstrosity's chest.

At the same moment, the massive bolt pistol clenched in the Heritor's left hand shot Gaunt through the heart.

NINETEEN

MOURNING GLORY

*'With this act we have richly denied the Darkness and made
trophies of its creatures. A dark lord is dead. So, this holy
crusade, blessed by the Emperor, is advanced with glory.'*
– Warmaster Macaroth, at Verghast

They came like ghosts at dusk. Phantom forms, impossibly large, underlit by the dying sun as they settled down through the smoke-filthy upper
atmosphere of Verghast. Warships, bulk troop transports, the might of
the Sabbat Worlds Crusade, the pride of the Segmentum Pacificus Navy.

It was the fiftieth day. Learning via the Astropathicus that Vervunhive
faced not an inconsequential rival hive but a hunted Chaos commander, Macaroth had made best speed for Verghast, arriving after
twenty-seven days of urgent transit through the warp.

The hazy sky was full of metal and looked like it should fall. The awesome power of the Imperium was there for every Verghastite to see:
ten thousand ships, some the size of cities, some bloated like ornate
oceanic turtles, some slender and serrated like airborne cathedrals.

Macaroth unleashed his might on the planet below: six million
Guardsmen, half a million tanks, squads drawn from three Chapters of the Adeptus Astartes, two Titan Legions. Troop dropships, bulk
machine-lifters and shuttles dropped in a swarm on the Hass valley.
For a while, the sky did fall.

Mass destruction followed, lasting for five days, thought it was brutally
one-sided. Heironymo's amulet had done its work and cut the insidious
chatter for all time. By the time the Warmaster's immense forces arrived,
the Zoicans were already in total rout. Aimless and lost, they broke off
the final assault. Many committed suicide or wandered blindly into the
defenders' fields of fire to be massacred. Millions of others woke as if from a
dream and stumbled, without purpose or motive, back into the grasslands.

Under Grizmund's command, the battered Imperial forces that had held Vervunhive for over a month reformed to drive the pitiful, bewildered invaders out. Narmenian and NorthCol tank brigades chased down and annihilated Zoican motorised units threading back across the grasslands towards their own hive. Guard infantry, co-ordinated by Colonel Corbec, Colonel Bulwar and Major Otte, utilising every troop-carrying machine they could raise, hunted out and slaughtered the fleeing troop elements in vast numbers. There was no question of mercy. Ferrozoica's taint had to be expunged.

By the time Macaroth's armada made orbit, the Zoicans had been driven back six hundred kilometres into the plains, leaving vehicles and equipment scattered and abandoned in their wake.

In the crippled hive itself, scratch companies slowly weeded out the last, feral pockets of Zoican resistance.

The Warmaster followed up with unstinting vigour. He politely but determinedly requested the assistance of the Iron Snakes Space Marines to overtake and neutralise the fleeing enemy. His armoured brigades poured down the main highways and decimated everything that lived. Skeletal Titans, shrieking like wraiths, stalked the grassland horizons, incinerating the retreating foe.

On the fifty-fourth day, crusade warships torched Ferrozoica Hive from low orbit. The blinding flame-flare filled the southern horizon.

But by then, the fight was out of the Zoicans and had been since the thirty-seventh day. Without the hypnotic chatter to unify their cause and drive them on, they had crumbled. Imperial Fists Space Marines ceremonially destroyed the Spike and incinerated the Heritor's corpse.

The final battle was one of humanitarian support. Intendant Banefail, along with the hive elders and noble houses, laboured to accommodate the millions of wounded and homeless. By day sixty, the true scale of the human cost was undeniable. Vervunhive was a necropolis: a city of the dead. Meeting with the surviving nobility, Macaroth signed the Dissolution Warrant that formally acknowledged Vervunhive's extinction. The hive was dead. All population elements were to be absorbed by the Northern Collectives or shipped to Ghasthive and the Isthmus Steeples. Two new hives were to be founded, one ruled by a clique of noble houses under House Anko, the other a collective governed by Houses Chass and Rodyin. Names would come later. It would be generations until these municipal structures would begin to establish themselves, and it would be decades before the bulk of the dispossessed population could be given new, permanent homes.

Lord Anko, siting his new hive's foundations higher up the Hass waters from dead Vervunhive, planned to exploit the prometheum reserves once controlled by Vannick. Lady Chass, the first woman to govern a collective on Vervunhive, set her foundation in the grasslands far to the south and turned to mining and servitor engineering. Their future rivalry and confrontation would be long and complex, but is not pertinent to this history.

At the time, an air of disillusion fell hard on the survivors of Vervunhive. Many felt they had given everything in defence of the city only to see the city abandoned anyway. When this mood was made known to the Warmaster, he spoke publicly about his decision and made law an Act of Consolation.

The Warmaster's staff faced a thousand duties as they tidied up the mess of the Vervunhive War. One of those was the prosecution of all those who had acted in a manner disloyal to the Emperor during that period of great hardship.

The reports of the Tanith Sergeant Varl, as logged by his commander, Gaunt, were sorted and processed by the Administratum during the latter stages of the purge. On day fifty-nine, prosecuting war-crime charges, Vervun Primary troops stormed the halls of Guild Worlin. Amchanduste Worlin was not to be found.

'They say he wants to see you,' Corbec said, leaning back against the sill of a vast stained-glass window in Medical Hall 67/mv.

'He can wait.'

'I'm sure he can,' Corbec grinned. 'He's only a Warmaster.'

'Feth. They're really abandoning the hive – after everything we did?'

'I think maybe because of everything we did. There's not much left standing.'

Ibram Gaunt heaved himself upright on his cot. The pain of his shoulder and thigh wounds had long since faded, but the burning ache in his chest still plagued him. He coughed blood, for the third time since Corbec had arrived.

'You should probably lie still, sir,' Corbec ventured.

'Probably,' returned Gaunt. It was the sixty-second day. He had been unconscious for most of the previous month and had undergone repeated surgery to repair the wound Heritor Asphodel had dealt him. Gaunt still didn't know – and never would – if it had been dumb luck or fate that had saved him. The Heritor's bolt had hit him directly on the steel rose Lord Chass had made him wear. Though the collapsing petals had been driven into his chest, it was certain he would not have survived otherwise.

'You heard about the Act of Consolation?'

'I heard. What of it?'

'Well, sir, you wouldn't believe the number of new Ghosts we've recruited.'

Under the terms of the Act of Consolation, any disillusioned Vervun-hiver anxious to leave Verghast to find a new life was offered the possibility of training for a place in the Imperial Guard. Upwards of forty thousand elected to do so. Some made their choice of unit a condition of their acceptance.

Motor convoys carried them north with the regular army to board bulk carriers that had put in at Kannak Port. Sergeant Agun Soric oversaw the embarkation of his brave Irregulars. All of them were yet to be issued with their Tanith fatigues and camo-capes. Soric moved past the ship's payload doors and greeted Sergeant Kolea, who had also joined up, along with most of his scratch company. Kolea was walking on crutches, his torso encased in mediplas bindings.

'We'll never see it again,' said Soric.

'What?'

'Verghast. Take a last look.'

'Nothing here for me now anyway,' Kolea said. Under his breath, he uttered a last goodbye to his lost wife and beloved children.

Half a kilometre away, Bragg supervised the loading of other Ghosts. Many, like Domor and Mkoll, were walking wounded. Along with the soldiers came the inevitable wave of camp followers, lugging their possessions: clerks, cooks, armourers, mechanics, women.

Bragg caught sight of Caffran leading a girl and two children up the ramp. One was just a babe in arms. He noticed that the girl, along with her piercings and surly look, wore the temporary badge of a Guard recruit. Another female trooper. Bad enough Kolea's fighting women had been given a place. Larkin would have a seizure.

Jumping down from his transit truck, Ban Daur took a last, wistful look at the land around him. He felt like a lost soul given one last chance to haunt the place that had raised him.

That was appropriate. He wasn't Captain Ban Daur of Vervun Primary any more. He was a Ghost.

'I kept these for a long while,' Ana Curth said. She held out the dog tags that had been in the pocket of her apron since Veyveyr Gate. 'I knew there would be no good time for you to see them, but maybe now...'

Dorden took the tags. He read them, sighing.

'Mikal Dorden. Infantryman. Yes, I... they told me...'

'I'm sorry, Dorden. Really I am.'

Dorden looked up from where he sat, his eyes wet with tears. 'So am I. You know I was the only Ghost to have a relative in the Tanith regiment? My son. A fragile, last link to the world we lost. And now... that's gone too.'

She held him to her as he shuddered and wept.

A door banged open and a guilder peered in at them. He was dressed in rich robes and had a driven intensity about his face.

'Whatever you're looking for, it isn't in here,' Curth told him, holding Dorden tightly.

'Surgeon Curth?'

'Yes? What?'

The guilder entered the swab-room. He smiled. 'I was looking for, erm, Surgeon Curth and Medic Dorden.' He unfolded a scrap of vellum. 'I had a request to talk to me... about that terrible incident at the carriage station weeks ago. God-Emperor, it was awful!'

Curth let go of Dorden and turned round to the guilder.

'I'm Curth,' she said, stepping forward. 'Thank you for coming. I need to know: what did you see?'

'I want Dorden here too, before I speak,' Worlin said.

'That's me,' Dorden said, rising and wiping his eyes.

'Both of you? Dorden and Curth?' Worlin grinned.

'Yes? What did you want to tell us? What did you see?'

Worlin pulled out his needle pistol and grinned. 'This.'

Dorden threw himself at Curth as Worlin opened fire. The first shot punched through Dorden's right hand, the second through his left thigh. The third hit Curth in the shoulder and threw her across the room.

Worlin advanced on Dorden, aiming the sleekly murderous pistol, eyes burning.

'Let's keep this between ourselves, doctor,' he hissed.

A bolt round blew Worlin's head off in matted chunks. Gaunt, gun raised, limped into the swab-room, supported by the bewildered Corbec.

'I heard shooting,' Gaunt said as he passed out.

TWENTY

NECROPOLIS

'Enough of this. Too many ghosts.'

— Ibram Gaunt, at Verghast

The outboards purred. The *Magnificat* lurched away from the dock into the middle of the Hass. It left behind a vast city-hulk still burning and smouldering. Folik steered them out, chasing the last tides of the day.

He left the bridge and dropped down onto the rear skirt of the old ferry, approaching the man in the long coat and peaked cap who leaned against the rail as if in pain. For a week, Folik had been ferrying Guardsmen to the north shore, the beginning of their long journey to who knew where next.

This was the very last run.

In the cabin seating, Dorden looked over at Curth, her shoulder bulked up by bandage.

'Are you sure about this, surgeon?'

'Utterly. I've given Verghast all I have.'

Dorden nodded.

'So have you, Tolin, and so much more than me. I want to repay the Guard. Don't tell me you can't use another medic.'

'Indeed not, Curth.'

She smiled sadly. 'I think, by now, it's all right for you to call me Ana.'

'It's a pleasure to have you aboard, sir,' Folik said to Gaunt. 'You being the People's Hero and all.'

'Are you sure you're not getting me mixed up with someone else?'

'I don't think so. You're Commissar Gaunt, aren't you?'

Gaunt nodded. He looked back across the Hass at the dead ruins of Vervunhive. They continued to burn in the low, morning light.

He took the shattered petals of the metal flower Dorden had cut out of his flesh and cast them out across the water.

IN REMEMBRANCE

To tell you the truth, it was a long time ago and I didn't really spend much time with them. It's pushing it to say I knew them at all, really. It was just a job, you see. A well paid commission between my more serious works. I never expected it to become... Well, the thing I am most famous for.

I doubt any of them remember me. I honestly doubt any of them are alive any more. It's been sixty years since the hive war on Verghast, and Imperial Guardsman is not a career with long-term prospects.

No, they're probably all long dead by now. If so, may the Emperor of Mankind rest them, every one. I had a friend who worked in the Munitorum at NorthCol who was kind enough to pass me copies of Imperial dispatches so I could follow their movements and fortunes. For a few years, it pleased me to keep track of them. When I read of their successes on Hagia and Phantine, I poured a glass of joiliq and sat in my studio, toasting their name.

But I stopped after a while. Sooner or later, I knew, the news would be bad. I have my memories, and they're enough.

I was a young man then. Just twenty-eight. I actually trained, would you believe it, in the Scholam Lapidae in Ferrozoica. Zoica, of all places! But by the time of the war I had been living and working in North-Col for about seven years. I'd visited Vervunhive half a dozen times, usually in regard of a commission, twice to consult with a fine toolmaker whose tungsten-nosed chisels I favoured. He died during the siege. A loss to my profession.

I well remember arriving in Vervunhive in the first days after the conflict. I barely recognised the place. War had smashed the majesty out of it and left it crumpled and deformed. It reminded me of nothing so much as a toppled statue; brought down, shattered, its scattered debris hinting at its former grace. You could trace what it had been from the wreckage but you could never put it back together again.

And they never did.

I remember getting off the transport in the gusting smoke and thinking that it didn't much look like a victory.

No matter where you went, there was smoke. Ash caked every surface, inside and out. Sooty flakes of it billowed in the air. The great bulk of the Main Spine was miserably buckled and punctured, and wept smoke from more holes than I could count. The sky was black. So very black. They said the smoke-storms roiling from Vervunhive could be seen from space.

I was utterly lost for a second. It had expected it to be bad, but this...

A voice started me out of my reverie. It said something like, 'What are you standing there for, you gakking fool?' Something like that, only more colourful. I found a VPHC officer glowering at me and realised I was standing in the middle of the transit concourse with floods of people moving around me, along with loaders, transports, troop trucks. I was pretty much in the way, gawping there like that, though to tell the truth only the VPHC staffer seemed to care. I showed him my papers.

He seemed contemptuous. I think he actually laughed at my explanation of why I was there. Then he pointed me over to the far side of the concourse, through the crowds, to where men were loading a grimy truck under a shrapnel-puckered awning.

'They're the ones you want,' he said.

I picked up my bag and walked across to them. My throat was already dry with the omnipresent smoke. Six men were working as a human chain to sling crates into the flatbed. They were all dressed in matt-black fatigues which were patched and ragged and in desperate need of boil washing. The men were uniformly black haired and pale skinned. Most had tattoos on their cheeks, brows or forearms, and silver studs in their ears. The biggest of them was a hairy brute with a fabulously tangled beard and huge arms like tree limbs. Blue spirals wound up through the black hair on those massive forearms. He was whistling a jaunty tune, but his lips were so dry and cracked, the noise was more like the whine of a weary dog.

His name was Colm Corbec, and he was, incredibly, the colonel.

'Who're you?' he said, hardly pausing in his work.

'Thoru. Jeshua Thoru. The... uh... artist.'

'Never heard of you.'

'Well,' I began, 'I'm not famous, as such... I never supposed you would have...'

He stopped his work suddenly and looked at me. The men behind him thumped to a halt, straining with boxes. 'I'm sure you're very good,' he said kindly, 'I meant no offence. Me and fine art, we're not, you know, close. I wouldn't know an oil painting if it came and bit me on the arse. You a painter?'

'No, I'm a sculptor.'

'A sculptor, eh?' he nodded at that, as if impressed, and resumed his labour, catching a carton and humping it off onto the truck. 'A sculptor. Fancy. You do statues, then?'

'Uh, yes. Actually, I specialise in bas-relief friezes and installations, but I...' I realised I was losing him fast. 'Yes, I do statues.'

'Good for you.'

'I've been commissioned,' I said.

'Me too, lad. I'm a colonel.'

'No, I...' I paused. The other men were looking at me like I was a madman. One of them, a good-looking, sharp-eyed man younger and smaller than his commander, flexed an augmetic shoulder and eyed me cautiously.

'I think he means artistically commissioned, chief,' he said.

'Does he now?' said Corbec.

'Yes,' I said. 'House Chass has paid me to produce a monument in honour of this... event.'

'What event?'

'The victory of Vervunhive,' I said.

'Ah,' said Corbec. He looked around, as if seeing for the first time the mutilated, burning city. 'So that's what this is.'

'My papers are official and up to date,' I said, producing them. He wasn't interested in looking. 'I've been granted permission to interview the Tanith First in order to... uhm... plan my work.'

'Us?' said the younger man with the augmetic shoulder.

'Yes,' I replied. 'Lady Chass was most specific. She wanted the Tanith First especially to be commemorated.'

'I've never been commemorated before,' said the younger man, a sergeant as it seemed from what was left of his rank pins.

'Keep working at that pace, Varl,' said Corbec, 'and I'll commemorate you myself. With the toe of me boot.'

They finished loading the truck and climbed aboard. I hesitated, not sure what to do. Corbec looked down from the cab at me. 'Well, lad,' he said. 'You'd better come with us, hadn't you?'

The Guard transport truck had clearly been wounded in the suspension during the fighting. We rattled down one street and the next, bone-shaken. I rode in the cab, squeezed in between Corbec and the sergeant. After a few minutes, the latter sniffed.

'Funny smell,' he said. 'Sweet, scenty.'

'Yeah,' said Corbec, also sniffing. I couldn't smell anything except the rank odour of unwashed bodies, old sweat and smoke. 'Have you had a bath today?' he asked me.

'Yes!' I said indignantly.

'That'd be it, then,' said Corbec.

'Lucky bastard,' said the other, Varl.

We joined a main arterial, slowing to skirt around burnt-out vehicles and sags of shelled rubble where building fronts had collapsed out over the roadway. Ahead, habbers were queuing for food and basic humanitarian supplies at a relief station set up in an old assembly plant. The arterial was almost a kilometre long, and the ragged queue lined it from end to end.

Corbec stared at them from the truck's filthy window as we drove by. The homeless, the bereaved, the hungry, the sick. Thin people with hollow faces and broken hopes, their eyes blank and sunken. Their skin was uniformly white, their clothing grey with ash and black with dirt. It was as if the world had become monochrome. He seemed fascinated.

'What is it?' I asked.

'They... they look like the old photopicts of me grandparents and kin,' he replied with surprising honesty. There was a terrible sadness in his tone. 'We had this great nalwood mantle over the kitchen hearth back home in County Pryze. Me mam stood the photopicts there, each one in a little frame. Uncles, aunts, distant cousins, weddings, baptisms. I always thought they looked so stiff and awkward, so soulless, you know? Black and white faces, like those out there.'

His words were mournful, and quite unlike anything I had ever expected to hear coming from such a hairy brute of a warrior. Lady Chass had asked me to try and capture the soul of the Tanith, and here, unexpectedly and without much searching, I seemed to have glimpsed it.

'Sometimes,' Corbec added, clearing his throat, 'and now would be one of those times, I wished I'd stuffed a few of those ragged old picts into me kitbag the morning I left home for the Founding Fields. They'd meant much to me, just relatives I'd barely met. Never met. Folks whose lives I knew nothing about. But now, if only I had them, they'd be like lifeline back to Tanith.'

'Where is Tanith?' I made the mistake of asking.

'Nowhere, Mister Artist, sir,' Corbec said, suddenly rousing out of his despond. 'It's dead and it's gone and we're all that's left. That's what makes us ghosts, you see.'

The long line of miserable faces continued to flicker past the cab windows.

'Let me get this straight... we won here, right, chief?' asked Sergeant Varl snidely. Varl was driving the truck, a contraband lho-stick dangling from his lips. The heady fumes filled the cab and made my eyes water, but Corbec seemed content to let it pass.

'Yeah, we won. Behold and marvel, this is what winning looks like.'

Varl pulled the truck into the loading dock of Medical Hall 67/mv. 'Stay here,' Corbec told him, climbing down from the cab. 'You can come with me, if you like,' he said to me as an afterthought and strode off towards the front steps of the battered building. I ran to catch up. Almost immediately, we were surrounded by children. Hab-urchins, refugees, all smeared in filth.

I didn't know what to do. Corbec had handed out the last of his dry rations and calorie packs days ago. The children mobbed him, pulling at his hands, tugging at his fatigues, ignoring his repeated murmur of apology.

The truck horn sounded. The kids looked round.

'Hey!' called Varl. 'Hey, over here! C'mon! Cake-bars!' He held up some of the foil-wrapped bars and waggled them.

The flock of children pulled away from us and swarmed around the truck, leaping to catch the cakes as Varl tossed them out from the carton on the seat.

Corbec watched for a moment and smiled. 'Varl and me scored the cake rations from a collapsed Munitorum storehouse. We'd intended them to be a treat for the Ghosts.' I realised he thought Varl had made a good call. This was more important.

We entered the Medical Hall. Inside the doorway was a stack of leaking sacks full of medical waste that lent the entrance a ghastly, pervasive fragrance. Beyond that was a train of linen carts, piled with soiled bedding. Two medics were fast asleep on the stacks of discoloured sheets. Even the roar of the incoming liberation warships hadn't woken them. They had worked until they had dropped. Someone had probably put them there.

Corbec knew the route to the room. He been visiting every day for over two weeks now, he said. He was looking for someone called Dorden.

'Doc? Doc?'

'He's sleeping,' said a woman quietly, coming in behind us.

Her name was Curth, Corbec told me later. He'd met her before a few times, but didn't know her at all well. A Verghastite local, a chief surgeon. Fething pretty, he said, if you liked small, well-made women with heart-shaped faces, and Corbec clearly did. But, he said emphatically, as if I was in any doubt, fancying Curth was like fancying the wife of a Sector Governor. He was a lowly spitball colonel and she was a senior civilian medic. Doc Dorden had the highest respect for her, and that was enough for a simple soul like Corbec. She'd proved herself here at Vervunhive. Corbec didn't think much of the idea of women in combat zones, but Curth was somebody the Ghosts could really use. He wondered if she'd heard about Warmaster Macaroth's Act of Consolation. Probably she had. There wasn't a chance in feth she'd take it up, in his opinion.

'Act of Consolation?' I had asked.

'A recruitment drive,' he had explained. 'A chance for brave Vervunhivers to become Ghosts like me.'

Anyway, she had appeared behind us, like a ghost herself.

'Is he alright?'

'He's stable, colonel,' said Curth.

'I meant the Doc, actually.'

'Oh.' She smiled. It was a damn fine smile, and I could tell Corbec enjoyed it. 'Yes, he's fine. Tired. He pulled three shifts straight and wasn't going to sleep even then. So I... I spiked his caffeine with aeldramol.'

She looked guilty, particularly with me there. Corbec sniggered.

'You zonked him out?'

'It was... ahm... medically necessary.'

'Excellent work, Surgeon Curth. My compliments. Dorden is a bugger when it comes to taking care of himself. Don't fret, I won't write you up.'

'Thank you, colonel.'

'Seeing as how you're not service, I think you can call me Colm.'

'Okay. You've come to see the patient, I presume?'

'I have. By the way, this is Mister Thoru. He's an artist, so he is.'

'An artist?' she said. 'Wait a minute... Thoru? The sculptor?'

'Yes,' I said, infinitely pleased.

'You did the frieze over the portico of the Imperial Hospice in NorthCol.'

'I did. Last year.'

'It was very good. I have friends on the hospice acquisition committee. They were very pleased with the work.'

'That's gratifying. Thank you.'

Curth pulled back the plastic tent screening the door and led us through into the intensive care room. Guided by some instinct, I held back and let Corbec go in ahead.

The patient lay on a hydraulic cot, tented in clear plastic. His body was laced with bio-feeds and life-support tubes. A chrome respirator puffed and wheezed beside the cot and a resuscitrex cart stood ready.

'Give me a minute, Mister Thoru, surgeon.'

'It's Ana, Colm.'

'Is it so?' Corbec smiled. 'Well, Ana. A moment, if you'd be so kind.'

'Of course.'

We backed off out and she slithered the plastic curtain back into place.

'Who is that?' I whispered to Curth.

'Ibram Gaunt. Colonel-commissar of the Tanith First-and-Only.'

The House Chass savants had briefed me about Gaunt. The hero of Vervunhive, they were calling him.

Gaunt had taken his wound destroying the abomination known as Heritor Asphodel. He'd been at the gates of death for three weeks, without regaining consciousness. I peered through the curtain. The sutures of his most recent thoracic surgery stood stark against his pale, tight flesh.

'So why are you here?' Curth asked me.

'I've been commissioned to create a memorial for the war. House Chass has hired me. They want something suitable and noble, and they arranged for me to tour with the Tanith for appropriate inspiration.'

'Good luck,' she said.

'Why? Am I looking in the wrong place?'

Curth shook her head. 'I just don't think there's very much nobility to be found in this misery. What little there is belongs to the Tanith Ghosts, and I doubt very much you could capture that.'

'Why?'

'Because it's very particular,' she said and walked away.

I looked back through the gap in the screen curtain.

'Hey, boss. It's Corbec. Just checking in.' Corbec sat himself down next to the cot.

'What's to tell? Well, it's a mess, basically. The hive is a mess. But you know what victory looks like, huh? The men are holding together. That old Tanith spirit. Varl asked me to ask you, if you die, can he have your coat? Heh! How about that? I think Baffels is shaping up well as a squad leader, but he needs a bit of a boost, confidence wise. Maybe you could take him on one side, when you're up and about again?'

The respirator puffed and sighed.

'The liberation is kicking off. The war-machines went through the outhabs yesterday afternoon, ready to head out into the salt grass-lands, hunting the last of the Zoicans. Feth me! Those Titans! They say there's Adeptus Astartes inbound too – Iron Snakes and Imperial Fists. The Warmaster ain't taking no chances.'

The vitals monitor continued to ping.

'They miss you, Ibram. The men. Me too. You gave us this victory and it's only right you share it. Don't go dying on us, you hear me?'

Corbec fell silent for a moment and stared down at the floor.

'You know, it's not fething fair,' he said finally. 'We won, but there are millions of civilians dying out there. Habbers, outhabbers, spiners. I saw some on my way in. It breaks my fething heart. You know what I thought? Well, I'll tell you, seeing as I have your undivided attention. I thought of Tanith. Yeah, Tanith. I thought of the millions we lost. My kin. My kind. My fething world. I looked at those pinched, fethed-up faces and I thought... Tanith. The folks of Tanith might have looked like this if we'd stayed and fought and won. Driven out the enemy. And you know what?'

The respirator thumped slowly.

'I'm glad. That's what. I'm glad it was all over and done with like that. Your call, Ibram, good call. I never really said it to you before, and I'm only saying it now because, feth knows, you can't hear me. But I'm glad we did what we did. Seeing this. I'd far rather that Tanith died quick and clean that suffer this kind of victory. My people deserved it. Not dying, I mean. But dying cleanly. This... this... crap, they wouldn't have deserved this. Better Tanith died, quick and complete, than...'

Corbec paused.

'You know what I mean. You've put troopers out of their pain too, I know it. It's better when it's quick. Better than this.'

Corbec got to his feet.

'Well, that's me for today. I've said my bit. You come back to us, you hear me? Come back to us.'

We went back out to the waiting truck and drove down to the billet where the Ghosts were stowed. Corbec seemed flat and quiet after his visit to the Medical Hall, and told me he was going to catch some rest. He put me into the care of massive trooper called Bragg.

'You detailed, Try?' Corbec asked. I didn't know at that point why Corbec called him 'Try'.

'Yes, chief. Outhab sweep.'

'Take him out for a tour,' he told Bragg, indicating me. 'Show him what it's all about. And look after him, okay?'

I was afraid of Bragg to begin with. He was just so imposing and big.

I quickly discovered he had a gentle heart that quite belied his ogrish appearance.

He gave me grey fatigues to wear in place of my rich blue civilian suit, and carefully strapped a spare ballistic vest around my torso. 'It should be quite enough, Mister Thoru,' he said. 'But you can never be too careful.' He had made a special effort to learn my name when we were introduced, and now used it respectfully. I felt I had been taken under his wing.

The men of his patrol assembled in the dusty air of the manufactory shed.

Bragg wasn't in charge. Lead fell to an older, bearded man called Baffels. Baffels was terribly serious about everything, like he had something to prove. I learned later he had only recently been promoted. There were eight others: a sniper called Larkin, a flame-trooper called Brostin, a scout called Doyl and five troopers called Domor, Milo, Feygor, Yael and Mktag.

They were an odd bunch, though they worked well together with the fluid ease that comes with shared experience. They all seemed to defer slightly to Larkin, the marksman, although he seemed to me a skinny, twitchy wretch liable to snap at the slightest provocation. They called him 'Larks' or 'Mad Larkin,' neither of which gave me any reassurance. They seemed to respect him, however. Bragg told me that Larkin had given the unit its name, dubbing them all Gaunt's Ghosts early on. I tried to talk to Larkin about that, but he said little. Just being close to him made me edgy. He radiated nervous energy and was forever fiddling with his weapon. After a while, I left him alone for the sake of my own sanity.

Doyl was a handsome man in his mid-twenties, the perfect subject for an uplifting statue. But he was even less forthcoming that Larkin.

'He's a scout,' Bragg told me, as if that explained everything. Brostin, stinking of promethium, was a rough-hewn oaf with a bad line in inappropriate jokes. Domor was a sound type, thoughtful and reserved. He sported augmetic eyes and the men called him 'Shoggy,' though they never told me why. His face and arms were pink with freshly healing burn tissue and this was his first patrol since he had been injured. I asked him how he had been hurt. Apparently a lasgun had exploded in his hands during close combat with Heritor Asphodel. I desperately wanted him to tell me more about that, but he wouldn't be drawn.

Mktag and Feygor were both in their thirties. Mktag was a cheery sort with a blue spiral tat around his left eye. Feygor was something else entirely. He had been wounded in the throat during the siege, and

862   DAN ABNETT

had fresh augmetics in his voice box. He was lean and surly, and, as it seemed to me, by far the most dangerous member of the unit.

Milo was the youngest, just a boy, really. Bragg told me Milo had only recently been awarded the rank of trooper. Before that he had been the only non-com to escape Tanith, saved by the colonel-commissar personally.

Yael wasn't much older. His lean adolescent body was just beginning to fill out with adult bulk. But there was a look in his eyes that showed he had grown up a long time since.

We went out into the southern outhabs. The purpose of the patrol, Bragg told me, was to smoke out the last vestiges of the Zoican host. They were lying low in the rubble mass, he said, dug in like splinters.

It all seemed alarmingly casual to me, but Bragg carried the sort of heavy autocannon that normally required a turret to mount it on, so I stuck close to him.

We left the city via what remained of the Hieronymo Sondar Gate. Several of the war's key battles had been fought here, and a few kilometres east along the vast, pock-marked curtain wall was Veyveyr Gate, the railhead that had seen the most savage engagement of the entire conflict.

The scale of the war was apparent to me now. Behind me stood the massive, spired bulk of Vervunhive, ringed by what remained of the great defensive curtain wall. In front, stretching out southwards as far as I could see, lay the outer habitats, the mining districts, the collieries, the manufactories, the great belt of urban structure that skirted the main hive itself. This was where the longest phase of the war had been fought, a relentless, invasive attrition, street to street, as the hosts of Zoica advanced towards the curtain wall and the inner hive. We passed beside the wreckage of some of the Zoican war machines: not just tanks and AFVs, but massive things shaped like spiders or crustaceans. Their colossal hulls were seared black from the fires that had consumed them.

It was a bright, sunny day, but the veils of smoke had stained the light almost green and settled a skein of haze across the middle distance like mist. A light wind from the southern grasslands lifted dust in little flurries and eddies. Speeders, drop-ships and shrieking Imperial interceptors crossed the sky back and forth, and the horizon to the south was flickering with flashes and tremors of light. Out in the grasslands, the fleeing remnants of the Zoican army were being hunted down to extinction.

For a while, there was activity everywhere. Columns of refugees, limping towards the city, laden with handcarts and baby carriages full of salvaged belongings. Foot patrols of Imperial Guardsmen. Trains of injured and, far worse, caravans of dead being shipped away for mass burial. Munitorum work crews and pioneer regiments engaged in the hopeless task of restoring some order to the carnage. I jumped with fright when a loud explosion roared through the manufactory block just west of us, but Bragg reassured me it was just an engineering detail blowing up some structure that was too dangerous to leave standing.

Narmenian tanks with dozer blades were clearing rubble and human debris from the main arterials, allowing light military convoys to speed more freely through the ruins. The Ghosts I was with had nothing but praise for the Narmenians, and saluted each tank that passed with waves and raised fists. From the reports I had read, Grizmund's Narmenian Armour had made a vital contribution to the victory, as had the Roane Deepers, the Vervun Primary and the 'scratch companies' of Vervunhive guerrillas. But Lady Chass had been quite specific. Gaunt's Ghosts were the ones she wished to celebrate. I wondered why her affections lay specifically with them. I supposed it was because of Gaunt himself. He had taken overall command at the crucial time, and secured the eventual victory almost personally.

I wished then I could have met him, rather than seeing his near-dead body in an infirmary bed.

The outhabs were terribly desolated. They had been pulverised by artillery so hard that barely a building was left standing. The ground was a tangle mass of shattered rockcrete and twisted metal spars. The air was thick with oily smoke, and where it wasn't, it was heavy with dust sifted off the rubble. There were fragments of human bone in the litter underfoot, white and burned clean. At first I thought they were shards of broken porcelain, until I saw one with an eye socket.

The piteous ruin that had befallen these worker habs was evident in every metre of the soil.

I began to feel unwell. This was upsetting, overwhelming. The genial Colonel Corbec had sent me on this trip deliberately. He obviously thought I could do with some sort of wake up call.

I resented that. I was fully awake to Vervunhive's misery. I didn't need to be shown it like this.

And there was no end to it. We crossed a sub-street that was littered with bodies. The air was noxious with corruption and full of flies. Corbec was a bastard, I decided. Whatever he thought of me and my commission, I wasn't looking for this kind of inspiration.

I realised Larkin was crying. It shook me to see it. And, though I know what you're thinking, it didn't diminish him in any way. I'd known from the first moment I saw him he was an emotionally vulnerable man. He didn't falter in his duty for a moment. He kept up the pace, covered all the angles he was asked to. He didn't even seem to be aware that he was crying. But he wept.

I have seen women weep. I have seen children weep. I have seen weak men sob.

I have never, in the sixty years since then, seen a soldier weep. That is the most aching sadness of all. Larkin's tears washed his filthy cheeks clean in long runnels. He kept about his business. To see a man trained and ready to kill cry for the fallen is to see true tragedy.

'Larkin... won't you shut the feth up?' Feygor said.

'I've... I've got something in my eye,' Larkin said. I wanted to step forward and speak up in his defence, but Feygor looked meaner than ever. Besides, he had a lasrifle.

'Just shut up with the fething sobbing,' Feygor said, his voice flat and toneless because of the augmetic larynx sewn into his throat.

'Leave him alone,' said Baffels.

'Yeah,' said Mktag. 'We'll all be crying if Gaunt dies.'

Feygor spat. 'He's dead already.'

'He is not!' Domor said. 'He's hurt bad, but he's not dead.'

'Like they'd tell us if he was,' Feygor commented.

'They would!' said Domor.

'Those eyes make you blind, Shoggy?' asked Brostin. 'We're just the poor, simple dog-soldiers. They wouldn't tell us until it mattered. Bad for morale.'

'Think what you want,' said Yael. 'I reckon they'd tell us.'

'Gaunt's not dead,' said Milo.

'How so?' asked Feygor.

'I visit him every day. He wasn't dead this morning.'

'Yeah,' said Brostin, 'but was he alive?'

Milo didn't reply.

'He was an hour ago,' I ventured.

'Who asked you?' Feygor spat.

'His name is Mister Thuro,' said Bragg. 'Be respectful.'

'Feth to respect,' said Feygor.

'Shut up, all of you!' Doyl hissed.

We took cover in an old bakery, the side of which had been blown out. Doyl, with Feygor, scouted forward. I began to be convinced that I shouldn't have come.

'This Act of Consolation thing,' Mktag said as we hunkered low. 'Do you think anybody will take it?'

'They'd be mad to,' said Yael.

'I think some will,' Domor disagreed.

'Yeah, some... the crazies...' said Brostin.

'Keep it down, will you?' Baffels called.

Brostin dropped his voice. 'You'd have to be mad to sign up. And these hivers, I don't know about them. Do we want their kind in our ranks?'

'I've seen them fight,' said Domor. 'The scratch companies. They're good. I'd be proud to have them with us.'

'They're not Tanith!' Brostin growled.

'No, they're not,' said Bragg. 'But I've seen them too. They fight like bastards.'

'Maybe, but would you be happy for them to take the Tanith colours? Eh?' Brostin asked. 'They're not Tanith! Feth this Act of Consolation... let them found their own regiment. They're not fething Tanith!'

'I was with Gaunt on the Spike raid, with a bunch of Verghast scratchers,' said Larkin suddenly. 'You were there too, Bragg. And you, Shoggy. The scratch company gave everything. That leader of theirs – what was his name?'

'Kolea,' said Bragg.

'Yeah... he was a piece of work. Totally driven.'

'Whatever.' Brostin said, unconvinced.

Doyl and Feygor returned to us. The way ahead was clear. We trawled forward through the landscape.

I think it was about then that I saved several lives. I had been looking at the devastation with a sculptor's eye for engineering. I said to Bragg: 'That way ahead. The slump of rockcrete looks like it's been disturbed.'

'How can you tell?' he asked.

I shrugged. 'I don't know. I just know from the feel of things how they should lie. That's not true. It's been drilled.'

Bragg called a halt. He tossed a rock onto the slumped slab and the resultant blast took out the ground and flung masonry debris through the air.

'Good call, Mister Thuro,' said Feygor.

'If you can't be anything except sarcastic, Feygor, shut the feth up!' Domor said.

'I'm not being sarcastic,' Feygor said, sarcastically.

'Shut the feth up!' several of them chorused.

'It's this thing! This thing!' Feygor insisted, rapping at the aug-unit in his throat with a dirty finger. 'It makes me sound fething sarcastic even when I'm not!'

It was perfectly true. The raspy monotone of the implant rendered every word he uttered in a deadpan flatness. He was going to be sarcastic for the rest of his life.

'Be fair, you're sarcastic most of the time anyway,' said Brostin.

'Not always.'

'How can we tell when you're not being sarcastic?' asked Yael.

'Maybe he could hold up a hand when he's actually being sarcastic for real,' Mktag suggested. 'Like a signal.'

'Oh, that's a good idea,' said Feygor.

Everyone looked at him. Slowly, reluctantly, he raised a hand.

I think we were all about to explode out laughing, even Feygor, but Doyl suddenly raised a hand himself, and the gesture had nothing to do with sarcasm.

We were all huddled low, and the dust from the booby-trap blast was still falling and settling. Wordlessly, Doyl pointed at two sites in the ruins ahead that seemed to me to be no different from the rest of the place. Then he made a couple of swift, deft hand signals.

Baffels nodded, and made a few gestures of his own. At once, Domor, Yael and Doyl slid to the left, crawling through the jumbled wasteland, and Feygor, Brostin and Milo went to the right.

'Keep low,' Bragg mouthed at me and I needed no encouragement. Damn House Chass should have paid me danger money for this. Bragg extended the bipod stand of his heavy weapon and nested it in pile of rubble. Mktag crouched beside him, unclasping ammo drums from his pack and feeding them to the munition port in the side of Bragg's support gun. Then he spread out the camouflage capes both he and Bragg were carrying and draped them out over their shoulders. Baffels was lying on his belly a few metres to the right, using a spotter periscope to survey out over the shattered brickwork. I realised I couldn't see Larkin. Then I realised he was immediately to my left, prone, with his sniper rifle raised in a firing position. Like the support gunners, he was draped in his camo-cape and though he was almost close enough for me to reach out and touch him, I had to look hard to see him. His concealment was extraordinary. I understand that is a trademark skill of the Tanith Ghosts.

I felt exposed, and entirely in the wrong place. I tried to curl up tighter against a cleft in the wall, but my feet dislodged loose stones and I got a dirty look from Larkin.

I could hear my own heart. I could smell brick dust and sweat, my own included. The sunlight seemed unpleasantly hot. There was the barest whisper of close-link vox exchanges.

Time seemed to slow down and stretch out, like a quiet, slow passage in a piece of music. It occurred to me then that I could never be a soldier. The waiting would kill me. It's ironic, I know. I can spend months on a work, whole weeks minutely carving some tiny part of it. I am obsessive with detail, and never care how long it takes to get something perfect, because the success of the whole might depend on one small part.

And this was the same, the same sort of meticulous craft. But here it was applied to war. The Guardsmen were singularly mindful to get this small preparation right, to have the patience to succeed. If a victory in war and a statue can be compared, and you'll forgive me but I'm not entirely sure they can, then achieving them, creating them, depends on detail and effort and patience. Curled up there in that out-hab ruin, cursing the wait and the intolerable delay, I was about to live through the worst ten minutes of my life. And I am utterly convinced that I would not be alive now if the Ghosts had rushed a second of it.

I'd never heard a las-weapon discharge before, not for real. I'd seen plenty of newsreels, of course, displaying our glorious soldiery in acts of staged victory, but I know now that the deep, resonating bangs of those weapons were dubbed on afterwards. Real guns make a sharp, cracking nose, like breaking sticks. It's thin, dry, and it doesn't sound at all important. I heard the cracking noise and wondered what it was. I was about to be educated.

I was about to be educated in all sorts of ways.

Baffels was suddenly whispering urgently into his vox. I knew something was happening, and then there was a very loud crack right next to me. Larkin had fired. He fired again, and I recognised my own stupidity. The cracking sounds I had been hearing was the fight already underway.

There was a strange strobing of the light around me, like the daylight was flickering. Dust kicked up from a half-fallen wall behind our position and several clumps of stone fell out. I realised we were being fired at. The flickering of the daylight was being caused by bright las-rounds passing over us, almost invisible against the hard glare of the sky. Then a shot stung by against the bricks and I saw it clearly. A dart of seething fire, tinged red, the size of a man's middle finger, so bright it hurt my eyes, so fast it was barely there.

Bragg's cannon woke up. It also didn't make the sound I was expecting. It rattled metallically like the rock drills I sometimes use on larger works. It burped out irregular bursts of hard, spitting bangs, strung together very fast and overlayed by the tinny rattle of the mechanism and the feeding ammunition belt. Spent cases rained down underneath the heavy weapon and made a tinkling, pinging sound as they bounced off the rocks.

Milo, Feygor and Brostin suddenly reappeared, running back frantically and throwing themselves down into cover with us. As soon as they were down, Feygor and Milo rose on their knees and started firing indiscriminate shots over the cover wall with their lasrifles.

Brostin was struggling with his flamer unit.

'What the feth's the problem?' Baffels cried.

'We came up on a gang of them. Maybe six or seven, and we had them cold, but Brostin's damn burner jammed!' Feygor rasped out the explanation as he continued with his firing. Heavier shots were falling around us now, each one making a dull, hollow sound as it exploded into the rubble.

'Get it working!' Baffels yelled.

'I'm trying!' Brostin replied. 'The igniter's dead.'

'Feth! They're coming!' Milo called. 'I see them moving!'

'Larkin!' Baffels almost screamed.

'Can't get a clear shot,' Larkin hissed.

'Fething thing!' said Baffels, now unscrewing the blackened cover of the flamer's nozzle. I dared to raise my head.

'Where's Doyl's group?' Milo asked.

'Dug in, under fire. They're pinned,' said Baffels. 'Where the feth is this heat coming from now?'

'To the left! There!' Feygor growled.

Bragg yanked his aim around and twisted the heavy cannon on its stand. Mktag tried to move with him. They were already onto their third drum of ammo.

Bragg fired in the direction Feygor had indicated.

'Try again, Bragg!' Feygor and Mktag cried out in unison. Now I understood the darkly ironic nickname.

Bragg fired another burst and then the belt ran out and Mktag was a few seconds late lining up the next box. Bragg shot a look in my direction. He smiled at me, trying to look reassuring. Try again, Bragg, I thought. Enemy fire was whipping all around him, and he just sat there, grinning a half-arsed grin that was supposed to perk me up and make me feel all right. Colonel Corbec had told him to look after me and he didn't want to let me down.

'It'll be okay,' he said. 'We'll be through this in a minute.'

Even today, sixty years later, I have a lasting memory of Trooper Bragg at that moment. His simplicity and his genuine sense of optimism. Simply his courage. I have no way of knowing what became of Trooper Bragg. I hope fate was kind to him.

'We need that flamer!' Baffels yelled, firing his weapon alongside Milo now. The heavy cannon opened up once more.

Brostin said something incomprehensible and tried to poke a cleaning rod down the mouth of the burner.

I crawled over to him. Though it was much bigger and heavier, the flamer resembled in principle the sort of heat-gun we sometimes used to work metals and ductile plastics. On a commission for House Anko two years before, I had been plagued by a heat-gun that had regularly refused to light.

'It's not the nozzle,' I said.

'It is so the fething nozzle!' spat Brostin. 'It's dust in the fething nozzle! Get the feth out of my face! You shouldn't even be here!'

'It's not the nozzle,' I repeated firmly. 'It's the secondary igniter. The fuel pipe is twisted or blocked and nothing's getting through to light the pilot.'

'Feth off and away with you!'

Ignoring him, I reached out and yanked the secondary fuel pipe out of its plug. Liquid fuel dribbled out over my hands.

'Get off it! Get him off me!' Brostin yelled. I was sure he was about to hit me.

I grabbed a cleaning rod and inserted it into the pipe, dragging out a fat plug of fuel-soaked matter. 'Now try it!'

Brostin looked murderously at me and reconnected the pipe. He squeezed the burner's heavy trigger bar and a small fireball coughed out of the nozzle. The igniter flame suddenly lit up: a hard, blue finger of heat.

'Feth me!' said Brostin.

'Don't mention it,' I said.

Brostin swung round with the active weapon and fired it over the barricade. Spurts of ferocious yellow fire swished over the rubble. I heard screams.

With the flamer firing, Milo, Feygor and Baffels dropped back into cover and fitted long, silver blades to their weapons.

'Is it going to come to that?' I asked the boy Milo.

'Who knows?' he said.

Baffels called out. Apparently there was now crossfire from Doyl's wing. The flamer had broken the deadlock. For all I could tell, the Emperor himself might just have arrived on a goat. I had no idea how they could read the chaotic situation like that, even with comlinks. It was just madness. Rocks and dust and flying jags of lethal, coherent light.

'Go!' said Baffels. I didn't know what 'go' meant, but suddenly Feygor, Milo, Brostin and Baffels were gone. They leapt up and charged into the smoke. I could hear furious cracking, and the breathy hush of the flamer.

Then Mktag rose from his prone position like he had been jerked up from behind by his webbing. He twisted and fell over. For a moment, I didn't understand what was happening. It seemed as if Mktag was just behaving stupidly, mucking around, kicking with his legs.

But Mktag had been shot. Right there in front of me. He fell at my feet, his heels drumming the ground, his hands spasming. A tiny plume of smoke spiraled up from the little black hole a las-round had made in his forehead. There was no blood. The shot had cauterised the entry wound and it didn't have enough power to exit his skull. Its heat and force had been expended getting into his cranium and incinerating his brain.

It was quite simply the most awful thing I have ever seen. His body thrashing, trying to live, the brain extinguished. I think if there had been more blood, more obvious physical damage, I could have coped better.

But it was just such a tiny hole.

And then he was utterly still, and that was the worst part of all.

I was still staring at Mktag when the others returned. Bragg had laid his cape over the corpse, and Larkin was crouched beside it, brokenly reading a rite of grace from the back pages of his Imperial Infantryman's Uplifting Primer. The battle was done, the pocket of Zoican resistance wiped out.

I never did see even a glimpse of the enemy.

It was dusk when we returned to the city. Doyl and Baffels carried Mktag all the way. Bragg and Brostin tried to buck me up, claiming my improvisation with the faulty flamer had saved the day. By the time we reached the curtain wall, their version of events had me as the hero, winning the entire encounter. They were generous souls, these Ghosts. Brostin in particular had no reason to admit I'd been right. They realised, I suppose, that I was a civilian and they'd taken me too far. They felt sorry for me. I'd survived their rite of passage and acquitted myself well.

I suppose I should have been flattered by the inclusion. Honoured to earn the respect of such warriors.

But Mktag's death had unsettled me profoundly. The memory of it had burned into my brain so deeply that I was sure it had left a little, smoking hole in my skull. I was no soldier, despite what Brostin and Bragg cheerfully said. I had no basis of experience with which to deal with this shock, no inoculation, no Fundamental Training brutalisation to take the sting away.

I was an artist, for the God-Emperor's sake! A soft, protected artist from a secure world where death happened behind closed doors or drawn curtains. For all I tried to make my work contain such eternal concepts as truth and grace, nobility and humanity, they were empty gestures. My work was empty. I despised everything I had ever done, all the artistic triumphs I had been so pleased with. They were nothing, barren, vapid. Devoid of any real human truth.

Real truth was out there in the shattered outhabs of Vervunhive. Real truth was waiting and silence, courage and stealth. Real truth was the ability to function in extremes. To fire a cannon and miss and try again. To fix a silver blade to the end of a las-weapon and leap from safety into a shroud of smoke, prepared as you did so to really use that makeshift spear.

Real truth was as real as a tiny hole in a man's forehead.

I had not been scared during the patrol. I had been bored, horrified, perplexed, impatient. But at no point had I actually succumbed to terror. Once we were back, fear consumed me. I shook. I could barely speak.

I sat, swathed in Bragg's camo-cape, in the doorway of the billet. Troopers moved around me, getting on with their work. I wondered why they didn't seem scared. If they were scared, and they were still just getting on with it, that was truly terrifying.

I saw Bragg talking with Corbec and pointing in my direction. Corbec disappeared, but a few moments later the young trooper, Milo, came to find me.

'Colonel Corbec wants me to take you to the Medical Hall.'

'I'm fine.'

'I know. But he wants the medics to check you out. You've had quite a day, Mister Thuro.'

We walked through the battered streets as night fell. The stars came out, fighting to shine through the smoke. High above, moonlight glinted on the hulls of the vast warships in low orbit.

'How do you do it?' I asked the boy.

'Do what, sir?'

'Shut it out? The fear? The trauma? Did they beat it out of you in basic training?'

Milo looked at me strangely. 'Who ever said we shut it out?' he asked.

'But you can't...' I began. 'You can't live like that. Continue to live, I mean, day in, day out, with that kind of stress, that kind of fear. You must cope somehow. Shut it out.'

He shook his head. 'I'm scared every minute of my life.'

'But how do you keep going?'

Milo shrugged. 'I've never thought about it. It's just what we do. What we're asked to do. We're Imperial Guard.'

I have never forgotten those words.

* * *

I had to wait an hour or so in the Medical Hall until I was seen. A kindly old doctor, the man Dorden that Corbec had been looking for, got to me eventually and pronounced me fit. He offered me something to calm me, but I turned him down. I asked after Gaunt, and he told me I could go and see for myself.

He led me through the wards of the Medical Hall. We passed the beds of soldiers, many of them Ghosts, wounded in the war. Dorden stopped frequently to check on them. He told me names – Mkoll, Bonin, Wheln, so many I forgot – and recounted the circumstances of their injuries.

I wanted to see Gaunt again before he died. I wanted to see him now I had seen the kind of men he had bred.

A group of men and women were waiting in the dim hallway outside his chamber when we arrived. A few Ghosts, but mostly Vervunhivers. Dorden knew them all. There was a big, grim-looking miner that Dorden called Mister Kolea; a one-eyed factory boss in declining years who introduced himself as Agun Soric; a badly wounded Vervun Primary Captain called Daur; a fierce-looking gang-girl called Criid who was accompanied by a young Tanith trooper.

'Why are they here?' I asked Dorden.

'They want to see Gaunt.'

'Why?'

'Because they've all accepted the Act of Consolation, them and hundreds like them,' Dorden whispered. 'They'll be joining our regiment and coming with us, God-Emperor help them.'

'Why have they come here?'

'To be close to Gaunt. He's the reason most of them have signed up. They want to be here of he lives... or if he dies. They've signed their lives to his cause. It matters to them.'

The motley band keeping the vigil outside Gaunt's room seemed content to wait there, but I went forward and slipped into his room. No one stopped me. The plastic drapes were drawn, and I was about to sweep them aside when I realised the beloved colonel-commissar already had company.

I paused in the doorway, peering in through the curtain. A lean, dangerous-looking man in black Tanith fatigues was sitting at Gaunt's bedside in the blue gloom. He was a major. Major Rawne, as I found out later.

I knew I shouldn't be there. I'd felt awkward that morning eavesdropping on Corbec, but this was far more invasive.

Still, I couldn't draw myself away.

I listened.

'You dare die,' Rawne was muttering at Gaunt. 'You dare die on me, you fething bastard. Die now and I'll never forgive you. It can't be this way. I won't let it.'

I started to back away, realising I had heard too much.

'If you're going to die, it's got to be me that kills you. Me, you hear, you bastard? Me. Otherwise, it isn't fair. I've got to be the one. I need to be the one. Not some Chaos bullet. You live, you bastard. You wake up and live so that I can kill you properly.'

He suddenly looked up and saw I was there. He rose and thundered towards me. 'What the feth are you doing?'

I backed off. He'd balled his fists and his face was readably furious despite the half-light. He was going to hurt me.

'Who the feth are you?' he snarled, slamming me against the wall.

'Great God-Emperor!' I stammered. 'Look–'

He turned. He saw what I saw.

Ibram Gaunt's eyes were open.

I never got to speak with Gaunt. Once he was well enough, they moved him to a medical frigate. And I barely saw any of the Tanith after that either. My transport back to NorthCol had been arranged, and a message from House Chass urged me to start on my work.

I missed three deadlines, and risked the wrath of Lady Chass. I scrapped five working models, and destroyed two works in the very last stages. They weren't right.

Eventually, the piece was cast in steel. I wasn't much satisfied with that either. To me, it had no truth, no real truth. But House Chass couldn't be denied any longer.

It stands today in the centre of what was once Vervunhive's Commercia. The hive has been levelled, and most of the land turned back to pasture and grassland. Shards of rock, bits of bone and spent shell cases can still be found on the windy slopes amongst the grasses.

It's become my most famous work. There's irony. To say I was really, truly pleased with it, I'd have to raise a hand, like Feygor. I've done so much since that seems to me more important. But you can't choose what you leave behind.

A single Imperial Guardsman, cast in steel rendered down from the broken weapons left in the ruins of the hive. It's not even specifically a Tanith Ghost, and it has no special likeness. One fist is raised, not in victory but in determination, a gesture like the one Baffels made. There is a set to the shoulders that resembles Colonel Corbec's relaxed stance, a set to the head that always reminds me of Trooper Bragg's reassuring backwards glance. There's Milo's honesty in it, I like to think, and Rawne's venom. It has, like all statues, Mktag's awful stillness.

It's called the Chass Memorial, and on the plinth it announces in large chiselled letters that House Chass paid for its construction in memory of the fallen of Vervunhive. In very much smaller letters, it says it is a work by Thuro of NorthCol. It stands on a grassy slope, guarding the necropolis that was once called Vervunhive. It may stand forever.

There's nothing of Gaunt himself in it, because I never knew him. Like I said, I never knew any of them, not really. But his men are in it, so I suppose he is too.

ABOUT THE AUTHORS

Dan Abnett has written over fifty novels, including
Anarch, the latest instalment in the acclaimed Gaunt's
Ghosts series. He has also written the Ravenor, Eisenhorn
and Bequin books, the most recent of which is *Penitent*.
For the Horus Heresy, he is the author of the Siege of
Terra novel *Saturnine*, as well as *Horus Rising*, *Legion*,
The Unremembered Empire, *Know No Fear* and *Prospero
Burns*, the last two of which were both *New York Times*
bestsellers. He also scripted *Macragge's Honour*, the first
Horus Heresy graphic novel, as well as numerous Black
Library audio dramas. Many of his short stories have been
collected into the volume *Lord of the Dark Millennium*. He
lives and works in Maidstone, Kent.

An extract from
The Warmaster
by Dan Abnett

They had so very nearly got away with it. Got away with it and survived to tell the tale.

So very nearly.

Hell and back. That's how someone had described the Salvation's
Reach mission. It sounded like the sort of thing Larkin or Varl would say.

Hell and back. They'd gone into hell and come out on the other side,
and not for the first time. But after everything they had endured, it
seemed as though they weren't going to make it home after all.

Four weeks out from the Rimworld Marginals, and the target rock
known as Salvation's Reach, the doughty old warship *Highness Ser
Armaduke* had begun to limp.

'How far are we from the intended destination?' Ibram Gaunt asked
the *Armaduke*'s shipmaster.

Spika, leaning back thoughtfully in his worn command seat, shrugged
his shoulders.

'The estimate is another fifteen days,' he replied, 'but I don't like the
look of the immaterium. Bad patterns ahead. I think we'll be riding out
a proper storm before nightfall, shiptime.'

'And that could slow us down?' asked Gaunt.

'By a margin of weeks, if we're unlucky,' said Spika.

'Still, you're saying the storm isn't the real problem?' Gaunt pressed.

'No,' said Spika. He held up a finger for quiet. 'You hear that?'

Gaunt listened, and heard many sounds: the chatter and chime of
the multiple cogitators ranked around the warship's bridge; the asth-
matic wheeze of the air-circulation system and environmental pumps;

the hum of the through-deck power hubs charging the strategium display; the deranged murmuring from the navigator's socket; the voxed back-chatter from the crew; footsteps on the deck plates; the deep, deep rumble of the warp drives behind everything else.

During the course of the Salvation's Reach mission, he had begun to learn the multifarious ambient running noises of the *Armaduke,* but not enough to become an expert.

'Not really,' he admitted.

'Not really?' asked Spika. 'No?' The shipmaster sounded disappointed. Though the life and the lifetime expectations of a Navy man were, quite literally, worlds away from those of a Guard officer, the two men had bonded during the mission tour, and had both gained insight into operational worlds quite alien from their own. They were not friends, but there was a measure of something that, nurtured, might one day resemble friendship. Clemensaw Spika seemed rather let down that Gaunt had grasped less shipboard nuance than he had expected.

'It's quite distinct,' Spika said, sadly. 'Number two drive. There's an arrhythmia in its generative pulse. The modulation is out of step. There. There. There. There.'

Like an orchestral conductor, he beat his finger to a pattern. It was a pattern that Ibram Gaunt did not have the experience of practice to discern.

It was Gaunt's turn to shrug.

Spika adjusted the brass levers on his armrests, and swept his command seat around. The entire chair, a metal-framed throne of worn leather with banks of control surfaces and levers set into each arm, sat upon a gilded carriage that connected it to a complex gimbal-jointed lifting arm. At a touch, Spika could hoist himself above the entire bridge, incline to share the point of view of any of the bridge stations below, or even raise himself up into the bridge dome to study hololithic star-map projections.

This more gentle adjustment merely turned the seat so he could dismount and lead Gaunt across the bridge to the bank of stations occupied by the Master of Artifice and his key functionaries.

'Output display, all engines,' Spika requested.

'Output display, all, aye,' the Master of Artifice answered. His hands – busy bionic spiders that dripped spots of oil and were attached to wrists made of rotator struts and looped cables jutting from the fine double-buttoned cuffs of his duty uniform – played across the main haptic panel of his console. Each finger-touch caused a separate and distinct electronic note, creating a little musical flurry like an atonal arpeggio. The Master of Artifice was not blind, for Gaunt could see the ochre-and-gold receptors in his enhanced pupils expanding and contracting his irises, but his attitude was that of a sightless pianist. He was not looking at what he was doing. His picture of the universe and the ship, which were, after all, the same thing, was being fed to him in a constantly updated flow through aural implants, and through data-trunks that ran up his neck like bulging arteries and entered the base of his skull through dermal sockets.

A hololithic display sprang up above the man's station. Side by side, in three dimensions, the rising and falling graph lines of the *Armaduke*'s engines were arranged for comparison. Gaunt's limited expertise was not found wanting now.

'I see,' Gaunt said. 'Clearly a problem.'

'Clearly,' replied Spika. 'Number two drive is operating at least thirty-five per cent below standard efficiency.'

'The yield is declining by the hour, shipmaster,' the Master of Artifice said.

'Are you examining it?' asked Gaunt.

'It's hard to examine a warp drive when it's active,' replied Spika. 'But, yes. Nothing conclusive yet. I believe this down-rate is the result of damage we sustained during the fight at Tavis Sun on the outward journey. Even a micro-impact or spalling on the inner liner might, over time, develop into this, especially given the demands we've made on principal artifice.'

'So this could be an old wound only now showing up?' asked Gaunt. Spika nodded.

'The Master of Artifice,' he said, 'prefers the theory that it is micro-particle damage taken during our approach to Salvation's Reach – ingested debris. This theory has some merit. The Reach was a particularly dense field.'

'What's the prognosis?' asked Gaunt.

'If we can effect repair, we're fine. If we can't, and the output continues to decline in this manner, we may be forced to exit the warp, and perhaps divert to a closer harbour.'

Gaunt frowned. They'd travelled non-stop since departing the Reach, except for one scheduled resupply halt at a secure depot, Aigor 991, a week earlier. It had not gone to plan. Resupply was urgently needed: the raid had expended a vast quantity of their munitions and perishable supplies, but they'd been obliged to abort and press on without restocking. Gaunt was reluctant to make another detour. He wanted to reach their destination as fast as possible.

'Worst case?' he asked.

'Worst case?' Spika replied. 'There are many kinds of worst case. The most obvious would be that the drive fails suddenly and we are thrown out of the warp. Thrown out of the warp... if we're lucky.'

'Is there anything,' Gaunt asked the shipmaster, 'which suggests to you that luck follows the occupants of this vessel around on any permanent or regular basis?'

'My dear colonel-commissar,' Spika replied, 'I've lived in this accursed galaxy long enough to believe that there's no such thing as luck at all.'